THE BIG BOOK OF
GHOST STORIES

THE BIG BOOK OF
Ghost Stories

EDITED AND WITH AN INTRODUCTION BY
OTTO PENZLER

VINTAGE CRIME/BLACK LIZARD
VINTAGE BOOKS
A DIVISION OF RANDOM HOUSE, INC.
NEW YORK

A VINTAGE CRIME/BLACK LIZARD ORIGINAL, SEPTEMBER 2012

Introductions and compilation copyright © 2012 by Otto Penzler

Library of Congress Cataloging-in-Publication Data
The big book of ghost stories / edited and with an introduction by Otto Penzler.
p. cm.
ISBN 978-0-307-47449-0
1. Ghost stories, English.   2. Ghost stories, American.   I. Penzler, Otto.
PR1309.G5B54 2012
823'.0873308—dc23
2012020265

Book design by Christopher M. Zucker
Cover design by Gregg Kulick

www.vintagebooks.com

Printed in the United States of America
10 9 8 7 6 5 4 3 2 1

For Edward Kastenmeier

With gratitude for your support

and commitment to my

Big

books

Contents

Introduction

OTTO PENZLER

TALES OF THE SUPERNATURAL have been a fixture of the storytelling tradition since preliterate times, and the most popular form they have taken is the ghost story. This should not be at all surprising, as the fear of death and its aftermath has abided in the breasts of humans ever since they became cognizant of what it meant to no longer be alive in the manner in which it is traditionally understood. Animals, down to the most primitive invertebrates, share this fear without precisely being aware of what it means in a conscious sense, but they nonetheless do all they can to stay alive. The question of what follows the extinguishing of life probably does not keep mosquitoes or squirrels awake at night, but more than a few *homo sapiens* have pondered their uncertain futures with trepidation in the dark of night.

All cultures on the planet have superstitions about the dead returning as spirits or phantoms—belief systems memorialized in drawings and writings from the very beginnings of civilization. In the Egyptian *Book of the Dead*, departed people are shown to return, not merely looking as they did in life, but dressed in similar garments. Therefore, apparently not only do dead people have the ability to materialize, making themselves visible again after they are gone, but so do textiles, leather, and metal.

In the Bible, the story of King Saul calling on the Witch of Endor to summon the spirit of Samuel has been recorded, as have the questions surrounding whether Jesus after his resurrection was a living being or a ghost. From ancient texts in Greek mythology, various types of ghosts are described in Homer's *Iliad* and *Odyssey*, and Romans, notably Plutarch and Pliny the Younger, wrote about haunted houses.

Literature of all eras abounds in ghosts stories. William Shakespeare often used ghosts in his plays, most famously in *Hamlet* and *Macbeth*, and Charles Dickens wrote the greatest pure ghost story of all time in *A Christmas Carol*. Others among the world's greatest authors who have written in the genre include Ben Jonson, Horace Walpole, Jane Austen, Nathaniel Hawthorne, Guy de Maupassant, Edgar Allan Poe, Wilkie Collins, Edward Bulwer-Lytton, Samuel Taylor Coleridge, Henry James, Edith Wharton, Oscar Wilde, Willa Cather, F. Scott Fitzgerald—well, really too many to continue.

What is the great attraction of supernatural fiction in general, and the ghost story in particular? From the time of childhood, we have a fear of the dark (and rightly so, as we don't know exactly what is lurking out there, wrapped in the black cloak of invisibility). Although it frightens them, children still love to hear scary stories at bedtime; just consider such fairy tales as Hansel and Gretel, Rapunzel, and Little Red Riding Hood. We never outgrow our love of fairy tales, even if in adulthood they take a more complex form as stories about vampires, serial killers, werewolves, or terrorists.

Ghost stories may be told in many different tones and styles, ranging from the excruciatingly horrific to the absurdly humorous. Ghosts, after all, may have widely divergent goals. Some return from the dead to wreak vengeance; others want to help a loved one. Some are the spirits of people who were murdered or committed suicide and so could not rest because their time officially had not yet come and therefore walked the earth instead of stretching out comfortably in their graves. Some were playful, enjoying the tricks and pranks their invisibility allowed them, while others delighted in their own cruelty, committing acts of violence and terror for the sheer inexplicable pleasure of it.

All these ghosts, and more, appear in this volume. You will meet ghosts who frighten you, who make you laugh, and for whom you will feel sorry. And they are true ghosts. I have tried to remain true to the notion that ghosts are spirits or specters of the dead. Some stories that frequently have appeared in other ghost story anthologies have nothing at all to do with ghosts. They may be trolls, or evil plants, vile fungi, monsters, or other creatures of that ilk. Rightly or not, I have attempted to be a bit of a narrow-minded purist about it all, not that it created a problem. There have been an astonishing number of outstanding ghost stories written by some of the finest authors who ever dared allow their dark creations to be set down on paper. It has been a confounding challenge to select the stories for this, the biggest collection of ghost stories ever compiled. It was tempting to include all the great classics but that would have filled to overflowing even this gigantic tome. It was equally tempting to stuff the pages with little-known stories, often every bit the equal of the cornerstone titles, but it is impossible to attempt to produce the definitive collection of ghost stories and omit M. R. James, Algernon Blackwood, H. P. Lovecraft, or Edith Wharton. Although I admire some of the supernatural tales of Henry James, especially "The Turn of the Screw," he won't be found here because that novella has been anthologized to death, is easy to find elsewhere, and is so long that a half-dozen other stories would have had to be sacrificed. Putting together an anthology is not a pure science, so there are contradictions galore. I've included "The Monkey's Paw," for example, which has also been anthologized to the point of being a cliché. Still, it's short, didn't use up too much space, and it is lively (unlike dear old Henry James—no offense). To make up for the very familiar stories, I've included some that you've never seen before, several of which appear in book form for the very first time. The Golden Age of the ghost story (the late Victorian and Edwardian eras) is fully represented, and so is the Golden Age of the pulp magazines (the 1920s and 1930s), while the contemporary masters have not been ignored.

Whether this collection is best enjoyed next to a summer campfire or a winter fireplace is up to you. On the other hand, it is so enormous that it may endure through several seasons. Whenever you read it, I hope you have a shiveringly good time with it. After all, in the dead of night, who would not believe in ghosts?

Although I read more than a thousand stories to find and identify those that I hope you will most enjoy, it would not have been possible to compile such a comprehensive and wide-reaching volume without the invaluable assistance of those who know a great deal more than I do. Sincere, if hopelessly inadequate, thanks are owed to Robert Weinberg, John Pelan, Chris Roden, Gardner Dozois, Joel Frieman, Harlan Ellison, John Knott, and those I'm forgetting who so freely and generously offered their assistance and expertise.

BUT I'M NOT DEAD YET

MR. ARCULARIS

Conrad Aiken

ALTHOUGH CONRAD POTTER AIKEN (1889–1973) wrote well-received novels and about forty short stories, it is his poetry that has provided his primary literary reputation. He wrote his first poem at the age of nine and, four years later, memorized a volume of Poe's poems, strongly influencing his early work. He was later devoted to the work of John Gould Fletcher and T. S. Eliot, changing his poetry to a more modern, Imagist style. His novels, notably *Blue Voyage* (1927), are reminiscent of James Joyce. Aiken's most important book was *The Selected Poems of Conrad Aiken* (1929), which won the Pulitzer Prize and the Shelley Memorial Award.

Born in Savannah, Georgia, he was the son of an old New England family and attended Harvard, then moved as a child to New Bedford, Massachusetts, later settling in Cambridge. His father, a brilliant but erratic doctor, took his young son to witness an eye operation and later killed his wife and himself while Conrad was still a boy. When World War I broke out, Conrad refused to serve, successfully insisting that writing poetry was an essential industry.

Among his most important prose works are the novel *King Coffin* (1935), in which a man plans the perfect crime because of his hatred for humanity, then fails to commit the act; the disturbing short story "Silent Snow, Secret Snow," in which the protagonist wages an internal battle with reality and frightening fantasy; and "Mr. Arcularis," both of which were published in his collection, *Among the Lost People* (1934).

"Mr. Arcularis" was originally published in the March 1931 issue of *Harper's;* Aiken later adapted it as a play, produced in 1949 and published in 1957 by Harvard University Press. It was further adapted for several television dramas, including as episodes of *Studio One in Hollywood* (June 25, 1956), *ITV Play of the Week* (September 8, 1959), *Great Ghost Tales* (July 6, 1961), and as a made-for-television film in West Germany, which aired April 8, 1967.

Mr. Arcularis

CONRAD AIKEN

MR. ARCULARIS STOOD AT the window of his room in the hospital and looked down at the street. There had been a light shower, which had patterned the sidewalks with large drops, but now again the sun was out, blue sky was showing here and there between the swift white clouds, a cold wind was blowing the poplar trees. An itinerant band had stopped before the building and was playing, with violin, harp, and flute, the finale of "Cavalleria Rusticana." Leaning against the window-sill—for he felt extraordinarily weak after his operation—Mr. Arcularis suddenly, listening to the wretched music, felt like crying. He rested the palm of one hand against a cold window-pane and stared down at the old man who was blowing the flute, and blinked his eyes. It seemed absurd that he should be so weak, so emotional, so like a child—and especially now that everything was over at last. In spite of all their predictions, in spite, too, of his own dreadful certainty that he was going to die, here he was, as fit as a fiddle—but what a fiddle it was, so out of tune!—with a long life before him. And to begin with, a voyage to England ordered by the doctor. What could be more delightful? Why should he feel sad about it and want to cry like a baby? In a few minutes Harry would arrive with his car to take him to the wharf; in an hour he would be on the sea, in two hours he would see the sunset behind him, where Boston had been, and his new life would be opening before him. It was many years since he had been abroad. June, the best of the year to come—England, France, the Rhine—how ridiculous that he should already be homesick!

There was a light footstep outside the door, a knock, the door opened, and Harry came in.

"Well, old man, I've come to get you. The old bus actually got here. Are you ready? Here, let me take your arm. You're tottering like an octogenarian!"

Mr. Arcularis submitted gratefully, laughing, and they made the journey slowly along the bleak corridor and down the stairs to the entrance hall. Miss Hoyle, his nurse, was there, and the Matron, and the charming little assistant with freckles who had helped to prepare him for the operation. Miss Hoyle put out her hand.

"Good-by, Mr. Arcularis," she said, "and *bon voyage.*"

"Good-by, Miss Hoyle, and thank you for everything. You were very kind to me. And I fear I was a nuisance."

The girl with the freckles, too, gave him her hand, smiling. She was very pretty, and it would have been easy to fall in love with her. She reminded him of some one. Who was it? He tried in vain to remember while he said good-by to her and turned to the Matron.

"And not too many latitudes with the young ladies, Mr. Arcularis!" she was saying.

Mr. Arcularis was pleased, flattered, by all this attention to a middle-aged invalid, and felt a joke taking shape in his mind, and no sooner in his mind than on his tongue.

"Oh, no latitudes," he said, laughing. "I'll leave the latitudes to the ship!"

"Oh, come now," said the Matron, "we don't seem to have hurt him much, do we?"

"I think we'll have to operate on him again and *really* cure him," said Miss Hoyle.

He was going down the front steps, between the potted palmettos, and they all laughed and waved. The wind was cold, very cold for June, and he was glad he had put on his coat. He shivered.

"Damned cold for June!" he said. "Why should it be so cold?"

"East wind," Harry said, arranging the rug over his knees. "Sorry it's an open car, but I believe in fresh air and all that sort of thing. I'll drive slowly. We've got plenty of time."

They coasted gently down the long hill toward Beacon Street, but the road was badly surfaced, and despite Harry's care Mr. Arcularis felt his pain again. He found that he could alleviate it a little by leaning to the right, against the arm-rest, and not breathing too deeply. But how glorious to be out again! How strange and vivid the world looked! The trees had innumerable green fresh leaves—they were all blowing and shifting and turning and flashing in the wind; drops of rainwater fell downward sparkling; the robins were singing their absurd, delicious little four-noted songs; even the street cars looked unusually bright and beautiful, just as they used to look when he was a child and had wanted above all things to be a motorman. He found himself smiling foolishly at everything, foolishly and weakly, and wanted to say something about it to Harry. It was no use, though—he had no strength, and the mere finding of words would be almost more than he could manage. And even if he should succeed in saying it, he would then most likely burst into tears. He shook his head slowly from side to side.

"Ain't it grand?" he said.

"I'll bet it looks good," said Harry.

"Words fail me."

"You wait till you get out to sea. You'll have a swell time."

"Oh, swell! . . . I hope not. I hope it'll be calm."

"Tut tut."

When they passed the Harvard Club Mr. Arcularis made a slow and somewhat painful effort to turn in his seat and look at it. It might be the last chance to see it for a long time. Why this sentimental longing to stare at it, though? There it was, with the great flag blowing in the wind, the Harvard seal now concealed by the swift folds and now revealed, and there were the windows in the library, where he had spent so many delightful hours reading—Plato, and Kipling, and the Lord knows what—and the balconies from which for so many years he had watched the Marathon. Old Talbot might be in there now, sleeping with a book on his knee, hoping forlornly to be interrupted by any one, for anything.

"Good-by to the old club," he said.

"The bar will miss you," said Harry, smiling with friendly irony and looking straight ahead.

"But let there be no moaning," said Mr. Arcularis.

"What's *that* a quotation from?"

"'The Odyssey.'"

In spite of the cold, he was glad of the wind on his face, for it helped to dissipate the feeling of vagueness and dizziness that came over him in a sickening wave from time to time. All of a sudden everything would begin to swim and dissolve, the houses would lean their heads together, he had to close his eyes, and there would be a curious and dreadful humming noise, which at regular intervals rose to a crescendo and then drawlingly subsided again. It was disconcerting. Perhaps he still had a trace of fever. When he got on the ship he would have a glass of whisky. . . . From one of these spells he opened his eyes and found that they were on the ferry, crossing to East Boston. It must have been the ferry's engines that he had heard. From another spell he woke to find himself on the wharf, the car at a standstill beside a pile of yellow packing-cases.

"We're here because we're here because we're here," said Harry.

"Because we're here," added Mr. Arcularis.

He dozed in the car while Harry—and what a good friend Harry was!—attended to all the details. He went and came with tickets and passports and baggage checks and porters. And at last he unwrapped Mr. Arcularis from the rugs and led him up the steep gangplank to the deck, and thence by devious windings to a small cold state-room with a solitary porthole like the eye of a cyclops.

"Here you are," he said, "and now I've got to go. Did you hear the whistle?"

"No."

"Well, you're half asleep. It's sounded the all-ashore. Good-by, old fellow, and take care of yourself. Bring me back a spray of edelweiss. And send me a picture post-card from the Absolute."

"Will you have it finite or infinite?"

"Oh, infinite. But with your signature on it. Now you'd better turn in for a while and have a nap. Cheerio!"

Mr. Arcularis took his hand and pressed it hard, and once more felt like crying. Absurd! Had he become a child again?

"Good-by," he said.

He sat down in the little wicker chair, with his overcoat still on, closed his eyes, and listened to the humming of the air in the ventilator. Hurried footsteps ran up and down the corridor. The chair was not too comfortable, and his pain began to bother him again, so he moved, with his coat still on, to the narrow berth and fell asleep. When he woke up, it was dark, and the porthole had been partly opened. He groped for the switch and turned on the light. Then he rang for the steward.

"It's cold in here," he said. "Would you mind closing the port?"

. . .

The girl who sat opposite him at dinner was charming. Who was it she reminded him of? Why, of course, the girl at the hospital, the girl with the freckles. Her hair was beautiful, not quite red, not quite gold, nor had it been bobbed; arranged with a sort of graceful untidiness, it made him think of a Melozzo da Forli angel. Her face was freckled, she had a mouth which was both humorous and voluptuous. And she seemed to be alone.

He frowned at the bill of fare and ordered the thick soup.

"No hors d'œuvres?" asked the steward.

"I think not," said Mr. Arcularis. "They might kill me."

The steward permitted himself to be amused and deposited the menu card on the table against the water-bottle. His eyebrows were lifted. As he moved away, the girl followed him with her eyes and smiled.

"I'm afraid you shocked him," she said.

"Impossible," said Mr. Arcularis. "These stewards, they're dead souls. How could they be stewards otherwise? And they think they've seen and known everything. They suffer terribly from the *déjà vu*. Personally, I don't blame them."

"It must be a dreadful sort of life."

"It's because they're dead that they accept it."

"Do you think so?"

"I'm sure of it. I'm enough of a dead soul myself to know the signs!"

"Well, I don't know what you mean by that!"

"But nothing mysterious! I'm just out of hospital, after an operation. I was given up for dead. For six months I had given *myself* up for dead. If you've ever been seriously ill you know the feeling. You have a posthumous feeling—a mild, cynical tolerance for everything and every one. What is there you haven't seen or done or understood? Nothing."

Mr. Arcularis waved his hands and smiled.

"I wish I could understand you," said the girl, "but I've never been ill in my life."

"Never?"

"Never."

"Good God!"

The torrent of the unexpressed and inexpressible paralyzed him and rendered him speechless. He stared at the girl, wondering who she was and then, realizing that he had perhaps stared too fixedly, averted his gaze, gave a little laugh, rolled a pill of bread between his fingers. After a second or two he allowed himself to look at her again and found her smiling.

"Never pay any attention to invalids," he said, "or they'll drag you to the hospital."

She examined him critically, with her head tilted a little to one side, but with friendliness.

"You don't *look* like an invalid," she said.

Mr. Arcularis thought her charming. His pain ceased to bother him, the disagreeable humming disappeared, or rather, it was dissociated from himself and became merely, as it should be, the sound of the ship's engines, and he began to think the voyage was going to be really delightful. The parson on his right passed him the salt.

"I fear you will need this in your soup," he said.

"Thank you. Is it as bad as that?"

The steward, overhearing, was immediately apologetic and solicitous. He explained that on the first day everything was at sixes and sevens. The girl looked up at him and asked him a question.

"Do you think we'll have a good voyage?" she said.

He was passing the hot rolls to the parson, removing the napkins from them with a deprecatory finger.

"Well, madam, I don't like to be a Jeremiah, but——"

"Oh, come," said the parson, "I hope we have no Jeremiahs."

"What do you mean?" said the girl.

Mr. Arcularis ate his soup with gusto—it was nice and hot.

"Well, maybe I shouldn't say it, but there's a corpse on board, going to Ireland; and I never yet knew a voyage with a corpse on board that we didn't have bad weather."

"Why, steward, you're just superstitious! What nonsense!"

"That's a very ancient superstition," said Mr. Arcularis. "I've heard it many times. Maybe it's true. Maybe we'll be wrecked. And what does it matter, after all?" He was very bland.

"Then let's be wrecked," said the parson coldly.

Nevertheless, Mr. Arcularis felt a shudder go through him on hearing the steward's remark. A corpse in the hold—a coffin? Perhaps it was true. Perhaps some disaster would befall them. There might be fogs. There might be icebergs. He thought of all the wrecks of which he had read. There was the *Titanic*, which he had read about in the warm newspaper room at the Harvard Club—it had seemed dreadfully real, even there. That band, playing "Nearer My God to Thee" on the after-deck while the ship sank! It was one of the darkest of his memories. And the *Empress of Ireland*—all those poor people trapped in the smoking-room, with only one door between them and life, and that door locked for the night by the deck-steward, and the deck-steward nowhere to be found! He shivered, feeling a draft, and turned to the parson.

"How do these strange delusions arise?" he said.

The parson looked at him searchingly, appraisingly—from chin to forehead, from forehead to chin—and Mr. Arcularis, feeling uncomfortable, straightened his tie.

"From nothing but fear," said the parson. "Nothing on earth but fear."

"How strange!" said the girl.

Mr. Arcularis again looked at her—she had lowered her face—and again tried to think of whom she reminded him. It wasn't only the little freckle-faced girl at the hospital—both of them had reminded him of some one else. Some one far back in his life: remote, beautiful, lovely. But he couldn't think. The meal came to an end, they all rose, the ship's orchestra played a feeble fox-trot, and Mr. Arcularis, once more alone, went to the bar to have his whisky. The room was stuffy, and the ship's engines were both audible and palpable. The humming and

throbbing oppressed him, the rhythm seemed to be the rhythm of his own pain, and after a short time he found his way, with slow steps, holding on to the walls in his moments of weakness and dizziness, to his forlorn and white little room. The port had been—thank God!—closed for the night: it was cold enough anyway. The white and blue ribbons fluttered from the ventilator, the bottle and glasses clicked and clucked as the ship swayed gently to the long, slow motion of the sea. It was all very peculiar—it was all like something he had experienced somewhere before. What was it? Where was it? . . . He untied his tie, looking at his face in the glass, and wondered, and from time to time put his hand to his side to hold in the pain. It wasn't at Portsmouth, in his childhood, nor at Salem, nor in the rose-garden at his Aunt Julia's, nor in the schoolroom at Cambridge. It was something very queer, very intimate, very precious. The jackstones, the Sunday-school cards which he had loved when he was a child . . . He fell asleep.

The sense of time was already hopelessly confused. One hour was like another, the sea looked always the same, morning was indistinguishable from afternoon—and was it Tuesday or Wednesday? Mr. Arcularis was sitting in the smoking-room, in his favorite corner, watching the parson teach Miss Dean to play chess. On the deck outside he could see the people passing and repassing in their restless round of the ship. The red jacket went by, then the black hat with the white feather, then the purple scarf, the brown tweed coat, the Bulgarian mustache, the monocle, the Scotch cap with fluttering ribbons, and in no time at all the red jacket again, dipping past the windows with its own peculiar rhythm, followed once more by the black hat and the purple scarf. How odd to reflect on the fixed little orbits of these things—as definite and profound, perhaps, as the orbits of the stars, and as important to God or the Absolute. There was a kind of tyranny in this fixedness, too—to think of it too much made one uncomfortable. He closed his eyes for a moment, to avoid seeing for the fortieth time the Bulgarian mustache and the pursuing monocle. The parson was explaining the movements of knights. Two forward and one to the side. Eight possible moves, always to the opposite color from that on which the piece stands. Two forward and one to the side: Miss Dean repeated the words several times with reflective emphasis. Here, too, was the terrifying fixed curve of the infinite, the creeping curve of logic which at last must become the final signpost at the edge of nothing. After that—the deluge. The great white light of annihilation. The bright flash of death. . . . Was it merely the sea which made these abstractions so insistent, so intrusive? The mere notion of *orbit* had somehow become extraordinarily naked; and to rid himself of the discomfort and also to forget a little the pain which bothered his side whenever he sat down, he walked slowly and carefully into the writing-room, and examined a pile of superannuated magazines and catalogues of travel. The bright colors amused him, the photographs of remote islands and mountains, savages in sampans or sarongs or both—it was all very far off and delightful, like something in a dream or a fever. But he found that he was too tired to read and was incapable of concentration. Dreams! Yes, that reminded him. That rather alarming business—sleepwalking!

Later in the evening—at what hour he didn't know—he was telling Miss Dean about it, as he had intended to do. They were sitting in deckchairs on the sheltered side. The sea was black, and there was a cold wind. He wished they had chosen to sit in the lounge.

Miss Dean was extremely pretty—no, beautiful. She looked at him, too, in a very strange and lovely way, with something of inquiry, something of sympathy, something of affection. It seemed as if, between the question and the answer, they had sat thus for a very long time, exchanging an unspoken secret, simply looking at each other quietly and kindly. Had an hour or two passed? And was it at all necessary to speak?

"No," she said, "I never have."

She breathed into the low words a note of interrogation and gave him a slow smile.

"That's the funny part of it. I never had either until last night. Never in my life. I hardly ever even dream. And it really rather frightens me."

"Tell me about it, Mr. Arcularis."

"I dreamed at first that I was walking, alone, in a wide plain covered with snow. It was growing dark, I was very cold, my feet were frozen and numb, and I was lost. I came then to a signpost—at first it seemed to me there was nothing on it. Nothing but ice. Just before it grew finally dark, however, I made out on it the one word 'Polaris.' "

"The Pole Star."

"Yes—and you see, I didn't myself know that. I looked it up only this morning. I suppose I must have seen it somewhere? And of course it rhymes with my name."

"Why, so it does!"

"Anyway, it gave me—in the dream—an awful feeling of despair, and the dream changed. This time, I dreamed I was standing *outside* my state-room in the little dark corridor, or *cul-de-sac,* and trying to find the door-handle to let myself in. I was in my pajamas, and again I was very cold. And at this point I woke up. . . . The extraordinary thing is that's exactly where I was!"

"Good heavens. How strange!"

"Yes. And now the question is, *where had I been?* I was frightened, when I came to—not unnaturally. For among other things I *did* have, quite definitely, the feeling that I *had been* somewhere. Somewhere where it was very cold. It doesn't sound very proper. Suppose I had been seen!"

"That might have been awkward," said Miss Dean.

"Awkward! It might indeed. It's very singular. I've never done such a thing before. It's this sort of thing that reminds one—rather wholesomely, perhaps, don't you think?"—and Mr. Arcularis gave a nervous little laugh—"how extraordinarily little we know about the workings of our own minds or souls. After all, what *do* we know?"

"Nothing—nothing—nothing—nothing," said Miss Dean slowly.

"*Absolutely* nothing."

Their voices had dropped, and again they were silent; and again they looked at each other gently and sympathetically, as if for the exchange of something unspoken and perhaps unspeakable. Time ceased. The orbit—so it seemed to Mr. Arcularis—once more became pure, became absolute. And once more he found himself wondering who it was that Miss Dean—Clarice Dean—reminded him of. Long ago and far away. Like those pictures of the islands and mountains. The little freckle-faced girl at the hospital was merely, as it were, the stepping-stone, the signpost, or, as in algebra, the "equals" sign. But what was it they both "equaled"? The jackstones came again into his mind and his Aunt Julia's rose-garden—at sunset; but this was ridiculous. It couldn't be simply that they reminded him of his childhood! And yet why not?

They went into the lounge. The ship's orchestra, in the oval-shaped balcony among faded palms, was playing the finale of "Cavalleria Rusticana," playing it badly.

"Good God!" said Mr. Arcularis, "can't I ever escape from that damned sentimental tune? It's the last thing I heard in America, and the last thing I *want* to hear."

"But don't you like it?"

"As music? No! It moves me too much, but in the wrong way."

"What, exactly, do you mean?"

"Exactly? Nothing. When I heard it at the hospital—when was it?—it made me feel like crying. Three old Italians tooting it in the rain. I suppose, like most people, I'm afraid of my feelings."

"Are they so dangerous?"

"Now then, young woman! Are you pulling my leg?"

The stewards had rolled away the carpets, and the passengers were beginning to dance. Miss Dean accepted the invitation of a young officer, and Mr. Arcularis watched them with envy. Odd, that last exchange of remarks—very odd; in fact, everything was odd. Was it possible that they were falling in love? Was that what it was all about—all these concealed references and recollections? He had read of such things. But at his age! And with a girl of twenty-two! It was ridiculous.

After an amused look at his old friend Polaris from the open door on the sheltered side, he went to bed.

The rhythm of the ship's engines was positively a persecution. It gave one no rest, it followed one like the Hound of Heaven, it drove one out into space and across the Milky Way and then back home by way of Betelgeuse. It was cold there, too. Mr. Arcularis, making the round trip by way of Betelgeuse and Polaris, sparkled with frost. He felt like a Christmas tree. Icicles on his fingers and icicles on his toes. He tinkled and spangled in the void, hallooed to the waste echoes, rounded the buoy on the verge of the Unknown, and tacked glitteringly homeward. The wind whistled. He was barefooted. Snowflakes and tinsel blew past him. Next time, by George, he would go farther still—for altogether it was rather a lark. Forward into the untrodden! as somebody said. Some intrepid explorer of his own backyard, probably, some middle-aged professor with an umbrella: those were the fellows for courage! But give us time, thought Mr. Arcularis, give us time, and we will bring back with us the night-rime of the Obsolute. Or was it Absolute? If only there weren't this perpetual throbbing, this iteration of sound, like a pain, these circles and repetitions of light—the feeling as of everything coiling inward to a centre of misery . . .

Suddenly it was dark, and he was lost. He was groping, he touched the cold, white, slippery woodwork with his fingernails, looking for an electric switch. The throbbing, of course, was the throbbing of the ship. But he was almost home—almost home. Another corner to round, a door to be opened, and there he would be. Safe and sound. Safe in his father's home.

It was at this point that he woke up: in the corridor that led to the dining saloon. Such pure terror, such horror, seized him as he had never known. His heart felt as if it would stop beating. His back was toward the dining saloon; apparently he had just come from it. He was in his pajamas. The corridor was dim, all but two lights having been turned out for the night, and—thank God!—deserted. Not a soul, not a sound. He was perhaps fifty yards from his room. With luck he could get to it unseen. Holding tremulously to the rail that ran along the wall, a brown, greasy rail, he began to creep his way forward. He felt very weak, very dizzy, and his thoughts refused to concentrate. Vaguely he remembered Miss Dean—Clarice—and the freckled girl, as if they were one and the same person. But he wasn't in the hospital, he was on the ship. Of course. How absurd. The Great Circle. Here we are, old fellow . . . steady round the corner . . . hold hard to your umbrella . . .

In his room, with the door safely shut behind him, Mr. Arcularis broke into a cold sweat. He had no sooner got into his bunk, shivering, than he heard the night watchman pass.

"But where—" he thought, closing his eyes in agony—"have I been? . . ."

A dreadful idea had occurred to him.

"It's nothing serious—how could it be anything serious? Of course it's nothing serious," said Mr. Arcularis.

"No, it's nothing serious," said the ship's doctor urbanely.

"I knew you'd think so. But just the same——"

"Such a condition is the result of worry," said the doctor. "Are you worried—do you mind telling me—about something? Just try to think."

"Worried?"

Mr. Arcularis knitted his brows. *Was* there something? Some little mosquito of a cloud disappearing into the southwest, the northeast? Some little gnat-song of despair? But no, that was all over. All over.

"Nothing," he said, "nothing whatever."

"It's very strange," said the doctor.

"Strange! I should say so. I've come to sea for a rest, not for a nightmare! What about a bromide?"

"Well, I can give you a bromide, Mr. Arcularis——"

"Then, please, if you don't mind, give me a bromide."

He carried the little phial hopefully to his state-room, and took a dose at once. He could see the sun through his porthole. It looked northern and pale and small, like a little peppermint, which was only natural enough, for the latitude was changing with every hour. But why was it that doctors were all alike? and all, for that matter, like his father, or that other fellow at the hospital? Smythe, his name was. Doctor Smythe. A nice, dry little fellow, and they said he was a writer. Wrote poetry, or something like that. Poor fellow—disappointed. Like everybody else. Crouched in there, in his cabin, night after night, writing blank verse or something—all about the stars and flowers and love and death; ice and the sea and the infinite; time and tide—well, every man to his own taste.

"But it's nothing serious," said Mr. Arcularis, later, to the parson. "How could it be?"

"Why, of course not, my dear fellow," said the parson, patting his back. "How could it be?"

"I know it isn't and yet I worry about it."

"It would be ridiculous to think it serious," said the parson.

Mr. Arcularis shivered: it was colder than ever. It was said that they were near icebergs. For a few hours in the morning there had been a fog, and the siren had blown—devastatingly—at three-minute intervals. Icebergs caused fog—he knew that.

"These things always come," said the parson, "from a sense of guilt. You feel guilty about something. I won't be so rude as to inquire what it is. But if you could rid yourself of the sense of guilt——"

And later still, when the sky was pink:

"But is it anything to worry about?" said Miss Dean. "Really?"

"No, I suppose not."

"Then don't worry. We aren't children any longer!"

"Aren't we? I wonder!"

They leaned, shoulders touching, on the deck-rail, and looked at the sea, which was multitudinously incarnadined. Mr. Arcularis scanned the horizon in vain for an iceberg.

"Anyway," he said, "the colder we are the less we feel!"

"I hope that's no reflection on *you*," said Miss Dean.

"Here . . . feel my hand," said Mr. Arcularis.

"Heaven knows it's cold!"

"It's been to Polaris and back! No wonder."

"Poor thing, poor thing!"

"Warm it."

"May I?"

"You can."

"I'll try."

Laughing, she took his hand between both of hers, one palm under and one palm over, and began rubbing it briskly. The decks were deserted, no one was near them, every one was dressing for dinner. The sea grew darker, the wind blew colder.

"I wish I could remember who you are," he said.

"And you—who are you?"

"Myself."

"Then perhaps *I* am yourself."

"Don't be metaphysical!"

"But I *am* metaphysical!"

She laughed, withdrew, pulled the light coat about her shoulders.

The bugle blew the summons for dinner—"The Roast Beef of Old England"—and they walked together along the darkening deck toward the door, from which a shaft of soft light fell across the deck-rail. As they stepped over the brass door-sill Mr. Arcularis felt the throb of the engines again; he put his hand quickly to his side.

"*Auf wiedersehen,*" he said. "*To-morrow and to-morrow and to-morrow.*"

Mr. Arcularis was finding it impossible, absolutely impossible, to keep warm. A cold fog surrounded the ship, had done so, it seemed, for days. The sun had all but disappeared, the transition from day to night was almost unnoticeable. The ship, too, seemed scarcely to be moving—it was as if anchored among walls of ice and rime. Monstrous, that merely because it was June, and supposed, therefore, to be warm, the ship's authorities should consider it unnecessary to turn on the heat! By day, he wore his heavy coat and sat shivering in the corner of the smoking-room. His teeth chattered, his hands were blue. By night, he heaped blankets on his bed, closed the porthole's black eye against the sea, and drew the yellow curtains across it, but in vain. Somehow, despite everything, the fog crept in, and the icy fingers touched his throat. The steward, questioned about it, merely said, "Icebergs." Of course—any fool knew that. But how long, in God's name, was it going to last? They surely ought to be past the Grand Banks by this time! And surely it wasn't necessary to sail to England by way of Greenland and Iceland!

Miss Dean—Clarice—was sympathetic.

"It's simply because," she said, "your vitality has been lowered by your illness. You can't expect to be your normal self so soon after an operation! When *was* your operation, by the way?"

Mr. Arcularis considered. Strange—he couldn't be quite sure. It was all a little vague—his sense of time had disappeared.

"Heavens knows!" he said. "Centuries ago. When I was a tadpole and you were a fish. I should think it must have been at about the time of the Battle of Teutoburg Forest. Or perhaps when I was a Neanderthal man with a club!"

"Are you sure it wasn't farther back still?"

What did she mean by that?

"Not at all. Obviously, we've been on this damned ship for ages—for eras—for æons. And even on this ship, you must remember, I've had plenty of time, in my nocturnal wanderings, to go several times to Orion and back. I'm thinking, by the way, of going farther still. There's a nice little star off to the left, as you round Betelgeuse, which looks as if it might be right at the edge. The last outpost of the finite. I think I'll have a look at it and bring you back a frozen rime-feather."

"It would melt when you got it back."

"Oh, no, it wouldn't—not on *this* ship!"

Clarice laughed.

"I wish I could go with you," she said.

"If only you would! If only——"

He broke off his sentence and looked hard at her—how lovely she was, and how desirable! No such woman had ever before come into his life; there had been no one with whom he had at once felt so profound a sympathy and understanding. It was a miracle, simply—a miracle. No need to put his arm around her or to kiss her—delightful as such small vulgarities would be. He had only to look at her, and to feel, gazing into those extraordinary eyes, that she knew him, had always known him. It was as if, indeed, she might be his own soul.

But as he looked thus at her, reflecting, he noticed that she was frowning.

"What is it?" he said.

She shook her head, slowly.

"I don't know."

"Tell me."

"Nothing. It just occurred to me that perhaps you weren't looking quite so well."

Mr. Arcularis was startled. He straightened himself up.

"What nonsense! Of course this pain bothers me—and I feel astonishingly weak——"

"It's more than that—much more than that. Something is worrying you horribly." She paused, and then with an air of challenging him, added, "Tell me, did you——"

Her eyes were suddenly asking him blazingly the question he had been afraid of. He flinched, caught his breath, looked away. But it was no use, as he knew: he would have to tell her. He had known all along that he would have to tell her.

"Clarice," he said—and his voice broke in spite of his effort to control it—"It's killing me, it's ghastly! Yes, I did."

His eyes filled with tears, he saw that her own had done so also. She put her hand on his arm.

"I knew," she said. "I knew. But tell me."

"It's happened twice again—*twice*—and each time I was farther away. The same dream of going round a star, the same terrible coldness and helplessness. That awful whistling curve . . ." He shuddered.

"And when you woke up—" she spoke quietly—"where were you when you woke up? Don't be afraid!"

"The first time I was at the farther end of the dining saloon. I had my hand on the door that leads into the pantry."

"I see. Yes. And the next time?"

Mr. Arcularis wanted to close his eyes in terror—he felt as if he were going mad. His lips moved before he could speak, and when at last he did speak it was in a voice so low as to be almost a whisper.

"I was at the bottom of the stairway that leads down from the pantry to the hold, past the refrigerating-plant. It was dark, and I was crawling on my hands and knees . . . *Crawling on my hands and knees! . . .*"

"Oh!" she said, and again, "Oh!"

He began to tremble violently; he felt the hand on his arm trembling also. And then he watched a look of unmistakable horror come slowly into Clarice's eyes, and a look of understanding, as if she saw . . . She tightened her hold on his arm.

"Do you think . . ." she whispered.

They stared at each other.

"I know," he said. "And so do you . . . Twice more—three times—and I'll be looking down into an empty . . ."

It was then that they first embraced—then, at the edge of the infinite, at the last signpost of the finite. They clung together desperately, forlornly, weeping as they kissed each other, staring hard one moment and closing their eyes the next. Passionately, passionately, she kissed him, as if she were indeed trying to give him her warmth, her life.

"But what nonsense!" she cried, leaning back, and holding his face between her hands, her hands which were wet with his tears. "What nonsense! It can't be!"

"It is," said Mr. Arcularis slowly.

"But how do you know? . . . How do you know where the——"

For the first time Mr. Arcularis smiled.

"Don't be afraid, darling—you mean the coffin?"

"How could you know where it is?"

"I don't need to," said Mr. Arcularis . . . "I'm already almost there."

Before they separated for the night, in the smoking-room, they had several whisky cocktails.

"We must make it gay!" Mr. Arcularis said. "Above all, we must make it gay. Perhaps even now it will turn out to be nothing but a nightmare from which both of us will wake! And even at the worst, at my present rate of travel, I ought to need two more nights! It's a long way, still, to that little star."

The parson passed them at the door.

"What! turning in so soon?" he said. "I was hoping for a game of chess."

"Yes, both turning in. But to-morrow?"

"To-morrow, then, Miss Dean! And good night!"

"Good night."

They walked once round the deck, then leaned on the railing and stared into the fog. It was thicker and whiter than ever. The ship was moving barely perceptibly, the rhythm of the engines was slower, more subdued and remote, and at regular intervals, mournfully, came the long reverberating cry of the foghorn. The sea was calm, and lapped only very tenderly against the side of the ship, the sound coming up to them clearly, however, because of the profound stillness.

"'On such a night as this—'" quoted Mr. Arcularis grimly.

"'On such a night as this——'"

Their voices hung suspended in the night, time ceased for them, for an eternal instant they were happy. When at last they parted it was by tacit agreement on a note of the ridiculous.

"Be a good boy and take your bromide!" she said.

"Yes, mother, I'll take my medicine!"

In his state-room, he mixed himself a strong potion of bromide, a very strong one, and got into bed. He would have no trouble in falling asleep: he felt more tired, more supremely exhausted, than he had ever been in his life; nor had bed ever seemed so delicious. And that long, magnificent, delirious swoop of dizziness . . . the Great Circle . . . the swift pathway to Arcturus . . .

It was all as before, but infinitely more rapid. Never had Mr. Arcularis achieved such phenomenal, such supernatural, speed. In no time at all he was beyond the moon, shot past the North Star as if it were standing still (which perhaps it was?), swooped in a long, bright curve round the Pleiades, shouted his frosty greetings to Betelgeuse, and was off to the little blue star which pointed the way to the Unknown. Forward into the untrodden! Courage, old man, and hold on to your umbrella! Have you got your garters on? Mind your hat! In no time at all we'll be back to Clarice with the frozen rime-feather, the rime-feather, the snowflake of the Absolute, the Obsolete. If only we don't wake . . . if only we needn't wake . . . if only we don't wake in that—in that—time and space . . . somewhere or nowhere . . . cold and dark . . . "Cavalleria Rusticana" sobbing among the palms; if a lonely . . . if only . . . the coffers of the poor—

not coffers, not coffers, not coffers, Oh, God, not coffers, but light, delight, supreme white and brightness, whirling lightness above all— and freezing—freezing—freezing . . .

At this point in the void the surgeon's last effort to save Mr. Arcularis's life had failed. He stood back from the operating table and made a tired gesture with a rubber-gloved hand.

"It's all over," he said. "As I expected."

He looked at Miss Hoyle, whose gaze was downward, at the basin she held. There was a moment's stillness, a pause, a brief flight of un-exchanged comment, and then the ordered life of the hospital was resumed.

AUGUST HEAT

William Fryer Harvey

POOR HEALTH PRETTY MUCH ruined the medical career of William Fryer Harvey (1885–1937) but it did give him the opportunity to become the writer of some of the most inventive horror stories of all time. Born into a very wealthy Quaker family in Yorkshire, he attended Balliol College at Oxford University, then received his medical degree from Leeds University. His frail condition sent him on a worldwide cruise and, on a stopover of several months in Australia, he began to write his first fiction pieces. Being a devotee of the works of Edgar Allan Poe clearly influenced his prose, which had similar overtones of dread. When England was drawn into World War I, Harvey joined a Friends' Ambulance unit and served as a surgeon-lieutenant in the Royal Navy. While heroically performing surgery in the boiler room of a destroyer as it was sinking, the fumes from burning oil damaged his lungs, earning Harvey the Albert Medal for Lifesaving and a lifelong debilitating lung condition, eventually costing him his life at the age of fifty-two. Oddly, despite his horrific stories, Harvey had the reputation of being an exceptionally kind, gentle, and jovial man, much loved by all who knew him.

His stories never enjoyed great success until he was "discovered" when *The Beast with Five Fingers* was filmed in 1946 with Robert Florey directing and Peter Lorre starring, inducing publishers on both sides of the Atlantic to collect the best of his horror fiction. "August Heat" served as the basis for an episode of a television series on three occasions: as episode one in the first season of *Danger,* airing on September 26, 1950; on *On Camera,* January 8, 1955, starring Patrick Macnee; and on *Great Ghost Tales,* August 3, 1961, starring James Broderick and Vincent Gardenia.

"August Heat" was first published in *Midnight House and Other Tales* (London, J. M. Dent, 1910).

August Heat

WILLIAM FRYER HARVEY

Phenistone Road, Clapham,

August 20th, 19—.

I HAVE HAD WHAT I believe to be the most remarkable day in my life, and while the events are still fresh in my mind, I wish to put them down on paper as clearly as possible.

Let me say at the outset that my name is James Clarence Withencroft.

I am forty years old, in perfect health, never having known a day's illness.

By profession I am an artist, not a very successful one, but I earn enough money by my black-and-white work to satisfy my necessary wants.

My only near relative, a sister, died five years ago, so that I am independent.

I breakfasted this morning at nine, and after glancing through the morning paper I lighted my pipe and proceeded to let my mind wander in the hope that I might chance upon some subject for my pencil.

The room, though door and windows were open, was oppressively hot, and I had just made up my mind that the coolest and most comfortable place in the neighbourhood would be the deep end of the public swimming bath, when the idea came.

I began to draw. So intent was I on my work that I left my lunch untouched, only stopping work when the clock of St. Jude's struck four.

The final result, for a hurried sketch, was, I felt sure, the best thing I had done.

It showed a criminal in the dock immediately after the judge had pronounced sentence. The man was fat—enormously fat. The flesh hung in rolls about his chin; it creased his huge, stumpy neck. He was clean shaven (perhaps I should say a few days before he must have been clean shaven) and almost bald. He stood in the dock, his short, clumsy fingers clasping the rail, looking straight in front of him. The feeling that his expression conveyed was not so much one of horror as of utter, absolute collapse.

There seemed nothing in the man strong enough to sustain that mountain of flesh.

I rolled up the sketch, and without quite knowing why, placed it in my pocket. Then with the rare sense of happiness which the knowledge of a good thing well done gives, I left the house.

I believe that I set out with the idea of calling upon Trenton, for I remember walking along Lytton Street and turning to the right along Gilchrist Road at the bottom of the hill where the men were at work on the new tram lines.

From there onwards I have only the vaguest recollection of where I went. The one thing of which I was fully conscious was the awful heat, that came up from the dusty asphalt pavement as an almost palpable wave. I longed for the thunder promised by the great banks of copper-coloured cloud that hung low over the western sky.

I must have walked five or six miles, when a small boy roused me from my reverie by asking the time.

It was twenty minutes to seven.

When he left me I began to take stock of my bearings. I found myself standing before a gate that led into a yard bordered by a strip of thirsty earth, where there were flowers, purple stock and scarlet geranium. Above the entrance was a board with the inscription—

CHAS. ATKINSON
MONUMENTAL MASON
WORKER IN ENGLISH AND ITALIAN MARBLES

From the yard itself came a cheery whistle, the noise of hammer blows, and the cold sound of steel meeting stone.

A sudden impulse made me enter.

A man was sitting with his back towards me, busy at work on a slab of curiously veined marble. He turned round as he heard my steps and I stopped short.

It was the man I had been drawing, whose portrait lay in my pocket.

He sat there, huge and elephantine, the sweat pouring from his scalp, which he wiped with a red silk handkerchief. But though the face was the same, the expression was absolutely different.

He greeted me smiling, as if we were old friends, and shook my hand.

I apologised for my intrusion.

"Everything is hot and glary outside," I said. "This seems an oasis in the wilderness."

"I don't know about the oasis," he replied, "but it certainly's hot, as hot as hell. Take a seat, sir!"

He pointed to the end of the gravestone on which he was at work, and I sat down.

"That's a beautiful piece of stone you've got hold of," I said.

He shook his head. "In a way it is," he answered; "the surface here is as fine as anything you could wish, but there's a big flaw at the back, though I don't expect you'd ever notice it. I could never make really a good job of a bit of marble like that. It would be all right in the summer like this; it wouldn't mind the blasted heat. But wait till the winter comes. There's nothing quite like frost to find out the weak points in stone."

"Then what's it for?" I asked.

The man burst out laughing.

"You'd hardly believe me if I was to tell you it's for an exhibition, but it's the truth. Artists have exhibitions: so do grocers and butchers; we have them too. All the latest little things in headstones, you know."

He went on to talk of marbles, which sort best withstood wind and rain, and which were easiest to work; then of his garden and a new sort of carnation he had bought. At the end of every other minute he would drop his tools, wipe his shining head, and curse the heat.

I said little, for I felt uneasy. There was something unnatural, uncanny, in meeting this man.

I tried at first to persuade myself that I had seen him before, that his face, unknown to me, had found a place in some out-of-the-way corner of my memory, but I knew that I was practising little more than a plausible piece of self-deception.

Mr. Atkinson finished his work, spat on the ground, and got up with a sigh of relief.

"There! what do you think of that?" he said, with an air of evident pride.

The inscription which I read for the first time was this—

SACRED TO THE MEMORY
OF
JAMES CLARENCE WITHENCROFT
BORN JAN. 18TH, 1860
HE PASSED AWAY VERY SUDDENLY
ON AUGUST 20TH, 19——

"In the midst of life we are in death."

For some time I sat in silence. Then a cold shudder ran down my spine. I asked him where he had seen the name.

"Oh, I didn't see it anywhere," replied Mr. Atkinson. "I wanted some name, and I put down the first that came into my head. Why do you want to know?"

"It's a strange coincidence, but it happens to be mine."

He gave a long, low whistle.

"And the dates?"

"I can only answer for one of them, and that's correct."

"It's a rum go!" he said.

But he knew less than I did. I told him of my morning's work. I took the sketch from my pocket and showed it to him. As he looked, the expression of his face altered until it became more and more like that of the man I had drawn.

"And it was only the day before yesterday," he said, "that I told Maria there were no such things as ghosts!"

Neither of us had seen a ghost, but I knew what he meant.

"You probably heard my name," I said.

"And you must have seen me somewhere and have forgotten it! Were you at Clacton-on-Sea last July?"

I had never been to Clacton in my life. We were silent for some time. We were both looking at the same thing, the two dates on the gravestone, and one was right.

"Come inside and have some supper," said Mr. Atkinson.

His wife is a cheerful little woman, with the flaky red cheeks of the country-bred. Her husband introduced me as a friend of his who was an artist. The result was unfortunate, for after the sardines and watercress had been removed, she brought out a Doré Bible, and I had to sit and express my admiration for nearly half an hour.

I went outside, and found Atkinson sitting on the gravestone smoking.

We resumed the conversation at the point we had left off.

"You must excuse my asking," I said, "but do you know of anything you've done for which you could be put on trial?"

He shook his head.

"I'm not a bankrupt, the business is prosperous enough. Three years ago I gave turkeys to some of the guardians at Christmas, but that's all I can think of. And they were small ones, too," he added as an afterthought.

He got up, fetched a can from the porch, and began to water the flowers. "Twice a day regular in the hot weather," he said, "and then the heat sometimes gets the better of the delicate ones. And ferns, good Lord! they could never stand it. Where do you live?"

I told him my address. It would take an hour's quick walk to get back home.

"It's like this," he said. "We'll look at the matter straight. If you go back home tonight, you take your chance of accidents. A cart may run over you, and there's always banana skins and orange peel, to say nothing of fallen ladders."

He spoke of the improbable with an intense seriousness that would have been laughable six hours before. But I did not laugh.

"The best thing we can do," he continued, "is for you to stay here till twelve o'clock. We'll go upstairs and smoke; it may be cooler inside."

To my surprise I agreed.

We are sitting now in a long, low room beneath the eaves. Atkinson has sent his wife to bed. He himself is busy sharpening some tools at a little oilstone, smoking one of my cigars the while.

The air seems charged with thunder. I am writing this at a shaky table before the open window. The leg is cracked, and Atkinson, who seems a handy man with his tools, is going to mend it as soon as he has finished putting an edge on his chisel.

It is after eleven now. I shall be gone in less than an hour.

But the heat is stifling.

It is enough to send a man mad.

I'LL LOVE YOU—FOREVER (OR MAYBE NOT)

THE SHADOWY THIRD AND THE PAST

Ellen Glasgow

THERE IS SUCH A strong sense of realism in the work of the noted Southern writer Ellen (Anderson Gholson) Glasgow (1873–1945) that it takes a little while to accept the notion that a story does, actually, have supernatural elements. Her portrayal of Southern life within its aristocracy and lower social levels had a particular emphasis on the relationship between Southern women and the men in their lives. She won accolades in the 1920s and 1930s as one of the enduring leaders of the literary renaissance of the South. In 1940 she was awarded the Howells Medal for Fiction by the American Academy of Arts and Letters and her 1941 novel, *In This Our Life,* won the Pulitzer Prize for fiction. She did not make many forays into supernatural fiction, but her sophisticated ghost stories have been frequently anthologized and were collected in *The Shadowy Third and Other Stories* (1923).

Born in Richmond, Virginia, Glasgow was a rather frail child and dropped out of school at the age of nine, teaching herself by reading from her father's substantial library. She lived briefly in New York where she began and then maintained a lengthy, long-distance affair with a married man (as recounted in her autobiography, *The Woman Within,* published posthumously in 1954), but soon returned to her birthplace where she continued to live and write, very much in solitude, in an old gray stone house in the middle of the city.

"The Shadowy Third" was first published in the December 1916 issue of *Scribner's Magazine.* "The Past" was first published in the October 1920 issue of *Good Housekeeping.* Both were collected in the author's *The Shadowy Third and Other Stories* (New York, Doubleday, Page, 1923).

23

The Shadowy Third

ELLEN GLASGOW

WHEN THE CALL CAME I remember that I turned from the telephone in a romantic flutter. Though I had spoken only once to the great surgeon, Roland Maradick, I felt on that December afternoon that to speak to him only once—to watch him in the operating-room for a single hour—was an adventure which drained the color and the excitement from the rest of life. After all these years of work on typhoid and pneumonia cases, I can still feel the delicious tremor of my young pulses; I can still see the

winter sunshine slanting through the hospital windows over the white uniforms of the nurses.

"He didn't mention me by name. Can there be a mistake?" I stood, incredulous yet ecstatic, before the superintendent of the hospital.

"No, there isn't a mistake. I was talking to him before you came down." Miss Hemphill's strong face softened while she looked at me. She was a big, resolute woman, a distant Canadian relative of my mother's, and the kind of nurse, I had discovered in the month since I had come up from Richmond, that Northern hospital boards, if not Northern patients, appear instinctively to select. From the first, in spite of her hardness, she had taken a liking—I hesitate to use the word "fancy" for a preference so impersonal—to her Virginia cousin. After all, it isn't every Southern nurse, just out of training, who can boast a kinswoman in the superintendent of a New York hospital. If experience was what I needed, Miss Hemphill, I judged, was abundantly prepared to supply it.

"And he made you understand positively that he meant me?" The thing was so wonderful that I simply couldn't believe it.

"He asked particularly for the nurse who was with Miss Hudson last week when he operated. I think he didn't even remember that you had a name—this isn't the South, you know, where people still regard nurses as human, not as automata. When I asked if he meant Miss Randolph, he repeated that he wanted the nurse who had been with Miss Hudson. She was small, he said, and cheerful-looking. This, of course, might apply to one or two others, but none of these was with Miss Hudson. Miss Maupin, the only nurse, except you, who went near her, is large and heavy."

"Then I suppose it is really true?" My pulses were tingling. "And I am to be there at six o'clock?"

"Not a minute later. The day nurse goes off duty at that hour, and Mrs. Maradick is never left by herself for an instant."

"It is her mind, isn't it? And that makes it all the stranger that he should select me, for I have had so few mental cases."

"So few cases of any kind." Miss Hemphill was smiling, and when she smiled I wondered if the other nurses would know her. "By the time you have gone through the treadmill in New York, Margaret, you will have lost a good many things besides your inexperience. I wonder how long you will keep your sympathy and your imagination? After all, wouldn't you have made a better novelist than a nurse?"

"I can't help putting myself into my cases. I suppose one ought not to?"

"It isn't a question of what one ought to do, but of what one must. When you are drained of every bit of sympathy and enthusiasm and have got nothing in return for it, not even thanks, you will understand why I try to keep you from wasting yourself."

"But surely in a case like this—for Doctor Maradick?"

"Oh, well, of course—for Doctor Maradick?" She must have seen that I implored her confidence, for, after a minute, she let fall almost carelessly a gleam of light on the situation. "It is a very sad case when you think what a charming man and a great surgeon Doctor Maradick is."

Above the starched collar of my uniform I felt the blood leap in bounds to my cheeks. "I have spoken to him only once," I murmured, "but he is charming, and, oh, so kind and handsome, isn't he?"

"His patients adore him."

"Oh, yes, I've seen that. Every one hangs on his visits." Like the patients and the other nurses, I, also, had come by delightful, if imperceptible, degrees to hang on the daily visits of Doctor Maradick. He was, I suppose, born to be a hero to women. Fate had selected him for the rôle, and it would have been sheer impertinence for a mortal to cross wills with the invisible Powers. From my first day in his hospital, from the moment when I watched, through closed shutters, while he stepped out of his car, I have never doubted that he was assigned to the great part in the play. If I had been ignorant of his spell— of the charm he exercised over his hospital—I should have felt it in the waiting hush, like a drawn breath, which followed his ring at the door and preceded his imperious footstep on the stairs. My first impression of him, even after the terrible events of the next year, records a memory that is both careless and splendid. At that moment, when, gazing through the chinks in the shutters, I watched him, in his coat of dark fur, cross the pavement over the pale streaks of sunshine, I knew beyond any doubt—I knew with a sort of infallible prescience—that my fate was irretrievably bound with his in the future.

I knew this, I repeat, though Miss Hemphill would still insist that my foreknowledge was merely a sentimental gleaning from indiscriminate novels. But it wasn't only first love, impressionable as my kinswoman believed me to be. It wasn't only the way he looked, handsome as he was. Even more than his appearance—more than the shining dark of his eyes, the silvery brown of his hair, the dusky glow in his face— even more than his charm and his magnificence, I think, the beauty and sympathy in his voice won my heart. It was a voice, I heard some one say afterward, that ought always to speak poetry.

So you will see why—if you do not understand at the beginning, I can never hope to make you believe impossible things!—so you will see why I accepted the call when it came as an imperative summons. I couldn't have stayed away after he sent for me. However much I may have tried not to go, I know that in the end I must have gone. In those days, while I was still hoping to write novels, I used to talk a great deal about "destiny" (I have learned since then how silly all such talk is), and I suppose it was my "destiny" to be caught in the web of Roland Maradick's personality. But I am not the first nurse to grow love-sick about a doctor who never gave her a thought.

"I am glad you got the call, Margaret. It may mean a great deal to you. Only try not to be too emotional about it." I remember that Miss Hemphill was holding a bit of rose-geranium in her hand while she spoke—one of the patients had given it to her from a pot she kept in her room, and the scent of the flower is still in my nostrils—or my memory. Since then—oh, long since then—I have wondered if she also had been caught in the web.

"I wish I knew more about the case." I was clearly pressing for light. "Have you ever seen Mrs. Maradick?"

"Oh, dear, yes. They have been married only a little over a year, and in the beginning she used to come sometimes to the hospital and wait outside while the doctor made his visits. She was a very sweet-looking woman then—not exactly pretty, but fair and slight, with the loveliest smile, I think, I have ever seen. In those first months she was so much in love that we used to laugh about it among ourselves. To see her face light up when the doctor came out of the hospital and crossed the pavement to his car, was as good as a play. We never got tired watching her—I wasn't superintendent then, so I had more time to look out of the window while I was on day duty. Once or twice she brought her little girl in to see one of the patients. The child was so much like her that you would have known them anywhere for mother and daughter."

I had heard that Mrs. Maradick was a widow, with one child, when she first met the doctor, and I asked now, still seeking an illumination I had not found: "There was a great deal of money, wasn't there?"

"A great fortune. If she hadn't been so attractive, people would have said, I suppose, that Doctor Maradick married her for her money. Only," she appeared to make an effort of memory, "I believe I've heard somehow that it was all left in trust away from Mrs. Maradick if she married again. I can't, to save my life, remember just how it was; but it was a queer will, I know, and Mrs. Maradick wasn't to come into the money unless the child didn't live to grow up. The pity of it—"

A young nurse came into the office to ask for something—the keys, I think, of the operating-room, and Miss Hemphill broke off inconclusively as she hurried out of the door. I was sorry that she left off just when she did. Poor Mrs. Maradick! Perhaps I was too emotional, but even before I saw her I had begun to feel her pathos and her strangeness.

My preparations took only a few minutes. In those days I always kept a suit-case packed and ready for sudden calls; and it was not yet six o'clock when I turned from 10th Street into Fifth Avenue, and stopped for a minute, before ascending the steps, to look at the house in which Doctor Maradick lived. A fine rain was falling, and I remember thinking, as I turned the corner, how depressing the weather must be for Mrs. Maradick. It was an old house, with damp-looking walls (though that may have been because of the rain) and a spindle-shaped iron railing which ran up the stone steps to the black door, where I noticed a dim flicker through the old-fashioned fan-light. Afterward I discovered that Mrs. Maradick had been born in the house—her maiden name was Calloran—and that she had never wanted to live anywhere else. She was a woman—this I found out when I knew her better—of strong attachments to both persons and places; and though Doctor Maradick had tried to persuade her to move up-town after her marriage, she had clung, against his wishes, to the old house in lower Fifth Avenue. I dare say she was obstinate about it in spite of her gentleness and her passion for the doctor. Those sweet, soft women, especially when they have always been rich, are sometimes amazingly obstinate. I have nursed so many of them since—women with strong affections and weak intellects—that I have come to recognize the type as soon as I set eyes upon it.

My ring at the bell was answered after a little delay, and when I entered the house I saw that the hall was quite dark except for the waning glow from an open fire which burned in the library. When I gave my name, and added that I was the night nurse, the servant appeared to think my humble presence unworthy of illumination. He was an old negro butler, inherited perhaps from Mrs. Maradick's mother, who, I learned afterward, had been from South Carolina; and while he passed me on his way up the staircase, I heard him vaguely muttering that he "wan't gwinter tu'n on dem lights twel de chile had done playin'."

To the right of the hall, the soft glow drew me into the library, and crossing the threshold timidly I stooped to dry my wet coat by the fire. As I bent there, meaning to start up at the first sound of a footstep, I thought how cosy the room was after the damp walls outside to which some bared creepers were clinging; and I was watching pleasantly the strange shapes and patterns the firelight made on the old Persian rug, when

the lamps of a slowly turning motor flashed on me through the white shades at the window. Still dazzled by the glare, I looked round in the dimness and saw a child's ball of red and blue rubber roll toward me out of the gloom of one of the adjoining rooms. A moment later, while I made a vain attempt to capture the toy as it spun past me, a little girl darted airily, with peculiar lightness and grace, through the door-way, and stopped quickly, as if in surprise at the sight of a stranger. She was a small child—so small and slight that her footsteps made no sound on the polished floor of the threshold; and I remember thinking while I looked at her that she had the gravest and sweetest face I had ever seen. She couldn't—I decided this afterward—have been more than six or seven, yet she stood there with a curious prim dignity, like the dignity of a very old person, and gazed up at me with enigmatical eyes. She was dressed in Scotch plaid, with a bit of red ribbon in her hair, which was cut in a fringe over her forehead and hung very straight to her shoulders. Charming as she was, from her uncurled brown hair to the white socks and black slippers on her little feet, I recall most vividly the singular look in her eyes, which appeared in the shifting light to be of an indeterminate color. For the odd thing about this look was that it was not the look of childhood at all. It was the look of profound experience, of bitter knowledge.

"Have you come for your ball?" I asked; but while the friendly question was still on my lips, I heard the servant returning. Even in my haste I made a second ineffectual grasp at the plaything, which rolled, with increased speed, away from me into the dusk of the drawing-room. Then, as I raised my head, I saw that the child also had slipped from the room; and without looking after her I followed the old negro into the pleasant study above, where the great surgeon awaited me.

Ten years ago, before hard nursing had taken so much out of me, I blushed very easily, and I was aware at the moment when I crossed Doctor Maradick's study that my cheeks were the color of peonies. Of course, I was a fool—no one knows this better than I do—but I had never been alone, even for an instant, with him before, and the man was more than a hero to me, he was—there isn't any reason now why I should blush over the confession—almost a god. At that age I was mad about the wonders of surgery, and Roland Maradick in the operating-room was magician enough to have turned an older and more sensible head than mine. Added to his great reputation and his marvellous skill, he was, I am sure of this, the most splendid-looking man, even at forty-five, that one could imagine. Had he been ungracious—had he been positively rude to me, I should still have adored him, but when he held out his hand, and greeted me in the charming way he had with women, I felt that I would have died for him. It is no wonder that a saying went about the hospital that every woman he operated on fell in love with him. As for the nurses—well, there wasn't a single one of them who had escaped his spell—not even Miss Hemphill, who could scarcely have been a day under fifty.

"I am glad you could come, Miss Randolph. You were with Miss Hudson last week when I operated?"

I bowed. To save my life I couldn't have spoken without blushing the redder.

"I noticed your bright face at the time. Brightness, I think, is what Mrs. Maradick needs. She finds her day nurse depressing." His eyes rested so kindly upon me that I have suspected since that he was not entirely unaware of my worship. It was a small thing, heaven knows, to flatter his vanity—a nurse just out of a training-school—but to some men no tribute is too insignificant to give pleasure.

"You will do your best, I am sure." He hesitated an instant—just long enough for me to perceive the anxiety beneath the genial smile on his face—and then added gravely: "We wish to avoid, if possible, having to send her away for treatment."

I could only murmur in response, and after a few carefully chosen words about his wife's illness, he rang the bell and directed the maid to take me up-stairs to my room. Not until I was ascending the stairs to the third story did it occur to me that he had really told me nothing. I was as perplexed about the nature of Mrs. Maradick's malady as I had been when I entered the house.

I found my room pleasant enough. It had been arranged—by Doctor Maradick's request, I think—that I was to sleep in the house, and after my austere little bed at the hospital I was agreeably surprised by the cheerful look of the apartment into which the maid led me. The walls were papered in roses, and there were curtains of flowered chintz at the window, which looked down on a small formal garden at the rear of the house. This the maid told me, for it was too dark for me to distinguish more than a marble fountain and a fir-tree, which looked old, though I afterward learned that it was replanted almost every season.

In ten minutes I had slipped into my uniform and was ready to go to my patient; but for some reason—to this day I have never found out what it was that turned her against me at the start—Mrs. Maradick refused to receive me. While I stood outside her door I heard the day nurse trying to persuade her to let me come in. It wasn't any use, however, and in the end I was obliged to go back to my room and wait until the poor lady got over her whim and consented to see me. That was long after dinner—it must have been nearer eleven than ten o'clock—and Miss Peterson was quite worn out by the time she came to fetch me.

"I'm afraid you'll have a bad night," she said as we went down-stairs together. That was her way, I soon saw, to expect the worst of everything and everybody.

"Does she often keep you up like this?"

"Oh, no, she is usually very considerate. I never knew a sweeter character. But she still has this hallucination—"

Here again, as in the scene with Doctor Maradick, I felt that the explanation had only deepened the mystery. Mrs. Maradick's hallucination, whatever form it assumed, was evidently a subject for evasion and subterfuge in the household. It was on the tip of my tongue to ask, "What is her hallucination?"—but before I could get the words past my lips we had reached Mrs. Maradick's door, and Miss Peterson motioned me to be silent. As the door opened a little way to admit me, I saw that Mrs. Maradick was already in bed, and that the lights were out except for a night-lamp burning on a candle-stand beside a book and a carafe of water.

"I won't go in with you," said Miss Peterson in a whisper; and I was on the point of stepping over the threshold when I saw the little girl, in the dress of Scotch plaid, slip by me from the dusk of the room into the electric light of the hall. She held a doll in her arms, and as she went by she dropped a doll's work-basket in the doorway. Miss Peterson must have picked up the toy, for when I turned in a minute to look for it I found that it was gone. I remember thinking that it was late for a child to be up—she looked delicate, too—but, after all, it was no business of mine, and four years in a hospital had taught me never to meddle in affairs that do not concern me. There is nothing a nurse learns quicker than not to try to put the world to rights in a day.

When I crossed the floor to the chair by Mrs. Maradick's bed, she turned over on her side and looked at me with the sweetest and saddest smile.

"You are the new night nurse," she said in a gentle voice; and from the moment she spoke I knew that there was nothing hysterical or violent about her mania—or hallucination, as they called it. "They told me your name, but I have forgotten it."

"Randolph—Margaret Randolph." I liked her from the start, and I think she must have seen it.

"You look very young, Miss Randolph."

"I am twenty-two, but I suppose I don't look quite my age. People usually think I am younger."

For a minute she was silent, and while I settled myself in the chair by the bed I thought how strikingly she resembled the little girl I had seen first in the afternoon, and then leaving her room a few moments ago. They had the same small, heart-shaped faces, colored ever so faintly; the same straight, soft hair, between brown and flaxen; and the same large, grave eyes, set very far apart under arched eyebrows. What surprised me most, however, was that they both looked at me with that enigmatical and vaguely wondering expression—only in Mrs. Maradick's face the vagueness seemed to change now and then to a definite fear—a flash, I had almost said, of startled horror.

I sat quite still in my chair, and until the time came for Mrs. Maradick to take her medicine not a word passed between us. Then, when I bent over her with the glass in my hand, she raised her head from the pillow and said in a whisper of suppressed intensity:

"You look kind. I wonder if you could have seen my little girl?"

As I slipped my arm under the pillow I tried to smile cheerfully down on her. "Yes, I've seen her twice. I'd know her anywhere by her likeness to you."

A glow shone in her eyes, and I thought how pretty she must have been before illness took the life and animation out of her features. "Then I know you're good." Her voice was so strained and low that I could barely hear it. "If you weren't good you couldn't seen her."

I thought this queer enough, but all I answered was: "She looked delicate to be sitting up so late."

A quiver passed over her thin features, and for a minute I thought she was going to burst into tears. As she had taken the medicine, I put the glass back on the candle-stand and, bending over the bed, smoothed the straight brown hair, which was as fine and soft as spun silk, back from her forehead. There was something about her—I don't know what it was—that made you love her as soon as she looked at you.

"She always had that light and airy way, though she was never sick a day in her life," she answered calmly after a pause. Then, groping for my hand, she whispered passionately: "You must not tell him—you must not tell any one that you have seen her!"

"I mustn't tell any one?" Again I had the impression that had come to me first in Doctor Maradick's study, and afterward with Miss Peterson on the staircase, that I was seeking a gleam of light in the midst of obscurity.

"Are you sure there isn't any one listening—that there isn't any one at the door?" she asked, pushing aside my arm and sitting up among the pillows.

"Quite, quite sure. They have put out the lights in the hall."

"And you will not tell him? Promise me that you will not tell him." The startled horror flashed from the vague wonder of her expression. "He doesn't like her to come back, because he killed her."

"Because he killed her!" Then it was that light burst on me in a blaze. So this was Mrs. Maradick's hallucination! She believed that her child was dead—the little girl I had seen with my own eyes leaving her room; and she believed that her husband—the great surgeon we worshipped in the hospital—had murdered her. No wonder they veiled the dreadful obsession in mystery! No wonder that even Miss Peterson had not dared to drag the horrid thing out into the light! It was the kind of hallucination one simply couldn't stand having to face.

"There is no use telling people things that nobody believes," she resumed slowly, still holding my hand in a grasp that would have hurt me if her fingers had not been so fragile. "Nobody believes that he killed her. Nobody believes that she comes back every day to the house. Nobody believes—and yet you saw her—"

"Yes, I saw her—but why should your husband have killed her?" I spoke soothingly, as one would speak to a person who was quite mad; yet she was not mad, I could have sworn this while I looked at her.

For a moment she moaned inarticulately, as if the horror of her thought were too great to pass into speech. Then she flung out her thin, bare arm with a wild gesture.

"Because he never loved me!" she said. "He never loved me!"

"But he married you," I urged gently after a moment in which I stroked her hair. "If he hadn't loved you, why should he have married you?"

"He wanted the money—my little girl's money. It all goes to him when I die."

"But he is rich himself. He must make a fortune from his profession."

"It isn't enough. He wanted millions." She had grown stern and tragic. "No, he never loved me. He loved some one else from the beginning—before I knew him."

It was quite useless, I saw, to reason with her. If she wasn't mad, she was in a state of terror and despondency so black that it had almost crossed the border-line into madness. I thought once of going up-stairs and bringing the child down from her nursery; but, after a moment's thought, I realized that Miss Peterson and Doctor Maradick must have long ago tried all these measures. Clearly, there was nothing to do except soothe and quiet her as much as I could; and this I did until she dropped into a light sleep which lasted well into the morning.

By seven o'clock I was worn out—not from work, but from the strain on my sympathy—and I was glad, indeed, when one of the maids came in to bring me an early cup of coffee. Mrs. Maradick was still sleeping—it was a mixture of bromide and chloral I had given her—and she did not wake until Miss Peterson came on duty an hour or two later. Then, when I went down-stairs, I found the dining-room deserted except for the old house-keeper, who was looking over the silver. Doctor Maradick, she explained to me presently, had his breakfast served in the morning-room on the other side of the house.

"And the little girl? Does she take her meals in the nursery?"

She threw me a startled glance. Was it, I questioned afterward, one of distrust or apprehension?

"There isn't any little girl. Haven't you heard?"

"Heard? No. Why, I saw her only yesterday."

The look she gave me—I was sure of it now—was full of alarm.

"The little girl—she was the sweetest child I ever saw—died just two months ago of pneumonia."

"But she couldn't have died." I was a fool to let this out, but the shock had completely unnerved me. "I tell you I saw her yesterday."

The alarm in her face deepened. "That is Mrs. Maradick's trouble. She believes that she still sees her."

"But don't you see her?" I drove the question home bluntly.

"No." She set her lips tightly. "I never see anything."

So I had been wrong, after all, and the explanation, when it came, only accentuated the terror. The child was dead—she had died of pneumonia two months ago—and yet I had seen her, with my own eyes, playing ball in the library; I had seen her slipping out of her mother's room, with her doll in her arms.

"Is there another child in the house? Could there be a child belonging to one of the servants?" A gleam had shot through the fog in which I was groping.

"No, there isn't any other. The doctors tried bringing one once, but it threw the poor lady into such a state she almost died of it. Besides, there wouldn't be any other child as quiet and sweet-looking as Dorothea. To see her skipping along in her dress of Scotch plaid used to make me think of a fairy, though they say that fairies wear nothing but white or green."

"Has any one else seen her—the child, I mean—any of the servants?"

"Only old Gabriel, the colored butler, who came with Mrs. Maradick's mother from South Carolina. I've heard that negroes often have a kind of second sight—though I don't know that that is just what you would call it. But they seem to believe in the supernatural by instinct, and Gabriel is so old and doty—he does no work except answer the door-bell and clean the silver—that nobody pays much attention to anything that he sees—"

"Is the child's nursery kept as it used to be?"

"Oh, no. The doctor had all the toys sent to the children's hospital. That was a great grief to Mrs. Maradick; but Doctor Brandon thought, and all the nurses agreed with him, that it was best for her not to be allowed to keep the room as it was when Dorothea was living."

"Dorothea? Was that the child's name?"

"Yes, it means the gift of God, doesn't it? She was named after the mother of Mrs. Maradick's first husband, Mr. Ballard. He was the grave, quiet kind—not the least like the doctor."

I wondered if the other dreadful obsession of Mrs. Maradick's had drifted down through the nurses or the servants to the house-keeper; but she said nothing about it, and since she was, I suspected, a garrulous person, I thought it wiser to assume that the gossip had not reached her.

A little later, when breakfast was over and I had not yet gone up-stairs to my room, I had my first interview with Doctor Brandon, the famous alienist who was in charge of the case. I had never seen him before, but from the first moment that I looked at him I took his measure, almost by intuition. He was, I suppose, honest enough—I have always granted him that, bitterly as I have felt toward him. It wasn't his fault that he lacked red blood in his brain, or that he had formed the habit, from long association with abnormal phenomena, of regarding all life as a disease. He was the sort of physician—every nurse will understand what I mean—who deals instinctively with groups instead of with individuals. He was long and solemn and very round in the face; and I hadn't talked to him ten minutes before I knew he had been educated in Germany, and that he had learned over there to treat every emotion as a pathological manifestation. I used to wonder what he got out of life—what any one got out of life who had analyzed away everything except the bare structure.

When I reached my room at last, I was so tired that I could barely remember either the questions Doctor Brandon had asked or the directions he had given me. I fell asleep, I know, almost as soon as my head touched the pillow;

and the maid who came to inquire if I wanted luncheon decided to let me finish my nap. In the afternoon, when she returned with a cup of tea, she found me still heavy and drowsy. Though I was used to night nursing, I felt as if I had danced from sunset to daybreak. It was fortunate, I reflected, while I drank my tea, that every case didn't wear on one's sympathies as acutely as Mrs. Maradick's hallucination had worn on mine.

Through the day, of course, I did not see Doctor Maradick, but at seven o'clock, when I came up from my early dinner on my way to take the place of Miss Peterson, who had kept on duty an hour later than usual, he met me in the hall and asked me to come into his study. I thought him handsomer than ever in his evening clothes, with a white flower in his buttonhole. He was going to some public dinner, the housekeeper told me, but, then, he was always going somewhere. I believe he didn't dine at home a single evening that winter.

"Did Mrs. Maradick have a good night?" He had closed the door after us, and, turning now with the question, he smiled kindly, as if he wished to put me at ease in the beginning.

"She slept very well after she took the medicine. I gave her that at eleven o'clock."

For a minute he regarded me silently, and I was aware that his personality—his charm—had been focussed upon me. It was almost as if I stood in the centre of converging rays of light, so vivid was my impression of him.

"Did she allude in any way to her—to her hallucination?" he asked.

How the warning reached me—what invisible waves of sense-perception transmitted the message—I have never known; but while I stood there, facing the splendor of the doctor's presence, every intuition cautioned me that the time had come when I must take sides in the household. While I stayed there I must stand either with Mrs. Maradick or against her.

"She talked quite rationally," I replied after a moment.

"What did she say?"

"She told me how she was feeling, that she missed her child, and that she walked a little every day about her room."

His face changed—how, I could not at first determine.

"Have you seen Doctor Brandon?"

"He came this morning to give me his directions."

"He thought her less well to-day. He has even advised me to send her to Rosedale."

I have never, even in secret, tried to account for Doctor Maradick. He may have been sincere. I tell only what I know—not what I believe or imagine—and the human is sometimes as inscrutable, as inexplicable, as the supernatural.

While he watched me I was conscious of an inner struggle, as if opposing angels warred somewhere in the depths of my being. When at last I made my decision, I was acting less from reason, I knew, than in obedience to the pressure of some secret current of thought. Heaven knows, even then, the man held me captive while I defied him.

"Doctor Maradick," I lifted my eyes for the first time frankly to his, "I believe that your wife is as sane as I am—or as you are."

He started. "Then she did not talk freely to you?"

"She may be mistaken, unstrung, piteously distressed in mind"—I brought this out with emphasis—"but she is not—I am willing to stake my future on it—a fit subject for an asylum. It would be foolish—it would be cruel to send her to Rosedale."

"Cruel, you say?" A troubled look crossed his face, and his voice grew very gentle. "You do not imagine that I could be cruel to her?"

"No, I do not think that." My voice also had softened.

"We will let things go on as they are. Perhaps Doctor Brandon may have some other suggestion to make." He drew out his watch and compared it with the clock—nervously, I observed, as if his action were a screen for his discomfiture or his perplexity. "I must be going now. We will speak of this again in the morning."

But in the morning we did not speak of it, and during the month that I nursed Mrs. Maradick I was not called again into her husband's study. When I met him in the hall or on the staircase, which was seldom, he was as charming as ever; yet, in spite of his courtesy, I had a persistent feeling that he had taken my measure on that evening, and that he had no further use for me.

As the days went by Mrs. Maradick seemed to grow stronger. Never, after our first night together, had she mentioned the child to me; never had she alluded by so much as a word to her dreadful charge against her husband. She was like any other woman recovering from a great sorrow, except that she was sweeter and gentler. It is no wonder that every one who came near her loved her; for there was a mysterious loveliness about her like the mystery of light, not of darkness. She was, I have always thought, as much of an angel as it is possible for a woman to be on this earth. And yet, angelic as she was, there were times when it seemed to me that she both hated and feared her husband. Though he never entered her room while I was there, and I never heard his name on her lips until an hour before the end, still I could tell by the look of terror in her face whenever his step passed down the hall that her very soul shivered at his approach.

During the whole month I did not see the child again, though one night, when I came suddenly into Mrs. Maradick's room, I found a little garden, such as children make out of pebbles and bits of box, on the window-sill. I did not mention it to Mrs. Maradick, and a little later, as the maid lowered the shades, I noticed that the garden had vanished. Since then I have often wondered if the child were invisible only to the rest of us, and if her mother still saw her. But there was no way of finding out except by questioning, and Mrs. Maradick was so well and patient that I hadn't the heart to question. Things couldn't have been better with her than they were, and I was beginning to tell myself that she might soon go out for an airing, when the end came suddenly.

It was a mild January day—the kind of day that brings the foretaste of spring in the middle of winter, and when I came down-stairs in the afternoon, I stopped a minute by the window at the end of the hall to look down on the box maze in the garden. There was an old fountain, bearing two laughing boys in marble, in the centre of the gravelled walk, and the water, which had been turned on that morning for Mrs. Maradick's pleasure, sparkled now like silver as the sunlight splashed over it. I had never before felt the air quite so soft and springlike in January; and I thought, as I gazed down on the garden, that it would be a good idea for Mrs. Maradick to go out and bask for an hour or so in the sunshine. It seemed strange to me that she was never allowed to get any fresh air except the air that came through her windows.

When I went into her room, however, I found that she had no wish to go out. She was sitting, wrapped in shawls, by the open window, which looked down on the fountain; and as I entered she glanced up from a little book she was reading. A pot of daffodils stood on the window-sill—she was very fond of flowers and we tried always to keep some growing in her room.

"Do you know what I was reading, Miss Randolph?" she asked in her soft voice; and then she read aloud a verse while I went over to the candle-stand to measure out a dose of medicine.

" 'If thou hast two loaves of bread, sell one and buy daffodils, for bread nourisheth the body, but daffodils delight the soul.' That is very beautiful, don't you think so?"

I said "Yes," that it was beautiful; and then I asked her if she wouldn't go down-stairs and walk about in the garden?

"He wouldn't like it," she answered; and it was the first time she had mentioned her husband to me since the night I came to her. "He doesn't want me to go out."

I tried to laugh her out of the idea; but it was no use, and after a few minutes I gave up and began talking of other things. Even then it did not occur to me that her fear of Doctor Maradick was anything but a fancy. I could see, of course, that she wasn't out of her head; but sane persons, I knew, sometimes have unaccountable prejudices, and I accepted her dislike as a mere whim or aversion. I did not understand then, and—I may as well confess this before the end comes—I do not understand any better to-day. I am writing down the things I actually saw, and I repeat that I have never had the slightest twist in the direction of the miraculous.

The afternoon slipped away while we talked— she talked brightly when any subject came up that interested her—and it was the last hour of day—that grave, still hour when the movement of life seems to droop and falter for a few precious minutes—that brought us the thing I had dreaded silently since my first night in the house. I remember that I had risen to close the window, and was leaning out for a breath of the mild air, when there was the sound of steps, consciously softened in the hall outside, and Doctor Brandon's usual knock fell on my ears. Then, before I could cross the room, the door opened, and the doctor entered with Miss Peterson. The day nurse, I knew, was a stupid woman; but she had never appeared to me so stupid, so armored and incased in her professional manner, as she did at that moment.

"I am glad to see that you have been taking the air." As Doctor Brandon came over to the window, I wondered maliciously what devil of contradictions had made him a distinguished specialist in nervous diseases.

"Who was the other doctor you brought this morning?" asked Mrs. Maradick gravely; and that was all I ever heard about the visit of the second alienist.

"Some one who is anxious to cure you." He dropped into a chair beside her and patted her hand with his long, pale fingers. "We are so anxious to cure you that we want to send you away to the country for a fortnight or so. Miss Peterson has come to help you get ready, and I've kept my car waiting for you. There couldn't be a nicer day for a little trip, could there?"

The moment had come at last. I knew at once what he meant, and so did Mrs. Maradick.

A wave of color flowed and ebbed in her thin cheeks, and I felt her body quiver when I moved from the window and put my arms on her shoulders. I was aware again, as I had been aware that evening in Doctor Maradick's study, of a current of thought that beat from the air around into my brain. Though it cost me my career as a nurse and my reputation for sanity, I knew that I must obey that invisible warning.

"You are going to take me to an asylum," said Mrs. Maradick.

He made some foolish denial or evasion; but before he had finished I turned from Mrs. Maradick and faced him impulsively. In a nurse this was flagrant rebellion, and I realized that the act wrecked my professional future. Yet I did not care—I did not hesitate. Something stronger than I was driving me on.

"Doctor Brandon," I said, "I beg you—I implore you to wait until to-morrow. There are things I must tell you."

A queer look came into his face, and I understood, even in my excitement, that he was mentally deciding in which group he should place me—to which class of morbid manifestations I must belong.

"Very well, very well, we will hear everything," he replied soothingly; but I saw him glance at Miss Peterson, and she went over to the wardrobe for Mrs. Maradick's fur coat and hat.

Suddenly, without warning, Mrs. Maradick threw the shawls away from her, and stood up. "If you send me away," she said, "I shall never come back. I shall never live to come back."

The gray of twilight was just beginning, and while she stood there, in the dusk of the room, her face shone out as pale and flower-like as the daffodils on the window-sill. "I cannot go away!" she cried in a sharper voice. "I cannot go away from my child!"

I saw her face clearly; I heard her voice; and then—the horror of the scene sweeps back over me!—I saw the door slowly open and the little girl run across the room to her mother. I saw her lift her little arms, and I saw the mother stoop and gather her to her bosom. So closely locked were they in that passionate embrace that their forms seemed to mingle in the gloom that enveloped them.

"After this can you doubt?" I threw out the words almost savagely—and then, when I turned from the mother and child to Doctor Brandon and Miss Peterson, I knew breathlessly—oh, there was a shock in the discovery!—that they were blind to the child. Their blank faces revealed the consternation of ignorance, not of conviction. They had seen nothing except the vacant arms of the mother and the swift, erratic gesture with which she stooped to embrace some phantasmal presence. Only my vision—and I have asked myself since if the power of sympathy enabled me to penetrate the web of material fact and see the spiritual form of the child—only my vision was not blinded by the clay through which I looked.

"After this can you doubt?" Doctor Brandon had flung my words back to me. Was it his fault, poor man, if life had granted him only the eyes of flesh? Was it his fault if he could see only half of the thing there before him?

But they couldn't see, and since they couldn't see I realized that it was useless to tell them. Within an hour they took Mrs. Maradick to the asylum; and she went quietly, though when the time came for parting from me she showed some faint trace of feeling. I remember that at the last, while we stood on the pavement, she lifted her black veil, which she wore for the child, and said: "Stay with her, Miss Randolph, as long as you can. I shall never come back."

Then she got into the car and was driven off, while I stood looking after her with a sob in my throat. Dreadful as I felt it to be, I didn't, of course, realize the full horror of it, or I couldn't have stood there quietly on the pavement. I didn't realize it, indeed, until several months afterward when word came that she had died in the asylum. I never knew what her illness was, though I vaguely recall that something was said about "heart failure"—a loose enough term. My own belief is that she died simply of the terror of life.

To my surprise Doctor Maradick asked me to stay on as his office nurse after his wife went to Rosedale; and when the news of her death came there was no suggestion of my leaving. I don't know to this day why he wanted me in the house. Perhaps he thought I should have less opportunity to gossip if I stayed under his roof; perhaps he still wished to test the power of his charm over me. His vanity was incredible in so great a man. I have seen him flush with pleasure when people turned to look at him in the street, and I know that he was not above playing on the sentimental weaknesses of his patients. But he was magnificent, heaven knows! Few men, I imagine, have been the objects of so many foolish infatuations.

The next summer Doctor Maradick went abroad for two months, and while he was away I took my vacation in Virginia. When we came back the work was heavier than ever—his reputation by this time was tremendous—and my days were so crowded with appointments, and hurried flittings to emergency cases, that I had scarcely a minute left in which to remember poor Mrs. Maradick. Since the afternoon when she went to the asylum the child had not been seen in the house; and at last I was beginning to persuade myself that the little figure had been an optical illusion—the effect of shifting lights in the gloom of the old rooms—not the apparition I had once believed it to be. It does not take long for a phantom to fade from the memory—especially when one leads the active and methodical life I was forced into that winter. Perhaps,—who knows?—(I remember telling myself) the doctors may have been right, after all, and the poor lady may have actually been out of her mind. With this view of the past, my judgment of Doctor Maradick insensibly altered. It ended, I think, in my acquitting him altogether. And then, just as he stood clear and splendid in my verdict of him, the reversal came so precipitately that I grow breathless now whenever I try to live it over again. The violence of the next turn in affairs left me, I often fancy, with a perpetual dizziness of the imagination.

It was in May that we heard of Mrs. Maradick's death, and exactly a year later, on a mild and fragrant afternoon, when the daffodils were blooming in patches around the old fountain in the garden, the house-keeper came into the office, where I lingered over some accounts, to bring me news of the doctor's approaching marriage.

"It is no more than we might have expected," she concluded rationally. "The house must be lonely for him—he is such a sociable man. But I can't help feeling," she brought out slowly after a pause in which I felt a shiver pass over me, "I can't help feeling that it is hard for that other woman to have all the money poor Mrs. Maradick's first husband left her."

"There is a great deal of money, then?" I asked curiously.

"A great deal." She waved her hand, as if words were futile to express the sum. "Millions and millions!"

"They will give up this house, of course?"

"That's done already, my dear. There won't be a brick left of it by this time next year. It's to be pulled down and an apartment-house built on the ground."

Again the shiver passed over me. I couldn't bear to think of Mrs. Maradick's old home falling to pieces.

"You didn't tell me the name of the bride," I said. "Is she some one he met while he was in Europe?"

"Dear me, no! She is the very lady he was engaged to before he married Mrs. Maradick, only she threw him over, so people said, because he wasn't rich enough. Then she married some lord or prince from over the water; but there was a divorce, and now she has turned again to her old lover. He is rich enough now, I guess, even for her!"

It was all perfectly true, I suppose; it sounded as plausible as a story out of a newspaper; and yet while she told me I was aware of a sinister, an impalpable hush in the atmosphere. I was nervous, no doubt; I was shaken by the suddenness with which the house-keeper had sprung her

news on me; but as I sat there I had quite vividly an impression that the old house was listening—that there was a real, if invisible, presence somewhere in the room or the garden. Yet, when an instant afterward I glanced through the long window which opened down to the brick terrace, I saw only the faint sunshine over the deserted garden, with its maze of box, its marble fountain, and its patches of daffodils.

The house-keeper had gone—one of the servants, I think, came for her—and I was sitting at my desk when the words of Mrs. Maradick on that last evening floated into my mind. The daffodils brought her back to me; for I thought, as I watched them growing, so still and golden in the sunshine, how she would have enjoyed them. Almost unconsciously I repeated the verse she had read to me.

"If thou hast two loaves of bread, sell one and buy daffodils"—and it was at that very instant, while the words were on my lips, that I turned my eyes to the box maze and saw the child skipping rope along the gravelled path to the fountain. Quite distinctly, as clear as day, I saw her come, with what children call the dancing step, between the low box borders to the place where the daffodils bloomed by the fountain. From her straight brown hair to her frock of Scotch plaid and her little feet, which twinkled in white socks and black slippers over the turning rope, she was as real to me as the ground on which she trod or the laughing marble boys under the splashing water. Starting up from my chair, I made a single step to the terrace. If I could only reach her—only speak to her—I felt that I might at last solve the mystery. But with my first call, with the first flutter of my dress on the terrace, the airy little form melted into the dusk of the maze. Not a breath stirred the daffodils, not a shadow passed over the sparkling flow of the water; yet, weak and shaken in every nerve, I sat down on the brick step of the terrace and burst into tears. I must have known that something terrible would happen before they pulled down Mrs. Maradick's home.

The doctor dined out that night. He was with

the lady he was going to marry, the house-keeper told me; and it must have been almost midnight when I heard him come in and go up-stairs to his room. I was down-stairs because I had been unable to sleep, and the book I wanted to finish I had left that afternoon in the office. The book—I can't remember what it was—had seemed to me very exciting when I began it in the morning; but after the visit of the child I found the romantic novel as dull as a treatise on nursing. It was impossible for me to follow the lines, and I was on the point of giving up and going to bed, when Doctor Maradick opened the front door with his latch-key and went up the staircase. "There can't be a bit of truth in it." I thought over and over again as I listened to his even step ascending the stairs. "There can't be a bit of truth in it." And yet, though I assured myself that "there couldn't be a bit of truth in it," I shrank, with a creepy sensation, from going through the house to my room in the third story. I was tired out after a hard day, and my nerves must have reacted morbidly to the silence and the darkness. For the first time in my life I knew what it was to be afraid of the unknown, of the invisible; and while I bent over my book, in the glare of the electric light, I became conscious presently that I was straining my senses for some sound in the spacious emptiness of the rooms overhead. The noise of a passing motor-car in the street jerked me back from the intense hush of expectancy; and I can recall the wave of relief that swept over me as I turned to my book again and tried to fix my distracted mind on its pages.

I was still sitting there when the telephone on my desk rang, with what seemed to my overwrought nerves a startling abruptness, and the voice of the superintendent told me hurriedly that Doctor Maradick was needed at the hospital. I had become so accustomed to these emergency calls in the night that I felt reassured when I had rung up the doctor in his room and had heard the hearty sound of his response. He had not yet undressed, he said, and would come down immediately while I ordered back his car, which must just have reached the garage.

"I'll be with you in five minutes!" he called as cheerfully as if I had summoned him to his wedding.

I heard him cross the floor of his room; and before he could reach the head of the staircase, I opened the door and went out into the hall in order that I might turn on the light and have his hat and coat waiting. The electric button was at the end of the hall, and as I moved toward it, guided by the glimmer that fell from the landing above, I instinctively lifted my eyes to the staircase, which climbed dimly, with its slender mahogany balustrade, as far as the third story. Then it was, at the very moment when the doctor, humming gayly, began his quick descent of the steps, that I distinctly saw—I will swear to this on my death-bed—a child's skipping-rope lying loosely coiled, as if it had dropped from a careless little hand, in the bend of the staircase. With a spring I had reached the electric button, flooding the hall with light; but as I did so, while my arm was still outstretched behind me, I heard the humming voice change to a cry of surprise or terror, and the figure on the staircase tripped heavily and stumbled with groping hands into emptiness. The scream of warning died in my throat while I watched him pitch forward down the long flight of stairs to the floor at my feet. Even before I bent over him, before I wiped the blood from his brow and felt for his silent heart, I knew that he was dead.

Something—it may have been, as the world believes, a misstep in the dimness, or it may have been, as I am ready to bear witness, a phantasmal judgment—something had killed him at the very moment when he most wanted to live.

The Past

ELLEN GLASGOW

I HAD NO SOONER entered the house than I knew something was wrong. Though I had never been in so splendid a place before—it was one of those big houses just off Fifth Avenue—I had a suspicion from the first that the magnificence covered a secret disturbance. I was always quick to receive impressions, and when the black iron doors swung together behind me, I felt as if I were shut inside a prison.

When I gave my name and explained that I was the new secretary, I was delivered into the charge of an elderly lady's-maid, who looked as if she had been crying. Without speaking a word, though she nodded kindly enough, she led me down the hall, and then up a flight of stairs at the back of the house to a pleasant bedroom in the third storey. There was a great deal of sunshine, and the walls, which were painted a soft yellow, made the room very cheerful. It would be a comfortable place to sit in when I was not working, I thought, while the sad-faced maid stood watching me remove my wraps and hat.

"If you are not tired, Mrs. Vanderbridge would like to dictate a few letters," she said presently, and they were the first words she had spoken.

"I am not a bit tired. Will you take me to her?" One of the reasons, I knew, which had decided Mrs. Vanderbridge to engage me was the remarkable similarity of our handwriting. We were both Southerners, and though she was now famous on two continents for her beauty, I couldn't forget that she had got her early education at the little academy for young ladies in Fredericksburg. This was a bond of sympathy in my thoughts at least, and, heaven knows, I needed to remember it while I followed the maid down the narrow stairs and along the wide hall to the front of the house.

In looking back after a year, I can recall every detail of that first meeting. Though it was barely four o'clock, the electric lamps were turned on in the hall, and I can still see the mellow light that shone over the staircase and lay in pools on the old pink rugs, which were so soft and fine that I felt as if I were walking on flowers. I remember the sound of music from a room somewhere on the first floor, and the scent of lilies and hyacinths that drifted from the conservatory. I remember it all, every note of music, every whiff of fragrance; but most vividly I remember Mrs. Vanderbridge as she looked round, when the door opened, from the wood fire into which she had been gazing. Her eyes caught me first. They were so wonderful that for a moment I couldn't see anything else; then I took in slowly the dark red of her hair, the clear pallor of her skin, and the long, flowing lines of her figure in a tea-gown of blue silk. There was a white bearskin rug under her feet, and while she stood there before the wood fire, she looked as if she had absorbed the beauty and colour of the house as a crystal vase absorbs the light. Only when she spoke to me, and I went nearer, did I detect the heaviness beneath her eyes and the nervous quiver of her mouth, which drooped a little at the corners. Tired and worn as she was, I never saw her afterwards—not even when she was dressed for the opera—look quite so lovely, so much like an exquisite flower, as she did on that first afternoon. When I knew her better, I discovered that she was a changeable beauty; there were days when all the colour seemed to go out of her, and she looked dull and haggard; but at her best no one I've ever seen could compare with her.

She asked me a few questions, and though she was pleasant and kind, I knew that she scarcely listened to my responses. While I sat down at the desk and dipped my pen into the ink, she flung herself on the couch before the fire with a movement which struck me as hopeless. I saw her feet tap the white fur rug, while she plucked nervously at the lace on the end of one of the gold-coloured sofa pillows. For an instant the thought flashed through my mind that she had been taking something—drug of some sort—and that she was suffering now from the effects of it. Then she looked at me steadily, almost as if she were reading my thoughts, and I knew that I was wrong. Her large radiant eyes were as innocent as a child's.

She dictated a few notes—all declining invitations—and then, while I still waited pen in hand, she sat up on the couch with one of her quick movements, and said in a low voice, "I am not dining out to-night, Miss Wrenn. I am not well enough."

"I am sorry for that." It was all I could think of to say, for I did not understand why she should have told me.

"If you don't mind, I should like you to come down to dinner. There will be only Mr. Vanderbridge and myself."

"Of course I will come if you wish it." I couldn't very well refuse to do what she asked me, yet I told myself, while I answered, that if I had known she expected me to make one of the family, I should never, not even at twice the salary, have taken the place. It didn't take me a minute to go over my slender wardrobe in my mind

and realize that I had nothing to wear that would look well enough.

"I can see you don't like it," she added after a moment, almost wistfully, "but it won't be often. It is only when we are dining alone."

This, I thought, was even queerer than the request—or command—for I knew from her tone, just as plainly as if she had told me in words, that she did not wish to dine alone with her husband.

"I am ready to help you in any way—in any way that I can," I replied, and I was so deeply moved by her appeal that my voice broke in spite of my effort to control it. After my lonely life I dare say I should have loved any one who really needed me, and from the first moment that I read the appeal in Mrs. Vanderbridge's face I felt that I was willing to work my fingers to the bone for her. Nothing that she asked of me was too much when she asked it in that voice, with that look.

"I am glad you are nice," she said, and for the first time she smiled—a charming, girlish smile with a hint of archness. "We shall get on beautifully, I know, because I can talk to you. My last secretary was English, and I frightened her almost to death whenever I tried to talk to her." Then her tone grew serious. "You won't mind dining with us. Roger—Mr. Vanderbridge—is the most charming man in the world."

"Is that his picture?"

"Yes, the one in the Florentine frame. The other is my brother. Do you think we are alike?"

"Since you've told me, I notice a likeness." Already I had picked up the Florentine frame from the desk, and was eagerly searching the features of Mr. Vanderbridge. It was an arresting face, dark, thoughtful, strangely appealing, and picturesque—though this may have been due, of course, to the photographer. The more I looked at it, the more there grew upon me an uncanny feeling of familiarity; but not until the next day, while I was still trying to account for the impression that I had seen the picture before, did there flash into my mind the memory of an old portrait of a Florentine nobleman in a loan collection last winter. I can't remember the name of the painter—I am not sure that it was known—but this photograph might have been taken from the painting. There was the same imaginative sadness in both faces, the same haunting beauty of feature, and one surmised that there must be the same rich darkness of colouring. The only striking difference was that the man in the photograph looked much older than the original of the portrait, and I remembered that the lady who had engaged me was the second wife of Mr. Vanderbridge and some ten or fifteen years younger, I had heard, than her husband.

"Have you ever seen a more wonderful face?" asked Mrs. Vanderbridge. "Doesn't he look as if he might have been painted by Titian?"

"Is he really so handsome as that?"

"He is a little older and sadder, that is all. When we were married it was exactly like him." For an instant she hesitated and then broke out almost bitterly, "Isn't that a face any woman might fall in love with, a face any woman—living or dead—would not be willing to give up?"

Poor child, I could see that she was overwrought and needed someone to talk to, but it seemed queer to me that she should speak so frankly to a stranger. I wondered why any one so rich and so beautiful should ever be unhappy—for I had been schooled by poverty to believe that money is the first essential of happiness—and yet her unhappiness was as evident as her beauty, or the luxury that enveloped her. At that instant I felt that I hated Mr. Vanderbridge, for whatever the secret tragedy of their marriage might be, I instinctively knew that the fault was not on the side of the wife. She was as sweet and winning as if she were still the reigning beauty in the academy for young ladies. I knew with a knowledge deeper than any conviction that she was not to blame, and if she wasn't to blame, then who under heaven could be at fault except her husband?

In a few minutes a friend came in to tea, and I went upstairs to my room, and unpacked the blue taffeta dress I had bought for my sister's wedding. I was still doubtfully regarding it when there was a knock at my door, and the maid with the sad face came in to bring me a pot of tea. After she had placed the tray on the table, she stood nervously twisting a napkin in her hands while she waited for me to leave my unpacking and sit down in the easy chair she had drawn up under the lamp.

"How do you think Mrs. Vanderbridge is looking?" she asked abruptly in a voice that held a breathless note of suspense. Her nervousness and the queer look in her face made me stare at her sharply. This was a house, I was beginning to feel, where everybody, from the mistress down, wanted to question me. Even the silent maid had found voice for interrogation.

"I think her the loveliest person I've ever seen," I answered after a moment's hesitation. There couldn't be any harm in telling her how much I admired her mistress.

"Yes, she is lovely—everyone thinks so—and her nature is as sweet as her face." She was becoming loquacious. "I have never had a lady who was so sweet and kind. She hasn't always been rich, and that may be the reason she never seems to grow hard and selfish, the reason she spends so much of her life thinking of other people. It's been six years now, ever since her marriage, that I've lived with her, and in all that time I've never had a cross word from her."

"One can see that. With everything she has she ought to be as happy as the day is long."

"She ought to be." Her voice dropped, and I saw her glance suspiciously at the door, which she had closed when she entered. "She ought to be, but she isn't. I have never seen any one so unhappy as she has been of late—ever since last summer. I suppose I oughtn't to talk about it, but I've kept it to myself so long that I feel as if it was killing me. If she was my own sister, I couldn't be any fonder of her, and yet I have to see her suffer day after day, and not say a word—not even to her. She isn't the sort of lady you could speak to about a thing like that."

She broke down, and dropping on the rug at my feet, hid her face in her hands. It was plain that she was suffering acutely, and while I patted her shoulder, I thought what a wonderful mistress Mrs. Vanderbridge must be to have attached a servant to her so strongly.

"You must remember that I am a stranger in the house, that I scarcely know her, that I've never so much as laid eyes on her husband," I said warningly, for I've always avoided, as far as possible, the confidences of servants.

"But you look as if you could be trusted." The maid's nerves, as well as the mistress's, were on edge, I could see. "And she needs somebody who can help her. She needs a real friend—somebody who will stand by her no matter what happens." Again, as in the room downstairs, there flashed through my mind the suspicion that I had got into a place where people took drugs or drink—or were all out of their minds. I had heard of such houses.

"How can I help her? She won't confide in me, and even if she did, what could I do for her?"

"You can stand by and watch. You can come between her and harm—if you see it." She had risen from the floor and stood wiping her reddened eyes on the napkin. "I don't know what it is, but I know it is there. I feel it even when I can't see it."

Yes, they were all out of their minds; there couldn't be any other explanation. The whole episode was incredible. It was the kind of thing, I kept telling myself, that did not happen. Even in a book nobody could believe it.

"But her husband? He is the one who must protect her."

She gave me a blighting look. "He would if he could. He isn't to blame—you mustn't think that. He is one of the best men in the world, but he can't help her. He can't help her because he doesn't know. He doesn't see it."

A bell rang somewhere, and catching up the tea-tray, she paused just long enough to throw me a pleading word, "Stand between her and harm, if you see it."

When she had gone I locked the door after her, and turned on all the lights in the room.

Was there really a tragic mystery in the house, or were they all mad, as I had first imagined? The feeling of apprehension, of vague uneasiness, which had come to me when I entered the iron doors, swept over me in a wave while I sat there in the soft glow of the shaded electric light. Something was wrong. Somebody was making that lovely woman unhappy, and who, in the name of reason, could this somebody be except her husband? Yet the maid had spoken of him as "one of the best men in the world," and it was impossible to doubt the tearful sincerity of her voice. Well, the riddle was too much for me. I gave it up at last with a sigh—dreading the hour that would call me downstairs to meet Mr. Vanderbridge. I felt in every nerve and fibre of my body that I should hate him the moment I looked at him.

But at eight o'clock, when I went reluctantly downstairs, I had a surprise. Nothing could have been kinder than the way Mr. Vanderbridge greeted me, and I could tell as soon as I met his eyes that there wasn't anything vicious or violent in his nature. He reminded me more than ever of the portrait in the loan collection, and though he was so much older than the Florentine nobleman, he had the same thoughtful look. Of course I am not an artist, but I have always tried, in my way, to be a reader of personality; and it didn't take a particularly keen observer to discern the character and intellect in Mr. Vanderbridge's face. Even now I remember it as the noblest face I have ever seen; and unless I had possessed at least a shade of penetration, I doubt if I should have detected the melancholy. For it was only when he was thinking deeply that this sadness seemed to spread like a veil over his features. At other times he was cheerful and even gay in his manner; and his rich dark eyes would light up now and then with irrepressible humour. From the way he looked at his wife I could tell that there was no lack of love or tenderness on his side any more than there was on hers. It was obvious that he was still as much in love with her as he had been before his marriage, and my immediate perception of this only deepened the mystery that enveloped them. If the fault wasn't his and wasn't hers, then who was responsible for the shadow that hung over the house?

For the shadow was there. I could feel it, vague and dark, while we talked about the war and the remote possibilities of peace in the spring. Mrs. Vanderbridge looked young and lovely in her gown of white satin with pearls on her bosom, but her violet eyes were almost black in the candlelight, and I had a curious feeling that this blackness was the colour of thought. Something troubled her to despair, yet I was as positive as I could be of anything I had ever told that she had breathed no word of this anxiety or distress to her husband. Devoted as they were, a nameless dread, fear, or apprehension divided them. It was the thing I had felt from the moment I entered the house; the thing I had heard in the tearful voice of the maid. One could scarcely call it horror, because it was too vague, too impalpable, for so vivid a name; yet, after all these quiet months, horror is the only word I can think of that in any way expresses the emotion which pervaded the house.

I had never seen so beautiful a dinner table, and I was gazing with pleasure at the damask and glass and silver—there was a silver basket of chrysanthemums, I remember, in the centre of the table—when I noticed a nervous movement of Mrs. Vanderbridge's head, and saw her glance hastily towards the door and the staircase beyond. We had been talking animatedly, and as Mrs. Vanderbridge turned away, I had just made a remark to her husband, who appeared to have fallen into a sudden fit of abstraction, and was gazing thoughtfully over his soup-plate at the white and yellow chrysanthemums. It occurred to me, while I watched him, that he was probably absorbed in some financial problem, and I regretted that I had been so careless as to speak to him. To my surprise, however, he replied immediately in a natural tone, and I saw, or imagined that I saw, Mrs. Vanderbridge throw me a glance of gratitude and relief. I can't remember what we were talking about, but I recall perfectly

that the conversation kept up pleasantly, without a break, until dinner was almost half over. The roast had been served, and I was in the act of helping myself to potatoes, when I became aware that Mr. Vanderbridge had again fallen into his reverie. This time he scarcely seemed to hear his wife's voice when she spoke to him, and I watched the sadness cloud his face while he continued to stare straight ahead of him with a look that was almost yearning in its intensity.

Again I saw Mrs. Vanderbridge, with her nervous gesture, glance in the direction of the hall, and to my amazement, as she did so, a woman's figure glided noiselessly over the old Persian rug at the door, and entered the dining-room. I was wondering why no one spoke to her, why she spoke to no one, when I saw her sink into a chair on the other side of Mr. Vanderbridge and unfold her napkin. She was quite young, younger even than Mrs. Vanderbridge, and though she was not really beautiful, she was the most graceful creature I had ever imagined. Her dress was of grey stuff, softer and more clinging than silk, and of a peculiar misty texture and colour, and her parted hair lay like twilight on either side of her forehead. She was not like any one I had ever seen before—she appeared so much frailer, so much more elusive, as if she would vanish if you touched her. I can't describe, even months afterwards, the singular way in which she attracted and repelled me.

At first I glanced inquiringly at Mrs. Vanderbridge, hoping that she would introduce me, but she went on talking rapidly in an intense, quivering voice, without noticing the presence of her guest by so much as the lifting of her eyelashes. Mr. Vanderbridge still sat there, silent and detached, and all the time the eyes of the stranger—starry eyes with a mist over them—looked straight through me at the tapestried wall at my back. I knew she didn't see me and that it wouldn't have made the slightest difference to her if she had seen me. In spite of her grace and her girlishness I did not like her, and I felt that this aversion was not on my side alone. I do not know how I received the impression that she hated Mrs. Vanderbridge—never once had she glanced in her direction—yet I was aware, from the moment of her entrance, that she was bristling with animosity, though animosity is too strong a word for the resentful spite, like the jealous rage of a spoiled child, which gleamed now and then in her eyes. I couldn't think of her as wicked any more than I could think of a bad child as wicked. She was merely wilful and un-disciplined and—I hardly know how to convey what I mean—selfish.

After her entrance the dinner dragged on heavily. Mrs. Vanderbridge still kept up her ner-vous chatter, but nobody listened, for I was too embarrassed to pay any attention to what she said, and Mr. Vanderbridge had never recov-ered from his abstraction. He was like a man in a dream, not observing a thing that happened be-fore him, while the strange woman sat there in the candlelight with her curious look of vague-ness and unreality. To my astonishment not even the servants appeared to notice her, and though she had unfolded her napkin when she sat down, she wasn't served with either the roast or the salad. Once or twice, particularly when a new course was served, I glanced at Mrs. Vander-bridge to see if she would rectify the mistake, but she kept her gaze fixed on her plate. It was just as if there were a conspiracy to ignore the pres-ence of the stranger, though she had been, from the moment of her entrance, the dominant fig-ure at the table. You tried to pretend she wasn't there, and yet you knew—you knew vividly that she was gazing insolently straight through you.

The dinner lasted, it seemed, for hours, and you may imagine my relief when at last Mrs. Vanderbridge rose and led the way back into the drawing-room. At first I thought the stranger would follow us, but when I glanced round from the hall she was still sitting there beside Mr. Vanderbridge, who was smoking a cigar with his coffee.

"Usually he takes his coffee with me," said Mrs. Vanderbridge, "but tonight he has things to think over."

"I thought he seemed absent-minded."

"You noticed it, then?" She turned to me with her straightforward glance, "I always won-der how much strangers notice. He hadn't been well of late, and he has these spells of depres-sion. Nerves are dreadful things, aren't they?"

I laughed. "So I've heard, but I've never been able to afford them."

"Well, they do cost a great deal, don't they?" She had a trick of ending her sentences with a question, "I hope your room is comfortable, and that you don't feel timid about being alone on that floor. If you haven't nerves, you can't get nervous, can you?"

"No, I can't get nervous." Yet while I spoke, I was conscious of a shiver deep down in me, as if my senses reacted again to the dread that perme-ated the atmosphere.

As soon as I could, I escaped to my room, and I was sitting there over a book, when the maid—her name was Hopkins, I had discovered—came in on the pretext of inquiring if I had everything I needed. One of the innumerable servants had al-ready turned down my bed, so when Hopkins ap-peared at the door, I suspected at once that there was a hidden motive underlying her ostensible purpose.

"Mrs. Vanderbridge told me to look after you," she began. "She is afraid you will be lonely until you learn the way of things."

"No, I'm not lonely," I answered. "I've never had time to be lonely."

"I used to be like that; but time hangs heavy on my hands now. That's why I've taken to knit-ting." She held out a grey yarn muffler. "I had an operation a year ago, and since then Mrs. Vanderbridge has had another maid—a French one—to sit up for her at night and undress her. She is always so fearful of overtaxing us, though there isn't really enough work for two lady's-maids, because she is so thoughtful that she never gives any trouble if she can help it."

"It must be nice to be rich," I said idly, as I turned a page of my book. Then I added almost before I realized what I was saying, "The other lady doesn't look as if she had so much money."

Her face turned paler if that were possible,

and for a minute I thought she was going to faint. "The other lady?"

"I mean the one who came down late to dinner—the one in the grey dress. She wore no jewels, and her dress wasn't low in the neck."

"Then you saw her?" There was a curious flicker in her face as if her pallor came and went.

"We were at the table when she came in. Has Mr. Vanderbridge a secretary who lives in the house?"

"No, he hasn't a secretary except at his office. When he wants one at the house, he telephones to his office."

"I wondered why she came, for she didn't eat any dinner, and nobody spoke to her—not even Mr. Vanderbridge."

"Oh, he never speaks to her. Thank God, it hasn't come to that yet."

"Then why does she come? It must be dreadful to be treated like that, and before the servants, too. Does she come often?"

"There are months and months when she doesn't. I can always tell by the way Mrs. Vanderbridge picks up. You wouldn't know her, she is so full of life—the very picture of happiness. Then one evening she—the Other One, I mean—comes back again, just as she did to-night, just as she did last summer, and it all begins over from the beginning."

"But can't they keep her out—the Other One? Why do they let her in?"

"Mrs. Vanderbridge tries hard. She tries all she can every minute. You saw her to-night?"

"And Mr. Vanderbridge? Can't he help her?"

She shook her head with an ominous gesture. "He doesn't know."

"He doesn't know she is there? Why, she was close by him. She never took her eyes off him except when she was staring through me at the wall."

"Oh, he knows she is there, but not in that way. He doesn't know that any one else knows."

I gave it up, and after a minute she said in an oppressed voice, "It seems strange that you should have seen her. I never have."

"But you know all about her."

"I know and I don't know. Mrs. Vanderbridge lets things drop sometimes—she gets ill and feverish very easily—but she never tells me anything outright. She isn't that sort."

"Haven't the servants told you about her—the Other One?"

At this, I thought, she seemed startled. "Oh, they don't know anything to tell. They feel that something is wrong; that is why they never stay longer than a week or two—we've had eight butlers since autumn—but they never see what it is."

She stooped to pick up the ball of yarn which had rolled under my chair. "If the time ever comes when you can stand between them, you will do it?" she asked.

"Between Mrs. Vanderbridge and the Other One?"

Her look answered me.

"You think, then, that she means harm to her?"

"I don't know. Nobody knows—but she is killing her."

The clock struck ten, and I returned to my book with a yawn, while Hopkins gathered up her work and went out, after wishing me a formal goodnight. The odd part about our secret conferences was that as soon as they were over, we began to pretend so elaborately to each other that they had never been.

"I'll tell Mrs. Vanderbridge that you are very comfortable," was the last remark Hopkins made before she sidled out of the door and left me alone with the mystery. It was one of those situations—I am obliged to repeat this over and over—that was too preposterous for me to believe in even while I was surrounded and overwhelmed by its reality. I didn't dare face what I thought, I didn't dare face even what I felt; but I went to bed shivering in a warm room, while I resolved passionately that if the chance ever came to me I would stand between Mrs. Vanderbridge and this unknown evil that threatened her.

In the morning Mrs. Vanderbridge went out shopping, and I did not see her until the evening, when she passed me on the staircase as she was going out to dinner and the opera. She was radiant in blue velvet, with diamonds in her hair and at her throat, and I wondered again how any one so lovely could ever be troubled.

"I hope you had a pleasant day, Miss Wrenn," she said kindly. "I have been too busy to get off any letters, but to-morrow we shall begin early." Then, as if from an afterthought, she looked back and added, "There are some new novels in my sitting-room. You might care to look over them."

When she had gone, I went upstairs to the sitting-room and turned over the books, but I couldn't, to save my life, force an interest in printed romances, after meeting Mrs. Vanderbridge and remembering the mystery that surrounded her. I wondered if "the Other One," as Hopkins called her, lived in the house, and I was still wondering this when the maid came in and began putting the table to rights.

"Do they dine out often?" I asked.

"They used to, but since Mr. Vanderbridge hasn't been so well, Mrs. Vanderbridge doesn't like to go without him. She only went to-night because he begged her to."

She had barely finished speaking when the door opened, and Mr. Vanderbridge came in and sat down in one of the big velvet chairs before the wood fire. He had not noticed us, for one of his moods was upon him, and I was about to slip out as noiselessly as I could when I saw that the Other One was standing in the patch of firelight on the hearthrug. I had not seen her come in, and Hopkins evidently was still unaware of her presence, for while I was watching, I saw the maid turn towards her with a fresh log for the fire. At the moment it occurred to me that Hopkins must be either blind or drunk, for without hesitating in her advance, she moved on the stranger, holding the huge hickory log out in front of her. Then, before I could utter a sound or stretch out a hand to stop her, I saw her walk straight through the grey figure and carefully place the log on the andirons.

So she isn't real, after all, she is merely a phantom, I found myself thinking, as I fled from the room, and hurried along the hall to the staircase. She is only a ghost, and nobody believes in ghosts any longer. She is something that I know doesn't exist, yet even though she can't possibly be, I can swear that I have seen her. My nerves were so shaken by the discovery that as soon as I reached my room I sank in a heap on the rug, and it was here that Hopkins found me a little later when she came to bring me an extra blanket.

"You looked so upset I thought you might have seen something," she said. "Did anything happen while you were in the room?"

"She was there all the time—every blessed minute. You walked right through her when you put the log on the fire. Is it possible that you didn't see her?"

"No, I didn't see anything out of the way." She was plainly frightened. "Where was she standing?"

"On the hearthrug in front of Mr. Vanderbridge. To reach the fire you had to walk straight through her, for she didn't move. She didn't give way an inch."

"Oh, she never gives way. She never gives way living or dead."

This was more than human nature could stand.

"In heaven's name," I cried irritably, "who is she?"

"Don't you know?" She appeared genuinely surprised. "Why, she is the other Mrs. Vanderbridge. She died fifteen years ago, just a year after they were married, and people say a scandal was hushed up about her, which he never knew. She isn't a good sort, that's what I think of her, though they say he almost worshipped her."

"And she still has this hold on him?"

"He can't shake it off, that's what's the matter with him, and if it goes on, he will end his days in an asylum. You see, she was very young, scarcely more than a girl, and he got the idea in his head that it was marrying him that killed her. If you want to know what I think, I believe she put it there for a purpose."

"You mean—?" I was so completely at sea that I couldn't frame a rational question.

"I mean she haunts him purposely in order to drive him out of his mind. She was always that sort, jealous and exacting, the kind that clutches and strangles a man, and I've often thought, though I've no head for speculation, that we carry into the next world the traits and feelings that have got the better of us in this one. It seems to me only common sense to believe that we're obliged to work them off somewhere until we are free of them. That is the way my first lady used to talk, anyhow, and I've never found anybody that could give me a more sensible idea."

"And isn't there any way to stop it? What has Mrs. Vanderbridge done?"

"Oh, she can't do anything now. It has got beyond her, though she has had doctor after doctor, and tried everything she could think of. But, you see, she is handicapped because she can't mention it to her husband. He doesn't know that she knows."

"And she won't tell him?"

"She is the sort that would die first—just the opposite from the Other One—for she leaves him free, she never clutches and strangles. It isn't her way." For a moment she hesitated, and then added grimly—"I've wondered if you could do anything?"

"If I could? Why, I am a perfect stranger to them all."

"That's why I've been thinking it. Now, if you could corner her some day—the Other One—and tell her up and down to her face what you think of her."

The idea was so ludicrous that it made me laugh in spite of my shaken nerves. "They would fancy me out of my wits! Imagine stopping an apparition and telling it what you think of it!"

"Then you might try talking it over with Mrs. Vanderbridge. It would help her to know that you see her also."

But the next morning, when I went down to Mrs. Vanderbridge's room, I found that she was too ill to see me. At noon a trained nurse came on the case, and for a week we took our meals together in the morning-room upstairs. She appeared competent enough, but I am sure that she didn't so much as suspect that there was anything wrong in the house except the influenza which had attacked Mrs. Vanderbridge the night of the opera. Never once during that week did I catch a glimpse of the Other One, though I felt her presence whenever I left my room and passed through the hall below. I knew all the time as well as if I had seen her that she was hidden there, watching, watching—

At the end of the week Mrs. Vanderbridge sent for me to write some letters, and when I went into her room, I found her lying on the couch with a tea-table in front of her. She asked me to make the tea because she was still so weak, and I saw that she looked flushed and feverish, and that her eyes were unnaturally large and bright. I hoped she wouldn't talk to me, because people in that state are apt to talk too much and then to blame the listener; but I had hardly taken my seat at the tea-table before she said in a hoarse voice—the cold had settled on her chest:

"Miss Wrenn, I have wanted to ask you ever since the other evening—did you—did you see anything unusual at dinner? From your face when you came out I thought—I thought—"

I met this squarely. "That I might have? Yes, I did see something."

"You saw her?"

"I saw a woman come in and sit down at the table, and I wondered why no one served her. I saw her quite distinctly."

"A small woman, thin and pale, in a grey dress?"

"She was so vague and—and misty, you know what I mean, that it is hard to describe her; but I should know her again anywhere. She wore her hair parted and drawn down over her ears. It was very dark and fine—as fine as spun silk."

We were speaking in low voices, and unconsciously we had moved closer together while my idle hands left the tea things.

"Then you know," she said earnestly, "that she really comes—that I am not out of my mind—that it is not an hallucination?"

"I know that I saw her. I would swear to it. But doesn't Mr. Vanderbridge see her also?"

"Not as we see her. He thinks that she is in his mind only." Then, after an uncomfortable silence, she added suddenly, "She is really a thought, you know. She is his thought of her—but he doesn't know that she is visible to the rest of us."

"And he brings her back by thinking of her?"

She leaned nearer while a quiver passed over her features and the flush deepened in her cheeks. "That is the only way she comes back—the only way she has the power to come back—as a thought. There are months and months when she leaves us in peace because he is thinking of other things, but of late, since his illness, she has been with him almost constantly." A sob broke from her, and she buried her face in her hands. "I suppose she is always trying to come—only she is too vague—and hasn't any form that we can see except when he thinks of her as she used to look when she was alive. His thought of her is like that, hurt and tragic and revengeful. You see, he feels that he ruined her life because she died when the child was coming—a month before it would have been born."

"And if he were to see her differently, would she change? Would she cease to be revengeful if he stopped thinking her so?"

"God only knows. I've wondered and wondered how I might move her to pity."

"Then you feel that she is really there? That she exists outside of his mind?"

"How can I tell? What do any of us know of the world beyond? She exists as much as I exist to you or you to me. Isn't thought all that there is—all that we know?"

This was deeper than I could follow; but in order not to appear stupid, I murmured sympathetically, "And does she make him unhappy when she comes?"

"She is killing him—and me. I believe that is why she does it."

"Are you sure that she could stay away? When he thinks of her isn't she obliged to come back?"

"Oh, I've asked that question over and over!

In spite of his calling her so unconsciously, I believe she comes of her own will, I have always the feeling—it has never left me for an instant—that she could appear differently if she would. I have studied her for years until I know her like a book, and though she is only an apparition, I am perfectly positive that she wills evil to us both. Don't you think he would change that if he could? Don't you think he would make her kind instead of vindictive if he had the power?"

"But if he could remember her as loving and tender?"

"I don't know. I give it up—but it is killing me."

It was killing her. As the days passed I began to realize that she had spoken the truth. I watched her bloom fade slowly and her lovely features grow pinched and thin like the features of a starved person. The harder she fought the apparition, the more I saw that the battle was a losing one, and that she was only wasting her strength. So impalpable yet so pervasive was the enemy that it was like fighting a poisonous odour. There was nothing to wrestle with, and yet there was everything. The struggle was wearing her out—was, as she had said, actually "killing her"; but the physician who dosed her daily with drugs—there was need now of a physician—had not the faintest idea of the malady he was treating. In those dreadful days I think that even Mr. Vanderbridge hadn't a suspicion of the truth. The past was with him so constantly—he was so steeped in the memories of it—that the present was scarcely more than a dream to him. It was, you see, a reverse of the natural order of things; the thought had become more vivid to his perceptions than any object. The phantom had been victorious so far, and he was like a man recovering from the effects of a narcotic. He was only half awake, only half alive to the events through which he lived and the people who surrounded him. Oh, I realize that I am telling my story badly!—that I am slurring over the significant interludes! My mind has dealt so long with external details that I have almost forgotten the words that express invisible things. Though the phantom in the house was more real to me than the bread I ate or the floor on which I trod, I can give you no impression of the atmosphere in which we lived day after day—of the suspense, of the dread of something we could not define, of the brooding horror that seemed to lurk in the shadows of the firelight, of the feeling always, day and night, that some unseen person was watching us. How Mrs. Vanderbridge stood it without losing her reason I have never known; and even now I am not sure that she could have kept her reason if the end had not come when it did. That I accidentally brought it about is one of the things in my life I am most thankful to remember.

It was an afternoon in late winter, and I had just come up from luncheon, when Mrs. Vanderbridge asked me to empty an old desk in one of the upstairs rooms. "I am sending all the furniture in that room away," she said; "it was bought in a bad period, and I want to clear it out and make room for the lovely things we picked up in Italy. There is nothing in the desk worth saving except some old letters from Mr. Vanderbridge's mother before her marriage."

I was glad that she could think of anything so practical as furniture, and it was with relief that I followed her into the dim, rather musty room over the library, where the windows were all tightly closed. Years ago, Hopkins had once told me, the first Mrs. Vanderbridge had used this room for a while, and after her death her husband had been in the habit of shutting himself up alone here in the evenings. This, I inferred, was the secret reason why my employer was sending the furniture away. She had resolved to clear the house of every association with the past.

For a few minutes we sorted the letters in the drawers of the desk, and then, as I expected, Mrs. Vanderbridge became suddenly bored by the task she had undertaken. She was subject to these nervous reactions, and I was prepared for them even when they seized her so spasmodically. I remember that she was in the very act of glancing over an old letter when she rose impatiently, tossed it into the fire unread, and picked up a magazine she had thrown down on a chair.

"Go over them by yourself, Miss Wrenn," she said, and it was characteristic of her nature that she should assume my trustworthiness. "If anything seems worth saving you can file it—but I'd rather die than have to wade through all this."

They were mostly personal letters, and while I went on, carefully filing them, I thought how absurd it was of people to preserve so many papers that were entirely without value. Mr. Vanderbridge I had imagined to be a methodical man, and yet the disorder of the desk produced a painful effect on my systematic temperament. The drawers were filled with letters evidently unsorted, for now and then I came upon a mass of business receipts and acknowledgements crammed in among wedding invitations or letters from some elderly lady, who wrote interminable pale epistles in the finest and most feminine of Italian hands. That a man of Mr. Vanderbridge's wealth and position should have been so careless about his correspondence amazed me until I recalled the dark hints Hopkins had dropped in some of her midnight conversations. Was it possible that he had actually lost his reason for months after the death of his first wife, during that year when he had shut himself alone with her memory? The question was still in my mind when my eyes fell on the envelope in my hand, and I saw that it was addressed to Mrs. Roger Vanderbridge. So this explained, in a measure at least, the carelessness and the disorder! The desk was not his, but hers, and after her death he had used it only during those desperate months when he barely opened a letter. What he had done in those long evenings when he sat alone here it was beyond me to imagine. Was it any wonder that the brooding should have permanently unbalanced his mind?

At the end of an hour I had sorted and filed the papers, with the intention of asking Mrs. Vanderbridge if she wished me to destroy the ones that seemed to be unimportant. The letters she had instructed me to keep had not come to my hand, and I was about to give up the search for them, when, in shaking the lock of one of the drawers, the door of a secret compartment fell open, and I discovered a dark object, which crumbled and dropped apart when I touched it. Bending nearer, I saw that the crumbled mass had once been a bunch of flowers, and that a streamer of purple ribbon still held together the frail structure of wire and stems. In this drawer someone had hidden a sacred treasure, and moved by a sense of romance and adventure, I gathered the dust tenderly in tissue paper, and prepared to take it downstairs to Mrs. Vanderbridge. It was not until then that some letters tied loosely together with a silver cord caught my eye, and while I picked them up, I remember thinking that they must be the ones for which I had been looking so long. Then, as the cord broke in my grasp and I gathered the letters from the lid of the desk, a word or two flashed back at me through the torn edges of the envelopes, and I realized that they were love letters written, I surmised, some fifteen years ago, by Mr. Vanderbridge to his first wife.

"It may hurt her to see them," I thought, "but I don't dare destroy them. There is nothing I can do except give them to her."

As I left the room, carrying the letters and the ashes of the flowers, the idea of taking them to the husband instead of to the wife flashed through my mind. Then—I think it was some jealous feeling about the phantom that decided me—I quickened my steps to a run down the staircase.

"They would bring her back. He would think of her more than ever," I told myself, "so he shall never see them. He shall never see them if I can prevent it." I believe it occurred to me that Mrs. Vanderbridge would be generous enough to give them to him—she was capable of rising above her jealousy, I knew—but I determined that she shouldn't do it until I had reasoned it

out with her. "If anything on earth would bring back the Other One for good, it would be his seeing these old letters," I repeated as I hastened down the hall.

Mrs. Vanderbridge was lying on the couch before the fire, and I noticed at once that she had been crying. The drawn look in her sweet face went to my heart, and I felt that I would do anything in the world to comfort her. Though she had a book in her hand, I could see that she had not been reading. The electric lamp on the table by her side was already lighted, leaving the rest of the room in shadow, for it was a grey day with a biting edge of snow in the air. It was all very charming in the soft light; but as soon as I entered I had a feeling of oppression that made me want to run out into the wind. If you have ever lived in a haunted house—a house pervaded by an unforgettable past—you will understand the sensation of melancholy that crept over me the minute the shadows began to fall. It was not in myself—of this I am sure, for I have naturally a cheerful temperament—it was in the space that surrounded us and the air we breathed.

I explained to her about the letters, and then, kneeling on the rug in front of her, I emptied the dust of the flowers into the fire. There was though I hate to confess it, a vindictive pleasure in watching it melt into the flames; and at the moment I believe I could have burned the apparition as thankfully. The more I saw of the Other One, the more I found myself accepting Hopkins's judgment of her. Yes, her behavior, living and dead, proved that she was not "a good sort."

My eyes were still on the flames when a sound from Mrs. Vanderbridge—half a sigh, half a sob—made me turn quickly and look up at her.

"But this isn't his handwriting," she said in a puzzled tone. "They are love letters, and they are to her—but they are not from him." For a moment or two she was silent, and I heard the pages rustle in her hands as she turned them impatiently. "They are not from him," she repeated presently, with an exultant ring in her voice. "They are written after her marriage, but they are from another man." She was as sternly tragic as an avenging fate. "She wasn't faithful to him while she lived. She wasn't faithful to him even while he was hers—"

With a spring I had risen from my knees and was bending over her.

"Then you can save him from her. You can win him back! You have only to show him the letters, and he will believe."

"Yes, I have only to show him the letters." She was looking beyond me into the dusky shadows of the firelight, as if she saw the Other One standing there before her, "I have only to show him the letters," I knew now that she was not speaking to me, "and he will believe."

"Her power over him will be broken," I cried out. "He will think of her differently. Oh, don't you see? Can't you see? It is the only way to make him think of her differently. It is the only way to break for ever the thought that draws her back to him."

"Yes, I see, it is the only way," she said slowly; and the words were still on her lips when the door opened and Mr. Vanderbridge entered.

"I came for a cup of tea," he began, and added with playful tenderness, "What is the only way?"

It was the crucial moment, I realized—it was the hour of destiny for these two—and while he sank wearily into a chair, I looked imploringly at his wife and then at the letters lying scattered loosely about her. If I had had my will I should have flung them at him with a violence which would have startled him out of his lethargy. Violence, I felt, was what he needed—violence, a storm, tears, reproaches—all the things he would never get from his wife.

For a minute or two she sat there, with the letters before her, and watched him with her thoughtful and tender gaze. I knew from her face, so lovely and yet so sad, that she was looking again at invisible things—at the soul of the man she loved, not at the body. She saw him, detached and spiritualized, and she saw also the

Other One—for while we waited I became slowly aware of the apparition in the firelight—of the white face and the cloudy hair and the look of animosity and bitterness in the eyes. Never before had I been so profoundly convinced of the malignant will veiled by that thin figure. It was as if the visible form were only a spiral of grey smoke covering a sinister purpose.

"The only way," said Mrs. Vanderbridge, "is to fight fairly even when one fights evil." Her voice was like a bell, and as she spoke, she rose from the couch and stood there in her glowing beauty confronting the pale ghost of the past. There was a light about her that was almost unearthly—the light of triumph. The radiance of it blinded me for an instant. It was like a flame, clearing the atmosphere of all that was evil, of all that was poisonous and deadly. She was looking directly at the phantom, and there was no hate in her voice—there was only a great pity, a great sorrow and sweetness.

"I can't fight you that way," she said, and I knew that for the first time she had swept aside subterfuge and evasion, and was speaking straight to the presence before her. "After all, you are dead and I am living, and I cannot fight you that way. I give up everything. I give him back to you. Nothing is mine that I cannot win and keep fairly. Nothing is mine that belongs really to you."

Then, while Mr. Vanderbridge rose, with a start of fear, and came towards her, she bent quickly, and flung the letters into the fire. When he would have stooped to gather the unburned pages, her lovely flowing body curved between his hands and the flames; and so transparent, so ethereal she looked, that I saw—or imagined that I saw—the firelight shine through her. "The only way, my dear, is the right way," she said softly.

The next instant—I don't know to this day how or when it began—I was aware that the apparition had drawn nearer, and that the dread and fear, the evil purpose, were no longer a part of her. I saw her clearly for a moment—saw her as I had never seen her before—young and gentle and—yes, this is the only word for it—loving. It was just as if a curse had turned into a blessing, for, while she stood there, I had a curious sensation of being enfolded in a kind of spiritual glow and comfort—only words are useless to describe the feeling because it wasn't in the least like anything else I had ever known in my life. It was light without heat, glow without light—and yet it was none of these things. The nearest I can come to it is to call it a sense of blessedness—of blessedness that made you at peace with everything you had once hated.

Not until afterwards did I realize that it was the victory of good over evil. Not until afterwards did I discover that Mrs. Vanderbridge had triumphed over the past in the only way that she could triumph. She had won, not by resisting, but by accepting; not by violence, but by gentleness; not by grasping, but by renouncing. Oh, long, long afterwards, I knew that she had robbed the phantom of power over her by robbing it of hatred. She had changed the thought of the past, in that lay her victory.

At the moment I did not understand this. I did not understand it even when I looked again for the apparition in the firelight, and saw that it had vanished. There was nothing there—nothing except the pleasant flicker of light and shadow on the old Persian rug.

David Morrell

WHEN DAVID MORRELL (1943–) wrote *First Blood* (1972), it was described as "the father of the modern adventure novel." It introduced the world to Rambo, who has gone on to become one of the most famous fictional characters in the world, largely through the movies that starred Sylvester Stallone. John Rambo (the famous name came from a variety of apple) is a Vietnam war vet, a troubled, violent, former Green Beret warrior trained in survival, hand-to-hand combat, and other special martial skills. The film series began with *First Blood* (1982), and has continued with *Rambo: First Blood Part II* (1985), *Rambo III* (1988), *Rambo* (2008), with perhaps more to come.

Morrell was born in Kitchener, Ontario, and was still a teenager when he decided to become a writer, inspired by the *Route 66* television scripts by Stirling Silliphant and encouraged by Philip Young, the Hemingway scholar at Penn State University, where he eventually received his M.A. and Ph. D. In 1970, he took a job as an English professor at the University of Iowa, and produced his initial novel, *First Blood*, two years later. He has enjoyed numerous other best-sellers in various genres among his twenty-nine novels, including *The Brotherhood of the Rose* (1984), which became a popular TV miniseries starring Robert Mitchum in 1989. In addition to his ambitious international thrillers, he has written highly popular horror fiction, notably *Creepers* (2005), which won the Bram Stoker Award from the Horror Writers association. He is also the cofounder of the International Thriller Writers association.

"But at My Back I Always Hear" was originally published in *Shadows 6*, edited by Charles L. Grant (New York, Doubleday, 1983).

But at My Back I Always Hear

DAVID MORRELL

SHE PHONED AGAIN LAST night. At 3 a.m. the way she always does. I'm scared to death. I can't keep running. On the hotel's register downstairs, I lied about my name, address, and occupation, hoping to hide from her. My real name's Charles Ingram. Though I'm here in Johnstown, Pennsylvania, I'm from Iowa City, Iowa. I teach—or used to teach until three days ago—creative writing at the University. I can't risk going back there. But I don't think I can hide much longer. Each night, she comes closer.

From the start, she scared me. I came to school at eight to prepare my classes. Through the side door of the English building I went up a stairwell to my third-floor office, which was isolated by a fire door from all the other offices. My colleagues used to joke that I'd been banished, but I didn't care, for in my far-off corner I could concentrate. Few students interrupted me. Regardless of the busy noises past the fire door, I sometimes felt there was no one else inside the building. And indeed at 8 a.m. I often *was* the only person in the building.

That day I was wrong, however. Clutching my heavy briefcase, I trudged up the stairwell. My scraping footsteps echoed off the walls of the pale-red cinderblock, the stairs of pale-green imitation marble. First floor. Second floor. The neon lights glowed coldly. Then the stairwell angled toward the third floor, and I saw her waiting on a chair outside my office. Pausing, I frowned up at her. I felt uneasy.

Eight a.m., for you, is probably not early. You've been up for quite a while so you can get to work on time or get your children off to school. But 8 a.m., for college students, is the middle of the night. They don't like morning classes. When their schedules force them to attend one, they don't crawl from bed until they absolutely have to, and they don't come stumbling into class until I'm just about to start my lecture.

I felt startled, then, to find her waiting ninety minutes early. She sat tensely: lifeless dull brown hair, a shapeless dingy sweater, baggy faded jeans with patches on the knees and frays around the cuffs. Her eyes seemed haunted, wild, and deep and dark.

I climbed the last few steps and, puzzled, stopped before her. "Do you want an early conference?"

Instead of answering, she nodded bleakly.

"You're concerned about a grade I gave you?"

This time, though, in pain she shook her head from side to side.

Confused, I fumbled with my key and opened the office, stepping in. The room was small and narrow: a desk, two chairs, a wall of bookshelves, and a window. As I sat behind the desk, I watched her slowly come inside. She glanced around uncertainly. Distraught, she shut the door.

That made me nervous. When a female student shuts the door, I start to worry that a colleague or a student might walk up the stairs and hear a female voice and wonder what's so private I want to keep the door closed. Though I should have told her to reopen it, her frantic eyes aroused such pity in me that I sacrificed my principle, deciding her torment was so personal she could talk about it only in strict secrecy.

"Sit down." I smiled and tried to make her feel at ease, though I myself was not at ease. "What seems to be the difficulty, Miss . . . ? I'm sorry, but I don't recall your name."

"Samantha Perry. I don't like 'Samantha,' though." She fidgeted. "I've shortened it to—"

"Yes? To what?"

"To 'Sam.' I'm in your Tuesday–Thursday class." She bit her lip. "You spoke to me."

I frowned, not understanding. "You mean what I taught seemed vivid to you? I inspired you to write a better story?"

"Mr. Ingram, no. I mean you *spoke* to me. You stared at me while you were teaching. You ignored the other students. You directed what you said to *me*. When you talked about Hemingway, how Frederic Henry wants to go to bed with Catherine"—she swallowed—"you were asking me to go to bed with you."

I gaped. To disguise my shock, I quickly lit a cigarette. "You're mistaken."

"But I *heard* you. You kept staring straight at *me*. I felt all the other students knew what you were doing."

"I was only lecturing. I often look at students' faces to make sure they pay attention. You received the wrong impression."

"You weren't asking me to go to bed with you?" Her voice sounded anguished.

"No. I don't trade sex for grades."

"But I don't care about a grade!"

"I'm married. Happily. I've got two children.

Anyway, suppose I did intend to proposition you. Would I do it in the middle of a class? I'd be foolish."

"Then you never meant to—" She kept biting her lip.

"I'm sorry."

"But you speak to me! Outside class I hear your voice! When I'm in my room or walking down the street! You talk to me when I'm asleep! You say you want to go to bed with me!"

My skin prickled. I felt frozen. "You're mistaken. Your imagination's playing tricks."

"But I hear your voice so clearly! When I'm studying or—"

"How? If I'm not there."

"You send your thoughts! You concentrate and put your voice inside my mind!"

Adrenaline scalded my stomach. I frantically sought an argument to disillusion her. "Telepathy? I don't believe in it. I've never tried to send my thoughts to you."

"Unconsciously?"

I shook my head from side to side. I couldn't bring myself to tell her: of all the female students in her class, she looked so plain, even if I wasn't married I'd never have wanted sex with her.

"You're studying too hard. You want to do so well you're preoccupied with me. That's why you think you hear my voice when I'm not there. I try to make my lectures vivid. As a consequence, you think I'm speaking totally to you."

"Then you shouldn't teach that way!" she shouted. "It's not fair! It's cruel! It's teasing!" Tears streamed down her face. "You made a fool of me!"

"I didn't mean to."

"But you did! You tricked me! You misled me!"

"No."

She stood so quickly I flinched, afraid she'd lunge at me or scream for help and claim I'd tried to rape her. That damned door. I cursed myself for not insisting she leave it open.

She rushed sobbing toward it. She pawed the knob and stumbled out, hysterically retreating down the stairwell.

Shaken, I stubbed out my cigarette, grabbing another. My chest tightened as I heard the dwindling echo of her wracking sobs, the awkward scuffle of her dimming footsteps, then the low deep rumble of the outside door.

The silence settled over me.

An hour later I found her waiting in class. She'd wiped her tears. The only signs of what had happened were her red and puffy eyes. She sat alertly, pen to paper. I carefully didn't face her as I spoke. She seldom glanced up from her notes.

After class I asked my graduate assistant if he knew her.

"You mean Sam? Sure, I know her. She's been getting Ds. She had a conference with me. Instead of asking how to get a better grade, though, all she did was talk about you, pumping me for information. She's got quite a thing for you. Too bad about her."

"Why?"

"Well, she's so plain, she doesn't have many friends. I doubt she goes out much. There's a problem with her father. She was vague about it, but I had the sense her three sisters are so beautiful that Daddy treats her as the ugly duckling. She wants very much to please him. He ignores her, though. He's practically disowned her. You remind her of him."

"Who? Of her father?"

"She admits you're ten years younger than him, but she says you look exactly like him."

I felt heartsick.

Two days later, I found her waiting for me—again at 8 a.m.—outside my office.

Tense, I unlocked the door. As if she heard my thought, she didn't shut it this time. Sitting before my desk, she didn't fidget. She just stared at me.

"It happened again," she said.

"In class I didn't even look at you."

"No, afterward, when I went to the library." She drew an anguished breath. "And later—I ate supper in the dorm. I heard your voice so clearly, I was sure you were in the room."

"What time was that?"

"Five-thirty."

"I was having cocktails with the Dean. Believe me, Sam, I wasn't sending messages to you. I didn't even *think* of you."

"I couldn't have imagined it! You wanted me to go to bed with you!"

"I wanted research money from the Dean. I thought of nothing else. My mind was totally involved in trying to convince him. When I didn't get the money, I was too annoyed to concentrate on anything but getting drunk."

"Your voice—"

"It isn't real. If I sent thoughts to you, wouldn't I admit what I was doing? When you asked me, wouldn't I confirm the message? Why would I deny it?"

"I'm afraid."

"You're troubled by your father."

"What?"

"My graduate assistant says you identify me with your father."

She went ashen. "That's supposed to be a secret!"

"Sam, I asked him. He won't lie to me."

"If you remind me of my father, if I want to go to bed with you, then I must want to go to bed with—"

"Sam—"

"—my father! You must think I'm disgusting!"

"No, I think you're confused. You ought to find some help. You ought to see a—"

But she never let me finish. Weeping again, ashamed, hysterical, she bolted from the room.

And that's the last I ever saw of her. An hour later, when I started lecturing, she wasn't in class. A few days later I received a drop-slip from the registrar, informing me she'd canceled all her classes.

I forgot her.

Summer came. Then fall arrived. November. On a rainy Tuesday night, my wife and I stayed up to watch the close results of the election, worried for our presidential candidate.

At 3 a.m. the phone rang. No one calls that late unless . . .

The jangle of the phone made me bang my head as I searched for a beer in the fridge. I rubbed my throbbing skull and swung alarmed as Jean, my wife, came from the living room and squinted toward the kitchen phone.

"It might be just a friend," I said. "Election gossip."

But I worried about our parents. Maybe one of them was sick or . . .

I watched uneasily as Jean picked up the phone.

"Hello?" She listened apprehensively. Frowning, she put her hand across the mouthpiece. "It's for you. A woman."

"What?"

"She's young. She asked for Mr. Ingram."

"Damn, a student."

"At 3 a.m.?"

I almost didn't think to shut the fridge. Annoyed, I yanked the pop-tab off the can of beer. My marriage is successful. I'll admit we've had our troubles. So has every couple. But we've faced those troubles, and we're happy. Jean is thirty-five, attractive, smart, and patient. But her trust in me was clearly tested at that moment. A woman had to know me awfully well to call at 3 a.m.

"Let's find out." I grabbed the phone. To prove my innocence to Jean, I roughly said, "Yeah, what?"

"I heard you." The female voice was frail and plaintive, trembling.

"Who *is* this?" I said angrily.

"It's me."

I heard a low-pitched crackle on the line.

"Who the hell is *me?* Just tell me what your name is."

"Sam."

My knees went weak. I slumped against the wall.

Jean stared. "What's wrong?" Her eyes narrowed with suspicion.

"Sam, it's 3 a.m. What's so damn important you can't wait to call me during office hours?"

"Three? It can't be. No, it's one."

"It's three. For God's sake, Sam, I know what time it is."

"Please, don't get angry. On my radio the news announcer said it was one o'clock."

"Where *are* you, Sam?"

"At Berkeley."

"California? Sam, the time-zone difference. In the Midwest it's two hours later. Here it's three o'clock."

". . . I guess I just forgot."

"But that's absurd. Have you been drinking? Are you drunk?"

"No, not exactly."

"What the hell does *that* mean?"

"Well, I took some pills. I'm not sure what they were."

"Oh, Jesus."

"Then I heard you. You were speaking to me."

"No. I told you your mind's playing tricks. The voice isn't real. You're imagining—"

"You called to me. You said you wanted me to go to bed with you. You wanted me to come to you."

"To Iowa? No. You've got to understand. Don't do it. I'm not sending thoughts to you."

"You're lying! Tell me why you're lying!"

"I don't want to go to bed with you. I'm glad you're in Berkeley. Stay there. Get some help. Lord, don't you realize? Those pills. They make you hear my voice. They make you hallucinate."

"I . . ."

"Trust me, Sam. Believe me. I'm not sending thoughts to you. I didn't even know you'd gone to Berkeley. You're two thousand miles away from me. What you're suggesting is impossible."

She didn't answer. All I heard was low-pitched static.

"Sam—"

The dial tone abruptly droned. My stomach sank. Appalled, I kept the phone against my ear. I swallowed dryly, shaking as I set the phone back on its cradle.

Jean glared. "Who was that? She wasn't any 'Sam.' She wants to go to bed with you? At 3 a.m.? What games have you been playing?"

"None." I gulped my beer, but my throat stayed dry. "You'd better sit. I'll get a beer for you."

Jean clutched her stomach.

"It's not what you think. I promise I'm not screwing anybody. But it's bad. I'm scared."

I handed Jean a beer.

"I don't know why it happened. But last spring, at 8 a.m., I went to school and . . ."

Jean listened, troubled. Afterward she asked for Sam's description, somewhat mollified to learn she was plain and pitiful.

"The truth?" Jean asked.

"I promise you."

Jean studied me. "You did nothing to encourage her?"

"I guarantee it. I wasn't aware of her until I found her waiting for me."

"But unconsciously?"

"Sam asked me that as well. I was only lecturing the best way I know how."

Jean kept her eyes on me. She nodded, glancing toward her beer. "Then she's disturbed. There's nothing you can do for her. I'm glad she moved to Berkeley. In your place, I'd have been afraid."

"I *am* afraid. She spooks me."

At a dinner party the next Saturday, I told our host and hostess what had happened, motivated more than just by need to share my fear with someone else, for while the host was both a friend and a colleague, he was married to a clinical psychologist. I needed professional advice.

Diane, the hostess, listened with slim interest

until halfway through my story, when she suddenly sat straight and peered at me.

I faltered. "What's the matter?"

"Don't stop. What else?"

I frowned and finished, waiting for Diane's reaction. Instead she poured more wine. She offered more lasagna.

"Something bothered you."

She tucked her long black hair behind her ears. "It could be nothing."

"I need to know."

She nodded grimly. "I can't make a diagnosis merely on the basis of your story. I'd be irresponsible."

"But hypothetically . . ."

"And *only* hypothetically. She hears your voice. That's symptomatic of a severe disturbance. Paranoia, for example. Schizophrenia. The man who shot John Lennon heard a voice. And so did Manson. So did Son of Sam."

"My God," Jean said. "Her name." She set her fork down loudly.

"The parallel occurred to me," Diane said. "Chuck, if she identifies you with her father, she might be dangerous to Jean and to the children."

"Why?"

"Jealousy. To hurt the equivalent of her mother and her rival sisters."

I felt sick; the wine turned sour in my stomach.

"There's another possibility. No more encouraging. If you continue to reject her, she could be dangerous to you. Instead of dealing with her father, she might redirect her rage and jealousy toward you. By killing you, she'd be venting her frustration toward her father."

I felt panicked. "For the *good* news."

"Understood, I'm speaking hypothetically. Possibly she's lying to you, and she doesn't hear your voice. Or, as you guessed, the drugs she takes might make her hallucinate. There could be many explanations. Without seeing her, without the proper tests, I wouldn't dare to judge her symptoms. You're a friend, so I'm compromising. Possibly she's homicidal."

"Tell me what to do."

"For openers, I'd stay away from her."

"I'm *trying*. She called from California. She's threatening to come back here to see me."

"Talk her out of it."

"I'm no psychologist. I don't know what to say to her."

"Suggest she get professional advice."

"I tried that."

"Try again. But if you find her at your office, don't go in the room with her. Find other people. Crowds protect you."

"But at 8 a.m. there's no one in the building."

"Think of some excuse to leave her. Jean, if she comes to the house, don't let her in."

Jean paled. "I've never seen her. How could I identify her?"

"Chuck described her. Don't take chances. Don't trust anyone who might resemble her, and keep a close watch on the children."

"*How?* Rebecca's twelve. Sue's nine. I can't insist they stay around the house."

Diane turned her wineglass, saying nothing.

". . . Oh, dear Lord," Jean said.

The next few weeks were hellish. Every time the phone rang, Jean and I jerked, startled, staring at it. But the calls were from our friends or from our children's friends or from some insulation/magazine/home-siding salesman. Every day I mustered courage as I climbed the stairwell to my office. Silent prayers were answered. Sam was never there. My tension dissipated. I began to feel she no longer was obsessed with me.

Thanksgiving came—the last day of peace I've known. We went to church. Our parents live too far away for us to share the feast with them. But we invited friends to dinner. We watched football. I helped Jean make the dressing for the turkey. I made both the pumpkin pies. The friends we'd invited were my colleague and his wife, the clinical psychologist. She asked if my student had continued to harass me. Shaking my head from side to side, I grinned and raised my glass in special thanks.

The guests stayed late to watch a movie with us. Jean and I felt pleasantly exhausted, mellowed by good food, good drink, good friends, when after midnight we washed all the dishes, went to bed, made love, and drifted wearily to sleep.

The phone rang, shocking me awake. I fumbled toward the bedside lamp. Jean's eyes went wide with fright. She clutched my arm and pointed toward the clock. It was 3 a.m.

The phone kept ringing.

"Don't," Jean said.

"Suppose it's someone else."

"You know it isn't."

"If it's Sam and I don't answer, she might come to the house instead of phoning."

"For God's sake, make her stop."

I grabbed the phone, but my throat wouldn't work.

"I'm coming to you," the voice wailed.

"Sam?"

"I heard you. I won't disappoint you. I'll be there soon."

"No. Wait. Listen."

"I've been listening. I hear you all the time. The anguish in your voice. You're begging me to come to you, to hold you, to make love to you."

"That isn't true."

"You say your wife's jealous of me. I'll convince her she isn't being fair. I'll make her let you go. Then we'll be happy."

"Sam, where are you? Still at Berkeley?"

"Yes. I spent Thanksgiving by myself. My father didn't want me to come home."

"You have to stay there, Sam. I didn't send my voice. You need advice. You need to see a doctor. Will you do that for me? As a favor?"

"I already did. But Dr. Campbell doesn't understand. He thinks I'm imagining what I hear. He humors me. He doesn't realize how much you love me."

"Sam, you have to talk to him again. You have to tell him what you plan to do."

"I can't wait any longer. I'll be there soon. I'll be with you."

My heart pounded frantically. I heard a roar in my head. I flinched as the phone was yanked away from me.

Jean shouted to the mouthpiece, "Stay away from us! Don't call again! Stop terrorizing—"

Jean stared wildly at me. "No one's there. The line went dead. I hear just the dial tone."

I'm writing this as quickly as I can. I don't have much more time. It's almost three o'clock.

That night, we didn't try to go back to sleep. We couldn't. We got dressed and went downstairs where, drinking coffee, we decided what to do. At eight, as soon as we'd sent the kids to school, we drove to the police.

They listened sympathetically, but there was no way they could help us. After all, Sam hadn't broken any law. Her calls weren't obscene; it was difficult to prove harassment; she'd made no overt threats. Unless she harmed us, there was nothing the police could do.

"Protect us," I insisted.

"How?" the sergeant said.

"Assign an officer to guard the house."

"How long? A day, a week, a month? That woman might not even bother you again. We're overworked and understaffed. I'm sorry—I can't spare an officer whose only duty is to watch you. I can send a car to check the house from time to time. No more than that. But if this woman does show up and bother you, then call us. We'll take care of her."

"But that might be too late."

We took the children home from school. Sam couldn't have arrived from California yet, but what else could we do? I don't own any guns. If all of us stayed together, we had some chance for protection.

That was Friday. I slept lightly. Three a.m., the phone rang. It was Sam, of course.

"I'm coming."

"Sam, where are you?"

"Reno."

"You're not flying."

"No, I can't."

"Turn back, Sam. Go to Berkeley. See that doctor."

"I can't wait to see you."

"Please—"

The dial tone was droning.

I phoned Berkeley information. Sam had mentioned Dr. Campbell. But the operator couldn't find him in the yellow pages.

"Try the University," I blurted. "Student Counseling."

I was right. A Dr. Campbell was a university psychiatrist. On Saturday I couldn't reach him at his office, but a woman answered his home. He wouldn't be available until the afternoon. At four o'clock I finally got through to him.

"You've got a patient named Samantha Perry," I began.

"I did. Not anymore."

"I know. She's left for Iowa. She wants to see me. I'm afraid. I think she might be dangerous."

"Well, you don't have to worry."

"She's not dangerous?"

"Potentially she was."

"But tell me what to do when she arrives. You're treating her. You'll know what I should do."

"No, Mr. Ingram, she won't come to see you. On Thanksgiving night, at 1 a.m., she killed herself. An overdose of drugs."

My vision failed. I clutched the kitchen table to prevent myself from falling. "That's impossible."

"I saw the body. I identified it."

"But she called that night."

"What time?"

"At 3 a.m. Midwestern time."

"Or one o'clock in California. No doubt after or before she took the drugs. She didn't leave a note, but she called you."

"She gave no indication—"

"She mentioned you quite often. She was morbidly attracted to you. She had an extreme, unhealthy certainty that she was telepathic, that you put your voice inside her mind."

"I know that! Was she paranoid or homicidal?"

"Mr. Ingram, I've already said too much. Although she's dead, I can't violate her confidence."

"But I don't think she's dead."

"I beg your pardon?"

"If she died on Thursday night, then tell me how she called again on *Friday* night."

The line hummed. I sensed the doctor's hesitation. "Mr. Ingram, you're upset. You don't know what you're saying. You've confused the nights."

"I'm telling you she called again on Friday!"

"And I'm telling you she died on *Thursday*. Either someone's tricking you, or else . . ." The doctor swallowed with discomfort.

"Or?" I trembled. "*I'm* the one who's hearing voices?"

"Mr. Ingram, don't upset yourself. You're honestly confused."

I slowly put the phone down, terrified. "I'm sure I heard her voice."

That night, Sam called again. At 3 a.m. From Salt Lake City. When I handed Jean the phone she heard just the dial tone.

"But you know the goddamn phone rang!" I insisted.

"Maybe a short circuit. Chuck, I'm telling you there was no one on the line."

Then Sunday. Three a.m. Cheyenne, Wyoming. Coming closer.

But she couldn't be if she was dead.

The student paper at the University subscribes to all the other major student papers. Monday, Jean and I left the children with friends and drove to its office. Friday's copy of the Berkeley campus paper had arrived. In desperation I searched its pages. "There!" A two-inch item. Sudden student death. Samantha Perry. Tactfully, no cause was given.

Outside in the parking lot, Jean said, "Now do you believe she's dead?"

"Then tell me why I hear her voice! I've got to be crazy if I think I hear a corpse!"

"You're feeling guilty that she killed herself because of you. You shouldn't. There was nothing you could do to stop her. You've been losing too much sleep. Your imagination's taking over."

"You admit you heard the phone ring!"

"Yes, it's true. I can't explain that. If the phone's broken, we'll have it fixed. To put your mind at rest, we'll get a new, unlisted number."

I felt better. After several drinks, I even got some sleep.

But Monday night, again the phone rang. Three a.m. I jerked awake. Cringing, I insisted Jean answer it. But she heard just the dial tone. I grabbed the phone. Of course, I heard Sam's voice.

"I'm almost there. I'll hurry. I'm in Omaha."

"This number isn't listed!"

"But you told me the new one. Your wife's the one who changed it. She's trying to keep us apart. I'll make her sorry. Darling, I can't wait to be with you."

I screamed. Jean jerked away from me.

"Sam, you've got to stop! I spoke to Dr. Campbell!"

"No. He wouldn't dare. He wouldn't violate my trust."

"He said you were dead!"

"I couldn't live without you. Soon we'll be together."

Shrieking, I woke the children, so hysterical Jean had to call an ambulance. Two interns struggled to sedate me.

Omaha was one day's drive from where we live. Jean came to visit me in the hospital on Tuesday.

"Are you feeling better?" Jean frowned, troubled.

"Please, you have to humor me," I said. "All right? Suspect I've gone crazy, but for God sake, humor me. I can't prove what I'm thinking, but I know you're in danger. I am too. You have to get the children and leave town. You have to hide somewhere. Tonight at 3 a.m. she'll reach the house."

Jean stared with pity.

"Promise me!" I said.

She saw the anguish on my face and nodded.

"Maybe she won't try the house," I said. "She might come here. I have to get away. I'm not sure how, but later, when you're gone, I'll find a way to leave."

Jean peered at me, distressed; her voice sounded totally discouraged. "Chuck."

"I'll check the house when I get out of here. If you're still there, you know you'll make me more upset."

"I promise. I'll take Susan and Rebecca, and we'll drive somewhere."

"I love you."

Jean began to cry. "I won't know where you are."

"If I survive this, I'll get word to you."

"But how?"

"The English department. I'll leave a message with the secretary."

Jean leaned down to kiss me, crying, certain I'd lost my mind.

I reached the house that night. As she'd promised, Jean had left with the children. I got in my sports car and raced to the Interstate.

A Chicago hotel where at 3 a.m. Sam called from Iowa. She'd heard my voice. She said I'd told her where I was, but she was hurt and angry. "Tell me why you're running."

I fled from Chicago in the middle of the night, driving until I absolutely had to rest. I checked in here at 1 a.m. In Johnstown, Pennsylvania. I can't sleep. I've got an awful feeling. Last night Sam repeated, "Soon you'll join me." In the desk I found this stationery.

God, it's 3 a.m. I pray I'll see the sun come up.

It's almost four. She didn't phone. I can't believe I escaped, but I keep staring at the phone.

·   ·   ·

It's four. Dear Christ, I hear the ringing.

Finally I've realized. Sam killed herself at one. In Iowa the time-zone difference made it three. But I'm in Pennsylvania. In the East. A different time zone. One o'clock in California would be *four* o'clock, not three, in Pennsylvania.

Now.

The ringing persists. But I've realized something else. This hotel's unusual, designed to seem like a home.

The ringing?

God help me, it's the doorbell.

THE FURNISHED ROOM

O. Henry

ONE OF THE MOST popular, beloved, and famous ghost stories of all time, "The Furnished Room" should not appear in an anthology of ghost stories because it tips off the surprise ending for which the author became famous. O. Henry, the pseudonym of William Sidney (later changed to Sydney) Porter (1862–1910), wrote more than six hundred short stories that once were as critically acclaimed as they were popular. Often undervalued today because of their sentimentality, many nonetheless remain iconic and familiar, notably such classics as "The Gift of the Magi," "The Last Leaf," "A Retrieved Reformation" (better known for its several stage and film versions as *Alias Jimmy Valentine*) and "The Ransom of Red Chief." *The O. Henry Memorial Award Prize Stories,* a prestigious annual anthology of the year's best short stories, has been published since 1919.

Several contemporary critics, including Stephen Leacock, called this story, probably the darkest O. Henry ever wrote, the best of all his work, even though the book in which it appeared, *The Four Million,* also contained such masterworks as "The Gift of the Magi," "The Cop and the Anthem," and "After Twenty Years." The book's title, by the way, was O. Henry's rebuttal to Ward McAllister, a prominent New Yorker, who averred that there were only four hundred people in the city worthy of consideration.

More than two hundred motion pictures and television programs were based on O. Henry's work, including the eponymous *O. Henry Playhouse,* so it is no surprise that "The Furnished Room" was frequently adapted—for radio broadcasts, a short silent film from Vitagraph in 1917, and an episode of television's *Great Mysteries* that starred Orson Welles and aired on February 24, 1974.

"The Furnished Room" was first published in the August 14, 1904, issue of the *New York Sunday World Magazine;* its first book appearance was in O. Henry's *The Four Million* (New York, McClure, Phillips, 1906).

The Furnished Room

O. HENRY

RESTLESS, SHIFTING, fugacious as time itself is a certain vast bulk of the population of the red brick district of the lower West Side. Homeless, they have a hundred homes. They flit from furnished room to furnished room, transients forever—transients in abode, transients in heart and mind. They sing "Home, Sweet Home" in ragtime; they carry their *lares et penates* in a bandbox; their vine is entwined about a picture hat; a rubber plant is their fig tree.

Hence the houses of this district, having had a thousand dwellers, should have a thousand tales to tell, mostly dull ones, no doubt; but it would be strange if there could not be found a ghost or two in the wake of all these vagrant guests.

One evening after dark a young man prowled among these crumbling red mansions, ringing their bells. At the twelfth he rested his lean hand-baggage upon the step and wiped the dust from his hatband and forehead. The bell sounded faint and far away in some remote, hollow depths.

To the door of this, the twelfth house whose bell he had rung, came a housekeeper who made him think of an unwholesome, surfeited worm that had eaten its nut to a hollow shell and now sought to fill the vacancy with edible lodgers.

He asked if there was a room to let.

"Come in," said the housekeeper. Her voice came from her throat; her throat seemed lined with fur. "I have the third floor, back, vacant since a week back. Should you wish to look at it?"

The young man followed her up the stairs. A faint light from no particular source mitigated the shadows of the halls. They trod noiselessly upon a stair carpet that its own loom would have forsworn. It seemed to have become vegetable; to have degenerated in that rank, sunless air to a lush lichen or spreading moss that grew in patches to the staircase and was viscid under the foot like organic matter. At each turn of the stairs were vacant niches in the wall. Perhaps plants had once been set within them. If so they had died in that foul and tainted air. It may be that statues of the saints had stood there, but it was not difficult to conceive that imps and devils had dragged them forth in the darkness and down to the unholy depths of some furnished pit below.

"This is the room," said the housekeeper, through her furry throat. "It's a nice room. It ain't often vacant. I had some most elegant people in it last summer—no trouble at all, and paid in advance to the minute. The water's at the end of the hall. Sprowls and Mooney kept it three months. They done a vaudeville sketch. Miss B'retta Sprowls—you may have heard of her— Oh, that was just the stage names—right there over the dresser is where the marriage certificate hung, framed. The gas is here, and you see there is plenty of closet room. It's a room everybody likes. It never stays idle long."

"Do you have many theatrical people rooming here?" asked the young man.

"They comes and goes. A proportion of my lodgers is connected with the theatres. Yes, sir, this is the theatrical district. Actor people never stays long anywhere. I get my share. Yes, they comes and they goes."

He engaged the room, paying for a week in advance. He was tired, he said, and would take possession at once. He counted out the money. The room had been made ready, she said, even to towels and water. As the housekeeper moved away he put, for the thousandth time, the question that he carried at the end of his tongue.

"A young girl—Miss Vashner—Miss Eloise Vashner—do you remember such a one among your lodgers? She would be singing on the stage, most likely. A fair girl, of medium height and slender, with reddish gold hair and a dark mole near her left eyebrow."

"No, I don't remember the name. Them stage people has names they change as often as their rooms. They comes and they goes. No, I don't call that one to mind."

No. Always no. Five months of ceaseless interrogation and the inevitable negative. So much time spent by day in questioning managers, agents, schools, and choruses; by night among the audiences of theatres from all-star casts down to music halls so low that he dreaded to find what he most hoped for. He who had loved her best had tried to find her. He was sure that since her disappearance from home this great, water-girt city held her somewhere, but it was like a monstrous quicksand, shifting its particles constantly, with no foundation, its upper granules of to-day buried to-morrow in ooze and slime.

The furnished room received its latest guest with a first glow of pseudo-hospitality, a hectic, haggard, perfunctory welcome like the specious smile of a demirep. The sophistical comfort came in reflected gleams from the decayed furniture, the ragged brocade upholstery of a couch and two chairs, a foot-wide cheap pier glass between the two windows, from one or two gilt picture frames and a brass bedstead in a corner.

The guest reclined, inert, upon a chair, while the room, confused in speech as though it were an apartment in Babel, tried to discourse to him of its divers tenantry.

A polychromatic rug like some brilliant-flowered rectangular, tropical islet lay surrounded by a billowy sea of soiled matting. Upon the gay-papered wall were those pictures that pursue the homeless one from house to house—The Huguenot Lovers, The First Quarrel, The Wedding Breakfast, Psyche at the Fountain. The mantel's chastely severe outline was ingloriously veiled behind some pert drapery drawn rakishly askew like the sashes of the Amazonian ballet. Upon it was some desolate flotsam cast aside by the room's marooned when a lucky sail had borne them to a fresh port—a trifling vase or two, pictures of actresses, a medicine bottle, some stray cards out of a deck.

One by one, as the characters of a cryptograph become explicit, the little signs left by the furnished room's procession of guests developed a significance. The threadbare space in the rug in front of the dresser told that lovely women had marched in the throng. Tiny finger prints on the wall spoke of little prisoners trying to feel their way to sun and air. A splattered stain, raying like the shadow of a bursting bomb, witnessed where a hurled glass or bottle had splintered with its contents against the wall. Across the pier glass had been scrawled with a diamond in staggering letters the name "Marie." It seemed that the succession of dwellers in the furnished room had turned in fury—perhaps tempted beyond forbearance by its garish coldness—and wreaked upon it their passions. The furniture was chipped and bruised; the couch, distorted by bursting springs, seemed a horrible monster that had been slain during the stress of some grotesque convulsion. Some more potent upheaval had cloven a great slice from the marble mantel. Each plank in the floor owned its particular cant and shriek as from a separate and individual agony. It seemed incredible that all this malice and injury had been wrought upon the room by those who had called it for a time their home; and yet it may have been the cheated home instinct surviving blindly, the resentful rage at false household gods that had kindled their wrath. A hut that is our own we can sweep and adorn and cherish.

The young tenant in the chair allowed these thoughts to file, soft-shod, through his mind, while there drifted into the room furnished sounds and furnished scents. He heard in one room a tittering and incontinent, slack laughter; in others the monologue of a scold, the rattling of dice, a lullaby, and one crying dully; above him a banjo tinkled with spirit. Doors banged somewhere; the elevated trains roared intermittently; a cat yowled miserably upon a back fence. And he breathed the breath of the house—a dank savor rather than a smell—a cold, musty effluvium as from underground vaults mingled with the reeking exhalations of linoleum and mildewed and rotten woodwork.

Then suddenly, as he rested there, the room was filled with the strong, sweet odor of mignonette. It came as upon a single buffet of wind with such sureness and fragrance and emphasis that it almost seemed a living visitant. And the man cried aloud: "What, dear?" as if he had been called, and sprang up and faced about. The rich odor clung to him and wrapped him around. He reached out his arms for it, all his senses for the time confused and commingled. How could one be peremptorily called by an odor? Surely it must have been a sound. But, was it not the sound that had touched, that had caressed him?

"She has been in this room," he cried, and he sprang to wrest from it a token, for he knew he would recognize the smallest thing that had belonged to her or that she had touched. This enveloping scent of mignonette, the odor that she had loved and made her own—whence came it?

The room had been but carelessly set in order. Scattered upon the flimsy dresser scarf were half a dozen hairpins—those discreet, indistinguishable friends of womankind, feminine of gender, infinite of mood and uncommunicative of tense. These he ignored, conscious of their triumphant lack of identity. Ransacking the drawers of the dresser he came upon a discarded, tiny, ragged handkerchief. He pressed it to his face. It was racy and insolent with heliotrope; he hurled it to the floor. In another drawer he found odd buttons, a theatre programme, a pawnbroker's card, two lost marshmallows, a book on the divination of dreams. In the last was a woman's black satin hair bow, which halted him, reached between ice and fire. But the black satin hair bow also is femininity's demure, impersonal, common ornament, and tells no tales.

And then he traversed the room like a hound on the scent, skimming the walls, considering the corners of the bulging matting on his hands and knees, rummaging mantel and tables, the curtains and hangings, the drunken cabinet in the corner, for a visible sign, unable to perceive that she was there beside, around, against, within, above him, clinging to him, wooing him, calling him so poignantly through the finer senses that even his grosser ones became cognizant of the call. Once again he answered loudly: "Yes, dear!" and turned, wild-eyed, to gaze on vacancy, for he could not yet discern form and color and love and outstretched arms in the odor of mignonette. Oh, God! Whence that odor, and since when have odors had a voice to call? Thus he groped.

He burrowed in crevices and corners, and found corks and cigarettes. These he passed in passive contempt. But once he found in a fold of the matting a half-smoked cigar, and this he ground beneath his heel with a green and trenchant oath. He sifted the room from end to end. He found dreary and ignoble small records of many a peripatetic tenant; but of her whom he sought, and who may have lodged there, and whose spirit seemed to hover there, he found no trace.

And then he thought of the housekeeper.

He ran from the haunted room downstairs and to a door that showed a crack of light. She came out to his knock. He smothered his excitement as best he could.

"Will you tell me, madam," he besought her, "who occupied the room I have before I came?"

"Yes, sir. I can tell you again. 'Twas Sprowls and Mooney, as I said. Miss B'retta Sprowls it was in the theatres, but Missis Mooney she was. My house is well known for respectability. The marriage certificate hung, framed, on a nail over—"

"What kind of a lady was Miss Sprowls—in looks, I mean?"

"Why, black-haired, sir, short, and stout, with a comical face. They left a week ago Tuesday."

"And before they occupied it?"

"Why, there was a single gentleman connected with the draying business. He left owing me a week. Before him was Missis Crowder and her two children, that stayed four months; and back of them was old Mr. Doyle, whose sons paid for him. He kept the room six months. That goes back a year, sir, and further I do not remember."

He thanked her and crept back to his room. The room was dead. The essence that had vivified it was gone. The perfume of mignonette had departed. In its place was the old, stale odor of mouldy house furniture, of atmosphere in storage.

The ebbing of his hope drained his faith. He sat staring at the yellow, singing gaslight. Soon he walked to the bed and began to tear the sheets into strips. With the blade of his knife he drove them tightly into every crevice around windows and door. When all was snug and taut he turned out the light, turned the gas full on again and laid himself gratefully upon the bed.

It was Mrs. McCool's night to go with the can for beer. So she fetched it and sat with Mrs. Purdy in one of those subterranean retreats where housekeepers foregather and the worm dieth seldom.

"I rented out my third floor, back, this evening," said Mrs. Purdy, across a fine circle of foam. "A young man took it. He went up to bed two hours ago."

"Now, did ye, Mrs. Purdy, ma'am?" said Mrs. McCool, with intense admiration. "You do be a wonder for rentin' rooms of that kind. And did ye tell him, then?" she concluded in a husky whisper, laden with mystery.

"Rooms," said Mrs. Purdy, in her furriest tones, "are furnished for to rent. I did not tell him, Mrs. McCool."

" 'Tis right ye are, ma'am; 'tis by renting rooms we kape alive. Ye have the rale sense for business, ma'am. There be many people will rayjict the rentin' of a room if they be tould a suicide has been after dyin' in the bed of it."

"As you say, we has our living to be making," remarked Mrs. Purdy.

"Yis, ma'am; 'tis true. 'Tis just one wake ago this day I helped ye lay out the third floor, back. A pretty slip of a colleen she was to be killin' herself wid the gas—a swate little face she had, Mrs. Purdy, ma'am."

"She'd a-been called handsome, as you say," said Mrs. Purdy, assenting but critical, "but for that mole she had a-growin' by her left eyebrow. Do fill up your glass again, Mrs. McCool."

Paul Ernst

UNLIKE MANY OF HIS contemporaries in the pulp-writing community, Paul (Frederick) Ernst (1899–1905) relied on his skill as a plotter and careful wordsmith to produce hundreds of thousands of words a year, rather than producing scenes of shocking violence to maintain interest in his stories. Like his contemporaries, however, he created works in a wide variety of genres, including mystery, horror, and adventure, most famously with his hero, the Avenger, written under the pseudonym Kenneth Robeson. The Robeson byline was used by Lester Dent for a long run of *Doc Savage* magazines, one of the most successful pulps of its time. Because of the tremendous sales recounting those adventures of "The Man of Bronze," the publisher convinced Ernst to write about the Avenger, "The Man of Steel." The author claimed it was the worst writing he ever did, though fans disagreed and his twenty-four novelettes were later reprinted as paperback books.

Ernst was a frequent contributor to *Weird Tales,* notably with his mid-1930s series about Dr. Satan, "the world's weirdest criminal," whose nemesis is the detective Ascott Keane. Ernst claimed that most of these stories, and other of his supernatural tales, came to him in dreams so perfectly constructed, remembered in the morning, that he merely had to sit down and transcribe them. A million-word-a-year man in his pulp-writing days, he gradually took his work to the better-paying slick magazines until he retired to Florida.

"Death's Warm Fireside" was originally published in the March 1936 issue of *Dime Mystery Magazine.*

Death's Warm Fireside

PAUL ERNST

OVER THE LIGHTS OF Newton a mile away an evening star glittered like blue ice with a lamp behind it. Blue-black was the early night sky; blue-white the thick drifts of snow that mantled the open countryside. That same snow crunched under Malcolm Slade's feet like singing particles of glass as he cut across the woodlot at the south end of the Slade farm and walked wearily, unsteadily, toward the house.

God, it was cold! It was blue-cold to the eye as well as paralyzingly chill to the senses. He shivered and thrust hands he could scarcely feel deeper into his coat pockets. He hunched his shoulders higher so that his coat collar should fit more closely around his neck.

Cold, cold, cold! And the house would be cold too—shut up and unoccupied for a little while, as it had been.

He shrugged philosophically. Well, that was his fault. The house wouldn't be shut, untenanted, if he hadn't lost that quick temper of his. With the passage of a little time he was ready to admit, now, that Claire had been right. He'd been a fool to fling himself angrily out of the house and leave her to go to her folks.

But he could see how still and black and dreary the house looked across the white-drifted fields. And that hurt. The house had been so homely and comfortable looking just a short while ago, before he had quarrelled with Claire. Now it looked . . .

"Never think it had been lived in," Malcolm Slade muttered laboriously. He felt that if he didn't talk aloud, do something like that, he would sink into the drifts and float off in the sleep that precedes freezing.

"Never think it had been lived in. But just a little while ago . . ."

It had been in the late fall that he'd left, scarcely six weeks before this period, the height of winter. The last of the leaves had been eddying in cheery piles before their porch. The big fireplace had been singing its message of warmth and benevolence for those fortunate enough to live in the old farm home.

Slade got to the meadow fence, with the black, bleak farm house only a hundred yards away. He climbed the fence, fell heavily on the other side in the snow. He had to fight his cold-drugged senses to make himself rise. And he groaned as he thought of what the house would be within. An empty house in winter always seems even more bitterly cold than the temperature outside.

Well, he'd light fires, get the thing going again. Then, he thought hazily, he'd get in touch with Claire and they'd pick up where they had left off. It was a nice little farm; they had proved that a good living could be taken from it. And it was perfect for the boy they were going to have. . . .

"Fool!" he mumbled, biting his lips to keep

his eyes from closing. "We have everything right in our hands, Claire and I. And I tossed it away. . . . But she'll come around. She won't let a few weeks break our whole lives. I'll tell her it was all my fault. . . ."

He went past the barn, staggering a little. And now he was so cold that his eyes were playing him tricks. He thought he saw the outlines of the old barn waver; thought he could see the stars through it in places.

"This is getting serious," he told himself, throwing his weary shoulders back and taking his hands from his pockets to beat them together. "God, I wish I was coming into a warm house instead of a freezing one. . . ."

And into a home instead of a bleak shell that looked, in the eerie moonlight, like a great, empty tomb, Slade went on with his thought.

He went to his knees in a drift near the front door of the dark house, got up again.

"Claire." he called, tongue thick, voice hoarse.

Then he got a grip on his wavering senses. This wouldn't do! Calling to Claire like that! As if, at his call, she would open the door and he would see her as he had seen her so many times in their life here: in a trim house dress, face flushed with heat from the coal range but beautiful nevertheless, arms opened to him. . . .

"But she'll be back again soon," Slade muttered. "I'll get the house warm, and things straightened again . . . place can go to pieces in a few weeks . . . she'll come back. . . ."

He climbed the porch. There were only three steps, but they were a hard struggle. He took them a step at a time, and leaned against a porch post and panted for a full minute after he had accomplished them.

Leaning there, he saw lights across the road, a few hundred yards away.

"New house," he muttered in surprise. "Well! Old Gleason got it built, did he? Put it up in a hurry when he did get started. Nice for Claire and me to have closer neighbors."

Mechanically, senselessly, he tried the door. It was locked, of course. Claire wouldn't leave

it unlocked when she left, after his abrupt and angry departure. And the other doors would be tightly fastened, too.

He walked along the porch to a window. It was one of the living room windows. He tried it with almost frozen fingers. It did not budge. Nailed shut, probably.

For a moment maudlin self-pity seized him. Coming through the freezing night like this, alone and cold, to a house that was nailed and locked against him, and that would be freezing within anyhow . . .

"Hell," he muttered. "It's your own fault it's like this. Now get in there and go to work."

There seemed no way short of violence for him to get in. He took off his felt hat, wadded it around his right hand, and smashed it through the window. Then he picked out the sharp pieces that clung to the sash, and slithered through.

Inside the living room he stood blanketed in total darkness.

Cold inside? Yes. But in this house that had known no heat for a time, the cold ate into his very heart. It sent ice needles through his flesh; attacked him like a living, bitter thing.

He searched through his pockets for matches, found them at last. Two dropped from his stiff fingers, but the third he managed to hold. He stared around in the dim light it cast.

He could see practically nothing, and he wondered for an instant if his eyeballs had frozen. He had heard of such things. But that was preposterous; the kind of thing that happened only in Arctic cold, not the zero weather of Ohio. The match threw a poor light, that was all.

Nevertheless, he shrank from the shadows its yellow flame produced; shadows that seemed to creep slowly toward him from all four sides of the room hemming him in, poising as though to leap.

He shuddered again, and now not entirely because of the cold. Then he started and dropped the match stub. Had that been a step upstairs?

He listened in the darkness, and heard it

again: a distinct creak as if a person's weight had been pressed against a board in the big bedroom.

For an instant a wild hope seized him. That was Claire! He was here! She . . .

"Fool! Here in this icy place with no light on and no fire going? It's a board creaking with the cold, that's all."

He walked toward the stairs off the little hall between living room and dining room. He didn't bother to light another match. He knew the way perfectly. He went slowly only because there might be some piece of furniture out of its accustomed place, between him and the hall.

The place was alive with memories of Claire. He kept seeing her in this hall doorway, calling him to dinner. He kept visioning the living room, warm and cheery, as she had furnished and arranged it. He kept seeing Claire and himself sitting before the leaping flames in the fireplace, talking of the boy that was to come. . . .

His steps resounded in the bleak house like giant drum-beats. He tried to walk on tiptoe, appalled by the noise. But he was too shaky with cold, and weariness from the distance he had walked, to make it. So he shuffled over the bare floor of the little hall and noisily climbed the stairs.

The second floor was, if anything, colder than the first. He realized that at last the bitter chill was really getting him. But even as he realized that, he found himself sinking to the top step.

He sat there, leaning against the newel post, chin on his chest.

"Got to get up," he said thickly, aloud.

But he made no move. It was so pleasant to sit, to give in for just a moment to his lassitude. He'd get up in a minute and get some fire going. With the living room stove red hot and the fireplace going, the first floor would warm up in a hurry. Have to get some wood in.

A sound from downstairs penetrated his stupor. And as he really heard it, he straightened quickly. This was not a fancied sound, nor one made by cold-contracting boards! It was real, and startling!

It was the sound of flames, the crackling of fire!

"My God, the matches I lit—" Slade thought.

He started drunkenly down the stairs. The little hall was already bright with the rosy glow of naked fire. He stumbled into the living room. . . .

There are moments too big, too marvelous, to be borne. And this one, as Slade stood in the living room doorway, was one of them.

Mouth open, eyes wide, he stared at the transformed room.

The fire that had sent its light into the hall was from the big fireplace; a great pile of wood was roaring there, with logs atop to send out even heat when the kindling had burned. The stove in the center of the room was already black-hot, and laving him with warmth. The bright lamps on the table near the front door were lit; and on the stove a pot was steaming that Slade knew contained hot rum.

And beside the stove stood Claire.

Her blue eyes were alight as she stared at him, though they were suspiciously moist. Her red young lips were half parted. Her heart was in her face, and staring at it, Slade knew he was already forgiven.

"Surprise—" Claire called, tears spilling from her eyes.

But Slade's knees were folding under him. He slid to the threshold and lay with his head inside the living room and his feet in the little hall.

Slade's head was in Claire's lap when he again became aware of things. She was holding him to her, calling him all the endearing terms they'd thought up during their five years of married life.

"Darling," she whispered, when his eyes opened. He saw fear in her own eyes, saw it fade into gladness when he looked at her.

"Mal! I was afraid. . . . You looked almost as if you were dead!"

"Kind of a shock," whispered Slade, staring at Claire's face as though he could not get his fill of it. "I didn't dream you were here too. It looked like no one was here. All cold and dark, like it was."

Claire's eyes, expressive as open books, lighted again.

"I wasn't here when you broke in, Mal. I was at Mr. Gleason's. I've been staying there, watching, waiting for you to come back. I saw a light in here—"

"I struck some matches to see my way around."

"I saw the light, dear, and came over. I came in as quietly as I could, and lit the fires. I wanted to surprise you."

Slade sat up. He didn't want to take his head from its comfortable position, but he was afraid Claire would think him ill or feeble from the cold if he lay where he was any longer.

"It was a surprise, all right!" he told her. "The most gorgeous one. . . . But it kind of knocked me out. So far from what I expected, and everything . . ."

They looked at each other for a long while. Then their two bodies, that had been so close so many times, swayed toward each other. They kissed, eyes closed, all quarrels melting in the wordless agreement.

"So you were waiting for me," marvelled Slade.

"I was waiting for you," nodded Claire. "It seemed a very long time, Mal."

"Well, now I'm home and we'll carry on. I'll get to work tomorrow and clear things up. . . . Claire, what did we quarrel about?"

She shook her head, smiling.

"I can't even remember. But it doesn't matter anyway. We won't quarrel again. You've come home, and so have I. Without the two of us, the place is just a house, cold and bleak and deserted. With us, it is a home again."

The flames in the fireplace leaped and roared. The stove behind them hummed with heat. Slade felt a little drowsy.

Claire handed him a glass of the hot rum that had steamed on the stove. He sipped at it. Floundering through snow drifts toward a house as cold and empty as his own heart had been since he left? Yes, he had been doing that, and only a little while ago. But it seemed years ago, now, in the light of his present warmth and comfort.

He was so warm, so comfortable! He let himself drift into a sort of dreamlike state, with Claire warm in his arms.

"You're kind of wonderful," he whispered to her.

And it was then that their bodies drew closer still, and he knew again the poignant sweetness of the woman he had married, and had been stupid enough to leave awhile ago.

Outside, a frigid wind began to moan over the blue-cold world. But the only effect it had in the warm room was to make the raw flame in the fireplace leap higher, and the warm stove hum more loudly.

"You've missed me?" he whispered at last, greedy for the look on her face to be translated into words.

"So much," she whispered back, running her young, smooth hands lightly down his stubbled cheek. "But now you're here. And I know you'll never leave again."

Curiously, now, a little chill stole down his spine. Her words were natural; the kind of thing she would tend to say. But there was something about her tone that struck him as a little odd. It had such extreme conviction in it. She *knew* he would never leave her again! She had said it as though he were now chained to her by some circumstance stronger than earthly will.

But the uneasy feeling faded soon. Why shouldn't she have conviction in her tone? She was right, wasn't she? He never would be separated from her again. Not while he was in his right mind!

So warm and comfortable before the fireplace. . . . So contented with Claire again by his side, in his arms. . . .

Malcolm Slade felt himself slide again into a sort of dreamlike trance.

"Kiss me," whispered Claire.

Dreamily, he kissed her.

"So glad I'm home," he said finally, eyes sagging closed as though weights pulled down the lids. "So glad . . ."

He dimly saw Claire smile. There was everything in her smile a man dreams of getting from a woman.

"You're sleepy, darling, aren't you? I don't blame you. The cold outside, the bitter, bitter cold inside before I got the fires going, your long walk, now this warmth. . . ." Her voice was a lullaby, closing his eyes more securely still.

"Sleep, Mal. Sleep. And know you'll never be away from me again. Sleep. . . ."

The fire was sending dim red even through his closed eyelids, carrying him off to unconsciousness with the feeling that all was right in a world that had not been too kind to him of late.

"Sleep. . . ."

Crackling fire, Claire, everything slipped into a slumber as comforting as it was profound.

The rather creditable Newton fire engine panted in the snow-packed lane beside the farm house. Its hose was out, and the volunteer firemen, half a dozen of them, were helmeted and in rubber slickers ready to attack the roaring blaze that soared through the roof twice as high as the house it was consuming.

But there was no way for them to attack it. There was no water in the well behind the house, and the nearby creek was frozen solid.

"Have to let 'er burn," said one of the men. "No loss, anyway."

A sedan slid up through the snow and stopped behind the fire engine. A man got out; the Newton doctor, Allen Lutz.

"Bill, you phoned there was a man here who needed me," he said.

The man he addressed shook his head a little.

"No work for you now, Doc. The guy died a few minutes after I phoned from Gleason's, without ever coming to."

The men parted. Lutz bent over a stark figure on a heap of coats in the snow. He felt the figure's chest.

"Dead, all right. Who is he?"

One of the others shrugged.

"Just some old tramp. None of us has ever seen him before. We found him lying in the burning house."

"In there?" said Doctor Lutz, staring incredulously at the almost demolished building. "In the roofless old ruin?"

"Yeah. I can't figure out why. 'I shouldn't think even an old drunk like this bum would try for shelter there. The house has been falling to pieces since I was a kid—ever since Mrs. Malcolm Slade died after her husband deserted her thirty years ago."

Andrew Klavan

BORN IN NEW YORK CITY as one of four sons of the popular liberal talk-show host Gene Klavan, who cohosted *Klavan and Finch* and then hosted *Klavan in the Morning*, Andrew Klavan (1954–) grew up and identified himself early in life as a liberal and a Jew, both of which changed as he grew older. He described himself as an agnostic for some years before converting to Christianity, and he is now an active writer and blogger with libertarian conservative views.

As a mystery writer, he has enjoyed both popular and critical success, with numerous Edgar Allan Poe nominations, two of which were winners: *Mrs. White* (1983), coauthored with his brother Laurence under the pseudonym Margaret Tracy, the basis for *White of the Eye*, a film released in 1987 starring David Keith and Cathy Moriarty, and *The Rain* (1988), under the pseudonym Keith Peterson. In 1992, he was nominated in the Best Novel category for *Don't Say a Word*, later a film was released in 2001 starring Michael Douglas, Sean Bean, and Brittany Murphy. His 1995 novel *True Crime* was filmed in 1999 with Clint Eastwood as the director and the star, along with Isaiah Washington, Lisa Gay Hamilton, and James Woods. Klavan wrote the screenplays for the Michael Caine vehicle *A Shock to the System* (1990), a mystery based on the novel by Simon Brett, and the horror film *One Missed Call* (2008). His most recent novels have been the political thrillers *Empire of Lies* (2008) and *The Identity Man* (2010).

"The Advent Reunion" began life as a video when the author decided to recapture the tradition of telling ghost stories at Christmas. Using a webcam, he filmed it in front of his fireplace, offering it as if it were a true story, and then posted it online. It was rewritten as a short story and published in the January 2011 issue of *Ellery Queen Mystery Magazine*.

The Advent Reunion

ANDREW KLAVAN

I. Ghost Hunter

I've wanted to tell this story for a long time. It began when I was a young man, during my junior year at Harvard.

To come, as I had, from a crumbling house on a sandy lane in a dying town just west of nowhere to the aged brick and history, high culture and customs, of one of the most prestigious universities in the country was a daunting journey for so inexperienced a boy. I spent my first year holed up in my room, buried in my books, working on my writing. Only after a very unpleasant summer break at home did I return to school determined to make friends.

I soon fell in with an aspiring composer named Jonathan Wilson, and through Jonathan, I found myself part of a little clique of brilliant artsy types—brilliant in our own minds, anyway. Among this group was a girl named Amanda Zane. She was blonde and willowy and had a dreamy, wistful quality about her. She wrote songs and played guitar and sang. Her voice was high and clear and sweet with a sad, yearning tone that just grabbed me by the heart. I was crazy about her pretty much on sight and, for some reason, she seemed to like me as well. We became a couple within the clique. It was the first truly happy time in my life.

No wonder, as the Christmas break approached, I began to dread the thought of going home again. And when Jonathan came up with

an alternative, I was delighted. His parents had decided to spend the holidays in Hawaii. Their house in a rural part of upstate New York was going to be empty. Jonathan invited our little gang to spend Christmas there with him. Five of us accepted the invitation, David, Lucy, Rosemary, Amanda, and I.

It was, it turned out, a perfect setting for Christmas. The house was enormous, stone and stately. It sat in a little valley with hills of forest on every side, everything white with snow as far as the eye could see. When we first arrived, we tried to behave with our usual pseudosophisticated pseudodetachment but the spirit of the season very quickly overwhelmed us. Within an hour of tumbling through the front door, we were laughing and shouting like the excited children we were. We found decorations in the attic and spread them all about the house. We found sleds in the garage and raced each other down the slopes. We found an axe in the cellar and cut down a large pine tree at the edge of the forest, tied it up with stout ropes and dragged it home over the snow. We hung ornaments on it and sang carols around the piano and basically had as much good, clean fun as it's legal to have.

We were having so much fun, in fact, that I didn't notice—none of us noticed—that Amanda had begun acting very strange. Shy and distracted at the best of times, she'd grown almost silent in our boisterous midst. More and more often, she withdrew from our festivities without excuse and went wandering on her own for hours.

Finally, one afternoon, when the others were planning a shopping excursion to the nearby mall, she asked me if I would remain behind. When we were alone together, she broke the news to me: she was pregnant.

What followed was both pitiful and predictable, knowing Amanda. She lived a little too much inside her own head. She had actually managed to convince herself I might be happy to hear about the child. But how could I be? I had no money. I had worked like a slave, year after year, to win my place at school. I had ambitions—big ambitions—to become a writer, a novelist—not exactly a very secure profession, not something you can count on, not in the beginning at least. I was in no position to take on the support of a wife and child.

Amanda only had to take one look at my face to read my thoughts. The next moment, she was in hysterical tears, raging at me. I had never seen her like that before. She screamed that I was selfish. I was thoughtless. I was this and that and the other. And when I tried to reason with her, when I suggested there might be another, better time for us to have a child together, she lost control completely, took it in the worst way, practically accused me of being some kind of homicidal maniac.

Thankfully, the worst of it was over by the time Jonathan and the others returned from their outing. When they burst through the door, shouting and laughing, I was in the living room, sitting alone in an armchair by the fireplace, staring into the flames, torn between panic and despair.

"Where's Amanda?" they all cried out at once. "We're going to play games! We're going to make cookies! We're going to play Ghost Hunter!"

I hesitated—but I finally managed to smile and tell them Amanda had gone to bed early with a headache. I didn't see the point of spoiling their good mood with the truth.

It was already evening, already dark. We all went into the kitchen and made popcorn and cookies, swilling wine and beer as we did. I forced myself to join in the fun with a show of enthusiasm. After an hour or so, we began our game of Ghost Hunter.

Ghost Hunter, if you've never played it, is really basically just hide n' seek in the dark. One person is designated the Ghost Hunter, then you turn off all the lights and everyone else scatters and hides. The Hunter moves through the house with a flashlight and if he leaves the room in which you're hiding without finding you, you're allowed to jump out and scare him. Each person who comes out of hiding then joins the hunt for the others.

I didn't want to sit out and ruin the game, but with everything that was weighing on my mind, I didn't know how long I could keep up the pretense of high spirits. I came up with what I thought was a brilliant idea. I hid down in the basement behind the boiler. It was, I felt sure, literally the last place anyone would look. The game could go on without me, and I would have time to brood on my troubles and think things through.

It was pitch dark down there, absolutely black. I could bring my hand within inches of my eyes and still not see it. I sat on the floor just behind the boiler, staring, blind, feeling sorry for myself. More than half an hour went by. All the while, I could hear the screams and giggles of my friends upstairs.

Finally, I heard the basement door open. A flashlight beam shone on the cellar stairs. Jonathan was the Ghost Hunter. He'd already collected all the others and I could hear them murmuring to each other.

"He must be here. Where else could he be?"

Laughing nervously, they came thumping down the stairs behind the flashlight beam. When they reached the bottom, Jonathan swept the light across the pitch darkness. It went over me once, then, a second later, snapped back to pick out my face.

"There you are! I see you!" they shouted together.

Someone—Rosemary, I think—said, "I'll get the lights."

The basement lights came on. And the next thing I knew, Rosemary let out a high, ragged, terrible scream. I lifted my eyes, following her horrified gaze. Then I started screaming too.

There, just above my head, Amanda's corpse hung dangling in the air, one end of a rope tied around a heating pipe in the ceiling, the other end pulled tight around her neck.

She had been there, right above me, the whole time I was sitting in the dark.

II. "She Haunts Us"

The aftermath of Amanda's death was ugly, especially for me. The coroner had no trouble deciding she'd committed suicide and he also had no trouble figuring out why. I was forced to tell the police the whole story: the pregnancy and our awful argument. This got back to Jonathan and the others, of course. I won't say they blamed me or anything, but they didn't exactly forgive me either. After that, we'd see each other around campus from time to time, and we were always pleasant enough with each other, but their underlying coldness toward me was unmistakable. To my great sorrow, the days of our true friendship were over.

When I graduated, I moved to New York City. I didn't see any of them again for a long time.

Seven years went by, in fact. Some hungry times, a lot of hard work, then I started to establish myself. My first couple of books came out. I scored some movie sales. I hit some bestseller lists. Things started to go well.

But all the while, I was aware that, in some way, what happened with Amanda continued to cast a shadow over my life. I had never been close with my family, but now I cut off communications with them altogether. I had girlfriends from time to time, but I never established another long-term relationship. Most of the people I called friends were really just casual acquain-

tances. Somehow, after Amanda, there was always a part of myself that I kept in reserve, that I was never quite willing to share with anyone else.

One day, in early December, I came home from a party to find a message on my answering machine. The message was from Jonathan Wilson. He said he was in New York and he wanted to meet with me. You would think I would be surprised to hear from him, but the truth was, I'd been expecting that call for some reason—expecting it for as long as I could remember.

The next evening, Jonathan and I met at my local tavern, McGlade's. It was a cold, drizzly day. I stepped into the bar and stood brushing the damp off my overcoat as I looked around for him. At first, I didn't see him. That is, I must have passed over him without recognizing him. Then I did. He was seated at a table in back by the brick fireplace. He was staring into a glass of red wine. He was a shocking sight. Only seven years had passed since I'd last seen him, but he seemed to have aged decades. He was thin and sallow and drawn.

I sat down with him. Ordered a drink. Before the waitress even returned with the glass, Jonathan had begun to tell me his story. Things had gone badly for him since school, he said. He'd been ill off and on. He'd abandoned his composing. Gone from job to job until he finally ended up at his father's investment firm, where he was doing only moderately well. The same was true of the others, he told me, the other three who'd been at his parents' house with us that Christmas. Rosemary had struggled with drugs and alcohol. David had been through an ugly divorce that left him depressed and nearly broke. Lucy had gone through a series of abusive relationships, including one that ended with her in the hospital with a couple of broken ribs.

"It's about her somehow," Jonathan told me. "It's about Amanda. We all feel it. She haunts us. She won't let us move on." Then, after a pause, he said, "I read about you in the papers all the time. You seem to be doing well."

It felt like an accusation. I was the one most closely connected to Amanda's death, after all. If anyone was responsible for it, obviously it was me. And I had my problems as I said, but basically he was right: I was doing well. And I said so.

Jonathan stared into his wine a long, silent moment. Then he looked up rather sharply and said, "We have to go back. We've all agreed. We're going to meet up at the house in a week. We're going to spend Christmas there again."

"What's that supposed to accomplish?" I asked him.

"I don't know. None of us knows. We just have to do it. Will you come?"

I said I would think about it. And I did think about it, all that night. And I thought: that time of my life, even that Christmas at the Wilson house before the tragedy—those were the happiest days I'd ever known. For all the success I'd had, nothing else had ever come close. I thought: Maybe they're right. Maybe if we could go back, if we could capture some of that spirit, lay our guilt about Amanda's death to rest . . . maybe we could be happy again.

I called Jonathan in the morning and told him I would drive up to the house next weekend.

III. A Voice in the Storm

I left the city on a gray Saturday morning and headed upstate. When I was about fifty miles north of Manhattan, it began to snow. Pretty soon, the grass by the side of the highway was dusted with white.

I pressed on. The snow kept getting heavier and heavier. The traveling wasn't all that bad as long as I was on the interstate, but once I got past Albany, once I got off the main roads and into the back country, the conditions deteriorated fast. Soon, the snow was falling so thickly I could barely see—and when I could see, leaning forward to peer through the windshield, all I could make out were the vague hulking shapes of the surrounding forest. The roads here had not been plowed. They wound perilously through narrower and narrower passages between higher and higher drifts. I probably should have pulled over someplace, tried to find a motel and wait out the storm. But the idea of this reunion had captured my imagination. I didn't want to get there late. I didn't want to miss anything.

I turned on the radio, hoping to hear the weather—news—any sound of civilization. Nothing came out of the speakers except a steady hiss of static. I hit the search button. The digital readout spun from number to number without stopping. A murmur of voices rose and faded. A whisper of music died beneath the unbroken wind-like sough.

Then, after another moment or two, the tuner seemed to catch hold of something. For several seconds, I could hear—soft beneath the interference—the wistful sound of an acoustic guitar. It was playing a sad, lilting melody I had never heard before. A woman's high, clear, sweet, and mournful voice was singing.

"I wait for you," she sang. "I wait for you."

I turned from the windshield and stared at the radio. That voice . . . It was far away, riddled with static . . . but I recognized it. . . .

Just then, the car went into a skid. I faced forward—but too late. I had lost control and was sliding, blind, through the whiteness.

Before I could get my bearings, the car dropped off the edge of the road and buried its front end in the deep drifts beneath the winter trees. I tried to rock it out, but the tires just whined uselessly. I couldn't get any traction. The car was stuck.

I sat back in my seat breathing hard as the full dimensions of the situation became clear to me. It was cold, very cold. I hadn't seen a building or a turnoff for miles. I had only about a quarter tank of gas. Maybe two hours of daylight left at most. If I stayed in the car, the engine would probably die right about the same time the light did. There was a real possibility I could freeze to death out here.

I decided to try to find help or shelter before nightfall. I stepped out of the car—and dropped into snow up to my knees. I stared around me into the blinding white. I saw nothing but the dim shadows of pine trees standing like sentinels watching me. I shouted for help. My voice was lost in the wind. Clutching my overcoat closed against the cold, I pushed forward until the snow grew more shallow and I could feel the road under my shoes. I followed the pavement as best I could up a small hill.

Just as I got to the top, something wonderful happened. A gust of wind pushed the snow aside like a curtain. The view cleared. There, nestled in an empty valley not a quarter of a mile away, stood the old Wilson mansion, the very place I was looking for.

I didn't go back to the car for my luggage. I was afraid of getting lost. I stumbled down the hill until the road wound round to the Wilson's long driveway. Then I shoved my way through the driveway's big drifts until I was at the front door. I pounded with the old iron knocker. No one came. Finally, shivering, I tried the knob. Thank God, the door opened. I spilled inside.

I shouted. No answer. It was clear the place was empty. I tried the lights. Nothing. The phones were out too. There wasn't much time before sunset. I had to find some supplies. Some matches; flashlights. Logs so I could start a fire.

Yet, I hesitated. I stood in the front room at the window, staring out at the falling snow. I watched the light grow dimmer and dimmer. Alone in that house with the night coming, all I could think about was that moment in the car just before I hit the final skid. That familiar voice lilting through the static on the radio. That song:

"I wait for you. I wait for you."

IV. Reunion

The day grew darker and darker at the windows. I made preparations to get through the night. I stacked some logs in the fireplace with old magazines for kindling. I rattled through every drawer I could find, searching for matches. Luckily, just as the last light was dying away, I opened a hall closet and found a flashlight on the top shelf. I followed the beam to the kitchen. But I stopped on the threshold.

I could see by the flashlight that the door leading from the kitchen down into the basement stood open, the cellar stairs disappearing into the blackness below. The open door unnerved me somehow. Alone in the dark house, my mind returned to that moment seven years ago when I saw Amanda's corpse dangling above me.

I stepped decisively to the basement door and swung it shut.

I took a second to calm myself. Then I searched the kitchen. I looked in the small pantry. Went through some more drawers. Finally, the flashlight beam picked out a box of wooden matches on a small shelf over the stove. I was reaching up to take hold of the box when my hand froze in midair.

I heard something, in the house. A guitar was playing. Slowly, I turned around, brought the flashlight around. The basement door was standing open again. A voice wafted up to me from below, singing softly, sadly.

"I wait for you. I wait for you."

I moved quickly back to the door, intending to shut it again. But just as I reached the top of the stairs, the singing stopped. The lightless basement fell silent. I stood there, staring down into the darkness. I felt a sour, burning fear rise in me as I realized I couldn't just close the door, I couldn't just walk away. I couldn't spend the night in this house wondering what was down there, not knowing.

I had to look. I started down the stairs, holding tight to the flashlight. The basement dark seemed to crawl up my sides and close around me. I reached the bottom. Immediately, I guided the beam to the place where I'd seen Amanda hanging. There was nothing there.

No. Wait. There was. The light picked out the shape of a rope. My hand trembled as I raised the beam to see that one end was tied around the heating pipe. My breath caught as I lowered the beam.

The bottom of the rope was tied in a noose. The noose hung empty. I started breathing again, relieved.

Then I lowered the flashlight and saw Amanda come walking toward me out of the darkness.

She was just as I'd seen her last. Her body was horribly bloated, her face disfigured, the eyes bulging, the skin bluish-green. In terror, I stumbled backwards. And the flashlight slipped out of my hands. It fell to the floor and went out. The blackness was complete.

I gave a strangled cry. I knew she was still coming toward me, but I couldn't see her. I couldn't see anything. With my hands out in front of me, I stumbled in what I hoped was the direction of the stairs. I found them. I grabbed the bannister. Started up. But in the darkness, I tripped. I went down on one knee.

Cold fingers wrapped themselves around my ankle.

I cried out and yanked myself free. I charged upward blindly, tripping, stumbling, but finally plunging through the doorway into the kitchen. I slammed the basement door behind me and looked desperately this way and that, lost in the darkness. I had to get back to the stove. To the matches on the shelf. I started moving—and, as I did, I heard her again. Through the basement door. Singing softly.

"I wait for you. I wait for you."

Her voice was growing louder as she slowly climbed the stairs.

I staggered across the kitchen. Bumped into the stove. Reached up, feeling for the box of matches. There it was. I grabbed it. I fumbled for a match, concentrating so hard that I barely noticed that the singing had stopped, that the darkness had grown silent again. I brought out a match. I struck it against the side of the box.

The flame flared and she was standing right in front of me, reaching for me with those dead hands.

I screamed and dropped the matches. Hurled myself headlong away from her. By sheer good luck, I bumped into the edge of the pantry door-

way. I rolled off into the pantry itself and shut the door fast. My hand still clutching the knob, I braced my shoulder against the door. The knob turned in my hand. I could feel her trying to push the door inward.

I held it shut.

V. I Wait for You

All night long, I heard her at the pantry door. Sometimes she rattled the knob, trying to get in. Sometimes she knocked softly or called my name in a laughing, teasing voice, trying to coax me out. I tried bracing my back against the door, covering my ears with my hands but I still heard her. I hugged my knees to myself, trembling. It was enough to drive me mad.

I knew what she wanted. Revenge. She'd been waiting for it for seven years. She would never forgive me for what I'd done. Not just getting her pregnant. Refusing to marry her, refusing to sacrifice my future, my whole life, to take care of her and a child. Not just for shouting at her so that she stormed off, crying.

I think she would've forgiven me for all that if I hadn't killed her.

But what else could I do? She never would have gotten an abortion. She would've had the child and used it against me. Forced me to come up with child support. Ruined any chance I had to be free, to be a success. I mean, deep down, Amanda was a very vindictive person. You can see that. You can see how long she'd waited to get back at me, nursing her bitterness all the while.

So anyway, I'd taken a rope—one of those stout ropes we'd used to haul the Christmas tree home from the woods. I went upstairs to her room. I pretended I wanted to make up with her so that she ran to me, put her arms around me. Then I slipped the rope around her neck and pulled it tight.

It took a long time. A long time. I don't like to think about it. Finally, she lost consciousness. I carried her down to the basement and strung her up on the heating pipe. That was kind of awful too because she woke up for a while and struggled, hanging up there, before it was finally over for good.

It really was a brilliant idea to hide downstairs in the basement during the game. It gave me a chance to collect myself—and to act surprised and scream in horror when they found her. And no one would believe I would just sit down there like that in the dark for so long, knowing she was with me all the while.

It had all worked out just as I imagined, just as I wanted. But Amanda had never forgiven me for it. She'd waited for me all this time.

All night long, she knocked and called outside the pantry door, trying to draw me out. But finally, I saw the first sunlight slip in under the door. I heard her voice grow softer and softer until it vanished.

I climbed unsteadily to my feet. I opened the door. Peeked out. She was gone. I breathed a prayer of thanks.

I rushed out of the house. The snow had stopped. The sun was shining. I was delighted to see that the road and the driveway had been plowed and sanded overnight. It was easy to get back to my car, easy in the daylight to push it free from the drift where it was stuck and get it back onto the road.

As I was driving away from the Wilson house, a Volvo came past me in the other direction. It was Jonathan. I don't think he saw me. He didn't stop.

When I reached the top of the hill, I looked back. I saw the Volvo go down the driveway to the house. A moment later, two more cars reached the drive from the opposite direction and joined the first. Jonathan got out and then David and Lucy and Rosemary. They all came together, hugging and kissing and shaking hands.

I left them to their reunion. Let them live in the past, not me. I wasn't going to waste my one and only life wallowing in remorse about Amanda.

Although I must admit, as the years go on, as I move toward the end of middle age, I find myself wondering about that sometimes. Whether this is, in fact, my one and only life, I mean. Death wasn't the end for Amanda, after all. Recently, more and more often, I hear her in the night, in the dark, in the distance, singing somewhere in that wistful voice:

"I wait for you. I wait for you."

I believe she does.

R. Murray Gilchrist

IF A PRE-RAPHAELITE PAINTING could be transmogrified from oil to words, the results would surely be one of the lush, weird stories of R(obert) Murray Gilchrist (1868–1917). His romantic, decadent stories are set in fantastical British landscapes of thick, decaying vegetation in the center of which may be found stone mansions, often with broken walls slowly disintegrating, much like the once wealthy aristocratic families that inhabited them in happier, brighter times. If his heroes survive at all, it is rarely in a manner for which they may have wished.

Born in Sheffield, Gilchrist was mainly privately educated before becoming an editor at *The National Observer* with the legendary William Ernest Henley. His literary career began at the age of twenty-two with the publication of a novel, *Passion the Plaything,* followed by a reasonably prolific body of work, the majority of which was novels and short stories set in Derbyshire and its Peak District, portraying the daily life of ordinary Derbyshire folks; he also produced several local histories. While these works were highly regarded in their time, they are all but forgotten today. What (too little) reputation Gilchrist has nowadays is due to his Gothic stories of the fantastic and supernatural, although his first collection of weird tales, *The Stone Dragon* (1894), was not successful and he did not often return to writing this type of fiction.

"The Return" was first published in *The National Observer* and was collected in *The Stone Dragon and Other Tragic Romances* (London, Methuen, 1894).

The Return

R. MURRAY GILCHRIST

FIVE MINUTES AGO I drew the window curtain aside and let the mellow sunset light contend with the glare from the girandoles. Below lay the orchard of Vernon Garth, rich in heavily flowered fruit-trees—yonder a medlar, here a pear, next a quince. As my eyes, unaccustomed to the day, blinked rapidly, the recollection came of a scene forty-five years past, and once more beneath the oldest tree stood the girl I loved, mischievously plucking yarrow, and, despite its evil omen, twining the snowy clusters in her black hair. Again her coquettish words rang in my ears:

"Make me thy lady! Make me the richest woman in England, and I promise thee, Brian, we shall be the happiest of God's creatures." And I remembered how the mad thirst for gold filled me: how I trusted in her fidelity, and without reasoning or even telling her that I would conquer fortune for her sake, I kissed her sadly and passed into the world. Then followed a complete silence until the *Star of Europe*, the greatest diamond discovered in modern times, lay in my hand—a rough unpolished stone not unlike the lumps of spar I had often seen lying on the sandy lanes of my native county. This should be Rose's own, and all the others that clanked so melodiously in their leather bulse should go towards fulfilling her ambition. Rich and happy I should be soon, and should I not marry an untitled gentlewoman, sweet in her prime? The twenty years' interval of work and sleep was

like a fading dream, for I was going home. The knowledge thrilled me so that my nerves were strung tight as iron ropes and I laughed like a young boy. And it was all because my home was to be in Rose Pascal's arms.

I crossed the sea and posted straight for Halkton village. The old hostelry was crowded. Jane Hopgarth, whom I remembered a ruddy-faced child, stood on the box-edged terrace, courtesying in matronly fashion to the departing mail-coach. A change in the sign-board drew my eye; the white lilies had been painted over with a mitre, and the name changed from the Pascal Arms to the Lord Bishop. Angrily aghast at this disloyalty, I cross-questioned the ostlers, who hurried to and fro, but failing to obtain any coherent reply I was fain to content myself with a mental denunciation of the times.

At last I saw Bow-Legged Jeffries, now bent double with age, sunning himself at his favourite place, the side of the horse-trough. As of old he was chewing a straw. No sign of recognition came over his face as he gazed at me, and I was shocked, because I wished to impart some of my gladness to a fellow-creature. I went to him, and after trying in vain to make him speak, held forth a gold coin. He rose instantly, grasped it with palsied fingers, and, muttering that the hounds were starting, hurried from my presence. Feeling half sad I crossed to the churchyard and gazed through the grated window of the Pascal burial chapel at the recumbent and undisturbed effigies of Geoffrey Pascal, gentleman, of Bretton Hall; and Margot Maltrevor his wife, with their quaint epitaph about a perfect marriage enduring for ever. Then, after noting the rankness of the docks and nettles, I crossed the worn stile and with footsteps surprisingly fleet passed towards the stretch of moorland at whose further end stands Bretton Hall.

Twilight had fallen ere I reached the cottage at the entrance of the park. This was in a ruinous condition: here and there sheaves in the thatched roof had parted and formed crevices through which smoke filtered. Some of the tiny windows had been walled up, and even where the glass remained snake-like ivy hindered any light from falling into their thick recesses.

The door stood open, although the evening was chill. As I approached, the heavy autumnal dew shook down from the firs and fell upon shoulders. A bat, swooping in an undulation, struck between my eyes and fell to the grass, moaning querulously. I entered. A withered woman sat beside the peat fire. She held a pair of steel knitting-needles which she moved without cessation. There was no thread upon them, and when they clicked her lips twitched as if she had counted. Some time passed before I recognised Rose's foster-mother, Elizabeth Carless. The russet colour of her cheeks had faded and left a sickly grey; those sunken, dimmed eyes were utterly unlike the bright black orbs that had danced so mirthfully. Her stature, too, had shrunk. I was struck with wonder. Elizabeth could not be more than fifty-six years old. I had been away twenty years; Rose was fifteen when I left her, and I had heard Elizabeth say that she was only twenty-one at the time of her darling's weaning. But what a change! She had such an air of weary grief that my heart grew sick.

Advancing to her side I touched her arm. She turned, but neither spoke nor seemed aware of my presence. Soon, however, she rose, and helping herself along by grasping the scanty furniture, tottered to a window and peered out. Her right hand crept to her throat; she untied the string of her gown and took from her bosom a pomander set in a battered silver case. I cried out; Rose had loved that toy in her childhood; thousands of times we played ball with it. . . . Elizabeth held it to her mouth and mumbled it, as if it were a baby's hand. Maddened with impatience, I caught her shoulder and roughly bade her say where I should find Rose. But something awoke in her eyes, and she shrank away to the other side of the house-place: I followed; she cowered on the floor, looking at me with a strange horror. Her lips began to move, but they made no sound. Only when I crossed to the threshold did she rise; and then her head moved wildly from side to side, and her hands pressed close to her breast, as if the pain there were too great to endure.

I ran from the place, not daring to look back. In a few minutes I reached the balustraded wall of the Hall garden. The vegetation there was wonderfully luxuriant. As of old, the great blue and white Canterbury bells grew thickly, and those curious flowers to which tradition has given the name of "Marie's Heart" still spread their creamy tendrils and blood-coloured bloom on every hand. But "Pascal's Dribble," the tiny spring whose water pulsed so fiercely as it emerged from the earth, has long since burst its bounds, and converted the winter garden into a swamp, where a miniature forest of queen-of-the-meadow filled the air with melancholy sweetness. The house looked as if no careful hand had touched it for years. The elements had played havoc with its oriels, and many of the latticed frames hung on single hinges. The curtain of the blue parlour hung outside, draggled and faded, and half hidden by a thick growth of bindweed.

With an almost savage force I raised my arm high above my head and brought my fist down upon the central panel of the door. There was no need for such violence, for the decayed fastenings made no resistance, and some of the rotten boards fell to the ground. As I entered the hall and saw the ancient furniture, once so fondly kept, now mildewed and crumbling to dust, quick sobs burst from my throat. Rose's spinet stood beside the door of the withdrawing-room. How many carols had we sung to its music! As I passed my foot struck one of the legs and the rickety structure groaned as if it were coming to pieces. I thrust out my hand to steady it, but at my touch the velvet covering of the lid came off and the tiny gilt ornaments rattled downwards. The moon was just rising and only half her disc was visible over the distant edge of the Hell Garden. The light in the room was very uncertain, yet I could see the keys of the instrument were stained brown, and bound together with thick cobwebs.

Whilst I stood beside it I felt an overpowering desire to play a country ballad with an overword of "Willow browbound." The words in strict accordance with the melody are merry and sad by turns: at one time filled with light happiness, at another bitter as the voice of one bereaved for ever of joy. So I cleared off the spiders and began to strike the keys with my forefinger. Many were dumb, and when I struck them gave forth no sound save a peculiar sigh; but still the melody rhythmed as distinctly as if a low voice crooned it out of the darkness. Wearied with the bitterness, I turned away.

By now the full moonlight pierced the window and quivered on the floor. As I gazed on the tremulous pattern it changed into quaint devices of hearts, daggers, rings, and a thousand tokens more. All suddenly another object glided amongst them so quickly that I wondered whether my eyes had been at fault—a tiny satin shoe, stained crimson across the lappets. A revulsion of feeling came to my soul and drove away all my fear. I had seen that selfsame shoe white and unsoiled twenty years before, when vain, vain Rose danced amongst her reapers at the harvest-home. And my voice cried out in ecstasy, "Rose, heart of mine! Delight of all the world's delights!"

She stood before me, wondering, amazed. Alas, so changed! The red-and-yellow silk shawl still covered her shoulders; her hair still hung in those eldritch curls. But the beautiful face had grown wan and tired, and across the fore-head lines were drawn like silver threads. She threw her arms round my neck and, pressing her bosom heavily on mine, sobbed so piteously that I grew afraid for her, and drew back the long masses of hair which had fallen forward, and kissed again and again those lips that were too lovely for simile. Never came a word of chiding from them. "Love," she said, when she had regained her breath, "the past struggle was sharp and torturing—the future struggle will be crueller still. What a great love yours was, to wait and trust for so long! Would that mine had been as powerful! Poor, weak heart that could not endure!"

The tones of a wild fear throbbed through all her speech, strongly, yet with insufficient power to prevent her feeling the tenderness of those moments. Often, timorously raising her head from my shoulder, she looked about and then turned with a soft, inarticulate, and glad murmur to hide her face on my bosom. I spoke fervently; told of the years spent away from her; how, when working in the diamond-fields she had ever been present in my fancy; how at night her name had fallen from my lips in my only prayer; how I had dreamed of her amongst the greatest in the land—the richest, and, I dare swear, the loveliest woman in the world. I grew warmer still: all the gladness which had been constrained for so long now burst wildly from my lips: a myriad of rich ideas resolved into words, which, being spoken, wove one long and delicious fit of passion. As we stood together, the moon brightened and filled the chamber with a light like the day's. The ridges of the surrounding moorland stood out in sharp relief.

Rose drank in my declarations thirstily, but soon interrupted me with a heavy sigh. "Come away," she said softly. "I no longer live in this house. You must stay with me to-night. This place is so wretched now: for time, that in you and me has only strengthened love, has wrought much ruin here."

Half leaning on me, she led me from the precincts of Bretton Hall. We walked in silence over the waste that crowns the valley of the Whitelands and, being near the verge of the rocks, saw the great pinewood sloping downwards, lighted near us by the moon, but soon lost in density. Along the mysterious line where the light changed into gloom, intricate shadows of withered summer bracken struck and receded in a mimic battle. Before us lay the Priests' Cliff. The moon was veiled by a grove of elms, whose ever-swaying branches alternately increased and lessened her brightness. This was a place of notoriety—a veritable Golgotha—a haunt fit only for demons. Murder and theft had been punished here; and to this day fireside stories are told of evil women dancing round that Druids' circle, carrying hearts plucked from gibbeted bodies.

"Rose," I whispered, "why have you brought me here?"

She made no reply, but pressed her head more closely to my shoulder. Scarce had my lips closed ere a sound like the hiss of a half-strangled snake vibrated amongst the trees. It grew louder and louder. A monstrous shadow hovered above.

Rose from my bosom murmured. "Love is strong as Death! Love is strong as Death!"

I locked her in my arms, so tightly that she grew breathless. "Hold me," she panted. "You are strong."

A cold hand touched our foreheads so that, benumbed, we sank together to the ground, to fall instantly into a dreamless slumber.

When I awoke the clear grey light of the early morning had spread over the country. Beyond the Hell Garden the sun was just bursting through the clouds, and had already spread a long golden haze along the horizon. The babbling of the streamlet that runs down to Halkton was so distinct that it seemed almost at my side. How sweetly the wild thyme smelt! Filled with tender recollections of the night, without turning, I called Rose Pascal from her sleep.

"Sweetheart, sweetheart, waken! waken! waken! See how glad the world looks—see the omens of a happy future."

No answer came. I sat up, and looking round me saw that I was alone. A square stone lay near. When the sun was high I crept to read the inscription carved thereon:—"*Here, at four cross-paths, lieth, with a stake through the bosom, the body of Rose Pascal, who in her sixteenth year wilfully cast away the life God gave.*"

Rudyard Kipling

WRITTEN IN 1885 but not published for three years, "The Phantom Rickshaw" is the first of the many and varied tales of the supernatural produced by (Joseph) Rudyard Kipling (1865–1936), all but one of which was written while he lived in India during the peak of England's colonial period under Queen Victoria. Born and raised in the care of Indians in Bombay until the age of six, he learned Hindustani concurrently with English and developed a love for the region and its people. After English schooling, he returned to India at eighteen, becoming a journalist and short story writer. By the end of the nineteenth century he was one of the world's most popular and highly regarded authors, becoming the first English-language author to win the Nobel Prize in Literature (1907). Many of his best-known works, most of which have been successfully filmed, are set in India, including his tales of "the soldiers three" in *Plain Tales from the Hills* (1888) and *Soldiers Three* (1888; the 1951 motion picture *Soldiers Three* starring Stewart Granger, David Niven, and Walter Pidgeon was loosely based on the stories); *The Jungle Books* (1894 & 1895; filmed in 1942 with Sabu as the Indian boy Mowgli; there was a live-action remake by Disney in 1994; a prequel was released in 1997); *Kim* (1901; filmed in 1950 with Errol Flynn and Dean Stockwell, remade in 1984 with Ravi Sheth and Peter O'Toole); and the familiar narrative poem "Gunga Din" (filmed in 1939 with Cary Grant, Victor McLaglen, and Douglas Fairbanks, Jr.). A dedicated colonialist, he is credited with inventing the phrase "the white man's burden" with a poem of that title, meant to reflect the responsibility of the British (and, presumably, other Anglo-Saxons) for their racial inferiors. In other settings, he produced such masterpieces as *The Light that Failed* (1890; filmed in 1939 with Ronald Colman, Ida Lupino, and Walter Huston) and *Captains Courageous* (1897; filmed in 1937 with Spencer Tracy, Lionel Barrymore, and Freddie Bartholomew; it was unmemorably remade in 1996), and "The Man Who Would Be King" (1888; wonderfully filmed in 1975 with Sean Connery, Michael Caine, and Christopher Plummer as Rudyard Kipling, who narrates the tale). "The Phantom Rickshaw" was televised as an episode of *Your Favorite Story* on February 8, 1953.

"The Phantom Rickshaw" was originally published in *The Phantom Rickshaw and Other Tales* (Allahabad, A. H. Wheeler, 1888).

The Phantom Rickshaw

RUDYARD KIPLING

May no ill dreams disturb my rest,
Nor Powers of Darkness me molest.

EVENING HYMN.

ONE OF THE FEW advantages that India has over England is a great Knowability. After five years' service a man is directly or indirectly acquainted with the two or three hundred Civilians in his Province, all the Messes of ten or twelve Regiments and Batteries, and some fifteen hundred other people of the nonofficial caste. In ten years his knowledge should be doubled, and at the end of twenty he knows, or knows something about, every Englishman in the Empire, and may travel anywhere and everywhere without paying hotel-bills.

Globe-trotters who expect entertainment as a right, have, even within my memory, blunted this open-heartedness, but none the less to-day, if you belong to the Inner Circle and are neither a Bear nor a Black Sheep, all houses are open to you, and our small world is very, very kind and helpful.

Rickett of Kamartha stayed with Polder of Kumaon some fifteen years ago. He meant to stay two nights, but was knocked down by rheumatic fever, and for six weeks disorganized Polder's establishment, stopped Polder's work, and nearly died in Polder's bedroom. Polder behaves as though he had been placed under eternal obligation by Rickett, and yearly sends the little Ricketts a box of presents and toys. It is the same everywhere. The men who do not take the trouble to conceal from you their opinion that you are an incompetent ass, and the women who blacken your character and misunderstand your wife's amusements, will work themselves to the bone in your behalf if you fall sick or into serious trouble.

Heatherlegh, the Doctor, kept, in addition to his regular practice, a hospital on his private account—an arrangement of loose boxes for Incurables, his friend called it—but it was really a sort of fitting-up shed for craft that had been damaged by stress of weather. The weather in India is often sultry, and since the tale of bricks is always a fixed quantity, and the only liberty allowed is permission to work overtime and get no thanks, men occasionally break down and become as mixed as the metaphors in this sentence. Heatherlegh is the dearest doctor that ever was, and his invariable prescription to all his patients is, "lie low, go slow, and keep cool." He says that more men are killed by overwork than the importance of this world justifies. He maintains that overwork slew Pansay, who died under his hands about three years ago. He has, of course, the right to speak authoritatively, and he laughs at my theory that there was a crack in Pansay's head and a little bit of the Dark World came through and pressed him to death. "Pansay went off the handle," says Heatherlegh, "after the stimulus of long leave at Home. He may or he may not have behaved like a blackguard to Mrs. Keith-Wessington. My notion is that the work of the Katabundi Settlement ran him off his legs, and that he took to brooding and making much of an ordinary P. & O. flirtation. He certainly was engaged to Miss Mannering, and

she certainly broke off the engagement. Then he took a feverish chill and all that nonsense about ghosts developed. Overwork started his illness, kept it alight, and killed him poor devil. Write him off to the System—one man to take the work of two and a half men."

I do not believe this. I used to sit up with Pansay sometimes when Heatherlegh was called out to patients, and I happened to be within claim. The man would make me most unhappy by describing in a low, even voice, the procession that was always passing at the bottom of his bed. He had a sick man's command of language. When he recovered I suggested that he should write out the whole affair from beginning to end, knowing that ink might assist him to ease his mind. When little boys have learned a new bad word they are never happy till they have chalked it up on a door. And this also is Literature.

He was in a high fever while he was writing, and the blood-and-thunder Magazine diction he adopted did not calm him. Two months afterward he was reported fit for duty, but, in spite of the fact that he was urgently needed to help an undermanned Commission stagger through a deficit, he preferred to die; vowing at the last that he was hag-ridden. I got his manuscript before he died, and this is his version of the affair, dated 1885:

My doctor tells me that I need rest and change of air. It is not improbable that I shall get both ere long—rest that neither the red-coated messenger nor the midday gun can break, and change of air far beyond that which any homeward-bound steamer can give me. In the meantime I am resolved to stay where I am; and, in flat defiance of my doctor's orders, to take all the world into my confidence. You shall learn for yourselves the precise nature of my malady; and shall, too, judge for yourselves whether any man born of woman on this weary earth was ever so tormented as I.

Speaking now as a condemned criminal might speak ere the drop-bolts are drawn, my story, wild and hideously improbable as it may appear, demands at least attention. That it will ever receive credence I utterly disbelieve. Two months ago I should have scouted as mad or drunk the man who had dared tell me the like. Two months ago I was the happiest man in India. Today, from Peshawur to the sea, there is no one more wretched. My doctor and I are the only two who know this. His explanation is, that my brain, digestion, and eyesight are all slightly affected; giving rise to my frequent and persistent "delusions." Delusions, indeed! I call him a fool; but he attends me still with the same unwearied smile, the same bland professional manner, the same neatly trimmed red whiskers, till I begin to suspect that I am an ungrateful, evil-tempered invalid. But you shall judge for yourselves.

Three years ago it was my fortune—my great misfortune—to sail from Gravesend to Bombay, on return from long leave, with one Agnes Keith-Wessington, wife of an officer on the Bombay side. It does not in the least concern you to know what manner of woman she was. Be content with the knowledge that, ere the voyage had ended, both she and I were desperately and unreasoningly in love with one another. Heaven knows that I can make the admission now without one particle of vanity. In matters of this sort there is always one who gives and another who accepts. From the first day of our ill-omened attachment, I was conscious that Agnes's passion was a stronger, a more dominant, and—if I may use the expression—a purer sentiment than mine. Whether she recognized the fact then, I do not know. Afterward it was bitterly plain to both of us.

Arrived at Bombay in the spring of the year, we went our respective ways, to meet no more for the next three or four months, when my leave and her love took us both to Simla. There we spent the season together; and there my fire of straw burned itself out to a pitiful end with the closing year. I attempt no excuse. I make no apology. Mrs. Wessington had given up much for my sake, and was prepared to give up all. From my own lips, in August 1882, she learned that I was sick of her presence, tired of her company, and

weary of the sound of her voice. Ninety-nine women out of a hundred would have wearied of me as I wearied of them; seventy-five of that number would have promptly avenged themselves by active and obtrusive flirtation with other men. Mrs. Wessington was the hundredth. On her neither my openly expressed aversion nor the cutting brutalities with which I garnished our interviews had the least effect.

"Jack, darling!" was her one eternal cuckoo cry: "I'm sure it's all a mistake—a hideous mistake; and we'll be good friends again some day. *Please* forgive me, Jack, dear."

I was the offender, and I knew it. That knowledge transformed my pity into passive endurance, and, eventually, into blind hate—the same instinct, I suppose, which prompts a man to savagely stamp on the spider he has but half killed. And with this hate in my bosom the season of 1882 came to an end.

Next year we met again at Simla—she with her monotonous face and timid attempts at reconciliation, and I with loathing of her in every fibre of my frame. Several times I could not avoid meeting her alone; and on each occasion her words were identically the same. Still the unreasoning wail that it was all a "mistake"; and still the hope of eventually "making friends." I might have seen had I cared to look, that that hope only was keeping her alive. She grew more wan and thin month by month. You will agree with me, at least, that such conduct would have driven any one to despair. It was uncalled for; childish; unwomanly. I maintain that she was much to blame. And again, sometimes, in the black, fever-stricken night-watches, I have begun to think that I might have been a little kinder to her. But that really is a "delusion." I could not have continued pretending to love her when I didn't; could I? It would have been unfair to us both.

Last year we met again—on the same terms as before. The same weary appeal, and the same curt answers from my lips. At least I would make her see how wholly wrong and hopeless were her attempts at resuming the old relationship.

As the season wore on, we fell apart—that is to say, she found it difficult to meet me, for I had other and more absorbing interests to attend to. When I think it over quietly in my sick-room, the season of 1884 seems a confused nightmare wherein light and shade were fantastically intermingled—my courtship of little Kitty Mannering; my hopes, doubts, and fears; our long rides together; my trembling avowal of attachment; her reply; and now and again a vision of a white face flitting by in the rickshaw with the black and white liveries I once watched for so earnestly; the wave of Mrs. Wessington's gloved hand; and, when she met me alone, which was but seldom, the irksome monotony of her appeal. I loved Kitty Mannering; honestly, heartily loved her, and with my love for her grew my hatred for Agnes. In August Kitty and I were engaged. The next day I met those accursed "magpie" *jhampanies* at the back of Jakko, and, moved by some passing sentiment of pity, stopped to tell Mrs. Wessington everything. She knew it already.

"So I hear you're engaged, Jack dear." Then, without a moment's pause: "I'm sure it's all a mistake—a hideous mistake. We shall be as good friends some day, Jack, as we ever were."

My answer might have made even a man wince. It cut the dying woman before me like the blow of a whip. "Please forgive me, Jack; I didn't mean to make you angry; but it's true, it's true!"

And Mrs. Wessington broke down completely. I turned away and left her to finish her journey in peace, feeling, but only for a moment or two, that I had been an unutterably mean hound. I looked back, and saw that she had turned her rickshaw with the idea, I suppose, of overtaking me.

The scene and its surroundings were photographed on my memory. The rain-swept sky (we were at the end of the wet weather), the sodden, dingy pines, the muddy road, and the black powder-riven cliffs formed a gloomy background against which the black and white liveries of the *jhampanies,* the yellow-paneled rickshaw and Mrs. Wessington's down-bowed golden head stood out clearly. She was holding her handkerchief in her left hand and was leaning back exhausted against the rickshaw cushions. I turned my horse up a bypath near the Sanjowlie Reservoir and literally ran away. Once I fancied I heard a faint call of "Jack!" This may have been imagination. I never stopped to verify it. Ten minutes later I came across Kitty on horseback; and, in the delight of a long ride with her, forgot all about the interview.

A week later Mrs. Wessington died, and the inexpressible burden of her existence was removed from my life. I went Plainsward perfectly happy. Before three months were over I had forgotten all about her, except that at times the discovery of some of her old letters reminded me unpleasantly of our bygone relationship. By January I had disinterred what was left of our correspondence from among my scattered belongings and had burned it. At the beginning of April of this year, 1885, I was at Simla—semi-deserted Simla—once more, and was deep in lover's talks and walks with Kitty. It was decided that we should be married at the end of June. You will understand, therefore, that, loving Kitty as I did, I am not saying too much when I pronounce myself to have been, at that time, the happiest man in India.

Fourteen delightful days passed almost before I noticed their flight. Then, aroused to the sense of what was proper among mortals circumstanced as we were, I pointed out to Kitty that an engagement ring was the outward and visible sign of her dignity as an engaged girl; and that she must forthwith come to Hamilton's to be measured for one. Up to that moment, I give you my word, we had completely forgotten so trivial a matter. To Hamilton's we accordingly went on the 15th of April, 1885. Remember that—whatever my doctor may say to the contrary—I was then in perfect health, enjoying a well-balanced mind and an absolute tranquil spirit. Kitty and I entered Hamilton's shop together, and there, regardless of the order of affairs, I measured Kitty for the ring in the presence of the amused assistant. The ring was a sapphire with two diamonds. We then rode out down the slope that leads to the Combermere Bridge and Peliti's shop.

While my Waler was cautiously feeling his way over the loose shale, and Kitty was laughing and chattering at my side—while all Simla, that is to say as much of it as had then come from the Plains, was grouped round the Reading-room and Peliti's veranda,—I was aware that some one, apparently at a vast distance, was calling me by my Christian name. It struck me that I had heard the voice before, but when and where I could not at once determine. In the short space it took to cover the road between the path from Hamilton's shop and the first plank of the Combermere Bridge I had thought over half a dozen people who might have committed such a solecism, and had eventually decided that it must have been singing in my ears. Immediately opposite Peliti's shop my eye was arrested by the sight of four *jhampanies* in "magpie" livery, pulling a yellow-paneled, cheap, bazar rickshaw. In a moment my mind flew back to the previous season and Mrs. Wessington with a sense of irritation and disgust. Was it not enough that the woman was dead and done with, without her black and white servitors reappearing to spoil the day's happiness? Whoever employed them now I thought I would call upon, and ask as a personal favor to change her *jhampanies'* livery. I would hire the men myself, and, if necessary, buy their coats from off their backs. It is impossible to say here what a flood of undesirable memories their presence evoked.

"Kitty," I cried, "there are poor Mrs. Wessington's *jhampanies* turned up again! I wonder who has them now?"

Kitty had known Mrs. Wessington slightly last season, and had always been interested in the sickly woman.

"What? Where?" she asked. "I can't see them anywhere."

Even as she spoke her horse, swerving from a laden mule, threw himself directly in front of the advancing rickshaw. I had scarcely time to utter a word of warning when, to my unutterable horror, horse and rider passed through men and carriage as if they had been thin air.

"What's the matter?" cried Kitty; "what made you call out so foolishly, Jack? If I *am* engaged I don't want all creation to know about it. There was lots of space between the mule and the veranda; and, if you think I can't ride—There!"

Whereupon wilful Kitty set off, her dainty little head in the air, at a hand-gallop in the direction of the Bandstand; fully expecting, as she herself afterward told me, that I should follow her. What was the matter? Nothing indeed. Either that I was mad or drunk, or that Simla was haunted with devils. I reined in my impatient cob, and turned round. The rickshaw had turned too, and now stood immediately facing me, near the left railing of the Combermere Bridge.

"Jack! Jack, darling!" (There was no mistake about the words this time: they rang through my brain as if they had been shouted in my ear.) "It's some hideous mistake, I'm sure. *Please* forgive me, Jack, and let's be friends again."

The rickshaw-hood had fallen back, and inside, as I hope and pray daily for the death I dread by night, sat Mrs. Keith-Wessington, handkerchief in hand, and golden head bowed on her breast.

How long I stared motionless I do not know. Finally, I was aroused by my syce taking the Waler's bridle and asking whether I was ill. From the horrible to the commonplace is but a step. I tumbled off my horse and dashed, half fainting, into Peliti's for a glass of cherry-brandy. There two or three couples were gathered round the coffee-tables discussing the gossip of the day. Their trivialities were more comforting to me just then than the consolations of religion could have been. I plunged into the midst of the conversation at once; chatted, laughed, and jested with a face (when I caught a glimpse of it in a mirror) as white and drawn as that of a corpse. Three or four men noticed my condition; and, evidently setting it down to the results of over-many pegs, charitably endeavoured to draw me apart from the rest of the loungers. But

I refused to be led away. I wanted the company of my kind—as a child rushes into the midst of the dinner-party after a fright in the dark. I must have talked for about ten minutes or so, though it seemed an eternity to me, when I heard Kitty's clear voice outside inquiring for me. In another minute she had entered the shop, prepared to roundly upbraid me for failing so signally in my duties. Something in my face stopped her.

"Why, Jack," she cried, "what *have* you been doing? What has happened? Are you ill?" Thus driven into a direct lie, I said that the sun had been a little too much for me. It was close upon five o'clock of a cloudy April afternoon, and the sun had been hidden all day. I saw my mistake as soon as the words were out of my mouth: attempted to recover it; blundered hopelessly and followed Kitty in a regal rage, out of doors, amid the smiles of my acquaintances. I made some excuse (I have forgotten what) on the score of my feeling faint; and cantered away to my hotel, leaving Kitty to finish the ride by herself.

In my room I sat down and tried calmly to reason out the matter. Here was I, Theobald Jack Pansay, a well-educated Bengal Civilian in the year of grace, 1885, presumably sane, certainly healthy, driven in terror from my sweetheart's side by the apparition of a woman who had been dead and buried eight months ago. These were facts that I could not blink. Nothing was further from my thought than any memory of Mrs. Wessington when Kitty and I left Hamilton's shop. Nothing was more utterly commonplace than the stretch of wall opposite Peliti's. It was broad daylight. The road was full of people; and yet here, look you, in defiance of every law of probability, in direct outrage of Nature's ordinance, there had appeared to me a face from the grave.

Kitty's Arab had gone *through* the rickshaw: so that my first hope that some woman marvelously like Mrs. Wessington had hired the carriage and the coolies with their old livery was lost. Again and again I went round this treadmill of thought; and again and again gave up baffled and in despair. The voice was as inexplicable as the apparition. I had originally some wild notion of confiding it all to Kitty; of begging her to marry me at once; and in her arms defying the ghostly occupant of the rickshaw. "After all," I argued, "the presence of the rickshaw is in itself enough to prove the existence of a spectral illusion. One may see ghosts of men and women, but surely never of coolies and carriages. The whole thing is absurd. Fancy the ghost of a hill-man!"

Next morning I sent a penitent note to Kitty, imploring her to overlook my strange conduct of the previous afternoon. My Divinity was still very wroth, and a personal apology was necessary. I explained, with a fluency born of night-long pondering over a falsehood, that I had been attacked with sudden palpitation of the heart—the result of indigestion. This eminently practical solution had its effect; and Kitty and I rode out that afternoon with the shadow of my first lie dividing us.

Nothing would please her save a canter round Jakko. With my nerves still unstrung from the previous night I feebly protested against the notion, suggesting Observatory Hill, Jutogh, the Boileaugunge road—anything rather than the Jakko round. Kitty was angry and a little hurt: so I yielded from fear of provoking further misunderstanding, and we set out together toward Chota Simla. We walked a greater part of the way, and, according to our custom, cantered from a mile or so below the Convent to the stretch of level road by the Sanjowlie Reservoir. The wretched horses appeared to fly, and my heart beat quicker and quicker as we neared the crest of the ascent. My mind had been full of Mrs. Wessington all the afternoon; and every inch of the Jakko road bore witness to our old-time walks and talks. The bowlders were full of it; the pines sang it aloud overhead; the rain-fed torrents giggled and chuckled unseen over the shameful story; and the wind in my ears chanted the iniquity aloud.

As a fitting climax, in the middle of the level men call the Ladies' Mile the Horror was awaiting me. No other rickshaw was in sight—only the four black and white *jhampanies*, the yellow-paneled carriage, and the golden head of the woman within—all apparently just as I had left them eight months and one fortnight ago! For an instant I fancied that Kitty *must* see what I saw—we were so marvelously sympathetic in all things. Her next words undeceived me—"Not a soul in sight! Come along, Jack, and I'll race you to the Reservoir buildings!" Her wiry little Arab was off like a bird, my Waler following close behind, and in this order we dashed under the cliffs. Half a minute brought us within fifty yards of the rickshaw. I pulled my Waler and fell back a little. The rickshaw was directly in the middle of the road; and once more the Arab passed through it, my horse following. "Jack! Jack dear! *Please* forgive me," rang with a wail in my ears, and, after an interval:—"It's a mistake, a hideous mistake!"

I spurred my horse like a man possessed. When I turned my head at the Reservoir works, the black and white liveries were still waiting—patiently waiting—under the grey hillside, and the wind brought me a mocking echo of the words I had just heard. Kitty bantered me a good deal on my silence throughout the remainder of the ride. I had been talking up till then wildly and at random. To save my life I could not speak afterward naturally, and from Sanjowlie to the Church wisely held my tongue.

I was to dine with the Mannerings that night, and had barely time to canter home to dress. On the road to Elysium Hill I overheard two men talking together in the dusk.—"It's a curious thing," said one, "how completely all trace of it disappeared. You know my wife was insanely fond of the woman (never could see anything in her myself), and wanted me to pick up her old rickshaw and coolies if they were to be got for love or money. Morbid sort of fancy I call it; but I've got to do what the Memsahib tells me. Would you believe that the man she hired it from tells me that all four of the men—they were brothers—died of cholera on the way to Hardwar, poor devils, and the rickshaw has been broken up by the man himself. Told me he never used a dead Memsahib's rickshaw. Spoiled his luck. Queer notion, wasn't it? Fancy poor little Mrs. Wessington spoiling any one's luck except her own!" I laughed aloud at this point; and my laugh jarred on me as I uttered it. So there *were* ghosts of rickshaws after all, and ghostly employments in the other world! How much did Mrs. Wessington give her men? What were their hours? Where did they go?

And for visible answer to my last question I saw the infernal Thing blocking my path in the twilight. The dead travel fast, and by short cuts unknown to ordinary coolies. I laughed aloud a second time and checked my laughter suddenly, for I was afraid I was going mad. Mad to a certain extent I must have been, for I recollect that I reined in my horse at the head of the rickshaw, and politely wished Mrs. Wessington "Good-evening." Her answer was one I knew only too well. I listened to the end; and replied that I had heard it all before, but should be delighted if she had anything further to say. Some malignant devil stronger than I must have entered into me that evening, for I have a dim recollection of talking the commonplaces of the day for five minutes to the Thing in front of me.

"Mad as a hatter, poor devil—or drunk. Max, try and get him to come home."

Surely *that* was not Mrs. Wessington's voice! The two men had overheard me speaking to the empty air, and had returned to look after me. They were very kind and considerate, and from their words evidently gathered that I was extremely drunk. I thanked them confusedly and cantered away to my hotel, there changed, and arrived at the Mannerings' ten minutes late. I pleaded the darkness of the night as an excuse; was rebuked by Kitty for my unlover-like tardiness; and sat down.

The conversation had already become general; and under cover of it, I was addressing some tender small talk to my sweetheart when I was aware that at the further end of the table a short red-whiskered man was describing, with much broidery, his encounter with a mad unknown that evening.

A few sentences convinced me that he was repeating the incident of half an hour ago. In the middle of the story he looked round for applause, as professional story-tellers do, caught my eye, and straightway collapsed. There was a moment's awkward silence, and the red-whiskered man muttered something to the effect that he had "forgotten the rest," thereby sacrificing a reputation as a good story-teller which he had built up for six seasons past. I blessed him from the bottom of my heart, and went on with my fish.

In the fullness of time that dinner came to an end; and with genuine regret I tore myself away from Kitty—as certain as I was of my own existence that It would be waiting for me outside the door. The red-whiskered man, who had been introduced to me as Doctor Heatherlegh, of Simla, volunteered to bear me company as far as our roads lay together. I accepted his offer with gratitude.

My instinct had not deceived me. It lay in readiness in the Mall, and, in what seemed devilish mockery of our ways, with a lighted head-lamp. The red-whiskered man went to the point at once, in a manner that showed he had been thinking over it all dinner time.

"I say, Pansay, what the deuce was the matter with you this evening on the Elysium road?" The suddenness of the question wrenched an answer from me before I was aware.

"That!" said I, pointing to It.

"*That* may be either D. T. or Eyes for aught I know. Now you don't liquor. I saw as much at dinner, so it can't be D. T. There's nothing whatever where you're pointing, though you're sweating and trembling with fright like a scared pony. Therefore, I conclude that it's Eyes. And I ought to understand all about them. Come along home with me. I'm on the Blessington lower road."

To my intense delight the rickshaw instead of waiting for us kept about twenty yards ahead—and this, too whether we walked, trotted, or cantered. In the course of that long night ride I had told my companion almost as much as I have told you here.

"Well, you've spoiled one of the best tales I've ever laid tongue to," said he, "but I'll forgive you for the sake of what you've gone through. Now come home and do what I tell you; and when I've cured you, young man, let this be a lesson to you to steer clear of women and indigestible food till the day of your death."

The rickshaw kept steady in front; and my red-whiskered friend seemed to derive great pleasure from my account of its exact whereabouts.

"Eyes, Pansay—all Eyes, Brain, and Stomach. And the greatest of these three is Stomach. You've too much conceited Brain, too little Stomach, and thoroughly unhealthy Eyes. Get your Stomach straight and the rest follows. And all that's French for a liver pill. I'll take sole medical charge of you from this hour! for you're too interesting a phenomenon to be passed over."

By this time we were deep in the shadow of the Blessington lower road and the rickshaw came to a dead stop under a pine-clad, over-hanging shale cliff. Instinctively I halted too, giving my reason. Heatherlegh rapped out an oath.

"Now, if you think I'm going to spend a cold night on the hillside for the sake of a stomach-*cum*-Brain-*cum*-Eye illusion. . . . Lord, ha' mercy! What's that?"

There was a muffled report, a blinding smother of dust just in front of us, a crack, the noise of rent boughs, and about ten yards of the cliff-side—pines, undergrowth, and all—slid down into the road below, completely blocking it up. The uprooted trees swayed and tottered for a moment like drunken giants in the gloom, and then fell prone among their fellows with a thunderous crash. Our two horses stood motionless and sweating with fear. As soon as the rattle of falling earth and stone had subsided, my companion muttered:—"Man, if we'd gone forward we should have been ten feet deep in our graves by now. 'There are more things in heaven and earth.'. . . Come home, Pansay, and thank God. I want a peg badly."

We retraced our way over the Church Ridge, and I arrived at Dr. Heatherlegh's house shortly after midnight.

His attempts toward my cure commenced almost immediately, and for a week I never left his sight. Many a time in the course of that week did I bless the good-fortune which had thrown me in contact with Simla's best and kindest doctor. Day by day my spirits grew lighter and more equable. Day by day, too, I became more and more inclined to fall in with Heatherlegh's "spectral illusion" theory, implicating eyes, brain, and stomach. I wrote to Kitty, telling her that a slight sprain caused by a fall from my horse kept me indoors for a few days; and that I should be recovered before she had time to regret my absence.

Heatherlegh's treatment was simple to a degree. It consisted of liver pills, cold-water baths, and strong exercise, taken in the dusk or at early dawn—for, as he sagely observed: "A man with a sprained ankle doesn't walk a dozen miles a day, and your young woman might be wondering if she saw you."

At the end of the week, after much examination of pupil and pulse, and strict injunctions as to diet and pedestrianism, Heatherlegh dismissed me as brusquely as he had taken charge of me. Here is his parting benediction: "Man, I can certify to your mental cure, and that's as much as to say I've cured most of your bodily ailments. Now, get your traps out of this as soon as you can; and be off to make love to Miss Kitty."

I was endeavoring to express my thanks for his kindness. He cut me short.

"Don't think I did this because I like you. I gather that you've behaved like a blackguard all through. But, all the same, you're a phenomenon, and as queer a phenomenon as you are a blackguard. No!"—checking me a second time—"not a rupee, please. Go out and see if you can find the eyes-brain-and-stomach business again. I'll give you a lakh for each time you see it."

Half an hour later I was in the Mannerings' drawing-room with Kitty—drunk with the intoxication of present happiness and the foreknowledge that I should never more be troubled with Its hideous presence. Strong in the sense of my new-found security, I proposed a ride at once; and, by preference, a canter round Jakko.

Never had I felt so well, so overladen with vitality and mere animal spirits, as I did on the afternoon of the 30th of April. Kitty was delighted at the change in my appearance, and complimented me on it in her delightfully frank and outspoken manner. We left the Mannerings' house together, laughing and talking, and cantered along the Chota Simla road as of old.

I was in haste to reach the Sanjowlie Reservoir and there make my assurance doubly sure. The horses did their best, but seemed all too slow to my impatient mind. Kitty was astonished at my boisterousness. "Why, Jack!" she cried at last, "you are behaving like a child. What are you doing?"

We were just below the Convent, and from sheer wantonness I was making my Waler plunge and curvet across the road as I tickled it with the loop of my riding-whip.

"Doing?" I answered; "nothing, dear. That's just it. If you'd been doing nothing for a week except lie up, you'd be as riotous as I.

" 'Singing and murmuring in your feastful
    mirth,
Joying to feel yourself alive;
Lord over Nature, Lord of the visible Earth,
Lord of the senses five.' "

My quotation was hardly out of my lips before we had rounded the corner above the Convent; and a few yards further on could see across to Sanjowlie. In the centre of the level road stood the black and white liveries, the yellow-paneled rickshaw, and Mrs. Keith-Wessington. I pulled up, looked, rubbed my eyes, and, I believe must have said something. The next thing I knew was that I was lying face downward on the road with Kitty kneeling above me in tears.

"Has it gone, child!" I gasped. Kitty only wept more bitterly.

"Has what gone, Jack dear? What does it all mean? There must be a mistake somewhere, Jack. A hideous mistake." Her last words brought me to my feet—mad—raving for the time being.

"Yes, there is a mistake somewhere," I repeated, "a hideous mistake. Come and look at It."

I have an indistinct idea that I dragged Kitty by the wrist along the road up to where It stood, and implored her for pity's sake to speak to It; to tell It that we were betrothed; that neither Death nor Hell could break the tie between us; and Kitty only knows how much more to the same effect. Now and again I appealed passionately to the Terror in the rickshaw to bear witness to all I had said, and to release me from a torture that was killing me. As I talked I suppose I must have told Kitty of my old relations with Mrs. Wessington, for I saw her listen intently with white face and blazing eyes.

"Thank you, Mr. Pansay," she said, "that's *quite* enough. *Syce ghora láo.*"

The syces, impassive as Orientals always are, had come up with the recaptured horses; and as Kitty sprang into her saddle I caught hold of the bridle, entreating her to hear me out and forgive. My answer was the cut of her riding-whip across my face from mouth to eye, and a word or two of farewell that even now I cannot write down. So I judged, and judged rightly, that Kitty knew all; and I staggered back to the side of the rickshaw. My face was cut and bleeding, and the blow of the riding-whip had raised a livid blue wheal on it. I had no self-respect. Just then, Heatherlegh, who must have been following Kitty and me at a distance, cantered up.

"Doctor," I said, pointing to my face, "here's Miss Mannering's signature to my order of dismissal and . . . I'll thank you for that lakh as soon as convenient."

Heatherlegh's face, even in my abject misery, moved me to laughter.

"I'll stake my professional reputation"—he began.

"Don't be a fool," I whispered. "I've lost my life's happiness and you'd better take me home."

As I spoke the rickshaw was gone. Then I lost all knowledge of what was passing. The crest of Jakko seemed to heave and roll like the crest of a cloud and fall in upon me.

Seven days later (on the 7th of May, that is to say) I was aware that I was lying in Heatherlegh's room as weak as a little child. Heatherlegh was watching me intently from behind the papers on his writing-table. His first words were not encouraging; but I was too far spent to be much moved by them.

"Here's Miss Kitty has sent back your letters. You corresponded a good deal, you young people. Here's a packet that looks like a ring, and a cheerful sort of a note from Mannering Papa, which I've taken the liberty of reading and burning. The old gentleman's not pleased with you."

"And Kitty?" I asked, dully.

"Rather more drawn than her father from what she says. By the same token you must have been letting out any number of queer reminiscences just before I met you. Says that a man who would have behaved to a woman as you did to Mrs. Wessington ought to kill himself out of sheer pity for his kind. She's a hot-headed little virago, your mash. Will have it too that you were suffering from D. T. when that row on the Jakko road turned up. Says she'll die before she ever speaks to you again."

I groaned and turned over to the other side.

"Now you've got your choice, my friend. This engagement has to be broken off; and the Mannerings don't want to be too hard on you. Was it broken through D. T. or epileptic fits? Sorry I can't offer you a better exchange unless you'd prefer hereditary insanity. Say the word and I'll tell 'em it's fits. All Simla knows about that scene on the Ladies' Mile. Come! I'll give you five minutes to think over it."

During those five minutes I believe that I explored thoroughly the lowest circles of the Inferno which it is permitted man to tread on earth. And at the same time I myself was watching myself faltering through the dark labyrinths of doubt, misery, and utter despair. I wondered, as Heatherlegh in his chair might have wondered, which dreadful alternative I should adopt. Presently I heard myself answering in a voice that I hardly recognized,—

"They're confoundedly particular about morality in these parts. Give 'em fits, Heatherlegh, and my love. Now let me sleep a bit longer."

Then my two selves joined, and it was only I (half crazed, devil-driven I) that tossed in my bed, tracing step by step the history of the past month.

"But I am in Simla," I kept repeating to myself. "I, Jack Pansay, am in Simla and there are no ghosts here. It's unreasonable of that woman to pretend there are. Why couldn't Agnes have left me alone? I never did her any harm. It might just as well have been me as Agnes. Only I'd never have come back on purpose to kill *her*. Why can't I be left alone—left alone and happy?"

It was high noon when I first awoke: and the sun was low in the sky before I slept—slept as the tortured criminal sleeps on his rack, too worn to feel further pain.

Next day I could not leave my bed. Heatherlegh told me in the morning that he had received an answer from Mr. Mannering, and that, thanks to his (Heatherlegh's) friendly offices, the story of my affliction had traveled through the length and breadth of Simla, where I was on all sides much pitied.

"And that's rather more than you deserve," he concluded, pleasantly, "though the Lord knows you've been going through a pretty severe mill. Never mind; we'll cure you yet, you perverse phenomenon."

I declined firmly to be cured. "You've been much too good to me already, old man," said I; "but I don't think I need trouble you further."

In my heart I knew that nothing Heatherlegh could do would lighten the burden that had been laid upon me.

With that knowledge came also a sense of hopeless, impotent rebellion against the unreasonableness of it all. There were scores of men no better than I whose punishments had at least been reserved for another world; and I felt that it was bitterly, cruelly unfair that I alone should have been singled out for so hideous a fate. This mood would in time give place to another where it seemed that the rickshaw and I were the only realities in a world of shadows; that Kitty was a ghost; that Mannering, Heatherlegh, and all the other men and women I knew were all ghosts; and the great, grey hills themselves but vain shadows devised to torture me. From mood to mood I tossed backward and forward for seven weary days; my body growing daily stronger and stronger, until the bedroom looking-glass told me that I had returned to everyday life, and was as other men once more. Curiously enough my face showed no signs of the struggle I had gone through. It was pale indeed, but as expressionless and commonplace as ever. I had expected some permanent alteration—visible evidence of the disease that was eating me away. I found nothing.

On the 15th of May, I left Heatherlegh's house at eleven o'clock in the morning; and the instinct of the bachelor drove me to the Club. There I found that every man knew my story as told by Heatherlegh, and was, in clumsy fashion, abnormally kind and attentive. Nevertheless I recognized that for the rest of my natural life I should be among but not of my fellows; and I envied very bitterly indeed the laughing coolies on the Mall below. I lunched at the Club, and at four o'clock wandered aimlessly down the Mall in the vague hope of meeting Kitty. Close to the Band-stand the black and white liveries joined me; and I heard Mrs. Wessington's old appeal at my side. I had been expecting this ever since I came out; and was only surprised at her delay. The phantom rickshaw and I went side by side along the Chota Simla road in silence. Close to the bazar, Kitty and a man on horseback overtook and passed us. For any sign she gave I might have been a dog in the road. She did not even pay me the compliment of quickening her pace; though the rainy afternoon had served for an excuse.

So Kitty and her companion, and I and my ghostly Light-o'-Love, crept round Jakko in couples. The road was streaming with water; the pines dripped like roof-pipes on the rocks below, and the air was full of fine, driving rain. Two or three times I found myself saying to myself almost aloud: "I'm Jack Pansay on leave at Simla—*at Simla!* Everyday, ordinary Simla. I mustn't forget that—I mustn't forget that." Then I would try to recollect some of the gossip I had heard at the Club: the prices of So-and-So's horses—anything, in fact, that related to the workaday Anglo-Indian world I knew so well. I even repeated the multiplication-table rapidly to myself, to make quite sure that I was not taking leave of my senses. It gave me much comfort; and must have prevented my hearing Mrs. Wessington for a time.

Once more I wearily climbed the Convent slope and entered the level road. Here Kitty and the man started off at a canter, and I was left alone with Mrs. Wessington. "Agnes," said I, "will you put back your hood and tell me what it all means?" The hood dropped noiselessly, and I was face to face with my dead and buried mistress. She was wearing the dress in which I had last seen her alive; carried the same tiny hand-kerchief in her right hand; and the same card-case in her left. (A woman eight months dead with a cardcase!) I had to pin myself down to the multiplication-table, and to set both hands on the stone parapet of the road, to assure myself that that at least was real.

"Agnes," I repeated, "for pity's sake tell me what it all means." Mrs. Wessington leaned forward, with that odd, quick turn of the head I used to know so well, and spoke.

If my story had not already so madly over-leaped the bounds of all human belief I should apologize to you now. As I know that no one—no, not even Kitty, for whom it is written as some sort of justification of my conduct—will believe me, I will go on. Mrs. Wessington spoke and I walked with her from the Sanjowlie road to the turning below the Commander-in-Chief's house as I might walk by the side of any living woman's rickshaw, deep in conversation. The second and most tormenting of my moods of sickness had

suddenly laid hold upon me, and like the Prince in Tennyson's poem, "I seemed to move amid a world of ghosts." There had been a garden-party at the Commander-in-Chief's, and we two joined the crowd of homeward-bound folk. As I saw them then it seemed that *they* were the shadows—impalpable, fantastic shadows—that divided for Mrs. Wessington's rickshaw to pass through. What we said during the course of that weird interview I cannot—indeed, I dare not—tell. Heatherlegh's comment would have been a short laugh and a remark that I had been "mash-ing a brain-eye-and-stomach chimera." It was a ghastly and yet in some indefinable way a mar-velously dear experience. Could it be possible, I wondered, that I was in this life to woo a second time the woman I had killed by my own neglect and cruelty?

I met Kitty on the homeward road—a shadow among shadows.

If I were to describe all the incidents of the next fortnight in their order, my story would never come to an end; and your patience would be exhausted. Morning after morning and eve-ning after evening the ghostly rickshaw and I used to wander through Simla together. Wher-ever I went there the four black and white liver-ies followed me and bore me company to and from my hotel. At the Theatre I found them amid the crowd or yelling *jhampanies;* outside the Club veranda, after a long evening of whist; at the Birthday Ball, waiting patiently for my reappearance; and in broad daylight when I went calling. Save that it cast no shadow, the rickshaw was in every respect as real to look upon as one of wood and iron. More than once, indeed, I have had to check myself from warn-ing some hard-riding friend against cantering over it. More than once I have walked down the Mall deep in conversation with Mrs. Wes-sington to the unspeakable amazement of the passers-by.

Before I had been out and about a week I learned that the "fit" theory had been discarded in favor of insanity. However, I made no change in my mode of life. I called, rode, and dined out as freely as ever. I had a passion for the society of my kind which I had never felt before; I hungered to be among the realities of life; and at the same time I felt vaguely unhappy when I had been separated too long from my ghostly companion. It would be almost impossible to describe my varying moods from the 15th of May up to to-day.

The presence of the rickshaw filled me by turns with horror, blind fear, a dim sort of pleasure, and utter despair. I dared not leave Simla; and I knew that my stay there was killing me. I knew, moreover, that it was my destiny to die slowly and a little every day. My only anxiety was to get the penance over as quietly as might be. Alternately I hungered for a sight of Kitty and watched her outrageous flirtations with my successor—to speak more accurately, my successors—with amused interest. She was as much out of my life as I was out of hers. By day I wandered with Mrs. Wessington almost content. By night I implored Heaven to let me return to the world as I used to know it. Above all these varying moods lay the sensation of dull, numbing wonder that the Seen and the Unseen should mingle so strangely on this earth to hound one poor soul to its grave.

August 27.—Heatherlegh has been indefatigable in his attendance on me; and only yesterday told me that I ought to send in an application for sick leave. An application to escape the company of a phantom! A request that the Government would graciously permit me to get rid of five ghosts and an airy rickshaw by going to England. Heatherlegh's proposition moved me to almost hysterical laughter. I told him that I should await the end quietly at Simla; and I am sure that the end is not far off. Believe me that I dread its advent more than any word can say; and I torture myself nightly with a thousand speculations as to the manner of my death.

Shall I die in my bed decently and as an English gentleman should die; or, in one last walk on the Mall, will my soul be wrenched from me to take its place forever and ever by the side of that ghastly phantasm? Shall I return to my old lost allegiance in the next world, or shall I meet Agnes loathing her and bound to her side through all eternity? Shall we two hover over the scene of our lives till the end of Time? As the day of my death draws nearer, the intense horror that all living flesh feels toward escaped spirits from beyond the grave grows more and more powerful. It is an awful thing to go down quick among the dead with scarcely one-half of your life completed. It is a thousand times more awful to wait as I do in your midst, for I know not what unimaginable terror. Pity me, at least on the score of my "delusion," for I know you will never believe what I have written here. Yet as surely as ever a man was done to death by the Powers of Darkness I am that man.

In justice, too, pity her. For as surely as ever woman was killed by man, I killed Mrs. Wessington. And the last portion of my punishment is ever now upon me.

Ambrose Bierce

DESCRIBED AS AMERICA'S GREATEST writer of horror fiction between Edgar Allan Poe and H. P. Lovecraft, Ambrose (Gwinnett) Bierce (1842–1914?) was born in Meigs County, Ohio, and grew up in Indiana with his mother and eccentric father; he was the tenth of thirteen children, all of whose names began with the letter "A." When the Civil War broke out, he volunteered and was soon commissioned a first lieutenant in the Union Army, seeing action in the Battle of Shiloh.

It seems that his entire life and every word he wrote was dark and cynical, earning him the sobriquet "Bitter Bierce." He became one of the most important and influential journalists in America, writing columns for William Randolph Hearst's *San Francisco Examiner*. His darkest book may be the devastating *Devil's Dictionary* (1906), in which he defined a saint as "a dead sinner revised and edited," befriend as "to make an ingrate," and birth as "the first and direst of all disasters." His most famous story is "An Occurrence at Owls Creek Bridge," in which a condemned prisoner believes he has been reprieved—just before the rope snaps his neck. It was filmed three times and was twice made for television, by Rod Serling and by Alfred Hitchcock.

In 1913, he accompanied Pancho Villa's army as an observer. He wrote a letter to a friend dated December 26, 1913. He then vanished—one of the most famous disappearances in history.

"The Moonlit Road" was first published in book form in *Can Such Things Be?* (New York, Cassell, 1893).

The Moonlit Road

AMBROSE BIERCE

I. Statement of Joel Hetman, Jr.

I am the most unfortunate of men. Rich, respected, fairly well educated and of sound health—with many other advantages usually valued by those having them and coveted by those who have them not—I sometimes think that I should be less unhappy if they had been denied me, for then the contrast between my outer and my inner life would not be continually demanding a painful attention. In the stress of privation and the need of effort I might sometimes forget the sombre secret ever baffling the conjecture that it compels.

I am the only child of Joel and Julia Hetman. The one was a well-to-do country gentleman, the other a beautiful and accomplished woman to whom he was passionately attached with what I now know to have been a jealous and exacting devotion. The family home was a few miles from Nashville, Tennessee, a large, irregularly built dwelling of no particular order of architecture, a little way off the road, in a park of trees and shrubbery.

At the time of which I write I was nineteen years old, a student at Yale. One day I received a telegram from my father of such urgency that in compliance with its unexplained demand I left at once for home. At the railway station in Nashville a distant relative awaited me to apprise me of the reason for my recall: my mother had been barbarously murdered—why and by whom none could conjecture, but the circumstances were these.

My father had gone to Nashville, intending to return the next afternoon. Something prevented his accomplishing the business in hand, so he returned on the same night, arriving just before the dawn. In his testimony before the coroner he explained that having no latchkey and not caring to disturb the sleeping servants, he had, with no clearly defined intention, gone round to the rear of the house. As he turned an angle of the building, he heard a sound as of a door gently closed, and saw in the darkness, indistinctly, the figure of a man, which instantly disappeared among the trees of the lawn. A hasty pursuit and brief search of the grounds in the belief that the trespasser was some one secretly visiting a servant proving fruitless, he entered at the unlocked door and mounted the stairs to my mother's chamber. Its door was open, and stepping into black darkness he fell headlong over some heavy object on the floor. I may spare myself the details; it was my poor mother, dead of strangulation by human hands!

Nothing had been taken from the house, the servants had heard no sound, and excepting those terrible finger-marks upon the dead woman's throat—dear God! that I might forget them!—no trace of the assassin was ever found.

I gave up my studies and remained with my father, who, naturally, was greatly changed. Always of a sedate, taciturn disposition, he now fell into so deep a dejection that nothing could hold his attention, yet anything—a footfall, the sudden closing of a door—aroused in him a fitful interest; one might have called it an apprehension. At any small surprise of the senses he would start visibly and sometimes turn pale, then relapse into a melancholy apathy deeper than before. I suppose he was what is called a "nervous wreck." As to me, I was younger then than now—there is much in that. Youth is Gilead, in which is balm for every wound. Ah, that I might again dwell in that enchanted land! Unacquainted with grief, I knew not how to appraise my bereavement; I could not rightly estimate the strength of the stroke.

One night, a few months after the dreadful event, my father and I walked home from the city. The full moon was about three hours above the eastern horizon; the entire countryside had the solemn stillness of a summer night; our footfalls and the ceaseless song of the katydids were the only sound, aloof. Black shadows of bordering trees lay athwart the road, which, in the short reaches between, gleamed a ghostly white. As we approached the gate to our dwelling, whose front was in shadow, and in which no light shone, my father suddenly stopped and clutched my arm, saying, hardly above his breath:

"God! God! what is that?"

"I hear nothing," I replied.

"But see—see!" he said, pointing along the road, directly ahead.

I said: "Nothing is there. Come, father, let us go in—you are ill."

He had released my arm and was standing rigid and motionless in the centre of the illuminated roadway, staring like one bereft of sense. His face in the moonlight showed a pallor and fixity inexpressibly distressing. I pulled gently at his sleeve, but he had forgotten my existence. Presently he began to retire backward, step by step, never for an instant removing his eyes from what he saw, or thought he saw. I turned half round to follow, but stood irresolute. I do not recall any feeling of fear, unless a sudden chill was its physical manifestation. It seemed as if an icy wind had touched my face and enfolded my body from head to foot; I could feel the stir of it in my hair.

At that moment my attention was drawn to a light that suddenly streamed from an upper window of the house: one of the servants, awakened by what mysterious premonition of evil who can say, and in obedience to an impulse that she was never able to name, had lit a lamp. When I turned to look for my father he was gone, and in all the years that have passed no whisper of his fate has come across the borderland of conjecture from the realm of the unknown.

II. Statement of Caspar Grattan

To-day I am said to live, to-morrow, here in this room, will lie a senseless shape of clay that all too long was I. If anyone lift the cloth from the face of that unpleasant thing it will be in gratification of a mere morbid curiosity. Some, doubtless, will go further and inquire, "Who was he?" In this writing I supply the only answer that I am able to make—Caspar Grattan. Surely, that should be enough. The name has served my small need for more than twenty years of a life of unknown length. True, I gave it to myself, but lacking another I had the right. In this world one must have a name; it prevents confusion, even when it does not establish identity. Some, though, are known by numbers, which also seem inadequate distinctions.

One day, for illustration, I was passing along a street of a city, far from here, when I met two men in uniform, one of whom, half pausing and looking curiously into my face, said to his companion, "That man looks like 767." Something in the number seemed familiar and horrible. Moved by an uncontrollable impulse, I sprang into a side street and ran until I fell exhausted in a country lane.

I have never forgotten that number, and always it comes to memory attended by gibbering obscenity, peals of joyless laughter, the clang of iron doors. So I say a name, even if self-bestowed, is better than a number. In the register of the potter's field I shall soon have both. What wealth!

Of him who shall find this paper I must beg a little consideration. It is not the history of my life; the knowledge to write that is denied me. This is only a record of broken and apparently unrelated memories, some of them as distinct and sequent as brilliant beads upon a thread, others remote and strange, having the character of crimson dreams with interspaces blank and black—witch-fires glowing still and red in a great desolation.

Standing upon the shore of eternity, I turn for a last look landward over the course by which I came. There are twenty years of footprints fairly distinct, the impressions of bleeding feet. They lead through poverty and pain, devious and unsure, as of one staggering beneath a burden—

Remote, unfriended, melancholy, slow.

Ah, the poet's prophecy of Me—how admirable, how dreadfully admirable!

Backward beyond the beginning of this via dolorosa—this epic of suffering with episodes of sin—I see nothing clearly; it comes out of a cloud. I know that it spans only twenty years, yet I am an old man.

One does not remember one's birth—one has to be told. But with me it was different; life came to me full-handed and dowered me with all my faculties and powers. Of a previous existence I know no more than others, for all have stammering intimations that may be memories and may be dreams. I know only that my first consciousness was of maturity in body and mind—a consciousness accepted without surprise or conjecture. I merely found myself walking in a forest, half-clad, footsore, unutterably weary and hungry. Seeing a farmhouse, I approached and asked for food, which was given me by one who inquired my name. I did not know, yet knew that all had names. Greatly embarrassed, I retreated, and night coming on, lay down in the forest and slept.

The next day I entered a large town which I shall not name. Nor shall I recount further incidents of the life that is now to end—a life of wandering, always and everywhere haunted by an overmastering sense of crime in punishment of wrong and of terror in punishment of crime. Let me see if I can reduce it to narrative.

I seem once to have lived near a great city, a prosperous planter, married to a woman whom I loved and distrusted. We had, it sometimes seems, one child, a youth of brilliant parts and promise. He is at all times a vague figure, never clearly drawn, frequently altogether out of the picture.

One luckless evening it occurred to me to test my wife's fidelity in a vulgar, commonplace way familiar to everyone who has acquaintance with the literature of fact and fiction. I went to the city, telling my wife that I should be absent until the following afternoon. But I returned before daybreak and went to the rear of the house, purposing to enter by a door with which I had secretly so tampered that it would seem to lock, yet not actually fasten. As I approached it, I heard it gently open and close, and saw a man steal away into the darkness. With murder in my heart, I sprang after him, but he had vanished without even the bad luck of identification. Sometimes now I cannot even persuade myself that it was a human being.

Crazed with jealousy and rage, blind and bestial with all the elemental passions of insulted manhood, I entered the house and sprang up the stairs to the door of my wife's chamber. It was closed, but having tampered with its lock also, I easily entered, and despite the black darkness soon stood by the side of her bed. My groping hands told me that although disarranged it was unoccupied.

"She is below," I thought, "and terrified by my entrance has evaded me in the darkness of the hall." With the purpose of seeking her I turned to leave the room, but took a wrong direction—the right one! My foot struck her, cowering in a corner of the room. Instantly my hands were at her throat, stifling a shriek, my knees were upon her struggling body; and there in the darkness, without a word of accusation or reproach,

I strangled her till she died! There ends the dream. I have related it in the past tense, but the present would be the fitter form, for again and again the sombre tragedy re-enacts itself in my consciousness—over and over I lay the plan, I suffer the confirmation, I redress the wrong. Then all is blank; and afterward the rains beat against the grimy windowpanes, or the snows fall upon my scant attire, the wheels rattle in the squalid streets where my life lies in poverty and mean employment. If there is ever sunshine I do not recall it; if there are birds they do not sing.

There is another dream, another vision of the night. I stand among the shadows in a moonlit road. I am aware of another presence, but whose I cannot rightly determine. In the shadow of a great dwelling I catch the gleam of white garments; then the figure of a woman confronts me in the road—my murdered wife! There is death in the face; there are marks upon the throat. The eyes are fixed on mine with an infinite gravity which is not reproach, nor hate, nor menace, nor anything less terrible than recognition. Before this awful apparition I retreat in terror—a terror that is upon me as I write. I can no longer rightly shape the words. See! they—

Now I am calm, but truly there is no more to tell: the incident ends where it began—in darkness and in doubt.

Yes, I am again in control of myself: "the captain of my soul." But that is not respite; it is another stage and phase of expiation. My penance, constant in degree, is mutable in kind: one of its variants is tranquillity. After all, it is only a life-sentence. "To Hell for life"—that is a foolish penalty: the culprit chooses the duration of his punishment. To-day my term expires.

To each and all, the peace that was not mine.

III. Statement of the Late Julia Hetman, through the Medium Bayrolles

I had retired early and fallen almost immediately into a peaceful sleep, from which I awoke with that indefinable sense of peril which is, I think, a common experience in that other, earlier life. Of its unmeaning character, too, I was entirely persuaded, yet that did not banish it. My husband, Joel Hetman, was away from home; the servants slept in another part of the house. But these were familiar conditions; they had never before distressed me. Nevertheless, the strange terror grew so insupportable that conquering my reluctance to move I sat up and lit the lamp at my bedside. Contrary to my expectation this gave me no relief; the light seemed rather an added danger, for I reflected that it would shine out under the door, disclosing my presence to whatever evil thing might lurk outside. You that are still in the flesh, subject to horrors of the imagination, think what a monstrous fear that must be which seeks in darkness security from malevolent existences of the night. That is to spring to close quarters with an unseen enemy—the strategy of despair!

Extinguishing the lamp I pulled the bedclothing about my head and lay trembling and silent, unable to shriek, forgetful to pray. In this pitiable state I must have lain for what you call hours—with us there are no hours, there is no time.

At last it came—a soft, irregular sound of footfalls on the stairs! They were slow, hesitant, uncertain, as of something that did not see its way; to my disordered reason all the more terrifying for that, as the approach of some blind and mindless malevolence to which is no appeal. I even thought that I must have left the hall lamp burning and the groping of this creature proved it a monster of the night. This was foolish and inconsistent with my previous dread of the light, but what would you have? Fear has no brains; it is an idiot. The dismal witness that it bears and the cowardly counsel that it whispers are unrelated. We know this well, we who have passed into the Realm of Terror, who skulk in eternal dusk among the scenes of our former lives, invisible even to ourselves, and one another, yet hiding forlorn in lonely places; yearning for speech with our loved ones, yet dumb, and as fearful of them as they of us. Sometimes the disability is removed, the law suspended: by the deathless power of love or hate we break the spell—we are seen by those whom we would warn, console, or punish. What form we seem to them to bear we know not; we know only that we terrify even those whom we most wish to comfort, and from whom we most crave tenderness and sympathy.

Forgive, I pray you, this inconsequent digression by what was once a woman. You who consult us in this imperfect way—you do not understand. You ask foolish questions about things unknown and things forbidden. Much that we know and could impart in our speech is meaningless in yours. We must communicate with you through a stammering intelligence in that small fraction of our language that you yourselves can speak. You think that we are of another world. No, we have knowledge of no world but yours, though for us it holds no sunlight, no warmth, no music, no laughter, no song of birds, nor any companionship. O God! what a thing it is to be a ghost, cowering and shivering in an altered world, a prey to apprehension and despair!

No, I did not die of fright: the Thing turned and went away. I heard it go down the stairs, hurriedly, I thought, as if itself in sudden fear. Then I rose to call for help. Hardly had my shaking hand found the door-knob when—merciful heaven!—I heard it returning. Its footfalls as it remounted the stairs were rapid, heavy and loud; they shook the house. I fled to an angle of the wall and crouched upon the floor. I tried to pray. I tried to call the name of my dear husband. Then I heard the door thrown open. There was an interval of unconsciousness, and when I revived I felt a strangling clutch upon my throat—felt my arms feebly beating against something that bore me backward—felt my tongue thrusting itself from between my teeth! And then I passed into this life.

No, I have no knowledge of what it was. The sum of what we knew at death is the measure of what we know afterward of all that went before. Of this existence we know many things, but no new light falls upon any page of that; in memory is written all of it that we can read. Here are no heights of truth overlooking the confused landscape of that dubitable domain. We still dwell in the Valley of the Shadow, lurk in its desolate places, peering from brambles and thickets at its mad, malign inhabitants. How should we have new knowledge of that fading past?

What I am about to relate happened on a night. We know when it is night, for then you retire to your houses and we can venture from our places of concealment to move unafraid about our old homes, to look in at the windows, even to enter and gaze upon your faces as you sleep. I had lingered long near the dwelling where I had been so cruelly changed to what I am, as we do while any that we love or hate remain. Vainly I had sought some method of manifestation, some way to make my continued existence and my great love and poignant pity understood by my husband and son. Always if they slept they would wake, or if in my desperation I dared approach them when they were awake, would turn toward me the terrible eyes of the living, frightening me by the glances that I sought from the purpose that I held.

On this night I had searched for them without success, fearing to find them; they were nowhere in the house, nor about the moonlit dawn. For, although the sun is lost to us for ever, the moon, full-orbed or slender, remains to us. Sometimes it shines by night, sometimes by day, but always it rises and sets, as in that other life.

I left the lawn and moved in the white light and silence along the road, aimless and sorrowing. Suddenly I heard the voice of my poor husband in exclamations of astonishment, with that of my son in reassurance and dissuasion; and there by the shadow of a group of trees they stood—near, so near! Their faces were toward me, the eyes of the elder man fixed upon mine. He saw me—at last, at last, he saw me! In the consciousness of that, my terror fled as a cruel dream. The death-spell was broken: Love had conquered Law! Mad with exultation I shouted—I must have shouted, "He sees, he sees: he will understand!" Then, controlling myself, I moved forward, smiling and consciously beautiful, to offer myself to his arms, to comfort him with endearments, and, with my son's hand in mine, to speak words that should restore the broken bonds between the living and the dead.

Alas! alas! his face went white with fear, his eyes were as those of a hunted animal. He backed away from me, as I advanced, and at last turned and fled into the wood—whither, it is not given to me to know.

To my poor boy, left doubly desolate, I have never been able to impart a sense of my presence. Soon he, too, must pass to this Life Invisible and be lost to me for ever.

THE STORY OF MING-Y AND YUKI-ONNA

Lafcadio Hearn

ALTHOUGH AS MULTINATIONAL as it was possible to be in the America of the nineteenth century, Patricio Lafcadio Tessima Carlos Hearn (1850–1904) is generally regarded as an American writer. He was born on the Ionian island of Santa Maura (now Lefcada), the son of a surgeon-major in the British army and his Greek wife, Rosa. He moved to Dublin at six, then studied in England and Paris before moving to America, where he worked in a print shop and as a journalist. He began to write grotesque tales, many with supernatural overtones, but earned a living by writing newspaper columns and features. When he became involved with a black woman, he lost his job and moved to New Orleans, where he wrote stories of Creole life and tried to learn Ghombo French (a Louisiana Negro dialect). In 1890, he journeyed to Japan, where he married a twenty-two-year-old woman of high samurai rank, and spent the rest of his life there.

His earliest books were translations of works by Gautier (1882), *Stray Leaves from Strange Literature* (1884), and collections of Creole Proverbs and Creole cuisine, but the bulk of his best work is in the form of transcriptions and retellings of Japanese and Chinese folktales, frequently of a ghostly or macabre nature. His spare, terse prose antedates that of Hemingway, though the similarities are not immediately apparent because of the large differences in tone. The two stories in this collection are similar to each other and to many other of the short stories that he fashioned from the legends and fairy tales of his adopted land and its neighbor.

"The Story of Ming-Y" was first published in *Some Chinese Ghosts* (Boston, Roberts Brothers, 1887). "Yuki-Onna" was first published in *Kwaidan: Stories and Studies of Strange Things* (Boston, Houghton Mifflin, 1904).

The Story of Ming-Y

LAFCADIO HEARN

THE ANCIENT WORDS OF Kouei—Master of Musicians in the Courts of the Emperor Yao:

When ye make to resound the stone melodious, the Ming-Khieou,—When ye touch the lyre that is called Kin, or the guitar that is called Ssé,—Accompanying their sound with song,—Then do the grandfather and the father return; Then do the ghosts of the ancestors come to hear.

THE STORY OF MING-Y

Sang the Poet Tching-Kou: "Surely the Peach-Flowers blossom over the tomb of Sië-Thao."

Do you ask me who she was,—the beautiful Sië-Thao? For a thousand years and more the trees have been whispering above her bed of stone. And the syllables of her name come to the listener with the lisping of the leaves; with the quivering of many-fingered boughs; with the fluttering of lights and shadows; with the breath, sweet as a woman's presence, of numberless savage flowers,—*Sië-Thao.* But, saving the whispering of her name, what the trees say cannot be understood; and they alone remember the years of Sië-Thao. Something about her you might, nevertheless, learn from any

of those *Kiang-kou-jin,*—those famous Chinese story-tellers, who nightly narrate to listening crowds, in consideration of a few *tsien,* the legends of the past. Something concerning her you may also find in the book entitled "Kin-Kou-Ki-Koan," which signifies in our tongue: "The Marvellous Happenings of Ancient and of Recent Times." And perhaps of all things therein written, the most marvellous is this memory of Sië-Thao:—

Five hundred years ago, in the reign of the Emperor Houng-Wou, whose dynasty was *Ming,* there lived in the City of Genii, the city of Kwang-tchau-fu, a man celebrated for his learning and for his piety, named Tien-Pelou. This Tien-Pelou had one son, a beautiful boy, who for scholarship and for bodily grace and for polite accomplishments had no superior among the youths of his age. And his name was Ming-Y.

Now when the lad was in his eighteenth summer, it came to pass that Pelou, his father, was appointed Inspector of Public Instruction at the city of Tching-tou; and Ming-Y accompanied his parents thither. Near the city of Tching-tou lived a rich man of rank, a high commissioner of the government, whose name was Tchang, and who wanted to find a worthy teacher for his children. On hearing of the arrival of the new Inspector of Public Instruction, the noble Tchang visited him to obtain advice in this matter; and happening to meet and converse with Pelou's accomplished son, immediately engaged Ming-Y as a private tutor for his family.

Now as the house of this Lord Tchang was situated several miles from town, it was deemed best that Ming-Y should abide in the house of his employer. Accordingly the youth made ready all things necessary for his new sojourn; and his parents, bidding him farewell, counselled him wisely, and cited to him the words of Lao-tseu and of the ancient sages:

"By a beautiful face the world is filled with love; but Heaven may never be deceived thereby. Shouldst thou behold a woman coming from the East, look thou to the West; shouldst thou perceive a maiden approaching from the West, turn thine eyes to the East."

If Ming-Y did not heed this counsel in after days, it was only because of his youth and the thoughtlessness of a naturally joyous heart.

And he departed to abide in the house of Lord Tchang, while the autumn passed, and the winter also.

When the time of the second moon of spring was drawing near, and that happy day which the Chinese call *Hoa-tchao,* or, "The Birthday of a Hundred Flowers," a longing came upon Ming-Y to see his parents; and he opened his heart to the good Tchang, who not only gave him the permission he desired, but also pressed into his hand a silver gift of two ounces, thinking that the lad might wish to bring some little memento to his father and mother. For it is the Chinese custom, on the feast of Hoa-tchao, to make presents to friends and relations.

That day all the air was drowsy with blossom perfume, and vibrant with the droning of bees. It seemed to Ming-Y that the path he followed had not been trodden by any other for many long years; the grass was tall upon it; vast trees on either side interlocked their mighty and moss-grown arms above him, beshadowing the way; but the leafy obscurities quivered with

bird-song, and the deep vistas of the wood were glorified by vapors of gold, and odorous with flower-breathings as a temple with incense. The dreamy joy of the day entered into the heart of Ming-Y; and he sat him down among the young blossoms, under the branches swaying against the violet sky, to drink in the perfume and the light, and to enjoy the great sweet silence. Even while thus reposing, a sound caused him to turn his eyes toward a shady place where wild peach-trees were in bloom; and he beheld a young woman, beautiful as the pinkening blossoms themselves, trying to hide among them. Though he looked for a moment only, Ming-Y could not avoid discerning the loveliness of her face, the golden purity of her complexion, and the brightness of her long eyes, that sparkled under a pair of brows as daintily curved as the wings of the silkworm butterfly outspread. Ming-Y at once turned his gaze away, and, rising quickly, proceeded on his journey. But so much embarrassed did he feel at the idea of those charming eyes peeping at him through the leaves, that he suffered the money he had been carrying in his sleeve to fall, without being aware of it. A few moments later he heard the patter of light feet running behind him, and a woman's voice calling him by name. Turning his face in great surprise, he saw a comely servant-maid, who said to him, "Sir, my mistress bade me pick up and return you this silver which you dropped upon the road." Ming-Y thanked the girl gracefully, and requested her to convey his compliments to her mistress. Then he proceeded on his way through the perfumed silence, athwart the shadows that dreamed along the forgotten path, dreaming himself also, and feeling his heart beating with strange quickness at the thought of the beautiful being that he had seen.

It was just such another day when Ming-Y, returning by the same path, paused once more at the spot where the gracious figure had momentarily appeared before him. But this time he was surprised to perceive, through a long vista of immense trees, a dwelling that had previously escaped his notice,—a country residence, not large, yet elegant to an unusual degree. The bright blue tiles of its curved and serrated double roof, rising above the foliage, seemed to blend their color with the luminous azure of the day; the green-and-gold designs of its carven porticos were exquisite artistic mockeries of leaves and flowers bathed in sunshine. And at the summit of terrace-steps before it, guarded by great porcelain tortoises, Ming-Y saw standing the mistress of the mansion,—the idol of his passionate fancy,—accompanied by the same waiting-maid who had borne to her his message of gratitude. While Ming-Y looked, he perceived that their eyes were upon him; they smiled and conversed together as if speaking about him; and, shy though he was, the youth found courage to salute the fair one from a distance. To his astonishment, the young servant beckoned him to approach; and opening a rustic gate half veiled by trailing plants bearing crimson flowers, Ming-Y advanced along the verdant alley leading to the terrace, with mingled feelings of surprise and timid joy. As he drew near, the beautiful lady withdrew from sight; but the maid waited at the broad steps to receive him, and said as he ascended:

"Sir, my mistress understands you wish to thank her for the trifling service she recently bade me do you, and requests that you will enter the house, as she knows you already by repute, and desires to have the pleasure of bidding you good-day."

Ming-Y entered bashfully, his feet making no sound upon a matting elastically soft as forest moss, and found himself in a reception-chamber vast, cool, and fragrant with scent of blossoms freshly gathered. A delicious quiet pervaded the mansion; shadows of flying birds passed over the bands of light that fell through the half-blinds of bamboo; great butterflies, with pinions of fiery color, found their way in, to hover a moment about the painted vases, and pass out again into the mysterious woods. And noiselessly as they, the young mistress of the mansion entered by another door, and kindly greeted the boy, who lifted his hands to his breast and bowed low in salutation. She was taller than he had deemed her, and supplely-slender as a beauteous lily; her black hair was interwoven with the creamy blossoms of the *chu-sha-kih;* her robes of pale silk took shifting tints when she moved, as vapors change hue with the changing of the light.

"If I be not mistaken," she said, when both had seated themselves after having exchanged the customary formalities of politeness, "my honored visitor is none other than Tien-chou, surnamed Ming-Y, educator of the children of my respected relative, the High Commissioner Tchang. As the family of Lord Tchang is my family also, I cannot but consider the teacher of his children as one of my own kin."

"Lady," replied Ming-Y, not a little astonished, "may I dare to inquire the name of your honored family, and to ask the relation which you hold to my noble patron?"

"The name of my poor family," responded the comely lady, "is *Ping,*—an ancient family of the city of Tching-tou. I am the daughter of a certain Sië of Moun-hao; Sië is my name, likewise; and I was married to a young man of the Ping family, whose name was Khang. By this marriage I became related to your excellent patron; but my husband died soon after our wedding, and I have chosen this solitary place to reside in during the period of my widowhood."

There was a drowsy music in her voice, as of the melody of brooks, the murmurings of spring; and such a strange grace in the manner of her speech as Ming-Y had never heard before. Yet, on learning that she was a widow, the youth would not have presumed to remain long in her presence without a formal invitation; and after having sipped the cup of rich tea presented to him, he arose to depart. Sië would not suffer him to go so quickly.

"Nay, friend," she said; "stay yet a little while in my house, I pray you; for, should your honored patron ever learn that you had been here, and that I had not treated you as a respected guest, and regaled you even as I would him, I know that he would be greatly angered. Remain at least to supper."

So Ming-Y remained, rejoicing secretly in his heart, for Sië seemed to him the fairest and sweetest being he had ever known, and he felt that he loved her even more than his father and his mother. And while they talked the long shadows of the evening slowly blended into one violet darkness; the great citron-light of the sunset faded out; and those starry beings that are called the Three Councillors, who preside over life and death and the destinies of men, opened their cold bright eyes in the northern sky. Within the mansion of Sië the painted lanterns were lighted; the table was laid for the evening repast; and Ming-Y took his place at it, feeling little inclination to eat, and thinking only of the charming face before him. Observing that he scarcely tasted the dainties laid upon his plate, Sië pressed her young guest to partake of wine; and they drank several cups together. It was a purple wine, so cool that the cup into which it was poured became covered with vapory dew; yet it seemed to warm the veins with strange fire. To Ming-Y, as he drank, all things became more luminous as by enchantment; the walls of the chamber appeared to recede, and the roof to heighten; the lamps glowed like stars in their chains, and the voice of Sië floated to the boy's ears like some far melody heard through the spaces of a drowsy night. His heart swelled; his tongue loosened; and words flitted from his lips that he had fancied he could never dare to utter. Yet Sië sought not to restrain him; her lips gave no smile; but her long bright eyes seemed to laugh with pleasure at his words of praise, and to return his gaze of passionate admiration with affectionate interest.

"I have heard," she said, "of your rare talent, and of your many elegant accomplishments. I know how to sing a little, although I cannot claim to possess any musical learning; and now that I have the honor of finding myself in the society of a musical professor, I will venture to lay modesty aside, and beg you to sing a few songs with me. I should deem it no small gratification if you would condescend to examine my musical compositions."

"The honor and the gratification, dear lady," replied Ming-Y, "will be mine; and I feel helpless to express the gratitude which the offer of so rare a favor deserves."

The serving-maid, obedient to the summons of a little silver gong, brought in the music and retired. Ming-Y took the manuscripts, and began to examine them with eager delight. The paper upon which they were written had a pale yellow tint, and was light as a fabric of gossamer; but the characters were antiquely beautiful, as though they had been traced by the brush of Heï-song Ché-Tchoo himself,—that divine Genius of Ink, who is no bigger than a fly; and the signatures attached to the compositions were the signatures of Youen-tchin, Kao-pien, and Thou-mou,—mighty poets and musicians of the dynasty of Thang! Ming-Y could not repress a scream of delight at the sight of treasures so inestimable and so unique; scarcely could he summon resolution enough to permit them to leave his hands even for a moment. "O Lady!" he cried, "these are veritably priceless things, surpassing in worth the treasures of all kings. This indeed is the handwriting of those great masters who sang five hundred years before our birth. How marvellously it has been preserved! Is not this the wondrous ink of which it was written: *Po-nien-jou-chi, i-tien-jou-ki*,—'After centuries I remain firm as stone, and the letters that I make like lacquer'? And how divine the charm of this composition!—the song of Kao-pien, prince of poets, and Governor of Sze-tchouen five hundred years ago!"

"Kao-pien! darling Kao-pien!" murmured Sië, with a singular light in her eyes. "Kao-pien is also my favorite. Dear Ming-Y, let us chant his verses together, to the melody of old,—the music of those grand years when men were nobler and wiser than to-day."

And their voices rose through the perfumed night like the voices of the wonder-birds,—of the Fung-hoang,—blending together in liquid sweetness. Yet a moment, and Ming-Y, overcome by the witchery of his companion's voice, could only listen in speechless ecstasy, while the lights of the chamber swam dim before his sight, and tears of pleasure trickled down his cheeks.

So the ninth hour passed; and they continued to converse, and to drink the cool purple wine, and to sing the songs of the years of Thang, until far into the night. More than once Ming-Y thought of departing; but each time Sië would begin, in that silver-sweet voice of hers, so wondrous a story of the great poets of the past, and of the women whom they loved, that he became as one entranced; or she would sing for him a song so strange that all his senses seemed to die except that of hearing. And at last, as she paused to pledge him in a cup of wine, Ming-Y could not restrain himself from putting his arm about her round neck and drawing her dainty head closer to him, and kissing the lips that were so much ruddier and sweeter than the wine. Then their lips separated no more;—the night grew old, and they knew it not.

The birds awakened, the flowers opened their eyes to the rising sun, and Ming-Y found himself at last compelled to bid his lovely enchantress farewell. Sië, accompanying him to the terrace, kissed him fondly and said, "Dear boy, come hither as often as you are able,—as often as your heart whispers you to come. I know that you are not of those without faith and truth, who betray secrets; yet, being so young, you might also be sometimes thoughtless; and I pray you never to forget that only the stars have been the witnesses of our love. Speak of it to no living person, dearest; and take with you this little souvenir of our happy night."

And she presented him with an exquisite and curious little thing,—a paper-weight in likeness of a couchant lion, wrought from a jade-stone yellow as that created by a rainbow in honor of Kong-fu-tze. Tenderly the boy kissed the gift and the beautiful hand that gave it. "May the Spirits punish me," he vowed, "if ever I knowingly give you cause to reproach me, sweetheart!" And they separated with mutual vows.

That morning, on returning to the house

of Lord Tchang, Ming-Y told the first falsehood which had ever passed his lips. He averred that his mother had requested him thenceforward to pass his nights at home, now that the weather had become so pleasant; for, though the way was somewhat long, he was strong and active, and needed both air and healthy exercise. Tchang believed all Ming-Y said, and offered no objection. Accordingly the lad found himself enabled to pass all his evenings at the house of the beautiful Sië. Each night they devoted to the same pleasures which had made their first acquaintance so charming: they sang and conversed by turns; they played at chess,—the learned game invented by Wu-Wang, which is an imitation of war; they composed pieces of eighty rhymes upon the flowers, the trees, the clouds, the streams, the birds, the bees. But in all accomplishments Sië far excelled her young sweetheart. Whenever they played at chess, it was always Ming-Y's general, Ming-Y's *tsiang*, who was surrounded and vanquished; when they composed verses, Sië's poems were ever superior to his in harmony of word-coloring, in elegance of form, in classic loftiness of thought. And the themes they selected were always the most difficult,—those of the poets of the Thang dynasty; the songs they sang were also the songs of five hundred years before,—the songs of Youen-tchin, of Thou-mou, of Kao-pien above all, high poet and ruler of the province of Sze-tchouen.

So the summer waxed and waned upon their love, and the luminous autumn came, with its vapors of phantom gold, its shadows of magical purple.

Then it unexpectedly happened that the father of Ming-Y, meeting his son's employer at Tching-tou, was asked by him: "Why must your boy continue to travel every evening to the city, now that the winter is approaching? The way is long, and when he returns in the morning he looks fordone with weariness. Why not permit him to slumber in my house during the season of snow?" And the father of Ming-Y, greatly astonished, responded: "Sir, my son has not visited the city, nor has he been to our house all this summer. I fear that he must have acquired wicked habits, and that he passes his nights in evil company,—perhaps in gaming, or in drinking with the women of the flower-boats." But the High Commissioner returned: "Nay! that is not to be thought of. I have never found any evil in the boy, and there are no taverns nor flower-boats nor any places of dissipation in our neighborhood. No doubt Ming-Y has found some amiable youth of his own age with whom to spend his evenings, and only told me an untruth for fear that I would not otherwise permit him to leave my residence. I beg that you will say nothing to him until I shall have sought to discover this mystery; and this very evening I shall send my servant to follow after him, and to watch whither he goes."

Pelou readily assented to this proposal, and promising to visit Tchang the following morning, returned to his home. In the evening, when Ming-Y left the house of Tchang, a servant followed him unobserved at a distance. But on reaching the most obscure portion of the road, the boy disappeared from sight as suddenly as though the earth had swallowed him. After having long sought after him in vain, the domestic returned in great bewilderment to the house, and related what had taken place. Tchang immediately sent a messenger to Pelou.

In the mean time Ming-Y, entering the chamber of his beloved, was surprised and deeply pained to find her in tears. "Sweetheart," she sobbed, wreathing her arms around his neck, "we are about to be separated forever, because of reasons which I cannot tell you. From the very first I knew this must come to pass; and nevertheless it seemed to me for the moment so cruelly sudden a loss, so unexpected a misfortune, that I could not prevent myself from weeping! After this night we shall never see each other again, beloved, and I know that you will not be able to forget me while you live; but I know also that you will become a great scholar, and that

honors and riches will be showered upon you, and that some beautiful and loving woman will console you for my loss. And now let us speak no more of grief; but let us pass this last evening joyously, so that your recollection of me may not be a painful one, and that you may remember my laughter rather than my tears."

She brushed the bright drops away, and brought wine and music and the melodious *kin* of seven silken strings, and would not suffer Ming-Y to speak for one moment of the coming separation. And she sang him an ancient song about the calmness of summer lakes reflecting the blue of heaven only, and the calmness of the heart also, before the clouds of care and of grief and of weariness darken its little world. Soon they forgot their sorrow in the joy of song and wine; and those last hours seemed to Ming-Y more celestial than even the hours of their first bliss.

But when the yellow beauty of morning came their sadness returned, and they wept. Once more Sië accompanied her lover to the terrace-steps; and as she kissed him farewell, she pressed into his hand a parting gift,—a little brush-case of agate, wonderfully chiselled, and worthy the table of a great poet. And they separated forever, shedding many tears.

Still Ming-Y could not believe it was an eternal parting. "No!" he thought, "I shall visit her tomorrow; for I cannot now live without her, and I feel assured that she cannot refuse to receive me." Such were the thoughts that filled his mind as he reached the house of Tchang, to find his father and his patron standing on the porch awaiting him. Ere he could speak a word, Pelou demanded: "Son, in what place have you been passing your nights?"

Seeing that his falsehood had been discovered, Ming-Y dared not make any reply, and remained abashed and silent, with bowed head, in the presence of his father. Then Pelou, striking the boy violently with his staff, commanded him to divulge the secret; and at last, partly through fear of his parent, and partly through fear of the law which ordains that *"the son refusing to obey his father shall be punished with one hundred blows of the bamboo,"* Ming-Y faltered out the history of his love.

Tchang changed color at the boy's tale. "Child," exclaimed the High Commissioner, "I have no relative of the name of Ping; I have never heard of the woman you describe; I have never heard even of the house which you speak of. But I know also that you cannot dare to lie to Pelou, your honored father; there is some strange delusion in all this affair."

Then Ming-Y produced the gifts that Sië had given him,—the lion of yellow jade, the brush-case of carven agate, also some original compositions made by the beautiful lady herself. The astonishment of Tchang was now shared by Pelou. Both observed that the brush-case of agate and the lion of jade bore the appearance of objects that had lain buried in the earth for centuries, and were of a workmanship beyond the power of living man to imitate; while the compositions proved to be veritable master-pieces of poetry, written in the style of the poets of the dynasty of Thang.

"Friend Pelou," cried the High Commissioner, "let us immediately accompany the boy to the place where he obtained these miraculous things, and apply the testimony of our senses to this mystery. The boy is no doubt telling the truth; yet his story passes my understanding." And all three proceeded toward the place of the habitation of Sië.

But when they had arrived at the shadiest part of the road, where the perfumes were most sweet and the mosses were greenest, and the fruits of the wild peach flushed most pinkly, Ming-Y, gazing through the groves, uttered a cry of dismay. Where the azure-tiled roof had risen against the sky, there was now only the blue emptiness of air; where the green-and-gold facade had been, there was visible only the flickering of leaves under the aureate autumn light;

and where the broad terrace had extended, could be discerned only a ruin,—a tomb so ancient, so deeply gnawed by moss, that the name graven upon it was no longer decipherable. The home of Sië had disappeared!

All suddenly the High Commissioner smote his forehead with his hand, and turning to Pelou, recited the well-known verse of the ancient poet Tching-Kou:—

"Surely the peach-flowers blossom over the tomb of SIË-THAO."

"Friend Pelou," continued Tchang, "the beauty who bewitched your son was no other than she whose tomb stands there in ruin before us! Did she not say she was wedded to Ping-Khang? There is no family of that name, but Ping-Khang is indeed the name of a broad alley in the city near. There was a dark riddle in all that she said. She called herself Sië of Moun-Hiao: there is no person of that name; there is no street of that name; but the Chinese characters *Moun* and *hiao*, placed together, form the character 'Kiao.' Listen! The alley Ping-Khang, situated in the street Kiao, was the place where dwelt the great courtesans of the dynasty of Thang! Did she not sing the songs of Kao-pien? And upon the brush-case and the paper-weight she gave your son, are there not characters which read, *'Pure object of art belonging to Kao, of the city of Pho-hai'*? That city no longer exists; but the memory of Kao-pien remains, for he was governor of the province of Sze-tchouen, and a mighty poet. And when he dwelt in the land of Chou, was not his favorite the beautiful wanton Sië,—Sië-Thao, unmatched for grace among all the women of her day? It was he who made her a gift of those manuscripts of song; it was he who gave her those objects of rare art. Sië-Thao died not as other women die. Her limbs may have crumbled to dust; yet something of her still lives in this deep wood,—her Shadow still haunts this shadowy place."

Tchang ceased to speak. A vague fear fell

upon the three. The thin mists of the morning made dim the distances of green, and deepened the ghostly beauty of the woods. A faint breeze passed by, leaving a trail of blossom-scent,—a last odor of dying flowers,—thin as that which clings to the silk of a forgotten robe; and, as it passed, the trees seemed to whisper across the silence, "*Sië-Thao*."

Fearing greatly for his son, Pelou sent the lad away at once to the city of Kwang-tchau-fu. And there, in after years, Ming-Y obtained high dignities and honors by reason of his talents and his learning; and he married the daughter of an illustrious house, by whom he became the father of sons and daughters famous for their virtues and their accomplishments. Never could he forget Sië-Thao; and yet it is said that he never spoke of her,—not even when his children begged him to tell them the story of two beautiful objects that always lay upon his writing-table: a lion of yellow jade, and a brush-case of carven agate.

Yuki-Onna

LAFCADIO HEARN

IN A VILLAGE OF Musashi Province, there lived two woodcutters: Mosaku and Minokichi. At the time of which I am speaking, Mosaku was an old man; and Minokichi, his apprentice, was a lad of eighteen years. Every day they went together to a forest situated about five miles from their village. On the way to that forest there is a wide river to cross; and there is a ferryboat. Several times a bridge was built where the ferry is; but the bridge was each time carried away by a flood. No common bridge can resist the current there when the river rises.

Mosaku and Minokichi were on their way home, one very cold evening, when a great snowstorm overtook them. They reached the ferry; and they found that the boatman had gone away, leaving his boat on the other side of the river. It was no day for swimming; and the woodcutters took shelter in the ferryman's hut,—thinking themselves lucky to find any shelter at all. There was no brazier in the hut, nor any place in which to make a fire: it was only a two-mat hut, with a single door, but no window. Mosaku and Minokichi fastened the door, and lay down to rest, with their straw rain-coats over them. At first they did not feel very cold; and they thought that the storm would soon be over.

The old man almost immediately fell asleep; but the boy, Minokichi, lay awake a long time, listening to the awful wind, and the continual slashing of the snow against the door. The river was roaring; and the hut swayed and creaked like a junk at sea. It was a terrible storm; and the air was every moment becoming colder; and Minokichi shivered under his raincoat. But at last, in spite of the cold, he too fell asleep.

He was awakened by a showering of snow in his face. The door of the hut had been forced open; and, by the snow-light (*yuki-akari*), he saw a woman in the room,—a woman all in white. She was bending above Mosaku, and blowing her breath upon him;—and her breath was like a bright white smoke. Almost in the same moment she turned to Minokichi, and stooped over him. He tried to cry out, but found that he could not utter any sound. The white woman bent down over him, lower and lower, until her face almost touched him; and he saw that she was very beautiful,—though her eyes made him afraid. For a little time she continued to look at him;—then she smiled, and she whispered:—"I intended to treat you like the other man. But I cannot help feeling some pity for you,—because you are so young. . . . You are a pretty boy, Minokichi; and I will not hurt you now. But, if you ever tell anybody—even your own mother about what you have seen this night, I shall know it; and then I will kill you. . . . Remember what I say!"

With these words, she turned from him, and passed through the doorway. Then he found himself able to move; and he sprang up, and looked out. But the woman was nowhere to be seen; and the snow was driving furiously into the hut. Minokichi closed the door, and secured it by fixing several billets of wood against it. He wondered if the wind had blown it open;—he thought that he might have been only dreaming, and might have mistaken the gleam of the snow-light in the doorway for the figure of a white woman: but he could not be sure. He called to Mosaku, and was frightened because the old man did not answer. He put out his hand in the dark, and touched Mosaku's face, and found that it was ice! Mosaku was stark and dead. . . .

By dawn the storm was over; and when the ferryman returned to his station, a little after sunrise, he found Minokichi lying senseless beside the frozen body of Mosaku. Minokichi was promptly cared for, and soon came to himself; but he remained a long time ill from the effects of the cold of that terrible night. He had been greatly frightened also by the old man's death; but he said nothing about the vision of the woman in white. As soon as he got well again, he returned to his calling, going alone every morning to the forest, and coming back at nightfall with his bundles of wood, which his mother helped him to sell.

One evening, in the winter of the following year, as he was on his way home, he overtook a girl who happened to be traveling by the same road. She was a tall, slim girl, very good-looking; and she answered Minokichi's greeting in a voice as pleasant to the ear as the voice of a song-bird. Then he walked beside her; and they began to talk. The girl said that her name was O-Yuki; that she had lately lost both of her parents; and that she was going to Yedo, where she happened to have some poor relations, who might help her to find a situation as servant. Minokichi soon felt charmed by this strange girl; and the more that he looked at her, the handsomer she appeared to be. He asked her whether she was yet betrothed; and she answered, laughingly, that she was free. Then, in her turn, she asked Minokichi whether he was married, or pledged to marry; and he told her that, although he had only a widowed mother to support, the question of an "honorable daughter-in-law" had not yet been considered, as he was very young. . . . After these confidences, they walked on for a long while without speaking; but, as the proverb declares, *Ki ga aréba, mé mo kuchi hodo ni mono wo iu:* "When the wish is there, the eyes can say as much as the mouth." By the time they reached the village, they had become very much pleased with each other; and then Minokichi asked O-Yuki to rest awhile at his house. After some shy hesitation, she went there with him; and his mother made her welcome, and prepared a warm meal for her. O-Yuki behaved so nicely that Minokichi's mother took a sudden fancy to her, and persuaded her to delay her journey to Yedo. And the natural end of the matter was that O-Yuki never went to Yedo at all. She remained in the house, as an "honorable daughter-in-law."

O-Yuki proved a very good daughter-in-law. When Minokichi's mother came to die,—some five years later,—her last words were words of affection and praise for the wife of her son. And O-Yuki bore Minokichi ten children, boys and girls,—handsome children all of them, and very fair of skin.

The country-folk thought O-Yuki a wonderful person, by nature different from themselves. Most of the peasant-women age early; but O-Yuki, even after having become the mother of ten children, looked as young and fresh as on the day when she had first come to the village.

One night, after the children had gone to sleep, O-Yuki was sewing by the light of a paper lamp; and Minokichi, watching her, said:—

"To see you sewing there, with the light on your face, makes me think of a strange thing that happened when I was a lad of eighteen. I then saw somebody as beautiful and white as you are now—indeed, she was very like you." . . .

Without lifting her eyes from her work, O-Yuki responded:—

"Tell me about her. . . . Where did you see her?"

Then Minokichi told her about the terrible night in the ferryman's hut,—and about the White Woman that had stooped above him, smiling and whispering,—and about the silent death of old Mosaku. And he said:—"Asleep or awake, that was the only time that I saw a being as beautiful as you. Of course, she was not a human being; and I was afraid of her,—very much afraid,—but she was so white I . . . Indeed, I have never been sure whether it was a dream that I saw, or the Woman of the Snow." . . .

O-Yuki flung down her sewing, and arose, and bowed above Minokichi where he sat, and shrieked into his face: "It was I—I—I! O-Yuki it was! And I told you then that I would kill you if you ever said one word about it! . . . But for those children asleep there, I would kill you this moment! And now you had better take very, very good care of them; for if ever they have reason to complain of you, I will treat you as you deserve!" . . .

Even as she screamed, her voice became thin, like a crying of wind;—then she melted into a bright white mist that spired to the roof-beams, and shuddered away through the smoke-hole. . . . Never again was she seen.

THIS OLD HOUSE

BRICKETT BOTTOM

Amyas Northcote

AS THE AUTHOR OF a single book of ghost stories, the rare *In Ghostly Company*, Amyas Northcote (1864–1923) has been a sadly neglected writer considering the excellence of the thirteen tales. A somewhat ghostly entity himself, very little is known of him.

He was born near Exeter and went to Eton, as most of his very distinguished family had before him. His father was Sir Stafford Northcote, Chancellor of the Exchequer during Benjamin Disraeli's six years as Prime Minister, later becoming the Leader of the House and the most important Tory in the House of Commons for ten years and serving as Foreign Secretary; after thirty years in Parliament, he stepped down and died on the same day. A statue was erected in his honor in 1887 in the vestibule of the House of Commons.

Amyas Northcote was at Eton at the same time that M. R. James was there, and they shared time at Oxford as well. Soon after his father died, Northcote moved to America to set up a business in Chicago and found time to write articles for various magazines. He returned to England about a decade later and moved into a house a mere few miles from M. R. James, where he commenced to write ghost stories in a style not unlike that of the master. The great scholar of supernatural fiction, Montague Summers, singled Northcote out for praise when he used "Brickett Bottom" in his landmark anthology, *The Supernatural Omnibus* (1931).

Whatever information about Amyas Northcote that has come to light is due to the remarkable scholarship of Richard Dalby, undertaken for his introduction to the 1997 Ash-Tree Press reprint of *In Ghostly Company*.

"Brickett Bottom" was originally published in *In Ghostly Company* (London, John Lane, 1922). Although 1922 was printed on the title page, the volume was actually released in November 1921 in time for the Christmas book-buying season. John Lane customarily added New York to its title pages but this volume was never distributed in the United States.

Brickett Bottom

AMYAS NORTHCOTE

THE REVEREND ARTHUR MAYDEW was the hard-working incumbent of a large parish in one of our manufacturing towns. He was also a student and a man of no strong physique, so that when an opportunity was presented to him to take an annual holiday by exchanging parsonages with an elderly clergyman, Mr. Roberts, the Squarson of the Parish of Overbury, and an acquaintance of his own, he was glad to avail himself of it.

Overbury is a small and very remote village in one of our most lovely and rural counties, and Mr. Roberts had long held the living of it.

Without further delay we can transport Mr. Maydew and his family, which consisted only of two daughters, to their temporary home. The two young ladies, Alice and Maggie, the heroines of this narrative, were at that time aged twenty-six and twenty-four years respectively. Both of them were attractive girls, fond of such society as they could find in their own parish and, the former especially, always pleased to extend the circle of their acquaintance. Although the elder in years, Alice in many ways yielded place to her sister, who was the more energetic and practical and upon whose shoulders the bulk of the family cares and responsibilities rested. Alice was inclined to be absent-minded and emotional and to devote more of her thoughts and time to speculations of an abstract nature than her sister.

Both of the girls, however, rejoiced at the prospect of a period of quiet and rest in a pleasant country neighbourhood, and both were gratified at knowing that their father would find in Mr. Roberts' library much that would entertain his mind, and in Mr. Roberts' garden an opportunity to indulge freely in his favourite game of croquet. They would have, no doubt, preferred some cheerful neighbours, but Mr. Roberts was positive in his assurances that there was no one in the neighbourhood whose acquaintance would be of interest to them.

The first few weeks of their new life passed pleasantly for the Maydew family. Mr. Maydew quickly gained renewed vigour in his quiet and congenial surroundings, and in the delightful air, while his daughters spent much of their time in long walks about the country and in exploring its beauties.

One evening late in August the two girls were returning from a long walk along one of their favourite paths, which led along the side of the Downs. On their right, as they walked, the ground fell away sharply to a narrow glen, named Brickett Bottom, about three-quarters of a mile in length, along the bottom of which ran a little-used country road leading to a farm, known as Blaise's Farm, and then onward and upward to lose itself as a sheep track on the higher Downs. On their side of the slope some scattered trees and bushes grew, but beyond the lane and running up over the farther slope of the glen was a thick wood, which extended away to Carew

Court, the seat of a neighbouring magnate, Lord Carew. On their left the open Down rose above them and beyond its crest lay Overbury.

The girls were walking hastily, as they were later than they had intended to be and were anxious to reach home. At a certain point at which they had now arrived the path forked, the right hand branch leading down into Brickett Bottom and the left hand turning up over the Down to Overbury.

Just as they were about to turn into the left hand path Alice suddenly stopped and pointing downwards exclaimed:

"How very curious, Maggie! Look, there is a house down there in the Bottom, which we have, or at least I have, never noticed before, often as we have walked up the Bottom."

Maggie followed with her eyes her sister's pointing finger.

"I don't see any house," she said.

"Why, Maggie," said her sister, "can't you see it! A quaint-looking, old-fashioned red brick house, there just where the road bends to the right, it seems to be standing in a nice, well-kept garden too."

Maggie looked again, but the light was beginning to fade in the glen and she was short-sighted to boot.

"I certainly don't see anything," she said. "But then I am so blind and the light is getting bad; yes, perhaps I do see a house," she added, straining her eyes.

"Well, it is there," replied her sister, "and to-morrow we will come and explore it."

Maggie agreed readily enough, and the sisters went home, still speculating on how they had happened not to notice the house before and resolving firmly on an expedition thither the next day. However, the expedition did not come off as planned, for that evening Maggie slipped on the stairs and fell, spraining her ankle in such a fashion as to preclude walking for some time.

Notwithstanding the accident to her sister, Alice remained possessed by the idea of making further investigations into the house she had looked down upon from the hill the evening be-fore; and the next day, having seen Maggie carefully settled for the afternoon, she started off for Brickett Bottom. She returned in triumph and much intrigued over her discoveries, which she eagerly narrated to her sister.

Yes. There was a nice, old-fashioned red brick house, not very large and set in a charming, old-world garden in the Bottom. It stood on a tongue of land jutting out from the woods, just at the point where the lane, after a fairly straight course from its junction with the main road half a mile away, turned sharply to the right in the direction of Blaise's Farm. More than that, Alice had seen the people of the house, whom she described as an old gentleman and a lady, presumably his wife. She had not clearly made out the gentleman, who was sitting in the porch, but the old lady, who had been in the garden busy with her flowers, had looked up and smiled pleasantly at her as she passed. She was sure, she said, that they were nice people and that it would be pleasant to make their acquaintance.

Maggie was not quite satisfied with Alice's story. She was of a more prudent and retiring nature than her sister; she had an uneasy feeling that, if the old couple had been desirable or attractive neighbours, Mr. Roberts would have mentioned them, and knowing Alice's nature she said what she could to discourage her vague idea of endeavouring to make acquaintance with the owners of the red brick house.

On the following morning, when Alice came to her sister's room to inquire how she did, Maggie noticed that she looked pale and rather absent-minded, and, after a few commonplace remarks had passed, she asked:

"What is the matter, Alice? You don't look yourself this morning."

Her sister gave a slightly embarrassed laugh.

"Oh, I am all right," she replied, "only I did not sleep very well. I kept on dreaming about the house. It was such an odd dream too: the house seemed to be home, and yet to be different."

"What, that house in Brickett Bottom?" said Maggie. "Why, what is the matter with you?— you seem to be quite crazy about the place."

"Well, it is curious, isn't it, Maggie, that we should have only just discovered it, and that it looks to be lived in by nice people? I wish we could get to know them."

Maggie did not care to resume the argument of the night before and the subject dropped, nor did Alice again refer to the house or its inhabitants for some little time. In fact, for some days the weather was wet and Alice was forced to abandon her walks, but when the weather once more became fine she resumed them, and Maggie suspected that Brickett Bottom formed one of her sister's favourite expeditions. Maggie became anxious over her sister, who seemed to grow daily more absent-minded and silent, but she refused to be drawn into any confidential talk, and Maggie was nonplussed.

One day, however, Alice returned from her afternoon walk in an unusually excited state of mind, of which Maggie sought an explanation. It came with a rush. Alice said that, that afternoon, as she approached the house in Brickett Bottom, the old lady, who as usual was busy in her garden, had walked down to the gate as she passed and had wished her good day.

Alice had replied and, pausing, a short conversation had followed. Alice could not remember the exact tenor of it, but, after she had paid a compliment to the old lady's flowers, the latter had rather diffidently asked her to enter the garden for a closer view. Alice had hesitated, and the old lady had said: "Don't be afraid of me, my dear, I like to see young ladies about me and my husband finds their society quite necessary to him." After a pause she went on: "Of course nobody has told you about us. My husband is Colonel Paxton, late of the Indian Army, and we have been here for many, many years. It's rather lonely, for so few people ever see us. Do come in and meet the Colonel."

"I hope you didn't go in," said Maggie rather sharply.

"Why not?" replied Alice.

"Well, I don't like Mrs. Paxton asking you in that way," answered Maggie.

"I don't see what harm there was in the in-

vitation," said Alice. "I didn't go in because it was getting late and I was anxious to get home; but—"

"But what?" asked Maggie.

Alice shrugged her shoulders.

"Well," she said, "I have accepted Mrs. Paxton's invitation to pay her a little visit tomorrow." And she gazed defiantly at Maggie.

Maggie became distinctly uneasy on hearing of this resolution. She did not like the idea of her impulsive sister visiting people on such slight acquaintance, especially as they had never heard them mentioned before. She endeavoured by all means, short of appealing to Mr. Maydew, to dissuade her sister from going, at any rate until there had been time to make some inquiries as to the Paxtons. Alice, however, was obdurate.

What harm could happen to her? she asked. Mrs. Paxton was a charming old lady. She was going early in the afternoon for a short visit. She would be back for tea and croquet with her father and, anyway, now that Maggie was laid up, long solitary walks were unendurable and she was not going to let slip the chance of following up what promised to be a pleasant acquaintance.

Maggie could do nothing more. Her ankle was better and she was able to get down to the garden and sit in a long chair near her father, but walking was still quite out of the question, and it was with some misgivings that on the following day she watched Alice depart gaily for her visit, promising to be back by half-past four at the very latest.

The afternoon passed quietly till nearly five, when Mr. Maydew, looking up from his book, noticed Maggie's uneasy expression and asked:

"Where is Alice?"

"Out for a walk," replied Maggie; and then after a short pause she went on: "And she has also gone to pay a call on some neighbours whom she has recently discovered."

"Neighbours," ejaculated Mr. Maydew, "what neighbours? Mr. Roberts never spoke of any neighbours to me."

"Well, I don't know much about them," answered Maggie. "Only Alice and I were out walking the day of my accident and saw or at least she saw, for I am so blind I could not quite make it out, a house in Brickett Bottom. The next day she went to look at it closer, and yesterday she told me that she had made the acquaintance of the people living in it. She says that they are a retired Indian officer and his wife, a Colonel and Mrs. Paxton, and Alice describes Mrs. Paxton as a charming old lady, who pressed her to come and see them. So she has gone this afternoon, but she promised me she would be back long before this."

Mr. Maydew was silent for a moment and then said:

"I am not well pleased about this. Alice should not be so impulsive and scrape acquaintance with absolutely unknown people. Had there been nice neighbours in Brickett Bottom, I am certain Mr. Roberts would have told us."

The conversation dropped; but both father and daughter were disturbed and uneasy and, tea having been finished and the clock striking half-past five, Mr. Maydew asked Maggie:

"When did you say Alice would be back?"

"Before half-past four at the latest, father."

"Well, what can she be doing? What can have delayed her? You say you did not see the house," he went on.

"No," said Maggie, "I cannot say I did. It was getting dark and you know how short-sighted I am."

"But surely you must have seen it at some other time," said her father.

"That is the strangest part of the whole affair," answered Maggie. "We have often walked up the Bottom, but I never noticed the house, nor had Alice till that evening. I wonder," she went on after a short pause, "if it would not be well to ask Smith to harness the pony and drive over to bring her back. I am not happy about her—I am afraid—"

"Afraid of what?" said her father in the irritated voice of a man who is growing frightened. "What can have gone wrong in this quiet place? Still, I'll send Smith over for her."

So saying he rose from his chair and sought out Smith, the rather dull-witted gardener-groom attached to Mr. Roberts' service.

"Smith," he said, "I want you to harness the pony at once and go over to Colonel Paxton's in Brickett Bottom and bring Miss Maydew home."

The man stared at him.

"Go where, sir?" he said.

Mr. Maydew repeated the order and the man, still staring stupidly, answered:

"I never heard of Colonel Paxton, sir. I don't know what house you mean."

Mr. Maydew was now growing really anxious.

"Well, harness the pony at once," he said; and going back to Maggie he told her of what he called Smith's stupidity, and asked her if she felt that her ankle would be strong enough to permit her to go with him and Smith to the Bottom to point out the house.

Maggie agreed readily and in a few minutes the party started off. Brickett Bottom, although not more than three-quarters of a mile away over the Downs, was at least three miles by road; and as it was nearly six o'clock before Mr. Maydew left the Vicarage, and the pony was old and slow, it was getting late before the entrance to Brickett Bottom was reached. Turning into the lane the cart proceeded slowly up the Bottom, Mr. Maydew and Maggie looking anxiously from side to side, whilst Smith drove stolidly on looking neither to the right nor left.

"Where is the house?" said Mr. Maydew presently. "At the bend of the road," answered Maggie, her heart sickening as she looked out through the failing light to see the trees stretching their ranks in unbroken formation along it. The cart reached the bend. "It should be here," whispered Maggie.

They pulled up. Just in front of them the road bent to the right round a tongue of land, which, unlike the rest of the right hand side of the road, was free from trees and was covered only by rough grass and stray bushes. A closer inspection disclosed evident signs of terraces having once been formed on it, but of a house there was no trace.

"Is this the place?" said Mr. Maydew in a low voice.

Maggie nodded.

"But there is no house here," said her father. "What does it all mean? Are you sure of yourself, Maggie? Where is Alice?"

Before Maggie could answer a voice was heard calling "Father! Maggie!" The sound of the voice was thin and high and, paradoxically, it sounded both very near and yet as if it came from some infinite distance. The cry was thrice repeated and then silence fell. Mr. Maydew and Maggie stared at each other.

"That was Alice's voice," said Mr. Maydew huskily, "she is near and in trouble, and is calling us. Which way did you think it came from, Smith?" he added, turning to the gardener.

"I didn't hear anybody calling," said the man.

"Nonsense!" answered Mr. Maydew.

And then he and Maggie both began to call "Alice. Alice. Where are you?" There was no reply and Mr. Maydew sprang from the cart, at the same time bidding Smith to hand the reins to Maggie and come and search for the missing girl. Smith obeyed him and both men, scrambling up the turfy bit of ground, began to search and call through the neighbouring wood. They heard and saw nothing, however, and after an agonised search Mr. Maydew ran down to the cart and begged Maggie to drive on to Blaise's Farm for help leaving himself and Smith to continue the search. Maggie followed her father's instructions and was fortunate enough to find Mr. Rumbold, the farmer, his two sons and a couple of labourers just returning from the harvest field. She explained what had happened, and the farmer and his men promptly volunteered to form a search party, though Maggie, in spite of her anxiety, noticed a queer expression on Mr. Rumbold's face as she told him her tale.

The party, provided with lanterns, now went down the Bottom, joined Mr. Maydew and Smith and made an exhaustive but absolutely fruitless search of the woods near the bend of the road. No trace of the missing girl was to be found, and after a long and anxious time the search was abandoned, one of the young Rumbolds volunteering to ride into the nearest town and notify the police.

Maggie, though with little hope in her heart, endeavoured to cheer her father on their homeward way with the idea that Alice might have returned to Overbury over the Downs whilst they were going by road to the Bottom, and that she had seen them and called to them in jest when they were opposite the tongue of land.

However, when they reached home there was no Alice and, though the next day the search was resumed and full inquiries were instituted by the police, all was to no purpose. No trace of Alice was ever found, the last human being that saw her having been an old woman, who had met her going down the path into the Bottom on the afternoon of her disappearance, and who described her as smiling but looking "queerlike."

This is the end of the story, but the following may throw some light upon it.

The history of Alice's mysterious disappearance became widely known through the medium of the Press and Mr. Roberts, distressed beyond measure at what had taken place, returned in all haste to Overbury to offer what comfort and help he could give to his afflicted friend and tenant. He called upon the Maydews and, having heard their tale, sat for a short time in silence. Then he said:

"Have you ever heard any local gossip concerning this Colonel and Mrs. Paxton?"

"No," replied Mr. Maydew, "I never heard their names until the day of my poor daughter's fatal visit."

"Well," said Mr. Roberts, "I will tell you all I can about them, which is not very much, I fear." He paused and then went on: "I am now nearly seventy-five years old, and for nearly seventy years no house has stood in Brickett Bottom. But when I was a child of about five there was an old-fashioned red brick house standing in a garden at the bend of the road, such as you have described. It was owned and lived in by a retired Indian soldier and his wife, a Colonel and Mrs. Paxton. At the time I speak of, certain events having taken place at the house and the old couple having died, it was sold by their heirs to Lord Carew, who shortly after pulled it down on the ground that it interfered with his shooting. Colonel and Mrs. Paxton were well known to my father, who was the clergyman here before me, and to the neighbourhood in general. They lived quietly and were not unpopular, but the Colonel was supposed to possess a violent and vindictive temper. Their family consisted only of themselves, their daughter and a couple of servants, the Colonel's old Army servant and his Eurasian wife. Well, I cannot tell you details of what happened, I was only a child; my father never liked gossip and in later years, when he talked to me on the subject, he always avoided any appearance of exaggeration or sensationalism. However, it is known that Miss Paxton fell in love with and became engaged to a young man to whom her parents took a strong dislike. They used every possible means to break off the match, and many rumours were set on foot as to their conduct—undue influence, even cruelty were charged against them. I do not know the truth, all I can say is that Miss Paxton died and a very bitter feeling against her parents sprang up. My father, however, continued to call, but was rarely admitted. In fact, he never saw Colonel Paxton after his daughter's death and only saw Mrs. Paxton once or twice. He described her as an utterly broken woman, and was not surprised at her following her daughter to the grave in about three months' time. Colonel Paxton became, if possible, more of a recluse than ever after his wife's death and himself died not more than a month after her under circumstances which pointed to suicide. Again a crop of rumours sprang up, but there was no one in particular to take action, the doctor certified Death from Natural Causes, and Colonel Paxton, like his wife and daughter, was buried in this churchyard. The property passed to a distant relative, who came down to it for one night shortly afterwards; he never came again,

having apparently conceived a violent dislike to the place, but arranged to pension off the servants and then sold the house to Lord Carew, who was glad to purchase this little island in the middle of his property. He pulled it down soon after he had bought it, and the garden was left to relapse into a wilderness."

Mr. Roberts paused.

"Those are all the facts," he added.

"But there is something more," said Maggie.

Mr. Roberts hesitated for a while.

"You have a right to know all," he said almost to himself; then louder he continued: "What I am now going to tell you is really rumour, vague and uncertain; I cannot fathom its truth or its meaning. About five years after the house had been pulled down a young maidservant at Carew Court was out walking one afternoon. She was a stranger to the village and a new-comer to the Court. On returning home to tea she told her fellow-servants that as she walked down Brickett Bottom, which place she described clearly, she passed a red brick house at the bend of the road and that a kind-faced old lady had asked her to step in for a while. She did not go in, not because she had any suspicions of there being anything uncanny, but simply because she feared to be late for tea.

"I do not think she ever visited the Bottom again and she had no other similar experience, so far as I am aware.

"Two or three years later, shortly after my father's death, a travelling tinker with his wife and daughter camped for the night at the foot of the Bottom. The girl strolled away up the glen to gather blackberries and was never seen or heard of again. She was searched for in vain—of course, one does not know the truth—and she may have run away voluntarily from her parents, although there was no known cause for her doing so.

"That," concluded Mr. Roberts, "is all I can tell you of either facts or rumours; all that I can now do is to pray for you and for her."

HOW FEAR DEPARTED FROM THE LONG GALLERY

E. F. Benson

ONE OF THREE BROTHERS who were all masters of ghost and horror stories, E(dward) F(rederic) Benson (1867–1940) was the most successful. Any of a dozen of his stories easily would have been welcome in the pages of this volume but "How Fear Departed from the Long Gallery" is unusual for him in that it has humor and has been slightly less frequently anthologized than such masterpieces as "Mrs. Amworth" and "The Room in the Tower."

Born in Wokingham, Berkshire, England, Fred Benson had early success with a society novel, *Dodo* (1893), which remained in print for more than eighty years. Its continued sales enabled him to devote full time to writing and he produced a prodigious amount of work in social satire, notably the series about Emmeline "Lucia" Lucas and Elizabeth Mapp, which was adapted for TV by London Weekend Television as *Mapp and Lucia,* (1985–1986). He also wrote highly regarded biographies, including the standard one at the time for Charlotte Brontë. In all, he wrote more than seventy books. While most of his novels of manners and society are now predictably dated, his frequent forays into the realm of supernatural and horror fiction remain high points in the literature. Among his novels in the fantasy genre are *The Judgement Books* (1895), *The Angel of Pain* (1905), *Across the Stream* (1919), *Colin: A Novel* (1923), *Colin II* (1925), *The Inheritor* (1930), and *Raven's Brood* (1934).

"How Fear Departed from the Long Gallery" was first published in the December 1911 issue of *The Windsor Magazine;* it was collected in *The Room in the Tower and Other Stories* (London, Mills & Boon, 1912).

How Fear Departed from the Long Gallery

E. F. BENSON

CHURCH-PEVERIL IS A HOUSE so beset and frequented by spectres, both visible and audible, that none of the family which it shelters under its acre and a half of green copper roofs takes psychical phenomena with any seriousness. For to the Peverils the appearance of a ghost is a matter of hardly greater significance than is the appearance of the post to those who live in more ordinary houses. It arrives, that is to say, practically every day, it knocks (or makes other noises), it is observed coming up the drive (or in other places). I myself, when staying there, have seen the present Mrs. Peveril, who is rather short-sighted, peer into the dusk, while we were taking our coffee on the terrace after dinner, and say to her daughter:

"My dear, was not that the Blue Lady who has just gone into the shrubbery. I hope she won't frighten Flo. Whistle for Flo, dear."

(Flo, it may be remarked, is the youngest and most precious of many dachshunds.)

Blanche Peveril gave a cursory whistle, and crunched the sugar left unmelted at the bottom of her coffee-cup between her very white teeth.

"Oh, darling, Flo isn't so silly as to mind," she said. "Poor blue Aunt Barbara is such a bore! Whenever I meet her she always looks as if she wanted to speak to me, but when I say, 'What is it, Aunt Barbara?' she never utters, but only points somewhere towards the house, which is so vague. I believe there was something she wanted to confess about two hundred years ago, but she has forgotten what it is."

Here Flo gave two or three short pleased barks, and came out of the shrubbery wagging her tail, and capering round what appeared to me to be a perfectly empty space on the lawn.

"There! Flo has made friends with her," said Mrs. Peveril. "I wonder why she dresses in that very stupid shade of blue."

From this it may be gathered that even with regard to psychical phenomena there is some truth in the proverb that speaks of familiarity. But the Peverils do not exactly treat their ghosts with contempt, since most of that delightful family never despised anybody except such people as avowedly did not care for hunting or shooting, or golf or skating. And as all of their ghosts are of their family, it seems reasonable to suppose that they all, even the poor Blue Lady, excelled at one time in field-sports. So far, then, they harbour no such unkindness or contempt, but only pity. Of one Peveril, indeed, who broke his neck in vainly attempting to ride up the main staircase on a thoroughbred mare after some monstrous and violent deed in the back-garden, they are very fond, and Blanche comes downstairs in the morning with an eye unusually bright when she can announce that Master Anthony was "very loud" last night. He (apart from the fact of his having been so foul a ruffian) was a tremendous fellow across country, and they like these indications of the continuance of his superb vitality. In fact, it is supposed to be a compliment, when you go to stay at Church-Peveril, to be assigned a bedroom which is frequented by defunct members of the family. It means that you are worthy to look on the august and villainous dead, and you will find yourself shown into some vaulted or tapestried chamber, without benefit of electric light, and are told that great-great-grandmamma Bridget occasionally has vague business by the fireplace, but it is better not to talk to her, and that you will hear Master Anthony "awfully well" if he attempts the front staircase any time before morning. There you are left for your night's repose, and, having quakingly undressed, begin reluctantly to put out your candles. It is draughty in these great chambers, and the solemn tapestry swings and bellows and subsides, and the firelight dances on the forms of huntsmen and warriors and stern pursuits. Then you climb into your bed, a bed so huge that you feel as if the desert of Sahara was spread for you, and pray, like the mariners who sailed with St. Paul, for day. And, all the time, you are aware that Freddy and Harry and Blanche and possibly even Mrs. Peveril are quite capable of dressing up and making disquieting tappings outside your door, so that when you open it some inconjecturable horror fronts you. For myself, I stick steadily to the assertion that I have an obscure valvular disease of the heart, and so sleep undisturbed in the new wing of the house where Aunt Barbara, and great-great-grandmamma Bridget and Master Anthony never penetrate. I forget the details of great-great-grandmamma Bridget, but she certainly cut the throat of some distant relation before she disembowelled herself with the axe that had been used at Agincourt. Before that she had led a very sultry life, crammed with amazing incident.

But there is one ghost at Church-Peveril at which the family never laugh, in which they feel no friendly and amused interest, and of which they only speak just as much as is necessary for the safety of their guests. More properly it should be described as two ghosts, for the "haunt" in question is that of two very young children, who were twins. These, not without reason, the family take very seriously indeed. The story of them, as told me by Mrs. Peveril, is as follows:

In the year 1602, the same being the last of Queen Elizabeth's reign, a certain Dick Peveril was greatly in favour at Court. He was brother to Master Joseph Peveril, then owner of the family house and lands, who two years previously, at the respectable age of seventy-four, became father of twin boys, first-born of his progeny. It is known that the royal and ancient virgin had said to handsome Dick, who was nearly forty years his brother's junior, " 'Tis pity that you are not master of Church-Peveril," and these words probably suggested to him a sinister design. Be that as it may, handsome Dick, who very adequately sustained the family reputation for wickedness, set off to ride down to Yorkshire, and found that, very conveniently, his brother Joseph had just been seized with an apoplexy, which appeared to be the result of a continued spell of hot weather combined with the necessity of quenching his thirst with an augmented amount of sack, and had actually died while handsome Dick, with God knows what thoughts in his mind, was journeying northwards. Thus it came about that he arrived at Church-Peveril just in time for his brother's funeral. It was with great propriety that he attended the obsequies, and returned to spend a sympathetic day or two of mourning with his widowed sister-in-law, who was but a faint-hearted dame, little fit to be mated with such hawks as these. On the second night of his stay, he did that which the Peverils regret to this day. He entered the room where the twins slept with their nurse, and quietly strangled the latter as she slept. Then he took the twins and put them into the fire which warms the long gallery. The weather, which up to the day of Joseph's death had been so hot, had changed suddenly to bitter cold, and the fire was heaped high with burning logs and was exultant with flame. In the core of this conflagration he

struck out a cremation-chamber, and into that he threw the two children, stamping them down with his riding-boots. They could just walk, but they could not walk out of that ardent place. It is said that he laughed as he added more logs. Thus he became master of Church-Peveril.

The crime was never brought home to him, but he lived no longer than a year in the enjoyment of his blood-stained inheritance. When he lay a-dying he made his confession to the priest who attended him, but his spirit struggled forth from its fleshly coil before Absolution could be given him. On that very night there began in Church-Peveril the haunting which to this day is but seldom spoken of by the family, and then only in low tones and with serious mien. For only an hour or two after handsome Dick's death, one of the servants passing the door of the long gallery heard from within peals of the loud laughter so jovial and yet so sinister which he had thought would never be heard in the house again. In a moment of that cold courage which is so nearly akin to mortal terror he opened the door and entered, expecting to see he knew not what manifestation of him who lay dead in the room below. Instead he saw two little white-robed figures toddling towards him hand in hand across the moon-lit floor.

The watchers in the room below ran upstairs startled by the crash of his fallen body, and found him lying in the grip of some dread convulsion. Just before morning he regained consciousness and told his tale. Then pointing with a trembling and ash-grey finger towards the door, he screamed aloud, and so fell back dead.

During the next fifty years this strange and terrible legend of the twin-babies became fixed and consolidated. Their appearance, luckily for those who inhabit the house, was exceedingly rare, and during these years they seem to have been seen four or five times only. On each occasion they appeared at night, between sunset and sunrise, always in the same long gallery, and always as two toddling children scarcely able to walk. And on each occasion the luckless individual who saw them died either speedily or terribly, or with both speed and terror, after the accursed vision had appeared to him. Sometimes he might live for a few months: he was lucky if he died, as did the servant who first saw them, in a few hours. Vastly more awful was the fate of a certain Mrs. Canning, who had the ill-luck to see them in the middle of the next century, or to be quite accurate, in the year 1760. By this time the hours and the place of their appearance were well known, and, as up till a year ago, visitors were warned not to go between sunset and sunrise into the long gallery.

But Mrs. Canning, a brilliantly clever and beautiful woman, admirer also and friend of the notorious sceptic M. Voltaire, wilfully went and sat night after night, in spite of all protestations, in the haunted place. For four evenings she saw nothing, but on the fifth she had her will, for the door in the middle of the gallery opened, and there came toddling towards her the ill-omened innocent little pair. It seemed that even then she was not frightened, but she thought good, poor wretch, to mock at them, telling them it was time for them to get back into the fire. They gave no word in answer, but turned away from her crying and sobbing. Immediately after they disappeared from her vision and she rustled downstairs to where the family and guests in the house were waiting for her, with the triumphant announcement that she has seen them both, and must needs write to M. Voltaire, saying that she had spoken to spirits made manifest. It would make him laugh. But when some months later the whole news reached him he did not laugh at all.

Mrs. Canning was one of the great beauties of her day, and in the year 1760 she was at the height and zenith of her blossoming. The chief beauty, if it is possible to single out one point where all was so exquisite, lay in the dazzling colour and incomparable brilliance of her complexion. She was now just thirty years of age, but, in spite of the excesses of her life, retained the snow and roses of girlhood, and she courted the bright light of day which other women shunned, for it but showed to great advantage the splendour of her skin. In consequence she was very considerably dismayed one morning, about a fortnight after her strange experience in the long gallery, to observe on her left cheek, an inch or two below her turquoise-coloured eyes, a little greyish patch of skin, about as big as a threepenny piece. It was in vain that she applied her accustomed washes and unguents: vain, too, were the arts of her fardeuse and of her medical adviser. For a week she kept herself secluded, martyring herself with solitude and unaccustomed physics, and for result at the end of the week she had no amelioration to comfort herself with: instead this woeful grey patch had doubled itself in size. Thereafter the nameless disease, whatever it was, developed in new and terrible ways. From the centre of the discoloured place there sprouted forth little lichen-like tendrils of greenish-grey, and another patch appeared on her lower lip. This, too, soon vegetated, and one morning, on opening her eyes to the horror of a new day, she found that her vision was strangely blurred. She sprang to her looking-glass, and what she saw caused her to shriek aloud with horror. From under her upper eye-lid a fresh growth had sprung up, mushroom-like, in the night, and its filaments extended downwards, screening the pupil of her eye. Soon after, her tongue and throat were attacked: the air passages became obstructed, and death by suffocation was merciful after such suffering.

More terrible yet was the case of a certain Colonel Blantyre who fired at the children with his revolver. What he went through is not to be recorded here.

It is this haunting, then, that the Peverils take quite seriously, and every guest on his arrival in the house is told that the long gallery must not be entered after nightfall on any pretext whatever. By day, however, it is a delightful room and intrinsically merits description, apart from the fact that the due understanding of its geography is necessary for the account that here follows. It is full eighty feet in length, and is lit by a row of six tall windows looking over the gardens at the back of the house. A door communicates with the landing at the top of the main staircase, and about half-way down the gallery in the wall facing the windows is another door communicating with the back staircase and servants' quarters, and thus the gallery forms a constant place of passage for them in going to the rooms on the first landing. It was through this door that the baby figures came when they appeared to Mrs. Canning, and on several other occasions they have been known to make their entry here, for the room out of which handsome Dick took them lies just beyond at the top of the back stairs. Further on again in the gallery is the fireplace into which he thrust them, and at the far end a large bow-window looks straight down the avenue. Above this fireplace there hangs with grim significance a portrait of handsome Dick, in the insolent beauty of early manhood, attributed to Holbein, and a dozen other portraits of great merit face the windows. During the day this is the most frequented sitting-room in the house, for its other visitors never appear there then, nor does it then ever resound with the harsh jovial laugh of handsome Dick, which sometimes, after dark has fallen, is heard by passers-by on the landing outside. But Blanche does not grow bright-eyed when she hears it: she shuts her ears and hastens to put a greater distance between her and the sound of that atrocious mirth.

But during the day the long gallery is frequented by many occupants, and much laughter in no wise sinister or saturnine resounds there. When summer lies hot over the land, those occupants lounge in the deep window seats, and when winter spreads his icy fingers and blows shrilly between his frozen palms, congregate round the fireplace at the far end, and perch, in companies of cheerful chatterers, upon sofa and chair, and chair-back and floor. Often have I sat there on long August evenings up till dressing-time, but never have I been there when anyone has seemed disposed to linger over-late without hearing the warning: "It is close on sunset: shall we go?" Later on in the shorter autumn days they often have tea laid there, and sometimes it has happened that, even while merriment was

most uproarious, Mrs. Peveril has suddenly looked out of the window and said, "My dears, it is getting so late: let us finish our nonsense downstairs in the hall." And then for a moment a curious hush always falls on loquacious family and guests alike, and as if some bad news had just been known, we all make our silent way out of the place.

But the spirits of the Peverils (of the living ones, that is to say) are the most mercurial imaginable, and the blight which the thought of handsome Dick and his doings casts over them passes away again with amazing rapidity.

A typical party, large, young, and peculiarly cheerful, was staying at Church-Peveril shortly after Christmas last year, and as usual on December 31, Mrs. Peveril was giving her annual New Year's Eve ball. The house was quite full, and she had commandeered as well the greater part of the Peveril Arms to provide sleeping-quarters for the overflow from the house. For some days past a black and windless frost had stopped all hunting, but it is an ill windlessness that blows no good (if so mixed a metaphor may be forgiven), and the lake below the house had for the last day or two been covered with an adequate and admirable sheet of ice. Everyone in the house had been occupied all the morning of that day in performing swift and violent manoeuvres on the elusive surface, and as soon as lunch was over we all, with one exception, hurried out again. This one exception was Madge Dalrymple, who had had the misfortune to fall rather badly earlier in the day, but hoped, by resting her injured knee, instead of joining the skaters again, to be able to dance that evening. The hope, it is true, was the most sanguine sort, for she could but hobble ignobly back to the house, but with the breezy optimism which characterises the Peverils (she is Blanche's first cousin), she remarked that it would be but tepid enjoyment that she could, in her present state, derive from further skating, and thus she sacrificed little, but might gain much.

Accordingly, after a rapid cup of coffee which was served in the long gallery, we left Madge comfortably reclined on the big sofa at right-angles to the fireplace, with an attractive book to beguile the tedium till tea. Being of the family, she knew all about handsome Dick and the babies, and the fate of Mrs. Canning and Colonel Blantyre, but as we went out I heard Blanche say to her, "Don't run it too fine, dear," and Madge had replied, "No; I'll go away well before sunset." And so we left her alone in the long gallery.

Madge read her attractive book for some minutes, but failing to get absorbed in it, put it down and limped across to the window. Though it was still but little after two, it was but a dim and uncertain light that entered, for the crystalline brightness of the morning had given place to a veiled obscurity produced by flocks of thick clouds which were coming sluggishly up from the north-east. Already the whole sky was overcast with them, and occasionally a few snow-flakes fluttered waveringly down past the long windows. From the darkness and bitter cold of the afternoon, it seemed to her that there was like to be a heavy snowfall before long, and these outward signs were echoed inwardly in her by that muffled drowsiness of the brain, which to those who are sensitive to the pressures and lightness of weather portends storm. Madge was peculiarly the prey of such external influences: to her a brisk morning gave an ineffable brightness and briskness of spirit, and correspondingly the approach of heavy weather produced a somnolence in sensation that both drowsed and depressed her.

It was in such mood as this that she limped back again to the sofa beside the log-fire. The whole house was comfortably heated by water-pipes, and though the fire of logs and peat, an adorable mixture, had been allowed to burn low, the room was very warm. Idly she watched the dwindling flames, not opening her book again, but lying on the sofa with face towards the fireplace, intending drowsily and not immediately to go to her own room and spend the hours, until the return of the skaters made gaiety in the house again, in writing one or two neglected letters. Still drowsily she began thinking over what she had to communicate: one letter several days overdue should go to her mother, who was immensely interested in the psychical affairs of the family. She would tell her how Master Anthony had been prodigiously active on the staircase a night or two ago, and how the Blue Lady, regardless of the severity of the weather, had been seen by Mrs. Peveril that morning, strolling about. It was rather interesting: the Blue Lady had gone down the laurel walk and had been seen by her to enter the stables, where, at the moment, Freddy Peveril was inspecting the frost-bound hunters. Identically then, a sudden panic had spread through the stables, and the horses had whinnied and kicked, and shied, and sweated. Of the fatal twins nothing had been seen for many years past, but, as her mother knew, the Peverils never used the long gallery after dark.

Then for a moment she sat up, remembering that she was in the long gallery now. But it was still but a little after half-past two, and if she went to her room in half an hour, she would have ample time to write this and another letter before tea. Till then she would read her book. But she found she had left it on the window-sill, and it seemed scarcely worth while to get it. She felt exceedingly drowsy.

The sofa where she lay had been lately recovered, in a greyish green shade of velvet, somewhat the colour of lichen. It was of a very thick soft texture, and she luxuriously stretched her arms out, one on each side of her body, and pressed her fingers into the nap. How horrible that story of Mrs. Canning was: the growth on her face was of the colour of lichen. And then without further transition or blurring of thought Madge fell asleep.

She dreamed. She dreamed that she awoke and found herself exactly where she had gone to sleep, and in exactly the same attitude. The flames from the logs had burned up again, and leaped on the walls, fitfully illuminating the picture of handsome Dick above the fireplace. In her dream she knew exactly what she had done to-day, and for what reason she was lying here now instead of being out with the rest of the skaters. She remembered also (still dreaming), that she was going to write a letter or two before tea, and prepared to get up in order to go to her room. As she half-rose she caught sight of her own arms lying out on each side of her on the grey velvet sofa.

But she could not see where her hands ended, and where the grey velvet began: her fingers seemed to have melted into the stuff. She could see her wrists quite clearly, and a blue vein on the backs of her hands, and here and there a knuckle. Then, in her dream, she remembered the last thought which had been in her mind before she fell asleep, namely the growth of the lichen-coloured vegetation on the face and the eyes and the throat of Mrs. Canning. At that thought the strangling terror of real nightmare began: she knew that she was being transformed into this grey stuff, and she was absolutely unable to move. Soon the grey would spread up her arms, and over her feet; when they came in from skating they would find here nothing but a huge misshapen cushion of lichen-coloured velvet, and that would be she. The horror grew more acute, and then by a violent effort she shook herself free of the clutches of this very evil dream, and she awoke.

For a minute or two she lay there, conscious only of the tremendous relief at finding herself awake. She felt again with her fingers the pleasant touch of the velvet, and drew them backwards and forwards, assuring herself that she was not, as her dream had suggested, melting into greyness and softness. But she was still, in spite of the violence of her awakening, very sleepy, and lay there till, looking down, she was aware that she could not see her hands at all. It was very nearly dark.

At that moment a sudden flicker of flame came from the dying fire, and a flare of burning gas from the peat flooded the room. The portrait of handsome Dick looked evilly down on her, and

her hands were visible again. And then a panic worse than the panic of her dreams seized her.

Daylight had altogether faded, and she knew that she was alone in the dark in the terrible gallery.

This panic was of the nature of nightmare, for she felt unable to move for terror. But it was worse than nightmare because she knew she was awake. And then the full cause of this frozen fear dawned on her; she knew with the certainty of absolute conviction that she was about to see the twin-babies.

She felt a sudden moisture break out on her face, and within her mouth her tongue and throat went suddenly dry, and she felt her tongue grate along the inner surface of her teeth. All power of movement had slipped from her limbs, leaving them dead and inert, and she stared with wide eyes into the blackness. The spurt of flame from the peat had burned itself out again, and darkness encompassed her.

Then on the wall opposite her, facing the windows, there grew a faint light of dusky crimson.

For a moment she thought it but heralded the approach of the awful vision, then hope revived in her heart, and she remembered that thick clouds had overcast the sky before she went to sleep, and guessed that this light came from the sun not yet quite sunk and set. This sudden revival of hope gave her the necessary stimulus, and she sprang off the sofa where she lay. She looked out of the window and saw the dull glow on the horizon. But before she could take a step forward it was obscured again. A tiny sparkle of light came from the hearth which did no more than illuminate the tiles of the fireplace, and snow falling heavily tapped at the window panes. There was neither light nor sound except these.

But the courage that had come to her, giving her the power of movement, had not quite deserted her, and she began feeling her way down the gallery. And then she found that she was lost. She stumbled against a chair, and, recovering herself, stumbled against another. Then a table barred her way, and, turning swiftly aside, she found herself up against the back of a sofa.

Once more she turned and saw the dim gleam of the firelight on the side opposite to that on which she expected it. In her blind gropings she must have reversed her direction. But which way was she to go now. She seemed blocked in by furniture. And all the time insistent and imminent was the fact that the two innocent terrible ghosts were about to appear to her.

Then she began to pray. "Lighten our darkness, O Lord," she said to herself. But she could not remember how the prayer continued, and she had sore need of it. There was something about the perils of the night. All this time she felt about her with groping, fluttering hands. The fire-glimmer which should have been on her left was on her right again; therefore she must turn herself round again. "Lighten our darkness," she whispered, and then aloud she repeated, "Lighten our darkness."

She stumbled up against a screen, and could not remember the existence of any such screen.

Hastily she felt beside it with blind hands, and touched something soft and velvety. Was it the sofa on which she had lain? If so, where was the head of it? It had a head and a back and feet—it was like a person, all covered with grey lichen. Then she lost her head completely. All that remained to her was to pray; she was lost, lost in this awful place, where no one came in the dark except the babies that cried. And she heard her voice rising from whisper to speech, and speech to scream. She shrieked out the holy words, she yelled them as if blaspheming as she groped among tables and chairs and the pleasant things of ordinary life which had become so terrible.

Then came a sudden and an awful answer to her screamed prayer. Once more a pocket of inflammable gas in the peat on the hearth was reached by the smouldering embers, and the room started into light. She saw the evil eyes of handsome Dick, she saw the little ghostly snow-flakes falling thickly outside. And she saw where she was, just opposite the door through which the terrible twins made their entrance.

Then the flame went out again, and left her in blackness once more. But she had gained something, for she had her geography now. The centre of the room was bare of furniture, and one swift dart would take her to the door of the landing above the main staircase and into safety. In that gleam she had been able to see the handle of the door, bright-brassed, luminous like a star. She would go straight for it; it was but a matter of a few seconds now.

She took a long breath, partly of relief, partly to satisfy the demands of her galloping heart.

But the breath was only half-taken when she was stricken once more into the immobility of nightmare.

There came a little whisper, it was no more than that, from the door opposite which she stood, and through which the twin-babies entered. It was not quite dark outside it, for she could see that the door was opening. And there stood in the opening two little white figures, side by side. They came towards her slowly, shufflingly. She could not see face or form at all distinctly, but the two little white figures were advancing. She knew them to be the ghosts of terror, innocent of the awful doom they were bound to bring, even as she was innocent. With the inconceivable rapidity of thought, she made up her mind what to do. She had not hurt them or laughed at them, and they, they were but babies when the wicked and bloody deed had sent them to their burning death. Surely the spirits of these children would not be inaccessible to the cry of one who was of the same blood as they, who had committed no fault that merited the doom they brought. If she entreated them they might have mercy, they might forebear to bring the curse on her, they might allow her to pass out of the place without blight, without the sentence of death, or the shadow of things worse than death upon her.

It was but for the space of a moment that she hesitated, then she sank down on to her knees, and stretched out her hands towards them.

"Oh, my dears," she said, "I only fell asleep. I have done no more wrong than that—"

She paused a moment, and her tender girl's heart thought no more of herself, but only of them, those little innocent spirits on whom so awful a doom was laid, that they should bring death where other children bring laughter, and doom for delight. But all those who had seen them before had dreaded and feared them, or had mocked at them.

Then, as the enlightenment of pity dawned on her, her fear fell from her like the wrinkled sheath that holds the sweet folded buds of Spring.

"Dears, I am so sorry for you," she said. "It is not your fault that you must bring me what you must bring, but I am not afraid any longer. I am only sorry for you. God bless you, you poor darlings."

She raised her head and looked at them. Though it was so dark, she could now see their faces, though all was dim and wavering, like the light of pale flames shaken by a draught. But the faces were not miserable or fierce—they smiled at her with shy little baby smiles. And as she looked they grew faint, fading slowly away like wreaths of vapour in frosty air.

Madge did not at once move when they had vanished, for instead of fear there was wrapped round her a wonderful sense of peace, so happy and serene that she would not willingly stir, and so perhaps disturb it. But before long she got up, and feeling her way, but without any sense of nightmare pressing her on, or frenzy of fear to spur her, she went out of the long gallery, to find Blanche just coming upstairs whistling and swinging her skates.

"How's the leg, dear," she asked. "You're not limping any more."

Till that moment Madge had not thought of it.

"I think it must be all right," she said; "I had forgotten it, anyhow. Blanche, dear, you won't be frightened for me, will you, but—but I have seen the twins."

For a moment Blanche's face whitened with terror.

"What?" she said in a whisper.

"Yes, I saw them just now. But they were kind, they smiled at me, and I was so sorry for them. And somehow I am sure I have nothing to fear."

It seems that Madge was right, for nothing has come to touch her. Something, her attitude to them, we must suppose, her pity, her sympathy, touched and dissolved and annihilated the curse.

Indeed, I was at Church-Peveril only last week, arriving there after dark. Just as I passed the gallery door, Blanche came out.

"Ah, there you are," she said: "I've just been seeing the twins. They looked too sweet and stopped nearly ten minutes. Let us have tea at once."

G. G. Pendarves

EMPLOYING THE PSEUDONYM G. G. Pendarves, Gladys Gordon Trenery (ca. 1885–1938), who also wrote under the pseudonym Marjory E. Lambe, became one of the few British writers to enjoy success in American pulp magazines. As a native of Cornwall, she used her native dark, forbidding, and lonely coastal region as the setting for many of her stories. Although she wrote a few stories for British periodicals, it is the nineteen stories she produced for *Weird Tales* that have kept her reputation alive. She was a popular second-tier contributor to the greatest of all horror and fantasy pulps, behind such greats as H. P. Lovecraft, Seabury Quinn, and Robert E. Howard. Occasionally she wrote for other pulps, such as *Oriental Stories* and *Magic Carpet*. These, as well as the *Weird Tales* stories, have been collected in *The Devil's Graveyard* (1988), *Thing of Darkness* (2005), and *Thirty Pieces of Silver* (2009) in small editions aimed at collectors and serious pulp aficionados.

As a student deeply involved with and knowledgeable about occultism, most of her stories reflect her belief in the existence and power of goodness. Her villainous characters, therefore, tend to be less fully fleshed out than her heroic figures, and it soon becomes fairly obvious that they are doomed because of their innate evil. There is a great sense of authenticity to her fiction, though there is little sense of wonder at even the most extraordinary supernatural occurrences.

"Thing of Darkness" was originally published in the August 1937 issue of *Weird Tales;* it has been collected in *Thing of Darkness* (Seattle, Midnight House, 2005), edited by Mike Ashley.

Thing of Darkness

G. G. PENDARVES

I

A long curving sweep of tall gray houses. At their feet the old parade, its worn seawall banked up against wind driven tides. Troon House, grayer, gaunter than the rest, stood empty. A signboard creaked on rusted hinges, advertising it For Sale or To Let.

Lonely. Lovely. Deserted.

Seagate was proud of Troon House. Seagate was afraid of it. People came by the score to see it, always in broad daylight. They were careful to keep in groups, silent, timid, turning a sharp corner, entering each unexplored room with that sudden jolt that a clumsily manipulated elevator gives to one's heart.

They stared at beautiful restorations, at blackened beams, at vast wall-cupboards, and at brick fireplaces whose ancient clay showed every tint of umber, rose, and purple-brown. They bunched together closely going up the last steep narrow stairs to the west attic. They looked at its deep recess, recently and fatally uncovered—looked and shuddered.

They went in close order downstairs again, escaped through low-roofed, retiled kitchens to a long untended garden behind the house and thence to a broad lane and main road at last. Shaken, nervously loquacious, they didn't speak of Troon until the old place was out of sight. Over tea and famous Seagate shrimps they exchanged impressions.

Going home after sunset, if they stayed so long, they glanced in passing along the road, at Troon's blank front windows, shivered, looked quickly away.

Troon—gray old house, left to hideous memories of the Thing of Darkness. Day by day, night by night, through the years, through the centuries Troon had stood. Old, forsaken, betrayed. Old Troon—shell of death—old Troon.

Low sullen clouds. A cold northwest wind. Fierce squalling gusts of rain. A high angry tide, gray-green flecked with bitter white, roaring up the estuary, Seagate was a mile of wet gray road and blank-faced houses. Wind and sea . . . wind and sea.

At the village-church of Keston, a fifteen minutes walk away on the hill behind, the broken body of Joe Dawlish with its staring tortured eyes and twisted face of fear was being buried. And in another grave, a sad small grave, the bones of Lizzy Werne were being laid to rest after three hundred years delay.

People thronged the small churchyard to its broad low moss-stained walls. From Seagate, from Keston, from all over the Wirral peninsula, and even from Liverpool and Chester they had come to witness this double funeral. Reporters, psychic investigators, university professors rubbed wet shoulders with fishermen, farmers, shop-keepers, and local gentry.

At the end, the very end when the last words of the service were said and it only remained for the gaping graves to be filled in, the vicar stood with uplifted hands. His somber gaze looked out over the crowd to tossing trees and lowering sky. His lined face, wet with rain, was worn and anxious.

Suddenly his voice rang out again, a cry from the heart of this shepherd of a stricken flock . . . "Deliver us, O Lord, from all assaults of the devil! In thine infinite mercy, protect and succor us! Stretch forth thy hand against this Thing of Darkness and set us free from fear! In the name of Him who died for us—Amen."

There was a murmurous response like water breaking on a distant shore. Then, slowly, silently, pelted by spiteful icy rain, the crowd dispersed.

At the lich-gate Doctor Dick Thornton was pushed up against two people he wanted to avoid: Edith and Alec Kinloch. Alec's heavy sallow face showed distinct traces of emotion. He looked quite appealingly at Doctor Dick.

"'Fraid I didn't take all this quite seriously before," he confessed. "I don't understand what it's all about, but—"

Edith put a restraining hand on his arm. He was having one of his emotional moments, she could see. Heaven knew what he might say! Probably he would double his already absurdly generous offer of five pounds to the widow. What a blessing she could count on herself never to lose her head! Queer sort of service it had been. These villagers adored emotional orgies. Well, poor things, they must have some pleasure in their dull stupid lives. Clever of the vicar to stage such a good show for them. He knew how to cater for a rural diocese.

To deflect her husband from possible weakness she turned to the young girl behind her.

"Lynneth, this is Doctor Thornton. He's a sort of uncle to all the fishermen of Seagate. Miss Lynneth Brey, Doctor Thornton. A connection of my husband's. She's going to spend a month or so with us—at Troon."

There, Edith thought, that'll let him know right off that they've not succeeded in scaring us. Her tactics were wasted. The doctor didn't

even hear her. He was looking down into Lynneth's uplifted rosy face. Black eyes, soft, sooty, heart-catching. Eyes made for tears and laughter and—oh, yes! he knew at once—made for love. He looked deep, deeper into them; young, radiant, kindled with recent deep emotion. Eyes to light a man's path, to draw him on and up, above life's dusty sordid clamor. Eyes that promised and withheld.

Doctor Dick's feet were treading air, his heart thumped with the beat-beat-beat of hooves on a hollow road, his head felt full of fizzy champagne. But no one guessed it. He heard his voice, it didn't seem to surprise anyone, replying to the introduction. He waited with parted lips, eyes a clear tender blue, listening—listening for her voice.

"Oh!" She considered him. A smile drew her lips in an adorable sideways quirk. "You make me feel homesick, although I've only been here a day. You speak like a Highlander."

"I am one. From Gairloch."

She put out a small hand to be enveloped in his close grip, and laughed in quick delight.

"That's my place. My own darling funny village. My mother's birthplace. We've got a cottage there. D'you remember it—the one like a brown loaf at the head of Glen Ruach?"

They drifted from the churchgate, away down the twisting road. The crowd of people might have been blown wet leaves. The two Kinlochs, left behind, exchanged long glances.

"Let 'em go." Alec took his wife's arm. "Birds of a feather—eh? She and Pills can keep each other amused. Looks like a case to me. You won't be bothered with her long."

"Really, Alec! There's the garage—what on earth are you dragging me on for? I'm certainly not going to hang about for that silly girl. Going off with a man she's just met, like that! She behaves like a child. No idea of appearances."

"What odds? Nobody's going to notice a kid like that."

"Nonsense! She's connected with us. D'you want him for a permanent relation?"

"Why not? Get the girl off your hands while

the going's good. She and Pills would run a dispensary or a nursing-home and be too busy to interfere with us. This yearly visit's beginning to pall."

She glanced shrewdly at him.

"Something in that. And even if he's queer, quite important people have taken him up. Come on, then. I'm perishing with cold. This sensed fuss! Seagate doesn't seem to have altered since Troon House was first built."

They clambered into their car and splashed down the lane to their bungalow by the marshes.

"Quite! Quite! However, there are always two sides to everything."

Mr. Alec Kinloch presented a large bulwark of flesh from behind which his schoolboy's mind issued bulletins to the outside world. He kept a store of such ready-made bulletins within, stereotyped responses calculated to give intimation of a subtle discerning intellect at work. He would employ such tactics indefinitely if conducting a conversation unaided. If his wife was with him she manned the big guns while he posed as an impregnable fortress.

Doctor Dick regarded the large dull pretentious creature with patience born of his profession rather than his temperament. Doctor Dick was a Highlander. Alec Kinloch a Lowland Scot. This, in itself, was a deep fixed gulf between them, apart from gulfs of breeding and intellect, and today the doctor found his host peculiarly trying. He'd made a point of calling when he knew Lynneth would not be at Sandilands. He wanted to spare her the grim tale he had to tell. It had been an effort, however, to miss a chance of seeing her, and his mood grew steadily darker.

"What," he demanded, "would you consider the other side of this horror at Troon?"

Baffled at such direct attack, Alec poked at his pipe with an air of grave reserve. He and Edith always were careful to be noncommittal in their attitude until they discovered the trend of popular feeling with reference to a new idea. This Troon ghost notion now! If Seagate took it seriously, and yesterday's funeral service seemed to indicate so, then they would follow suit. Alec

had been swayed by the vicar yesterday. Now, however, he knew Edith's view was the really intelligent and logical one. The vicar had been simply playing up, doing what the villagers expected of him. Jolly good thing no one but his wife knew that he'd actually got the wind up yesterday. The "Thing of Darkness!" Uh! Nasty phrase that! He'd felt like chucking up everything—selling Troon to any fool who wanted the old place. Well, he could laugh at himself and his fears now.

But this young Pills! He seemed officious. Trying to interfere. Pulling all this stuff about haunts and devils at Troon. Warning him that the workmen restoring the old house were in danger and that he and Edith ought to give up all idea of living there. Damned young whippersnapper, sitting there at his ease and telling a man of the world what was what! He'd tell him where he got off all right!

The door opened to admit his wife. Alec crossed his legs, resumed his pipe, took up the fortress-pose as Doctor Dick rose to his feet. Edith Kinloch progressed with ceremony to a chair.

"How nice of you to call again—so soon, Doctor Thornton."

"Doctor Dick" corrected the visitor. "My father is still in practice here. We have to make a distinction."

"Oh! How awkward for you!"

Edith was slim and tall and neat. She was invariably bright and kind too. It was part of her chosen role to stoop kindly to her inferiors. The Lady Bountiful was her favorite part, to be gracious, to condescend. She'd been these things infuriatingly and increasingly ever since she cut free from her decent but quite uneducated family at the age of fourteen. Alec never knew to this day that her mother had a fish-and-chips shop in Edgware road, that her father was crippled and on the dole, that her younger sisters were working in a glue factory.

"My wife," Alec would tell you, believing it to be a fact, "lost both her parents—died in India when she was a child. Friends made themselves responsible for her education" (the Local Educational Council as represented by Edith's adaptable mind) "a branch of the Dorsetshire Frome-Stoddarts, you know. Good old family but improverished—impoverished."

Edith smiled brightly on the two men sitting before the study fire.

"I'm sure you must be cold and hungry, Doctor—Dick, if you insist on the familiarity. I just went to tell cook she must drop everything and make some of her famous hot cakes for tea. Cook is so difficult, but really I find the best thing is to alter her routine every now and then. I do it on principle."

She proceeded to stage-manage a background for an afternoon-tea act. Doctor Dick was used as scene-shifter. Edith directed him with firm smiling competence. He pulled up tables and pushed away chairs. She conveyed atmospherically that he was young and insignificant enough to do these things rather than Alec.

"And now do let's go on with all that too adorable tale you were telling us about Troon just now. So like a story of Edgar Allan Poe's. Now don't say you finished that tale while I was out of the room! No? That's right!"

She beamed approval.

"Now. We're all settled. Tea—and put on another log, Alec, the basket's beside you there— a real Christmas fire to warm you up, Doctor Dick. And eat up the scones; you must be needing something. No use calling at teatime and not taking advantage of the fact."

Glittering gracious hostess. Her varnished toffee-brown eyes shone in the firelight. She addressed the doctor as if he were a schoolboy out for a treat. She was convinced he'd arranged purposely to call at their tea hour. So lean and hungry-looking! She plumed herself on the observation which thus misread Doctor Dick's rigidly disciplined muscular body.

"This is the only time I can call," the doctor was young enough to feel not amused at her patronage. "I pass this bungalow on my way up to Keston. Due at the hospital at five, you know."

Edith smiled her best worldly understanding smile. Let the young man get away with his excuses, poor dear. She didn't grudge him his tea. Pity Lynneth was out. It would have been easy then to sidetrack him from the mission he felt he had concerning Troon and its restoration. She must make things plain, perfectly plain, once and for all. She leaned forward. Her glistening eyes, her perfectly smooth face, her small ungenerous mouth registered smiling cordiality.

"Now do tell me all about it."

Doctor Dick's blue eyes grew black and gray as the November afternoon. He told her. Told her details of Joe Dawlish's death. Told her of daily increasing peril at Troon. Implored her to give up the whole thing, to leave the gray haunted old house to its evil.

"The men are in hourly danger—horrible danger. You are letting loose forces that have been pent up in the place for centuries. The men should come off the job at once."

At his increasingly urgent manner, Alec and Edith Kinloch stiffened simultaneously. After all, dash it all, the house is mine, ran Alec's thoughts, and there's a limit to the interference one can stand! Edith's eyes answered his unspoken protest, agreeing with it.

Alec voiced his ideas. His tone was a subtle reproach.

"Was this Joe Dawlish working on the house when he died?"

"He was." The doctor's clipped reply roused all Alec's fathomless obstinacy.

"I suppose he was insured."

Alec's own instant perception of the vital core of this queer fuss about Dawlish gratified him enormously. He was moved, without waiting for his wife's lead, to make a gesture.

"Well, I might give the wife a little extra. Ten pounds would pay for the funeral—handsomely. These people love a ghoulish sort of feast, don't they? 'Buried him with ham'—what!"

"Ham? Er, yes . . . quite. Ham."

Doctor Dick looked his host up and down as if he saw some connection between him and the word he reiterated. He got to his feet.

He was out of the room, out of the little entrance-hall, out of the house—stalking like a longlegged bird down the garden and on to the road almost before Edith and Alec could reply to his swift farewell. He'd been so quick, so cumbered with hat, stick, and a knobby untidy parcel, that he didn't even shake hands.

Alec threw himself down in his armchair by the fire, took up a brass toasting fork and began to warm up the remaining scones. Edith watched him absent-mindedly.

"Shut Pills up, didn't I?" he spoke with his mouth full of scone. "Nothing like getting down to brass tacks with these fellows. Driveling about spooks and Troon! Neat dodge for collecting for Dawlish's widow. Better do the thing handsomely, as we're strangers here. Living at the big house, we'll be obliged to play up a bit."

Edith continued her pursuit of abstract thought.

"Well?"

"Yes, dear."

She came out of her trance, sat forward inelegantly, a thin hand on either knee. Strong emotion did occasionally uncover the past.

"Alec, there's more in this than meets the eye. Mark my words, there's someone else after Troon. They want to turn us out, force us to sell. I dare say they've found how old and much more valuable the property is than they believed. Let 'em try!"

He wolfed the last scone, pulled out a large white linen handkerchief, polished his lips, arranged his mustache, hitched up his trousers at the knee, and lighted a fresh pipe.

"Let 'em!" he echoed in profound sepulchral tones.

Six o'clock on a late November evening. Rain and a squalling wind from the east. A high tide slapping and hissing against the mile-long ancient seawall.

Jim Sanderson drove at his job in the cold drafty house with nervous hurry. A highly intelligent able workman was Jim, the best workman of the gang at Troon House.

Well over three hundred years old the house was. Of late it had fallen into bad disrepair. Its landlord lived in Ireland and had rented his fine old derelict to one careless tenant after another until roof and walls let in as much weather as they kept out.

The Liverpool agent happened to love the house. He had done his best, wrested small sums from its owner for patching here and patching there for forty odd years. But he and Troon could bluff no longer.

Would-be tenants kept on coming, for a genuine old Seagate house for sale was rare. Their verdict was unanimous. Damp! Rain drove in through deep cracks and faulty windows. Salt water used in the cement made ugly discolorations everywhere. Timbers were rotting. One roof had curvature of the spine. Toads and spiders had taken over ruined outbuildings and kitchens. Weeds, coarse grass, overgrown hedges, and dumps of rubbish made a desert of the long garden at Troon's back.

At last, the agent had put up enormous startling bills in each of Troon's front windows. And, suddenly, he sold the house.

The two Kinlochs had seen it. They had money. They needed an old and mellow background. They got a first-class architect to vet the place, found a reasonable sum would make it weatherproof, beat the Irish landlord down a little—very little, for he was savage as a cornered rat. Followed a flurry of contracts, plans, and agreements, then parleyings with the local council, who mistrusted haste and people with money to spend on a damp derelict house in Seagate. And the Kinlochs were in a hurry: they wanted to settle in before Christmas.

At last Troon House legally changed hands. The Kinlochs rented a bungalow lurking a mile away by the marshes. Troon was delivered up to the builders and decorators.

And so we return to Jim Sanderson on this gloomy November evening.

He had an electric torch, for no light was yet installed in the house. By its beam he prodded furiously at a patch of decayed timber by the hearthstone. A specimen was demanded by the Mycology Section of the Forest Products Research Laboratory. Dry rot was suspected in this large front room on the ground floor. Sanderson had to send his specimen by that night's post. The other workmen were gone. He was working overtime—alone.

Clap! Clap! Clap!

Somewhere in the drafty darkness upstairs a door banged persistently. It got on his nerves. He was a sensitive man in spite of his big muscular frame. Temperament, imagination, nerves were part of his quick flexible intelligence. He hated this night job. He felt queer and jumpy.

Clap! Clap! Clap!

There! The damned door had shut itself at last. He heaved a sigh of relief. Then his scalp prickled. Was someone up there? Had they shut the door? Was that someone coming down the broken creaking staircase?

The whites of his eyes showed like those of a frightened horse as he glanced up at the rain-blurred glass of a large bay-window on his right. Impulse seized him to dash himself at the panes, to escape to the friendly old parade just outside. Overwhelmingly he wanted to be out in the open—to exchange this dusty, musty shelter for rain and salt wind and flying scuds of foam.

He'd had enough. Things had got worse ever since Joe Dawlish had pulled down the cupboard in the big west attic a week ago. The wall and chimney-breast had crumbled and broken with its removal. A few stout blows, and the whole false facade had come down, revealing a deep recess reaching from rafters halfway to floor. On the broad stone shelf thus formed, a skeleton lay.

The bones of a child. Skull smashed in. A staple and chain padlocked round the bone of the left arm. The padlock was the strangest thing of all, of black smooth heavy stone with queer red markings chalked on it.

The vicar had been summoned in a hurry. He'd brought Doctor Dick with him. They were in a great taking about the affair, and carried off the poor little bones for burial.

From that hour things had gone wrong at Troon. Joe, who'd found the bones, was dead and buried inside a week—and what a week, too!

Sanderson's big brown hands fumbled as he tugged and strained at the flooring. He felt suddenly hot and weak. There was a flurry in his brain. He wrenched out the piece of wood he needed, stowed it roughly away in a torn capacious pocket of his old coat. Still on his knees, he gathered up his tools.

He rattled and banged things about, trying to shut out other sounds . . . sounds on the stairs . . .

The breath seemed to stop in his big body.

Creak. Creak. Creak.

It was someone cautiously stealing downstairs.

Crack!

He knew that sound. It was a broken step, third from the bottom. He tried to call out. It must be that damned oaf, Walter! The fool must have gone to sleep up there. Sanderson couldn't make his stiff dry tongue obey him. He couldn't hail whoever it was out there. He couldn't—he daren't.

His hunted eyes sought the window. Power to move, to jump for it, had left him. He knelt there, powerful shoulders hunched, hands on the floor for support, crouched like a big frightened animal. He fought to prevent himself looking over his shoulder at the door behind. He knew it was opening. He heard stealthy fingers on the old loose knob. He heard the harsh scrape of wood on wood as the sagging door was pushed back.

Ice-cold wind blew in, rustled bits of paper and shavings on the floor.

Sanderson's head jerked back to look. The door stood widely open. His eyes, filmed with terror, focused achingly on the gap between door and wall. Darkness moved there. A Thing Of Darkness. On the threshold it bulked in shapeless moving menace. Darkness made visible . . . blotting out everything . . . blotting out life itself.

The crash of a small wooden crate on which his heavy hand rested saved Sanderson from fainting. He leaped for the window. Glass cracked and fell in sharp tinkling showers. A thick cloth cap protected his lowered head. He was through. He fell on the strip of trampled grass outside, among a tangle of ladders and buckets. He vaulted the pointed iron railing and was in the road—running—running—breath coming in deep sobbing gusts—deathly face splashed with rain and blood.

Ahead shone the cheerful red and white lamp of the Three Mariners. He went straight for it as a fox for a familiar burrow.

Mr. and Mrs. Burden—old Tom and old Mary to most—who kept the Three Mariners were sitting in their vast red-tiled kitchen before a blazing fire. Black hand-made rugs were spread. Oil lamps of heavy brass hung from massive black oak rafters. At a round walnut table covered with a crimson cloth, Mrs. Burden was working placidly through a pile of stockings to be mended. Solomon, a great tawny Persian cat, dozed with its leonine head on her instep. Mr. Burden, smoking a long churchwarden, sat in a wide Windsor chair glossy with age and use, his stockinged feet on a gleaming wrought-brass stool.

Doctor Dick sprawled on a settle near by. Two or three fishermen, warming up before the tide turned and they put out for their night's catch, completed the little company of friends.

They all looked up at the loud bang of the outer door. Every face was turned toward the kitchen entrance when Jim Sanderson burst in.

"For God's sake—a drink!"

He collapsed into a big chair and sat with head down on his hands, shivering and gasping before the hot fire. Doctor Dick was at his side in a moment. Mrs. Burden ran for a drink. Mr. Burden dropped his favorite pipe and stared.

The fishermen sat forward, hands on knees, consternation on their weathered red-brown faces. Solomon stood with arched back, great feathery tail waving nervously, before seeking shelter under a distant chair to await developments.

Sanderson told his experience in jerks between sips of the Three Mariners' best Jamaica rum. His audience blinked, muttered, stared. Doctor Dick, that brilliant modern young man, listened with flattering and tremendous concentration, sea-blue eyes and keen face losing every trace of their habitual friendly good-humor.

Mrs. Burden sat immobile. She had, as always, a flavor of the wild, of a remote and more instinctive age, of ancient beliefs and wisdom. She moved like a feather in a draft of wind—so light, so frail, so incalculable. She always seemed curiously unrelated to furniture and rooms and human dwelling-places in spite of making the Three Mariners the coziest inn in the whole county of Cheshire. She had the quality of some dear deep peatbrown river, nourishing the earth and nourished by it.

Her husband, rocklike as she was fluid and quick, turned to her now.

"What d'yer say to that, old woman? That there Troon house was always what you might say queer-like. I reckon it's had queer folk in it and all. But I never heard tell of anything out and out bad."

"No? Well, I did, then."

Doctor Dick leaned forward, pipe in hand, his eyes bright as blue steel in the lamp-glow.

"Now this isn't treating me on the level, old Mary." He waved his pipe in reproach. "You know very well the vicar and I are trying to rake up Troon's past history. I've been here for the last hour and you've never let out one solitary squeak."

"No, and I wouldn't have done it if Jim hadn't seen what he has seen this night." Her bright dark eyes flashed round the intent faces.

"I've been thinking over that business you've been telling about, Doctor Dick, that skeleton Joe dug out of the walls last week. Seems like as if that must have been her skeleton."

No one contradicted this dark surmise.

"I'll tell you the story as my grandfeyther's grandfeyther wrote it. He was a scholar. Kept village school up at Keston. He'd got an old book with everything put down that happened since Seagate began. I read this story when I was a girl and never forgot a word. I can get the book from my uncle's niece by marriage that works in a big library up to London to prove I'm right."

Chairs were hitched up, pipes relit. Old Tom flung a log that roused the fire to crackling flame. Solomon emerged, paced majestically back to his mistress, stretched at her feet with his yellow chin supported on them.

"The year 1600 saw Troon put up at the end of the parade, only a low seawall then. Course Troon was naught but a little tavern then: Troon Tavern. Even for those rough times it was a bad place. They had miners over from Flint across the water—dark little devils, those Welsh men, always scrapping and more handy with knives than a butcher himself. Mostly it was miners went to Troon Tavern. The man that built it was Thomas Werne, a Seagate man that got hold of money somehow. Smuggling, most like.

"Werne, the book said, was nothing but a block brute of a man. Treated his young wife wors'n a dog. When she died he got downright savage, and the child, Lizzy, left to him, came in for it all. I'm not going to harrow your feelings nor my own by telling what that innocent suffered. Laws weren't much then when it came to looking after poor people's children.

"But there was a gentleman came to stay here at this very inn, the Three Mariners, and he was that angry when he saw Lizzy and learned about her from Seagate talk, he threatened he'd have Werne put in prison. The gentleman went back to London after that and told Werne he'd hear more about it. Well, next thing that happened was—Lizzy Werne disappeared."

"Ah!" Doctor Dick's voice poignantly expressed his thought.

"Yes. Every one was certain sure Werne had done it, same as you're thinking yourself," responded old Mary. "But nothing could be proved. The body of the child, not much more of it than bones Joe found, never turned up, search though they might and did! The law made a great fuss when it was too late. The gentleman from London came back and he stayed for weeks, he was that set on getting Werne hanged for murder."

"And he walled the child up in his own house, then!" Doctor Dick's eyes blazed.

"Aye. After three hundred years we've found what Werne did, I b'lieve!"

"Eh, think of that!" Old Tom spat into the red fire. "And what did the murderin' fellow say had happened to the child? What did he tell 'em?"

"Said she was drowned. No one ever knew whether or not she was, the tides being mortal quick and dangerous here at Seagate. An' 'twas worse then. There were quicksands down by the marshes, and more than Werne's Lizzy had been caught and drowned. No one believed Werne's tale, only nothing could be done to him because Lizzy's body was never found."

"Quite. What I don't see," put in Doctor Dick, "is why he walled the body up. After smashing her skull, why not have taken the corpse out to sea and dropped it overboard one dark night?"

Old Mary shook her head.

"You mean he hadn't a boat?"

"No, I don't mean that, Doctor Dick. All the Seagate men had boats in those days, same as you and me have a pair of shoes. Reckon you're the only one here doesn't know why he couldn't put that body in the sea."

There were confirmatory nods all round the silent spellbound circle. Doctor Dick frowned in bewilderment.

"Why?"

"Well, seeing you don't know, I'll say the verse that was in the old book my grandfeyther's grandfeyther wrote out;

*"A murdered body cast to sea
May never there lie quietly,*

But every night is washed ashore,
And standing by the murderer's door
It cries to be let in.

"Of course that's put in rhyme and it's not quite right about the tides, not being a high tide every night anyhow. But the tide or no tide, the ghost would come back to the man who did the murder every night of his life."

Jim Sanderson shivered and looked with haunted eyes at the old woman.

"You reckon I saw her then—the ghost?"

"No. There's one, and it's a downright dangerous one. The child escaped, thanks be! But Werne's caught himself now and he's going to make people suffer for it."

She turned to Doctor Dick.

"That padlock you told me about, with the red marks on it. Magic that was, black magic to keep the child's soul a prisoner all these years. Sold her to the devil, did her father! Just so long as the child was promised, Werne himself was free."

Sanderson made an abrupt movement.

"I don't know as I get your meaning, old Mary."

"Plain enough. He'd sold his child to the devil, same as you'd bind an apprentice. The devil, he taught Werne how to lock her up safe so as her little ghost couldn't escape and go wandering round, making people suspect. Well, that spell was broken when Joe Dawlish broke down the wall and the padlock and chain."

"As far as that goes," Doctor Dick's crisp voice interrupted the old woman's uncomfortably clear exposition, "the vicar and I are equally to blame."

"And Werne's not going to forget it," warned old Mary. "Now Lizzie's bones lie in the churchyard all safe and sound there'll be trouble—black trouble. That's how I see it, anyways."

Jim sucked in his breath on a long tremulous hiss. The fishermen got to their feet.

"Reckon the tide's right enough now," said one.

"Wait! I'll come along." Jim lunged clumsily in the wake of the retreating men. "You're going my road and I'll be glad of company tonight."

Old Mary's serious withdrawn look followed the group out. As the heavy outer door banged to, she shook her head.

"Jim Sanderson's in for it," she said in a low voice. "After sunset it's asking for trouble to set foot in Troon. He'll go like Joe Dawlish went. Poor fellow . . . poor fellow!"

The next afternoon, Troon stood in a blaze of sunlight. The sky was mother-of-pearl. A slow full tide gleamed like gray satin. Troon confronted it—cold, indifferent, implacable.

Inside its strong walls an army of workmen went about like busy scurrying ants. They were desperate to finish this job. Work that would ordinarily have lingered on for weeks was being rushed through at treble speed. One week more would see painting and decorations complete. Even the long wilderness of a garden was being dug and planted and trimmed and sown at a pace contrary to all Seagate tradition.

Doctor Dick lingered outside the strip of grass and iron rail protecting Troon's tall front windows on the ground floor. Lynneth had told him she was coming with the Kinlochs about three o'clock this afternoon. Elaborate juggling with his day's appointments brought him to Troon on the stroke of the hour.

"Afternoon, doctor!"

A joiner called Frost touched his cap. He carried a big woven basket of tools over his shoulder. His face looked bleached. He glanced back over his shoulder as he stepped from Troon's front door and blinked in the clear light outside the house.

"Knocking off already?"

"Aye, sir. Not worth going to fetch more tools for half an hour."

Doctor Dick stared. Laughed.

"You don't mean your day finishes at three-thirty, Frost? I envy you."

"There's none of us works there," he jerked a backward thumb, "after three-thirty, sir. Not these short days. All of us goes at three-thirty—before dusk," he added with significance.

"I see. How do you square that up with regulations?"

"We begins at seven 'stead of eight o' mornings, sir. That's how we does it. The boss is agreeable so long as we does a regular day all told."

"Leave before sundown. Yes, I see."

"We've got good reasons for it."

"I believe you."

"Aye. Not a man would stay in Troon after dusk. No—not for a ransom, not since Jim Sanderson went. A cruel death! Went like Joe Dawlish—just the same."

Seeing the doctor's grave expression, Frost began speaking again.

"Mark my words, sir, if them two iggerant foreigners—if you'll excuse me putting it so bald-like—wot are renting the bungalow over by the marshes—"

"Mr. and Mrs. Kinloch?"

"Aye. If them two move into Troon next week, all I say is they'd do better to go down marsh-walk and be drowned comfortable. Might as well die natural deaths like! That's wot I says and wot I sticks to."

Doctor Dick took this with gratifying seriousness. He went to his car and fiddled about with it for a minute or so to gain time, then returned with a thought he appeared to have found under the car's hood.

"Look here, Frost! Believing in anything makes it real. If the Kinlochs have no faith at all in old Werne and his power to hurt them, well, perhaps he can not."

Frost poked his head forward like a turtle emerging from its shell.

"Noa," his north-country accent marked strong emotion, "I doan't hold wi' thot and thee doesn't neether, Doctor Dick! Thot oogly Thing a-grinnin' and a-murderin' there in the dark like, it's naught to it what we b'lieves! It just bides quiet—same as a beast or summat—and then——"

The man's gesture, brawny fist smashing downward, was eloquent.

Other workmen began to emerge from Troon. They mounted a fleet of bicycles leaning up against the iron railing and made for home and tea. Doctor Dick frowned. Surely the Kinlochs wouldn't—yes. There they were.

"Good afternoon, Doctor Thornton. Oh, I mean Doctor Dick—it's so difficult to bring myself to say that. In town, of course, one's so much more formal. D'you remember Doctor de Tourville, Alice? Imagine if we'd called him Doctor Henry! Of course he was really a consultant. A very big man. A personal friend of ours."

Doctor Dick let Edith's flow gush right over his head. She'd thought out her speech carefully in order to make two distinct impressions; first as to his regrettable lack of professional dignity, second as to the standing she and Alec had enjoyed in Liverpool. She saw him turn to Lynneth. His rising color she attributed to having got home with her two little stabs. It was always inconceivable to Edith that anyone could just ignore her. She gave them credit for ordinary intelligence.

"You're not—not going over the house so late?"

Doctor Dick had eyes and ears for Lynneth only. Alec, on his way to the front door, turned back and surveyed the doctor with a dull eye of one whose liver is perpetually ill-treated.

"So late!" he echoed. "Late for what? Was old Werne expecting us earlier?"

He burst into a high-pitched laugh, disconcerting in a man of his size. Doctor Dick's glance went to the windows of the house before which they stood. He thought he heard a louder, gruffer laugh within—a workman, perhaps. Yes, something dark passed one of the bedroom windows at that moment.

Edith ran forward to the front door, all girlish abandon to take up her husband's witty remark. She lifted the knocker and gave a smart rat-tat-tat.

"We'll ask him if he'll give us tea."

She cast a glassy brown look over the shoulder of her ponyskin coat. Alec, fumbling for his key, laughed again, louder and longer. Edith gave vent to a selection of well-rehearsed "outbursts of merriment." Doctor Dick, alert and listening with painful intentness now, was convinced he heard a hoarse, coarse echo within the walls of Troon. It must be a workman—and—yet—. As he stood there, wondering how on earth he was going to prevent Lynneth from following the two Kinlochs inside, a further shock assaulted his nerves. Alec was still clumsily rooting for his mislaid key.

The heavy front door swung silently, widely open without a touch.

Edith blinked, frowned, assumed a bright tone of playfulness.

"We are invited for tea!" she laughed. "I suppose the men didn't pull the door to. How careless! I shall report it tomorrow to the foreman. These country yokels! Oh, well, one must be patient, I suppose."

Alec followed his wife inside. Doctor Dick drew Lynneth back.

"Look here—no right to interfere with you and all that—but don't go in!"

Her eyes were fathomless, shining. In the golden dusk her vivid eager face had a transparent look, as if it were wrought glass, golden-tinted, exquisite, through which rare wine sparkled and bubbled and gleamed.

"I—but why do you ask that?"

"Because it's dangerous. It's deadly. Your cousins don't or won't believe anything against Troon. But I tell you the truth. The place is haunted. There's a devil in it."

She looked at him very straightly under the fine beautiful arch of her brows. She knew truth when she heard it. She trusted this man. More than trusted—much, much more than that. For a moment her whole heart responded. Her hands were gripped in his.

"Lynneth! Oh, my dear!" he breathed.

"But—but—" she stammered in surprise. "Is it like this—like this? To feel so sure, when only yesterday—"

The front door banged violently. For a second their startled eyes questioned each other. Then they rushed forward. They had no key.

Doctor Dick plied the knocker. Lynneth ran back to the front of the house to peer through the long windows. She returned to Doctor Dick.

"It's all right. Alec's there. He's talking to Edith from the hall. She must be upstairs."

They looked together. Yes, Alec was there safe and sound. He seemed annoyed. Under the hanging unshaded light his face was unhealthily sallow and fretful. His head was flung back. He was talking to someone above, but no sound was audible to the watchers.

They felt a queer chill of apprehension. His side of the conversation seemed acrimonious, to judge by his expression. His frown became a sullen scowl. He turned from the stairway up which he'd been looking, jammed his hat down, stalked away. Next moment he came outside, leaving the front door open behind him.

"Too damned cold in there to hang about. Edith's as obstinate as—"

He scowled at them, pulled out a pipe, clamped strong yellow teeth on its stem, and began to fill the bowl. After a few puffs he relaxed. Recent and surprising discomfort urged him to speech.

"Chill on my liver or something," he vouchsafed, "Edith insisted—well, you know what she is!" He turned to the girl. "Today's plans included a visitation here," he jerked a thumb inelegantly. "No consideration for my health—must go over the place. Doesn't matter that the house reeks of gas or something. And colder than a tomb. Damn it all, if she must see it, she'll see it without my company!"

Lynneth stared. Never, no, never had she heard him come so near a criticism of his wife. Even when absent in the flesh, her mind ruled his, subjugated it to her opinions. He must be extraordinarily upset.

Inside Troon's heavy old walls, Edith went confidently to and fro, snapping on lights, snapping off lights, rubbing a finger on surfaces of wood, raising an eyebrow at a pile of tools and shavings in the middle of a bathroom floor, opening every door in order that air should circulate. The house seemed strangely stuffy, although windows and ventilators were all opened this mild day to dry up paint and varnish and new plaster. And how much colder it was indoors than out! A great golden sun flung a path of light across five miles of sea and sand. Its clear shining reached Troon's gray western face. Six tall west windows met the golden light—and repelled it.

"But how absurd!"

Edith stared about with indignation. Her high heels clicked smartly on woodblock floors as she tried another room. Her room, the room she meant to call her boudoir. The most perfectly preserved in the whole lovely house with its south and west windows, its beams, its old, old corner fireplace so laboriously restored.

"What have they been doing—idiots!" The toffee-brown eyes took on a glaze of anger. "I told them vita-glass in this room. Do they think they can fob off this gray clouded stuff on me? I'd make them come back and change it right away if I were in charge. I shall ring up the contractor tonight. The very idea! These country bumpkins—tiresome things!"

The windows darkened and darkened as she glared about her. So angry was she that a voice from the doorway behind did not startle her at all; it merely represented a person on whom she could vent her vicious mood.

At sight of the big hulking weatherbeaten figure in stained ragged jersey and sea-boots, she let fly:

"You're not a workman here?"

The grizzled ugly head made a gesture of denial.

"I'm Mrs. Kinloch."

The man stared, unenlightened by the great news. He was like some great dark bull with his lowered head and bloodshot savage eyes. Edith caught sight of the trail of leaf-mold, mud, and dust that marked the intruder's path across polished flooring beyond the doorway.

"Look at the mess you've made. How dare you come tramping about here? Who are you?"

"Thomas Werne."

"Werne! Werne! Why, that's the same name as some unpleasant old man who's supposed to have lived here centuries ago! The one there's such a silly fuss about."

The man appeared uninterested.

"Well! You can go away—at once! D'you hear? Don't imagine because you've the same name as that creature that you've a right of entry to these premises. Be off at once."

He regarded her with a fixed glare. Abruptly he burst into a loud long hoarse laugh. It echoed and reechoed through the hollow rooms.

Edith drew up her thin person in disgust.

"Really!" She soliloquized without troubling to lower her voice. "Must be a half-wit. These fisherman are the limit. Unpleasant dirty animals. Phew! How dark it's getting. I wish I hadn't stayed after all."

Her glance took in the blank windows, frowned at them. It was almost like an eclipse of the sun, something so queer and sudden and unnatural was in the gloom that spread . . . and spread.

She looked beyond the burly figure in the doorway. An immense skylight was set in the roof above the staircase. When she'd come up only ten minutes ago, clear strong light had shone down. She remembered thinking how well the oak-grain of the steep old stairs showed up after treatment. Now, a wall of impenetrable darkness lay behind the intruder.

Secret inadmissable fear lent a barb to her tongue. Baffled, furious, uncertain, she tried to assume the glacial manner of an aristocrat as she conceived one.

"I don't wish to get you into trouble, my good man, but unless you go—at once—I shall feel it my duty to report you to the police."

A noisy bellow answered her. "Report old Tom Werne, eh! Thot's a good 'un—a reet down dom good 'un!"

His great bulk shook like a jelly. Walls and floor and windows—the whole structure of old Troon seemed to strain and shake and quiver with its uncontrollable amusement.

She stamped her high-heeled shoe, so neat and polished.

"Oh, how dare you! Impertinent—I shall send Mr. Kinloch back to speak to you."

She took a few steps in the gray gloom toward the darker gloom outside, and stopped short. Raging inwardly, she was forced to realize that she couldn't, she positively couldn't make up her mind to go nearer that unpleasant filthy chuckling old beast in the doorway. Should she throw up a window and call to Alec? It would put her in a perfectly idiotic light. Infuriating impasse! She hesitated, summoned her reserves.

"I shall certainly give you in charge," she began. "The moment I—I—"

She blinked, stuttered. Was she mad, or blind, or ill?

Through the windows, golden sun streamed in across the floor, long gleaming ladders of light upon the beautiful wood. The landing outside shone in a yellow haze of cross-lights from open doors on every side. The doorway was empty before her. Empty! The flooring beyond was bare of every trace of dust or leaves.

She stood shivering, spellbound in the quiet sunset glow. Downstairs a door banged like a gun going off. Heavy feet resounded on the red-brick yard at the side of the house. They echoed, died away, swallowed up in the green shadowy depths of the long garden beyond.

Released from a spell, she ran downstairs, out the front door, and pulled it after her with an angry bang. She poured out to the waiting three her recent experience. Gesture and phrasing harked back to pre-Lady Bountiful days. Doctor Dick recognized hysteria. Lynneth recognized that sub-Edith she'd always felt but never heard before. Alec did not recognize anything. He regarded her with mulish lack-luster eye.

"You would go over the house! You are so damned obstinate! Must have been old Werne himself you were up there chatting to."

Edith's laugh rose shrill in the cool winter dusk.

"I can believe the doctor might say a thing like that. But you, Alec! Really! What are we coming to!"

"That's what I think. Old Werne himself. I've changed my mind since I went in just now. Not been in such a funk since I was a kid."

"So you left me to face it!"

"I did not. You did all the leaving part. Skipped up the stairs and left me cold. And cold's the word, too. I told you not to go. I knew something beastly was prowling around. Damn it all, you've got nerves of chromium-plated steel."

"Alec! How can you be so silly and so vulgar! Actually using language—in the public street—and to your own wife!"

The shock of it pulled her together quite effectually. She shot across the wide road and began to canter homeward. Alec turned to the doctor and grinned, a shamefaced but quite a human friendly grin.

"See you again, my boy. Looks as if you'd be needed at Troon to give us all nerve tonics and soothing-powders. Well—so long!"

He looked down at Lynneth. One of his more perceptive moments dawned.

"Better get a spot of walk after that scene, my child. I'll toddle home and see to Edith."

He lumbered off, a burly blot of all-British respectability against a sheet of silver water. Doctor Dick turned, eager, ready to make the most of every precious moment. The girl was standing with flower-like face entranced, lips parted, her whole attention absorbed.

"Lynneth! Lynneth darling! What are you looking at inside that horrible old house?"

She did not reply, did not seem to hear. She stood as in a dream, her hands gripping the pointed arrowheads that tipped the iron railing.

"What on earth—?"

He went to her side and peered in through dark blank panes of glass to Troon's lower floor. Darkness. Shadowy darkness.

Chill touched the leaping flame of joy in his heart. He put a hand on hers. She did not move.

"Lynneth! Lynneth!"

The shining of a street lamp showed her face clearly. It was smiling in happy wonder. She seemed intent on some marvel, some vision beyond the big blank windowpanes.

He hesitated. Short of force he couldn't wrench away those small hands that clutched the iron railing. He put an arm about her shoulders, tried to draw her to him, but she did not yield an inch. Her slim soft body might have been one of the iron uprights of the railing. Her eyes didn't flicker from their rapt gaze.

He made up his mind, put out his arms to exert full force, to drag her from Troon, from whatever she saw inside its haunted wall. Abruptly she sighed, loosed her grip, her eyes faded to disappointment, to sick misery.

"Oh, it's gone! The lovely, lovely thing! I can't tell you how lovely. But it's gone. It won't come back. Not now. But I'll watch for it again. I must see it soon again."

The man froze. His blood turned to ice. What deadly perilous thing had she seen? A trap—a snare had been set. For Lynneth—for Lynneth! Oh, God!

To all his anguished questioning she shook her head. Her eyes were sad, full of longing. Remote, distraught, she walked beside him.

"There are no words for it. I can't tell, even if I would. Clouds . . . clouds . . . and a new lovely world. I must go back there—go back—"

He shivered. A devil's trick. Old Werne had played a devil's trick to get her fast. She'd been afraid before. She would have been on guard. Now she only longed to be inside that cursed place, dreamed of it as a wanderer dreams of home.

Their precious hour together was a grim ordeal to him. She, withdrawn and silent, he sick with fear for her. And the end of the nightmare walk was as strange as any of it.

At the black and white gate of Sandilands the two took formal farewell. A rising moon lighted the dark road. On one side of it crouched the little bungalow, looking like a child's toy with its gables, and its fir-trees on either side of the straight formal garden-path. Opposite the odd little dwelling stretched a long meadow. Beyond lay half-drowned marshes—beyond them sand and shining pools left by the tide where seabirds clamored in the moonlight.

Doctor Dick strode away from the gate. He hadn't dreamed such black despair was possible. A voice called him.

"Dick! Dick! I want you. Come back!"

Next moment he had her in his arms. So close, so safe against his heart, it seemed nothing could hurt her again. She put him away at last, laughing, tears gleaming in her eyes.

"What happened to you—darling—darling?" she whispered. "I feel as if I'd waked from a nightmare. Kiss me! Again! Oh, Dick, you do care after all!"

II

"There now, Doctor Dick! Sit down and make yourself at home. It's a week since you've been in. What's worrying you, sir? Tom—a glass of sherry for the doctor."

The host, in blue striped shirtsleeves, apron girt about his beaver waistcoat, clattered off across the red-tiled room. Mrs. Burden looked with keen old eyes at her guest's shadowed face.

"Nothing wrong, so far?"

"No."

His monosyllable dropped like a stone into a deep well. "Nothing. And it's unbearable. The suspense. Waiting—waiting—"

He sprang up, paced to and fro in the leaping firelight, stopped before the quiet watchful old woman, his hands clasped behind his back, legs astride, head thrust forward. She met his searching look and answered his agonized unspoken question in her unhurried fashion.

"Aye. There is danger for the lass every hour she's there. But there's just a gleam of hope to my mind, too."

"For Lynneth! You think so? Why, Mary?"

"That great dark Thing at Troon seems as if it settles on one at a time."

He frowned, stared.

"Then, if so—if so it's Mrs. Kinloch who's in the line of fire. I told you that she saw him—old Werne—and insists he was a drunken fisherman."

Old Mary was emphatic. "It was him. He came with the darkness that's part of him."

"Yes. Mrs. Kinloch admitted the darkness—at first. Went back on it later, though. Said she'd only imagined it got dark."

"She saw Werne. It's my belief she'll go next. Then you can take your lass away."

"But, good heavens! D'you mean I'm to wait until that devil murders Mrs. Kinloch?"

"What other way is there?"

Her calm matter-of-factness roused in him a sudden hysterical desire to roar with laughter. And after all, he had to wait! If that obstinate woman—

"I've asked her a dozen times to leave Troon. She's on the point of forbidding me the house," he admitted.

"Waste no more words," advised the old woman. "They'll take you nowhere. Your job is to save the lass. Never mind fretting over them as are blind and deaf as stones."

Old Tom returned and poured the wine. Doctor Dick sat down, glass in hand.

"How about the servant lassies at Troon?" asked Mr. Burden.

"From Liverpool," the doctor said. "They've heard nothing so far, Dressed up-town girls, too superior to be friendly with Seagate fishermen. They've only one complaint so far."

"Aye!"

"They say Troon's dark. Grumble about the windows—that the glass is always gray and clouded even when the sun's shining outside."

"Darkness. 'Thing of Darkness'—that's what parson called it the day he buried Joe Dawlish."

"Thing of Darkness." Doctor Dick rose. His face was drawn and stern. "Well, I must be off. I'm dining at Troon. A housewarming. I'll call in again after it's over. It's likely to be a housewarming that leaves me cold."

The heavy door clanged behind him.

"He'll not come back this night." Mrs. Burden turned a solemn face to her husband. He sat in his favorite chair, drawing on his churchwarden. "Friday, 'tis! And full moon. And—I didn't tell Doctor Dick purposely—he's enough on his mind—but it's the anniversary of the day Lizzie Werne disappeared. It's written in that old book I told you of. December 2nd, 1636."

"You think old Werne'll—?"

"Aye. I think he will."

"You must excuse this picnic meal." Edith's eyes were ablaze with triumph. Hard bright color dyed her thin cheeks. "I warned you it would be a case of roughing it. The maids have done their best, but you know what they are!"

Four sat at the gate-legged table of Jacobean oak for dinner that night, the seventh night of the Kinloch's arrival at Troon. Edith had worked like a beaver, had driven cook and housemaid before her whirl of energy like galley-slaves. The big gaunt house was furnished from wide shadowy attics to scrubbed and scoured kitchens and pantries.

Doctor Dick remembered the Biblical story of the man possessed of a devil, who swept and garnished his house. He remembered and shivered.

He made the reply his hostess expected of him. The well-pointed table, the gleaming silver and dinner service chosen to harmonize with the house, the five-course dinner, the well-trained maids imported from town, were all elaborate and overemphatic in perfection. Not the natural and dignified background of a well-bred hostess, but a show. Herself the blatant complacent showman!

"Alone I did it," her voice, manner, and conversation implied.

"You know," she reproached the visitor, "I really believe you're disappointed. I think I see—yes, I'm sure I do—a sort of 'I'd rather that my friend should die than my prediction prove a lie' expression on your face."

Alec intervened. He, at least, had the advantage of early discipline that had planted certain fixed rules of conduct in him. Doctor Dick looked ill at ease. He must be soothed. Hang it all, you didn't rub things in at your own dinner-table! Edith was a bit above herself to-night. She'd got her way. They were living at Troon. Things were all right too—at least—He brushed away suspicion. Just an effect of lighting. He wasn't used to the queer old house yet.

"Noticed the fireplace?" he asked. "It's part of the original tavern. Sort of bakehouse. The whole inglenook, arches and chimney-breast and the little iron door to shove ashes through, were covered up by a kitchen range. Lovely old stuff that brick—three hundred years old."

Thankfully, the guest accepted the diversion.

"Makes a wonderful dining room. That window too, I like the square panes—different from the silly imitations they make. Set in that battered old framework it's—hello! Who's that looking in? D'you keep a gardener working at this hour?"

Edith glanced up quickly, wished she'd drawn the curtains after all. She'd decided, on such a romantic moonlight night, that the vista of garden enhanced the room's perfection. Impatiently she tinkled a small copper bell at her hand. No one answered it. She rang again, waited. No sound from outside.

Lynneth ventured a suggestion. She was in one of the strange dreamy moods that the doctor dreaded—moods that had recurred again and again since that night of her "vision," as she called it. Her dinner-gown of smoke-gray velvet with its gleam of gold thread, the jewel—Tiger's Tear—glinting tawny-yellow on her breast, the thick shining hair like folded wings about her head, all gave Doctor Dick a pang of terror and dismay. She looked unreal tonight, held in dreams, unaware of evil, of danger coming stealthily nearer as she slept.

"I think," the girl's voice was only a whisper, "I think they've gone away. Someone—came for them."

Edith's answer was sharp with vexation. "My dear girl, what an idea! Go away in the middle of my dinner party? Why? They don't know a soul here. Really, Lynneth! You look half asleep. You'd better go and look for them. It might rouse you."

Doctor Dick sprang to his feet. "No. Let me go, please!"

Edith raised resigned exasperated brows. He would behave like this. How irritating these unconventional people were! He seemed to think this was a picnic, after all. Taken her literally. So stupid! Spoiling the whole tone of her dinner. Now they'd all have to get up. She and Alec couldn't sit still and let a guest chase about the house.

She rose, stood with finger-tips on the table, lifted her chin, looked around from under lowered lids in what she knew to be a really compelling pose. Her Queen Elizabeth look, she termed it privately. More privately still, she was sure there was some strain of royal blood in her. Some ancestor of hers had been—er—naughty! Oh, she was sure. How else did she come by the profound conviction of her own superiority? She knew she was different—an aristocrat deep down.

"I will go myself," she pronounced. "I insist. The maids are my province, after all."

Lynneth was unmoved by majesty's withdrawal. She seemed to be listening to some far-off entrancing sound. The two men looked uncertainly at each other. Alec assumed a boisterous hearty manner.

"Drink up, drink up! Fill your glass, my boy, and pass the claret along. The girls are new to Seagate. Heard something and dashed out to investigate, I expect. You know how pin-headed they are."

Minutes passed. No sound from hall or kitchens. Then came the tap-tap of high heels just overhead.

"Edith! Girls must've gone upstairs, not outside. I wonder—"

"We ought to go up, too."

Doctor Dick was on his feet. Alec, puzzled and uncomfortably disturbed by something he did not begin to understand, rose also. They made for the door. The doctor turned back, to see Lynneth sitting peacefully at the table, dreaming, indifferent.

"Stay there. Don't move from this room," he called back. "Lynneth! Lynneth!"

She responded with a vague absent smile. Doctor Dick followed his host with a last anxious look of love at the girl. A sense of mortal deadly peril threatened. The whole house seemed growing dark and suffocating and evil.

A cry came from above. Every light dimmed, went out. Thick choking darkness muffled Troon from kitchens to attics. Blindly, Doctor Dick fought his way up.

"Where are you?" he called.

From the stairs above, he heard Alec's voice, muffled, cursing.

"What's wrong? What are you doing? Can't you answer me, man?"

"I'm trying—to—get down."

Alec's voice came thicker, fainter now. A stumble. Curses and sound of hoarse hurried breathing in the darkness above. Then there was a yell—the crack of splintering wood—a heavy body came slithering and sprawling down the stairs as if flung with immense force. It knocked against Doctor Dick as he was stumbling upward, and he fell too, slipping down until an angle in the wall stopped him. Winded, uninjured, uncertain what to do next, he called out.

"Lynneth! Lynneth! Are you all right? Can you find matches? I left my lighter in my overcoat."

No answer from the profound darkness below.

"Lynneth!"

A voice, a vague faint echo of the girl's clear tone, floated down from above, it seemed to him. He made his way up the steep narrow old stairs again. "Lynneth! Lynneth!"

Edith Kinloch, cinnamon-brown silk flounces rustling her indignation, pursued her search. The kitchens, the pantries, were ablaze with light. And the hall. And the landing upstairs. She looked quickly into the rooms on the ground floor. No one there. But every room was brilliantly lighted.

She stamped her annoyance. Was this some low silly joke? Had the two maids gone off for some reason, leaving on all the lights merely to upset her? But why? Why? There had been no trouble over anything. Later perhaps, when they knew she did not intend to get more help—

She ran upstairs. Here again all lights were on. Every bedroom door was flung widely open. The blood rose to her head. In a rage now, she went up the last steep twisting staircase to the attics, and once more found the same silly prank had been played. True the lights were less brilliant. Fifteens were good enough for maids to waste! They'd only read in bed and be late in the morning if she gave them stronger lamps.

She hadn't thought fifteens were quite so poor though. Why, one candle would give more light than these things. Must be faulty bulbs. She'd ring up and complain tomorrow. They seemed to be getting dimmer as she looked at them. One died right out overhead. The one over the stairwell. She'd turn her ankle getting down again.

But where were those fools of girls? She stalked across to the wardrobe. There hung the tweed coats they wore, and a lot of other clothes. They couldn't have run off. They must be in the garden. She'd go down and send Alec out to find them.

Lynneth would have to make coffee and serve it, to cover the gap. Thank heaven, they'd finished the last course, anyhow. She turned about on the square landing, a mere three-foot platform, from which the attics opened.

In the big west room a sound brought her head about with a jerk.

"Who's there? Is that you, Beasley? Parkes?"

A shuffle. A heavy tread. She went back to the room. A light clicked off in the room as she entered it. She wheeled with a little squeal of anger.

"How dare you—"

In the darkness, a blacker deadlier darkness moved. Held rigid in sudden cold fear, her eyes accustomed themselves to the gloom. The window stood widely open. No. Not open. She looked at the thing. No window or even frame was there. Merely a ruinous irregular break in the crumbling wall.

She went to it, dizzy, sick, her nostrils filled with dusty choking stench. Her eyes followed the swelling shapeless Thing of Darkness that moved in the moonlit darkness of the room. A sudden red light shone from a foul little lantern that stood on a stone shelf formed by the chimney-breast's irregularities. Bare crumbling brick, the chimney was.

"But this"—she spoke aloud in a hoarse amazed voice—"this is what it was before we restored it. This isn't our Troon!"

"No. It's mine."

Loud voice and louder laughter answered her. She recognized them. In the smoking lamplight, she saw the vast ugly bulk, the bloated face, the small cruel eyes set under matted hair.

"You! You here again! I thought I told you—"

Her voice died. Her cold hands flew to her throat. She pressed back—back against the dirty old wall behind. The other attic was darkened now; her frightened eyes glanced across to it. She was up here in the dark, shut up with this brutal mad old man. It was a trick! Those servants! She'd have them punished. A monstrous experience! How dare they let her be subjected to it!

Ah!—he was moving nearer—nearer—darkness, thick black choking darkness, rolled forward like a tidal wave.

Now it touched her. She shrieked. Ice-cold, wet, like rotting slime, it touched her—closer about her—closer! Backward she went before the stifling death—back to the gaping ruinous wall. If she could get to that—call for help! Yes! Yes! She was on her knees on the dusty uneven broken flooring. With desperate effort she twisted, thrust her head outside.

"Help! Help!" she shrieked. "Help!"

The word choked in her throat. She was drawn back, as if the room were a quicksand into which she sank—down—down—silken flounces ripped—hair fallen all about her face of idiot terror—down—down—through the door of life—down through hell's dark gates—down—down—the Thing of Darkness pressed closer—closer still. . . .

It seemed to Doctor Dick, fighting his way in the unnatural darkness, as if he struggled up through clouds of poisonous gas whose fumes took strength from his limbs, sight from his eyes. Gasping. Dragging himself up one stair at a time. A cold numbness invaded him.

Then a frightful bubbling shriek pierced his senses. It came from above. Another—and more horrible cry. He groaned. He couldn't hurry. He felt consciousness being blotted out. Darkness pressed on him like solid walls. A stench of rotted decay filled his nostrils, choked the breath in his throat . . . it failed him . . . he fell forward.

Darkness flowed over him like the river of death itself.

He opened his eyes to find himself lying on the stairs just below the first-floor landing. Electric lights winked on all sides. Gray dawn met his aching bewildered eyes through a vast skylight overhead.

He tried to think, to remember as he struggled to rise. How had he come there? Why did such heavy desperate weariness weigh him down?

Sick, trembling with effort, he stood clinging to the baluster rail. Below, under the glare of a droplight, he caught sight of a man sprawled untidily across a glowing Persian rug. Groaning, he stumbled down to investigate.

It was Alec who lay there. Doctor Dick's professional instinct pricked him from lethargy as he examined the man. "Broken leg, slight concussion," he murmured. Suddenly full recollection flashed in his clouded mind.

"Lynneth! Lynneth!" he called aloud.

He made for the dining-room where he had left her last night. The place was deserted. Lights gleamed dismally in the half daylight. The dinner-table's bravery of silver and glass mocked his distraught gaze. He searched the lower rooms. No one.

He passed Alec as if he'd been part of the

hall furniture, and went upstairs. Lights burned everywhere. The air was chill but clean. Empty room after empty room greeted him vacantly. Only the last narrow stairs now to the wide attics above.

"Lynneth!"

He sprang up the topmost flight, and crouched beside the crumpled heap of gray velvet.

Her dark head was against the wall, blood stained her face, her soft white neck, the bosom of her dress. The Tiger's Tear had fallen back against her parted lips—gleaming golden bauble.

Wild meaningless phrases shot into his distraught mind. Bits of Ecclesiastes: "The silver cord is loosed . . . the golden bowl—"

He touched her, bent closer. Ah, it was not death after all! Not death. He was all physician now. The healer. Dare he lift her to examine further? That head wound was very deep—blood still welling. His eyes grew cold with fear once more as he explored it. The skull was crushed at one place. How could he move her from that awkward corner? It would be fatal to jolt her wounded head.

He hesitated only a moment. He must do it, of course. He daren't leave her alone in Troon while he got help. And every second counted. If ever he thanked heaven for his strength, it was now. When, with infinite care he'd laid her down at last on a bed in the nearest room on the floor below the attics, he went to the bathroom.

From an elaborately fitted-out medicine chest there, on which Edith had greatly plumed herself, he dug out what he could. Gray dawn brightened to day as he fought to save Lynneth. He used what makeshift medicaments he had. Dark hair he'd cut away was strewn on a pale costly rug beside the bed. The girl's face looked carved from frozen snow beneath its bandages. Her pulse beat ominously beneath his touch.

Her life hung balanced by a thread, and he watched with increasing fear. She must lie undisturbed now for another twenty-four hours at least. There was a slim, a very slim chance of life—no chance at all if she moved.

But there was another night to face—another night at Troon. How could he protect her? What weapons could a man use against the Thing of Darkness? Brooding, pondering, dazed with the terrific strain of the past hours, he sat. A creaking sound startled him.

It was Mrs. Burden. She was coming upstairs. He took her hands, kissed her withered cheek, tears of relief in his eyes at the sight of the old woman's calm face and faithful eyes.

"You're a miracle. No one in the world but you would have come. Now perhaps—"

He poured out in brief hurried whispers what he'd seen and heard last night.

"Servants gone. Kinloch's smashed up. Edith Kinloch's gone. I couldn't look for her. I daren't leave Lynneth alone for a minute in this house."

"Best look now, sir. I'll bide with your lass."

She settled down beside the patient like a little brown bird, watching the unconscious girl, taking in the room with clear thoughtful old eyes.

Doctor Dick went upstairs to begin his search. She heard him coming slowly down at last; heard his heavy breathing as if he carried some awkward weight. He had to pass the open door of the room where she sat. She saw what it was he carried.

Its broken neck revealed what once had been a human face—now a darkened dreadful mask. A few tattered wisps of silk clung to the broken body. Jeweled rings glittered on limp and dusty hands.

Doctor Dick passed on, went into a room near by. When he came in to her again he looked like an old man.

"You saw—it?"

Mrs. Burden nodded solemnly.

"Wait here, sir. Coffee laced with brandy is what you need. We'll talk when you're better, my lamb—sir, I mean—begging your pardon!"

"Wait!" His hoarse voice detained her. "There's Kinloch, poor chap! Help me lift him. I don't think he's seriously hurt.

"There's no way out. We've got to spend this coming night at Troon. The chances are we'll go"—Doctor Dick made a gesture to the bedroom across the landing—"like . . . that!"

"No. Not like that. Whatever comes, not like that. It's true, as you said, 'tis no good letting any other body come inside this place. 'Tis for you and me—this night's work. No one else can help. Even the vicar himself couldn't. 'Tis for you and me. But no one of us will go—the way she did! No. If we have to die, I can take the three of us an easier road than that."

Day faded. Its last gold shone above the distant hills. A gleaming path lay across the water. The gold dimmed, and died. Darkness began to fall. Shadows thickened within the walls of Troon.

Mrs. Burden got up from her chair, beckoned the doctor to the door of Lynneth's room.

"You must leave things to me from this hour on. Keep your door fast bolted inside. Don't open it, not even if you think you hear my own voice call. 'Twould be a trick of old Werne that—to get you out of here. For God's sake, Doctor Dick, heed what I'm telling you. Stay inside until daylight comes. Bide with your lass here, if you want her to live, and want to live yourself."

"If you'd only tell me what you're up to, Mary! It's horrible to shut you out, to leave you alone—with that devilish thing."

"Eh, haven't we talked enough o' that? All the day long you've argued wi' me, Doctor Dick, and I tell you mind's made up. I'm old, too old to fear death. And I know things—things I can't tell you, sir. Bolt the door—and leave it fast till daylight."

Moving with sure unhurried purpose outside the bolted door, Mrs. Burden went to and fro among the shifting looming shadows. She had all prepared. She made no mistake.

There was only one way to shut out a damned soul. The cross itself. A cross of living flesh and blood.

In the wood-frame of the door, outside, four great hooks had been screwed in by Doctor Dick that day. Iron hooks that Mrs. Burden had brought prepared for her purpose, two at the top corners of the cross-piece, and one on ei-

ther side of the door. From these hooks she hung four plaited loops of hair and hempen rope—two long loops from the top, two very short ones on either side.

She stood with back against door and slipped the long right-hand loop beneath her left armpit, and the long left-hand loop beneath her right armpit. Then, supported so that fatigue should not make her fall, she thrust her hands through the small handcuff loops on either side to keep her arms straight out from her body.

So she stood, a small light bird-like figure. Through the big roof-window, glimmering stars and rising moon showed her in the dusk, a human crucifix past which the Thing of Darkness might not go.

Facing Troon and its evil. Frail old body. Staunch old soul.

Daylight. Daylight and Lynneth had passed the crisis! She was safe. Doctor Dick opened the door. The light worn body of Old Mary hung there still.

It was an empty shrine, too old, too tired to survive the night's long vigil and shock of battle—an empty shrine, but not marred, not touched by hurt or evil. The Thing of Darkness had left no shadow in the calm sightless eyes, no lines of terror or dismay on the peaceful worn face; only deep exhaustion. A victor fallen at the goal.

A victor. Yes, Doctor Dick knew that. For long minutes he looked at the frail triumphant figure, assurance of her victory deep in his heart; giving homage to the dead, giving thanks for her divine courage.

His eyes, blinded with tears, lifted to see something else at last. A hulking black-haired man stood against an opposite wall. As the doctor stared, red sunrise dyed the skylight window above, touched the ugly brutal figure with flame.

It shrank, quivered. Its purple lips opened in soundless rage. Its dark bulk glowed like molten metal. White-hot . . . sullen red . . . dissolving . . . writhing . . . twisting in the sun's merciless fire to inhuman appalling decay—to a rag and wisp of a thing—to a shriveled black mummy that grinned in age-old death.

That too dissolved and was split like sand and running through an hourglass. It lay on the jade-green Chinese carpet, a drift of gray dust, last grim symbol of mortality.

The shadow-life that Werne had bargained for was finished. Soul, will, poisonous hate were blotted out. The blackest magic could perpetuate his borrowed existence no longer. The deepest hell could offer no shelter for his furious ghost. Werne—Thing of Darkness—was no more.

But the old house still fronts sea and sky hills. Troon—old Troon. Shell of death. Desolate. Betrayed.

THE HOUSE OF THE NIGHTMARE

Edward Lucas White

IT IS HIS HISTORICAL novels that Edward Lucas White (1866–1934) regarded as his most important work, but he is remembered today for his horror stories, which he claimed came to him in dreams and nightmares. Born in Bergen, New Jersey, he attended Johns Hopkins University in Baltimore and spent the rest of his life in that city, mainly as a teacher at the University School for Boys, where he taught from 1915 to 1930. He wrote a history book, *Why Rome Fell* (1927), in addition to the historical novels *El Supremo: A Romance of the Great Dictator of Paraguay* (1916), *The Unwilling Vestal: A Tale of Rome Under the Caesars* (1918), *Andivius Hedulio: Adventures of a Roman Nobleman in the Days of the Empire* (1921), and *Helen* (1925). His magnum opus was to be a giant utopian science fiction novel, *Plus Ultra,* which he began in 1885, destroyed, and began anew in 1901; at an estimated half-million words, it was never published.

While he wrote enough supernatural and fantasy fiction to fill two volumes, *The Song of the Sirens and Other Stories* (1919) and *Lukundoo and Other Stories* (1927), only two stories are much read today, the present one and "Lukundoo," one of the great classics of horror fiction. In this chilling tale, an African witch doctor casts a curse on an explorer who begins to find his body covered with pustules, which he quickly notices are the heads of tiny African men who viciously gesticulate and threaten him. He cuts off their heads but they relentlessly emerge anew, causing him to kill himself. The author, a longtime sufferer of migraine headaches, also committed suicide, on the seventh anniversary of his wife's death.

"The House of the Nightmare" was originally published in the September 1906 issue of *Smith's Magazine;* it was first collected in *Lukundoo and Other Stories* (New York, Doran, 1927).

The House of the Nightmare

EDWARD LUCAS WHITE

I FIRST CAUGHT SIGHT of the house from the brow of the mountain as I cleared the woods and looked across the broad valley several hundred feet below me, to the low sun sinking toward the far blue hills. From that momentary viewpoint I had an exaggerated sense of looking almost vertically down. I seemed to be hanging over the checker-board of roads and fields, dotted with farm buildings, and felt the familiar deception that I could almost throw a stone upon the house. I barely glimpsed its slate roof.

What caught my eyes was the bit of road in front of it, between the mass of dark-green trees about the house and the orchard opposite. Perfectly straight it was, bordered by an even row of trees, through which I made out a cinder side path and a low stone wall.

Conspicuous on the orchard side between two of the flanking trees was a white object, which I took to be a tall stone, a vertical splinter of one of the tilted lime-stone reefs with which the fields of the region are scarred.

The road itself I saw plain as a box-wood ruler on a green baize table. It gave me a pleasurable anticipation of a chance for a burst of speed. I had been painfully traversing closely forested, semimountainous hills. Not a farmhouse had I passed, only wretched cabins by the road, more than twenty miles of which I had found very bad and hindering. Now, when I was not many miles from my expected stopping-place, I looked forward to better going, and to that straight, level bit in particular.

As I sped cautiously down the sharp beginning of the long descent the trees engulfed me again, and I lost sight of the valley. I dipped into a hollow, rose on the crest of the next hill, and again saw the house, nearer, and not so far below.

The tall stone caught my eye with a shock of surprise. Had I not thought it was opposite the house next the orchard? Clearly it was on the left-hand side of the road toward the house. My self-questioning lasted only the moment as I passed the crest. Then the outlook was cut off again; but I found myself gazing ahead, watching for the next chance at the same view.

At the end of the second hill I only saw the bit of road obliquely and could not be sure, but, as at first, the tall stone seemed on the right of the road.

At the top of the third and last hill I looked down the stretch of road under the over-arching trees, almost as one would look through a tube. There was a line of whiteness which I took for the tall stone. It was on the right.

I dipped into the last hollow. As I mounted the farther slope I kept my eyes on the top of the road ahead of me. When my line of sight sur-

163

mounted the rise I marked the tall stone on my right hand among the serried maples. I leaned over, first on one side, then on the other, to inspect my tyres, then I threw the lever.

As I flew forward, I looked ahead. There was the tall stone—on the left of the road! I was really scared and almost dazed. I meant to stop dead, take a good look at the stone, and make up my mind beyond peradventure whether it was on the right or the left—if not, indeed, in the middle of the road.

In my bewilderment I put on the highest speed. The machine leaped forward; everything I touched went wrong; I steered wildly, slewed to the left, and crashed into a big maple.

When I came to my senses, I was flat on my back in the dry ditch. The last rays of the sun sent shafts of golden-green light through the maple boughs overhead. My first thought was an odd mixture of appreciation of the beauties of nature and disapproval of my own conduct in touring without a companion—a fad I had regretted more than once. Then my mind cleared and I sat up. I felt myself from the head down. I was not bleeding; no bones were broken; and, while much shaken, I had suffered no serious bruises.

Then I saw the boy. He was standing at the edge of the cinderpath, near the ditch. He was so stocky and solidly built; barefoot, with his trousers rolled up to his knees; wore a sort of butternut shirt, open at the throat; and was coatless and hatless. He was tow-headed, with a shock of tousled hair; was much freckled, and had a hideous harelip. He shifted from one foot to the other, twiddled his toes, and said nothing whatever, though he stared at me intently.

I scrambled to my feet and proceeded to survey the wreck. It seemed distressingly complete. It had not blown up, nor even caught fire; but otherwise the ruin appeared hopelessly thorough. Everything I examined seemed worse smashed than the rest. My two hampers, alone, by one of those cynical jokes of chance, had escaped—both had pitched clear of the wreckage and were unhurt, not even a bottle broken.

During my investigations the boy's faded eyes followed me continuously, but he uttered no word. When I had convinced myself of my helplessness I straightened up and addressed him:

"How far is it to a blacksmith's shop?"

"Eight mile," he answered. He had a distressing case of cleft palate and was scarcely intelligible.

"Can you drive me there?" I inquired.

"Nary team on the place," he replied; "nary horse, nary cow."

"How far to the next house?" I continued.

"Six mile," he responded.

I glanced at the sky. The sun had set already. I looked at my watch: it was going—seven thirty-six.

"May I sleep in your house tonight?" I asked.

"You can come in if you want to," he said, "and sleep if you can. House all messy; ma's been dead three year, and dad's away. Nothin' to eat but buckwheat flour and rusty bacon."

"I've plenty to eat," I answered, picking up a hamper. "Just take that hamper, will you?"

"You can come in if you've a mind to," he said, "but you got to carry your own stuff." He did not speak gruffly or rudely, but appeared mildly stating an inoffensive fact.

"All right," I said, picking up the other hamper; "lead the way."

The yard in front of the house was dark under a dozen or more immense ailanthus trees. Below them many smaller trees had grown up, and beneath these a dank underwood of tall, rank suckers out of the deep, shaggy, matted grass. What had once been, apparently, a carriage-drive, left a narrow, curved track, disused and grass-grown, leading to the house. Even here were some shoots of the ailanthus, and the air was unpleasant with the vile smell of the roots and suckers and the insistent odour of their flowers.

The house was of grey stone, with green shutters faded almost as grey as the stone. Along its front was a veranda, not much raised from the ground, and with no balustrade or railing. On it were several hickory splint rockers.

There were eight shuttered windows toward the porch, and midway of them a wide door, with small violet panes on either side of it and a fan-light above.

"Open the door," I said to the boy.

"Open it yourself," he replied, not unpleasantly nor disagreeably, but in such a tone that one could not but take the suggestion as a matter of course.

I put down the two hampers and tried the door. It was latched but not locked, and opened with a rusty grind of its hinges, on which it sagged crazily, scraping the floor as it turned. The passage smelt mouldy and damp. There were several doors on either side; the boy pointed to the first on the right.

"You can have that room," he said.

I opened the door. What with the dusk, the interlacing trees outside, the piazza roof, and the closed shutters, I could make out little.

"Better get a lamp," I said to the boy.

"Nary lamp," he declared cheerfully. "Nary candle. Mostly I get abed before dark."

I returned to the remains of my conveyance. All four of my lamps were merely scrap metal and splintered glass. My lantern was mashed flat. I always, however, carried candles in my valise. This I found split and crushed, but still holding together. I carried it to the porch, opened it, and took out three candles.

Entering the room, where I found the boy standing just where I had left him, I lit the candle. The walls were white-washed, the floor bare. There was a mildewed, chilly smell, but the bed looked freshly made up and clean, although it felt clammy.

With a few drops of its own grease I stuck the candle on the corner of a mean, rickety little bureau. There was nothing else in the room save two rush-bottomed chairs and a small table. I went out on the porch, brought in my valise, and put it on the bed. I raised the sash of each window and pushed open the shutter. Then I asked the boy, who had not moved or spoken, to show me the way to the kitchen. He led me straight through the hall to the back of the house. The kitchen was large, and had no furniture save some pine chairs, a pine bench, and a pine table.

I stuck two candles on opposite corners of the table. There was no stove or range in the kitchen, only a big hearth, the ashes in which smelt and looked a month old. The wood in the woodshed was dry enough, but even it had a cel-lary, stale smell. The axe and hatchet were both rusty and dull, but usable, and I quickly made a big fire. To my amazement, for the mid-June evening was hot and still, the boy, a wry smile on his ugly face, almost leaned over the flame, hands and arms spread out, and fairly roasted himself.

"Are you cold?" I inquired.

"I'm allus cold," he replied, hugging the fire closer than ever, till I thought he must scorch.

I left him toasting himself while I went in search of water. I discovered the pump, which was in working order and not dry on the valves; but I had a furious struggle to fill the two leaky pails I had found. When I had put water to boil I fetched my hampers from the porch.

I brushed the table and set out my meal—cold fowl, cold ham, white and brown bread, olives, jam, and cake. When the can of soup was hot and the coffee made I drew up two chairs to the table and invited the boy to join me.

"I ain't hungry," he said; "I've had supper."

He was a new sort of boy to me; all the boys I knew were hearty eaters and always ready. I had felt hungry myself, but somehow when I came to eat I had little appetite and hardly relished the food. I soon made an end of my meal, covered the fire, blew out the candles, and returned to the porch, where I dropped into one of the hickory rockers to smoke. The boy followed me silently and seated himself on the porch floor, leaning against a pillar, his feet on the grass outside.

"What do you do," I asked, "when your father is away?"

"Just loaf 'round," he said. "Just fool 'round."

"How far off are your nearest neighbours?" I asked.

"Don't no neighbours never come here," he stated. "Say they're afeared of the ghosts."

I was not at all startled; the place had all those aspects which lead to a house being called haunted. I was struck by his odd matter-of-fact way of speaking—it was as if he had said they were afraid of a cross dog.

"Do you ever see any ghosts around here?" I continued.

"Never see 'em," he answered, as if I had mentioned tramps or partridges. "Never hear 'em. Sort o' feel 'em 'round sometimes."

"Are you afraid of them?" I asked.

"Nope," he declared. "I ain't skeered o' ghosts; I'm skeered o' nightmares. Ever have nightmares?"

"Very seldom," I replied.

"I do," he returned. "Allus have the same nightmare—big sow, big as a steer, trying to eat me up. Wake up so skeered I could run to never. Nowheres to run to. Go to sleep, and have it again. Wake up worse skeered than ever. Dad says it's buckwheat cakes in summer."

"You must have teased a sow some time," I said.

"Yep," he answered. "Teased a big sow wunst, holding up one of her pigs by the hind leg. Teased her too long. Fell in the pen and got bit up some. Wisht I hadn't a' teased her. Have that nightmare three times a week sometimes. Worse'n being burnt out. Worse'n ghosts. Say, I sorter feel ghosts around now."

He was not trying to frighten me. He was as simply stating an opinion as if he had spoken of bats or mosquitoes. I made no reply, and found myself listening involuntarily. My pipe went out. I did not really want another, but felt disinclined for bed as yet, and was comfortable where I was, while the smell of the ailanthus blossoms was very disagreeable. I filled my pipe again, lit it, and then, as I puffed, somehow dozed off for a moment.

I awoke with a sensation of some light fabric trailed across my face. The boy's position was unchanged.

"Did you do that?" I asked sharply.

"Ain't done nary thing," he rejoined. "What was it?"

"It was like a piece of mosquito-netting brushed over my face."

"That ain't netting," he asserted; "that's a veil. That's one of the ghosts. Some blow on you; some touch you with their long, cold fingers. That one with the veil she drags acrosst your face—well, mostly I think it's ma."

He spoke with the unassailable conviction of the child in *We Are Seven*. I found no words to reply, and rose to go to bed.

"Good night," I said.

"Good night," he echoed. "I'll sit out here a spell yet."

I lit a match, found the candle I had stuck on the corner of the shabby little bureau, and undressed. The bed had a comfortable husk mattress, and I was soon asleep.

I had the sensation of having slept some time when I had a nightmare—the very nightmare the boy had described. A huge sow, big as a dray horse, was reared up with her forelegs over the foot-board of the bed, trying to scramble over to me. She grunted and puffed, and I felt I was the food she craved. I knew in the dream that it was only a dream, and strove to wake up.

Then the gigantic dream-beast floundered over the foot-board, fell across my shins, and I awoke.

I was in darkness as absolute as if I were sealed in a jet vault, yet the shudder of the nightmare instantly subsided, my nerves quieted; I realised where I was, and felt not the least panic. I turned over and was asleep again almost at once. Then I had a real nightmare, not recognisable as a dream, but appallingly real—an unutterable agony of reasonless horror.

There was a Thing in the room; not a sow, nor any other nameable creature, but a Thing. It was as big as an elephant, filled the room to the ceiling, was shaped like a wild boar, seated on its haunches, with its forelegs braced stiffly in front of it. It had a hot, slobbering, red mouth, full of big tusks, and its jaws worked hungrily. It shuffled and hunched itself forward, inch by inch, till its vast forelegs straddled the bed.

The bed crushed up like wet blotting-paper, and I felt the weight of the Thing on my feet, on my legs, on my body, on my chest. It was hungry, and I was what it was hungry for, and it meant to begin on my face. Its dripping mouth was nearer and nearer.

Then the dream-helplessness that made me unable to call or move suddenly gave way, and I yelled and awoke. This time my terror was positive and not to be shaken off.

It was near dawn: I could descry dimly the cracked, dirty window-panes. I got up, lit the stump of my candle and two fresh ones, dressed hastily, strapped my ruined valise, and put it on the porch against the wall near the door. Then I called the boy. I realised quite suddenly that I had not told him my name or asked his.

I shouted, "Hello!" a few times, but won no answer. I had had enough of that house. I was still permeated with the panic of the nightmare. I desisted from shouting, made no search, but with two candles went out to the kitchen. I took a swallow of cold coffee and munched a biscuit as I hustled my belongings into my hampers. Then, leaving a silver dollar on the table, I carried the hampers out on the porch and dumped them by my valise.

It was now light enough to see the walk, and I went out to the road. Already the night-dew had rusted much of the wreck, making it look more hopeless than before. It was, however, entirely undisturbed. There was not so much as a wheel-track or a hoof-print on the road. The tall, white stone, uncertainty about which had caused my disaster, stood like a sentinel opposite where I had upset.

I set out to find that blacksmith shop. Before I had gone far the sun rose clear from the horizon, and was almost at once scorching. As I footed it along I grew very much heated, and it seemed more like ten miles than six before I reached the first house. It was a new frame house, neatly painted and close to the road, with a whitewashed fence along its garden front.

I was about to open the gate when a big black dog with a curly tail bounded out of the bushes. He did not bark but stood inside the gate wagging his tail and regarding me with a friendly eye; yet I hesitated with my hand on the latch and considered. The dog might not be as friendly as he looked, and the sight of him made me realise that except for the boy I had seen no creature about the house where I had spent the night; no dog or cat; not even a toad or bird. While I was ruminating upon this a man came from behind the house.

"Will your dog bite?" I asked.

"Naw," he answered; "he don't bite. Come in."

I told him I had had an accident to my automobile, and asked if he could drive me to the blacksmith shop and back to my wreckage.

"Cert," he said. "Happy to help you. I'll hitch up foreshortly. Wher'd you smash?"

"In front of the grey house about six miles back," I answered.

"That big stone-built house?" he queried.

"The same," I assented.

"Did you go a-past here?" he inquired astonished. "I didn't hear ye."

"No," I said; "I came from the other direction."

"Why," he meditated, "you must'a' smashed about sun-up. Did you come over them mountains in the dark?"

"No," I replied; "I came over them yesterday evening. I smashed up about sunset."

"Sundown!" he exclaimed. "Where in thunder've ye been all night?"

"I slept in the house where I broke down."

"In that big stone-built house in the trees?" he demanded.

"Yes," I agreed.

"Why," he answered excitedly, "that there house is haunted! They say if you have to drive past it after dark, you can't tell which side of the road the big white stone is on."

"I couldn't tell even before sunset," I said.

"There!" he exclaimed. "Look at that, now! And you slep' in that house! Did you sleep, honest?"

"I slept pretty well," I said. "Except for a nightmare, I slept all night."

"Well," he commented, "I wouldn't go in that there house for a farm, nor sleep in it for my salvation. And you slep'! How in thunder did you get in?"

"The boy took me in," I said.

"What sort of boy?" he queried, his eyes fixed on me with a queer, countrified look of absorbed interest.

"A thick-set, freckle-faced boy with a harelip," I said.

"Talk like his mouth was full of mush?" he demanded.

"Yes," I said; "bad case of cleft palate."

"Well!" he exclaimed. "I never did believe in ghosts, and I never did half believe that house was haunted, but I know it now. And you slep'!"

"I didn't see any ghosts," I retorted irritably.

"You seen a ghost for sure," he rejoined solemnly. "That there harelip boy's been dead six months."

Hector Bolitho

A BIOGRAPHER OF THE British royal family for decades, (Henry) Hector Bolitho (1898–1974) was born in Auckland, New Zealand, and settled in England in 1922. He traveled extensively to every part of the world, including the Antipodes at twenty-one with the Prince of Wales (later the Duke of Windsor), and claimed to prefer America to all the rest "because the people are honest and comparatively true." He served in the military in both world wars, on the home front in New Zealand at eighteen and later with the Royal Air Force Volunteer Reserve as an intelligence officer. He began his writing career as a journalist at seventeen, produced his first novel at twenty-five, and went on to write more than thirty volumes as a sort of unofficial biographer and historian of the royal family. His biography of Queen Victoria's husband, *Albert the Good and the Victorian Reign* (1932) is regarded as one of the greatest of all works about the royal family. He also edited the letters of Queen Victoria and Prince Albert.

Bolitho once publicly declared that he was free of ambition and content to be a second-rate writer because he found *life* to be far more interesting than anything he could create with his pen. His early fiction took the form of historical adventure novels and short stories, few of which are remembered today.

"The House in Half Moon Street" was first published in his collection *The House in Half Moon Street* (London, Cobden-Sanderson, 1935).

The House in Half Moon Street

HECTOR BOLITHO

I

Michael Stranger was born on Christmas Day, in a small, half-timbered house called *The Hollies*, on the outskirts of the town of Reading. There is no record of his birth in the parish register, but it seems, when we read his uncle Benjamin's letters and from his own diaries, that Michael was born in the early 'teens of the nineteenth century. Among the papers which were found in his room after his death was a water-colour drawing of *The Hollies*.

The lattice windows of the house opened upon a lawn and standing upon the grass were two yew trees, trimmed into the shape of peacocks. In the little drawing, which is still kept among Michael Stranger's papers, the peacocks stare at each other across a flagged path.

In summer, the windows of the house were open so that the muslin curtains blew out, fluttering for a moment against the glass, until they were caught on the hollyhocks. The scents of rose and clover came in from the white orchard where Michael played jungle games in the grass. When he was no more than five years old, the cool green arches under the apple trees had been haunted by lions and tigers of his own invention. Sometimes he would be tired of stalking the elephant which was, in truth, a wheelbarrow: then he would lie in the long grass, digging his teeth into an apple and dreaming of the broad and exciting world which existed beyond the horizon of the Berkshire fields.

Michael's dream of jungles was confused with the stories which were told to him of his wonderful uncle who lived in London. He knew that his uncle lived in Half Moon Street and he imagined him fighting his way into Piccadilly, over the dead bodies of the lions he had killed. There was never a whole apple lying in the grass of *The Hollies* orchard. Even if the birds had pecked them or if the wasps had burrowed into them, the apples were crisp and sweet. When he had taken one big bite, he would throw the apple at the shrill-voiced turkey gobblers who screeched and flaunted their dusty tails on the low brick wall. Michael Stranger spoke of these happy days of his childhood many times in the later years, when he came to live in London.

When he was almost twenty-one, on a day when the scents had died from the garden and when the two yew peacocks wore bonnets and capes of snow, Michael's sister asked him to come to her sitting-room. He had expected some unusual announcement when he saw her dress, a precious, rustling, black silk, with big sleeves and bands of black velvet ribbon laced across the bodice. There was a stiff, surprised bow of ribbon in her hair: a bow which never appeared except for a birth, a wedding, or a great occasion.

Michael sat on the edge of the chair, looking out at the yew peacocks now becoming whiter and whiter under the snow. He thought that they were like his sister, on the cold days when she wore her white shawl. She opened a folded letter: her spiky fingers held the broad black edges of the paper. "I have received a letter from your uncle Benjamin," she said. "It concerns you, Michael, and the unhappy time when you must leave me and go out into the world. I shall read it to you!"

Half Moon Street,
London,
October 26th.

Dear Niece,

The time has now come when we must consider the future life of your brother, Master Michael, or Mister Michael as he will no doubt wish to be named, since his years must now number one and twenty. My own years now number seventy-two, so it is all the more an urgent matter that I should see him established in my Counting House according to his merits, before I pass hence, to join my lamented wife and your noble aunt Florence in that Blessed Land where she awaits me. As you know, my dear niece, I live the life of a lonely widower in my house here, proceeding to my office in Mincing Lane upon most days, when the weather and my gout permit of my making the journey. My gout gives me monstrous pain and obliges me to remain in my rooms upon days when the weather is inclement. In the evening, I repair to the solitude of my dinner and my hearth, having permitted no visitor since the death of your aunt and the beginning of my own desolate life as a widower. It will therefore be most suitable for your brother Michael to live in bachelor's chambers which I shall engage for him in Jermyn Street, a fashionable and respectable vicinity, where he will be near enough to take luncheon with me on Sundays, after Church, which I trust he will attend with me when the weather allows of my attempting the outing. He will also dine with me upon one night each week, when I may aid him with the religious and moral guidance, together with advice in commerce and social manners, which will be indispensable to a young country boy embarking for the first time upon life in London. The rent for his chambers will be paid each quarter by my clerk and he will receive a remuneration which will permit his enjoyment of the comforts and amenities of a young Christian gentleman, at the same time obliging him to observe those economies which are a defense against extravagance, loose living, and lounging in coffee-houses, from which I hear many stories of peril to the young.

It will be pleasant and suitable that he should arrive in London to eat Christmas dinner with me, on the twenty-fifth day of December. I observe by a memorandum sent to me this day that the coach from your part of Berkshire arrives in Kensington on the evening of December 24th, one day before I shall require his presence at dinner, as I shall myself be engaged at Bath upon that day, in matters relating to the estate of my late partner. Master Michael's room in Jermyn Street cannot be made ready for him until the following day as a gentleman lately returned from the Indies will still be in possession. I shall therefore arrange for his reception for one night at the Goat and Compasses Inn, Kensington, wherein my old butler and his Kentish wife are established and where the young gentleman will come to no harm nor be faced by aught of temptation.

I see, in the miniature which you sent me, a likeness between the boy and my lamented wife, his aunt Florence, and if his moral character and talents are a tithe of those with which she was so liberally endowed, I shall be happy in the opportunity of his acquaintance. If you concur with these prospects for the future of your brother, I would ask him to address me in his own hand and thus embark upon that relationship and confidence which I hope to awaken in his young heart.

I am,
Your affectionate uncle and obedient servant,
Benjamin Grinling.

The snow fell softly as Michael listened to his sister's voice. The flakes tumbled from the backs of the yew peacocks like moulting feathers. He, Michael Stranger, was to live in London! He was to live in his own rooms, near to his wonderful uncle, who worked in offices in Mincing Lane, where he dealt in tea and spices and cloves and ginger, brought from the far-away places of the world. He would travel to London by the coach which swung down the Thames Valley, from Reading to Maidenhead and from Maidenhead to London. In the days that followed, Michael read his uncle's letter many times, thinking out the words of his answer, which was to open the way to the first adventure of his life. After much scratching upon the sheets of paper, and moulding of phrases, many questions to his sister's knowledge and frowning over the words he used, Michael dispatched an answer to his uncle's letter.

The Hollies,
Three miles from Reading,
November 3rd.

My dear Uncle Grinling,
My sister has read me your letter and I have read it myself also, many times, so as to be fully aware of its contents and import before embarking upon the happy task of penning you my answer. I am grateful beyond earthly measure for the opportunities and good fortune you offer me and I shall be obedient to your wishes in proceeding from Reading to London by the coach which will bring me to the Goat and Compasses Inn, upon the night of December the twenty-fourth. There I shall await your orders and wishes. My sister instructs me to say that my wardrobe is sparse, being that of a young man accustomed to country pursuits, but she wishes me to acquaint you with the fact that I shall travel to London with the sum of twenty pounds sterling, which she has saved for the purpose of my equipment in whatever manner you may direct. I trust, dear uncle, that I shall merit the honour put upon me and the trust you demonstrate in so admitting me to your Counting House. I shall endeavour to

earn the kindness so generously expressed in your letter.

With my duty to you, Sir,

I beg to remain,
Your affectionate nephew and humble servant,
Michael Joseph Stranger,
Aged twenty-one years.

November passed and December came. The little tailor came out from Reading, with his pins and his chalk, to make a plum-coloured coat for Michael, and a waistcoat, upon which his father's cut steel buttons were sewn. On the morning of Christmas Eve, Michael stood at the door of the house, watching the servant walk down through the snow, carrying his carpet bag and his hat-box.

His sister came to him then. The gaunt woman softened a little as she led him to the sitting-room to say good-bye. Beside the window was a glass-topped table which Michael had always known but had never dared to open. In it were a hundred treasures, lying on a bed of faded blue velvet. There was a little silver watering-can, and a gilt carriage, on wheels. When he was very young, Michael had wondered whether the wheels would move if he touched them: but he had never dared to lift the lid and learn for himself. There were two of his father's medals and a lock of his mother's hair, arranged in a gold locket, in the shape of a flower. There were three seals, a coin salvaged from a wreck, a model of St. Peter's in ivory, four rings, and some small *papier mâché* boxes. His sister opened the top of the table and lifted a tortoise-shell snuff box and a cornelian, set in a ring, from the bed of velvet. They had belonged to Michael's father.

"You will take these, Michael, because he intended that you should have them. Our father used this snuff box to the end of his life and the cornelian ring was upon his hand when he died."

The ring was too big for Michael's finger, so his sister wrapped some cotton around the heavy gold shaft, tying the ends into a neat knot. Michael's mouth fumbled with the hard edge of her cheek, in a shy attempt to kiss her. Then he too walked down the white path, towards the gate.

Within half-an-hour the high coach was rolling on towards Maidenhead and London. Michael pressed his feet against his carpet bag and he closed his hand so that the cotton could not be seen upon the ring. He sat, stiff and nervous, watching the occasional stretches of the river, the rafts of ice floating down, and, in one place, a perplexed swan beating her white wings upon a frozen pond. The trees were white and the earth was hard and silent.

The coach passed through Maidenhead and came to a fork in the road. The old man sitting next to Michael pointed to the grey outline of the castle on the hill at Windsor. "They say the King's pet giraffe died not so very long ago, and that he was as unhappy about it as if it had been his own Royal lady," said the stranger.

"A giraffe, the King's giraffe?"

"Aye, the King's giraffe; it's lived at the castle these many months, and its dying has broken His Majesty's heart, they say. A great funeral it had, and it was buried in the castle garden. A ghost walks there, they say, but the King is no ghost. They tell me he's so fat that the leeches have to bleed him before his Christmas dinner."

Michael Stranger opened his eyes a little wider. Rumours of the ways of kings seldom drifted as far as *The Hollies.* Surely, now, he was coming into the great world. The lash of the whip danced in the air; they passed an inn where Dick Turpin used to sleep and the stranger told him a story of the highwaymen at Hounslow. Late in the day, the coach came to the outskirts of Kensington.

Kensington and Westminster were still parted by a greensward: only a few years before there had been a turnpike at Hyde Park Corner. Indeed, the little stretch of open country had been so treacherous in Benjamin Grinling's boyhood that when he crossed it, he always walked in the middle of the road, peering hard at the shadows which might spring to life and become footpads in hiding.

Michael went to the inn to which his uncle had directed him: he walked shyly through the taproom and asked for his bedroom. The wife of his uncle's old butler, a heavy-hipped woman from Kent, brought him his food: slices of beef with potatoes and cucumber and then plum pudding. She stayed with him for a little while, talking of the old days when her husband served Benjamin Grinling. "And you've never even seen your uncle! Well, indeed! He's a fine gentleman, sir, is Mr. Grinling, a fine gentleman. A quiet gentleman, mind you sir, but very kind."

As she stood before him, she rested one swollen red hand on her breast, and with the other, she pointed out of the window. "If you lean far out, sir, you'll see Kensington Palace," she said. "There's little to see at this time of the year, for the gentry shut themselves up in the winter, like bugs in a rug. Or they are off to their fine houses in the country. All except your uncle, sir, and he's such a solitary gentleman. But when the spring comes, it's all flowers and you will see the young Princess Victoria: she's the daughter of the Duke of Kent that died from getting his feet wet, you know. I have seen her many a day, with her big hat, toddling with two of the biggest footmen you ever saw. Some days I used to see them lift her on to a donkey by the Round Pond, and there is an old man following her always. They say he worships the very ground she walks on. A busy young person, they say, playing the piano and making paint pictures. She's pretty as a rose, and I've seen her toddling down the path with a watering can in her hand, and sitting on the terrace in the summer mornings, with her mother, eating her bread and milk."

"And is she a *great* Princess?" asked Michael Stranger.

"Great, maybe. The King's her uncle, and it isn't all of us whose uncles are kings. But I'm not complaining. And there are noises downstairs as if somebody's come and wanting something, so if you'll bang the stick three times on the floor when you've finished, I'll be up to bring you your pudding."

She waddled out of the room and later, through the darkness which had come, Michael went down into the taproom and asked for a glass of Madeira, which was the only wine he had known in his sister's house.

The taproom was filled with happy, noisy people and with Christmas as their excuse for merry-making, they mixed hot punch and called on Michael to drink with them. He held the glass in his hand and slowly sipped the punch. Alarmed by the drowsiness and contentment which came over him, he walked out into the cold air of Kensington. The road was white and a few late robins, frightened from the trees, shook their wings and scattered the snow into showers. Bells were ringing, and the window of a big house was open so that Michael could see people dancing within. A tall man came out on to the balcony, a slim, dark form against the inner brillance of chandeliers and gilt. He threw coins down to some children who were singing in the street. Michael walked past them.

"A merry Christmas to you, stranger," somebody called, from a doorstep.

"A merry Christmas, sir," Michael answered.

He walked on until he came to a big, dark building set back in a park. There must have been fifty windows, sleepy, dark windows, with the curtains drawn. He stood before the park railings for a long time, so long that the night-watchman passed him twice and peered into his face.

"Is that Kensington Palace?" he asked.

"It is," the watchman answered.

They stood together in the snow, and as they talked, more bells rang, more and more bells, so that the cold air was alive with them. It was so dark now that all the robins had gone to sleep. As Michael looked up to the dark palace, one window—two windows—suddenly became alive with light. "There must be somebody there," Michael said to the watchman.

"*Somebody!* Why don't you know what *that* is?" asked the night-watchman. "Lor, you must be a country bumpkin. That's the room where the young Princess sleeps."

"Princess Victoria? That's the one the woman at the inn where I'm staying, told me about."

"Yes," answered the watchman. "I've heard tell—of course you never know about these things, because in my line of profession, you hear a tidy bit of gossip—I've heard tell that some day, when she grows up, that self-same Princess may be made Queen of England."

II

Michael's uncle lived in Half Moon Street. Benjamin Grinling's origin was a mystery, even to the family into which he had married. The frowns of doubt had been smoothed away when he married Michael's aunt Florence: the shadow over his origin had been forgotten when the rich comforts of his house in Half Moon Street were revealed. Room upon room, paintings by Canaletto in the drawing-room, curtains so thick and rich that they hung in sumptuous curves, resting their hems upon Aubusson carpets and rare Persian rugs, which Grinling had brought with him from the East.

His fair wife had shone in the dark house in Half Moon Street for little more than a year. She had been unhappy in the noisy gloom and had pined for the open fields about her old home in Reading. The red stains upon her cheeks had become sharper as the first London winter pressed in upon her, and one dull, grey December day, she had died in Benjamin's arms, her golden hair tumbling about his hands as he held her. For seventeen years Benjamin Grinling had lived alone in the beautiful Queen Anne house, venturing out every day to his warehouse in Mincing Lane, and returning every evening to his lonely dinner, his glass of port, and the silent hour beside the fire, when he read books about the countries he had visited as a younger man. He was a cultivated and a travelled gentleman. He had seen the Great Wall of China and he had ridden all the way from Jerusalem to Jericho on a donkey so that he could bathe in the Dead Sea. He had clapped his hands in the echo room in the palace in Würzburg and he had seen the chattering apes climbing up the rocky slopes of Gibraltar. Dim prints upon the walls and books bound in dark brown leather were all that he possessed now to awaken pictures of the more sprightly days . . . they alone could make his thoughts stray from the limited rooms of his house, into the greater spaces of the world which he had known when he was a boy.

A little of the old spring came into Benjamin Grinling's walk upon this Christmas morning, when he set out to drive across the green from Piccadilly to Kensington, to meet his nephew from Reading. He had engaged chambers for the boy in Jermyn Street. A faint suggestion in an earlier letter from his niece, that Michael might perhaps be allowed to live with his uncle, in Half Moon Street, had so frightened the old gentleman that he wondered now if even Jermyn Street were not a little too near. By this time, Benjamin Grinling has become jealous of his loneliness and alarmed by any attempt to intrude upon it. No visitors ever crossed the threshold of the house in Half Moon Street: indeed, the only caller in ten years who was admitted to enter beyond the hall was his old and trusted clerk. Five years before on Michael's sixteenth birthday, Benjamin's niece had sent him a miniature of the boy. And there had been a silhouette, but by an itinerant artist who had passed through Reading in 1816. Benjamin Grinling had observed them, seeking the face of his beloved wife in the likeness. Then he had put them away in a drawer to wait until the day when he could see his nephew in the flesh.

Benjamin Grinling's carriage moved out into the wider space of Piccadilly. Hyde Park Corner was a white field . . . it might have been a country green, with its snow men and its urchins, and the last carts making their way home, with berries and torn holly leaves in the cracks between their floor boards.

When the carriage stopped before the Goat and Compasses Inn, Benjamin Grinling did not move from beneath his rug. Michael was brought out to him, and, with his carpet bag and his hat-box, he was packed in and driven to his uncle's house. His wide brown eyes opened in wonder. The houses of Piccadilly were so high that their chimneys seemed to touch the sky.

Benjamin Grinling sat back. Shyness tied the old man's tongue, but he turned again and again and watched the face of the boy beside him. There *was* a likeness which startled and pained him. He saw Michael's long lashes and his country-coloured cheeks. He saw his heavy hands and the cornelian. He saw the roughly made clothes, the meagre carpet bag and the hat-box in which Michael's belongings were packed. To himself, Benjamin Grinling said, "His face is like that of my beloved Flossie. But he is a raw fellow. Yet I shall make him into a gentleman. Good clothes and good food will drain the yokel out of him."

Michael Stranger's feelings did not assume the form of words. He turned his ring round upon his finger, hiding the cotton with his left hand. He leaned forward upon the edge of the seat, with the shy self-consciousness of one who has never driven in a sumptuous carriage before. When he came to his uncle's house in Half Moon Street, when the servant took his hat and his coat and opened the door of the sitting-room, Michael was amazed. He walked on tip-toes.

The furniture in the room made it seem like the cemetery of the old man's happiness. Upon a table was the box of ivory spillikins which Benjamin had bought for *her* in Paris. Above this hung a painting of the Doge's Palace by Canaletto, as they had seen it together when they came into Venice from the sea. The picture glowed with gold-pink light. Behind the sofa was a Chippendale fire-screen, its embroidered basket of flowers incomplete, with the needle and the strand of green silk, just as Florence Grinling had left them. The realisation that Michael was her nephew and of the same blood, teased Benjamin's memory and awakened a picture of her moving across the room in a heliotrope silk dress. Once, he remembered, she had come down to dinner and she had stood upon the polar bear rug. They had been married only four weeks then, but his love for her had already reached fullness and quiet. He had been sitting by the fire when he heard the rustle of her dress. He had looked up and had seen her with her heliotrope skirt billowing upon the white fur rug.

"Dear Flossie," he had said, "you look just like an autumn crocus blossoming in the snow."

She had laughed as she said: "But, my dear, my dress is heliotrope and an autumn crocus is saffron. And autumn crocuses do *not* bloom in the snow, Benjamin. Oh yes, and I am *sure* that they are saffron."

"Then it's the light," he had answered.

"But it's very poetical of you," she had said, coming over to him from her raft of white fur, and resting her hands upon his coat. "Very poetical!"

It was their first foolish little joke. "Oh, you remember the night when you were poetical?" Florence would say, and they would laugh, neither Heaven nor themselves knowing why.

When she died, the emptiness of the white rug hurt Benjamin so much that he removed it. Once, ten years afterwards, when he went to the Wolfgangsee and saw the late crocuses, he had gone back to his room and cried like a child.

Benjamin Grinling touched his nephew's arm and led him to the fire. The servant came in with a tray, two glasses and a decanter of sherry wine. Benjamin filled the glasses and lifting his own, he smiled at his nephew and said, "You have the look of your aunt in your eyes, my boy, and for this alone you are endeared to me. You must not be afraid of me, nephew. Give me your arm and let us stand thus before the fire, where *she* used to stand. We are going to be great friends . . . yes, we are going to be great friends."

III

At nine o'clock Michael walked out of his uncle's house, into the snow. He had dined well: his tongue had been loosened and his misgivings dispelled by his share of a bottle of burgundy and a decanter of port. Half Moon Street was a floor of snow, walled in by the dark houses. They shielded the snow from light and sound. His uncle's servant had walked ahead with Michael's traps, so he was free to swing his arms as he passed the dark doorways, his feet sinking four inches into the snow, his breath making a turbulent cloud in the milky grey light.

As Michael came near to Piccadilly, he saw an open door and a wedge of light coming from inside, making a gold-white path across the pavement. When he came to the light, he paused to observe the inner, warm scene of furniture, stairs, and carpet. As he became used to the outer silence, his ears were sensitive enough to hear sounds within the house. They seemed to come from the first room, the door of which opened into the hall, which he could see. The sounds of human movements stopped; Michael heard somebody screaming and then groaning. The groans ended in a thud. Michael walked into the house. He paused when his feet touched the carpet, but he heard the groans again and he walked nearer to the door of the room. As he passed the table in the hall, he saw a big print upon the wall. It bore the title *Coronation of Queen Victoria, 1839.*

In the second during which he peered at it, in passing, Michael thought this strange, for the year in which he lived was 1832 and he knew that Princess Victoria was still a child, walking in the gardens of Kensington Palace. Three paces more and he stood before the open door of the sitting-room. The scene astounded him. The snow fell in the street, but here, in the house, the room was full of sunshine. Hyacinths and daffodils were in bronze urns, upon the tables. Lying upon the floor was a woman in a light summer dress, and bent over her was a man, pressing his thumbs viciously into her throat. The woman's head was turned towards the door, and her white face was framed in a tangle of red-gold hair. Her hands had clutched the green rug so that it was drawn up about her body. As Michael watched her, she released the rug and it fell back from her hands. Then the white fingers lay still and limp among the scattered primroses and snowdrops which had fallen from a broken vase. The man weakened his hold upon the woman's throat and then he stood erect.

The sunshine made every object in the room alive with light. The furniture was of a fashion unknown to Michael. There were bunches of stiff flowers beneath glass shades, lace mats upon the chairs and dyed pampas grass in the grate, for, despite the winter outside, the room was warm and there was no fire.

The man was still unaware of Michael's presence. Michael saw him take the hyacinths and daffodils from the vases and scatter them over the girl's body: he saw him scatter the white snowdrops upon her red-golden hair.

Michael sped out of the house, into the street. The wedge of light still made a pathway across the snow. He turned and ran down towards Piccadilly. The wide white expanse was scored by carriages and befouled by the feet of the pedestrians. But all had gone now: the street was dead and there was no night-watchman. Piccadilly seemed to yawn with emptiness. Michael turned and ran up the street again, towards his uncle's house. His hands were already raised, to beat wildly upon the door for help. There were eight houses between the corner stone and the house from which he had seen the wedge of light. When he was twelve yards away, the light disappeared from the snow. He came to the door and found that it was closed. Upon the upper panel was the number. The darkness of the windows was deepened by the shutters, which were closed. Michael leaned against the railings, his face held forward, towards the black velvet shadow of the lower window. It was the window of the room which he had seen two minutes before, filled with sunshine and spring flowers. He walked back a few paces to the steps. Upon the railings, he saw the outline of a board. He knelt down in the snow, and, by holding his face near enough, with the aid of the faint moonlight and the reflection of the snow, he deciphered the words *For Sale.*

Ashamed and bewildered, Michael walked down the street again. The picture of the room tumbled and changed in his brain. As he trudged on, the snow growing thicker and thicker upon his heels and then falling off again, he forced his memory back to every detail of the furniture and the white face upon the carpet. He crossed Piccadilly and then he turned down St. James's Street. By this time, his uncle's servant had come back and, walking beside him, the man guided him to Jermyn Street. Incredulity and the fear of seeming ridiculous made Michael hold his tongue, but he asked the man if any of the houses in Half Moon Street were unused. "Oh, no, sir, but most people are away in their country houses this time of the year, you know, so the shutters is up and they seem to be empty, sir."

"And are none of the houses for sale?" Michael asked.

"Not that I know of, sir," he answered. "Except of course, sir, the cursed house."

"The cursed house! Which one is that?"

"Well, sir, it's half way between Mr. Grinling's house and the corner of Piccadilly. I don't know the story, sir, but some says that unhappiness comes to whoever lives there. It's been empty for a long time. There's a *For Sale* board upon the railings . . . you might notice it, sir, if ever you chanced to look in the daytime. But I suppose these stories spread because nobody's ever lived there in all the years I have been with Mr. Grinling, and that's eight years coming Whitsuntide, sir."

Michael and the servant had come to the corner of Jermyn Street. The dark form of St. James's Palace loomed up against the low sky line. From the corner opposite, the sound of voices and hammering came to them. "Goings on at Brooks's, sir, being Christmas. They are unscrewing the knocker from their neighbour's house. It's a custom, sir, with the gentry."

Jermyn Street was narrow and dark. They came to Michael's chambers where he was given two rooms on the second floor. The servant had already unpacked his carpet bag and his nightshirt was warming upon the fire guard. A brass can of hot water, shrouded in a towel, stood upon the washing stand. Michael prepared for bed, undressing, washing, pushing his head through the neck of his white flannel nightshirt, half conscious of his own movements. For a moment or two it seemed that the scene of the spring flowers and the murderous man belonged to a story he had read. Or to a picture upon the wall. He stood warming his toes before the fire, his hands upon the mantelpiece. The clock before him caught the light of the fire. One hand covered the other: they pointed to twelve o'clock. The twelve muted bells sounded from within the black marble body and announced the end of his first day in London.

Michael went over to the bed and took up the lighted candle from the table near by. He walked about the room, lifting the flame to each picture. One was a coloured print, named *The Buck's Toilet*. Five servants attended a figure sitting upon a chair. A man in striped trousers read from a book, before the fire. Then there was a print called *A Quadrille at Almack's*, showing twenty or more people dancing within an ornate room. Beside the bed was another picture called *A Forced Entry by Broker's Men*, showing still another self-indulgent Buck sitting upon a chair. But in this picture, four miscreants had invaded the fellow's room and his lady was in a swoon beside the fire. Michael tried to believe that these prints were windows to his new life. He tried to peer past the lattice casement of the house in Reading and to see something more than the two yew peacocks upon the lawn. He wondered if ever he too would become a dandy and, sitting upon a chair, have his stockings brought by one servant and his shoes by another while a scented, crimped barber dressed his hair. Michael went to bed. He snuffed the candle and when his eyes were accustomed to the dark, he watched the big, blue-grey square of the window light. For an hour he lay awake, building up the picture in the house in Half Moon Street. At moments the scene was not more than phantasy. Then it became so real that the scent of the spring flowers was sweet in his nostrils, here in his London room. Through all the pictures tumbling in his brain, the face of the girl persisted, still and white. Contemplating it, he at last turned upon his pillow and went to sleep.

IV

In the weeks which followed Christmas, Michael came to know his uncle as his friend. The older man withheld the moral lectures and advice which he had promised his nephew. They walked together on Sundays and they ate together one night each week. Michael once cajoled his uncle into dining early so that they could go to the Theatre Royal, in Drury Lane. Among the wonders of the entertainment was the appearance of Mr. Wilson, who rode a cycle along a tight rope, stretched between the edge of the stage and the dress circle. Another novelty was the representation of Niagara Falls, in a grand panorama, with lighting and mechanical effects "so devised as to give a realistic impression of the noble spectacle." Benjamin Grinling had seen Niagara Falls during his visit to America in 1806, and when the old man and his nephew returned to Half Moon Street at the end of the entertainment, Benjamin surprised his servant by pressing Michael to stay for yet another hour, to drink a bottle of wine and to see the album of fine prints which he had collected when abroad upon his American journey. In this way their friendship ripened. After luncheon at Half Moon Street on Sundays, uncle and nephew would walk towards the fresh air and open grassland of Edgeware Road, or towards the river. One Sunday, Benjamin Grinling waited upon Carlton House Terrace for almost an hour while his more agile nephew climbed the staircase within the pillar which had been erected in memory of the Duke of York. The old man had bent his head back, watching the bronze figure with its spiked lightning conductors, apparently swaying against the blue sky; he was anxious lest Michael should come to harm in his foolhardiness. There were journeys to Hampton Court, to see the long lines of trees which King William had planted, and excursions to Roehampton and Kew. In all these adventures, Michael joined eagerly in his uncle's wish for reminiscence and talk. But, behind the pictures which passed through his brain, pictures of the past and of the present, there remained with him the face of the fair victim in the house in Half Moon Street. Whether ghost or illusion, the face was as clear to Michael as the reflection of his own features in the

looking glass. Haunted thus by his experience, Michael at last decided to share his secret with his uncle. He chose the moment with care, for Benjamin Grinling was a man of sense, prone to neither visions nor dreams. He pooh-poohed Michael's tale and when the boy had gone, he charged his servant to be more tardy in pouring wine into the boy's glass during dinner.

V

In his thirtieth year, Michael had lost all the gaucherie of his simple life in Reading: indeed, he was something of a *beau* by this time, frequenting a merchant's club, to which he had been elected through his uncle's encouragement. In the beginning, he had been without friends, looking wistfully through the windows of London at the lights and signs of happiness within. He would sit alone of an evening, ill at ease in his new, fashionable clothes, or he would repair to his room. Here, before the fire, he would take his letter case upon his knee and write to his sister; sometimes a record of his work in his uncle's counting house; sometimes a sad story of his loneliness. Once he wrote to his sister:

> *In London anything may be had for money; and one thing may be had there in perfection without it. That one thing is solitude. Take up your abode in the deepest glen or on the wildest heath, in the remotest province of the kingdom, where the din of commerce is not heard and where the wheels of pleasure make no trace, even there humanity will find you, and sympathy, under some of its varied aspects, will creep beneath the humble roof. Travellers' curiosity will be excited to gaze upon the recluse, or the village pastor will come to offer his religious consolation to the heart-chilled solitary, or some kind spinster who is good to the poor, will proffer her kindly aid in medicine for sickness, or in some shape of relief for poverty. But in the mighty metropolis, where myriads*

*of human hearts are throbbing—where all
that is busy in commerce, all that is elegant in
manners, all that is mighty in power, all that
is dazzling in splendour, all that is brilliant
in genius, all that is benevolent in feeling, is
congregated together—there the solitary may
feel the depth of solitude. From morn to night
he may pensively pace the streets, the world
may be busy and cheerful and noisy around
him, but no sympathy shall reach him.*

Michael's first months in London were spent
in lounging in the coffee rooms for his amusement. He was bewildered by the throbbing life
of the great city, carriages, the tumult of the
streets and the big houses. His loneliness passed
in time, for he met the rich merchants in his
uncle's counting house. He was bidden to dine
in the new houses which were covering the once
open fields and swards.

Michael had eaten his luncheon with his
uncle on the day of Queen Victoria's Coronation. The old man was now so feeble that he
observed Michael and his life with dim, lethar-
gic eyes. For an hour or two each day, he was
brought down to the sitting-room, his gnarled,
shaking hands grasping two ivory-topped sticks,
his mumbling voice recalling scenes of his life in
such confusion that his servant no longer com-
prehended what he said. For the most part, he
lay in his bed, muttering a story about an autumn when the crocuses bloomed in the snow.
He was helpless now as a child.

On the morning of the Coronation, a fine
June morning, when there was neither rain nor
heat to mar London's happiness, Michael walked
from his rooms through the decorated streets, to
call upon his uncle. On the way up St. James's
Street, where he always paused to see the hats
and the tobacco jars, the pictures and the silver
trophies in the windows of the shops, he came
upon an especially grand display in a print-
seller's window. The shop was decorated with
flags and in the centre was a new print of Queen
Victoria, elegantly displayed in a gold frame
upon an easel. She was splendid in her Corona-

tion robes. Her pale, girlish face seemed to be
weighed down by the gorgeous crown which she
wore; her hand too frail to hold the sceptre. Michael gasped as he beheld the picture. It was the
same as that which he had seen in the house in
Half Moon Street, seven years before. Michael
did not attempt to explain the mystery to himself, nor did he seek help from his uncle when
he sat with him at luncheon. Some fantastic
twist in time had shown him the picture of the
Queen, even before it was certain that she would
rule the land. Day after day, during the week of
festivity and change which followed the Coronation, Michael went to the shop to see the print.
Sometimes there would be a group of loiterers,
looking into the window. He would wait until he
was alone. Then he would stare at the date underneath, wondering more and more. In the end,
Michael bought the picture and ordered it to be
framed in gilt, for his room in Jermyn Street.
There it hung for some months, above the black
marble clock. With a candle raised level with his
eyes, he would look at it, night after night, until
he came to know every detail of the picture, the
looped curtains behind the throne, the number
of steps leading up to the tiny feet of the Queen,
the folds of her robes and the intricacy of the design of the crown and the sceptre.

One night when Michael returned to his
room from the Club, befuddled with too much
wine and entranced because he was to proceed
to the country for a holiday on the morrow, he
found the picture upon the floor. Its cord was
snapped: the glass was broken into a hundred
pieces and scattered in the fender and upon the
hearth rug. The ill omen of a fallen picture had
not left him. He remembered a day when a picture fell in the sitting room of *The Hollies*, before the day of his father's death. Recalling the
incident, he picked up the frame and the print
and, placing them behind the tallboy, he never
looked at them again.

Now that he was a man of authority in his
uncle's office, Michael met the prosperous merchants, among them a gentleman named John
Merryweather, who had been his uncle's friend

and companion in many business adventures. John Merryweather was younger than Benjamin Grinling, and therefore able to help Michael with advice and patronage, long after the older man had retired to the dim shadows of his house. Merryweather was a jovial man, loving good food, frivolous puns, and verses. The friendship between himself and Michael was nurtured over games of whist and hazard, played at the club. The friendship was sealed when Merryweather asked his young companion to accompany him to his country place at Penn. Here, within sight of Windsor's high towers and near to the cool shade of Burnham Beeches, John Merryweather had built himself a fine house, in the fashion of the time. The new age was already abandoning the simple straight lines of the Regency. Early Victorian houses had sprung up in London and in the countryside. Old red brick houses of Queen Anne's day were embellished with new decoration and hidden behind stucco: old furniture was carried up to the dim attics and chairs and sofas, sideboards and tables were designed to satisfy the new spirit. Shawls were spread over the straight-backed sofas: the new chairs were covered with Genoa velvet and they were edged with deep fringes. Mantelpieces were shrouded in draperies, worked in wool and silk: curtains were looped and looped again over the windows. Tables were laden with daguerreotypes in velvet frames, work-boxes decorated with mother-of-pearl, and wax flowers, stiff and gay, beneath glass shades.

John Merryweather had made such a house for his wife and daughter, among the oaks and beeches of a field in Penn. Alice Merryweather, a buxom mother in a rustling black silk dress, and her daughter Felicity moved through the rooms of the new house, stirring the *potpourri* in the china bowls, spreading the crocheted antimacassars upon the fine new chairs, with almost as much delight as if they had been walking through Paradise.

Erratic hummocks of mist lay in the fields of the Thames valley. John Merryweather had chosen this way to Penn, because Michael wished to awaken again the pictures of the first journey he had made from Reading, in the coach, nine years before. In some places, the mist was so thick that it hid the distance and shut the carriage in, so that it seemed to be swimming in a tide. The fences were ghostly vague, the houses visible only because of the dim topaz light of the lamps in their window, placed there to guide the farmers home from their early morning husbandry. Sometimes there were gaps in the mist, showing the high, green pinnacles of pine trees, the lines of cabbages and cauliflowers, leading up to trim cottages. One of these was guarded by shaped yew trees which reminded Michael of the house in which he had lived when he was a boy. He saw the house in Reading dimly now, as if his childhood and his sister's anxiety over him were but a story he had read in a book; or a picture, seen dimly, when he was young.

In the afternoon, after a mighty lunch of beef, fruit tart, and beer, in a roadside inn, Merryweather and his guest came to Penn and within a few minutes they had passed the new Gothic lodge and the gates which it guarded. They were at *Springfields* at last and Mrs. Merryweather was greeting them before the drawing-room fire. Here indeed was happiness for Michael. He enjoyed the big new rooms, with their fashionable furniture, the fat glass of sherry wine, the crisp biscuits and the warm comfort, after the cold air and the endless road.

Over the mantelpiece was a portrait of Mrs. Merryweather, painted before her body had succumbed to the pleasant round lines of motherhood and domesticity. She smiled down from a gilt frame: a tall, slim figure, in a milky dress. Her right elbow rested upon a pedestal, her left hand hung down, trailing a sprig of lilac against her skirt. At her feet, a plump spaniel gambolled, his feet raised in the air as if he were waiting patiently for the painter to allow him to rest them upon the ground again. Below the tall, painted figure of Mrs. Merryweather was the mantelpiece, hung in maroon plush with a fringe of maroon and gold; Venetian glass vases with their diamond pendants, Dresden figures, a white marble and ormolu clock, and two big china cats fought for room upon the mantelpiece; in the centre was a bunch of wax convolvulus, crowned by a gay butterfly. These lived safely within a glass dome. Michael turned his back upon the fire and saw the rich expanses of the room, the great painting above the piano of Greek maidens carrying pitchers and baskets of fruit across an alabaster floor. Painted peacocks swept their tails between the porphyry pillars: beyond the painted window was a bay, leading up to a ruined castle upon a hill.

Michael discussed the beauties of travel with Mrs. Merryweather and then, passing his eyes over a gold harp, draped with a Spanish shawl, he saw the innumerable small tables, the bunches of feather flowers beneath glass, and the bowl of real flowers, picked that morning.

"My daughter Felicity arranged the flowers, Mr. Stranger," said Mrs. Merryweather. Michael turned to commend their beauty to his hostess: she interrupted him and said: "Oh, but here she is. Come, Felicity, and meet Mr. Stranger."

Michael looked up to the door and there he saw the face of Felicity Merryweather, delicate and shy. His wine glass shook in his hand. He stepped back, almost as if he would fall into the fire. Felicity moved, her pink dress rippling as she came nearer to him. He held out his hand with dim knowledge of what he was doing and he muttered an answer to her welcome. But he was too sick and faint to hear the voice of his host bidding him sit down. He only looked into Felicity's turquoise eyes, knowing, with alarm, that it was her face which he had seen upon the floor of the house in Half Moon Street, and that it was her golden hair he had seen spun into a halo about her dead face, as the murderer scattered the daffodils and hyacinths over her body, nine years before.

From the moment in which he first saw Felicity Merryweather walk into the room, Michael's heart and mind were in a tempest of anxiety and discontent. In the afternoon, he walked with her in the orchard, telling her of his sister's fruit trees in Reading. They looked up among the branches, to the new, young apples which were no more than small jade knobs among the leaves. This was the first time that he had walked thus among fruit trees, since the days in Reading, before he went to London. A hundred little memories were awakened by the sight of a wheelbarrow leaning against a garden wall, a ladder disappearing among the branches of an apple tree, and by the smell of earth and wet grass. For most of the time, Michael did not speak. He was afraid to allow his tumbled ideas to shape themselves into words. Later in the afternoon, Mrs. Merryweather suggested that Felicity should take Michael to the stables; so they set off, with hands full of sugar lumps and four wizened apples. Michael watched the horses nuzzling their dark noses in Felicity's little hand. But more often he found himself unable to resist the wish to stare at her face. The lines of her chin and nose were so well known to him now. She would turn as he stared and then look away again, conscious of his eyes.

John Merryweather and Michael talked of many things over their Madeira after dinner. When Mr. and Mrs. Merryweather were alone in their bedroom that night, Mrs. Merryweather moving across the green carpet in a vast nightdress of pink flannelette, tightly tied about her neck, her husband said to her, "Well, my dear, what do you think of him?"

"I like him very much, John," she answered. "He is well-mannered and handsome and, as you say, his uncle's heir."

"But not only that, my dear. He is a good boy with character and prospects before him. Most suitable, I should think."

"Yes, I would face losing my dear child, if I thought he were the right young man to make her happy. But there is plenty of time yet."

"Your mother said that, my dear, but we did not agree with her."

Then Mrs. Merryweather sighed and crept into the big bed, dragging the loose, wide hem of her nightdress in after her. John Merryweather followed her, sitting up to suck a lozenge, before he leaned over, snuffed the candle, and lay back to sleep.

"If he made her as happy as you have made me, John, I would be contented," Mrs. Merryweather whispered.

John Merryweather leaned over and kissed her cheek. "God bless you, my dear," he said.

"God bless you," she answered. Then they went to sleep.

VI

On Sunday morning, Mr. and Mrs. Merryweather, Felicity, and Michael drove to the little stone church at Penn. Here Michael seemed to find the first quiet hour in which he could weave some shape out of his confusion of ideas. For he had paced up and down his room the night before, until the candle had burned down and left him to creep into bed in the dark. Sitting in the pew, Michael half listened to the voice of the preacher,

> Give ear to my words, O Lord, consider my
>   meditation.
> Hearken unto the voice of my cry, my King,
>   and my God: for unto thee will I pray.
> My voice shalt thou hear in the morning, O
>   Lord; in the morning will I direct my prayer
>   unto thee and will look up.
> For thou art not a God that hath pleasure in
>   wickedness: neither shall evil dwell with
>   thee. . . .

Michael half understood the words which came to him. But he knew that evil was dwelling with him, in his memory of the unhappy night of his arrival in London. He tried to shake off the weight of his melancholy and he straightened his back, as if to strengthen himself. He looked towards Felicity. He had never seen anybody so beautiful. As if in answer to his wish, the memory of the first time that he saw her face vanished from his mind. Felicity had never lived in London, beyond a month or so every year, so her cheeks were rosy as apples from the country air. Her eyes were blue and the hair beneath her grey and lavender hat was golden. Michael watched her shyly, glancing now and then towards Mrs. Merryweather, anxious lest his look should be detected. Sometimes Felicity sat back in the pew, watching the preacher. Her gloved hands rested upon her prayer book, which was white, with a golden cross upon it. Her lips would part as if she wished to speak: the movement of her mouth excited Michael, so that he looked down again to the pattern of his trousers or to the pattern of the carpet. It was not until they were leaving the church, when her eyes closed, as the light from the window dazzled her, that he again felt the shudder of fear which came every time he recalled the house in Half Moon Street. Her eyes, closed like this, awakened the picture and then his terror. Once as she walked, the light through the stained glass window coloured her hair and her cheek and she seemed like a saint to him. When they came to the stretch of grass and the path before the church, Felicity paused to greet her friends.

Michael did not speak as they drove back to *Springfields*. But he turned many times to watch Felicity's face, her eyes showing with their brightness how much she enjoyed the air and the scene which spread about them. As the carriage rolled on, her face moved too, against the background of trees, the white cottages in the fields and the deep hollows, gay with the flowers of spring.

When Michael went to his room to wash his hands before luncheon, he stood before his looking glass. He stretched his arms above his head, then out and then down to his sides. He swelled his chest as if to assure himself of his own strength. He said, almost aloud, "If any man hurts her, I shall kill him. I may have been mad on that Christmas night. I do not know. It may have been no more than an evil dream. But if any man dares to hurt her, I shall be the death of him."

Confident of his own strength, he went down to the dining room and found himself able to talk with more ease to Felicity. After luncheon, they sat upon a sofa, looking at stereoscopic views of Venice and of the Taj Mahal. They said how pleasant it would be to travel. Michael asked, "And tell me, Miss Merryweather, which country do you wish most to see?"

Felicity told him that she had always dreamed of Italy. From that moment, Michael dreamed of Italy too.

In May of 1845, Mrs. Merryweather had closed the house at Penn and had come up to their London house which was in North Street, Westminster. With the coming of the Merryweathers to London, Michael's life changed in many ways. He forsook his club of an evening, he forsook the coffee shops and his own chambers, to ring the Merryweather's bell in North Street, upon any pretext his love-sick imagination could invent. The way from Jermyn Street to North Street became a path of air for him to tread. He would set out in the late afternoon, when his hands were washed free of the smudges from his work in the office: a slim, quick-walking figure of a man, fashionable now, dressed in a suit of Garter blue which was the mode at this time. It fitted him so that his young body gave its own lines to the cloth which covered him. His waistcoat was of ivory silk, speckled with minute blue flowers. He was gallant to look upon as he walked along St. James's to buy a nosegay. They were so fashionable now, since the Queen carried one every night when she went to the opera. Thus armed with his excuse for intruding upon the Merryweathers, he would walk down past St. James's Palace, across the green stretches of the park and past the high, noble towers of Westminster. Once he walked into the Abbey as he passed this way, drawn into the shadows and the holy quiet by the faint notes of the organ. The Abbey seemed to him to smell of death and the organ played a song of the glory that was to come. He was too impatient to stay. He turned again into the sunshine, walking in the full glory of what was with him now: he was in love with the world.

Michael came to know the way to North Street so well that he foresaw the number of steps he must take from one point to another: three hundred and sixteen anxious strides from the end of Jermyn Street to the end of St. James's. The number of steps across the park varied, much to his chagrin, because of the carriages which impeded his way, or lines of guardsmen marching to Buckingham Palace, or market wagons trundling home from Covent Garden on their way to the cool countryside. But the number of paces between the corner of North Street and the door of Merryweather's house was assured. Thirty-four, with one mighty stride as he placed his right foot upon the step and raised his hand to ring the bell. The nosegay was for Mrs. Merryweather, but the shy glances, almost as he pressed the flowers into her hands, were for the younger figure near to the window. One day John Merryweather was in the drawing-room when Michael called with his flowers.

"Michael, Michael," he said, with his jovial voice, which seemed to be so full of port, "what is this? Flowers for my wife upon three days in one week! I shall begin to suspect you of being a cuckoo in my happy nest, my son. Wife, you must not encourage him."

"You must not tease Michael, John. It is very kind of him to bring me flowers. Take no heed of the naughty man, Michael," she said.

While they spoke, Felicity clutched the fold of the window curtain in her hand, trembling under the waves of faintness and ecstasy which disturbed her.

VII

It seems that we have not brought Felicity Merryweather close enough for us to see her clearly in this record. One has hesitated, in consideration of her own shyness, to talk of the diary which she kept at this time: the diary which ended so sadly before another year was to pass. Eight little books remain, with Michael Stranger's letters, in a morocco box which is still owned by the descendants of the Merryweather family. The eight volumes of Felicity's diary begin with the spring of 1838. I have dipped into their pages many times, during Sundays when it was raining, almost afraid of stirring the shy secrets which she wrote in them. One opens the first volume with the record of Felicity's first visit to London. She was sixteen then. She had been allowed to see Mrs. Graham's famous balloon descend at Hampton and she had been allowed to drink tea once at the Flora Tea Gardens in Bayswater. Here she had seen the wonderful Ducrow perform upon his horses and she had seen the sable sky above Bayswater radiant with the light of fireworks and rockets. She had seen Madame Saqui walking upon a tight rope at Vauxhall and she had heard Madame Vestris sing *Cherry Ripe*. It is difficult to read on through these fragrant pages when one is aware of the end. I know no diaries so sweet with childhood as these. Felicity had been reared upon beauty and kindliness. There is no mean judgment or carping note in any day's story. It is not until the summer of 1844 that Michael Stranger is mentioned. Then we read uncompromising records of his calls.

"Michael Stranger came to-day and drank tea with Mother," she wrote.

"Michael arrived upon the doorstep with Father, just as I was leaving the house with Thorpe to accompany me, to pay my call upon Mrs. Duff in Cowley Street, which is near by. He seemed embarrassed as we encountered. Why, I dare not tell."

Two months pass before we come upon an entry which pleases us, in our search through Felicity's sad story.

"*June 14th.* This has been a happy day for me, but with much pain. It was the pain which is sweet for a young woman to bear, for I know now what M. feels for me, as I have known for so long what feelings I have entertained for him. This morning I awakened in a trice, feeling suddenly refreshed and happy as I saw the sunshine burst into the room when Thorpe drew the curtains. I even suspected a new note of kindness in her voice when she said, 'Good morning, Miss Felicity, I hope you have slept well.' But this must have been my imagination, for she was cross as ever as she combed my hair. I do believe she would rap me with the brush, if she dared. And yet I love her. Father says that her early morning tempers come from her stomach and when I spoke of her crossness at breakfast this morning, he shocked Mother and made her quite angry by saying that Thorpe required some rhubarb, in a strong dose, to set her to rights. I would take Thorpe with me, if I married, for all her scoldings. I do believe she has teased and scolded me more than Mother has ever done. Dear Father has never been cross with me once. Sometimes I think that if Mother were not married to Father, I would wish to marry him myself. He is such a kind man and so full of comical sayings. But I suppose that would be impossible. We would be so happy together. And yet I do not know if this is true any longer, for to-day has shown me my error and my joy. In the afternoon, Mother said to me, 'Are you going out, Felicity? Thorpe must accompany you—but I want you to stay because Michael is coming to call upon us about five o'clock.'

"I answered with much confusion which I could not hide, that I wished to go to the Abbey for the evening service. And then, to my shame and confusion, I said, 'He comes to see you, Mother, there is no need that I should be here.'

"The words stumbled out, one upon the heels of the other. I blushed and turned towards the door. Mother was too dear and tender. She came up to me and placed her hands upon my shoulders, without turning me about to search my blushes. 'Dear Felicity,' she said, 'I do not know the feminine word for *knave*, unless it is *witch*. And I am sure you are not a little witch. But you are either a female knave or a little goose. Which is it?'

"I said that I did not know.

"And then Father came into the drawing room and I wished to escape. To my eternal confusion he argued Mother into repeating her question to him. 'Knave or goose?' he said. 'I should think my Felicity was a goose once, but now she is a mixture of both.'

"With this I *ran* out of the room and up the stairs as if this were a mad-house. I sat here in my bedroom for ten minutes to compose myself for the ordeal of walking through the busy streets with Thorpe at my side.

"I proceeded to the shops in St. James's to order a fine new hat for riding at Penn, my old one being a shabby sight since the day when I rode to Stoke Poges and it blew into the coppice. Father consoled me for my loss and pressed a sovereign into my hand for a new one. There were many fine people in the shop, and I saw Lord Melbourne *walking* in the park as I crossed the lawns on my way home. He was talking to a dark gentleman who seemed to be a foreigner from his antics and his dress. Father says that Lord Melbourne is a very wicked man, but I saw no signs of his worldliness upon his smiling face. As we came to the open square before the Abbey, Thorpe said to me, 'We are ten minutes late for the beginning of the service, Miss Felicity.' This I knew, I confess, for I had tarried in the hatter's shop trying on this hat, its shape being monstrously new and fashionable.

"Since we were so late, we proceeded immediately here, which was my plan.

"My feet were like leaden weights as I came down to the drawing-room door. Dear Michael was standing there. I dare to write of him thus, and not as Mr. S. or Michael S., as of yore, for my heart has told me its secret and I can no longer deny it. Michael was sitting beside Mother upon the sofa, and they were talking of politics which do not interest me very much, try as I may. M. stood up from the sofa and came across the room to me. Father came into the room and said, 'Ah, let me see,' by which I always know that a plot is afoot. I only wished to die and I could not look into Michael's eyes as he took my hand and wished me 'good afternoon.' He seemed so strong and so brave and so beautiful with his fashionable clothes and his hair shining. I almost snatched my hand from his, which was *gauche* of me, so terrified was I at the realisation of how the touch of him burned me and distressed me. All other secrets I have shared with Mother, who

has always been sweet and dear to me. But this I cannot share with any living being. Unless it be Michael himself. I walked across the room and sat upon a chair, so that the light was not upon my face. I was wearing my violet silk dress which is truly paler than violet. A pretty colour which I chose myself. I trembled again and when I looked up, I saw Father leave the room and then Mother followed him. I thought I must forget all manners and propriety and run to Father's arms for protection from myself. But I did not. I stayed. Mother closed the door behind her and I realised that I was alone with Michael. I looked up a little, still keeping my head lowered so that he would not suspect my intention. But he detected me and our eyes met. Mother has always said that it is as immodest to blush as it is to give cause for blushing. But I felt the flame stealing over my cheek. He came over to me, and standing near to my chair, he said, 'Felicity, I have been speaking upon a serious matter with your mother and your father.'

"I had no answer, but I knew what the matter was. He said, 'I have always loved you, Felicity, from the first day when I met you at Penn. I remember every hour with you, for everything which has happened to me since then has been more beautiful for me. I cannot tell you of my love in beautiful words, Felicity, but I *do* love you. I suppose my declaration will be a surprise to you for I have tried to hide my feelings lest they should disturb you.' (At this place in the conversation, I could well have thrown caution aside and have told him the truth, for I was *not surprised*, but merely *embarrassed*.) He continued and, coming nearer to my chair, he said, 'Felicity, look up at me, and let me know a little of what you are thinking from your eyes, before I say any more.' I looked up at him and I beheld heaven in his eyes for they were tender and smiling and noble as they looked down at me. Then he said, 'Will you marry me, Felicity? I have spoken to your mother and to your father and they agree. Will you marry me?'

"Oh, that I had somebody to cry upon now as I write. Perhaps modesty should have bidden me to look down towards the floor at his question. I only looked at his eyes and answered, with calm which surprised me, 'Yes, Michael, I love you too.' Then he fell upon his knees beside me and he held both my hands in his and kissed them . . . I looked down upon his dear head. I am afraid that two foolish tears welled up in my eyes and sped down my cheeks. My hands were imprisoned in his and I could do naught to hide my foolishness. Then he looked up and I knew, as I looked into his eyes, something of the happiness angels must feel when they look into the eyes of God.

"I cannot sleep this night. I write on and on. I stood for ten minutes before the window and watched the high towers of Westminster Abbey piercing the low clouds. There is a moon, but it must struggle with many clouds to-night. I thought of this afternoon, when I was so deceitful about going to the service at the Abbey. And I wondered if God would be angry or whether he would hurt me for my treachery against Him. But as I wondered, the clouds moved away from the moon so that it shone down on the world and made everything beautiful. I closed my eyes and when I opened them, the face on the moon was smiling, as if it were an answer to my fear. God is not angry with me. I shall go to church always now, even when I do not want to, to thank Him for Michael's love.

"*June 15th*. Michael came again this afternoon. He brought *two* bunches of flowers, one for Mother and one for me. I cannot write any more to-day. My words tumble out . . . Oh, I am very happy. That is all.

"*June 16th*. This morning I was so ill with fever that Thorpe placed her hand on my cheek when she called me, and she felt my pulse. 'You stay in bed to-day,' she said. I was angry and I proceeded to rise from my bed in defiance. She took my slippers and my robe and went out of the room. Presently Mother came and there was much fuss at my state. They have elected to drive me down to Penn this very day and I am not to see Michael for five days. Thus is my happiness snatched from me. I heard Father pleading for

me and he came to my room in his anxiety, but partially dressed, which was unusual and surprising. Men wear strange clothes beneath their suits. He said, 'Leave the poor child alone.' But Mother won, as she always does when some dull virtuous good to me is involved. I leave for Penn in one hour. I tried to vent my temper upon Thorpe when she brought my breakfast. I called her some vile names, such as *beast* and *martinet*. She did not answer me and as she went from my room I saw a smile upon her face which I considered most impertinent to my dignity as a betrothed woman."

VIII

Upon the evening of the day when Felicity was taken to Penn, Michael sat in his rooms, writing his first love letter. From five to six, from six to seven o'clock, he wrote. There seemed so few words in the world with which to say so much. When the letter was finished, he sent it to the post and, when he had washed and dressed again, he walked to Half Moon Street to call upon his uncle.

The hush of death had already come to Benjamin Grinling's house. The furniture in the drawing-room was covered: the gilt frames of the paintings were shrouded in sheets of black paper. The butler seemed to creak as if risen from the dead, as he came to the door when Michael rang the bell.

"The old gentleman is not so well to-day, Master Michael," he said. "He was poorly this morning and I was for sending you a note, sir, but he would have none of it. When I told him you were coming this evening he seemed to be more happy, sir. It will be a rare tonic for him, I am thinking, for he has not seen you these four days."

Michael climbed the stairs slowly. He tapped lightly upon his uncle's door and then he walked into the darkened room, upon the tips of his toes. One candle burned behind a shade, upon a table beside the bed. Benjamin Grinling lay back, withered and still, his eyes open and turned towards Michael. "I knew you would come, my boy," he said. Michael drew a chair up to the side of the bed, and as he sat down he leaned over the figure of the old man. "Yes, Uncle Benjamin, I have come," he said. "I would come every day if I thought you would not be tired with talking to me."

"There will not be many days now, Michael, so you need not spare me. I lie here all day thinking of the things I have not said to you. But there it is."

Michael was silent.

"You have something to tell me, Michael, I know. You have something to tell me, my boy. I can see it in your eyes."

"Yes, Uncle, I have, and I do hope you will not be angry with me."

"Ah, I know, I know. You think because I am an old man that I am a fool. Oh, no!" A little chuckle came into his voice and he raised himself. "Give me another pillow . . . there . . . on the chair."

Michael placed the pillow behind his head. Benjamin Grinling chuckled again. "You think you can surprise an old man! I passed surprising many a long year ago, Michael. Many a long year ago. I know, yes, I know. You are in love with Felicity Merryweather and you have asked her to marry you?"

"Yes, Uncle."

"And has she said you 'Yes' or 'No'?"

"She has said 'Yes,' Uncle."

"Well, well! If John Merryweather and I are not a clever pair of old cronies! I suppose you think you did it all by yourself. Oh no, Michael, my son. We planned it all five years ago. Ha! Ha! What a clever pair of cronies we were."

"But, Uncle, I . . . I . . ." Michael spluttered and remained silent.

"You shall have all, my boy. All. My blessing you have now. My blessing you have always had, for you have been a good boy, Michael. Ever since that day. Do you remember . . . the inn, and our glasses of sherry before the fire? Our

first glasses of sherry together! Well, there won't be any more sherry together now for us. But the cellar is full of good wine for you to drink the health of a younger generation, my son. All is for you, Michael. All is for you."

Benjamin Grinling lay still for a moment. Michael stretched out his hand and he touched the older man's thin fingers as they lay on the cover of the bed. He spoke once more. "Now you must go, Michael, for I am tired. Bring Felicity to me some day soon, before I die. Because she will live in this house with you when I am gone. Or perhaps you will want another house and not wish to remember this. Some day, Michael, buy Felicity a dress of heliotrope silk, a full flowing skirt of heliotrope and ask her to stand upon the white rug, the skin of the polar bear, in the drawing-room. They have rolled it up now because I do not use the room any longer. Ask her to stand there, Michael, and remember that your Aunt Florence stood there like an autumn crocus in the snow. Yes, like an autumn crocus in the snow. I have seen them, Michael, heliotrope or saffron, it does not matter. That was a little joke between your Aunt Flossie and me, Michael. Always have your little jokes, because they are like the autumn crocuses, the last beauty of the year. Does Felicity laugh at little jokes, not only big jokes, but little, *silly* jokes?"

"Yes, Uncle."

"Then you will be happy, my boy. Goodnight."

When he returned to his rooms, Michael wrote still another letter to Felicity.

Uncle Benjamin has said "Yes," my dearest. And he has supported his spiritual blessing with more worldly promises which matter to me only in that they will make you more comfortable and happy. But I fear that he will not live very long. The thought of his death is the only sadness in my wonderful happiness.

Michael paused then, before he signed his name to the letter. He had walked down Half

Moon Street only twenty minutes before, past the house of which he was once afraid. He no longer embraced the memory of his first night in London. The practical man in him made it possible for him to turn away from the old dread. He saw Felicity now as the living symbol of his contentment, not as the figure of his dream. He had taught himself to call the experience a *dream* and in this word he sought and found his comfort. The house had been still and quiet. The old *For Sale* notice was still upon the railings, an almost unreadable notice now. He braced his shoulders as the signal of his victory and he wrote at the end of the letter, *Your devoted and loving Michael.*

IX

Benjamin Grinling died at four o'clock in the afternoon of the twenty-third of December. Michael was busy at the counting house, for he was to travel to Penn next morning and there was much to do. A messenger came to him with the news and he hurried across London, a London of white streets and pitiless winter wind. Half Moon Street seemed to be hushed in the knowledge of death. The snow was piled high against the railings: a boy with a torch shambled down the cleared way between the banks of snow, whistling. But he stopped his clamour as he came to Benjamin Grinling's house. The door was open, and within, Michael was standing at the foot of the stairs, listening to the servant's story. "He died in my arms, sir. I had just taken up his beef tea, sir, which the physic man ordered for him. He called me, sir; it was my name he said at the last, sir. He just called, 'Sadler, I feel very weak now. Come near to me, Sadler.' Those were his last words, sir. I went over and lifted him for he had fallen low in the bed, sir. As I lifted him, he died, just like a baby, with never a murmur."

Michael went to his uncle's room. The awful secret of death held him beside the body for a long time. He stood against the bed, looking down at the old, peaceful face. The lines of agitation and thought were already faded away and Benjamin Grinling looked younger. There was too a serene smile about the mouth, as if some new and wonderful knowledge had already come to him. Beside the bed was a Bible. Michael had always seen it near to his uncle and he touched it now, as a tangible souvenir of the living man. He picked it up and ran his finger along the edge of the pages. They fell open in his hand and, from inside the back cover, three dry and faded autumn crocuses fell at his feet.

Michael left the house about seven o'clock and went to his club. He dined quickly and returned to Half Moon Street, for there was much to do. He noticed a change as he passed towards his uncle's house. The *For Sale* notice on the house of his early adventure was removed from the railings and a newly painted board was suspended on a bracket from the first floor window. Michael remained in his uncle's house until half-past eleven. The dismal servitors of death came to him, and there were letters to write; one to John Merryweather and one to Felicity. Their marriage must wait now. Despair over his misfortune took the place of Michael's sorrow for a little time. And even the glow of acquiring possessions struggled with the other emotions which came to him. He lifted the black paper cover of the big Canaletto picture in the drawing-room. It was his now. He dismissed the realisation as being an offence against the solemnity of the moment. But the confidence of being a man with his own estate already touched him, lightly. When he went upstairs, in the last moment, to see his uncle's body again, all feelings but those of remorse and desolation left him. He had loved the old man more than as his benefactor. Michael took his hat and coat from the hall with a weight of desolation upon him. He closed the door behind him and walked out into the snow.

It was upon such a night as this that he had dined with his uncle Benjamin fifteen years ago. The expanse of snow was the same; the stillness, the filth marks of other feet, leaving deep shadows in the white. The sameness of the scene drew a string of memories before Michael's eyes—a conglomeration of fruit trees in the orchard at Reading, the wheelbarrow leaning against the apple tree, the firescreen in his uncle's room, the ink pot on the table in his office, the faint tap his pen made when he dipped it, the inn at Knightsbridge and the cylinder of cucumber upon his plate for his first meal in London—one scene tumbling at the heels of the other—the drive to his uncle's house, the dinner, and the snow in Half Moon Street, afterwards, like this, white and silent.

Michael looked up. A more searching light would have shown his whitened face and his eyes, wide with terror. For there lay across the path in front of him, the same wedge of yellow light, coming from the open door of the house which was "for sale." He stumbled quickly into the light as if it were part of him, as if it were inevitably waiting for him. He leaned one hand upon the railing and, when he had looked beside him, he leaned forward and peered through the open door, to the lighted hall inside. All was the same. The carpet, the pictures on the wall, the sunlight which beat so incongruously against the night darkness outside. Michael stepped nearer. He saw the carpeted stairs leading to the upper part of the house. For here also the sunlight came. As Michael took one more pace into the full tide of the light from within, he heard the sound of human groaning, coming from the lower room. Fifteen years faded from him. He was here again, younger, afraid. The groaning ceased and again he heard the long pitiful scream. This time he knew the voice. Even in its terror, it was the voice of Felicity, calling to him. He rushed into the house. The print of Queen Victoria and the year printed upon it found a place in the phantasmagoria as he passed to the door of the evil room. There he paused. He could not move: he could not raise his hands to help or protest. He looked back, over his shoulder, towards the open, outer door: the snow was falling again. Here in the room there were no candles. Sunlight touched

the hyacinths and daffodils in the bronze urns upon the tables. Lying upon the floor was the form of Felicity in a light summer dress. Bent over her was the same man, pressing his thumbs into her throat. Michael saw her face turn and he saw again, this time in terror, the face he knew so well, white, framed in the tangle of red-gold hair. He saw her hands clutch the rug as before, drawing it up towards her body. The white fingers released the rug and they fell, weak and limp, among the primroses and snowdrops which had fallen from a broken vase. He saw the man weaken his hold upon Felicity's throat and then stand erect. He leaned over to a vase, and taking the hyacinths and daffodils from the water, he scattered them over Felicity's body. He scattered the snowdrops upon her red-golden hair. Thus far Michael had observed the horrible scene before. He waited now. The murderer knelt down and seemed to peer into Felicity's eyes: then he turned for the first time, and looked towards the door. Michael fell back against the wall and then he ran into the white silent street, for it had been his own face that looked at him from the sunlit room.

He ran towards his uncle's house. It seemed dark and empty. He beat his hands against the door, but nobody came to him. He beat them against the brass knocker until they bled. His feet pounded the snow into a mess. Michael called, "Uncle Benjamin! Oh, Jesus! Oh, Uncle Benjamin! Jesus in Heaven help me!" He whimpered and fell on to the doorstep, all strength and protest abandoning him in his melancholy.

A night watchman found Michael's body upon the doorstep, when the first light of the morning was coming to Half Moon Street. The snow had almost covered him and his face was buried deep in the drift against the door. They carried him into the house and placed him before the fire. But he was dead and neither the flames nor Sadler's warm hands could awaken life in him again. When the lawyer came in the evening, he found a letter upon the table, which Michael had not seen or opened. Felicity had written to him:

Springfields,
Penn,
Tuesday.

My Darling Michael,

You must come down to stay with us for Saturday and Sunday, no matter how your wicked office holds you away from me. Father came home last night with a plan for us. He has found a house which he thinks could be made comfortable and beautiful and it is near to your uncle's house. It is actually in *Half Moon Street,* but Michael, there is a silly story which has frightened people from living in it for many years. It has been kept in good order, but superstition says that the house is haunted. We are proof against such nonsense, aren't we? Mother has not one good word to say for the scheme as she says people should live in an atmosphere of happiness. But I told her that if the ghost were a kind ghost, we would not mind him staying with us and that if he were an unkind *ghost our love would drive him away.*

Father is in two minds about the whole matter and I feel that the plan will not come to anything now. But we must see the haunted house, mustn't we? I am in a flutter of shopping lists which Mother makes me prepare in duplicate. I said to her yesterday that if I had known being married involved so much list making, I would have remained a spinster for the rest of my life. She says that I must not be facetious about sacred things. But you *would* have known that it was only one of those silly little jokes, wouldn't you? So you must throw down your horrid pen and come to us for Saturday: desert the pen you love for the Penn I love. You see! That is another little joke, darling Michael, in case you are so busy with your horrid office that you do not see little jokes in the morning.

With all my love, to my Dearest Michael,

Your Felicity.

A NIGHT OF HORROR

Dick Donovan

ALTHOUGH ONE OF THE most successful authors of Victorian and Edwardian detective stories and a regular contributor to the same *Strand* magazine in which Sherlock Holmes found fame, the pseudonymous Dick Donovan's mysteries are seldom read today. His melodramatic, sensational plots featured physically active detectives—the most popular being Dick Donovan in first-person narratives—taking on secret societies, master villains, and innocent people coerced into crime while hypnotized or under the influence of sinister drugs. The lack of texture in his prose, the sparseness of background context, and the stick-figure characters all contributed to the diminishment of his reputation. Although he wrote more than fifty volumes of detective stories and novels, James Edward Preston Muddock (later changed to Joyce Emmerson Preston Muddock) (1842–1934) claimed in his autobiography, *Pages from an Adventurous Life* (1907), to be disappointed in their popularity, preferring his historical and nongenre fiction (much as Arthur Conan Doyle lamented the adulation given his Sherlock Holmes stories).

Born in Southampton, Muddock traveled extensively throughout Asia, the Pacific, and Europe as a special correspondent to *The London Daily News* and the *Hour* and as a regular contributor to other periodicals. When he turned to writing mystery stories, he named his Glasgow detective Dick Donovan after a famous eighteenth-century Bow Street Runner. The stories became so popular that he took it for his pseudonym.

The town of Flin Flon, Manitoba, takes its name from a character in Donovan's lost race novel, *The Sunless City* (1905), in which Flintabbatey Flonatin discovers a world through an underwater gold-lined cavern. When a copper-lined cavern was discovered in Canada, the subsequent mine was named for the protagonist in a (blessedly) shortened form.

"A Night of Horror" was first published in *Tales of Terror* (London, Chatto & Windus, 1899).

A Night of Horror

DICK DONOVAN

Bleak Hill Castle

"*My dear old Chum,—Before you leave England for the East I claim the redemption of a promise you made to me some time ago that you would give me the pleasure of a week or two of your company. Besides, as you may have already guessed, I have given up the folly of my bachelor days, and have taken unto myself the sweetest, dearest little woman that ever walked the face of the earth. We have been married just six months, and are as happy as the day is long. And then this place is entirely after your own heart. It will excite all your artistic fancies, and appeal with irresistible force to your romantic nature. To call the building a castle is somewhat preten-*

tious, but I believe it has been known as the Castle ever since it was built, more than two hundred years ago. Hester—need I say that Hester is my better half!—is just delighted with it, and if either of us was in the least degree superstitious, we might see or hear ghosts every hour of the day. Of course, as becomes a castle, we have a haunted room, though my own impression is that it is haunted by nothing more fearsome than rats. Anyway, it is such a picturesque, curious sort of chamber that if it hasn't a ghost it ought to have. But I have no doubt, old chap, that you will make one of us, for, as I remember, you have always had a love for the eerie and creepy, and you cannot forget how angry you used to get with me sometimes for chaffing you about your avowed belief in the occult and supernatural, and what you were pleased to term the 'unexplainable phenomena of psychomancy.' However, it is possible you have got over some of the errors of your youth but whether or not, come down, dear boy, and rest assured that you will meet with the heartiest of welcomes.

"Your old pal,
"DICK DIRCKMAN."

The above letter was from my old friend and college chum, who, having inherited a substantial fortune, and being passionately fond of the country and country pursuits, had thus the means of gratifying his tastes to their fullest bent. Although Dick and I were very differently constituted, we had always been greatly attached to each other. In the best sense of the term he was what is generally called a hard-headed, practical man. He was fond of saying he never believed in anything he couldn't see, and even that which he could see he was not prepared to accept as truth without due investigation. In short, Dick was neither romantic, poetical, nor, I am afraid, artistic, in the literal sense. He preferred facts to fancies, and was possessed of what the world generally calls "an unimpressionable nature." For nearly four years I had lost sight of my friend, as I had

been wandering about Europe as tutor and companion to a delicate young nobleman. His death had set me free; but I had no sooner returned to England than I was offered and accepted a lucrative appointment in the service of his Highness the Nizam of Chundlepore, in Northern India, and there was every probability of my being absent for a number of years.

On returning home I had written to Dick to the chambers he had formerly occupied, telling him of my appointment, and expressing a fear that unless we could snatch a day or two in town I might not be able to see him, as I had so many things to do. It was true I had promised that when opportunity occurred I should do myself the pleasure of accepting his oft-proffered hospitality which I knew to be lavish and generous. I had not heard of his marriage; his letter gave me the first intimation of that fact, and I confess that when I got his missive I experienced some curiosity to know the kind of lady he had succeeded in captivating. I had always had an idea that Dick was cut out for a bachelor, for there was nothing of the ladies' man about him, and he used at one time to speak of the gentler sex with a certain levity and brusqueness of manner that by no means found favour with the majority of his friends. And now Dick was actually married, and living in a remote region, where most town-bred people would die of ennui.

It will be gathered from the foregoing remarks that I did not hesitate about accepting Dick's cordial invitation. I determined to spare a few days at least of my somewhat limited time, and duly noted Dick to that effect, giving him the date of my departure from London, and the hour at which I should arrive at the station nearest to his residence.

Bleak Hill Castle was situated in one of the most picturesque parts of Wales; consequently, on the day appointed I found myself comfortably ensconced in a smoking carriage of a London and North-Western train. And towards the close of the day—the time of the year was May—I was the sole passenger to alight at the wayside station, where Dick awaited me with a smart dog-cart. His greeting was hearty and robust, and when his man had packed in my traps he gave the handsome little mare that drew the cart the reins, and we spanked along the country roads in rare style. Dick always prided himself on his knowledge of horseflesh, and with a sense of keen satisfaction he drew my attention to the points of the skittish little mare which bowled along as if we had been merely featherweights.

A drive of eight miles through the bracing Welsh air so sharpened our appetites that the smell of dinner was peculiarly welcome; and telling me to make a hurried toilet, as his cook would not risk her reputation by keeping a dinner waiting, Dick handed me over to the guidance of a natty chambermaid. As it was dark when we arrived I had no opportunity of observing the external characteristics of Bleak Hill Castle; but there was nothing in the interior that suggested bleakness. Warmth, comfort, light, held forth promise of carnal delights.

Following my guide up a broad flight of stairs, and along a lofty and echoing corridor, I found myself in a large and comfortably-furnished bedroom. A bright wood fire burned upon the hearthstone, for although it was May the temperature was still very low on the Welsh hills. Hastily changing my clothes, I made my way to the dining-room, where Mrs. Dirckman emphasised the welcome her husband had already given me. She was an exceedingly pretty and rather delicate-looking little woman, in striking contrast to her great, bluff, busy husband. A few neighbours had been gathered together to meet me, and we sat down, a dozen all told, to a dinner that from a gastronomic point of view left nothing to be desired. The viands were appetising, the wines perfect, and all the appointments were in perfect consonance with the good things that were placed before us.

It was perhaps natural, when the coffee and cigar stage had arrived, that conversation should turn upon our host's residence, by way of affording me—a stranger to the district—some information. Of course, the information was conveyed to me in a scrappy way, but I gathered in substance that Bleak Hill Castle had originally belonged to a Welsh family, which was chiefly distinguished by the extravagance and gambling propensities of its male members. It had gone through some exciting times, and numerous strange and startling stories had come to centre round it. There were stories of wrong, and shame, and death, and more than a suggestion of dark crimes. One of these stories turned upon the mysterious disappearance of the wife and daughter of a young scion of the house, whose career had been somewhat shady. His wife was considerably older than he, and it was generally supposed that he had married her for money. His daughter, a girl of about twelve, was an epileptic patient, while the husband and father was a gloomy, disappointed man. Suddenly the wife and daughter disappeared. At first no surprise was felt; but, then some curiosity was expressed to know where they had gone to and curiosity led to wonderment, and wonderment to rumour—for people will gossip, especially in a country district. Of course, Mr. Greeta Jones, the husband, had to submit to much questioning as to where his wife and child were staying. But being sullen and morose of temperament he contented himself by brusquely and tersely saying, "They had gone to London." But as no one had seen them go, and no one had heard of their going, the statement was accepted as a perversion of fact. Nevertheless, incredible as it may seem, no one thought it worth his while to insist upon an investigation, and a few weeks later Greeta Jones himself went away—and to London, as was placed beyond doubt. For a long time Bleak Hill Castle was shut up, and throughout the country side it began to be whispered that sights and sounds had been seen and heard at the castle which were suggestive of things unnatural, and soon it became a crystallised belief in men's minds that the place was haunted.

On the principle of giving a dog a bad name you have only to couple ghosts with the name of an old country residence like this castle for it to fall into disfavour, and to be generally shunned. As might have been expected in such a region the castle was shunned; no tenant could be found for it. It was allowed to go to ruin, and for a long time was the haunt of smugglers. They were cleared out in the process of time, and at last hard-headed, practical Dick Dirckman heard of the place through a London agent, went down to see it, took a fancy to it, bought it for an old song, and, having taste and money, he soon converted the half-ruined building into a country gentleman's home, and thither he carried his bride.

Such was the history of Bleak Hill Castle as I gathered it in outline during the postprandial chat on that memorable evening.

On the following day I found the place all that my host had described it in his letter to me. Its situation was beautiful in the extreme; and there wasn't one of its windows that didn't command a magnificent view of landscape and sea. He and I rambled about the house, he evinced a keen delight in showing me every nook and corner, in expatiating on the beauties of the locality generally, and of the advantages of his dwelling-place in particular. Why he reserved taking me to the so-called haunted chamber until the last I never have known; but so it was; and as he threw open the heavy door and ushered me into the apartment he smiled ironically and remarked:

"Well, old man, this is the ghost's den; and as I consider that a country mansion of this kind should, in the interests of all tradition and of fiction writers, who, under the guise of truth, he like Ananias, have its haunted room, I have let this place go untouched, except that I have made it a sort of lumber closet for some antique and mouldering old furniture which I picked up a bargain in Wardour Street, London. But I needn't tell you that I regard the ghost stories as rot."

I did not reply to my friend at once, for the room absorbed my attention. It was unquestionably the largest of the bedrooms in the house, and, while in keeping with the rest of the house, had characteristics of its own. The walls were panelled with dark oak, the floor was oak, polished. There was a deep V-shaped bay, formed

by an angle of the castle, and in each side of the bay was a diamond-paned window, and under each window an oak seat, which was also a chest with an ancient iron lock. A large wooden bedstead with massive hangings stood in one corner, and the rest of the furniture was of a very nondescript character, and calls for no special mention. In a word, the room was picturesque, and to me it at once suggested the *mise-en-scène* for all sorts of dramatic situations of a weird and eerie character. I ought to add that there was a very large fireplace with a most capacious hearthstone, on which stood a pair of ponderous and rusty steel dogs. Finally, the window commanded superb views, and altogether my fancy was pleased, and my artistic susceptibilities appealed to in an irresistible manner, so that I replied to my friend thus:

"I like this room, Dick, awfully. Let me occupy it, will you?"

He laughed.

"Well, upon my word, you are an eccentric fellow to want to give up the comfortable den which I have assigned to you for this mouldy, draughty, dingy old lumber room. However"—here he shrugged his shoulders—"there is no accounting for tastes, and as this is liberty hall, my friends do as they like; so I'll tell the servants to put the bed in order, light a fire, and cart your traps from the other room."

I was glad I had carried my point, for I frankly confess to having romantic tendencies. I was fond of old things, old stories and legends, old furniture, and anything that was removed above the dull level of commonplaceness. This room in a certain sense, was unique, and I was charmed with it.

When pretty little Mrs. Dirckman heard of the arrangements she said, with a laugh that did not conceal a certain nervousness, "I am sorry you are going to sleep in that wretched room. It always makes me shudder, for it seems so uncomfortable. Besides, you know, although Dick laughs at me and calls me a little goose, I am inclined to believe there may be some foundation for the current stories. Anyway, I wouldn't sleep in the room for a crown of gold. I hope you will be comfortable, and not be frightened to death or into insanity by gruesome apparitions."

I hastened to assure my hostess that I should be comfortable enough, while as for apparitions, I was not likely to be frightened by them.

The rest of the day was spent exploring the country round about, and after a *recherché* dinner Dick and I played billiards until one o'clock, and then having drained a final "peg," I retired to rest. When I reached the haunted chamber I found that much had been done to give an air of cheerfulness and comfort to the place. Some rugs had been laid about the floor, a modern chair or two introduced, a wood fire blazed on the hearth. On a little "occasional table" that stood near the fire was a silver jug, filled with hot water, and an antique decanter containing spirits, together with lemon and sugar, in case I wanted a final brew. I could not but feel grateful for my host and hostess's thoughtfulness, and, having donned my dressing-gown and slippers, I drew a chair within the radius of the wood fire's glow, and proceeded to fill my pipe for a few whiffs previous to tumbling into bed. This was a habit of mine—a habit of years and years of growth, and, while perhaps an objectionable one in some respects, it afforded me solace and conduced to restful sleep. So I lit my pipe, and fell to pondering and trying to see if I could draw any suggestiveness as to my future from the glowing embers. Suddenly a remarkable thing happened. My pipe was drawn gently from my lips and laid upon the table, and at the same moment I heard what seemed to me to be a sigh. For a moment or two I felt confused, and wondered whether I was awake or dreaming. But there was the pipe on the table, and I could have taken the most solemn oath that to the best of my belief it had been placed there by unseen hands.

My feelings, as may be imagined, were peculiar. It was the first time in my life that I had ever been the subject of a phenomenon which was capable of being attributed to supernatural agency. After a little reflection, and some

reasoning with myself, however, I tried to believe that my own senses had made a fool of me, and that in a half-somnolent and dreamy condition I had removed the pipe myself, and placed it on the table. Having come to this conclusion I divested myself of my clothing, extinguished the two tall candles, and jumped into bed. Although usually a good sleeper, I did not go to sleep at once, as was my wont, but lay thinking of many things, and mingling with my changing thoughts was a low, monotonous undertone—nature's symphony—of booming sea on the distant beach, and a bass piping—rising occasionally to a shrill and weird upper note—of the wind. From its situation the house was exposed to every wind that blew, hence its name "Bleak Hill Castle," and probably a south-east gale would have made itself felt to an uncomfortable degree in this room, which was in the south-east angle of the building. But now the booming sea and wind had a lullaby effect, and my nerves sinking into restful repose I fell asleep. How long I slept I do not know, and never shall know; but I awoke suddenly, and with a start, for it seemed as if a stream of ice-cold water was pouring over my face. With an impulse of indefinable alarm I sprang up in bed, and then a strange, awful, ghastly sight met my view.

I don't know that I could be described as a nervous man in any sense of the word. Indeed, I think I may claim to be freer from nerves than the average man, nor would my worst enemy, if he had a regard for truth, accuse me of lacking courage. And yet I confess here, frankly, that the sight I gazed upon appalled me. Yet was I fascinated with a horrible fascination, that rendered it impossible for me to turn my eyes away. I seemed bound by some strange weird spell. My limbs appeared to have grown rigid; there was a sense of burning in my eyes; my mouth was parched and dry; my tongue swollen, so it seemed. Of course, these were mere sensations, but they were sensations I never wish to experience again. They were sensations that tested my sanity. And the sight that held me in the thrall was truly calculated to test the nerves of the strongest.

There, in mid-air, between floor and ceiling, surrounded or made visible by a trembling nebulous light, that was weird beyond the power of any words to describe, was the head and bust of a woman. The face was paralysed into an unutterably awful expression of stony horror; the long black hair was tangled and dishevelled, and the eyes appeared to be bulging from the head. But this was not all. Two ghostly hands were visible. The fingers of one were twined savagely in the black hair, and the other grasped a long-bladed knife, and with it hacked, and gashed, and tore, and stabbed at the bare white throat of the woman, and the blood gushed forth from the jagged wounds, reddening the spectre hand and flowing in one continuous stream to the oak floor, where I heard it drip, drip, drip until my brain seemed as if it would burst, and I felt as if I was going raving mad. Then I saw with my strained eyes the unmistakable sign of death pass over the woman's face; and next, the devilish hands flung the mangled remnants away, and I *heard* a low chuckle of satisfaction—heard, I say, and swear it, as plainly as I have ever heard anything in this world. The light had faded; the vision of crime and death I had gone, and yet the spell held me. Although the night was cold, I believe I was bathed in perspiration. I think I tried to cry out—nay, I am sure I did—but no sound came from my burning, parched lips; my tongue refused utterance; it clove to the roof of my mouth. Could I have moved so much as a joint of my little finger, I could have broken the spell; at least, such was the idea that occupied my half-stunned brain. It was a nightmare of waking horror, and I shudder now, and shrink within myself as I recall it all. But the revelation—for revelation it was—had not yet reached its final stage. Out of the darkness was once more evolved a faint, phosphorescent glow, and in the midst of it appeared the dead body of a beautiful girl with the throat all gashed and bleeding, the red blood flowing in a crimson blood

over her night-robe, which only partially concealed her young limbs; and the cruel, spectral hands, dyed with her blood, appeared again, and grasped her, and lifted her, and bore her along. Then that vision faded, and a third appeared. This time I seemed to be looking into a gloomy, damp, arched cave or cellar, and the horror that froze me was intensified as I saw the hands busy preparing a hole in the wall at one end of the cave; and presently they lifted two bodies—the body of the woman, and the body of the young girl—all gory and besmirched; and the hands crushed them into the hole in the wall, and then proceeded to brick them up.

All these things I saw as I have described them, and this I solemnly swear to be the truth as I hope for mercy at the Supreme Judgment.

It was a vision of crime; a vision of merciless, pitiless, damnable murder. How long it all lasted I don't know. Science has told us that dreams which seem to embrace a long series of years, last but seconds; and in the few moments of consciousness that remain to the drowning man his life's scroll is unrolled before his eyes. This vision of mine, therefore, may only have lasted seconds, but it seemed to me hours, years, nay, an eternity. With that final stage in the ghostly drama of blood and death, the spell was broken, and flinging my arms wildly about, I know that I uttered a great cry as I sprang up in bed.

"Have I been in the throes of a ghastly nightmare?" I asked myself.

Every detail of the horrific vision I recalled, and yet somehow it seemed to me that I had been the victim of a hideous nightmare. I felt strangely ill. I was wet and clammy with perspiration, and nervous to a degree that I had never before experienced in my existence. Nevertheless, I noted everything distinctly. On the hearthstone there was still a mass of glowing red embers. I heard the distant booming of the sea, and round the house the wind moaned with a peculiar, eerie, creepy sound.

Suddenly I sprang from the bed, impelled thereto by an impulse I was bound to obey, and by the same impulse was drawn towards the door. I laid my hand on the handle. I turned it, opened the door, and gazed into the long dark corridor. A sigh fell upon my ears. An unmistakable human sigh, in which was expressed all intensity of suffering and sorrow that thrilled me to the heart. I shrank back, and was about to close the door, when out of the darkness was evolved the glowing figure of a woman clad in blood-stained garments and with dishevelled hair. She turned her white corpse-like face towards me, and her eyes pleaded with a pleading that was irresistible, while she pointed the index finger of her left hand downwards, and then beckoned me. Then I followed whither she led. I could no more resist than the unrestrained needle can resist the attracting magnet. Clad only in my night apparel, and with bare feet and legs, I followed the spectre along the corridor, down the broad oak stairs, traversing another passage to the rear of the building until I found myself standing before a heavy barred door. At that moment the spectre vanished, and I retraced my steps like one who walked in a dream. I got back to my bedroom, but how I don't quite know; nor have any recollection of getting into bed. Hours afterwards I awoke. It was broad daylight. The horror of the night came back to me with overwhelming force, and made me faint and ill. I managed, however, to struggle through with my toilet, and hurried from that haunted room. It was a beautifully fine morning. The sun was shining brightly, and the birds carolled blithely in every tree and bush. I strolled out on to the lawn, and paced up and down. I was strangely agitated, and asked myself over and over again if what I had seen or dreamed about had any significance.

Presently my host came out. He visibly started as he saw me.

"Hullo, old chap. What's the matter with you?" he exclaimed. "You look jolly queer; as though you had been having a bad night of it."

"I have had a bad night."

His manner became more serious and grave.

"What—seen anything?"

"Yes."

"The deuce! You don't mean it, really!"

"Indeed I do. I have gone through a night of horror such as I could not live through again. But let us have breakfast first, and then I will try and make you understand what I have suffered, and you shall judge for yourself whether any significance is to be attached to my dream, or whatever you like to call it."

We walked, without speaking, into the breakfast room, where my charming hostess greeted me cordially; but she, like her husband, noticed my changed appearance, and expressed alarm and anxiety. I reassured her by saying I had had a rather restless night, and didn't feel particularly well, but that it was a mere passing ailment. I was unable to partake of much breakfast, and both my good friend and his wife again showed some anxiety, and pressed me to state the cause of my distress. As I could not see any good cause that was to be gained by concealment, and even at the risk of being laughed at by my host, I recounted the experience I had gone through during the night of terror.

So far from my host showing any disposition to ridicule me, as I quite expected he would have done, he became unusually thoughtful, and presently said:

"Either this is a wild phantasy of your own brain, or there is something in it. The door that the ghost of the woman led you to is situated on the top of a flight of stone steps, leading to a vault below the building, which I have never used, and have never even had the curiosity to enter, though I did once go to the bottom of the steps; but the place was so exceedingly suggestive of a tomb that I mentally exclaimed, 'I've no use for this dungeon,' and so I shut it up, bolted and barred the door, and have never opened it since."

I answered that the time had come when he must once more descend into that cellar or vault, whatever it was. He asked me if I would accompany him, and, of course, I said I would. So he summoned his head gardener, and after much searching about, the key of the door was found; but even then the door was only opened with difficulty, as lock and key alike were foul with rust.

As we descended the slimy, slippery stone steps, each of us carrying a candle, a rank, mouldy smell greeted us, and a cold noisome atmosphere pervaded the place. The steps led into a huge vault, that apparently extended under the greater part of the building. The roof was arched, and was supported by brick pillars. The floor was the natural earth, and was soft and oozy. The miasma was almost overpowering, notwithstanding that there were ventilating slits in the wall in various places.

We proceeded to explore this vast cellar, and found that there was an air shaft which apparently communicated with the roof of the house; but it was choked with rubbish, old boxes, and the like. The gardener cleared this away, and then looking up, we could see the blue sky overhead.

Continuing our exploration, we noted that in a recess formed by the angle of the walls was a quantity of bricks and mortar. Under other circumstances this would not, perhaps, have aroused our curiosity or suspicions. But in this instance it did; and we examined the wall thereabouts with painful interest, until the conviction was forced upon us that a space of over a yard in width, and extending from door to roof, had recently been filled in. I was drawn towards the new brickwork by some subtle magic, some weird fascination. I examined it with an eager, critical, curious interest, and the thoughts that passed through my brain were reflected in the faces of my companions. We looked at each other, and each knew by some unexplainable instinct what was passing in his fellow's mind.

"It seems to me we are face to face with some mystery," remarked Dick, solemnly. Indeed, throughout all the years I had known him I had never before seen him so serious. Usually his expression was that of good-humoured cynicism,

but now he might have been a judge about to pass the doom of death on a red-handed sinner.

"Yes," I answered, "there is a mystery, unless I have been tricked by my own fancy."

"Umph! it is strange," muttered Dick to himself.

"Well, sir," chimed in the gardener, "you know there have been some precious queer stories going about for a long time. And before you come and took the place plenty of folks round about used to say they'd seen some uncanny sights. I never had no faith in them stories myself; but, after all, maybe there's truth in 'em."

Dick picked up half a brick and began to tap the wall with it where the new work was, and the taps gave forth a hollow sound, quite different from the sound produced when the other parts of the wall were struck.

"I say, old chap," exclaimed my host, with a sorry attempt at a smile, "upon my word, I begin to experience a sort of uncanny kind of feeling. I'll be hanged if I am not getting as superstitious as you are."

"You may call me superstitious if you like, but either I have seen what I have seen, or my senses have played the fool with me. Anyway, let us put it to the test."

"How?"

"By breaking away some of that new brickwork."

Dick laughed a laugh that wasn't a laugh, as he asked:

"What do you expect to find?" I hesitated what to say, and he added the answer himself—"Mouldering bones, if our ghostly visitor hasn't deceived you."

"Mouldering bones!" I echoed involuntarily.

"Gardener, have you got a crowbar amongst your tools?" Dick asked.

"Yes, sir."

"Go up and get it."

The man obeyed the command.

"This is a strange sort of business altogether," Dick continued, after glancing round the vast and gloomy cellar. "But, upon my word, to tell you the truth, I'm half ashamed of myself for yielding to anything like superstition. It strikes me that you'll find you are the victim of a trick of the imagination, and that these bogey fancies of yours have placed us in rather a ridiculous position."

In answer to this I could not possibly resist reminding Dick that even scientists admitted that there were certain phenomena—they called them "natural phenomena"—that could not be accounted for by ordinary laws.

Dick shrugged his shoulders and remarked with assumed indifference:

"Perhaps—perhaps it is so." He proceeded to fill his pipe with tobacco, and having lit it he smoked with a nervous energy quite unusual with him.

The gardener was only away about ten minutes, but it seemed infinitely longer. He brought both a pickaxe and a crowbar with him, and in obedience to his master's orders he commenced to hack at the wall. A brick was soon dislodged. Then the crowbar was inserted in the hole, and a mass prized out. From the opening came forth a sickening odour, so that we all drew back instinctively, and I am sure we all shuddered, and I saw the pipe fall from Dick's lips; but he snatched it up quickly and puffed at it vigorously until a cloud of smoke hung in the fœtid and stagnant air. Then picking up a candle from the ground, where it had been placed, he approached the hole, holding the candle in such a position that its rays were thrown into the opening. In a few moments he started back with an exclamation:

"My God! the ghost hasn't lied," he said, and I noticed that his face paled. I peered into the hole and so did the gardener, and we both drew back with a start, for sure enough in that recess were decaying human remains.

"This awful business must be investigated," said Dick. "Come, let us go."

We needed no second bidding. We were only too glad to quit that place of horror, and get into the fresh air and bright sunlight. We verily felt that we had come up out of a tomb, and we knew

that once more the adage, "Murder will out," had proved true.

Half an hour later Dick and I were driving to the nearest town to lay information of the awful discovery we had made, and the subsequent search carried out by the police brought two skeletons to light. Critical medical examination left not the shadow of a doubt that they were the remains of a woman and a girl and each had been brutally murdered. Of course it became necessary to hold an inquest, and the police set to work to collect evidence as to the identity of the bodies hidden in the recess in the wall.

Naturally all the stories which had been current for so many years throughout the country were revived, and the gossips were busy in retelling all they had heard, with many additions of their own, of course. But the chief topic was that of the strange disappearance of the wife and daughter of the once owner of the castle, Greeta Jones. This story had been touched upon the previous night, during the after dinner chat in my host's smoking room. Morgan, as was remembered had gambled his fortune away, and married a lady much older than himself, who bore him a daughter who was subject to epileptic fits. When this girl was about twelve she and her mother disappeared from the neighbourhood, and, according to the husband's account, they had gone to London.

Then he left, and people troubled themselves no more about him and his belongings.

A quarter of a century had passed since that period, and Bleak Hill Castle had gone through many vicissitudes until it fell into the hands of my friend Dick Dirckman. The more the history of Greeta Jones was gone into the more it was made clear that the remains which had been bricked up in the cellar were those of his wife and daughter. That the unfortunate girl and woman had been brutally and barbarously murdered there wasn't a doubt. The question was, who murdered them? After leaving Wales Greeta Jones—as was brought to light—led a wild life in London. One night, while in a state of intoxication, he was knocked down by a cab, and so seriously injured that he died while being carried to the hospital; and with him his secret, for could there be any reasonable doubt that, even if he was not the actual murderer, he had connived at the crime. But there was reason to believe that he killed his wife and child with his own hand, and that with the aid of a navvy, whose services he bought, he bricked the bodies up in the cellar. It was remembered that a navvy named Howell Williams had been in the habit of going to the castle frequently, and that suddenly he became

possessed of what was, for him, a considerable sum of money. For several weeks he drank hard; then being a single man, he packed up his few belongings and gave out that he was going to California, and all efforts to trace him failed.

So much for this ghastly crime. As to the circumstances that led to its discovery, it was curious that I should have been selected as the medium for bringing it to light. Why it should have been so I cannot and do not pretend to explain. I have recorded facts as they occurred; I leave others to solve the mystery.

THE BURNED HOUSE

Vincent O'Sullivan

LOST TRAVELERS ARE IDEAL victims of supernatural events and horrific entities, whether vampires, monsters, or ghosts, and even those who escape unscathed have a scary story to tell, like the late night perambulator in this excellent little story. Vincent O'Sullivan (1868–1940) was born to a wealthy family in New York City and attended Columbia Grammar School, then moved to England and graduated from Oscott Roman Catholic College before attending Oxford.

In 1894, he began to contribute stories and poems to *The Senate* magazine, resulting in a collection of the poems; in 1896, *A Book of Bargains*, one of the most important early collections of supernatural fiction, was published by his friend Leonard Smithers, a key figure in the *Yellow Book* decade of the 1890s. O'Sullivan was the only American of significance in the Aesthetic Movement, which was led by Aubrey Beardsley, Oscar Wilde, Ernest Dowson, and Arthur Symons. Like so many of his circle, O'Sullivan's work was filled with morbidity and decadence. In later years, his style reflected changing tastes and he wrote with clarity and precision. O'Sullivan used his means to help friends, notably Wilde after his release from prison, and his wealth was eventually dissipated. Of his friend O'Sullivan, Wilde once wrote that he is "really very pleasant, for one who treats life from the standpoint of the tomb." There was strong negative reaction to his support of the despised Wilde, resulting in a largely closed market for O'Sullivan's work. He was reduced to dire poverty late in life and died in a pauper's ward in Paris shortly after the German occupation.

"The Burned House" was first published in the October 1916 issue of *The Century Magazine;* it appears to have remained uncollected until the publication of *Master of Fallen Years: The Complete Supernatural Stories of Vincent O'Sullivan* (London, Ghost Story Press, 1995).

The Burned House

VINCENT O'SULLIVAN

ONE NIGHT AT THE end of dinner, the last time I crossed the Atlantic, somebody in our group remarked that we were just passing over the spot where the *Lusitania* had gone down. Whether this were the case or not, the thought of it was enough to make us rather grave, and we dropped into some more or less serious discussion about the emotions of men and women who see all hope gone, and realise that they are going to sink with the vessel.

From that the talk wandered to the fate of the drowned. Was not theirs, after all, a fortunate end? Somebody related details from the narratives of those who had been all-but drowned in the accident of the war. A Scotch lady inquired fancifully if the ghosts of those who are lost at sea ever appear above the waters and come aboard ships. Would there be danger of seeing one when the light was turned out in her cabin? This put an end to all seriousness, and most of us laughed. But a little, tight-faced man, bleak and iron-grey, who had been listening attentively, did not laugh. The lady noticed his decorum, and appealed to him for support.

"You are like me—you believe in ghosts!" she asked lightly.

He hesitated, thinking it over.

"In ghosts?" he repeated slowly. "N-no, I don't know as I do. I've never had any personal experience that way. I've never seen the ghost of anyone I knew. Has anybody here?"

No one replied. Instead, most of us laughed again—a little uneasily, perhaps.

"All the same, strange enough things happen in life," resumed the man, "even if you leave out ghosts, that you can't clear up by laughing. You laugh till you've had some experience big enough to shock you, and then you don't laugh any more. It's like being thrown out of a car—"

At this moment there was a blast on the whistle, and everybody rushed up on deck. As it turned out, we had only entered into a belt of fog. On the upper deck I fell in again with the little man, smoking a cigar and walking up and down. We took a few turns together, and he referred to the conversation at dinner. Our laughter evidently rankled in his mind.

"So many strange things happen in life that you can't account for," he protested. "You go on laughing at faith-healing, and at dreams, and this and that, and then something comes along that you just can't explain. You have got to throw up your hands and allow that it doesn't answer to any tests our experience has provided us with. Now, I'm as matter-of-fact a man as any of those folks down there; but once I had an experience which I had to conclude was out of the ordinary. Whether other people believe it or not, or whether they think they can explain it, don't matter. It happened to me, and I could no more doubt it than I could doubt having had a tooth pulled after the dentist had done it. If you will sit down here with me in this corner, out of the wind, I'll tell you how it was.

"Some years ago I had to be for several months in the North of England. I was before the courts; it does not signify now what for, and it is all forgotten by this time. But it was a long and worrying case, and it aged me by twenty years. Well, sir, all through the trial, in that grimy Manchester court-room, I kept thinking and thinking of a fresh little place I knew in the Lake district, and it helped to get through the hours by thinking that if things went well with me I'd go there at once. And so it was that on the very next morning after I was acquitted I boarded the north-bound train.

"It was the early autumn; the days were closing in, and it was night and cold when I arrived. The village was very dark and deserted; they don't go out much after dark in those parts, anyhow, and the keen mountain wind was enough to quell any lingering desire. The hotel was not one of those modern places which are equipped and upholstered like the great city hotels. It was one of the real old-fashioned taverns, about as uncomfortable places as there are on earth, where the idea is to show the traveller that travelling is a penitential state, and that, morally and physically, the best place for him is home. The landlord brought me a kind of supper, with his hat on and a pipe in his mouth. The room was chilly, but when I asked for a fire, he said he guessed he couldn't go out to the woodshed till morning. There was nothing else to do, when I had eaten my supper, but to go outside, both to get the smell of the lamp out of my nose and to warm myself by a short walk.

"As I did not know the country well, I did not mean to go far. But although it was an overcast night, with a high north-east wind and an occasional flurry of rain, the moon was up, and, even concealed by clouds as it was, it yet lit the night with a kind of twilight grey—not vivid, like the open moonlight, but good enough to see some distance. On account of this, I prolonged my stroll, and kept walking on and on till

I was a considerable way from the village, and in a region as lonely as anywhere in the country. Great trees and shrubs bordered the road, and many feet below was a mountain stream. What with the passion of the wind pouring through the high trees and the shout of the water racing among the boulders, it seemed to me sometimes like the noise of a crowd of people. Sometimes the branches of the trees became so thick that I was walking as if in a black pit, unable to see my hand close to my face. Then, coming out from the tunnel of branches, I would step once more into a grey clearness which opened the road and surrounding country a good way on all sides.

"I suppose it might be some three-quarters of an hour I had been walking when I came to a fork of the road. One branch ran downward, getting almost on a level with the bed of the torrent; the other mounted in a steep hill, and this, after a little idle debating, I decided to follow. After I had climbed for more than half a mile, thinking that if I should happen to lose track of one of the landmarks I should be very badly lost, the path—for it was now no more than that— curved, and I came out on a broad plateau. There, to my astonishment, I saw a house. It was a good-sized house, three storeys high, with a verandah round two sides of it, and from the elevation on which it stood it commanded a far stretch of country.

"There were a few great trees at a little distance from the house, and behind it, a stone's-throw away, was a clump of bushes. Still, it looked lonely and stark, offering its four sides unprotected to the winds. For all that, I was very glad to see it. 'It does not matter now,' I thought, 'whether I have lost my way or not. The people in the house will set me right.'

"But when I came up to it I found that it was, to all appearance, uninhabited. The shutters were closed on all the windows; there was not a spark of light anywhere. There was something about it, something sinister and barren, that gave me the kind of shiver you have at the door of a room where you know that a dead man lies inside, or if you get thinking hard about dropping over the rail into that black waste of waters out there. This feeling, you know, isn't altogether unpleasant; you relish all the better your present security. It was the same with me standing before that house. I was not *really* frightened. I was alone up there, miles from any kind of help, at the mercy of whoever might be lurking behind the shutters of that sullen house; but I felt that by all the chances I was perfectly alone and safe. My sensation of the uncanny was due to the effect on the nerves produced by wild scenery and the unexpected sight of a house in such a very lonely situation. Thus I reasoned, and, instead of following the road farther, I walked over the grass till I came to a stone wall, perhaps two hundred and fifty yards in front of the house, and rested my arms on it, looking forth at the scene.

"On the crests of the hills far away a strange light lingered, like the first touch of dawn in the sky on a rainy morning or the last glimpse of twilight before night comes. Between me and the hills was a wide stretch of open country. On my right hand was an apple orchard, and I observed that a stile had been made in the wall of piled stones to enable the house people to go back and forth.

"Now, after I had been there leaning on the wall some considerable time, I saw a man coming towards me through the orchard. He was walking with a good, free stride, and as he drew nearer I could see that he was a tall, sinewy fellow between twenty-five and thirty, with a shaven face, wearing a slouch hat, a dark woollen shirt, and gaiters. When he reached the stile and began climbing over it I bade him goodnight in neighbourly fashion. He made no reply, but he looked me straight in the face, and the look gave me a qualm. Not that it was an evil face, mind you—it was a handsome, serious face—but it was ravaged by some terrible passion: stealth was on it, ruthlessness, and a deadly resolution, and at the same time such a look as a man driven by some uncontrollable power might throw on surrounding things, asking for comprehension

and mercy. It was impossible for me to resent his churlishness, his thoughts were so certainly elsewhere. I doubt if he even saw me.

"He could not have gone by more than a quarter of a minute when I turned to look after him. He had disappeared. The plateau lay bare before me, and it seemed impossible that, even if he had sprinted like an athlete, he could have got inside the house in so little time. But I have always made it a rule to attribute what I cannot understand to natural causes that I have failed to observe. I said to myself that no doubt the man had gone back into the orchard by some other opening in the wall lower down, or there might be some flaw in my vision owing to the uncertain and distorting light.

"But even as I continued to look towards the house, leaning my back now against the wall, I noticed that there were lights springing up in the windows behind the shutters. They were flickering lights, now bright—now dim, and had a ruddy glow like firelight. Before I had looked long I became convinced that it was indeed firelight—the house was on fire. Black smoke began to pour from the roof; the red sparks flew in the wind. Then at a window above the roof of the verandah the shutters were thrown open, and I heard a woman shriek. I ran towards the house as hard as I could, and when I drew near I could see her plainly.

"She was a young woman; her hair fell in disorder over her white nightgown. She stretched out her bare arms, screaming. I saw a man come behind and seize her. But they were caught in a trap. The flames were licking round the windows, and the smoke was killing them. Even now the part of the house where they stood was caving in.

"Appalled by this horrible tragedy which had thus suddenly risen before me, I made my way still nearer the house, thinking that if the two could struggle to the side of the house not bounded by the verandah they might jump, and I might break the fall. I was shouting this at them; I was right up close to the fire; and then I was struck by—I noticed for the first time an astonishing thing—the flames had no heat in them!

"I was standing near enough to the fire to be singed by it, and yet I felt no heat. The sparks were flying about my head; some fell on my hands, and they did not burn. And now I perceived that, although the smoke was rolling in columns, I was not choked by the smoke, and that there had been no smell of smoke since the fire broke out. Neither was there any glare against the sky.

"As I stood there stupefied, wondering how these things could be, the whole house was swept by a very tornado of flame, and crashed down in a red ruin.

"Stricken to the heart by this abominable catastrophe, I made my way uncertainly down the hill, shouting for help. As I came to a little wooden bridge spanning the torrent, just beyond where the roads forked, I saw what appeared to be a rope in loose coils lying there. I saw that part of it was fastened to the railing of the bridge and hung outside, and I looked over. There was a man's body swinging by the neck between the road and the stream. I leaned over still farther, and then I recognised him as the man I had seen coming out of the orchard. His hat had fallen off, and the toes of his boots just touched the water.

"It seemed hardly possible, and yet it was certain. That was the man, and he was hanging there. I scrambled down at the side of the bridge, and put out my hand to seize the body, so that I might lift it up and relieve the weight on the rope. I succeeded in clutching hold of his loose shirt, and for a second I thought that it had come away in my hand. Then I found that my hand had closed on nothing, I had clutched nothing but air. And yet the figure swung by the neck before my eyes!

"I was suffocated with such horror that I feared for a moment I must lose consciousness. The next minute I was running and stumbling along that dark road in mortal anxiety, my one idea being to rouse the town, and bring men to the bridge. That, I say, was my intention; but the fact is that when I came at last in sight of the village I slowed down instinctively and began to reflect. After all, I was unknown there; I had just gone through a disagreeable trial in Manchester, and rural people were notoriously given to groundless suspicion. I had had enough of the law, and of arrests without sufficient evidence. The wisest thing would be to drop a hint or two before the landlord, and judge by his demeanour whether to proceed.

"I found him sitting where I had left him, smoking, in his shirtsleeves, with his hat on.

"'Well,' he said slowly, 'I didn't know where you had got to.'

"I told him I had been taking a walk. I went on to mention casually the fork in the road, the hill, and the plateau.

"'And who lives in that house?' I asked with a good show of indifference, 'on top of the hill?'

"He stared.

"'House? There ain't no house up there,' he said positively. 'Old Joe Snedeker, who owns the land, says he's going to build a house up there for his son to live in when he gets married; but he ain't begun yet, and some folks reckon he never will.'

"'I feel sure I *saw* a house,' I protested feebly. But I was thinking—no heat in the fire, no substance in the body. I had not the courage to dispute.

"The landlord looked at me not unkindly. 'You seem sort of done up,' he remarked. 'What you want is to go to bed.'"

The man who was telling me the story paused, and for a moment we sat silent, listening to the pant of the machinery, the thrumming of the wind in the wire stays, and the lash of the sea. Some voices were singing on the deck below. I considered him with the shade of contemptuous superiority we feel, as a rule, towards those who tell us their dreams or what some fortune-teller has predicted.

"Hallucinations," I said at last, with reassuring indulgence. "Trick of the vision, toxic opthalmia. After the long strain of your trial your nerves were shattered."

"That's what I thought myself," he replied shortly, "especially after I had been out to the plateau the next morning, and saw no sign that a house had ever stood there."

"And no corpse at the bridge?" I said; and laughed.

"And no corpse at the bridge."

He tried to get a light for another cigar. This took him some little time, and when at last he managed it, he got out of his chair and stood looking down at me.

"Now listen. I told you that the thing happened several years ago. I'd got almost to forget it; if you can only persuade yourself that a thing is a freak of imagination, it pretty soon gets dim inside your head. Delusions have no staying power once it is realised that they are delusions. Whenever it did come back to me, I used to think how near I had once been to going out of my mind. That was all.

"Well, last year, being up north, I went up to that village again. I went to the same hotel, and found the same landlord. He remembered me at once as 'the feller who stayed with him and thought he saw a house,' 'I believe you had the jim-jams,' he said.

"We laughed, and the landlord went on:

"'There's been a house there since, though.'

"'Has there?'

"'Yes; an' it ha' been as well if there never had been. Old Snedeker built it for his son, a fine big house with a verandah on two sides. The son, young Joe, got courting Mabel Elting from Windermere. She'd gone down to work in a shop somewhere in Liverpool. Well, sir, she used to get carrying on with another young feller 'bout here, Jim Travers, and Jim was wild about her; used to save up his wages to go down to see her. But she chucked him in the end, and married Joe; I suppose because Joe had the house, and the old man's money to expect. Well, poor Jim must ha' gone quite mad. What do you think he did? The very first night the new-wed pair spent in that house he burned it down. Burned the two of them in their bed, and he was as nice and quiet a feller as you want to see. He may ha' been full of whisky at the time.'

"'No, he wasn't,' I said.

"The landlord looked surprised.

"'You've heard about it?'

"'No; go on.'

"'Yes, sir, he burned them in their bed. And then what do you think he did? He hung himself at the little bridge half a mile below. Do you remember where the road divides? Well, it was there. I saw his body hanging there myself the next morning. The toes of his boots were just touching the water.'"

KIDS WILL BE KIDS

Rosemary Timperley

THE AUTHOR OF MORE than sixty novels and several hundred short stories, Rosemary (Kenyon) Timperley (1920–1988) was a twentieth-century woman who wrote with a Victorian sensibility. Along with an enormous amount of general fiction, she produced scores of ghost stories that tend to be charming and gentle in tone, rather than terrifying.

Born in London, she worked as a schoolteacher and journalist before becoming a full-time writer in 1960, though she had sold her first story in 1946 to *Illustrated* magazine. She became a regular contributor to numerous periodicals, including the London *Evening News*, *London Mystery Selection*, *Good Housekeeping*, *Reveille*, etc. It was when one of her stories, "Christmas Meeting," was selected for *The Second Ghost Book* (1952), the prestigious series edited by Cynthia Asquith, that she began to acquire a reputation as one of Great Britain's foremost ghost story writers. She went on to become the editor of the *Ghost Books* for five years (1969–1973).

Several of her novels have been adapted for telecasts on the BBC, including *The Velvet Smile* (1961), *Yesterday's Voices* (1961), and *Juliet* (1974). Many of her short stories have also been adapted for radio by the BBC, and she has written several original radio dramas.

"Harry," perhaps her most famous story, has twice been adapted for film, first in 1960 as an episode of the Canadian television series *First Person*, then as a short American film titled *Twice Removed* in 2003. It was originally published in *The Third Ghost Book*, edited by Cynthia Asquith (London, James Barrie, 1955).

There's one sure place where old kin and friends can get together—forever.

Harry

ROSEMARY TIMPERLEY

SUCH ORDINARY THINGS make me afraid. Sunshine. Sharp shadows on grass. White roses. Children with red hair. And the name—Harry. Such an ordinary name.

Yet the first time Christine mentioned the name, I felt a premonition of fear.

She was five years old, due to start school in three months' time. It was a hot, beautiful day and she was playing alone in the garden, as she often did. I saw her lying on her stomach in the grass, picking daisies and making daisy-chains with laborious pleasure. The sun burned on her pale red hair and made her skin look very white. Her big blue eyes were wide with concentration.

Suddenly she looked towards the bush of

white roses, which cast its shadow over the grass, and smiled.

"Yes, I'm Christine," she said. She rose and walked slowly towards the bush, her little plump legs defenceless and endearing beneath the too short blue cotton skirt. She was growing fast.

"With my mummy and daddy," she said clearly. Then, after a pause, "Oh, but *they* are my mummy and daddy."

She was in the shadow of the bush now. It was as if she'd walked out of the world of light into darkness. Uneasy, without quite knowing why, I called her:

"Chris, what are you doing?"

"Nothing." The voice sounded too far away.

"Come indoors now. It's too hot for you out there."

"Not too hot."

"Come indoors, Chris."

She said: "I must go in now. Goodbye," then walked slowly towards the house.

"Chris, who were you talking to?"

"Harry," she said.

"Who's Harry?"

"Harry."

I couldn't get anything else out of her, so I just gave her some cake and milk and read to her until bedtime. As she listened, she stared out at the garden. Once she smiled and waved. It was a relief finally to tuck her up in bed and feel she was safe.

When Jim, my husband, came home I told him about the mysterious "Harry." He laughed.

"Oh, she's started that lark, has she?"

"What do you mean, Jim?"

"It's not so very rare for only children to have an imaginary companion. Some kids talk to their dolls. Chris has never been keen on her dolls. She hasn't any brothers or sisters. She hasn't any friends her own age. So she imagines someone."

"But why has she picked that particular name?"

He shrugged. "You know how kids pick things up. I don't know what you're worrying about, honestly I don't."

"Nor do I really. It's just that I feel extra re-sponsible for her. More so than if I were her real mother."

"I know, but she's all right. Chris is fine. She's a pretty healthy, intelligent little girl. A credit to you."

"And to you."

"In fact, we're thoroughly nice parents!"

"And so modest."

We laughed together and he kissed me. I felt consoled.

Until next morning.

Again the sun shone brilliantly on the small, bright lawn and white roses. Christine was sitting on the grass, cross-legged, staring towards the rose bush, smiling.

"Hello," she said. "I hoped you'd come. . . . Because I like you. How old are you? . . . I'm only five and a piece. . . . I'm *not* a baby! I'm going to school soon and I shall have a new dress. A green one. Do you go to school? . . . What do you do then?" She was silent for a while, nodding, listening, absorbed.

I felt myself going cold as I stood there in the kitchen. "Don't be silly. Lots of children have an imaginary companion," I told myself desperately. "Just carry on as if nothing were happening. Don't listen. Don't be a fool."

But I called Chris in earlier than usual for her midmorning milk.

"Your milk's ready, Chris. Come along."

"In a minute." This was a strange reply. Usually she rushed in eagerly for her milk and the special sandwich cream biscuits, over which she was a little gourmande.

"Come now, darling," I said.

"Can Harry come too?"

"No!" The cry burst from me harshly, surprising me.

"Goodbye, Harry. I'm sorry you can't come in but I've got to have my milk," Chris said, then ran towards the house.

"Why can't Harry have some milk too?" she challenged me.

"Who *is* Harry, darling?"

"Harry's my brother."

"But Chris, you haven't got a brother. Daddy

and mummy have only got one child, one little girl, that's you. Harry can't be your brother."

"Harry's my brother. He says so." She bent over the glass of milk and emerged with a smeary top lip. Then she grabbed at the biscuits. At least "Harry" hadn't spoilt her appetite!

After she'd had her milk, I said, "We'll go shopping now, Chris. You'd like to come to the shops with me, wouldn't you?"

"I want to stay with Harry."

"Well you can't. You're coming with me."

"Can Harry come too?"

"No."

My hands were trembling as I put on my hat and gloves. It was chilly in the house nowadays, as if there were a cold shadow over it in spite of the sun outside. Chris came with me meekly enough, but as we walked down the street, she turned and waved.

I didn't mention any of this to Jim that night. I knew he'd only scoff as he'd done before. But when Christine's "Harry" fantasy went on day after day, it got more and more on my nerves. I came to hate and dread those long summer days. I longed for grey skies and rain. I longed for the white roses to wither and die. I trembled when I heard Christine's voice prattling away in the garden. She talked quite unrestrainedly to "Harry" now.

One Sunday, when Jim heard her at it, he said:

"I'll say one thing for imaginary companions, they help a child on with her talking. Chris is talking much more freely than she used to."

"With an accent," I blurted out.

"An accent?"

"A slight cockney accent."

"My dearest, every London child gets a slight cockney accent. It'll be much worse when she goes to school and meets lots of other kids."

"We don't talk cockney. Where does she get it from? Who can she be getting it from except Ha——" I couldn't say the name.

"The baker, the milkman, the dustman, the coalman, the window cleaner—want any more?"

"I suppose not." I laughed ruefully. Jim made me feel foolish.

"Anyway," said Jim, "I haven't noticed any cockney in her voice."

"There isn't when she talks to us. It's only when she's talking to—to him."

"To Harry. You know, I'm getting quite attached to young Harry. Wouldn't it be fun if one day we looked out and saw him?"

"Don't," I cried. "Don't say that! It's my nightmare. My waking nightmare. Oh, Jim, I can't bear it much longer."

He looked astonished. "This Harry business is really getting you down, isn't it?"

"Of course it is! Day in, day out, I hear nothing but 'Harry this,' 'Harry that,' 'Harry says,' 'Harry thinks,' 'Can Harry have some?' 'Can Harry come too?'—it's all right for you out at the office all day, but I have to live with it: I'm—I'm afraid of it, Jim. It's so queer."

"Do you know what I think you should do to put your mind at rest?"

"What?"

"Take Chris along to see old Dr. Webster tomorrow. Let him have a little talk with her."

"Do you think she's ill—in her mind?"

"Good heavens, no! But when we come across something that's beyond us, it's as well to take professional advice."

Next day I took Chris to see Dr. Webster. I left her in the waiting-room while I told him briefly about Harry. He nodded sympathetically, then said:

"It's a fairly unusual case, Mrs. James, but by no means unique. I've had several cases of children's imaginary companions becoming so real to them that the parents got the jitters. I expect she's rather a lonely little girl, isn't she?"

"She doesn't know any other children. We're new to the neighbourhood, you see. But that will be put right when she starts school."

"And I think you'll find that when she goes to school and meets other children, these fantasies will disappear. You see, every child needs company of her own age, and if she doesn't get it, she invents it. Older people who are lonely talk to themselves. That doesn't mean that they're crazy, just that they need to talk to someone. A child is more practical. Seems silly to talk to oneself, she thinks, so she invents someone to talk to. I honestly don't think you've anything to worry about."

"That's what my husband says."

"I'm sure he does. Still, I'll have a chat with Christine as you've brought her. Leave us alone together."

I went to the waiting-room to fetch Chris. She was at the window. She said: "Harry's waiting."

"Where, Chris?" I said quietly, wanting suddenly to see him with her eyes.

"There. By the rose bush."

The doctor had a bush of white roses in his garden.

"There's no-one there," I said. Chris gave me a glance of unchildlike scorn. "Dr. Webster wants to see you now, darling," I said shakily. "You remember him, don't you? He gave you sweets when you were getting better from chicken pox."

"Yes," she said and went willingly enough to the doctor's surgery. I waited restlessly. Faintly I heard their voices through the wall, heard the doctor's chuckle, Christine's high peal of laughter. She was talking away to the doctor in a way she didn't talk to me.

When they came out, he said: "Nothing wrong with her whatever. She's just an imaginative little monkey. A word of advice, Mrs. James. Let her talk about Harry. Let her become accustomed to confiding in you. I gather you've shown some disapproval of this 'brother' of hers so she doesn't talk much to you about him. He makes wooden toys, doesn't he, Chris?"

"Yes, Harry makes wooden toys."

"And he can read and write, can't he?"

"And swim and climb trees and paint pictures. Harry can do everything. He's a wonderful brother." Her little face flushed with adoration.

The doctor patted me on the shoulder and said: "Harry sounds a very nice brother for her. He's even got red hair like you, Chris, hasn't he?"

"Harry's got red hair," said Chris proudly, "redder than my hair. And he's nearly as tall as daddy, only thinner. He's as tall as you, mummy. He's fourteen. He says he's tall for his age. What *is* tall for his age?"

"Mummy will tell you about that as you walk home," said Dr. Webster. "Now, goodbye, Mrs. James. Don't worry. Just let her prattle. Goodbye, Chris. Give my love to Harry."

"He's there," said Chris, pointing to the doctor's garden. "He's been waiting for me."

Dr. Webster laughed. "They're incorrigible, aren't they?" he said. "I know one poor mother whose children invented a whole tribe of imaginary natives whose rituals and taboos ruled the household. Perhaps you're lucky, Mrs. James!"

I tried to feel comforted by all this, but I wasn't. I hoped sincerely that when Chris started school this wretched Harry business would finish.

Chris ran ahead of me. She looked up as if at someone beside her. For a brief, dreadful second, I saw a shadow on the pavement alongside her own—a long, thin shadow—like a boy's shadow. Then it was gone. I ran to catch her up and held her hand tightly all the way home. Even in the comparative security of the house— the house so strangely cold in this hot weather— I never let her out of my sight. On the face of it she behaved no differently towards me, but in reality she was drifting away. The child in my house was becoming a stranger.

For the first time since Jim and I had adopted Chris, I wondered seriously: Who is she? Where does she come from? Who were her real parents? Who is this little loved stranger I've taken as a daughter? Who *is* Christine?

Another week passed. It was Harry, Harry all the time. The day before she was to start school, Chris said:

"Not going to school."

"You're going to school tomorrow, Chris.

You're looking forward to it. You know you are. There'll be lots of other little girls and boys."

"Harry says he can't come too."

"You won't want Harry at school. He'll—" I tried hard to follow the doctor's advice and appear to believe in Harry—"He'll be too old. He'd feel silly among little boys and girls, a great lad of fourteen."

"I won't go to school without Harry. I want to be with Harry." She began to weep, loudly, painfully.

"Chris, stop this nonsense! Stop it!" I struck her sharply on the arm. Her crying ceased immediately. She stared at me, her blue eyes wide open and frighteningly cold. She gave me an adult stare that made me tremble. Then she said:

"You don't love me. Harry loves me. Harry wants me. He says I can go with him."

"I will not hear any more of this!" I shouted, hating the anger in my voice, hating myself for being angry at all with a little girl—*my* little girl—mine——

I went down on one knee and held out my arms.

"Chris, darling, come here."

She came, slowly. "I love you," I said. "I love you, Chris, and I'm real. School is real. Go to school to please me."

"Harry will go away if I do."

"You'll have other friends."

"I want Harry." Again the tears, wet against my shoulder now. I held her closely.

"You're tired, baby. Come to bed."

She slept with the tear stains still on her face.

It was still daylight. I went to the window to draw her curtains. Golden shadows and long strips of sunshine in the garden. Then, again, like a dream, the long thin clear-cut shadow of a boy near the white roses. Like a mad woman I opened the window and shouted:

"Harry! Harry!"

I thought I saw a glimmer of red among the roses, like close red curls on a boy's head. Then there was nothing.

When I told Jim about Christine's emotional outburst he said: "Poor little kid. It's always

a nervy business, starting school. She'll be all right once she gets there. You'll be hearing less about Harry too, as time goes on."

"Harry doesn't want her to go to school."

"Hey! You sound as if you believe in Harry yourself!"

"Sometimes I do."

"Believing in evil spirits in your old age?" he teased me. But his eyes were concerned. He thought I was going "round the bend" and small blame to him!

"I don't think Harry's evil," I said. "He's just a boy. A boy who doesn't exist, except for Christine. And who *is* Christine?"

"None of that!" said Jim sharply. "When we adopted Chris we decided she was to be our own child. No probing into the past. No wondering and worrying. No mysteries. Chris is as much ours as if she'd been born of our flesh. Who is Christine indeed! She's our daughter—and just you remember that!"

"Yes, Jim, you're right. Of course you're right."

He'd been so fierce about it that I didn't tell him what I planned to do the next day while Chris was at school.

Next morning Chris was silent and sulky. Jim joked with her and tried to cheer her, but all she would do was look out of the window and say: "Harry's gone."

"You won't need Harry now. You're going to school," said Jim.

Chris gave him that look of grown-up contempt she'd given me sometimes.

She and I didn't speak as I took her to school. I was almost in tears. Although I was glad for her to start school, I felt a sense of loss at parting with her. I suppose every mother feels that when she takes her ewe-lamb to school for the first time. It's the end of babyhood for the child, the beginning of life in reality, life with its cruelty, its strangeness, its barbarity. I kissed her good-bye at the gate and said:

"You'll be having dinner at school with the other children, Chris, and I'll call for you when school is over, at three o'clock."

"Yes, Mummy." She held my hand tightly. Other nervous little children were arriving with equally nervous parents. A pleasant young teacher with fair hair and a white linen dress appeared at the gate. She gathered the new children towards her and led them away. She gave me a sympathetic smile as she passed and said: "We'll take good care of her."

I felt quite light-hearted as I walked away, knowing that Chris was safe and I didn't have to worry.

Now I started on my secret mission. I took a bus to town and went to the big, gaunt building I hadn't visited for over five years. Then, Jim and I had gone together. The top floor of the building belonged to the Greythorne Adoption Society. I climbed the four flights and knocked on the familiar door with its scratched paint. A secretary whose face I didn't know let me in.

"May I see Miss Cleaver? My name is Mrs. James."

"Have you an appointment?"

"No, but it's very important."

"I'll see." The girl went out and returned a second later. "Miss Cleaver will see you, Mrs. James."

Miss Cleaver, a tall, thin, grey-haired woman with a charming smile, a plain, kindly face and a very wrinkled brow, rose to meet me. "Mrs. James. How nice to see you again. How's Christine?"

"She's very well. Miss Cleaver, I'd better get straight to the point. I know you don't normally divulge the origin of a child to its adopters and vice versa, but I must know who Christine is."

"Sorry, Mrs. James," she began, "our rules . . ."

"Please let me tell you the whole story, then you'll see I'm not just suffering from vulgar curiosity."

I told her about Harry.

When I finished, she said: "It's very queer. Very queer indeed. Mrs. James, I'm going to break my rule for once. I'm going to tell you in strict confidence where Christine came from.

"She was born in a very poor part of London. There were four in the family, father, mother, son and Christine herself."

"Son?"

"Yes. He was fourteen when—when it happened."

"When what happened?"

"Let me start at the beginning. The parents hadn't really wanted Christine. The family lived in one room at the top of an old house which should have been condemned by the Sanitary Inspector in my opinion. It was difficult enough when there were only three of them, but with a baby as well life became a nightmare. The mother was a neurotic creature, slatternly, unhappy, too fat. After she'd had the baby she took no interest in it. The brother, however, adored the little girl from the start. He got into trouble for cutting school so he could look after her.

"The father had a steady job in a warehouse, not much money, but enough to keep them alive. Then he was sick for several weeks and lost his job. He was laid up in that messy room, ill, worrying, nagged by his wife, irked by the baby's crying and his son's eternal fussing over the child—I got all these details from neighbours afterwards, by the way. I was also told that he'd had a particularly bad time in the war and had been in a nerve hospital for several months before he was fit to come home at all after his demob. Suddenly it all proved too much for him.

"One morning, in the small hours, a woman in the ground floor room saw something fall past her window and heard a thud on the ground. She went out to look. The son of the family was there on the ground. Christine was in his arms. The boy's neck was broken. He was dead. Christine was blue in the face but still breathing faintly.

"The woman woke the household, sent for the police and the doctor, then they went to the top room. They had to break down the door, which was locked and sealed inside. An overpowering smell of gas greeted them, in spite of the open window.

"They found husband and wife dead in bed and a note from the husband saying:

'I can't go on. I am going to kill them all. It's the only way.'

"The police concluded that he'd sealed up door and windows and turned on the gas when his family were asleep, then lain beside his wife until he drifted into unconsciousness, and death. But the son must have wakened. Perhaps he struggled with the door but couldn't open it. He'd be too weak to shout. All he could do was pluck away the seals from the window, open it, and fling himself out, holding his adored little sister tightly in his arms.

"Why Christine herself wasn't gassed is rather a mystery. Perhaps her head was right under the bedclothes, pressed against her brother's chest—they always slept together. Anyway, the child was taken to hospital, then to the home where you and Mr. James first saw her . . . and a lucky day that was for little Christine!"

"So her brother saved her life and died himself?" I said.

"Yes. He was a very brave man."

"Perhaps he thought not so much of saving her as of keeping her with him. Oh dear! That sounds ungenerous. I didn't mean to be. Miss Cleaver, what was his name?"

"I'll have to look that up for you." She referred to one of her many files and said at last: "The family's name was Jones and the fourteen-year-old brother was called 'Harold.'"

"And did he have red hair?" I murmured.

"That I don't know, Mrs. James."

"But it's Harry. The boy was Harry. What does it mean? I can't understand it."

"It's not easy, but I think perhaps deep in her unconscious mind Christine has always remembered Harry, the companion of her babyhood. We don't think of children as having much memory, but there must be images of the past tucked away somewhere in the little heads. Christine doesn't *invent* this Harry. She *remembers* him. So clearly that she's almost brought him to life again. I know it sounds far-fetched, but the whole story is so odd that I can't think of any other explanation."

"May I have the address of the house where they lived?"

She was reluctant to give this information, but I persuaded her and set out at last to find No. 13 Canver Row, where the man Jones had tried to kill himself and his whole family and almost succeeded.

The house seemed deserted. It was filthy and derelict. But one thing made me stare and stare. There was a tiny garden. A scatter of bright uneven grass splashed the bald brown patches of earth. But the little garden had one strange glory that none of the other houses in the poor sad street possessed—a bush of white roses. They bloomed gloriously. Their scent was overpowering.

I stood by the bush and stared up at the top window.

A voice startled me: "What are you doing here?"

It was an old woman, peering from the ground floor window.

"I thought the house was empty," I said.

"Should be. Been condemned. But they can't get me out. Nowhere else to go. Won't go. The others went quickly enough after it happened. No-one else wants to come. They say the place is haunted. So it is. But what's the fuss about? Life and death. They're very close. You get to know that when you're old. Alive or dead. What's the difference?"

She looked at me with yellowish, bloodshot eyes and said: "I saw him fall past my window. That's where he fell. Among the roses. He still comes back. I see him. He won't go away until he gets her."

"Who—who are you talking about?"

"Harry Jones. Nice boy he was. Red hair. Very thin. Too determined though. Always got his own way. Loved Christine too much, I thought. Died among the roses. Used to sit down here with her for hours, by the roses. Then died there. Or do people die? The church ought to give us an answer, but it doesn't. Not one you can believe. Go away, will you? This place isn't for you. It's for the dead who aren't dead, and the living who aren't alive. Am I alive or dead? You tell me. I don't know."

The crazy eyes staring at me beneath the matted white fringe of hair frightened me. Mad people are terrifying. One can pity them, but one is still afraid. I murmured:

"I'll go now. Goodbye," and tried to hurry across the hard hot pavements although my legs felt heavy and half-paralysed, as in a nightmare.

The sun blazed down on my head, but I was hardly aware of it. I lost all sense of time or place as I stumbled on.

Then I heard something that chilled my blood.

A clock struck three.

At three o'clock I was supposed to be at the school gates, waiting for Christine.

Where was I now? How near the school? What bus should I take?

I made frantic enquiries of passers-by, who looked at me fearfully, as I had looked at the old woman. They must have thought I was crazy.

At last I caught the right bus and, sick with dust, petrol fumes and fear, reached the school. I ran across the hot, empty playground. In a classroom, the young teacher in white was gathering her books together.

"I've come for Christine James. I'm her mother. I'm so sorry I'm late. Where is she?" I gasped.

"Christine James?" The girl frowned, then said brightly: "Oh, yes, I remember, the pretty little red-haired girl. That's all right, Mrs. James. Her brother called for her. How alike they are, aren't they? And so devoted. It's rather sweet to see a boy of that age so fond of his baby sister. Has your husband got red hair, like the two children?"

"What did—her brother—say?" I asked faintly.

"He didn't say anything. When I spoke to him, he just smiled. They'll be home by now, I should think. I say, do you feel all right?"

"Yes, thank you. I must go home."

I ran all the way home through the burning streets.

"Chris! Christine, where are you! Chris! Chris!" Sometimes even now I hear my own voice of the past screaming through the cold house. "Christine! Chris! Where are you? Answer me! Chrrriiiiiss!" Then: "Harry! Don't take her away! Come back! Harry! Harry!"

Demented, I rushed out into the garden. The sun struck me like a hot blade. The roses glared whitely. The air was so still I seemed to stand in timelessness, placelessness. For a moment, I seemed very near to Christine, although I couldn't see her. Then the roses danced before my eyes and turned red. The world turned red. Blood red. Wet red. I fell through redness to blackness to nothingness—to almost death.

For weeks I was in bed with sunstroke which turned to brain fever. During that time Jim and the police searched for Christine in vain. The futile search continued for months. The papers were full of the strange disappearance of the red-haired child. The teacher described the "brother" who had called for her. There were newspaper stories of kidnapping, baby-snatching, child-murders.

Then the sensation died down. Just another unsolved mystery in police files.

And only two people knew what had happened. An old crazed woman living in a derelict house, and myself.

Years have passed. But I walk in fear.

Such ordinary things make me afraid. Sunshine. Sharp shadows on grass. White roses. Children with red hair. And the name—Harry. Such an ordinary name!

Michael Reaves

WORKING IN NUMEROUS GENRES and media, (James) Michael Reaves (1950–) has written more than two dozen books, five of which have been on *The New York Times* bestseller list, and has collaborated with several colleagues on novels, including Steve Perry on *Hellstar* (1984), *Dome* (1987), and *The Omega Cage* (1988); Byron Preiss on *Dragonworld* (1979); and Steven-Elliot Altman on *Batman: Fear Itself* (2007). He also cowrote the young adult novel *InterWorld* (2007) with Neil Gaiman.

Among his several hundred scripts for various television series are episodes of *Star Trek: The Next Generation*, *The Twilight Zone*, *Sliders*, *The Flash*, *Father Dowling Mysteries*, and Disney's *Gargoyles*. He won an Emmy and was nominated for a second one as a story editor and writer on *Batman: The Animated Series*, created and coproduced the syndicated series *The Lost Continent*, and was a writer and producer of *Invasion America*, which was produced by Steven Spielberg and Harve Bennett. His screenplay credits include *Batman: Mask of the Phantasm*, *Batman: Mystery of the Batwoman*, and *Full Eclipse*, an HBO original movie. Reaves has had short stories published in *The Magazine of Fantasy and Science Fiction*, *Twilight Zone Magazine*, *Heavy Metal*, and *Cemetery Dance*. His short story "The Night People" (in the July 1985 issue of *Twilight Zone Magazine*) was named the best horror story of 1985 and is included in *The Century's Best Horror Fiction* (2012), edited by John Pelan.

"Make-Believe" is based, up to a point, on a true incident from the author's childhood; it was originally published in the March/April 2010 issue of *The Magazine of Fantasy and Science Fiction*.

Make-Believe

MICHAEL REAVES

I AM A VERY lucky man. The reason for my saying this is obvious: I'm standing before you, accepting this award for Outstanding Alumnus. But the reason behind the reason is that I became what I wanted to be.

I'm lucky because, for as far back as I can remember, I've wanted to be a writer. Ever since I was a kid, five years old, sitting down in front of our new black-and-white TV to watch *The Adventures of Superman*. I was hooked the first time I saw George Reeves leap into the air and fly. Actually, he was lying on a board in front of a cyclorama screen with a wind machine blowing his hair and cape, but I didn't know that at the time, of course. I do remember wondering even back then, however, why he always leveled off at a cruising altitude of 30,000 feet even when he was just going a couple of city blocks away.

I'm not what you would call a mainstream writer. I have an unabashed preference for genre fiction—specifically, horror. And, like most horror writers, I've drawn most of my stories from childhood fears and experiences. I grew up in this town—you wouldn't think a place on the edge of the desert would be particularly spooky or atmospheric, but you'd be wrong. The desert can be a terrifying place.

If you'll indulge me, I'd like to tell you about one of those childhood experiences. Oddly enough, I've never written about it, or even spoken of it, before now. I'm not sure why. Perhaps my reasons will become clear—to me as well as you—during the telling. After all, good fiction is supposed to illuminate as well as entertain, isn't it?

I was seven years old, and this took place in 1955. It is probably impossible to convey to you all how totally different a time it was. It was, first and foremost, a much simpler time. You all have console games that tremble on the edge of virtual reality; we had Winky Dink. You have cell phones that can video and text and Twitter; we had party lines. And, of course, you have computers capable of processing gigabytes that you can hold in one hand, and we had UNIVAC.

But it wasn't just the technology that was simpler. It was a more *trusting* time. Back then, parents thought nothing of letting their kids roam all over the neighborhood, as long as they were home in time for dinner. Somehow or other, adults back then were much better at protecting the young from fearful realities. It's true that we were aware of those realities—ever hear of "duck and cover"? But kids were allowed to be kids back then. They weren't exposed to the rampant cynicism and smut that you all imbibed along with your baby food. Don't get me started.

It was spring, I remember, around the end of April or the beginning of May—you'd think that, considering what happened, the date would be burned into my memory. It had to have been a Saturday, because school wasn't out yet. I was playing with a couple of friends—Tom Harper and Malcolm James. We'd gone up into the hills a few blocks from my house to play cowboys and Indians. We were armed and ready for trouble.

When I say "armed," I mean something different than what the word might connote today. I was carrying my trusty McRepeater Rifle, which made a very satisfactory bang when the wheel atop the stock was turned. Tom had a deadly Daisy 1101 Thunderbird, and in addition was packing twin cap pistols. And Malcolm . . . well, Malcolm was carrying his Johnny Eagle *Magumba* Big Game Rifle, which he'd insisted on bringing even though he had a perfectly good Fanner 50 cap gun back in his bedroom. Some people just won't get with the program.

We were hunting Indians, or, as we called them, "Injuns." The term "political correctness," let alone the concept, wasn't exactly widespread back then. It was the middle of the afternoon and, though it was early in the year, it was already hot enough to raise shimmers of heat waves from the dirt road. The hills were still green, but you could see that slowly the vegetation was dying. Another month, and brown would be the dominant color, announcing the beginning of the fire season.

For now, however, it was still pleasant, or as pleasant as those hills ever became. We were walking cautiously through the Badlands of our fantasy, alert for the slightest sound that might betray an Apache ambush. This was more difficult than it might seem, because every few minutes Malcolm would drop into a crouch and spin around, spraying the mesquite with imaginary bullets and going "*Kachow!! Kachow!!*" Tom Harper finally grew tired of this, and demanded to know how we were going to get the drop on the bad guys with Malcolm constantly announcing our presence to everyone in the county. To which Malcolm replied that it was only make-believe, and that the most we might hope to flush from the underbrush was a rabbit or coyote.

We knew that, of course. We all knew that. It's important to keep this in mind.

"Knock it off," Tom finally said, exasperated, "or I'll drop-kick your ass into next week."

That got the desired result. Tom Harper's right leg ended in a stump just above the knee—legacy of a car accident. He wore a prosthetic, a hinged contraption made of wood, metal, and plastic, and when he ran, he used a sort of half-skip in his locomotion which the rest of us found very amusing. We were careful not to show it, however, because Tom could turn that half-skip into a devastating kick that could easily deliver the recipient as far up the calendar as Tom wanted. Malcolm said nothing more that in any way damaged the fantasy *gemütlichkeit* we had constructed. And again, it's important to remember that we knew what we were doing.

Malcolm was going on eight, with a seborrheic head of densely black hair and horn-rimmed glasses the exact same shade. He was built like a concentration camp inmate, all sharp, acute angles, with an Adam's apple that leapt about like the bouncing ball in a Fleischer sing-along cartoon. Not surprisingly, he had few friends. Tom had just turned eight; he was handsome, if somewhat bland in appearance, and looked like a future gridiron star—until he began to walk or run with that characteristic hitching limp. I remember once, when we were both younger and I was at his sixth birthday party, seeing his father's eyes fill with tears as he watched his son skip-run across the back yard.

We knew what we were doing. It was play, make-believe. Nothing more.

We were wandering along a dirt road, not far from the ranger station. The shadows were starting to grow longer, and the light more sanguine, as the sun neared the smoggy horizon. "We should maybe turn around," Malcolm said. "We're gettin' too near the cave."

There was no need to stipulate which cave. There was only one in the area—Arrowhead Cave, so named because of the dozens of chipped flint relics found there over the years. It was a tectonic cave, not one formed by gradual erosion. It had come into being thousands of years ago, when an earthquake had shattered a sandstone outcrop and deposited the fragments at the bottom of a ravine. Over the centuries talus and dirt had covered it, and eventually solidified into a roof. It hadn't been a particularly impressive cave, according to rumor, but it had served the local Indians well as shelter for centuries before the valley was settled. It was even less impressive now, after the tragedy of 1938, when four young boys—out, like us, for play—had become lost in the cave.

I never did learn the specifics of the story—when I was a child, the adults had been very tight-lipped about it, even almost two decades later. All I knew—all any kid knew—was that the four boys had died in Arrowhead Cave. A few days later the City Council, acting with an alacrity hard to believe for anyone familiar with local government, had authorized several construction workers to blow up the cave's entrance with dynamite, closing it for good.

Tom and I looked at each other after Malcolm's statement. Neither of us wanted to be thought cowardly. On the other hand, neither of us particularly wanted to get any closer to Arrowhead Cave, as it was supposedly haunted. There had been another minor temblor last week as well, and none of us relished the thought of being near the cave, or—worse—in it, should another quake hit.

As the three of us stood there, momentarily paralyzed by indecision, we—or I, at least—became aware of just how *quiet* it was. I know it's a cliché—I knew it even back then—to speak of an ominous, brooding silence holding dominion over the scene. How many times had I lain on the threadbare rug in our living room, chin cupped in my hands, staring at a black-and-white image of somebody wearing a pith helmet, standing in front of a sarcophagus and saying grimly, "It's quiet—*too* quiet"? Usually this particular trope was immediately followed by the hero being seized around the throat and throttled by an ancient hand wrapped in dry, dusty cerements.

Still, cliché or no, I could suddenly feel my heart pounding. The light had taken on a shimmering, glassine quality, and the air seemed *dead*. It was impossible to get a lungful, no matter how deeply I breathed. There was no nourishment to it.

It would be easy, I suppose, to speculate that we all passed through some sort of *transition* then—a portal to another reality, I guess you could call it. It's tempting to use such a device as an explanation of a sort for what we did next. But the truth, as it usually is, was much more banal. We did what we did because that's what kids did back then.

I started to say something, even though I was somehow convinced that the leaden air would not convey my words. Before I could try, however, a voice shouted, "*Hands up!*"

Now, this is the point. It was fantasy. Make-believe. And we *knew* that. But unless you can remember, *really* remember, those Bradbury days of childhood, the unspoken social norms that we all lived by then, the secret lives and inviolate rules that bound us as fully and completely as office politics and the laws of church and state circumscribed our parents' lives—well, then I have no real hope of making you understand why we did what we did. It wasn't even something we thought about—we just did it. They had the drop on us, after all. They'd caught us, fair and square.

So, all three of us dropped our toy guns and reached for the sky.

"They" were four boys our age, armed with toy guns like ours. They'd come up on us from behind and nailed us good. The tallest one, a kid my age, was wearing bib overalls over a flannel shirt. There seemed to be something odd about his weapon—a carbine, with no manufacturer's stamp apparent—but it was obviously a toy. He gestured with the barrel, a peremptory jerk obviously intended to move us along, while the other three picked up our weapons.

"Let's go," he said. "Shag it."

Arms still upraised, we stumbled along down the road, our captors herding us toward an unknown destination.

Even though these lads represented "the Enemy" (Apaches, space aliens, Nazis, gangsters, the heathen Chinee, or a hundred and one other incarnations of Bad Guys), there was nothing in our childhood rules of engagement that prohibited discourse. Consequently, Malcolm attempted conversation. "Where d'you guys go to school?" he asked. "I haven't seen you around—"

"Quiet," one of them, a tall fellow with hair as red as Malcolm's was black, and a face mottled with more freckles than the moon has craters, hissed. And yes, I know it's bad writing to use anything other than "said"—but you weren't there. Trust me; there was less humanity in that one word as spoken by him than there was in a snake's sibilance.

We marched on in silence. And I started to wonder just how they'd managed to catch us so thoroughly off-guard. We'd been standing on the crest of a small hill; if they'd come along the road from either direction we'd have seen them, and there was no way they could've climbed up the side, through the dry creosote, without making enough noise to wake the dead.

. . . to wake the dead . . . There are certain phrases that we use a thousand times without thinking, until one day you realize just how hideously appropriate they are.

We went around a bluff's shoulder, down a steep trail, and found ourselves in a high-walled ravine; almost a box canyon. A quarter of the way up the rear wall, at the top of a pile of talus, was what had once been the mouth of Arrowhead Cave. It was little more than a lacuna now, the dynamite having closed it off seventeen years ago. Two of our four captors urged us up the ten-foot slope.

"Hey, guys?" The nasal quality of Malcolm's voice was rising, a sure barometer of anxiety. "It's gettin' dark—my dad'll hide me if I miss dinner—"

"Zip it," one of them—short and rotund, with wire-rim specs—said. I got a good look at the clothes he was wearing as I passed him— knee pants and suspenders, a sweater and a flat, button-down cap. There was definitely something anachronistic about the apparel, but what really caught my eye was the toy gun he was brandishing. It was unlike any kids' gun I'd ever seen, and after looking at it for a minute, I real-

ized why. I didn't have the words to describe it at the time, but looking back on it, I realize it was made of stamped metal. It was black, with a red barrel, and on the butt was a stylized sketch of the Lone Ranger. A legend ran in curved script along the bottom of the image; I can't recall the exact phrase, but it was something about listening to Brace Beemer as the Lone Ranger, every Friday.

Why "listen"? Why not "watch"? And who was Brace Beemer? Everyone knew the Lone Ranger was played by Clayton Moore.

As big of a puzzle as that gun represented, however, the one held by the third boy was even more so. It, too, was made out of some material which I didn't immediately recognize. When I did realize what it was, it was enough to make me stop and stare, open-mouthed.

His gun was made of cardboard.

There was a slogan inscribed on the side of it, as well—I couldn't read all of it, because his hand partly obscured it. The part I could read proclaimed Geyser Flour to be "America's *top* self-rising flour!"

The boy saw me staring at his paper gun. "Shut yer bazoo, yegg," he instructed me, raising the toy as he did so.

And a strange feeling possessed me; I suppose it made sense in light of later developments, but at the time it was as inexplicable as it was overwhelming. I was, abruptly and totally, *terrified* of that ridiculous cardboard gun. So terrified that I felt in danger of soiling my corduroys.

He reached out and put a hand on my shoulder, pushing me up the slope, and his hand was *cold.* I could feel it through the fabric of my T-shirt.

As we climbed the steep slope, I watched both of my comrades, and knew they'd come to the same conclusion I had about our captors. Tom's face was set in the utter blankness of denial, his gaze as uncomprehending as that of an abused animal. Malcolm's was a hundred and eighty degrees opposite, full of growing realization and horror.

By the time the three of us had clambered up into the shallow remnant of the cave's former entrance, Malcolm had lost it. He was sobbing, babbling incoherently, snot drooling from his nose. I wasn't doing much better myself, but I at least managed to keep a somewhat braver face on. Tom seemed outwardly calm also, but his face was the same sallow hue as that of his prosthetic's plastic skin.

We sat on the sandstone lip that hung above the declivity for what seemed like hours, but was in reality scarcely more than forty-five minutes; just long enough for the sun to disappear behind the western slope of the ravine. I watched our captors. I was only seven, and so I had no idea that all of them were dressed in Depression-era, poor white trash clothes, or that their toy weapons were relics of those same long-gone days. I only knew that there was something profoundly *wrong* about every aspect of them—even the way they moved, and sat, and talked amongst themselves.

I say they talked, but, even though I could clearly see them address each other; could even, until the light faded too much, see their lips moving, I heard nothing. It was deathly quiet in the ravine—even Malcolm's crying had, for a time, subsided—and I knew that sound rose with great clarity in still air. But it was like watching TV with the sound off.

"Gh-ghosts," Malcolm blubbered. "Th-they're *ghosts*. They were kuh-*killed* in the cave—"

"Bullshit," Tom muttered.

"—twenty years ago—"

"Stop it." Tom's voice was level and icy, but it was thin ice, covering black depths of hysteria. He stood and faced Malcolm.

Malcolm stood as well. "You *know* it's true! You nuh-know it's—"

"Shut up."

"Shouldn't've let 'em get us, should've *run,* now they're gonna—"

Tom hit him.

It was a short, hard jab, brought up from his waist into the pit of Malcolm's stomach, and

it let the air out of him like a nail in a tire. He stared at Tom in utter shock, mouth gaping, making vaguely piscine sounds.

Then he turned, staggered toward the edge of the rocky shelf, and before either of us could try to stop him, he fell.

He rolled down the declivity a few feet before he managed to stop himself. Then he looked up, and Tom and I both heard his moan of terror when he saw the four boys—or whatever they were—surrounding him. His face had been scratched during his fall, and a red streak of blood stood out vividly against his chalk-white skin.

"Please," I heard him say. "Please—I'm late for dinner—"

And they laughed.

I guess it was laughter, though it was the most mirthless, soulless sound I've ever heard. It was the sort of laughter something dead for a long time, long enough to completely forget any connection it had had with life, would make, if it were to somehow be amused.

They laughed, and they moved closer to him. Malcolm made a high, keening noise, a sound of utter despair.

Tom shouted, "You *bastards!* Leave him *alone!*" And he jumped off the ledge.

I don't know what he thought he could possibly do. I doubt he thought about it at all. He just went to Malcolm's rescue—or tried to. He might have been successful, somehow, if he'd had two good legs. I don't know if he forgot that one was artificial, or if he just didn't care.

It was a magnificent jump; it carried him to within five feet of them. He plowed into the loose stone and gravel, and his right leg buckled beneath him; he lost his balance and fell.

He struggled to stand, but before he could, the one with the cardboard gun looked up at him. He was grinning, and it might have just been a trick of the fading light, but for one awful instant it looked like the grin of a naked skull. He raised the gun and pointed it at Tom's chest.

And, softly, but somehow very clearly, I heard him say, "Bang."

That was all; just "Bang," in a quiet voice. There was no puff of smoke, no recoil from the paper muzzle.

But Tom's back erupted in a spray of blood.

He fell backward.

I screamed.

All four heads swiveled up toward me. Their eyes were like spiders' eyes: black and gleaming.

I knew that following Tom and Malcolm would only get me killed—or worse. There was only one other direction that I could go—back into the cave.

I'd seen before-and-after photos of Arrowhead Cave. The City Fathers had ordered it sealed off, and sealed off it had been, with a vengeance. What had been a dark, mysterious opening into the underworld had been reduced to a pile of rubble, leaving an overhang barely a yard deep.

But there was no place else to hide. I pressed against the unyielding stone, feeling a distant wetness as my bladder let go. I could hear them scrabbling up the slope after me. I turned frantically from side to side, seeking an impossible escape—

And saw, six inches above my head, a lateral crack in the rock.

It was barely wider than my body, and beyond it was unrelieved blackness, yet to me it looked like the gates of Heaven. I jumped, grabbed the flat sandstone lip, pulled myself up and into it, kicking and squirming. There was barely enough room for me to wriggle between the two slabs of rock; I had to breathe shallowly to do so. But I kept crawling.

To this day I've no idea how that providential escape route came to be there. Perhaps it had been overlooked after the blast; perhaps it had been deemed too small to worry about. Or perhaps that temblor we'd had a week earlier had had something to do with opening it. All I know is that, after a lifetime of frantic crawling, I saw light up ahead.

I redoubled my efforts, scooted forward— and felt a cold hand close around my ankle.

I didn't have the breath to scream—it came out as a thin, mewling cry. Whichever one of those things had me began dragging me relentlessly back, down into the darkness. I felt my fingernails splinter on the rock. I kicked back frantically with my free leg, felt my shoe strike what had to be the head of the one that had grabbed me. I gritted my teeth, drew my leg up, and kicked backward with every bit of strength I had left.

His head *splintered*. I felt his skull cave in. But his grip did not slacken.

Sobbing obscenities, I swung my free leg against my other one, as hard as I could. Among the injuries that would be counted up later was a hairline fracture of my ankle—but at the time I felt nothing but a fierce joy when that cold grip loosened for a moment.

I lunged forward, panting, and came to the end of the passage, so abruptly that I tumbled out before I could stop myself. I caught a brief, dizzying glimpse of a hillside below me, scrub bushes barely illuminated by the crepuscular twilight—then I fell. Pain exploded in my head like a roman candle, and I must have passed out.

My last thought before I lost consciousness was: *They're still coming for me.*

And now most of you are wondering a few different things, I imagine—such as, *Why did he waste our time with this silliness?* or, *He's got quite an imagination,* or even, *Where are the men with white coats and butterfly nets?*

For those of you who wish to know the end of the story—I wish I could tell you. There was front-page material in the local paper the day after that day in 1955, documenting the discovery of Tom Harper's body near Arrowhead Cave. No bullet or gun was ever found, but something very powerful had punched a hole clean through him.

They never found Malcolm.

Me they found at the bottom of the next ravine over from Arrowhead Cave. I had a concussion, and was in a coma for nearly two weeks. When I finally came out of it, I told everyone who asked—and many did, believe me—that I remembered nothing. Which was the truth. My recollection of the events of that long-ago day has come back to me piecemeal, during the course of many a long and sleepless night. I stopped seeing therapists after one diagnosed me with PTSD, and wondered why a writer with no military history was so afflicted.

I suppose it's possible that I imagined the whole thing, in an attempt to supply a story that fit the necessary particulars. If it hadn't been for the finding of Tom's body, I would have no reason not to assume that wasn't true. Which, of course, asks the question: What could pos-sibly have happened that was so horrible that I might have made up such a story to normalize the reality?

In any event, I must admit lying to you at the start of my speech. I said I had always known that I wanted to be a writer. That's not strictly true; until I was seven years old, I had no idea what I wanted to be. But after that night, there was no doubt in my mind.

It's how I deal with it.

So, in conclusion, to those of you out there who know without question what you want to be when you grow up, I say congratulations—and be careful what you wish for.

A. M. Burrage

AS A MEMBER OF a family noted for writing juvenile fiction, A(lfred) M(cLelland) Burrage (1889–1956) followed in their footsteps, selling his first story to the prestigious children's magazine, *Chums*, when he was only sixteen. Although he was prolific in this genre, producing numerous stories in the "Tufty" series under the pseudonym Frank Lelland, and, under his own name, selling stories to such magazines as *Boys' Friend Weekly*, *Boys Herald*, and *Comic Life*, his father, Alfred Sherrington Burrage, and his uncle, Edwin Harcourt Burrage, were even more successful, the former credited with hundreds of stories for boys' magazines and the latter with twenty-eight hardcover books.

However, it is for his ghost stories that A. M. Burrage is mainly remembered today, especially those collected in *Some Ghost Stories* (1927) and *Someone in the Room* (1931), written under the pseudonym Ex-Private X, under which name he also wrote a bitter war memoir, *War Is War* (1930). Burrage also wrote an occult novel of black magic, *Seeker to the Dead* (1942), based on the life and work of Aleister Crowley. Among his most famous stories are "The Green Scarf" (1927), "Between the Minute and the Hour" (1927), and "The Waxwork" (1931), which twice was filmed as an episode of a television series: on *Lights Out* in 1950 starring John Beal and on *Alfred Hitchcock Presents* in 1959 starring Barry Nelson.

"Playmates" was first published in *Some Ghost Stories* (London, Cecil Palmer, 1927). It appeared as an episode of three half-hour television series: *Gruen Guild Theatre* (1952), *The Schaefer Century Theatre* (1952), and *The Pepsi–Cola Playhouse* (1954), starring Natalie Wood and Alan Napier.

Playmates

A. M. BURRAGE

I

Although everybody who knew Stephen Everton agreed that he was the last man under Heaven who ought to have been allowed to bring up a child, it was fortunate for Monica that she fell into his hands; else she had probably starved or drifted into some refuge for waifs and strays. True her father, Sebastian Threlfall the poet, had plenty of casual friends. Almost everybody knew him slightly, and right up to the time of his fatal attack of *delirium tremens* he contrived to look one of the most interesting of the regular frequenters of the Café Royal. But people are generally not hasty to bring up the children of casual acquaintances, particularly when such children may be suspected of having inherited more than a fair share of human weaknesses.

Of Monica's mother literally nothing was known. Nobody seemed able to say if she were dead or alive. Probably she had long since deserted Threlfall for some consort able and willing to provide regular meals.

Everton knew Threlfall no better than a hundred others knew him, and was ignorant of his daughter's existence until the father's death was a new topic of conversation in literary and artistic circles. People vaguely wondered what would become of "the kid"; and while they were still wondering, Everton quietly took possession of her.

Who's Who will tell you the year of Everton's birth, the names of his *Almae Matres* (Win-chester and Magdalen College, Oxford), the titles of his books and of his predilections for skating and mountaineering; but it is necessary to know the man a little less superficially. He was then a year or two short of fifty and looked ten years older. He was a tall, lean man, with a delicate pink complexion, an oval head, a Roman nose, blue eyes which looked out mildly through strong glasses, and thin straight lips drawn tightly over slightly protruding teeth. His high forehead was bare, for he was bald to the base of his skull. What remained of his hair was a neutral tint between black and grey, and was kept closely cropped. He contrived to look at once prim and irascible, scholarly and acute; Sherlock Holmes, perhaps, with a touch of old-maidishness.

The world knew him for a writer of books on historical crises. They were cumbersome books with cumbersome titles, written by a scholar for scholars. They brought him fame and not a little money. The money he could have afforded to be without, since he was modestly wealthy by inheritance. He was essentially a cold-blooded animal, a bachelor, a man of regular and temperate habits, fastidious, and fond of quietude and simple comforts.

Nobody is ever likely to know why Everton adopted the orphan daughter of a man whom he knew but slightly and neither liked nor respected. He was no lover of children, and his humours were sardonic rather than sentimental.

I am only hazarding a guess when I suggest that, like so many childless men, he had theories of his own concerning the upbringing of children, which he wanted to see tested. Certain it is that Monica's childhood, which had been extraordinary enough before, passed from the tragic to the grotesque.

Everton took Monica from the Bloomsbury "apartments" house, where the landlady, already nursing a bad debt, was wondering how to dispose of the child. Monica was then eight years old, and a woman of the world in her small way. She had lived with drink and poverty and squalor; had never played a game nor had a playmate; had seen nothing but the seamy side of life; and had learned skill in practising her father's petty shifts and mean contrivances. She was grave and sullen and plain and pale, this child who had never known childhood. When she spoke, which was as seldom as possible, her voice was hard and gruff. She was, poor little thing, as unattractive as her life could have made her.

She went with Everton without question or demur. She would no more have questioned anybody's ownership than if she had been an inanimate piece of luggage left in a cloak-room. She had belonged to her father. Now that he was gone to his own place she was the property of whomsoever chose to claim her. Everton took her with a cold kindness in which was neither love nor pity; in return she gave him neither love nor gratitude, but did as she was desired after the manner of a paid servant.

Everton disliked modern children, and for what he disliked in them he blamed modern schools. It may have been on this account that he did not send Monica to one; or perhaps he wanted to see how a child would contrive its own education. Monica could already read and write and, thus equipped, she had the run of his large library, in which was almost every conceivable kind of book from heavy tomes on abstruse subjects to trashy modern novels bought and left there by Miss Gribbin. Everton barred nothing, recommended nothing, but watched the tree grow naturally, untended and unpruned.

Miss Gribbin was Everton's secretary. She was the kind of hatchet-faced, flat-chested, middle-aged sexless woman who could safely share the home of a bachelor without either of them being troubled by the tongue of Scandal. To her duties was now added the instruction of Monica in certain elementary subjects. Thus Monica learned that a man named William the Conqueror arrived in England in 1066; but to find out what manner of man this William was, she had to go to the library and read the conflicting accounts of him given by the several historians. From Miss Gribbin she learned bare irrefutable facts; for the rest she was left to fend for herself. In the library she found herself surrounded by all the realms of reality and fancy, each with its door invitingly ajar.

Monica was fond of reading. It was, indeed, almost her only recreation, for Everton knew no other children of her age, and treated her as a grown-up member of the household. Thus she read everything from translations of the *Iliad* to Hans Andersen, from the Bible to the love-gush of the modern female fiction-mongers.

Everton, although he watched her closely, and plied her with innocent-sounding questions, was never allowed a peep into her mind. What muddled dreams she may have had of a strange world surrounding the Hampstead house—a world of gods and fairies and demons, and strong silent men making love to sloppy-minded young women—she kept to herself. Reticence was all that she had in common with normal childhood, and Everton noticed that she never played.

Unlike most young animals, she did not take naturally to playing. Perhaps the instinct had been beaten out of her by the realities of life while her father was alive. Most lonely children improvise their own games and provide themselves with a vast store of make-believe. But Monica, as sullen-seeming as a caged animal, devoid alike of the naughtiness and the charms of childhood, rarely crying and still more rarely laughing, moved about the house sedate to the verge of being wooden. Occasionally Everton, the experimentalist, had twinges of conscience and grew half afraid. . . .

II

When Monica was twelve Everton moved his establishment from Hampstead to a house remotely situated in the middle of Suffolk, which was part of a recent legacy. It was a tall, rectangular, Queen Anne house standing on a knoll above marshy fields and wind-bowed beech woods. Once it had been the manor house, but now little land went with it. A short drive passed between rank evergreens from the heavy wrought-iron gate to a circle of grass and flower beds in front of the house. Behind was an acre and a half of rank garden, given over to weeds and marigolds. The rooms were high and well lighted, but the house wore an air of depression as if it were a live thing unable to shake off some ancient fit of melancholy.

Everton went to live in the house for a variety of reasons. For the most part of a year he had been trying in vain to let or sell it, and it was when he found that he would have no difficulty in disposing of his house at Hampstead that he made up his mind. The old house, a mile distant from a remote Suffolk village, would give him all the solitude he required. Moreover he was anxious about his health—his nervous system had never been strong—and his doctor had recommended the bracing air of East Anglia.

He was not in the least concerned to find that the house was too big for him. His furniture filled the same number of rooms as it had filled at Hampstead, and the others he left empty. Nor did he increase his staff of three indoor servants and gardener. Miss Gribbin, now less dispensable than ever, accompanied him; and with them came Monica to see another aspect of life, with the same wooden stoicism which Everton had remarked in her upon the occasion of their first meeting.

As regarded Monica, Miss Gribbin's duties were then becoming more and more of a sinecure. "Lessons" now occupied no more than half an hour a day. The older Monica grew, the better she was able to grub for her education in the great library. Between Monica and Miss Gribbin there was neither love nor sympathy, nor was there any affectation of either. In their common duty to Everton they owed and paid certain duties to each other. Their intercourse began and ended there.

Everton and Miss Gribbin both liked the house at first. It suited the two temperaments which were alike in their lack of festivity. Asked if she too liked it, Monica said simply "Yes," in a tone which implied stolid and complete indifference.

All three in their several ways led much the same lives as they had led at Hampstead. But a slow change began to work in Monica, a change so slight and subtle that weeks passed before Everton or Miss Gribbin noticed it. It was late on an afternoon in early spring when Everton first became aware of something unusual in Monica's demeanor.

He had been searching in the library for one of his own books—*The Fall of the Commonwealth of England*—and having failed to find it went in search of Miss Gribbin and met Monica instead at the foot of the long oak staircase. Of her he casually inquired about the book, and she jerked up her head brightly, to answer him with an unwonted smile:

"Yes, I've been reading it. I expect I left it in the schoolroom. I'll go and see."

It was a long speech for her to have uttered, but Everton scarcely noticed that at the time. His attention was directed elsewhere.

"*Where* did you leave it?" he demanded.

"In the schoolroom," she repeated.

"I know of no schoolroom," said Everton coldly. He hated to hear anything miscalled, even were it only a room. "Miss Gribbin generally takes you for your lessons in either the library or the dining-room. If it is one of those rooms, kindly call it by its proper name."

Monica shook her head.

"No, I mean the schoolroom—the big empty room next to the library. That's what it's called."

Everton knew the room. It faced north, and seemed darker and more dismal than any other room in the house. He had wondered idly why Monica chose to spend so much of her time in a room bare of furniture, with nothing better to sit on than uncovered boards or a cushionless window-seat; and put it down to her genius for being unlike anybody else.

"Who calls it that?" he demanded.

"*It's* its name," said Monica smiling.

She ran upstairs, and presently returned with the book, which she handed to him with another smile. He was already wondering at her. It was surprising and pleasant to see her run, instead of the heavy and clumsy walk which generally moved her when she went to obey a behest. And she had smiled two or three times in the short space of a minute. Then he realized that for some little while she had been a brighter, happier creature than she had ever been at Hampstead.

"How did you come to call that room the schoolroom?" he asked, as he took the book from her hand.

"It *is* the schoolroom," she insisted, seeking to cover her evasion by laying stress on the verb.

That was all he could get out of her. As he questioned further the smiles ceased and the pale, plain little face became devoid of any expression. He knew then that it was useless to press her, but his curiosity was aroused. He inquired of Miss Gribbin and the servant, and learned that nobody was in the habit of calling the long, empty apartment the schoolroom.

Clearly Monica had given it its name. But why? She was so altogether remote from school and schoolrooms. Some germ of imagination was active in her small mind. Everton's interest was stimulated. He was like a doctor who remarks in a patient some abnormal symptom.

"Monica seems a lot brighter and more alert than she used to be," he remarked to Miss Gribbin.

"Yes," agreed the secretary. "I have noticed that. She is learning to play."

"To play what? The piano?"

"No, no. To play childish games. Haven't you heard her dancing about and singing?"

Everton shook his head and looked interested.

"I have not," he said. "Possibly my presence acts as a check upon her—er—exuberance."

"I hear her in that empty room which she insists upon calling the schoolroom. She stops when she hears my step. Of course, I have not interfered with her in any way, but I could wish that she would not talk to herself. I don't like people who do that. It is somehow—uncomfortable."

"I didn't know she did," said Everton slowly.

"Oh, yes, quite long conversations. I haven't actually heard what she talks about, but sometimes you would think she was in the midst of a circle of friends."

"In that same room?"

"Generally," said Miss Gribbin, with a nod.

Everton regarded his secretary with a slow, thoughtful smile.

"Development," he said, "is always extremely interesting. I am glad the place seems to suit Monica. I think it suits all of us."

There was a doubtful note in his voice as he uttered the last words, and Miss Gribbin agreed with him with the same lack of conviction in her tone. As a fact, Everton had been doubtful of late if his health had been benefited by the move from Hampstead. For the first week or two his nerves had been the better for the change of air; but now he was conscious of the beginning of a relapse. His imagination was beginning to play him tricks, filling his mind with vague, distorted fancies. Sometimes when he sat up late, writing—he was given to working at night on strong coffee—he became a victim of the most distressing nervous symptoms, hard to analyze and impossible to combat, which invariably drove him to bed with a sense of defeat.

That same night he suffered one of the variations of this common experience.

It was close upon midnight when he felt stealing over him a sense of discomfort which he was compelled to classify as fear. He was working in a small room leading out of the drawing-room which he had selected for his study. At first he was scarcely aware of the sensation. The effect was always cumulative; the burden was laid upon him straw by straw.

It began with his being oppressed by the silence of the house. He became more and more acutely conscious of it, until it became like a thing tangible, a prison of solid walls growing around him.

The scratching of his pen at first relieved the tension. He wrote words and erased them again for the sake of that comfortable sound. But presently that comfort was denied him, for it seemed to him that this minute and busy noise was attracting attention to himself. Yes, that was it. He was being watched.

Everton sat quite still, the pen poised an inch above the half-covered sheet of paper. This had become a familiar sensation. He was being watched. And by what? And from what corner of the room?

He forced a tremulous smile to his lips. One moment he called himself ridiculous; the next, he asked himself hopelessly how a man could argue with his nerves. Experience had taught him that the only cure—and that a temporary one—was to go to bed. Yet he sat on, anxious to learn more about himself, to coax his vague imaginings into some definite shape.

Imagination told him that he was being watched, and although he called it imagination he was afraid. That rapid beating against his ribs was his heart, warning him of fear. But he sat rigid, anxious to learn in what part of the room his fancy would place these imaginary "watchers"—for he was conscious of the gaze of more than one pair of eyes being bent upon him.

At first the experiment failed. The rigidity of his pose, the hold he was keeping upon himself, acted as a brake upon his mind. Presently he realized this and relaxed the tension, striving to give his mind that perfect freedom which might have been demanded by a hypnotist or one experimenting in telepathy.

Almost at once he thought of the door. The eyes of his mind veered round in that direction as the needle of a compass veers to the magnetic north. With these eyes of his imagination he saw the door. It was standing half open, and the aperture was thronged with faces. What kind of faces he could not tell. They were just faces; imagination left it at that. But he was aware that these spies were timid; that they were in some ways as fearful of him as he was of them; that to scatter them he had but to turn his head and gaze at them with the eyes of his body.

The door was at his shoulder. He turned his head suddenly and gave it one swift glance out of the tail of his eye.

However imagination deceived him, it had not played him false about the door. It was standing half open although he could have sworn that he had closed it on entering the room. The aperture was empty. Only darkness, solid as a pillar, filled the space between floor and lintel. But although he saw nothing as he turned his head, he was dimly conscious of something vanishing, a scurrying noiseless and incredibly swift, like the flitting of trout in clear, shallow water.

Everton stood up, stretched himself, and brought his knuckles up to his strained eyes. He told himself that he must go to bed. It was bad enough that he must suffer these nervous attacks; to encourage them was madness.

But as he mounted the stairs he was still conscious of not being alone. Shy, timorous, ready to melt into the shadows of the walls if he turned his head, *they* were following him, whispering noiselessly, linking hands and arms, watching him with the fearful, awed curiosity of—Children.

III

The Vicar had called upon Everton. His name was Parslow, and he was a typical country parson of the poorer sort, a tall, rugged, shabby, worried man in the middle forties, obviously embarrassed by the eternal problem of making ends meet on an inadequate stipend.

Everton received him courteously enough, but with a certain coldness which implied that he had nothing in common with his visitor. Parslow was evidently disappointed because "the new people" were not church-goers nor likely to take much interest in the parish. The two men made half-hearted and vain attempts to find common ground. It was not until he was on the point of leaving that the Vicar mentioned Monica.

"You have, I believe, a little girl?" he said.

"Yes. My small ward."

"Ah! I expect she finds it lonely here. I have a little girl of the same age. She is at present away at school, but she will be home soon for the Easter holidays. I know she would be delighted if your little—er—ward would come down to the Vicarage and play with her sometimes."

The suggestion was not particularly welcome to Everton, and his thanks were perfunctory. This other small girl, although she was a vicar's daughter, might carry the contagion of other modern children and infect Monica with the pertness and slanginess which he so detested. Altogether he was determined to have as little to do with the Vicarage as possible.

Meanwhile the child was becoming to him a study of more and more absorbing interest. The change in her was almost as marked as if she had just returned after having spent a term at school. She astonished and mystified him by using expressions which she could scarcely have learned from any member of the household. It was not the jargon of the smart young people of the day which slipped easily from her lips, but the polite family slang of his own youth. For instance, she remarked one morning that Mead, the gardener, was a whale at pruning vines.

A whale! The expression took Everton back a very long way down the level road of the spent years; took him, indeed, to a nursery in a solid respectable house in a Belgravian square, where he had heard the word used in that same sense for the first time. His sister Gertrude, aged ten, notorious in those days for picking up loose expressions, announced that she was getting to be a whale at French. Yes, in those days an expert was "whale" or a "don"; not, as he is to-day, a "stout fellow." But who was a "whale" nowadays? It was years since he had heard the term.

"Where did you learn to say that?" he demanded in so strange a tone that Monica stared at him anxiously.

"Isn't it right?" she asked eagerly. She might have been a child at a new school, fearful of not having acquired the fashionable phraseology of the place.

"It is a slang expression," said the purist coldly. "It used to mean a person who was proficient in something. How did you come to hear it?"

She smiled without answering, and her smile was mysterious, even coquettish after a childish fashion. Silence had always been her refuge, but it was no longer a sullen silence. She was changing rapidly, and in a manner to bewilder her guardian. He failed in an effort to cross-examine her, and, later in the day, consulted Miss Gribbin.

"That child," he said, "is reading something that we know nothing about."

"Just at present," said Miss Gribbin, "she is glued to Dickens and Stevenson."

"Then where on earth does she get her expressions?"

"I don't know," the secretary retorted testily, "any more than I know how she learned to play Cat's Cradle."

"What? That game with string? Does she play that?"

"I found her doing something quite complicated and elaborate the other day. She wouldn't tell me how she learned to do it. I took the trouble to question the servants, but none of them had shown her."

Everton frowned.

"And I know of no book in the library which tells how to perform tricks with string. Do you think she has made a clandestine friendship with any of the village children?"

Miss Gribbin shook her head.

"She is too fastidious for that. Besides, she seldom goes into the village alone."

There, for the time, the discussion ended. Everton, with all the curiosity of the student, watched the child as carefully and closely as he was able without at the same time arousing her suspicions. She was developing fast. He had known that she must develop, but the manner of her doing so amazed and mystified him, and, likely as not, denied some preconceived theory. The untended plant was not only growing but showed signs of pruning. It was as if there were outside influences at work on Monica which could have come neither from him nor from any other member of the household.

Winter was dying hard, and dark days of rain kept Miss Gribbin, Monica, and Everton within doors. He lacked no opportunities of keeping the child under observation, and once, on a gloomy afternoon, passing the room which she had named the schoolroom, he paused and listened until he became suddenly aware that his conduct bore an unpleasant resemblance to eavesdropping. The psychologist and the gentleman engaged in a brief struggle in which the gentleman temporarily got the upper hand. Everton approached the door with a heavy step and flung it open.

The sensation he received, as he pushed open the door, was vague but slightly disturbing, and it was by no means new to him. Several times of late, but generally after dark, he had entered an empty room with the impression that it had been occupied by others until the very moment of his crossing the threshold. His coming disturbed not merely one or two, but a crowd. He felt rather than heard them scattering, flying swiftly and silently as shadows to incredible hiding-places, where they held breath and watched and waited for him to go. Into the same atmosphere of tension he now walked, and looked about him as if expecting to see more than only the child who held the floor in the middle of the room, or some tell-tale trace of other children in hiding. Had the room been furnished he must have looked involuntarily for shoes protruding from under tables or settees, for ends of garments unconsciously left exposed.

The long room, however, was empty save for Monica from wainscot to wainscot and from floor to ceiling. Fronting him were the long high windows starred by fine rain. With her back to the white filtered light Monica faced him, looking up to him as he entered. He was just in time to see a smile fading from her lips. He also saw by a slight convulsive movement of her shoulders that she was hiding something from him in the hands clasped behind her back.

"Hullo," he said, with a kind of forced geniality, "what are you up to?"

She said: "Nothing," but not as sullenly as she would once have said it.

"Come," said Everton, "that is impossible. You were talking to yourself, Monica. You should not do that. It is an idle and very, very foolish habit. You will go mad if you continue to do that."

She let her head droop a little.

"I wasn't talking to myself," she said in a low, half playful but very deliberate tone.

"That's nonsense. I heard you."

"I wasn't talking to myself."

"But you must have been. There is nobody else here."

"There isn't—now."

"What do you mean? Now?"

"They've gone. You frightened them, I expect."

"What do you mean?" he repeated, advancing a step or two towards her. "And whom do you call 'they'?"

Next moment he was angry with himself. His tone was so heavy and serious and the child was half laughing at him. It was as if she were triumphant at having inveigled him into taking a serious part in her own game of make-believe.

"You wouldn't understand," she said.

"I understand this—that you are wasting your time and being a very silly little girl. What's that you're hiding behind your back?"

She held out her right hand at once, unclenched her fingers and disclosed a thimble. He looked at it and then into her face.

"Why did you hide that from me?" he asked. "There was no need."

She gave him a faint secretive smile—that new smile of hers—before replying.

"We were playing with it. I didn't want you to know."

"*You* were playing with it, you mean. And why didn't you want me to know?"

"About them. Because I thought you wouldn't understand. You *don't* understand."

He saw that it was useless to affect anger or show impatience. He spoke to her gently, even with an attempt at displaying sympathy.

"Who are 'they'?" he asked.

"They're just them. Other girls."

"I see. And they come and play with you, do they? And they run away whenever I'm about, because they don't like me. Is that it?"

She shook her head.

"It isn't that they don't like you. I think they like everybody. But they're so shy. They were shy of me for a long, long time. I knew they were there, but it was weeks and weeks before they'd come and play with me. It was weeks before I even saw them."

"Yes? Well, what are they like?"

"Oh, they're just girls. And they're awfully, awfully nice. Some are a bit older than me and some are a bit younger. And they don't dress like other girls you see to-day. They're in white with longer skirts and they wear sashes."

Everton inclined his head gravely. "She got that out of the illustrations of books in the library," he reflected.

"You don't happen to know their names, I suppose?" he asked, hoping that no quizzical note in his voice rang through the casual but sincere tone which he intended.

"Oh, yes. There's Mary Hewitt—I think I love her best of all—and Elsie Power and——"

"How many of them altogether?"

"Seven. It's just a nice number. And this is the schoolroom where we play games. I love games. I wish I'd learned to play games before."

"And you've been playing with the thimble?"

"Yes. Hunt-the-thimble they call it. One of us hides it, and then the rest of us try to find it, and the one who finds it hides it again."

"You mean you hide it yourself, and then go and find it."

The smile left her face at once, and the look in her eyes warned him that she was done with confidences.

"Ah!" she exclaimed. "You don't understand after all. I somehow knew you wouldn't."

Everton, however, thought he did. His face wore a sudden smile of relief.

"Well, never mind," he said. "But I shouldn't play too much if I were you."

With that he left her. But curiosity tempted him, not in vain, to linger and listen for a moment on the other side of the door which he had closed behind him. He heard Monica whisper:

"Mary! Elsie! Come on. It's all right. He's gone now."

At an answering whisper, very unlike Monica's, he started violently and then found himself grinning at his own discomfiture. It was natural that Monica, playing many parts, should try to change her voice with every character. He went downstairs sunk in a brown study which brought him to certain interesting conclusions. A little later he communicated these to Miss Gribbin.

"I've discovered the cause of the change in Monica. She's invented for herself some imaginary friends—other little girls, of course."

Miss Gribbin started slightly and looked up from the newspaper which she had been reading.

"Really?" she exclaimed. "Isn't that rather an unhealthy sign?"

"No, I should say not. Having imaginary friends is quite a common symptom of childhood, especially among young girls. I remember my sister used to have one, and was very angry when none of the rest of us would take the matter seriously. In Monica's case I should say it was perfectly normal—normal, but interesting. She must have inherited an imagination from that father of hers, with the result that she has seven imaginary friends, all properly named, if you please. You see, being lonely, and having no friends of her own age, she would naturally invent more than one 'friend.' They are all nicely and primly dressed, I must tell you, out of Victorian books which she has found in the library."

"It can't be healthy," said Miss Gribbin, pursing her lips. "And I can't understand how she has learned certain expressions and a certain style of talking and games——"

"All out of books. And pretends to herself that 'they' have taught her. But the most interesting part of the affair is this: it's given me my first practical experience of telepathy, of the existence of which I have hitherto been rather sceptical. Since Monica invented this new game, and before I was aware that she had done so, I have had at different times distinct impressions of there being a lot of little girls about the house."

Miss Gribbin started and stared. Her lips parted as if she were about to speak, but it was as if she had changed her mind while framing the first word she had been about to utter.

"Monica," he continued smiling, "invented these 'friends,' and has been making me telepathically aware of them, too. I have lately been most concerned about the state of my nerves."

Miss Gribbin jumped up as if in anger, but her brow was smooth and her mouth dropped at the corners.

"Mr. Everton," she said, "I wish you had not told me all this." Her lips worked. "You see," she added unsteadily, "I don't believe in telepathy."

IV

Easter, which fell early that year, brought little Gladys Parslow home for the holidays to the Vicarage. The event was shortly afterwards signalized by a note from the Vicar to Everton, inviting him to send Monica down to have tea and play games with his little daughter on the following Wednesday.

The invitation was an annoyance and an embarrassment to Everton. Here was the disturbing factor, the outside influence, which might possibly thwart his experiment in the upbring-

ing of Monica. He was free, of course, simply to decline the invitation so coldly and briefly as to make sure that it would not be repeated; but the man was not strong enough to stand on his own feet impervious to the winds of criticism. He was sensitive and had little wish to seem churlish, still less to appear ridiculous. Taking the line of least resistance he began to reason that one child, herself no older than Monica, and in the atmosphere of her own home, could make but little impression. It ended in his allowing Monica to go.

Monica herself seemed pleased at the prospect of going but expressed her pleasure in a discreet, restrained, grown-up way. Miss Gribbin accompanied her as far as the Vicarage doorstep, arriving with her punctually at half-past three on a sullen and muggy afternoon, and handed her over to the woman-of-all-work who answered the summons at the door.

Miss Gribbin reported to Everton on her return. An idea which she conceived to be humorous had possession of her mind, and in talking to Everton she uttered one of her infrequent laughs.

"I only left her at the door," she said, "so I didn't see her meet the other little girl. I wish I'd stayed to see that. It must have been funny."

She irritated Everton by speaking exactly as if Monica were a captive animal which had just been shown, for the first time in its life, another of its own kind. The analogy thus conveyed to Everton was close enough to make him wince. He felt something like a twinge of conscience, and it may have been then that he asked himself for the first time if he were being fair to Monica.

It had never once occurred to him to ask himself if she were happy. The truth was that he understood children so little as to suppose that physical cruelty was the one kind of cruelty from which they were capable of suffering. Had he ever before troubled to ask himself if Monica were happy, he had probably given the question a curt dismissal with the thought that she had no right to be otherwise. He had given her a good home, even luxuries, together with every opportunity to develop her mind. For companions she had himself, Miss Gribbin, and, to a limited extent, the servants. . . .

Ah, but that picture, conjured up by Miss Gribbin's words with their accompaniment of unreasonable laughter! The little creature meeting for the first time another little creature of its own kind and looking bewildered, knowing neither what to do nor what to say. There was pathos in that—uncomfortable pathos for Everton. Those imaginary friends—did they really mean that Monica had needs of which he knew nothing, of which he had never troubled to learn?

He was not an unkind man, and it hurt him to suspect that he might have committed an unkindness. The modern children whose behavior and manners he disliked, were perhaps only obeying some inexorable law of evolution. Suppose in keeping Monica from their companionship he were actually flying in the face of Nature? Suppose, after all, if Monica were to be natural, she must go unhindered on the tide of her generation?

He compromised with himself, pacing the little study. He would watch Monica much more closely, question her when he had the chance. Then, if he found she was not happy, and really needed the companionship of other children, he would see what could be done.

But when Monica returned home from the Vicarage it was quite plain that she had not enjoyed herself. She was subdued, and said very little about her experience. Quite obviously the two little girls had not made very good friends. Questioned, Monica confessed that she did not like Gladys—much. She said this very thoughtfully with a little pause before the adverb.

"Why don't you like her?" Everton demanded bluntly.

"I don't know. She's so funny. Not like other girls."

"And what do you know about other girls?" he demanded, faintly amused.

"Well, she's not a bit like——"

Monica paused suddenly and lowered her gaze.

"Not like your 'friends,' you mean?" Everton asked.

She gave him a quick, penetrating little glance and then lowered her gaze once more.

"No," she said, "not a bit."

She wouldn't be, of course. Everton teased the child with no more questions for the time being, and let her go. She ran off at once to the great empty room, there to seek that uncanny companionship which had come to suffice her.

For the moment Everton was satisfied. Monica was perfectly happy as she was, and had no need of Gladys, or, probably any other child friends. His experiment with her was shaping successfully. She had invented her own young friends, and had gone off eagerly to play with the creations of her own fancy.

This seemed very well at first. Everton reflected that it was just what he would have wished, until he realized suddenly with a little shock of discomfort that it was not normal and it was not healthy.

V

Although Monica plainly had no great desire to see any more of Gladys Parslow, common civility made it necessary for the Vicar's little daughter to be asked to pay a return visit. Most likely Gladys Parslow was as unwilling to come as was Monica to entertain her. Stern discipline, however, presented her at the appointed time on an afternoon prearranged by correspondence, when Monica received her coldly and with dignity, tempered by a sort of grownup graciousness.

Monica bore her guest away to the big empty room, and that was the last of Gladys Parslow seen by Everton or Miss Gribbin that afternoon. Monica appeared alone when the gong sounded for tea, and announced in a subdued tone that Gladys had already gone home.

"Did you quarrel with her?" Miss Gribbin asked quickly.

"No-o."

"Then why has she gone like this?"

"She was stupid," said Monica, simply. "That's all."

"Perhaps it was you who was stupid. Why did she go?"

"She got frightened."

"Frightened!"

"She didn't like my friends."

Miss Gribbin exchanged glances with Everton.

"She didn't like a silly little girl who talks to herself and imagines things. No wonder she was frightened."

"She didn't think they were real at first, and laughed at me," said Monica, sitting down.

"Naturally!"

"And then when she saw them——"

Miss Gribbin and Everton interrupted her simultaneously, repeating in unison and with well-matched astonishment, her two last words.

"And when she saw them," Monica continued, unperturbed, "she didn't like it. I think she was frightened. Anyhow, she said she wouldn't stay and went straight off home. I think she's a stupid girl. We all had a good laugh about her after she was gone."

She spoke in her ordinary matter-of-fact tones, and if she were secretly pleased at the state of perturbation into which her last words had obviously thrown Miss Gribbin she gave no sign of it. Miss Gribbin immediately exhibited outward signs of anger.

"You are a very naughty child to tell such untruths. You know perfectly well that Gladys couldn't have *seen* your 'friends.' You have simply frightened her by pretending to talk to people who weren't there, and it will serve you right if she never comes to play with you again."

"She won't," said Monica. "And she *did* see them, Miss Gribbin."

"How do you know?" Everton asked.

"By her face. And she spoke to them too, when she ran to the door. They were very shy at first because Gladys was there. They wouldn't come for a long time, but I begged them, and at last they did."

Everton checked another outburst from Miss Gribbin with a look. He wanted to learn more, and to that end he applied some show of patience and gentleness.

"Where did they come from?" he asked. "From outside the door?"

"Oh, no. From where they always come."

"And where's that?"

"I don't know. They don't seem to know themselves. It's always from some direction where I'm not looking. Isn't it strange?"

"Very! And do they disappear in the same way?"

Monica frowned very seriously and thoughtfully.

"It's so quick you can't tell where they go. When you or Miss Gribbin come in——"

"They always fly on our approach, of course. But why?"

"Because they're dreadfully, dreadfully shy. But not so shy as they were. Perhaps soon they'll get used to you and not mind at all."

"That's a comforting thought!" said Everton with a dry laugh.

When Monica had taken her tea and departed, Everton turned to his secretary.

"You are wrong to blame the child. These creatures of her fancy are perfectly real to her. Her powers of suggestion have been strong enough to force them to some extent on me. The little Parslow girl, being younger and more receptive, actually *sees* them. It is a clear case of telepathy and autosuggestion. I have never studied such matters, but I should say that these instances are of some scientific interest."

Miss Gribbin's lips tightened and he saw her shiver slightly.

"Mr. Parslow will be angry," was all she said.

"I really cannot help that. Perhaps it is all for the best. If Monica does not like his little daughter they had better not be brought together again."

For all that, Everton was a little embarrassed when on the following morning he met the Vicar out walking. If the Rev. Parslow knew that his little daughter had left the house so unceremoniously on the preceding day, he would either wish to make an apology, or perhaps require one, according to his view of the situation. Everton did not wish to deal in apologies one way or the other, he did not care to discuss the vagaries of children, and altogether he wanted to have as little to do with Mr. Parslow as was conveniently possible. He would have passed with a brief acknowledgment of the Vicar's existence, but, as he had feared, the Vicar stopped him.

"I had been meaning to come and see you," said the Rev. Parslow.

Everton halted and sighed inaudibly, thinking that perhaps this casual meeting out of doors might after all have saved him something.

"Yes?" he said.

"I will walk in your direction if I may." The Vicar eyed him anxiously. "There is something you must certainly be told. I don't know if you guess, or if you already know. If not, I don't know how you will take it. I really don't."

Everton looked puzzled. Whichever child the Vicar might blame for the hurried departure of Gladys, there seemed no cause for such a portentous face and manner.

"Really?" he asked. "Is it something serious?"

"I think so, Mr. Everton. You are aware, of course, that my little girl left your house yesterday afternoon with some lack of ceremony."

"Yes, Monica told us she had gone. If they could not agree it was surely the best thing she could have done, although it may sound inhospitable of me to say it. Excuse me, Mr. Parslow, but I hope you are not trying to embroil me in a quarrel between children?"

The Vicar stared in his turn.

"I am not," he said, "and I am unaware that there was any quarrel. I was going to ask you to forgive Gladys. There was some excuse for her lack of ceremony. She was badly frightened, poor child."

"Then it is my turn to express regret. I had Monica's version of what happened. Monica has been left a great deal to her own resources, and, having no playmates of her own age, she seems to have invented some."

"Ah!" said the Rev. Parslow, drawing a deep breath.

"Unfortunately," Everton continued, "Monica has an uncomfortable gift for impressing her fancies on other people. I have often thought I felt the presence of children about the house, and so, I am almost sure, has Miss Gribbin. I am afraid that when your little girl came to play with her yesterday afternoon, Monica scared her by introducing her invisible 'friends' and by talking to imaginary and therefore invisible little girls."

The Vicar laid a hand on Everton's arm.

"There is something more in it than that. Gladys is not an imaginative child; she is, indeed, a practical little person. I have never yet known her to tell me a lie. What would you say, Mr. Everton, if I were to tell you that Gladys positively asserts that she *saw* those other children?"

Something like a cold draught went through Everton. An ugly suspicion, vague and almost shapeless, began to move in dim recesses of his mind. He tried to shake himself free of it, to smile and to speak lightly.

"I shouldn't be in the least surprised. Nobody knows the limits of telepathy and autosuggestion. If I can feel the presence of children whom Monica has created out of her own imagination, why shouldn't your daughter, who is probably more receptive and impressionable than I am, be able to see them?"

The Rev. Parslow shook his head.

"Do you really mean that?" he asked. "Doesn't it seem to you a little far-fetched?"

"Everything we don't understand must seem far-fetched. If one had dared to talk of wireless thirty years ago——"

"Mr. Everton, do you know that your house was once a girl's school?"

Once more Everton experienced that vague feeling of discomfiture.

"I didn't know," he said, still indifferently.

"My aunt, whom I never saw, was there. Indeed she died there. There were seven who died. Diphtheria broke out there many years ago. It ruined the school which was shortly afterwards closed. Did you know that, Mr. Everton? My aunt's name was Mary Hewitt——"

"Good God!" Everton cried out sharply. "Good God!"

"Ah!" said Parslow. "Now do you begin to see?"

Everton, suddenly a little giddy, passed a hand across his forehead.

"That is—one of the names Monica told me," he faltered. "How could she know?"

"How indeed? Mary Hewitt's great friend was Elsie Power. They died within a few hours of each other."

"That name too . . . she told me . . . and there were seven. How could she have known? Even the people around here wouldn't have remembered names after all these years."

"Gladys knew them. But that was only partly why she was afraid. Yet I think she was more awed than afraid, because she knew instinctively that the children who came to play with little Monica, although they were not of this world, were good children, blessed children."

"What are you telling me?" Everton burst out.

"Don't be afraid, Mr. Everton. You are not afraid, are you? If those whom we call dead still remain close to us, what more natural than these children should come back to play with a lonely little girl who lacked human playmates? It may seem inconceivable, but how else explain it? How could little Monica have invented those two names? How could she have learned that seven little girls once died in your house? Only the very old people about here remember it, and even they could not tell you how many died or the name of any one of the little victims. Haven't you noticed a change in your ward since first she began to—imagine them, as you thought?"

Everton nodded heavily.

"Yes," he said, almost unwittingly, "she learned all sorts of tricks of speech, childish gestures she never had before, and games. . . . I couldn't understand. Mr. Parslow, what in God's name am I to do?"

The Rev. Parslow still kept a hand on Everton's arm.

"If I were you I should send her off to school. It may not be very good for her."

"Not good for her! But the children, you say——"

"Children? I might have said angels. *They* will never harm her. But Monica is developing a gift of seeing and conversing with—with beings that are invisible and inaudible to others. It is not a gift to be encouraged. She may in time see and converse with others—wretched souls who are not God's children. She may lose the faculty if she mixes with others of her age. Out of her need, I am sure, these came to her."

"I must think," said Everton.

He walked on dazedly. In a moment or two the whole aspect of life had changed, had grown clearer, as if he had been blind from birth and was now given the first glimmerings of light. He looked forward no longer into the face of a blank and featureless wall, but through a curtain beyond which life manifested itself vaguely but at least perceptibly. His footfalls on the ground beat out the words: "There is no death. There is no death."

VI

That evening after dinner he sent for Monica and spoke to her in an unaccustomed way. He was strangely shy of her, and his hand, which he rested on one of her slim shoulders, lay there awkwardly.

"Do you know what I'm going to do with you, young woman?" he said. "I'm going to pack you off to school."

"O-oh!" she stared at him, half smiling. "Are you really?"

"Do you want to go?"

She considered the matter, frowning and staring at the tips of her fingers.

"I don't know. I don't want to leave *them*."

"Who?" he asked.

"Oh, you know!" she said, and turned her head half shyly.

"What? Your—friends, Monica?"

"Yes."

"Wouldn't you like other playmates?"

"I don't know. I love *them,* you see. But they said—they said I ought to go to school if you ever sent me. They might be angry with me if I was to ask you to let me stay. They wanted me to play with other girls who aren't—that aren't like they are. Because you know, they are *different* from children that everybody can see. And Mary told me not to—not to encourage anybody else who was different, like them."

Everton drew a deep breath.

"We'll have a talk tomorrow about finding a school for you, Monica," he said. "Run off to bed, now. Good-night, my dear."

He hesitated, then touched her forehead with his lips. She ran from him, nearly as shy as Everton himself, tossing back her long hair, but from the door she gave him the strangest little brimming glance, and there was that in her eyes which he had never seen before.

Late that night Everton entered the great empty room which Monica had named the schoolroom. A flag of moonlight from the window lay across the floor, and it was empty to the gaze. But the deep shadows hid little shy presences of which some unnamed and undeveloped sense in the man was acutely aware.

"Children!" he whispered. "Children!"

He closed his eyes and stretched out his hands. Still they were shy and held aloof, but he fancied that they came a little nearer.

"Don't be afraid," he whispered. "I'm only a very lonely man. Be near me after Monica is gone."

He paused, waiting. Then as he turned away he was aware of little caressing hands upon his arm. He looked around at once, but the time had not yet come for him to see. He saw only the barred window, the shadows on either wall, and the flag of moonlight.

Ramsey Campbell

HEAVILY INFLUENCED BY THE work of H. P. Lovecraft, John Ramsey Campbell (1946-) published three short story collections in a similar style before producing his first novel, *The Doll Who Ate His Mother* (1976; revised edition 1985). The following year, 1977, he wrote the novelizations of three films (*The Bride of Frankenstein, Dracula's Daughter,* and *The Wolfman*) as Carl Dreadstone, a house name under which three additional novels were written by others. He was successful in bringing a pulpy style that evoked those classic films. Among the best of his later novels are *The Face That Must Die* (1979), *Incarnate* (1983), *Ancient Images* (1989), *Midnight Sun* (1991), and *Grin of the Dark* (2008). Among the many accolades Campbell has received are six World Fantasy nominations (four winners), sixteen British Fantasy Society nominations (ten winners), and two Bram Stoker Award nominations (both winners). He has been named the Lifetime President of the British Fantasy Society. Often described by critics and fellow writers as the greatest stylist of the contemporary horror genre, Campbell was born in Liverpool. He set many of his novels and stories there and in the fictional city of Brichester in the same region. While much of his work is explicitly violent, Campbell's use of metaphor, symbolism, and imagery allows a poetic tone to suffuse his prose, suggesting horrors that remain in the memory long after the initial shock of a starkly brutal occurrence has passed.

"Just Behind You" was first published in *Poe's Progeny*, edited by Gary Fry (Bradford, U.K., Gray Friar Press, 2005).

Just Behind You

RAMSEY CAMPBELL

I'VE HARDLY SLAMMED the car door when Mr. Holt trots out of the school. "Sorry we're late, head," I tell him.

"Don't send yourself to my office, Paul. It was solid of you to show up." He elevates his bristling eyebrows, which tug his mottled round face blank. "I'd have laid odds on you if I were a betting man."

"You don't mean no one else has come."

"None of your colleagues. You're their repre-

sentative. Don't worry, I'll make sure it goes on your record somehow."

I want to keep this job, whatever memories the school revives, but now it looks as if I'm attending his son's party to ingratiate myself rather than simply assuming it was expected; the invitations were official enough. I'm emitting a diffident sound when Mr. Holt clasps his pudgy hands behind his back. "And let me guess, this is your son," he says, lowering his face at Tom as if his joviality is weighing it down. "What's the young man's name?"

I'm afraid Tom may resent being patronised, but he struggles to contain a grin as he says "Tom."

"Tom Francis, hey? Good strong name. You could go to bat for England with a name like that. The birthday boy's called Jack. I expect you're eager to meet him."

Tom hugs the wrapped computer game as if he's coveting it all over again, and I give him a frown that's both a warning and a reminder that his mother promised we'd buy him one for Christmas. "I don't mind," he says.

"Not done to show too much enthusiasm these days, is it, Paul? Cut along there, Tom, and the older men will catch you up."

As Tom marches alongside the elongated two-storey red brick building as if he's determined to leave more of his loathed chubbiness behind, Mr. Holt says, "I think we can say it's a success. A couple of the parents are already talking about hiring the school for their parties. Do let me know if you have any wheezes for swelling the funds."

I'm distracted by the notion that a boy is pacing Tom inside the ground-floor classrooms. It's his reflection, of course, and now I can't even see it in the empty sunlit rooms. "It was tried once before," I'm confused enough to remark. "Hiring the place out."

"Before my time," the headmaster says so sharply he might be impressing it on someone who doesn't know. "There was a tragedy, I gather. Was it while you were a pupil here?"

Although I'm sure he doesn't mean to sound accusing, he makes me feel accused. I might almost not have left the school and grown up, and the prospect ahead doesn't help—the school-yard occupied by people I've never seen before. The adults and most of the boys have taken plastic cups from a trestle table next to one laden with unwrapped presents. "I'm afraid I was," I say, which immediately strikes me as an absurd turn of phrase.

"Can we start now, dad?" the fattest boy shouts. "Who else are we supposed to be waiting for?"

"I think you've just got one new friend, Jack."

I hope it's only being told it that makes him scowl at Tom. "Who are you? Did you have to come?"

"I'm sure he wanted to," Mr. Holt says, though I think he may have missed the point of the question, unless he's pretending. "This is Paul Francis and his son Tom, everyone. Paul is proving to be the loyallest of my staff."

Some of the adults stand their cups on the table to applaud while others raise a polite cheer. "Is that my present?" Jack Holt is asking Tom. "What have you got me?"

"I hope you like it," Tom says and yields it up. "I would."

Jack tears off the wrapping and drops it on the concrete. A woman who has been dispensing drinks utters an affectionate tut as she swoops to retrieve it and consign it to the nearest bin. "Thank you, dear," Mr. Holt says, presumably identifying her as his wife. "Even if it's your birthday, Jack—"

"I'll see if it's any good later," Jack tells Tom, and as Tom's face owns up to hoping he can have a turn, adds, "When I get home."

"Do pour Paul some bubbly, dear. Not precisely champers, Paul, but I expect you can't tell on your salary."

As a driver I should ask for lemonade, but I don't think I'll be able to bear much more of the afternoon without a stronger drink or several. As Mrs. Holt giggles at the foam that swells out of my cup, her husband claps his hands. "Well, boys, I think it's time for games."

"I want to eat first." With a slyness I'm surely not alone in noticing Jack says, "You wouldn't like all the food mother made to go stale."

I take rather too large a gulp from my cup. His behaviour reminds me of Jasper, and I don't care to remember just now, especially while Tom is on the premises. I look around for distraction, and fancy that I glimpsed someone ducking out of sight behind the schoolyard wall closest to the building. I can do without such notions, and so I watch Mrs. Holt uncover the third table. The flourish with which she whips off its paper shroud to reveal plates of sandwiches and sausage rolls and a cake armed with eleven candles falters, however, and a corner of the paper scrapes the concrete. "Dear me," she comments. "Don't say this was you, Jack."

"It wasn't me," Jack protests before he even looks.

Someone has taken a bite out of a sandwich from each platter and sampled the sausage rolls as well, though the cake has survived the raid. Jack stares at Tom as if he wants to blame him, but must realise Tom had no opportunity. "Who's been messing with my food?" he demands at a pitch that hurts my ears.

"Now, Jack, don't spoil your party," his mother says. "Someone must have sneaked in when we all went to welcome your guests."

"I don't want it any more. I don't like the look of it."

"We'll just put the food that's been nibbled out for the birds, shall we? Then it won't be wasted, and I'm certain the rest will be fine."

I do my best to share her conviction for Tom's sake, although the bite marks in the food she lays on top of the wall closest to the sports field look unpleasantly discoloured. Jack seems determined to maintain his aversion until the other boys start loading their paper plates, and then he elbows Tom aside and grabs handfuls to heap his own plate. I tell myself that Tom will have to survive worse in his life as I promise mentally to make up to him for the afternoon. If I'd come alone I wouldn't be suffering quite so much.

I let Mrs. Holt refill my cup as an aid to conversing with the adult guests. I've already spoken to a magistrate and a local councillor and an accountant and a journalist. Their talk is so small it's close to infinitesimal, except when it's pointedly personal. Once they've established that this is my first job at a secondary school, and how many years I attended night classes

to upgrade my qualifications, and that my wife doesn't teach since she was attacked by a pupil, except I'd call her nursery work teaching, they seem to want me and Tom to feel accepted. "He certainly knows how to enjoy himself," says the magistrate, and the councillor declares, "He's a credit to his parents." The accountant contributes, "He's a generous chap," and it's only when the journalist responds, "Makes everybody welcome even if he doesn't know them" that I realise they're discussing not my son but Jack. The relentlessly sparkling wine helps me also understand they're blind to anything here that they don't want to see. I refrain from saying so for Tom's sake and quite possibly my job's. I do my best not to be unbearably aware of Tom's attempts to stay polite while Jack boasts how superior his private school is to this one. When Jack asks Tom if his parents can't afford to send him to a better school than he's admitted to attending, my retort feels capable of heading off Tom's. It's Mrs. Holt who interrupts, however. "If everyone has had sufficient, let's bring on the cake."

If she meant to cater for the adults, Jack has seen off their portions, either gobbling them or mauling them on his plate. He dumps it on the pillaged table as his mother elevates the cake and his father touches a lighter to the candles. Once all the pale flames are standing up to the July sun, Mr. Holt sets about "Happy birthday to you" as if it's one of the hymns we no longer sing in school. Everybody joins in, with varying degrees of conviction; one boy is so out of tune that he might be poking fun at the song. At least it isn't Tom; his mouth is wide open, whereas the voice sounds muffled, almost hidden. The song ends more or less in unison before I can locate the mocking singer, and Jack plods to blow out the candles. As he takes a loud moist breath they flutter and expire. "Sorry," says his father and relights them.

Jack performs another inhalation as a prelude to lurching at the cake so furiously that for an instant I think his movement has blown out the candles. "Who's doing that?" he shouts.

He glares behind him at the schoolyard wall and then at his young guests. His gaze lingers on Tom, who responds, "Looks like someone doesn't want you to have a birthday."

Jack's stare hardens further. "Well, they'd better play their tricks on someone else or my dad'll make them wish they had."

"I'm sure it's just these candles," Mrs. Holt says with a reproachful blink at her husband and holds out the cake for him to apply the lighter. "Have another try, Jack. Big puff."

The boy looks enraged by her choice of words. He ducks to the candles the moment they're lit and extinguishes them, spraying the cake with saliva. I won't pretend I'm disappointed that the adults aren't offered a slice. I can tell that Tom accepts one out of politeness, because he dabs the icing surreptitiously with a paper napkin. Mrs. Holt watches so closely to see all the cake is consumed that it's clear she would take anything less as an insult to her or her son. "That's the idea. Build up your vim," she says and blinks across the yard. "Those birds must have been quick. I didn't see them come or go, did you?"

Mr. Holt hardly bothers to shake his head at the deserted field. "All right, boys, no arguments this time. Let's work off some of that energy."

I suspect that's a euphemism for reducing Jack's weight, unless Mr. Holt and his wife are determined to be unaware of it. I'm wondering what I may have let Tom in for when Mr. Holt says "Who's for a race around the field?"

"I don't mind," says Tom.

"Go on then. We'll watch," Jack says, and the rest of the boys laugh.

"How about a tug of war?" the magistrate suggests as if she's commuting a sentence.

"I don't think that would be fair, would it?" the councillor says. "There'd be too many on one side."

Jack's entourage all stare at Tom until the accountant says, "How do you come up with that? Twelve altogether, that was twice six when I went to school."

"I mustn't have counted the last chap. I hope it won't lose me your vote," the councillor says

to me and perhaps more facetiously to Tom, and blames her drink with a comical grimace.

"I don't care. It's supposed to be my party for me. It's like she said, if we have games it isn't fair unless I win," Jack complains, and I can't avoid remembering any longer. Far too much about him reminds me of Jasper.

I didn't want to go to Jasper's party either. I only accepted the invitation because he made me feel I was the nearest to a friend he had at his new school. I mustn't have been alone in taking pity on him, because all his guests turned out to be our classmates; there was nobody from his old school. His mother had remarried, and his stepfather had insisted on moving him to a state school, where he could mix with ordinary boys like us. I expected him to behave himself in front of his family, but whenever he saw the opportunity he acted even worse than usual, accusing the timidest boy of taking more than his share of the party food, and well-nigh wailing when someone else was offered whichever slices of the cake Jasper had decided were his, and arguing with his parents over who'd won the various games they organised unless he was the winner, and refusing to accept that he hadn't caught us moving whenever he swung around while we were trying to creep up on him unnoticed. Now I remember we played that game among ourselves when the adults went to search for him. As if I've communicated my thoughts Tom says, "How about hide and seek?"

I could almost imagine that someone has whispered the suggestion in his ear. He looks less than certain of his inspiration even before Jack mimics him. "How about it?"

"Give it a try," Mrs. Holt urges. "It'll be fun. I'm sure Mr. Francis must have played it when he was your age. I know I did."

Why did she single me out? It brings memories closer and a grumble from Jack. As his allies echo him, his father intervenes. "Come on, chaps, give your new friend a chance. He's made an effort on your behalf."

I wonder whether Mr. Holt has any sense of how much. Perhaps Jack takes the comment as an insult; he seems still more resentful. I can't help hoping he's about to say something to Tom that will provide us with an excuse to leave. Despite his scowl he says only, "You've got to be It, then."

"You see, you did know how to play," his mother informs him.

This aggravates his scowl, but it stays trained on Tom. "Go over by the wall," he orders, "and count to a hundred so we can hear you. Like this. One. And. Two. And. Three, and don't dare look."

Tom stands where he's directed—overlooking the sports field—and rests his closed eyes on his folded arms on top of the bare wall. As soon as Tom begins to count, Jack waddles unexpectedly fast and with a stealth I suspect is only too typical of him out of the yard, beckoning his cronies to follow. There must be a breeze across the field; Tom's hair is standing up, and he seems restless, though I can't feel the wind or see evidence of it elsewhere. I'm distracted by Mr. Holt's shout. "Boys, don't go—"

Either it's too late or it fails to reach them, unless they're pretending not to hear. All of them vanish into the school. Mrs. Holt puts a finger to her lips and nods at Tom, who's counting in a loud yet muffled voice that sounds as if somebody is muttering in unison with him—it must be rebounding from the wall. I take Mrs. Holt not to want the game to be spoiled. "They won't come to any harm in there, will they?" she murmurs.

Jasper didn't, I'm forced to recall: he was on the roof until he fell off. Mr. Holt tilts his head as though his raised eyebrow has altered the balance. "I'm sure they know not to get into any mischief."

Tom shouts a triumphant hundred as he straightens up. He seems glad to retreat from the wall. Without glancing at anyone, even at me, he runs out of the yard. Either he overheard the Holts or his ears are sharper than mine, since he heads directly for the school. Someone peers out to watch his approach and dodges back in. I don't hear the door then, nor as Tom disappears into the school. It's as if the building has joined in the general stealth.

I remember the silence that met all the shouts of Jasper's name. For years I would wonder why he was so determined not to be found: because he didn't want to be It, or on the basis that we couldn't play any games without him? In that case he was wrong about us. As the calls shrank into and around the school, we played at creeping up on one another while he wasn't there to ruin it for us. It was my turn to catch the others out when I heard his mother cry "Jasper" in the distance—nothing else, not so much as a thud. The desperation in her voice made me turn to see what my friends made of it. Could I really have expected to find Jasper at my back, grinning at the trick he'd worked on us and on his parents, or was that only a dream that troubled my sleep for weeks?

He must have resolved not to be discovered even by his parents; perhaps he didn't want them to know he'd been on the roof. I assume he tried to scramble out of sight. We didn't abandon our game until we heard the ambulance, and by the time we reached the front of the school, Jasper was covered up on a stretcher and his parents were doing their best to suppress their emotions until they were behind closed doors. As the ambulance pulled away it emitted a wail that I didn't immediately realise belonged to Jasper's mother. The headmaster had emerged from his office, where no doubt he'd hoped to be only nominally in charge of events, and put us to work at clearing away the debris of the party and storing Jasper's presents in his office; we never knew what became of them. Then he sent us home without quite accusing us of anything, and on Monday told the school how it had lost a valued pupil and warned everyone against playing dangerous games. I couldn't help taking that as at least a hint of an accusation. If we hadn't carried on with our game, might we have spotted Jasper on the roof or caught him as he fell?

It seems unlikely, and I don't want to brood about it now. I attempt to occupy my mind by helping Mrs. Holt clear up. This time she doesn't leave any food on the wall for whatever stole away with it, but drops the remains in the bin. From thanking me she graduates to saying, "You're so kind" and "He's a treasure," none of which helps me stay alert. It's the magistrate who enquires, "What do we think they're up to?"

"Who?"

She answers Mr. Holt's tone with an equally sharp glance before saying "Shouldn't some of them have tried to get back to base by now?"

At once I'm sure that Jack has organised his friends in some way against Tom. I'm trying to decide if I should investigate when Mr. Holt says "They should be in the fresh air where it's healthier. Come with me, Paul, and we'll flush them out."

"Shall we tag along?" says the accountant.

"Two members of staff should be adequate, thank you," Mr. Holt tells her and trots to catch me up. We're halfway along the flagstoned path to the back entrance when he says, "You go this way and I'll deal with the front, then nobody can say they didn't know the game was over."

As he rounds the corner of the building at a stately pace I make for the entrance through which all the boys vanished. I grasp the metal doorknob and experience a twinge of guilt: suppose we call a halt to the game just as Tom is about to win? He should certainly be able to outrun Jack. This isn't the thought that seems to let the unexpected chill of the doorknob spread up my arm and shiver through me. I'm imagining Tom as he finds someone who's been hiding—someone who turns to show him a face my son should never see.

It's absurd, of course. Just the sunlight should render it ridiculous. If any of the boys deserves such an encounter it's Jack, not my son. I can't help opening my mouth to say as much, since nobody will hear, but then I'm shocked by what I was about to do, however ineffectual it would be. Jack's just a boy, for heaven's sake—a product of his upbringing, like Jasper. He's had no more chance to mature than Jasper ever will have, whereas I've had decades and should be-

have like it. Indeed, it's mostly because I'm too old to believe in such things that I murmur "Leave Tom alone and the rest of them as well. If you want to creep up on anyone, I'm here." I twist the knob with the last of my shiver and let myself into the school.

The empty corridor stretches past the cloakroom and the assembly hall to the first set of fire doors, pairs of which interrupt it all the way to the front of the building. My thoughts must have affected me more than I realised; I feel as though it's my first day at school, whether as a pupil or a teacher hardly matters. I have a notion that the sunlight propped across the corridor from every window won't be able to hold the place quiet for much longer. Of course it won't if the boys break cover. I scoff at my nerves and start along the corridor.

Am I supposed to be making a noise or waiting until Mr. Holt lets himself be heard? For more reasons than I need articulate I'm happy to be unobtrusive, if that's what I am. Nobody is hiding in a corner of the cloakroom. I must have glimpsed a coat hanging down to the floor, except that there aren't any coats—a shadow, then, even if I can't locate it now. I ease open the doors of the assembly hall, where the ranks of folding chairs resemble an uproar held in check. The place is at least as silent as the opposite of the weekday clamour. As the doors fall shut they send a draught to the fire doors, which quiver as though someone beyond them is growing impatient. Their panes exhibit a deserted stretch of corridor, and elbowing them aside shows me that nobody is crouching out of sight. The gymnasium is unoccupied except for an aberrant reverberation of my footsteps, a noise too light to have been made by even the smallest of the boys; it's more like the first rumble of thunder or a muted drum-roll. The feeble rattle of the parallel bars doesn't really sound like a puppet about to perform, let alone bones. Another set of fire doors brings me alongside the art room. Once I'm past I wonder what I saw in there: one of the paintings displayed on the wall must have made especially free with its subject—I wouldn't have called the dark blotchy peeling piebald mass a face apart from its grin, and that was too wide. As I hurry past classrooms with a glance into each, that wretched image seems to have lodged in my head; I keep being left with a sense of having just failed to register yet another version of the portrait that was pressed against the window of the door at the instant I looked away. The recurrences are progressively more detailed and proportionately less appealing. Of course only my nerves are producing them, though I've no reason to be nervous or to look back. I shoulder the next pair of doors wide and peer into the science room. Apparently someone thought it would be amusing to prop up a biology aid so that it seems to be watching through the window onto the corridor. It's draped with a stained yellowish cloth that's so tattered I can distinguish parts of the skull beneath, plastic that must be discoloured with age. While I'm not sure of all this because of the dazzle of sunlight, I've no wish to be surer. I hasten past and hear movement behind me. It has to be one if not more of the boys from Jack's party, but before I can turn I see a figure beyond the last set of fire doors. It's the headmaster.

The sight is more reassuring than I would have expected until he pushes the doors open. The boy with him is my son, who looks as if he would rather be anywhere else. I'm about to speak Tom's name as some kind of comfort when I hear the doors of the assembly hall crash open and what could well be the sound of almost a dozen boys charging gleefully out of the school. "I take it you were unable to deal with them," says Mr. Holt.

"They were all hiding together," Tom protests.

Since Mr. Holt appears to find this less than pertinent, I feel bound to say, "They must have been well hidden, Tom. I couldn't find them either."

"I'm afraid Master Francis rather exceeded himself."

"I was only playing." Perhaps out of resentment at being called that, Tom adds, "I thought I was supposed to play."

Mr. Holt doesn't care for the addition. With all the neutrality I'm able to muster I ask, "What did Tom do?"

"I discovered him in my passage."

Tom bites his lip, and I'm wondering how sternly I'm expected to rebuke him when I gather that he's fighting to restrain a burst of mirth. At once Mr. Holt's choice of words strikes me as almost unbearably hilarious, and I wish I hadn't met Tom's eyes. My nerves and the release of tension are to blame. I shouldn't risk speaking, but I have to. "He wouldn't have known it was out of bounds," I blurt, which sounds at least as bad and disintegrates into a splutter.

Tom can't contain a snort as the headmaster stares at us. "I don't believe I've ever been accused of lacking a sense of humour, but I fail to see what's so amusing."

That's worse still. Tom's face works in search of control until I say, "Go on, Tom. You should be with the others" more sharply than he deserves. "Sorry, head. Just a misunderstanding," I offer Mr. Holt's back as I follow them both, and then I falter. "Where's—"

There's no draped skull at the window of the science room. I grab the clammy doorknob and jerk the door open and dart into the room. "Someone was in here," I insist.

"Well, nobody is now. If you knew they were, why didn't you deal with them as I asked?"

"I didn't see them. They've moved something, that's how I know."

"Do show me what and where."

"I can't," I say, having glared around the room. Perhaps the item is in one of the cupboards, but I'm even less sure than I was at the time what I saw. All this aggravates my nervousness, which is increasingly on Tom's behalf. I don't like the idea of his being involved in whatever is happening. I'll deal with it on Monday if there's anything to deal with, but just now I'm more concerned to deliver him safely home.

"Would you be very unhappy if we cut our visit short?"

"I'm ready," says Tom.

I was asking Mr. Holt, who makes it clear I should have been. "I was about to propose some noncompetitive games," he says.

I don't know if that's meant to tempt Tom or as a sly rebuke. "To tell you the truth"—which to some extent I am—"I'm not feeling very well."

Mr. Holt gazes at Tom, and I'm more afraid than makes any sense that he'll invite him to stay even if I leave. "I'll need to take him with me," I say too fast, too loud.

"Very well, I'll convey your apologies. A pity, though. Jack was just making friends."

A hint of ominousness suggests that my decision may affect my record. I'm trailing after the headmaster, though I've no idea what I could say to regain his approval, when he says, "We'll see you on Monday, I trust. Go out the front. After all, you're staff."

It feels more like being directed to a tradesman's entrance. Tom shoves one fire door with his fist and holds it open for me. It thuds shut behind us like a lid, then stirs with a semblance of life. Perhaps Mr. Holt has sent a draught along the corridor. "Let's get out of his passage," I say, but the joke is stale. I unlatch the door opposite his office and step into the sunlight, and don't release my grip on the door until I hear it lock.

My Fiat is the smallest of the cars parked outside. I watch the door of the school in the driving mirror until Tom has fastened his seat belt, and then I accelerate with a gnash of gravel. We're nearly at the gates when Tom says, "Hadn't I better go back?"

I halt the car just short of the dual carriageway that leads home. I'm hesitating mostly because of the traffic. "Not unless you want to," I tell him.

"I don't much."

"Then we're agreed," I say and send the car into a gap in the traffic.

A grassy strip planted with trees divides the road, two lanes on each side. The carriageway curves back and forth for three miles to our home. Tom doesn't wait for me to pick up speed before he speaks again. "Wouldn't it help if I did?"

I'm distracted by the sight of a Volkswagen several hundred yards back in the outer lane. It's surely too small to contain so many children; it looks positively dangerous, especially at that speed. "Help what?"

"You to stay friends with the headmaster."

This may sound naïve, but it's wise enough, and makes me doubly uncomfortable. As the Volkswagen overtakes me I observe that it contains fewer boys than I imagined. "I don't need to use you to do that, Tom. I shouldn't have used you at all."

"I don't mind if it helps now mother hasn't got such a good job."

The next car—an Allegro—to race along the outer lane has just one boy inside. He's in the back, but not strapped in, if he's even seated. As he leans forward between the young couple in front I have the disconcerting impression that he's watching me. I don't know how I can, since I'm unable to distinguish a single detail within the dark blotch of his face. I force my attention away from the mirror and strive to concentrate on the road ahead. Until I brake I'm too close to a bus. "Look, Tom," I hear myself say, "I know you mean well, but just now you're not helping, all right? I've got enough on my mind. Too much."

With scant warning the bus halts at a stop. The Allegro flashes its lights to encourage me to pull out. Its young passenger is unquestionably watching me; he has leaned further forward between the seats, though his face still hasn't emerged into the light. The trouble is that the man and woman in front of him are middle-aged or older. It isn't the same car. This confuses me so badly that as I make to steer around the bus I stall the engine. The Allegro hurtles past with a blare of its horn, and I have a clear view of the occupants. Unless the boy has crouched out of view, the adults are the only people in the car.

The starter motor screams as I twist the key an unnecessary second time. I'm tailing the bus at more than a safe distance while cars pass us when Tom says, "Are you sure you're all right to drive, dad? We could park somewhere and come back for it later."

"I'll be fine if you just shut up." I would be more ashamed of my curtness if I weren't so aware of a Mini that's creeping up behind us in the inner lane. The old man who's driving it is on his own, or is he? No, a silhouette about Tom's size but considerably thinner and with holes in it has reared up behind him. It leans over his shoulder, and I'm afraid of what may happen if he notices it, unless I'm the only person who can see it. I tramp on the accelerator to send the Fiat past the bus, only just outdistancing an impatient Jaguar. "I mean," I say to try and recapture Tom's companionship, "let's save talking till we're home."

He deserves more of an apology, but I'm too preoccupied by realising that it wasn't such a good idea to overtake the bus. The only person on board who's visible to me is the driver. At least I can see that he's alone in the cabin, but who may be behind him out of sight? Suppose he's distracted while he's driving? A woman at a bus stop extends a hand as if she's attempting to warn me, and to my relief, the bus coasts to a halt. The Mini wavers into view around it and trundles after my car. I put on as much speed as I dare and risk a glance in the mirror to see whether there was anything I needed to leave behind. The old man is on his own. Tom and I aren't, however.

My entire body stiffens to maintain my grip on the wheel and control of the steering. I struggle not to look over my shoulder or in the mirror, and tell myself that the glimpse resembled a damaged old photograph, yellowed and blotchy and tattered, hardly identifiable as a face. It's still in the mirror at the edge of my determinedly lowered vision, and I wonder what it may do to regain my attention—and then I have a worse thought. If Tom sees it, will it transfer its revenge to him? Was this its intention ever since it saw us? "Watch the road," I snarl.

At first Tom isn't sure I mean him. "What?" he says without much enthusiasm.

"Do it for me. Tell me if I get too close to anything."

"I thought you didn't want me to talk."

"I do now. Grown-ups can change their minds, you know. This is your first driving lesson. Never get too close."

I hardly know what I'm saying, but it doesn't matter so long as he's kept unaware of our passenger. I tread on the accelerator and come up fast behind a second bus. I can't avoid noticing that the object in the mirror has begun to grin so widely that the remnants of its lips are tearing, exposing too many teeth. The car is within yards of the bus when Tom says nervously "Too close?"

"Much too. Don't wait so long next time or you won't like what happens."

My tone is even more unreasonable than that, but I can't think what else to do. I brake and swerve around the bus, which involves glancing in the mirror. I'm barely able to grasp that the Fiat is slower than the oncoming traffic, because the intruder has leaned forward to show me the withered blackened lumps it has for eyes. I fight to steady my grip on the wheel as my shivering leg presses the accelerator to the floor. "Keep it up," I urge and retreat into the inner lane ahead of the bus. "I'm talking to you, Tom."

I will him not to wonder who else I could have been addressing. "Too close," he cries soon enough. I scarcely know whether I'm driving like this to hold his attention or out of utter panic. "Too close," I make him shout several times, and at last, "Slow down, dad. Here's our road."

What may I be taking home? I'm tempted to drive past the junction and abandon the car, but I've no idea what that would achieve beyond leaving Tom even warier of me. I brake and grapple with the wheel, swinging far too widely into the side road, almost mounting the opposite kerb. Perhaps the lumps too small for eyes are spiders, because they appear to be inching out of the sockets above the collapsed shrivelled nose and protruding grin. I try to tell myself it's a childish trick as the car speeds between the ranks of mutually supportive red-brick semis to our house, the farther half of the sixth pair on the right. As I swing the car into the driveway, barely missing one concrete gatepost, Tom protests, "You don't park like this, dad. You always back in."

"Don't tell me how to drive," I blurt and feel shamefully irrational.

As soon as we halt alongside Wendy's Honda he springs his belt and runs to the house, losing momentum when his mother opens the front door. She's wiping her hands on a cloth multicoloured with ink from drawing work cards for the nursery. "You're early," she says. "Wasn't it much of a party?"

"I wish I hadn't gone," Tom declares and runs past her into the house.

"Oh dear," says Wendy, which is directed at least partly at me, but I'm busy. Reversing into the driveway would have entailed looking in the mirror or turning in my seat, and now I do both. I have to release my seat belt and crane over the handbrake to convince myself that the back seat and the floor behind me are empty. "Done your worst, have you?" I mutter as I drag myself out of the car.

This isn't meant for Wendy to hear, but she does. "What are you saying about Tom?" she says with a frown and a pout that seem to reduce her already small and suddenly less pretty face.

"Not him. It was—" Of course I can't continue, except with a frustrated sigh. "I was talking to myself."

The sigh has let her smell my breath. "Have you been drinking? How much have you drunk?"

"Not a great deal under the circumstances."

"Which are those?" Before I can answer, however incompletely, she says, "You know I don't like you drinking and driving, especially with Tom in the car."

"I wasn't planning to drive so soon."

"Was it really that awful? Should I have come to support you?"

"Maybe." It occurs to me that her presence might have kept the unwelcome passenger out of my car, but I don't want her to think I'm blaming her. "I wasn't going to make an issue of it," I say. "You didn't seem very eager."

"I'm not completely terrified of school, you know."

Despite the sunlight and the solidity of our house, I abruptly wonder if my tormentor is listening. "Me neither," I say louder than I should.

"I hope not, otherwise we'll never survive. Come inside, Paul. No need for anyone to hear our troubles."

"All I was trying to say was I've already made one person feel they had to tag along with me that shouldn't have."

"I expect one of you will get around to telling me about it eventually." Wendy gazes harder at me without relinquishing her frown. "Taking him with you didn't put him at risk, did it? But driving like that did. He's the best thing we've made together, the only one that really counts. Don't endanger him again or I'll have to think what needs to be done to protect him."

"What's that, a threat? Believe me, you've no idea what you're talking about." The sense that I'm not rid of Jasper is letting my nerves take control of my speech. "Look, I'm sorry. You're right, we shouldn't be discussing this now. Leave it till we've both calmed down," I suggest and dodge past her into the hall.

I need to work out what to say to Tom. I hurry upstairs and take refuge in Wendy's and my room. As I stare at the double bed while Tom and Wendy murmur in the kitchen, I have the notion that my fate is somehow in the balance. Now there's silence, which tells me nothing. No, there's a faint noise—the slow stealthy creak of a stair, and then of a higher one. An intruder is doing its best not to be heard.

I sit on the bed and face the dressing-table mirror. It frames the door, which I didn't quite shut. I'll confront whatever has to be confronted now that I'm on my own. I'll keep it away from my family however I have to. The creaks come to an end, and I wonder if they were faint only because so little was climbing the stairs. How much am I about to see? After a pause during which my breath seems to solidify into a painful lump in my chest, the door in the mirror begins to edge inwards. I manage to watch it advance several inches before I twist around, crumpling the summer quilt. "Get away from us," I say with a loathing that's designed to overcome my panic. "Won't you be happy till you've destroyed us, you putrid little—"

The door opens all the way, revealing Tom. His mouth strives not to waver as he flees into his room. I stumble after him as far as the landing and see Wendy gazing up from the hall. "He wanted to say he was sorry if he put you off your driving," she says in a low flat voice. "I don't know why. I wouldn't have." Before I can speak she shuts herself in the front room, and I seem to hear a muffled snigger that involves the clacking of rotten teeth. Perhaps it's fading into the distance. Perhaps Jasper has gone, but I'm afraid far more has gone than him.

ADAM AND EVE AND PINCH ME

A. E. Coppard

COMBINING REALISM WITH THE supernatural does not come easily to most authors of horror and fantastic fiction, as they are, by definition, diametrically opposed to one another. Nonetheless, the British poet and short story writer A(lfred) E(dgar) Coppard (1878–1957) managed this as well, or better, than most of his more famous contemporaries, smoothly slipping back and forth in his narrative between the mundane world and the ethereal one. In how many tales of terror and suspense do the characters need to worry about earning a living or think about filling their bellies? This foothold in reality is commonplace for many of the characters in Coppard's stories, even while they are enmeshed in occult happenings.

Having to work in a tailor shop at the age of nine, Coppard was totally self-educated, learning to be an accountant for an ironworks firm in Oxford until he became a full-time writer in his forties. He went on to write more than a hundred short stories, which he preferred to call modern folk tales, as well as poetry and children's stories. He was proud of his stories, going so far as to write a descriptive bibliography of his own work, and often inserted his own "fictive self," as he described it, into it.

In 1967, the British television series *Omnibus* filmed *The World of Coppard*, which adapted three of his stories: "The Field of Mustard," "Dusky Ruth," and "Adam and Eve and Pinch Me," which was produced and directed by Jack Gold and adapted by Kit Coppard.

"Adam and Eve and Pinch Me" was first published in *Adam and Eve and Pinch Me Tales* (Waltham Saint Lawrence, Berskshire, U.K., Golden Cockerel Press, 1921).

Adam and Eve and Pinch Me

A. E. COPPARD

AND IN THE WHOLE of his days, vividly at the end of the afternoon—he repeated it again and again to himself—the kind country spaces had *never* absorbed *quite* so rich a glamour of light, so miraculous a bloom of clarity. He could feel streaming in his own mind, in his bones, the same crystalline brightness that lay upon the land. Thoughts and images went flowing through him as easily and amiably as fish swim in their pools; and as idly, too, for one of his speculations took up the theme of his family name. There was such an agreeable oddness about it, just as there was about all the luminous sky today, that it touched him as just a little remarkable. What *did* such a name connote, signify, or symbolize? It was a rann of a name, but it had euphony! Then again, like the fish, his ambulating fancy flashed into other shallows, and he giggled as he paused, peering at the buds in the brake. Turning back towards his house again he could see, beyond its roofs, the spire of the Church tinctured richly as the vane: all round him was a new grandeur upon the grass of the fields, and the spare trees had shadows below that seemed to support them in the manner of a plinth, more real than themselves, and the dykes and any chance heave of the level fields were underlined, as if for special emphasis, with long shades of mysterious blackness.

With a little drift of emotion that had at other times assailed him in the wonder and ecstasy of pure light, Jaffa Codling pushed through the slit in the back hedge and stood within his own garden. The gardener was at work. He could hear the voices of the children about the lawn at the other side of the house. He was very happy, and the place was beautiful, a fine white many-windowed house rising from a lawn bowered with plots of mould, turretted with shrubs, and overset with a vast walnut tree. This house had deep clean eaves, a roof of faint coloured slates that, after rain, glowed dully, like onyx or jade, under the red chimneys, and half-way up at one end was a balcony set with black balusters. He went to a French window that stood open and stepped into the dining room. There was no-one within, and, on that lonely instant, a strange feeling of emptiness dropped upon him. The clock ticked almost as if it had been caught in some indecent act; the air was dim and troubled after that glory outside. Well, now, he would go up at once to the study and write down for his new book the ideas and images he had accumulated—beautiful rich thoughts they were—during that wonderful afternoon. He went to mount the stairs and he was passed by one of the maids; humming a silly song she brushed past him rudely, but he was an easy-going man—

maids were unteachably tiresome—and reaching the landing he sauntered towards his room. The door stood slightly open and he could hear voices within. He put his hand upon the door . . . it would not open any further. What the devil . . . he pushed—like the bear in the tale—and he pushed, and he pushed—was there something against it on the other side? He put his shoulder to it . . . some wedge must be there, and *that* was extraordinary. Then his whole apprehension was swept up and whirled as by an avalanche—Mildred, his wife, was in there; he could hear her speaking to a man in fair soft tones and the rich phrases that could be used only by a woman yielding a deep affection for him. Codling kept still. Her words burned on his mind and thrilled him as if spoken to himself. There was a movement in the room, then utter silence. He again thrust savagely at the partly open door, but he could not stir it. The silence within continued. He beat upon the door with his fists, crying: "Mildred, Mildred!" There was no response, but he could hear the rocking arm chair commence to swing to and fro. Pushing his hand round the edge of the door he tried to thrust his head between the opening. There was not space for this, but he could just peer into the corner of a mirror hung near, and this is what he saw: the chair at one end of its swing, a man sitting in it, and upon one arm of it Mildred, the beloved woman, with her lips upon the man's face, caressing him with her hands. Codling made another effort to get into the room—as vain as it was violent. "Do you hear me, Mildred?" he shouted. Apparently neither of them heard him; they rocked to and fro while he gazed stupefied. What, in the name of God, . . . What this . . . was she bewitched . . . were there such things after all as magic, devilry!

He drew back and held himself quite steadily. The chair stopped swaying, and the room grew awfully still. The sharp ticking of the clock in the hall rose upon the house like the tongue of some perfunctory mocker. Couldn't they hear the clock? . . . Couldn't they hear his heart? He had to put his hand upon his heart, for, surely, in that great silence inside there, they would hear its beat, growing so loud now that it seemed almost to stun him! Then in a queer way he found himself reflecting, observing, analysing his own actions and intentions. He found some of them to be just a little spurious, counterfeit. He felt it would be easy, so perfectly easy to flash in one blast of anger and annihilate the two. He would do nothing of the kind. There was no occasion for it. People didn't really do that sort of thing, or, at least, not with a genuine passion. There was no need for anger. His curiosity was satisfied, quite satisfied, he was certain, he had not the remotest interest in the man. A welter of unexpected thoughts swept upon his mind as he stood there. As a writer of books he was often stimulated by the emotions and impulses of other people, and now his own surprise was beginning to intrigue him, leaving him, O, quite unstirred emotionally, but interesting him profoundly.

He heard the maid come stepping up the stairway again, humming her silly song. He did not want a scene, or to be caught eavesdropping, and so turned quickly to another door. It was locked. He sprang to one beyond it; the handle would not turn. "Bah! what's *up* with 'em?" But the girl was now upon him, carrying a tray of coffee things. "O, Mary!" he exclaimed casually, "I . . ." To his astonishment the girl stepped past him as if she did not hear or see him, tapped open the door of his study, entered, and closed the door behind her. Jaffa Codling then got really angry. "Hell! were the blasted servants in it!" He dashed to the door again and tore at the handle. It would not even turn, and, though he wrenched with fury at it, the room was utterly sealed against him. He went away for a chair with which to smash the effrontery of that door. No, he wasn't angry, either with his wife or this fellow—Gilbert, she had called him—who had a strangely familiar aspect as far as he had been able to take it in; but when one's servants . . . faugh!

The door opened and Mary came forth

smiling demurely. He was a few yards further along the corridor at that moment. "Mary!" he shouted, "leave the door open!" Mary carefully closed it and turned her back on him. He sprang after her with bad words bursting from him as she went towards the stairs and flitted lightly down, humming all the way as if in derision. He leaped downwards after her three steps at a time, but she trotted with amazing swiftness into the kitchen and slammed the door in his face. Codling stood, but kept his hands carefully away from the door, kept them behind him. "No, no," he whispered cunningly, "there's something fiendish about door handles today, I'll go and get a bar, or a butt of timber," and, jumping out into the garden for some such thing, the miracle happened to him. For it was nothing else than a miracle, the unbelievable, the impossible, simple and laughable if you will, but having as much validity as any miracle can ever invoke. It was simple and laughable because by all the known physical laws he should have collided with his gardener, who happened to pass the window with his wheelbarrow as Codling jumped out on to the path. And it was unbelievable that they should not, and impossible that they *did* not collide; and it was miraculous, because Codling stood for a brief moment in the garden path and the wheelbarrow of Bond, its contents, and Bond himself passed apparently through the figure of Codling as if he were so much air, as if he were not a living breathing man but just a common ghost. There was no impact, just a momentary breathlessness. Codling stood and looked at the retreating figure going on utterly unaware of him. It is interesting to record that Codling's first feelings were mirthful. He giggled. He was jocular. He ran along in front of the gardener, and let him pass through him once more; then after him again; he scrambled into the man's barrow, and was wheeled about by this incomprehensible thick-headed gardener who was dead to all his master's efforts to engage his attention. Presently he dropped the wheelbarrow and went away, leaving Codling to cogitate upon the occurrence. There was

no room for doubt, some essential part of him had become detached from the obviously not less vital part. He felt he was essential because he was responding to the experience, he was re-acting in the normal way to normal stimuli, although he happened for the time being to be invisible to his fellows and unable to communicate with them. How had it come about—this queer thing? How could he discover what part of him had cut loose, as it were? There was no question of this being death; death wasn't funny, it wasn't a joke; he had still all his human instincts. You didn't get angry with a faithless wife or joke with a fool of a gardener if you were dead, certainly not! He had realized enough of himself to know he was the usual man of instincts, desires, and prohibitions, complex and contradictory; his family history for a million or two years would have denoted that, not explicitly—obviously impossible—but suggestively. He had found himself doing things he had no desire to do, doing things he had a desire *not* to do, thinking thoughts that had no contiguous meaning, no meanings that could be related to his general experience. At odd times he had been chilled—aye, and even agreeably surprised—at the immense potential evil in himself. But still, this was no mere Jekyll and Hyde affair, that a man and his own ghost should separately inhabit the same world was a horse of quite another colour. The other part of him was alive and active somewhere . . . as alive . . . as alive . . . yes, as *he* was, but dashed if he knew where! What a lark when they got back to each other and compared notes! In his tales he had brooded over so many imagined personalities, followed in the track of so many psychological enigmas that he *had* felt at times a stranger to himself. What if, after all, that brooding had given him the faculty of projecting this figment of himself into the world of men. Or was he some unrealized latent element of being without its natural integument, doomed now to drift over the ridge of the world for ever. Was it his personality, his spirit? Then how was the dashed thing working? Here was he with the most wonderful happening in human experience, and he couldn't differentiate or disinter things. He was like a new Adam flung into some old Eden.

There was Bond tinkering about with some plants a dozen yards in front of him. Suddenly his three children came round from the other side of the house, the youngest boy leading them, carrying in his hand a small sword which was made, not of steel, but of some more brightly shining material; indeed it seemed at one moment to be of gold, and then again of flame, transmuting everything in its neighbourhood into the likeness of flame, the hair of the little girl Eve, a part of Adam's tunic; and the fingers of the boy Gabriel as he held the sword were like pale tongues of fire. Gabriel, the youngest boy, went up to the gardener and gave the sword into his hands, saying: "Bond, is this sword any good?" Codling saw the gardener take the weapon and examine it with a careful sort of smile; his great gnarled hands became immediately transparent, the blood could be seen moving diligently about the veins. Codling was so interested in the sight that he did not gather in the gardener's reply. The little boy was dissatisfied and repeated his question, "No, but Bond, *is* this sword any good?" Codling rose, and stood by invisible. The three beautiful children were grouped about the great angular figure of the gardener in his soiled clothes, looking up now into his face, and now at the sword, with anxiety in all their puckered eyes. "Well, Marse Gabriel," Codling could hear him reply, "as far as a sword goes, it may be a good un, or it may be a bad un, but, good as it is, it can never be anything but a bad thing." He then gave it back to them; the boy Adam held the haft of it, and the girl Eve rubbed the blade with curious fingers. The younger boy stood looking up at the gardener with unsatisfied gaze. "But, Bond, *can't* you say if this sword's any *good?*" Bond turned to his spade and trowels. "Mebbe the shape of it's wrong, Marse Gabriel, though it seems a pretty handy size." Saying this he moved off across the lawn. Gabriel turned to his brother and sister and took the sword from them; they all followed

after the gardener and once more Gabriel made enquiry: "Bond, is this sword any *good?*" The gardener again took it and made a few passes in the air like a valiant soldier at exercise. Turning then, he lifted a bright curl from the head of Eve and cut it off with a sweep of the weapon. He held it up to look at it critically and then let it fall to the ground. Codling sneaked behind him and, picking it up, stood stupidly looking at it. "Mebbe, Marse Gabriel," the gardener was saying, "it ud be better made of steel, but it has a smartish edge on it." He went to pick up the barrow but Gabriel seized it with a spasm of anger, and cried out: "No, no, Bond, will you say, just yes or no, Bond, is this sword any *good?*" The gardener stood still, and looked down at the little boy, who repeated his question—"just yes or no, Bond!" "No, Marse Gabriel!" "Thank you, Bond!" replied the child with dignity, "That's all we wanted to know," and calling to his mates to follow him, he ran away to the other side of the house.

Codling stared again at the beautiful lock of hair in his hand, and felt himself grow so angry that he picked up a strange looking flower pot at his feet and hurled it at the retreating gardener. It struck Bond in the middle of the back and, passing clean through him, broke on the wheel of his barrow, but Bond seemed to be quite unaware of this catastrophe. Codling rushed after, and, taking the gardener by the throat, he yelled, "Damn you, will you tell me what all this means?" But Bond proceeded calmly about his work unnoticing, carrying his master about as if he were a clinging vapour, or a scarf hung upon his neck. In a few moments, Codling dropped exhausted to the ground. "What . . . O Hell . . . what, what am I to do?" he groaned. "What has happened to me? What shall I *do?* What *can* I do?" He looked at the broken flower pot. "Did I invent that?" He pulled out his watch. "That's a real watch, I hear it ticking, and it's six o'clock." Was he dead or disembodied or mad? What was this infernal lapse of identity? And who the devil, yes, who was it upstairs with Mildred? He jumped to his feet and hurried to the window; it was shut; to

259

the door, it was fastened; he was powerless to open either. Well! well! this was experimental psychology with a vengeance, and he began to chuckle again. He'd have to write to McDougall about it. Then he turned and saw Bond wheeling across the lawn towards him again. "*Why* is that fellow always shoving that infernal green barrow around?" he asked, and, the fit of fury seizing him again, he rushed towards Bond, but, before he reached him, the three children danced into the garden again, crying, with great excitement, "Bond, O Bond!" The gardener stopped and set down the terrifying barrow; the children crowded about him, and Gabriel held out another shining thing, asking: "Bond, is this box any good?" The gardener took the box and at once his eyes lit up with interest and delight. "O, Marse Gabriel, where'd ye get it? Where'd ye get it?" "Bond," said the boy impatiently, "Is the box any *good?*" "Any good?" echoed the man, "Why, Marse Gabriel, Marse Adam, Miss Eve, look yere!" Holding it down in front of them, he lifted the lid from the box and a bright coloured bird flashed out and flew round and round above their heads. "O," screamed Gabriel with delight, "It's a kingfisher!" "That's what it is," said Bond, "a kingfisher!" "Where?" asked Adam. "Where?" asked Eve. "There it flies—round the fountain—see it? see it!" "No," said Adam. "No," said Eve.

"O, do, do, see it," cried Gabriel, "here it comes, it's coming!" and, holding his hands on high, and standing on his toes, the child cried out as happy as the bird which Codling saw flying above them.

"I can't see it," said Adam.

"Where is it, Gaby?" asked Eve.

"O, you stupids," cried the boy, "*There* it goes. There it goes . . . there . . . it's gone!"

He stood looking brightly at Bond, who replaced the lid.

"What shall we do now?" he exclaimed eagerly. For reply, the gardener gave the box into his hand, and walked off with the barrow. Gabriel took the box over to the fountain. Codling, unseen, went after him, almost as excited as the

boy; Eve and her brother followed. They sat upon the stone tank that held the falling water. It was difficult for the child to unfasten the lid; Codling attempted to help him, but he was powerless. Gabriel looked up into his father's face and smiled. Then he stood up and said to the others:

"Now, *do* watch it this time."

They all knelt carefully beside the water. He lifted the lid and, behold, a fish like a gold carp, but made wholly of fire, leaped from the box into the fountain. The man saw it dart down into the water, he saw the water bubble up behind it, he heard the hiss that the junction of fire and water produced, and saw a little track of steam follow the bubbles about the tank until the figure of the fish was consumed and disappeared. Gabriel, in ecstasies, turned to his sister with blazing happy eyes, exclaiming:

"There! Evey!"

"What was it?" asked Eve, nonchalantly, "I didn't see anything."

"More didn't I," said Adam.

"Didn't you see that lovely fish?"

"No," said Adam.

"No," said Eve.

"O, stupids," cried Gabriel, "it went right past the bottom of the water."

"Let's get a fishin' hook," said Adam.

"No, no, no," said Gabriel, replacing the lid of the box. "O no."

Jaffa Codling had remained on his knees staring at the water so long that, when he looked around him again, the children had gone away. He got up and went to the door, and that was closed; the windows, fastened. He went moodily to a garden bench and sat on it with folded arms. Dusk had begun to fall into the shrubs and trees, the grass to grow dull, the air chill, the sky to muster its gloom. Bond had overturned his barrow, stalled his tools in the lodge, and gone to his home in the village. A curious cat came round the house and surveyed the man who sat chained to his seven-horned dilemma. It grew dark and fearfully silent. Was the world empty now? Some small thing, a snail, perhaps, crept among the dead leaves in the hedge, with a sharp, irritating noise. A strange flood of mixed thoughts poured through his mind until at last one idea disentangled itself, and he began thinking with tremendous fixity of little Gabriel. He wondered if he could brood or meditate, or "will" with sufficient power to bring him into the garden again. The child had just vaguely recognized him for a moment at the waterside. He'd try that dodge, telepathy was a mild kind of a trick after so much of the miraculous. If he'd lost his blessed body, at least the part that ate and smoked and talked to Mildred . . . He stopped as his mind stumbled on a strange recognition. . . . What a joke, of course . . . idiot . . . not to have seen *that*. He stood up in the garden with joy . . . of course, *he* was upstairs with Mildred, it was himself, the other bit of him, that Mildred had been talking to. What a howling fool he'd been.

He found himself concentrating his mind on the purpose of getting the child Gabriel into the garden once more, but it was with a curious mood that he endeavoured to establish this relationship. He could not fix his will into any calm intensity of power, or fixity of purpose, or pleasurable mental ecstasy. The utmost force seemed to come with a malicious threatening splenetic "entreaty." That damned snail in the hedge broke the thread of his meditation; a dog began to bark sturdily from a distant farm; the faculties of his mind became joggled up like a child's picture puzzle, and he brooded unintelligibly upon such things as skating and steam engines, and Elizabethan drama so lapped about with themes like jealousy and chastity. Really now, Shakespeare's Isabella was the most consummate snob in . . . He looked up quickly to his wife's room and saw Gabriel step from the window to the balcony as if he were fearful of being seen. The boy lifted up his hands and placed the bright box on the rail of the balcony. He looked up at the faint stars for a moment or two, and then carefully released the lid of the box. What came out of it and rose into the air appeared to Codling to be just a piece of floating light, but as it soared above the roof he saw it grow to be a little ancient ship, with its hull and fully set sails and its three masts all of faint primrose flame colour. It cleaved through the air, rolling slightly as a ship through the wave, in widening circles above the house, making a curving ascent until it lost the shape of a vessel and became only a moving light hurrying to some sidereal shrine. Codling glanced at the boy on the balcony, but in that brief instant something had happened, the ship had burst like a rocket and released three coloured drops of fire which came falling slowly, leaving beautiful grey furrows of smoke in their track. Gabriel leaned over the rail with outstretched palms, and, catching the green star and the blue one as they drifted down to him, he ran with a rill of laughter back into the house. Codling sprang forward just in time to catch the red star; it lay vividly blasting his own palm for a monstrous second, and then, slipping through, was gone. He stared at the ground, at the balcony, the sky, and then heard an exclamation . . . his wife stood at his side.

"Gilbert! How you frightened me!" she cried, "I thought you were in your room; come along in to dinner." She took his arm and they walked up the steps into the dining room together. "Just a moment," said her husband, turning to the door of the room. His hand was upon the handle, which turned easily in his grasp, and he ran upstairs to his own room. He opened the door. The light was on, the fire was burning brightly, a smell of cigarette smoke about, pen and paper upon his desk, the Japanese book-knife, the gilt matchbox, everything all right, no one there. He picked up a book from his desk. . . . *Monna Vanna*. His bookplate was in it—*Ex Libris—Gilbert Cannister*. He put it down beside the green dish; two yellow oranges were in the green dish, and two most deliberately green Canadian apples rested by their side. He went to the door and swung it backwards and forwards quite easily. He sat on his desk trying to piece the thing together, glaring at the print and the book-knife and the smart matchbox, until his wife came up behind him exclaiming: "Come along, Gilbert!"

"Where are the kids, old man?" he asked her, and, before she replied, he had gone along to the nursery. He saw the two cots, his boy in one, his girl in the other. He turned whimsically to Mildred, saying, "There *are* only two, *are* there?" Such a question did not call for reply, but he confronted her as if expecting some assuring answer. She was staring at him with her bright beautiful eyes.

"Are there?" he repeated.

"How strange you should ask me that now!" she said. . . . "If you're a very good man . . . perhaps . . ."

"Mildred!"

She nodded brightly.

He sat down in the rocking chair, but got up again saying to her gently—"We'll call him Gabriel."

"But, suppose——"

"No, no," he said, stopping her lovely lips, "I know all about him." And he told her a pleasant little tale.

THE LOST BOY OF THE OZARKS

Steve Friedman

A LIFELONG AFICIONADO OF ghost stories who used to scare his charges while a camp counselor by telling them tales of supernatural beings that go bump in the night, Steve Friedman (1955-) was born in St. Louis, Missouri, and graduated from Stanford University. He left his graduate work at the University of Missouri School of Journalism to take a job at the Columbia (Missouri) *Daily Tribune,* where he worked for five years before becoming editor in chief at *St. Louis Magazine* and then senior editor at *GQ.* He has been a full-time writer since 1997, his work appearing in such publications as *Esquire, Outside,* and *The New York Times;* he is a writer-at-large for *Runner's World, Bicycling,* and *Backpacker.* Many of his stories have been anthologized in *The Best American Travel Writing, The Best of* Outside, and, eight times, in *The Best American Sports Writing.* He has written five books, including *Driving Lessons* (2011) and *Lost on Treasure Island: A Memoir of Longing, Love, and Lousy Choices in New York City* (2011).

"The Lost Boy of the Ozarks" is the first piece of fiction ever to appear in *Backpacker* magazine. When the editors requested a story with the only guideline being that it had to be mysterious and have something to do with the outdoors, Friedman combined his affection for ghost stories with a book he was reading at the time, Tana French's *Into the Woods,* from which he (admittedly) stole the powerful idea of two children walking into the woods and never returning. Adding his own experiences as a journalist completed the tale.

"The Lost Boy of the Ozarks" was originally published in the November 2009 issue of *Backpacker.*

The Lost Boy of the Ozarks

STEVE FRIEDMAN

GOODNIGHT HOLLOW, MISSOURI—
A boy walked into the woods and no one worried. In those days, five-year-olds skinned squirrels and giggled and a child could open a sow's throat with a single steady swipe. Before they were taught figures, daughters learned how to season steaming possum meat. Sons of slaves

plowed the rocky soil and mothers bled to death in childbirth and if a little girl cut her finger, and the cut oozed green and the finger swelled, then her father measured the child and he started nailing together a tidy box of pine.

In the hidden hollows of Missouri's Ozark Mountains, which is where the boy lived, times were hard. It was 1903 and the boy had just turned eight, but there was game to hunt, hogs to butcher, and there was no pine box or preacher or slab of limestone to mark the boy's passing, because there was no boy. The woods had claimed him. Adults paid respect in private, on sagging elm porches, late at night, over lonely, guttering flames. They remembered the child's pale green eyes, the coonskin cap he always wore. They remarked that his stutter must have made his short childhood more difficult than most. Wives murmured to husbands that the missing boy was surely in a happier place, but what they remembered was that their own children had avoided the boy the way pack animals avoided the diseased and the crippled; that ever since the boy was born, he had carried in his downcast gaze something ghostly and damned.

Time passed, and when visitors from nearby Chestnutridge and Reeds Spring and Abesville found themselves walking in the woods where the boy had disappeared, they remembered beatings they had suffered when they were young and worse, they suddenly thought of the welts they had left on their children's flesh. They conjured visions of their little boys' and girls' quivering lips. Mothers looked up through the thick, fetid canopy toward a sunny and benign forgiveness they longed for but which the woods made them doubt, and they blinked back tears. Fathers heard the wind make ghastly, forlorn noises in the trees and the men felt cold, and then the strangers hurried out of the woods and after awhile, very few walked in those woods at all, though no one could explain exactly why. More time passed, and then the only reminder of what had happened was the way some of the stooped, white-haired waitresses at Gus's Diner, hard on State Highway 176, would squeeze their lips together whenever a family with a little boy with brown hair and pale green eyes would sit down at a table. And sometimes if the boy giggled, one of the ancient waitresses would have to take a cigarette break, and tourists would see her outside, sitting on a pine bench, her shoulders silently convulsing.

Then even the old waitresses died off and

mountains of Oklahoma dust swirled over the land and noontime turned to night. The Great Depression came and engineers built Bagnell Dam and, later, developers carved Branson out of the state's blood-soaked red soil and Midwestern millionaires started flocking to The Lake of the Ozarks and in the midst of violin-playing Japanese and joke-telling Russians and cigarette-shaped speedboats that cost hundreds of thousands of dollars, people forgot all about the little boy who walked into the woods and never came out.

Time passed and life wasn't as hard anymore, and a family from Eureka Springs, Arkansas, just across Missouri's southern border, drove north to St. Louis to visit relatives, and after an hour on the road, the father, who was behind the wheel, pulled over at a shady spot and he announced to his wife and two children that The Gateway to the West could wait a couple days, because they were going on a little adventure first. The kids groaned and the man's wife smiled a hidden smile—she was in on the plan and she loved her husband's belief in the healing properties of the outdoors.

The little girl, five years old, had long red hair and freckles and wore sandals with sunflowers separating her big and second toes. The brown-haired, green-eyed boy was wearing blue shorts and a blue T-shirt and blue sneakers. He had just turned eight. They were bareheaded, so mom slathered them with sunscreen while dad pulled backpacks and sleeping bags from the trunk.

Fifteen minutes into the woods, the boy cried out. He shouted that something had grabbed his hand and tried to pull him into the bushes. Dad chuckled and told the child that it was probably a branch—it was mid-April, and the woods were lush—and that even if it wasn't, if the boy stayed on the trail, none of the monsters in the wood could get to him, because wood monsters didn't like trails, and that outraged the boy, who said it wasn't just a branch, it was a skinny kid in a furry hat, and why did no one ever believe him, it wasn't fair! He said the skinny kid had been following them ever since they walked into the woods.

"He's right, I saw him, too," the little girl said, and the mother decided the children were hungry and it might be a good idea to stop and have some fruits and nuts. But the father thought that children should not be catered to—that certainly their fears should not be indulged—so he insisted they walk another fifteen minutes into the woods. The mother bit her lip and went along—starting an argument wouldn't help things—and she made sure she kept the kids in sight, because now she was sure her son and daughter were fatigued, too, and when they were hungry and tired, they tended to hit each other, and then, for no reason at all, she remembered hitting her little sister when she was barely old enough to talk, and she thought about the last argument they had, and before she knew it, she felt a sob lodged in her throat and she squeezed her eyes shut to get hold of herself. When she opened them, she caught a glimpse of movement sneaky and swift in the bushes next to her child and she yelped, which made both kids scream.

Mom broke out the fruit and nuts, and the family sat in a tight little circle on the trail and no matter how much they ate, and no matter how many times the father told the kids about the great marshmallows they would roast that night, and how they would be able to look up and see stars, the kids wouldn't stop crying. The wind was picking up, too, and it was getting colder. Mom took her husband's hand and she squeezed it and she raised her eyebrows, and he knew what that meant. They walked back to the car and all of them felt something chilly and damp on the back of their necks, like something was watching them. Maybe next year they would sleep under the stars.

They drove a few minutes, around a bend, and stopped at Gus's Diner for lunch, and while mom and dad drank iced tea and discussed mom's no-good shiftless ex-husband and argued about how much time they had to spend with him and his sleazy, chain-smoking cocktail waitress girlfriend in St. Louis, the little boy said he

was bored. Take your sister and go look at the fish in the stream just outside the backdoor, the father said, because he wanted the kids to forget about whatever had given them such a fright in the woods. Fifteen minutes later, after mom and dad had reached an uneasy peace about her no-good ex and his shiftless girlfriend—who had invited the whole family up to St. Louis for a let's-get-to-know-each-other-better visit, after all—a woman at another table screamed. The visitors from Eureka Springs looked up and there was their little girl, staring into the jukebox. She was barefoot, rocking back and forth, humming. Her parents thought an animal had climbed onto her head, but then they looked closer and they saw it was just a coonskin cap. But what had happened to her sandals? Why was she humming? Was that mud on her legs, and why was it red? And where was her big brother?

This time, the cops were called. Times had changed, even in the Ozarks, so of course sex offenders were interviewed. Television crews drove from Kansas City and Springfield and St. Louis, and the hoteliers and restaurateurs of nearby Branson refused to appear on camera, because a missing kid was terrible, but business was business. A newspaper editor in Columbia, in central Missouri, saw one of the spots about "Little Boy Blue," as the missing child was already being called, on the 5 p.m. KSDK news show from St. Louis, and it made her think of something. She had taken a class in "Rural Anthropology and Folklore" at the University of Missouri before she became a newspaperwoman and the news reminded her of a lecture she had heard—an obscure tall tale about a mysterious little boy in a coonskin cap. That excited her, in the way that missing children and creepy coincidences excited newspaper editors, especially back then, in 1980, when newspapering was an exciting thing to do. She pulled her ace cops reporter, a gregarious and chain-smoking Irishman named Kevin Gerrity who typed with two fingers, off his beat and told him to work the search angle hard. She took the statehouse reporter, a bookish second generation Armenian named Edward Alouisious Dorian who wore heavily starched white shirts and spoke with a formality the other reporters snickered about, and whom they all called Deadline Ed behind his back, and she told him she wanted to know everything there was to know about the missing kid's family, that Deadline should pack a toothbrush and be in Eureka Springs by dinnertime. The editor wanted something on the creepy historical angle, too, and some local color on the woods and the rednecks who lived there, but the only person she had left to send anywhere was a cub reporter with an overactive imagination and a nasty drinking habit, a dreamy mope she had been thinking of firing almost since the day she had hired him.

That's where I come in.

I covered the animal beat. I wrote stories about trick pigs and clever ferrets. I covered jumping frog contests and birthday parties for overweight cats. If there was a fire, and a pet, and survivors, it was my byline on the piece. ("Snuffy the rabbit smelled smoke and bleated. And in that magical moment, with that simple utterance, Snuffy was forever transformed from mere friend to beloved and immortal big-eared hero.")

Animals didn't talk, so I didn't have to interview them. Animals didn't sue, so I didn't have to worry too much about getting facts straight. The animal beat provided a safe place for a reporter like me, who, in his first two weeks on the job, had misspelled a city councilman's name, reported that a chamber of commerce director had been sued for sexual harassment when he hadn't, and who had shown up for work late and hungover four times. I had been at the *Columbia Daily Tribune* for just a year and was already, barely twenty-five, a floridly failing cub reporter. I suspect that Carolyn "Sissy" White, the editor, was hoping I'd become so humiliated at writing about hamsters and puppies that I'd quit. She overestimated my sense of personal dignity.

"I want atmosphere," she said, after she had summoned me to her office.

"Got it," I said. "Can do."

"And leave out the telepathic Shih Tzus, okay?"

"Hey, c'mon, my *Jim the Wonder Dog* feature won second place in the Boone County Press Asso——"

"All I want is a mood piece. A solid mood piece. With actual facts. No animals."

"Got it, boss. Can do."

"And no drinking. If I even suspect you've been juicing, you're going to *wish* you were writing about mind-reading squirrels. You think the animal beat's bad? I find out you're hitting the bottle, you're going to be interviewing farmers at the state fair about their prize-winning giant vegetables."

"You're not going to regret this, Sissy. I'm gonna give you thirty inches of gold."

"Just get your ass down there, and don't screw up."

"Can do. Hold page one, above the fold," I said, and Sissy sighed.

I drove through long stretches of flat land and grey, hard sky. The roads were newly paved, but the houses alongside were sagging, peeling. I crossed two rivers, listened to a local call-in show where a listener drove the host to sputtering by insisting that Christmas was nothing but a pagan ritual with roots "that had nothing to do with baby Jesus and everything to do with cold, dark, and frightened losers who badly wanted some grog and song." I reached for the six-pack I always kept underneath the front seat, until I remembered that I hadn't brought it this time.

I had the road mostly to myself, and the occasional hawk circling overhead, and gangs of large black crows that descended, picked at some unlucky skunk's remains, then flapped heavily away. The few cars I passed could have come from the same church service, bought their cars at the same used car lot, descended from the same bitter, wind-beaten pioneers. The children in the backseat were blonde, puffy, moon-faced. I counted eight cars in one hundred twenty miles.

Eight weary and resentful, vaguely malevolent-looking families. They all squinted. By the time I arrived at Gus's diner, I needed a drink.

Instead, I ordered a burger and a cup of coffee. I said "please" and "thank you" to the waitress, who didn't say anything back, or call me "hon" or do anything I thought rural waitresses were supposed to do. She was slim and had pale blue eyes and I wondered if she had been working when the couple from Eureka Springs lost their son. I wondered what they said when they saw their daughter, with blood-smeared legs. I wondered what song was playing on the juke box, whether the freaked-out little girl had even heard the music. I wondered what kind of tests the cops had done on the coonskin cap and if anyone besides me and my folklore-loving editor knew about the spooky kid from 1903. I didn't ask the waitress any questions, just ate my burger and drank my coffee and looked around the place. I saw Formica tables, and knotty wood walls and in back a bald man in a dirty white T-shirt muttering and moving jars from shelf to shelf. I made a note to myself to find out what kind of wood the walls were made of. That would help with the atmosphere.

It was dusk, and the gravel parking lot was fading into nothingness and the only sounds were a gentle breeze slithering through the woods outside, and, occasionally, the whispery rubber of a car passing on the highway. When that happened, the bald man and the waitress would both look out the front window, and then—was it my imagination?—they would both check over their shoulders, toward the back of the restaurant, and the river, and the woods beyond.

The waitress refilled my mug.

"Best not go in there" she said, jerking her head toward the back of the restaurant, toward the woods.

"What?!??"

"Anything else?" she asked, in a normal, pleasant, I'm-just-a-waitress-and-not-some-hillbilly-from-a-horror-movie voice.

"Don't go in where? Why? What's going on?" I said.

She stared at me.

I noticed her looking at the counter and I followed her gaze. She was gazing at my hands, which were trembling.

"Are you okay?" she asked.

"Yeah, yeah, fine, I'm fine," I lied. Then, because I needed to say something and because I didn't think it was the best time to be revealing the real reason for my visit—that I was here to investigate a missing little boy, and to tie it to another child's disappearance that happened almost one hundred years ago and while I was at it to write a story and to reclaim a prematurely wrecked career and oh, yeah, somehow stop drinking—I told her I was down for some rest and relaxation, and that I was looking for a place to stay.

"Only place to stay around here is Gus's," she said.

"I thought this was Gus's."

"This is Gus's diner. I mean Gus's hotel, a hundred feet up the highway, just 'round that corner. Easy to miss, so look out for the sign," she said.

The peeling sign said "rooms" and I asked for one.

"A-yup," said Gus, or Gus's employee, as he pulled a key from a wooden slot behind him. Knotty pine? Walnut? Elm? I would have to check that out.

"Pretty country here," I said, trying to establish my wilderness bona fides, which I sorely lacked, having spent exactly one night outdoors, when I was a Cub Scout. I contracted poison oak on that trip, and my mother yanked me from the organization, right when I was on the verge of becoming a Webelo. That's when I started my clarinet lessons.

"Some times," said Gus.

"People go hiking around here?"

Gus looked like he had just eaten a piece of bad squirrel meat.

"You plannin' to go into the woods, mister?"

No one had ever called me mister.

"Maybe," I said. (I had promised Sissy I would spend a night in the woods. We knew I wasn't going to find the kid, who had been gone for three days now. But we also knew that missing children moved product.)

"Not so smart."

"Why do you say that, Gus?"

"Ain't Gus," he said.

"You're not Gus?"

He spat something behind the counter. "Ain't no Gus," he said. "Ain't been no Gus for a long time. People call me BC."

I didn't sleep well that night. It wasn't the cars passing on the highway, or the way their headlights cut through my flimsy puke green curtains and flooded my second-floor room with light. It wasn't the shakes—I had learned to live with the shakes from the other times I'd gone on the wagon. It wasn't even the tinny, desolate sounds of BC's television set drifting from behind the counter, up the stairs.

It was the noise from the woods: It was the river gurgling, and twigs rustling, and the wind through the trees, and creaking. It was a hiss and crack that made me think of a bullwhip snapping, and a low, soft moaning. It was a thin, reedy whimpering that haunts me to this day, an eerie and primal noise that I wish I would have listened to more closely. If I had, if I had been able to comprehend what the thing in the woods was saying, would things have turned out differently?

"Huh huh huh," the thing from the woods cried. "Huh huh huh huh."

There was longing in the sound, and anger, and fear. It sounded like a person, urgently alive, and yet there was something inhuman about it, too, something older than the sky, sadder than the wind.

Or maybe this is what the Ozarks sounded like, particularly to someone detoxing from too much booze. I put my pillow over my ears, but it was no use. The sound continued.

"Huh huh huh. Huh huh huh huh."

I called the newsroom the next day morning.

"What have you got?" Sissy asked.

I didn't mention the sounds.

"Great stuff," I lied. "Lots of local color, and some fascinating characters. Plus, some local mysteries. There's a place called Gus's, without a Gus, and a restaurant where the waitress and the dishwasher—or maybe he's the owner—look at the woods every time a car goes by and . . . ."

"Have you been drinking?"

"No, I told you. I'm done . . . "

"Have you been anywhere other than your hotel and the place you've been eating?"

"You said you wanted a mood piece, right? I'm gathering mood."

"Where was the last place the kid was seen?"

"He was walking out the diner, toward the river."

"And what's next to the river?"

I didn't like where this conversation was going. I didn't like it at all.

"The woods?" I said. It came out as a question.

"You planning to go there?"

"Well, of course I'm planning to go there. But I need to find a guide, and I need to bone up on some of the local law enforcement angles. And I want to survey the land for . . . ."

"Call me by the end of the week," she said. "You better have a story about camping out where the kid disappeared."

I walked to the diner to consider my options, and to have some pancakes and coffee. Option one: Cozy up to BC, pull some town gossip out of him, and call Sissy on Friday with some tales of tight-lipped, flinty-eyed locals and the sad knowledge they shared. I had made it a point whenever I was writing about people in towns of less than 5,000, or owners of trick pigs and/or telepathic dogs, to refer to them as "locals." Or "folks." But instead of "shared," I would make it "bound them together." That would be good. But it would also be dangerous. What if Sissy liked my mood piece and sent a photographer down to snap pictures of some of the bound-together-by-sad-knowledge folks and those folks mentioned, that a-nope, that coffee-drinking fella with the little notebook didn't take one step into the woods, that he barely made it off the stool one single time, but a-yup, he sure could put away a lot of flapjacks. Option two: Take my waterproof matches and my poncho and down coat that I had packed and cross the shallow stream and then tromp into the leafy dense hilly woods on the other side. Spend a night in the land where even from my hotel room I had heard all manner of screams and moans and what sounded like a bullwhip. That would certainly provide some local color. Downside: I would probably die. Option three: Have a beer. Then another beer. Then another one. And a few more.

I chose option four. I always chose option four. Option four had long been my fallback option. Option four took some time, but it bought time. Option number four was my speciality: More research and reporting.

When the blue-eyed waitress brought me my pancakes, I asked if I could ask her a question.

"You're a reporter," she said. "Isn't that what you do?"

"How'd you know I was a reporter?"

"Everyone around here knows you're a reporter. Since that poor child went missing, that's the only people been coming round here. Ain't no tourists anymore. Certainly not any families."

"Yeah," I said. "I'm a reporter. Have you heard anything about what might have happened to the ki— . . . to the little boy?"

"Probably got lost in the woods. It happens."

"It does?"

"You're funny, Mr. Reporter," she said. "You think you're going to find that little boy, do you?"

"No, I'm just here to do a moo— . . . I mean, to write something about the area. You know any place within a few miles that might sell trail maps of the area?"

I heard a sharp hacking noise and looked into the back of the restaurant. There was the dishwasher/owner/bald hairy armed guy, bent over and coughing. Or laughing.

"No trail maps around here," Blue Eyes told me. "You want to know about trails, or anything

to do with those woods, you need to talk to Mrs. Loomis, the retired librarian who lives down in Goodnight Hollow, not far from Walnut Shade.

I pictured a grey-haired, muffin-faced crone. I saw piles of knitting needles and gangs of house cats.

"How do I get in touch with her?" I asked.

"You don't have to," the waitress said. "I already did."

The river road was empty and quiet, and I drove through patches of blinding sun and shade dark as night, until the notion of a sunny day seemed a distant, hazy memory. I saw the hand-lettered sign for Country Road EE, and pulled off the pot-holed, single-lane pavement onto what looked like a driveway, but was another paved road. That gave way to gravel and the gravel to dirt. The dirt was hard-packed, and ahead smoke curled up out of the brick chimney. Dead petunias were scattered on the side of a white frame house.

She opened the door without looking through any peephole that I could see, or asking who had knocked, or doing any of the other things that might have been prudent for a woman living in a region where kids went missing and things cried in the night.

She had braces and slim ankles, and the rest of her was covered in a long navy blue skirt and an expensive-looking black cashmere sweater. She could have been thirty-five, or forty-five. She turned the corners of her mouth up, and showed just a little bit of metal and tooth, but I wouldn't call it a smile. She had brown bangs as fashionable as any magazine model I'd ever seen in a magazine, and they framed high cheekbones and hazel eyes. In the white of her left eye was a popped blood vessel that made a tiny explosion of red, perfectly matching her lipstick.

I was staring at the flash of red in her eye when she said something.

"What?"

"I said, 'Can I help you with something?' "

She didn't know who I was.

"I'm the reporter," I said.

"The reporter?"

"Uh," I said, "the one who's reporting the disappearance of the little boy?"

She coughed. Or was she stifling a giggle?

"Oh, yes," she said. "Beatrice called me about you. I've been out of sorts. I had meant to have some things to show you, but my prints were late, and, well, you can imagine. Can I get you something to drink? English Breakfast tea? Coffee?"

She turned, did something to a vase on a table. The hair at the back of her neck had been hacked off.

She turned again, put her hands on her hips and smiled. Her eyes were like marbles—lovely, cold, and lifeless.

"What do you think?" she asked, flouncing what hair was left.

"It's great," I lied.

"You're lying, but that's okay." Before I could answer, she'd taken my hand and pulled me toward the kitchen. "Let's have some tea before we talk," she said.

I told her tea would be fine, as I wondered what had been getting her out of sorts, besides disappearing children and spooky woods. I also wondered what prints she was talking about, and what a nice looking woman with braces and tea was doing living in the muddy, malodorous backwoods of the Show Me state. And where was Mr. Loomis?

"You like being a reporter?" she asked, as we sat down.

"Yeah, for the most part," I said. It was my standard answer to people who didn't know me or my work, equal parts world-weariness, sensitivity to others' pain, and a doomed but undying determination to make the world a better place. I didn't mention Jim the Wonder Dog, or Snuffy the Miracle Rabbit.

She smiled, but her eyes were still inert hazel aggies. I tried to smile back, but there was sweat beading on my forehead. I wiped it away with my left hand and almost gagged. I smelled something rotting and maggoty. It was a humid odor, ripe, like a body left too long in a hothouse, or a swamp. Was it coming from the librarian, or my hand, that she had held? "This will make you feel better," she said, as she pushed a steaming mug toward me.

"I had a long night," I said, "and I've been putting in some long hours on this story."

"Ah, yes," she said, "the story. Have you found the little boy yet?"

"No, and I'm not going to. I'm not here to find the lit——"

"What if I could lead you to him?"

Maybe that's the moment I should have called the local cops, or at least checked in with Deadline Ed, or Kev. Maybe I should have called Sissy. Maybe I should have told the weird librarian she scared me, and I didn't know what she was talking about, and the hacked hair and dead flowers and all the print talk and the bad smell in her house was starting to creep me out, and I should just leave her alone and get back to town. And maybe if I had done any of that, things wouldn't have turned out how they did. I've always pondered the maybes of my life. It's never helped.

"Lead me to him? Sure, lead me to him. Right. Let's go."

She took my hand and pulled me out the back door. Black clouds had piled upon each other and they sat, bullying and sullen, on the western horizon. We walked around the farmhouse, to a small path in the woods that abutted the backyard. My shirt stuck to my back. Streaks of lightning cut through the clouds, but I heard no thunder.

I watched her walk ahead of me.

"My ex said I was hallucinating," she said. "He told me no one lived in the woods, that it was just coyotes. He told me I was hearing what I wanted to hear."

She said this in the same tone of voice she'd used to tell me that she was waiting on her prints. I looked at the back of her haircut. What was the deal with that? That's when I heard the *huh-huh-huh* sound again.

We had walked fifty yards down the path. What had seemed like a cute little trail had turned into an overgrown, weed-choked passage into a dark, dank jungle. I knew there couldn't be a jungle in mid-Missouri. I knew that the *huh-huh-huh* couldn't be a monster's growl, that it was more likely the mating grunt of some smallish Ozarks rodent. In a minute, Mrs. Loomis would show me the animal and I would note its fuzzy ears and its cute wet nose and its funny little paws. It would help my mood piece.

Sweat dripped into my eyes. The jungle was getting darker, and more dank. The *huh-huh-huh* was getting louder. This was more mood than I needed.

After a quarter mile, the trail ended at a small pile of ash, what looked like a rudimentary barbecue pit, at the northern tip of an oblong clearing twenty feet by fifteen feet.

I saw blood. I smelled meat.

The wind had picked up. I thought I heard small and not so small animals chattering and shrieking. I tried to get a fix on the clouds, but the horizon had disappeared. We were deeper into the forest than I'd thought. Fat, cold drops of water fell on us. I had never felt such heavy rain.

"*Huh-huh-huh-huh*," the woods cried. I heard movement in the bushes.

She grasped my hand again. When I turned toward her, she was peering into the woods. I followed her eyes and thought I saw a flash of fur, a shy, greenish quivering.

"What's that?" I croaked.

"What?"

"In the woods."

She turned to me. What was the expression on her face? Amusement? Regret? Despair?

"It's okay," she said.

"What?"

"Everything will be okay. Don't worry."

She took my face in her hands. They were like ice. I couldn't remember why I was here. Why had we come this way? Why was she looking at me so strangely? The rain continued, heavy as

sin, loud as a guilty conscience. Cutting through the sound of rain, something worse. Something remorseless: "*Huh-huh-huh HUH.*"

There was rattling behind the tree, then primal, urgent moaning.

"We'd better go," she said. "Leave him be."

The dizziness got worse, until I thought I might fall into the ashes, and I clung to her hand. I followed her down the path, out of the woods.

That night, as the dank haze of the Ozarks gave way to thick blackness, I laid down in bed, and listened to BC's television. It was a sitcom, and canned laughter had never made me feel so sad, or lonely, especially the way the metallic chuckles and machine-generated hilarity bounced off the lobby's walls. Knotty pine? Birch? I had to check that out. I tried to think of what I might do the next day, but couldn't come up with a plan. I tried to think of what I would do when I got back to Columbia, but all I could see in my mind's eye were watermelon-eating coyotes and salamanders who liked bluegrass music. Just as I had worked myself into a hopeless despair about my future, I heard something that drove out any emotion other than reflexive, unthinking terror. It came from the woods.

"*Huh Huh Huh Huh . . . .*"

The next morning, as I was stumbling through the lobby on my way to the diner, BC looked up from behind the desk, then thrust a lumpy brown envelope into my hands. There were no stamps and no return address. Scrawled across the front of the envelope, in what looked like brown chalk, was "*Reporter.*" The printing had been done by someone old and arthritic. Or a kindergartener.

I asked BC where it had come from and he gave me the bad-squirrel-meat look again.

"No idea. It was leaning against the door this morning."

When I opened it, a puff of dust floated out and settled on the counter, just missing my flapjacks. Inside I found a black, leather-bound notebook, 8½ by 11, thin as a hymnal at a failing church. In faded red type, across the cover: "Oral Traditions and Folk Lore among the Early Settlers of the Missouri Ozarks."

I read chapter one, *The Weeping Woman*, the tale of a grey-haired wraith in a nightgown who wandered the hollows and hillsides, pitifully calling for her baby, who had died from smallpox decades earlier. In chapter two, I made the acquaintance of *The Old Man of the Ozarks*, a petty thief who was imprisoned for vagrancy and then, when the town jail was torn down as part of some ill-conceived urban renewal program, was promptly forgotten, and lived out his years trapped in the rubble, feeding only on rats and cockroaches and the occasional small child who got too close to the condemned property. I flipped through other ghost stories, skimmed legends, read more nonsense that had brought shudders of delight to any kid who has ever spent a night at sleepover camp.

I passed the morning shoveling forkfuls of Bea's excellent pancakes into my mouth, drinking her strong coffee and enjoying the exploits of *The McDonald County Backbreaker*, *The Stranger at The Door*, and *The Man with the Hook*. I met *The James Strangler*, the slithery and lithe creature who lurked at the bottom of the nearby James River, and wriggled and writhed until curious fishermen waded in after it,—only to be found later washed up on the shore, terror in their empty, staring eyes (in some versions of the tale, their brains had been sucked out through the ears). As I mopped up syrup, I chuckled and felt myself relax. The missing kid from Eureka Springs was sad, of course, tragic even, but it wasn't my job to find him. My role was simply to write something evocative. If there's one thing an animal beat guy needs to be good at, it's evocative. These stories from this odd little book would help.

I was going to give the *Tribune* readers a mood piece, all right. I would etch some portraits of BC, and Beatrice the sexy waitress and certainly the wackjob of a librarian. I'd throw in *The Old Man of the Ozarks*, too. I would describe the knotty pine walls (or maple, or whatever they turned out to be). I would leave out the bloody meat in the ashes, and the crying I heard in the woods at night, because no one would believe that stuff. Plus, for the purposes of authorial credibility, I needed to maintain a certain flinty-eyed persona. So definitely no *huh-huh-huh*s. But mood? Oh, yeah. With a capital M.

I returned to the book, read in the afterword how tall tales had been part of the Ozarks culture for as long as anyone could remember, how "these tales have been handed down for generations, used as instructional devices to impart lessons about human nature and to dissuade children from societally unacceptable and risky activity."

I asked Bea for more coffee. The spooky yarn as pedagogy? Interesting. I sped through the stories again. The weeping woman wasn't just a scary old hag; she provided a cautionary example of what happened to someone who failed to come to terms with grief, who could not let go of a loved one who had died. *The Old Man of the Ozarks?* More than a crotchety old cannibal, he was the bogeyman who kept kids from deserted buildings. And any little boy or girl who heard about the *James Strangler* would surely not get too close to the river's edge. Too bad the kids from Eureka Springs hadn't been told that one.

Whomever had left the book at BC's door had done me a favor. He or she had made me realize that ghost stories were just that—stories. I thought of the sound from the woods and my weird walk with the librarian with the bad haircut and I felt myself blush, right there at the counter of Gus's Diner. Odd and creepy rural folk? Definitely. Supernatural? Negative. It was good to have regained some reportorial perspective.

I was composing the lede in my head—"If you want a long life for your kids, you might consider scaring the wee ones to death"—when I noticed something sticking out of the back of the book. It was a single sheet of single-spaced paper, yellowed and crackling. Typed across the top of the sheet, "The Curious and Disturbing Case of Ukiah Clemons."

I read it while I drank more coffee. The story was different from the others. It read more like a police report than a tall tale. There was no obvious anthropological value in the text. And, according to the property records attached, there definitively *was* a Ukiah Clemons. He was the fourth oldest of eight, the son of a blacksmith. By the only accounts that could be trusted—and there weren't many of those—the Clemons family was, like many rural Missouri clans of that era, poor and desperately invested in survival. The blacksmith was a moonshiner and drunk who barely made ends meet. His wife was highstrung, prone to long bouts of silence interrupted by episodes of screaming and minor violence, always directed at one child or another. There was chronic sickness and relentless hunger. Young Ukiah was a lonely child, and other schoolchildren shunned him. It might have been because he tended to cling to his mother's skirts, or because he wept easily. It might have been because he was always so hungry; other children reported seeing him in the woods at all hours, digging in the dirt, at times chewing on wriggling, squealing things that looked like squirrels, or snakes he hadn't even bothered to kill. People said that when Ukiah's father discovered the boy eating a snake in bed one night, he tied him to a tree and used his bullwhip. After that night, people said, Ukiah stuttered. He stuttered until the day he disappeared.

"The exact date that Ukiah walked into the woods is still disputed," the paper said. "What is beyond doubt—from school records, from tax rolls, and from birth and death certificates—is that after his eighth birthday, there was never a documented sighting of him again."

According to the yellowing manuscript, some stories said he didn't even make it to the woods. One account had him dying at home of pneumonia. Another legend had him bleeding to death from wounds suffered at his father's bullwhip.

The most grisly account presented Ukiah, mad from hunger, suffocating and then cutting up and eating his baby sister, then being chased into the woods by his mother, who hung herself from a Sumac tree that very night.

I heard a clattering noise from the counter and looked down. My hands were shaking again. I dropped my fork, continued reading.

"Why such a gruesome and apparently pointless narrative has endured for so long," wrote the nameless author of the paper, "and why it still pops up from time to time, is a mystery greater than the fate of Ukiah himself."

I stuck the paper back in the book, and walked back to the hotel. Had the insane librarian dropped the book off? Was the waitress just playing a joke on me? Back at the hotel, BC informed me that a woman named Sissy had called me five times this morning, that it was urgent I call her back.

I walked up the steps to my room and started making notes for my mood piece. Maybe I *would* use the strange sounds in the woods. "The eerie moans have haunted visitors to this area for decades," I wrote. That was probably true. I described the flapjacks, "friendly, hearty, reassuring fare that offers stark contrast to the terrible mystery that occurred down by the river and through the woods." I had a lot, but I needed more. I knew that if I didn't spend a night in the woods, then I'd be back on the Animal Beat faster than someone could say "Pork chop city for the trick pig." I didn't plan to call Sissy back until I had my piece ready.

I walked back down to the desk, asked BC where I could hire a guide to take me camping.

"I can do it today," he told me.

"Today?" I squeaked.

He told me to be ready in an hour.

"But what about food, and water, and equipment, and a tent and . . . ."

"I'll take care of it."

An hour later, a little after noon, we drove toward the librarian's. After twenty minutes, just when I was wondering with a chill whether he was taking me back to the chattering thing by the ash pit, BC jerked his wheel and we lurched left and into the undergrowth. Dark branches whipped the windshield and I might have squealed, or screamed, because BC said, "Hold on now." We drove another thirty minutes, though "drove" isn't the right word, because most of the time we were bumping and lurching. We stopped long after we had left anything that anyone might refer to as a road. The air was thick and sour and all around was a low, insect whine. This was way too much mood.

I got out and sunk to my shins in muck. BC reached into the bed of his pickup and grabbed two backpacks.

"Here," he said, throwing one at me. "Put this on."

We walked for at least two hours. We walked up muddy hills and across streams and we walked through patches of witch hazel and clouds of black flies. We walked until I didn't think I could walk any more.

We stopped at a treeless patch of dirt, a rough circle surrounded by dogwood and maple trees. (I asked BC; he told me.)

"I'll set up camp here," BC said. "Why don't you relax?"

I sat down heavily.

"I'm thirsty," I said.

"I got something," BC said. "But first we gotta eat. It's dangerous to be hungry out here."

I vaguely remembered reading that people could live a long time without food, that in fact it was riskier to be thirsty. But BC seemed to know what he was doing, so I leaned on my backpack, and the next thing I knew, BC was shaking my shoulder and it was dark. He had a fire going, was stirring two cans with a stick.

"Grub's ready," he said.

"What's that sound?" I said. It was like a woodpecker, but more human. It sounded like the *Huh-huh-huh* sound at the librarian's house, but now it said, *Duh-duh-duh-doe, duh-duh-duh doe.* It came from deep in the woods, from the direction we had hiked in from. Is this what sobriety was like? Was I going to be hearing that damned noise as long as I didn't drink?

BC looked at me and laughed. I had never heard laughter sound so cruel.

"Lots of sounds in the woods, boy," he said. "Here, eat up." He thrust a can of pork and beans at me.

I didn't like how he had called me "boy," but I was ravenous. I hadn't realized how ravenous until I smelled the pork and beans. I ate until my stomach hurt.

"Can we have some water now?" I asked. I couldn't remember ever being so thirsty.

"Got something better," BC said and thrust a plastic bottle filled with yellowish liquid into my hand. "Take a pull on this, you won't worry about no mountain sounds."

I took a drink and spat it out.

"I don't drink alcohol anymore," I said.

"Better start," BC said.

I was angry for just a moment. He didn't know any better. And I was thirsty. And no one ever needed to know about tonight. It was just me and BC and the noise, the *Duh-duh-duh-doe.* Maybe a couple swigs would make it shut up.

I took a pull from the bottle and suddenly the woods seemed safer and softer. I took another pull and another, and I decided that life was good, and the Ozarks were a rugged but wonderful place, and that I would definitely ask the blue-eyed waitress out on a date when I had flapjacks tomorrow. I resolved that Beatrice and I might make a life together. I decided that we *deserved* a life together. I had another pull and the *Duh Duh Duh DOE* turned into a scream, a relentless, urgent scream, but I couldn't be bothered with it; Why had I ever stopped drinking? Every swig made me more relaxed, and happy, and I was definitely a boozer again, and I wondered why I had ever thought I wasn't a boozer and I took another pull and I was going to clap BC on the back and thank him for being such a good hotel manager, and faithful guide, for being my friend, and then I passed out.

I woke in a puddle of vomit. I could see the glowing embers of the dying fire, but BC wasn't on his bedroll. My eyes adjusted to the darkness. I saw a shape at the edge of the fire circle. It was BC and he was doing something on a rock. It looked like he was sharpening a knife.

DUH-DUH-DUH-DOE! The noise was behind me and I turned, startled. It was a strangled cry. Now I saw a light, too. The light was dancing, in the same location as the cry. I looked back at BC, but he kept doing what he was doing. I wasn't drunk anymore, and I wasn't stupider than usual. Asking for BC's help might have been my most reasonable next move. Staying put would have made sense, too. I wish I could tell you why I followed the light into the woods, but I can't. All I can tell you is that I did follow it.

I crawled on my belly the first fifty yards.

When my head bumped into a log, I stood up. I didn't feel hungover. I didn't feel quite sober either. I felt like I was floating, like I had spent my life in these woods. I followed the light over hills and through ravines. My feet must have hit the ground, but I couldn't feel them. It was more like I was leaping, or dancing. As I moved, I breathed, and as I breathed, I could feel the woods breathe. I was one with the woods, and with the thing I was following. As I was floating through the woods, I heard eating sounds—I don't know how else to describe them. Lip-smacking, chewing, tearing exclamations, and wet grunts, and soft sobbing. I don't know how long I followed the sounds and the light, only that it was so long that the embers from the campfire were gone before I came to another clearing, one we had not passed before. Now the sound was everywhere. The eating, and the sobbing, and the screaming. Then slobbering and then the scream again and then it was deafening, a shrill, witless screaming.

I knew that the sounds were impossible. Maybe hitting my head on the log had affected my hearing. I shook my head, but the sounds grew louder. At the clearing, I realized the sounds weren't all around me—they were coming from the edge of the woods on the other side of the treeless circle. I walked into the clearing, and the light on the other side didn't move. I saw

a shape in front of the light. The noise was coming from the shape.

I moved closer. It wasn't tall enough to be a bear, but it was upright. It had to be a wolf, or some kind of feral dog, on its hind legs, with its forelegs resting on some slim branch I couldn't see. But it was so skinny . . . so bony, like an undersized, malnourished chimpanzee, or ground sloth. Its head was shaking from side to side, chewing. Was it looking at me?

I moved closer. Its head was large and angular, and covered with fur, and its eyes were moist and ravenous.

I moved closer and saw that the fur covered only the head, and that the face was pink, and that the forelegs weren't leaning on anything. They were holding something. And they weren't forelegs. They were arms, covered in ragged, torn scraps.

I moved closer, until I was only ten feet away. Closer.

It couldn't be. It couldn't possibly be.

"*DUH DUH DUH DUH DOE,*" the little boy said.

I stopped breathing.

It could not be a little boy. It could not be a little boy holding a kerosene lamp. I told myself I would never ever *ever* drink again.

"*DUH DUH DUH DUH DOE,*" the little boy said. He put down the kerosene lamp. He was wearing a coonskin hat. There was something wrong with his mouth, something messy. I should have run. I should have screamed. But I did nothing. I was one with the woods. I couldn't feel my feet. The boy walked closer. I realized what was wrong with his mouth; his lips were smeared with blood. He was holding something wet and dripping.

"*DUH DUH DUH DUH DOE,*" the boy screamed.

"What?" I said, and he moved toward me and I saw what he was holding. It was a hand, a tiny little fist, a baby's fist. Two fingers had already been chewed off.

"*DUH DUH DUH DUH DON'T TRUST HIM,*" the little boy cried. "*Duh Duh duh

DON'T TRUST THE BAD MAN WITH THE KNIFE."

And then the little boy reached out his hand and he took mine and his hand was colder than death, slick with blood. *"I-I-I-I'm your fuh-fuh-fuh-fuh-friend,"* he bawled.

I heard a high, keening wail, an awful shriek of pain, and terror. The little boy in the coonskin cap stared at me with dead eyes, and the shrieking wouldn't stop, and then I realized the shrieking was coming from me.

A large man with the sad, liquid eyes of an otter slapped me.

"What?" I tried to say, but what came out was "Wulb!"

"He's alive," the large man said, then wrote something on a clipboard he was carrying.

"Wuh-wuh-wuh-wulb?" I said.

I was at the Cox Medical Center, the doctor told me, in Springfield. Fishermen headed to the James River had found me at dawn, passed out at the edge of Highway 176. They had brought me here. Doctors suspected alcohol poisoning, which turned out to be true, but when they ran tests, they also found large amounts of Ibogaine, a powerful hallucinogen used by certain tribes in South America. They also found LSD, horse tranquilizers, Ecstasy, and methamphetamines.

I thought of BC and the drink he had given me.

"You're lucky you're alive," the otter-eyed doctor told me. "Having fun with happy pills at home's one thing, but in the woods? That's plain dumb."

"But," I tried to say but what came out was "Blib."

After he left, a nurse came in and whispered to me.

"Your girlfriend's been calling," she said. "She sounds angry."

"My girlfriend?"

"Sissy."

"Why haven't you been returning my calls?" Sissy said, when I got her on the phone.

"I've been calling you for two days! We found him."

"What? Who? No, I found him. He . . ."

"Little Boy Blue, you boozing, animal-loving, mood-piece happy idiot! He never disappeared into the woods. His mom's no-good ex snatched him. Kevin's source in the highway patrol fed him the inside dope, told him everything. And Deadline Ed got the cops in Eureka Springs to fill in the gaps. The ex's cocktail waitress girl-friend wanted a kid, but she wasn't so keen on being pregnant. She convinced the no-good ex that kidnapping was a great solution. So they invited Little Boy Blue and his sister and their folks to St. Louis, then hired one hillbilly from Branson to trail the car and to call another hill-billy to grab the kid when he saw a chance. He saw the chance when the kids were playing by the stream outside Gus's Diner. It was the second hillbilly's idea to smear raccoon blood on the little girl and tell her if she said anything, he'd come back and snatch her, too. He took her shoes, too, so she wouldn't get back to the res-taurant as fast."

My head hurt. My eyes hurt. My feet hurt. I wanted to stop hurting. I wondered what time it was. I wondered if there was a bar nearby.

"And the coonskin hat?"

"Weird thing about that. No one knows where that came from. After the boy was found, the little girl kept babbling about a stutter-ing child in the woods, how he was hungry but didn't want to hurt anyone. She said he gave her the hat. She kept crying and yelling to the cops that they had to go back and save the kid. Fi-nally, a paramedic gave her a sedative to shut her up. She'll probably sleep for a week."

I would find the bar, and I would treat myself to a beer and I would drink until I didn't hurt anymore. I would remind myself that scared lit-tle girls make up stories every day and that hallu-cinogenic drugs make even flinty-eyed imbecilic cub reporters imagine things, and I would drink some more and I would go back to school and I would become an accountant. I would drink lots and lots of beer.

"So Little Boy Blue's okay?"

"Yep. Home sweet home. A pizza delivery guy saw his picture on the news and spotted him at the no-good ex's house. The no good ex and his shifty gal pal are going away for a long, long time. Deadline says the cops are still looking for the first hillbilly. But Kev's working on a piece about how they arrested the second one yesterday, the snatcher. They caught him in the woods near Goodnight Hollow. A nasty piece of work, that one. Top suspect in five or six murders down there in Deliveranceland, but they never had enough evidence to convict him. He liked knives, though, everyone knows that. It's funny, huh?"

"Funny? What's funny?"

"A psycho like that, with all those knives, running a hotel."

I thought I was going to throw up.

"What did you say his name was?"

"Clemons."

"His first name?"

"Balthazar, though everyone down there called him BC."

I shut my eyes, saw the man by the rock, backlit by fire. I saw the man in the woods, sharpening his knife. The bad man.

"Hey!" Sissy said. "Are you still there? Or are you tripping your juicehead wonderdog skull off?"

"No, I mean yeah. I'm still here."

I could hear her sigh.

"Right. Sure you are. The nurse told me all about your pharmaceutical celebration in the trees. I wish I could say I was surprised. Get your ass back to town. We got a kids' turtle race that needs to be written up. And then it's time for the state fair and the Biggest Pumpkin in Boone County contest. Guess who's covering it?"

Kev and Deadline won state reporting awards for their Little Boy Blue coverage and got raises. Sissy spiked my mood piece. She told me no one cared about local legends, or spooky dishwash-ers, or librarians with emotional problems. (It turns out that Mrs. Loomis was bipolar, that after she miscarried, which led to her divorce, she started seeing forest children and was institutionalized briefly, and that shortly before the kid from Eureka Springs was grabbed, the librarian had gone off her meds and joined a coven of Wiccans. That explained the dead flowers and the haircut.)

Back on the beat where I had always belonged, I wrote a story about a singing guinea pig named Tess and its owner, a stockbroker I referred to as "jolly and portly, if a slight bit socially retarded." How was I supposed to know that Tess's owner was country-club buddies with the *Tribune* publisher? The publisher had a talk with Sissy, who, when it came to the subject of me, didn't need much talking to. Sissy called me into her office on a bright, spring Friday afternoon, a full year after my trip to the Ozarks.

"As the great poet wrote," she said, "April is the cruelest month."

"Huh," I said, and then she told me that even though I'd always struggled with facts, she liked my way with words and admired my imagination and wished me nothing but the best. Then she told me to clean out my desk.

I took a road trip, because I didn't know what else to do. I pointed my car toward Northern California, where I had always imagined quiet, friendly little streams and springy meadows and people with good skin and strong handshakes, but somehow I ended up behind a plate of flapjacks and a steaming cup of coffee, next to a twisting stream, hard on Missouri State Highway 176. A little voice had been whispering to me ever since the otter-eyed doctor had wakened me, telling me to slow down, telling me that if I wanted happiness, happiness was waiting for me, that peace was slinging hash, that serenity had blue eyes, and that her name was Beatrice. As usual, the little voice was feeding me a line.

Bea and I dated for a few months, until she told me she was sick to death of the country, and of the Ozarks, and she wanted to move to the big city, and what was wrong with me, and would

I ever grow up and stop looking for things that never were?

I don't know if I ever did. I don't know if I ever have.

Little Boy Blue was lost, and then he was found, and now he's an adult, older than I was when I walked into the woods and the woods claimed me. You don't know about him because he stopped doing interviews a long time ago. He wants people to forget about him. I don't blame him.

Sometimes I wish I could forget about him. I'm different now. The world is different. Things have changed, even in the hidden hollows of southern Missouri. Millionaires still haul their fancy speedboats to the Lake of the Ozarks, and they tie up together and drink too much and the girls take off their shirts but now you can see it all on the Internet. Missing kids—especially cute white ones—are gone for an hour now and you can see them on the Internet, too. The only people who walk into the Ozarks' hidden hollows these days wear Gore-Tex and carry mesh baskets and likely as not, they're hunting for morel mushrooms and ginseng, which they sell to the fancy restaurants where the millionaires like to eat and where possum meat's not on the menu. Gus's Hotel is gone, and there's a Walmart where it used to be. The diner's a parking lot. If a five-year-old skinned a squirrel, he'd probably get his own reality TV show. No one writes mood pieces anymore.

I think about my failed mood piece sometimes. I think about BC, too, and four or five times every year I call the Missouri State Penitentiary, in Jefferson City, to make sure he's still locked up, and to see when his next parole hearing is, so that I can drive to The Big House, which is what folks here call the institution, and suggest it not be granted. I think about Bea, too. More often than I'd like to admit, if you want the truth. I think about her late at night, when I'm lying in bed. But I don't ever talk about her. That wouldn't be the right thing to do, not to Rachael. That's Mrs. Loomis' first name. Rachael and I have been living together for thirty

years now, in the house at the end of the gravel road, just a few miles from Walnut Shade, next to the James River, deep in the shadows of Goodnight Hollow.

I'm a middle-aged man now, recently retired from twenty-nine years of teaching fifth grade. I haven't had a drink since that last pull of drug-laced moonshine in the clearing, next to the fire. Rachael takes her meds and I go to AA meetings and we read local history books together and we sit on lawn chairs on the banks of the James River and we fish and our sun-freckled shoulders touch. Sometimes on a warm spring afternoon we even drive up to St. Louis, to take in a Cardinals baseball game and to sit on the hood of our cherry red Buick Skylark afterward and breathe in the city smells while we slurp our vanilla milkshakes at Ted Drewes Frozen Custard Stand on Grand Avenue. And when we get home, while I'm inside measuring coffee for the morning and tidying up, Rachael makes a trip to the little ash mound down the path behind the house. She calls it her "constitutional." I followed her once, many years ago, to see what she was doing and I saw her gently place a raw chicken, still bloody and freshly butchered, on the little pile of ashes. That was the last time I followed her.

I think of Bea and BC and baseball games and frozen custard late at night, when Rachael is sleeping and I'm trying not to think of other things. I try not to think about the thing I saw in the woods, the thing I couldn't possibly have seen. I try not to think about the baby's fist with the missing fingers. I try not to think about the terrible fate of that little boy from another time.

Trying not to think about things keeps a man awake at night. It keeps me awake. So do the sounds, the sounds from the woods next to the river. They're still there, the rustling and the creaking, the sighing of the wind. Sometimes, in the stillness of the predawn darkness I tell myself that I have grown used to them. But then the silence will be broken—by soft weeping, by the fierce whisper of the whip, by a low, soft moaning.

"*Huh-huh-huh,*" the reedy, haunted voice says, and then louder, "*HUH-HUH-HUH*" and I don't even bother to put a pillow over my ears, because I know it won't help.

"*HUH-HUH-HUH-HUNGRY!*" the lost little boy screams. And then comes the rattling in the woods, the urgent scuttling. Then there is a tearing and chewing as the ghostly, damned thing in the woods falls upon its bloody sustenance, and then there is a horrible, savage slurping and then an ecstatic lip-smacking.

The silence comes then, and I always wish it would go on forever, but it never does. After the silence comes a sigh, night after night, week after week, decade after endless decade, a sigh lonelier than the wind, sadder than the ageless river. And then, after the sigh, the last thing I hear every night, before I finally fall into an uneasy sleep. It is the sound of death, and the horror that comes after.

"Fuh-fuh-fuh friends," the lost little boy says. "Muh-muh-muh my friends."

THERE'S SOMETHING
FUNNY AROUND HERE

A GHOST'S STORY

Mark Twain

WHETHER WRITING ABOUT CRIME, romance, religion, or ghosts, Samuel Langhorne Clemens (1835–1910) thought it was all just hilarious and his satiric wit often elevated the most ordinary tales into minor masterpieces. He is justly famous as a great, perhaps *the* great, American novelist, with such masterpieces to his credit as *The Adventures of Tom Sawyer* (1876), *The Prince and the Pauper* (1882), *Life on the Mississippi* (1883), and *Adventures of Huckleberry Finn* (1884), but he also savored the notion of taking genre fiction and skewing it until it became uniquely his.

He wrote frequently in the mystery genre but reserved much of his prodigious inventiveness for tales of science fiction, fantasy, and the supernatural. He employs the notion of time travel wonderfully in *A Connecticut Yankee in King Arthur's Court* (1889), handles afterlife fantasy in *Captain Stormfield's Visit to Heaven* (1909), and explores Gothic themes and medieval settings in *The Mysterious Stranger* (1916). Many short stories also contains fantastic elements, such as the present tale about the Cardiff Giant, "A Horse's Tale" (1906) about a talking horse, and "The Canvasser's Tale" (1876) about a man who collects echoes.

"A Ghost's Story" (sometimes published as "A Ghost's Tale") was first published in *Werner's Readings and Recitations* (New York, Edgar S. Werner Company, 1888).

A Ghost's Story

MARK TWAIN

I TOOK A LARGE room, far up Broadway, in a huge old building whose upper stories had been wholly unoccupied for years until I came. The place had long been given up to dust and cobwebs, to solitude and silence. I seemed groping among the tombs and invading the privacy of the dead, that first night I climbed up to my quarters. For the first time in my life a super-stitious dread came over me; and as I turned a dark angle of the stairway and an invisible cob-web swung its hazy woof in my face and clung there, I shuddered as one who had encountered a phantom.

I was glad enough when I reached my room and locked out the mold and the darkness. A cheery fire was burning in the grate, and I sat down before it with a comforting sense of relief. For two hours I sat there, thinking of bygone times; recalling old scenes, and summoning half-forgotten faces out of the mists of the past; listening, in fancy, to voices that long ago grew silent for all time, and to once familiar songs that nobody sings now. And as my reverie softened down to a sadder and sadder pathos, the shrieking of the winds outside softened to a wail, the angry beating of the rain against the panes diminished to a tranquil patter, and one by one the noises in the street subsided, until the hurrying footsteps of the last belated straggler died away in the distance and left no sound behind.

The fire had burned low. A sense of loneliness crept over me. I arose and undressed, moving on tiptoe about the room, doing stealthily what I had to do, as if I were environed by sleeping enemies whose slumbers it would be fatal to break. I covered up in bed, and lay listening to the rain and wind and the faint creaking of distant shutters, till they lulled me to sleep.

I slept profoundly, but how long I do not know. All at once I found myself awake, and filled with a shuddering expectancy. All was still. All but my own heart—I could hear it beat. Presently the bedclothes began to slip away slowly toward the foot of the bed, as if some one were pulling them! I could not stir; I could not speak. Still the blankets slipped deliberately away, till my breast was uncovered. Then with a great effort I seized them and drew them over my head. I waited, listened, waited. Once more that steady pull began, and once more I lay torpid a century of dragging seconds till my breast was naked again. At last I roused my energies and snatched the covers back to their place and held them with a strong grip. I waited. By and by I felt a faint tug, and took a fresh grip. The tug strengthened to a steady strain—it grew stronger and stronger. My hold parted, and for the third time the blankets slid away. I groaned. An answering groan came from the foot of the bed! Beaded drops of sweat stood upon my forehead. I was more dead than alive. Presently I heard a heavy footstep in my room—the step of an ele-

phant, it seemed to me—it was not like anything human. But it was moving from me—there was relief in that. I heard it approach the door—pass out without moving bolt or lock—and wander away among the dismal corridors, straining the floors and joists till they creaked again as it passed—and then silence reigned once more.

When my excitement had calmed, I said to myself, "This is a dream—simply a hideous dream." And so I lay thinking it over until I convinced myself that it was a dream, and then a comforting laugh relaxed my lips and I was happy again. I got up and struck a light; and when I found that the locks and bolts were just as I had left them, another soothing laugh welled in my heart and rippled from my lips. I took my pipe and lit it, and was just sitting down before the fire, when—down went the pipe out of my nerveless fingers, the blood forsook my cheeks, and my placid breathing was cut short with a gasp! In the ashes on the hearth, side by side with my own bare footprint, was another, so vast that in comparison mine was but an infant's! Then I had had a visitor, and the elephant tread was explained.

I put out the light and returned to bed, palsied with fear. I lay a long time, peering into the darkness, and listening.—Then I heard a grating noise overhead, like the dragging of a heavy body across the floor; then the throwing down of the body, and the shaking of my windows in response to the concussion. In distant parts of the building I heard the muffled slamming of doors. I heard, at intervals, stealthy footsteps creeping in and out among the corridors, and up and down the stairs. Sometimes these noises approached my door, hesitated, and went away again. I heard the clanking of chains faintly, in remote passages, and listened while the clanking grew nearer—while it wearily climbed the stairways, marking each move by the loose surplus of chain that fell with an accented rattle upon each succeeding step as the goblin that bore it advanced. I heard muttered sentences; half-uttered screams that seemed smothered violently; and the swish of invisible garments, the rush of invisible wings. Then I became conscious that my chamber was invaded—that I was not alone. I heard sighs and breathings about my bed, and mysterious whisperings. Three little spheres of soft phosphorescent light appeared on the ceiling directly over my head, clung and glowed there a moment, and then dropped—two of them upon my face and one upon the pillow. They spattered, liquidly, and felt warm. Intuition told me they had turned to gouts of blood as they fell—I needed no light to satisfy myself of that. Then I saw pallid faces, dimly luminous, and white uplifted hands, floating bodiless in the air—floating a moment and then disappearing. The whispering ceased, and the voices and the sounds, and a solemn stillness followed. I waited and listened. I felt that I must have light or die. I was weak with fear. I slowly raised myself toward a sitting posture, and my face came in contact with a clammy hand! All strength went from me apparently, and I fell back like a stricken invalid. Then I heard the rustle of a garment—it seemed to pass to the door and go out.

When everything was still once more, I crept out of bed, sick and feeble, and lit the gas with a hand that trembled as if it were aged with a hundred years. The light brought some little cheer to my spirits. I sat down and fell into a dreamy contemplation of that great footprint in the ashes. By and by its outlines began to waver and grow dim. I glanced up and the broad gas flame was slowly wilting away. In the same moment I heard that elephantine tread again. I noted its approach, nearer and nearer, along the musty halls, and dimmer and dimmer the light waned. The tread reached my very door and paused—the light had dwindled to a sickly blue, and all things about me lay in a spectral twilight. The door did not open, and yet I felt a faint gust of air fan my cheek, and presently was conscious of a huge, cloudy presence before me. I watched it with fascinated eyes. A pale glow stole over the Thing; gradually its cloudy folds took shape—an arm appeared, then legs, then a body, and last a great sad face looked out of the vapor. Stripped of its filmy housings, naked, muscular

and comely, the majestic Cardiff Giant loomed above me!

All my misery vanished—for a child might know that no harm could come with that benignant countenance. My cheerful spirits returned at once, and in sympathy with them the gas flamed up brightly again. Never a lonely outcast was so glad to welcome company as I was to greet the friendly giant. I said:

"Why, is it nobody but you? Do you know, I have been scared to death for the last two or three hours? I am most honestly glad to see you. I wish I had a chair—Here, here, don't try to sit down in that thing—"

But it was too late. He was in it before I could stop him and down he went—I never saw a chair shivered so in my life.

"Stop, stop, you'll ruin ev—"

Too late again. There was another crash, and another chair was resolved into its original elements.

"Confound it, haven't you got any judgment at all? Do you want to ruin all the furniture in the place? Here, here, you petrified fool—"

But it was no use. Before I could arrest him he had sat down on the bed, and it was a melancholy ruin.

"Now what sort of a way is that to do? First you come lumbering about the place bringing a legion of vagabond goblins along with you to worry me to death, and then when I overlook an indelicacy of costume which would not be tolerated anywhere by cultivated people except in a respectable theater, and not even there if the nudity were of your sex, you repay me by wrecking all the furniture you can find to sit down on. And why will you? You damage yourself as much as you do me. You have broken off the end of your spinal column, and littered up the floor with chips of your hams till the place looks like a marble yard. You ought to be ashamed of yourself—you are big enough to know better."

"Well, I will not break any more furniture. But what am I to do? I have not had a chance to sit down for a century." And the tears came into his eyes.

"Poor devil," I said, "I should not have been so harsh with you. And you are an orphan, too, no doubt. But sit down on the floor here—nothing else can stand your weight—and besides, we cannot be sociable with you away up there above me; I want you down where I can perch on this high counting-house stool and gossip with you face to face." So he sat down on the floor, and lit a pipe which I gave him, threw one of my red blankets over his shoulders, inverted my sitz-bath on his head, helmet fashion, and made himself picturesque and comfortable. Then he crossed his ankles, while I renewed the fire, and exposed the flat, honeycombed bottoms of his prodigious feet to the grateful warmth.

"What is the matter with the bottom of your feet and the back of your legs, that they are gouged up so?"

"Infernal chilblains—I caught them clear up to the back of my head, roosting out there under Newell's farm. But I love the place; I love it as one loves his old home. There is no peace for me like the peace I feel when I am there."

We talked along for half an hour, and then I noticed that he looked tired, and spoke of it.

"Tired?" he said. "Well, I should think so. And now I will tell you all about it, since you have treated me so well. I am the spirit of the Petrified Man that lies across the street there in the museum. I am the ghost of the Cardiff Giant. I can have no rest, no peace, till they have given that poor body burial again. Now what was the most natural thing for me to do, to make men satisfy this wish? Terrify them into it! haunt the place where the body lay! So I haunted the museum night after night. I even got other spirits to help me. But it did no good, for nobody ever came to the museum at midnight. Then it occurred to me to come over the way and haunt this place a little. I felt that if I ever got a hearing I must succeed, for I had the most efficient company that perdition could furnish. Night after night we have shivered around through these mildewed halls, dragging chains, groaning, whispering, tramping up and down stairs, till, to tell you the

truth, I am almost worn out. But when I saw a light in your room to-night I roused my energies again and went at it with a deal of the old freshness. But I am tired out—entirely fagged out. Give me, I beseech you, give me some hope!"

I lit off my perch in a burst of excitement, and exclaimed:

"This transcends everything! everything that ever did occur! Why you poor blundering old fossil, you have had all your trouble for nothing—you have been haunting a plaster cast of yourself—the real Cardiff Giant is in Albany! [A fact. The original was ingeniously and fraudulently duplicated and exhibited in New York as the "only genuine" Cardiff Giant (to the unspeakable disgust of the owners of the real colossus) at the very same time that the real giant was drawing crowds at a museum in Albany.] Confound it, don't you know your own remains?"

I never saw such an eloquent look of shame, of pitiable humiliation, overspread a countenance before.

The Petrified Man rose slowly to his feet, and said:

"Honestly, is that true?"

"As true as I am sitting here."

He took the pipe from his mouth and laid it on the mantel, then stood irresolute a moment (unconsciously, from old habit, thrusting his hands where his pantaloons pockets should have been, and meditatively dropping his chin on his breast); and finally said:

"Well—I never felt so absurd before. The Petrified Man has sold everybody else, and now the mean fraud has ended by selling its own ghost! My son, if there is any charity left in your heart for a poor friendless phantom like me, don't let this get out. Think how you would feel if you had made such an ass of yourself."

I heard his stately tramp die away, step by step down the stairs and out into the deserted street, and felt sorry that he was gone, poor fellow—and sorrier still that he had carried off my red blanket and my bath-tub.

IN AT THE DEATH

Donald E. Westlake

THERE CAN BE LITTLE dispute that the funniest mystery writer who ever lived was Donald Edwin Westlake (1933–2008). But he also wrote a very hard-boiled series about the tough professional thief Parker, using the pen name Richard Stark, and a poignant series featuring Mitch Tobin, under the pseudonym Tucker Coe. Born in Brooklyn, he lived in the New York City area most of his adult life and set the majority of his books and stories there. A prolific writer, especially early in his career when he wrote more than two dozen soft-core porn novels under various pseudonyms, short stories in the science fiction and mystery genres, and hard-boiled crime novels, the first being *The Mercenaries* (1960), he produced more than a hundred books. It is for his complex and hilarious caper novels, mainly about the unlucky criminal genius John Dortmunder, for whom every perfectly planned burglary goes woefully wrong, that Westlake has been most honored, notably by the Mystery Writers of America, which named him a Grand Master for lifetime achievement in 1993. He also won Edgars in three different categories (Best Novel for *God Save the Mark*, 1968; Best Short Story for "Too Many Crooks," 1990; and Best Motion Picture for *The Grifters*, 1991). Numerous films have been made from his novels, most notably *The Hot Rock* (1970, filmed in 1972 with Robert Redford), *The Hunter* (1962, filmed as *Point Blank* in 1967 with Lee Marvin, and remade in 1999 as *Payback* with Mel Gibson), and *Bank Shot* (1972, filmed in 1974 with George C. Scott). His 1992 novel, *Humans*, is about an angel.

"In at the Death" was originally published in *The 13th Ghost Book*, edited by James Hale (London, Barrie & Jenkins, 1977).

In at the Death

DONALD E. WESTLAKE

IT'S HARD NOT TO believe in ghosts when you are one. I hanged myself in a fit of truculence—stronger than pique, but not so dignified as despair—and regretted it before the thing was well begun. The instant I kicked the chair away, I wanted it back, but gravity was turning my former wish to its present command; the chair would not right itself from where it lay on the floor, and my 193 pounds would not cease to urge downward from the rope thick around my neck.

There was pain, of course, quite horrible pain centered in my throat, but the most astounding thing was the way my cheeks seemed to swell. I could barely see over their round red hills, my eyes staring in agony at the door, *willing* someone to come in and rescue me, though I knew there was no one in the house, and in any event the door was carefully locked. My kicking legs caused me to twist and turn, so that sometimes I faced the door and sometimes the window, and my shivering hands struggled with the rope so deep in my flesh I could barely find it and most certainly could not pull it loose.

I was frantic and terrified, yet at the same time my brain possessed a cold corner of aloof observation. I seemed now to be everywhere in the room at once, within my writhing body but also without, seeing my frenzied spasms, the thick rope, the heavy beam, the mismatched pair of lit bedside lamps throwing my convulsive double shadow on the walls, the closed locked door, the white-curtained window with its shade drawn all the way down. *This is death*, I thought, and I no longer wanted it, now that the choice was gone forever.

My name is—was—Edward Thornburn, and my dates are 1938–1977. I killed myself just a month before my fortieth birthday, though I don't believe the well-known pangs of that milestone had much if anything to do with my action. I blame it all (as I blamed most of the errors and failures of my life) on my sterility. Had I been able to father children my marriage would have remained strong, Emily would not have been unfaithful to me, and I would not have taken my own life in a final fit of truculence.

The setting was the guest room in our house in Barnstaple, Connecticut, and the time was just after seven p.m.; deep twilight, at this time of year. I had come home from the office—I was a realtor, a fairly lucrative occupation in Connecticut, though my income had been falling off recently—shortly before six, to find the note on the kitchen table: "Antiquing with Greg. Afraid you'll have to make your own dinner. Sorry. Love, Emily."

Greg was the one; Emily's lover. He owned an antique shop out on the main road toward New York, and Emily filled a part of her days as his ill-paid assistant. I knew what they did together in the back of the shop on those long midweek afternoons when there were no tourists, no antique collectors to disturb them. I knew, and I'd known for more than three years, but I had never decided how to deal with my knowledge. The fact was, I blamed myself, and therefore I had no way to *behave* if the ugly subject were ever to come into the open.

So I remained silent, but not content. I was discontent, unhappy, angry, resentful—truculent.

I'd tried to kill myself before. At first with the car, by steering it into an oncoming truck (I swerved at the last second, amid howling horns) and by driving it off a cliff into the Connecticut River (I slammed on the brakes at the very brink, and sat covered in perspiration for half an hour before backing away), and finally by stopping athwart one of the few level crossings left in this neighborhood. But no train came for twenty minutes, and my truculence wore off, and I drove home.

Later I tried to slit my wrists, but found it impossible to push sharp metal into my own skin. Impossible. The vision of my naked wrist and that shining steel so close together washed my truculence completely out of my mind. Until the next time.

With the rope; and then I succeeded. Oh, totally, oh, fully I succeeded. My legs kicked at air, my fingernails clawed at my throat, my bulging eyes stared out over my swollen purple cheeks, my tongue thickened and grew bulbous in my mouth, my body jigged and jangled like a toy at the end of a string, and the pain was excruciating, horrible, not to be endured. I can't endure it, I thought, it can't be endured. Much worse than knife slashings was the knotted strangled pain in my throat, and my head ballooned with pain, pressure outward, my face turning black, my eyes no longer human, the pressure in my head building and building as though I would explode. Endless horrible pain, not to be endured, but going on and on.

My legs kicked more feebly. My arms sagged, my hands dropped to my sides, my fingers twisted uselessly against my sopping trouser legs, my head hung at an angle from the rope, I turned more slowly in the air, like a broken wind

chime on a breezeless day. The pains lessened, in my throat and head, but never entirely stopped.

And now I saw that my distended eyes had become lusterless, gray. The moisture had dried on the eyeballs, they were as dead as stones. And yet I could see them, my own eyes, and when I widened my vision I could *see* my entire body, turning, hanging, no longer twitching, and with horror I realized I was dead.

But *present.* Dead, but still present, with the scraping ache still in my throat and the bulging pressure still in my head. Present, but no longer in that used-up clay, that hanging meat; I was suffused through the room, like indirect lighting, everywhere present but without a source. What happens now? I wondered, dulled by fear and strangeness and the continuing pains, and I waited, like a hovering mist, for whatever would happen next.

But nothing happened. I waited; the body became utterly still; the double shadow on the wall showed no vibration; the bedside lamps continued to burn; the door remained shut and the window shade drawn; and nothing happened.

What *now*? I craved to scream the question aloud, but I could not. My throat ached, but I had no throat. My mouth burned, but I had no mouth. Every final strain and struggle of my body remained imprinted in my mind, but I had no body and no brain and no *self,* no substance. No power to speak, no power to move myself, no power to *remove* myself from this room and this suspended corpse. I could only wait here, and wonder, and go on waiting.

There was a digital clock on the dresser opposite the bed, and when it first occurred to me to look at it the numbers were 7:21—perhaps twenty minutes after I'd kicked the chair away, perhaps fifteen minutes since I'd died. Shouldn't something happen, shouldn't some *change* take place?

The clock read 9:11 when I heard Emily's Volkswagen drive around to the back of the house. I had left no note, having nothing I wanted to say to anyone and in any event believing my own dead body would be eloquent enough, but I hadn't thought I would be *present* when Emily found me. I was justified in my action, however much I now regretted having taken it, I was justified, I knew I was justified, but I didn't want to see her face when she came through that door. She had wronged me, she was the cause of it, she would have to know that as well as I, but I didn't want to see her face.

The pains increased, in what had been my throat, in what had been my head. I heard the back door slam, far away downstairs, and I stirred like air currents in the room, but I didn't leave, I couldn't leave.

"Ed? Ed? It's me, hon!"

I know it's you. I must go away now, I can't stay here, I must go away. Is there a God? Is this my soul, this hovering presence? *Hell* would be better than this, take me away to Hell or wherever I'm to go, don't leave me here!

She came up the stairs, calling again, walking past the closed guest room door. I heard her go into our bedroom, heard her call my name, heard the beginnings of apprehension in her voice. She went by again, out there in the hall, went downstairs, became quiet.

What was she doing? Searching for a note perhaps, some message from me. Looking out the window, seeing again my Chevrolet, knowing I must be home. Moving through the rooms of this old house, the original structure a barn nearly two hundred years old, converted by some previous owner just after the Second World War, bought by me twelve years ago, furnished by Emily—and Greg—from their interminable, damnable, awful antiques. Shaker furniture, Colonial furniture, hooked rugs and quilts, the old yellow pine tables, the faint sense always of being in some slightly shabby minor museum, this house that I had bought but never loved. I'd bought it for Emily, I did everything for Emily, because I knew I could never do the one thing for Emily that mattered. I could never give her a child.

She was good about it, of course. Emily *is* good, I never blamed her, never completely blamed *her* instead of myself. In the early days of our marriage she made a few wistful references, but I suppose she saw the effect they had on me, and for a long time she has said nothing. But I have known.

The beam from which I had hanged myself was a part of the original building, a thick hand-hewed length of aged timber eleven inches square, chevroned with the marks of the hatchet that had shaped it. A strong beam, it would support my weight forever. It would support my weight until I was found and cut down. Until I was found.

The clock read 9:23 and Emily had been in the house twelve minutes when she came upstairs again, her steps quick and light on the old wood, approaching, pausing, stopping. "Ed?"

The doorknob turned.

The door was locked, of course, with the key on the inside. She'd have to break it down, have to call someone else to break it down, perhaps she wouldn't be the one to find me after all. Hope rose in me, and the pains receded.

"Ed? Are you in there?" She knocked at the door, rattled the knob, called my name several times more, then abruptly turned and ran away downstairs again, and after a moment I heard her voice, murmuring and unclear. She had called someone, on the phone.

Greg, I thought, and the throat-rasp filled me, and I wanted this to be the end. I wanted to be taken away, dead body and living soul, taken away. I wanted everything to be finished.

She stayed downstairs, waiting for him, and I stayed upstairs, waiting for them both. Perhaps she already knew what she'd find up here, and that's why she waited below.

I didn't mind about Greg, about being present when he came in. I didn't mind about *him*. It was Emily I minded.

The clock read 9:44 when I heard tires on the gravel at the side of the house. He entered, I heard them talking down there, the deeper male voice slow and reassuring, the lighter female voice quick and frightened, and then they came up together, neither speaking. The doorknob turned, jiggled, rattled, and Greg's voice called, "Ed?"

After a little silence Emily said, "He wouldn't—He wouldn't *do* anything, would he?"

"Do anything?" Greg sounded almost annoyed at the question. "What do you mean, do anything?"

"He's been so depressed, he's—Ed!" And forcibly the door was rattled, the door was shaken in its frame.

"Emily, don't. Take it easy."

"I shouldn't have called you," she said. "Ed, *please!*"

"Why not? For heaven's sake, Emily—"

"Ed, *please* come out, don't scare me like this!"

"*Why shouldn't* you call me, Emily?"

"Ed isn't stupid, Greg. He's—"

There was then a brief silence, pregnant with the hint of murmuring. They thought me still alive in here, they didn't want me to hear Emily say, "He *knows*, Greg, he knows about us."

The murmurings sifted and shifted, and then Greg spoke loudly, "That's ridiculous. Ed? Come out, Ed, let's talk this over." And the doorknob rattled and clattered, and he sounded annoyed when he said, "We must get in, that's all. Is there another key?"

"I think all the locks up here are the same. Just a minute."

They were. A simple skeleton key would open any interior door in the house. I waited, listening, knowing Emily had gone off to find another key, knowing they would soon come in together, and I felt such terror and revulsion for Emily's entrance that I could feel myself shimmer in the room, like a reflection in a warped mirror. Oh, can I at least stop seeing? In life I had eyes, but also eyelids, I could shut out the intolerable, but now I was only a presence, a total presence, I *could not* stop my awareness.

The rasp of key in lock was like rough metal edges in my throat; my memory of a throat. The pain flared in me, and through it I heard Emily asking what was wrong, and Greg answering. "The key's in it, on the other side."

"Oh, dear God! Oh, Greg, what has he done?"

"We'll have to take the door off its hinges," he told her. "Call Tony. Tell him to bring the toolbox."

"Can't you push the key through?"

Of course he could, but he said, quite determinedly, "Go *on*, Emily," and I realized then he had no intention of taking the door down. He simply wanted her away when the door was first opened. Oh, very good, *very* good!

"All right," she said doubtfully, and I heard her go away to phone Tony. A beetle-browed young man with great masses of black hair and olive complexion, Tony lived in Greg's house and was a kind of handyman. He did work around the house and was also (according to Emily) very good at restoration of antique furniture; stripping paint, reassembling broken parts, that sort of thing.

There was now a renewed scraping and rasping at the lock, as Greg struggled to get the door open before Emily's return. I found myself feeling unexpected warmth and liking toward Greg. He wasn't a bad person. Would he marry her now? They could live in this house, he'd had more to do with its furnishing than I. Or would this room hold too grim a memory, would Emily have to sell the house, live elsewhere? She might have to sell at a low price; as a realtor, I knew the difficulty in selling a house where a suicide has taken place. No matter how much they may joke about it, people are still afraid of the supernatural. Many of them would believe this room was haunted.

It was then I finally realized the room *was* haunted. With me! *I'm a ghost*, I thought, thinking the word for the first time, in utter blank astonishment. I'm a ghost.

Oh, how dismal! To hover here, to be a boneless fleshless aching *presence* here, to be a kind of ectoplasmic mildew seeping through the days and nights, alone, unending, a stupid pain-racked misery-filled observer of the comings and goings of strangers—she *would* sell the house, she'd have to, I was sure of that. Was this my punishment? The punishment of the suicide, the solitary hell of him who takes his own life. To remain forever a sentient nothing, bound by a force greater than gravity itself to the place of one's finish.

I was distracted from this misery by a sudden agitation in the key on this side of the lock. I saw it quiver and jiggle like something alive, and then it popped out—it seemed to *leap* out, itself a suicide leaping from a cliff—and clattered to the floor, and an instant later the door was pushed open and Greg's ashen face stared at my own purple face, and after the astonishment and horror, his expression shifted to revulsion— and contempt?—and he backed out, slamming the door. Once more the key turned in the lock, and I heard him hurry away downstairs.

The clock read 9:58. *Now* he was telling her. *Now* he was giving her a drink to calm her. *Now* he was phoning the police. *Now* he was talking to her about whether or not to admit their affair to the police; what would they decide?

"Noooooooooo!"

The clock read 10:07. What had taken so long? Hadn't he even called the police yet?

She was coming up the stairs, stumbling and rushing, she was pounding on the door, screaming my name. I shrank into the corners of the room, I *felt* the thuds of her fists against the door, I cowered from her. She can't come in, dear God don't let her in! I don't care what she's done, I don't care about anything, just don't let her see me! *Don't let me see her!*

Greg joined her. She screamed at him, he persuaded her, she raved, he argued, she demanded, he denied. "Give me the key. Give me the key."

Surely he'll hold out, surely he'll take her away, surely he's stronger, more forceful.

He gave her the key.

No. *This* cannot be endured. *This* is the horror beyond all else. She came in, she walked into the room, and the sound she made will always live inside me. That cry wasn't human; it was the howl of every creature that has ever despaired. *Now* I know what despair is, and why I called my own state mere truculence.

Now that it was too late, Greg tried to restrain her, tried to hold her shoulders and draw her from the room, but she pulled away and crossed the room toward—not toward *me.* I was everywhere in the room, driven by pain and remorse, and Emily walked toward the carcass. She looked at it almost tenderly, she even reached up and touched its swollen cheek. "Oh, Ed," she murmured.

The pains were as violent now as in the moments before my death. The slashing torment in my throat, the awful distension in my head, they made me squirm in agony all over again; but I *could not* feel her hand on my cheek.

Greg followed her, touched her shoulder again, spoke her name, and immediately her face dissolved, she cried out once more and wrapped her arms around the corpse's legs and clung to it, weeping and gasping and uttering words too quick and broken to understand. Thank *God* they were too quick and broken to understand!

Greg, that fool, did finally force her away, though he had great trouble breaking her clasp on the body. But he succeeded, and pulled her out of the room and slammed the door, and for a little while the body swayed and turned, until it became still once more.

That was the worst. Nothing could be worse than that. The long days and nights here—how long must a stupid creature like myself *haunt* his death-place before release?—would be horrible, I knew that, but not so bad as this. Emily would survive, would sell the house, would slowly forget. (Even I would slowly forget.) She and Greg could marry. She was only thirty-six, she could still be a mother.

For the rest of the night I heard her wailing, elsewhere in the house. The police did come at last, and a pair of grim silent white-coated men from the morgue entered the room to cut me— it—down. They bundled it like a broken toy into a large oval wicker basket with long wooden handles, and they carried it away.

I had thought I might be forced to stay with the body, I had feared the possibility of being buried with it, of spending eternity as a thinking nothingness in the black dark of a casket, but the body left the room and I remained behind.

A doctor was called. When the body was carried away the room door was left open, and now I could plainly hear the voices from downstairs. Tony was among them now, his characteristic surly monosyllable occasionally rumbling, but the main thing for a while was the doctor. He was trying to give Emily a sedative, but she kept wailing, she kept speaking high hurried frantic sentences as though she had too little time to say it all. "I did it!" she cried, over and over. "I did it! I'm to blame!"

Yes. That was the reaction I'd wanted, and expected, and here it was, and it was horrible. Everything I had desired in the last moments of my life had been granted to me, and they were all ghastly beyond belief. I *didn't* want to die! I *didn't* want to give Emily such misery! And more than all the rest I didn't want to be here, seeing and hearing it all.

They did quiet her at last, and then a policeman in a rumpled blue suit came into the room with Greg, and listened while Greg described everything that had happened. While Greg talked, the policeman rather grumpily stared at the remaining length of rope still knotted around the beam, and when Greg had finished the policeman said, "You're a close friend of his?"

"More of his wife's. She works for me. I own The Bibelot, an antique shop out on the New York road."

"Mmm. Why on earth did you let her in here?"

Greg smiled; a sheepish embarrassed expression. "She's stronger than I am," he said. "A more forceful personality. That's always been true."

It was with some surprise I realized it *was* true. Greg was something of a weakling, and Emily was very strong. (*I* had been something of a weakling, hadn't I? Emily was the strongest of us all.)

The policeman was saying, "Any idea why he'd do it?"

"I think he suspected his wife was having an affair with me." Clearly Greg had rehearsed this sentence, he'd much earlier come to the decision to say it and had braced himself for the moment. He blinked all the way through the statement, as though standing in a harsh glare.

The policeman gave him a quick shrewd look. "Were you?"

"Yes."

"She was getting a divorce?"

"No. She doesn't love me, she loved her husband."

"Then why sleep around?"

"Emily wasn't sleeping *around,*" Greg said, showing offense only with that emphasized word. "From time to time, and not very often, she was sleeping with me."

"Why?"

"For comfort." Greg too looked at the rope around the beam, as though it had become me and he was awkward speaking in its presence. "Ed wasn't an easy man to get along with," he said carefully. "He was moody. It was getting worse."

"Cheerful people don't kill themselves," the policeman said.

"Exactly. Ed was depressed most of the time, obscurely angry now and then. It was affecting his business, costing him clients. He made Emily miserable but she wouldn't leave him, she loved him. I don't know what she'll do now."

"You two won't marry?"

"Oh, no." Greg smiled, a bit sadly. "Do you think we murdered him, made it look like suicide so we could marry?"

"Not at all," the policeman said. "But what's the problem? You already married?"

"I am homosexual."

The policeman was no more astonished than I. He said, "I don't get it."

"I live with my friend; that young man downstairs. I am—capable—of a wider range, but my preferences are set. I am very fond of Emily, I felt sorry for her, the life she had with Ed. I told you our physical relationship was infrequent. And often not very successful."

Oh, Emily. Oh, poor Emily.

The policeman said, "Did Thornburn know you were, uh, that way?"

"I have no idea. I don't make a public point of it."

"All right." The policeman gave one more half-angry look around the room, then said, "Let's go."

They left. The door remained open, and I heard them continue to talk as they went downstairs, first the policeman asking, "Is there somebody to stay the night? Mrs. Thornburn shouldn't be alone."

"She has relatives in Great Barrington. I phoned them earlier. Somebody should be arriving within the hour."

"You'll stay until then? The doctor says she'll probably sleep, but just in case—"

"Of course."

That was all I heard. Male voices murmured awhile longer from below, and then stopped. I heard cars drive away.

How complicated men and women are. How stupid are simple actions. I had never understood anyone, least of all myself.

The room was visited once more that night, by Greg, shortly after the police left. He entered, looking as offended and repelled as though the body were still here, stood the chair up on its legs, climbed on it, and with some difficulty untied the remnant of rope. This he stuffed partway into his pocket as he stepped down again to the floor, then returned the chair to its usual spot in the corner of the room, picked the key off the floor and put it in the lock, switched off both bedside lamps, and left the room, shutting the door behind him.

Now I was in darkness, except for the faint line of light under the door, and the illuminated numerals of the clock. How long one minute is! That clock was my enemy, it dragged out every minute, it paused and waited and paused and waited till I could stand it no more, and then it waited longer, and *then* the next number dropped into place. Sixty times an hour, hour after hour, all night long. I couldn't stand one night of this, how could I stand eternity?

And how could I stand the torment and torture inside my brain? That was much worse now than the physical pain, which never entirely left me. I had been right about Emily and Greg, but at the same time I had been hopelessly brainlessly wrong. I had been right about my life, but wrong; right about my death, but wrong. How *much* I wanted to make amends, and how impossible it was to do anything anymore, anything at all. My actions had all tended to this, and ended with this: black remorse, the most dreadful pain of all.

I had all night to think, and to feel the pains, and to wait without knowing what I was waiting for or when—or if—my waiting would ever end. Faintly I heard the arrival of Emily's sister and brother-in-law, the murmured conversation, then the departure of Tony and Greg. Not long afterward the guest room door opened, but almost immediately closed again, no one having entered, and a bit after that the hall light went out, and now only the illuminated clock broke the darkness.

When next would I see Emily? Would she ever enter this room again? It wouldn't be as horrible as the first time, but it would surely be horror enough.

Dawn grayed the window shade, and gradually the room appeared out of the darkness, dim and silent and morose. Apparently it was a sunless day, which never got very bright. The day went on and on, featureless, each protracted minute marked by the clock. At times I dreaded someone's entering this room, at other times I prayed for something, anything—even the presence of Emily herself—to break this unending boring *absence*. But the day went on with no event, no sound, no activity anywhere—they must be keeping Emily sedated through this first day—and it wasn't until twilight, with the digital clock reading 6:52, that the door again opened and a person entered.

At first I didn't recognize him. An angry-looking man, blunt and determined, he came in with quick ragged steps, switched on both bedside lamps, then shut the door with rather more force than necessary, and turned the key in the lock. Truculent, his manner was, and when he turned from the door I saw with incredulity that he was *me*. Me! I wasn't dead, I was alive! But how could that be?

And what was that he was carrying? He picked up the chair from the corner, carried it to the middle of the room, stood on it—

No! No!

He tied the rope around the beam. The noose was already in the other end, which he slipped over his head and tightened around his neck.

Good God, *don't!*

He kicked the chair away.

The instant I kicked the chair away I wanted it back, but gravity was turning my former wish to its present command; the chair would not right itself from where it lay on the floor, and my 193 pounds would not cease to urge downward from the rope thick around my neck.

There was pain, of course, quite horrible pain centered in my throat, but the most astounding thing was the way my cheeks seemed to swell. I could barely see over their round red hills, my eyes staring in agony at the door, *willing* someone to come in and rescue me, though I knew there was no one in the house, and in any event the door was carefully locked. My kicking legs caused me to twist and turn, so that sometimes I faced the door and sometimes the window, and my shivering hands struggled with the rope so deep in my flesh I could barely find it and most certainly could not pull it loose.

I was frantic and horrified, yet at the same time my brain possessed a cold corner of aloof observation. I seemed now to be everywhere in the room at once, within my writhing body but also without, seeing my frenzied spasms, the thick rope, the heavy beam, the mismatched pair of lit bedside lamps throwing my convulsive double shadow on the walls, the closed locked door, the white-curtained window with its shade drawn all the way down. *This is death.*

THE GHOST OF DR. HARRIS

Nathaniel Hawthorne

GENERALLY RANKED AT OR near the top of every list of the greatest American novelists, Nathaniel Hawthorne (born Hathorne) (1804–1864)
endowed most of his major work with classic elements of occult happenings,
superstition, allegory, horror, and the supernatural. He was born in Salem, Massachusetts, the great-great-grandson of a judge in the Salem witch trials. He was
extremely solitary as a child, a state which endured throughout most of his life.
His masterpiece, *The Scarlet Letter* (1850), is filled with such fantastic elements
as a great glowing "A" in the sky, and another apparently burned into the chest
of the cowardly minister. *The House of the Seven Gables* (1851) also contains
numerous if nuanced overtones of Gothic fantasy, including a well whose water
turns foul when an injustice is done, the hereditary curse of a wizard, a skeleton
with a missing hand, and a portrait that seems to change expressions. In his short
stories, especially those collected in *Twice-Told Tales* (1837; expanded in 1842),
Mosses from an Old Manse (1846), and *The Snow Image and Other Twice-Told Tales*
(1852), otherworldly creatures such as ghosts, demons, witches, etc., abound,
though they are often rationalized or made to seem as no more than entities in
dreams. In his finest short story, "Young Goodman Brown," the title character
encounters a witch, a coven attended by virtually everyone he knows, and the
devil himself—or, in fact, he encounters no one, having either fantasized the
episode or dreamed it; Hawthorne does not resolve whether or not it occurred,
leaving it to the reader to decide.

"The Ghost of Dr. Harris" was written in a single day on August 17, 1856,
but remained unpublished until a small printing of a chapbook in 1900. Hawthorne claimed the story to be a true account of his own real-life experience.

The Ghost of Dr. Harris

NATHANIEL HAWTHORNE

I AM AFRAID THIS ghost story will be a very faded aspect when transferred to paper. Whatever effect is had on you, or whatever charm it retains in your memory, is perhaps to be attributed to the favorable circumstances under which it was originally told.

We were sitting, I remember, late in the evening, in your drawing-room, where the lights of the chandelier were so muffled as to produce a delicious obscurity through which the fire diffused a dim red glow. In this rich twilight the feelings of the party had been properly attuned by some tales of English superstition, and the lady of Smithills Hall had just been describing that Bloody Footstep which marks the threshold of her old mansion, when your Yankee guest (zealous for the honour of his country, and desirous of proving that his dead compatriots have the same ghostly privileges as other dead people, if they think it worth while to use them) began a story of something wonderful that long ago happened to himself. Possibly in the verbal narrative he may have assumed a little more licence than would be allowable in a written record. For the sake of the artistic effect, he may then have thrown in, here and there, a few slight circumstances which he will not think it proper to retain in what he now puts forth as the sober statement of a veritable fact.

A good many years ago (it must be as many as fifteen, perhaps more, and while I was still a bachelor) I resided at Boston, in the United States. In that city there is a large and long-established library, styled the Athenaeum, connected with which is a reading-room, well supplied with foreign and American periodicals and newspapers. A splendid edifice has since been erected by the proprietors of the institution; but, at the period I speak of, it was contained within a large old mansion, formerly the town residence of an eminent citizen of Boston. The reading-room (a spacious hall, with the group of the Laocoon at one end, and the Belvedere Apollo at the other) was frequented by not a few elderly merchants, retired from business, by clergymen and lawyers, and by such literary men as we had amongst us. These good people were mostly old, leisurely, and somnolent, and used to nod and doze for hours together, with the newspapers before them, ever and anon recovering themselves as far as to read a word or two of the politics of the day, sitting, as as it were, on the boundary of the Land of Dreams, and having little to do with this world, except through the newspapers which they so tenaciously grasped.

One of these worthies, whom I occasionally saw there, was the Reverend Doctor Harris, a Unitarian clergyman of considerable repute and eminence. He was very far advanced in life, not less than eighty years old, and probably more; and he resided, I think, at Dorchester, a suburban village in the immediate vicinity of Boston.

I had never been personally acquainted with this good old clergyman, but had heard of him all my life as a noteworthy man; so that when he was first pointed out to me I looked at him with a certain specialty of attention, and always subsequently eyed him with a degree of interest whenever I happened to see him at the Athenaeum or elsewhere. He was a small, withered, infirm, but brisk old gentleman, with snow-white hair, a somewhat stooping figure, but yet a remarkable alacrity of movement. I remember it was in the street that I first noticed him. The Doctor was plodding along with a staff, but turned smartly about on being addressed by the gentleman who was with me, and responded with a good deal of vivacity.

"Who is he?" I inquired, as soon as he had passed. "The Reverend Doctor Harris, of Dorchester," replied my companion; and from that time I often saw him, and never forgot his aspect. His especial haunt was the Athenaeum. There I used to see him daily, and almost always with a newspaper—the *Boston Post*, which was the leading journal of the Democratic Party in the Northern States. As old Doctor Harris had been a noted Democrat during his more active life, it was a very natural thing that he should still like to read the *Boston Post*. There his reverend figure was accustomed to sit day after day, in the self-same chair by the fireside; and, by degrees, seeing him there so constantly, I began to look towards him as I entered the reading-room, and felt that a kind of acquaintance, at least on my part, was established. Not that I had any reason (as long as this venerable person remained in the body) to suppose that he ever noticed me; but by some subtle connection, that small, white-haired, infirm, yet vivacious figure of an old clergyman became associated with my idea and recollection of the place. One day especially (about noon, as was generally his hour) I am perfectly certain that I had seen this figure of old Doctor Harris, and taken my customary note of him, although I remember nothing in his appearance at all different from what I had seen on many previous occasions.

But, that very evening, a friend said to me: "Did you hear that old Doctor Harris is dead?" "No," said I very quietly, "and it cannot be true; for I saw him at the Athenaeum to-day." "You must be mistaken," rejoined my friend. "He is certainly dead!" and confirmed the fact with such special circumstances that I could no longer doubt it. My friend has often since assured me that I seemed much startled at the intelligence; but, as well as I can recollect, I believe that I was very little disturbed, if at all, but set down the apparition as a mistake of my own, or, perhaps, the interposition of a familiar idea into the place and amid the circumstances with which I had been accustomed to associate it.

The next day, as I ascended the steps of the Athenaeum, I remember thinking within myself: "Well, I never shall see old Doctor Harris again!" With this thought in my mind, as I opened the door of the reading-room, I glanced towards the spot and chair where Doctor Harris usually sat, and there, to my astonishment, sat the grey, infirm figure of the deceased Doctor, reading the newspaper as was his wont! His own death must have been recorded, that very morning, in that very newspaper! I have no recollection of being greatly discomposed at the moment, or indeed that I felt any extraordinary emotion whatever. Probably, if ghosts were in the habit of coming among us, they would coincide with the ordinary train of affairs, and melt into them so familiarly that we should not be shocked at their presence. At all events, so it was in this instance. I looked through the newspapers as usual, and turned over the periodicals, taking about as much interest in their contents as at other times. Once or twice, no doubt, I may have lifted my eyes from the page to look again at the venerable Doctor, who ought then to have been lying in his coffin dressed out for the grave, but who felt such interest in the *Boston Post* as to come back from the other world to read it the morning after his death. One might have supposed that he would have cared more about the novelties of the sphere to which he had just been introduced than about the politics he had left behind him! The apparition took no notice of me, nor behaved otherwise in any respect than on any previous day. Nobody but myself seemed to notice him, and yet the old gentlemen round about the fire, beside his chair, were his lifelong acquaintances, who were perhaps thinking of his death, and who in a day or two would deem it a proper courtesy to attend his funeral.

I have forgotten how the ghost of Doctor Harris took its departure from the Athenaeum on this occasion, or, in fact, whether the ghost or I went first. This equanimity, and almost indifference, on my part—the careless way in which I glanced at so singular a mystery and left it aside—is what now surprises me as much as anything else in the affair.

From that time, for a long time thereafter—for weeks at least, and I know not but for months—I used to see the figure of Doctor Harris quite as frequently as before his death. It grew to be so common that at length I regarded the venerable defunct no more than any other of the old fogies who basked before the fire and dozed over the newspapers.

It was but a ghost—nothing but thin air—not tangible nor appreciable, nor demanding any attention from a man of flesh and blood! I cannot recollect any cold shudderings, any awe, any repugnance, any emotion whatever, such as would be suitable and decorous on beholding a visitant from the spiritual world. It is very strange, but such is the truth. It appears excessively odd to me now that I did not adopt such means as I readily might to ascertain whether the appearance had solid substance, or was merely gaseous and vapoury. I might have brushed against him, have jostled his chair, or have trodden accidentally on his poor old toes. I might have snatched the *Boston Post*—unless that were an apparition, too—out of his shadowy hands. I might have tested him in a hundred ways; but I did nothing of the kind.

Perhaps I was loath to destroy the illusion, and to rob myself of so good a ghost story, which might probably have been explained in some very commonplace way. Perhaps, after all, I had a secret dread of the old phenomenon, and therefore kept within my limits, with an instinctive caution which I mistook for indifference. Be this as it may, here is the fact. I saw the figure, day after day, for a considerable space of time, and took no pains to ascertain whether it was a ghost or no. I never, to my knowledge, saw him come into the reading-room or depart from it. There sat Doctor Harris in his customary chair, and I can say little else about him.

After a certain period—I really know not how long—I began to notice, or to fancy, a peculiar regard in the old gentleman's aspect towards myself. I sometimes found him gazing at me, and, unless I deceived myself, there was a sort of expectancy in his face. His spectacles, I think, were shoved up, so that his bleared eyes might meet my own. Had he been a living man I should have flattered myself that good Doctor Harris was, for some reason or other, interested in me and desirous of a personal acquaintance. Being a ghost, and amenable to ghostly laws, it was natural to conclude that he was waiting to be spoken to before delivering whatever message he wished to impart. But, if so, the ghost had shown the bad judgement common among the spiritual brotherhood, both as regarded the place of interview and the person whom he had selected as the recipient of his communications. In the reading-room of the Athenaeum conversation is strictly forbidden, and I could not have addressed the apparition without drawing the instant notice and indignant frowns of the slumberous old gentlemen around me. I myself, too, at that time, was shy as any ghost, and followed the ghosts' rule never to speak first. And what an absurd figure should I have made, solemnly and awfully addressing what must have appeared, in the eyes of all the rest of the company, an empty chair! Besides, I had never been introduced to Doctor Harris, dead or alive, and I am not aware that social regulations are to be abrogated by the accidental fact of one of the parties hav-

ing crossed the imperceptible line which separates the other party from the spiritual world. If ghosts throw off all conventionalism among themselves, it does not therefore follow that it can be safely dispensed with by those who are still hampered with flesh and blood.

For such reasons as these—and reflecting, moreover, that the deceased Doctor might burden me with some disagreeable task, with which I had no business nor wish to be concerned— I stubbornly resolved to have nothing to say to him. To this determination I adhered; and not a syllable ever passed between the ghost of Doctor Harris and myself.

To the best of my recollection, I never observed the old gentleman either enter the reading-room or depart from it, or move from his chair, or lay down the newspaper, or exchange a look with any person in the company, unless it were myself. He was not by any means invariably in his place. In the evening, for instance, though often at the reading-room myself, I never saw him. It was at the brightest noontide that I used to behold him, sitting within the most comfortable focus of the glowing fire, as real and lifelike an object (except that he was so very old, and of an ashen complexion) as any other in the room. After a long while of this strange intercourse, if such it can be called, I remember—once at least, and I know not but oftener—a sad, wistful, disappointed gaze, which the ghost fixed upon me from beneath his spectacles; a melancholy look of helplessness, which, if my heart had not been as hard as a paving-stone, I could hardly have withstood. But I did withstand it; and I think I saw him no more after this last appealing look, which still dwells in my memory as perfectly as while my own eyes were encountering the dim and bleared eyes of the ghost. And whenever I recall this strange passage of my life, I see the small, old withered figure of Doctor Harris, sitting in his accustomed chair, the *Boston Post* in his hand, his spectacles shoved upwards, and gazing at me as I close the door of the reading-room, with that wistful, appealing, hopeless, helpless look. It is too late now: his grave has been grass-grown this many and many a year; and I hope he has found rest in it without any aid from me.

I have only to add that it was not until long after I had ceased to encounter the ghost that I became aware how very odd and strange the whole affair had been; and even now I am made sensible of its strangeness chiefly by the wonder and incredulity of those to whom I tell the story.

THE EVERLASTING CLUB

"Ingulphus"

TAKING THE NAME OF a Saxon abbot of Crowland Abbey, Sir Arthur Gray (1852–1940) spent virtually his entire life at Jesus College, Cambridge, first as a student, then a fellow, then a tutor, and finally as Master of the College, becoming the first non-ordained man in its four-hundred-year history to hold that position. He wrote very little fiction, mostly published in college magazines, especially *Cambridge Review,* but his stories are almost uniformly distinguished supernatural tales set in or around Jesus College. As a well-known scholar with numerous books to his credit, notably on local Cambridge history and about William Shakespeare, Gray used the pseudonym "Ingulphus" for his fiction, which often was thought to be the work of his fellow Cambridge scholar and ghost story writer M. R. James. Gray's identity remained secret until his stories were collected with the understated title *Tedious Brief Tales of Granta and Gramarye* in 1919. Of the nine stories in the slim (and rare) volume, six are supernatural tales, including such acknowledged masterpieces as "The Burden of Dead Books," in which a man discovers the secret of everlasting life by simply inhabiting a new body when the old one wears out; "The Necromancer," where the title character is able to wander the streets of his town at night as a cat during his lifetime—and after; and "The True History of Anthony Fryar," in which an alchemist *almost* succeeds in developing a cure for all human ailments.

"The Everlasting Club" was originally published in the October 27, 1910, issue of the *Cambridge Review;* it was collected in *Tedious Brief Tales of Granta and Gramarye* (Cambridge, Heffer & Sons, 1919).

The Everlasting Club

"INGULPHUS"

THERE IS A CHAMBER in Jesus College the existence of which is probably known to few who are now resident, and fewer still have penetrated into it or even seen its interior. It is on the right hand of the landing on the top floor of the precipitous staircase which for some forgotten story connected with it is traditionally called "Cow Lane." The padlock which secures its massive oaken door is very rarely unfastened, for the room is bare and unfurnished. Once it served as a place of deposit for superfluous kitchen ware, but even that ignominious use has passed from it, and it is now left to undisturbed solitude and darkness. For I should say that it is entirely cut off from the light of the outer day by the walling up, some time in the eighteenth century, of its single window, and such light as ever reaches it comes from the door, when rare occasion causes it to be opened.

Yet at no extraordinarily remote day this chamber has evidently been tenanted, and, before it was given up to the darkness, was comfortably fitted, according to the standard of comfort which was known in college in the days of George II. There is still a roomy fireplace before which legs have been stretched and wine and gossip have circulated in the days of wigs and brocade. For the room is spacious and, when it was lighted by the window looking eastward over the fields and common, it must have been a cheerful place for the sociable don.

Let me state in brief, prosaic outline the circumstances which account for the gloom and solitude in which this room has remained now for nearly a century and a half.

In the second quarter of the eighteenth century the University possessed a great variety of clubs of a social kind. There were clubs in college parlours and clubs in private rooms, or in inns and coffee-houses: clubs flavoured with politics, clubs clerical, clubs purporting to be learned and literary. Whatever their professed particularity, the aim of each was convivial. Some of them, which included undergraduates as well as seniors, were dissipated enough, and in their limited provincial way aped the profligacy of such clubs as the Hell Fire Club of London notoriety.

Among these last was one which was at once more select and of more evil fame than any of its fellows. By a singular accident, presently to be explained, the Minute Book of this Club, including the years from 1738 to 1766, came into the hands of the Master of Jesus College, and though, so far as I am aware, it is no longer extant, I have before me a transcript of it which, though it is in a recent handwriting, presents in a bald shape such a singular array of facts that I must ask you to accept them as veracious. The original book is described as a stout duodecimo volume bound in red leather and fastened with red silken strings. The writing in it occupied some forty pages, and ended with the date November 2, 1766.

The Club in question was called the Everlasting Club—a name sufficiently explained by its rules, set forth in the pocket-book. Its number was limited to seven, and it would seem that its members were all young men, between twenty-two and thirty. One of them was a Fellow-Commoner of Trinity: three of them were Fellows of Colleges, among whom I should especially mention a Fellow of Jesus, named Charles Bellasis, another was a landed proprietor in the county, and the sixth was a young Cambridge physician. The Founder and President of the Club was the Honorable Alan Dermot, who, as the son of an Irish peer, had obtained a nobleman's degree in the University, and lived in idleness in the town. Very little is known of his life and character, but that little is highly in his disfavour. He was killed in a duel in Paris in the year 1743, under circumstances which I need not particularise, but which point to an exceptional degree of cruelty and wickedness in the slain man.

I will quote from the first page of the Minute Book some of the laws of the Club, which will explain its constitution:—

"1. This Society consisteth of seven Everlastings, who may be Corporeal or Incorporeal, as Destiny may determined.
2. The rules of the Society, as herein written, are immutable and Everlasting.
3. None shall hereafter be chosen into the Society and none shall cease to be members.
4. The Honorable Alan Dermot is the Everlasting President of the Society.
5. The Senior Corporeal Everlasting, not being President, shall be the Secretary of the Society, and in the Book of Minutes shall record its transactions, the date at which any Everlasting shall cease to be Corporeal, and all fines due to the Society. And when such Senior Everlasting shall cease to be Corporeal he shall, either in person or by some sure hand, deliver this Book of Minutes to him who shall be next Senior and at the time Corporeal, and he shall in like

manner record the transactions therein and transmit it to the next Senior. The neglect of these provisions shall be visited by the President with fine or punishment according to his discretion.
6. On the Second day of November in every year, being the Feast of All Souls, at ten o'clock post meridiem, the Everlastings shall meet at supper in the place of residence of that Corporeal member of the Society to whom it shall fall in order of rotation to entertain them, and they shall all subscribe in this Book of Minutes their names and present place of abode.
7. It shall be the obligation of every Everlasting to be present at the yearly entertainment of the Society, and none shall allege for excuse that he has not been invited thereto. If any Everlasting shall fail to attend the yearly meeting, or in his turn shall fail to provide entertainment for the Society, he shall be mulcted at the discretion of the President.
8. Nevertheless, if in any year, in the month of October and not less than seven days before the Feast of All Souls, the major part of the Society, that is to say, four at least, shall meet and record in writing in these Minutes that it is their desire that no entertainment be given in that year, then, notwithstanding the two rules rehearsed, there shall be no entertainment in that year, and no Everlasting shall be mulcted on the ground of his absence."

The rest of the rules are either too profane or too puerile to be quoted here. They indicate the extraordinary levity with which the members entered on their preposterous obligations. In particular, to the omission of any regulation as to the transmission of the Minute Book after the last Everlasting ceased to be "Corporeal," we owe the accident that it fell into the hands of one who was not a member of the society, and the consequent preservation of its contents to the present day.

Low as was the standard of morals in all

classes of the University in the first half of the eighteenth century, the flagrant defiance of public decorum by the members of the Everlasting Society brought upon it the stern censure of the authorities, and after a few years it was practically dissolved and its members banished from the University. Charles Bellasis, for instance, was obliged to leave the college, and, though he retained his fellowship, he remained absent from it for nearly twenty years. But the minutes of the society reveal a more terrible reason for its virtual extinction.

Between the years of 1738 and 1743 the minutes record many meetings of the Club, for it met on other occasions besides that of All Souls Day. Apart from a great deal of impious jocularity on the part of the writers, they are limited to the formal record of the attendance of the members, fines inflicted, and so forth. The meeting on November 2 in the latter year is the first about which there is any departure from the stereotyped forms. The supper was given in the house of the physician. One member, Henry Davenport, the former Fellow-Commoner of Trinity, was absent from the entertainment, as he was then serving in Germany, in the Dettingen campaign. The minutes contain an entry, "Mulctatus propter absentiam per Presidentem, Hen. Davenport." An entry on the next page of the book runs, "Henry Davenport by a cannon-shot became an Incorporeal Member, November 3, 1743."

The minutes give in their handwriting, under date November 2, the names and addresses of the six other members. First in the list, in a large bold hand, is the autograph of "Alan Dermot, President, at the Court of His Royal Highness." Now in October Dermot had certainly been in attendance on the Young Pretender at Paris, and doubtless the address which he gave was understood at the time by the other Everlastings to refer to the fact. But on October 28, five days before the meeting of the Club, he was killed, as I have already mentioned, in a duel. The news of his death cannot have reached Cambridge on November 2, for the Secretary's record of it is placed below that of Davenport, and with the date of November 10: "this day was reported that the President was become an Incorporeal by the hands of a french chevalier." And in a sudden ebullition, which is in glaring contrast with his previous profanities, he has dashed down, "The Good God shield us from ill."

The tidings of the President's death scattered the Everlastings like a thunderbolt. They left Cambridge and buried themselves in widely parted regions. But the Club did not cease to exist. The Secretary was still bound to his hateful records; the five survivors did not dare to neglect their fatal obligations. Horror of the presence of the President made the November gathering once and for ever impossible: but the horror, too, forbade them to neglect the meeting in October of every year to put in writing their objection to the celebration. For five years five names are appended to that entry in the minutes, and that is all the business of the Club. Then another member died, who was not the Secretary.

For eighteen more years four miserable men met once each year to deliver the same formal protest. During those years we gather from the signatures that Charles Bellasis returned to Cambridge, now, to appearance, chastened and decorous. He occupied the rooms which I have described on the staircase on the corner of the cloister.

Then in 1766 comes a new handwriting and an altered minute: "Jan. 27, on this day Francis Witherington, Secretary, became an Incorporeal member. The same day this Book was delivered to me, James Harvey." Harvey lived only a month, and a similar entry on March 7 states that the book has descended, with the same mysterious celerity, to William Catherton. Then, on May 18, Charles Bellasis writes that on that day, being the day of Catherton's decease, the Minute Book has come to him as the last surviving Corporeal of the Club.

As it is my purpose to record fact only I shall not attempt to describe the feelings of the unhappy Secretary when he penned that fatal record. When Witherington died it must have come home to the three survivors that after twenty-three years' intermission the ghastly entertainment must be annually renewed, with the addition of fresh Incorporeal guests, or that they must undergo the pitiless censure of the President. I think it likely that the terror of the alternative, coupled with the mysterious delivery of the Minute Book, was answerable for the speedy decease of the first two successors to the Secretaryship. Now that the alternative was offered to Bellasis alone, he was firmly resolved to bear the consequences, whatever they might be, of an infringement of the Club rules.

The graceless days of George II had passed away from the University. They were succeeded by times of outward respectability, when religion and morals were no longer publicly challenged. With Bellasis, too, the petulance of youth had passed: he was discreet, perhaps exemplary. The scandal of his early conduct was unknown to most of the new generation, condoned by the few survivors who had witnessed it.

On the night of November 2, 1766, a terrible event revived in the older inhabitants of the College the memory of those evil days. From ten o'clock to midnight a hideous uproar went on in the chamber of Bellasis. Who were his companions none knew. Blasphemous outcries and ribald songs, such as had not been heard for twenty years past, aroused from sleep or study the occupants of the court; but among the voices was not that of Bellasis. At twelve a sudden silence fell upon the cloisters. But the Master lay awake all night, troubled at the relapse of a respected colleague and the horrible example of libertinism set to his pupils.

In the morning all remained quiet about Bellasis' chamber. When his door was opened, soon after daybreak, the early light creeping through the drawn curtains revealed a strange scene. About the table were drawn seven chairs, but some of them had been overthrown, and the furniture was in chaotic disorder, as after some wild orgy. In the chair at the foot of the table sat the lifeless figure of the Secretary, his head bent over his folded arms, as though he would shield his eyes from some horrible sight. Before him on the table lay pen, ink, and the red Minute Book. On the last inscribed page, under the date of November 2nd, were written, for the first time since 1742, the autographs of the seven members of the Everlasting Club, but without address. In the same strong hand in which the President's name was written there was appended below the signatures the note "Mulctus per Presidentem propter neglectum obsonii, Car. Bellasis."

The Minute Book was secured by the Master of the College and I believe that he alone was acquainted with the nature of its contents. The scandal reflected on the College by the circumstances revealed in it caused him to keep the knowledge rigidly to himself. But some suspicion of the nature of the occurrences must have percolated to students and servants, for there was a long-abiding belief in the College that annually on the night of November 2 sounds of unholy revelry were heard to issue from the chamber of Charles Bellasis. I cannot learn that the occupants of the adjoining rooms have ever been disturbed by them. Indeed, it is plain from the minutes that owing to their improvident drafting no provision was made for the perpetuation of the All Souls entertainment after the last Everlasting ceased to Corporeal. Such superstitious belief must be treated with contemptuous incredulity. But whether for that cause or another the rooms were shut up, and have remained tenantless from that day to this.

Isaac Asimov and James MacCreigh

BORN ISAAK YUDOVICH OSIMOV in Petrograd, the young Isaac Asimov (1920–1992) grew up in Brooklyn and retained his New York accent for his entire life. A precocious genius, he began writing for pulp magazines at the age of nineteen, the same age at which he received his master's degree from Columbia University. He had an academic career at Boston University as associate professor in the field of biochemistry, but his quick and profound success as an author of science fiction (he is regarded as one of the three greatest science fiction writers of the twentieth century, along with Arthur C. Clarke and Robert A. Heinlein) curtailed his teaching activities. Prolific in both fictional works and nonfiction, with more than three hundred books to his credit, he is remembered for such enduring, groundbreaking classics as *I, Robot* (1950), *Foundation* (1951), and the short story "Nightfall" (1941), selected by the Science Fiction Writers of America as the best science fiction story ever written.

James MacCreigh is the pseudonym of Frederik (George) Pohl, Jr. (1919–), who, under his own name and at least a dozen pseudonyms, has written steadily and successfully for more than seventy years. He also has been an influential editor, holding that position at *Super Science Stories* and *Astonishing Stories* (1939–1943) and at *Galaxy* and *if* for more than a decade (1959–1969), winning three Nebula Awards for Best Editor. His writing has also earned him numerous Hugo and Nebula awards, including Grand Master. His 1980 novel, *Jem*, received the National Book Award.

"Legal Rites" was originally published in the September 1950 issue of *Weird Tales*.

Legal Rites

ISAAC ASIMOV AND JAMES MACCREIGH

I

Already the stars were out, though the sun had just dipped under the horizon, and the sky of the west was a blood-stuck gold behind the Sierra Nevadas.

"Hey!" squawked Russell Harley. "Come back!"

But the one-lunged motor of the old Ford was making too much noise; the driver didn't hear him. Harley cursed as he watched the old car careen along the sandy ruts on its half-flat tires. Its taillight was saying a red *no* to him. *No, you can't get away tonight; no, you'll have to stay here and fight it out.*

Harley grunted and climbed back up the porch stairs of the old wooden house. It was well made, anyhow. The stairs, though half a century old, neither creaked beneath him nor showed cracks.

Harley picked up the bags he'd dropped when he experienced his abrupt change of mind—fake leather and worn out, they were—and carted them into the house. He dumped them on a dust-jacketed sofa and looked around.

It was stifling hot, and the smell of the desert outside had permeated the room. Harley sneezed.

"Water," he said out loud. "That's what I need."

He'd prowled through every room on the ground floor before he stopped still and smote his head. Plumbing—naturally there'd be no plumbing in this hole eight miles out on the desert! A well was the best he could hope for—

If that.

It was getting dark. No electric lights either, of course. He blundered irritatedly through the dusky rooms to the back of the house. The screen door shrieked metallically as he opened it. A bucket hung by the door. He picked it up, tipped it, shook the loose sand out of it. He looked over the "back yard"—about thirty thousand visible acres of hilly sand, rock, and patches of sage and flame-tipped ocotillo.

No well.

The old fool got water from somewhere, he thought savagely. Obstinately he climbed down the back steps and wandered out into the desert. Overhead the stars were blinding, a million billion of them, but the sunset was over already and he could see only hazily. The silence was murderous. Only a faint whisper of breeze over the sand, and the slither of his shoes.

He caught a glimmer of starlight from the nearest clump of sage and walked to it. There was a pool of water, caught in the angle of two enormous boulders. He stared at it doubtfully, then shrugged. It was water. It was better than nothing. He dipped the bucket in the little pool. Knowing nothing of the procedure, he filled it with a quart of loose sand as he scooped it along the bottom. When he lifted it, brimful, to his lips, staggering under the weight of it, he spat out the first mouthful and swore vividly.

Then he used his head. He set the bucket down, waited a second for the sand grains to settle, cupped water in his hands, lifted it to his lips. . . .

Pat. HISS. Pat. HISS. Pat. HISS—

"What the hell!" Harley stood up, looked around in abrupt puzzlement. It sounded like water dripping from somewhere, onto a red-hot stove, flashing into sizzling steam. He saw nothing, only the sand and the sage and the pool of tepid, sickly water.

Pat. HISS—

Then he saw it, and his eyes bulged. Out of nowhere it was dripping, a drop a second, a sticky, dark drop that was thicker than water, that fell to the ground lazily, in slow defiance of gravity. And when it struck each drop sizzled and skittered about, and vanished. It was perhaps eight feet from him, just visible in the starlight.

And then, "Get off my land!" said the voice from nowhere.

Harley got. By the time he got to Rebel Butte three hours later, he was barely managing to walk, wishing desperately that he'd delayed long enough for one more good drink of water, despite all the fiends of hell. But he'd run the first three miles. He'd had plenty of encouragement. He remembered with a shudder how the clear desert air had taken milky shape around the incredible trickle of dampness and had advanced on him threateningly.

And when he got to the first kerosene-lighted saloon of Rebel Butte, and staggered inside, the saloonkeeper's fascinated stare at the front of his shoddy coat showed him strong evidence that he hadn't been suddenly taken with insanity, or drunk on the unaccustomed sensation of fresh desert air. All down the front of him it was, and the harder he rubbed the harder it stayed, the stickier it got. Blood!

"Whiskey!" he said in a strangled voice, tottering to the bar. He pulled a threadbare dollar bill from his pocket, flapped it onto the mahogany.

The blackjack game at the back of the room had stopped. Harley was acutely conscious of the eyes of the players, the bartender, and the tall, lean man leaning on the bar. All were watching him.

The bartender broke the spell. He reached for a bottle behind him without looking at it, placed it on the counter before Harley. He poured a glass of water from a jug, set it down with a shot glass beside the bottle.

"I could of told you that would happen," he said casually. "Only you wouldn't of believed me. You had to meet Hank for yourself before you'd believe he was there."

Harley remembered his thirst and drained the glass of water, then poured himself a shot of the whiskey and swallowed it without waiting for the chaser to be refilled. The whiskey felt good going down, almost good enough to stop his internal shakes.

"What are you talking about?" he said finally. He twisted his body and leaned forward across the bar to partly hide the stains on his coat. The saloonkeeper laughed.

"Old Hank," he said. "I knowed who you was right away even before Tom came back and told me where he'd took you. I knowed you was Zeb Harley's no-good nephew, come to take Harley Hall an' sell it before he was cold in his grave."

The blackjack players were still watching him, Russell Harley saw. Only the lean man farther along the bar seemed to have dismissed him. He was pouring himself another drink quite occupied with his task.

Harley flushed. "Listen," he said, "I didn't come in here for advice. I wanted a drink. I'm paying for it. Keep your mouth out of this."

The saloonkeeper shrugged. He turned his back and walked away to the blackjack table. After a couple of seconds one of the players turned too, and threw a card down. The others followed suit.

Harley was just getting set to swallow his pride and talk to the saloonkeeper again—he seemed to know something about what Harley'd been through, and might be helpful—when the lean man tapped his shoulder. Harley whirled

and almost dropped his glass. Absorbed and jumpy, he hadn't seen him come up.

"Young man," said the lean one, "my name's Nicholls. Come along with me, sir, and we'll talk this thing over. I think we may be of service to each other."

Even the twelve-cylinder car Nicholls drove jounced like a haywagon over the sandy ruts leading to the place old Zeb had—laughingly— named "Harley Hall."

Russell Harley twisted his neck and stared at the heap of paraphernalia in the open rumble seat. "I don't like it," he complained. "I never had anything to do with ghosts. How do I know this stuff'll work?"

Nicholls smiled. "You'll have to take my word for it. I've had dealings with ghosts before. You could say that I might qualify as a ghost exterminator, if I chose."

Harley growled. "I still don't like it."

Nicholls turned a sharp look on him. "You like the prospect of owning Harley Hall, don't you? And looking for all the money your late uncle is supposed to have hidden around somewhere?" Harley shrugged. "Certainly you do," said Nicholls, returning his eyes to the road. "And with good reason. The local reports put the figure pretty high, young man."

"That's where you come in, I guess," Harley said sullenly. "I find the money—that I own anyhow—and give some of it to you. How much?"

"We'll discuss that later," Nicholls said. He smiled absently as he looked ahead.

"We'll discuss it right now!"

The smile faded from Nicholls' face. "No," he said. "We won't. I'm doing you a favor, young Harley. Remember that. In return—you'll do as I say, all the way!"

Harley digested that carefully, and it was not a pleasant meal. He waited a couple of seconds before he changed the subject.

"I was out here once when the old man was

alive," he said. "He didn't say nothing about any ghost."

"Perhaps he felt you might think him—well, peculiar," Nicholls said. "And perhaps you would have. When were you here?"

"Oh, a long time ago," Harley said evasively. "But I was here a whole day, and part of the night. The old man was crazy as a coot, but he didn't keep any ghosts in the attic."

"This ghost was a friend of his," Nicholls said. "The gentleman in charge of the bar told you that, surely. Your late uncle was something of a recluse. He lived in this house a dozen miles from nowhere, came into town hardly ever, wouldn't let anyone get friendly with him. But he wasn't exactly a hermit. He had Hank for company."

"Fine company."

Nicholls inclined his head seriously. "Oh, I don't know," he said. "From all accounts they got on well together. They played pinochle and chess—Hank's supposed to have been a great pinochle player. He was killed that way, according to the local reports. Caught somebody dealing from the bottom and shot it out with him. He lost. A bullet pierced his throat and he died quite bloodily." He turned the wheel, putting his weight into the effort, and succeeded in twisting the car out of the ruts of the "road," sent it jouncing across unmarked sand to the old frame house to which they were going.

"That," he finished as he pulled up before the porch, "accounts for the blood that accompanies his apparition."

Harley opened the door slowly and got out, looking uneasily at the battered old house. Nicholls cut the motor, got out, and walked at once to the back of the car.

"Come on," he said, dragging things out of the compartment. "Give me a hand with this. I'm not going to carry this stuff all by myself."

Harley came around reluctantly, regarded the curious assortment of bundles of dried faggots, lengths of colored cord, chalk pencils, ugly little bunches of wilted weeds, bleached bones of small animals, and a couple of less pleasant things without pleasure.

Pat. HISS. Pat. HISS—

"He's here!" Harley yelped. "Listen! He's someplace around here watching us."

"Ha!"

The laugh was deep, unpleasant, and—bodiless. Harley looked around desperately for the tell-tale trickle of blood. And he found it; from the air it issued, just beside the car, sinking gracefully to the ground and sizzling, vanishing, there.

"I'm watching you, all right," the voice said grimly. "Russell, you worthless piece of corruption, I've got no more use for you than you used to have for me. Dead or alive, this is my land! I shared it with your uncle, you young scalawag, but I won't share it with you. Get out!"

Harley's knees weakened and he tottered dizzily to the rear bumper, sat on it. "Nicholls—" he said confusedly.

"Oh, brace up," Nicholls said with irritation. He tossed a ball of gaudy twine, red and green, with curious knots tied along it, to Harley. Then he confronted the trickle of blood and made a few brisk passes in the air before it. His lips were moving silently, Harley saw, but no words came out.

There was a gasp and a chopped-off squawk from the source of the blood drops. Nicholls clapped his hands sharply, then turned to young Harley.

"Take that cord you have in your hands and stretch it around the house," he said. "All the way around, and make sure it goes right across the middle of the doors and windows. It isn't much, but it'll hold him till we can get the good stuff set up."

Harley nodded, then pointed a rigid finger at the drops of blood, now sizzling and fuming more angrily than before. "What about *that?*" he managed to get out.

Nicholls grinned complacently. "It'll hold him here till the cows come home," he said. "Get moving!"

Harley inadvertently inhaled a lungful of noxious white smoke and coughed till the tears rolled down his cheeks. When recovered he looked at Nicholls, who was reading silently from a green leather book with dog-eared pages. He said, "Can I stop stirring this now?"

Nicholls grimaced angrily and shook his head without looking at him. He went on reading, his lips contorting over syllables that were not in any language Harley had ever heard, then snapped the book shut and wiped his brow.

"Fine," he said. "So far, so good." He stepped over to leeward of the boiling pot Harley was stirring on the hob over the fireplace, peered down into it cautiously.

"That's about done," he said. "Take it off the fire and let it cool a bit."

Harley lifted it down, then squeezed his aching biceps with his left hand. The stuff was the consistency of sickly green fudge.

Nicholls didn't answer. He looked up in mild surprise at the sudden squawk of triumph from outside, followed by the howling of a chill wind.

"Hank must be loose," he said casually. "He can't do us any harm, I think, but we'd better get a move on." He rummaged in the dwindled pile of junk he'd brought from the car, extracted a paint-brush. "Smear this stuff around all the windows and doors. All but the front door. For that I have something else." He pointed to what seemed to be the front axle of an old Model-T. "Leave that on the doorsill. Cold iron. You can just step over it, but Hank won't be able to pass it. It's been properly treated already with the very best thaumaturgy."

"Step over it," Harley repeated. "What would I want to step over it for? *He's* out there."

"He won't hurt you," said Nicholls. "You will carry an amulet with you—that one, there—that will keep him away. Probably he couldn't really hurt you anyhow, being a low-order ghost who can't materialize to any great density. But just to take no chances, carry the amulet and don't stay out too long. It won't hold him off forever, not for more than half an hour. If you ever have to go out and stay for any length of time, tie that bundle of herbs around your neck." Nicholls smiled. "That's only for emergencies, though. It works on the asafoetida principle. Ghosts can't

come anywhere near it—but you won't like it much yourself. It has—ah—a rather definite odor."

He leaned gingerly over the pot again, sniffing. He sneezed.

"Well, that's cool enough," he said. "Before it hardens, get moving. Start spreading the stuff upstairs—and make sure you don't miss any windows."

"What are you going to do?"

"I," said Nicholls sharply, "will be here. Start."

But he wasn't. When Harley finished his disagreeable task and came down he called Nicholls' name, but the man was gone. Harley stepped to the door and looked out; the car was gone too.

He shrugged. "Oh, well," he said, and began taking the dust-clothes off the furniture.

II

Somewhere within the cold, legal mind of Lawyer Turnbull, he weighed the comparative likeness of nightmare and insanity.

He stared at the plush chair facing him, noted with distinct uneasiness how the strangely weightless, strangely sourceless trickle of redness disappeared as it hit the floor, but left long, mud-ochre streaks matted on the upholstery. The sound was unpleasant too; *Pat. HISS. Pat. HISS—*

The voice continued impatiently, "Damn your human stupidity! I may be a ghost, but heaven knows I'm not trying to haunt you. Friend, you're not that important to me. Get this—I'm here on business."

Turnbull learned that you cannot wet lips with a dehydrated tongue. "Legal business?"

"Sure. The fact that I was once killed by violence, and have to continue my existence on the astral plane, doesn't mean I've lost my legal right. Does it?"

The lawyer shook his head in bafflement. He said, "This would be easier on me if you weren't invisible. Can't you do something about it?"

There was a short pause. "Well, I could materialize for a minute," the voice said. "It's hard work—damn hard, for me. There are a lot of us astral entities that can do it easy as falling out of bed, but—Well, if I have to I shall try to do it once."

There was a shimmering in the air above the armchair, and a milky, thick smoke condensed into an intangible seated figure. Turnbull took no delight in noting that, through the figure, the outlines of the chair were still hazily visible. The figure thickened. Just as the features took form—just as Turnbull's bulging eyes made out a prominent hooked nose and a crisp beard—it thinned and exploded with a soft pop.

The voice said weakly, "I didn't think I was that bad. I'm way out of practice. I guess that's the first daylight materialization I've made in seventy-five years."

The lawyer adjusted his rimless glasses and coughed. *Hell's hinges,* he thought, *the worst thing about this is that I'm believing it!*

"Oh, well," he said aloud. Then he hurried on before the visitor could take offense: "Just what did you want? I'm just a small-town lawyer, you know. My business is fairly routine—"

"I know all about your business," the voice said. "You can handle my case—it's a land affair. I want to sue Russell Harley."

"Harley?" Turnbull fingered his cheek. "Any relation to Zeb Harley?"

"His nephew—and his heir too."

Turnbull nodded. "Yes, I remember now. My wife's folks live in Rebel Butte, and I've been there. Quite a coincidence you should come to me—"

The voice laughed. "It was no coincidence," it said softly.

"Oh." Turnbull was silent for a second. Then, "I see," he said. He cast a shrewd glance at the chair. "Lawsuits cost money, Mr.—I don't think you mentioned your name?"

"Hank Jenkins," the voice prompted. "I know that. Would—let's see. Would six hundred and fifty dollars be sufficient?"

Turnbull swallowed. "I think so," he said in a relatively unemotional tone—relative to what he was thinking.

"Then suppose we call that your retainer. I happen to have cached a considerable sum in gold when I was—that is to say, before I became an astral entity. I'm quite certain it hasn't been disturbed. You will have to call it treasure trove, I guess, and give half of it to the state, but there's thirteen hundred dollars altogether."

Turnbull nodded judiciously. "Assuming we can locate your trove," he said, "I think that would be quite satisfactory." He leaned back in his chair and looked legal. His aplomb had returned.

And half an hour later he said slowly, "I'll take your case."

Judge Lawrence Gimbel had always liked his job before. But his thirteen honorable years on the bench lost their flavor for him as he grimaced wearily and reached for his gavel. This case was far too confusing for his taste.

The clerk made his speech, and the packed courtroom sat down en masse. Gimbel held a hand briefly to his eyes before he spoke.

"Is the counsel for the plaintiff ready?"

"I am, your honor." Turnbull, alone at his table, rose and bowed.

"The counsel for the defendant?"

"Ready, your honor!" Fred Wilson snapped. He looked with a hard flicker of interest at Turnbull and his solitary table, then leaned over and whispered in Russell Harley's ear. The youth nodded glumly, then shrugged.

Gimbel said, "I understand the attorneys for both sides have waived jury trial in this case of Henry Jenkins versus Russell Joseph Harley."

Both lawyers nodded. Gimbel continued, "In view of the unusual nature of this case, I imagine it will prove necessary to conduct it with a certain amount of informality. The sole purpose of this court is to arrive at the true facts at issue, and to deliver a verdict in accord with the laws pertaining to these facts. I will not stand on ceremony. Nevertheless, I will not tolerate any disturbances or unnecessary irregularities. The spectators will kindly remember that they are here on privilege. Any demonstration will result in the clearing of the court."

He looked severely at the white faces that gleamed unintelligently up at him. He suppressed a sigh as he said, "The counsel for the plaintiff will begin."

Turnbull rose quickly to his feet, faced the judge.

"Your honor," he said, "we propose to show that my client, Henry Jenkins, has been deprived of his just rights by the defendant. Mr. Jenkins, by virtue of a sustained residence of more than twenty years in the house located on Route 22, eight miles north of the town of Rebel Butte, with the full knowledge of its legal owner, has acquired certain rights. In legal terminology we define these as the rights of adverse possession. The laymen would call them common-law rights—squatters' rights."

Gimbel folded his hands and tried to relax. Squatters' rights—for a ghost! He sighed, but listened attentively as Turnbull went on.

"Upon the death of Zebulon Harley, the owner of the house involved—it is better known, perhaps, as Harley Hall—the defendant inherited title to the property. We do not question his right to it. But my client has an equity in Harley Hall; the right to free and full occupation of it for the duration of his existence. The defendant has forcefully evicted my client, by means which have caused my client great mental distress, and have even endangered his very existence."

Gimbel nodded. If the case only had a precedent somewhere. . . . But it hadn't; he remembered grimly the hours he'd spent thumbing through all sorts of unlikely law books, looking for anything that might bear on the case. It had been his better judgment that he throw the case out of court outright—a judge couldn't afford to have himself laughed at, not if he were ambitious. And public laughter was about the only

certainty there was to this case. But Wilson had put up such a fight that the judge's temper had taken over. He never did like Wilson, anyhow.

"You may proceed with your witnesses," he said.

Turnbull nodded. To the clerk he said, "Call Henry Jenkins to the stand."

Wilson was on his feet before the clerk opened his mouth.

"Objection!" he bellowed. "The so-called Henry Jenkins cannot qualify as a witness!"

"Why not?" demanded Turnbull.

"Because he's dead!"

The judge clutched his gavel with one hand, forehead with the other. He banged on the desk to quiet the courtroom.

Turnbull stood there, smiling. "Naturally," he said, "you'll have proof of that statement."

Wilson snarled. "Certainly." He referred to his brief. "The so-called Henry Jenkins is the ghost, spirit, or specter of one Hank Jenkins, who prospected for gold in this territory a century ago. He was killed by a bullet through the throat from the gun of one Long Tom Cooper, and was declared legally dead on September 14, 1850. Cooper was hanged for his murder. No matter what hocus-pocus you produce for evidence to the contrary now, that status of legal death remains completely valid."

"What evidence have you of the identity of my client with this Hank Jenkins?" Turnbull asked grimly.

"Do you deny it?"

Turnbull shrugged. "I deny nothing. I'm not being cross-examined. Furthermore, the sole prerequisite of a witness is that he understand the value of an oath. Henry Jenkins was tested by John Quincy Fitzjames, professor of psychology at the University of Southern California. The results—I have Dr. Fitzjames' sworn statement of them here, which I will introduce as an exhibit—show clearly that my client's intelligence quotient is well above normal, and that a psychiatric examination discloses no important aberrations which would injure his validity as a witness. I insist that my client be allowed to testify on his own behalf."

"But he's dead!" squawked Wilson. "He's invisible right now!"

"My client," said Turnbull stiffly, "is not present just now. Undoubtedly that accounts for what you term his invisibility."

He paused for the appreciative murmur that swept through the court. Things were breaking perfectly, he thought, smiling. "I have here another affidavit," he said. "It is signed by Elihu James and Terence MacRae, who respectively head the departments of physics and biology at the same university. It states that my client exhibits all the vital phenomena of life. I am prepared to call all three of my expert witnesses to the stand, if necessary."

Wilson scowled but said nothing. Judge Gimbel leaned forward.

"I don't see how it is possible for me to refuse the plaintiff the right to testify," he said. "If the three experts who prepared these reports will testify on the stand to the facts contained in them, Henry Jenkins may then take the stand."

Wilson sat down heavily. The three experts spoke briefly—and dryly. Wilson put them through only the most formal of cross-examinations.

The judge declared a brief recess. In the corridor outside, Wilson and his client lit cigarettes, and looked unsympathetically at each other.

"I feel like a fool," said Russell Harley. "Bringing suit against a ghost."

"The ghost brought the suit," Wilson reminded him. "If only we'd been able to hold fire for a couple more weeks, till another judge came on the bench, I could've got this thing thrown right out of court."

"Well, why couldn't we wait?"

"Because you were in such a damn hurry!" Wilson said. "You and that idiot Nicholls—so confident that it would never come to trial."

Harley shrugged, and thought unhappily of their failure in completely exorcising the ghost of Hank Jenkins. That had been a mess. Jenkins had somehow escaped from the charmed circle they'd drawn around him, in which they'd hoped to keep him till the trial was forfeited by nonappearance.

"That's another thing," said Wilson. "Where is Nicholls?"

Harley shrugged again. "I dunno. The last I saw of him was in your office. He came around to see me right after the deputy slapped the showcause order on me at the house. He brought me down to you—said you'd been recommended to him. Then you and him and I talked about the case for a while. He went out, after he lent me a little money to help meet your retainer. Haven't seen him since."

"I'd like to know who recommended me to him," Wilson said grimly. "I don't think he'd ever recommend anybody else. I don't like this case—and I don't much like you."

Harley growled but said nothing. He flung his cigarette away. It tasted of the garbage that hung around his neck—everything did. Nicholls had told no lies when he said Harley wouldn't much like the bundle of herbs that would ward off the ghost of old Jenkins. They smelled.

The court clerk was in the corridor, bawling something, and people were beginning to trickle back in. Harley and his attorney went with them.

When the trial had been resumed, the clerk said, "Henry Jenkins!"

Turnbull was on his feet at once. He opened the door of the judge's chamber, said something in a low tone. Then he stepped back, as if to let someone through.

Pat, HISS. Pat. HISS—

There was a concerted gasp from the spectators as the weirdly appearing trickle of blood moved slowly across the open space to the witness chair. This was the ghost—the plaintiff in the most eminently absurd case in the history of jurisprudence.

"All right, Hank," Turnbull whispered. "You'll have to materialize long enough to let the clerk swear you in."

The clerk drew back nervously at the pillar of milky fog that appeared before him, vaguely humanoid in shape. A phantom hand, half transparent, reached out to touch the Bible. The clerk's voice shook as he administered the oath, and heard the response come from the heart of the cloud-pillar.

The haze drifted into the witness chair, bent curiously at about hip-height, and popped into nothingness.

The judge banged his gavel wildly. The buzz of alarm that had arisen from the spectators died out.

"I'll warn you again," he declared, "that unruliness will not be tolerated. The counsel for the plaintiff may proceed."

Turnbull walked to the witness chair and addressed its emptiness.

"Your name?"

"My name is Henry Jenkins."

"Your occupation?"

There was a slight pause. "I have none. I guess you'd say I'm retired."

"Mr. Jenkins, just what connection have you with the building referred to as Harley Hall?"

"I have occupied it for ninety years."

"During this time, did you come to know the late Zebulon Harley, owner of the Hall?"

"I knew Zeb quite well."

Turnbull nodded. "When did you make his acquaintance?" he asked.

"In the spring of 1907. Zeb had just lost his wife. After that, you see, he made Harley Hall his year-round home. He became—well, more or less of a hermit. Before that we had never met, since he was only seldom at the Hall. But we became friendly then."

"How long did this friendship last?"

"Until he died last fall. I was with him when he died. I still have a few keepsakes he left me then." There was a distinct nostalgic sigh from the witness chair, which by now was liberally spattered with muddy red liquid. The falling drops seemed to hesitate for a second, and their sizzling noise was muted as with a strong emotion.

Turnbull went on, "Your relations with him were good, then?"

"I'd call them excellent," the emptiness replied firmly. "Every night we sat up together.

When we didn't play pinochle or chess or cribbage, we just sat and talked over the news of the day. I still have the book we used to keep records of the chess and pinochle games. Zed made the entries himself, in his own handwriting."

Turnbull abandoned the witness for a moment. He faced the judge with a smile. "I offer in evidence," he said, "the book mentioned. Also a ring given to the plaintiff by the late Mr. Harley, and a copy of the plays of Gilbert and Sullivan. On the flyleaf of this book is inscribed, 'To Old Hank,' in Harley's own hand."

He turned again to the empty, blood-leaking witness chair.

He said, "In all your years of association, did Zebulon Harley ever ask you to leave, or to pay rent?"

"Of course not. Not Zeb!"

Turnbull nodded. "Very good," he said. "Now, just one or two more questions. Will you tell in your own words what occurred, after the death of Zebulon Harley, that caused you to bring this suit?"

"Well, in January young Harley—"

"You mean Russell Joseph Harley, the defendant?"

"Yes. He arrived at Harley Hall on January fifth. I asked him to leave, which he did. On the next day he returned with another man. They placed a talisman upon the threshold of the main entrance, and soon after sealed every threshold and window sill in the Hall with a substance which is noxious to me. These activities were accompanied by several of the most deadly spells in the Ars Magicorum. He further added an Exclusion Circle with a radius of a little over a mile, entirely surrounding the Hall."

"I see," the lawyer said. "Will you explain to the court the effects of these activities?"

"Well," the voice said thoughtfully, "it's a little hard to put in words. I can't pass the Circle without a great expenditure of energy. Even if I did I couldn't enter the building because of the talisman and the seals."

"Could you enter by air? Through a chimney, perhaps?"

"No. The exclusion Circle is really a sphere. I'm pretty sure the effort would destroy me."

"In effect, then, you are entirely barred from the house you have occupied for ninety years, due to the wilful acts of Russell Joseph Harley, the defendant, and an unnamed accomplice of his."

"That is correct."

Turnbull beamed. "Thank you. That's all."

He turned to Wilson, whose face had been a study in dourness throughout the entire examination. "Your witness," he said.

Wilson snapped to his feet and strode to the witness chair.

He said belligerently, "You say your name is Henry Jenkins?"

"Yes."

"That is your name now, you mean to say. What was your name before?"

"Before?" There was surprise in the voice that emanated from above the trickling blood-drops. "Before when?"

Wilson scowled. "Don't pretend ignorance," he said sharply. "Before you *died*, of course."

"Objection!" Turnbull was on his feet, glaring at Wilson. "The counsel for the defense has no right to speak of some hypothetical death of my client!"

Gimbel raised a hand wearily and cut off the words that were forming on Wilson's lips. "Objection sustained," he said. "No evidence has been presented to identify the plaintiff as the prospector who was killed in 1850—or anyone else."

Wilson's mouth twisted into a sour grimace. He continued on a lower key.

"You say, Mr. Jenkins, that you occupied Harley Hall for ninety years."

"Ninety-two years next month. The Hall wasn't built—in its present form, anyhow—until 1876, but I occupied the house that stood on the site previously."

"What did you do before then?"

"Before then?" The voice paused, then said doubtfully, "I don't remember."

"You're under oath!" Wilson flared.

The voice got firmer. "Ninety years is a long time," it said. "I don't remember."

"Let's see if I can't refresh your memory. Is it true that ninety-one years ago, in the very year in which you claim to have begun your occupancy of Harley Hall, Hank Jenkins was killed in a gun duel?"

"That may be true, if you say so. I don't remember."

"Do you remember that the shooting occurred not fifty feet from the present site of Harley Hall?"

"It may be."

"Well, then," Wilson thundered, "is it not a fact that when Hank Jenkins died by violence his ghost assumed existence? That it was then doomed to haunt the site of its slaying throughout eternity?"

The voice said evenly, "I have no knowledge of that."

"Do you deny that it is well known throughout that section that the ghost of Hank Jenkins haunts Harley Hall?"

"Objection!" shouted Turnbull. "Popular opinion is not evidence."

"Objection sustained. Strike the question from the record."

Wilson, badgered, lost his control. In a dangerously uneven voice, he said, "Perjury is a criminal offense. Mr. Jenkins, do you deny that you are the ghost of Hank Jenkins?"

The tone was surprised. "Why, certainly."

"You *are* a ghost, aren't you?"

Stiffly, "I'm an entity on the astral plane."

"That, I believe, is what is called a ghost?"

"I can't help what it's called. I've heard you called a lot of things. Is that proof?"

There was a surge of laughter from the audience. Gimbel slammed his gavel down on the bench.

"The witness," he said, "will confine himself to answering questions."

Wilson bellowed, "In spite of what you say, it's true, isn't it, that you are merely the spirit of a human being who had died through violence?"

The voice from above the blood drops retorted. "I repeat that I am an entity of the astral plane. I am not aware that I was ever a human being."

The lawyer turned an exasperated face to the bench.

"Your honor," he said, "I ask that you instruct the witness to cease playing verbal hide-and-seek. It is quite evident that the witness is a ghost, and that he is therefore the relict of some human being, ipso facto. Circumstantial evidence is strong that he is the ghost of the Hank Jenkins who was killed in 1850. But this is a non-essential point. What is definite is that he is the ghost of someone who is dead, and hence is unqualified to act as witness! I demand his testimony be stricken from the record!"

Turnbull spoke up at once. "Will the counsel for the defense quote his authority for branding my client a ghost—in the face of my client's repeated declaration that he is an entity of the astral plane? What is the legal definition of a ghost?"

Judge Gimbel smiled. "Counsel for the defense will proceed with the cross-examination," he said.

Wilson's face flushed dark purple. He mopped his brow with a large bandanna, then glared at the dropping, sizzling trickle of blood.

"Whatever you are," he said, "answer me this question. Can you pass through a wall?"

"Why, yes. Certainly." There was a definite note of surprise in the voice from nowhere. "But it isn't as easy as some people think. It definitely requires a lot of effort."

"Never mind that. You can do it?"

"Yes."

"Could you be bound by any physical means? Would handcuffs hold you? Or ropes, chains, prison walls, a hermetically sealed steel chest?"

Jenkins had no chance to answer. Turnbull, scenting danger, cut in hastily. "I object to this line of questioning. It is entirely irrelevant."

"On the contrary," Wilson cried loudly, "it bears strongly on the qualifications of the so-called Henry Jenkins as a witness! I demand that he answer the question."

Judge Gimbel said, "Objection overruled. Witness will answer the question."

The voice from the air said superciliously, "I don't mind answering. Physical barriers mean nothing to me, by and large."

The counsel for the defense drew himself up triumphantly.

"Very good," he said with satisfaction. "*Very* good." Then to the judge, the words coming sharp and fast, "I claim, your honor, that the so-called Henry Jenkins has no legal status as a witness in court. There is clearly no value in understanding the nature of an oath if a violation of the oath can bring no punishment in its wake. The statements of a man who can perjure himself freely have no worth. I demand they be stricken from the record!"

Turnbull was at the judge's bench in two strides.

"I had anticipated that, your honor," he said quickly. "From the very nature of the case, however, it is clear that my client can be very definitely restricted in his movements—spells, pentagrams, talismans, amulets, Exclusion Circles, and what-not. I have here—which I am prepared to deliver to the bailiff of the court—a list of the various methods of confining an astral entity to a restricted area for periods ranging from a few moments to all eternity. Moreover, I have also signed a bond for five thousand dollars, prior to the beginning of the trial, which I stand ready to forfeit should my client be confined and make his escape, if found guilty of any misfeasance as a witness."

Gimbel's face, which had looked startled for a second, slowly cleared. He nodded. "The court is satisfied with the statement of the counsel for the plaintiff," he declared. "There seems no doubt that the plaintiff can be penalized for any misstatements, and the motion of the defense is denied."

Wilson looked choleric, but shrugged. "All right," he said. "That will be all."

"You may step down, Mr. Jenkins," Gimbel directed, and watched in fascination as the blood-dripping column rose and floated over the floor, along the corridor, out the door.

Turnbull approached the judge's bench again. He said, "I would like to place in evidence these notes, the diary of the late Zebulon Harley. It was presented to my client by Harley himself last fall. I call particular attention to the entry for April sixth, 1917, in which he mentions the entrance of the United States into the First World War, and records the results of a series of eleven pinochle games played with a personage identified as 'Old Hank.' With the court's permission, I will read the entry for that day, and also various other entries for the next four years. Please note the references to someone known variously as 'Jenkins,' 'Hank Jenkins,' and—in one extremely significant passage—'Old Invisible.'"

Wilson stewed silently during the slow reading of Harley's diary. There was anger on his face, but he paid close attention, and when the reading was over he leaped to his feet.

"I would like to know," he asked, "if the counsel for the plaintiff is in possession of any diaries *after* 1920?"

Turnbull shook his head. "Harley apparently never kept a diary, except during the four years represented in this."

"Then I demand that the court refuse to admit this diary as evidence on two counts," Wilson said. He raised two fingers to tick off the points. "In the first place, the evidence presented is frivolous. The few vague and unsatisfactory references to Jenkins nowhere specifically describe him as what he is—ghost, astral entity, or what you will. Second, the evidence, even were the first point overlooked, concerns only the years up to 1921. The case concerns itself only with the supposed occupation of Harley Hall by the so-called Jenkins in the last twenty years—*since* '21. Clearly, the evidence is therefore irrelevant."

Gimbel looked at Turnbull, who smiled calmly.

"The reference to 'Old Invisible' is far from vague," he said. "It is a definite indication of the astral character of my client. Furthermore, evidence as to the friendship of my client with the late Mr. Zebulon Harley before 1921 is entirely relevant, as such a friendship, once established, would naturally be presumed to have continued indefinitely. Unless of course, the defense is able to present evidence to the contrary."

Judge Gimbel said, "The diary is admitted as evidence."

Turnbull said, "I rest my case."

There was a buzz of conversation in the courtroom while the judge looked over the diary, and then handed it to the clerk to be marked and entered.

Gimbel said, "The defense may open its case."

Wilson rose. To the clerk he said, "Russell Joseph Harley."

But young Harley was recalcitrant. "Nix," he said, on his feet, pointing at the witness chair. "That thing's got blood all over it! You don't expect me to sit down in that large puddle of blood, do you?"

Judge Gimbel leaned over to look at the chair. The drip-drop trickle of blood from the apparition who'd been testifying had left its mark. Muddy brown all down the front of the chair. Gimbel found himself wondering how the ghost managed to replenish its supply of the fluid, but gave it up.

"I see your point," he said. "Well, it's getting a bit late anyhow. The clerk will take away the present witness chair and replace it. In the interim, I declare the court recessed till tomorrow morning at ten o'clock."

III

Russell Harley noticed how the elevator boy's back registered repulsion and disapproval, and scowled. He was not a popular guest in the hotel, he knew well. Where he made his mistake, though, was in thinking that the noxious bundle of herbs about his neck was the cause of it. His odious personality had a lot to do with the chilly attitude of the management and his fellow guests.

He made his way to the bar, ignoring the heads that turned in surprise to follow the reeking comet-tail of his passage. He entered the red-leather-and-chromium drinking room, and stared about for Lawyer Wilson.

And blinked in surprise when he saw him. Wilson wasn't alone. In the booth with him was a tall, dark figure, with his back to Harley. The back alone was plenty of recognition. Nicholls!

Wilson had seen him. "Hello, Harley," he said, all smiles and affability in the presence of the man with the money. "Come on and sit down. Mr. Nicholls dropped in on me a little while ago, so I brought him over."

"Hello," Harley said glumly, and Nicholls nodded. The muscles of his cheeks pulsed, and he seemed under a strain, strangely uncomfortable in Harley's presence. Still there was a twinkle in the look he gave young Harley, and his voice was friendly enough—though supercilious—as he said:

"Hello, Harley. How is the trial going?"

"Ask him," said Harley, pointing a thumb at Wilson as he slid his knees under the booth's table and sat down. "He's the lawyer. He's supposed to know these things."

"Doesn't he?"

Harley shrugged and craned his neck for the waitress. "Oh, I guess so. . . . Rye and water!" He watched the girl appreciatively as she nodded and went off to the bar, then turned his attention back to Nicholls. "The trouble is," he said, "Wilson may think he knows, but I think he's all wet."

Wilson frowned. "Do you imply—" he began, but Nicholls put up a hand.

"Let's not bicker," said Nicholls. "Suppose you answer my question. I have a stake in this, and I want to know. How's the trial going?"

Wilson put on his most open-faced expression. "Frankly," he said, "not too well. I'm afraid

the judge is on the other side. If you listened to me and stalled till another judge came along—"

"I had no time to stall," said Nicholls. "I have to be elsewhere within a few days. Even now, I should be on my way. Do you think we might lose the case?"

Harley laughed sharply. As Wilson glared at him he took his drink from the waitress' tray and swallowed it. The smile remained on his face as he listened to Wilson say smoothly:

"There is a good deal of danger, yes."

"Hum." Nicholls looked interestedly at his fingernails. "Perhaps I chose the wrong lawyer."

"Sure you did." Harley waved at the waitress, ordered another drink. "You want to know what else I think? I think you picked the wrong client; spelled s-t-o-o-g-e. I'm getting sick of this. This damn thing around my neck smells bad. How do I know it's any good, anyhow? Far as I can see, it just smells bad and that's all."

"It works." Nicholls said succinctly. "I wouldn't advise you to go without it. The late Hank Jenkins is not a very strong ghost—a strong one would tear you apart and chew up your herbs for dessert—but without the protection of what you wear about your neck, you would become a very uncomfortable human as soon as Jenkins heard you'd stopped wearing it."

He put down the glass of red wine he'd been inhaling without drinking, looked intently at Wilson. "I've put the money on this," he said. "I had hoped you'd be able to handle the legal end. I see I'll have to do more. Now listen intently because I have no intention of repeating this. There's an angle to this case that's got right by your blunted legal acumen. Jenkins claims to be an astral entity, which he undoubtedly is. Now, instead of trying to prove him a ghost, and legally dead, and therefore unfit to testify, which you should have been doing, suppose you do this. . . ."

He went on to speak rapidly and to the point.

And when he left them a bit later, and Wilson took Harley up to his room and poured him into bed, the lawyer felt happy for the first time in days.

Russell Joseph Harley, a little hung over and a lot nervous, was called to the stand as first witness in his own behalf.

Wilson said, "Your name?"

"Russell Joseph Harley."

"You are the nephew of the late Zebulon Harley, who bequeathed the residence known as Harley Hall to you?"

"Yes."

Wilson turned to the bench. "I offer this copy of the late Mr. Zebulon Harley will in evidence. All his possessions are left to his nephew and only living kin, the defendant."

Turnbull spoke from his desk. "The plaintiff in no way disputes the defendant's equity in Harley Hall."

Wilson continued, "You passed part of your childhood in Harley Hall, did you not, and visited it as a grown man on occasion?"

"Yes."

"At any time, has anything in the shape of a ghost, specter, or astral entity manifested itself to you in Harley Hall?"

"No. I'd remember it."

"Did your late uncle ever mention any such manifestation to you?"

"Him? No."

"That's all."

Turnbull came up for the cross-examination. "When, Mr. Harley, did you last see your uncle before his death?"

"It was in 1938. In September, some time—around the tenth or eleventh of the month."

"How long a time did you spend with him?"

Harley flushed unaccountably. "Ah—just one day," he said.

"When before that did you see him?"

"Well, not since I was quite young. My parents moved to Pennsylvania in 1920."

"And since then—except for that one-day visit in 1938—has any communication passed between your uncle and yourself?"

"No, I guess not. He was a rather queer duck—solitary. A little bit balmy, I think."

"Well, you're a loving nephew. But in view of what you've just said, does it sound surprising that your uncle never told you of Mr. Jenkins? He never had much chance to, did he?"

"He had a chance in 1938, but he didn't," Harley said defiantly.

Turnbull shrugged. "I'm finished," he said.

Gimbel began to look bored. He had anticipated something more in the way of fireworks. He said, "Has the defense any further witnesses?"

Wilson smiled grimly. "Yes, your honor," he said. This was his big moment, and he smiled again as he said gently, "I would like to call Mr. Henry Jenkins to the stand."

In the amazed silence that followed, Judge Gimbel leaned forward. "You mean you wish to call the plaintiff as a witness for the defense?"

Serenely, "Yes, your honor."

Gimbel grimaced. "Call Henry Jenkins," he said wearily to the clerk, and sank back in his chair.

Turnbull was looking alarmed. He bit his lip, trying to decide whether to object to this astonishing procedure, but finally shrugged as the clerk bawled out the ghost's name.

Turnbull sped down the corridor, out the door. His voice was heard in the anteroom, then he returned more slowly. Behind him came the trickle of blood drops; *Pat. HISS. Pat. HISS—*

"One moment," said Gimbel, coming to life again. "I have no objection to your testifying, Mr. Jenkins, but the State should not be subjected to the needless expense of reupholstering its witness chair every time you do. Bailiff, find some sort of a rug or something to throw over the chair before Mr. Jenkins is sworn in."

A tarpaulin was hurriedly procured and adjusted to the chair; Jenkins materialized long enough to be sworn in, then sat.

Wilson began in an amiable enough tone.

"Tell me, Mr. Jenkins," he said, "just how many 'astral entities'—I believe that is what you call yourself—are there?"

"I have no way of knowing. Many billions."

"As many, in other words, as there have been human beings to die by violence?"

Turnbull rose to his feet in sudden agitation, but the ghost neatly evaded the trap. "I don't know. I only know there are billions."

The lawyer's cat-who-ate-canary smile remained undimmed. "And all these billions are constantly about us, everywhere, only remaining invisible. Is that it?"

"Oh, no. Very few remain on Earth. Of those, still fewer have anything to do with humans. Most humans are quite boring to us."

"Well, how many would you say are on Earth? A hundred thousand?"

"Even more, maybe. But that's a good guess."

Turnbull interrupted suddenly. "I would like to know the significance of these questions. I object to this whole line of questioning as being totally irrelevant."

Wilson was a study in legal dignity. He retorted, "I am trying to elicit some facts of major value, your honor. This may change the entire character of the case. I ask your patience for a moment or two."

"Counsel for the defense may continue," Gimbel said curtly.

Wilson showed his canines in a grin. He continued to the blood-dripping before him. "Now, the contention of your counsel is that the late Mr. Harley allowed an 'astral entity' to occupy his home for twenty years or more, with his full knowledge and consent. That strikes me as being entirely improbable, but shall we for the moment assume it to be the case?"

"Certainly! It's the truth."

"Then tell me, Mr. Jenkins, have you fingers?"

"Have I—what?"

"You heard me!" Wilson snapped. "Have you fingers, flesh-and-blood fingers, capable of making an imprint?"

"Why, no. I—"

Wilson rushed on. "Or have you a photograph of yourself—or specimens of your handwriting—or any sort of material identification? Have you any of these?"

The voice was definitely querulous. "What do you mean?"

Wilson's voice became harsh, menacing. "I mean, can you prove that *you* are the astral entity alleged to have occupied Zebulon Harley's home. Was it you—or was it another of the featureless, faceless, intangible unknowns—one of the hundreds of thousands of them that, by your own admission, are all over the face of the earth, rambling where they choose, not halted by any locks or bars? Can you prove that *you* are anyone in particular?"

"Your honor!" Turnbull's voice was almost a shriek as he found his feet at last. "My client's identity was never in question!"

"It is now!" roared Wilson. "The opposing counsel has presented a personage whom he styles 'Henry Jenkins.' Who is this Jenkins? What is he? Is he even an individual—or a corporate aggregation of these mysterious 'astral entities' which we are to believe are everywhere, but which we never see? If he is an individual, is he *the* individual? And how can we know that even if he says he is? Let him produce evidence—photographs, a birth certificate, fingerprints. Let him bring in identifying witnesses who have known both ghosts, and are prepared to swear that these ghosts are the same ghost. Failing this, there is no case! Your honor, I demand the court declare an immediate judgment in favor of the defendant!"

Judge Gimbel stared at Turnbull. "Have you anything to say?" he asked. "The argument of the defense would seem to have every merit with it. Unless you can produce some sort of evidence as to the identity of your client, I have no alternative but to find for the defense."

For a moment there was a silent tableau. Wilson triumphant, Turnbull furiously frustrated.

How could you identify a ghost?

And then came the quietly amused voice from the witness chair.

"This thing has gone far enough," it said above the sizzle and splatter of its own leaking blood. "I believe I can present proof that will satisfy the court."

Wilson's face fell with express-elevator speed. Turnbull held his breath, afraid to hope.

Judge Gimbel said, "You are under oath. Proceed."

There was no other sound in the courtroom as the voice said, "Mr. Harley, here, spoke of a visit to his uncle in 1938. I can vouch for that. They spent a night and a day together. They weren't alone. I was there."

No one was watching Russell Harley, or they might have seen the sudden sick pallor that passed over his face.

The voice, relentless, went on, "Perhaps I shouldn't have eavesdropped as I did, but old Zeb never had any secrets from me anyhow. I listened to what they talked about. Young Harley was working for a bank in Philadelphia at the time. His first big job. He needed money, and needed it bad. There was a shortage in his department. A woman named Sally—"

"Hold on!" Wilson yelled. "This has nothing to do with your identification of yourself. Keep to the point!"

But Turnbull had begun to comprehend. He was shouting too, almost too excited to be coherent. "Your honor, my client must be allowed to speak. If he shows knowledge of an intimate conversation between the late Mr. Harley and defendant, it would be certain proof that he enjoyed the late Mr. Harley's confidence, and thus, Q.E.D., that he is no other than the astral entity who occupied Harley Hall for so long!"

Gimbel nodded sharply. "Let me remind counsel for defense that this is his own witness. Mr. Jenkins, continue."

The voice began again. "As I was saying, the woman's name—"

"Shut up, damn you!" Harley yelled. He sprang upright, turned beseechingly toward the judge. "He's twisting it! Make him stop! Sure, I knew my uncle had a ghost. He's it, all right, curse his black soul! He can have the house if he wants it—I'll clear out. I'll clear out of the whole damned state!" He broke off into babbling and turned about wildly. Only the intervention of a marshal kept him from hurtling out of the courtroom.

Banging of the gavel and hard work by the court clerk and his staff restored order in the courtroom. When the room had returned almost to normalcy, Judge Gimbel, perspiring and annoyed, said, "As far as I am concerned, identification of the witness is complete. Has the defense any further evidence to present?"

Wilson shrugged morosely. "No, your honor."

"Counsel for the plaintiff?"

"Nothing, your honor. I rest my case."

Gimbel plowed a hand through his sparse hair and blinked. "In that case," he said, "I find for the plaintiff. An order is entered hereby that the defendant, Russell Joseph Harley, shall remove from the premises of Harley Hall all spells, pentagrams, talismans, and other means of exorcism employed; that he shall cease and desist from making any attempts, of whatever nature, to evict the tenant in the future; and that Henry Jenkins, the plaintiff, shall be permitted the full use and occupancy of the premises designated as Harley Hall for the full term of his natural—ah—existence."

The gavel banged. "The case is closed."

"Don't take it so hard," said a mild voice behind Russell Harley. He whirled surlily. Nicholls was coming up the street after him from the courthouse, Wilson in tow.

Nicholls said, "You lost the case, but you've still got your life. Let me buy you a drink. In here, perhaps."

He herded them into a cocktail lounge, sat them down before they had a chance to object. He glanced at his expensive wrist watch. "I have a few minutes," he said. "Then I really must be off. It's urgent."

He hailed a barman, ordered for all. Then he looked at young Harley and smiled broadly as he dropped a bill on the counter to pay for the drinks.

"Harley," he said, "I have a motto that you would do well to remember at times like these. I'll make you a present of it, if you like."

"What is it?"

"The worst is yet to come."

Harley snarled and swallowed his drink without replying. Wilson said, "What gets me is why didn't they come to us before the trial with that stuff about this charmingly illicit client you wished on me? We'd have had to settle out of court."

Nicholls shrugged. "They had their reasons," he said. "After all one case of exorcism, more or less, doesn't matter. But lawsuits set precedents. You're a lawyer, of sorts, Wilson; do you see what I mean?"

"Precedents?" Wilson looked at him slackjawed for a moment; then his eyes widened.

"I see you understand me." Nicholls nodded. "From now on in this state—and by virtue of the full-faith-and-credence clause of the Constitution, in *every* state of the country—a ghost has a legal right to haunt a house!"

"Good Lord!" said Wilson. He began to laugh, not loud, but from the bottom of his chest.

Harley stared at Nicholls. "Once and for all," he whispered, "tell me—what's your angle on all this?"

Nicholls smiled again.

"Think about it awhile," he said lightly. "You'll begin to understand." He sniffed his wine once more, then sat the glass down gently—

And vanished.

Albert E. Cowdrey

IN WHAT MUST BE a nearly unprecedented display of loyalty (unless there is a darker explanation), all of Albert E(dward) Cowdrey's (1933–) more than forty short stories have been published exclusively in *The Magazine of Fantasy and Science Fiction*. The first, "The Lucky People," appeared in the February 1968 issue under the pseudonym Chet Arthur.

Born in New Orleans, Cowdrey received his B.A. from Tulane University, then an M.A. from Johns Hopkins University. He served in the U.S. Army from 1957 to 1959, then in the Army Reserves from 1960 to 1963. He has written numerous histories of the army, including *The Delta Engineers: A History of the United States Army Corps of Engineers in the New Orleans District* (1971), *A City for the Nation: The Army Engineers and the Building of Washington, D.C., 1790–1967* (1979), and *Fighting for Life: American Military Medicine in World War II* (1994). His first published book was *Elixir of Life* (1965), a historical novel set in New Orleans. His single science fiction novel, *Crux* (2004), tells of the resettling on space colonies by Earth's survivors in the twenty-fifth century after the devastating wars of the twenty-first century in which twelve billion people died. Cowdrey's novella "Queen for a Day," which appeared in the October/November 2001 issue of *The Magazine of Fantasy and Science Fiction*, won the World Fantasy Award for Best Short Story.

"Death Must Die" was originally published in the November/December 2010 issue of *The Magazine of Fantasy and Science Fiction*.

Death Must Die*

ALBERT E. COWDREY

ON A DULL NOVEMBER DAY, I was seated in the office of my firm—Martin & Martin, Psychic Investigators—gazing at the dark, brooding sky beyond the window, when the door opened and a client entered.

He wore a three-piece charcoal suit and carried a briefcase for which an alligator had paid the highest possible price. His card identified him as Stephen Preston James, attorney at law, with offices in Greenwood Falls, Virginia. I like clients whose friends include the Brothers Brooks, and waved him to my most comfortable chair.

"I bet you run seven miles every morning," I said, noting his lean bronzed face and fleshless form.

"Bicycle. Less stress on the knee cartilage. And it's more like ten."

"Wow," I marveled. "I have a stationary bike in my bathroom, but I just hang towels on it. So why do you need a Psychic Investigator?"

"Look, I don't believe in spirits," he said defiantly.

"Generally speaking, that's wise. I spend a lot of time telling people they're not living in Amityville, the problem's just squirrels in the attic. I give a lot of business to Animal Control."

"Well," he said, "I don't live in Amityville, but I *do* live at 419 Merritt Street."

"Ah," said I with quickening interest. "I begin to understand."

He nodded glumly. "I see you know about the house. In fact, it turns out everybody in this goddamn burg knew about it but Alsatia and me."

"Alsatia?"

"Wife," he said, handing me a gold-initialed cowskin folder with pictures of a woman and kids in it. They looked exactly like everybody else's wife and kids.

"Nice family," I said tactfully, handing it back.

"Thank you. It's the kids I'm worried about. They haven't yet seen the, uh—the, uh—" He choked on the word *ghost*, so I gave him a hand.

"The manifestation," I suggested, and he looked relieved.

"Exactly. The manifestation. And I'd rather they didn't. So far it's only showed up around midnight, when they're in bed, but who knows what's next. Any chance you can get rid of it?"

"I can but try. I charge fifty dollars an hour," I added, expecting and receiving a glance of contempt. Stephen Preston James probably charged two-fifty at least.

"That's high," he lied, "but there seems to be remarkably few people in your profession, despite all the stuff I see about ghost hunters on TV. So I suppose I'm stuck."

*By George Martin, P.I., in *Journal of Psychical Research*, Vol. XCII, No. 2. Reprinted by permission.

I gave him a copy of my standard contract. He read every word twice, then opened the alligator, took out a checkbook, and paid my minimum (eight hours). I asked if tonight would be a convenient time for me to check out the manifestation, and he said well, not tonight—he and Alsatia were giving a wine and cheese party for a group of clients.

"It's not work I particularly want," he added. "No real money in it, but it would be great publicity if the case went to the Supreme Court."

"Who are you representing?"

"A bunch called Death Must Die. They're trying to get the death penalty declared cruel and unusual punishment. Back in '76 the justices decided it was, then later they reversed themselves and decided it wasn't."

"You're attorney for an anti-death-penalty group?"

"Right. So maybe you'd better come tomorrow night instead."

Politely I showed him to the door, all the time thinking, *Wow, will Wellington Meeks be pissed!*

Living all my life in Greenwood Falls, I've had plenty of time to check out its reputed spooks. Most have the serious defect of being nonexistent, but a few have proved to be what I call Nonpersons of Interest. I still keep an eye on them.

There's Lizzie M'Luhan (deceased 1907), whose love for a local butcher named Gavrilo Princip ended in tragedy when his jealous wife used a cleaver to divide Lizzie more or less in two. A multilevel parking garage now sprawls over the site of the shop amid whose tripe trays and hanging hams Lizzie and Gavrilo once reveled in the throes of fornication. If you're lucky you can spot her on Level A after midnight, her bifurcated form flitting among the parked SUVs, searching either for the man she loved or else for sirloin at 1907 prices, who knows which.

Then there's Bennie Marx (deceased 1955). Determined to become the new Houdini at whatever risk, Bennie had some friends shackle

him to the engine block of a retired 2½-ton truck and throw him into the Potomac River. The fact that he was no good at picking padlocks soon became apparent. His wraith is one of the saddest I've ever observed, hovering over the seething currents of Great Falls on moonlit nights and blowing bubbles that burst with the sound of sobs.

And there's Paul Vincent Obol (deceased 1978), an equestrian who loved his mare Fleetfoot not wisely but too well. He was standing on an upended bucket in his stable, jodhpurs at half mast, engaged in an act of interspecies amour, when Fleetfoot—up to then the most docile of animals—had one of those lightning changes of mood so typical of females, and kicked him to death. Nowadays he flits through local riding schools, uttering deep sighs of rejected love.

I could cite other examples, but why bother? The point is that most of our local manifestations are losers who come back only to whine about their unhappy lives. Wellington Meeks is the great exception—a citizen whose life exuded Presbyterian work ethic and solid albeit modest success. In his day suburbs grew around railroad tracks, not highways. When he moved into Greenwood Falls in 1910, its little wooden depot was new and the future burb was mostly lush, rolling countryside populated by meditative cows rather than frenetic Washington go-getters. Meeks built himself a house near the depot for convenience in reaching D.C.'s Union Station, where—he told his housekeeper, a respectable widow who promptly told everyone else—he boarded trains for "business trips" throughout the mid-Atlantic states.

At home he dwelt in bachelor seclusion, tended by the widow, who cleaned and cooked and saw to it that his shirts and detachable collars were always the way he wanted them, stiff with starch and as uncomfortable as possible. Local people found him affable but cool. His next-door neighbor recalled that conversing with him was like playing tennis with an opponent who catches your ball and keeps it, instead of hitting it back. Curiosity about what he did for a living went unrewarded until 1927, when he died of complications following gall-bladder surgery. Then the executor of his will paid a vanity publisher to bring out his memoirs. Wisely, the editor changed the title that Meeks had chosen for his opus ("My Thirty Years of Public Service") to one he would surely have vetoed, had he been in a condition to do so. A man so respectable could hardly have wished to be commemorated by a tome entitled *I, the Hangman.*

Yes, that was the secret of Wellington Meeks—his business trips all had been to penitentiaries that required his services. The new title was sufficiently striking to win the book a modest success, delighting the ladies of the Women's Christian Temperance Union, who received the author's royalties to carry on their noble though hopeless task of drying out America. Decades later, I came across a battered copy of the book in a flea market, and found it (if I may be pardoned a pun) a treasury of totally unconscious gallows humor.

Meeks believed firmly in the necessity of his profession, pointing to some truly atrocious criminals he had dispatched. Yet he acknowledged that most of his victims were simple, uneducated men who had bashed or shot somebody on a momentary impulse, and whose souls were consequently salvageable. He saw himself posted at the gateway between life and death, with a Christian duty to treat the somber ceremony over which he presided with dignity, and those he dispatched with compassion.

"Every public executioner," he wrote, "should have always before his mind the adage *There, but for the grace of God, go I.* After the wrists and ankles of the condemned man have been tied, the black hood put over his head, and the stout noose properly aligned behind his left ear, a murmured word of encouragement— *Tonight, brother, you sleep in Paradise*—a pat on the back, or the simple word 'Courage!' uttered in a firm yet friendly tone, will do much to ease the Great Transition he faces."

The smugness of such passages caused limerick writers throughout the then forty-eight states to reach for their fountain pens or uncover their manual typewriters. As one versifier put it,

Mr. Meeks I greatly admire—
Of hanging he never does tire.
He arranges the drop,
Hears the vertebrae pop,
Then goes home to his seat by the fire.

Meeks apparently began manifesting early in 1933. At any rate, that was when the weekly *Greenwood Falls Standard* started to report strange goings-on at 419, always in the coy jokey way that journalists have of saying, "Just kidding, folks!" There were headlines like *Hangman Still Hanging Around* and *Merritt Street Ghost Anything but Meek.* Bad jokes aside, it soon became clear that a theme ran through the dead man's appearances. He loved the house he'd built and occupied, and when activities happened there that his Puritanical soul disapproved of, he came to scare the current occupants straight.

A lifelong Republican, his early visits resulted from the election of Franklin D. Roosevelt and the repeal of Prohibition. (His appearance during one of the President's Fireside Chats garnered the headline *GOP Ghost Haunts FDR Broadcast.*) Any sign of inebriation, debauchery, or Democracy was guaranteed to bring his greenish ghost out of the netherworld, grimly dangling the noose by which he'd earned his living. *Not the Ghost of a Cocktail for Me, Thanks,* chuckled the *Standard,* and—after Roosevelt crushed Alf Landon in the 1936 election—*Only the Dead Like Alf.*

At one point in the sixties, the house was occupied by four hippies, all devotees of Sex, Drugs, and Rock 'n' Roll. They didn't last long—indeed, one was so shaken by his experience with the ghost that he had to be lobotomized. I'm not sure Meeks ought to be blamed for that, however. Tests showed that the young man had ingested a near-lethal dose of LSD, so maybe that was the cause of his breakdown, and the ghost's appearance merely the trigger.

Other occupants came and went, none staying

for long. And then, beginning in the early eighties, all the manifestations ceased. A spinster schoolteacher, Miss Angela Groening, lived at 419 comfortably for almost twenty years, without ever seeing anything out of the way. She had the house painted, maintained it in perfect condition, and grew prizewinning antique roses in the garden. She was Meeks's kind of tenant, and he wouldn't have dreamed of disturbing her. Since Miss Groening was known to drink one glass of pale sherry every day at six p.m., people speculated that under her benign influence the ghost was, at long last, mellowing out on the subject of Prohibition. Whatever, a whole generation of local people grew up believing that the legends about the house were only that—legends.

By the turn of the millennium, the older houses in our community—once taken by hippies and schoolteachers simply because they couldn't afford anything newer—had become fashionably retro dwellings. They were especially favored by well-to-do, conservative people who scorned the bloated palaces of the *nouveaux riches*, yet wanted the convenience of a Washington suburb with easy access to the Beltway. Stephen Preston James was a perfect example of the breed, and Meeks's midnight manifestations as a glowing face suspended over the booze locker probably were meant only to warn him and Alsatia against taking too many nightcaps.

But what the ghost might do when he found people meeting in his house, swilling liquor, denouncing his profession, and vowing to abolish it forever—well, it's no exaggeration to say that I shuddered to think. Events soon proved that I had plenty to shudder about.

Stephen Preston James had one of those names that work equally well forward and backward, so when he called me early next morning, saying abruptly, "This is James," I recollected his name as James Preston Stevens, and thought he wanted to get on a first-name basis.

"What can I do for you, Jim?" I inquired.

About ten minutes went by before we got this unsnarled, which did nothing to calm his already jangled nerves.

"So," I said when things at last became clear, "I gather Wellington Meeks manifested himself at the meeting of Death Must Die."

"Did he ever! Alsatia was almost hysterical, to say nothing of my clients and, to be perfectly honest, me. God, how I wish there was somebody I could sue."

His wife chose to blame him for the fiasco, and issued a *fatwa*. "She's taking the kids to her mother's in Timonium, Maryland, even though that means we'll be separated at Thanksgiving. I have three months to get rid of 419 and find an unhaunted house, or she'll file for divorce."

"Nasty situation."

"I'd say so. What can I do?"

"I'll be there in twenty minutes. Be prepared to give a full and objective account of last night's proceedings. You may not know this, Jim—"

"Steve."

"Whoever you are. You may not know this, but Meeks in his memoirs boasts of executing over three hundred men and five women in the course of his long, busy career. He's not to be trifled with. I'll need the facts, all the facts, and nothing but the facts."

"You mean I'm going to be deposed."

"Unless we can pacify Meeks, that's not the worst that'll happen to you."

When I arrived at 419 Merritt, a sharp-featured lady I recognized from the photograph was herding two whining children into a white Infiniti, in which they roared away. I entered the house—I'd never actually been inside before—to find Steve sitting in a repro Victorian parlor chair and looking like, as the saying goes, death warmed over.

"And I'm even afraid to take a drink," he complained, after I'd shaken his flaccid hand.

"I've brought a recorder," I said, displaying the palm-sized digital device and pulling up a repro Lincoln rocker to sit on. "Since you're an attorney, I'm sure there's no need to advise you about the protocol."

He nodded and, after a moment's thought, began to speak with professional lucidity, giving his name, the location, date, and time, then launching into the following narrative:

Last night sixteen people, members of the organization Death Must Die, gathered here for an informal conference with wine and cheese. White wines were more popular than red, and the munchies included hothouse grapes, Wafer-Thins, and a wheel of Brie. Thank God, my children were staying the night at friends' houses.

Most members of the group proved to be nice sensible people whose opposition to the death penalty followed traditional lines. Some said the state shouldn't take away a life, since if the individual is later proved innocent, it can't return what it has taken. Others cited the dozens of cases in which DNA evidence has caused condemned men to be released from Death Row. Still others pointed to the bad company in which the United States finds itself—bracketed with Russia, China, Iran, and Saudi Arabia, and separated from most of the civilized world. An African-American gentleman spoke scathingly about the disproportionate number of blacks who have been condemned to death.

Only one lady, a widow named Letitia (Letty) Loos, turned out to be the sort of enthusiast I'd feared might constitute the norm for Death Must Die. In a strident voice she kept repeating that each and every precious human life without a single exception is of infinite value, leading me to wonder if she included such precious lives as that of Adolf Hitler among the infinitely valuable.

None of this had much to do with the legal and constitutional question of what exactly constitutes cruel and unusual punishment, a subject almost as debatable as what constitutes truth or beauty. I had just begun trying to focus the group on the issues that might conceivably get us a hearing before the Supreme Court, when the lamps in the room grew dim. Since I am somewhat given to worst-case scenarios, my first thought was that I had a brain tumor and was going blind. Then several others commented on the phenomenon, causing me to blame the power company instead. It was only when Alsatia said there was smoke in the room that I realized the light wasn't weakening—instead, the air was, so to speak, growing denser.

The darkening continued for several minutes, with increasing dismay among my wife, our guests, and myself. Then, from the shadowy hallway that leads to the bedrooms, appeared—shut off the goddamn recorder!

My client's face had turned the color of fresh spackle. I jumped up, threw open a repro antique cellaret, and—Wellington Meeks or no Wellington Meeks—poured Steve a healthy shot of brandy. He swallowed it too fast, went into a choking fit, had to be pounded on the back, etc. But at last he was restored to a condition closely resembling normal, except for streaming eyes that he wiped with a monogrammed handkerchief.

"Sorry about that," he muttered.

I assured him that his reaction was perfectly normal—indeed, he wouldn't have been normal if he'd failed to have it. "Only psychopaths," I told him, "are truly fearless, and that's only because they're wired wrong."

He nodded, and after a second shot of brandy—this time mixed with soda, and sipped quietly and slowly—he signaled for me to turn the recorder back on. The interview (or as he called it, the deposition) continued as follows:

Out of the darkness emerged a figure more appalling than a mere nightmare—a huge shambling man wearing baggy trousers, a collarless shirt, and a dangling noose.

His hands were like the stumps of small trees, with crooked fingers for roots. His face was a head-sized lump of damp putty with holes where the eyes, nostrils, and mouth ought to have been. His whole form exuded a sickly greenish light, as if luminous bacteria had colonized his flesh. As he approached, two members of Death Must Die thrust themselves violently away, tipping over their chairs, and lay on their backs with legs working spasmodically like those of poisoned roaches, in a hapless imitation of flight.

The horror was not yet complete. The monster began to speak—and in such a voice! I've heard more human sounds emerge from the business end of a concrete mixer. Yet the words were clearly audible, as the thing confessed to a career of gruesome and appalling murders done merely for pleasure, giving details that caused members of the group to clamp their hands over their ears. I tried that too, but it didn't work—his confession distilled within my brain as clearly as ever, all the way to the end. Then the monster lurched to the opposite wall, passed through it, and vanished, only to have its place taken by an elderly woman.

Or rather, hag. She too wore a noose, and her voice reminded me of a malicious child swinging on a gate with rusty hinges, back and forth, back and forth. She had been a nurse running a home for the aged and infirm, whom she murdered one by one with every incident of cruelty—she particularly favored a poison called corrosive sublimate, which I gathered was a household cleanser of times gone by. Her reward? The pathetic belongings of her victims, which often consisted of no more than old clothes and perhaps a cheap ring or two. She ended with such a laugh as I hope never to hear again—a long cackling shriek that caused two wine goblets to shatter.

Finally, when we'd all been reduced more or less to jelly, Meeks himself emerged. He looked a bit like Herbert Hoover—double-breasted suit, stiff high collar, sparse hair slicked down and neatly parted in the middle. He carried his noose instead of wearing it, and headed straight for the widow Letty Loos. Suspending the rope before her face

while she quailed and gibbered, he spoke in a cold, controlled, distant voice, a bit shrill and squeaky like some sort of primitive recording machine. He had a slight Elmer Fudd–ish speech impediment, and what he said shocked me more than anything I'd heard so far.

"I wespect you, madam, for you have murdered your husband. Unlike these other fools, you have good weason to oppose capital punishment, knowing that you too—like the monsters I've just shown you—deserve to die."

So saying, he placed the glowing image of the rope around her neck, and vanished instantly, in perfect silence. The rope dissolved more slowly, like the grin of the Cheshire Cat in Alice in Wonderland, lingering for a long minute or two while Mrs. Loos uttered squeaks and mewlings of dismay. Then she jumped up and fled into the night, followed by the other members of Death Must Die.

"A remarkable document," I said, warmly. "I don't think I've ever heard an account of a manifestation more convincingly put."

"Easy for you to say," Steve replied. His voice was grim. "I'm going to get sued all to hell and gone. Those people will have tame doctors swearing they've been traumatized for life, and what can I say? That ghosts were at fault? I'm going to be divorced and impoverished. And I'll still be living at 419 Merritt, because when this story gets around, nobody in his right mind will buy it."

"Now, now, now," I said, patting his bony shoulder. "You forget that the plaintiffs will be as reluctant as you are to give testimony about what they saw last night. They won't want to look like lunatics either."

"Well . . . yeah," he acknowledged. His face brightened a little.

"And you certainly have nothing to fear from Letty Loos. A mere mention of the ghost's accusation in the media, and voilà! Her husband's case might be reopened."

"Rrrrr . . . ight," he admitted, smiling a crocodilian lawyer's grin, which of itself indicated that he was recovering his nerve.

"Try to avoid drunkenness and blasphemy for a while, and if you must oppose the death penalty, do so only in your office. Meantime I'll strike at Wellington Meeks where he lives."

"Meeks is dead," Steve reminded me.

"So," I informed him, "is the person I intend to send after him."

Alas, that person was not my dad. Though at one time he'd been the senior member of the firm, he had failed to survive death—surely an ironic fate for a talented medium! But dying, like birth, is a major trauma, and you have to be pretty tightly wrapped to go through it in one piece. Dad lacked intense views on most issues, and even when he believed strongly in something (e.g., the hapless Washington Senators) was always ready to flip-flop in the presence of a stronger personality. As a result, the poor fellow delaminated at the hour of death—that is, he dispersed, his elements returning to the Cosmic All.

Fortunately, my mom—who passed over soon after Dad—was made of stronger stuff, and quickly became my favorite Spirit Guide. Back at home, I mixed her a large Old Fashioned, being sure to muddle it with a cinnamon stick, *not* with a spoon. I placed the glass on a little table beside my La-Z-Boy, pulled the curtains to exclude the dull light of the November day, sat down, lolled back, and closed my eyes. I fixed my thoughts upon the last sight I had of Mom—lying in her coffin, a serene smile on her face, her pale hands holding a spray of baby's breath and resurrection fern—and within ten minutes she manifested herself. Not, of course, in the crude, Tales-from-the-Crypt manner of the Hangman. Instead, her well-known voice distilled—a good word that Steve had used in a similar case—inside my brain, with no need to pass through my ears to get there.

"Yes, Honey?" she said. "Problems?"

I explained the situation—only to have her flatly refuse to help.

"Death Must Die," she sneered, "sounds to me like a bunch of cowards. What in the world is wrong with being dead? Anybody with any sense knows it's better than living in one of those horrible prisons."

Tactfully I agreed, adding, "Still, it's rough, Steve and his wife not being able to entertain whoever they please in their own home."

Mom has always been very strong for property rights and the sanctity of the American home, and she responded instantly to my ploy.

"Well, of course you're right there. I remember the first time your dad and I entertained a Negro. He was Dr. Dent from the college, and that night some hooligan threw eggs on our porch. If I'd caught him," she added grimly, "he would have scrubbed that porch on his hands and knees."

"I just bet he would have."

"Using his toothbrush!"

"Would've served him right. So Mom, what can I do about Wellington Meeks? He won't admit that 419 isn't his house any longer, or that the current owners have the right to live their lives in peace."

"I'll ask around," she said. "See if I can locate him. Maybe he just needs a good talking to. What's he look like? I was a little tiny girl when he died, so I've no personal recollection of him."

Briefly I repeated Steve's description, adding, "He's a Prohibitionist."

She snorted. Mom is the only manifestation I've ever heard snort. "He sounds like a real drip," she said. "These old bachelors! I bet he wore one-piece underwear and worried about his bowels. Probably a couch potato, too."

"Mom, I'm an old bachelor. *And* a couch potato."

"You're different," she replied, with true maternal love and irrationality. "I'll see what I can do."

She signed off and I opened my eyes. The Old Fashioned had been consumed, right down to the maraschino cherry. Some spirits like spirits, I reflected. Some don't.

. . .

A week passed. Nobody sued Steve. Another hopeful sign: his mother-in-law in Timonium spoiled her grandchildren rotten and kept interfering with Alsatia's attempts to discipline them. Soon his wife was calling him two or three times a day to complain about her mama. Steve told me he thought she'd be home in a flash, except for her fear that Meeks might manifest himself to the children and scare them into autism.

"That's absurd," I told him. "Meeks has never frightened a child. Actually, being a bachelor, he's probably afraid of *them*."

"Maybe you'd like to explain that to Alsatia."

Cautiously, I said I didn't want to get between a man and his wife. In no place on Earth, save perhaps Afghanistan, is the danger to non-combatants greater. Instead, I assured him that if we could only hold out long enough, Meeks would gradually weaken and lose his power to make trouble.

"You're telling me that ghosts"—this time he used the G-word without a quiver—"are mortal, like the rest of us?"

"Nothing is truly immortal except Nature, and of course God, if there is one. A few ghosts delaminate and all of them, given enough time, fade away."

"How long does the fading take?"

"Depends on the strength of the personality. Sometimes only a few weeks. Sometimes centuries."

"Oh, *great*," he said. *"Centuries."*

He added a string of four-letter words that I considered unworthy of a professional man, not knowing that the time was fast approaching when Meeks would make me lapse into vulgarity myself.

Next day began badly, then got worse. The digital *Standard* showed up on my Hewlett-Packard carrying on Page One an all too circumstantial account of Meeks's last appearance. The article (*Death Protesters Meet the Real Thing*) three times referred to 419 Merritt Street as "the Hangman's House." I could almost feel Steve's real estate agent shudder. About ten o'clock the man himself phoned to add to the quota of bad news. His maid Annunciata had called his office to report that a huckster who did bus tours of Historic Greenwood Falls was at that moment parked across Merritt Street, haranguing his passengers about the ghost.

"I'm filing for an injunction to stop him," said Steve, his voice shaking with anger. He directed some rather harsh remarks at me for failing to solve his problem, but most of his rage was directed at Wellington Meeks.

"Goddamn him," he growled, audibly grinding his teeth, "I'm gonna go home tonight and get sloshed. I'm gonna change my registration from Republican to Democrat. I'm gonna take the anti-death-penalty case pro bono and fight it all the way to the Supreme Court. I'm gonna find Meeks's goddamn grave and piss on it. I—"

Clearly the fellow needed to vent, so I let him. When he quieted down, I warned him that fighting the dead was a fool's game. What could he possibly do to Meeks, compared to what Meeks could do to him? Steve grunted and growled some more, but finally rang off. I hated to hurry Mom, but the situation left me no choice. So I mixed her a drink, returned to the La-Z-Boy, and put in a call. Her voice, when she responded, sounded less confident than I could ever remember it. She'd located Meeks, but found him immovable.

"He's a tough nut," she admitted. "I've known some pigheaded people in my time, but that man takes the cake. I told him, 'Here you've survived death, you've finally got time to relax and enjoy yourself, and what do you do? You waste it scaring people back on Earth.'"

"What did he say?"

"He just got this terribly annoying smug look on his face and said that a pwinciple—as he put it—was at stake. And get this: women don't understand these things. According to him, that's why he never married. He never found a woman who was up to his standards."

"What a shit. Sorry, Mom. The word just slipped out."

"There's a time for everything, dear, including the S-word, and this is as good a time as any. Oh! That *man*."

I'd really expected Mom to handle the Hangman for me, and now felt somewhat at a loss for a strategy. I tossed the notion of exorcism at once. What could more certainly arouse the scorn of a confirmed Presbyterian than the sight of a Catholic priest doing his mumbo-jumbo? As for holding a séance, forget it—the problem with the Hangman was not to make him manifest himself, but to stop him from doing so. I was still wrestling with the problem when, at ten-thirty that evening, the phone rang. The instant I lifted it, I knew that Steve was in trouble—more trouble.

He was drunk, his normally crisp diction gone all mushy. "God, you should shee it," he maundered. "You should *shee* it. God, it'sh *horrible.*"

"Get a grip," I said. "I'll be there in two shakes." (Not, perhaps, the best thing to say to a man so badly shaken.)

When I arrived his porch light was on, but the house was dark. Walking up the neat path of herringbone brick to the front door, I could see through the windows a dim, slowly moving, rather unpleasant greenish glow—the kind of thing that any ten-year-old knows means a haunting, and any adult knows means the luminescence of decay. In this case, I thought while ringing the bell, both would be right.

Steve was in bad shape. The porch light showed his expensive tailored shirt stained with booze. His breath exhaled both the odor of brandy and a sickly undertone suggesting he had recently thrown up. He didn't say anything as he let me in. Didn't have to. Give the devil his due—Wellington Meeks had staged one of the most remarkable manifestations I've ever witnessed.

The whole house seemed to be filled with suspended, gently swaying greenish-yellow corpses. Occasionally one would go through a series of jerky motions that I took to be postmortem muscular spasms. The hoods worn by the hanged men had become partly transpar-

ent, like stocking masks, and behind the veils every eye was wide and bulging, every jaw hanging, every tongue protruding. Ropy drool glued cloth to chin. With great reluctance, I stepped into that chamber of horrors, passed through a body, and heard the loathsome gurgle of its entrails releasing waste—as they must, when the body is suspended and at the mercy of gravity. Fortunately, Meeks's prissiness caused him to omit the appalling smell of the real thing.

"At least," I muttered, "he spared us that."

Then the hanging bodies began to fade—dislimn—evaporate. Five minutes later the room was an ordinary early twentieth-century parlor, filled with the shades not of dead people but of imitation antiques. The lamps returned to life, their beams strengthening until a homey, comfortable radiance dispelled the dark. While Steve collapsed on the sofa and passed out, I went to the cellaret, selected a clean glass, and poured myself the last finger of brandy remaining in a bottle of Rémy Martin. I downed it at a gulp, fetched a blanket from the master bedroom, and spread it over my client's recumbent form. Then, turning off all the lamps but one, I went home to bed. For the life of me, I couldn't think of anything else to do.

Yet, as I lay with the covers drawn up to my chin, a steely resolution took form. I am, after all, my mother's son. I found it simply insufferable that a decent man should have to endure this kind of persecution in his own home.

"Wellington Meeks," I exclaimed aloud, "this time you've gone too far! Prepare to take the consequences!"

Sheer bravado, of course. Yet I slept soundly that night, knowing that this was no longer a merely professional problem. It was a fight, and I was in it to the finish.

Sometimes going to bed is the best medicine. I woke promptly at my usual hour—seven—with a plan of action in mind. Maybe my subconscious is smarter than my waking self, or maybe I'd received inspiration while snoring. Whatever, I felt ready for a warm shower, followed by eggs and coffee, followed by action.

At nine o'clock I was in my recliner, and by nine-twenty Mom had responded to my call. I told her briefly about last night's manifestation, then inquired if she could access certain decedents I wished to talk to.

"If they survived dying, I can find them," she replied confidently. "When and where do you want them?"

"Today, I want them here. Tonight, I'll want them at 419 Merritt Street."

"Fix me a drinky, dear," she replied, "and give me an hour."

By ten-twenty I was back in my chair, the Old Fashioned on the table, the curtains closed. Soon, out of the darkness wavering forms—at first mere sketchy outlines, then fuller and more convincing figures—began to emerge. All were male, which did not surprise me, for Southern chivalry guaranteed that none but the most appalling murderesses were hanged. My guests chose to appear, not in their striped prison uniforms—which they probably were anxious to forget—but in the garments they'd worn as free men. Some wore the battered top hats of chimney sweeps, some the white canvas of painters, some the bib overalls of farmers. Most wore the generic clothing of the working poor, collarless shirts and rough trousers held up by suspenders they probably called galluses. Their faces were strong and bony—the faces of the frontiersmen their grandparents had been. In the darkened room their eyes looked pale, especially those of the blacks who formed at least half the contingent.

"Men," I said aloud, "can you hear me?" There was a general nodding of heads.

"Do I understand that each and every one of you died at the hands of Wellington Meeks?"

A black man spoke up, his voice distilling in the usual fashion inside my head. "Yessuh. Mr. Meeks done done us all, I do believe."

Tight-lipped smiles passed around the group. A white man of particularly craggy appearance said, "That sumbitch. I asked the judge to give me death, but—"

"You *asked* for death?" I interrupted.

"Yes, sir, I did. I shot my own brother in a argyment over cards, when both of us was full of white lightning. I reckoned I deserved to die and the judge, he agreed with me. So there I was, the rope around my neck, all ready to apologize to pore Bubba when I met him on the other side. Only Meeks, instead of pulling the leever and getting it over with, starts giving me this sermon—nasty little voice he's got, too—'bout how I ought to wepent and go to sleep in the arms of Jesus. As if I hadn't just heard aplenty of that guff from the preacher while he was walking me to the gallows!

"I got mad—I mean, hell, the hanging was *my* show, not his—and inside that black hood I raised my voice and told Meeks what he could do to himself and what he could do it with. So he shortened the rope—Goddamn him, I felt him pull on it. And because of that, when he drapped me my neck didn't break, and I danced on air for maybe five minutes before I blacked out."

Suddenly I recalled the twitching and jerking figures in Steve's house last night. Post-mortem spasms? Or the writhing of men that Meeks had deliberately allowed to strangle on the rope? I used to think of the Hangman as a quaint, rather absurd figure, who belonged in the comic pages of the twenties alongside Foxy Grandpa and Tillie the Toiler. Steadily that view had darkened as I watched his persecution of my client. Now I saw him as a sort of devil, all the worse for his smug self-righteousness.

I asked the men to join me later that evening— Mom would show them the way—specifying what they should bring with them. They responded with grim chuckles. I added that, while I couldn't reward them as they deserved, I *could* offer them a drink. The result was a curious sound—a rush and rustle like an autumn wind moving through a field of dying cornstalks. After a moment, I realized it must be applause. Well, they'd been dry a long time, poor fellows.

Next I called Steve, and for a while he seemed likely to miss his own party. In a voice gone all weak and whiny, he told me he was packing up to abandon 419 and stay at a motel. I asked sharply if he was too much of a coward to fight for his home and family. That got him spluttering with rage—a good sign—so I begged his pardon, and after some more palaver we arranged to meet in his house that evening at ten o'clock. He promised he'd try to persuade some members of Death Must Die to attend, though holding out little hope that all would do so, and none that Letty Loos would return to the place where Meeks had outed her.

"Oh, one more thing," I said. "Lay in a good supply of Kentucky straight bourbon. Say five or six liters. Just open the bottles and leave them out."

"I *hate* bourbon," he growled.

"You won't be the one drinking it," I told him, and signed off.

Seldom do I have reason to feel like a soldier. My long-ago military service was spent as a draftee at Fort Jackson, South Carolina, where the bloodthirstiest enemies I encountered were the gnats. My life today is even more quiet and withdrawn than Meeks's, for he at least was always taking little trips here and there to do his dirty work, while I never leave the Old Dominion except to shop or eat an overpriced meal in Georgetown. And yet, as I set out for 419 Merritt that evening, I had the Hemingwayish feelings of a combat soldier—the dry throat, the accelerated and uneven heartbeat, the taste of pennies in my mouth. Fighting a devil, even a little devil, is no laughing matter, though I counted on my allies and felt the justice of our cause.

I found awaiting me eight members of Death Must Die, who'd bravely returned to the house they must have remembered with horror and revulsion. As conversation began, I learned why they'd come. Nobody likes to be terrorized, and Meeks had made these folks very, very angry. Also, given their beliefs on the subject of the death penalty, he'd come across as the personification of everything they were fighting against. So, while half the original membership cravenly stayed home, the stronger half returned to confront their own fears, and the Hangman as well.

I encouraged them to vent their feelings, then took a seat in the Lincoln rocker a few paces back from the group. The discussion began quietly, but as the Chardonnay passed from hand to hand, turned decidedly vigorous. They were like battered women who find in a support group the courage to denounce their abusers. Soon Meeks was being described in language more appropriate to a town meeting on medical care than to Steve's respectable house. If Meeks never before heard himself described as a scumbag, swine, and sadist, he heard it that night. The three women present were just as frank as the men, a white-haired member of the First Families of Virginia even declaring, in the tones of an avenging fury, that "the little bastard ought to be hanged!"

I was not surprised when the lights began to grow dim. Indeed, I had been expecting it. Leaning back in Mr. Lincoln's comfortable chair, I closed my eyes and put in a call to Mom. When I opened them, the room was dark save for the now familiar corpse-light manifested by the dead and gone. Deploying from the dark hallway that led to the bedrooms a grim array of monstrous images advanced, while around me a second army gathered as if to do battle.

But Meeks's creatures—as I had deduced—were not, had never been, the actual dead, over whom he had no power. Rather they were his projected memories or perverse imaginings. *My* ghosts, on the other hand, were as real as thunder, and they moved forward with purpose, each and every man of them lifting the vivid, glowing memory of the noose he had died by.

We the living had become irrelevant. The specters passed through us as we might have passed through smoke. Yet I could see through them, so that even amid the throng the enemy remained dimly visible. I was able to watch Meeks's fearsome fantasies shrivel and fade as his terror mounted, leaving only the pathetic Hangman himself to confront his victims. They closed in around him; he gave a strangled outcry; they were so thick upon him that he vanished for a moment.

And then forever. With a flicker, pop, and squelch, like the explosion of a damp firecracker, he delaminated and rejoined the Cosmic All—which, as far as anyone living or dead cared, was welcome to him. We the living rose and clasped hands, noting only then that the six bottles of bourbon Steve had set out were now entirely empty.

Comment from the Editors of the JPR

We present the foregoing account—discovered on Mr. Martin's computer by the executor of his will—with a certain degree of hesitancy, not to say trepidation.

The author was a Life Member of this society, well known to all of us as a person of unimpeachable veracity. Back copies of the *Greenwood Falls Standard* confirm the existence of stories about the Hangman's House, exactly as reported in his account.

Yet "Stephen Preston James" (a pseudonym) refuses to comment on Mr. Martin's essay, and threatens a lawsuit if we print either his real name or the actual address of his house. Members of the group Death Must Die follow their attorney's lead, stating that if they become known as "kooks" their attempt to have the death penalty abolished will suffer. Efforts to reach the widow Letitia Loos have been unavailing, since she has left the country, and is believed to be living in Rio de Janeiro.

So confirmatory testimony is lacking. Yet the Editors feel constrained to publish this account, not only because of its intrinsic interest, but also as a memorial to Mr. Martin. Following the tumultuous events here recounted, our old friend and colleague returned home, sat down to rest in his La-Z-Boy, and passed over in his sleep, a victim of cardiovascular disease associated with his age and sedentary lifestyle. A curious final note has been added by the appearance, on the CD-ROM containing his account, of a few lines not present when the disc was first viewed at our offices. Perhaps a sort of spirit message, like those received by mediums of past times on sealed writing slates? This postscript to the story—perhaps (or perhaps not) the last words we shall ever receive from George Martin—reads as follows:

I don't know how long I slept after the excitement of last evening. I do remember having a brief, unpleasant dream of some sort, before a familiar voice woke me.

"Hi, Mom," I said, rising from the chair toward the ceiling. "It'll be really nice, being with you again at Thanksgiving."

THE TRANSFERRED GHOST

Frank Stockton

A WRITER OF CHILDREN'S books laced with fantasy and popular fiction, mostly of a humorous nature, Frank Stockton (1834–1902) is remembered almost exclusively today for a few satiric ghost stories and the great American classic "The Lady, or the Tiger?" This most famous of all riddle stories was originally titled "The King's Arena" when Stockton read it aloud at a party. It drew such enthusiastic response that he expanded it, changed the title, and sold it to *Century Magazine* (November 1882). Two years later, it became the title story of his most successful collection of short stories.

Born in Philadelphia, Stockton started out as a wood engraver, inventing an important engraving tool. He began writing at an early age, starting with children's stories and sketches, continuing with popular stories for most of the important magazines of the time; he also served as the assistant editor of the very successful *St. Nicholas Magazine*. His novels of humor, notably *Rudder Grange* (1879) and *The Rudder Grangers Abroad* (1891), which made him famous, were unusual for their time as they used neither colloquialisms nor dialect—then a staple of comic writing in America. His other contributions to the fantasy and supernatural genre include *The Christmas Wreck and Other Stories* (1886), *The Bee-Man of Orn and Other Fanciful Tales* (1887), *A Story-Teller's Pack* (1897), and *The Queen's Museum and Other Fanciful Tales* (1906).

"The Transferred Ghost" was first collected in *The Lady or the Tiger? And Other Stories* (New York, Scribner's, 1884).

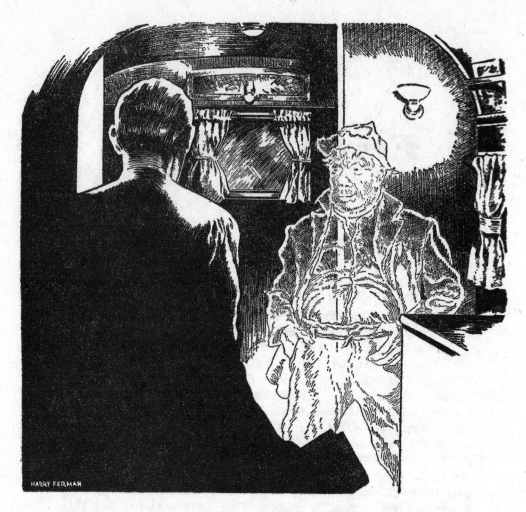

The Transferred Ghost

FRANK STOCKTON

THE COUNTRY RESIDENCE OF Mr. John Hinckman was a delightful place to me, for many reasons. It was the abode of a genial, though somewhat impulsive, hospitality. It had a broad, smooth-shaven lawn and towering oaks and elms; there were bosky shades at several points, and not far from the house there was a little rill spanned by a rustic bridge with the bark on; there were fruits and flowers, pleasant people, chess, billiards, rides, walks, and fishing. These were great attractions; but none of them, nor all of them together, would have been sufficient to hold me to the place very long. I had been invited for the trout season, but should, probably, have finished my visit early in the summer had it not been that upon fair days, when the grass was dry, and the sun was not too hot, and there was but little wind, there strolled beneath the lofty elms, or passed lightly through the bosky shades, the form of my Madeline.

This lady was not, in very truth, my Madeline. She had never given herself to me, nor had I, in any way, acquired possession of her. But as I considered her possession the only sufficient reason for the continuance of my existence, I called her, in my reveries, mine. It may have been that I would not have been obliged to confine the use of this possessive pronoun to my reveries had I confessed the state of my feelings to the lady.

But this was an unusually difficult thing to do. Not only did I dread, as almost all lovers dread, taking the step which would in an instant put an end to that delightful season which may be termed the ante-interrogatory period of love, and which might at the same time terminate all intercourse or connection with the object of my passion; but I was also dreadfully afraid of John Hinckman. This gentleman was a good friend of mine, but it would have required a bolder man than I was at that time to ask him for the gift of his niece, who was the head of his household, and, according to his own frequent statement, the main prop of his declining years. Had Madeline acquiesced in my general views on the subject, I might have felt encouraged to open the matter to Mr. Hinckman; but, as I said before, I had never asked her whether or not she would be mine. I thought of these things at all hours of the day and night, particularly the latter.

I was lying awake one night, in the great bed in my spacious chamber, when, by the dim light of the new moon, which partially filled the room, I saw John Hinckman standing by a large chair near the door. I was very much surprised at this for two reasons. In the first place, my host had never before come into my room; and, in the second place, he had gone from home that morning, and had not expected to return for several days. It was for this reason that I had been able that evening to sit much later with Madeline on the moonlit porch. The figure was

certainly that of John Hinckman in his ordinary dress, but there was a vagueness and indistinctness about it which presently assured me that it was a ghost. Had the good old man been murdered? and had his spirit come to tell me of the deed, and to confide to me the protection of his dear—? My heart fluttered at what I was about to think, but at this instant the figure spoke.

"Do you know," he said, with a countenance that indicated anxiety, "if Mr. Hinckman will return to-night?"

I thought it well to maintain a calm exterior, and I answered:

"We do not expect him."

"I am glad of that," he said, sinking into the chair by which he stood. "During the two years and a half that I have inhabited this house, that man has never before been away for a single night. You can't imagine the relief it gives me."

And as he spoke he stretched out his legs, and leaned back in the chair. His form became less vague, and the colours of his garments more distinct and evident, while an expression of gratified relief succeeded to the anxiety of his countenance.

"Two years and a half!" I exclaimed. "I don't understand you."

"It is fully that length of time," said the ghost, "since I first came here. Mine is not an ordinary case. But before I say any more about it, let me ask you again if you are sure that Mr. Hinckman will not return to-night."

"I am as sure of it as I can be of anything," I answered. "He left to-day for Bristol, two hundred miles away."

"Then I will go on," said the ghost, "for I am glad to have the opportunity of talking to someone who will listen to me; but if John Hinckman should come in and catch me here, I should be frightened out of my wits."

"This is all very strange," I said, greatly puzzled by what I heard. "Are you the ghost of Mr. Hinckman?"

This was a bold question, but my mind was so full of other emotions that there seemed to be no room for that of fear.

"Yes, I am his ghost," my companion replied, "and yet I have no right to be. And this is what makes me so uneasy, and so much afraid of him. It is a strange story, and, I truly believe, without precedent. Two years and a half ago, John Hinckman was dangerously ill in this very room. At one time he was so far gone that he was really believed to be dead. It was in consequence of too precipitate a report in regard to this matter that I was, at that time, appointed to be his ghost. Imagine my surprise and horror, sir, when, after I had accepted the position and assumed its responsibilities, that old man revived, became convalescent, and eventually regained his usual health. My situation was now one of extreme delicacy and embarrassment. I had no power to return to my original unembodiment, and I had no right to be the ghost of a man who was not dead. I was advised by my friends to quietly maintain my position, and was assured that, as John Hinckman was an elderly man, it could not be long before I could rightfully assume the position for which I had been selected. But I tell you, sir," he continued, with animation, "the old fellow seems as vigorous as ever, and I have no idea how much longer this annoying state of things will continue. I spend my time trying to get out of that old man's way. I must not leave this house, and he seems to follow me everywhere. I tell you, sir, he haunts me."

"That is truly a queer state of things," I remarked. "But why are you afraid of him? He couldn't hurt you."

"Of course he couldn't," said the ghost. "But his very presence is a shock and terror to me. Imagine, sir, how you would feel, if my case were yours."

I could not imagine such a thing at all. I simply shuddered.

"And if one must be a wrongful ghost at all," the apparition continued, "it would be much pleasanter to be the ghost of some man other than John Hinckman. There is in him an irascibility of temper, accompanied by a facility of invective, which is seldom met with. And what would happen if he were to see me, and find out, as I am sure he would, how long and why I have inhabited his house, I can scarcely conceive. I have seen him in his bursts of passion; and, although he did not hurt the people he stormed at any more than he would hurt me, they seemed to shrink before him."

All this I knew to be very true. Had it not been for this peculiarity of Mr. Hinckman, I might have been more willing to talk to him about his niece.

"I feel sorry for you," I said, for I really began to have a sympathetic feeling toward this unfortunate apparition. "Your case is indeed a hard one. It reminds me of those persons who have had doubles, and I suppose a man would often be very angry indeed when he found that there was another being who was personating himself."

"Oh! the cases are not similar at all," said the ghost. "A double or *doppelgänger* lives on the earth with a man; and, being exactly like him, he makes all sorts of trouble, of course. It is very different with me. I am not here to live with Mr. Hinckman. I am here to take his place. Now, it would make John Hinckman very angry if he knew that. Don't you know it would?"

I assented promptly.

"Now that he is away I can be easy for a little while," continued the ghost; "and I am so glad to have the opportunity of talking to you. I have frequently come into your room, and watched you while you slept, but did not dare to speak to you for fear that if you talked with me Mr. Hinckman would hear you, and come into the room to know why you were talking to yourself."

"But would he not hear you?" I asked.

"Oh, no!" said the other: "there are times when anyone may see me, but no one hears me except the person to whom I address myself."

"But why did you wish to speak to me?" I asked.

"Because," replied the ghost, "I like occasionally to talk to people, and especially to someone like yourself, whose mind is so troubled and perturbed that you are not likely to be frightened by a visit from one of us. But I particularly wanted to ask you to do me a favour. There is every probability, so far as I can see, that John Hinckman will live a long time, and my situation is becoming insupportable. My great object at present is to get myself transferred, and I think that you may, perhaps, be of use to me."

"Transferred!" I exclaimed. "What do you mean by that?"

"What I mean," said the other, "is this: Now that I have started on my career I have got to be the ghost of somebody, and I want to be the ghost of a man who is really dead."

"I should think that would be easy enough," I said. "Opportunities must continually occur."

"Not at all! Not at all!" said my companion quickly. "You have no idea what a rush and pressure there is for situations of this kind. Whenever a vacancy occurs, if I may express myself in that way, there are crowds of applications for the ghostship."

"I had no idea that such a fate of things existed," I said, becoming quite interested in the matter. "There ought to be some regular system, or order of precedence, by which you could all take your turns like customers in a barber's shop."

"Oh, dear, that would never do at all!" said the other. "Some of us would have to wait for ever. There is always a great rush whenever a good ghostship offers itself—while, as you know, there are some positions that no one would care for. And it was in consequence of my being in too great a hurry on an occasion of the kind that I got myself into my present disagreeable predicament, and I have thought that it might be possible that you would help me out of it. You might know of a case where an opportunity for a ghostship was not generally expected, but which might present itself at any moment. If you would give me a short notice, I know I could arrange for a transfer."

"What do you mean?" I exclaimed. "Do you want me to commit suicide? Or to undertake a murder for your benefit?"

"Oh, no, no, no!" said the other, with a vapoury smile. "I mean nothing of that kind. To be sure, there are lovers who are watched with

considerable interest, such persons having been known, in moments of depression, to offer very desirable ghostships; but I did not think of anything of that kind in connection with you. You were the only person I cared to speak to, and I hoped that you might give me some information that would be of use; and, in return, I shall be very glad to help you in your love affair."

"You seem to know that I have such an affair," I said.

"Oh, yes!" replied the other, with a little yawn. "I could not be here so much as I have been without knowing all about that."

There was something horrible in the idea of Madeline and myself having been watched by a ghost, even, perhaps, when we wandered together in the most delightful and bosky places. But, then, this was quite an exceptional ghost, and I could not have the objections to him which would ordinarily arise in regard to beings of his class.

"I must go now," said the ghost, rising. "But I will see you somewhere to-morrow night. And remember—you help me, and I'll help you."

I had doubts the next morning as to the propriety of telling Madeline anything about this interview, and soon convinced myself that I must keep silent on the subject. If she knew there was a ghost about the house, she would probably leave the place instantly. I did not mention the matter, and so regulated my demeanour that I am quite sure Madeline never suspected what had taken place. For some time I had wished that Mr. Hinckman would absent himself, for a day at least, from the premises. In such case I thought I might more easily nerve myself up to the point of speaking to Madeline on the subject of our future collateral existence; and, now that the opportunity for such speech really occurred, I did not feel ready to avail myself of it. What would become of me if she refused me?

I had an idea, however, that the lady thought that, if I were going to speak at all, this was the time. She must have known that certain sentiments were afloat within me, and she was not unreasonable in her wish to see the matter settled one way or the other. But I did not feel like taking a bold step in the dark. If she wished me to ask her to give herself to me, she ought to offer me some reason to suppose that she would make the gift. If I saw no probability of such generosity, I would prefer that things should remain as they were.

That evening I was sitting with Madeline in the moonlit porch. It was nearly ten o'clock, and ever since supper-time I had been working myself up to the point of making an avowal of my sentiments. I had not positively determined to do this, but wished gradually to reach the proper point, when, if the prospect looked bright, I might speak. My companion appeared to understand the situation—at least, I imagined that the nearer I came to a proposal the more she seemed to expect it. It was certainly a very critical and important epoch in my life. If I spoke, I should make myself happy or miserable for ever, and if I did not speak I had every reason to believe that the lady would not give me another chance to do so.

Sitting thus with Madeline, talking a little, and thinking very hard over these momentous matters, I looked up and saw the ghost, not a dozen feet away from us. He was sitting on the railing of the porch, one leg thrown up before him, the other dangling down as he leaned against a post. He was behind Madeline, but almost in front of me, as I sat facing the lady. It was fortunate that Madeline was looking out over the landscape, for I must have appeared very much startled. The ghost had told me that he would see me some time this night, but I did not think he would make his appearance when I was in the company of Madeline. If she should see the spirit of her uncle, I could not answer for the consequences. I made no exclamation, but the ghost evidently saw that I was troubled.

"Don't be afraid," he said, "I shall not let her see me; and she cannot hear me speak unless I address myself to her, which I do not intend to do."

I suppose I looked grateful.

"So you need not trouble yourself about that," the ghost continued; "but it seems to me that you are not getting along very well with your affair. If I were you, I should speak without waiting any longer. You will never have a better chance. You are not likely to be interrupted; and, so far as I can judge, the lady seems disposed to listen to you favourably; that is, if she ever intends to do so. There is no knowing when John Hinckman will go away again; certainly not this summer. If I were in your place, I should never dare to make love to Hinckman's niece if he were anywhere about the place. If he should catch anyone offering himself to Miss Madeline, he would then be a terrible man to encounter."

I agreed perfectly to all this.

"I cannot bear to think of him!" I ejaculated aloud.

"Think of whom?" asked Madeline, turning quickly toward me.

Here was an awkward situation. The long speech of the ghost, to which Madeline paid no attention, but which I heard with perfect distinctness, had made me forget myself.

It was necessary to explain quickly. Of course, it would not do to admit that it was of her dear uncle that I was speaking, and so I mentioned hastily the first name I thought of.

"Mr. Vilars," I said.

This statement was entirely correct, for I never could bear to think of Mr. Vilars, who was a gentleman who had, at various times, paid much attention to Madeline.

"It is wrong for you to speak in that way of Mr. Vilars," she said. "He is a remarkably well-educated and sensible young man, and has very pleasant manners. He expects to be elected to the legislature this autumn, and I should not be surprised if he made his mark. He will do well in a legislative body, for whenever Mr. Vilars has anything to say he knows just how and when to say it."

This was spoken very quietly, and without any show of resentment, which was all very natural, for if Madeline thought at all favourably of me she could not feel displeased that I should have disagreeable emotions in regard to a possible rival. The concluding words contained a hint which I was not slow to understand. I felt very sure that if Mr. Vilars were in my present position he would speak quickly enough.

"I know it is wrong to have such ideas about a person," I said, "but I cannot help it."

The lady did not chide me, and after this she seemed even in a softer mood. As for me, I felt considerably annoyed, for I had not wished to admit that any thought of Mr. Vilars had ever occupied my mind.

"You should not speak aloud that way," said the ghost, "or you may get yourself into trouble. I want to see everything go well with you, because then you may be disposed to help me, especially if I should chance to be of any assistance to you, which I hope I shall be."

I longed to tell him that there was no way in which he could help me so much as by taking his instant departure. To make love to a young lady with a ghost sitting on the railing near by, and that ghost the apparition of a much-dreaded uncle, the very idea of whom in such a position and at such a time made me tremble, was a difficult, if not an impossible, thing to do; but I forbore to speak, although I may have looked my mind.

"I suppose," continued the ghost, "that you have not heard anything that might be of advantage to me? Of course, I am very anxious to hear; but if you have anything to tell me, I can wait until you are alone. I will come to you to-night in your room, or I will stay here until the lady goes away."

"You need not wait here," I said; "I have nothing at all to say to you."

Madeline sprang to her feet, her face flushed and her eyes ablaze.

"Wait here!" she cried. "What do you suppose I am waiting for? Nothing to say to me, indeed!—I should think so! What should you have to say to me?"

"Madeline!" I exclaimed, stepping toward her, "let me explain."

But she was gone.

Here was the end of the world for me! I turned fiercely to the ghost.

"Wretched existence!" I cried, "you have ruined everything. You have blackened my whole life. Had it not been for you—"

But here my voice faltered. I could say no more.

"You wrong me," said the ghost. "I have not injured you. I have tried only to encourage and assist you, and it is your own folly that has done this mischief. But do not despair. Such mistakes as these can be explained. Keep up a brave heart. Good-bye."

And he vanished from the railing like a bursting soap-bubble.

I went gloomily to bed, but I saw no apparitions that night except those of despair and misery which my wretched thoughts called up. The words I had uttered had sounded to Madeline like the basest insult. Of course, there was only one interpretation she could put upon them.

As to explaining my ejaculations, that was impossible. I thought the matter over and over again as I lay awake that night, and I determined that I would never tell Madeline the facts of the case. It would be better for me to suffer all my life than for her to know that the ghost of her uncle haunted the house. Mr. Hinckman was away, and if she knew of his ghost she could not be made to believe that he was not dead. She might not survive the shock! No, my heart could bleed, but I would never tell her.

The next day was fine, neither too cool nor too warm; the breezes were gentle, and Nature smiled. But there were no walks or rides with Madeline. She seemed to be much engaged during the day, and I saw but little of her. When we met at meals she was polite, but very quiet and reserved. She had evidently determined on a course of conduct and had resolved to assume that, although I had been very rude to her, she did not understand the import of my words. It would be quite proper, of course, for her not to know what I meant by my expressions of the night before.

I was downcast and wretched, and said but little, and the only bright streak across the black horizon of my woe was the fact that she did not appear to be happy, although she affected an air of unconcern. The moonlit porch was deserted that evening, but wandering about the house I found Madeline in the library alone. She was reading, but I went in and sat down near her. I felt that, although I could not do so fully, I must in a measure explain my conduct of the night before. She listened quietly to a somewhat laboured apology I made for the words I had used.

"I have not the slightest idea what you meant," she said, "but you were very rude."

I earnestly disclaimed any intention of rudeness, and assured her, with a warmth of speech that must have made some impression upon her, that rudeness to her would be an action impossible to me. I said a great deal upon the subject, and implored her to believe that if it were not for a certain obstacle I could speak to her so plainly that she would understand everything.

She was silent for a time, and then she said, rather more kindly, I thought, than she had spoken before:

"Is that obstacle in any way connected with my uncle?"

"Yes," I answered, after a little hesitation, "it is, in a measure, connected with him."

She made no answer to this, and sat looking at her book, but not reading. From the expression of her face, I thought she was somewhat softened toward me. She knew her uncle as well as I did, and she may have been thinking that, if he were the obstacle that prevented my speaking (and there were many ways in which he might be that obstacle), my position would be such a hard one that it would excuse some wildness of speech and eccentricity of manner. I saw, too, that the warmth of my partial explanations had had some effect on her, and I began to believe that it might be a good thing for me to speak my mind without delay. No matter how she would receive my proposition, my relations with her could not be worse than they had been the previous night and day, and there was something in her face which encouraged me to hope that she might forget my foolish exclamations of the evening before if I began to tell her my tale of love.

I drew my chair a little nearer to her, and as I did so the ghost burst into the room from the doorway behind her. I say burst, although no door flew open and he made no noise. He was wildly excited, and waved his arms above his head. The moment I saw him, my heart fell within me. With the entrance of that impertinent apparition, every hope fled from me. I could not speak while he was in the room.

I must have turned pale; and I gazed steadfastly at the ghost, almost without seeing Madeline, who sat between us.

"Do you know," he cried, "that John Hinckman is coming up the hill? He will be here in fifteen minutes; and if you are doing anything in the way of lovemaking, you had better hurry it up. But this is not what I came to tell you. I have glorious news! At last I am transferred! Not forty minutes ago a Russian nobleman was murdered by the Nihilists. Nobody ever thought of him in connection with an immediate ghostship. My friends instantly applied for the situation for me, and obtained my transfer. I am off before that horrid Hinckman comes up the hill. The moment I reach my new position, I shall put off his hated semblance. Good-bye. You can't imagine how glad I am to be at last the real ghost of somebody."

"Oh!" I cried, rising to my feet, and stretching out my arms in utter wretchedness, "I would to Heaven you were mine!"

"I *am* yours," said Madeline, raising to me her tearful eyes.

THE CANTERVILLE GHOST

Oscar Wilde

ALTHOUGH HIS PRODIGIOUS LITERARY talent appears at first glance to be too much of its time, with its elaborate style, rococo embellishments, and focus on descriptions of rare jewels, exotic scents, and other flamboyant excesses, the stories of Oscar (Fingal O'Flahertie Wills) Wilde (1854–1900) remain wonderfully readable today, just as his plays are imbued with wit and charm that remain clever and entertaining. Born in Dublin, he attended Trinity College and Oxford University, selling his first poems while still in school. He affected bohemian styles and mannerisms that were despised by some but fascinated others. After dabbling at various literary endeavors in his early years, he produced work at a prodigious rate in the late 1880s, including fairy tales for adults in *The Happy Prince and Other Tales* (1888), short stories in *Lord Arthur Savile's Crime and Other Stories* (1891), the iconic horror novel *The Picture of Dorian Gray* (1891), and the plays that gave him financial independence and still enjoy large audiences today, including *Lady Windemere's Fan* (1892), *A Woman of No Importance* (1893), *An Ideal Husband* (1895), and *The Importance of Being Earnest* (1895). His writing career and life were cut short when he was sent to jail for two years because of his homosexuality. Released in 1897, his health damaged, he moved to France, taking the name Sebastian Melmoth, and died three years later.

"The Canterville Ghost" was originally published in *The Court and Society Review* in 1887; it was first collected in *Lord Arthur Savile's Crime and Other Stories* (London, Osgood, McIlvaine, 1891). It has been adapted for motion pictures several times, most significantly in 1944 starring Charles Laughton, in a 1985 made-for-TV film with Richard Kiley, and in a more elaborate made-for-TV film in 1987 starring John Gielgud; it also was adapted for TV dramas in the United States and in Great Britain more than a half dozen times.

The Canterville Ghost

OSCAR WILDE

I

When Mr. Hiram B. Otis, the American Minister, bought Canterville Chase, every one told him he was doing a very foolish thing, as there was no doubt at all that the place was haunted. Indeed, Lord Canterville himself, who was a man of the most punctilious honour, had felt it his duty to mention the fact to Mr. Otis when they came to discuss terms.

"We have not cared to live in the place ourselves," said Lord Canterville, "since my grandaunt, the Dowager Duchess of Bolton, was frightened into a fit, from which she never really recovered, by two skeleton hands being placed on her shoulders as she was dressing for dinner, and I feel bound to tell you, Mr. Otis, that the ghost has been seen by several living members of my family, as well as by the rector of the parish, the Rev. Augustus Dampier, who is a Fellow of King's College, Cambridge. After the unfortunate accident to the Duchess, none of our younger servants would stay with us, and Lady Canterville often got very little sleep at night, in consequence of the mysterious noises that came from the corridor and the library."

"My Lord," answered the Minister, "I will take the furniture and the ghost at a valuation. I have come from a modern country, where we have everything that money can buy; and with all our spry young fellows painting the Old World red, and carrying off your best actors and prima-donnas, I reckon that if there were such a thing as a ghost in Europe, we'd have it at home in a very short time in one of our public museums, or on the road as a show."

"I fear that the ghost exists," said Lord Canterville, smiling, "though it may have resisted the overtures of your enterprising impresarios. It has been well known for three centuries, since 1584 in fact, and always makes its appearance before the death of any member of our family."

"Well, so does the family doctor for that matter, Lord Canterville. But there is no such thing, sir, as a ghost, and I guess the laws of Nature are not going to be suspended for the British aristocracy."

"You are certainly very natural in America," answered Lord Canterville, who did not quite understand Mr. Otis's last observation, "and if you don't mind a ghost in the house, it is all right. Only you must remember I warned you."

A few weeks after this, the purchase was concluded, and at the close of the season the Minister and his family went down to Canterville Chase. Mrs. Otis, who, as Miss Lucretia R. Tappan, of West 53d Street, had been a celebrated New York belle, was now a very handsome, middle-aged woman, with fine eyes, and a superb profile. Many American ladies on leaving their native land adopt an appearance of chronic ill-health, under the impression that it is a form of European refinement, but Mrs. Otis had never fallen into this error. She had a magnificent constitution, and a really wonderful amount of animal spirits. Indeed, in many respects, she was quite English, and was an excellent example of the fact that we have really everything in common with America nowadays, except, of course, language. Her eldest son, christened Washington by his parents in a moment of patriotism, which he never ceased to regret, was a fair-haired, rather good-looking young man, who had qualified himself for American diplomacy by leading the German at the Newport Casino for three successive seasons, and even in London was well known as an excellent dancer. Gardenias and the peerage were his only weaknesses. Otherwise he was extremely sensible. Miss Virginia E. Otis was a little girl of fifteen, lithe and lovely as a fawn, and with a fine freedom in her large blue eyes. She was a wonderful Amazon, and had once raced old Lord Bilton on her pony twice round the park, winning by a length and a half, just in front of the Achilles statue, to the huge delight of the young Duke of Cheshire, who proposed for her on the spot, and was sent back to Eton that very night by his guardians, in floods of tears. After Virginia came the twins, who were usually called "The Stars and Stripes," as they were always getting swished. They were delightful boys, and, with the exception of the worthy Minister, the only true republicans of the family.

As Canterville Chase is seven miles from Ascot, the nearest railway station, Mr. Otis had telegraphed for a waggonette to meet them, and they started on their drive in high spirits. It was a lovely July evening, and the air was delicate with the scent of the pinewoods. Now and then they heard a wood-pigeon brooding over its own sweet voice, or saw, deep in the rustling fern, the burnished breast of the pheasant. Little squirrels peered at them from the beech-trees as they went by, and the rabbits scudded away through the brushwood and over the mossy knolls, with their white tails in the air. As they entered the avenue of Canterville Chase, however, the sky became suddenly overcast with clouds, a curious stillness seemed to hold the atmosphere, a great flight of rooks passed silently over their heads, and, before they reached the house, some big drops of rain had fallen.

Standing on the steps to receive them was an old woman, neatly dressed in black silk, with a white cap and apron. This was Mrs. Umney, the housekeeper, whom Mrs. Otis, at Lady Canterville's earnest request, had consented to keep in her former position. She made them each a low curtsey as they alighted, and said in a quaint, old-fashioned manner, "I bid you welcome to Canterville Chase." Following her, they passed through the fine Tudor hall into the library, a long, low room, panelled in black oak, at the end of which was a large stained glass window. Here they found tea laid out for them, and, after taking off their wraps, they sat down and began to look round, while Mrs. Umney waited on them.

Suddenly Mrs. Otis caught sight of a dull red stain on the floor just by the fireplace, and, quite unconscious of what it really signified, said to Mrs. Umney, "I am afraid something has been spilt there."

"Yes, madam," replied the old housekeeper in a low voice, "blood has been spilt on that spot."

"How horrid!" cried Mrs. Otis; "I don't at all care for blood-stains in a sitting-room. It must be removed at once."

The old woman smiled, and answered in the same low, mysterious voice, "It is the blood of Lady Eleanore de Canterville, who was murdered on that very spot by her own husband, Sir Simon de Canterville, in 1575. Sir Simon survived her nine years, and disappeared suddenly under very mysterious circumstances. His body has never been discovered, but his guilty spirit still haunts the Chase. The blood-stain has been much admired by tourists and others, and cannot be removed."

"That is all nonsense," cried Washington Otis; "Pinkerton's Champion Stain Remover and Paragon Detergent will clean it up in no time," and before the terrified housekeeper could interfere, he had fallen upon his knees, and was rapidly scouring the floor with a small stick of what looked like a black cosmetic. In a few moments no trace of the blood-stain could be seen.

"I knew Pinkerton would do it," he exclaimed, triumphantly, as he looked round at his admiring family; but no sooner had he said these words than a terrible flash of lightning lit up the sombre room, a fearful peal of thunder made them all start to their feet, and Mrs. Umney fainted.

"What a monstrous climate!" said the American Minister, calmly, as he lit a long cheroot. "I guess the old country is so overpopulated that they have not enough decent weather for everybody. I have always been of opinion that emigration is the only thing for England."

"My dear Hiram," cried Mrs. Otis, "what can we do with a woman who faints?"

"Charge it to her like breakages," answered the Minister; "she won't faint after that"; and in a few moments Mrs. Umney certainly came to. There was no doubt, however, that she was extremely upset, and she sternly warned Mr. Otis to beware of some trouble coming to the house.

"I have seen things with my own eyes, sir," she said, "that would make any Christian's hair stand on end, and many and many a night I have not closed my eyes in sleep for the awful things that are done here." Mr. Otis, however, and his wife warmly assured the honest soul that they were not afraid of ghosts, and, after invoking the blessings of Providence on her new master and mistress, and making arrangements for an increase of salary, the old housekeeper tottered off to her own room.

II

The storm raged fiercely all that night, but nothing of particular note occurred. The next morning, however, when they came down to breakfast, they found the terrible stain of blood once again on the floor. "I don't think it can be the fault of the Paragon Detergent," said Washington, "for I have tried it with everything. It must be the ghost." He accordingly rubbed out the stain a second time, but the second morning it appeared again. The third morning also it was there, though the library had been locked up at night by Mr. Otis himself, and the key carried up-stairs. The whole family were now quite interested; Mr. Otis began to suspect that he had been too dogmatic in his denial of the existence of ghosts, Mrs. Otis expressed her intention of joining the Psychical Society, and Washington prepared a long letter to Messrs. Myers and Podmore on the subject of the Permanence of Sanguineous Stains when connected with Crime. That night all doubts about the objective existence of phantasmata were removed for ever.

The day had been warm and sunny; and, in the cool of the evening, the whole family went out to drive. They did not return home till nine o'clock, when they had a light supper. The conversation in no way turned upon ghosts, so there were not even those primary conditions of receptive expectations which so often precede the presentation of psychical phenomena. The subjects discussed, as I have since learned from Mr. Otis, were merely such as form the ordinary conversation of cultured Americans of the better class, such as the immense superiority of Miss Fanny Devonport over Sarah Bernhardt as an actress; the difficulty of obtaining green corn, buckwheat cakes, and hominy, even in the best English houses; the importance of Boston in the development of the world-soul; the advantages of the baggage-check system in railway travelling; and the sweetness of the New York accent as compared to the London drawl. No mention at all was made of the supernatural, nor was Sir Simon de Canterville alluded to in any way. At eleven o'clock the family retired, and by half-past all the lights were out. Some time after, Mr. Otis was awakened by a curious noise in the corridor, outside his room. It sounded like the clank of metal, and seemed to be coming nearer every moment. He got up at once, struck a match, and looked at the time. It was exactly one o'clock. He was quite calm, and felt his pulse, which was not at all feverish. The strange noise still continued, and with it he heard distinctly the sound of footsteps. He put on his slippers, took a small oblong phial out of his dressing-case, and opened the door. Right in front of him he saw, in the wan moonlight, an old man of terrible aspect. His eyes were as red burning coals; long grey hair fell over his shoulders in matted coils; his garments, which were of antique cut, were soiled and ragged, and from his wrists and ankles hung heavy manacles and rusty gyves.

"My dear sir," said Mr. Otis, "I really must insist on your oiling those chains, and have brought you for that purpose a small bottle of the Tammany Rising Sun Lubricator. It is said to be completely efficacious upon one application, and there are several testimonials to that effect on the wrapper from some of our most eminent native divines. I shall leave it here for you by the bedroom candles, and will be happy to supply you with more, should you require it." With these words the United States Minister laid the bottle down on a marble table, and, closing his door, retired to rest.

For a moment the Canterville ghost stood quite motionless in natural indignation; then, dashing the bottle violently upon the polished floor, he fled down the corridor, uttering hollow groans, and emitting a ghastly green light. Just, however, as he reached the top of the great oak staircase, a door was flung open, two little white-robed figures appeared, and a large pillow whizzed past his head! There was evidently no time to be lost, so, hastily adopting the Fourth dimension of Space as a means of escape, he vanished through the wainscoting, and the house became quite quiet.

On reaching a small secret chamber in the left wing, he leaned up against a moonbeam to recover his breath, and began to try and realize his position. Never, in a brilliant and uninterrupted career of three hundred years, had he been so grossly insulted. He thought of the Dowager Duchess, whom he had frightened into a fit as she stood before the glass in her lace and diamonds; of the four housemaids, who had gone into hysterics when he merely grinned at them through the curtains on one of the spare bedrooms; of the rector of the parish, whose candle he had blown out as he was coming late one night from the library, and who had been under the care of Sir William Gull ever since, a perfect martyr to nervous disorders; and of old Madame de Tremouillac, who, having wakened up one morning early and seen a skeleton seated in an armchair by the fire reading her diary, had been confined to her bed for six weeks with an attack of brain fever, and, on her recovery, had become reconciled to the Church, and broken off her connection with that notorious sceptic, Monsieur de Voltaire. He remembered the terrible night when the wicked Lord Canterville was found choking in his dressing-room, with the knave of diamonds half-way down his throat, and confessed, just before he died, that he had cheated Charles James Fox out of £50,000 at Crockford's by means of that very card, and swore that the ghost had made him swallow it. All his great achievements came back to him again, from the butler who had shot himself in the pantry because he had seen a green hand tapping at the window-pane, to the beautiful Lady Stutfield, who was always obliged to wear a black velvet band round her throat to hide the mark of five fingers burnt upon her white skin, and who drowned herself at last in the carp-pond at the end of the King's Walk. With the enthusiastic egotism of the true artist, he went over his most celebrated performances, and smiled bitterly to himself as he recalled to mind his last appearance as "Red Reuben, or the Strangled Babe," his *début* as "Guant Gibeon, the Blood-sucker of Bexley Moor," and the *furore* he had excited one lovely June evening by merely playing ninepins with his own bones upon the lawn-tennis ground. And after all this some wretched modern Americans were to come and offer him the Rising Sun Lubricator, and throw pillows at his head! It was quite unbearable. Besides, no ghost in history had ever been treated in this manner. Accordingly, he determined to have vengeance, and remained till daylight in an attitude of deep thought.

III

The next morning, when the Otis family met at breakfast, they discussed the ghost at some length. The United States Minister was naturally a little annoyed to find that his present had not been accepted. "I have no wish," he said, "to do the ghost any personal injury, and I must say that, considering the length of time he has been in the house, I don't think it is at all polite to throw pillows at him,"—a very just remark, at which, I am sorry to say, the twins burst into shouts of laughter. "Upon the other hand," he continued, "if he really declines to use the Rising Sun Lubricator, we shall have to take his chains from him. It would be quite impossible to sleep, with such a noise going on outside the bedrooms."

For the rest of the week, however, they were undisturbed, the only thing that excited any attention being the continual renewal of the blood-stain on the library floor. This certainly was very strange, as the door was always locked at night by Mr. Otis, and the windows kept closely barred. The chameleon-like colour, also, of the stain excited a good deal of comment. Some mornings it was a dull (almost Indian) red, then it would be vermilion, then a rich purple, and once when they came down for family prayers, according to the simple rites of the Free American Reformed Episcopalian Church, they found it a bright emerald-green. These kaleidoscopic changes naturally amused the party very much, and bets on the subject were freely made every evening. The only person who did not enter into the joke was little Virginia, who, for some unexplained reason, was always a good deal distressed at the sight of the blood-stain, and very nearly cried the morning it was emerald-green.

The second appearance of the ghost was on Sunday night. Shortly after they had gone to bed they were suddenly alarmed by a fearful crash in the hall. Rushing down-stairs, they found that a large suit of old armour had become detached from its stand, and had fallen on the stone floor, while seated in a high-backed chair was the Canterville ghost, rubbing his knees with an expression of acute agony on his face. The twins, having brought their pea-shooters with them, at once discharged two pellets on him, with that accuracy of aim which can only be attained by long and careful practice on a writing-master, while the United States Minister covered him with his revolver, and called upon him, in accordance with Californian etiquette, to hold up his hands! The ghost started up with a wild shriek of rage, and swept through them like a mist, extinguishing Washington Otis's candle as he passed, and so leaving them all in total darkness. On reaching the top of the staircase he recovered himself, and determined to give his celebrated peal of demoniac laughter. This he had on more than one occasion found extremely useful. It was said to have turned Lord Raker's wig grey in a single night, and had certainly made three of Lady Canterville's French governesses give warning before their month was up. He accordingly laughed his most horrible laugh, till the old vaulted roof rang and rang again, but hardly had the fearful echo died away when a door opened, and Mrs. Otis came out in a light blue dressing-gown. "I am afraid you are far from well," she said, "and have brought you a bottle of Doctor Dobell's tincture. If it is indigestion, you will find it a most excellent remedy." The ghost glared at her in fury, and began at once to make preparations for turning himself into a large black dog, an accomplishment for which he was justly renowned, and to which the family doctor always attributed the permanent idiocy of Lord Canterville's uncle, the Hon. Thomas Horton. The sound of approaching footsteps, however, made him hesitate in his fell purpose, so he contented himself with becoming faintly phosphorescent, and vanished with a deep churchyard groan, just as the twins had come up to him.

On reaching his room he entirely broke down, and became a prey to the most violent agitation. The vulgarity of the twins, and the gross materialism of Mrs. Otis, were naturally extremely annoying, but what really distressed him most was that he had been unable to wear the suit of mail. He had hoped that even modern Americans would be thrilled by the sight of a Spectre in armour, if for no more sensible reason, at least out of respect for their natural poet Longfellow, over whose graceful and attractive poetry he himself had whiled away many a weary hour when the Cantervilles were up in town. Besides it was his own suit. He had worn it with great success at the Kenilworth tournament, and had been highly complimented on it by no less a person than the Virgin Queen herself. Yet when he had put it on, he had been completely overpowered by the weight of the huge breastplate and steel casque, and had fallen heavily on the stone pavement, barking both his knees severely, and bruising the knuckles of his right hand.

For some days after this he was extremely ill, and hardly stirred out of his room at all, except to keep the blood-stain in proper repair. However, by taking great care of himself, he recovered, and resolved to make a third attempt to frighten the United States Minister and his family. He selected Friday, August 17th, for his appearance, and spent most of that day in looking over his wardrobe, ultimately deciding in favour of a large slouched hat with a red feather, a winding-sheet frilled at the wrists and neck, and a rusty dagger. Towards evening a violent storm of rain came on, and the wind was so high that all the windows and doors in the old house shook and rattled. In fact, it was just such weather as he loved. His plan of action was this. He was to make his way quietly to Washington Otis's room, gibber at him from the foot of the bed, and stab himself three times in the throat to the sound of low music. He bore Washington a special grudge, being quite aware that it was he who was in the habit of removing the famous Canterville blood-stain by means of Pinkerton's Paragon Detergent. Having reduced the reckless and foolhardy youth to a condition of abject terror, he was then to proceed to the room occupied by the United States Minister and his wife, and there to place a clammy hand on Mrs. Otis's forehead, while he hissed into her trembling husband's ear the awful secrets of the charnel-house. With regard to little Virginia, he had not quite made up his mind. She had never insulted him in any way, and was pretty and gentle. A few hollow groans from the wardrobe, he thought, would be more than sufficient, or, if that failed to wake her, he might grabble at the counterpane with palsy-twitching fingers. As for the twins, he was quite determined to teach them a lesson. The first thing to be done was, of course, to sit upon their chests, so as to produce the stifling sensation of nightmare. Then, as their beds were quite close to each other, to stand between them in the form of a green, icy-cold corpse, till they became paralyzed with fear, and finally, to throw off the winding-sheet, and crawl round the room, with white, bleached bones and one rolling eyeball, in the character of "Dumb Daniel, or the Suicide's Skeleton," a *rôle* in which he had on more than one occasion produced a great effect, and which he considered quite equal to his famous part of "Martin the Maniac, or the Masked Mystery."

At half-past ten he heard the family going to bed. For some time he was disturbed by wild shrieks of laughter from the twins, who, with the light-hearted gaiety of schoolboys, were evidently amusing themselves before they retired to rest, but at a quarter-past eleven all was still, and, as midnight sounded, he sallied forth. The owl beat against the window-panes, the raven croaked from the old yew-tree, and the wind wandered moaning round the house like a lost soul; but the Otis family slept unconscious of their doom, and high above the rain and storm he could hear the steady snoring of the Minister for the United States. He stepped stealthily out of the wainscoting, with an evil smile on his cruel, wrinkled mouth, and the moon hid her face in a cloud as he stole past the great oriel window, where his own arms and those of his murdered wife were blazoned in azure and gold. On and on he glided, like an evil shadow, the very darkness seeming to loathe him as he passed. Once he thought he heard something call, and stopped; but it was only the baying of a dog from the Red Farm, and he went on, muttering strange sixteenth-century curses, and ever and anon brandishing the rusty dagger in the midnight air. Finally he reached the corner of the passage that led to luckless Washington's room. For a moment he paused there, the wind blowing his long grey locks about his head, and twisting into grotesque and fantastic folds the nameless horror of the dead man's shroud. Then the clock struck the quarter, and he felt the time was come. He chuckled to himself, and turned the corner; but no sooner had he done so than, with a piteous wail of terror, he fell back, and hid his blanched face in his long, bony hands. Right in front of him was standing a horrible spectre, motionless as a carven image, and monstrous as a madman's dream! Its head was bald and burnished; its face round, and fat, and white; and hideous laughter seemed to have writhed its features into an eternal grin. From the eyes streamed rays of scarlet light, the mouth was a wide well of fire, and a hideous garment, like to his own, swathed with its silent snows the Titan form. On its breast was a placard with strange writing in antique characters, some scroll of shame it seemed, some record of wild sins, some awful calendar of crime, and, with its right hand, it bore aloft a falchion of gleaming steel.

Never having seen a ghost before, he naturally was terribly frightened, and, after a second hasty glance at the awful phantom, he fled back to his room, tripping up in his long winding-sheet as he sped down the corridor, and finally dropping the rusty dagger into the Minister's jack-boots, where it was found in the morning by the butler. Once in the privacy of his own apartment, he flung himself down on a small pallet-bed, and hid his face under the clothes. After a time, however, the brave old Canterville spirit asserted itself, and he determined to go and speak to the other ghost as soon as it was daylight. Accordingly, just as the dawn was touching the hills with silver, he returned towards the spot where he had first laid eyes on the grisly phantom, feeling that, after all, two ghosts were better than

one, and that, by the aid of his new friend, he might safely grapple with the twins. On reaching the spot, however, a terrible sight met his gaze. Something had evidently happened to the spectre, for the light had entirely faded from its hollow eyes, the gleaming falchion had fallen from its hand, and it was leaning up against the wall in a strained and uncomfortable attitude. He rushed forward and seized it in his arms, when, to his horror, the head slipped off and rolled on the floor, the body assumed a recumbent posture, and he found himself clasping a white dimity bed-curtain, with a sweeping-brush, a kitchen cleaver, and a hollow turnip lying at his feet! Unable to understand this curious transformation, he clutched the placard with feverish haste, and there, in the grey morning light, he read these fearful words:—

YE OTIS GHOSTE
YE ONLIE TRUE AND ORIGINALE SPOOK,
BEWARE OF YE IMITATIONES.
ALL OTHERS ARE COUNTERFEITE.

The whole thing flashed across him. He had been tricked, foiled, and out-witted! The old Canterville look came into his eyes; he ground his toothless gums together; and, raising his withered hands high above his head, swore according to the picturesque phraseology of the antique school, that, when Chanticleer had sounded twice his merry horn, deeds of blood would be wrought, and murder walk abroad with silent feet.

Hardly had he finished this awful oath when, from the red-tiled roof of a distant homestead, a cock crew. He laughed a long, low, bitter laugh, and waited. Hour after hour he waited, but the cock, for some strange reason, did not crow again. Finally, at half-past seven, the arrival of the housemaids made him give up his fearful vigil, and he stalked back to his room, thinking of his vain oath and baffled purpose. There he consulted several books of ancient chivalry, of which he was exceedingly fond, and found that, on every occasion on which this oath had been used, Chanticleer had always crowed a second time. "Perdition seize the naughty fowl," he muttered, "I have seen the day when, with my stout spear, I would have run him through the gorge, and made him crow for me an 'twere in death!" He then retired to a comfortable lead coffin, and stayed there till evening.

IV

The next day the ghost was very weak and tired. The terrible excitement of the last four weeks was beginning to have its effect. His nerves were completely shattered, and he started at the slightest noise. For five days he kept his room, and at last made up his mind to give up the point of the blood-stain on the library floor. If the Otis family did not want it, they clearly did not deserve it. They were evidently people on a low, material plane of existence, and quite incapable of appreciating the symbolic value of sensuous phenomena. The question of phantasmic apparitions, and the development of astral bodies, was of course quite a different matter, and really not under his control. It was his solemn duty to appear in the corridor once a week, and to gibber from the large oriel window on the first and third Wednesdays in every month, and he did not see how he could honourably escape from his obligations. It is quite true that his life had been very evil, but, upon the other hand, he was most conscientious in all things connected with the supernatural. For the next three Saturdays, accordingly, he traversed the corridor as usual between midnight and three o'clock, taking every possible precaution against being either heard or seen. He removed his boots, trod as lightly as possible on the old worm-eaten boards, wore a large black velvet cloak, and was careful to use the Rising Sun Lubricator for oiling his chains. I am bound to acknowledge that it was with a good deal of difficulty that he brought himself to adopt this last mode of protection. However, one night, while the family were at dinner, he slipped into Mr. Otis's bedroom and carried off the bottle. He felt a little humiliated at first, but afterwards was sensible enough to see that there was a great deal to be said for the invention, and, to a certain degree, it served his purpose. Still in spite of everything he was not left unmolested. Strings were continually being stretched across the corridor, over which he tripped in the dark, and on one occasion, while dressed for the part of "Black Isaac, or the Huntsman of Hogley Woods," he met with a severe fall, through treading on a butter-slide, which the twins had constructed from the entrance of the Tapestry Chamber to the top of the oak staircase. This last insult so enraged him, that he resolved to make one final effort to assert his dignity and social position, and determined to visit the insolent young Etonians the next night in his celebrated character of "Reckless Rupert, or the Headless Earl."

He had not appeared in this disguise for more than seventy years; in fact, not since he had so frightened pretty Lady Barbara Modish by means of it, that she suddenly broke off her engagement with the present Lord Canterville's grandfather, and ran away to Gretna Green with handsome Jack Castletown, declaring that nothing in the world would induce her to marry into a family that allowed such a horrible phantom to walk up and down the terrace at twilight. Poor Jack was afterwards shot in a duel by Lord Canterville on Wandsworth Common, and Lady Barbara died of a broken heart at Tunbridge Wells before the year was out, so, in every way, it had been a great success. It was, however, an extremely difficult "make-up," if I may use such a theatrical expression in connection with one of the greatest mysteries of the supernatural, or, to employ a more scientific term, the higher-natural world, and it took him fully three hours to make his preparations. At last everything was ready, and he was very pleased with his appearance. The big leather riding-boots that went with the dress were just a little too large for him, and he could only find one of the two horse-pistols, but, on the whole, he was quite satisfied, and at a quarter-past one he glided out of the wainscoting and crept down the corridor. On reaching the room occupied by the twins, which I should mention was called the Blue Bed Chamber, on account of the colour of its hangings, he found the door just ajar. Wishing to make an effective entrance, he flung it wide open, when a heavy jug of water fell right down on him, wetting him to the skin, and just missing his left shoulder by a couple of inches. At the same moment he heard stifled shrieks of laughter proceeding from the four-post bed. The shock to his nervous system was so great that he fled back to his room as hard as he could go, and the next day he was laid up with a severe cold. The only thing that at all consoled him in the whole affair was the fact that he had not brought his head with him, for, had he done so, the consequences might have been very serious.

He now gave up all hope of ever frightening this rude American family, and contented himself, as a rule, with creeping about the passages in list slippers, with a thick red muffler round his throat for fear of draughts, and a small arquebuse, in case he should be attacked by the twins. The final blow he received occurred on the 19th of September. He had gone down-stairs to the great entrance-hall, feeling sure that there, at any rate, he would be quite unmolested, and was amusing himself by making satirical remarks on the large Saroni photographs of the United States Minister and his wife which had now taken the place of the Canterville family pictures. He was simply but neatly clad in a long shroud, spotted with churchyard mould, had tied up his jaw with a strip of yellow linen, and carried a small lantern and a sexton's spade. In fact, he was dressed for the character of "Jonas the Graveless, or the Corpse-Snatcher of Chertsey Barn," one of his most remarkable impersonations, and one which the Cantervilles had every reason to remember, as it was the real origin of their quarrel with their neighbour, Lord Rufford. It was about a quarter-past two o'clock in the morning, and, as far as he could ascertain, no one was stirring. As he was strolling towards the library, however, to see if there were any traces left of the blood-stain, suddenly there leaped out on him from a dark corner two figures, who waved their arms wildly above their heads, and shrieked out "BOO!" in his ear.

Seized with a panic, which, under the circumstances, was only natural, he rushed for the staircase, but found Washington Otis waiting for him there with the big garden-syringe, and being thus hemmed in by his enemies on every side, and driven almost to bay, he vanished into the great iron stove, which, fortunately for him, was not lit, and had to make his way home through the flues and chimneys, arriving at his own room in a terrible state of dirt, disorder, and despair.

After this he was not seen again on any nocturnal expedition. The twins lay in wait for him on several occasions, and strewed the passages with nutshells every night to the great annoyance of their parents and the servants, but it was of no avail. It was quite evident that his feelings were so wounded that he would not appear. Mr. Otis consequently resumed his great work on the history of the Democratic Party, on which he had been engaged for some years; Mrs. Otis organized a wonderful clam-bake, which amazed the whole county; the boys took to lacrosse, euchre, poker, and other American national games, and Virginia rode about the lanes on her pony, accompanied by the young Duke of Cheshire, who had come to spend the last week of his holidays at Canterville Chase. It was generally assumed that the ghost had gone away, and, in fact, Mr. Otis wrote a letter to that effect to Lord Canterville, who, in reply, expressed his great pleasure at the news, and sent his best congratulations to the Minister's worthy wife.

The Otises, however, were deceived, for the ghost was still in the house, and though now almost an invalid, was by no means ready to let matters rest, particularly as he heard that among the guests was the young Duke of Cheshire, whose grand-uncle, Lord Francis Stilton, had once bet a hundred guineas with Colonel Carbury that he would play dice with the Canterville ghost, and was found the next morning lying on the floor of the card-room in such a helpless paralytic state that, though he lived on to a great age, he was never able to say anything again but "Double Sixes." The story was well known at the time, though, of course, out of respect to the feelings of the two noble families, every attempt was made to hush it up, and a full account of all the circumstances connected with it will be found in the third volume of Lord Tattle's *Recollections of the Prince Regent and His Friends*. The ghost, then, was naturally very anxious to show that he had not lost his influence over the Stiltons, with whom, indeed, he was distantly connected, his own first cousin having been married *en secondes noces* to the Sieur de Bulkeley, from whom, as every one knows, the Dukes of Cheshire are lineally descended. Accordingly, he made arrangements for appearing to Virginia's little lover in his celebrated impersonation of "The Vampire Monk, or the Bloodless Benedictine," a performance so horrible that when old Lady Startup saw it, which she did on one fatal New Year's Eve, in the year 1764, she went off into the most piercing shrieks, which culminated in violent apoplexy, and died in three days, after disinheriting the Cantervilles, who were her nearest relations, and leaving all her money to her London apothecary. At the last moment, however, his terror of the twins prevented his leaving his room, and the little Duke slept in peace under the great feathered canopy in the Royal Bedchamber, and dreamed of Virginia.

V

A few days after this, Virginia and her curly-haired cavalier went out riding on Brockley meadows, where she tore her habit so badly in getting through a hedge that, on their return home, she made up her mind to go up by the back staircase so as not to be seen. As she was running past the Tapestry Chamber, the door of which happened to be open, she fancied she saw some one inside, and thinking it was her mother's maid, who sometimes used to bring her work there, looked in to ask her to mend her habit. To her immense surprise, however, it was the Canterville Ghost himself! He was sitting by the window, watching the ruined gold of the yellowing trees fly through the air, and the red leaves dancing madly down the long avenue. His head was leaning on his hand, and his whole attitude was one of extreme depression. Indeed, so forlorn, and so much out of repair did he look, that little Virginia, whose first idea had been to run away and lock herself in her room, was filled with pity, and determined to try and comfort him. So light was her footfall, and so deep his melancholy, that he was not aware of her presence till she spoke to him.

"I am so sorry for you," she said, "but my brothers are going back to Eton to-morrow, and then, if you behave yourself, no one will annoy you."

"It is absurd asking me to behave myself," he answered, looking round in astonishment at the pretty little girl who had ventured to address him, "quite absurd. I must rattle my chains, and groan through keyholes, and walk about at night, if that is what you mean. It is my only reason for existing."

"It is no reason at all for existing, and you know you have been very wicked. Mrs. Umney told us, the first day we arrived here, that you had killed your wife."

"Well, I quite admit it," said the Ghost, petulantly, "but it was a purely family matter, and concerned no one else."

"It is very wrong to kill any one," said Virginia, who at times had a sweet puritan gravity, caught from some old New England ancestor.

"Oh, I hate the cheap severity of abstract ethics! My wife was very plain, never had my ruffs properly starched, and knew nothing about cookery. Why, there was a buck I had shot in Hogley Woods, a magnificent pricket, and do you know how she had it sent to table? However, it is no matter now, for it is all over, and I don't think it was very nice of her brothers to starve me to death, though I did kill her."

"Starve you to death? Oh, Mr. Ghost—I mean Sir Simon, are you hungry? I have a sandwich in my case. Would you like it?"

"No, thank you, I never eat anything now; but it is very kind of you, all the same, and you are much nicer than the rest of your horrid, rude, vulgar, dishonest family."

"Stop!" cried Virginia, stamping her foot, "it is you who are rude, and horrid, and vulgar, and as for dishonesty, you know you stole the paints out of my box to try and furbish up that ridiculous blood-stain in the library. First you took all my reds, including the vermilion, and I couldn't do any more sunsets, then you took the emerald-green and the chrome-yellow, and finally I had nothing left but indigo and Chinese white, and could only do moonlight scenes, which are always depressing to look at, and not at all easy to paint. I never told on you, though I was very much annoyed, and it was most ridiculous, the whole thing; for who ever heard of emerald-green blood?"

"Well, really," said the Ghost, rather meekly, "what was I to do? It is a very difficult thing to get real blood nowadays, and, as your brother began it all with his Paragon Detergent, I certainly saw no reason why I should not have your paints. As for colour, that is always a matter of taste: the Cantervilles have blue blood, for instance, the very bluest in England; but I know you Americans don't care for things of this kind."

"You know nothing about it, and the best thing you can do is to emigrate and improve your mind. My father will be only too happy to give you a free passage, and though there is a heavy duty on spirits of every kind, there will be no difficulty about the Custom House, as the officers are all Democrats. Once in New York, you are sure to be a great success. I know lots of people there who would give a hundred thousand dollars to have a grandfather, and much more than that to have a family ghost."

"I don't think I should like America."

"I suppose because we have no ruins and no curiosities," said Virginia, satirically.

"No ruins! no curiosities!" answered the Ghost; "you have your navy and your manners."

"Good evening; I will go and ask papa to get the twins an extra week's holiday."

"Please don't go, Miss Virginia," he cried; "I am so lonely and so unhappy, and I really don't know what to do. I want to go to sleep and I cannot."

"That's quite absurd! You have merely to go to bed and blow out the candle. It is very difficult sometimes to keep awake, especially at church, but there is no difficulty at all about sleeping. Why, even babies know how to do that, and they are not very clever."

"I have not slept for three hundred years," he said sadly, and Virginia's beautiful blue eyes opened in wonder; "for three hundred years I have not slept, and I am so tired."

Virginia grew quite grave, and her little lips trembled like rose-leaves. She came towards him, and kneeling down at his side, looked up into his old withered face.

"Poor, poor Ghost," she murmured; "have you no place where you can sleep?"

"Far away beyond the pine-woods," he answered, in a low, dreamy voice, "there is a little garden. There the grass grows long and deep, there are the great white stars of the hemlock flower, there the nightingale sings all night long. All night long he sings, and the cold crystal moon looks down, and the yew-tree spreads out its giant arms over the sleepers."

Virginia's eyes grew dim with tears, and she hid her face in her hands.

"You mean the Garden of Death," she whispered.

"Yes, death. Death must be so beautiful. To lie in the soft brown earth, with the grasses waving above one's head, and listen to silence. To have no yesterday, and no to-morrow. To forget time, to forget life, to be at peace. You can help me. You can open for me the portals of death's house, for love is always with you, and love is stronger than death is."

Virginia trembled, a cold shudder ran through

her, and for a few moments there was silence. She felt as if she was in a terrible dream.

Then the ghost spoke again, and his voice sounded like the sighing of the wind.

"Have you ever read the old prophecy on the library window?"

"Oh, often," cried the little girl, looking up; "I know it quite well. It is painted in curious black letters, and is difficult to read. There are only six lines:

> '*When a golden girl can win*
> *Prayer from out the lips of sin,*
> *When the barren almond bears,*
> *And a little child gives away its tears,*
> *Then shall all the house be still*
> *And peace come to Canterville.*'

"But I don't know what they mean."

"They mean," he said, sadly, "that you must weep with me for my sins, because I have no tears, and pray with me for my soul, because I have no faith, and then, if you have always been sweet, and good, and gentle, the angel of death will have mercy on me. You will see fearful shapes in darkness, and wicked voices will whisper in your ear, but they will not harm you, for against the purity of a little child the powers of Hell cannot prevail."

Virginia made no answer, and the ghost wrung his hands in wild despair as he looked down at her bowed golden head. Suddenly she stood up, very pale, and with a strange light in her eyes. "I am not afraid," she said firmly, "and I will ask the angel to have mercy on you."

He rose from his seat with a faint cry of joy, and taking her hand bent over it with old-fashioned grace and kissed it. His fingers were as cold as ice, and his lips burned like fire, but Virginia did not falter, as he led her across the dusky room. On the faded green tapestry were broidered little huntsmen. They blew their tasselled horns and with their tiny hands waved to her to go back. "Go back! little Virginia," they cried, "go back!" but the ghost clutched her

hand more tightly, and she shut her eyes against them. Horrible animals with lizard tails and goggle eyes blinked at her from the carven chimneypiece, and murmured, "Beware! little Virginia, beware! we may never see you again," but the Ghost glided on more swiftly, and Virginia did not listen. When they reached the end of the room he stopped, and muttered some words she could not understand. She opened her eyes, and saw the wall slowly fading away like a mist, and a great black cavern in front of her. A bitter cold wind swept round them, and she felt something pulling at her dress. "Quick, quick," cried the Ghost, "or it will be too late," and in a moment the wainscoting had closed behind them, and the Tapestry Chamber was empty.

VI

About ten minutes later, the bell rang for tea, and, as Virginia did not come down, Mrs. Otis sent up one of the footmen to tell her. After a little time he returned and said that he could not find Miss Virginia anywhere. As she was in the habit of going out to the garden every evening to get flowers for the dinner-table, Mrs. Otis was not at all alarmed at first, but when six o'clock struck, and Virginia did not appear, she became really agitated, and sent the boys out to look for her, while she herself and Mr. Otis searched every room in the house. At half-past six the boys came back and said that they could find no trace of their sister anywhere. They were all now in the greatest state of excitement, and did not know what to do, when Mr. Otis suddenly remembered that, some few days before, he had given a band of gipsies permission to camp in the park. He accordingly at once set off for Blackfell Hollow, where he knew they were, accompanied by his eldest son and two of the farm-servants. The little Duke of Cheshire, who was perfectly frantic with anxiety, begged hard to be allowed to go too, but Mr. Otis would not allow him, as he was afraid there might be a scuffle. On arriving at the spot, however, he found that the gipsies had gone, and it was evident that their departure had been rather sudden, as the fire was still burning, and some plates were lying on the grass. Having sent off Washington and the two men to scour the district, he ran home, and despatched telegrams to all the police inspectors in the county, telling them to look out for a little girl who had been kidnapped by tramps or gipsies. He then ordered his horse to be brought round, and, after insisting on his wife and the three boys sitting down to dinner, rode off down the Ascot road with a groom. He had hardly, however, gone a couple of miles, when he heard somebody galloping after him, and, looking round, saw the little Duke coming up on his pony, with his face very flushed, and no hat. "I'm awfully sorry, Mr. Otis," gasped out the boy, "but I can't eat any dinner as long as Virginia is lost. Please don't be angry with me; if you had let us be engaged last year, there would never have been all this trouble. You won't send me back, will you? I can't go! I won't go!"

The Minister could not help smiling at the handsome young scapegrace, and was a good deal touched at his devotion to Virginia, so leaning down from his horse, he patted him kindly on the shoulders, and said, "Well, Cecil, if you won't go back, I suppose you must come with me, but I must get you a hat at Ascot."

"Oh, bother my hat! I want Virginia!" cried the little Duke, laughing, and they galloped on to the railway station. There Mr. Otis inquired of the station-master if any one answering to the description of Virginia had been seen on the platform, but could get no news of her. The station-master, however, wired up and down the line, and assured him that a strict watch would be kept for her, and, after having bought a hat for the little Duke from a linen-draper, who was just putting up his shutters, Mr. Otis rode off to Bexley, a village about four miles away, which he was told was a well-known haunt of the gipsies, as there was a large common next to it. Here they roused up the rural policeman, but could get no information from him, and, after riding all over

the common, they turned their horses' heads homewards, and reached the Chase about eleven o'clock, dead-tired and almost heart-broken. They found Washington and the twins waiting for them at the gate-house with lanterns, as the avenue was very dark. Not the slightest trace of Virginia had been discovered. The gipsies had been caught on Brockley meadows, but she was not with them, and they had explained their sudden departure by saying that they had mistaken the date of Chorton Fair, and had gone off in a hurry for fear they should be late. Indeed, they had been quite distressed at hearing of Virginia's disappearance, as they were very grateful to Mr. Otis for having allowed them to camp in his park, and four of their number had stayed behind to help in the search. The carp-pond had been dragged, and the whole Chase thoroughly gone over, but without any result. It was evident that, for that night at any rate, Virginia was lost to them; and it was in a state of the deepest depression that Mr. Otis and the boys walked up to the house, the groom following behind with the two horses and the pony. In the hall they found a group of frightened servants, and lying on a sofa in the library was poor Mrs. Otis, almost out of her mind with terror and anxiety, and having her forehead bathed with eau de cologne by the old housekeeper. Mr. Otis at once insisted on her having something to eat, and ordered up supper for the whole party. It was a melancholy meal, as hardly any one spoke, and even the twins were awestruck and subdued, as they were very fond of their sister. When they had finished, Mr. Otis, in spite of the entreaties of the little Duke, ordered them all to bed, saying that nothing more could be done that night, and that he would telegraph in the morning to Scotland Yard for some detectives to be sent down immediately. Just as they were passing out of the dining-room, midnight began to boom from the clock tower, and when the last stroke sounded they heard a crash and a sudden shrill cry; a dreadful peal of thunder shook the house, a strain of unearthly music floated through the air, a panel at the top of the staircase flew back with a loud noise, and out on the landing, looking very pale and white, with a little casket in her hand, stepped Virginia. In a moment they had all rushed up to her. Mrs. Otis clasped her passionately in her arms, the Duke smothered her with violent kisses, and the twins executed a wild war-dance round the group.

"Good heavens! child, where have you been?" said Mr. Otis, rather angrily, thinking that she had been playing some foolish trick on them. "Cecil and I have been riding all over the country looking for you, and your mother has been frightened to death. You must never play these practical jokes any more."

"Except on the Ghost! except on the Ghost!" shrieked the twins, as they capered about.

"My own darling, thank God you are found; you must never leave my side again," murmured Mrs. Otis, as she kissed the trembling child, and smoothed the tangled gold of her hair.

"Papa," said Virginia, quietly, "I have been with the Ghost. He is dead, and you must come and see him. He had been very wicked, but he was really sorry for all that he had done, and he gave me this box of beautiful jewels before he died."

The whole family gazed at her in mute amazement, but she was quite grave and serious; and, turning round, she led them through the opening in the wainscoting down a narrow secret corridor, Washington following with a lighted candle, which he had caught up from the table. Finally, they came to a great oak door, studded with rusty nails. When Virginia touched it, it swung back on its heavy hinges, and they found themselves in a little low room, with a vaulted ceiling, and one tiny grated window. Imbedded in the wall was a huge iron ring, and chained to it was a gaunt skeleton, that was stretched out at full length on the stone floor, and seemed to be trying to grasp with its long fleshless fingers an old-fashioned trencher and ewer, that were placed just out of its reach. The jug had evidently been once filled with water, as it was covered inside with green mould. There was nothing on the trencher but a pile of dust. Virginia knelt down beside the skeleton, and, folding her little hands together, began

to pray silently, while the rest of the party looked on in wonder at the terrible tragedy whose secret was now disclosed to them.

"Hallo!" suddenly exclaimed one of the twins, who had been looking out of the window to try and discover in what wing of the house the room was situated. "Hallo! the old withered almond-tree has blossomed. I can see the flowers quite plainly in the moonlight."

"God has forgiven him," said Virginia, gravely, as she rose to her feet, and a beautiful light seemed to illumine her face.

"What an angel you are!" cried the young Duke, and he put his arm round her neck, and kissed her.

VII

Four days after these curious incidents, a funeral started from Canterville Chase at about eleven o'clock at night. The hearse was drawn by eight black horses, each of which carried on its head a great tuft of nodding ostrich-plumes, and the leaden coffin was covered by a rich purple pall, on which was embroidered in gold the Canterville coat-of-arms. By the side of the hearse and the coaches walked the servants with lighted torches, and the whole procession was wonderfully impressive. Lord Canterville was the chief mourner, having come up specially from Wales to attend the funeral, and sat in the first carriage along with little Virginia. Then came the United States Minister and his wife, then Washington and the three boys, and in the last carriage was Mrs. Umney. It was generally felt that, as she had been frightened by the ghost for more than fifty years of her life, she had a right to see the last of him. A deep grave had been dug in the corner of the churchyard, just under the old yew-tree, and the service was read in the most impressive manner by the Rev. Augustus Dampier. When the ceremony was over, the servants, according to an old custom observed in the Canterville family, extinguished their torches, and, as the coffin was being lowered into the grave,

Virginia stepped forward, and laid on it a large cross made of white and pink almond-blossoms. As she did so, the moon came out from behind a cloud, and flooded with its silent silver the little churchyard, and from a distant copse a nightingale began to sing. She thought of the ghost's description of the Garden of Death, her eyes became dim with tears, and she hardly spoke a word during the drive home.

The next morning, before Lord Canterville went up to town, Mr. Otis had an interview with him on the subject of the jewels the ghost had given to Virginia. They were perfectly magnificent, especially a certain ruby necklace with old Venetian setting, which was really a superb specimen of sixteenth-century work, and their value was so great that Mr. Otis felt considerable scruples about allowing his daughter to accept them.

"My lord," he said, "I know that in this country mortmain is held to apply to trinkets as well as to land, and it is quite clear to me that these jewels are, or should be, heirlooms in your family. I must beg you, accordingly, to take them to London with you, and to regard them simply as a portion of your property which has been restored to you under certain strange conditions. As for my daughter, she is merely a child, and has as yet, I am glad to say, but little interest in such appurtenances of idle luxury. I am also informed by Mrs. Otis, who, I may say, is no mean authority upon Art,—having had the privilege of spending several winters in Boston when she was a girl,—that these gems are of great monetary worth, and if offered for sale would fetch a tall price. Under these circumstances, Lord Canterville, I feel sure that you will recognize how impossible it would be for me to allow them to remain in the possession of any member of my family; and, indeed, all such vain gauds and toys, however suitable or necessary to the dignity of the British aristocracy, would be completely out of place among those who have been brought up on the severe, and I believe immortal, principles of Republican simplicity. Perhaps I should mention that Virginia is very anxious that you should allow her to retain the box, as a memento of your unfortunate but misguided ancestor. As it is extremely old, and consequently a good deal out of repair, you may perhaps think fit to comply with her request. For my own part, I confess I am a good deal surprised to find a child of mine expressing sympathy with mediævalism in any form, and can only account for it by the fact that Virginia was born in one of your London suburbs shortly after Mrs. Otis had returned from a trip to Athens."

Lord Canterville listened very gravely to the worthy Minister's speech, pulling his grey moustache now and then to hide an involuntary smile, and when Mr. Otis had ended, he shook him cordially by the hand, and said: "My dear sir, your charming little daughter rendered my unlucky ancestor, Sir Simon, a very important service, and I and my family are much indebted to her for her marvellous courage and pluck. The jewels are clearly hers, and, egad, I believe that if I were heartless enough to take them from her, the wicked old fellow would be out of his grave in a fortnight, leading me the devil of a life. As for their being heirlooms, nothing is an heirloom that is not so mentioned in a will or legal document, and the existence of these jewels has been quite unknown. I assure you I have no more claim on them than your butler, and when Miss Virginia grows up, I dare say she will be pleased to have pretty things to wear. Besides, you forget, Mr. Otis, that you took the furniture and the ghost at a valuation, and anything that belonged to the ghost passed at once into your possession, as, whatever activity Sir Simon may have shown in the corridor at night, in point of law he was really dead, and you acquired his property by purchase."

Mr. Otis was a good deal distressed at Lord Canterville's refusal, and begged him to reconsider his decision, but the good-natured peer was quite firm, and finally induced the Minister to allow his daughter to retain the present the ghost had given her, and when, in the spring of 1890, the young Duchess of Cheshire was presented at the Queen's first drawing-room on the occasion of her marriage, her jewels were the universal theme of admiration. For Virginia received the coronet, which is the reward of all good little American girls, and was married to her boy-lover as soon as he came of age. They were both so charming, and they loved each other so much, that every one was delighted at the match, except the old Marchioness of Dumbleton, who had tried to catch the Duke for one of her seven unmarried daughters, and had given no less than three expensive dinner-parties for that purpose, and, strange to say, Mr. Otis himself. Mr. Otis was extremely fond of the young Duke personally, but, theoretically, he objected to titles, and, to use his own words, "was not without apprehension lest, amid the enervating influences of a pleasure-loving aristocracy, the true principles of Republican simplicity should be forgotten." His objections, however, were completely overruled, and I believe that when he walked up the aisle of St. George's, Hanover Square, with his daughter leaning on his arm, there was not a prouder man in the whole length and breadth of England.

The Duke and Duchess, after the honeymoon was over, went down to Canterville Chase, and on the day after their arrival they walked over in the afternoon to the lonely churchyard by the pine-woods. There had been a great deal of difficulty at first about the inscription on Sir Simon's tombstone, but finally it had been decided to engrave on it simply the initials of the old gentleman's name, and the verse from the library window. The Duchess had brought with her some lovely roses, which she strewed upon the grave, and after they had stood by it for some time they strolled into the ruined chancel of the old abbey. There the Duchess sat down on a fallen pillar, while her husband lay at her feet smoking a cigarette and looking up at her beautiful eyes. Suddenly he threw his cigarette away, took hold of her hand, and said to her, "Virginia, a wife should have no secrets from her husband."

"Dear Cecil! I have no secrets from you."

"Yes, you have," he answered, smiling, "you have never told me what happened to you when you were locked up with the ghost."

"I have never told any one, Cecil," said Virginia, gravely.

"I know that, but you might tell me."

"Please don't ask me, Cecil, I cannot tell you. Poor Sir Simon! I owe him a great deal. Yes, don't laugh, Cecil, I really do. He made me see what Life is, and what Death signifies, and why Love is stronger than both."

The Duke rose and kissed his wife lovingly.

"You can have your secret as long as I have your heart," he murmured.

"You have always had that, Cecil."

"And you will tell our children some day, won't you?"

Virginia blushed.

A NEGATIVE
TRAIN OF THOUGHT

PACIFIC 421

August Derleth

APART FROM HIS SUPERNATURAL fiction and Solar Pons stories, August Derleth (1909–1971) is not widely read today, which would undoubtedly have surprised those familiar with his early writing career. Already an accomplished writer while still in his teens, he was given accolades by such contemporaries as the novelist Sinclair Lewis, the poet Edgar Lee Masters, the great editor of Hemingway and Fitzgerald, Maxwell Perkins, and was awarded a prestigious Guggenheim Fellowship. In addition to being a prolific short story writer, Derleth was a novelist, poet, essayist, historian, biographer, dramatist, critic, and children's book writer.

It may well be, however, that his greatest legacy in the world of literature is the founding, with Donald Wandrei, of Arkham House. Created in 1939 to preserve the work of H. P. Lovecraft's magazine stories in hardcover book form, this little publishing house almost single-handedly defined the development of horror fiction in America. Although Derleth wrote Lovecraftian stories using the landscape and many of the characters of the first great American horror writer of the twentieth century, they were designed to maintain interest in what became known as the Cthulhu mythos and were not very good. Derleth preferred the more traditional kind of supernatural and ghost story as practiced by M. R. James and produced many tales of that type, suspenseful and proficient enough so that they are relentlessly anthologized today.

"*Pacific 421*" was originally published in the September 1944 issue of *Weird Tales.*

Pacific 421

By
AUGUST DERLETH

Pacific 421

AUGUST DERLETH

JUST TO BE ON the safe side, I wouldn't spend too much time over the hill at the far end of your property," said the agent with an apologetic smile.

Colley took the keys and pocketed them. "That's an odd thing to say. Why not?"

"Around mid-evening especially," continued the agent.

"Oh, come—why not?"

"That's just what I've been told. Something strange there, I'd guess. Give yourself time to become used to the place first."

Albert Colley had every intention of doing that. He had not bought a place in the country just out of a village on the Pacific line without the determination to become used to it before he invited his stepfather down—if he could screw up courage enough to have the old curmudgeon around for a week or so. If it were not for the old man's money—well, if it were not for that, and the fact that Albert Colley was his only legal heir, he would have been free of the old man long before this. Even as it was, Philander Colley was a trial that made itself felt in the remotest atom of Albert's being.

Of course, the agent's off-hand reference had been a mistake. Few people, in any case, are qualified to judge just how any given man will act, especially on such short acquaintance as there had been between Colley and the agent for the Parth house two miles out of that Missouri town. Colley was a cool customer, cooler than the agent guessed him to be. Colley apprehended at once that there was something a little strange about the far end of the property he had bought—a good forty-acre piece, with the house right up next to the road in a little clump of trees there, and, as he understood it from that old map in the county surveyor's office, a portion of the Pacific line cutting across the far edge of his property, over a little gully there. From the road and the house, his property stretched through a garden, then through a dense belt of woods to an open place beyond which there was a little knoll, politely called "the hill," and past this, the railroad and the termination of Colley's newly-acquired property at the foot of a steeper slope, likewise for the most part wooded.

And, being a cool customer, Colley went that first evening for a tour of exploration, half expecting some denizened beast to spring at him out of the woods, but not afraid, for all that. He walked down to the point where the railroad crossed the trestle over the gully and then turned to look down the tracks, this way and that; the railroad came around a curve, crossed the trestle and the edge of his property, and disappeared around a further curve to westward. He stood for a while on the trestle, smoking a cigar, and taking pleasure in the sound of nighthawks swooping and sky-coasting in the evening sky. He looked at his watch. Almost nine o'clock. Well, that was as close to mid-evening as a man would want, he thought.

He left the trestle and was beginning to walk leisurely back to the house when he heard the whistle and rumble of an approaching locomotive. He turned there on the edge of his woods to look. Yes, it was coming, brightly lit; so he stood and watched the powerful, surging force of the train thunder across the trestle, eight passenger cars streaming speedily along behind the locomotive—*Pacific 421*—on the way to the west coast. Like most men, he had always had a kind of affinity for trains; he liked to see them, ride on them, hear them. He watched this one out of sight and turned.

But at that moment there fell upon his ears the most frightful explosion of sound— a screaming of steel on steel, a splintering of wood, a great rush of steam, the roar of flames crackling, and the shrill, horrible screaming of people in agony. For a moment he was paralyzed with shock; then he realized that the train must have leaped the tracks or crashed into an eastbound train, and, without stopping to think that he ought to telephone for help, he sped back to the tracks and raced down as fast as he could to round the curve of the hill there to westward.

It was just as well that he did not summon help first.

There was nothing, nothing at all on the tracks beyond the curve!

For a moment Colley thought that the train must be found farther along, over the horizon; but that was impossible, for the tracks stretched away under the stars to join a greater network of railroads beyond, and there was nothing whatever on them. The evening train had gone through, and he—well, he had undoubtedly suffered a kind of auditory hallucination. But it jarred him still; for an hallucination, the experience had been shakingly convincing, and it was a somewhat subdued Albert Colley who made his way back along the tracks and into his property once more.

He thought about it all night.

In the morning he might have forgotten it but for the fact that he took a look at the village weekly he had had delivered to his house by the rural postman and his eye caught sight of train schedules; trains leaving for the west on the Pacific line were scheduled at 6:07 and at 11:23. Their numbers were different, too—there was no *Pacific 421* among them.

Colley was sharp. He had not been engaged in dubious business practices for some years without becoming shrewd about little matters. It did not take much to figure out that something was very much wrong. He read the railroad schedule over carefully and deliberately, and then got up and took a quick walk down through the garden, through the woods to the railroad tracks.

Their appearance under the sun was puzzling, to put it mildly. They were rusted and gave every evidence of deterioration under disuse. Wild roses, fox grass, evening primroses, weeds grew between the ties, and bushes climbed the embankment. The ties and the trestle were in good shape, but the fact remained that the railroad did not have the look of being in use. He crossed the trestle and walked for over a mile until he came to the double track which was certainly the main line. Then he walked back until he came to the tracks of the main line far around the slope of the hill on the other side. The cut-off spur across his property was not more than five miles in length, all told.

It was well past noon when he returned to the house. He made himself a light lunch and sat down to think the matter over.

Very peculiar. Then there had been the agent's half-hearted warning. A faint prickling made itself felt at the roots of his scalp, but something turning over in his scheming mind was stronger.

It was Saturday afternoon, or he would have made it a point to drive into the village and call on the agent; but the agent would be out of his office; the trip would be futile. What he could and would do, however, was to walk down through the garden and the woods, over the hill to the railroad embankment in mid-evening and keep an eye out for the *Pacific 421*.

It was not without some trepidation that he made his way through the woods to the railroad that night. He was filled with a certain uneasy

anticipation, but he would not yield to his inner promptings to return to the house and forget what he had seen. He took up his stand at the foot of an old cottonwood tree and lit a cigar, the aromatic smoke of which mingled with the pleasant, sweet foliage fragrance to make a pleasant cloud of perfume around him.

As nine o'clock drew near, he grew restive. He looked at his watch several times, but the time passed with execrable slowness. The train was manifestly late.

Nine-fifteen, nine-thirty, nine-forty-five—and at last ten. No train.

Colley was more mystified than ever, and he returned to the house that night determined to repeat his experiment on the morrow.

But on Sunday night he saw no more than he had seen the previous day. No locomotive whistled and roared across the trestle and away around the curve of the hill, drawing its passenger cars, brilliantly alight, after it—nothing at all. Only the wind sighed and whispered at the trestle, and a persistent owl hooted from the hillside beyond the ravine bridged by the trestle. Colley was puzzled, and, yes, a little annoyed.

He went into the village on Monday and paid a call on the agent.

"Tell me," he said affably, "doesn't the old *Pacific 421* run out of here anymore?"

The agent gave him an odd glance. "Not since the accident. I think even the number's been discontinued. Let me see—the accident took place about seven years ago, when that spur across your land was still part of the main line."

"Oh, it's no longer in use, then?"

"No, it hasn't been for years—ever since the accident." He coughed. "You haven't seen anything, have you?"

It was at this point that Colley made his fatal mistake. He was too clever for his own good. Because his thoughts were several leaps and bounds ahead of the agent's, he said gravely, "No. Why?"

The agent sighed his relief. "Well, some people have laid claim to seeing a ghost there." He laughed. "A ghost train, if you can believe it!"

"Interesting," said Colley dryly, his skin at the back of his neck chilling.

"That wreck occurred on a Friday evening, and it's usually on Friday that the so-called apparition is seen. And then it seems to have its limitations; I've never seen it myself; nor have very many people. I did have the experience of being with someone who claimed to be seeing it. But I never heard ghost, man or train, which could be seen and heard by one person and not by someone standing beside him, did you?"

"Never," agreed Colley gravely.

"Well, there you are. I was afraid you, too, might have seen something. I was just a little nervous about it."

"I suppose that's what you meant . . ."

"Yes. Maybe I shouldn't have said anything."

"No harm done," said Colley, smiling good-naturedly.

He was really not paying much attention to what the agent was saying, for he was busy with his own thoughts. His own thoughts would have been of considerable interest to his stepfather, for they concerned him very much indeed. Philander Colley had a weak heart, and it had occurred to Albert Colley that with a careful build-up and the sudden exposure of the old man to that ghost train some Friday night, the old man's heart might give out on him, and that would leave Albert, as the old man's only heir, in sound financial shape.

He had expected the agent to put the matter more or less as he did. Incredible as it seemed, the idea of a phantom train was not entirely beyond the bounds of possibility. Of course, curiously, Colley did not actually believe in the phantom train as anything supernatural—doubtless there was some kind of scientific explanation for it, he felt, thus betraying a juvenile faith in one kind of superstition as opposed to another. But as long as something came rushing along there and wrecked itself, repeating the catastrophe of that Friday evening seven years ago, it might as well be put to his own use. After all, that train, whatever its status, did cross his land, and he had a certain proprietary right in it.

Forthwith he wired his stepfather that he had got settled, and the old man might like to come down from his place in Wisconsin and take a look around Colley's place in the Missouri country.

The old man came, with dispatch.

If Albert Colley had his dark side, the old man was cantankerous enough to match his stepson any day, any time, any place. He was the sort of crotchety old devil who would argue about anything under the sun, at scarcely the shadow of a provocation. Small wonder Colley wanted to get rid of him!

Colley lost no time in setting the stage. He told the old man that it was his regular habit to walk down to the end of his property every evening, and would like the old man to accompany him.

Bitterly complaining, the old man went along.

As they approached the railroad tracks—it was Wednesday night, and nothing was likely to happen—Colley coughed unctuously and said that the stretch of abandoned tracks before them had the reputation of being haunted.

"Haunted?" repeated the old man, with a sarcastic laugh. "By what?"

"A train that was wrecked here about seven years ago. *Pacific 421*."

"Cock and bull story," snapped Philander.

"There *are* people who claim to have seen it."

"Out of their minds. Or drunk. You ought to know what you can see when you're drunk, Albert. I remember that time you saw alligators all over your room."

"Still, you know," said Albert, trying his best to be patient, "one ought not to dismiss such stories too casually. After all, things happen, and science cannot always explain them satisfactorily."

"Things! What things? Optical illusions, hallucinations—such like. No, my boy, you never were very bright in school, but I never thought it would come to this—a belief in ghosts. And what a ghost, to be specific!" He turned on him almost fiercely. "Have you seen it yourself?"

"N-no," faltered Albert.

"Well, then!" snorted the old man.

That ended the conversation about the phantom train for that evening. Albert was just a little disappointed, but not too badly; after all, he must go slowly; the groundwork for Friday night's hoped-for fatal apparition must be laid carefully. What he could not accomplish on Wednesday, he might well be able to do on the following evening. And then,—then, on Friday . . . Ah, but Friday was still two days away!

So, on Thursday evening they walked down to the tracks again. The old man wanted to go out onto the trestle, and there he stood, talking about trestles in Wisconsin from which he had fished as a boy—quite a long time before he had married Albert's mother. Albert had a hard time bringing the conversation around to the phantom train, and he had hardly mentioned it before the old man cut him off with his customary rudeness.

"Still going on about that ghost train, eh?"

"The fact is, there seems to be some question about the story both ways."

"I should think there would be!" he snorted. "I can't figure out how a sane, normal, healthy young man would want to even think of such drivel, let alone go on about it the way you do."

"Keep an open mind, Philander," said Albert with ill-concealed asperity.

"My mind's been open all my life," retorted the old man. "But not to a lot of silly superstitions and womanish fears."

"I can't recall having expressed fear of any kind," said Albert frigidly.

"No, but you sound like it."

"I'm not in the habit of being afraid of something I've never seen," said Albert.

"Oh, most people are afraid of the dark." He strove to peer through the gloom into the gully. "Tell me—sand or rock on the sides down there?"

"Rock for the most part. The sand's been washed away."

"Look to be some trees growing down there."

"Young ones—just a few."

Poor Albert! He lost ten minutes talking about rocks, trees, declivities, angles, degrees, and erosion of wind as against that of water, and by that time he was almost too exhausted to bring up the subject of the phantom train again. But he strove manfully and came up with a weak question.

"Tell me, Philander—what would you do if you saw that train coming at us?"

"That ghost train?"

"Yes, the one some people believe in."

"Why, close my eyes till she went past," said the old man promptly.

"Then you would be afraid of it," charged Albert.

"If there were any such thing, you're darn' tootin' I would!"

That was something—in the way of a hopeful sign, at least, thought Albert, walking slowly back at his stepfather's side. Well, tomorrow night would tell the story. And if somehow it failed, there was always Friday night a week hence. Patience and fortitude, Albert, my boy! he told himself, meanwhile contemplating with pleasure his acquisition of his stepfather's material possessions. He resolved to time their visit with the utmost care tomorrow night.

All that day he went out of his way to be nice to the old man, on the theory that those who are about to die deserve such little pleasures as it is possible to give; and he was unnaturally ready to forgive the old man his cantankerousness and irritability—which startled Philander because it was an attitude for which Albert had never won any medals. If the old man had not been so selfish himself, he might have thought about this change in his stepson; but he opined that perhaps Albert was in need of money and was about to make a touch, and took pleasure for hours thinking up ways in which to rebuff Albert.

As for Albert, he grew hourly more elated as that fateful Friday passed on its way. Time went heavy-footed, but Albert could be patient. After all, Philander's money drew closer moment by moment, and it was of proportions worth waiting for, even if the old man were not exactly what a man might call "rich."

For some reason, all the signs were auspicious. That is to say, along about mid-afternoon, the old man began to recall tales of hauntings he had heard in his youth, and waxed quite garrulous. Albert considered this virtually a sign from—well, not heaven, of course; heaven would hardly be giving him a green light. Anyway, it was a sign, a kind of portent that all was destined to happen as Albert had planned it.

So that evening he gave Philander one of his best cigars, lit it for him jovially, and set out with him for the railroad tracks. He had had a few moments of ghastly fear that the old man might not accompany him, but there was no stopping him. He had in fact taken over Albert's little walk, and called it his "constitutional."

"This is the night, you know, that ghost train is said to appear," said Albert cautiously.

"Friday, eh?"

"Yes, it was on Friday that the accident took place."

"Funny thing—how methodical ghosts and suchlike can be, eh?"

Albert agreed, and then very subtly, according to plan, discredited the entire narrative, from beginning to end. It would not do to appear too gullible, when the old man knew very well he was not.

He had hoped they might be able to take up a stand at the edge of the woods, so that Philander might get the best possible view and the maximum shock at sight of that speeding spectre, but the old man insisted upon walking farther. Indeed, he ventured out upon the embankment, he walked along the tracks, he even crossed the trestle. This was not quite in accordance with Albert's plans, but he had to yield to it; he followed his stepfather across the trestle, observing in some dismay that the hour must be close to nine.

Even as he thought this, the sound of a thin, wailing whistle burst upon his ears, and almost immediately thereafter came the rumble of the approaching train. Ahead of them the light of the locomotive swung around and bore down on them; it was the ghost train, rushing at them with the speed of light, it seemed, with a kind of demoniac violence wholly in keeping with the shattering end to which it was destined to come.

Even in the sudden paroxysm of fright that struck him, Albert did not forget to act natural; this was as he had planned it—to pretend he saw nothing; all he did was to step off the tracks to one side. Then he turned to look at his step-father. What he saw filled him with complete dismay.

The old man stood in the middle of the right-of-way relighting his cigar. Not a hair of his head had turned, and his eyes were not closed. Yet he appeared to be gazing directly at the approaching train. Albert remembered with sickening chagrin that the agent had said many people could not see the train.

But if Philander Colley could not see the spectral train, he was nevertheless not immune. For at the moment that the phantom locomotive came into contact with the material person of the old man, Philander was knocked up and catapulted into the gully with terrific force, while the agent of his disaster went on its destined way, its lighted coaches streaming by, vanishing around the hill, and ending up, as before, in a horrific din of wreckage.

Albert had to take a minute or two to collect himself. Then he ran as best he could down the slope to where his stepfather lay.

Philander Colley was very thoroughly dead. He had been crushed and broken—just as if he had been struck by a locomotive! Albert did not give him a second thought; however, it had been done, Philander's end had been accomplished. He set off at a rapid trot for the car to run into the village and summon help.

Unfortunately for Albert Colley, the villagers were wholly devoid of imagination. A ghost train, indeed! There was plenty of evidence from Wisconsin that Albert Colley and his stepfather had not got along at all well. And Albert was the old man's only heir, too! An open and shut matter, in the opinion of the officials. If there were any such thing as a phantom train, why hadn't Albert Colley said something about it before? The agent could testify he had not. It was plain as a pikestaff that Albert had beaten up the old man and probably pushed him off the trestle. With commendable dispatch Albert Colley was arrested, tried, and hanged.

Robert Weinberg

ONE OF THE WORLD'S foremost experts in the world of pulp magazines, science fiction, horror, and fantasy, Robert (Bob) Weinberg (1947–) was a successful bookseller in those fields for many years while writing and editing on a part-time basis. He sold his first story in 1967 and went on to write seventeen novels, the most popular being the trilogy Masquerade of the Red Death (1995/1996), and two short story collections. He created the character Sidney (Sid) Taine, known as "the psychic detective," who appeared in the novel *The Black Lodge* (1991) and short stories collected in *The Occult Detective* (2005). The Marvel comic book series *Nightside* (2001), which Weinberg created and wrote, featured the further exploits of Taine.

Among Weinberg's nonfiction books, the best known and most significant are *The Weird Tales Story* (1977), *A Biographical Dictionary of Science Fiction and Fantasy Authors* (1988), *Horror of the 20th Century* (2000), and, with Louis H. Gresh, *The Science of James Bond* (2006). He has edited more than 150 anthologies in the pulp, horror, science fiction, western, and mystery genres, often in collaboration with Stefan R. Dziemianowicz and/or Martin H. Greenberg. Among Weinberg's numerous honors are two Bram Stoker Awards, two World Fantasy Awards, and a Lifetime Achievement Award from the Horror Writers Association.

"The Midnight El" was originally published in *Return to the Twilight Zone*, edited by Carol Serling (New York, DAW Books, 1994).

The Midnight El

ROBERT WEINBERG

COLD AND ALONE, Sidney Taine waited for the Midnight El. Collar pulled up close around his neck, he shivered as the frigid Chicago wind attacked his exposed skin. Not even the usual drunks haunted the outdoor subway platforms on nights like these. With temperatures hovering only a few degrees above zero, the stiff breeze off Lake Michigan plunged the wind chill factor to twenty below. Fall asleep outside in the darkness and you never woke up.

Taine hated the cold. Though he had lived in Chicago for more than a year, he had yet to adjust to the winter weather. Originally from San Francisco, he delighted his hometown friends when he groused that he never realized what the phrase "chilled to the bone" meant until he moved to the Windy City.

Six feet four inches tall, weighing a bit more than two hundred and thirty pounds, Taine resembled a professional football player. Yet he moved with the grace of a stalking tiger and, for his size, was incredibly light on his feet. A sly grin and dark, piercing eyes gave him a sardonic, slightly mysterious air. An image he strived hard to cultivate.

Like his father and grandfather before him, Taine worked as a private investigator. Though he had opened his office in Chicago only fourteen months ago, he was already well known throughout the city. Dubbed by one of the major urban newspapers as "The New-Age Detective," Taine used both conventional techniques and occult means to solve his cases. While his unusual methods caused a few raised eyebrows, no one mocked his success rate. Specializing in missing-person investigations, Taine rarely failed to locate his quarry. He had his doubts, though, about tonight's assignment.

Before leaving his office this evening, Taine had mixed, then drunk, an elixir with astonishing properties. According to the famous grimoire, *The Key of Solomon,* the potion enabled the user to see the spirits of the dead. Its effects only lasted till dawn. Which was more than enough time for Taine. If he failed tonight, there would be no second chance.

The detective glanced down at his watch for the hundredth time. The glowing hands indicated five minutes to twelve. According to local legends, it was nearly the hour for the Midnight El to start its run.

No one knew how or when the stories began. A dozen specialists in urban folklore supplied the detective with an equal number of fabled origins. One and all, they were of the opinion that the tales dated back to the first decades of the century, when the subway first debuted in Chicago.

A few old-timers, mostly retired railway conductors and engineers, claimed the Midnight El continued an even older tradition—the Phantom Train, sometimes called the Death's Head Locomotive. Despite the disagreements, several elements remained constant in all the accounts. The Midnight El hit the tracks exactly at the stroke of twelve. Its passengers consisted of those who had died that day in Chicago. The train traversed the entire city, starting at the station closest to the most deaths of the day, and working its way along from there.

Knowing that fact, Taine waited on a far south side platform. Earlier in the day, twelve people had died in a flash fire only blocks from this location. There was little question that this would be the subway's first stop.

Slowly, the seconds ticked past. A harsh west wind wailed off the lake, like some dread banshee warning Taine of his peril. With it came the doleful chiming of a distant church bell striking the hour. Midnight—the end of one day, start of another.

The huge train came hurtling along the track rumbling like distant thunder. Emerging ghostlike out of thin air, dark and forbidding, blacker than the night, it lumbered into the station. Lights flashed red and yellow as it slowed to a stop. Taine caught a hurried vision inside a half-dozen cars as they rumbled past. Pale, vacant, *dead* faces stared out into the night. Riders from another city, or another day, he wasn't sure which, and he had no desire to know. Young and old, black and white, men and women, all hungering for a glimpse of life.

Hissing loudly, double doors swung open on each car. A huge, shadowy figure clad in a conductor's uniform emerged from midway along the train. In his right hand he held a massive silver pocket watch, hooked by a glittering chain to his vest. Impatiently, he stood there, waiting for new arrivals.

The conductor's gaze swept the station, rested on Taine for a moment, then continued by. The ghost train and all its passengers were invisible to mortal eyes. There was no way for him to know that the man on the platform could actually see him. Nor suspect what Taine planned to do.

Once he had been a ferryman. The ancient Greeks knew him as Charon. To the Egyptians, he had been Anubis, the Opener of the Way. A hundred other cultures named him a hundred different ways. But always his task remained the same—transporting the newly dead to their final destination.

They came with the wind. Not there, then suddenly there. Each one stopped to face the conductor for an instant before being allowed to pass. The breath froze in Taine's throat as he watched them file by. Those who had died that day.

His hands clenched into fists when he sighted three pajama-clad black children. The detective recognized the trio immediately. Today's newspapers had been filled with all the grisly details of that sudden tenement fire that had resulted in their deaths. None of them had been over six years old.

Wordlessly, the last of the three turned. Lonely, mournful eyes stared deep into Taine's for an instant. The detective remained motionless. If he reacted now, it might warn the conductor. An instant passed, and then the child and all the other passengers were gone. Disappeared into the Midnight El.

The conductor stepped back into the doorway. Raising one hand, he signaled to some unseen engineer to continue. Seeing his chance, Taine acted.

Moving incredibly fast for a man his size, the detective darted at, then around, the astonished doorman. Before the shadowy figure could react, Taine was past him and into the subway. Ignoring the restless dead on all sides, the detective headed for the front of the car.

"Come back here," demanded the conductor, swinging aboard. Behind him, the doors thudded shut. An instant later, the car jerked forward as the engine came to life. Outside scenery blurred as the train gained speed. The floor shook with a gentle, rocking motion. The Midnight El was off to its next stop.

Taine relaxed, letting his pursuer catch up to him. Surprise had enabled him to board the ghostly train. Getting off might not prove so easy.

"You do not belong on the Midnight El, Mr.

Taine," said the conductor. He spoke calmly, without any trace of accent. Listening closely, Taine caught the barest hint of amusement in the phantom's voice. "At least, not yet. Your time is not for years and years."

"You know my name, and the instant of my death?" asked Taine, not the least bit intimidated by the imposing bulk of the other. Surrounded by shadows, the ticket taker towered over Taine by a head. His face, though human, appeared cut from weathered marble. Only his black, black eyes burned with life.

"Of course," answered the conductor. His body swayed gracefully with every motion of the subway car. "Past, present, future mean nothing to me. One look at a man is all I need to review his entire life history, from the moment of his birth to the last breath he takes. It's part of my job, supervising the Midnight El."

"For what employer?" asked Taine, casually.

"Someday you'll learn the answer," replied the conductor, with a chuckle. "But it won't matter much then."

The phantom reached into his vest pocket and pulled out the silver pocket watch. "Thirteen minutes to the next stop. This train, unlike most, always runs on time. You shall exit there, Mr. Taine."

"And if I choose not to," said Taine.

The conductor frowned. "You must. I cannot harm you. Such action is strictly forbidden under the terms of my contract. However, I appeal to your sense of compassion. A living presence on this train upsets the other passengers. Think of the pain you are inflicting on them."

Darkness gathered around the railroad man. He no longer looked so human. His black coal eyes burned into Taine's with inhuman intensity. "Leave them to their rest, Mr. Taine. You do not belong here."

"Nor does one other," replied the detective.

The conductor sighed, his rock-hard features softening in sorrow. "I should have guessed. You came searching for Maria Hernandez. Why?"

"Her husband hired me. He read about my services in the newspapers. I'm the final resort for those who refuse to give up hope.

"Victor told me what little he knew. My knowledge of the occult filled in the blanks. Combined together, the facts led me here."

"All trails end at the Midnight El," declared the conductor solemnly. "Though I'm surprised that you realized that."

"After examining the information, it was the only possible solution," said Taine. "Maria disappeared two weeks ago. She vanished without a trace from an isolated underground subway platform exactly at midnight. No one else recognized the significance of the time.

"The police admitted they were completely baffled. The ticket seller remembered Maria taking the escalator down to the station a few minutes before twelve. A transit patrolman spoke to her afterward. He remembered looking up at the clock and noting the lateness of the hour. But when he looked around, the woman was no longer there. Somehow, she disappeared in the blink of an eye. Searching the tunnels for her body turned up nothing."

Taine paused. "Victor Hernandez considered me his last and only chance. I promised him I would do my best. I never mentioned the Midnight El."

"My thanks to you for that," said the conductor, nodding his understanding. "Suicides cause me the greatest pain. Especially those who sacrifice themselves to join the one they love."

"She meant a great deal to him," said Taine. "They were only married a few months. It seemed quite unfair."

"The world is unfair, Mr. Taine," said the conductor, shrugging his massive shoulders. "Or so I have been told by many of my passengers. Again and again, for centuries beyond imagining."

"She wasn't dead," said Taine. "If I don't belong here, then neither does she."

The conductor grimaced, his black eyes narrowing. He looked down at his great silver watch and shook his head. "There's not enough time to explain," he said. "Our schedule is too tight for long talks. Please understand my position."

"The Greeks considered Charon the most honorable of the gods," said Taine, sensing his host's inner conflict. "Of course, that was thousands of years ago."

"Spare me the dramatics," said the conductor. A bitter smile crossed his lips. He nodded to himself, as if making an important decision. Slowly, ever so slowly, he twisted the stem on the top of his watch.

All motion ceased. The subway car no longer shook with motion. Outside, the blurred features of the city solidified into grotesque, odd shapes, faintly resembling the Chicago skyline.

Taine grunted in surprise. "You can stop time?"

"For a little while," said the conductor. "Don't forget, the Midnight El visits every station in the city and suburbs within the space of a single night. On a hot summer night in a violent city like this, we often need extra minutes for all the passengers. Thus my watch. Twisting a little more produces a timeless state."

"The scenery?" asked Taine, not wanting to waste his questions, but compelled to ask by the alienness of the landscape.

"All things exist in time as well as space," said the conductor. "Take away that fourth dimension and the other three seem twisted."

The phantom turned and beckoned with his other hand. "Maria Hernandez. Attend me."

A short, slender woman in her early twenties pushed her way forward through the ranks of the dead. Long brown hair, knotted in a single thick braid, dropped down her back almost to her waist. Wide, questioning eyes looked at the detective. Unlike all the others on the train, a spark of color still touched Maria's cheeks. And her chest rose and fell with her every breath.

"Tell Mr. Taine how you missed the subway two weeks ago," said the conductor. He glanced over at Taine, almost as if checking to make sure the detective was paying attention.

"There was a shortage in one of the drawers at closing time," began Maria Hernandez, her voice calm, controlled. "My superior asked me to do a crosscheck. It was merely a mathematical error, but it took nearly twenty minutes to find. By then, I was ten minutes late for my train."

She hesitated, as if remembering something particularly painful. "I was in a hurry to get home. It was our six-month anniversary. When I left that morning for the bank, my husband, Victor, promised me a big surprise when I returned. I loved surprises."

"Yes, I know," said the conductor, his voice gentle. "He bought you tickets to the theater. But that is incidental to the story. Please continue."

"Usually, I have to wait a few minutes for my train," said Maria. "Not that night. It arrived exactly on schedule. When I reached the el platform, the conductor was signaling to close the doors. The next subway wasn't for thirty minutes. So, I ran."

Again, she paused. "I would have made it, too, if it wasn't for my right heel." She looked down at her shoes. "It caught in a crack in the cement. Wedged there so tight I couldn't pull my foot loose. By the time I wrenched free, the train had already left."

"Two weeks ago," said Taine, comprehension dawning. "The day of the big subway crash in the Loop."

"Correct," said the conductor. "Four minutes after Mrs. Hernandez missed her train, it crashed headlong into another, stalled on the tracks ahead. Fourteen people died when several of the cars sandwiched together. *Fifteen* should have perished."

"Fate," said Taine.

"She was destined to die," replied the conductor, as if explaining the obvious. "It was woven in the threads. A mistake was made somewhere. Her heel should have missed that crack. There was probably a knot in the twine. I assure you her name was on my passenger list. Maria was scheduled to ride the Midnight El."

"So, when she didn't, you decided to correct

that mistake on your own," said Taine, his temper rising. Mrs. Hernandez stood silent, as if frozen in place. Her story told, the conductor ignored her. "I thought a living person on board disturbed the dead?"

"With effort, the rules can be bent," said the conductor. He sighed. "It grows so boring here, Taine. You cannot imagine how terribly boring. I desired company, someone to talk to. Someone alive, someone with feelings, emotions. The dead no longer care about anything. They are so dull.

"The Three Sisters had to unravel a whole section of the cloth. They needed to weave a new destiny for Mrs. Hernandez to cover up their mistake. Meanwhile, Maria should have been dead but was still alive. Her spirit belonged to neither plane of existence. It took no great effort to bring her on the train as a passenger. And here she will remain, for all eternity, neither living nor dead but in a state between the two. Immortal, undying, unchanging—exactly like me. Forever."

Taine's fist clenched in anger. "Who gave you the power to decide her fate? That's not your job. You're only the ferryman, nothing more. She doesn't belong here. I won't allow you to do this."

"Your opinion means nothing to me, Mr. Taine," said the conductor, his features hardening. His left hand rested on the stem of the pocket watch. "There is nothing you can do to stop me."

"Like hell," said the detective, and leaped forward.

A big, powerfully built man, he moved with astonishing speed. Once tonight he had caught the conductor by surprise. This time, he did not.

The phantom's left hand shot out and caught Taine by the throat. Without effort, he raised the detective into the air, so that the man's feet dangled inches off the floor.

"I am not fooled so easily a second time," he declared.

Taine flailed wildly with both hands at the conductor. Not one of his punches connected. Desperately, the detective lashed out one foot, hitting the other in the chest. The phantom didn't even flinch. He hardly seemed to notice Taine's struggles.

"In my youth," said the conductor, "I wrestled with Atlas and Hercules. Your efforts pale before theirs, Mr. Taine."

The conductor's attention focused entirely on the detective. Neither man nor spirit noticed Mrs. Hernandez cautiously reaching for the silver pocket watch the trainman held negligently in his other hand. Not until she suddenly grabbed it away.

"What!" bellowed the conductor, dropping Taine and whirling about. "You . . . you . . ."

"Just because I obeyed your commands," said Mrs. Hernandez, "didn't mean that I no longer possessed a will of my own. I was waiting for the right opportunity." She gestured with her head at the crowds of the dead all around them. "I'm not like them. I'm alive."

She held the pocket watch tightly, one hand on the stem. "If you try to take this away, I'll break it. Don't make me do that."

Taine, his throat and neck burning with pain, staggered to Mrs. Hernandez's side. "Let us go. Otherwise, we'll remain here forever, frozen in time."

"Nonsense," said the conductor. "I told you the rules can only be bent so far. Sooner or later, the strain would become too great and snap this train back to the real world."

"But if Maria breaks your watch," said Taine, "what then? You admitted needing its powers. Think of the problems maintaining your schedule without it."

"True enough," admitted the conductor. He paused for a moment, as if in thought. "Listen, I am willing to offer this compromise. Maria cannot leave this train without my permission. The Fates will not spin her a new destiny as long as she remains on the El. Return the watch to me and I'll give her a chance to return to her husband. And resume her life on Earth."

"A chance?" said the detective, suspiciously. "What exactly do you mean by that?"

"A gamble, a bet, *a wager*, Mr. Taine," said the conductor. "Relieve my boredom. Ask me a question, any question. If I cannot answer, you and Mrs. Hernandez go free. If I guess correctly, then both of you remain here for all eternity—not dead but no longer among the living—on the Midnight El. It will take a great deal of effort, but I can manage. Take it or leave it. I refuse to bend any further."

"Both of us?" said Taine. "You raised the stakes. And what about disturbing the dead? A little while ago you were anxious for me to leave."

"As I stated before, the rules can be bent. After all, I am the ferryman. And," continued Charon, the faintest trace of a smile on his lips, "what better way to sharpen your wits, Mr. Taine, than to put your own future at peril?"

"But," said the detective, "according to your earlier remarks, there's nothing in the world you don't know."

"There is only one omniscient presence," said the conductor. "Man or spirit, we are mere reflections of his glory. Still," he added, almost in afterthought, "the universe holds few mysteries for me."

Shadows gathered around the phantom. He extended one huge hand. "Make your decision. Now. Before I change my mind." His eyes burned like two flaming coals. "No tricks, either. An answer must exist for your question."

"Give him the watch," Taine said to Maria Hernandez.

"Then you agree?" asked the conductor.

"I agree," replied the detective, calmly.

Chuckling, the conductor twisted the stem of his great silver watch. Immediately, the scenery shifted and the subway car started shaking. They were back in the real world.

"We arrive at the next station in a few minutes," Charon announced smugly. "You have until then to frame your question, Mr. Taine."

Maria Hernandez gasped, raising her hands to her face. "But . . . but . . . that's cheating."

"Not true," said the conductor. "I promised no specific length of time for our challenge." He glanced down at his watch. "Your time is ticking by quickly. Better think fast."

Taine took a deep breath. Not all questions depended on facts for their answer. He prayed that the ferryman would not renege on their bargain once he realized his mistake. "You trapped yourself," said the detective. "I'm ready now."

"You are?" said the conductor, frowning. He sounded surprised.

"Of course," said Taine. "Are you prepared to accept defeat?"

"Impossible," replied the conductor, bewildered. "I know the answer to every question."

"Then tell me," said Taine, "the answer to the question raised when I first boarded the train. When is the exact moment of my death?"

"You will perish . . ." began the conductor, then stopped. He stood silent, mouth open in astonishment. Slowly, the fire left his eyes. The phantom shook his head in dismay. "Caught by my own words."

Not exactly sure what the conductor meant, Maria Hernandez directed her attention to Taine. "I don't understand. Caught? How?"

"The conductor bragged earlier that he knew the date of my death," said Taine. "If he answers correctly, then he wins our bet."

"And," continued Maria, comprehension dawning, "by the terms of the agreement, you must remain on the Midnight El forever."

"Thus making his prediction false," finished Taine, "since I cannot die when he predicts. On the other hand, if he says that I will never die, then he does not know the date of my death. Which means he cannot answer the question. So, whatever he says, I am the winner. The bet is ours."

With a sigh, the conductor pocketed his watch. "You would have made good company, Mr. Taine." Metal screeched on metal as the Midnight El pulled into the next station. "This is your stop. Farewell."

They were outside. Alone. On a deserted subway station. With a cold wind blowing, but neither of them noticed.

Tears filled Maria Hernandez's eyes. "Are we free? Really free?"

Taine nodded, his thoughts drifting. Already, he searched for an explanation for Maria's disappearance that would satisfy both the police and her husband.

"As free as any man or woman can be," he answered somberly. "In the end, we all have a date to keep with the Midnight El."

STOP—YOU'RE SCARING ME

Frederick Cowles

ALTHOUGH HIS WORK HAS sometimes been accused of being derivative, perhaps owing too much to M. R. James, Frederick (Ignatius) Cowles (1900–1948) has, nonetheless, produced numerous classic works in the supernatural genre, including "The Vampire of Kaldenstein" (1938), "Princess of Darkness" (1993), and "The Horror of Abbot's Grange" (1936). Born in Cambridge, England, he graduated from Emmanuel College, Cambridge, and worked for a time at the library of Trinity College, but then moved in 1927 to become chief librarian at Swinton and Pendlebury in Lancashire, a position he held until the end of his life. There, the bibliophilic Cowles edited the library *Bulletin,* for which he wrote occasional ghost stories. Two collections of supernatural stories were published during his lifetime, *The Horror of Abbot's Grange* (1936), which contained his first published story, "The Headless Leper," and *The Night Wind Howls* (1938).

The fact that his grandmother was a gypsy may help account for his many wanderings throughout the British Isles as he researched a series of travel books, including *Dust of Years: Pilgrimages in Search of the Ancient Shrines of England* (1933), *'Neath English Skies* (1933), *The Magic of Cornwall* (1934), *Not Far from the Smoke* (1935), and *Vagabond Pilgrimage* (1948), all of which were illustrated by his talented wife, Doris. After World War II ended, he published his most famous book, *This Is England* (1946). He also wrote children's books, including *The Magic Map* (1934) and one for his son, *Michael in Bookland* (1936).

"Punch and Judy" was originally published in book form in *Star Book of Horror No. 1* (London, Star, 1975); it was first collected in *Fear Walks the Night: The Complete Ghost Stories of Frederick Cowles* (London, Ghost Story Press, 1993).

Punch and Judy

FREDERICK COWLES

I

I came upon him in a green lane near Lewes. My attention was attracted by a long, oblong affair, covered with a shabby waterproof sheet and mounted on a kind of two-wheeled trolley. On one side of this contraption was some faded lettering which, as I drew nearer, I made out to be: *Prof. Jack Smith. The Oldest Show in the World.* A crude painting of Punch confirmed that this was the set-up of a travelling Punch and Judy showman. Snores from under the hedge revealed the presence of the Professor, who was sprawled on the grass in a most inelegant attitude. An empty bottle by an outstretched hand indicated the source of the gentleman's profound slumber.

Something urged me to hurry on, for there was an indefinable unpleasantness about the sleeping man. I caught a glimpse of a cruel mouth, the bristly stubble of an unshaven chin, and dirty, greying hair under a dilapidated felt hat. There was even something sinister, I felt, about that oblong article on wheels. Yet there is always an attraction about a Punch and Judy show and I suppose the glamour is shared, in some measure, by the man who operates the puppets. I hesitated just a moment too long. The Professor awakened, struggled into a sitting posture, and regarded me through bleary, bloodshot eyes which were set so close in his head that they gave him a foxy appearance.

"Good afternoon," I said, feeling that the conventions must at least be satisfied.

"Good afternoon to you," he replied in a hoarse voice. "Are yer making for Lewes?"

I told him I had just left the town and was out for a country walk.

"Too bloody 'ot fer walkin'," he said. "I'm fagged out with wheelin' that there barrer. The blarsted thing gets 'eavier with every mile. I'm gettin' past this game."

He dragged himself to his feet, picked up the empty bottle, regarded it ruefully, and threw it into the hedge. It was evident that he had once been a fine figure of a man. But the broad shoulders were stooped, there was an unhealthy look about his flabby limbs, and I fancied there was a hunted look in his eyes. He must have realised I was weighing him up for, as if following on his last remark, he shot out at me: "How old do yer think I am?"

I tried to be kind and hazarded a guess at fifty-six. "So that's what yer think," he said with a mirthless laugh. "Well you're a long way out. Knock off ten an' you're still on the wrong side. I'm only forty-five, but I've 'ad enough worry these last few days to put me in me grave. It's a poor case when the only way of gettin' sleep is ter drink it out of a bottle. An' with whisky the price it is an' not so easy to git, there's too many hours to a day an' far too many to a night."

I made sympathetic noises and, to change the subject, said something about the show.

"Aye," he replied. "The oldest show on earth. All about a murder and a 'anging. It's queer 'ow folks likes a murder, even if it's only old Punch knocking Judy's brains out with 'is stick." He looked towards the barrow and quickly turned back to me. It was then I knew for certain that he was afraid. Stark naked fear lurked in those shifty, bloodshot eyes. His hand clutched my arm and he spoke in an urgent whisper. "Tell me, guv'ner. Tell me the truth as Gord's yer maker. Can you see a little dorg—a little white dorg with a black marking on its left ear, a-sittin' on that barrer?"

I looked in the direction indicated and replied sharply. "There's no dog there. It must be the whisky making you see things."

"Not this time it ain't, guv'ner. It's bin there fer three days now." He began to babble something about a sailor, a dog, and a newspaper. I couldn't make head or tail of what he was saying. Then, with a desperate effort, he seemed to pull himself together and spoke more rationally.

"They all likes the Punch and Judy show an' that means they likes a good murder. You likes it, mister, an' knows as it's true ter life. I'm frightened, guv'ner, an' that's Gord's truth. I've got ter tell someone about it else I shall go crackers." He began babbling again and, convinced I had a madman to deal with, I decided it safer to humour him.

"Tell me what you like," I said, "if it is going to help you at all. Only, for heaven's sake, pull yourself together man, if you expect me to listen to you."

He sat down again and I perched myself on a handy tree stump, ready to make off if he showed any signs of becoming violent. It isn't an exactly pleasant sensation to know that you are alone in an unfrequented lane with a fellow who may be a dangerous maniac.

II

"Now all this 'appened over ten years ago," began the Professor. "I was a bit better lookin' in them days than wot I am now, an' there was a girl. 'Er name was Daisy—Daisy Greening—an' I met 'er at Maidstone. She liked the show an' she liked me, an' so we became friendly an' started walkin' out together. I was makin' good money an' it wasn't so long before we decided to get spliced. We got a cottage at Detling fer five bob a week, an' furnished it with a few odds and ends as I picked up in me travels. It was to 'ave been a proper little love nest. But things don't always turn out the way they are planned, an' Daisy as a sweetheart an' Daisy as a wife was two different things. I soon found out that she 'ad the temper of a bitch, an' I set meself out to cure it, for I always did 'old as a man should be master in 'is own 'ouse. Well, ter make a long story short, within twelve months she took out a summons agin me fer cruelty, an' the bleedin' magistrates made a separation order under which I was ter pay 'er ten bob a week.

"I wasn't the sort of chap to take all that lyin' down, mister. Most of the time I was away with me show. But in betweens I was in Maidstone an' I kept me eye on little Daisy who'd gorn back ter live with 'er dear mother. It wasn't so long before I found out there was another chap in the offing—a sailor, name of Ted Richards. When 'e was on leaf they'd go orf into the country tergether just like a couple of love-birds, an me 'aving ter pay me ten bob into the Court every week.

"Well, I bided me time. I took good care they never ran into me 'cause I didn't want 'im ter know what I looked like. I let it go on fer nearly a year, an' I might 'ave let 'em carry on even longer but for the fact I discovered by accident as they was plannin' ter set up 'ouse together when 'is next leaf come round. It didn't matter much for, by then, I was ready ter put an end ter their love dreams. Wouldn't you feel the same, guv'ner, if yer wife was carryin' on with another man an' you was still 'avin' ter keep 'er out of yer 'ard-earned money?"

He gave me a nasty leer and I hurriedly agreed. I felt a physical repulsion for the man, but I dared not attempt to leave him.

"It was on a day in November when 'er precious Ted's ship docked at Sheerness. I knew which pub 'e'd make for as soon as 'e came ashore, an' I was there ready for 'im. It was easy enough ter get pally. A few drinks an' we was bosom friends. I 'ad a little shed down in Blue Town—a shack I rented fer storing me show. I told the sailor I'd some whisky there an' 'e didn't think twice about comin' along with me. 'E wasn't expecting a blow between the eyes with a lump of lead piping. But that's what 'e got an' it split 'is skull like an egg-shell. Later I packed 'im all nice an' comfortable into my little booth, covered it with the mackintosh sheet, an' left 'im fer the night.

"Perhaps yer knows the Isle of Sheppey an' perhaps yer don't. Sheerness is the only place of any size on the island, but there are a number of villages where a Punch and Judy man could always be certain of a few bob. I used ter work 'em pretty regular, an' I knew the whole island like the palm of me 'and. There is a part of the coast, between Minster and Leysdown, where the mud cliffs are always givin' way—or they used ter be always tumblin' down in them days. Usually only small falls took place, but sometimes a whole great chunk just toppled over into the sea. Once a blinkin' church disappeared in a night. I had explored those cliffs fer days on end an' knew all the most dangerous places.

"There was a light railway which ran to the different villages—a ragtime sort of affair where the drive 'ad ter get out at every level-crossin' to open the gates, an' then wait fer the guard to shut 'em again after they 'ad driven through.

"The next morning I wheeled my show down to the railway station. I 'ad a little dorg then—a black and white terrier what took part in the show, an' I remember 'ow the animal whimpered at my 'eels as I pushed the barrer through the streets. The guard, who knew me quite well, passed the usual joke about the 'coffin on wheels,' little thinkin' that this time 'e was nearer the truth than 'e guessed. I travelled in 'is van so as ter keep me eyes on the barrer an', all the way, that blarsted dorg whimpered and yapped, although I nearly kicked the guts out of it.

"It was barely eight o'clock when we got to Leysdown an' nobody seemed to take any interest in me or me barrer. I wheeled it out to the cliffs an' along the sea path 'til I reached the spot I 'ad chosen. It was a tiny bay where the waves 'ad washed away the under part of the cliff, makin' a kind of cave. There was no one about an' it didn't take me long to unload the body, drop it to the beach, an' drag it into the 'ole. An' then that damned dorg started 'owling loud enough to be 'eard in Sheerness. I grabbed 'old of it, bashed its 'ead against a rock, an' chucked it in to keep the sailor company. I'd brought a couple of crowbars with me an' struck them into the top of the cliff. By using them as levers I soon managed to dislodge about ten tons of soil an' Daisy's lover was beneath it.

"I went back to Leysdown an' gave a show for the kids at the school. I also gave shows that day at Eastchurch and Minster, an' only one person asked me where me little dorg 'ad gorn." He glanced uneasily towards the barrow and started to his feet with a cry. "There 'e is, there 'e is," he whimpered, pointing with a shaking hand. "Can't you see 'im now, mister, sittin' on the barrer?"

I assured him that no dog was visible to me. But, I must confess, I was badly frightened and ready to take to my heels at any moment. The man seemed to gain control of himself again and came closer to me.

"It all 'appened ten years ago," he croaked, "an' now they've both got out. I daren't set up me show 'cause, when I did it last Monday at Cranbrook, the sailor an' the dorg both got inside with me an' nearly sent me screamin' mad." He looked towards the barrow again and gripped my arm. "Tell me, 'onest, guv'ner," he pleaded. "Can't yer see that bleedin' dorg sittin' there an' grinnin' at me?"

Once again I told him that no dog was to be seen and tried to soothe him.

"You bloody liar," the Professor yelled. "You can see the dorg all right an' yer think I don't know. It's been there ever since I read that bit in the paper four days ago. An' I'll tell yer somethin' else." He came closer and I recoiled from his foetid breath. "The sailor's inside the booth an' I daresn't open it. Now I've got to push them both around for the rest of me life." Wild bursts of hideous laughter broke from his throat. "It's a good joke, ain't it?" he screamed. "Ted Richards is livin' at Chatham with my wife. The sailor killed wasn't 'im at all."

Still laughing wildly he rushed across to the barrow, seized the handles, and went pelting off down the lane as if the devil was after him.

III

Chief Inspector Stanton, of the Sussex Constabulary, is an old friend of mine, and I suppose I should have gone to him at once with my story. But I hate to be laughed at and, on reflection, the tale seemed most improbable. The Professor was obviously the victim of delusions induced by alcoholic excesses.

More than twenty-four hours passed before I mentioned the business to Stanton and I only did so then because we happened to meet at the club. I could see a gleam of interest flicker in his eyes as soon as I began the tale of my encounter. He listened quietly whilst I described the ramblings of the Punch and Judy man, and then he said, "I suppose there was a name painted on the barrow and I dare wager it happened to be Jack Smith."

"True enough," I replied. "You don't mean to say you've nabbed him already."

"Not exactly. He hanged himself last night in an old barn on the Brighton road."

"Good Lord!" I exclaimed. "Then the man *was* mad and his delusions got the better of him."

"I'm not so certain about the delusions. We managed to trace his wife this afternoon and she is living at Chatham with a sailor called Edward Richards. That part of the tale was true enough and so was the bit about the murder. We found this in Smith's pocket. It was evidently torn from one of the East Kent newspapers and is about five days old."

He extracted a dirty slip of printed paper from his notebook and handed it over to me. It was a short paragraph recounting the fall of a portion of the cliffs near Leysdown, on Sheppey, and the subsequent discovery of the skeleton of a man with the bones of a dog at his side. "From an identity disc found near the remains," the report concluded, "there is reason to believe that the unfortunate person was a seaman. The police have the matter in hand and we are given to understand there is suspicion of foul play."

"Then he did get the wrong man?" I said, handing back the slip of paper.

"That's about the sum of it," replied Stanton in his laconic manner. "But there are a couple of points about the suicide which puzzle me. In the soft earth under the body were the marks of a dog's paws and, from the state of Smith's trousers and legs, it was obvious that the animal had been jumping up at him as he swung from the beam. The paw-marks were only in that one spot and we haven't found any traces of a stray dog. I suppose you are certain there wasn't a terrier with him yesterday afternoon."

"There was no dog there," I stated without hesitation. "Smith swore he could see one, but it wasn't visible to my eyes."

"Curious," said Stanton. "The other thing is even more mysterious. When we came to examine the booth it was saturated with water and mud, and a most unholy stench hung around it. The doctor says the dampness was undoubtedly caused by sea water, and maintains that the smell was that of a decomposing corpse."

THE FIREPLACE

Henry S. Whitehead

THE FIRST PUBLISHED STORY of Reverend Henry St. Clair White-
head (1882–1932) was "The Intarsia Box," which appeared in *Adventure* in
1923, and he began a lifelong connection to *Weird Tales* with the publication
of "Tea Leaves" the following year. He developed a steady correspondence and
friendship with H. P. Lovecraft, with whom he collaborated on a story, "The
Trap," in 1931. In his relatively brief career of less than a decade, he published
more than forty pulp stories, twenty-five for *Weird Tales*. Two collections of his
stories were published posthumously, *Jumbee and Other Uncanny Tales* (1944)
and *West India Lights* (1946).

Born in Elizabeth, New Jersey, he graduated from Harvard University, where
he played football and studied with the poet and philosopher George Santayana,
earning a doctorate in philosophy in 1904. He became a newspaper editor and
served as the commissioner of the Amateur Athletic Union, then went to the
Berkeley Divinity School in Middletown, Connecticut. He was ordained a dea-
con in the Episcopal Church in 1912, serving in a series of increasingly important and responsible positions, progressing from rector and children's pastor
to the post of Archdeacon to the Virgin Islands in the West Indies from 1921
to 1929. He wrote frequently of ecclesiastical matters and, while living on St.
Croix, gathered ideas and background material on voodoo and native legends
and superstitions for the fiction he was to write for such pulp magazines as
Adventure, Weird Tales, and *Strange Tales.*

"The Fireplace" was originally published in the January 1925 issue of *Weird
Tales;* it was first collected in *Jumbee and Other Uncanny Tales* (Sauk City, Wisconsin, Arkham House, 1944).

The Fireplace

HENRY S. WHITEHEAD

WHEN THE PLANTER'S HOTEL in Jackson, Mississippi, burned to the ground in the notable fire of 1922, the loss to that section of the South could not be measured in terms of that ancient hostelry's former grandeur. The days had indeed long passed when a Virginia ham was therein stewed in no medium meaner than good white wine; and as the rambling old building was heavily insured, the owners suffered no great material loss. The real loss was the community's, in the deaths by fire of two of its prominent citizens, Lieutenant-Governor Frank Stacpoole and Mayor Cassius L. Turner. These gentlemen, just turning elderly, had been having a reunion in the hotel with two of their old associates, Judge Varney J. Baker of Memphis,

Tennessee, and the Honorable Valdemar Peale, a prominent Georgian, from Atlanta. Thus, two other Southern cities had a share in the mourning, for Judge Baker and Mr. Peale both likewise perished in the flames. The fire took place just before Christmas on the twenty-third of December, and among the many sympathetic and regretful comments which ensued upon this holocaust was the many-times-repeated conjecture that these gentlemen had been keeping a kind of Christmas anniversary, a fact which added no little to the general feeling of regret and horror.

On the request of these prominent gentlemen, the hotel management had cleared out and furnished a second floor room with a great fireplace, a room for long used only for storage, but for which, the late mayor and lieutenant-governor had assured them, the four old cronies cherished a certain sentiment. The fire, which gained headway despite the truly desperate efforts of the occupants of the room, had its origin in the fireplace, and it was believed that the four, who were literally burned to cinders, had been trapped. The fire had started, it appeared, about half an hour before midnight, when everybody else in the hotel had retired. No other occupant of the house suffered from its effects, beyond a few incidental injuries sustained in the hurried departure at dead of night from the blazing old firetrap.

Some ten years before this regrettable incident ended the long and honorable career of this one-time famous hostelry, a certain Mr. James Callender, breaking a wearisome journey north at Jackson, turned into the hospitable vestibule of the Planter's, with a sigh of relief. He had been shut up for nine hours in the mephitic atmosphere of a soft-coal train. He was tired, hungry, thirsty, and begrimed with soot.

Two grinning negro porters deposited his ample luggage, toted from the railway station in the reasonable hope of a large emolument, promised by their patron's prosperous appear-

ance and the imminence of the festival season of Christmas. They received their reward and left Mr. Callender in the act of signing the hotel register.

"Can you let me have number twenty-eight?" he required of the clerk. "That, I believe, is the room with the large fireplace, is it not? My friend, Mr. Tom Culbertson of Sweetbriar, recommended it to me in case I should be stopping here."

Number twenty-eight was fortunately vacant, and the new guest was shortly in occupation, a great fire, at his orders, roaring up the chimney, and he himself engaged in preparing for the luxury of a hot bath.

After a leisurely dinner of the sort for which the old hotel was famous, Mr. Callender first sauntered slowly through the lobby, enjoying the first fragrant whiffs of a good cigar. Then, seeing no familiar face which gave promise of a conversation, he ascended to his room, replenished the fire, and got himself ready for a solitary evening. Soon, in pajamas, bathrobe, and comfortable slippers, he settled himself in a comfortable chair at just the right distance from the fire and began to read a new book which he had brought with him. His dinner had been a late one, and it was about half-past nine when he really settled to his book. It was Arthur Machen's *House of Souls*, and Mr. Callender soon found himself absorbed in the eery ecstasy of reading for the first time a remarkable work which transcended all his previous secondhand experiences of the occult. It had, he found, anything but a soporific effect upon him. He was reading carefully, well into the book, with all his faculties alert, when he was interrupted by a knock on the door of his room.

Mr. Callender stopped reading, marked his place, and rose to open the door. He was wondering who should summon him at such an hour. He glanced at his watch on the bureau in passing and was surprised to note that it was eleven-twenty. He had been reading for nearly two hours, steadily. He opened the door, and was surprised to find no one in the corridor. He stepped through the doorway and glanced right and then left. There were, he observed, turns in both directions at short distances from his door, and Mr. Callender, whose mind was trained in the sifting of evidence, worked out an instantaneous explanation in his mind. The occupant of a double room (so he guessed) had returned late, and, mistaking the room, had knocked to apprize his fellow occupant of his return. Seeing at once that he had knocked prematurely, on the wrong door, the person had bolted around one of the corners to avoid an awkward explanation!

Mr. Callender, smiling at this whimsical idea of his, turned back into his room and shut the door behind him.

A gentleman was sitting in the place he had vacated. Mr. Callender stopped short and stared at this intruder. The man who had appropriated his comfortable chair was a few years older than himself, it appeared—say about thirty-five. He was tall, well-proportioned, and very well dressed, although there seemed to Mr. Callender's hasty scrutiny something indefinably odd about his clothes.

The two men looked at each other appraisingly for the space of a few seconds, in silence, and then abruptly Mr. Callender saw what was wrong with the other's appearance. He was dressed in the fashion of about fifteen years back, in the style of the late nineties. No one was wearing such a decisive-looking piccadilly collar, nor such a huge puff tie which concealed every vestige of the linen except the edges of the cuffs. These, on Mr. Callender's uninvited guest, were immaculate and round, and held in place by a pair of large, round, cut-cameo black buttons.

The strange gentleman, without rising, broke the silence in a well-modulated voice with a deprecatory wave of a very well kept hand.

"I owe you an apology, sir. I trust that you will accept what amends I can make. This room has for me a peculiar interest which you will understand if you will allow me to speak further, but for the present I confine myself to asking your pardon."

This speech was delivered in so frank and pleasing a fashion that Mr. Callendar could take no offense at the intrusion of the speaker.

"You are quite welcome, sir, but perhaps you will be good enough to continue, as you suggest. I confess to being mightily puzzled as to the precise manner in which you came to be here. The only way of approach is through the door, and I'll take my oath no one came through it. I heard a knock, went to the door, and there was no one there."

"I imagine I would do well to begin at the beginning," said the stranger, gravely. "The facts are somewhat unusual, as you will see when I have related them; otherwise I should hardly be here, at this time of night, and trespassing upon your good nature. That this is no mere prank I beg that you will believe."

"Proceed, sir, by all means," returned Mr. Callender, his curiosity aroused and keen. He drew up another chair and seated himself on the side of the fireplace opposite the stranger, who at once began his explanation.

"My name is Charles Bellinger, a fact which I will ask you kindly to note and keep well in mind. I come from Biloxi, down on the Gulf, and, unlike yourself, I am a Southerner, a native of Mississippi. You see, sir, I know something about you, or at least who you are."

Mr. Callender inclined his head, and the stranger waved his hand again, this time as if to express acknowledgment of an introduction.

"I may as well add to this, since it explains several matters, though in itself sounding somewhat odd, that actually I am dead."

Mr. Bellinger, at this astounding statement, met Mr. Callender's facial expression of amazement with a smile clearly meant to be reassuring, and again, with a kind of unspoken eloquence, waved his expressive hand.

"Yes, sir, what I tell you is the plain truth. I passed out of this life in this room where we are sitting almost exactly sixteen years ago. My death occurred on the twenty-third of December. That will be precisely sixteen years ago the day after tomorrow. I came here tonight for the express purpose of telling you the facts, if you will bear with me and suspend your judgment as to my sanity. It was I who knocked at your door, and I passed through it, and, so to speak, through you, my dear sir!

"On the late afternoon of the day I have mentioned I arrived in this hotel in company with Mr. Frank Stacpoole, an acquaintance, who still lives here in Jackson. I met him as I got off the train, and invited him to come here with me for dinner. Being a bachelor, he made no difficulty, and just after dinner we met in the lobby another man named Turner—Cassius L. Turner, also a Jacksonian—who proposed a game of cards and offered to secure two more gentlemen to complete the party. I invited him to bring them here to my room, and Stacpoole and I came up in advance to get things ready for an evening of poker.

"Shortly afterwards Mr. Turner and the two other gentlemen arrived. One of them was named Baker, the other was Mr. Valdemar Peale, of Atlanta, Georgia. You recognize his name, I perceive, as I had expected you would. Mr. Peale is now a very prominent man. He has gone far since that time. If you happened to be better acquainted here you would know that Stacpoole and Turner are also men of very considerable prominence. Baker, who lives in Memphis, Tennessee, is likewise a well-known man in his community and state.

"Peale, it appeared, was Stacpoole's brother-in-law, a fact which I had not previously known, and all four were well acquainted with each other. I was introduced to the two newcomers and we commenced to play poker.

"Somewhat to my embarrassment, since I was both the host and the 'stranger' of the party, I won steadily from the very beginning. Mr. Peale was the heaviest loser, and although as the evening wore on he sat with compressed lips and made no comment, it was plain that he was taking his considerable losses rather hardly.

"Not long after eleven o'clock a most unfortunate incident took place. I had in no way suspected that I was not among gentlemen. I had begun, you see, by knowing only Stacpoole, and even with him my acquaintance was only casual.

"At the time I mention there began a round of jack-pots, and the second of these I opened with a pair of kings and a pair of fours. Hoping to better my hand I discarded the fours, with the odd card, and drew to the pair of kings, hoping for a third. I was fortunate. I obtained not only the third king but with it a pair of eights. Thus, equipped with a full house, I considered my hand likely to be the best, and when, within two rounds of betting, the rest had laid down their hands, the pot lay between Peale and me. Peale, I noticed, had also thrown down three cards, and every chance indicated that I had him beaten. I forced him to call me after a long series of raises back and forth; and when he laid down his hand he was holding four fours!

"You see? He had picked up my discard.

"Wishing to give Peale the benefit of any possible doubt, I declared the matter at once, for one does not lightly accuse a gentleman of cheating at cards, especially here in the South. It was possible, though far from likely, that there had been a mistake. The dealer might for once have laid down his draw on the table, although he had consistently handed out the cards as we dealt in turn all the evening. To imply further that I regarded the matter as nothing worse than a mistake, I offered at once to allow the considerable pot, which I had really won, to lie over to the next hand.

"I had risen slightly out of my chair as I spoke, and before anyone could add a word, Peale leaned over the table and stabbed me with a bowie knife which I had not even seen him draw, so rapid was his action. He struck upwards, slantingly, and the blade, entering my body just below the ribs, cut my right lung nearly in two. I sank down limp across the table, and within a few seconds had coughed myself almost noiselessly to death.

"The actual moment of dissolution was painful to a degree. It was as if the permanent part of me, 'myself'—my soul, if you will—snapped abruptly away from that distorted thing which sprawled prone across the disordered table and which no longer moved.

"Dispassionately, then, the something which continued to be myself (though now, of course, dissociated from what had been my vehicle of expression, my body) looked on and apprehended all that followed.

"For a few moments there was utter silence. Then Turner, in a hoarse, constrained voice, whispered to Peale: 'You've done for yourself now, you unmentionable fool!'

"Peale sat in silence, the knife, which he had automatically withdrawn from the wound, still grasped in his hand, and what had been my life's blood slowly dripping from it and gradually congealing as it fell upon a disarranged pile of cards.

"Then, quite without warning, Baker took charge of the situation. He had kept very quiet and played a very conservative game throughout the evening.

"'This affair calls for careful handling,' he drawled, 'and if you will take my advice I think it can be made into a simple case of disappearance. Bellinger comes from Biloxi. He is not well known here.' Then, rising and gathering the attention of the others, he continued: 'I am going down to the hotel kitchen for a short time. While I am gone, keep the door shut, keep quiet, and clear up the room, leaving *this* (he indicated my body) where it lies. You, Stacpoole, arrange the furniture in the room as nearly as you can remember how it looked when you first came in. You, Turner, make up a big fire. You needn't begin that just yet,' he threw at Peale, who had begun nervously to cleanse the blade of his knife on a piece of newspaper; and with this cryptic remark he disappeared through the door and was gone.

"The others, who all appeared somewhat dazed, set about their appointed tasks silently. Peale, who seemed unable to leave the vicinity of the table, at which he kept throwing glances, straightened up the chairs, replaced them where

they had been, and then gathered up the cards and other debris from the table, and threw these into the now blazing fire which Turner was rapidly feeding with fresh wood.

"Within a few minutes Baker returned as unobtrusively as he had left, and after carefully fastening the door and approaching the table, gathered the three others about him and produced from under his coat an awkward and hastily-wrapped package of newspapers. Unfastening this he produced three heavy kitchen knives.

"I saw that Turner went white as Baker's idea dawned upon his consciousness. I now understood what Baker had meant when he told Peale to defer the cleansing of his bowie knife! It was, as plans go, a very practical scheme which he had evolved. The body—the *corpus delicti*, as I believe you gentlemen of the law call it—was an extremely awkward fact. It was a fact which had to be accounted for, unless—well, Baker had clearly perceived that *there must be no* corpus delicti!

"He held a hurried, low-voiced conversation with the others, from the immediate effect of which all, even Peale, at first drew back. I need not detail it to you. You will have already apprehended what Baker had in mind. There was the roaring fire in the fireplace. That was his means of making certain that there would remain no *corpus delicti* in that room when the others left. Without such evidence, that is, the actual body of the murdered man, there could be, as you are of course well aware, no prosecution, because there would be no proof that the murder had even been committed. I should simply have 'disappeared.' He had seen all that, and the opportunity which the fireplace afforded for carrying out his plan, all at once. But the fireplace, while large, was not large enough to accommodate the body of a man intact. Hence his hurried and stealthy visit to the hotel kitchen.

"The men looked up from their conference. Peale was trembling palpably. The sweat streamed from Turner's face. Stacpoole seemed unaffected, but I did not fail to observe that the hand which he reached out for one of the great meat knives shook violently, and that he was first to turn his head aside when Baker, himself pale and with set face, gingerly picked up from the table one of the stiffening hands. . . .

"Within an hour and a quarter (for the fireplace drew as well then as it does tonight) there was not a vestige left of the *corpus delicti*, except the teeth.

"Baker appeared to think of everything. When the fire had pretty well burned itself out, and consumed what had been placed within it piecemeal, he remade it, and within its heart placed such charred remnants of the bones as had not been completely incinerated the first time. Eventually all the incriminating evidence had been consumed. It was as if I had never existed!

"My clothes, of course, had been burned. When the four, now haggard with their ordeal, had completed the burning process, another clearing-up and final re-arrangement of the room was undertaken. Various newspapers which they had been carrying in their coat pockets were used to cleanse the table. The knives, including Peale's, were washed and scrubbed, the water poured out and the wash-basin thoroughly scoured. No blood had got upon the carpet.

"My not inconsiderable winnings, as well as the coin and currency which had been in my possession, were then cold-bloodedly divided among these four rascals, for such I had for some time now recognized them as being. There arose then the problem of the disposal of my other belongings. There was my watch, pocket-knife, and several old seals which had belonged to my grandfather and which I had been accustomed to wear on the end of the chain in the pocket opposite that in which I carried my watch. There were my studs, scarf-pin, cuff-buttons, two rings, and lastly, my teeth. These had been laid aside at the time when Baker had carefully raked the charred but indestructible teeth out of the embers of the first fire."

At this point in his narrative, Mr. Bellinger paused and passed one of his eloquent hands through the hair on top of his head in a reflective gesture. Mr. Callender observed what he had not before clearly noted, that his guest possessed a pair of extraordinarily long, thin hands, very muscular, the hands of an artist and also of a man of determination and action. He particularly observed that the index fingers were almost if not quite as long as the middle fingers. The listener, who had been unable to make up his mind upon the question of the sanity of him who had presented this extraordinary narrative in so calm and convincing a fashion, viewed these hands indicative of so strong a character with the greatest interest. Mr. Bellinger resumed his narrative.

"There was some discussion about the disposal of all these things. The consensus was that they must be concealed, since they could not easily be destroyed. If I had been one of those men I should have insisted upon throwing them into the river at the earliest opportunity. They could have been carried out of the room by any one of the group with the greatest ease and with no chance of detection, since all together they took up very little room, but this simple plan seemed not to occur to them. Perhaps they had exhausted their ingenuity in the horrible task just finished and were over-anxious to depart. They decided only upon the necessity of disposal of these trinkets, and the actual disposition was haphazard. This was by a method which I need not describe because I think it desirable to show them to you."

Mr. Bellinger rose and led the way to a corner of the room, closely followed by the amazed Callender. Bellinger pointed to the precise corner.

"Although I am for the present materialized," he remarked, "you will probably understand that this whole proceeding is in the nature of a severe psychic strain upon me and my resources. It is quite out of the question for me to do certain things. Managing to knock at the door took it out of me, rather, but I wished to give you as much warning of my presence as I could. Will you kindly oblige me by lifting the carpet at this point?"

Mr. Callender worked his fingers nervously under the corner of the carpet and pulled. The tacks yielded after several hard pulls, and the corner of the carpet came up, revealing a large piece of heavy tin which had been tacked down over an ancient rat-hole.

"Pull up the tin, too, if you please," requested Mr. Bellinger. The tin presented a more difficult task than had the carpet, but Mr. Callender, now thoroughly intrigued, made short work of it, though at the expense of two broken blades of his pocket-knife. At Mr. Bellinger's further direction, inserting his hand, he found and drew out a packet of cloth, which proved on examination to have been fabricated out of a trousers pocket lining. The cloth was rotted and brittle, and Mr. Callender carried it carefully over to the table and laid it down, and, emptying it out between them, checked off the various articles which Mr. Bellinger had named. The round cuff-buttons came last, and as he held these in his hand, he looked at Mr. Bellinger's wrists. Mr. Bellinger smiled and pulled down his cuffs, holding out his hands in the process, and Mr. Callender again noted carefully their peculiarities, the long, muscular fingers being especially conspicuous, thus seen under the direct light of the electric lamp. The cuff-buttons, he noted, were absolutely identical.

"Perhaps you will oblige me by putting the whole collection in your pocket," suggested Mr. Bellinger. Then, smiling, as Mr. Callender, not unnaturally, hesitated: "Take them, my dear man, take them freely. They're really mine to give, you know!"

Mr. Callender stepped over to the wardrobe where his clothes hung, and placed the packet in his coat pocket. When he returned to the vicinity of the fireplace, his guest had already resumed his seat.

"I trust," he said, "that despite the very singular—I may say, *bizarre*—character of my narrative and especially the statement with which I thought best to begin it, you will have given me your credence. It is uncommon to be confronted with the recital of such an experience as I have related to you, and it is not everybody who is—may I say privileged?—to carry on an extended conversation with a man who has been dead sixteen years!

"My object may possibly have suggested itself to you. These men have escaped all consequences of their act. They are, as I think you will not deny, four thorough rascals. They are at large and even in positions of responsibility, trust, and prominence in their several communities. You are a lawyer, a man held in high esteem for your professional skill and personal integrity. I ask you, then, will you undertake to bring these men to justice? You should be able to reproduce the salient points of my story. You have even proofs in the shape of the articles now in your coat pocket. There is the fact of my disappearance. That made a furor at the time, and has never been explained or cleared up. You have the evidence of the hotel register for my being here on that date and it would not be hard to prove that these men were in my company. But above all else, I would pin my faith for a conviction upon the mere recounting in the presence of these four, duly subpoenaed, of my story as I have told it to you. That would fasten their guilt upon them to the satisfaction of any judge and jury. They would be crying aloud for mercy and groveling in abject superstitious fear long before you had finished the account of precisely what they had done. Or, three of them could be confronted with an alleged confession made by the other. Will you undertake to right this festering wrong, Mr. Callender, and give me peace? Your professional obligation to promote justice and set wrong right should conspire with your character to cause you to agree."

"I will do so, with all my heart," replied Mr. Callender, holding out his hand.

But before the other could take it, there came another knocking on the door of the hotel room. Slightly startled, Mr. Callender went to the door and threw it open. One of the hotel servants reminded him that he had asked to be called, and that it was the hour specified. Mr. Callender thanked and freed the man, and turning back into the room found himself alone.

He went to the fireplace and sat down. He looked fixedly at the smoldering fire in the grate. He went over to the wardrobe and felt in his coat pocket in search of negative evidence that he had been dreaming, but his hand encountered the bag which had been the lining of a trousers pocket. He drew it out and spread a second time that morning on the table the various articles which it contained.

After an early breakfast Mr. Callender asked for permission to examine the register for the year 1896. He found that Charles Bellinger of Biloxi had registered on the afternoon of the twenty-third of December and had been assigned room twenty-eight. He had no time for further enquiries, and, thanking the obliging clerk, he hastened to the railway station and resumed his journey north.

During the journey his mind refused to occupy itself with anything except his strange experience. He reached his destination in a state of profound preoccupation.

As soon as his professional engagements allowed him the leisure to do so, he began his enquiries by having looked up the owners of those names which were deeply imprinted in his memory. He was obliged to stop there because an unprecedented quantity of new legal business claimed his more immediate attention. He was aware that this particular period in his professional career was one vital to his future, and he slaved painstakingly at the affairs of his clients. His diligence was rewarded by a series of conspicuous legal successes, and his reputation became greatly enhanced. This heavy preoccupation could not fail to dull somewhat the sharp impression which the adventure in the hotel bedroom had made upon his mind, and the contents of the trousers pocket remained locked in his safe-deposit box undisturbed while he settled the affairs of the Rockland Oil Corporation

and fought through the Appellate Division the conspicuous case of *Burnet vs. De Castro, et al.*

It was in the pursuit of a vital piece of evidence in this last-named case that his duties called him South again. Having obtained the evidence, he started home, and again found it expedient to break the long journey northward, at Jackson. It was not, though, until he was actually signing the register that he noted that it was the twenty-third of December, the actual date with which Mr. Bellinger's singular narrative had been concerned.

He did not ask for any particular room this time. He felt a chill of vague apprehension, as if there awaited him an accounting for some laxity, a feeling which recalled the occasional lapses of his remote childhood. He smiled, but this whimsical idea was quickly replaced by a sombre apprehension which he could not shake off, and which emanated from the realization that the clerk by some strange fatality had again assigned him room twenty-eight—the room with the fireplace. He thought of asking for another room, but could not think of any reasonable excuse. He sighed and felt a positive sinking at the heart when he saw the figures written down at the edge of the page; but he said nothing. If he shrank from this room's occupancy, this room with its frightful secret shared by him alone of this world's company with the four guilty men who were still at large because of his failure to keep his promise, he was human enough and modern enough in his ideas to shrink still more from the imputation of oddity which his refusal of the room on no sensible grounds would inevitably suggest.

He went up to his room, and, as it was a cold night outside, ordered the fire to be made up. . . .

When the hotel servant rapped on his door in the morning there was no answer, and after several attempts to arouse the occupant the man reported his failure at the office. Later another attempt was made, and, this proving equally ineffectual, the door was forced with the assistance of a locksmith.

Mr. Callender's body was found lying with the head in the grate. He had been, it appeared, strangled, for the marks of a pair of hands were deeply imprinted on his throat. The fingers had sunk deeply into the bluish, discolored flesh, and the coroner's jury noted the unusual circumstance when they sent out a description of the murderer confined to this peculiarity, that these marks indicated that the murderer (who was never discovered) possessed very long thin fingers, the index fingers being almost or quite as long as the middle fingers.

THE NIGHT WIRE

H. F. Arnold

MANY STRUGGLING PULP WRITERS went on to fame and fortune and became household names (assuming the household is literate). The novels and stories of Erle Stanley Gardner, Robert E. Howard, Dashiell Hammett, Louis L'Amour, Raymond Chandler, and others still resonate, long after they, and the magazines for which they wrote, expired.

Others, and one might say the vast majority of others, remained mired in obscurity, frequently because they were not very talented, turning out hack work for a penny a word or less, and sometimes because they did not write very much.

One of the latter appears to have been (H)enry (F)erris Arnold (1901/1902–1963), who, as nearly as can be ascertained, as so little is known of him (including whether this is really his name), wrote only three stories in his career. Probably born and raised in Illinois, he moved to Hollywood to become a press agent in the 1920s and 1930s, and he was almost certainly a newspaperman, as the tone and minor details of the present story will attest. "The Night Wire" was his first story and was a great favorite of H. P. Lovecraft's, who called it one of the six best stories ever to appear in *Weird Tales*, an opinion shared by fans of the magazine, acclaiming it as possibly the most popular story ever to appear in its pages. He also wrote a two- part serial, "The City of Iron Cubes" for the *Weird Tales* issues of March and April 1929.

"The Night Wire" was first published in the September 1926 issue of *Weird Tales.*

The Night Wire

H. F. ARNOLD

NEW YORK, SEPTEMBER 30 CP FLASH

Ambassador Holliwell died here today. The end came suddenly as the ambassador was alone in his study. . . .

THERE IS SOMETHING UNGODLY about these night wire jobs. You sit up here on the top floor of a skyscraper and listen in to the whispers of a civilization. New York, London, Calcutta, Bombay, Singapore—they're your next-door neighbors after the streetlights go dim and the world has gone to sleep.

Alone in the quiet hours between two and four, the receiving operators doze over their sounders and the news comes in. Fires and disasters and suicides. Murders, crowds, catastrophes. Sometimes an earthquake with a casualty list as long as your arm. The night wire man takes it down almost in his sleep, picking it off on his typewriter with one finger.

Once in a long time you prick up your ears and listen. You've heard of some one you knew in Singapore, Halifax, or Paris, long ago. Maybe they've been promoted, but more probably they've been murdered or drowned. Perhaps they just decided to quit and took some bizarre way out. Made it interesting enough to get in the news.

But that doesn't happen often. Most of the time you sit and doze and tap, tap on your typewriter and wish you were home in bed.

Sometimes, though, queer things happen. One did the other night, and I haven't got over it yet. I wish I could.

You see, I handle the night manager's desk in a western seaport town; what the name is, doesn't matter.

There is, or rather was, only one night operator on my staff, a fellow named John Morgan, about forty years of age, I should say, and a sober, hard-working sort.

He was one of the best operators I ever knew, what is known as a "double" man. That means he could handle two instruments at once and type the stories on different typewriters at the same time. He was one of the three men I ever knew who could do it consistently, hour after hour, and never make a mistake.

Generally, we used only one wire at night, but sometimes, when it was late and the news was coming fast, the Chicago and Denver stations would open a second wire, and then Morgan would do his stuff. He was a wizard, a mechanical automatic wizard which functioned marvelously but was without imagination.

On the night of the sixteenth he complained of feeling tired. It was the first and last time I had ever heard him say a word about himself, and I had known him for three years.

It was just three o'clock and we were running only one wire. I was nodding over the reports at my desk and not paying much attention to him, when he spoke.

"Jim," he said, "does it feel close in here to you?"

"Why, no, John," I answered, "but I'll open a window if you like."

"Never mind," he said. "I reckon I'm just a little tired."

That was all that was said, and I went on working. Every ten minutes or so I would walk over and take a pile of copy that had stacked up neatly beside the typewriter as the messages were printed out in triplicate.

It must have been twenty minutes after he spoke that I noticed he had opened up the other wire and was using both typewriters. I thought it was a little unusual, as there was nothing very "hot" coming in. On my next trip I picked up the copy from both machines and took it back to my desk to sort out the duplicates.

The first wire was running out the usual sort of stuff and I just looked over it hurriedly. Then I turned to the second pile of copy. I remembered it particularly because the story was from a town I had never heard of: "Xebico." Here is the dispatch. I saved a duplicate of it from our files:

XEBICO, SEPT 16 CP BULLETIN

The heaviest mist in the history of the city settled over the town at 4 o'clock yesterday afternoon. All traffic has stopped and the mist hangs like a pall over everything. Lights of ordinary intensity fail to pierce the fog, which is constantly growing heavier.

Scientists here are unable to agree as to the cause, and the local weather bureau states that the like has never occurred before in the history of the city.

At 7 p.m. last night the municipal authorities . . . (more)

That was all there was. Nothing out of the ordinary at a bureau headquarters, but, as I say, I noticed the story because of the name of the town.

It must have been fifteen minutes later that I went over for another batch of copy. Morgan was slumped down in his chair and had switched his green electric light shade so that the gleam missed his eyes and hit only the top of the two typewriters.

Only the usual stuff was in the righthand pile, but the lefthand batch carried another story from Xebico. All press dispatches come in "takes," meaning that parts of many different stories are strung along together, perhaps with but a few paragraphs of each coming through at a time. This second story was marked "add fog." Here is the copy:

At 7 p.m. the fog had increased noticeably. All lights were now invisible and the town was shrouded in pitch darkness.

As a peculiarity of the phenomenon, the fog is accompanied by a sickly odor, comparable to nothing yet experienced here.

Below that in customary press fashion was the hour, 3:27, and the initials of the operator, JM.

There was only one other story in the pile from the second wire. Here it is:

2ND ADD XEBICO FOG

Accounts as to the origin of the mist differ greatly. Among the most unusual is that of the sexton of the local church, who groped his way to headquarters in a hysterical condition and declared that the fog originated in the village churchyard.

"It was first visible as a soft gray blanket clinging to the earth above the graves," he stated. "Then it began to rise, higher and higher. A subterranean breeze seemed to blow it in billows, which split up and then joined together again.

"Fog phantoms, writhing in anguish, twisted the mist into queer forms and figures. And then, in the very thick midst of the mass, something moved.

"I turned and ran from the accursed spot. Behind me I heard screams coming from the houses bordering on the grave-yard."

Although the sexton's story is gener-ally discredited, a party has left to inves-tigate. Immediately after telling his story, the sexton collapsed and is now in a local hospital, unconscious.

Queer story, wasn't it. Not that we aren't used to it, for a lot of unusual stories come in over the wire. But for some reason or other, perhaps be-cause it was so quiet that night, the report of the fog made a great impression on me.

It was almost with dread that I went over to the waiting piles of copy. Morgan did not move, and the only sound in the room was the tap-tap of the sounders. It was ominous, nerve-racking.

There was another story from Xebico in the pile of copy. I seized on it anxiously.

NEW LEAD XEBICO FOG CP

The rescue party which went out at 11 p.m. to investigate a weird story of the origin of a fog which, since late yesterday, has shrouded the city in darkness has failed to return. Another and larger party has been dispatched.

Meanwhile, the fog has, if possible, grown heavier. It seeps through the cracks in the doors and fills the atmosphere with a depressing odor of decay. It is oppres-sive, terrifying, bearing with it a subtle impression of things long dead.

Residents of the city have left their homes and gathered in the local church, where the priests are holding services of prayer. The scene is beyond description. Grown folk and children are alike terrified and many are almost beside themselves with fear.

Amid the whisps of vapor which partly veil the church auditorium, an old priest is praying for the welfare of his flock. They alternately wail and cross them-selves.

From the outskirts of the city may be heard cries of unknown voices. They echo through the fog in queer uncadenced minor keys. The sounds resemble noth-ing so much as wind whistling through a gigantic tunnel. But the night is calm and there is no wind. The second rescue party . . . (more)

I am a calm man and never in a dozen years spent with the wires have I been known to be-come excited, but despite myself I rose from my chair and walked to the window.

Could I be mistaken, or far down in the can-yons of the city beneath me did I see a faint trace of fog? Pshaw! It was all imagination.

In the pressroom the click of the sounders seemed to have raised the tempo of their tune. Morgan alone had not stirred from his chair. His head sunk between his shoulders, he tapped the dispatches out on the typewriters with one fin-ger of each hand.

He looked asleep, but no; endlessly, efficiently, the two machines rattled off line after line, as re-lentlessly and effortlessly as death itself. There was something about the monotonous move-ment of the typewriter keys that fascinated me. I walked over and stood behind his chair, reading over his shoulder the type as it came into being, word by word.

Ah, here was another:

FLASH XEBICO CP

There will be no more bulletins from this office. The impossible has happened. No messages have come into this room for twenty minutes. We are cut off from the outside and even the streets below us.

I will stay with the wire until the end.

It is the end, indeed. Since 4 p.m. yesterday the fog has hung over the city. Following reports from the sexton of the local church, two rescue parties were sent out to investigate conditions on the outskirts of the city. Neither party has ever returned nor was any word received from them. It is quite certain now that they will never return.

From my instrument I can gaze down on the city beneath me. From the position of this room on the thirteenth floor, nearly the entire city can be seen. Now I can see only a thick blanket of blackness where customarily are lights and life.

I fear greatly that the wailing cries heard constantly from the outskirts of the city are the death cries of the inhabitants. They are constantly increasing in volume and are approaching the center of the city.

The fog yet hangs over everything. If possible, it is even heavier than before, but the conditions have changed. Instead of an opaque, impenetrable wall of odorous vapor, there now swirls and writhes a shapeless mass in contortions of almost human agony. Now and again the mass parts and I catch a brief glimpse of the streets below.

People are running to and fro, screaming in despair. A vast bedlam of sound flies up to my window, and above all is the immense whistling of unseen and unfelt winds.

The fog has again swept over the city and the whistling is coming closer and closer.

It is now directly beneath me.

God! An instant ago the mist opened and I caught a glimpse of the streets below.

The fog is not simply vapor—it lives! By the side of each moaning and weeping human is a companion figure, an aura of strange and vari-colored hues. How the shapes cling! Each to a living thing!

The men and women are down. Flat on their faces. The fog figures caress them lovingly. They are kneeling beside them. They are—but I dare not tell it.

The prone and writhing bodies have been stripped of their clothing. They are being consumed—piecemeal.

A merciful wall of hot, steaming vapor has swept over the whole scene. I can see no more.

Beneath me the wall of vapor is changing colors. It seems to be lighted by internal fires. No, it isn't. I have made a mistake. The colors are from above, reflections from the sky.

Look up! Look up! The whole sky is in flames. Colors as yet unseen by man or demon. The flames are moving; they have started to intermix; the colors are rearranging themselves. They are so brilliant that my eyes burn, yet they are a long way off.

Now they have begun to swirl, to circle in and out, twisting in intricate designs and patterns. The lights are racing each with each, a kaleidoscope of unearthly brilliance.

I have made a discovery. There is nothing harmful in the lights. They radiate force and friendliness, almost cheeriness. But by their very strength, they hurt.

As I look, they are swinging closer and closer, a million miles at each jump. Millions of miles with the speed of light. Aye, it is light of quintessence of all light. Beneath it the fog melts into a jeweled mist radiant, rainbow-colored of a thousand varied spectra.

I can see the streets. Why, they are filled with people! The lights are coming closer. They are all around me. I am enveloped. I . . .

The message stopped abruptly. The wire to Xebico was dead. Beneath my eyes in the narrow circle of light from under the green lamp-shade, the black printing no longer spun itself, letter by letter, across the page.

The room seemed filled with a solemn quiet, a silence vaguely impressive, powerful.

I looked down at Morgan. His hands had dropped nervelessly at his sides, while his body had hunched over peculiarly. I turned the lamp-shade back, throwing light squarely in his face. His eyes were staring, fixed.

Filled with a sudden foreboding, I stepped beside him and called Chicago on the wire. After a second the sounder clicked its answer.

Why? But there was something wrong. Chicago was reporting that Wire Two had not been used throughout the evening.

"Morgan!" I shouted. "Morgan! Wake up, it isn't true. Some one has been hoaxing us. Why . . ." In my eagerness I grasped him by the shoulder.

His body was quite cold. Morgan had been dead for hours. Could it be that his sensitized brain and automatic fingers had continued to record impressions even after the end?

I shall never know, for I shall never again handle the night shift. Search in a world atlas discloses no town of Xebico. Whatever it was that killed John Morgan will forever remain a mystery.

Fritz Leiber

NOW FAMOUS FOR THE wide range of his writings and for the frequently poetic quality of his prose, Fritz (Reuter) Leiber, Jr. (1910–1992), sold his first short story, "Two Sought Adventure," for the August 1939 issue of *Unknown*, thereby creating two of the most popular characters in the history of the "Sword and Sorcery" genre—a form of fantasy literature that he named. The two were the giant Fafhrd, nearly seven feet tall with long, shaggy red hair, who carried an enormous broadsword and was one of the greatest swordsmen the world has ever seen, and his friend and companion, the diminutive and accomplished thief Gray Mouser, an equally adept swordsman with Scalpel, his shorter weapon. The two adventurers were actually conceived by Leiber's friend Harry Otto Fischer, though Leiber was the sole author of virtually all the stories over a period of fifty years. The authors claimed that Fafhrd was based on Leiber and the Mouser on Fischer.

Sword and sorcery fantasy tales were only one element of Leiber's fiction. His early horror fiction had been heavily influenced by H. P. Lovecraft, and among his eight Hugo Awards and two Nebula Awards are such science fiction classics as *The Big Time* (1957) and *The Wanderer* (1964). His best-known work is probably the voodoo/witchcraft novel *The Conjure Wife* (1943), which was filmed three times, most memorably under the title *Burn Witch Burn* (1962) with a chilling script by George Baxt, Charles Beaumont, and Richard Matheson, and starring Janet Blair and Peter Wyngarde; it had previously been adapted as *Weird Woman* (1944) and again later as *Witches' Brew* (1980).

"Smoke Ghost" was originally published in the October 1941 issue of *Unknown*.

Smoke Ghost

FRITZ LEIBER

MISS MILLICK WONDERED JUST what had happened to Mr. Wran. He kept making the strangest remarks when she took dictation. Just this morning he had quickly turned around and asked, "Have you ever seen a ghost, Miss Millick?" And she had tittered nervously and replied, "When I was a girl there was a thing in white that used to come out of the closet in the attic bedroom when I slept there, and moan. Of course it was just my imagination. I was frightened of lots of things." And he had said, "I don't mean that kind of ghost. I mean a ghost from the world today, with the soot of the factories on its face and the pounding of machinery in its soul. The kind that would haunt coal yards and slip around at night through deserted office buildings like this one. A real ghost. Not something out of books." And she hadn't known what to say.

He'd never been like this before. Of course he might be joking, but it didn't sound that way. Vaguely Miss Millick wondered whether he mightn't be seeking some sort of sympathy from her. Of course, Mr. Wran was married and had a little child, but that didn't prevent her from having daydreams. The daydreams were not very exciting, still they helped fill up her mind. But now he was asking her another of those unprecedented questions.

"Have you ever thought what a ghost of our times would look like, Miss Millick? Just picture it. A smoky composite face with the hungry anxiety of the unemployed, the neurotic restlessness of the person without purpose, the jerky tension of the high-pressure metropolitan worker, the uneasy resentment of the striker, the callous opportunism of the scab, the aggressive whine of the panhandler, the inhibited terror of the bombed civilian, and a thousand other twisted emotional patterns. Each one overlying and yet blending with the other, like a pile of semi-transparent masks?"

Miss Millick gave a little self-conscious shiver and said, "That would be terrible. What an awful thing to think of."

She peered furtively across the desk. Was he going crazy? She remembered having heard that there had been something impressively abnormal about Mr. Wran's childhood, but she couldn't recall what it was. If only she could do something—laugh at his mood or ask him what was really wrong. She shifted the extra pencils in her left hand and mechanically traced over some of the shorthand curlicues in her notebook.

"Yet, that's just what such a ghost or vitalized projection would look like, Miss Millick," he continued, smiling in a tight way. "It would grow out of the real world. It would reflect all the tangled, sordid, vicious things. All the loose ends. And it would be very grimy. I don't think it would seem white or wispy or favour graveyards. It wouldn't moan. But it would mutter unintelligibly, and twitch at your sleeve. Like a sick, surly ape. What would such a thing want from a person, Miss Millick? Sacrifice? Worship? Or just fear? What could you do to stop it from troubling you?"

Miss Millick giggled nervously. There was an expression beyond her powers of definition in Mr. Wran's ordinary, flat-cheeked, thirtyish face, silhouetted against the dusty window. He turned away and stared out into the grey downtown atmosphere that rolled in from the railroad yards and the mills. When he spoke again his voice sounded far away.

"Of course, being immaterial, it couldn't hurt you physically—at first. You'd have to be peculiarly sensitive even to see it, or be aware of it at all. But it would begin to influence your actions. Make you do this. Stop you from doing that. Although only a projection, it would gradually get its hooks into the world of things as they are. Might even get control of suitably vacuous minds. Then it could hurt whomever it wanted."

Miss Millick squirmed and read back her shorthand, like the books said you should do when there was a pause. She became aware of the failing light and wished Mr. Wran would ask her to turn on the overhead. She felt scratchy, as if soot were sifting down onto her skin.

"It's a rotten world, Miss Millick," said Mr. Wran, talking at the window. "Fit for another morbid growth of superstition. It's time the ghosts, or whatever you call them, took over and began a rule of fear. They'd be no worse than men."

"But"—Miss Millick's diaphragm jerked, making her titter inanely—"of course there aren't any such things as ghosts."

Mr. Wran turned around.

"Of course there aren't Miss Millick," he said in a loud, patronizing voice, as if she had been doing the talking rather than he. "Science and common sense and psychiatry all go to prove it."

She hung her head and might even have blushed if she hadn't felt so all at sea. Her leg muscles twitched, making her stand up, although she hadn't intended to. She aimlessly rubbed her hand back and forth along the edge of the desk.

"Why, Mr. Wran, look what I got off your desk," she said, showing him a heavy smudge.

There was a note of clumsily playful reproof in her voice. "No wonder the copy I bring you always gets so black. Somebody ought to talk to those scrubwomen. They're skimping on your room."

She wished he would make some normal joking reply. But instead he drew back and his face hardened.

"Well, to get back to that business of the second class mailing privileges," he rapped out harshly, and began to dictate.

When she was gone he jumped up, dabbed his finger experimentally at the smudged part of the desk, frowned worriedly at the almost inky smears. He jerked open a drawer, snatched out a rag, hastily swabbed off the desk, crumpled the rag into a ball and tossed it back. There were three or four other rags in the drawer, each impregnated with soot.

Then he strode over to the window and peered out anxiously through the gathering dusk, his eyes searching the panorama of roofs, fixing on each chimney and water tank.

"It's a neurosis. Must be compulsions. Hallucinations," he muttered to himself in a tired, distraught voice that would have made Miss Millick gasp. "It's that damned mental abnormality cropping up in a new form. Can't be any other explanation. But it's so damned real. Even the soot. Good thing I'm seeing the psychiatrist. I don't think I could force myself to get on the elevated tonight . . ." His voice trailed off, he rubbed his eyes, and his memory automatically started to grind.

It had all begun on the elevated. There was a particular little sea of roofs he had grown into the habit of glancing at just as the packed car carrying him homeward lurched around a turn. A dingy, melancholy little world of tar-paper, tarred gravel, and smoky brick. Rusty tin chimneys with odd conical hats suggested abandoned listening posts. There was a washed-out advertisement of some ancient patent medicine on the nearest wall. Superficially it was like ten thousand other drab city roofs. But he always saw it around dusk, either in the smoky half-light, or

tinged with red by the flat rays of a dirty sunset, or covered by ghostly wind-blown white sheets of rain-splash, or patched with blackish snow; and it seemed unusually bleak and suggestive, almost beautifully ugly, though in no sense picturesque; dreary, but meaningful. Unconsciously it came to symbolize for Catesby Wran certain disagreeable aspects of the frustrated, frightened century in which he lived, the jangled century of hate and heavy industry and total wars. The quick, daily glance into the half-darkness became an integral part of his life. Oddly, he never saw it in the morning, for it was then his habit to sit on the other side of the car, his head buried in the paper.

One evening toward winter he noticed what seemed to be a shapeless black sack lying on the third roof from the tracks. He did not think about it. It merely registered as an addition to the well-known scene and his memory stored away the impression for further reference. Next evening, however, he decided he had been mistaken in one detail. The object was a roof nearer than he had thought. Its colour and texture, and the grimy stains around it, suggested that it was filled with coal dust, which was hardly reasonable. Then, too, the following evening it seemed to have been blown against a rusty ventilator by the wind—which could hardly have happened if it were at all heavy. Perhaps it was filled with leaves. Catesby was surprised to find himself anticipating his next daily glance with a minor note of apprehension. There was something unwholesome in the posture of the thing that stuck in his mind—a bulge in the sacking that suggested a misshapen head peering around the ventilator. And his apprehension was justified, for that evening the thing was on the nearest roof, though on the farther side, looking as if it had just flopped down over the low brick parapet.

Next evening the sack was gone. Catesby was annoyed at the momentary feeling of relief that went through him, because the whole matter seemed too unimportant to warrant feelings of any sort. What difference did it make if his imagination had played tricks on him, and he'd fancied that the object was crawling and hitching itself slowly closer across the roofs? That was the way any normal imagination worked. He deliberately chose to disregard the fact that there were reasons for thinking his imagination was by no means a normal one. As he walked home from the elevated, however, he found himself wondering whether the sack was really gone. He seemed to recall a vague, smudgy trail leading across the gravel to the nearer side of the roof, which was marked by a parapet. For an instant an unpleasant picture formed in his mind—that of an inky humped creature crouched behind the parapet, waiting. Then he dismissed the whole subject.

The next time he felt the familiar grating lurch of the car, he caught himself trying not to look out. That angered him. He turned his head quickly. When he turned it back his compact face was definitely pale. There had only been time for a fleeting rearward glance at the escaping roof. Had he actually seen in silhouette the upper part of a head of some sort peering over the parapet? Nonsense, he told himself. And even if he had seen something, there were a thousand explanations which did not involve the supernatural or even true hallucination. Tomorrow he would take a good look and clear up the whole matter. If necessary, he would visit the roof personally, though he hardly knew where to find it and disliked in any case the idea of pampering a silly fear.

He did not relish the walk home from the elevated that evening, and visions of the thing disturbed his dreams and were in and out of his mind all next day at the office. It was then that he first began to relieve his nerves by making jokingly serious remarks about the supernatural to Miss Millick, who seemed properly mystified. It was on the same day, too, that he became aware of a growing antipathy to grime and soot. Everything he touched seemed gritty, and he found himself mopping and wiping at his desk like an old lady with a morbid fear of germs. He reasoned that there was no real change in his office, and that he'd just now become sensitive to the

dirt that had always been there, but there was no denying an increasing nervousness. Long before the car reached the curve, he was straining his eyes through the murky twilight, determined to take in every detail.

Afterward he realized that he must have given a muffled cry of some sort, for the man beside him looked at him curiously, and the woman ahead gave him an unfavourable stare. Conscious of his own pallor and uncontrollable trembling, he stared back at them hungrily, trying to regain the feeling of security he had completely lost. They were the usual reassuringly wooden-faced people everyone rides home with on the elevated. But suppose he had pointed out to one of them what he had seen—that sodden, distorted face of sacking and coal dust, that boneless paw which waved back and forth, unmistakably in his direction, as if reminding him of a future appointment—he involuntarily shut his eyes tight. His thoughts were racing ahead to tomorrow evening. He pictured this same windowed oblong of light and packed humanity surging around the curve—then an opaque monstrous form leaping out from the roof in a parabolic swoop—an unmentionable face pressed close against the window, smearing it with wet coal dust—huge paws fumbling sloppily at the glass—

Somehow he managed to turn off his wife's anxious inquiries. Next morning he reached a decision and made an appointment for that evening with a psychiatrist a friend had told him about. It cost him a considerable effort, for Catesby had a well-grounded distaste for anything dealing with psychological abnormality. Visiting a psychiatrist meant raking up an episode in his past which he had never fully described even to his wife. Once he had made the decision, however, he felt considerably relieved. The psychiatrist, he told himself, would clear everything up. He could almost fancy him saying, "Merely a bad case of nerves. However, you must consult the oculist whose name I'm writing down for you, and you must take two of these pills in water every four hours," and so on.

It was almost comforting, and made the coming revelation he would have to make seem less painful.

But as the smoky dust rolled in, his nervousness returned and he let his joking mystification of Miss Millick run away with him until he realized that he wasn't frightening anyone but himself.

He would have to keep his imagination under better control, he told himself, as he continued to peer out restlessly at the massive, murky shapes of the downtown office buildings. Why, he had spent the whole afternoon building up a kind of neo-medieval cosmology of superstition. It wouldn't do. He realized then that he had been standing at the window much longer than he'd thought, for the glass panel in the door was dark and there was no noise coming from the outer office. Miss Millick and the rest must have gone home.

It was then he made the discovery that there would have been no special reason for dreading the swing around the curve that night. It was, as it happened, a horrible discovery. For, on the shadowed roof across the street and four stories below, he saw the thing huddle and roll across the gravel and, after one upward look of recognition, merge into the blackness beneath the water tank.

As he hurriedly collected his things and made for the elevator, fighting the panicky impulse to run, he began to think of hallucination and mild psychosis as very desirable conditions. For better or for worse, he pinned all his hopes on the psychiatrist.

"So you find yourself growing nervous and ... er ... jumpy, as you put it," said Dr. Trevethick, smiling with dignified geniality. "Do you notice any more definite physical symptoms? Pain? Headache? Indigestion?"

Catesby shook his head and wet his lips. "I'm especially nervous while riding in the elevated," he murmured swiftly.

"I see. We'll discuss that more fully. But I'd like you first to tell me about something you mentioned earlier. You said there was something about your childhood that might predispose you to nervous ailments. As you know, the early years are critical ones in the development of an individual's behaviour pattern."

Catesby studied the yellow reflections of frosted globes in the dark surface of the desk. The palm of his left hand aimlessly rubbed the thick nap of the armchair. After a while he raised his head and looked straight into the doctor's small brown eyes.

"From perhaps my third to my ninth year," he began, choosing the words with care, "I was what you might call a sensory prodigy."

The doctor's expression did not change. "Yes?" he inquired politely.

"What I mean is that I was supposed to be able to see through walls, read letters through envelopes and books through their covers, fence and play ping-pong blindfolded, find things that were buried, read thoughts." The words tumbled out.

"And could you?" The doctor's expression was toneless.

"I don't know. I don't suppose so," answered Catesby, long-lost emotions flooding back into his voice. "It's all confused now. I thought I could, but then they were always encouraging me. My mother ... was ... well ... interested in psychic phenomena. I was ... exhibited. I seem to remember seeing things other people couldn't. As if most opaque objects were transparent. But I was very young. I didn't have any scientific criteria for judgement."

He was reliving it now. The darkened rooms. The earnest assemblages of gawking, prying adults. Himself sitting alone on a little platform, lost in a straight-backed wooden chair. The black silk handkerchief over his eyes. His mother's coaxing, insistent questions. The whispers. The gasps. His own hate of the whole business, mixed with hunger for the adulation of adults. Then the scientists from the university, the experiments, the big test. The reality of those memories engulfed him and momentarily made him forget the reason why he was disclosing them to a stranger.

"Do I understand that your mother tried to make use of you as a medium for communicating with the . . . er . . . other world?"

Catesby nodded eagerly.

"She tried to, but she couldn't. When it came to getting in touch with the dead, I was a complete failure. All I could do—or thought I could do—was see real, existing, three-dimensional objects beyond the vision of normal people. Objects anyone could have seen except for distance, obstruction, or darkness. It was always a disappointment to mother."

He could hear her sweetish patient voice saying, "Try again, dear, just this once. Katie was your aunt. She loved you. Try to hear what she's saying." And he had answered, "I can see a woman in a blue dress standing on the other side of Dick's house." And she replied, "Yes, I know, dear. But that's not Katie. Katie's a spirit. Try again. Just this once, dear." The doctor's voice gently jarred him back into the softly gleaming office.

"You mentioned scientific criteria for judgement, Mr. Wran. As far as you know, did anyone ever try to apply them to you?"

Catesby's nod was emphatic.

"They did. When I was eight, two young psychologists from the university got interested in me. I guess they did it for a joke at first, and I remember being very determined to show them I amounted to something. Even now I seem to recall how the note of polite superiority and amused sarcasm drained out of their voices. I suppose they decided at first that it was very clever trickery, but somehow they persuaded mother to let them try me out under controlled conditions. There were lots of tests that seemed very businesslike after mother's slipshod little exhibitions. They found I was clairvoyant—or so they thought. I got worked up and on edge. They were going to demonstrate my super-normal sensory powers to the university psychology faculty. For the first time I began to worry about whether I'd come through. Perhaps they kept me going at too hard a pace, I don't know. At any rate, when the test came, I couldn't do a thing. Everything became opaque. I got desperate and made things up out of my imagination. I lied. In the end I failed utterly, and I believe the two young psychologists got into a lot of hot water as a result."

He could hear the brusque, bearded man saying, "You've been taken in by a child, Flaxman, a mere child. I'm greatly disturbed. You've put yourself on the same plane as common charlatans. Gentlemen, I ask you to banish from your minds this whole sorry episode. It must never be referred to." He winced at the recollection of his feeling of guilt. But at the same time he was beginning to feel exhilarated and almost light-hearted. Unburdening his long-repressed memories had altered his whole viewpoint. The episodes on the elevated began to take on what seemed their proper proportions as merely the bizarre workings of overwrought nerves and an overly suggestible mind. The doctor, he anticipated confidently, would disentangle the obscure subconscious causes, whatever they might be. And the whole business would be finished off quickly, just as his childhood experience—which was beginning to seem a little ridiculous now—had been finished off.

"From that day on," he continued, "I never exhibited a trace of my supposed powers. My mother was frantic and tried to sue the university. I had something like a nervous breakdown. Then the divorce was granted, and my father got custody of me. He did his best to make me forget it. We went on long outdoor vacations and did a lot of athletics, associated with normal, matter-of-fact people. I went to business college eventually. I'm in advertising now. But," Catesby paused, "now that I'm having nervous symptoms, I've wondered if there mightn't be a connection. It's not a question of whether I really was clairvoyant or not. Very likely my mother taught me a lot of unconscious deceptions, good enough to fool even young psychology instructors. But don't you think it may have some important bearing on my present condition?"

For several moments the doctor regarded him with a slightly embarrassing professional frown. Then he said quietly, "And is there some . . . er . . . more specific connection between your experiences then and now? Do you by any chance find that you are once again beginning to . . . er . . . see things?"

Catesby swallowed. He had felt an increasing eagerness to unburden himself of his fears, but it was not easy to make a beginning, and the doctor's shrewd question rattled him. He forced himself to concentrate. The thing he thought he had seen on the roof loomed up before his inner eye with unexpected vividness. Yet it did not frighten him. He groped for words.

Then he saw that the doctor was not looking at him but over his shoulder. Colour was draining out of the doctor's face and his eyes did not seem so small. Then the doctor sprang to his feet, walked past Catesby, threw open the window, and peered into the darkness.

As Catesby rose, the doctor slammed down the window and said in a voice whose smoothness was marred by a slight, persistent gasping, "I hope I haven't alarmed you. I must have frightened him, for he seems to have gotten out of sight in a hurry. Don't give it another thought. Doctors are frequently bothered by voyeurs . . . er . . . Peeping Toms."

"A Negro?" asked Catesby, moistening his lips.

The doctor laughed nervously. "I imagine so, though my first odd impression was that it was a white man in blackface. You see, the colour didn't seem to have any brown in it. It was dead-black."

Catesby moved toward the window. There were smudges on the glass. "It's quite all right, Mr. Wran." The doctor's voice had acquired a sharp note of impatience, as if he were trying hard to reassume his professional authority. "Let's continue our conversation. I was asking you if you were"—he made a face—"seeing things."

Catesby's whirling thoughts slowed down and locked into place. "No, I'm not seeing anything

that other people don't see, too. And I think I'd better go now. I've been keeping you too long." He disregarded the doctor's half-hearted gesture of denial. "I'll phone you about the physical examination. In a way you've already taken a big load off my mind." He smiled woodenly. "Good night, Dr. Trevethick."

Catesby Wran's mental state was a peculiar one. His eyes searched every angular shadow, he glanced sideways down each chasm-like alley and barren basement passageway, and kept stealing looks at the irregular line of the roofs, yet he was hardly conscious of where he was going. He pushed away the thoughts that came into his mind, and kept moving. He became aware of a slight sense of security as he turned into a lighted street where there were people and high buildings and blinking signs. After a while he found himself in the dim lobby of the structure that housed his office. Then he realized why he couldn't go home—because he might cause his wife and baby to see it, just as the doctor had seen it.

"Hello, Mr. Wran," said the night elevator man, a burly figure in blue overalls, sliding open the grillwork door to the old-fashioned cage. "I didn't know you were working nights now."

Catesby stepped in automatically. "Sudden rush of orders," he murmured inanely. "Some stuff that has to be gotten out."

The cage creaked to a stop at the top floor. "Be working very late, Mr. Wran?"

He nodded vaguely, watched the car slide out of sight, found his keys, swiftly crossed the outer office, and entered his own. His hand went out to the light switch, but then the thought occurred to him that the two lighted windows, standing out against the dark bulk of the building, would indicate his whereabouts and serve as a goal toward which something could crawl and climb. He moved his chair so that the back was against the wall and sat down in the semi-darkness. He did not remove his overcoat.

For a long time he sat there motionless, listening to his own breathing and the faraway sounds from the streets below: the thin metallic surge of the crosstown streetcar, the farther one of the elevated, faint lonely cries and honkings, indistinct rumblings. Words he had spoken to Miss Millick in nervous jest came back to him with the bitter taste of truth. He found himself unable to reason critically or connectedly, but by their own volition thoughts rose up into his mind and gyrated slowly and rearranged themselves, with the inevitable movement of planets.

Gradually his mental picture of the world was transformed. No longer a world of material atoms and empty space, but a world in which the bodiless existed and moved according to its own obscure laws or unpredictable impulses. The new picture illumined with dreadful clarity certain general facts which had always bewildered and troubled him and from which he had tried to hide: the inevitability of hate and war, the diabolically timed machines which wrecked the best of human intentions, the walls of willful misunderstanding that divided one man from another, the eternal vitality of cruelty and ignorance and greed. They seemed appropriate now, necessary parts of the picture. And superstition only a kind of wisdom.

Then his thoughts returned to himself, and the question he had asked Miss Millick came back, "What would such a thing want from a person? Sacrifice? Worship? Or just fear? What could you do to stop it from troubling you?" It had become a practical question.

With an explosive jangle, the phone began to ring. "Cate, I've been trying everywhere to get you," said his wife. "I never thought you'd be at the office. What are you doing? I've been worried."

He said something about work.

"You'll be home right away?" came the faint anxious question. "I'm a little frightened. Ronny just had a scare. It woke him up. He kept pointing to the window saying 'Black man, black man.' Of course it's something he dreamed. But I'm frightened. You will be home? What's that, dear? Can't you hear me?"

"I will. Right away," he said. Then he was out

of the office, buzzing the night bell and peering down the shaft.

He saw it peering up the shaft at him from the deep shadows three floors below, the sacking face pressed against the iron grillwork. It started up the stair at a shockingly swift, shambling gait, vanishing temporarily from sight as it swung into the second corridor below.

Catesby clawed at the door to the office, realized he had not locked it, pushed it in, slammed and locked it behind him, retreated to the other side of the room, cowered between the filing cases and the wall. His teeth were clicking. He heard the groan of the rising cage. A silhouette darkened the frosted glass of the door, blotting out part of the grotesque reverse of the company name. After a little the door opened.

The big-globed overhead light flared on and, standing just inside the door, her hand on the switch, he saw Miss Millick.

"Why, Mr. Wran," she stammered vacuously, "I didn't know you were here. I'd just come in to do some extra typing after the movie. I didn't . . . but the lights weren't on. What were you—"

He stared at her. He wanted to shout in relief, grab hold of her, talk rapidly. He realized he was grinning hysterically.

"Why, Mr. Wran, what's happened to you?" she asked embarrassedly, ending with a stupid titter. "Are you feeling sick? Isn't there something I can do for you?"

He shook his head jerkily, and managed to say, "No, I'm just leaving. I was doing some extra work myself."

"But you *look* sick," she insisted, and walked over toward him. He inconsequentially realized she must have stepped in mud, for her high-heeled shoes left neat black prints.

"Yes, I'm sure you must be sick. You're so terribly pale." She sounded like an enthusiastic, incompetent nurse. Her face brightened with a sudden inspiration. "I've got something in my bag that'll fix you up right away," she said. "It's for indigestion."

She fumbled at her stuffed oblong purse. He

noticed that she was absent-mindedly holding it shut with one hand while she tried to open it with the other. Then, under his very eyes, he saw her bend back the thick prongs of metal locking the purse as if they were tinfoil, or as if her fingers had become a pair of steel pliers.

Instantly his memory recited the words he had spoken to Miss Millick that afternoon. "It couldn't hurt you physically—at first . . . gradually get its hooks into the world . . . might even get control of suitably vacuous minds. Then it could hurt whomever it wanted." A sickish, cold feeling came to a focus inside him. He began to edge toward the door.

But Miss Millick hurried ahead of him.

"You don't have to wait, Fred," she called. "Mr. Wran's decided to stay awhile longer."

The door to the cage shut with a mechanical rattle. The cage creaked. Then she turned around in the door.

"Why, Mr. Wran," she gurgled reproachfully, "I just couldn't think of letting you go home now. I'm sure you're terribly unwell. Why, you might collapse in the street. You've just got to stay here until you feel different."

The creaking died away. He stood in the centre of the office motionless. His eyes traced the course of Miss Millick's footprints to where she stood blocking the door. A sound that was almost a scream was wrenched out of him.

"Why, Mr. Wran," she said, "you're acting as if you were crazy. You must lie down for a little while. Here, I'll help you off with your coat."

The nauseously idiotic and rasping note was the same; only it had been intensified. As she came toward him he turned and ran through the storeroom, clattered a key desperately at the lock of the second door to the corridor.

"Why, Mr. Wran," he heard her call, "are you having some kind of fit? You must let me help you."

The door came open and he plunged out into the corridor and up the stairs immediately ahead. It was only when he reached the top that he realized the heavy steel door in front of him led to the roof. He jerked up the catch.

"Why, Mr. Wran, you mustn't run away. I'm coming after you."

Then he was out on the gritty gravel of the roof, the night sky was clouded and murky, with a faint pinkish glow from the neon signs. From the distant mills rose a ghostly spurt of flame. He ran to the edge. The street lights glared dizzily upward. Two men walking along were round blobs of hat and shoulders. He swung around.

The thing was in the doorway. The voice was no longer solicitous but moronically playful, each sentence ending in a titter.

"Why, Mr. Wran, why have you come up here? We're all alone. Just think, I might push you off."

The thing came slowly toward him. He moved backward until his heels touched the low parapet. Without knowing why or what he was going to do, he dropped to his knees. The face he dared not look at came nearer, a focus for the worst in the world, a gathering point for poisons from everywhere. Then the lucidity of terror took possession of his mind, and words formed on his lips.

"I will obey you. You are my god," he said. "You have supreme power over man and his animals and his machines. You rule this city and all others. I recognize that."

Again the titter, closer. "Why, Mr. Wran, you never talked like this before. Do you mean it?"

"The world is yours to do with as you will, save or tear to pieces." He answered fawningly, as the words automatically fitted themselves together into vaguely liturgical patterns. "I recognize that. I will praise, I will sacrifice. In smoke and soot and flame I will worship you for ever."

The voice did not answer. He looked up. There was only Miss Millick, deathly pale and swaying drunkenly. Her eyes were closed. He caught her as she wobbled toward him. His knees gave way under the added weight and they sank down together on the edge of the roof.

After a while she began to twitch. Small noises came from her throat, and her eyelids edged open.

"Come on, we'll go downstairs," he murmured jerkily, trying to draw her up. "You're feeling bad."

"I'm terribly dizzy," she whispered. "I must have fainted. I didn't eat enough. And then I'm so nervous lately, about the war and everything, I guess. Why, we're on the roof! Did you bring me up here to get some air? Or did I come up without knowing it? I'm awfully foolish. I used to walk in my sleep, my mother said."

As he helped her down the stairs, she turned and looked at him. "Why, Mr. Wran," she said, faintly, "you've got a big black smudge on your forehead. Here, let me get it off for you." Weakly she rubbed at it with her handkerchief. She started to sway again and he steadied her.

"No, I'll be all right," she said. "Only I feel cold. What happened, Mr. Wran? Did I have some sort of fainting spell?"

He told her it was something like that.

Later, riding home in an empty elevated car, he wondered how long he would be safe from the thing. It was a purely practical problem. He had no way of knowing, but instinct told him he had satisfied the brute for some time. Would it want more when it came again? Time enough to answer that question when it arose. It might be hard, he realized, to keep out of an insane asylum. With Helen and Ronny to protect, as well as himself, he would have to be careful and tight-lipped. He began to speculate as to how many other men and women had seen the thing or things like it.

The elevated slowed and lurched in a familiar fashion. He looked at the roofs again, near the curve. They seemed very ordinary, as if what made them impressive had gone away for a while.

Wyatt Blassingame

AFTER GRADUATING FROM THE University of Alabama, Wyatt (Rainey) Blassingame (1909–1985) was eager to travel, so he hit the road and was given the nickname "Hobo." He got a job with a newspaper but lost it within a year because of the Depression. He eventually found his way to New York City in 1933, where his brother Lurton, a literary agent, showed the young writer a stack of pulp magazines and told him to take them home and study them, as they were buying stories. Six weeks later, Wyatt, who had never even heard of the pulps, sold his first story. A slower writer than many of his contemporaries, he nonetheless sold four hundred stories to the pulps before serving as an officer in the U.S. Navy during World War II, and about six hundred throughout his career. The service gave him background for several books, and he graduated to the better-paying slick magazines like *The Saturday Evening Post, Collier's, American,* and *Redbook.* When the fiction markets began to dry up, he turned to writing nonfiction articles, mainly on travel, and children's books, mostly about animals and American history. His only book of mystery fiction was a short story collection, *John Smith Hears Death Walking* (1944). Perhaps his best-known mystery character was Joe Gee (a short name he liked because he could type it quickly but which still counted as two words), who couldn't sleep while he was on a case. He also wrote many pulp stories under the pseudonym William B. Rainey.

"Song of the Dead" was first published in the March 1935 issue of *Dime Mystery Magazine.*

Song of the Dead

WYATT BLASSINGAME

Chapter One

Deadly Doggerel

You may say I'm crazy, but if you look at me you won't laugh while you say it. You will turn away from me, shutting your eyes tightly, shaking your head in an effort to forget. It's not that I'm deformed, and my face is not hideous. But you will see in my eyes some shadow of the things I have seen—and you will want to forget.

For me there is no forgetting, and it is not a pretty thing to live as I do, remembering the things which I must remember, and knowing already the misery which death holds for me. It is not a pretty thing to look into the mirror of a morning and see in your own eyes the things which I have seen in mine, the things which you may turn away from, clenching your teeth.

We first saw Saba Island from St. Martin's. We had anchored in what goes for a harbor and rowed into the little Dutch town of Phillipsburg. Our schooner was the only vessel in the harbor and looking back at it we could see the Caribbean stretch blue and purple to where a big rock formation rose like a tall blue cone, badly rumpled on one side, out of the sea. Silver clouds hid the top of the cone. Mary Wayne nodded and asked, "What island is that?"

There were several Negroes standing around gaping at us the way they do at strangers. I pointed toward the cloud-topped island and repeated Mary's question.

"Dot's Saba," one of them answered.

"Saba." Mary spoke the word slowly. "I never heard of it."

"It's on the chart," John Wayne said. "That's all I know."

Carl Hammer said, "I've heard about it. It's Dutch. Not many persons live there; it's just an extinct volcano sticking out of the sea. Practically nobody ever touches there."

Behind us the Negroes made a little shuffling noise and began to whisper among themselves. I turned toward them. "What sort of place is Saba?" I asked.

They continued to shuffle uneasily. At last one said, "You sailors?"

"We're sailing that schooner," I answered.

The Negro said, "Sailors don't go 'shore in Saba."

John Wayne's triangular-shaped blond eyebrows went up. "Why?"

"Well, they—they . . ." The Negro hesitated.

"They scared of Bill Wales," another of them blurted suddenly.

That was all we could get out of them, that sailors were afraid of Bill Wales. But the place sounded interesting and we decided to go.

Reaching Saba, we found Fort Bay, the only anchorage, wasn't really a bay at all. The whole island rises sheer out of the water and the Bay was merely a place where it was possible to drag a small boat ashore. We could see a pathway leading up the mountain, circling along the edge of a deep gorge. There was one small house at the foot of the path, but no sign of life. "The

other houses must be hidden back in the mountain somewhere," Mary said.

We anchored about a hundred and fifty yards off shore. There was an unusually heavy swell and the schooner dipped and rolled. Hammer and Wayne had gone forward to lower our one boat, when I saw the man on the shore. He was standing almost at the water's edge looking out at us. I can't explain it, but the instant I saw him I knew that something was wrong. I felt as if the wind had suddenly turned colder and I shivered.

At first I couldn't tell what there was strange about him. He seemed to be dressed in blue denim work clothes such as sailors or the natives on the islands often wear. It was too far to see his face, yet looking at him I found myself swallowing hard and my lips working. The sun was still an hour high, hot and intense. It made the water a glittering blue and where it lashed about the rocky shore the foam was startlingly white. I hardly noticed these things, however, looking at the man.

And then, all at once, I knew what was wrong with him. *I could see straight through him!* He was standing there looking out at us, and yet I had the impression I could see the rocks directly behind him. It was like a thick mist which has body and substance but which you can look through and on the other side of which you can see things.

Mary's heels made a clicking sound on the deck behind me and I turned quickly. "Come here," I said. "Look!"

She stared at me and began to smile. "What's the trouble? Seen a ghost?"

"I don't know. You look." I turned and pointed toward the shore where the man had been. He was gone.

Mary said, "I don't see anything but a lot of rocks. I don't even see how we're going to get ashore."

I took a deep breath, searching the shore. The man might have ducked behind one of the rocks or he might have reached the little house by running, but where he had stood there was only warm sunlight. "It must have been some trick of light and shadow that made him look that way," I thought.

"All right," John Wayne called. "You two come forward if you're going to the isle of Saba."

Pete, the Negro cook, was standing amidships as we went toward the small boat. "Would you like to go ashore and climb that mountain?" Mary asked him.

He said, "No, ma'am. Hit looks too steep fer me."

Mary laughed. "Well, you can guard the schooner," she said. I helped her over the side and followed her into the small boat with Carl Hammer and John Wayne.

It was a strange crew we had on the *Sink or Swim*, our dilapidated old two-masted schooner. I had often wondered how John Wayne, Carl Hammer, and I ever got together and just what the common bond was that made us such close friends. We didn't have much in common except a desire to ramble; yet for five years we had been together almost constantly and any one of us would have gladly gone through hell for the other two.

Hammer—it was an odd trick we had of calling each other by the last name—was an artist whose pictures brought him in just enough money to let him keep moving. They were strange pictures, going deep into metaphysics, and the man himself was strange. He was thin and dark, with glittering black eyes, sharp features, a thin mouth, and long, slim fingers that moved quickly and nervously. Sometimes when he was painting one of those strange, physic pictures of his the light in his black eyes wasn't human. Wayne and I had often said his mind was set on a hair trigger and he was likely to go crazy very suddenly, breaking the way a stretched cord may break.

John Wayne was the biggest man in the group. Tall, heavy shouldered, and blond, sunburned but with a slight redness to his nose caused by almost constant attention to the bottle, he was one of the best-natured men I have ever known.

And one of the most worthless, from the world's point of view. He had never done a day's work in his life, except on hunting and fishing trips and things of that sort. There had never been any need for him to work otherwise. He had several million dollars, I don't think he knew exactly how much. He was the man who had actually bought the *Sink or Swim*, though Hammer and I had contributed and had insisted, therefore, on the ship being a cheap one. You would have known Wayne anywhere because he always had a bottle in one hand—or very close to it—and a big grin on his face.

Mary was Wayne's sister and the one thing I had ever cared enough about to try for—and the one thing which always had seemed utterly impossible of attainment. She had been very much in love with some fellow in New York and he'd thrown her over just before we left for the West Indies. She'd been pretty badly broken up about it and Wayne had suggested we bring her along.

I had never understood how anybody could help but be in love with her. She wasn't tall, but she gave that impression until you were close to her. She was slim, with high, round breasts and a waist that curved as delicately as a flower into full thighs, and her legs were long and slim and well turned. Her hair was almost as blond as her brother's but with a trace of gold in it. Here eyes were wide set and very blue. Her mouth was a little too big to be classical, but to me it had always seemed the perfect mouth for kissing, though I had never kissed it.

Carl Hammer often said there was only one more worthless man in the world than John Wayne, and that was I. I had been left enough income to live on if I lived cheaply, so I spent my life moving from one cheap part of the world to another.

There you have the four of us who rowed ashore. Hammer was at the tiller, Wayne and I at the oars. He had to slide right in between two boulders to the small, rocky beach, but we made it.

I still had my back to the shore when I saw that strange look come over Hammer's face. Without asking, I knew what he had seen. His black eyes had suddenly grown very wide in his lean face. His thin, dark lips had parted. For a moment he stopped breathing; then over the beat of the surf I heard the air hiss through his nostrils. I believe he could see, even then, with that almost mystic power of his, what was coming. During that long minute he sat in the stern and stared, he must have recognized the thing at which he was looking.

Wayne noticed the expression on his face and said, "What the hell, Hammer? What the hell?" He went over the side then, without waiting for an answer, and began to tug the boat onto the shore. The surf was heavy and I should have gone to help him, but for some reason I couldn't.

I had shipped the oars and I began to turn slowly. The muscles in my neck seemed very cold. I heard Wayne's voice, sounding far away. "Damn it, get out and give me a hand."

Then I was looking at the shore and at the man standing there. As I looked he moved, caught the prow of the boat and tugged. I knew that he was the same man I had seen from the ship. He was tall, in his early thirties, and very sunburned; yet under the darkness of his skin there was a strange pallor. It was the shade of thin brown paper held up to the sun. I thought, suddenly, of a well-embalmed corpse and of the pallor beneath the paint on its cheeks. I had got the impression of seeing through the man when I looked at him from the ship, but now, while he kept moving and tugging at the boat, I lost that impression. In that first moment I saw nothing strange about him except the color of his skin. His face was dirty and with little wrinkles around the corners of his eyes as if from looking into the sun. He wore an old cap so that I couldn't see the color of his hair and with his face half turned I couldn't look into his eyes.

I went over the side then and helped them tug the boat onto the shore. Mary clambered out, threw back her head and looked up at the mountain which towered over us. Hammer was still sitting in the stern, staring at the man, but his breathing was more natural. Slowly he came forward and got out.

Wayne turned toward the man who had helped him beach the boat. "Where's the town?" he asked.

The man kept moving, stepping from rock to rock and back again, yet he did it with a slow calmness that did not seem at all nervous. I wondered then why he kept moving. As he stepped from one rock to another he nodded toward the path which led upward. "Up the hill about half a mile," he said. He talked with a distinctly English accent.

From directly behind me Hammer spoke. His voice was breathless, rapid. "What's your name?"

The man turned quickly and looked at Hammer. When he did I saw his eyes and instinctively I stepped to one side. His eyes were like those of a fish, an utterly lifeless blue. Like those of a corpse, I thought. And in the second that he stood motionless, staring at Hammer, I once more had the weird impression that I was looking through a figure made of mist and that directly beyond it I could see the rocks of the shore.

Then the man moved sideways, calmly. He grinned and said, "My name's Bill—just Bill—to sailors like yourselves."

Wayne said, "Well, Bill, we'll find the town if we go right up this path?"

"I'll show you," Bill said. "Got nothing else to do myself." He turned and started up the path.

Wayne made a quick duck into the prow of the rowboat and pulled out a bottle of red wine. "It looks like a long climb to go thirsty," he said. He started up the mountain. Mary went next and I followed her. Where the path was wide enough I stepped up beside her. Carl Hammer brought up the rear.

I was thinking that the name Bill on this island should have some special significance, but I couldn't remember what. I kept staring at the man, wondering what had given me the impression of seeing *through* him, but now he was moving steadily up the mountain and most of the time both Mary and Wayne stood between us. Watching the liquid movement of Mary's white linen skirt across her hips I forgot about the man called Bill . . .

We had climbed for nearly ten minutes when Bill began to hum. The sun was low now, but it was still hot and the climb and the heat had the rest of us panting heavily; yet there was no hint of exhaustion in Bill's breathing. After a moment his humming changed to a low singing. At first I couldn't understand what he was singing, then, as his voice grew louder, I began to catch the words.

"Oh, the first man died in a fall from the cliff,
And the second man died the same.
The third man went to a watery grave.
And the woman died from shame."

It had the swing of a sea chantey and he sang the same lines over and over, his voice gradually getting louder. We kept climbing.

The path rose sharply, clinging to the canyon wall. On our right the sheer drop grew deeper and deeper. The mountain above us was matted with big rocks, a thick wide-bladed grass I had never seen before, and mango trees. Small goats wandered about among the rocks and bleated mournfully. I noticed that when we came near one he would whirl, stare at us for a moment, and then go bounding away in terror.

"It's odd," I said to Mary. "Those goats shouldn't be that wild."

Behind us Hammer said, "It's not us they stare at. It's Bill." His voice sounded strange.

We both turned to look at him and it was in that second that it happened. Bill's voice had risen high and booming on the final line, *"And the woman died from shame."* As he had started the stanza again his tone changed, dropped and took on a weird tenseness, *"Oh, the first man died in a fall from the cliff."* That one line and no more. His voice went out as sharply as a light and left a silence thick as darkness.

Wayne made a choked, half-screaming sound.

"You—you—" Mary and I were spinning to look at him.

He was at the very edge of the cliff, reeling backward. The bottle of wine was held stiffly in front of him as if to guard himself from the thing he had seen. His eyes were bulging, his mouth twisted with incredulous fear. His left hand was chest high, and shaking. I couldn't see Bill and I thought that he must have rounded the sharp curve ahead.

The whole thing happened in a half second. Wayne went reeling backward while the three of us stared, spellbound. Then his left foot went over the cliff's edge and he toppled. Mary screamed, "John!" and leaped. I went past her in a rush.

It was too late. Wayne was falling, his face still upward—and I could see the fear-twisted mouth, the bulging eyes. Then he was out of sight below the brink of the cliff. I heard the crash of underbrush, the sickening thud as his body struck. There was a rattling, rumbling sound as rocks and body tumbled downward.

I was still kneeling at the edge of the cliff, my right hand stretched out over it helplessly, and Mary was standing close behind me, body rigid, face blank with amazement, when Carl Hammer passed us. He reached the bend in the path moving fast, and ripped around it. I heard the skid of his shoes as he stopped.

He came back just as I was getting slowly to my feet. Mary was still motionless, looking out over the canyon where Wayne had fallen. Hammer said dully, "Bill Wales has vanished."

Chapter Two

"The First Man Died in a Fall from the Cliff"

The dead call the dying
And finger at the doors.

—HOUSMAN

I looked at him blankly. "Who?" I asked.

He said, "Bill Wales." His voice sounded hopeless, beaten.

Even then I didn't remember. Perhaps I would have, had not Mary suddenly begun to sob. I caught her quickly in my arms. "Don't worry," I said, knowing even at the moment how foolish I sounded.

I turned to Hammer. "We've got to get him, quick!"

Hammer nodded, but his black eyes held that wild, spiritual look I had seen in them when he was painting. I don't believe he knew exactly what I said.

The cliff was too steep where Wayne had fallen for us to go over. We had to run back a hundred yards or more, then work our way down gradually. It was hard going, but we found Wayne lying half between a huge stone and a mango tree. He was on his back, his face bleeding from two long gashes and a bad bruise on his right cheek. He still held the neck of the broken bottle in his right hand.

When I knelt beside him I saw that his eyes were wide open and he was still breathing. He recognized me and tried to grin, but there was more than pain twisting his mouth. There was fear and a dull groping for understanding. His voice was a whisper. "He never touched me. He was just there and then—then I—I was afraid. But he never touched—"

"That's all right," I said. "You just keep steady. You'll be all right. You'll be—"

I had to stop. I was about to cry. I wasn't ashamed but I didn't want Wayne to see me.

Hammer and I made a stretcher of our linen coats and our shirts, using a couple of limbs we tore from the mango trees. As we worked I could see Hammer's thin lips twisting, see him blinking his dark eyes to keep back the tears; for one look at Wayne had shown us both that he was badly injured. The mystic, frightened expression had gone from Hammer's face, though he must have known then what lay in store for him and how utterly impossible it was to avoid.

It wasn't easy to carry Wayne up the cliff side. Before we reached the path we heard the excited voices, the pounding of shoes.

"Mary must have gone to the village for help," Hammer said.

From the cot Wayne whispered, "I'm hurting deep in my belly. I'd sure like a drink." He paused, then the whispering started again. "He never touched me, just—"

"Don't talk, fellow," I said. "Just take it easy."

"I'd like a drink."

"You damned sot," Hammer said. There was a little sob in his voice.

Then, all at once, men were around us and helping us lift the stretcher to the path, and carrying it up the mountain to a little village cuddled in what must have been the crater of an old volcano. A doctor had cut Wayne's clothes from him and set a broken leg and several ribs and put him to bed in the small government hospital. There weren't any other patients.

Wayne was still under the ether and Mary was sitting beside the cot, her thin brown hands holding one of his, her blond head bowed, when the doctor called Hammer and me outside. The doctor was a Negro, the only doctor on the island but his work had seemed very competent. Now he looked from Hammer to me.

"Well?" I asked.

The doctor spoke softly. "He may come through. There's a chance, but a small one. He'll have to be kept very quiet. Any exertion . . ." He made a short gesture.

"We'll keep him still," Hammer said.

The doctor hesitated. His very white teeth slid out over his lower lip. "While he was under the ether he kept saying, 'He never touched me. He just turned around and—I was afraid.' I think you two had best come down to the police station and explain how this happened."

"We'll come," Hammer said. That strange look was in his black eyes again and his dark lips were very thin across his teeth.

We finished our report. There wasn't much we could say. The Brigadier, as they call the chief of the five-man police force, was a sleek, very black Negro. He stood beside his desk looking at us and we looked at him. Almost suddenly Carl Hammer said, "Tell us about Bill Wales."

No surprise showed on the Brigadier's face. Instead there was an abrupt show of fear. Then the muscles about his mouth tightened, leaving no emotion at all.

"It's a very old story around here," he said. He spoke crisply and very precisely as if conscious of his office and that he should speak correctly. He kept his face masklike; so calm it gave me the impression he was afraid to be natural lest belief should show in his eyes.

"Bill Wales," the Brigadier said, "was supposed to be an English sailor marooned on Saba years ago. His ship had stayed here for a while and he'd married one of the native girls. The captain took Bill's girl and left him here. The next few ships that came—only one every six months or so in those days—were low on water or food, couldn't get any on this island and refused to take him. He went crazy and died swearing he'd kill every sailor and every sailor's sweetheart that landed here."

"And has he"—Hammer's voice was slow, deliberate—"kept his vow?"

The Brigadier looked nervous. "Of course I—I don't believe the story. But sailors *are* afraid of this island. A number of them have been killed accidentally here. The natives claim that if Bill Wales fails to kill them the first time, he comes back and makes good. The local boatmen always keep a cross in the back of their rowboats, claim it keeps Wales from going with them out to the ships. And—and—" The muscles around the Negro's mouth relaxed, trembled for one moment, then froze hard again. He tried to smile. "And it's true that as long as sailors stay ashore they keep meeting accidents. Of course, the walks around here are dangerous, if one is not used to them."

We thanked him and left. Once outside the building I said, "That was a swell story he told," and laughed.

Hammer looked at me without speaking and the laughter died in my throat. His face was like that of a man who looks at certain death and watches it coming toward him.

We ate supper at the little hospital and afterward all three of us sat around Wayne's bed. He was conscious now and suffering terribly. Whenever he caught one of us looking at him he tried to grin, but at other times there was a strange, drawn expression on his face. Not pain exactly, but bewilderment and something very close to fear. It was the same look that had been on his face when we reached him at the foot of the cliff. I kept remembering the thing he had said: "He never touched me. He just turned and I—I was afraid."

And I kept wondering what had happened to our guide. He'd never shown up, and our description had been too vague for the Brigadier to tell who he might be.

Mary got up from her chair beside the bed and tiptoed to a small window. "There's a moon just over the mountain-top," she said.

I didn't say anything and in the silence I could hear Hammer's breathing. It wasn't natural and I turned to look at him. He was leaning forward, black eyes glittering, head cocked to one side.

"Listen," he said. The word quivered in the room.

I said, "I don't hear anything."

Hammer didn't make a sound but his thin lips were moving, framing the words, "If he fails, he comes back and makes good."

Wayne stirred on the bed then, and we all turned to look at him. His head was raised, his shoulders almost off the pillow. At first he seemed to be listening, but slowly his face changed. The corners of his mouth began to tremble, his eyes to dilate. Even as I looked beads of sweat started to break out on his forehead.

"God!" he whispered. *"It's him!"*

Mary came toward him with a rush. "John! John!" she was saying. "Lie still! What is it, John?"

Wayne whispered again, *"It's him."* His whole life seemed to go into those words.

And then I heard it, still soft and barely audible, drifting in with the breeze through the open window. At first there was only the tune, the rhythm of the sea chantey. Then I began to catch an occasional word. "*. . . first . . . died . . . second . . . went to a watery grave.*"

I didn't move when I first heard those words. They were like cold iron bands around my chest, stopping my lungs. I just sat there and I could see my hands tightening around the arms of the chair. All at once I knew that I was afraid.

I shook myself then and stood up quickly. "I'm acting like a kid," I thought, "getting afraid of stories."

Mary had her arms about Wayne now, her fingers on his mouth, but he was saying, "You'll *have* to leave the island. You'll have to!"

"Be quiet," Mary said. "Just lie still . . ." She stopped, her head raised, her eyes growing wide. She too had heard the song.

"I'll go see that fellow," I muttered. I turned toward the door. Not until I reached the small porch did I realize that Hammer and Mary were following me.

Moonlight flooded softly over the village, showing the small white houses and their red roofs like dim shadows. We could see the stone walls that separated most of the houses, low and dark. A breadfruit tree made a rustling sound in the wind.

"*Oh, the first man died in a fall from the cliff.*"

The line rang loud, clear. There was something horribly vicious about the sound, something undefinable yet deadly, the way there is in the burr of a rattlesnake. But there was more than that in these words. They weren't earthly.

Then I saw the man who had called himself Bill. He was standing just beyond the left corner of the stone wall around the hospital. He was dressed as he had been in the afternoon, the cap pulled down over his temples, the ragged blue overalls. His head was thrown back, bathed in moonlight, mouth open as he sang. And even now I could see the strange pallor of his face, and his eyes, as utterly lifeless as those of a fish, showed palely blue. Even at that second I won-

dered why I could see his eyes so plainly by the moonlight.

"*And the second man died the same.*"

The words broke, each as clear and distinct as a glass ball. They hammered at my ears with a terrible meaningfulness. They jerked at my nerves, sent fear and anger flooding through me.

"*The third man went to a watery grave.*"

The man had never moved, but stood, head thrown back, singing. And even then I had the weird impression that I was looking *through* him and seeing the moonlight spilling over the ground beyond.

"Oh God!" Mary cried. "Stop him! Stop him!"

"I'll stop him," I said. I didn't know then why I was so angry or why I was so afraid, but I went off the porch with a rush and down the path toward the gate. Behind me I heard Hammer and Mary running.

"*And the woman died from shame!*"

I went through the gate moving fast, stumbled where the path dropped to the sidewalk, caught myself and whirled toward the left.

I took three steps, still running, before I could stop. My eyes were getting big in my face. I could feel the eyelids stretching. Perhaps I had stopped breathing altogether. I took one long step and reached the corner of the wall.

The man had vanished!

There was no sound for a long time—utterly no sound in the whole world. Even the moonlight had taken on a stiff frigidity. It lay on the leaves of the breadfruit tree, stiff and cold. The little white hospital with its red roof seemed frozen, taut, waiting for something to happen.

After a long while I heard breathing behind me and turned. Mary and Hammer were standing at the end of the stone wall, staring at the place where the man had been. And in Mary's face was reflected the look I had seen in Hammer's. Her hair seemed as white as the moonlight, as white as her cheeks, and very still.

Then suddenly she moved. "Oh God!" she said. "John! Alone . . . !" She was turning even as she spoke.

We heard the voice before she could finish turning, before she could take one step. It wasn't the booming voice that had sung the other lines. It was low and tense. It was clear, hideously clear, yet it was little more than a whisper.

"Oh, the first man died in a fall from the cliff."

That one line and no more. Not even a ghost moved in this world of death.

Something made a jarring noise inside the hospital. Mary and Hammer were running along the walk toward the gate. I was jumping the wall, in the air, striking the ground, running. The porch boomed under my steps, the door banged. I stopped just inside the room where John Wayne lay.

I never heard Mary and Hammer come up behind me. I don't know if Mary cried out at first; but before she reached him, moving slowly, stiffly, she knew he was dead. He lay there beside the bed, his body bent in a half circle, the sheets tangled about him, and his face turned upward with the eyes wide, the mouth open, fear showing in every stiffening muscle. Carl Hammer knew it and I knew it. We stood in the door motionless, watching.

After a minute Mary knelt beside him, began to sob, very quietly. I went and put my arms around her and lifted her up and carried her out of the room. Hammer must have gone for the doctor, for he came soon and gave Mary a sedative and got her to sleep.

It was the fall from the bed, he said, which had killed John Wayne.

We buried Wayne at sea the next day. He'd always said, the big, good-natured grin showing on his face, that he wanted to be buried at sea. He liked liquid and he wanted to spend eternity in it.

We rowed out in the small boat, Mary sitting beside the body, a priest in the stern. Before we reached the schooner we could see Pete, the Negro cook, standing at the rail. We told him Wayne had fallen from a cliff accidentally. Then we upped anchor, sailed out about a quarter of the way to St. Eustatius, and slid the body overboard. We went back and dropped anchor off Fort Bay.

Hammer and I were forward, ready to lower the small boat and row the priest ashore, when I said, "I'm going to wander around that island for a while. I'm going to find the fellow that does the singing."

Both the priest and Hammer turned swiftly to look at me. Hammer said, "You fool."

The priest was a small man with a face all angles and lean, wrinkled fingers. For a moment the fingers twisted the crucifix about his neck. He said slowly, "I advise you to leave the island—without coming ashore."

"And you believe that legend?" I demanded scornfully.

The priest looked down at the deck and his wrinkled fingers kept twisting the beads, toying with the cross. Almost suddenly he looked up.

"If I didn't believe in a life after death, I wouldn't be a priest," he said simply. "All religion is founded on an after-life. Man has believed in it from the dawn of history. The Bible has innumerable references to 'The Spirit' of a departed person, and that can be only what we call a ghost today. A number of your scientists believe also. There are things which they can't explain otherwise. Conan Doyle always believed. The German physicist Von Bernuth came to that belief after years of study. Your own Dr. Tillingham in California, probably the greatest of American scientists, has recently come to believe in the life after death."

I made a grunting sound and gestured with both hands as if I thought the man a fool. And yet there was a cold hollow deep in my chest. I couldn't believe that the man we had seen was the ghost of Bill Wales, and yet . . . How else was one to explain what had happened? I think that even then the awful certainty was forming itself in my brain, but I had laughed at the idea for so many years that now it was almost impossible to believe.

Hammer spoke then, his voice bitterly contemptuous. "You don't believe in spirits because you don't understand them. It's like saying there can't be a radio because you can't understand how it works. And you don't understand because you've never tried, you've never thought. You were told once that what you call a 'ghost' could not be, and you've shut your mind to any other belief, closed your eyes against the evidence which every day of your life piles up around you. It's only those of us who study, who face the problem . . ." He was looking now as I had seen him look while painting, the muscles in his dark face grown taut, his lips thin across white teeth, his black eyes glittering as though they saw a thing great and awful beyond human vision.

Seeing him made fear crawl along my back. The muscles in my throat began to tighten. But even then I wouldn't believe. *There weren't any ghosts!* I shut my mind on that idea, tightly, refused to look beyond. Sometimes now, gazing into the mirror, seeing the thing that is reflected there and remembering that moment while I still had a chance to escape, I feel like tearing my own throat. But I did not know then what was to happen.

"You're both crazy," I said. "I'm going ashore and finding the man that killed Wayne."

Part of the life went out of Carl Hammer then. He raised his right hand with its thin, long fingers halfway to my arm, stopped. His lips twitched. "All right," he said. "If you're going, I'll go along."

We dropped the boat over, helped the priest in, followed him. We were halfway to the shore when, looking back, I saw that Mary had come up from the cabin and was standing in the cockpit. The Negro cook was on the deck amidships, gazing out after us.

I didn't have any idea where to look for the man who bellowed a sea chantey before death struck. I had an eerie feeling that he would come

looking for me and the thought made my heart contract. But Hammer and I followed the priest all the way up to the Bottom, the misnamed little village situated eight hundred feet up that rocky mountain-side, without anything happening.

It was late afternoon by then. We told the priest good-bye. "Maybe we better start back now," I said to Hammer. "We don't want to leave Mary alone too long."

Hammer nodded, but he didn't speak. I don't believe he could have spoken at that moment. The skin on his face was as taut as parchment and wet with perspiration. I could see a vein beating in his throat. His mouth was thin, but the left corner kept twitching. All at once I remembered what Wayne used to say as he watched Hammer painting: "That man has a hair trigger brain. He'll go off it some day."

There wasn't anybody along the narrow winding steps that lead down to the sea. The sun was out of sight below the mountain, but the tops of the cliffs were white gold. Goats bleated from above and below us. The path went downward, one edge against the cliff, the other sometimes above a gradual slope, sometimes bordered by a sheer drop of two hundred feet or more. The wind had died and there was no sound except for the mournful cry of the goats.

It may have been the twilight, it may have been the silence, it may have been some premonition of the thing which was about to happen that made me feel the way I did. With each step toward the point where Wayne had fallen, the feeling grew on me. I was having to draw my breath consciously and the effort hurt my throat and lungs. It was hot and it was hard exercise going down that precipitous path; but the sweat that broke out on my shoulders was cold.

All at once I noticed that the goats were not bleating anymore. There was no sound except the scuff of our shoes as we went downward. I had several Dutch quarter-gilders in my pocket and in the silence I could hear them clinking as I walked. Ahead of me Carl Hammer was moving stiff-kneed. He seemed to force each leg the way a man does who is wading upstream. His back was rigid, head high. His long fingers were held stiffly at his side and I saw a bead of sweat slide from one to make a dark spot on the ground.

And then I heard it!

Chapter Three

"And the Second Man Died the Same"

It was very soft at first, more a stirring of the wind than a whispering of leaves, not as loud as the murmur of the sea heard from far away, or the notes of a death march dying into thick twilight.

It seemed to me that Carl Hammer's body grew more stiff than ever. His fingers seemed to get longer and more rigid at his side. The motion of his legs was heavier, pushing through the thick current of fear which flowed about him. But he did not hesitate, did not look around.

The sound grew slowly, becoming more distinct as the wind puffs and fades and puffs again, coming more strongly each time until the hurricane strikes. Hardly knowing that I did so I glanced to the left of the path. It dropped away for a hundred feet or more, straight down.

"We must be near the spot where Wayne fell." I heard the words without knowing I had spoken them. Hammer did not pause, did not look around.

The tune was very distinct now. It seemed to keep an eerie, death-march time with the crunching of our steps. I didn't hear the words, but I knew them.

"Hammer," I said. "Hammer!" I stopped. It couldn't have been long since I first heard the sound and yet it seemed like years that I had walked straight toward it, moving like a somnambulist without realizing I was walking.

Carl Hammer kept going, moving with that awkward motion like pushing his way through water or against a heavy wind. "Hammer," I said again. He kept going and never turned his head.

"Carl Hammer!" I screamed the words.

He hesitated, swayed as though drunk. The fingers at his side were clenched. Veins stood high on them and the knuckles showed white. Little muscles jerked in his wrist. Then he stepped forward again.

Ahead of us the song was a booming volley, sweeping down on us, crashing about our ears.

"And the woman died from shame!"

Then came the silence. It seemed to creep on cold and brittle feet through eternity. It froze me standing there on the brink between life and death, standing there motionless and watching the man ahead of me.

There was a sharp bend in the path. Hammer went toward it. He was there when I remembered.

It was here that Wayne had plunged over!

"Hammer!" I screamed.

He took two more short, awkward steps. They brought him to the curve and half around it.

"And the second man died the same!"

Even before it happened I knew then there was no stopping it; I knew that a power beyond life, beyond the touch of a human being, had control of us, was closing about us. I knew that one of us would die quickly, for that last line had been as tense and low and soft as the hiss of a snake.

Carl Hammer was half around the curve when he stopped. For one half second he stood there. Then he reeled. His hands, stiff and claw-like, came up in front of his chest. He staggered backward.

"Hammer!" In the silence that had followed the last line my cry boomed like a gun. And with the boom, Hammer turned.

He came like a fury, black hair slithering back from a lean face and eyes that were crackling madness above a dark and twisted mouth where teeth gleamed white. He came snarling, the breath husking in his nostrils, saliva drooling from his mouth. He came head first, lean shoulders driving—a man who had forced himself to the edge of death, going first to take the place of the friend who followed, but whose nerves had broken at the last step, flinging him backward and insane.

I threw up my hands and he crashed into me. We went over, hard. It seemed that we fell a long time and all that while through utter silence. Then we struck the path.

The breath jumped from my lungs and I heard Carl Hammer sob. I was teetering, rolling; my legs were swinging out into space and my fingers were clawing at the path while I hung there, almost like a bird who has stopped, wings outspread and motionless for a long second. Then I heard Hammer sob again, far away and below me; and I was pulling myself back on the path when I heard the crash of his body. There was the tinkling of rocks, the rustle of stilling leaves after the body passed through, and then there was silence.

I lay on my back on the path and did not move. High above me I could see the broad gold beam of the sunlight. It was like a clear river, flowing deep and strong. It touched the mountain-top and soaked it in warmth and flowed around it without movement, without ever a ripple.

Far off a goat bleated lugubriously.

I got to my feet then. My hands were grimy from clawing at the path and one fingernail was broken. It hurt but the pain seemed totally removed from my body. It was as if I were watching someone else nursing a broken fingernail, knowing that it hurt them, but unmoved, unsympathetic.

I went to the curve in the path and looked around it. The steps led twistingly downward. A ragged cliff on the left stuck out far enough to hide the sea.

During the whole time that I struggled down to Carl Hammer's body I was in that dazed, almost unconscious condition. It was seeing him lying there, one leg bent under him, the bone sticking out through his linen trousers, the bone unbearably clean and white, whiter than the linen through which it stuck, that brought feeling back to me. I didn't cry, yet there were tears sliding from my eyes. I kept trying to get the lump out of my throat and I began to curse, slowly, completely. Letting each word stand on my tongue, mouthing the full harshness of it, letting it fall slowly before I said the next one, I cursed myself.

Carl Hammer had known all the while what was coming. He had tried to tell me, but I had refused to listen. And then, because he had known, he had come ashore with me and had walked to his death ahead of me, standing between me and the thing which no human being could fight.

After a while I got the body up in my arms. There was blood on it and the blood felt clammy on my arms. I fought my way through the brush and the cactus trying to shield his body with my own, remembering always how he had shielded me and that the gesture I was making now was only absurd, yet forcing myself to do it, cursing at the pain of the thorns and cactus.

The sun was down when I reached Fort Bay, but in the east there was a flaming rose of piled clouds. I made my way through the big rocks to the water's edge and stopped. The rowboat was gone. Looking out to the anchored schooner I could see the shadow of the boat bobbing at its side.

"Oh God!" I said aloud. "He couldn't—couldn't—" I swallowed hard,

"And the woman died from shame."

The line stabbed suddenly through my mind.

Still holding Hammer's body in my arms I began to shout, "Pete! Pete! Mary!" A shadow moved on the deck. It was the Negro cook.

"Bring me that boat!" I yelled.

For a moment he didn't answer. Then I heard his voice, soft in the twilight. "Boat?"

"You're damn' right, the boat!" I shouted. "It's tied forward."

He went to the rail, looked over. Then he went forward and climbed over and into the boat.

There's always a heavy surf around Saba, probably the roughest seas in the West Indies. I don't know how Pete ever got the boat ashore by himself. I didn't watch. I stretched Hammer out on the ground, straightened his leg as best I could, covered his face with my coat. Then I began to wash the blood from myself—I didn't want to frighten Mary any worse than need be. But I did these things almost unconsciously, for my brain was clamped cold with fear. Who had rowed that boat out to the ship?

I tried to think of something else, knowing that guessing would do me no good. But I couldn't shake the thought from my mind. Mary couldn't have swum ashore and rowed back. Who had carried the boat out to the schooner? And why?

I heard the boat grate on the beach and looked up. Pete had gone over in water waist deep and, waiting until a wave came in, heaved the boat higher. He came up on the rock and turned toward me. All at once he noticed Hammer's body. He stopped and even in the twilight I could see his eyes growing wider, the whites seeming to spread across his face.

"What—what dat?" he asked.

"Mr. Hammer fell over the cliff," I said.

Pete began to stammer, to ask questions, but I stopped him. "Who rowed the boat out to the schooner?" I asked.

The words seemed to come to him slowly and far apart. As he listened his mouth dripped open; the pupils of his eyes contracted until they were invisible in the rolling whites. "I ain't goin' back on dat ship," he said at last. "Naw, Sur, not yit. I—I'se goin' where dere's folks."

He began to back away from me, up the path. I watched him go without speaking. It didn't seem important to me then. For a long moment nothing seemed important. And then, abruptly, I thought of Mary.

She was on the schooner—alone or—with Bill Wales!

I caught Hammer's body in my arms, carried it to the boat and put it in. I shoved the boat off and began to row. It's strange that I didn't capsize in that sea. I don't even remember the passage. But I remember tying the boat to the schooner. Then I was crawling over the rail with Hammer's body in my arms.

It was dark now. Just over the sea to the east the sky was growing white and gold from the rising moon, but now I could hardly see the length of the deck, the dark shadow of the boat-house and the cockpit. I laid Hammer on the deck and went aft. There was no sound except the lap of the water against the schooner, the dull echo of the surf booming on the rocky shore. No light came up from the cabin into the cockpit.

I stood on the deck for a long minute, gazing down into the darkness, scarcely breathing. My heart ached against my ribs. I could feel a nerve twitching at the right corner of my mouth. On the seat of the cockpit I could see the pale blur of a box of writing paper. Evidently Mary had been there during the afternoon.

I hadn't thought much of Mary during the last twenty-four hours. I had believed Wayne's death an accident and since Hammer's sudden madness and death I had been too shocked to think. But now the full significance of the song which rang as a death knell came to me.

*"The third man went to a watery grave.
And the woman died from shame."*

Standing there, looking down into the silent darkness of the cockpit, seeing the black square of doorway which led into the cabin, those words kept beating through my mind.

I was the third man, and Mary . . .

Chapter Four

"And the Woman . . ."

My fists knotted suddenly and I jerked a great breath into my lungs. By God! I wouldn't go down without fighting. Nothing would touch Mary until—My fingers relaxed and the breath slid in a sickening gasp from my nostrils. Fighting—how could I fight this thing? It had killed twice without ever touching its victim. At last I knew what I was facing, *and I knew that no human being could hope to withstand it.*

How long I stood beside the dark cockpit I don't know, but with each moment I grew more afraid. There was only darkness and silence in the cabin. Suppose I called to Mary and she didn't answer. Where would she be? What would have happened to her? What horrible thing . . .

And then I couldn't stand it any longer. I heard my voice calling out, calling frantically, "Mary? Mary!"

For a long while there was nothing. The water lapping against the schooner took on an awful roaring. My breath congealed in my nostrils. And then, "What is it, Tom?"

"Thank God!" I said aloud.

I went down into the cabin with a rush. I flicked a match across the doorsill, lit a storm lantern, and turned. Mary was sitting on the edge of Wayne's bunk. Her hands were folded in her lap, fingers motionless. Her hair was golden in the light and hung very still around cheeks as pale as those of a corpse. Her blue eyes were wide and large, and in them an expression which took the joy out of seeing her. It was as if she were looking into the face of death and waiting, waiting quietly, knowing absolutely there was no escape.

"Mary," I said. I found myself wondering if it had already happened. Had she—but I put the thought from my mind.

Her voice was like her face, emotionless, dead. "He killed Carl like he did Wayne. I saw him."

I made a gasping sound, then stiffened my muscles. "Where did you see him? On the ship?"

She shook her head slowly. "No. I didn't see Bill Wales. I saw Carl fall from the cliff."

"But—but Mary . . ." I was close to her now, kneeling in front of her, holding her folded hands. "How did you get ashore?" At the same time I could feel hope coming up through my chest, spreading out like a soft flame. That meant she was the person who had rowed the boat out to the schooner.

"I didn't go ashore," Mary said. "I was trying to write a letter, sitting in the cockpit. I saw it from there."

My hands tightened savagely about hers. "You *couldn't* have seen it from the ship. There's a cliff in the way, and—"

"I saw it," Mary said. "I was in the cockpit. I just—just saw it. I knew just when it happened."

I didn't say anything. I had heard of persons who had visions of things which happened miles away. It did not seem strange to me now. Nothing seemed impossible anymore.

But one thought did keep growing in my mind: if Mary had not rowed the boat out to the schooner someone else had. And the only other person . . .

I stood up. Mary did not move. She sat with her hands folded, looking off into space. I took the storm lantern from its bracket and made a slow circuit of the cabin. Nothing there. I went into the small cabin where Mary stayed, found nothing. I searched all the ship below-decks that I could reach from the cockpit. Everything was exactly as it had been.

Leaving the lantern with Mary, I went on deck.

The moon had swung up out of the sea now. It was a silver bubble and a shimmering path led from it to the schooner. The water was a rolling blackness where now and then white foam glimmered and vanished as the wind whipped the top from a wave. On the port side Saba rose in a great, dark shadow into the sky.

What I intended to do if I found Bill Wales, I didn't know. But somehow it seemed that I had to find him. Perhaps I thought I could do something which would help Mary to escape; I don't know. But I went toward the forward hatch, intending to enter it. I had the tarpaulin off when I stopped, rigid, staring.

I was on the starboard side of the hatch, looking out across the empty deck to the port rail. The deck showed clearly in the moonlight and little shadows rippled up and down it as the schooner rocked.

I was looking at the spot where I had placed Carl Hammer's body—and it was gone!

. . .

It was a long time before I began to laugh, a half crazy, guttural laughter. Carl Hammer had gone overboard, without a Christian burial; and he had believed in a hereafter . . .

"There was only one before," I said, and my voice had a ringing, insane note, "but now there're two." I kept holding to the edge of the uncovered hatch and laughing. The sound grew higher, wilder, madder. My shoulders began to shake. Madness clawed through me and burst out with the laughter.

"Tom! Tom!" Mary was calling to me from the cockpit.

My hands tightened on the hatch. I jerked at it, shook it and shook myself. The laughter choked in my throat.

"Steady," I said to myself. "Steady. You've got to help Mary." I turned and went aft, conscious of the fingernails biting into my palms, the pain from the one I had broken.

Mary was standing in the cockpit. The moonlight made her hair and cheeks seem very white and her eyes were dark pools of shadow. "I have never seen her quite so beautiful," I thought. "And soon . . ."

"What—what was that laughing, Tom?" she asked.

I dropped into the cockpit beside her, put my arms around her. It was the first time I had ever held her that way except when dancing. Her body was warm and firm. "It was me," I said. "I think I—I was going crazy."

She pulled away just enough to tilt back her head and look at me. She smiled, a pitifully brave smile with her lips trembling. "You can't do that," she said. "I had given up for a while, but we can't. Carl and—" a shadow of pain came in her eyes before she said her brother's name "—and John wouldn't want us to give up. They fought it out."

I pulled her close, held her there, her breasts flattened against my chest. I had loved this woman for five years and never held her this way until now, and now . . . Her hair brushed softly against my chin and mouth. "We won't give up," I said. "I'll get you out of this some way. There's got to be a way. Got to be!"

After a few minutes we went back into the cabin, sat side by side on what had been Wayne's bunk. I rested elbows on knees, hands clenched in front, head bowed, thinking. There had to be some way. If I could only be certain whether or not the thing was on board. If I could get him ashore . . . But Mary couldn't sail the schooner alone. If I could get her ashore, and sail off, carrying the thing with me . . .

"The third man went to a watery grave."

That was the line he'd sung and I was the third man. Well, I wasn't afraid of drowning, if I could save Mary. When the Brigadier had told us the story he'd said the local boatmen never left shore without a cross in the back of their boats.

All at once I sat up straight and stiff. That was it! I'd row Mary ashore, forcing the thing to stay on the ship. Then I'd come back and sail away. If I drowned, why . . .

"What is it, Tom?" Mary asked.

"I'm going to get you out of this," I said. "Listen—"

And then, as if in answer to the word I'd spoken, I heard the sound. In the half second after I said, "Listen," and paused to draw a breath, there was no noise except the lap of the water against the wooden hull of the schooner. But before I could speak again the sound came.

It came softly, gently, like the very lapping of the water, like waves striking one after another against the side of the ship, each coming a little faster and a little harder than the one before and yet maintaining a perfect rhythm, a growing cadence. The sound started in silence and yet it was a visible, audible silence like a current of water revolving slowly, and it grew louder as the current grew, whirling up, up until it crashed and roared about us.

"Oh, the first man died in a fall from the cliff,
And the second man died the same.
The third man went to a watery grave—"

The sound boomed and whirled around us like a giant wave, filling the cabin, coming from nowhere and everywhere. Mary and I turned, slowly, like puppets on a string, until we faced the companionway to the cockpit. The light of the storm lantern spilled out into the darkness and faded. I got to my feet. *"And the woman died from shame."*

There was a silence in which the world died. Mary and I had stopped breathing. I believe the water quit lapping against the ship. My ears were aching for some tiny sound, screaming into the silence.

And then, standing in the light of the companionway, motionless and grinning horribly, was Bill Wales. And beyond him, *straight through him,* I could see the light spilling out into the darkness of the cockpit, and fading.

It seemed an eternity that no one spoke, no one moved. And in that long silence I could feel myself plunging downward, downward. I was like a man falling from a cliff, living aeons of time in the seconds that it takes him to reach the bottom, waiting for the next line of Bill Wales' song, powerless to move.

"And the third man . . ." Destruction whirled up. I thought of Wayne, seeing it coming.

"Went to a watery . . ."

Something moved in the light that slid through Bill Wales' body, some shadow that at first I could not believe. The last line of Wales' song was never uttered. It was jerked from his mouth. He whirled, crouched and snarling. He stepped backward into the full glow of the light.

The shadow in the cockpit moved again. It was a man, but I could see *through* him as I had seen through Wales; and then the light was on him as he stood in the doorway, and I was looking at the blood-smeared face of Carl Hammer.

"Now there are two of them," I said half aloud. On the bunk Mary did not move.

Bill Wales quit snarling and for a long while there was no movement in the cabin. Then he began to laugh, softly. It was a quiet laugh, but terrible in its quietness. If ever there was a sound of absolute confidence, it rang in that cabin.

Still laughing, Bill Wales stepped toward the cabin door, his eyes—which showed no mirth, no light, no life—fixed on Hammer's bloody face. There was no sound in the cabin except the laughter.

Wales was very near him when Hammer stepped backward. Wales followed, laughing. The light from the storm lamp fell on his face, the lifeless blue eyes, the twisted mouth. And then he had passed through the door and he was only a shadow among shadows, and that shadow moved again and vanished.

From the deck overhead the laughter kept flowing, softly, horribly. It glided forward and toward the starboard. It grew fainter, more distant, but not for one instant did it lose that note of dreadful certainty.

Then there was only silence.

Slowly, my muscles feeling cold and sluggish, I turned my head until I was looking at Mary. She still sat on the edge of the bunk and her hands were still folded in her lap. Her mouth was slightly open, her eyes open, but when I saw them I shuddered and turned away.

It had been very quiet in the cabin for perhaps a minute when the idea came to me. Bill Wales was not on the ship now. If we left there might be no way for him to follow! I plunged down into our small engine-room, started the auxiliary. I don't know how I ever got the anchor up alone, but I did. Then I sprinted back to the wheel in the cockpit, set a course for St. Kitts, lashed the wheel and went back into the cabin.

Mary sat as I had left her, mouth open, eyes staring. I don't think she'd moved at all. I felt sick when I went toward her. I took her hand and said gently, "Come out in the cockpit, darling. It's cooler there."

She didn't answer. She just quivered and sat still.

I bit my lip. It wasn't easy to look at her, remembering how beautiful she'd been a few hours before. I said, "They've gone now. There's nothing to be afraid of."

"No," she said. "They haven't gone." There was no hope, no emotion in her voice. It was as cold and certain as death.

"They have gone!" I said. "They have gone!" I think I screamed the words.

"No," she repeated. But she let me lead her out to the cockpit. I pushed out of her way the box of letter paper she'd left, and she sat down.

The schooner was running before the wind and making good time. There was a big swell and she ran up the waves and dropped down the far side of them. The wake trailed behind, pale and greenish in the moonlight.

"You'll feel better soon," I told Mary.

But she only answered, in that bleak, dead voice, "No, they haven't gone."

I opened my mouth to scream at her, to say they had gone, they had gone and would never come back, but I didn't speak. It was her face in the moonlight that stopped me first. The light was falling cold and clear and soft into the cockpit. Her mouth was slightly open, her eyes open and blank. She looked exactly as she had when I turned to her in the cabin.

And then I saw the difference. I was standing at the wheel, hands clenched around it, or I would

have fallen. I wanted to run and I couldn't. Every muscle in my body was motionless with cold.

Crawling through the night, shivering cold and soft and horrible, was the laughter. It took me a long time to raise my eyes. The moonlight came down strong on the deck. Bill Wales was standing near the forward mast. Between us, straight and motionless, was Carl Hammer.

"Look in the cabin," Wales called.

"Look in the cabin." His voice was part of the pounding of the sea. It was in the trade wind that ruffled my hair and it came with the throb of the motor throughout the schooner; it was the blood that beat hard in my temples.

But I did not look in the cabin. I can't bring myself to that, though I know what I should find there. I have sat here in the cockpit, writing on the paper that Mary left. It must already have happened, then, before I got to the ship. But not till just now did she—

My muscles keep jerking me toward the cabin, but I won't go. I don't want to look at Mary, yet at times my eyes turn toward her and I am unable to stop them. And then I see her mouth, still open, her eyes still staring; and I see her blond hair around her face, hair which the trade wind does not ruffle. And straight through her I see the edge of the cockpit.

I MUST BE DREAMING

Wilkie Collins

THE INVENTOR OF WHAT became known as the "sensation" novel and one of the most popular and highest paid of all Victorian novelists, (William) Wilkie Collins (1824–1889) was a friend and frequent collaborator of Charles Dickens's and author of two of the greatest novels in the history of mystery fiction, *The Woman in White* (1860) and *The Moonstone* (1868).

Born in London, the son of the very successful landscape painter William Collins, a member of the Royal Academy, Collins received a law degree but never practiced, deciding to become a full-time writer instead. Over the course of his life, he published twenty-five novels, fifteen plays, more than fifty short stories, and over a hundred nonfiction articles. He met Dickens in 1851 and soon cowrote a play with him, *The Frozen Deep*, then collaborated with him on short stories, articles, etc. When Dickens founded a magazine, *All the Year Round*, in 1859, Collins assured its success by serializing *The Woman in White* in its pages. He later wrote Christmas stories for the periodical, and serialized the long novel *No Name* (1862) and, in 1868, the classic *The Moonstone*, which T. S. Eliot described as "the first, the longest, and the best" detective novel of all time. Collins adapted *The Woman in White* for the stage in 1871; it has been filmed frequently, beginning with a Pathe silent in 1917 but most memorably in 1948 with Alexis Smith, Eleanor Parker, Gig Young, and Sydney Greenstreet as the evil Count Fosco. *The Moonstone* was also dramatized by Collins, opening in 1877; it has been filmed at least five times, first as a 1909 silent, followed by a 1915 silent, then as a lackluster 1934 low-budget film, as a garrulous five-hour BBC production in 1972, and again as a BBC production in 1997.

"The Dream Woman" was originally published in the Christmas 1855 issue of *Household Words* with the title "The Ostler"; it was first collected in *The Queen of Hearts* (London, Hurst & Blackett, 1859) with the title "Brother Morgan's Story of the Dream Woman."

The Dream Woman

A MYSTERY IN FOUR NARRATIVES

WILKIE COLLINS

The First Narrative

**Introductory Statement of the Facts
by Percy Fairbank**

I

"Hullo, there! Hostler! Hullo-o-o!"

"My dear! why don't you look for the bell?"

"I *have* looked—there is no bell."

"And nobody in the yard. How very extraordinary! Call again, dear."

"Hostler! Hullo, there! Hostler-r-r!"

My second call echoes through empty space, and rouses nobody—produces, in short, no visible result. I am at the end of my resources—I don't know what to say or what to do next. Here I stand in the solitary inn yard of a strange town, with two horses to hold, and a lady to take care of. By way of adding to my responsibilities, it so happens that one of the horses is dead lame, and that the lady is my wife.

Who am I?—you will ask.

There is plenty of time to answer the question. Nothing happens; and nobody appears to receive us. Let me introduce myself and my wife.

I am Percy Fairbank—English gentleman—age (let us say) forty—no profession—moderate politics—middle height—fair complexion—easy character—plenty of money.

My wife is a French lady. She was Mademoiselle Clotilde Delorge—when I was first presented to her at her father's house in France. I fell in love with her—I really don't know why. It might have been because I was perfectly idle, and had nothing else to do at the time. Or it might have been because all my friends said she was the very last woman whom I ought to think of marrying. On the surface, I must own, there is nothing in common between Mrs. Fairbank and me. She is tall; she is dark; she is nervous, excitable, romantic; in all her opinions she proceeds to extremes. What could such a woman see in me? what could I see in her? I know no more than you do. In some mysterious manner we exactly suit each other. We have been man and wife for ten years, and our only regret is that we have no children. I don't know what *you* may think; I call that—upon the whole—a happy marriage.

So much for ourselves. The next question is—what has brought us into the inn yard? and why am I obliged to turn groom, and hold the horses?

We live for the most part in France—at the country house in which my wife and I first met. Occasionally, by way of variety, we pay visits to my friends in England. We are paying one of those visits now. Our host is an old college friend of mine, possessed of a fine estate in Somersetshire; and we have arrived at his house—called Farleigh Hall—toward the close of the hunting season.

On the day of which I am now writing—des-tined to be a memorable day in our calendar—the hounds meet at Farleigh Hall. Mrs. Fairbank and I are mounted on two of the best horses in my friend's stables. We are quite unworthy of that distinction; for we know nothing and care nothing about hunting. On the other hand, we delight in riding, and we enjoy the breezy Spring morning and the fair and fertile English landscape surrounding us on every side. While the hunt prospers, we follow the hunt. But when a check occurs—when time passes and patience is sorely tried; when the bewildered dogs run hither and thither, and strong language falls from the lips of exasperated sportsmen—we fail to take any further interest in the proceedings. We turn our horses' heads in the direction of a grassy lane, delightfully shaded by trees. We trot merrily along the lane, and find ourselves on an open common. We gallop across the common, and follow the windings of a second lane. We cross a brook, we pass through a village, we emerge into pastoral solitude among the hills. The horses toss their heads, and neigh to each other, and enjoy it as much as we do. The hunt is forgotten. We are as happy as a couple of children; we are actually singing a French song—when in one moment our merriment comes to an end. My wife's horse sets one of his forefeet on a loose stone, and stumbles. His rider's ready hand saves him from falling. But, at the first attempt he makes to go on, the sad truth shows itself—a tendon is strained; the horse is lame.

What is to be done? We are strangers in a lonely part of the country. Look where we may, we see no signs of a human habitation. There is nothing for it but to take the bridle road up the hill, and try what we can discover on the other side. I transfer the saddles, and mount my wife on my own horse. He is not used to carrying a lady; he misses the familiar pressure of a man's legs on either side of him; he fidgets, and starts, and kicks up the dust. I follow on foot, at a respectful distance from his heels, leading the lame horse. Is there a more miserable object on the face of creation than a lame horse? I have seen lame men and lame dogs who were cheerful creatures; but I never yet saw a lame horse who didn't look heartbroken over his own misfortune.

For half an hour my wife capers and curvets sideways along the bridle road. I trudge on behind her; and the heartbroken horse halts behind me. Hard by the top of the hill, our melancholy procession passes a Somersetshire peasant at work in a field. I summon the man to approach us; and the man looks at me stolidly, from the middle of the field, without stirring a step. I ask at the top of my voice how far it is to Farleigh Hall. The Somersetshire peasant answers at the top of *his* voice:

"Vourteen mile. Gi' oi a drap o' zyder."

I translate (for my wife's benefit) from the Somersetshire language into the English language. We are fourteen miles from Farleigh Hall; and our friend in the field desires to be rewarded, for giving us that information, with a drop of cider. There is the peasant, painted by himself! Quite a bit of character, my dear! Quite a bit of character!

Mrs. Fairbank doesn't view the study of agricultural human nature with my relish. Her fidgety horse will not allow her a moment's repose; she is beginning to lose her temper.

"We can't go fourteen miles in this way," she says. "Where is the nearest inn? Ask that brute in the field!"

I take a shilling from my pocket and hold it up in the sun. The shilling exercises magnetic virtues. The shilling draws the peasant slowly toward me from the middle of the field. I inform him that we want to put up the horses and to hire a carriage to take us back to Farleigh Hall. Where can we do that? The peasant answers (with his eye on the shilling):

"At Oonderbridge, to be zure." (At Underbridge, to be sure.)

"Is it far to Underbridge?"

The peasant repeats, "Var to Oonderbridge?"—and laughs at the question. "Hoo-hoo-hoo!" (Underbridge is evidently close by—if we could only find it.) "Will you show us the way, my man?" "Will you gi' oi a drap of zyder?" I courteously bend my head, and point

to the shilling. The agricultural intelligence exerts itself. The peasant joins our melancholy procession. My wife is a fine woman, but he never once looks at my wife—and, more extraordinary still, he never even looks at the horses. His eyes are with his mind—and his mind is on the shilling.

We reach the top of the hill—and, behold on the other side, nestling in a valley, the shrine of our pilgrimage, the town of Underbridge! Here our guide claims his shilling, and leaves us to find out the inn for ourselves. I am constitutionally a polite man. I say "Good morning" at parting. The guide looks at me with the shilling between his teeth to make sure that it is a good one. "Marnin!" he says savagely—and turns his back on us, as if we had offended him. A curious product, this, of the growth of civilization. If I didn't see a church spire at Underbridge, I might suppose that we had lost ourselves on a savage island.

II

Arriving at the town, we had no difficulty in finding the inn. The town is composed of one desolate street; and midway in that street stands the inn—an ancient stone building sadly out of repair. The painting on the sign-board is obliterated. The shutters over the long range of front windows are all closed. A cock and his hens are the only living creatures at the door. Plainly, this is one of the old inns of the stage-coach period, ruined by the railway. We pass through the open arched doorway, and find no one to welcome us. We advance into the stable yard behind; I assist my wife to dismount—and there we are in the position already disclosed to view at the opening of this narrative. No bell to ring. No human creature to answer when I call. I stand helpless, with the bridles of the horses in my hand. Mrs. Fairbank saunters gracefully down the length of the yard and does what all women do, when they find themselves in a strange place. She opens every door as she passes it, and peeps in. On my side, I have just recovered my breath, I am on the point of shouting for the hostler for the third and last time, when I hear Mrs. Fairbank suddenly call to me:

"Percy! come here!"

Her voice is eager and agitated. She has opened a last door at the end of the yard, and has started back from some sight which has suddenly met her view. I hitch the horses' bridles on a rusty nail in the wall near me, and join my wife. She has turned pale, and catches me nervously by the arm.

"Good heavens!" she cries; "look at that!"

I look—and what do I see? I see a dingy little stable, containing two stalls. In one stall a horse is munching his corn. In the other a man is lying asleep on the litter.

A worn, withered, woebegone man in a hostler's dress. His hollow wrinkled cheeks, his scanty grizzled hair, his dry yellow skin, tell their own tale of past sorrow or suffering. There is an ominous frown on his eyebrows—there is a painful nervous contraction on the side of his mouth. I hear him breathing convulsively when I first look in; he shudders and sighs in his sleep. It is not a pleasant sight to see, and I turn round instinctively to the bright sunlight in the yard. My wife turns me back again in the direction of the stable door.

"Wait!" she says. "Wait! he may do it again."

"Do what again?"

"He was talking in his sleep, Percy, when I first looked in. He was dreaming some dreadful dream. Hush! he's beginning again."

I look and listen. The man stirs on his miserable bed. The man speaks in a quick, fierce whisper through his clinched teeth. "Wake up! Wake up, there! Murder!"

There is an interval of silence. He moves one lean arm slowly until it rests over his throat; he shudders, and turns on his straw; he raises his arm from his throat, and feebly stretches it out; his hand clutches at the straw on the side toward which he has turned; he seems to fancy that he is grasping at the edge of something. I see his lips begin to move again; I step softly into the stable;

my wife follows me, with her hand fast clasped in mine. We both bend over him. He is talking once more in his sleep—strange talk, mad talk, this time.

"Light gray eyes" (we hear him say), "and a droop in the left eyelid—flaxen hair, with a gold-yellow streak in it—all right, mother! fair, white arms with a down on them—little, lady's hand, with a reddish look round the fingernails—the knife—the cursed knife—first on one side, then on the other—aha, you she-devil! where is the knife?"

He stops and grows restless on a sudden. We see him writhing on the straw. He throws up both his hands and gasps hysterically for breath. His eyes open suddenly. For a moment they look at nothing, with a vacant glitter in them—then they close again in deeper sleep. Is he dreaming still? Yes; but the dream seems to have taken a new course. When he speaks next, the tone is altered; the words are few—sadly and imploringly repeated over and over again. "Say you love me! I am so fond of *you*. Say you love me! say you love me!" He sinks into deeper and deeper sleep, faintly repeating those words. They die away on his lips. He speaks no more.

By this time Mrs. Fairbank has got over her terror; she is devoured by curiosity now. The miserable creature on the straw has appealed to the imaginative side of her character. Her illimitable appetite for romance hungers and thirsts for more. She shakes me impatiently by the arm.

"Do you hear? There is a woman at the bottom of it, Percy! There is love and murder in it, Percy! Where are the people of the inn? Go into the yard, and call to them again."

My wife belongs, on her mother's side, to the South of France. The South of France breeds fine women with hot tempers. I say no more. Married men will understand my position. Single men may need to be told that there are occasions when we must not only love and honor—we must also obey—our wives.

I turn to the door to obey *my* wife, and find myself confronted by a stranger who has stolen on us unawares. The stranger is a tiny, sleepy, rosy old man, with a vacant pudding-face, and a shining bald head. He wears drab breeches and gaiters, and a respectable square-tailed ancient black coat. I feel instinctively that here is the landlord of the inn.

"Good morning, sir," says the rosy old man. "I'm a little hard of hearing. Was it you that was a-calling just now in the yard?"

Before I can answer, my wife interposes. She insists (in a shrill voice, adapted to our host's hardness of hearing) on knowing who that unfortunate person is sleeping on the straw. "Where does he come from? Why does he say such dreadful things in his sleep? Is he married or single? Did he ever fall in love with a murderess? What sort of a looking woman was she? Did she really stab him or not? In short, dear Mr. Landlord, tell us the whole story!"

Dear Mr. Landlord waits drowsily until Mrs. Fairbank has quite done—then delivers himself of his reply as follows:

"His name's Francis Raven. He's an Independent Methodist. He was forty-five year old last birthday. And he's my hostler. That's his story."

My wife's hot southern temper finds its way to her foot, and expresses itself by a stamp on the stable yard.

The landlord turns himself sleepily round, and looks at the horses. "A fine pair of horses, them two in the yard. Do you want to put 'em in my stables?" I reply in the affirmative by a nod. The landlord, bent on making himself agreeable to my wife, addresses her once more. "I'm a-going to wake Francis Raven. He's an Independent Methodist. He was forty-five year old last birthday. And he's my hostler. That's his story."

Having issued this second edition of his interesting narrative, the landlord enters the stable. We follow him to see how he will wake Francis Raven, and what will happen upon that. The stable broom stands in a corner; the landlord takes it—advances toward the sleeping hostler—and coolly stirs the man up with a broom as if he was a wild beast in a cage. Francis Raven

starts to his feet with a cry of terror—looks at us wildly, with a horrid glare of suspicion in his eyes—recovers himself the next moment—and suddenly changes into a decent, quiet, respectable serving-man.

"I beg your pardon, ma'am. I beg your pardon, sir."

The tone and manner in which he makes his apologies are both above his apparent station in life. I begin to catch the infection of Mrs. Fairbank's interest in this man. We both follow him out into the yard to see what he will do with the horses. The manner in which he lifts the injured leg of the lame horse tells me at once that he understands his business. Quickly and quietly, he leads the animal into an empty stable; quickly and quietly, he gets a bucket of hot water, and puts the lame horse's leg into it. "The warm water will reduce the swelling, sir. I will bandage the leg afterwards." All that he does is done intelligently; all that he says, he says to the purpose.

Nothing wild, nothing strange about him now. Is this the same man whom we heard talking in his sleep?—the same man who woke with that cry of terror and that horrid suspicion in his eyes? I determine to try him with one or two questions.

III

"Not much to do here," I say to the hostler.

"Very little to do, sir," the hostler replies.

"Anybody staying in the house?"

"The house is quite empty, sir."

"I thought you were all dead. I could make nobody hear me."

"The landlord is very deaf, sir, and the waiter is out on an errand."

"Yes; and *you* were fast asleep in the stable. Do you often take a nap in the daytime?"

The worn face of the hostler faintly flushes. His eyes look away from my eyes for the first time. Mrs. Fairbank furtively pinches my arm.

Are we on the eve of a discovery at last? I repeat my question. The man has no civil alternative but to give me an answer. The answer is given in these words:

"I was tired out, sir. You wouldn't have found me asleep in the daytime but for that."

"Tired out, eh? You had been hard at work, I suppose?"

"No, sir."

"What was it, then?"

He hesitates again, and answers unwillingly, "I was up all night."

"Up all night? Anything going on in the town?"

"Nothing going on, sir."

"Anybody ill?"

"Nobody ill, sir."

That reply is the last. Try as I may, I can extract nothing more from him. He turns away and busies himself in attending to the horse's leg. I leave the stable to speak to the landlord about the carriage which is to take us back to Farleigh Hall. Mrs. Fairbank remains with the hostler, and favors me with a look at parting. The look says plainly, "I mean to find out why he was up all night. Leave him to Me."

The ordering of the carriage is easily accomplished. The inn possesses one horse and one chaise. The landlord has a story to tell of the horse, and a story to tell of the chaise. They resemble the story of Francis Raven—with this exception, that the horse and chaise belong to no religious persuasion. "The horse will be nine year old next birthday. I've had the shay for four-and-twenty year. Mr. Max, of Underbridge, he bred the horse; and Mr. Pooley, of Yeovil, he built the shay. It's my horse and my shay. And that's their story!" Having relieved his mind of these details, the landlord proceeds to put the harness on the horse. By way of assisting him, I drag the chaise into the yard. Just as our preparations are completed, Mrs. Fairbank appears. A moment or two later the hostler follows her out. He has bandaged the horse's leg, and is now ready to drive us to Farleigh Hall. I observe signs of agitation in his face and manner, which suggest that my wife has found her way into his confidence. I put the question to her privately in a corner of the yard. "Well? Have you found out why Francis Raven was up all night?"

Mrs. Fairbank has an eye to dramatic effect. Instead of answering plainly, Yes or No, she suspends the interest and excites the audience by putting a question on her side.

"What is the day of the month, dear?"

"The day of the month is the first of March."

"The first of March, Percy, is Francis Raven's birthday."

I try to look as if I was interested—and don't succeed.

"Francis was born," Mrs. Fairbank proceeds gravely, "at two o'clock in the morning."

I begin to wonder whether my wife's intellect is going the way of the landlord's intellect. "Is that all?" I ask.

"It is *not* all," Mrs. Fairbank answers. "Francis Raven sits up on the morning of his birthday because he is afraid to go to bed."

"And why is he afraid to go to bed?"

"Because he is in peril of his life."

"On his birthday?"

"On his birthday. At two o'clock in the morning. As regularly as the birthday comes round."

There she stops. Has she discovered no more than that? No more thus far. I begin to feel really interested by this time. I ask eagerly what it means. Mrs. Fairbank points mysteriously to the chaise—with Francis Raven (hitherto our hostler, now our coachman) waiting for us to get in. The chaise has a seat for two in front, and a seat for one behind. My wife casts a warning look at me, and places herself on the seat in front.

The necessary consequence of this arrangement is that Mrs. Fairhank sits by the side of the driver during a journey of two hours and more. Need I state the result? It would be an insult to your intelligence to state the result. Let me offer you my place in the chaise. And let Francis Raven tell his terrible story in his own words.

The Second Narrative

The Hostler's Story—Told by Himself

IV

It is now ten years ago since I got my first warning of the great trouble of my life in the Vision of a Dream.

I shall be better able to tell you about it if you will please suppose yourselves to be drinking tea along with us in our little cottage in Cambridgeshire, ten years since.

The time was the close of day, and there were three of us at the table, namely, my mother, myself, and my mother's sister, Mrs. Chance. These two were Scotchwomen by birth, and both were widows. There was no other resemblance between them that I can call to mind. My mother had lived all her life in England, and had no more of the Scotch brogue on her tongue than I have. My aunt Chance had never been out of Scotland until she came to keep house with my mother after her husband's death. And when *she* opened her lips you heard broad Scotch, I can tell you, if you ever heard it yet!

As it fell out, there was a matter of some consequence in debate among us that evening. It was this: whether I should do well or not to take a long journey on foot the next morning.

Now the next morning happened to be the day before my birthday; and the purpose of the journey was to offer myself for a situation as groom at a great house in the neighboring county to ours. The place was reported as likely to fall vacant in about three weeks' time. I was as well fitted to fill it as any other man. In the prosperous days of our family, my father had been manager of a training stable, and he had kept me employed among the horses from my boyhood upward. Please to excuse my troubling you with these small matters. They all fit into my story further on, as you will soon find out. My poor mother was dead against my leaving home on the morrow.

"You can never walk all the way there and all the way back again by to-morrow night," she says. "The end of it will be that you will sleep away from home on your birthday. You have never done that yet, Francis, since your father's death, I don't like your doing it now. Wait a day longer, my son—only one day."

For my own part, I was weary of being idle, and I couldn't abide the notion of delay. Even one day might make all the difference. Some other man might take time by the forelock, and get the place.

"Consider how long I have been out of work," I says, "and don't ask me to put off the journey. I won't fail you, mother. I'll get back by to-morrow night, if I have to pay my last sixpence for a lift in a cart."

My mother shook her head. "I don't like it, Francis—I don't like it!" There was no moving her from that view. We argued and argued, until we were both at a deadlock. It ended in our agreeing to refer the difference between us to my mother's sister, Mrs. Chance.

While we were trying hard to convince each other, my aunt Chance sat as dumb as a fish, stirring her tea and thinking her own thoughts. When we made our appeal to her, she seemed as it were to wake up. "Ye baith refer it to my puir judgment?" she says, in her broad Scotch. We both answered Yes. Upon that my aunt Chance first cleared the tea-table, and then pulled out from the pocket of her gown a pack of cards.

Don't run away, if you please, with the notion that this was done lightly, with a view to amuse my mother and me. My aunt Chance seriously believed that she could look into the future by telling fortunes on the cards. She did nothing herself without first consulting the cards. She could give no more serious proof of her interest in my welfare than the proof which she was offering now. I don't say it profanely; I only mention the fact—the cards had, in some incomprehensible way, got themselves jumbled up together with her religious convictions. You meet with people nowadays who believe in spirits working by way of tables and chairs. On the same principle (if there is any principle in it) my aunt Chance believed in Providence working by way of the cards.

"Whether *you* are right, Francie, or your mither—whether ye will do weel or ill, the morrow, to go or stay—the cairds will tell it. We are a' in the hands of Proavidence. The cairds will tell it."

Hearing this, my mother turned her head aside, with something of a sour look in her face. Her sister's notions about the cards were little better than flat blasphemy to her mind. But she kept her opinion to herself. My aunt Chance, to own the truth, had inherited, through her late husband, a pension of thirty pounds a year. This was an important contribution to our housekeeping, and we poor relations were bound to treat her with a certain respect. As for myself, if my poor father never did anything else for me before he fell into difficulties, he gave me a good education, and raised me (thank God) above superstitions of all sorts. However, a very little amused me in those days; and I waited to have my fortune told, as patiently as if I believed in it too!

My aunt began her hocus pocus by throwing out all the cards in the pack under seven. She shuffled the rest with her left hand for luck; and then she gave them to me to cut. "Wi' yer left hand, Francie. Mind that! Pet your trust in Proavidence—but dinna forget that your luck's in yer left hand!" A long and roundabout shifting of the cards followed, reducing them in number until there were just fifteen of them left, laid out neatly before my aunt in a half circle. The card which happened to lie outermost, at the right-hand end of the circle, was, according to rule in such cases, the card chosen to represent Me. By way of being appropriate to my situation as a poor groom out of employment, the card was— the King of Diamonds.

"I tak' up the King o' Diamants," says my aunt. "I count seven cairds fra' richt to left; and I humbly ask a blessing on what follows." My aunt shut her eyes as if she was saying grace before meat, and held up to me the seventh card. I called the seventh card—the Queen of Spades. My aunt opened her eyes again in a hurry, and cast a sly look my way. "The Queen o' Spades means a dairk woman. Ye'll be thinking in secret, Francie, of a dairk woman?"

When a man has been out of work for more than three months, his mind isn't troubled much with thinking of women—light or dark. I was thinking of the groom's place at the great house, and I tried to say so. My aunt Chance wouldn't listen. She treated my interpretation with contempt. "Hoot-toot! there's the caird in your hand! If ye're no thinking of her the day, ye'll be thinking of her the morrow. Where's the harm of thinking of a dairk woman! I was ance a dairk woman myself, before my hair was gray. Haud yer peace, Francie, and watch the cairds."

I watched the cards as I was told. There were seven left on the table. My aunt removed two from one end of the row and two from the other, and desired me to call the two outermost of the three cards now left on the table. I called the Ace of Clubs and the Ten of Diamonds. My aunt Chance lifted her eyes to the ceiling with a look of devout gratitude which sorely tried my mother's patience. The Ace of Clubs and the Ten of Diamonds, taken together, signified—first, good news (evidently the news of the groom's place); secondly, a journey that lay before me (pointing plainly to my journey to-morrow!); thirdly and lastly, a sum of money (probably the groom's wages!) waiting to find its way into my pockets. Having told my fortune in these encouraging terms, my aunt declined to carry the experiment any further. "Eh, lad! it's a clean tempting o' Proavidence to ask mair o' the cairds than the cairds have tauld us noo. Gae yer ways to-morrow to the great hoose. A dairk woman will meet ye at the gate; and she'll have a hand in getting ye the groom's place, wi' a' the gratifications and pairquisites appertaining to the same. And, mebbe, when yer poaket's full o' money, ye'll no' be forgetting yer aunt Chance, maintaining her ain unblemished widowhood—wi' Proavidence assisting—on thratty punds a year!"

I promised to remember my aunt Chance

(who had the defect, by the way, of being a terribly greedy person after money) on the next happy occasion when my poor empty pockets were to be filled at last. This done, I looked at my mother. She had agreed to take her sister for umpire between us, and her sister had given it in my favor. She raised no more objections. Silently, she got on her feet, and kissed me, and sighed bitterly—and so left the room. My aunt Chance shook her head. "I doubt, Francie, yer puir mither has but a heathen notion of the vairtue of the cairds!"

By daylight the next morning I set forth on my journey. I looked back at the cottage as I opened the garden gate. At one window was my mother, with her handkerchief to her eyes. At the other stood my aunt Chance, holding up the Queen of Spades by way of encouraging me at starting. I waved my hands to both of them in token of farewell, and stepped out briskly into the road. It was then the last day of February. Be pleased to remember, in connection with this, that the first of March was the day, and two o'clock in the morning the hour of my birth.

V

Now you know how I came to leave home. The next thing to tell is, what happened on the journey.

I reached the great house in reasonably good time considering the distance. At the very first trial of it, the prophecy of the cards turned out to be wrong. The person who met me at the lodge gate was not a dark woman—in fact, not a woman at all—but a boy. He directed me on the way to the servants' offices; and there again the cards were all wrong. I encountered, not one woman, but three—and not one of the three was dark. I have stated that I am not superstitious, and I have told the truth. But I must own that I did feel a certain fluttering at the heart when I made my bow to the steward, and told him what business had brought me to the house.

His answer completed the discomfiture of aunt Chance's fortune-telling. My ill-luck still pursued me. That very morning another man had applied for the groom's place, and had got it.

I swallowed my disappointment as well as I could, and thanked the steward, and went to the inn in the village to get the rest and food which I sorely needed by this time.

Before starting on my homeward walk I made some inquiries at the inn, and ascertained that I might save a few miles, on my return, by following a new road. Furnished with full instructions, several times repeated, as to the various turnings I was to take, I set forth, and walked on till the evening with only one stoppage for bread and cheese. Just as it was getting toward dark, the rain came on and the wind began to rise; and I found myself, to make matters worse, in a part of the country with which I was entirely unacquainted, though I guessed myself to be some fifteen miles from home. The first house I found to inquire at was a lonely roadside inn, standing on the outskirts of a thick wood. Solitary as the place looked, it was welcome to a lost man who was also hungry, thirsty, footsore, and wet. The landlord was civil and respectable-looking; and the price he asked for a bed was reasonable enough. I was grieved to disappoint my mother. But there was no conveyance to be had, and I could go no farther afoot that night. My weariness fairly forced me to stop at the inn.

I may say for myself that I am a temperate man. My supper simply consisted of some rashers of bacon, a slice of home-made bread, and a pint of ale. I did not go to bed immediately after this moderate meal, but sat up with the landlord, talking about my bad prospects and my long run of ill-luck, and diverging from these topics to the subjects of horse-flesh and racing. Nothing was said, either by myself, my host, or the few laborers who strayed into the tap-room, which could, in the slightest degree, excite my mind, or set my fancy—which is only a small fancy at the best of times—playing tricks with my common sense.

At a little after eleven the house was closed. I went round with the landlord, and held the candle while the doors and lower windows were being secured. I noticed with surprise the strength of the bolts, bars, and iron-sheathed shutters.

"You see, we are rather lonely here," said the landlord. "We never have had any attempts to break in yet, but it's always as well to be on the safe side. When nobody is sleeping here, I am the only man in the house. My wife and daughter are timid, and the servant girl takes after her missuses. Another glass of ale, before you turn in?—No!—Well, how such a sober man as you comes to be out of a place is more than I can understand for one.—Here's where you're to sleep. You're the only lodger to-night, and I think you'll say my missus has done her best to make you comfortable. You're quite sure you won't have another glass of ale?—Very well. Good night."

It was half-past eleven by the clock in the passage as we went upstairs to the bedroom. The window looked out on the wood at the back of the house.

I locked my door, set my candle on the chest of drawers, and wearily got me ready for bed. The bleak wind was still blowing, and the solemn, surging moan of it in the wood was very dreary to hear through the night silence. Feeling strangely wakeful, I resolved to keep the candle alight until I began to grow sleepy. The truth is, I was not quite myself. I was depressed in mind by my disappointment of the morning; and I was worn out in body by my long walk. Between the two, I own I couldn't face the prospect of lying awake in the darkness, listening to the dismal moan of the wind in the wood.

Sleep stole on me before I was aware of it; my eyes closed, and I fell off to rest, without having so much as thought of extinguishing the candle.

The next thing that I remember was a faint shivering that ran through me from head to foot, and a dreadful sinking pain at my heart, such as I had never felt before. The shivering only disturbed my slumbers—the pain woke me instantly. In one moment I passed from a state of sleep to a state of wakefulness—my eyes wide open—my mind clear on a sudden as if by a miracle. The candle had burned down nearly to the last morsel of tallow, but the unsnuffed wick had just fallen off, and the light was, for the moment, fair and full.

Between the foot of the bed and the closet door, I saw a person in my room. The person was a woman, standing looking at me, with a knife in her hand. It does no credit to my courage to confess it—but the truth *is* the truth. I was struck speechless with terror. There I lay with my eyes on the woman; there the woman stood (with the knife in her hand) with *her* eyes on *me.*

She said not a word as we stared each other in the face; but she moved after a little—moved slowly toward the left-hand side of the bed.

The light fell full on her face. A fair, fine woman, with yellowish flaxen hair, and light gray eyes, with a droop in the left eyelid. I noticed these things and fixed them in my mind, before she was quite round at the side of the bed. Without saying a word; without any change in the stony stillness of her face; without any noise following her footfall, she came closer and closer; stopped at the bed-head; and lifted the knife to stab me. I laid my arm over my throat to save it; but, as I saw the blow coming, I threw my hand across the bed to the right side, and jerked my body over that way, just as the knife came down, like lightning, within a hair's breadth of my shoulder.

My eyes fixed on her arm and her hand—she gave me time to look at them as she slowly drew the knife out of the bed. A white, well-shaped arm, with a pretty down lying lightly over the fair skin. A delicate lady's hand, with a pink flush round the fingernails.

She drew the knife out, and passed back again slowly to the foot of the bed; she stopped there for a moment looking at me; then she came on without saying a word; without any change in the stony stillness of her face; without any noise following her footfall—came on to the side of the bed where I now lay.

Getting near me, she lifted the knife again, and I drew myself away to the left side. She struck, as before right into the mattress, with a swift downward action of her arm; and she missed me, as before; by a hair's breadth. This time my eyes wandered from *her* to the knife. It was like the large clasp knives which laboring men use to cut their bread and bacon with. Her delicate little fingers did not hide more than two thirds of the handle; I noticed that it was made of buckhorn, clean and shining as the blade was, and looking like new.

For the second time she drew the knife out of the bed, and suddenly hid it away in the wide sleeve of her gown. That done, she stopped by the bedside watching me. For an instant I saw her standing in that position—then the wick of the spent candle fell over into the socket. The flame dwindled to a little blue point, and the room grew dark.

A moment, or less, if possible, passed so—and then the wick flared up, smokily, for the last time. My eyes were still looking for her over the right-hand side of the bed when the last flash of light came. Look as I might, I could see nothing. The woman with the knife was gone.

I began to get back to myself again. I could feel my heart beating; I could hear the woeful moaning of the wind in the wood; I could leap up in bed, and give the alarm before she escaped from the house. "Murder! Wake up there! Murder!"

Nobody answered to the alarm. I rose and groped my way through the darkness to the door of the room. By that way she must have got in. By that way she must have gone out.

The door of the room was fast locked, exactly as I had left it on going to bed! I looked at the window. Fast locked too!

Hearing a voice outside, I opened the door. There was the landlord, coming toward me along the passage, with his burning candle in one hand, and his gun in the other.

"What is it?" he says, looking at me in no very friendly way.

I could only answer in a whisper, "A woman, with a knife in her hand. In my room. A fair, yellow-haired woman. She jabbed at me with the knife, twice over."

He lifted his candle, and looked at me steadily from head to foot. "She seems to have missed you—twice over."

"I dodged the knife as it came down. It struck the bed each time. Go in, and see."

The landlord took his candle into the bedroom immediately. In less than a minute he came out again into the passage in a violent passion.

"The devil fly away with you and your woman with the knife! There isn't a mark in the bedclothes anywhere. What do you mean by coming into a man's place and frightening his family out of their wits by a dream?"

A dream? The woman who had tried to stab me, not a living human being like myself? I began to shake and shiver. The horrors got hold of me at the bare thought of it.

"I'll leave the house," I said. "Better be out on the road in the rain and dark, than back in that room, after what I've seen in it. Lend me the light to get my clothes by, and tell me what I'm to pay."

The landlord led the way back with his light into the bedroom. "Pay?" says he. "You'll find your score on the slate when you go downstairs. I wouldn't have taken you in for all the money you've got about you, if I had known your dreaming, screeching ways beforehand. Look at the bed—where's the cut of a knife in it? Look at the window—is the lock bursted? Look at the door (which I heard you fasten yourself)—is it broke in? A murdering woman with a knife in my house! You ought to be ashamed of yourself!"

My eyes followed his hand as it pointed first to the bed—then to the window—then to the door. There was no gainsaying it. The bed sheet was as sound as on the day it was made. The window was fast. The door hung on its hinges as steady as ever. I huddled my clothes on without speaking. We went downstairs together. I looked at the clock in the bar-room. The time was twenty minutes past two in the morning. I paid my bill, and the landlord let me out. The rain had ceased; but the night was dark, and the wind was bleaker than ever. Little did the darkness, or the cold, or the doubt about the way home matter to *me*. My mind was away from all these things. My mind was fixed on the vision in the bedroom. What had I seen trying to murder me? The creature of a dream? Or that other creature from the world beyond the grave, whom men call ghost? I could make nothing of it as I walked along in the night; I had made nothing by it by midday—when I stood at last, after many times missing my road, on the doorstep of home.

VI

My mother came out alone to welcome me back. There were no secrets between us two. I told her all that had happened, just as I have told it to you. She kept silence till I had done. And then she put a question to me.

"What time was it, Francis, when you saw the Woman in your Dream?"

I had looked at the clock when I left the inn, and I had noticed that the hands pointed to twenty minutes past two. Allowing for the time consumed in speaking to the landlord, and in getting on my clothes, I answered that I must have first seen the Woman at two o'clock in the morning. In other words, I had not only seen her on my birthday, but at the hour of my birth.

My mother still kept silence. Lost in her own thoughts, she took me by the hand, and led me into the parlor. Her writing-desk was on the table by the fireplace. She opened it, and signed to me to take a chair by her side.

"My son! your memory is a bad one, and mine is fast failing me. Tell me again what the Woman looked like. I want her to be as well known to both of us, years hence, as she is now."

I obeyed; wondering what strange fancy might be working in her mind. I spoke; and she wrote the words as they fell from my lips:

"Light gray eyes, with a droop in the left eyelid. Flaxen hair, with a golden-yellow streak in it. White arms, with a down upon them. Little,

lady's hands, with a rosy-red look about the fingernails."

"Did you notice how she was dressed, Francis?"

"No, mother."

"Did you notice the knife?"

"Yes. A large clasp knife, with a buckhorn handle, as good as new."

My mother added the description of the knife. Also the year, month, day of the week, and hour of the day when the Dream Woman appeared to me at the inn. That done, she locked up the paper in her desk.

"Not a word, Francis, to your aunt. Not a word to any living soul. Keep your Dream a secret between you and me."

The weeks passed, and the months passed. My mother never returned to the subject again. As for me, time, which wears out all things, wore out my remembrance of the Dream. Little by little, the image of the Woman grew dimmer and dimmer. Little by little, she faded out of my mind.

VII

The story of the warning is now told. Judge for yourself if it was a true warning or a false, when you hear what happened to me on my next birthday.

In the Summer time of the year, the Wheel of Fortune turned the right way for me at last. I was smoking my pipe one day, near an old stone quarry at the entrance to our village, when a carriage accident happened, which gave a new turn, as it were, to my lot in life. It was an accident of the commonest kind—not worth mentioning at any length. A lady driving herself; a runaway horse; a cowardly man-servant in attendance, frightened out of his wits; and the stone quarry too near to be agreeable—that is what I saw, all in a few moments, between two whiffs of my pipe. I stopped the horse at the edge of the quarry, and got myself a little hurt by the shaft of the chaise. But that didn't matter. The lady declared I had saved her life; and her husband, coming with her to our cottage the next day, took me into his service then and there. The lady happened to be of a dark complexion; and it may amuse you to hear that my aunt Chance instantly pitched on that circumstance as a means of saving the credit of the cards. Here was the promise of the Queen of Spades performed to the very letter, by means of "a dark woman," just as my aunt had told me. "In the time to come, Francis, beware o' pettin' yer ain blinded intairpretation on the cairds. Ye're ower ready, I trow, to murmur under dispensation of Proavidence that ye canna fathom—like the Eesraelites of auld. I'll say nae mair to ye. Mebbe when the mony's powering into yer poakets, ye'll no forget yer aunt Chance, left like a sparrow on the housetop, wi a sma' annuitee o' thratty punds a year."

I remained in my situation (at the West-end of London) until the Spring of the New Year. About that time, my master's health failed. The doctors ordered him away to foreign parts, and the establishment was broken up. But the turn in my luck still held good. When I left my place, I left it—thanks to the generosity of my kind master—with a yearly allowance granted to me, in remembrance of the day when I had saved my mistress's life. For the future, I could go back to service or not, as I pleased; my little income was enough to support my mother and myself.

My master and mistress left England toward the end of February. Certain matters of business to do for them detained me in London until the last day of the month. I was only able to leave for our village by the evening train, to keep my birthday with my mother as usual. It was bedtime when I got to the cottage; and I was sorry to find that she was far from well. To make matters worse, she had finished her bottle of medicine on the previous day, and had omitted to get it replenished, as the doctor had strictly directed. He dispensed his own medicines, and I offered to go and knock him up. She refused to let me do this; and, after giving me my supper, sent me away to my bed.

I fell asleep for a little, and woke again. My mother's bed-chamber was next to mine. I heard my aunt Chance's heavy footsteps going to and fro in the room, and, suspecting something wrong, knocked at the door. My mother's pains had returned upon her; there was a serious necessity for relieving her sufferings as speedily as possible, I put on my clothes, and ran off, with the medicine bottle in my hand, to the other end of the village, where the doctor lived. The church clock chimed the quarter to two on my birthday just as I reached his house. One ring of the night bell brought him to his bedroom window to speak to me. He told me to wait, and he would let me in at the surgery door. I noticed, while I was waiting, that the night was wonderfully fair and warm for the time of year. The old stone quarry where the carriage accident had happened was within view. The moon in the clear heavens lit it up almost as bright as day.

In a minute or two the doctor let me into the surgery. I closed the door, noticing that he had left his room very lightly clad. He kindly pardoned my mother's neglect of his directions, and set to work at once at compounding the medicine. We were both intent on the bottle; he filling it, and I holding the light—when we heard the surgery door suddenly opened from the street.

VIII

Who could possibly be up and about in our quiet village at the second hour of the morning?

The person who opened the door appeared within range of the light of the candle. To complete our amazement, the person proved to be a woman! She walked up to the counter, and standing side by side with me, lifted her veil. At the moment when she showed her face, I heard the church clock strike two. She was a stranger to me, and a stranger to the doctor. She was also, beyond all comparison, the most beautiful woman I have ever seen in my life.

"I saw the light under the door," she said. "I want some medicine."

She spoke quite composedly, as if there was nothing at all extraordinary in her being out in the village at two in the morning, and following me into the surgery to ask for medicine! The doctor stared at her as if he suspected his own eyes of deceiving him. "Who are you?" he asked. "How do you come to be wandering about at this time in the morning?"

She paid no heed to his questions. She only told him coolly what she wanted. "I have got a bad toothache. I want a bottle of laudanum."

The doctor recovered himself when she asked for the laudanum. He was on his own ground, you know, when it came to a matter of laudanum; and he spoke to her smartly enough this time.

"Oh, you have got the toothache, have you? Let me look at the tooth."

She shook her head, and laid a two-shilling piece on the counter. "I won't trouble you to look at the tooth," she said. "There is the money. Let me have the laudanum, if you please."

The doctor put the two-shilling piece back again in her hand. "I don't sell laudanum to strangers," he answered. "If you are in any distress of body or mind, that is another matter. I shall be glad to help you."

She put the money back in her pocket. "*You* can't help me," she said, as quietly as ever. "Good morning."

With that, she opened the surgery door to go out again into the street. So far, I had not spoken a word on my side. I had stood with the candle in my hand (not knowing I was holding it)—with my eyes fixed on her, with my mind fixed on her like a man bewitched. Her looks betrayed, even more plainly than her words, her resolution, in one way or another, to destroy herself. When she opened the door, in my alarm at what might happen I found the use of my tongue.

"Stop!" I cried out. "Wait for me. I want to speak to you before you go away." She lifted her eyes with a look of careless surprise and a mocking smile on her lips.

"What can *you* have to say to me?" She stopped, and laughed to herself. "Why not?" she said. "I have got nothing to do, and nowhere to go." She turned back a step, and nodded to me. "You're a strange man—I think I'll humor you—I'll wait outside." The door of the surgery closed on her. She was gone.

I am ashamed to own what happened next. The only excuse for me is that I was really and truly a man bewitched. I turned me round to follow her out, without once thinking of my mother. The doctor stopped me.

"Don't forget the medicine," he said. "And if you will take my advice, don't trouble yourself about that woman. Rouse up the constable. It's his business to look after her—not yours."

I held out my hand for the medicine in silence: I was afraid I should fail in respect if I trusted myself to answer him. He must have seen, as I saw, that she wanted the laudanum to poison herself. He had, to my mind, taken a very heartless view of the matter. I just thanked him when he gave me the medicine—and went out.

She was waiting for me as she had promised; walking slowly to and fro—a tall, graceful, solitary figure in the bright moonbeams. They shed over her fair complexion, her bright golden hair, her large gray eyes, just the light that suited them best. She looked hardly mortal when she first turned to speak to me.

"Well?" she said. "And what do you want?"

In spite of my pride, or my shyness, or my better sense—whichever it might be—all my heart went out to her in a moment. I caught hold of her by the hands, and owned what was in my thoughts, as freely as if I had known her for half a lifetime.

"You mean to destroy yourself," I said. "And I mean to prevent you from doing it. If I follow you about all night, I'll prevent you from doing it."

She laughed. "You saw yourself that he wouldn't sell me the laudanum. Do you really care whether I live or die?" She squeezed my hands gently as she put the question: her eyes searched mine with a languid, lingering look in them that ran through me like fire. My voice died away on my lips; I couldn't answer her.

She understood, without my answering. "You

have given me a fancy for living, by speaking kindly to me," she said. "Kindness has a wonderful effect on women, and dogs, and other domestic animals. It is only men who are superior to kindness. Make your mind easy—I promise to take as much care of myself as if I was the happiest woman living! Don't let me keep you here, out of your bed. Which way are you going?"

Miserable wretch that I was, I had forgotten my mother—with the medicine in my hand! "I am going home," I said. "Where are you staying? At the inn?"

She laughed her bitter laugh, and pointed to the stone quarry. "There is *my* inn for to-night," she said. "When I got tired of walking about, I rested there."

We walked on together, on my way home. I took the liberty of asking her if she had any friends.

"I thought I had one friend left," she said, "or you would never have met me in this place. It turns out I was wrong. My friend's door was closed in my face some hours since; my friend's servants threatened me with the police. I had nowhere else to go, after trying my luck in your neighborhood; and nothing left but my two-shilling piece and these rags on my back. What respectable innkeeper would take me into his house? I walked about, wondering how I could find my way out of the world without disfiguring myself, and without suffering much pain. You have no river in these parts. I didn't see my way out of the world, till I heard you ringing at the doctor's house. I got a glimpse at the bottles in the surgery, when he let you in, and I thought of the laudanum directly. What were you doing there? Who is that medicine for? Your wife?"

"I am not married!"

She laughed again. "Not married! If I was a little better dressed there might be a chance for me. Where do you live? Here?"

We had arrived, by this time, at my mother's door. She held out her hand to say good-by. Houseless and homeless as she was, she never asked me to give her a shelter for the night. It was *my* proposal that she should rest, under my

roof, unknown to my mother and my aunt. Our kitchen was built out at the back of the cottage: she might remain there unseen and unheard until the household was astir in the morning. I led her into the kitchen, and set a chair for her by the dying embers of the fire. I dare say I was to blame—shamefully to blame, if you like. I only wonder what you would have done in my place. On your word of honor as a man, would you have let that beautiful creature wander back to the shelter of the stone quarry like a stray dog? God help the woman who is foolish enough to trust and love you, if you would have done that!

I left her by the fire, and went to my mother's room.

IX

If you have ever felt the heartache, you will know what I suffered in secret when my mother took my hand, and said, "I am sorry, Francis, that your night's rest has been disturbed through me." I gave her the medicine; and I waited by her till the pains abated: My aunt Chance went back to her bed; and my mother and I were left alone. I noticed that her writing-desk, moved from its customary place, was on the bed by her side. She saw me looking at it. "This is your birthday, Francis," she said. "Have you anything to tell me?" I had so completely forgotten my Dream, that I had no notion of what was passing in her mind when she said those words. For a moment there was a guilty fear in me that she suspected something. I turned away my face, and said, "No, mother; I have nothing to tell." She signed to me to stoop down over the pillow and kiss her. "God bless you, my love!" she said; "and many happy returns of the day." She patted my hand, and closed her weary eyes, and, little by little, fell off peaceably into sleep.

I stole downstairs again. I think the good influence of my mother must have followed me down. At any rate, this is true: I stopped with my hand on the closed kitchen door, and said to myself: "Suppose I leave the house, and leave the village, without seeing her or speaking to her more?"

Should I really have fled from temptation in this way, if I had been left to myself to decide? Who can tell? As things were, I was not left to decide. While my doubt was in my mind, she heard me, and opened the kitchen door. My eyes and her eyes met. That ended it.

We were together, unsuspected and undisturbed, for the next two hours. Time enough for her to reveal the secret of her wasted life. Time enough for her to take possession of me as her own, to do with me as she liked. It is needless to dwell here on the misfortunes which had brought her low; they are misfortunes too common to interest anybody.

Her name was Alicia Warlock. She had been born and bred a lady. She had lost her station, her character, and her friends. Virtue shuddered at the sight of her; and Vice had got her for the rest of her days. Shocking and common, as I told you. It made no difference to *me*. I have said it already—I say it again—I was a man bewitched. Is there anything so very wonderful in that? Just remember who I was. Among the honest women in my own station in life, where could I have found the like of *her*? Could *they* walk as she walked? and look as she looked? When *they* gave me a kiss, did their lips linger over it as hers did? Had *they* her skin, her laugh, her foot, her hand, her touch? *She* never had a speck of dirt on her: I tell you her flesh was a perfume. When she embraced me, her arms folded round me like the wings of angels; and her smile covered me softly with its light like the sun in heaven. I leave you to laugh at me, or to cry over me, just as your temper may incline. I am not trying to excuse myself—I am trying to explain. You are gentle-folks; what dazzled and maddened *me*, is everyday experience to *you*. Fallen or not, angel or devil, it came to this—she was a lady; and I was a groom.

Before the house was astir, I got her away (by the workmen's train) to a large manufacturing town in our parts.

Here—with my savings in money to help her—she could get her outfit of decent clothes and her lodging among strangers who asked no questions so long as they were paid. Here—now on one pretense and now on another—I could visit her, and we could both plan together what our future lives were to be. I need not tell you that I stood pledged to make her my wife. A man in my station always marries a woman of her sort.

Do you wonder if I was happy at this time? I should have been perfectly happy but for one little drawback. It was this: I was never quite at my ease in the presence of my promised wife.

I don't mean that I was shy with her, or suspicious of her, or ashamed of her. The uneasiness I am speaking of was caused by a faint doubt in my mind whether I had not seen her somewhere, before the morning when we met at the doctor's house. Over and over again, I found myself wondering whether her face did not remind me of some other face—what other I never could tell. This strange feeling, this one question that could never be answered, vexed me to a degree that you would hardly credit. It came between us at the strangest times—oftenest, however, at night, when the candles were lit. You have known what it is to try and remember a forgotten name—and to fail, search as you may, to find it in your mind. That was my case. I failed to find my lost face, just as you failed to find your lost name.

In three weeks we had talked matters over, and had arranged how I was to make a clean breast of it at home. By Alicia's advice, I was to describe her as having been one of my fellow-servants during the time I was employed under my kind master and mistress in London. There was no fear now of my mother taking any harm from the shock of a great surprise. Her health had improved during the three weeks' interval. On the first evening when she was able to take her old place at tea time, I summoned my courage, and told her I was going to be married. The poor soul flung her arms round my neck, and burst out crying for joy. "Oh, Francis!" she says, "I am so glad you will have somebody to comfort you and care for you when I am gone!"

As for my aunt Chance, you can anticipate what she did, without being told. Ah, me! If there had really been any prophetic virtue in the cards, what a terrible warning they might have given us that night! It was arranged that I was to bring my promised wife to dinner at the cottage on the next day.

X

I own I was proud of Alicia when I led her into our little parlor at the appointed time. She had never, to my mind, looked so beautiful as she looked that day. I never noticed any other woman's dress—I noticed hers as carefully as if I had been a woman myself! She wore a black silk gown, with plain collar and cuffs, and a modest lavender-colored bonnet, with one white rose in it placed at the side. My mother, dressed in her Sunday best, rose up, all in a flutter, to welcome her daughter-in-law that was to be. She walked forward a few steps, half smiling, half in tears—she looked Alicia full in the face—and suddenly stood still. Her cheeks turned white in an instant; her eyes stared in horror; her hands dropped helplessly at her sides. She staggered back, and fell into the arms of my aunt, standing behind her. It was no swoon—she kept her senses. Her eyes turned slowly from Alicia to me. "Francis," she said, "does that woman's face remind you of nothing?"

Before I could answer, she pointed to her writing-desk on the table at the fireside. "Bring it!" she cried, "bring it!"

At the same moment I felt Alicia's hand on my shoulder, and saw Alicia's face red with anger—and no wonder!

"What does this mean?" she asked. "Does your mother want to insult me?"

I said a few words to quiet her; what they were I don't remember—I was so confused and astonished at the time. Before I had done, I heard my mother behind me.

My aunt had fetched her desk. She had opened it; she had taken a paper from it. Step by step, helping herself along by the wall, she came nearer and nearer, with the paper in her hand. She looked at the paper—she looked in Alicia's face—she lifted the long, loose sleeve of her gown, and examined her hand and arm. I saw fear suddenly take the place of anger in Alicia's eyes. She shook herself free of my mother's grasp. "Mad!" she said to herself, "and Francis never told me!" With those words she ran out of the room.

I was hastening out after her, when my mother signed to me to stop. She read the words written on the paper. While they fell slowly, one by one, from her lips, she pointed toward the open door.

"Light gray eyes, with a droop in the left eyelid. Flaxen hair, with a golden-yellow streak in it. White arms, with a down upon them. Little, lady's hand, with a rosy-red look about the fingernails. The Dream Woman, Francis! The Dream Woman!"

Something darkened the parlor window as those words were spoken. I looked sidelong at the shadow. Alicia Warlock had come back! She was peering in at us over the low window blind. There was the fatal face which had first looked at me in the bedroom of the lonely inn. There, resting on the window blind, was the lovely little hand which had held the murderous knife. I *had* seen her before we met in the village. The Dream Woman! The Dream Woman!

XI

I expect nobody to approve of what I have next to tell of myself. In three weeks from the day when my mother had identified her with the Woman of the Dream, I took Alicia Warlock to church, and made her my wife. I was a man bewitched. Again and again I say it—I was a man bewitched!

During the interval before my marriage, our little household at the cottage was broken up. My mother and my aunt quarreled. My mother, believing in the Dream, entreated me to break off my engagement. My aunt, believing in the cards, urged me to marry.

This difference of opinion produced a dispute between them, in the course of which my aunt Chance—quite unconscious of having any superstitious feelings of her own—actually set out the cards which prophesied happiness to me in my married life, and asked my mother how anybody but "a blinded heathen could be fule enough, after seeing those cairds, to believe in a dream!" This was, naturally, too much for my mother's patience; hard words followed on either side; Mrs. Chance returned in dudgeon to her friends in Scotland. She left me a written statement of my future prospects, as revealed by the cards, and with it an address at which a post-office order would reach her. "The day was not that far off," she remarked, "when Francie might remember what he owed to his aunt Chance, maintaining her ain unbleemished widowhood on thratty punds a year."

Having refused to give her sanction to my marriage, my mother also refused to be present at the wedding, or to visit Alicia afterwards. There was no anger at the bottom of this conduct on her part. Believing as she did in this Dream, she was simply in mortal fear of my wife. I understood this, and I made allowances for her. Not a cross word passed between us. My one happy remembrance now—though I did disobey her in the matter of my marriage—is this: I loved and respected my good mother to the last.

As for my wife, she expressed no regret at the estrangement between her mother-in-law and herself. By common consent, we never spoke on that subject. We settled in the manufacturing town which I have already mentioned, and we kept a lodging-house. My kind master, at my request, granted me a lump sum in place of my annuity. This put us into a good house, decently furnished. For a while things went well enough. I may describe myself at this time of my life as a happy man.

My misfortunes began with a return of the complaint with which my mother had already suffered. The doctor confessed, when I asked him the question, that there was danger to be dreaded this time. Naturally, after hearing this, I was a good deal away at the cottage. Naturally also, I left the business of looking after the house, in my absence, to my wife. Little by little, I found her beginning to alter toward me. While my back was turned, she formed acquaintances with people of the doubtful and dissipated sort. One day, I observed something in her manner which forced the suspicion on me that she had been drinking. Before the week was out, my suspicion was a certainty. From keeping company with drunkards, she had grown to be a drunkard herself.

I did all a man could do to reclaim her. Quite useless! She had never really returned the love I felt for her: I had no influence; I could do nothing. My mother, hearing of this last worse trouble, resolved to try what her influence could do. Ill as she was, I found her one day dressed to go out.

"I am not long for this world, Francis," she said. "I shall not feel easy on my deathbed, unless I have done my best to the last to make you happy. I mean to put my own fears and my own feelings out of the question, and go with you to your wife, and try what I can do to reclaim her. Take me home with you, Francis. Let me do all I can to help my son, before it is too late."

How could I disobey her? We took the railway to the town: it was only half an hour's ride. By one o'clock in the afternoon we reached my house. It was our dinner hour, and Alicia was in the kitchen. I was able to take my mother quietly into the parlor and then to prepare my wife for the visit. She had drunk but little at that early hour; and, luckily, the devil in her was tamed for the time.

She followed me into the parlor, and the meeting passed off better than I had ventured to forecast; with this one drawback, that my mother—though she tried hard to control herself—shrank from looking my wife in the face when she spoke to her. It was a relief to me when Alicia began to prepare the table for dinner.

She laid the cloth, brought in the bread tray,

and cut some slices for us from the loaf. Then she returned to the kitchen. At that moment, while I was still anxiously watching my mother, I was startled by seeing the same ghastly change pass over her face which had altered it in the morning when Alicia and she first met. Before I could say a word, she started up with a look of horror.

"Take me back!—home, home again, Francis! Come with me, and never go back more!"

I was afraid to ask for an explanation; I could only sign her to be silent, and help her quickly to the door. As we passed the bread tray on the table, she stopped and pointed to it.

"Did you see what your wife cut your bread with?" she asked.

"No, mother; I was not noticing. What was it?"

"Look!"

I did look. A new clasp knife, with a buckhorn handle, lay with the loaf in the bread tray. I stretched out my hand to possess myself of it. At the same moment, there was a noise in the kitchen, and my mother caught me by the arm.

"The knife of the Dream! Francis, I'm faint with fear—take me away before she comes back!"

I couldn't speak to comfort or even to answer her. Superior as I was to superstition, the discovery of the knife staggered me. In silence, I helped my mother out of the house; and took her home.

I held out my hand to say good-by. She tried to stop me.

"Don't go back, Francis! don't go back!"

"I must get the knife, mother. I must go back by the next train." I held to that resolution. By the next train I went back.

XII

My wife had, of course, discovered our secret departure from the house. She had been drinking. She was in a fury of passion. The dinner in the kitchen was flung under the grate; the cloth was off the parlor table. Where was the knife?

I was foolish enough to ask for it. She refused to give it to me. In the course of the dispute between us which followed, I discovered that there was a horrible story attached to the knife. It had been used in a murder—years since—and had been so skillfully hidden that the authorities had been unable to produce it at the trial. By help of some of her disreputable friends, my wife had been able to purchase this relic of a bygone crime. Her perverted nature set some horrid unacknowledged value on the knife. Seeing there was no hope of getting it by fair means, I determined to search for it, later in the day, in secret. The search was unsuccessful. Night came on, and I left the house to walk about the streets. You will understand what a broken man I was by this time, when I tell you I was afraid to sleep in the same room with her!

Three weeks passed. Still she refused to give up the knife; and still that fear of sleeping in the same room with her possessed me. I walked about at night, or dozed in the parlor, or sat watching by my mother's bedside. Before the end of the first week in the new month, the worst misfortune of all befell me—my mother died. It wanted then but a short time to my birthday. She had longed to live till that day. I was present at her death. Her last words in this world were addressed to me. "Don't go back, my son—don't go back!"

I was obliged to go back, if it was only to watch my wife. In the last days of my mother's illness she had spitefully added a sting to my grief by declaring she would assert her right to attend the funeral. In spite of all that I could do or say, she held to her word. On the day appointed for the burial she forced herself, inflamed and shameless with drink, into my presence, and swore she would walk in the funeral procession to my mother's grave.

This last insult—after all I had gone through already—was more than I could endure. It maddened me. Try to make allowances for a man beside himself. I struck her.

The instant the blow was dealt, I repented it. She crouched down, silent, in a corner of the room, and eyed me steadily. It was a look that cooled my hot blood in an instant. There was no time now to think of making atonement. I could only risk the worst, and make sure of her till the funeral was over. I locked her into her bedroom.

When I came back, after laying my mother in the grave, I found her sitting by the bedside, very much altered in look and bearing, with a bundle on her lap. She faced me quietly; she spoke with a curious stillness in her voice—strangely and unnaturally composed in look and manner.

"No man has ever struck me yet," she said. "My husband shall have no second opportunity. Set the door open, and let me go."

She passed me, and left the room. I saw her walk away up the street. Was she gone for good?

All that night I watched and waited. No footstep came near the house. The next night, overcome with fatigue, I lay down on the bed in my clothes, with the door locked, the key on the table, and the candle burning. My slumber was not disturbed. The third night, the fourth, the fifth, the sixth, passed, and nothing happened. I lay down on the seventh night, still suspicious of something happening; still in my clothes; still with the door locked, the key on the table, and the candle burning.

My rest was disturbed. I awoke twice, without any sensation of uneasiness. The third time, that horrid shivering of the night at the lonely inn, that awful sinking pain at the heart, came back again, and roused me in an instant. My eyes turned to the left-hand side of the bed. And there stood, looking at me—

The Dream Woman again? No! My wife. The living woman, with the face of the Dream—in the attitude of the Dream—the fair arm up; the knife clasped in the delicate white hand.

I sprang upon her on the instant; but not quickly enough to stop her from hiding the knife. Without a word from me, without a cry from her, I pinioned her in a chair. With one hand I felt up her sleeve; and there, where the Dream Woman had hidden the knife, my wife had hidden it—the knife with the buckhorn handle, that looked like new.

What I felt when I made that discovery I could not realize at the time, and I can't describe now. I took one steady look at her with the knife in my hand. "You meant to kill me?" I said.

"Yes," she answered; "I meant to kill you." She crossed her arms over her bosom, and stared me coolly in the face. "I shall do it yet," she said. "With that knife."

I don't know what possessed me—I swear to you I am no coward; and yet I acted like a coward. The horrors got hold of me. I couldn't look at her—I couldn't speak to her. I left her (with the knife in my hand), and went out into the night.

There was a bleak wind abroad, and the smell of rain was in the air. The church clocks chimed the quarter as I walked beyond the last house in the town. I asked the first policeman I met what hour that was, of which the quarter past had just struck.

The man looked at his watch, and answered, "Two o'clock." Two in the morning. What day of the month was this day that had just begun? I reckoned it up from the date of my mother's funeral. The horrid parallel between the dream and the reality was complete—it was my birthday!

Had I escaped the mortal peril which the dream foretold? or had I only received a second warning? As that doubt crossed my mind I stopped on my way out of the town. The air had revived me—I felt in some degree like my own self again. After a little thinking, I began to see plainly the mistake I had made in leaving my wife free to go where she liked and to do as she pleased.

I turned instantly, and made my way back to the house. It was still dark. I had left the candle burning in the bed-chamber. When I looked up to the window of the room now, there was no light in it. I advanced to the house door. On going away, I remembered to have closed it; on trying it now, I found it open.

I waited outside, never losing sight of the house till daylight. Then I ventured indoors—listened, and heard nothing—looked into the kitchen, scullery, parlor, and found nothing—went up at last into the bedroom. It was empty.

A picklock lay on the floor, which told me how she had gained entrance in the night. And that was the one trace I could find of the Dream Woman.

XIII

I waited in the house till the town was astir for the day, and then I went to consult a lawyer. In the confused state of my mind at the time, I had one clear notion of what I meant to do: I was determined to sell my house and leave the neighborhood. There were obstacles in the way which I had not counted on. I was told I had creditors to satisfy before I could leave—I, who had given my wife the money to pay my bills regularly every week! Inquiry showed that she had embezzled every farthing of the money I had intrusted to her. I had no choice but to pay over again.

Placed in this awkward position, my first duty was to set things right, with the help of my lawyer. During my forced sojourn in the town I did two foolish things. And, as a consequence that followed, I heard once more, and heard for the last time, of my wife.

In the first place, having got possession of the knife, I was rash enough to keep it in my pocket. In the second place, having something of importance to say to my lawyer, at a late hour of the evening, I went to his house after dark—alone and on foot. I got there safely enough. Returning, I was seized on from behind by two men, dragged down a passage, and robbed—not only of the little money I had about me, but also of the knife. It was the lawyer's opinion (as it was mine) that the thieves were among the disreputable acquaintances formed by my wife, and that they had attacked me at her instigation. To confirm this view I received a letter the next day, without date or address, written in Alicia's hand. The first line informed me that the knife was back again in her possession. The second line reminded me of the day when I struck her. The

third line warned me that she would wash out the stain of that blow in my blood, and repeated the words, "I shall do it with the knife!"

These things happened a year ago. The law laid hands on the men who had robbed me; but from that time to this, the law has failed completely to find a trace of my wife.

My story is told. When I had paid the creditors and paid the legal expenses, I had barely five pounds left out of the sale of my house; and I had the world to begin over again. Some months since—drifting here and there—I found my way to Underbridge. The landlord of the inn had known something of my father's family in times past. He gave me (all he had to give) my food, and shelter in the yard. Except on market days, there is nothing to do. In the coming winter the inn is to be shut up, and I shall have to shift for myself. My old master would help me if I applied to him—but I don't like to apply: he has done more for me already than I deserve. Besides, in another year who knows but my troubles may all be at an end? Next winter will bring me nigh to my next birthday, and my next birthday may be the day of my death. Yes! it's true I sat up all last night; and I heard two in the morning strike: and nothing happened. Still, allowing for that, the time to come is a time I don't trust. My wife has got the knife—my wife is looking for me. I am above superstition, mind! I don't say I believe in dreams; I only say Alicia Warlock is looking for me. It is possible I may be wrong. It is possible I may be right. Who can tell?

The Third Narrative

The Story Continued by Percy Fairbank

XIV

We took leave of Francis Raven at the door of Farleigh Hall, with the understanding that he might expect to hear from us again.

The same night Mrs. Fairbank and I had a discussion in the sanctuary of our own room. The topic was "The Hostler's Story"; and the question in dispute between us turned on the measure of charitable duty that we owed to the hostler himself.

The view I took of the man's narrative was of the purely matter-of-fact kind. Francis Raven had, in my opinion, brooded over the misty connection between his strange dream and his vile wife, until his mind was in a state of partial delusion on that subject. I was quite willing to help him with a trifle of money, and to recommend him to the kindness of my lawyer, if he was really in any danger and wanted advice. There my idea of my duty toward this afflicted person began and ended.

Confronted with this sensible view of the matter, Mrs. Fairbank's romantic temperament rushed, as usual, into extremes. "I should no more think of losing sight of Francis Raven when his next birthday comes round," says my wife, "than I should think of laying down a good story with the last chapters unread. I am positively determined, Percy, to take him back with us when we return to France, in the capacity of groom. What does one man more or less among the horses matter to people as rich as we are?" In this strain the partner of my joys and sorrows ran on, perfectly impenetrable to everything that I could say on the side of common sense. Need I tell my married brethren how it ended? Of course I allowed my wife to irritate me, and spoke to her sharply.

Of course my wife turned her face away indignantly on the conjugal pillow, and burst into tears. Of course upon that, "Mr." made his excuses, and "Mrs." had her own way.

Before the week was out we rode over to Underbridge, and duly offered to Francis Raven a place in our service as supernumerary groom.

At first the poor fellow seemed hardly able to realize his own extraordinary good fortune. Recovering himself, he expressed his gratitude modestly and becomingly. Mrs. Fairbank's ready sympathies overflowed, as usual, at her lips. She talked to him about our home in France, as if the worn, gray-headed hostler had

been a child. "Such a dear old house, Francis; and such pretty gardens! Stables! Stables ten times as big as your stables here—quite a choice of rooms for you. You must learn the name of our house—Maison Rouge. Our nearest town is Metz. We are within a walk of the beautiful River Moselle. And when we want a change we have only to take the railway to the frontier, and find ourselves in Germany."

Listening, so far, with a very bewildered face, Francis started and changed color when my wife reached the end of her last sentence. "Germany?" he repeated.

"Yes. Does Germany remind you of anything?"

The hostler's eyes looked down sadly on the ground. "Germany reminds me of my wife," he replied.

"Indeed! How?"

"She once told me she had lived in Germany—long before I knew her—in the time when she was a young girl."

"Was she living with relations or friends?"

"She was living as governess in a foreign family."

"In what part of Germany?"

"I don't remember, ma'am. I doubt if she told me."

"Did she tell you the name of the family?"

"Yes, ma'am. It was a foreign name, and it has slipped my memory long since. The head of the family was a wine grower in a large way of business—I remember that."

"Did you hear what sort of wine he grew? There are wine growers in our neighborhood. Was it Moselle wine?"

"I couldn't say, ma'am, I doubt if I ever heard."

There the conversation dropped. We engaged to communicate with Francis Raven before we left England, and took our leave. I had made arrangements to pay our round of visits to English friends, and to return to Maison Rouge in the Summer. On the eve of departure, certain difficulties in connection with the management of some landed property of mine in Ireland obliged us to alter our plans. Instead of getting back to our house in France in the Summer, we only returned a week or two before Christmas. Francis Raven accompanied us, and was duly established, in the nominal capacity of stable keeper, among the servants at Maison Rouge.

Before long, some of the objections to taking him into our employment, which I had foreseen and had vainly mentioned to my wife, forced themselves on our attention in no very agreeable form. Francis Raven failed (as I had feared he would) to get on smoothly with his fellow-servants. They were all French; and not one of them understood English. Francis, on his side, was equally ignorant of French. His reserved manners, his melancholy temperament, his solitary ways—all told against him. Our servants called him the "English Bear." He grew widely known in the neighborhood under his nickname. Quarrels took place, ending once or twice in blows. It became plain, even to Mrs. Fairbank herself, that some wise change must be made. While we were still considering what the change was to be, the unfortunate hostler was thrown on our hands for some time to come by an accident in the stables. Still pursued by his proverbial ill-luck, the poor wretch's leg was broken by a kick from a horse.

He was attended to by our own surgeon, in his comfortable bedroom at the stables. As the date of his birthday drew near, he was still confined to his bed.

Physically speaking, he was doing very well. Morally speaking, the surgeon was not satisfied. Francis Raven was suffering under some mysterious mental disturbance, which interfered seriously with his rest at night. Hearing this, I thought it my duty to tell the medical attendant what was preying on the patient's mind. As a practical man, he shared my opinion that the hostler was in a state of delusion on the subject of his Wife and his Dream. "Curable delusion, in my opinion," the surgeon added, "if the experiment could be fairly tried."

"How can it be tried?" I asked. Instead of re-plying, the surgeon put a question to me, on his side.

"Do you happen to know," he said, "that this year is Leap Year?"

"Mrs. Fairbank reminded me of it yesterday," I answered. "Otherwise I might not have known it."

"Do you think Francis Raven knows that this year is Leap Year?"

(I began to see dimly what my friend was driving at.)

"It depends," I answered, "on whether he has got an English almanac. Suppose he has not got the almanac—what then?"

"In that case," pursued the surgeon, "Francis Raven is innocent of all suspicion that there is a twenty-ninth day in February this year. As a necessary consequence—what will he do? He will anticipate the appearance of the Woman with the Knife, at two in the morning of the twenty-ninth of February, instead of the first of March. Let him suffer all his superstitious terrors on the wrong day. Leave him, on the day that is really his birthday, to pass a perfectly quiet night, and to be as sound asleep as other people at two in the morning. And then, when he wakes comfortably in time for his breakfast, shame him out of his delusion by telling him the truth."

I agreed to try the experiment. Leaving the surgeon to caution Mrs. Fairbank on the subject of Leap Year, I went to the stables to see Mr. Raven.

XV

The poor fellow was full of forebodings of the fate in store for him on the ominous first of March. He eagerly entreated me to order one of the men servants to sit up with him on the birthday morning. In granting his request, I asked him to tell me on which day of the week his birthday fell. He reckoned the days on his fingers; and proved his innocence of all suspicion that it was Leap Year, by fixing on the twenty-ninth of February, in the full persuasion that it was the first of March. Pledged to try the surgeon's experiment, I left his error uncorrected, of course. In so doing, I took my first step blindfold toward the last act in the drama of the Hostler's Dream.

The next day brought with it a little domestic difficulty, which indirectly and strangely associated itself with the coming end.

My wife received a letter, inviting us to assist in celebrating the "Silver Wedding" of two worthy German neighbors of ours—Mr. and Mrs. Beldheimer. Mr. Beldheimer was a large wine grower on the banks of the Moselle. His house was situated on the frontier line of France and Germany; and the distance from our house was sufficiently considerable to make it necessary for us to sleep under our host's roof. Under these circumstances, if we accepted the invitation, a comparison of dates showed that we should be away from home on the morning of the first of March. Mrs. Fairbank—holding to her absurd resolution to see with her own eyes what might, or might not, happen to Francis Raven on his birthday—flatly declined to leave Maison Rouge. "It's easy to send an excuse," she said, in her off-hand manner.

I failed, for my part, to see any easy way out of the difficulty. The celebration of a "Silver Wedding" in Germany is the celebration of twenty-five years of happy married life; and the host's claim upon the consideration of his friends on such an occasion is something in the nature of a royal "command." After considerable discussion, finding my wife's obstinacy invincible, and feeling that the absence of both of us from the festival would certainly offend our friends, I left Mrs. Fairbank to make her excuses for herself, and directed her to accept the invitation so far as I was concerned. In so doing, I took my second step, blindfold, toward the last act in the drama of the Hostler's Dream.

A week elapsed; the last days of February were at hand. Another domestic difficulty happened; and, again, this event also proved to be strangely associated with the coming end.

My head groom at the stables was one Joseph Rigobert. He was an ill-conditioned fellow, inordinately vain of his personal appearance, and by no means scrupulous in his conduct with women. His one virtue consisted of his fondness for horses, and in the care he took of the animals under his charge. In a word, he was too good a groom to be easily replaced, or he would have quitted my service long since. On the occasion of which I am now writing, he was reported to me by my steward as growing idle and disorderly in his habits. The principal offense alleged against him was that he had been seen that day in the city of Metz, in the company of a woman (supposed to be an Englishwoman), whom he was entertaining at a tavern, when he ought to have been on his way back to Maison Rouge. The man's defense was that "the lady" (as he called her) was an English stranger, unacquainted with the ways of the place, and that he had only shown her where she could obtain some refreshments at her own request. I administered the necessary reprimand, without troubling myself to inquire further into the matter. In failing to do this, I took my third step, blindfold, toward the last act in the drama of the Hostler's Dream.

On the evening of the twenty-eighth, I informed the servants at the stables that one of them must watch through the night by the Englishman's bedside. Joseph Rigobert immediately volunteered for the duty—as a means, no doubt, of winning his way back to my favor. I accepted his proposal.

That day the surgeon dined with us. Toward midnight he and I left the smoking room, and repaired to Francis Raven's bedside. Rigobert was at his post, with no very agreeable expression on his face. The Frenchman and the Englishman had evidently not got on well together so far. Francis Raven lay helpless on his bed, waiting silently for two in the morning and the Dream Woman.

"I have come, Francis, to bid you good night," I said, cheerfully. "To-morrow morning

I shall look in at breakfast time, before I leave home on a journey."

"Thank you for all your kindness, sir. You will not see me alive to-morrow morning. She will find me this time. Mark my words—she will find me this time."

"My good fellow! she couldn't find you in England. How in the world is she to find you in France?"

"It's borne in on my mind, sir, that she will find me here. At two in the morning on my birthday I shall see her again, and see her for the last time."

"Do you mean that she will kill you?"

"I mean that, sir, she will kill me—with the knife."

"And with Rigobert in the room to protect you?"

"I am a doomed man. Fifty Rigoberts couldn't protect me."

"And you wanted somebody to sit up with you?"

"Mere weakness, sir. I don't like to be left alone on my deathbed."

I looked at the surgeon. If he had encouraged me, I should certainly, out of sheer compassion, have confessed to Francis Raven the trick that we were playing him. The surgeon held to his experiment; the surgeon's face plainly said—"No."

The next day (the twenty-ninth of February) was the day of the "Silver Wedding." The first thing in the morning, I went to Francis Raven's room. Rigobert met me at the door.

"How has he passed the night?" I asked.

"Saying his prayers, and looking for ghosts," Rigobert answered. "A lunatic asylum is the only proper place for him."

I approached the bedside. "Well, Francis, here you are, safe and sound, in spite of what you said to me last night."

His eyes rested on mine with a vacant, wondering look.

"I don't understand it," he said.

"Did you see anything of your wife when the clock struck two?"

"No, sir."

"Did anything happen?"

"Nothing happened, sir."

"Doesn't this satisfy you that you were wrong?"

His eyes still kept their vacant, wondering look. He only repeated the words he had spoken already: "I don't understand it."

I made a last attempt to cheer him. "Come, come, Francis! keep a good heart. You will be out of bed in a fortnight."

He shook his head on the pillow. "There's something wrong," he said. "I don't expect you to believe me, sir. I only say there's something wrong—and time will show it."

I left the room. Half an hour later I started for Mr. Beldheimer's house; leaving the arrangements for the morning of the first of March in the hands of the doctor and my wife.

XVI

The one thing which principally struck me when I joined the guests at the "Silver Wedding" is also the one thing which it is necessary to mention here. On this joyful occasion a noticeable lady present was out of spirits. That lady was no other than the heroine of the festival, the mistress of the house!

In the course of the evening I spoke to Mr. Beldheimer's eldest son on the subject of his mother. As an old friend of the family, I had a claim on his confidence which the young man willingly recognized.

"We have had a very disagreeable matter to deal with," he said; "and my mother has not recovered the painful impression left on her mind. Many years since, when my sisters were children, we had an English governess in the house. She left us, as we then understood, to be married. We heard no more of her until a week or ten days since, when my mother received a letter, in which our ex-governess described herself as being in a condition of great poverty and distress. After much hesitation she had ventured—at the suggestion of a lady who had been kind to her—to write to her former employers, and to appeal to their remembrance of old times. You know my mother; she is not only the most kind-hearted, but the most innocent of women—it is impossible to persuade her of the wickedness that there is in the world. She replied by return of post, inviting the governess to come here and see her, and inclosing the money for her traveling expenses. When my father came home, and heard what had been done, he wrote at once to his agent in London to make inquiries, inclosing the address on the governess' letter. Before he could receive the agent's reply the governess arrived. She produced the worst possible impression on his mind. The agent's letter, arriving a few days later, confirmed his suspicions. Since we had lost sight of her, the woman had led a most disreputable life. My father spoke to her privately: he offered—on condition of her leaving the house—a sum of money to take her back to England. If she refused, the alternative would be an appeal to the authorities and a public scandal. She accepted the money, and left the house. On her way back to England she appears to have stopped at Metz. You will understand what sort of woman she is when I tell you that she was seen the other day in a tavern with your handsome groom, Joseph Rigobert."

While my informant was relating these circumstances, my memory was at work. I recalled what Francis Raven had vaguely told us of his wife's experience in former days as governess in a German family. A suspicion of the truth suddenly flashed across my mind. "What was the woman's name?" I asked.

Mr. Beldheimer's son answered: "Alicia Warlock."

I had but one idea when I heard that reply—to get back to my house without a moment's needless delay. It was then ten o'clock at night—the last train to Metz had left long since. I arranged with my young friend—after duly informing him of the circumstances—that I should go by the first train in the morning, instead of staying to breakfast with the other guests who slept in the house.

At intervals during the night I wondered uneasily how things were going on at Maison Rouge. Again and again the same question occurred to me, on my journey home in the early morning—the morning of the first of March. As the event proved, but one person in my house knew what really happened at the stables on Francis Raven's birthday. Let Joseph Rigobert take my place as narrator, and tell the story of the end to You—as he told it, in times past, to his lawyer and to Me.

Fourth (and Last) Narrative

Statement of Joseph Rigobert: Addressed to the Advocate Who Defended Him at His Trial

Respected Sir,—On the twenty-seventh of February I was sent, on business connected with the stables at Maison Rouge, to the city of Metz. On the public promenade I met a magnificent woman. Complexion, blond. Nationality, English. We mutually admired each other; we fell into conversation. (She spoke French perfectly—with the English accent.) I offered refreshment; my proposal was accepted. We had a long and interesting interview—we discovered that we were made for each other. So far, Who is to blame?

Is it my fault that I am a handsome man—universally agreeable as such to the fair sex? Is it a criminal offense to be accessible to the amiable weakness of love? I ask again, Who is to blame? Clearly, nature. Not the beautiful lady—not my humble self.

To resume. The most hard-hearted person living will understand that two beings made for each other could not possibly part without an appointment to meet again.

I made arrangements for the accommodation of the lady in the village near Maison Rouge. She consented to honor me with her company at supper, in my apartment at the stables, on the night of the twenty-ninth. The time fixed on was the time when the other servants were accustomed to retire—eleven o'clock.

Among the grooms attached to the stables was an Englishman, laid up with a broken leg. His name was Francis. His manners were repulsive; he was ignorant of the French language. In the kitchen he went by the nickname of the "English Bear." Strange to say, he was a great favorite with my master and my mistress. They even humored certain superstitious terrors to which this repulsive person was subject—terrors into the nature of which I, as an advanced freethinker, never thought it worth my while to inquire.

On the evening of the twenty-eighth the Englishman, being a prey to the terrors which I have mentioned, requested that one of his fellow-servants might sit up with him for that night only. The wish that he expressed was backed by Mr. Fairbank's authority. Having already incurred my master's displeasure—in what way, a proper sense of my own dignity forbids me to relate—I volunteered to watch by the bedside of the English Bear. My object was to satisfy Mr. Fairbank that I bore no malice, on my side, after what had occurred between us. The wretched Englishman passed a night of delirium. Not understanding his barbarous language, I could only gather from his gesture that he was in deadly fear of some fancied apparition at his bedside. From time to time, when this madman disturbed my slumbers, I quieted him by swearing at him. This is the shortest and best way of dealing with persons in his condition.

On the morning of the twenty-ninth, Mr. Fairbank left us on a journey. Later in the day, to my unspeakable disgust, I found that I had not done with the Englishman yet. In Mr. Fairbank's absence, Mrs. Fairbank took an incomprehensible interest in the question of my delirious fellow-servant's repose at night. Again, one or the other of us was to watch at his bedside, and report it, if anything happened. Expecting my fair friend to supper, it was necessary to make

sure that the other servants at the stables would be safe in their beds that night. Accordingly, I volunteered once more to be the man who kept watch. Mrs. Fairbank complimented me on my humanity. I possess great command over my feelings. I accepted the compliment without a blush.

Twice, after nightfall, my mistress and the doctor (the last staying in the house in Mr. Fairbank's absence) came to make inquiries. Once before the arrival of my fair friend—and once after. On the second occasion (my apartment being next door to the Englishman's) I was obliged to hide my charming guest in the harness room. She consented, with angelic resignation, to immolate her dignity to the servile necessities of my position. A more amiable woman (so far) I never met with!

After the second visit I was left free. It was then close on midnight. Up to that time there was nothing in the behavior of the mad Englishman to reward Mrs. Fairbank and the doctor for presenting themselves at his bedside. He lay half awake, half asleep, with an odd wondering kind of look in his face. My mistress at parting warned me to be particularly watchful of him toward two in the morning. The doctor (in case anything happened) left me a large hand bell to ring, which could easily be heard at the house.

Restored to the society of my fair friend, I spread the supper table. A pate, a sausage, and a few bottles of generous Moselle wine composed our simple meal. When persons adore each other, the intoxicating illusion of Love transforms the simplest meal into a banquet. With immeasurable capacities for enjoyment, we sat down to table. At the very moment when I placed my fascinating companion in a chair, the infamous Englishman in the next room took that occasion, of all others, to become restless and noisy once more. He struck with his stick on the floor; he cried out, in a delirious access of terror, "Rigobert! Rigobert!"

The sound of that lamentable voice, suddenly

assailing our ears, terrified my fair friend. She lost all her charming color in an instant. "Good heavens!" she exclaimed. "Who is that in the next room?"

"A mad Englishman."

"An Englishman?"

"Compose yourself, my angel. I will quiet him." The lamentable voice called out on me again, "Rigobert! Rigobert!"

My fair friend caught me by the arm. "Who is he?" she cried. "What is his name?"

Something in her face struck me as she put that question. A spasm of jealousy shook me to the soul. "You know him?" I said.

"His name!" she vehemently repeated; "his name!"

"Francis," I answered.

"Francis—*what?*"

I shrugged my shoulders. I could neither remember nor pronounce the barbarous English surname. I could only tell her it began with an "R."

She dropped back into the chair. Was she going to faint? No: she recovered, and more than recovered, her lost color. Her eyes flashed superbly. What did it mean? Profoundly as I understand women in general, I was puzzled by this woman!

"You know him?" I repeated.

She laughed at me. "What nonsense! How should I know him? Go and quiet the wretch."

My looking-glass was near. One glance at it satisfied me that no woman in her senses could prefer the Englishman to Me. I recovered my self-respect. I hastened to the Englishman's bedside.

The moment I appeared he pointed eagerly toward my room. He overwhelmed me with a torrent of words in his own language. I made out, from his gestures and his looks, that he had, in some incomprehensible manner, discovered the presence of my guest; and, stranger still, that he was scared by the idea of a person in my room. I endeavored to compose him on the system which I have already mentioned—that is to say, I swore at him in my language. The result not proving satisfactory, I own I shook my fist in his face, and left the bed-chamber.

Returning to my fair friend, I found her walking backward and forward in a state of excitement wonderful to behold. She had not waited for me to fill her glass—she had begun the generous Moselle in my absence. I prevailed on her with difficulty to place herself at the table. Nothing would induce her to eat. "My appetite is gone," she said. "Give me wine."

The generous Moselle deserves its name—delicate on the palate, with prodigious "body." The strength of this fine wine produced no stupefying effect on my remarkable guest. It appeared to strengthen and exhilarate her—nothing more. She always spoke in the same low tone, and always, turn the conversation as I might, brought it back with the same dexterity to the subject of the Englishman in the next room. In any other woman this persistency would have offended me. My lovely guest was irresistible; I answered her questions with the docility of a child. She possessed all the amusing eccentricity of her nation. When I told her of the accident which confined the Englishman to his bed, she sprang to her feet. An extraordinary smile irradiated her countenance. She said, "Show me the horse who broke the Englishman's leg! I must see that horse!" I took her to the stables. She kissed the horse—on my word of honor, she kissed the horse! That struck me. I said. "You do know the man; and he has wronged you in some way." No! she would not admit it, even then. "I kiss all beautiful animals," she said. "Haven't I kissed you?" With that charming explanation of her conduct, she ran back up the stairs. I only remained behind to lock the stable door again. When I rejoined her, I made a startling discovery. I caught her coming out of the Englishman's room.

"I was just going downstairs again to call you," she said. "The man in there is getting noisy once more."

The mad Englishman's voice assailed our ears once again. "Rigobert! Rigobert!"

He was a frightful object to look at when I saw him this time. His eyes were staring wildly; the perspiration was pouring over his face. In a panic of terror he clasped his hands; he pointed up to heaven. By every sign and gesture that a man can make, he entreated me not to leave him again. I really could not help smiling. The idea of my staying with him, and leaving my fair friend by herself in the next room!

I turned to the door. When the mad wretch saw me leaving him he burst out into a screech of despair—so shrill that I feared it might awaken the sleeping servants.

My presence of mind in emergencies is proverbial among those who know me. I tore open the cupboard in which he kept his linen—seized a handful of his handkerchiefs—gagged him with one of them, and secured his hands with the others. There was now no danger of his alarming the servants. After tying the last knot, I looked up.

The door between the Englishman's room and mine was open. My fair friend was standing on the threshold—watching him as he lay helpless on the bed; watching me as I tied the last knot.

"What are you doing there?" I asked. "Why did you open the door?"

She stepped up to me, and whispered her answer in my ear, with her eyes all the time upon the man on the bed:

"I heard him scream."

"Well?"

"I thought you had killed him."

I drew back from her in horror. The suspicion of me which her words implied was sufficiently detestable in itself. But her manner when she uttered the words was more revolting still. It so powerfully affected me that I started back from that beautiful creature as I might have recoiled from a reptile crawling over my flesh.

Before I had recovered myself sufficiently to reply, my nerves were assailed by another shock. I suddenly heard my mistress's voice calling to me from the stable yard.

There was no time to think—there was only time to act. The one thing needed was to keep Mrs. Fairbank from ascending the stairs, and discovering—not my lady guest only—but the Englishman also, gagged and bound on his bed. I instantly hurried to the yard. As I ran down the stairs I heard the stable clock strike the quarter to two in the morning.

My mistress was eager and agitated. The doctor (in attendance on her) was smiling to himself, like a man amused at his own thoughts.

"Is Francis awake or asleep?" Mrs. Fairbank inquired.

"He has been a little restless, madam. But he is now quiet again. If he is not disturbed" (I added those words to prevent her from ascending the stairs), "he will soon fall off into a quiet sleep."

"Has nothing happened since I was here last?"

"Nothing, madam."

The doctor lifted his eyebrows with a comical look of distress. "Alas, alas, Mrs. Fairbank!" he said. "Nothing has happened! The days of romance are over!"

"It is not two o'clock yet," my mistress answered, a little irritably.

The smell of the stables was strong on the morning air. She put her handkerchief to her nose and led the way out of the yard by the north entrance—the entrance communicating with the gardens and the house. I was ordered to follow her, along with the doctor. Once out of the smell of the stables she began to question me again. She was unwilling to believe that nothing had occurred in her absence. I invented the best answers I could think of on the spur of the moment; and the doctor stood by laughing. So the minutes passed till the clock struck two. Upon that, Mrs. Fairbank announced her intention of personally visiting the Englishman in his room. To my great relief, the doctor interfered to stop her from doing this.

"You have heard that Francis is just falling asleep," he said. "If you enter his room you may disturb him. It is essential to the success of my experiment that he should have a good night's rest, and that he should own it himself, before I tell him the truth. I must request, madam, that you will not disturb the man. Rigobert will ring the alarm bell if anything happens."

My mistress was unwilling to yield. For the next five minutes, at least, there was a warm discussion between the two. In the end Mrs. Fairbank was obliged to give way—for the time. "In half an hour," she said, "Francis will either be sound asleep, or awake again. In half an hour I shall come back." She took the doctor's arm. They returned together to the house.

Left by myself, with half an hour before me, I resolved to take the Englishwoman back to the village—then, returning to the stables, to remove the gag and the bindings from Francis, and to let him screech to his heart's content. What would his alarming the whole establishment matter to me after I had got rid of the compromising presence of my guest?

Returning to the yard I heard a sound like the creaking of an open door on its hinges. The gate of the north entrance I had just closed with my own hand. I went round to the west entrance, at the back of the stables. It opened on a field crossed by two footpaths in Mr. Fairbank's grounds. The nearest footpath led to the village. The other led to the highroad and the river.

Arriving at the west entrance I found the door open—swinging to and fro slowly in the fresh morning breeze. I had myself locked and bolted that door after admitting my fair friend at eleven o'clock. A vague dread of something wrong stole its way into my mind. I hurried back to the stables.

I looked into my own room. It was empty. I went to the harness room. Not a sign of the woman was there. I returned to my room, and approached the door of the Englishman's bedchamber. Was it possible that she had remained there during my absence? An unaccountable reluctance to open the door made me hesitate, with my hand on the lock. I listened. There

was not a sound inside. I called softly. There was no answer. I drew back a step, still hesitating. I noticed something dark moving slowly in the crevice between the bottom of the door and the boarded floor. Snatching up the candle from the table, I held it low, and looked. The dark, slowly moving object was a stream of blood!

That horrid sight roused me. I opened the door. The Englishman lay on his bed—alone in the room. He was stabbed in two places—in the throat and in the heart. The weapon was left in the second wound. It was a knife of English manufacture, with a handle of buckhorn as good as new.

I instantly gave the alarm. Witnesses can speak to what followed. It is monstrous to suppose that I am guilty of the murder. I admit that I am capable of committing follies: but I shrink from the bare idea of a crime. Besides, I had no motive for killing the man. The woman murdered him in my absence. The woman escaped by the west entrance while I was talking to my mistress. I have no more to say. I swear to you what I have here written is a true statement of all that happened on the morning of the first of March.

Accept, sir, the assurance of my sentiments of profound gratitude and respect.

Joseph Rigobert.

Last Lines—Added by Percy Fairbank

Tried for the murder of Francis Raven, Joseph Rigobert was found Not Guilty; the papers of the assassinated man presented ample evidence of the deadly animosity felt towards him by his wife.

The investigations pursued on the morning when the crime was committed showed that the murderess, after leaving the stable, had taken the footpath which led to the river. The river was dragged—without result. It remains doubtful to this day whether she died by drowning or not.

The one thing certain is—that Alicia Warlock was never seen again.

So—beginning in mystery, ending in mystery—the Dream Woman passes from your view. Ghost; demon; or living human creature—say for yourselves which she is. Or, knowing what unfathomed wonders are around you, what unfathomed wonders are in you, let the wise words of the greatest of all poets be explanation enough:

> *We are such stuff*
> *As dreams are made of, and our little life*
> *Is rounded with a sleep.*

Washington Irving

KNOWN WITH GOOD REASON as the "Father of American Literature," Washington Irving (1783–1859) was the first author to produce uniquely American stories, frequently based on local legends, that were read and applauded abroad. He was born in New York City and studied law in a desultory manner, even working (in a minor role) on Aaron Burr's trial for treason. He was still a teenager when he began contributing to the *Morning Chronicle*. In 1807, he, his brother William, and James Kirk Paulding began writing sketches collected as *Salmagundi*, a forerunner of Dickens's *Pickwick Papers*. He followed this with *A History of New York*, purportedly by Diedrich Knickerbocker (1809), the first significant American literary work of humor, and, after several lesser works, *The Sketch Book of Geoffrey Crayon, Gent*, published in 1819 and 1820, which contains two of the most famous short stories in American literature, though they are based on German legends. In "Rip Van Winkle," the title character is kind to a dwarf, who gives him a special drink and Rip falls asleep, waking twenty years later. "The Legend of Sleepy Hollow," which has scared children at Halloween for nearly two centuries, features a headless horseman. Other fantasy stories by Irving were set in the Dutch communities of New York's mid-Hudson Valley and in Spain, whose legends provided fodder for some of his most chilling supernatural stories.

"The Adventure of the German Student" (also published as "The Lady of the Velvet Collar") was originally published in *Tales of a Traveller* (London, John Murray, 1824).

The Adventure of the German Student

WASHINGTON IRVING

IN A STORMY NIGHT, in the tempestuous times of the French Revolution, a young German was returning to his lodgings, at a late hour, across the old part of Paris. The lightning gleamed, and the loud claps of thunder rattled through the lofty narrow streets—but I should first tell you something about this young German.

Gottfried Wolfgang was a young man of good family. He had studied for some time at Göttingen, but being of a visionary and enthusiastic character, he had wandered into those wild and speculative doctrines which have so often bewildered German students. His secluded life, his intense application, and the singular nature of his studies had an effect on both mind and body. His health was impaired; his imagination diseased. He had been indulging in fanciful speculations on spiritual essences, until, like Swedenborg, he had an ideal world of his own around him. He took up a notion, I do not know from what cause, that there was an evil influence hanging over him; an evil genius or spirit seeking to ensnare him and ensure his perdition. Such an idea working on his melancholy temperament produced the most gloomy effects. He became haggard and desponding. His friends discovered the mental malady preying upon him, and determined that the best cure was a change of scene; he was sent, therefore, to finish his studies amidst the splendors and gayeties of Paris.

Wolfgang arrived at Paris at the breaking out of the revolution. The popular delirium at first caught his enthusiastic mind, and he was captivated by the political and philosophical theories of the day; but the scenes of blood which followed shocked his sensitive nature, disgusted him with society and the world, and made him more than ever a recluse. He shut himself up in a solitary apartment in the *Pays Latin,* the quarter of students. There, in a gloomy street not far from the monastic walls of the Sorbonne, he pursued his favorite speculations. Sometimes he spent hours altogether in the great libraries of Paris, those catacombs of departed authors, rummaging among their hoards of dusty and obsolete works in quest of food for his unhealthy appetite. He was, in a manner, a literary ghoul, feeding in the charnel-house of decayed literature.

Wolfgang, though solitary and recluse, was of an ardent temperament, but for a time it operated merely upon his imagination. He was too shy and ignorant of the world to make any advances to the fair, but he was a passionate admirer of female beauty, and in his lonely chamber would often lose himself in reveries on forms and faces which he had seen, and his

470

fancy would deck out images of loveliness far surpassing the reality.

While his mind was in this excited and sublimated state, a dream produced an extraordinary effect upon him. It was of a female face of transcendent beauty. So strong was the impression made, that he dreamt of it again and again. It haunted his thoughts by day, his slumbers by night; in fine, he became passionately enamoured of this shadow of a dream. This lasted so long that it became one of those fixed ideas which haunt the minds of melancholy men, and are at times mistaken for madness.

Such was Gottfried Wolfgang, and such his situation at the time I mentioned. He was returning home late one stormy night, through some of the old and gloomy streets of the *Marais*, the ancient part of Paris. The loud claps of thunder rattled among the high houses of the narrow streets. He came to the Place de Grève, the square where public executions are performed. The lightning quivered about the pinnacles of the ancient Hôtel de Ville, and shed flickering gleams over the open space in front. As Wolfgang was crossing the square, he shrank back with horror at finding himself close by the guillotine. It was the height of the reign of terror, when this dreadful instrument of death stood ever ready, and its scaffold was continually running with the blood of the virtuous and the brave. It had that very day been actively employed in the work of carnage, and there it stood in grim array, amidst a silent and sleeping city, waiting for fresh victims.

Wolfgang's heart sickened within him, and he was turning shuddering from the horrible engine, when he beheld a shadowy form, cowering as it were at the foot of the steps which led up to the scaffold. A succession of vivid flashes of lightning revealed it more distinctly. It was a female figure, dressed in black. She was seated on one of the lower steps of the scaffold, leaning forward, her face hid in her lap; and her long dishevelled tresses hanging to the ground, streaming with the rain which fell in torrents. Wolfgang paused. There was something awful in this solitary monument of woe. The female had the appearance of being above the common order. He knew the times to be full of vicissitude, and that many a fair head, which had once been pillowed on down, now wandered houseless. Perhaps this was some poor mourner whom the dreadful axe had rendered desolate, and who sat here heart-broken on the strand of existence, from which all that was dear to her had been launched into eternity.

He approached, and addressed her in the accents of sympathy. She raised her head and gazed wildly at him. What was his astonishment at beholding, by the bright glare of the lightning, the very face which had haunted him in his dreams. It was pale and disconsolate, but ravishingly beautiful.

Trembling with violent and conflicting emotions, Wolfgang again accosted her. He spoke something of her being exposed at such an hour of the night, and to the fury of such a storm, and offered to conduct her to her friends. She pointed to the guillotine with a gesture of dreadful signification.

"I have no friend on earth!" said she.

"But you have a home," said Wolfgang.

"Yes—in the grave!"

The heart of the student melted at the words.

"If a stranger dare make an offer," said he, "without danger of being misunderstood, I would offer my humble dwelling as a shelter; myself as a devoted friend. I am friendless myself in Paris, and a stranger in the land; but if my life could be of service, it is at your disposal, and should be sacrificed before harm or indignity should come to you."

There was an honest earnestness in the young man's manner that had its effect. His foreign accent, too, was in his favor; it showed him not to be a hackneyed inhabitant of Paris. Indeed, there is an eloquence in true enthusiasm that is not to be doubted. The homeless stranger confided herself implicitly to the protection of the student.

He supported her faltering steps across the Pont Neuf, and by the place where the statue of

Henry the Fourth had been overthrown by the populace. The storm had abated, and the thunder rumbled at a distance. All Paris was quiet; that great volcano of human passion slumbered for a while, to gather fresh strength for the next day's eruption. The student conducted his charge through the ancient streets of the *Pays Latin,* and by the dusky walls of the Sorbonne, to the great dingy hotel which he inhabited. The old portress who admitted them stared with surprise at the unusual sight of the melancholy Wolfgang, with a female companion.

On entering his apartment, the student, for the first time, blushed at the scantiness and indifference of his dwelling. He had but one chamber—an old-fashioned saloon—heavily carved, and fantastically furnished with the remains of former magnificence, for it was one of those hotels in the quarter of the Luxembourg palace, which had once belonged to nobility. It was lumbered with books and papers, and all the usual apparatus of a student, and his bed stood in a recess at one end.

When lights were brought, and Wolfgang had a better opportunity of contemplating the stranger, he was more than ever intoxicated by her beauty. Her face was pale, but of a dazzling fairness, set off by a profusion of raven hair that hung clustering about it. Her eyes were large and brilliant, with a singular expression approaching almost to wildness. As far as her black dress permitted her shape to be seen, it was of perfect symmetry. Her whole appearance was highly striking, though she was dressed in the simplest style. The only thing approaching to an ornament which she wore, was a broad black band round her neck, clasped by diamonds.

The perplexity now commenced with the student how to dispose of the helpless being thus thrown upon his protection. He thought of abandoning his chamber to her, and seeking shelter for himself elsewhere. Still, he was so fascinated by her charms, there seemed to be such a spell upon his thoughts and senses, that he could not tear himself from her presence. Her manner, too, was singular and unaccountable. She spoke no more of the guillotine. Her grief had abated. The attentions of the student had first won her confidence, and then, apparently, her heart. She was evidently an enthusiast like himself, and enthusiasts soon understand each other.

In the infatuation of the moment, Wolfgang avowed his passion for her. He told her the story of his mysterious dream, and how she had possessed his heart before he had even seen her. She was strangely affected by his recital, and acknowledged to have felt an impulse towards him equally unaccountable. It was the time for wild theory and wild actions. Old prejudices and superstitions were done away; everything was under the sway of the "Goddess of Reason." Among other rubbish of the old times, the forms and ceremonies of marriage began to be considered superfluous bonds for honorable minds. Social compacts were the vogue. Wolfgang was too much of a theorist not to be tainted by the liberal doctrines of the day.

"Why should we separate?" said he; "our hearts are united; in the eye of reason and honor we are as one. What need is there of sordid forms to bind high souls together?"

The stranger listened with emotion: she had evidently received illumination at the same school.

"You have no home nor family," continued he; "let me be everything to you, or rather let us be everything to one another. If form is necessary, form shall be observed—there is my hand. I pledge myself to you forever."

"Forever?" said the stranger, solemnly.

"Forever!" repeated Wolfgang.

The stranger clasped the hand extended to her. "Then I am yours," murmured she, and sank upon his bosom.

The next morning the student left his bride sleeping, and sallied forth at an early hour to seek more spacious apartments suitable to the change in his situation. When he returned, he found the stranger lying with her head hanging over the bed, and one arm thrown over it. He spoke to her, but received no reply. He advanced to awaken her from her uneasy posture. On taking her hand, it was cold—there was no pulsation—her face was pallid and ghastly. In a word, she was a corpse.

Horrified and frantic, he alarmed the house. A scene of confusion ensued. The police were summoned. As the officer of police entered the room, he started back on beholding the corpse.

"Great heaven!" cried he, "how did this woman come here?"

"Do you know anything about her?" said Wolfgang eagerly.

"Do I?" exclaimed the officer; "she was guillotined yesterday."

He stepped forward; undid the black collar round the neck of the corpse, and the head rolled on the floor!

The student burst into a frenzy. "The fiend! the fiend has gained possession of me!" shrieked he; "I am lost forever."

They tried to soothe him, but in vain. He was possessed with the frightful belief that an evil spirit had reanimated the dead body to ensnare him. He went distracted, and died in a mad-house.

A SÉANCE, YOU SAY?

Joseph Shearing

GABRIELLE MARGARET VERE LONG (née Campbell) (1886–1952) used at least six pseudonyms (though several sources speculate that it might have been ten or more), the most famous of which are Marjorie Bowen (see "The Avenging of Ann Leete" in this collection) and, later, Joseph Shearing. Almost all the books written under the Shearing byline are historical novels, usually based on real-life criminal cases. While her other noms de plume have faded into obscurity, the Bowen and Shearing names endure, the former for the many outstanding ghost stories produced under that name and the latter for the novels of murder set in other times.

Among her best-known crime novels as Shearing are *Moss Rose* (1934; released on film in 1947, starring Peggy Cummins, Victor Mature, Ethel Barrymore, and Vincent Price), set in late Victorian-era London; *Blanche Fury* (1939; released in 1948, starring Valerie Hobson and Stewart Granger), a Gothic romance based on the infamous early nineteenth-century Rush murder, in which the dazzlingly stupid Rush blew the head off his stepfather and forged a note by a man well known to be illiterate; *Airing in a Closed Carriage* (1943; released in 1947 as *The Mark of Cain*, starring Sally Gray, Eric Portman, and Patrick Holt, with a screenplay by the great detective fiction writer Christianna Brand); and *For Her to See*, published in the United States as *So Evil My Love* (1947; released as *So Evil My Love* in England in 1948 and released in the United States as *The Obsessed*, starring Ann Todd, Ray Milland, and Geraldine Fitzgerald), a psychological thriller set in England in 1876. Her short story "The Silk Petticoat" was televised as an episode of *Alfred Hitchcock Presents* in 1962; it starred Antoinette Bower and Michael Rennie.

"They Found My Grave" was originally published in the author's short story collection *Orange Blossoms* (London, Heinemann, 1938).

They Found My Grave

JOSEPH SHEARING

ADA TRIMBLE WAS BORED with the sittings. She had been persuaded to attend against her better judgment, and the large dingy Bloomsbury house depressed and disgusted her; the atmosphere did not seem to her in the least spiritual and was always tainted with the smell of stale frying.

The medium named herself Astra Destiny. She was a big, loose woman with a massive face expressing power and cunning. Her garments were made of upholstery material and round her cropped yellowish curls she wore a tinsel belt. Her fat feet bulged through the straps of cheap gilt shoes.

She had written a large number of books on subjects she termed "esoteric" and talked more nonsense in half an hour than Ada Trimble had heard in a lifetime. Yet Madame gave an impression of shrewd sense and considerable experience; a formidable and implacable spirit looked through her small grey eyes and defied anyone to pierce the cloud of humbug in which she chose to wrap herself.

"I think she is detestable," said Ada Trimble; but Helen Trent, the woman who had introduced her to the big Bloomsbury Temple, insisted that, odious as the setting was, odd things did happen at the sittings.

"It sounds like hens," said Miss Trimble, "but séances are worse."

"Well, it is easy to make jokes. And I know it is pretty repulsive. But there are *unexplained* things. They puzzle me. I should like your opinion on them."

"I haven't seen anything yet I can't explain; the woman is a charlatan, making money out of fools. She suspects us and might get unpleasant, I think."

But Helen Trent insisted: "Well, if you'd been going as often as I have, and noticing carefully, as I've been noticing . . ."

"Helen—why *have* you been interested in this nonsense?"

The younger woman answered seriously: "Because I *do* think there is something in it."

Ada Trimble respected her friend's judgment; they were both intelligent, middle-aged, cheerful, and independent in the sense that they had unearned incomes. Miss Trimble enjoyed every moment of her life and therefore grudged those spent in going from her Knightsbridge flat to the grubby Bloomsbury Temple. Not even Helen's persistency could induce Ada to continue the private sittings that wasted money as well as time. Besides, Miss Trimble really disliked being shut up in the stuffy, ugly room while Madame Destiny sat in a trance and the control, a Red Indian called Purple Stream, babbled in her voice and in pidgin English about the New Atlantis, the brotherhood of man, and a few catch phrases that could have been taken from any cheap handbook on philosophy or the religions of the world.

But Helen persuaded her to join in some experiments in what were termed typtology and lucidity that were being conducted by Madame Destiny and a circle of choice friends. These experiments proved to be what Ada Trimble had called in her youth "table turning." Five people were present, besides Ada and Madame Destiny. The table moved, gave raps, and conversations with various spirits followed. A code was used, the raps corresponding in number to the letters of the alphabet, one for "a" and so on to twenty-six for "z." The method was tedious, and nothing, Miss Trimble thought, could have

been more dull. All manner of unlikely spirits appeared: a Fleming of the twelfth century; a President of a South American Republic, late nineteenth century; an Englishman who had been clerk to residency at Tonkin, and who had been killed by a tiger a few years before; a young schoolmaster who had thrown himself in front of a train in Devonshire; a murderer who announced in classic phrase that he had "perished on the scaffold"; a factory hand who had died of drink in Manchester; and a retired schoolmistress recently "passed over."

The spirit of a postman and that of a young girl "badly brought up, who had learnt to swear," said the medium, also spoke through the rap code. These people gave short accounts of themselves and of their deaths, and some vague generalizations about their present state. "I am happy." "I am unhappy." "It is wonderful here." "God does not die." "I remain a Christian." "When I first died it was as if I was stunned. Now I am used to it—" and so on.

They were never asked about the future, who would win the Derby, the results of the next election, or anything of that kind. "It wouldn't be fair," smiled Madame Destiny. "Besides, they probably don't know."

The more important spirits were quickly identified by references to the *Dictionary of National Biography* for the English celebrities and Larousse for the foreign. The Temple provided potted editions of each work. These reliable tomes confirmed all that the spirits said as to their careers and ends. The obscure spirits, if they gave dates and place names, were traced by enquiries of town clerks and registrars. This method always worked out, too.

Madame Destiny sometimes showed the letters that proved that the spirits had once had, as she hideously quoted, "a local habitation and name."

"I can't think why you are interested," said Ada Trimble to Helen Trent as they drove home together. "It is such an easy fraud. Clever, of course, but she has only to keep all the stuff in her head."

"You mean that she looks up the references first?"

"Of course." Ada Trimble was a little surprised that Helen should ask so simple a question. "And those postmen and servant girls could be got up, too, quite easily."

"It would be expensive. And she doesn't charge much."

"She makes a living out of it," said Ada Trimble sharply. "Between the lectures, the healings, the services, the sittings, the lending library, and those ninepenny teas, I think the Temple of Eastern Psycho-Physiological Studies does pretty well. . . ." She looked quickly at her companion and in a changed voice asked: "You're not getting—drawn in—are you, Helen?"

"Oh, no! At least I don't think so, but last year, when you were in France, I was rather impressed—it was the direct voice. I wish it would happen again, I should like your opinion—" Helen Trent's voice faltered and stopped; it was a cold night, she drew her collar and scarf up more closely round her delicate face. The smart comfortable little car was passing over the bridge. The two women looked out at the street and ink-blue pattern of the Serpentine, the bare trees on the banks, the piled buildings beyond, stuck with vermilion and orange lights. The November wind struck icy across Ada Trimble's face.

"I don't know why I forgot the window," she said, rapidly closing it. "I suggest that we leave Madame Destiny alone, Helen. I don't believe that sort of thing is any good; it might easily get on one's nerves."

"Well," said Helen irrelevantly, "what are dreams, anyway?"

Ada remembered how little she knew of the early life of her cultured, elegant friend, and how much she had forgotten of her own youthful experiences that had once seemed so warm, so important, so terrible.

"Come next Tuesday, at least," pleaded Helen as she left the car for the wet pavement. "She has promised the direct voice."

"I ought to go, because of Helen," thought Ada Trimble. "She is beginning to be affected by this nonsense. Those rogues know that she has money."

So on the Tuesday the two charming women in their rich, quiet clothes, with their tasteful veils, handbags, furs, and posies of violets and gardenias were seated in the upper room in the Bloomsbury Temple with the queer shoddy folk who made up Madame Destiny's audience.

Ada Trimble settled into her chair; it was comfortable like all the chairs in the Temple, and she amused herself by looking round the room. The Victorian wallpaper had been covered by dark serge clumsily pinned up; dusty crimson chenille curtains concealed the tall windows. Worn linoleum was on the floor; the table stood in the centre of the room and on it was a small, old-fashioned gramophone with a horn. By it was a small red lamp; this and the light from the cheerful gas fire were the only illumination in the room.

A joss stick smoldered in a brass vase on the mantelpiece but this sickly perfume could not disguise the eternal smell of stew and onions that hung about the Temple.

"I suppose they live on a permanent hot-pot," thought Ada Trimble vaguely, as she looked round on the gathered company.

The medium lay sprawled in the largest chair; she appeared to be already in a trance; her head was sunk on her broad breast, and her snorting breath disturbed the feather edging on her brocade robe. The cheap belt round her head, the cheap gilt shoes, exasperated Ada Trimble once more. "For a woman of sense—" she thought.

Near the medium was a husband, who called himself Lemoine. He was a turnip-coloured, nondescript man, wearing a dirty collar and slippers; his manner hesitated between the shamefaced and the insolent. He was not very often seen, but Ada sometimes suspected him of being the leader of the whole concern.

She speculated with a shudder, and not for the first time, on the private lives of this repulsive couple. What were they like when they were alone together? What did they say when they dropped the gibberish and the posing?

Were they ever quite sincere or quite clean? She had heard they lived in a "flat" at the top of the house and had turned a bleak Victorian bathroom into a kitchen, and that they had "difficulties" with servants.

Beside Mr. Lemoine was Essie Clark, a stringy, cheerful woman, who was Madame Destiny's secretary, and, as Ada Trimble supposed, maid-of-all-work too. She had been "caught" sweeping the stairs, and Ada thought that she mixed the permanent stew.

Essie's taste had stopped, dead as a smashed clock, in childhood, and she wore straight gowns of faded green that fifty years before had been termed "artistic" by frustrated suburban spinsters, and bunches of little toys and posies made of nuts and leather.

The circle was completed by the people well known to Ada: a common, overdressed little woman who called spiritualism her "hobby," and who was on intimate terms with the spirit of her late husband, and a damp, depressed man, Mr. Maple, who had very little to say for himself beyond an occasional admission that he was "investigating and couldn't be sure."

The little woman, Mrs. Penfleet, said cheerfully: "I am certain dear Arthur will come today. I dreamed of him last night," and she eyed the trumpet coyly.

"We don't know who will come, if anyone," objected Mr. Maple gloomily. "We've got to keep open minds."

Mr. Lemoine begged for silence, and Miss Clark put on a disc that played "Rock of Ages."

Ada Trimble's mind flashed to the consumptive Calvinist who had written that hymn; she felt slightly sick and glanced at Helen—dreamy, elegant, sunk in her black velvet collar.

Ada looked at the trumpet, at the medium, and whispered "Ventriloquism," as she bent to drop and pick up her handkerchief, but Helen whispered back "Wait."

Essie Clark took off the record and returned to her chair with a smile of pleased expectancy. It was all in the day's work for her, like cheapening the food off the barrows in the Portobello Road.

Ada Trimble kept her glance from the fire and the lamp, lest, comfortable and drowsy as she was, she should be hypnotized with delusions— "Though I don't think it likely here," she said to herself, "in these sordid surroundings."

There was a pause; the obviously dramatic prelude to the drama. Madame Destiny appeared to be unconscious. Ada thought: "There ought to be a doctor here to make sure." A humming sound came from the painted horn that had curled-back petals like a metallic flower. "Arthur!" came from Mrs. Penfleet and "Hush!" from Mr. Maple. Ada felt dull, a party to a cheap, ignoble fraud. "How dare they," she thought indignantly, "fool with such things—supposing one of the dead *did* return!" The gramophone was making incoherent noises, hummings and sighings.

"The psychic force is manifest," whispered Mr. Lemoine reverently, in familiar phrase.

There was another pause; Ada Trimble's attention wandered to obtrusive details—the pattern of the braid encircling Madame Destiny's bent head, a dull yellow in the lamp's red glow, and the firmness with which her podgy fingers gripped the pad and pencil, even though she was supposed to be in a state of trance.

Suddenly a deep masculine voice said:

"*Beatus qui intelligit super egenum et pauperem.*"

Ada was utterly startled; she felt as if another personality was in the room; she sat forward and looked around; she felt Helen's cold fingers clutch hers; she had not more than half understood the Latin; nor, it seemed, had anyone else. Only Mr. Lemoine remained cool, almost indifferent. Leaning forward he addressed the gramophone.

"That is a proverb or quotation?"

The deep voice replied:

"It is my epitaph."

"It is, perhaps, on your tomb?" asked Mr. Lemoine gently.

"Yes."

"Where is your tomb?"

"I do not choose to disclose." The voice was

speaking with a marked accent. It now added in French: "Is there no one here that speaks my language?"

"Yes," said Ada Trimble, almost without her own volition. French was very familiar to her and she could not disregard the direct appeal.

"*Eh, bien!*" the voice which had always an arrogant, scornful tone, seemed gratified, and ran on at once in French. "I have a very fine tomb—a monument, I should say, shaded with chestnut trees. Every year, on my anniversary, it is covered with wreaths."

"Who are you?" asked Ada Trimble faintly, but Mr. Lemoine gently interposed:

"As the other members of our circle don't speak French," he told the gramophone, "will you talk in English?"

"Any language is easy to me," boasted the voice in English, "but I prefer my own tongue."

"Thank you," said Mr. Lemoine. "The lady asked you who you were—will you tell us?"

"Gabriel Letourneau."

"Would you translate your epitaph?"

"Blessed is he who understands the poor and has pity on the unfortunate."

"What were you?"

"Many things."

"When did you die?"

"A hundred years ago. May 12th, 1837."

"Will you tell us something more about yourself?"

The voice was harsh and scornful.

"It would take a long time to relate my exploits. I was a professor, a peer, a philosopher, a man of action. I have left my many works behind me."

"Please give the titles." Mr. Lemoine, who had always been so effaced and who looked so incompetent, was proving himself cool and skilful at this question-and-answer with the voice.

"There are too many."

"You had pupils?"

"Many famous men."

"Will you give the names?"

"You continually ask me to break your rules," scolded the voice.

"What rules?"

"The rules spirits have to obey."

"You are a Christian?"

"I have never been ashamed to call myself so."

"Where—in the Gospels—is the rule of which you speak?" asked Mr. Lemoine sharply. "There are special rules for spirits?"

"Yes."

So the dialogue went on, more or less on orthodox lines, but Ada Trimble was held and fascinated by the quality and accent of the voice. It was rough, harsh, intensely masculine, with a definite foreign accent. The tone was boastful and arrogant to an insufferable extent. Ada Trimble detested this pompous, insistent personality; she felt odd, a little dazed, a little confused; the orange glow of the gas fire, the red glow of the lamp, the metallic gleams on the horn fused into a fiery pattern before her eyes. She felt as if she were being drawn into a void in which nothing existed but the voice.

Even Mr. Lemoine's thin tones, faintly questioning, seemed a long way off, a thread of sound compared to the deep boom of the voice. The conversation was like a ball being deftly thrown to and fro. Mr. Lemoine asked: "What do you understand by faith?" And the voice, steadily rising to a roar, replied: "The Faith as taught by the Gospel."

"Does not the Gospel contain moral precepts rather than dogma?"

"Why that remark?"

"Because narrow or puerile practices have been built on this basis."

"A clear conscience sees further than practices."

"I see that you are a believer," said Mr. Lemoine placidly. "What is your present situation?"

"Explain!" shouted the voice.

"Are you in Heaven, Hell, or Purgatory?" rapped out Mr. Lemoine.

"I am in Heaven!"

"How is it that you are in Heaven and here at the same time?"

"You are a fool," said the voice stridently. "Visit my grave and you will understand more about me."

"Once more, where is your grave?"

The horn gave a groan of derision and was silent; Mr. Lemoine repeated his question, there was no answer; he then wiped his forehead and turned to his wife who was heaving back to consciousness.

"That is all for today," he smiled round the little circle; no one save Ada and Helen seemed affected by the experience; Mr. Maple made some gloomy sceptical remarks; Mrs. Penfleet complained because Arthur had not spoken, and Essie Clark indifferently and efficiently put away the gramophone and the records.

When the red lamp was extinguished and the light switched on, Ada looked at Madame Destiny who was rubbing her eyes and smiling with an exasperating shrewd blandness.

"It was Gabriel Letourneau," her husband told her mildly. "You remember I told you he came some months ago?" He glanced at Ada. "The medium never knows what spirit speaks."

Ada glanced at Helen who sat quiet and downcast, then mechanically gathered up her gloves and handbag.

"Did you find this person in Larousse?" she asked.

"No. We tried other sources too, but never could discover anything. Very likely he is a liar; quite a number of them are, you know. I always ask him the same questions, but as you heard, there is no satisfaction to be got."

"He always boasts so," complained Mr. Maple, "and particularly about his grave."

"Oh," smiled Mr. Lemoine, rising to indicate that the sitting was at an end. "He is a common type, a snob. When he was alive he boasted about his distinctions, visits to court, and so on; now he is dead he boasts of having seen God, being in Heaven, and the marvels of his grave."

When they were out in the wind-swept evening Helen clasped Ada's arm.

"Now, what do you make of that? Ventriloquism? It is a personality."

"It is odd, certainly. I was watching the woman. Her lips didn't move—save just for snorting or groaning now and then."

"Oh, I dare say it *could* be done," said Helen impatiently. "But I don't think it is a trick. I can't feel that it is. Can you? That is what I wanted you to hear. There have been other queer things, but this is the queerest. What do *you* think?"

"Oh, Helen dear, I don't know!" Ada was slightly trembling. "I never thought that I could be moved by anything like this."

"That is it, isn't it?" interrupted Helen, clinging to her as they passed along the cold street. "*Moved*—and what by?"

"Intense dislike—the man is loathsome!"

"There! You said *man*. It was a voice only!"

"Oh, Helen!"

They walked in silence to the waiting car and when inside began to talk again in low tones, pressed together. No, there was no explanation possible; any attempt at one landed you in a bog of difficulties.

"He spoke to me," sighed Ada Trimble, "and, you know that I forgot he wasn't *there*—I wish that I could have gone on talking to him, I feel that I should have been sufficiently insistent—"

"To—what, Ada?"

"To make him say something definite about himself—"

"It's crazy, Ada! It lets loose all kinds of dreadful thoughts. He might be here, now, riding with us."

"Well, he can't talk without the trumpet." Then both women laughed uneasily.

"My dear, we are getting foolish!" said Helen, and Ada answered: "Yes. Foolish either way—to talk of it at all if we think it was a fraud—and not be more serious if we don't think it a fraud."

But as people usually will when in this kind of a dilemma, they compromised; they discussed the thing and decided to put it to the test once again.

They became frequent visitors to the Bloomsbury Temple, and began to pay to have private sittings with the direct voice.

Busy as they were, Madame Destiny and Mr.

Lemoine "fitted in" a good number of these, and the harsh voice that called itself Gabriel Letourneau usually spoke, though there were annoying occasions when Persian sages, Polish revolutionaries, and feeble-minded girls of unknown nationality insisted on expounding colourless views.

By the spring the personality of Gabriel Letourneau was complete to Ada and Helen. They had been able to build him up, partly from details he had supplied himself and partly out of their own uneasy imaginations. He had been—or was now, but they dared not speculate upon his present shape—a tall, dark, gaunt Frenchman, with side whiskers and a blue chin, the kind of brown eyes known as "piercing," and a fanatical, grim expression.

Ada had often spoken to him in French, but she could never penetrate his identity. A professor, a peer in the reign of Louis Philippe? It was impossible for her to attempt to trace so elusive a person. At first she did not try; she told herself that she had other things to do and she tried to keep the thing out of her mind, or at least to keep it reduced to proper proportions. But this soon proved impossible, and sensible, charming, broad-minded Ada Trimble at length found herself in the grip of an obsession.

The voice and her hatred of the voice. It was useless for her to tell herself, as she frequently did, that the voice was only that of the woman who called herself Astra Destiny and not a personality at all. This was hopeless; she *believed* in Gabriel Letourneau. He had, she was sure, a bad effect on her character and on that of Helen. But opposite effects. Whereas Helen became limp, distracted, nervous, and talked vaguely of being "haunted," Ada felt as if active evil was clouding her soul.

Why should she hate the voice? She had always been afraid of hatred. She knew that the person who hates, not the person who is hated, is the one who is destroyed. When she disliked a person or a thing she had always avoided it, making exceptions only in the cases of cruelty and fanaticism. There she had allowed hate to impel her to exertions foreign to her reserved

nature. And now there was hatred of Gabriel Letourneau possessing her like a poison. He hated her, too. When she spoke to him he told her in his rapid French that Helen could not follow, his scornful opinion of her; he called her an "aging woman"; he said she was pretentious, facile, a silly little atheist, while "I am in Heaven."

He made acid comments on her carefully-chosen clothes, on her charmingly-arranged hair, her little armory of wit and culture, on her delicate illusions and vague, romantic hopes. She felt stripped and defaced after one of the dialogues in which she could not hold her own. Sometimes she tried to shake herself out of "this nonsense." She would look sharply at the entranced medium; Ada had never made the mistake of undervaluing the intelligence of Astra Destiny, and surely the conversation of Gabriel Letourneau was flavoured with feminine malice?

Out in the street with Helen she would say, "We really *are* fools! It is only an out-of-date gramophone."

"Is it?" asked Helen bleakly. "And ventriloquism?" Then she added: "Where does she—that awful woman—get that fluent French?"

"Oh, when you begin asking questions!" cried Ada.

She examined the subject from all angles, she went to people who, she thought, "ought to know," but she could get no satisfaction; it was a matter on which the wisest said the least.

"If only he wouldn't keep boasting!" she complained to Helen. "His grave—that now—he says it is a marvellous monument and that people keep putting wreaths on it, that they make pilgrimages to it—and Helen, why should I *mind*? I ought to be pleased that he has that satisfaction or—at least be indifferent—but I'm not."

"He's been hateful to you, to us," said Helen simply. "I loathe him, too—let us try to get away from him."

"I can't."

Helen went; she drifted out of Ada's life with a shivering reluctance to leave her, but with a definite inability to face the situation created by Gabriel Letourneau. She wrote from Cairo, and presently did not write at all. Ada, left alone with her obsession, no longer struggled against it; she pitted herself deliberately against the voice. Sometimes, as she came and went in the Bloomsbury Temple, she would catch a glint in the dull eyes of Mr. Lemoine or the flinty eyes of Madame Destiny that made her reflect on how many guineas she had paid them. But even these flashes of conviction that she was being the worst type of fool did not save her; she had reached the point where she had to give rein to her fortune.

In September she went to France; countless friends helped her to search archives; there was no member of the Chamber of Peers under Louis Philippe named Letourneau. She wrote to the keepers of the famous cemeteries, she visited these repulsive places herself; there were Letourneaus, not a few, but none with pre-name Gabriel, or with the inscription quoted by the voice. Nor was there anywhere an imposing monument, covered with wreaths and visited by pilgrims, to a professor-peer who had died in 1837.

"Fraud," she kept telling herself, "that wretched couple just practised a very clever fraud on me. But why? What an odd personality for people like that to invent! And the deep masculine voice and the idiomatic French—clever is hardly the word. I suppose they got the data from Larousse." The courteous friends helped her to make enquiries at the Sorbonne. No professors of that name there, or at any of the other big universities.

Ada Trimble believed that she was relieved from her burden of credulity and hate; perhaps if she kept away from the Bloomsbury Temple the thing would pass out of her mind. She was in this mood when she received an answer to a letter she had written to the keeper of the cemetery at Sceaux. She had written to so many officials, and it had been so long since she had written to Sceaux, and she had such little expectation of any result from her enquiries, that she scarcely took much interest in opening the letter.

It read thus:

Madame, in reply to your letter of November 30th, I have the honour to inform you that I have made a search for the Letourneau tomb, which fortunately I found, and I have copied the epitaph cut on the tomb.

Gabriel Letourneau
Man of Letters
Died at Sceaux June 10th, 1858
Beatus qui intelligit
Super egenum et pauperem.

This neglected grave was in a miserable condition covered by weeds; in order to send you the above information it was necessary to undertake cleaning that occupied an hour, and this merely on the portion that bears the inscription. According to the register, this Letourneau was a poor tutor; his eccentric habits are still remembered in the quarter where he lived. He has become a legend—and "he boasts like a Gabriel Letourneau" is often said of a braggart. He has left no descendants and no one has visited his grave. He left a small sum of money to pay for the epitaph.

(signed) Robert, Keeper of the Cemetery at Sceaux, 231 Rue Louis le Grand, Sceaux (Seine)

Ada Trimble went at once to Sceaux. She arrived there on a day of chill, small rain, similar to that on which she had first heard the voice in the Bloomsbury Temple. There was a large, black cemetery, a row of bare chestnut-trees overlooking the walls, an ornate gate. The conscientious keeper, M. Robert, conducted her to the abandoned grave in the corner of the large graveyard; the rotting, dank rubbish of last year's weeds had been cut away above the inscription that Ada had first heard in the Bloomsbury Temple a year ago.

She gazed and went away, full of strange terror. What was the solution of the miserable problem? There were many ways in which the Lemoine couple might have chanced to hear of the poor tutor of Sceaux, but how had they come to know of the epitaph for years concealed behind ivy, bramble, and moss? M. Robert, who was so evidently honest, declared that he never remembered anyone making enquiries about the Letourneau grave, and he had been years in this post. He doubted, he said, whether even the people to whom the name of the eccentric was a proverb knew of the existence of his grave. Then, the shuffling of the dates, 1858 instead of 1837, the lies about the state of the grave and the position that Letourneau had held in life.

Ada had a sickly qualm when she reflected how this fitted in with the character she had been given of a slightly unhinged braggart with egomania. A peerage, the Sorbonne, the monument—all lies?

Ada returned to England and asked Madame Destiny to arrange another sitting for her with the direct voice. She also asked for as large a circle as possible to be invited, all the people who had ever heard Gabriel Letourneau.

"Oh, that will be a large number," said Madame Destiny quickly; "he is one of the spirits who visits us most frequently."

"Never mind, the large room, please, and I will pay all expenses. I think I have found out something about that gentleman."

"How interesting," said Madame Destiny, with civil blankness.

"Can she possibly know where I have been?" thought Ada Trimble, but it seemed absurd to suppose that this hard-up couple, existing by shifts, should have the means to employ spies and detectives. The meeting was arranged, and as all the seats were free, the room was full.

The gramophone was on a raised platform; it was placed on a table beside which sat Madame Destiny to the right and her husband to the left. The red lamp was in place. A dark curtain, badly pinned up, formed the back cloth. Save for the gas fire, the room—a large Victorian *salon*—was in darkness. Ada Trimble sat on one of the Bentwood chairs in the front row. "He won't come," she thought. "I shall never hear the voice again. And the whole absurdity will be over."

But the medium was no sooner twitching in a trance than the voice came rushing from the tin horn. It spoke directly to Ada Trimble, and she felt her heart cleave with horror as she heard the cringing tone.

"Good evening, madame, and how charming you are tonight! Your travels have improved you—you recall my little jokes, my quips? Only to test your wit, dear lady, I have always admired you so much—"

Ada could not reply; the one thought beat in her mind, half paralysing her, "He knows what I found out—he is trying to flatter me so that I don't give him away."

The voice's opening remarks had been in French and for this Mr. Lemoine called him to order; the usual verbal duel followed, Lemoine pressing the spirit to give proof of his identity, the spirit arrogantly defending his secrets. The audience that had heard this parrying between Lemoine and Letourneau before so often was not interested, and Ada Trimble did not hear anything; she was fiercely concerned with her own terror and bewilderment. Then the voice, impatiently breaking off the bitter sparring, addressed her directly in oily, flattering accents.

"What a pleasure that we meet again; how charming to see you here! The time has been very long since I saw you last."

Ada roused herself; she began to speak in a thick voice that she could scarcely have recognised as her own.

"Yes, one is drawn to what one dislikes as surely as towards what one hates. I have been too much concerned with you, I hope now that I shall be free."

"Miss Trimble," protested Mr. Lemoine, "there are others present; pray speak in English. I think you said you had been able to identify this spirit quite precisely."

In French the gramophone harshly whispered, "Take care."

"Well," said Mr. Lemoine briskly, "this lady says she found your grave; what have you to say to that?"

"I beg the lady not to talk of my private affairs"; voice and accent were alike thick, with agitation, perhaps despair.

"But you have often spoken of your tomb, the wreaths, the pilgrimages; you have talked of your peerage, your professorship, your pupils. As you would never give us corroborative details, this lady took the trouble to find them out."

"Let her give them," said the voice, "when we are alone—she and I."

"What would be the sense of that?" demanded Mr. Lemoine. "All these people know you well, they are interested—now, Miss Trimble."

"I found the grave in Sceaux cemetery," began Ada.

The voice interrupted her furiously: "You are doing a very foolish thing!"

"I see," said Mr. Lemoine coolly, "you are still an earthbound spirit. You are afraid that something hurtful to your vanity is about to be revealed."

"You should be free from this material delusion. We," added the turnip-faced man pompously, "are neither noble nor learned. We shall not think the less of you if it is true you have boasted."

"I am not a boaster!" stormed the voice.

"Your grave is in the cemetery at Sceaux," said Ada Trimble rapidly. "You died in 1858, not 1837; you were neither peer nor professor—no one visits your grave. It is miserable, neglected, covered with weeds. It took the keeper an hour's work even to cut away the rubbish sufficiently to see your epitaph."

"Now we know that," said Mr. Lemoine smoothly, "we can help you to shake off these earthly chains."

"These are lies." The voice rose to a hum like the sound of a spinning top. "Lies—"

"No," cried Ada. "You have lied; you have never seen God, either."

"You may," suggested Mr. Lemoine, "have seen a fluid personage in a bright illumination, but how can you have been sure it was God?"

The humming sound grew louder; then the horn flew over, as if wrenched off, and toppled onto the table, then onto the floor. Mr. Le-

moine crossed the platform and switched on the light.

"An evil spirit," he said in his routine voice. "Now that he has been exposed I don't suppose that he will trouble us again." And he congratulated Ada on her shrewd and careful investigations, though the stare he gave her through his glasses seemed to express a mild wonder as to why she had taken so much trouble. The meeting broke up; there was coffee for a few chosen guests upstairs in the room lined with books on the "occult"; no one seemed impressed by the meeting; they talked of other things; only Ada Trimble was profoundly moved.

This was the first time she had come to these banal coffee-drinkings. Hardly knowing what she did, she had come upstairs with these queer, self-possessed people who seemed to own something she had not got. They were neither obsessed nor afraid. Was she afraid? Had not Gabriel Letourneau vanished for ever? Had he not broken the means of communication between them? Undoubtedly she had exorcized him; she would be free now of this miserable, humiliating, and expensive obsession. She tried to feel triumphant, released, but her spirit would not soar. In the back of her mind surged self-contempt. "Why did I do it? There was no need. His lies hurt no one. To impress these people was his one pleasure—perhaps he is in hell, and that was his one freedom from torment—but I must think sanely."

This was not easy to do; she seemed to have lost all will-power, all judgment. "I wish Helen had not escaped." She used the last word unconsciously; her fingers were cold round the thick cup, her face in the dingy mirror above the fireplace looked blurred and odd. She tried to steady herself by staring at the complacent features of Astra Destiny, who was being distantly gracious to a circle of admirers, and then by talking to commonplace Mr. Lemoine, whose indifference was certainly soothing. "Oh, yes," he said politely, "we get a good deal of that sort of thing. Malicious spirits—evil influences—"

"Aren't you afraid?" asked Ada faintly.

"Afraid?" asked Mr. Lemoine, as if he did not know what the word meant. "Oh, dear no, we are quite safe—" he added, then said: "Of course, if one was afraid, if one didn't quite believe, there might be danger. Any weakness on one's own part always gives the spirits a certain power over one—"

All this was, Ada knew, merely "patter"; she had heard it, and similar talk, often enough, and never paid much attention to it; now it seemed to trickle through her inner consciousness like a flow of icy water. She was afraid, she didn't quite believe; yet how could she even but think that? Now she must believe. Astra Destiny could not have "faked" Gabriel Letourneau. Well, then, he was a real person—a real spirit? Ada Trimble's mind that had once been so cool and composed, so neat and tidy, now throbbed in confusion.

"Where do they go?" she asked childishly. "These evil spirits? I mean—today—will he come again?"

"I don't suppose so, not here. He will try to do all he can elsewhere. Perhaps he will try to impose on other people. I am afraid he has wasted a good deal of our time."

"How can you say 'wasted'!" whispered Ada Trimble bleakly. "He *proves* that the dead return."

"We don't need such proof," said Mr. Lemoine, meekly confident and palely smiling.

"I had better go home now," said Ada; she longed to escape and yet dreaded to leave the warmth, the light, the company; perhaps these people were protected, and so were safe from the loathed, prowling, outcast spirit. She said good-bye to Madame Destiny, who was pleasant, as usual, without being effusive, and then to the others. She could not resist saying to Essie Clark: "Do you think that I did right?"

"Right?" the overworked woman smiled mechanically, the chipped green coffee-pot suspended in her hand.

"In exposing—the voice—the spirit?"

"Oh, *that!* Of course. You couldn't have done anything else, could you?" And Miss Clark poured her coffee and handed the cup, with a tired pleasantry, to a tall Indian who was the only elegant looking person present. Ada Trimble went out on to the landing; the smell of frying, of stew, filled the gaunt stairway; evidently one of the transient servants was in residence; through the half-open door behind her Ada could hear the babble of voices, then another voice, deep, harsh, that whispered in her ear: "*Canaille!*"

She started forward, missed her foot-hold, and fell.

Mr. Lemoine, always efficient, was the first to reach the foot of the stairs. Ada Trimble had broken her neck.

"A pure accident," said Astra Destiny, pale, but mistress of the situation. "Everyone is witness that she was quite alone at the time. She has been very nervous lately, and those high heels . . ."

Edgar Jepson

IT IS LIKELY THAT the most widely read works of Edgar (Alfred) Jepson (1863–1938) are not the rather dull, lightweight detective novels he began to write soon after the turn of the nineteenth century, nor the pedestrian adventure novels with which he began his career as a novelist, but his translations from the French of novels and stories by Maurice Leblanc, for whom he brought to the English reading public many of the famous Arsene Lupin adventures, and the once-popular novel *The Man with the Black Feather* (1912) by Gaston Leroux.

Born in London, Jepson graduated from Baliol College, Oxford, then spent five years in Barbados before returning to take a job as editor at *Vanity Fair,* where he worked with Richard Middleton and the libidinous Frank Harris. He became involved, albeit tangentially, with members of the Decadent Movement, such as Ernest Dawson, John Gawsworth (with whom he collaborated on several short stories), and Arthur Machen. The first novel he wrote under his own name, *Sibyl Falcon* (1895), features a female adventurer, and he followed this with such fantasy novels as *The Horned Shepherd* (1904), which features the worship of Pan, and *No. 19* (1910; published in the United States as *The Garden at 19*), in which a Londoner brings to life a statue of Pan. Among his better thrillers are *The Mystery of the Myrtles* (1909), which involves human sacrifice, and *The Moon Gods* (1930), a lost race novel. His son, Selwyn Jepson, was a prolific mystery writer, and his granddaughter is the noted British novelist Fay Weldon.

"Mrs. Morrel's Last Séance" was originally published in the February 1912 issue of *The London Magazine.*

Mrs. Morrel's Last Séance

EDGAR JEPSON

I HAD ATTENDED ALL the séances of Mrs. Joaquine Morrel during the two previous winters; and of all the mediums I have sat with, in the States or in Europe, she was the best. Sometimes, of course, she was not in the right mood or condition, or whatever it is; and the phenomena were trivial; sometimes we got mere trickery, and that poorly done. Like most other mediums, public or even private, if real phenomena did not come, Mrs. Morrel would do her best to produce imitations. Sometimes she would quite deliberately use trickery rather than endure the exhaustion and nausea which always followed the genuine exercise of her powers.

But often at her séances I had seen phenomena which I did not believe to have been produced by trickery. I did not profess to be able to find any explanation of them; and I was profoundly sceptical about their having anything to do with the spirits of the dead. I inclined to the theory that they were produced by the obscure and mysterious action of the subconscious, or, if you prefer it, the subliminal self. But whatever their cause, I saw phenomena which I accounted genuine; and, as I say, after these Mrs. Morrel was in a state of utter prostration. She seemed not only to have lost vital force, but actually to have lost blood, so weak and pale and shrunken was she.

I came to the séance on the fourth of last December with no great expectations: for it was a mere chance whether the phenomena would be interesting, or more or less trickery. Besides, the night was very cold, and the weather had been abominable; and that was against Mrs. Morrel's being in a favourable condition for the best exercise of her powers. But I had not been in the room with her three minutes before I was sure that she was in uncommonly good spirits; and I began to expect a good sitting.

I was the first to arrive; and we chatted for a few minutes about what she had been doing since the last séance I had attended, and about the members of the circle which was to sit that night. I became aware that one of the reasons of her good spirits was that she was wearing a new dress, a black, watered silk. I complimented her on it; and she made me feel the material, what a good, thick, serviceable silk it was. She was plainly so proud of it that I again complimented her on her taste, and congratulated her on having got so exactly what she wanted and such an excellent fit. Indeed, the dress suited her very well, for she was a dark, almost swarthy, black-haired, biggish woman, and stout, weighing over eleven stone. Her rather heavy face lighted up and grew quite animated at my compliments.

Then the other members of the circle began to arrive, singly or two at a time. There was Eric Magnus, who was even more sceptical than I, though for the last year he had ceased to deny, in anything like his old tone of conviction, that we did sometimes get genuine, inexplicable phenomena at Mrs. Morrel's séances. There were Harold Beveridge and Walters, the Professor of Mathematics, both of them very careful and shrewd observers of psychical phenomena; and there were Dr. and Mrs. Paterson, Mrs. Grant, Admiral Norton, and a man of the name of Thompson of whom I knew very little, since he had only lately attended the séances. These five were of the credulous type which sees, or makes itself see, anything, and were of very little account in matters psychical.

Of course, the circle was rather too large. I have always seen the best phenomena when the circle has been composed of three men and two women.

Last of all came two strangers, who, I gathered, had never sat with Mrs. Morrel, or with anyone else—a Mr. and Mrs. Longridge. Longridge was a man of about forty-five, of a short, square, stout figure, clean-shaven, with a heavy, masterful jaw, thin lips, and keen black eyes, deep-set under projecting brows. He looked a man of uncommon force of character; and I hoped that Mrs. Morrel would keep off trickery, for he was the very man, if he detected it, to make a row. I fancied that I had seen his face among a set of portraits of captains of industry in a magazine.

His wife was a very pretty, even beautiful, woman of about twenty-eight, with large, dark-brown eyes and dark-brown hair. Her cheeks were pale and she looked fragile; she gave me the impression of having been broken down by some great trouble. It was plain that she was strung up to the highest pitch; her eyes were restless and excited, and her lips kept twitching. Longridge looked rather bored.

Mrs. Morrel welcomed them with great deference, and Mrs. Longridge came into the room wearing a cloak of sables over her black evening gown. All the members of the circle, except Professor Walters, are rich people, but not to the point of being able to pay two thousand pounds for a sable cloak. I took it that Longridge was a millionaire. When his wife found that the room was quite warm, she gave him the cloak, and he laid it on the little writing-table, against the wall, by the door.

We were all assembled by a quarter to nine; and I explained to the Longridges the conditions of the séance, especially begging them on no account, whatever happened, to break the circle by loosing the hand of the person on either side of them. Then we settled down on our chairs in a half-circle before the cabinet, which was formed by a curtain hung on a rod across a corner of the room. The curtain was drawn back and it was quite plain that but for Mrs. Morrel's chair the cabinet was empty.

Mrs. Morrel went into it and drew the curtain. Magnus turned out two of the gas-jets of the chandelier, and left the third burning about three-quarters of an inch. It gave less light than a candle would have done.

We joined hands, and Mrs. Grant went to the piano and began to play softly. We talked quietly. I had placed myself between Mr. and Mrs. Longridge. Magnus sat on the other side of Longridge. I realised even more clearly that Mrs. Longridge was strung up to a pitch of extraordinary tenseness. She answered my occasional remarks to her in strained tones; and her hand was rigid, and so cold that it kept mine chilled. Two or three times I begged her to let herself relax, but it was no use.

Every now and then I felt her quiver. Longridge was relaxed enough; he was leaning back in his chair, his hand was warm and limp in mine, and two or three times I heard him sigh impatiently. It was plain that he had only come to please his wife, and expected nothing.

We sang the hymn "Lead, Kindly Light," and then we went on talking. It was about half an hour after we had sat down that I heard in the cabinet the sound of scratching which always preceded Mrs. Morrel's going into a trance.

The talk died down in a momentary hush; Mrs. Grant left the piano and sat down on her chair at the end of the half-circle nearest the piano; and Mrs. Longridge said, in a shaky whisper:

"Is it going to begin?"

"Very soon," I said, and I felt that she was quivering, or, to be exact, trembling violently; and after that she was trembling most of the time.

The first phenomenon was a ball of light. It began in a faint luminousness about three feet from the floor in front of the curtain of the cabinet, and grew stronger and stronger till it was a ball of greenish, phosphorescent light, some six inches in diameter, and about the strength of the light given out by those marine *animalculae* which are called sea-stars; not, that is, as bright as the light of a glow-worm. Longridge sat upright in his chair.

The ball of light disappeared suddenly, and from beyond the end of the half-circle a voice began to speak, the voice of Thomas. We were familiar with it; sometimes he would materialise and move about the room, an odd, dwarfish figure; sometimes we only heard his voice. Mrs. Longridge was still, no longer trembling, but breathing quickly.

I knew that we were going to have an interesting sitting. But it seemed to me that the atmosphere was different from that of any other sitting at which I had been present. There was a sense of strain in it, rather oppressive and unnerving. I thought Mrs. Longridge's emotion had infected me.

Two or three lights floated across the room and faded; as one of them passed it, I caught a glimpse of Thomas's rather impish face—only his face.

He talked for a while, the usual aimless, trivial, and rather tiresome talk, chiefly to Admiral Norton, who wanted to know what would be the upshot of a naval scandal which was agitating the public mind. Thomas's views on it were those of a schoolboy of fourteen.

Then he said: "Sister Sylvia is coming."

There came from the cabinet the figure of a nun, a familiar figure at Mrs. Morrel's séances. She went by the name of Sister Sylvia. She talked to one and another of us. There was very little more to her talk than to that of Thomas. Mrs. Longridge was panting softly, and holding my hand tighter; Longridge, too, had tightened his grip, and was leaning forward.

There was a breath of cold air (a very common phenomenon at séances), then Sister Sylvia said: "There's a little girl here. She wants——"

I heard Mrs. Longridge gasp, and without finishing her sentence, Sister Sylvia went back into the cabinet with quite unusual swiftness. It was almost, if one might say so, as if she had been sucked back into it.

Another light floated across the room and faded. Then the rings of the curtain grated softly along the rod, and there came out of the cabinet the figure of a child, a little girl. Then I saw that the curtain was half-drawn, a thing which had never happened at one of Mrs. Morrel's séances before, and I could see dimly the figure of Mrs. Morrel on her chair in the cabinet.

The child came straight to Mrs. Longridge. Mrs. Longridge sank back in her chair, gasping painfully, and her nerveless hand would have slipped from mine had I not held it firmly.

The child stood before her, and said in a faint, shrill voice: "Oh, Mummy!"

Mrs. Longridge burst out sobbing, tried vainly to tear her hand from mine, and cried wildly: "Oh, Maisie! Maisie!"

I heard Mrs. Morrel shuffle in the cabinet. Then suddenly Longridge's hand gripped mine with a vicelike, crushing grip. He said hoarsely: "Don't go back, Maisie! Stay with us—try to stay with us—hard!" Then he hissed: "Will her to stay, Grace! Hold her! Will her to stay!"

He crouched forward, and I saw the glimmer of his eyes staring at the dim figure of Mrs. Morrel.

Mrs. Longridge and the child were murmuring to one another in broken, staccato voices, just repeating one another's names. When Longridge had spoken, Mrs. Longridge was silent. She seemed to stiffen, and her breathing was slower, coming in long-drawn gasps; plainly she was concentrating herself in the effort of will.

Longridge was crushing my hand; I thought that the bones would go. The pain was confusing. I thought that the child had her arms round Mrs. Longridge's neck.

There were some seconds, perhaps fifteen, of tense stillness. It seemed to me that the air of the room grew more and more oppressive with the sense of a straining, silent struggle, but that feeling might have been caused by the pain of Longridge's grip. Then I felt rather than saw that the child was being drawn back to the cabinet. Longridge crouched forward in his intense effort, never stirred, never loosened his crushing grip.

Mrs. Grant burst out crying; Magnus cried in a high-pitched, squeaky whisper: "Keep still! Keep still! Don't break the circle!" I heard the Admiral rap out an oath; then I saw that Mrs. Morrel was swaying on her chair.

The child seemed to be about two feet from Mrs. Longridge, bent forward as though her arms were round her neck and she was holding on to it.

Then Mrs. Morrel rose from her chair, swaying, clutching at the air with twisting arms; then she pitched forward on her face, half in the cabinet and half out of it.

As she came to the ground the child cried in quite another voice, a deeper, louder voice:

"I can't get back!"

We were all on our feet at once.

Longridge cried: "Come along! Come along!" thrust me aside, and picked up the child.

Magnus sprang to the gas, but in his excitement, instead of turning it up, he turned it off, and we were in pitch darkness. The door opened; a sheet of light from the hall fell into the room, and in it I saw Longridge's face, very white and glistening with sweat. He was carrying the child in his arms, wrapped in his wife's sable cloak. I only caught a glimpse of them as he hurried out of the room. His wife followed him quickly, and slammed the door after her.

I made for the door. I ran into a chair; then I ran into Professor Walters. Just as my hand touched the wall I heard the house door bang.

The Admiral struck a match. I opened the door, ran down the hall, and opened the house door. A big, closed motor-car was gliding swiftly down the street.

I came quickly back to the room. The gas had been lighted, and everyone was talking at once, wildly. I hurried to Mrs. Morrel, who still lay where she had fallen, and raised her. To my amazement it was no more than if I were lifting a child of twelve. As I laid her on the sofa my sleeve-link caught in her dress. It tore a patch out of that strong new silk as if it had been tissue-paper. The bodice had fitted like a glove; it hung about her shrunken bust in great wrinkles. Her face was bloodless and shrunken; her black hair and eyebrows were a curious, dead, lustreless white; and, oddest of all, the iris, and even the black pupils of her eyes, had gone grey, as if the colour had been bleached out of them.

Mrs. Grant had a bottle of strong smelling-salts, the Admiral got some brandy from the servant, and we tried our best to revive her. Our efforts were useless. She was dead.

We sent for a doctor. He could do nothing. He talked about heart-failure, and seemed to have it firmly in his mind that Mrs. Morrel was an albino.

Eric Magnus and I were the last to leave, and we came away together.

As we turned up the street he said:

"It was a good thing that I noticed the draught when the door of the room was opened to let the child slip in."

"I noticed a breath of cold air; in fact, I noticed several during the evening," I said. "But if the door was opened, why didn't the light from the hall lamp fall into the room? It was burning brightly."

"Oh, it was turned down, and then up again," he said confidently.

"It might have been," said I; and for the next twenty yards he said nothing.

Then he broke out:

"It was a splendid fake—splendid! I never saw a better! What accomplices! It was first-rate acting—absolutely first-rate!"

"Yes; acting that turned the lady's hands icy.

And accomplices? An accomplice of Mrs. Morrel's in a two-thousand-pound sable cloak! That is a bit hard to swallow," I said.

"Hired, my dear fellow—hired," he said confidently.

"It might be," I said. "A hired cloak and a form of heart disease which turns a swarthy woman into an albino."

"Oh, yes, that was odd; but I have no doubt that it sometimes acts like that."

"Haven't you?" I said.

We separated at the end of the street, and I was glad to be rid of him. I wanted to think it out quietly. I could not; my mind was in a whirl, and it would not clear.

The next day I set about trying to find out something about the Longridges. I was quite unsuccessful; I could not find a trace of them. They were unknown in spiritist circles by name; no medium of my acquaintance recognised either of them from my description. Also, I could find no one of the name of Longridge among our captains of industry. I was forced to the conclusion that, like so many other people, they had come to the séance under false names. So many people are ashamed of their interest in spiritism.

NIGHT-SIDE

Joyce Carol Oates

ARGUABLY THE GREATEST LIVING writer in the world to have not yet been awarded the Nobel Prize for Literature (she has been regarded as a favorite by readers, critics, and bookies for about twenty-five years), Joyce Carol Oates (1938–) has enjoyed a career known for its excellence, popularity, and prolificacy. Born in Lockport, New York, in the northwestern part of the state, she began to write as a young child, attended Syracuse University on scholarship, and won a *Mademoiselle* magazine short story award at nineteen. Her first novel, *With Shuddering Fall* (1964), has been followed by more than a hundred books, including fifty novels, thirty-six short story collections, three children's books, five young adult novels, ten volumes of poetry, fourteen collections of essays and criticism, and eight volumes of plays; eleven of her novels of suspense were released under the pseudonyms Rosamond Smith and Lauren Kelly. An overwhelming number of her novels and short stories feature such subjects as violence, sexual abuse, murder, racial tensions, and class conflicts. Many of her fictional works have been based on real-life incidents, including violent crimes.

As prolific as her writing career has been, so, too, has been the extraordinary number of major literary prizes and honors awarded to her, including a National Book Award for *them* (1969), as well as five other nominations; three Pulitzer Prize nominations; two O. Henry Awards for short stories; and a Bram Stoker Award for the novel *Zombie* (1995). Her bestselling books have been *We Were the Mulvaneys* (1995; aired on television in 2002 with Beau Bridges and Blythe Danner), an Oprah Book Club selection; and *Blonde* (2000; made for television in 2001 with Poppy Montgomery), a novel based on the life of Marilyn Monroe. The 1996 film *Foxfire* (starring Cathy Moriarty, Hedy Burress, and Angelina Jolie) was an adaptation of Oates's 1993 novel *Foxfire: Confessions of a Girl Gang*.

"Night-Side" was first published in the collection *Night-Side* (New York, Vanguard, 1977).

Night-Side

JOYCE CAROL OATES

6 February 1887. Quincy, Massachusetts.
Montague House.

Disturbing experience at Mrs. A——'s home
yesterday evening. Few theatrics—comfortable though rather pathetically shabby surroundings—an only mildly sinister atmosphere
(especially in contrast to the Walpurgis Night

presented by that shameless charlatan in Portsmouth: the Dwarf Eustace who presumed to
introduce me to Swedenborg himself, under the
erroneous impression that I am a member of the
Church of the New Jerusalem—*I!*). Nevertheless I came away disturbed, and my conversation
with Dr. Moore afterward, at dinner, though
dispassionate and even, at times, a bit flippant,

did not settle my mind. Perry Moore is of course a hearty materialist, an Aristotelian-Spencerian with a love of good food and drink, and an appreciation of the more nonsensical vagaries of life; when in his company I tend to support that general view, as I do at the University as well—for there is a terrific pull in my nature toward the gregarious that I cannot resist. (That I do not wish to resist.) Once I am alone with my thoughts, however, I am accursed with doubts about my own position and nothing seems more precarious than my intellectual "convictions."

The more hardened members of our Society, like Perry Moore, are apt to put the issue bluntly: Is Mrs. A—— of Quincy a conscious or unconscious fraud? The conscious frauds are relatively easy to deal with; once discovered, they prefer to erase themselves from further consideration. The unconscious frauds are not, in a sense, "frauds" at all. It would certainly be difficult to prove criminal intention. Mrs. A——, for instance, does not accept money or gifts so far as we have been able to determine, and both Perry Moore and I noted her courteous but firm refusal of the Judge's offer to send her and her husband (presumably ailing?) on holiday to England in the spring. She is a mild, self-effacing, rather stocky woman in her mid-fifties who wears her hair parted in the center, like several of my maiden aunts, and whose sole item of adornment was an old-fashioned cameo brooch; her black dress had the appearance of having been homemade, though it was attractive enough, and freshly ironed. According to the Society's records she has been a practicing medium now for six years. Yet she lives, still, in an undistinguished section of Quincy, in a neighborhood of modest frame dwellings. The A——s' house is in fairly good condition, especially considering the damage routinely done by our winters, and the only room we saw, the parlor, is quite ordinary, with overstuffed chairs and the usual cushions and a monstrous horsehair sofa and, of course, the oaken table; the atmosphere would have been so conventional as to have seemed disappointing had not Mrs. A—— made an attempt to brighten it, or perhaps to give it a glamourously occult air, by hanging certain watercolors about the room. (She claims that the watercolors were "done" by one of her contact spirits, a young Iroquois girl who died in the seventeen seventies of smallpox. They are touchingly garish—mandalas and triangles and stylized eyeballs and even a transparent Cosmic Man with Indian-black hair.)

At last night's sitting there were only three persons in addition to Mrs. A——. Judge T—— of the New York State Supreme Court (now retired); Dr. Moore; and I, Jarvis Williams. Dr. Moore and I came out from Cambridge under the aegis of the Society for Psychical Research in order to make a preliminary study of the kind of mediumship Mrs. A—— affects. We did not bring a stenographer along this time though Mrs. A—— indicated her willingness to have the sitting transcribed; she struck me as being rather warmly cooperative, and even interested in our formal procedures, though Perry Moore remarked afterward at dinner that she had struck him as "noticeably reluctant." She was, however, flustered at the start of the séance and for a while it seemed as if we and the Judge might have made the trip for nothing. (She kept waving her plump hands about like an embarrassed hostess, apologizing for the fact that the spirits were evidently in a "perverse uncommunicative mood tonight.")

She did go into trance eventually, however. The four of us were seated about the heavy round table from approximately 6:50 p.m. to 9 p.m. For nearly forty-five minutes Mrs. A—— made abortive attempts to contact her Chief Communicator and then slipped abruptly into trance (dramatically, in fact: her eyes rolled back in her head in a manner that alarmed me at first), and a personality named Webley appeared. "Webley's" voice appeared to be coming from several directions during the course of the sitting. At all times it was at least three yards from Mrs. A——; despite the semi-dark of the parlor I believe I could see the woman's mouth and throat clearly enough, and I could not detect any obvious signs of ventriloquism. (Perry Moore, who is more experienced than I in psychical research, and rather more casual about the whole phenomenon, claims he has witnessed feats of ventriloquism that would make poor Mrs. A—— look quite shabby in comparison.) "Webley's" voice was raw, sing-song, peculiarly disturbing. At times it was shrill and at other times so faint as to be nearly inaudible. Something brattish about it. Exasperating. "Webley" took care to pronounce his final *g*'s in a self-conscious manner, quite unlike Mrs. A——. (Which could be, of course, a deliberate ploy.)

This Webley is one of Mrs. A——'s most frequent manifesting spirits, though he is not the most reliable. Her Chief Communicator is a Scots patriarch who lived "in the time of Merlin" and who is evidently very wise; unfortunately he did not choose to appear yesterday evening. Instead, Webley presided. He is supposed to have died some seventy-five years ago at the age of nineteen in a house just up the street from the A——s'. He was either a butcher's helper or an apprentice tailor. He died in a fire—or by a "slow dreadful crippling disease"—or beneath a horse's hooves, in a freakish accident; during the course of the sitting he alluded self-pityingly to his death but seemed to have forgotten the exact details. At the very end of the evening he addressed me directly as Dr. Williams of Harvard University, saying that since I had influential friends in Boston I could help him with his career—it turned out he had written hundreds of songs and poems and parables but none had been published; would I please find a publisher for his work? Life had treated him so unfairly. His talent—his genius—had been lost to humanity. I had it within my power to help him, he claimed, was I not *obliged* to help him . . . ? He then sang one of his songs, which sounded to me like an old ballad; many of the words were so shrill as to be unintelligible, but he sang it just the same, repeating the verses in a haphazard order:

This ae nighte, this ae nighte,
* —Every nighte and alle,*
Fire and fleet and candle-lighte,
* And Christe receive thy saule.*

When thou from hence away art past,
* —Every nighte and alle,*
To Whinny-muir thou com'st at last:
* And Christe receive thy saule.*

From Brig o' Dread when thou may'st pass,
* —Every nighte and alle,*
The whinnes sall prick thee to the bare bane:
* And Christe receive thy saule.*

The elderly Judge T—— had come up from New York City in order, as he earnestly put it, to "speak directly to his deceased wife as he was never able to do while she was living"; but Webley treated the old gentleman in a high-handed, cavalier manner, as if the occasion were not at all serious. He kept saying, "Who is there tonight? *Who* is there? Let them introduce themselves again—I don't *like* strangers! I tell you I don't *like* strangers!" Though Mrs. A—— had informed us beforehand that we would witness no physical phenomena, there were, from time to time, glimmerings of light in the darkened room, hardly more than the tiny pulsations of light made by fireflies; and both Perry Moore and I felt the table vibrating beneath our fingers. At about the time when Webley gave way to the spirit of Judge T——'s wife, the temperature in the room seemed to drop suddenly and I remember being gripped by a sensation of panic—but it lasted only an instant and I was soon myself again. (Dr. Moore claimed not to have noticed any drop in temperature and Judge T—— was so rattled after the sitting that it would have been pointless to question him.)

The séance proper was similar to others I have attended. A spirit—or a voice—laid claim to being the late Mrs. T——; this spirit addressed the survivor in a peculiarly intense, urgent manner, so that it was rather embarrassing to be present. Judge T—— was soon weeping.

His deeply creased face glistened with tears like a child's.

"Why Darrie! *Darrie!* Don't cry! Oh don't cry!" the spirit said. "No one is dead, Darrie. There is no death. No death! . . . Can you hear me, Darrie? Why are you so frightened? So upset? No need, Darrie, no need! Grandfather and Lucy and I are together here—happy together. Darrie, look up! Be brave, my dear! My poor frightened dear! We never knew each other, did we? My poor dear! My love! . . . I saw you in a great transparent house, a great burning house; poor Darrie, they told me you were ill, you were weak with fever; all the rooms of the house were aflame and the staircase was burnt to cinders, but there were figures walking up and down, Darrie, great numbers of them, and you were among them, dear, stumbling in your fright—so clumsy! Look up, dear, and shade your eyes, and you will see me. Grandfather helped me—did you know? Did I call out his name at the end? My dear, my darling, it all happened so quickly—we never knew each other, did we? Don't be hard on Annie! Don't be cruel! Darrie? Why are you crying?" And gradually the spirit voice grew fainter; or perhaps something went wrong and the channels of communication were no longer clear. There were repetitions, garbled phrases, meaningless queries of "Dear? Dear?" that the Judge's replies did not seem to placate. The spirit spoke of her gravesite, and of a trip to Italy taken many years before, and of a dead or unborn baby, and again of Annie— evidently Judge T——'s daughter; but the jumble of words did not always make sense and it was a great relief when Mrs. A—— suddenly woke from her trance.

Judge T—— rose from the table, greatly agitated. He wanted to call the spirit back; he had not asked her certain crucial questions; he had been overcome by emotion and had found it difficult to speak, to interrupt the spirit's monologue. But Mrs. A—— (who looked shockingly tired) told him the spirit would not return again that night and they must not make any attempt to call it back.

"The other world obeys its own laws," Mrs. A—— said in her small, rather reedy voice.

We left Mrs. A——'s home shortly after 9:00 p.m. I too was exhausted; I had not realized how absorbed I had been in the proceedings.

Judge T—— is also staying at Montague House, but he was too upset after the sitting to join us for dinner. He assured us, though, that the spirit was authentic—the voice had been his wife's, he was certain of it, he would stake his life on it. She had never called him "Darrie" during her lifetime, wasn't it odd that she called him "Darrie" now?—and was so concerned for him, so loving?—and concerned for their daughter as well? He was very moved. He had a great deal to think about. (Yes, he'd had a fever some weeks ago—a severe attack of bronchitis and a fever; in fact, he had not completely recovered.) What was extraordinary about the entire experience was the wisdom revealed: There is no death.

There is no death.

Dr. Moore and I dined heartily on roast crown of lamb, spring potatoes with peas, and buttered cabbage. We were served two kinds of bread—German rye and sour-cream rolls; the hotel's butter was superb; the wine excellent; the dessert—crepes with cream and toasted almonds—looked marvelous, though I had not any appetite for it. Dr. Moore was ravenously hungry. He talked as he ate, often punctuating his remarks with rich bursts of laughter. It was his opinion, of course, that the medium was a fraud—and not a very skillful fraud, either. In his fifteen years of amateur, intermittent investigations he had encountered far more skillful mediums. Even the notorious Eustace with his levitating tables and hobgoblin chimes and shrieks was cleverer than Mrs. A——; one knew of course that Eustace was a cheat, but one was hard pressed to explain his method. Whereas Mrs. A—— was quite transparent.

Dr. Moore spoke for some time in his amiable, dogmatic way. He ordered brandy for both of us, though it was nearly midnight when we finished our dinner and I was anxious to get to bed. (I hoped to rise early and work on a lecture dealing with Kant's approach to the problem of Free Will, which I would be delivering in a few days.) But Dr. Moore enjoyed talking and seemed to have been invigorated by our experience at Mrs. A——'s.

At the age of forty-three Perry Moore is only four years my senior, but he has the air, in my presence at least, of being considerably older. He is a second cousin of my mother's, a very successful physician with a bachelor's flat and office in Louisburg Square; his failure to marry, or his refusal, is one of Boston's perennial mysteries. Everyone agrees that he is learned, witty, charming, and extraordinarily intelligent. Striking rather than conventionally handsome, with a dark, lustrous beard and darkly bright eyes, he is an excellent amateur violinist, an enthusiastic sailor, and a lover of literature—his favorite writers are Fielding, Shakespeare, Horace, and Dante. He is, of course, the perfect investigator in spiritualist matters since he is detached from the phenomena he observes and yet he is indefatigably curious; he has a positive love, a mania, for facts. Like the true scientist he seeks facts that, assembled, may possibly give rise to hypotheses: he does not set out with a hypothesis in mind, like a sort of basket into which certain facts may be tossed, helter-skelter, while others are conveniently ignored. In all things he is an empiricist who accepts nothing on faith.

"If the woman is a fraud, then," I say hesitantly, "you believe she is a self-deluded fraud? And her spirits' information is gained by means of telepathy?"

"Telepathy indeed. There can be no other explanation," Dr. Moore says emphatically. "By some means not yet known to science . . . by some uncanny means she suppresses her conscious personality . . . and thereby releases other, secondary personalities that have the power of seizing upon others' thoughts and memories. It's done in a way not understood by science at the present time. But it will be understood eventually. Our investigations into the unconscious powers of the human mind are just beginning; we're on the threshold, really, of a new era."

"So she simply picks out of her clients' minds whatever they want to hear," I say slowly. "And from time to time she can even tease them a little—insult them, even: she can unloose a creature like that obnoxious Webley upon a person like Judge T—— without fear of being discovered. Telepathy. . . . Yes, that would explain a great deal. Very nearly everything we witnessed tonight."

"*Everything*, I should say," Dr. Moore says.

In the coach returning to Cambridge I set aside Kant and my lecture notes and read Sir Thomas Browne: *Light that makes all things seen, makes some things invisible. The greatest mystery of Religion is expressed by adumbration.*

19 March 1887. Cambridge. 11 p.m.

Walked ten miles this evening; must clear cobwebs from mind.

Unhealthy atmosphere. Claustrophobic. Last night's sitting in Quincy—a most unpleasant experience.

(Did not tell my wife what happened. Why is she so curious about the Spirit World?—about Perry Moore?)

My body craves more violent physical activity. In the summer, thank God, I will be able to swim in the ocean: the most strenuous and challenging of exercises.

Jotting down notes re the Quincy experience:

I. Fraud

Mrs. A——, possibly with accomplices, conspires to deceive: she does research into her clients' lives beforehand, possibly bribes servants. She is either a very skillful ventriloquist or works with someone who is. (Husband? Son? The husband is a retired cabinet-maker said to be in poor health;

possibly consumptive. The son, married, lives in Waterbury.)

Her stated wish to avoid publicity and her declining of payment may simply be ploys; she may intend to make a great deal of money at some future time.

(Possibility of blackmail?—might be likely in cases similar to Perry Moore's.)

II. Non-fraud
Naturalistic
1. Telepathy. She reads minds of clients.
2. "Multiple personality" of medium. Aspects of her own buried psyche are released as her conscious personality is suppressed. These secondary beings are in mysterious rapport with the "secondary" personalities of the clients.

Spiritualistic
1. The controls are genuine communicators, intermediaries between our world and the world of the dead. These spirits give way to other spirits, who then speak through the medium; or
2. These spirits *influence* the medium, who relays their messages using her own vocabulary. Their personalities are then filtered through and limited by hers.
3. The spirits are not those of the deceased; they are perverse, willful spirits. (Perhaps demons? But there are no demons.)

III. Alternative hypothesis
Madness: the medium is mad, the clients are mad, even the detached, rationalist investigators are mad.

Yesterday evening at Mrs. A——'s home, the second sitting Perry Moore and I observed together, along with Miss Bradley, a stenographer from the Society, and two legitimate clients—a Brookline widow, Mrs. P——, and her daughter Clara, a handsome young woman in her early twenties. Mrs. A—— exactly as she appeared to us in February; possibly a little stouter. Wore black dress and cameo brooch. Served Lapsang tea, tiny sandwiches, and biscuits when we arrived shortly after 6 p.m. Seemed quite friendly to Perry, Miss Bradley, and me; fussed over us, like any hostess; chattered a bit about the cold spell. Mrs. P—— and her daughter arrived at six-thirty and the sitting began shortly thereafter.

Jarring from the very first. A babble of spirit voices. Mrs. A—— in trance, head flung back, mouth gaping, eyes rolled upward. Queer. Unnerving. I glanced at Dr. Moore but he seemed unperturbed, as always. The widow and her daughter, however, looked as frightened as I felt.

Why are we here, sitting around this table?

What do we believe we will discover?

What are the risks we face . . . ?

"Webley" appeared and disappeared in a matter of minutes. His shrill, raw, aggrieved voice was supplanted by that of a creature of indeterminate sex who babbled in Gaelic. This creature in turn was supplanted by a hoarse German, a man who identified himself as Felix; he spoke a curiously ungrammatical German. For some minutes he and two or three other spirits quarreled. (Each declared himself Mrs. A——'s Chief Communicator for the evening.) Small lights flickered in the semi-dark of the parlor and the table quivered beneath my fingers and I felt, or believed I felt, something brushing against me, touching the back of my head. I shuddered violently but regained my composure at once. An unidentified voice proclaimed in English that the Spirit of our Age was Mars: there would be a catastrophic war shortly and most of the world's population would be destroyed. All atheists would be destroyed. Mrs. A—— shook her head from side to side as if trying to wake. Webley appeared, crying "Hello? Hello? I can't see anyone! Who is there? Who has called me?" but was again supplanted by another spirit who shouted long strings of words in a foreign language. [Note: I discovered a few days later that this language was Walachian, a Romanian dialect. Of course Mrs. A——, whose ancestors are English, could not possibly have known Walachian, and I rather doubt that the woman has even heard of the Walachian people.]

The sitting continued in this chaotic way for some minutes. Mrs. P—— must have been quite disappointed, since she had wanted to be put in contact with her deceased husband. (She needed advice on whether or not to sell certain pieces of property.) Spirits babbled freely in English, German, Gaelic, French, even in Latin, and at one point Dr. Moore queried a spirit in Greek, but the spirit retreated at once as if not equal to Dr. Moore's wit. The atmosphere was alarming but at the same time rather manic; almost jocular. I found myself suppressing laughter. Something touched the back of my head and I shivered violently and broke into perspiration, but the experience was not altogether unpleasant; it would be very difficult for me to characterize it.

And then—

And then, suddenly, everything changed. There was complete calm. A spirit voice spoke gently out of a corner of the room, addressing Perry Moore by his first name in a slow, tentative, groping way. "Perry? Perry . . . ?" Dr. Moore jerked about in his seat. He was astonished; I could see by his expression that the voice belonged to someone he knew.

"Perry . . . ? This is Brandon. I've waited so long for you, Perry, how could you be so selfish? I forgave you. Long ago. You couldn't help your cruelty and I couldn't help my innocence. Perry? My glasses have been broken—I can't see. I've been afraid for so long, Perry, please have mercy on me! I can't bear it any longer. I didn't *know* what it would be like. There are crowds of people here, but we can't see one another, we don't know one another, we're strangers, there is a universe of strangers—I can't see anyone clearly—I've been lost for twenty years, Perry, I've been waiting for you for twenty years! You don't dare turn away again, Perry! Not again! Not after so long!"

Dr. Moore stumbled to his feet, knocking his chair aside.

"No—Is it—I don't believe—"

"Perry? Perry? Don't abandon me again, Perry! Not again!"

"What is this?" Dr. Moore cried.

He was on his feet now; Mrs. A—— woke from her trance with a groan. The women from Brookline were very upset and I must admit that I was in a mild state of terror, my shirt and my underclothes drenched with perspiration.

The sitting was over. It was only seven-thirty.

"Brandon?" Dr. Moore cried. "Wait. Where are—? Brandon? Can you hear me? Where are you? Why did you do it, Brandon? Wait! Don't leave! Can't anyone call him back—Can't anyone help me—"

Mrs. A—— rose unsteadily. She tried to take Dr. Moore's hands in hers but he was too agitated.

"I heard only the very last words," she said. "They're always that way—so confused, so broken—the poor things—Oh, what a pity! It wasn't murder, was it? Not murder! Suicide—? I believe suicide is even worse for them! The poor broken things, they wake in the other world and are utterly, utterly lost—they have no guides, you see—no help in crossing over—They are completely alone for eternity—"

"Can't you call him back?" Dr. Moore asked wildly. He was peering into a corner of the parlor, slightly stooped, his face distorted as if he were staring into the sun. "Can't someone help me? . . . Brandon? Are you here? Are you here somewhere? For God's sake can't someone help!"

"Dr. Moore, please, the spirits are gone—the sitting is over for tonight—"

"You foolish old woman, leave me alone! Can't you see I—I—I must not lose him—Call him back, will you? I insist! I insist!"

"Dr. Moore, please—You mustn't shout—"

"I said call him back! At once! *Call him back!*"

Then he burst into tears. He stumbled against the table and hid his face in his hands and wept like a child; he wept as if his heart had been broken.

And so today I have been reliving the séance. Taking notes, trying to determine what happened. A brisk windy walk of ten miles. Head buzzing with ideas. Fraud? Deceit? Telepathy? Madness?

What a spectacle! Dr. Perry Moore calling after a spirit, begging it to return—and then crying, afterward, in front of four astonished witnesses.

Dr. Perry Moore of all people.

My dilemma: whether I should report last night's incident to Dr. Rowe, the president of the Society, or whether I should say nothing about it and request that Miss Bradley say nothing. It would be tragic if Perry's professional reputation were to be damaged by a single evening's misadventure; and before long all of Boston would be talking.

In his present state, however, he is likely to tell everyone about it himself.

At Montague House the poor man was unable to sleep. He would have kept me up all night had I had the stamina to endure his excitement.

There *are* spirits! There have always been spirits!

His entire life up to the present time has been misspent!

And of course, most important of all—there is no death!

He paced about my hotel room, pulling at his beard nervously. At times there were tears in his eyes. He seemed to want a response of some kind from me but whenever I started to speak he interrupted; he was not really listening.

"Now at last I know. I can't undo my knowledge," he said in a queer hoarse voice. "Amazing, isn't it, after so many years . . . so many wasted years. . . . Ignorance has been my lot, darkness . . . and a hideous complacency. My God, when I consider my deluded smugness! I am so ashamed, so ashamed. All along people like Mrs. A—— have been in contact with a world of such power . . . and people like me have been toiling in ignorance, accumulating material achievements, expending our energies in idiotic transient things. . . . But all that is changed now. Now I know. I *know*. There is no death, as the Spiritualists have always told us."

"But, Perry, don't you think—Isn't it possible that—"

"I *know*," he said quietly. "It's as clear to me as if I had crossed over into that other world myself. Poor Brandon! He's no older now than he was *then*. The poor boy, the poor tragic soul! To think that he's still living after so many years. . . . Extraordinary. . . . It makes my head spin," he said slowly. For a moment he stood without speaking. He pulled at his beard, then absently touched his lips with his fingers, then wiped at his eyes. He seemed to have forgotten me. When he spoke again his voice was hollow, rather ghastly. He sounded drugged. "I . . . I had been thinking of him as . . . as dead, you know. As dead. Twenty years. Dead. And now, tonight, to be forced to realize that . . . that he isn't dead after all. . . . It was laudanum he took. I found him. His rooms on the third floor of Weld Hall. I found him, I had no real idea, none at all, not until I read the note . . . and of course I destroyed the note . . . I had to, you see: for his sake. For his sake more than mine. It was because he realized there could be no . . . no hope. . . . Yet he called me cruel! You heard him, Jarvis, didn't you? Cruel! I suppose I was. Was I? I don't know what to think. I must talk with him again. I . . . I don't know what to . . . what to think. I . . . ."

"You look awfully tired, Perry. It might be a good idea to go to bed," I said weakly.

" . . . recognized his voice at once. Oh at once: no doubt. None. What a revelation! And my life so misspent. . . . Treating people's *bodies*. Absurd. I know now that nothing matters except that other world . . . nothing matters except our dead, our beloved dead . . . who are *not dead*. What a colossal revelation . . . ! Why, it will change the entire course of history. It will alter men's minds throughout the world. You were there, Jarvis, so you understand. You were a witness. . . ."

"But—"

"You'll bear witness to the truth of what I am saying?"

He stared at me, smiling. His eyes were bright and threaded with blood.

I tried to explain to him as courteously and sympathetically as possible that his experience at Mrs. A——'s was not substantially different from the experiences many people have had at séances. "And always in the past psychical researchers have taken the position—"

"You were *there*," he said angrily. "You heard Brandon's voice as clearly as I did. Don't deny it!"

"—have taken the position that—that the phenomenon can be partly explained by the telepathic powers of the medium—"

"That was Brandon's *voice*," Perry said. "I felt his presence, I tell you! *His*. Mrs. A—— had nothing to do with it—nothing at all. I feel as if . . . as if I could call Brandon back by myself. . . . I feel his presence even now. Close about me. He isn't dead, you see; no one is dead, there's a universe of . . . of people who are not dead. . . . Parents, grandparents, sisters, brothers, everyone . . . everyone. . . . How can you deny, Jarvis, the evidence of your own senses? You were there with me tonight and you know as well as I do. . . ."

"Perry, I don't *know*. I did hear a voice, yes, but we've heard voices before at other sittings, haven't we? There are always voices. There are always 'spirits.' The Society has taken the position that the spirits could be real, of course, but that there are other hypotheses that are perhaps more likely—"

"Other hypotheses indeed!" Perry said irritably. "You're like a man with his eyes shut tight who refuses to open them out of sheer cowardice. Like the cardinals refusing to look through Galileo's telescope! And you have pretensions of being a man of learning, of science. . . . Why, we've got to destroy all the records we've made so far; they're a slander on the world of the spirits. Thank God we didn't file a report yet on Mrs. A——! It would be so embarrassing to be forced to call it back. . . ."

"Perry, please. Don't be angry. I want only to remind you of the fact that we've been present at other sittings, haven't we?—and we've witnessed others responding emotionally to certain phenomena. Judge T——, for instance. He was convinced he'd spoken with his wife. But you must remember, don't you, that you and I were not at all convinced . . . ? It seemed to us more likely that Mrs. A—— is able, through extrasensory powers we don't quite understand, to read the minds of her clients, and then to project certain voices out into the room so that it sounds as if they are coming from other people. . . . You even said, Perry, that she wasn't a very skillful ventriloquist. You said—"

"What does it matter what, in my ignorance, I said?" he cried. "Isn't it enough that I've been humiliated? That my entire life has been turned about? Must you insult me as well—sitting there so smugly and insulting *me*? I think I can make claim to being someone whom you might respect."

And so I assured him that I did respect him. And he walked about the room, wiping at his eyes, greatly agitated. He spoke again of his friend, Brandon Gould, and of his own ignorance, and of the important mission we must undertake to inform men and women of the true state of affairs. I tried to talk with him, to reason with him, but it was hopeless. He scarcely listened to me.

". . . must inform the world . . . crucial truth. . . . There is no death, you see. Never was. Changes civilization, changes the course of history. Jarvis?" he said groggily. "You see? *There is no death*."

25 March 1887. Cambridge.

Disquieting rumors re Perry Moore. Heard today at the University that one of Dr. Moore's patients (a brother-in-law of Dean Barker) was extremely offended by his behavior during a consultation last week. Talk of his having been drunk—which I find incredible. If the poor man appeared to be excitable and not his customary self, it was not because he was *drunk*, surely.

Another far-fetched tale told me by my wife, who heard it from her sister Maude: Perry Moore went to church (St. Aidan's Episcopal

Church on Mount Street) for the first time in a decade, sat alone, began muttering and laughing during the sermon, and finally got to his feet and walked out, creating quite a stir. *What delusions! What delusions!*—he was said to have muttered.

I fear for the poor man's sanity.

31 March 1887. Cambridge. 4 a.m.

Sleepless night. Dreamed of swimming . . . swimming in the ocean . . . enjoying myself as usual when suddenly the water turns thick . . . turns to mud. Hideous! Indescribably awful. I was swimming nude in the ocean, by moonlight, I believe, ecstatically happy, entirely alone, when the water turned to mud. . . . Vile, disgusting mud; faintly warm; sucking at my body. Legs, thighs, torso, arms. Horrible. Woke in terror. Drenched with perspiration: pajamas wet. One of the most frightening nightmares of my adulthood.

A message from Perry Moore came yesterday just before dinner. Would I like to join him in visiting Mrs. A—— sometime soon, in early April perhaps, on a noninvestigative basis . . . ? He is uncertain now of the morality of our "investigating" Mrs. A—— or any other medium.

4 April 1887. Cambridge.

Spent the afternoon from two to five at William James's home on Irving Street, talking with Professor James of the inexplicable phenomenon of consciousness. He is robust as always, rather irreverent, supremely confident in a way I find enviable; rather like Perry Moore before his conversion. (Extraordinary eyes—so piercing, quick, playful; a graying beard liberally threaded with white; close-cropped graying hair; a large, curving, impressive forehead; a manner intelligent and graceful and at the same time rough-edged, as if he anticipates or perhaps even hopes for recalcitration in his listeners.) We both find conclusive the ideas set forth in Binét's *Alterations of Personality* . . . unsettling as these ideas may be to the rationalist position. James speaks

of a *peculiarity* in the constitution of human nature: that is, the fact that we inhabit not only our ego-consciousness but a wide field of psychological experience (most clearly represented by the phenomenon of memory, which no one can adequately explain) over which we have no control whatsoever. In fact, we are not generally aware of this field of consciousness.

We inhabit a lighted sphere, then; and about us is a vast penumbra of memories, reflections, feelings, and stray uncoordinated thoughts that "belong" to us theoretically, but that do not seem to be part of our conscious identity. (I was too timid to ask Professor James whether it might be the case that we do not inevitably own these aspects of the personality—that such phenomena belong as much to the objective world as to our subjective selves.) It is quite possible that there is an element of some indeterminate kind: oceanic, timeless, and living, against which the individual being constructs temporary barriers as part of an ongoing process of unique, particularized survival; like the ocean itself, which appears to separate islands that are in fact not "islands" at all, but aspects of the earth firmly joined together below the surface of the water. Our lives, then, resemble these islands. . . . All this is no more than a possibility, Professor James and I agreed.

James is acquainted, of course, with Perry Moore. But he declined to speak on the subject of the poor man's increasingly eccentric behavior when I alluded to it. (It may be that he knows even more about the situation than I do—he enjoys a multitude of acquaintances in Cambridge and Boston.) I brought our conversation round several times to the possibility of the *naturalness* of the conversion experience in terms of the individual's evolution of self, no matter how his family, his colleagues, and society in general viewed it, and Professor James appeared to agree; at least he did not emphatically disagree. He maintains a healthy skepticism, of course, regarding Spiritualist claims, and all evangelical and enthusiastic religious movements, though he is, at the same time, a highly articulate foe of the "rationalist" position and he believes that psychical research of the kind some of us are attempting will eventually unearth riches—revealing aspects of the human psyche otherwise closed to our scrutiny.

"The fearful thing," James said, "is that we are at all times vulnerable to incursions from the 'other side' of the personality. . . . We cannot determine the nature of the total personality simply because much of it, perhaps most, is hidden from us. . . . When we are invaded, then, we are overwhelmed and surrender immediately. Emotionally charged intuitions, hunches, guesses, even ideas may be the least aggressive of these incursions; but there are visual and auditory hallucinations, and forms of automatic behavior not controlled by the conscious mind. . . . Ah, you're thinking I am simply describing insanity?"

I stared at him, quite surprised.

"No. Not at all. Not at all," I said at once.

Reading through my grandfather's journals, begun in East Anglia many years before my birth. Another world then. Another language, now lost to us. *Man is sinful by nature. God's justice takes precedence over His mercy.* The dogma of Original Sin: something brutish about the innocence of that belief. And yet consoling. . . .

Fearful of sleep since my dreams are so troubled now. The voices of impudent spirits (Immanuel Kant himself come to chide me for having made too much of his categories—!), stray shouts and whispers I cannot decipher, the faces of my own beloved dead hovering near, like carnival masks, insubstantial and possibly fraudulent. Impatient with my wife, who questions me too closely on these personal matters; annoyed from time to time, in the evenings especially, by the silliness of the children. (The eldest is twelve now and should know better.) Dreading to receive another lengthy letter—sermon, really—from Perry Moore re his "new position," and yet perversely hoping one will come soon.

I must know.
(Must know *what* . . . ?)
I must know.

10 April 1887. Boston. St. Aidan's Episcopal Church.

Funeral service this morning for Perry Moore; dead at forty-three.

17 April 1887. Seven Hills, New Hampshire.

A weekend retreat. No talk. No need to think.

Visiting with a former associate, author of numerous books. Cartesian specialist. Elderly. Partly deaf. Extraordinarily kind to me. (Did not ask about the Department or about my work.) Intensely interested in animal behavior now, in observation primarily; fascinated with the phenomenon of hibernation.

He leaves me alone for hours. He sees something in my face I cannot see myself.

The old consolations of a cruel but just God: ludicrous today.

In the nineteenth century we live free of God. We live in the illusion of freedom-of-God.

Dozing off in the guest room of this old farmhouse and then waking abruptly. *Is someone here? Is someone here?* My voice queer, hushed, childlike. *Please: is someone here?*

Silence.

Query: Is the penumbra outside consciousness all that was ever meant by "God"?

Query: Is inevitability all that was ever meant by "God"?

God—the body of fate we inhabit, then; no more and no less.

God pulled Perry down into the body of fate: into Himself. (Or Itself.) As Professor James might say, Dr. Moore was "vulnerable" to an assault from the other side.

At any rate he is dead. They buried him last Saturday.

25 April 1887. Cambridge.

Shelves of books. The sanctity of books. Kant, Plato, Schopenhauer, Descartes, Hume, Hegel, Spinoza. The others. All. Nietzsche, Spencer, Leibnitz (on whom I did a torturous Master's thesis). Plotinus. Swedenborg. *The Transactions of the American Society for Psychical Research.* Voltaire. Locke. Rousseau. And Berkeley: the good Bishop adrift in a dream.

An etching by Halbrech above my desk, *The Thames 1801.* Water too black. Inky-black. Thick with mud . . . ? Filthy water in any case.

Perry's essay, forty-five scribbled pages. "The Challenge of the Future." Given to me several weeks ago by Dr. Rowe, who feared rejecting it for the *Transactions* but could not, of course, accept it. I can read only a few pages at a time, then push it aside, too moved to continue. Frightened also.

The man had gone insane.

Died insane.

Personality broken: broken bits of intellect.

His argument passionate and disjointed, with no pretense of objectivity. Where some weeks ago he had taken the stand that it was immoral to investigate the Spirit World, now he took the stand that it was imperative we do so. We are on the brink of a new age . . . new knowledge of the universe . . . comparable to the stormy transitional period between the Ptolemaic and the Copernican theories of the universe. . . . More experiments required. Money. Donations. Subsidies by private institutions. All psychological research must be channeled into a systematic study of the Spirit World and the ways by which we can communicate with that world. Mediums like Mrs. A—— must be brought to centers of learning like Harvard and treated with the respect their genius deserves. Their value to civilization is, after all, beyond estimation. They must be rescued from arduous and routine lives

where their genius is drained off into vulgar pursuits . . . they must be rescued from a clientele that is mainly concerned with being put into contact with deceased relatives for utterly trivial, self-serving reasons. Men of learning must realize the gravity of the situation. Otherwise we will fail, we will stagger beneath the burden, we will be defeated, ignobly, and it will remain for the twentieth century to discover the existence of the Spirit Universe that surrounds the Material Universe, and to determine the exact ways by which one world is related to another.

Perry Moore died of a stroke on the eighth of April; died instantaneously on the steps of the Bedford Club shortly after 2 p.m. Passers-by saw a very excited, red-faced gentleman with an open collar push his way through a small gathering at the top of the steps—and then suddenly fall, as if shot down.

In death he looked like quite another person: his features sharp, the nose especially pointed. Hardly the handsome Perry Moore everyone had known.

He had come to a meeting of the Society, though it was suggested by Dr. Rowe and by others (including myself) that he stay away. Of course he came to argue. To present his "new position." To insult the other members. (He was contemptuous of a rather poorly organized paper on the medium Miss E—— of Salem, a young woman who works with objects like rings, articles of clothing, locks of hair, et cetera; and quite angry with the evidence presented by a young geologist that would seem to discredit, once and for all, the claims of Eustace of Portsmouth. He interrupted a third paper, calling the reader a "bigot" and an "ignorant fool.")

Fortunately the incident did not find its way into any of the papers. The press, misunderstanding (deliberately and maliciously) the Society's attitude toward Spiritualism, delights in ridiculing our efforts.

There were respectful obituaries. A fine

eulogy prepared by Reverend Tyler of St. Aidan's. Other tributes. *A tragic loss. . . . Mourned by all who knew him. . . .* (I stammered and could not speak. I cannot speak of him, of it, even now. Am I mourning, am I aggrieved? Or merely shocked? Terrified?) Relatives and friends and associates glossed over his behavior these past few months and settled upon an earlier Perry Moore, eminently sane, a distinguished physician and man of letters. I did not disagree, I merely acquiesced; I could not make any claim to have really known the man.

And so he has died, and so he is dead. . . .

Shortly after the funeral I went away to New Hampshire for a few days. But I can barely remember that period of time now. I sleep poorly, I yearn for summer, for a drastic change of climate, of scene. It was unwise for me to take up the responsibility of psychical research, fascinated though I am by it; my classes and lectures at the University demand most of my energy.

How quickly he died, and so young: so relatively young.

No history of high blood pressure, it is said.

At the end he was arguing with everyone, however. His personality had completely changed. He was rude, impetuous, even rather profane; even poorly groomed. (Rising to challenge the first of the papers, he revealed a shirt-front that appeared to be stained.) Some claimed he had been drinking all along, for years. Was it possible . . . ? (He had clearly enjoyed the wine and brandy in Quincy that evening, but I would not have said he was intemperate.) Rumors, fanciful tales, outright lies, slander. . . . It is painful, the vulnerability death brings.

Bigots, he called us. Ignorant fools. Unbelievers—atheists—traitors to the Spirit World—heretics. Heretics! I believe he looked directly at me as he pushed his way out of the meeting room: his eyes glaring, his face dangerously flushed, no recognition in his stare.

After his death, it is said, books continue to arrive at his home from England and Europe. He spent a small fortune on obscure, out-of-print volumes—commentaries on the Kabbala, on Plotinus, medieval alchemical texts, books on astrology, witchcraft, the metaphysics of death. Occult cosmologies. Egyptian, Indian, and Chinese "wisdom." Blake, Swedenborg, Cozad. *The Tibetan Book of the Dead.* Datsky's *Lunar Mysteries.* His estate is in chaos because he left not one but several wills, the most recent made out only a day before his death, merely a few lines scribbled on scrap paper, without witnesses. The family will contest, of course. Since in this will he left his money and property to an obscure woman living in Quincy, Massachusetts, and since he was obviously not in his right mind at the time, they would be foolish indeed not to contest.

Days have passed since his sudden death. Days continue to pass. At times I am seized by a sort of quick, cold panic; at other times I am inclined to think the entire situation has been exaggerated. In one mood I vow to myself that I will never again pursue psychical research because it is simply too dangerous. In another mood I vow I will never again pursue it because it is a waste of time and my own work, my own career, must come first.

Heretics, he called us. Looking straight at me.

Still, he was mad. And is not to be blamed for the vagaries of madness.

19 June 1887. Boston.

Luncheon with Dr. Rowe, Miss Madeleine van der Post, young Lucas Matthewson; turned over my personal records and notes re the mediums Dr. Moore and I visited. (Destroyed jottings of a private nature.) Miss van der Post and Matthewson will be taking over my responsibilities. Both are young, quick-witted, alert, with a certain ironic play about their features; rather like Dr. Moore in his prime. Matthewson is a former seminary student now teaching physics at the Boston University. They questioned me about Perry Moore, but I avoided answering frankly. Asked if we were close, I said *No*. Asked if I had heard a bizarre tale making the rounds of Boston salons—that a spirit claiming to be Perry Moore has intruded upon a number of séances in the area—I said honestly that I had not; and I did not care to hear about it.

Spinoza: *I will analyze the actions and appetites of men as if it were a question of lines, of planes, and of solids.*

It is in this direction, I believe, that we must move. Away from the phantasmal, the vaporous, the unclear; toward lines, planes, and solids.

Sanity.

8 July 1887. Mount Desert Island, Maine.

Very early this morning, before dawn, dreamed of Perry Moore: a babbling gesticulating spirit, bearded, bright-eyed, obviously mad. Jarvis? Jarvis? Don't deny me! he cried. I am so . . . so bereft. . . .

Paralyzed, I faced him: neither awake nor asleep. His words were not really *words* so much as unvoiced thoughts. I heard them in my own voice; a terrible raw itching at the back of my throat yearned to articulate the man's grief.

Perry?

You don't dare deny me! Not now!

He drew near and I could not escape. The dream shifted, lost its clarity. Someone was shouting at me. Very angry, he was, and baffled—as if drunk—or ill—or injured.

Perry? I can't hear you—

—our dinner at Montague House, do you remember? Lamb, it was. And crepes with almond for dessert. You remember! You remember! You can't deny me! We were both nonbelievers then, both abysmally ignorant—you can't deny me!

(I was mute with fear or with cunning.)

—that idiot Rowe, how humiliated he will be! All of them! All of you! The entire rationalist bias, the—the conspiracy of—of fools—bigots—In a few years—In a few short years—Jarvis, where are you? Why can't I see

you? Where have you gone?—My eyes can't focus: will someone help me? I seem to have lost my way. Who is here? Who am I talking with? You remember me, don't you?

(He brushed near me, blinking helplessly. His mouth was a hole torn into his pale ravaged flesh.)

Where are you? Where is everyone? I thought it would be crowded here but—but there's no one—I am forgetting so much! My name—what was my name? Can't see. Can't remember. Something very important—something very important I must accomplish—can't remember—Why is there no God? No one here? No one in control? We drift this way and that way, we come to no rest, there are no landmarks—no way of judging—everything is confused—disjointed—Is someone listening? Would you read to me, please? Would you read to me?—anything!—that speech of Hamlet's—*To be or not*—a sonnet of Shakespeare's—any sonnet, anything—*That time of year thou may in me behold*—is that it?—is that how it begins? *Bare ruin'd choirs where the sweet birds once sang*. How does it go? Won't you tell me? I'm lost—there's nothing here to see, to touch—isn't anyone listening? I thought there was someone nearby, a friend: isn't anyone here?

(I stood paralyzed, mute with caution: he passed by.)

—*When in the chronicle of wasted time—the wide world dreaming of things to come*—is anyone listening?—can anyone help?—I am forgetting so much—my name, my life—my life's work—to penetrate the mysteries—the veil—to do justice to the universe of—of what—what had I intended?—am I in my place of repose now, have I come home? Why is it so empty here? Why is no one in control? My eyes—my head—mind broken and blown about—slivers—shards—annihilating all that's made to a—a green thought—a green shade—Shakespeare? Plato? Pascal? Will someone read me Pascal again? I seem to have lost my way—I am being blown about—Jarvis, was it? My dear young friend Jarvis? But I've forgotten your last name—I've forgotten so much—

(I wanted to reach out to touch him—but could not move, could not wake. The back of my throat ached with sorrow. Silent! Silent! I could not utter a word.)

—my papers, my journal—twenty years—a key somewhere hidden—where?—ah yes: the bottom drawer of my desk—do you hear?—my desk—house—Louisburg Square—the key is hidden there—wrapped in a linen handkerchief—the strongbox is—the locked box is—hidden—my brother Edward's house—attic—trunk—steamer trunk—initials R. W. M. —Father's trunk, you see—strongbox hidden inside—my secret journals—life's work—physical and spiritual wisdom—must not be lost—are you listening?—is anyone listening? I am forgetting so much, my mind is in shreds—but if you could locate the journal and read it to me—if you could salvage it—me—I would be so very grateful—I would forgive you anything, all of you—Is anyone there? Jarvis? Brandon? No one?—My journal, my soul: will you salvage it? Will—

(He stumbled away and I was alone again.)

Perry—?

But it was too late: I awoke drenched with perspiration.

Nightmare.

Must forget.

Best to rise early, before the others. Mount Desert Island lovely in July. Our lodge on a hill above the beach. No spirits here: wind from the northeast, perpetual fresh air, perpetual waves. Best to rise early and run along the beach and plunge into the chilly water.

Clear the cobwebs from one's mind.

How beautiful the sky, the ocean, the sunrise!

No spirits here on Mount Desert Island. Swimming: skillful exertion of arms and legs.

Head turned this way, that way. Eyes half shut. The surprise of the cold rough waves. One yearns almost to slip out of one's human skin at such times . . . ! Crude blatant beauty of Maine. Ocean. Muscular exertion of body. How alive I am, how living, how invulnerable; what a triumph in my every breath. . . .

Everything slips from my mind except the present moment. I am living, I am alive, I am immortal. Must not weaken: must not sink. Drowning? No. Impossible. Life is the only reality. It is not extinction that awaits but a hideous dreamlike state, a perpetual groping, blundering—far worse than extinction—incomprehensible: so it is life we must cling to, arm over arm, swimming, conquering the element that sustains us.

Jarvis? someone cried. *Please hear me—*

How exquisite life is, the turbulent joy of life contained in flesh! I heard nothing except the triumphant waves splashing about me. I swam for nearly an hour. Was reluctant to come ashore for breakfast, though our breakfasts are always pleasant rowdy sessions: my wife and my brother's wife and our seven children thrown together for the month of July. Three boys, four girls: noise, bustle, health, no shadows, no spirits. No time to think. Again and again I shall emerge from the surf, face and hair and body streaming water, exhausted but jubilant, triumphant. Again and again the children will call out to me, excited, from the dayside of the world that they inhabit.

I will not investigate Dr. Moore's strongbox and his secret journal; I will not even think about doing so. The wind blows words away. The surf is hypnotic. I will not remember this morning's dream once I sit down to breakfast with the family. I will not clutch my wife's wrist and say *We must not die! We dare not die!*—for that would only frighten and offend her.

Jarvis? she is calling at this very moment.

And I say *Yes—? Yes, I'll be there at once.*

CLASSICS

"OH, WHISTLE AND I'LL COME TO YOU, MY LAD"

M. R. James

REMEMBERED TODAY AS ARGUABLY the greatest writer of ghost stories who ever lived, Montague Rhodes James (1862–1936) admitted to being heavily influenced by the work of J. Sheridan Le Fanu, especially when it came to tales of walking corpses. He was born in Kent and moved to Suffolk at the age of three, where he lived at the rectory in Great Livermere for many years, setting several of his ghost stories there. He studied at Cambridge University, living there as an undergraduate, then as a don and provost at King's College, also setting several stories there. It became an annual custom to gather a group of friends and colleagues to a room on Christmas Eve where he would tell his latest ghost story, taking great pleasure in acting out all the roles.

In addition to becoming the first name of his time in supernatural fiction, he was also a medieval scholar of prodigious knowledge and productivity, having cataloged many of the libraries of Cambridge and Oxford and being responsible, after the discovery of a manuscript fragment, of rediscovering the graves of several twelfth-century abbots. Among his scholarly publications are several about the Apocrypha.

His greatest macabre stories are generally regarded to have been published in his first two collections, *Ghost Stories of an Antiquary* (1904) and *More Ghost Stories of an Antiquary* (1911). Also published in his lifetime were *A Thin Ghost and Others* (1919), *A Warning to the Curious and Other Ghost Stories* (1925), *Wailing Well* (1928), and *The Collected Ghost Stories of M. R. James* (1931).

" 'Oh, Whistle and I'll Come to You, My Lad' " was first published in *Ghost Stories of an Antiquary* (London, Edward Arnold, 1904).

"Oh, Whistle and I'll Come To You, My Lad"

M. R. JAMES

I

"I suppose you will be getting away pretty soon, now. Full term is over, Professor," said a person not in the story to the Professor of Ontography, soon after they had sat down next to each other at a feast in the hospitable hall of St. James's College.

The Professor was young, neat, and precise in speech.

"Yes," he said; "my friends have been making me take up golf this term, and I mean to go to the East Coast—in point of fact to Burnstow—(I dare say you know it) for a week or ten days, to improve my game. I hope to get off to-morrow."

"Oh, Parkins," said his neighbour on the other side, "if you are going to Burnstow, I wish you would look at the site of the Templars' preceptory, and let me know if you think it would be any good to have a dig there in the summer."

It was, as you might suppose, a person of antiquarian pursuits who said this, but, since he merely appears in this prologue, there is no need to give his entitlements.

"Certainly," said Parkins, the Professor; "if you will describe to me whereabouts the site is, I will do my best to give you an idea of the lie of the land when I get back; or I could write to you about it, if you would tell me where you are likely to be."

"Don't trouble to do that, thanks. It's only that I'm thinking of taking my family in that direction in the Long, and it occurred to me that, as very few of the English preceptories have ever been properly planned, I might have an opportunity of doing something useful on off-days."

The Professor rather sniffed at the idea that planning out a preceptory could be described as useful. His neighbour continued:

"The site—I doubt if there is anything showing above ground—must be down quite close to the beach now. The sea has encroached tremendously, as you know, all along that bit of coast. I should think, from the map, that it must be about three-quarters of a mile from the Globe Inn, at the north end of the town. Where are you going to stay?"

"Well, *at* the Globe Inn, as a matter of fact," said Parkins; "I have engaged a room there. I couldn't get in anywhere else; most of the lodging-houses are shut up in winter, it seems; and, as it is, they tell me that the only room of any size I can have is really a double-bedded one, and that they haven't a corner in which to store the other bed, and so on. But I must have a fairly large room, for I am taking some books down, and mean to do a bit of work; and though I don't quite fancy having an empty bed—not to speak of two—in what I may call for the time being my study, I suppose I can manage to rough it for the short time I shall be there."

"Do you call having an extra bed in your room roughing it, Parkins?" said a bluff person opposite. "Look here, I shall come down and occupy it for a bit; it'll be company for you."

The Professor quivered, but managed to laugh in a courteous manner.

"By all means, Rogers; there's nothing I should like better. But I'm afraid you would find it rather dull; you don't play golf, do you?"

"No, thank Heaven!" said rude Mr. Rogers.

"Well, you see, when I'm not writing I shall most likely be out on the links, and that, as I say, would be rather dull for you, I'm afraid."

"Oh, I don't know! There's certain to be somebody I know in the place; but, of course, if you don't want me, speak the word, Parkins; I shan't be offended. Truth, as you always tell us, is never offensive."

Parkins was, indeed, scrupulously polite and strictly truthful. It is to be feared that Mr. Rogers sometimes practised upon his knowledge of these characteristics. In Parkins's breast there was a conflict now raging, which for a moment or two did not allow him to answer. That interval being over, he said:

"Well, if you want the exact truth, Rogers, I was considering whether the room I speak of would really be large enough to accommodate us both comfortably; and also whether (mind, I shouldn't have said this if you hadn't pressed me) you would not constitute something in the nature of a hindrance to my work."

Rogers laughed loudly.

"Well done, Parkins!" he said. "It's all right. I promise not to interrupt your work; don't you disturb yourself about that. No, I won't come if you don't want me; but I thought I should do so nicely to keep the ghosts off." Here he might have been seen to wink and to nudge his next neighbour. Parkins might also have been seen to become pink. "I beg pardon, Parkins," Rogers continued; "I oughtn't to have said that. I forgot you didn't like levity on these topics."

"Well," Parkins said, "as you have mentioned the matter, I freely own that I do *not* like careless talk about what you call ghosts. A man in my position," he went on, raising his voice a little, "cannot, I find, be too careful about appearing to sanction the current beliefs on such subjects. As you know, Rogers, or as you ought to know; for I think I have never concealed my views—"

"No, you certainly have not, old man," put in Rogers *sotto voce*.

"—I hold that any semblance, any appearance of concession to the view that such things might exist is equivalent to a renunciation of all that I hold most sacred. But I'm afraid I have not succeeded in securing your attention."

"Your *undivided* attention, was what Dr. Blimber actually *said*," Rogers interrupted, with every appearance of an earnest desire for accuracy. "But I beg your pardon, Parkins; I'm stopping you."

"No, not at all," said Parkins. "I don't remember Blimber; perhaps he was before my time. But I needn't go on. I'm sure you know what I mean."

"Yes, yes," said Rogers, rather hastily—"just so. We'll go into it fully at Burnstow, or somewhere."

In repeating the above dialogue I have tried to give the impression which it made on me, that Parkins was something of an old woman—rather henlike, perhaps, in his little ways; totally destitute, alas! of the sense of humour, but at the same time dauntless and sincere in his convictions, and a man deserving of the greatest respect. Whether or not the reader has gathered so much, that was the character which Parkins had.

On the following day Parkins did, as he had hoped, succeed in getting away from his college, and in arriving at Burnstow. He was made welcome at the Globe Inn, was safely installed in the large double-bedded room of which we have heard, and was able before retiring to rest to arrange his materials for work in apple-pie order upon a commodious table which occupied the outer end of the room, and was surrounded on three sides by windows looking out seaward; that is to say, the central window looked straight out to sea, and those on the left and right commanded prospects along the shore to the north and south respectively. On the south you saw the village of Burnstow. On the north no houses were to be seen, but only the beach and the low cliff backing it. Immediately in front was a strip—not considerable—of rough grass, dotted with old anchors, capstans, and so forth; then a broad path; then the beach. Whatever may have been the original distance between the Globe Inn and the sea, not more than sixty yards now separated them.

The rest of the population of the inn was, of course, a golfing one, and included few elements that call for a special description. The most conspicuous figure was, perhaps, that of an *ancien militaire* secretary of a London club, and possessed of a voice of incredible strength, and of views of a pronouncedly Protestant type. These were apt to find utterance after his attendance upon the ministrations of the Vicar, an estimable man with inclinations towards a picaresque ritual, which he gallantly kept down as far as he could out of deference to East Anglian tradition.

Professor Parkins, one of whose principal characteristics was pluck, spent the greater part of the day following his arrival at Burnstow in what he had called improving his game, in company with this Colonel Wilson; and during the afternoon—whether the process of improvement were to blame or not, I am not sure—the Colonel's demeanour assumed a colouring so lurid that even Parkins jibbed at the thought of walking home with him from the links. He determined, after a short and furtive look at that bristling moustache and those incarnadined features, that it would be wiser to allow the influences of tea and tobacco to do what they could with the Colonel before the dinner-hour should render a meeting inevitable.

"I might walk home to-night along the beach," he reflected; "yes, and take a look—there will be light enough for that—at the ruins of which Disney was talking. I don't exactly know

where they are, by the way; but I expect I can hardly help stumbling on them."

This he accomplished, I may say, in the most literal sense, for in picking his way from the links to the shingle beach his foot caught, partly in a gorse-root and partly in a biggish stone, and over he went. When he got up and surveyed his surroundings, he found himself in a patch of somewhat broken ground covered with small depressions and mounds. These latter, when he came to examine them, proved to be simply masses of flints embedded in mortar and grown over with turf. He must, he quite rightly concluded, be on the site of the preceptory he had promised to look at. It seemed not unlikely to reward the spade of the explorer; enough of the foundations was probably left at no great depth to throw a good deal of light on the general plan. He remembered vaguely that the Templars, to whom this site had belonged, were in the habit of building round churches, and he thought a particular series of the humps or mounds near him did appear to be arranged in something of a circular form. Few people can resist the temptation to try a little amateur research in a department quite outside their own, if only for the satisfaction of showing how successful they would have been had they only taken it up seriously. Our Professor, however, if he felt something of this mean desire, was also truly anxious to oblige Mr. Disney. So he paced with care the circular area he had noticed, and wrote down its rough dimensions in his pocket-book. Then he proceeded to examine an oblong eminence which lay east of the centre of the circle, and seemed to his thinking likely to be the base of a platform or altar. At one end of it, the northern, a patch of the turf was gone—removed by some boy or other creature *feræ naturæ*. It might, he thought, be as well to probe the soil here for evidences of masonry, and he took out his knife and began scraping away the earth. And now followed another little discovery: a portion of soil fell inward as he scraped, and disclosed a small cavity. He lighted one match after another to help him to see of what nature the hole was, but the wind was too strong for them all. By tapping and scratching the sides with his knife, however, he was able to make out that it must be an artificial hole in masonry. It was rectangular, and the sides, top, and bottom, if not actually plastered, were smooth and regular. Of course it was empty. No! As he withdrew the knife he heard a metallic clink, and when he introduced his hand it met with a cylindrical object lying on the floor of the hole. Naturally enough, he picked it up, and when he brought it into the light, now fast fading, he could see that it, too, was of man's making—a metal tube about four inches long, and evidently of some considerable age.

By the time Parkins had made sure that there was nothing else in this odd receptacle, it was too late and too dark for him to think of undertaking any further search. What he had done had proved so unexpectedly interesting that he determined to sacrifice a little more of the daylight on the morrow to archæology. The object which he now had safe in his pocket was bound to be of some slight value at least, he felt sure.

Bleak and solemn was the view on which he took a last look before starting homewards. A faint yellow light in the west showed the links, on which a few figures moving towards the club-house were still visible, the squat martello tower, the lights of Aldsey village, the pale ribbon of sands intersected at intervals by black wooden groynes, the dim and murmuring sea. The wind was bitter from the north, but was at his back when he set out for the Globe. He quickly rattled and clashed through the shingle and gained the sand, upon which, but for the groynes which had to be got over every few yards, the going was both good and quiet. One last look behind, to measure the distance he had made since leaving the ruined Templars' church, showed him a prospect of company on his walk, in the shape of a rather indistinct personage, who seemed to be making great efforts to catch up with him, but made little, if any, progress. I mean that there was an appearance of running about his movements, but that the distance between him and Parkins did not seem materially to lessen. So,

at least, Parkins thought, and decided that he almost certainly did not know him, and that it would be absurd to wait until he came up. For all that, company, he began to think, would really be very welcome on that lonely shore, if only you could choose your companion. In his unenlightened days he had read of meetings in such places which even now would hardly bear thinking of. He went on thinking of them, however, until he reached home, and particularly of one which catches most people's fancy at some time of their childhood. "Now I saw in my dream that Christian had gone but a very little way when he saw a foul fiend coming over the field to meet him." "What should I do now," he thought, "if I looked back and caught sight of a black figure sharply defined against the yellow sky, and saw that it had horns and wings? I wonder whether I should stand or run for it. Luckily, the gentleman behind is not of that kind, and he seems to be about as far off now as when I saw him first. Well, at this rate he won't get his dinner as soon as I shall; and, dear me! it's within a quarter of an hour of the time now. I must run!"

Parkins had, in fact, very little time for dressing. When he met the Colonel at dinner, Peace—or as much of her as that gentleman could manage—reigned once more in the military bosom; nor was she put to flight in the hours of bridge that followed dinner, for Parkins was a more than respectable player. When, therefore, he retired towards twelve o'clock, he felt that he had spent his evening in quite a satisfactory way, and that, even for so long as a fortnight or three weeks, life at the Globe would be supportable under similar conditions—"especially," thought he, "if I go on improving my game."

As he went along the passages he met the boots of the Globe, who stopped and said:

"Beg your pardon, sir, but as I was a-brushing your coat just now there was somethink fell out of the pocket. I put it on your chest of drawers, sir, in your room, sir—a piece of a pipe or something of that, sir. Thank you, sir. You'll find it on your chest of drawers, sir—yes, sir. Good night, sir."

The speech served to remind Parkins of his little discovery of that afternoon. It was with some considerable curiosity that he turned it over by the light of his candles. It was of bronze, he now saw, and was shaped very much after the manner of the modern dog-whistle; in fact it was—yes, certainly it was—actually no more nor less than a whistle. He put it to his lips, but it was quite full of a fine, caked-up sand or earth, which would not yield to knocking, but must be loosened with a knife. Tidy as ever in his habits, Parkins cleared out the earth on to a piece of paper, and took the latter to the window to empty it out. The night was clear and bright, as he saw when he had opened the casement, and he stopped for an instant to look at the sea and note a belated wanderer stationed on the shore in front of the inn. Then he shut the window, a little surprised at the late hours people kept at Burnstow, and took his whistle to the light again. Why, surely there were marks on it, not merely marks, but letters! A very little rubbing rendered the deeply-cut inscription quite legible, but the Professor had to confess, after some earnest thought, that the meaning of it was as obscure to him as the writing on the wall to Belshazzar. There were legends both on the front and on the back of the whistle. The one read thus:

FLA
FUR FLE
BIS

The other:

卐 QUIS EST ISTE QUI UENIT 卐

"I ought to be able to make it out," he thought; "but I suppose I am a little rusty in my Latin. When I come to think of it, I don't believe I even know the word for a whistle. The long one does seem simple enough. It ought to mean, 'Who is this who is coming?' Well, the best way to find out is evidently to whistle for him."

He blew tentatively and stopped suddenly, startled and yet pleased at the note he had elicited. It had a quality of infinite distance in it, and, soft as it was, he somehow felt it must be audible for miles round. It was a sound, too, that seemed to have the power (which many scents possess) of forming pictures in the brain. He saw quite clearly for a moment a vision of a wide, dark expanse at night, with a fresh wind blowing, and in the midst a lonely figure—how employed, he could not tell. Perhaps he would have seen more had not the picture been broken by the sudden surge of a gust of wind against his casement, so sudden that it made him look up, just in time to see the white glint of a sea-bird's wing somewhere outside the dark panes. The sound of the whistle had so fascinated him that he could not help trying it once more, this time more boldly. The note was little, if at all, louder than before, and repetition broke the illusion—no picture followed, as he had half hoped it might. "But what is this? Goodness! what force the wind can get up in a few minutes! What a tremendous gust! There! I knew that window-fastening was no use! Ah! I thought so—both candles out. It's enough to tear the room to pieces."

The first thing was to get the window shut. While you might count twenty Parkins was struggling with the small casement, and felt almost as if he were pushing back a sturdy burglar, so strong was the pressure. It slackened all at once and the window banged to and latched itself. Now to relight the candles and see what damage, if any, had been done. No, nothing seemed amiss; no glass even was broken in the casement. But the noise had evidently roused at least one member of the household: the Colonel was to be heard stumping in his stockinged feet on the floor above, and growling.

Quickly as it had risen, the wind did not fall at once. On it went, moaning and rushing past the house, at times rising to a cry so desolate that, as Parkins disinterestedly said, it might have made fanciful people feel quite uncomfortable; even the unimaginative, he thought after a quarter of an hour, might be happier without it.

Whether it was the wind, or the excitement of golf, or of the researches in the preceptory that kept Parkins awake, he was not sure. Awake he remained, in any case, long enough to fancy (as I am afraid I often do myself under such conditions) that he was the victim of all manner of fatal disorders: he would lie counting the beats of his heart, convinced that it was going to stop work every moment, and would entertain grave suspicions of his lungs, brain, liver, etc.—suspicions which he was sure would be dispelled by the return of daylight, but which until then refused to be put aside. He found a little vicarious comfort in the idea that someone else was in the same boat. A near neighbour (in the darkness it was not easy to tell his direction) was tossing and rustling in his bed, too.

The next stage was that Parkins shut his eyes and determined to give sleep every chance. Here again over-excitement asserted itself in another form—that of making pictures. *Experto crede*, pictures do come to the closed eyes of one trying to sleep, and are often so little to his taste that he must open his eyes and disperse them.

Parkins's experience on this occasion was a very distressing one. He found that the picture which presented itself to him was continuous. When he opened his eyes, of course, it went; but when he shut them once more it framed itself afresh, and acted itself out again, neither quicker nor slower than before. What he saw was this:

A long stretch of shore—shingle edged by sand, and intersected at short intervals with black groynes running down to the water—a scene, in fact, so like that of his afternoon's walk that, in the absence of any landmark, it could not be distinguished therefrom. The light was obscure, conveying an impression of gathering storm, late winter evening, and slight cold rain. On this bleak stage at first no actor was visible. When, in the distance, a bobbing black object appeared; a moment more, and it was a man running, jumping, clambering over the groynes, and every few seconds looking eagerly back. The nearer he came the more obvious it was that he was not only anxious, but even terribly frightened, though his face was not to be distinguished. He was, moreover, almost at the end of his strength. On he came; each successive obstacle seemed to cause him more difficulty than the last. "Will he get over this next one?" thought Parkins; "it seems a little higher than the others." Yes; half climbing, half throwing himself, he did get over, and fell all in a heap on the other side (the side nearest to the spectator). There, as if really unable to get up again, he remained crouching under the groyne, looking up in attitude of painful anxiety.

So far no cause whatever for the fear of the runner had been shown; but now there began to be seen, far up the shore, a little flicker of something light-coloured moving to and fro with great swiftness and irregularity. Rapidly growing larger, it, too, declared itself as a figure in pale, fluttering draperies, ill-defined. There was something about its motion which made Parkins very unwilling to see it at close quarters. It would stop, raise arms, bow itself toward the sand, then run stooping across the beach to the water-edge and back again; and then, rising upright, once more continue its course forward at a speed that was startling and terrifying. The moment came when the pursuer was hovering about from left to right only a few yards beyond the groyne where the runner lay in hiding. After two or three ineffectual castings hither and thither it came to a stop, stood upright, with arms raised high, and then darted straight forward towards the groyne.

It was at this point that Parkins always failed in his resolution to keep his eyes shut. With many misgivings as to incipient failure of eyesight, overworked brain, excessive smoking, and so on, he finally resigned himself to light his candle, get out a book, and pass the night waking, rather than be tormented by this persistent panorama, which he saw clearly enough could only be a morbid reflection of his walk and his thoughts on that very day.

The scraping of match on box and the glare of light must have startled some creatures of the night—rats or what not—which he heard scurry across the floor from the side of his bed with much rustling. Dear, dear! the match is out!

Fool that it is! But the second one burnt better, and a candle and book were duly procured, over which Parkins pored till sleep of a wholesome kind came upon him, and that in no long space. For about the first time in his orderly and prudent life he forgot to blow out the candle, and when he was called next morning at eight there was still a flicker in the socket and a sad mess of guttered grease on the top of the little table.

After breakfast he was in his room, putting the finishing touches to his golfing costume—fortune had again allotted the Colonel to him for a partner—when one of the maids came in.

"Oh, if you please," she said, "would you like any extra blankets on your bed, sir?"

"Ah! thank you," said Parkins. "Yes, I think I should like one. It seems likely to turn rather colder."

In a very short time the maid was back with the blanket.

"Which bed should I put it on, sir?" she asked.

"What? Why, that one—the one I slept in last night," he said, pointing to it.

"Oh yes! I beg your pardon, sir, but you seemed to have tried both of 'em; leastways, we, had to make 'em both up this morning."

"Really? How very absurd!" said Parkins. "I certainly never touched the other, except to lay some things on it. Did it actually seem to have been slept in?"

"Oh yes, sir!" said the maid. "Why, all the things was crumpled and throwed about all ways, if you'll excuse me, sir, quite as if anyone 'adn't passed but a very poor night, sir."

"Dear me," said Parkins. "Well, I may have disordered it more than I thought when I unpacked my things. I'm very sorry to have given you the trouble, I'm sure. I expect a friend of mine soon, by the way—a gentleman from Cambridge—to come and occupy it for a night or two. That will be all right, I suppose, won't it?"

"Oh yes, to be sure, sir. Thank you, sir. It's no trouble, I'm sure," said the maid, and departed to giggle with her colleagues.

Parkins set forth, with a stern determination to improve his game.

I am glad to be able to report that he succeeded so far in this enterprise that the Colonel, who had been rather repining at the prospect of a second day's play in his company, became quite chatty as the morning advanced; and his voice boomed out over the flats, as certain also of our own minor poets have said, "like some great bourdon in a minster tower."

"Extraordinary wind, that, we had last night," he said. "In my old home we should have said someone had been whistling for it."

"Should you, indeed!" said Parkins. "Is there a superstition of that kind still current in your part of the country?"

"I don't know about superstition," said the Colonel. "They believe in it all over Denmark and Norway, as well as on the Yorkshire coast; and my experience is, mind you, that there's generally something at the bottom of what these country-folk hold to, and have held to for generations. But it's your drive" (or whatever it might have been: the golfing reader will have to imagine appropriate digressions at the proper intervals). When conversation was resumed, Parkins said, with a slight hesitancy: "Apropos of what you were saying just now, Colonel, I think I ought to tell you that my own views on such subjects are very strong. I am, in fact, a convinced disbeliever in what is called the 'supernatural.' "

"What!" said the Colonel, "do you mean to tell me you don't believe in second-sight, or ghosts, or anything of that kind?"

"In nothing whatever of that kind," returned Parkins firmly.

"Well," said the Colonel, "but it appears to me at that rate, sir, that you must be little better than a Sadducee."

Parkins was on the point of answering that, in his opinion, the Sadducees were the most sensible sons he had ever read of in the Old Testament; but, feeling some doubt as to whether much mention of them was to be found in that work, he preferred to laugh the accusation off.

"Perhaps I am," he said; "but—Here, give

me my cleek, boy!—Excuse me one moment, Colonel." A short interval. "Now, as to whistling for the wind, let me give you my theory about it. The laws which govern winds are really not at all perfectly known—to fisher-folk and such, of course, not known at all. A man or woman of eccentric habits, perhaps, or a stranger, is seen repeatedly on the beach at some unusual hour, and is heard whistling. Soon afterwards a violent wind rises; a man who could read the sky perfectly or who possessed a barometer could have foretold that it would. The simple people of a fishing-village have no barometers, and only a few rough rules for prophesying weather. What more natural than that the eccentric personage I postulated should be regarded as having raised the wind, or that he or she should clutch eagerly at the reputation of being able to do so? Now, take last night's wind: as it happens, I myself was whistling. I blew a whistle twice, and the wind seemed to come absolutely in answer to my call. If anyone had seen me—"

The audience had been a little restive under this harangue, and Parkins had, I fear, fallen somewhat into the tone of a lecturer; but at the last sentence the Colonel stopped.

"Whistling, were you?" he said. "And what sort of whistle did you use? Play this stroke first." Interval.

"About that whistle you were asking, Colonel. It's rather a curious one. I have it in my—No; I see I've left it in my room. As a matter of fact, I found it yesterday."

And then Parkins narrated the manner of his discovery of the whistle, upon hearing which the Colonel grunted, and opined that, in Parkins's place, he should himself be careful about using a thing that had belonged to a set of Papists, of whom, speaking generally, it might be affirmed that you never knew what they might not have been up to. From this topic he diverged to the enormities of the Vicar, who had given notice on the previous Sunday that Friday would be the Feast of St. Thomas the Apostle, and that there would be service at eleven o'clock in the church. This and other similar proceedings constituted

in the Colonel's view a strong presumption that the Vicar was a concealed Papist, if not a Jesuit; and Parkins, who could not very readily follow the Colonel in this region, did not disagree with him. In fact, they got on so well together in the morning that there was no talk on either side of their separating after lunch.

Both continued to play well during the afternoon, or, at least, well enough to make them forget everything else until the light began to fail them. Not until then did Parkins remember that he had meant to do some more investigating at the preceptory; but it was of no great importance, he reflected. One day was as good as another; he might as well go home with the Colonel.

As they turned the corner of the house, the Colonel was almost knocked down by a boy who rushed into him at the very top of his speed, and then, instead of running away, remained hanging on to him and panting. The first words of the warrior were naturally those of reproof and objurgation, but he quickly discerned that the boy was almost speechless with fright. Inquiries were useless at first. When the boy got his breath he began to howl, and still clung to the Colonel's legs. He was at last detached, but continued to howl.

"What in the world *is* the matter with you? What have you been up to? What have you seen?" said the two men.

"Ow, I seen it wive at me out of the winder," wailed the boy, "and I don't like it."

"What window?" said the irritated Colonel. "Come, pull yourself together, my boy."

"The front winder it was, at the 'otel," said the boy.

At this point Parkins was in favour of sending the boy home, but the Colonel refused; he wanted to get to the bottom of it, he said; it was most dangerous to give a boy such a fright as this one had had, and if it turned out that people had been playing jokes, they should suffer for it in some way. And by a series of questions he made out this story: The boy had been playing about on the grass in front of the Globe with some others; then they had gone home to their teas, and he was just going, when he happened to look up at the front winder and see it a-wiving at him. *It* seemed to be a figure of some sort, in white as far as he knew—couldn't see its face; but it wived at him, and it warn't a right thing—not to say not a right person. Was there a light in the room? No, he didn't think to look if there was a light. Which was the window? Was it the top one or the second one? The seckind one it was—the big winder what got two little uns at the sides.

"Very well, my boy," said the Colonel, after a few more questions. "You run away home now. I expect it was some person trying to give you a start. Another time, like a brave English boy, you just throw a stone—well, no, not that exactly, but you go and speak to the waiter, or to Mr. Simpson, the landlord, and—yes—and say that I advised you to do so."

The boy's face expressed some of the doubt he felt as to the likelihood of Mr. Simpson's lending a favourable ear to his complaint, but the Colonel did not appear to perceive this, and went on:

"And here's a sixpence—no, I see it's a shilling—and you be off home, and don't think any more about it."

The youth hurried off with agitated thanks, and the Colonel and Parkins went round to the front of the Globe and reconnoitred. There was only one window answering to the description they had been hearing.

"Well, that's curious," said Parkins; "it's evidently my window the lad was talking about. Will you come up for a moment, Colonel Wilson? We ought to be able to see if anyone has been taking liberties in my room."

They were soon in the passage, and Parkins made as if to open the door. Then he stopped and felt in his pockets.

"This is more serious than I thought," was his next remark. "I remember now that before I started this morning I locked the door. It is locked now, and, what is more, here is the key." And he held it up. "Now," he went on, "if the servants are in the habit of going into one's room

during the day when one is away, I can only say that—well, that I don't approve of it at all." Conscious of a somewhat weak climax, he busied himself in opening the door (which was indeed locked) and in lighting candles. "No," he said, "nothing seems disturbed."

"Except your bed," put in the Colonel.

"Excuse me, that isn't my bed," said Parkins. "I don't use that one. But it does look as if someone had been playing tricks with it."

It certainly did: the bed-clothes were bundled up and twisted together in a most tortuous confusion. Parkins pondered.

"That must be it," he said at last: "I disordered the clothes last night in unpacking, and they haven't made it since. Perhaps they came in to make it, and that boy saw them through the window; and then they were called away and locked the door after them. Yes, I think that must be it."

"Well, ring and ask," said the Colonel, and this appealed to Parkins as practical.

The maid appeared, and, to make a long story short, deposed that she had made the bed in the morning when the gentleman was in the room, and hadn't been there since. No, she hadn't no other key. Mr. Simpson he kep' the keys; he'd be able to tell the gentleman if anyone had been up.

This was a puzzle. Investigation showed that nothing of value had been taken, and Parkins remembered the disposition of the small objects on tables and so forth well enough to be pretty sure that no pranks had been played with them. Mr. and Mrs. Simpson furthermore agreed that neither of them had given the duplicate key of the room to any person whatever during the day. Nor could Parkins, fair-minded man as he was, detect anything in the demeanour of master, mistress, or maid that indicated guilt. He was much more inclined to think that the boy had been imposing on the Colonel.

The latter was unwontedly silent and pensive at dinner and throughout the evening. When he bade good night to Parkins, he murmured in a gruff undertone:

"You know where I am if you want me during the night."

"Why, yes, thank you, Colonel Wilson, I think I do; but there isn't much prospect of my disturbing you, I hope. By the way," he added, "did I show you that old whistle I spoke of? I think not. Well, here it is."

The Colonel turned it over gingerly in the light of the candle.

"Can you make anything of the inscription?" asked Parkins, as he took it back.

"No, not in this light. What do you mean to do with it?"

"Oh, well, when I get back to Cambridge I shall submit it to some of the archæologists there, and see what they think of it; and very likely, if they consider it worth having, I may present it to one of the museums."

"'M!" said the Colonel. "Well, you may be right. All I know is that, if it were mine, I should chuck it straight into the sea. It's no use talking, I'm well aware, but I expect that with you it's a case of live and learn. I hope so, I'm sure, and I wish you a good night."

He turned away, leaving Parkins in act to speak at the bottom of the stair, and soon each was in his own bedroom.

By some unfortunate accident, there were neither blinds nor curtains to the windows of the Professor's room. The previous night he had thought little of this, but to-night there seemed every prospect of a bright moon rising to shine directly on his bed, and probably wake him later on. When he noticed this he was a good deal annoyed, but, with an ingenuity which I can only envy, he succeeded in rigging up, with the help of a railway-rug, some safety-pins, and a stick and umbrella, a screen which, if it only held together, would completely keep the moonlight off his bed. And shortly afterwards he was comfortably in that bed. When he had read a somewhat solid work long enough to produce a decided wish for sleep, he cast a drowsy glance round the room, blew out the candle, and fell back upon the pillow.

He must have slept soundly for an hour or more, when a sudden clatter shook him up in a most unwelcome manner. In a moment he realized what had happened: his carefully-constructed screen had given way, and a very bright frosty moon was shining directly on his face. This was highly annoying. Could he possibly get up and reconstruct the screen? or could he manage to sleep if he did not?

For some minutes he lay and pondered over the possibilities; then he turned over sharply, and with his eyes open lay breathlessly listening. There had been a movement, he was sure, in the empty bed on the opposite side of the room. To-morrow he would have it moved, for there must be rats or something playing about in it. It was quiet now. No! the commotion began again. There was a rustling and shaking: surely more than any rat could cause.

I can figure to myself something of the Professor's bewilderment and horror, for I have in a dream thirty years back seen the same thing happen; but the reader will hardly, perhaps, imagine how dreadful it was to him to see a figure suddenly sit up in what he had known was an empty bed. He was out of his own bed in one bound, and made a dash towards the window, where lay his only weapon, the stick with which he had propped his screen. This was, as it turned out, the worst thing he could have done, because the personage in the empty bed, with a sudden motion, slipped from the bed and took up a position, with outspread arms, between the two beds, and in front of the door. Parkins watched it in a horrid perplexity. Somehow, the idea of getting past it and escaping through the door was intolerable to him; he could not have borne—he didn't know why—to touch it; and as for its touching him, he would sooner dash himself through the window than have that happen. It stood for the moment in a band of dark shadow, and he had not seen what its face was like. Now it began to move, in a stooping posture, and all at once the spectator realized, with some horror and some relief, that it must be blind, for it seemed to feel about it with its muffled arms in a groping and random fashion.

Turning half away from him, it became suddenly conscious of the bed he had just left, and darted towards it, and bent over and felt the pillows in a way which made Parkins shudder as he had never in his life thought it possible. In a very few moments it seemed to know that the bed was empty, and then, moving forward into the area of light and facing the window, it showed for the first time what manner of thing it was.

Parkins, who very much dislikes being questioned about it, did once describe something of it in my hearing, and I gathered that what he chiefly remembers about it is a horrible, an intensely horrible, face *of crumpled linen*. What expression he read upon it he could not or would not tell, but that the fear of it went nigh to maddening him is certain.

But he was not at leisure to watch it for long. With formidable quickness it moved into the middle of the room, and, as it groped and waved, one corner of its draperies swept across Parkins's face. He could not—though he knew how perilous a sound was—he could not keep back a cry of disgust, and this gave the searcher an instant clue. It leapt towards him upon the instant, and the next moment he was half-way through the window backwards, uttering cry upon cry at the utmost pitch of his voice, and the linen face was thrust close into his own. At this, almost the last possible second, deliverance came, as you will have guessed: the Colonel burst the door open, and was just in time to see the dreadful group at the window. When he reached the figures only one was left. Parkins sank forward into the room in a faint, and before him on the floor lay a tumbled heap of bed-clothes.

Colonel Wilson asked no questions, but busied himself in keeping everyone else out of the room and in getting Parkins back to his bed; and himself, wrapped in a rug, occupied the other bed for the rest of the night. Early on the next day Rogers arrived, more welcome than he would have been a day before, and the three of them held a very long consultation in the Professor's room. At the end of it the Colonel left the hotel door carrying a small object between his finger and thumb, which he cast as far into the sea as a very brawny arm could send it. Later on the smoke of a burning ascended from the back premises of the Globe.

Exactly what explanation was patched up for the staff and visitors at the hotel I must confess I do not recollect. The Professor was somehow cleared of the ready suspicion of delirium tremens, and the hotel of the reputation of a troubled house.

There is not much question as to what would have happened to Parkins if the Colonel had not intervened when he did. He would either have fallen out of the window or else lost his wits. But it is not so evident what more the creature that came in answer to the whistle could have done than frighten. There seemed to be absolutely nothing material about it save the bed-clothes of which it had made itself a body. The Colonel, who remembered a not very dissimilar occurrence in India, was of opinion that if Parkins had closed with it it could really have done very little, and that its one power was that of frightening. The whole thing, he said, served to confirm his opinion of the Church of Rome.

There is really nothing more to tell, but, as you may imagine, the Professor's views on certain points are less clear cut than they used to be. His nerves, too, have suffered: he cannot even now see a surplice hanging on a door quite unmoved, and the spectacle of a scarecrow in a field late on a winter afternoon has cost him more than one sleepless night.

THE MONKEY'S PAW AND THE TOLL-HOUSE

W. W. Jacobs

READERS OF THE TWO stories that follow will not find it easy to believe that W(illiam) W(ymark) Jacobs (1863–1943) gained his fame and fortune as a writer of humorous tales, sketches, and plays, as it will be difficult to find hints of hilarity in his ghost stories. Born in Wapping, London, he lived close to the sea and his father was the manager of a wharf in South Devon, which helps to explain why so many of his stories were about sailors and others connected to the shipping world. A famously quiet, self-effacing man, he took a job as a civil servant and, in his spare time, began in 1885 to write humorous sketches for *Blackfriar's, Punch,* and *The Strand.* They were popular enough to be collected in *Many Cargoes* in 1896, quickly followed by the novel *The Skipper's Wooing* (1897) and another collection, *Sea Urchins* (1898). With financial burdens eased, he married the suffragette Agnes Eleanor Williams in 1900. Although quite prolific for two decades, his last book, *Night Watches,* appeared in 1914; subsequent titles were largely of previously published stories.

"The Monkey's Paw" is one of the most frequently anthologized stories of all time, as well as one of the most bone-chilling. It has been adapted relentlessly: for radio, as a 1907 play, in motion pictures (several silent films as well as a 1933 talkie and a 1948 remake), for television as episodes of *Suspense* (May 17, 1949, and again on October 3, 1950), *Great Ghost Tales* (July 20, 1961), *The Alfred Hitchcock Hour* (April 19, 1965), and *Great Mysteries* (November 10, 1973), and for three operas. Somewhat less familiar is "The Toll-House," which ranks a close second in its ability to turn the blood chilly.

"The Monkey's Paw" was first published in the September 1902 issue of *Harper's Monthly;* it was collected in *The Lady of the Barge* (London, Harper & Brothers, 1902). "The Toll-House" was first published in the April 1907 issue of *The Strand;* it was collected in *Sailors' Knots* (London, Methuen, 1909).

The Monkey's Paw

W. W. JACOBS

I

Without, the night was cold and wet, but in the small parlour of Laburnam Villa the blinds were drawn and the fire burned brightly. Father and son were at chess, the former, who possessed ideas about the game involving radical changes, putting his king into such sharp and unnecessary perils that it even provoked comment from the white-haired old lady knitting placidly by the fire.

"Hark at the wind," said Mr. White, who, having seen a fatal mistake after it was too late, was amiably desirous of preventing his son from seeing it.

"I'm listening," said the latter, grimly surveying the board as he stretched out his hand. "Check."

"I should hardly think that he'd come to-night," said his father, with his hand poised over the board.

"Mate," replied the son.

"That's the worst of living so far out," bawled Mr. White, with sudden and unlooked-for violence; "of all the beastly, slushy, out-of-the-way places to live in, this is the worst. Pathway's a bog, and the road's a torrent. I don't know what people are thinking about. I suppose because only two houses on the road are let, they think it doesn't matter."

"Never mind, dear," said his wife soothingly; "perhaps you'll win the next one."

Mr. White looked up sharply, just in time to intercept a knowing glance between mother and son. The words died away on his lips, and he hid a guilty grin in his thin grey beard.

"There he is," said Herbert White, as the gate banged to loudly and heavy footsteps came toward the door.

The old man rose with hospitable haste, and opening the door, was heard condoling with the new arrival. The new arrival also condoled with himself, so that Mrs. White said, "Tut, tut!" and coughed gently as her husband entered the room, followed by a tall burly man, beady of eye and rubicund of visage.

"Sergeant-Major Morris," he said, introducing him.

The sergeant-major shook hands, and taking the proffered seat by the fire, watched contentedly while his host got out whisky and tumblers and stood a small copper kettle on the fire.

At the third glass his eyes got brighter, and he began to talk, the little family circle regarding with eager interest this visitor from distant parts, as he squared his broad shoulders in the chair and spoke of strange scenes and doughty deeds; of wars and plagues and strange peoples.

"Twenty-one years of it," said Mr. White, nodding at his wife and son. "When he went away he was a slip of a youth in the warehouse. Now look at him."

"He don't look to have taken much harm," said Mrs. White, politely.

"I'd like to go to India myself," said the old man, "just to look round a bit, you know."

"Better where you are," said the sergeant-major, shaking his head. He put down the empty glass, and sighing softly, shook it again.

"I should like to see those old temples and fakirs and jugglers," said the old man. "What was that you started telling me the other day about a monkey's paw or something, Morris?"

"Nothing," said the soldier hastily. "Leastways, nothing worth hearing."

"Monkey's paw?" said Mrs. White curiously.

"Well, it's just a bit of what you might call magic, perhaps," said the sergeant-major off-handedly.

His three listeners leaned forward eagerly. The visitor absentmindedly put his empty glass to his lips and then set it down again. His host filled it for him.

"To look at," said the sergeant-major, fumbling in his pocket, "it's just an ordinary little paw, dried to a mummy."

He took something out of his pocket and proffered it. Mrs. White drew back with a grimace, but her son, taking it, examined it curiously.

"And what is there special about it?" inquired Mr. White, as he took it from his son and, having examined it, placed it upon the table.

"It had a spell put on it by an old fakir," said the sergeant-major, "a very holy man. He wanted to show that fate ruled people's lives, and that those who interfered with it did so to their sorrow. He put a spell on it so that three separate men could each have three wishes from it."

His manner was so impressive that his hearers were conscious that their light laughter jarred somewhat.

"Well, why don't you have three, sir?" said Herbert White cleverly.

The soldier regarded him in the way that middle age is wont to regard presumptuous youth. "I have," he said quietly, and his blotchy face whitened.

"And did you really have the three wishes granted?" asked Mrs. White.

"I did," said the sergeant-major, and his glass tapped against his strong teeth.

"And has anybody else wished?" inquired the old lady.

"The first man had his three wishes, yes," was the reply. "I don't know what the first two were, but the third was for death. That's how I got the paw."

His tones were so grave that a hush fell upon the group.

"If you've had your three wishes, it's no good to you now, then, Morris," said the old man at last. "What do you keep it for?"

The soldier shook his head. "Fancy, I suppose," he said slowly.

"If you could have another three wishes," said the old man, eyeing him keenly, "would you have them?"

"I don't know," said the other. "I don't know."

He took the paw, and dangling it between his front finger and thumb, suddenly threw it upon the fire. White, with a slight cry, stooped down and snatched it off.

"Better let it burn," said the soldier solemnly.

"If you don't want it, Morris," said the old man, "give it to me."

"I won't," said his friend doggedly. "I threw it on the fire. If you keep it, don't blame me for what happens. Pitch it on the fire again, like a sensible man."

The other shook his head and examined his new possession closely. "How do you do it?" he inquired.

"Hold it up in your right hand and wish aloud," said the sergeant-major, "but I warn you of the consequences."

"Sounds like the Arabian Nights," said Mrs. White, as she rose and began to set the supper. "Don't you think you might wish for four pairs of hands for me?"

Her husband drew the talisman from his pocket and then all three burst into laughter as the sergeant-major, with a look of alarm on his face, caught him by the arm.

"If you must wish," he said gruffly, "wish for something sensible."

Mr. White dropped it back into his pocket, and placing chairs, motioned his friend to the table. In the business of supper the talisman was partly forgotten, and afterward the three sat listening in an enthralled fashion to a second instalment of the soldier's adventures in India.

"If the tale about the monkey paw is not more truthful than those he has been telling us," said Herbert, as the door closed behind their guest, just in time for him to catch the last train, "we shan't make much out of it."

"Did you give him anything for it, father?" inquired Mrs. White, regarding her husband closely.

"A trifle," said he, colouring slightly. "He didn't want it, but I made him take it. And he pressed me again to throw it away."

"Likely," said Herbert, with pretended horror. "Why, we're going to be rich, and famous, and happy. Wish to be an emperor, father, to begin with; then you can't be henpecked."

He darted round the table, pursued by the maligned Mrs. White armed with an antimacassar.

Mr. White took the paw from his pocket and eyed it dubiously. "I don't know what to wish for, and that's a fact," he said slowly. "It seems to me I've got all I want."

"If you only cleared the house, you'd be quite happy, wouldn't you?" said Herbert, with his hand on his shoulder. "Well, wish for two hundred pounds, then; that'll just do it."

His father, smiling shamefacedly at his own credulity, held up the talisman, as his son, with a solemn face somewhat marred by a wink at his mother, sat down at the piano and struck a few impressive chords.

"I wish for two hundred pounds," said the old man distinctly.

A fine crash from the piano greeted the words, interrupted by a shuddering cry from the old man. His wife and son ran toward him.

"It moved," he cried, with a glance of disgust at the object as it lay on the floor. "As I wished it twisted in my hands like a snake."

"Well, I don't see the money," said his son, as he picked it up and placed it on the table, "and I bet I never shall."

"It must have been your fancy, father," said his wife, regarding him anxiously.

He shook his head. "Never mind, though; there's no harm done, but it gave me a shock all the same."

They sat down by the fire again while the two men finished their pipes. Outside, the wind was higher than ever, and the old man started nervously at the sound of a door banging upstairs. A silence unusual and depressing settled upon all three, which lasted until the old couple rose to retire for the night.

"I expect you'll find the cash tied up in a big bag in the middle of your bed," said Herbert, as he bade them good-night, "and something horrible squatting up on top of the wardrobe watching you as you pocket your ill-gotten gains."

He sat alone in the darkness, gazing at the dying fire, and seeing faces in it. The last face was so horrible and so simian that he gazed at it in amazement. It got so vivid that, with a little uneasy laugh, he felt on the table for a glass containing a little water to throw over it. His hand grasped the monkey's paw, and with a little shiver he wiped his hand on his coat and went up to bed.

II

In the brightness of the wintry sun next morning as it streamed over the breakfast table Herbert laughed at his fears. There was an air of prosaic wholesomeness about the room which it had lacked on the previous night, and the dirty, shrivelled little paw was pitched on the sideboard with a carelessness which betokened no great belief in its virtues.

"I suppose all old soldiers are the same," said Mrs. White. "The idea of our listening to such nonsense! How could wishes be granted in these days? And if they could, how could two hundred pounds hurt you, father?"

"Might drop on his head from the sky," said the frivolous Herbert.

"Morris said the things happened so naturally," said his father, "that you might if you so wished attribute it to coincidence."

"Well, don't break into the money before I come back," said Herbert, as he rose from the table. "I'm afraid it'll turn you into a mean, avaricious man, and we shall have to disown you."

His mother laughed, and following him to the door, watched him down the road, and returning to the breakfast table, was very happy at the expense of her husband's credulity. All of which did not prevent her from scurrying to the door at the postman's knock, nor prevent her from referring somewhat shortly to retired sergeant-majors of bibulous habits when she found that the post brought a tailor's bill.

"Herbert will have some more of his funny remarks, I expect, when he comes home," she said, as they sat at dinner.

"I dare say," said Mr. White, pouring himself out some beer; "but for all that, the thing moved in my hand; that I'll swear to."

"You thought it did," said the old lady soothingly.

"I say it did," replied the other. "There was no thought about it; I had just—What's the matter?"

His wife made no reply. She was watching the mysterious movements of a man outside, who, peering in an undecided fashion at the house, appeared to be trying to make up his mind to enter. In mental connection with the two hundred pounds, she noticed that the stranger was well dressed and wore a silk hat of glossy newness. Three times he paused at the gate, and then walked on again. The fourth time he stood with his hand upon it, and then with sudden resolution flung it open and walked up the path. Mrs. White at the same moment placed her hands behind her, and hurriedly unfastening the strings of her apron, put that useful article of apparel beneath the cushion of her chair.

She brought the stranger, who seemed ill at ease, into the room. He gazed at her furtively, and listened in a preoccupied fashion as the old lady apologized for the appearance of the room, and her husband's coat, a garment which he usually reserved for the garden. She then waited as patiently as her sex would permit, for him to broach his business, but he was at first strangely silent.

"I—was asked to call," he said at last, and stooped and picked a piece of cotton from his trousers. "I come from Maw and Meggins."

The old lady started. "Is anything the matter?" she asked breathlessly. "Has anything happened to Herbert? What is it? What is it?"

Her husband interposed. "There, there, mother," he said hastily. "Sit down, and don't jump to conclusions. You've not brought bad news, I'm sure, sir," and he eyed the other wistfully.

"I'm sorry—" began the visitor.

"Is he hurt?" demanded the mother.

The visitor bowed in assent. "Badly hurt," he said quietly, "but he is not in any pain."

"Oh, thank God!" said the old woman, clasping her hands. "Thank God for that! Thank—"

She broke off suddenly as the sinister meaning of the assurance dawned upon her and she saw the awful confirmation of her fears in the other's averted face. She caught her breath, and turning to her slower-witted husband, laid her trembling old hand upon his. There was a long silence.

"He was caught in the machinery," said the visitor at length, in a low voice.

"Caught in the machinery," repeated Mr. White, in a dazed fashion, "yes."

He sat staring blankly out at the window, and taking his wife's hand between his own, pressed it as he had been wont to do in their old courting days nearly forty years before.

"He was the only one left to us," he said, turning gently to the visitor. "It is hard."

The other coughed, and rising, walked slowly to the window. "The firm wished me to convey their sincere sympathy with you in your great loss," he said, without looking round. "I beg that you will understand I am only their servant and merely obeying orders."

There was no reply; the old woman's face was white, her eyes staring, and her breath inaudible; on the husband's face was a look such as his friend the sergeant might have carried into his first action.

"I was to say that Maw and Meggins disclaim all responsibility," continued the other. "They admit no liability at all, but in consideration of your son's services they wish to present you with a certain sum as compensation."

Mr. White dropped his wife's hand, and rising to his feet, gazed with a look of horror at his visitor. His dry lips shaped the words, "How much?"

"Two hundred pounds," was the answer.

Unconscious of his wife's shriek, the old man smiled faintly, put out his hands like a sightless man, and dropped, a senseless heap, to the floor.

III

In the huge new cemetery, some two miles distant, the old people buried their dead, and came back to a house steeped in shadow and silence. It was all over so quickly that at first they could hardly realize it, and remained in a state of expectation as though of something else to happen—something else which was to lighten this load, too heavy for old hearts to bear.

But the days passed, and expectation gave place to resignation—the hopeless resignation of the old, sometimes miscalled apathy. Sometimes they hardly exchanged a word, for now they had nothing to talk about, and their days were long to weariness.

It was about a week after that that the old man, waking suddenly in the night, stretched out his hand and found himself alone. The room was in darkness, and the sound of subdued weeping came from the window. He raised himself in bed and listened.

"Come back," he said tenderly. "You will be cold."

"It is colder for my son," said the old woman, and wept afresh.

The sound of her sobs died away on his ears.

The bed was warm, and his eyes heavy with sleep. He dozed fitfully, and then slept until a sudden wild cry from his wife awoke him with a start.

"The paw!" she cried wildly. "The monkey's paw!"

He started up in alarm. "Where? Where is it? What's the matter?"

She came stumbling across the room toward him. "I want it," she said quietly. "You've not destroyed it?"

"It's in the parlour, on the bracket," he replied, marvelling. "Why?"

She cried and laughed together, and bending over, kissed his cheek.

"I only just thought of it," she said hysterically. "Why didn't I think of it before? Why didn't you think of it?"

"Think of what?" he questioned.

"The other two wishes," she replied rapidly. "We've only had one."

"Was not that enough?" he demanded fiercely.

"No," she cried, triumphantly; "we'll have one more. Go down and get it quickly, and wish our boy alive again."

The man sat up in bed and flung the bedclothes from his quaking limbs. "Good God, you are mad!" he cried aghast.

"Get it," she panted; "get it quickly, and wish—Oh, my boy, my boy!"

Her husband struck a match and lit the candle. "Get back to bed," he said, unsteadily. "You don't know what you are saying."

"We had the first wish granted," said the old woman, feverishly; "why not the second."

"A coincidence," stammered the old man.

"Go and get it and wish," cried the old woman, quivering with excitement.

The old man turned and regarded her, and his voice shook. "He has been dead ten days, and besides he—I would not tell you else, but—I could only recognize him by his clothing. If he was too terrible for you to see then, how now?"

"Bring him back," cried the old woman, and

THE MONKEY'S PAW

dragged him toward the door. "Do you think I fear the child I have nursed?"

He went down in the darkness, and felt his way to the parlour, and then to the mantelpiece. The talisman was in its place, and a horrible fear that the unspoken wish might bring his mutilated son before him ere he could escape from the room seized upon him, and he caught his breath as he found that he had lost the direction of the door. His brow cold with sweat, he felt his way round the table, and groped along the wall until he found himself in the small passage with the unwholesome thing in his hand.

Even his wife's face seemed changed as he entered the room. It was white and expectant, and to his fears seemed to have an unnatural look upon it. He was afraid of her.

"Wish!" she cried, in a strong voice.

"It is foolish and wicked," he faltered.

"Wish!" repeated his wife.

He raised his hand. "I wish my son alive again."

The talisman fell to the floor, and he regarded it fearfully. Then he sank trembling into a chair as the old woman, with burning eyes, walked to the window and raised the blind.

He sat until he was chilled with the cold, glancing occasionally at the figure of the old woman peering through the window. The candle end, which had burnt below the rim of the china candlestick, was throwing pulsating shadows on the ceiling and walls, until, with a flicker larger than the rest, it expired. The old man, with an unspeakable sense of relief at the failure of the talisman, crept back to his bed, and a minute or two afterward the old woman came silently and apathetically beside him.

Neither spoke, but both lay silently listening to the ticking of the clock. A stair creaked, and a squeaky mouse scurried noisily through the wall. The darkness was oppressive, and after lying for some time screwing up his courage, the husband took the box of matches, and striking one, went downstairs for a candle.

At the foot of the stairs the match went out, and he paused to strike another, and at the same moment a knock, so quiet and stealthy as to be scarcely audible, sounded on the front door.

The matches fell from his hand. He stood motionless, his breath suspended until the knock was repeated. Then he turned and fled swiftly back to his room, and closed the door behind him. A third knock sounded through the house.

"What's that?" cried the old woman, starting up.

"A rat," said the old man, in shaking tones— "a rat. It passed me on the stairs."

His wife sat up in bed listening. A loud knock resounded through the house.

"It's Herbert!" she screamed. "It's Herbert!"

She ran to the door, but her husband was before her, and catching her by the arm, held her tightly.

"What are you going to do?" he whispered hoarsely.

"It's my boy; it's Herbert!" she cried, struggling mechanically. "I forgot it was two miles away. What are you holding me for? Let go. I must open the door."

"For God's sake, don't let it in," cried the old man trembling.

"You're afraid of your own son," she cried, struggling. "Let me go. I'm coming, Herbert; I'm coming."

There was another knock, and another. The old woman with a sudden wrench broke free and ran from the room. Her husband followed to the landing, and called after her appealingly as she hurried downstairs. He heard the chain rattle back and the bottom bolt drawn slowly and stiffly from the socket. Then the old woman's voice, strained and panting.

"The bolt," she cried loudly. "Come down. I can't reach it."

But her husband was on his hands and knees groping wildly on the floor in search of the paw. If he could only find it before the thing outside got in. A perfect fusillade of knocks reverberated through the house, and he heard the scraping

531

of a chair as his wife put it down in the passage against the door. He heard the creaking of the bolt as it came slowly back, and at the same moment he found the monkey's paw, and frantically breathed his third and last wish.

The knocking ceased suddenly, although the echoes of it were still in the house. He heard the chair drawn back and the door opened. A cold wind rushed up the staircase, and a long loud wail of disappointment and misery from his wife gave him courage to run down to her side, and then to the gate beyond. The street lamp flickering opposite shone on a quiet and deserted road.

The Toll-House

W. W. JACOBS

"IT'S ALL NONSENSE," said Jack Barnes. "Of course people have died in the house; people die in every house. As for the noises—wind in the chimney and rats in the wainscot are very convincing to a nervous man. Give me another cup of tea, Meagle."

"Lester and White are first," said Meagle, who was presiding at the tea-table of the Three Feathers Inn. "You've had two."

Lester and White finished their cups with irritating slowness, pausing between sips to sniff the aroma, and to discover the sex and dates of arrival of the "strangers" which floated in some numbers in the beverage. Mr. Meagle served them to the brim, and then, turning to the grimly expectant Mr. Barnes, blandly requested him to ring for hot water.

"We'll try and keep your nerves in their present healthy condition," he remarked. "For my part I have a sort of half-and-half belief in the supernatural."

"All sensible people have," said Lester. "An aunt of mine saw a ghost once."

White nodded.

"I had an uncle that saw one," he said.

"It always is somebody else that sees them," said Barnes.

"Well, there is the house," said Meagle, "a large house at an absurdly low rent, and nobody will take it. It has taken toll of at least one life of every family that has lived there—however short the time—and since it has stood empty caretaker after caretaker has died there. The last caretaker died fifteen years ago."

"Exactly," said Barnes. "Long enough ago for legends to accumulate."

"I'll bet you a sovereign you won't spend the night there alone, for all your talk," said White suddenly.

"And I," said Lester.

"No," said Barnes slowly. "I don't believe in ghosts nor in any supernatural things whatever; all the same, I admit that I should not care to pass a night there alone."

"But why not?" inquired White.

"Wind in the chimney," said Meagle, with a grin.

"Rats in the wainscot," chimed in Lester.

"As you like," said Barnes, colouring.

"Suppose we all go?" said Meagle. "Start after supper, and get there about eleven? We have been walking for ten days now without an adventure—except Barnes's discovery that ditch-water smells longest. It will be a novelty, at any rate, and, if we break the spell by all surviving, the grateful owner ought to come down handsome."

"Let's see what the landlord has to say about it first," said Lester. "There is no fun in passing a night in an ordinary empty house. Let us make sure that it is haunted."

He rang the bell, and, sending for the landlord, appealed to him in the name of our common humanity not to let them waste a night watching in a house in which spectres and hobgoblins had no part. The reply was more than reassuring, and the landlord, after describing with considerable art the exact appearance of a head which had been seen hanging out of a window in the moonlight, wound up with a polite but urgent request that they would settle his bill before they went.

"It's all very well for you young gentlemen to have your fun," he said indulgently; "but, supposing as how you are all found dead in the morning, what about me? It ain't called the Toll-House for nothing, you know."

"Who died there last?" inquired Barnes, with an air of polite derision.

"A tramp," was the reply. "He went there for the sake of half-a-crown, and they found him next morning hanging from the balusters, dead."

"Suicide," said Barnes. "Unsound mind."

The landlord nodded. "That's what the jury brought it in," he said slowly; "but his mind was sound enough when he went in there. I'd known him, off and on, for years. I'm a poor man, but I wouldn't spend the night in that house for a hundred pounds."

He repeated this remark as they started on their expedition a few hours later. They left as the inn was closing for the night; bolts shot noisily behind them, and, as the regular customers trudged slowly homewards, they set off at a brisk pace in the direction of the house. Most of the cottages were already in darkness, and lights in others went out as they passed.

"It seems rather hard that we have got to lose a night's rest in order to convince Barnes of the existence of ghosts," said White.

"It's in a good cause," said Meagle. "A most worthy object; and something seems to tell me that we shall succeed. You didn't forget the candles, Lester?"

"I have brought two," was the reply; "all the old man could spare."

There was but little moon, and the night was cloudy. The road between high hedges was dark, and in one place, where it ran through a wood, so black that they twice stumbled in the uneven ground at the side of it.

"Fancy leaving our comfortable beds for this!" said White again. "Let me see; this desirable residential sepulchre lies to the right, doesn't it?"

"Farther on," said Meagle.

They walked on for some time in silence, broken only by White's tribute to the softness, the cleanliness, and the comfort of the bed which was receding farther and farther into the distance. Under Meagle's guidance they turned off at last to the right, and, after a walk of a quarter of a mile, saw the gates of the house before them.

The lodge was almost hidden by over-grown shrubs and the drive was choked with rank growths. Meagle leading, they pushed through it until the dark pile of the house loomed above them.

"There is a window at the back where we can get in, so the landlord says," said Lester, as they stood before the hall door.

"Window?" said Meagle. "Nonsense. Let's do the thing properly. Where's the knocker?"

He felt for it in the darkness and gave a thundering rat-tat-tat at the door.

"Don't play the fool," said Barnes crossly.

"Ghostly servants are all asleep," said Meagle gravely, "but I'll wake them up before I've done with them. It's scandalous keeping us out here in the dark."

He plied the knocker again, and the noise volleyed in the emptiness beyond. Then with a sudden exclamation he put out his hands and stumbled forward.

"Why, it was open all the time," he said, with an odd catch in his voice. "Come on."

"I don't believe it was open," said Lester, hanging back. "Somebody is playing us a trick."

"Nonsense," said Meagle sharply. "Give me a candle. Thanks. Who's got a match?"

Barnes produced a box and struck one, and Meagle, shielding the candle with his hand, led the way forward to the foot of the stairs. "Shut the door, somebody," he said; "there's too much draught."

"It is shut," said White, glancing behind him.

Meagle fingered his chin. "Who shut it?" he inquired, looking from one to the other. "Who came in last?"

"I did," said Lester, "but I don't remember shutting it—perhaps I did, though."

Meagle, about to speak, thought better of it, and, still carefully guarding the flame, began to explore the house, with the others close behind. Shadows danced on the walls and lurked in the corners as they proceeded. At the end of the passage they found a second staircase, and ascending it slowly gained the first floor.

"Careful!" said Meagle, as they gained the landing.

He held the candle forward and showed where the balusters had broken away. Then he peered curiously into the void beneath.

"This is where the tramp hanged himself, I suppose," he said thoughtfully.

"You've got an unwholesome mind," said White, as they walked on. "This place is quite creepy enough without you remembering that. Now let's find a comfortable room and have a little nip of whisky apiece and a pipe. How will this do?"

He opened a door at the end of the passage and revealed a small square room. Meagle led the way with the candle, and, first melting a drop or two of tallow, stuck it on the mantelpiece. The others seated themselves on the floor and watched pleasantly as White drew from his pocket a small bottle of whisky and a tin cup.

"H'm! I've forgotten the water," he exclaimed.

"I'll soon get some," said Meagle.

He tugged violently at the bell-handle, and the rusty jangling of a bell sounded from a distant kitchen. He rang again.

"Don't play the fool," said Barnes roughly.

Meagle laughed. "I only wanted to convince you," he said kindly. "There ought to be, at any rate, one ghost in the servants' hall."

Barnes held up his hand for silence.

"Yes?" said Meagle, with a grin at the other two. "Is anybody coming?"

"Suppose we drop this game and go back," said Barnes suddenly. "I don't believe in spirits, but nerves are outside anybody's command. You may laugh as you like, but it really seemed to me that I heard a door open below and steps on the stairs."

His voice was drowned in a roar of laughter.

"He is coming round," said Meagle, with a smirk. "By the time I have done with him he will be a confirmed believer. Well, who will go and get some water? Will you, Barnes?"

"No," was the reply.

"If there is any it might not be safe to drink after all these years," said Lester. "We must do without it."

Meagle nodded, and taking a seat on the floor held out his hand for the cup. Pipes were lit, and the clean, wholesome smell of tobacco filled the room. White produced a pack of cards; talk and laughter rang through the room and died away reluctantly in distant corridors.

"Empty rooms always delude me into the belief that I possess a deep voice," said Meagle. "To-morrow I—"

He started up with a smothered exclamation as the light went out suddenly and something struck him on the head. The others sprang to their feet. Then Meagle laughed.

"It's the candle," he exclaimed. "I didn't stick it enough."

Barnes struck a match, and re-lighting the candle, stuck it on the mantelpiece, and sitting down took up his cards again.

"What was I going to say?" said Meagle. "Oh, I know; to-morrow I—"

"Listen!" said White, laying his hand on the other's sleeve. "Upon my word I really thought I heard a laugh."

"Look here!" said Barnes. "What do you say to going back? I've had enough of this. I keep fancying that I hear things too; sounds of something moving about in the passage outside. I know it's only fancy, but it's uncomfortable."

"You go if you want to," said Meagle, "and we will play dummy. Or you might ask the tramp to take your hand for you, as you go downstairs."

Barnes shivered and exclaimed angrily. He got up, and, walking to the half-closed door, listened.

"Go outside," said Meagle, winking at the other two. "I'll dare you to go down to the hall door and back by yourself."

Barnes came back, and, bending forward, lit his pipe at the candle.

"I am nervous, but rational," he said, blowing out a thin cloud of smoke. "My nerves tell me that there is something prowling up and down the long passage outside; my reason tells me that that is all nonsense. Where are my cards?"

He sat down again, and, taking up his hand, looked through it carefully and led.

"Your play, White," he said, after a pause.

White made no sign.

"Why, he is asleep," said Meagle. "Wake up, old man. Wake up and play."

Lester, who was sitting next to him, took the sleeping man by the arm and shook him, gently at first and then with some roughness, but White, with his back against the wall and his head bowed, made no sign. Meagle bawled in his ear, and then turned a puzzled face to the others.

"He sleeps like the dead," he said, grimacing. "Well, there are still three of us to keep each other company."

"Yes," said Lester, nodding. "Unless—Good Lord! suppose—"

He broke off, and eyed them, trembling.

"Suppose what?" inquired Meagle.

"Nothing," stammered Lester. "Let's wake him. Try him again. White! WHITE!"

"It's no good," said Meagle seriously; "there's something wrong about that sleep."

"That's what I meant," said Lester; "and if he goes to sleep like that, why shouldn't—"

Meagle sprang to his feet. "Nonsense," he said roughly. "He's tired out; that's all. Still, let's take him up and clear out. You take his legs and Barnes will lead the way with the candle. Yes? Who's that?"

He looked up quickly towards the door. "Thought I heard somebody tap," he said, with a shamefaced laugh. "Now, Lester, up with him. One, two—Lester! Lester!"

He sprang forward too late; Lester, with his face buried in his arms, had rolled over on the floor fast asleep, and his utmost efforts failed to awake him.

"He—is—asleep," he stammered. "Asleep!"

Barnes, who had taken the candle from the mantelpiece, stood peering at the sleepers in silence and dropping tallow over the floor.

"We must get out of this," said Meagle. "Quick!"

Barnes hesitated. "We can't leave them here—" he began.

"We must," said Meagle, in strident tones. "If you go to sleep I shall go—Quick! Come!"

He seized the other by the arm and strove to drag him to the door. Barnes shook him off, and, putting the candle back on the mantelpiece, tried again to arouse the sleepers.

"It's no good," he said at last, and, turning from them, watched Meagle. "Don't you go to sleep," he said anxiously.

Meagle shook his head, and they stood for some time in uneasy silence. "May as well shut the door," said Barnes at last.

He crossed over and closed it gently. Then at a scuffling noise behind him he turned and saw Meagle in a heap on the hearthstone.

With a sharp catch in his breath he stood motionless. Inside the room the candle, fluttering in the draught, showed dimly the grotesque attitudes of the sleepers. Beyond the door there seemed to his overwrought imagination a strange and stealthy unrest. He tried to whistle, but his lips were parched, and in a mechanical fashion he stooped, and began to pick up the cards which littered the floor.

He stopped once or twice and stood with bent head listening. The unrest outside seemed to increase; a loud creaking sounded from the stairs.

"Who is there?" he cried loudly.

The creaking ceased. He crossed to the door, and, flinging it open, strode out into the corridor. As he walked his fears left him suddenly.

"Come on!" he cried, with a low laugh. "All of you! All of you! Show your faces—your infernal ugly faces! Don't skulk!"

He laughed again and walked on; and the heap in the fireplace put out its head tortoise fashion and listened in horror to the retreating footsteps. Not until they had become inaudible in the distance did the listener's features relax.

"Good Lord, Lester, we've driven him mad," he said, in a frightened whisper. "We must go after him."

There was no reply. Meagle sprang to his feet.

"Do you hear?" he cried. "Stop your fooling now; this is serious. White! Lester! Do you hear?"

He bent and surveyed them in angry bewilderment. "All right," he said, in a trembling voice. "You won't frighten me, you know."

He turned away and walked with exaggerated carelessness in the direction of the door. He even went outside and peeped through the crack, but the sleepers did not stir. He glanced into the blackness behind, and then came hastily into the room again.

He stood for a few seconds regarding them. The stillness in the house was horrible; he could not even hear them breathe. With a sudden resolution he snatched the candle from the mantelpiece and held the flame to White's finger. Then as he reeled back stupefied, the footsteps again became audible.

He stood with the candle in his shaking hand, listening. He heard them ascending the farther staircase, but they stopped suddenly as he went to the door. He walked a little way along the passage, and they went scurrying down the stairs and then at a jog-trot along the corridor below. He went back to the main staircase, and they ceased again.

For a time he hung over the balusters, listening and trying to pierce the blackness below; then slowly, step by step, he made his way downstairs, and, holding the candle above his head, peered about him.

"Barnes!" he called. "Where are you?"

Shaking with fright, he made his way along the passage, and summoning up all his courage, pushed open doors and gazed fearfully into empty rooms. Then, quite suddenly, he heard the footsteps in front of him.

He followed slowly for fear of extinguishing

the candle, until they led him at last into a vast bare kitchen, with damp walls and a broken floor. In front of him a door leading into an inside room had just closed. He ran towards it and flung it open, and a cold air blew out the candle. He stood aghast.

"Barnes!" he cried again. "Don't be afraid! It is I—Meagle!"

There was no answer. He stood gazing into the darkness, and all the time the idea of something close at hand watching was upon him. Then suddenly the steps broke out overhead again.

He drew back hastily, and passing through the kitchen groped his way along the narrow passages. He could now see better in the darkness, and finding himself at last at the foot of the staircase, began to ascend it noiselessly. He reached the landing just in time to see a figure disappear round the angle of a wall. Still careful to make no noise, he followed the sound of the steps until they led him to the top floor, and he cornered the chase at the end of a short passage.

"Barnes!" he whispered. "Barnes!"

Something stirred in the darkness. A small circular window at the end of the passage just softened the blackness and revealed the dim outlines of a motionless figure. Meagle, in place of advancing, stood almost as still as a sudden horrible doubt took possession of him. With his eyes fixed on the shape in front he fell back slowly, and, as it advanced upon him, burst into a terrible cry.

"Barnes! For God's sake! Is it you?"

The echoes of his voice left the air quivering, but the figure before him paid no heed. For a moment he tried to brace his courage up to endure its approach, then with a smothered cry he turned and fled.

The passages wound like a maze, and he threaded them blindly in a vain search for the stairs. If he could get down and open the hall door—

He caught his breath in a sob; the steps had begun again. At a lumbering trot they clattered up and down the bare passages, in and out, up and down, as though in search of him. He stood appalled, and then as they drew near entered a small room and stood behind the door as they rushed by. He came out and ran swiftly and noiselessly in the other direction, and in a moment the steps were after him. He found the long corridor and raced along it at top speed. The stairs he knew were at the end, and with the steps close behind he descended them in blind haste. The steps gained on him, and he shrank to the side to let them pass, still continuing his headlong flight. Then suddenly he seemed to slip off the earth into space.

Lester awoke in the morning to find the sunshine streaming into the room, and White sitting up and regarding with some perplexity a badly-blistered finger.

"Where are the others?" inquired Lester.

"Gone, I suppose," said White. "We must have been asleep."

Lester arose, and, stretching his stiffened limbs, dusted his clothes with his hands and went out into the corridor. White followed. At the noise of their approach a figure which had been lying asleep at the other end sat up and revealed the face of Barnes. "Why, I've been asleep," he said, in surprise. "I don't remember coming here. How did I get here?"

"Nice place to come for a nap," said Lester severely, as he pointed to the gap in the balusters. "Look there! Another yard and where would you have been?"

He walked carelessly to the edge and looked over. In response to his startled cry the others drew near, and all three stood staring at the dead man below.

AFTERWARD

Edith Wharton

MORE FAMOUS AS A writer of literary, mainstream fiction than of supernatural stories, Edith (Newbold) Wharton, née Jones (1862–1937), was the first woman to win a Pulitzer Prize, for her novel *The Age of Innocence* (1920); yet her superb ghost stories spanned virtually her entire career.

Born to enormous wealth in New York City, she rebelled against her privileged life among high society in New York, Paris, and Newport, Rhode Island, by writing fiction, which her family regarded as an eccentricity that was best ignored. Her earliest stories were written for *Scribner's Magazine* and, when the editor requested a serial novel "in six months," she wrote her first big bestseller for him, *The House of Mirth* (1905). Six years later she published what many regard as her masterpiece, *Ethan Frome* (1911), ultimately writing forty-seven books.

Her first ghost story was "The Lady Maid's Bell" (1902) in which the spirit of a long-dead maid still answers a summoning bell. Her last was the chilling "All Souls," written the year she died. Her ghost stories were collected in *Tales of Men and Ghosts* (1910), *Xingu and Other Stories* (1916), *Here and Beyond* (1926), and *Ghosts* (1937).

"Afterward" was filmed for the PBS television series *Mystery!* as part of the *Shades of Darkness* series; it aired on June 17, 1983, and starred Kate Harper and Michael Shannon. It was originally published in the January 1910 issue of *The Century Magazine;* it was collected in *Tales of Men and Ghosts* (New York, Charles Scribner's Sons, 1910).

Afterward

EDITH WHARTON

I

"Oh, there *is* one, of course, but you'll never know it."

The assertion, laughingly flung out six months earlier in a bright June garden, came back to Mary Boyne with a new perception of its significance as she stood, in the December dusk, waiting for the lamps to be brought into the library.

The words had been spoken by their friend Alida Stair, as they sat at tea on her lawn at Pangbourne, in reference to the very house of which the library in question was the central, the pivotal "feature." Mary Boyne and her husband, in quest of a country place in one of the southern or southwestern counties, had, on their arrival in England, carried their problem straight to Alida Stair, who had successfully solved it in her own case; but it was not until they had rejected, almost capriciously, several practical and judicious suggestions that she threw out: "Well, there's Lyng, in Dorsetshire. It belongs to Hugo's cousins, and you can get it for a song."

The reason she gave for its being obtainable on these terms—its remoteness from a station, its lack of electric light, hot-water pipes, and other vulgar necessities—were exactly those pleading in its favour with two romantic Americans perversely in search of the economic drawbacks which were associated, in their tradition, with unusual architectural felicities.

"I should never believe I was living in an old house unless I was thoroughly uncomfortable," Ned Boyne, the more extravagant of the two, had jocosely insisted; "the least hint of 'convenience' would make me think it had been bought out of an exhibition, with the pieces numbered, and set up again." And they had proceeded to enumerate, with humorous precision, their various doubts and demands, refusing to believe that the house their cousin recommended was *really* Tudor till they learned it had no heating system, or that the village church was literally in the grounds till she assured them of the deplorable uncertainty of the water-supply.

"It's too uncomfortable to be true!" Edward Boyne had continued to exult as the avowal of each disadvantage was successively wrung from her; but he had cut short his rhapsody to ask, with a relapse to distrust: "And the ghost? You've been concealing from us the fact that there is no ghost!"

Mary, at the moment, had laughed with him, yet almost with her laugh, being possessed of several sets of independent perceptions, had been struck by a note of flatness in Alida's answering hilarity.

"Oh, Dorsetshire's full of ghosts, you know."

"Yes, yes; but that won't do. I don't want to have to drive ten miles to see somebody else's ghost. I want one of my own on the premises. *Is* there a ghost at Lyng?"

His rejoinder had made Alida laugh again,

and it was then that she had flung back tantalisingly: "Oh, there *is* one, of course, but you'll never know it."

"Never know it?" Boyne pulled her up. "But what in the world constitutes a ghost except the fact of its being known for one?"

"I can't say. But that's the story."

"That there's a ghost, but that nobody knows it's a ghost?"

"Well—not till afterward, at any rate."

"Till afterward?"

"Not till long, long afterward."

"But if it's once been identified as an unearthly visitant, why hasn't its *signalement* been handed down in the family? How has it managed to preserve its incognito?"

Alida could only shake her head. "Don't ask me. But it has."

"And then suddenly—" Mary spoke up as if from cavernous depths of divination—"suddenly, long afterward, one says to one's self *'That was it?'* "

She was startled at the sepulchral sound with which her question fell on the banter of the other two, and she saw the shadow of the same surprise flit across Alida's pupils. "I suppose so. One just has to wait."

"Oh, hang waiting!" Ned broke in. "Life's too short for a ghost who can only be enjoyed in retrospect. Can't we do better than that, Mary?"

But it turned out that in the event they were not destined to, for within three months of their conversation with Mrs. Stair they were settled at Lyng, and the life they had yearned for, to the point of planning it in advance in all its daily details, had actually begun for them.

It was to sit, in the thick December dusk, by just such a wide-hooded fireplace, under just such black oak rafters, with the sense that beyond the mullioned panes the downs were darkened to a deeper solitude: it was for the ultimate indulgence of such sensations that Mary Boyne, abruptly exiled from New York by her husband's business, had endured for nearly fourteen years the soul-deadening ugliness of a Middle Western town, and that Boyne had ground on doggedly at his engineering till, with a suddenness that still made her blink, the prodigious windfall of the Blue Star Mine had put them at a stroke in possession of life and the leisure to taste it. They had never for a moment meant their new state to be one of idleness; but they meant to give themselves only to harmonious activities. She had her vision of painting and gardening (against a background of grey walls), he dreamed of the production of his long-planned book on the "Economic Basis of Culture"; and with such absorbing work ahead no existence could be too sequestered: they could not get far enough from the world, or plunge deep enough into the past.

Dorsetshire had attracted them from the first by an air of remoteness out of all proportion to its geographical position. But to the Boynes it was one of the ever-recurring wonders of the whole incredibly compressed island—a nest of counties, as they put it—that for the production of its effects so little of a given quality went so far: that so few miles made a distance, and so short a distance a difference.

"It's that," Ned had once enthusiastically explained, "that gives such depth to their effects, such relief to their contrasts. They've been able to lay the butter so thick on every delicious mouthful."

The butter had certainly been laid on thick at Lyng: the old house hidden under a shoulder of the downs had almost all the finer marks of commerce with a protracted past. The mere fact that it was neither large nor exceptional made it, to the Boynes, abound the more completely in its special charm—the charm of having been for centuries a deep dim reservoir of life. The life had probably not been of the most vivid order: for long periods, no doubt, it had fallen as noiselessly into the past as the quiet drizzle of autumn fell, hour after hour, into the fish-pond between the yews; but these backwaters of existence sometimes breed, in their sluggish depths, strange acuities of emotion, and Mary Boyne had felt from the first the mysterious stir of intenser memories.

The feeling had never been stronger than on

this particular afternoon when, waiting in the library for the lamps to come, she rose from her seat and stood among the shadows of the hearth. Her husband had gone off, after luncheon, for one of his long tramps on the downs. She had noticed of late that he preferred to go alone; and, in the tried security of their personal relations, had been driven to conclude that his book was bothering him, and that he needed the afternoons to turn over in solitude the problems left from the morning's work. Certainly the book was not going as smoothly as she had thought it would, and there were lines of perplexity between his eyes such as had never been there in his engineering days. He had often, then, looked fagged to the verge of illness, but the native demon of "worry" had never branded his brow. Yet the few pages he had so far read to her—the introduction, and a summary of the opening chapter—showed a firm hold on his subject, and an increasing confidence in his powers.

The fact threw her into deeper perplexity, since, now that he had done with "business" and its disturbing contingencies, the one other possible source of anxiety was eliminated. Unless it were his health, then? But physically he had gained since they had come to Dorsetshire, grown robuster, ruddier, and fresher-eyed. It was only within the last week that she had felt in him the undefinable change which made her restless in his absence, and as tongue-tied in his presence as though it were *she* who had a secret to keep from him!

The thought that there *was* a secret somewhere between them struck her with a sudden rap of wonder, and she looked about her down the long room.

"Can it be the house?" she mused.

The room itself might have been full of secrets. They seemed to be piling themselves up, as evening fell, like the layers and layers of velvet shadow dropping from the low ceiling, the rows of books, the smoke-blurred sculpture of the hearth.

"Why, of course—the house is haunted!" she reflected.

The ghost—Alida's imperceptible ghost—after figuring largely in the banter of their first month or two at Lyng, had been gradually left aside as too ineffectual for imaginative use. Mary had, indeed, as became the tenant of a haunted house, made the customary inquiries among her rural neighbours, but, beyond a vague "They dü say so, Ma'am," the villagers had nothing to impart. The elusive spectre had apparently never had sufficient identity for a legend to crystallise about it, and after a time the Boynes had set the matter down to their profit-and-loss account, agreeing that Lyng was one of the few houses good enough in itself to dispense with supernatural enhancements.

"And I suppose, poor ineffectual demon, that's why it beats its beautiful wings in vain in the void," Mary had laughingly concluded.

"Or, rather," Ned answered in the same strain, "why, amid so much that's ghostly, it can never affirm its separate existence as *the* ghost." And thereupon their invisible housemate had finally dropped out of their references, which were numerous enough to make them soon unaware of the loss.

Now, as she stood on the hearth, the subject of their earlier curiosity revived in her with a new sense of its meaning—a sense gradually acquired through daily contact with the scene of the lurking mystery. It was the house itself, of course, that possessed the ghost-seeing faculty, that communed visually but secretly with its own past; if one could only get into close enough communion with the house, one might surprise its secret, and acquire the ghost-sight on one's own account. Perhaps, in his long hours in this very room, where she never trespassed till the afternoon, her husband *had* acquired it already, and was silently carrying about the weight of whatever it had revealed to him. Mary was too well versed in the code of the spectral world not to know that one could not talk about the ghosts one saw: to do so was almost as great a breach of taste as to name a lady in a club. But this explanation did not really satisfy her. "What, after all, except for the fun of the shudder," she reflected, "would he really care for any of their old ghosts?" And thence she was thrown back once more on the fundamental dilemma: the fact that one's greater or less susceptibility to spectral influences had no particular bearing on the case, since, when one *did* see a ghost at Lyng, one did not know it.

"Not till long afterward," Alida Stair had said. Well, supposing Ned *had* seen one when they first came, and had known only within the last week what had happened to him? More and more under the spell of the hour, she threw back her thoughts to the early days of their tenancy, but at first only to recall a lively confusion of unpacking, settling, arranging of books, and calling to each other from remote corners of the house as, treasure after treasure, it revealed itself to them. It was in this particular connection that she presently recalled a certain soft afternoon of the previous October, when, passing from the first rapturous flurry of exploration to a detailed inspection of the old house, she had pressed (like a novel heroine) a panel that opened on a flight of corkscrew stairs leading to a flat ledge of the roof—the roof which, from below, seemed to slope away on all sides too abruptly for any but practised feet to scale.

The view from this hidden coign was enchanting, and she had flown down to snatch Ned from his papers and give him the freedom of her discovery. She remembered still how, standing at her side, he had passed his arm about her while their gaze flew to the long tossed horizon-line of the downs, and then dropped contentedly back to trace the arabesque of yew hedges about the fish-pond, and the shadow of the cedar on the lawn.

"And now the other way," he had said, turning her about within his arm; and closely pressed to him, she had absorbed, like some long satisfying draught, the picture of the grey-walled court, the squat lions on the gates, and the lime-avenue reaching up to the highroad under the downs.

It was just then, while they gazed and held each other, that she had felt his arm relax, and heard a sharp "Hullo!" that made her turn to glance at him.

Distinctly, yes, she now recalled that she had seen, as she glanced, a shadow of anxiety, of perplexity, rather, fall across his face; and, following his eyes, had beheld the figure of a man—a man in loose greyish clothes, as it appeared to her—who was sauntering down the lime-avenue to the court with the doubtful gait of a stranger who seeks his way. Her short-sighted eyes had given her but a blurred impression of slightness and greyishness, with something foreign, or at least unlocal, in the cut of the figure or its dress; but her husband had apparently seen more—seen enough to make him push past her with a hasty "Wait!" and dash down the stairs without pausing to give her a hand.

A slight tendency to dizziness obliged her, after a provisional clutch at the chimney against which they had been leaning, to follow him first more cautiously; and when she had reached the landing she paused again, for a less definite reason, leaning over the banister to strain her eyes through the silence of the brown sun-flecked depths. She lingered there till, somewhere in those depths, she heard the closing of a door; then, mechanically impelled, she went down the shallow flights of steps till she reached the lower hall.

The front door stood open on the sunlight of the court, and hall and court were empty. The library door was open, too, and after listening in vain for any sound of voices within, she crossed the threshold, and found her husband alone, vaguely fingering the papers on his desk.

He looked up, as if surprised at her entrance, but the shadow of anxiety had passed from his face, leaving it even, as she fancied, a little brighter and clearer than usual.

"What was it? Who was it?" she asked.

"Who?" he repeated, with the surprise still all on his side.

"The man we saw coming toward the house."

He seemed to reflect. "The man? Why, I thought I saw Peters; I dashed after him to say a word about the stable drains, but he had disappeared before I could get down."

"Disappeared? But he seemed to be walking so slowly when we saw him."

Boyne shrugged his shoulders. "So I thought; but he must have got up steam in the interval. What do you say to our trying a scramble up Meldon Steep before sunset?"

That was all. At the time the occurrence had been less than nothing, had, indeed, been immediately obliterated by the magic of their first vision from Meldon Steep, a height which they had dreamed of climbing ever since they had first seen its bare spine rising above the roof of Lyng. Doubtless it was the mere fact of the other incident's having occurred on the very day of their ascent to Meldon that had kept it stored away in the fold of memory from which it now emerged; for in itself it had no mark of the portentous. At the moment there could have been nothing more natural than that Ned should dash himself from the roof in the pursuit of dilatory tradesmen. It was the period when they were always on the watch for one or the other of the specialists employed about the place; always lying in wait for them, and rushing out at them with questions, reproaches, or reminders. And certainly in the distance the grey figure had looked like Peters.

Yet now, as she reviewed the scene, she felt her husband's explanation of it to have been invalidated by the look of anxiety on his face. Why had the familiar appearance of Peters made him anxious? Why, above all, if it was of such prime necessity to confer with him on the subject of the stable drains, had the failure to find him produced such a look of relief? Mary could not say that any one of these questions had occurred to her at the time, yet, from the promptness with which they now marshalled themselves at her summons, she had a sense that they must all along have been there, waiting their hour.

II

Weary with her thoughts, she moved to the window. The library was now quite dark, and she was surprised to see how much faint light the outer world still held.

As she peered out into it across the court, a figure shaped itself far down the perspective of bare limes: it looked a mere blot of deeper grey in the greyness, and for an instant, as it moved toward her, her heart thumped to the thought "It's the ghost!"

She had time, in that long instant, to feel suddenly that the man of whom, two months earlier, she had had a distant vision from the roof, was now, at his predestined hour, about to reveal himself as *not* having been Peters; and her spirit sank under the impending fear of the disclosure. But almost with the next tick of the clock the figure, gaining substance and character, showed itself even to her weak sight as her husband's; and she turned to meet him, as he entered, with the confession of her folly.

"It's really too absurd," she laughed out, "but I never *can* remember!"

"Remember what?" Boyne questioned as they drew together.

"That when one sees the Lyng ghost one never knows it."

Her hand was on his sleeve, and he kept it there, but with no response in his gesture or in the lines of his preoccupied face.

"Did you think you'd seen it?" he asked, after an appreciable interval.

"Why, I actually took *you* for it, my dear, in my mad determination to spot it!"

"Me—just now?" His arm dropped away, and he turned from her with a faint echo of her laugh. "Really, dearest, you'd better give it up, if that's the best you can do."

"Oh, yes, I give it up. Have *you?*" she asked, turning round on him abruptly.

The parlour-maid had entered with letters and a lamp, and the light struck up into Boyne's face as he bent above the tray she presented.

"Have *you?*" Mary perversely insisted, when the servant had disappeared on her errand of illumination.

"Have I what?" he rejoined absently, the light

bringing out the sharp stamp of worry between his brows as he turned over the letters.

"Given up trying to see the ghost." Her heart beat a little at the experiment she was making.

Her husband, laying his letters aside, moved away into the shadow of the hearth.

"I never tried," he said, tearing open the wrapper of a newspaper.

"Well, of course," Mary persisted, "the exasperating thing is that there's no use trying, since one can't be sure till so long afterward."

He was unfolding the paper as if he had hardly heard her; but after a pause, during which the sheets rustled spasmodically between his hands, he looked up to ask, "Have you any idea *how long?*"

Mary had sunk into a low chair beside the fireplace. From her seat she glanced over, startled, at her husband's profile, which was projected against the circle of lamplight.

"No; none. Have *you?*" she retorted, repeating her former phrase with an added stress of intention.

Boyne crumpled the paper into a bunch, and then, inconsequently, turned back with it toward the lamp.

"Lord, no! I only meant," he explained, with a faint tinge of impatience, "is there any legend, any tradition, as to that?"

"Not that I know of," she answered; but the impulse to add "What makes you ask?" was checked by the reappearance of the parlour-maid, with tea and a second lamp.

With the dispersal of shadows, and the repetition of the daily domestic office, Mary Boyne felt herself less oppressed by that sense of something mutely imminent which had darkened her afternoon. For a few moments she gave herself to the details of her task, and when she looked up from it she was struck to the point of bewilderment by the change in her husband's face. He had seated himself near the farther lamp, and was absorbed in the perusal of his letters; but was it something he had found in them, or merely the shifting of her own point

of view, that had restored his features to their normal aspect? The longer she looked the more definitely the change affirmed itself. The lines of tension had vanished, and such traces of fatigue as lingered were of the kind easily attributable to steady mental effort. He glanced up, as if drawn by her gaze, and met her eyes with a smile.

"I'm dying for my tea, you know; and here's a letter for you," he said.

She took the letter he held out in exchange for the cup she proffered him, and, returning to her seat, broke the seal with the languid gesture of the reader whose interests are all enclosed in the circle of one cherished presence.

Her next conscious motion was that of starting to her feet, the letter falling to them as she rose, while she held out to her husband a newspaper clipping.

"Ned! What's this? What does it mean?"

He had risen at the same instant, almost as if hearing her cry before she uttered it; and for a perceptible space of time he and she studied each other, like adversaries watching for an advantage, across the space between her chair and his desk.

"What's what? You fairly made me jump!" Boyne said at length, moving toward her with a sudden half-exasperated laugh. The shadow of apprehension was on his face again, not now a look of fixed foreboding, but a shifting vigilance of lips and eyes that gave her the sense of his feeling himself invisibly surrounded.

Her hand shook so that she could hardly give him the clipping.

"This article—from the *Waukesha Sentinel*—that a man named Elwell has brought suit against you—that there was something wrong about the Blue Star Mine. I can't understand more than half."

They continued to face each other as she spoke, and to her astonishment she saw that her words had the almost immediate effect of dissipating the strained watchfulness of his look.

"Oh, *that!*" He glanced down the printed slip, and then folded it with the gesture of one who handles something harmless and familiar. "What's the matter with you this afternoon, Mary? I thought you'd got bad news."

She stood before him with her undefinable terror subsiding slowly under the reassurance of his tone.

"You knew about this, then—it's all right?"

"Certainly I knew about it; and it's all right."

"But what *is* it? I don't understand. What does this man accuse you of?"

"Pretty nearly every crime in the calendar." Boyne had tossed the clipping down, and thrown himself into an arm-chair near the fire. "Do you want to hear the story? It's not particularly interesting—just a squabble over interests in the Blue Star."

"But who is this Elwell? I don't know the name."

"Oh, he's a fellow I put into it—gave him a hand up. I told you all about him at the time."

"I daresay. I must have forgotten." Vainly she strained back among her memories. "But if you helped him, why does he make this return?"

"Probably some shyster lawyer got hold of him and talked him over. It's all rather technical and complicated. I thought that kind of thing bored you."

His wife felt a sting of compunction. Theoretically, she deprecated the American wife's detachment from her husband's professional interests, but in practise she had always found it difficult to fix her attention on Boyne's report of the transactions in which his varied interests involved him. Besides, she had felt during their years of exile, that, in a community where the amenities of living could be obtained only at the cost of efforts as arduous as her husband's professional labours, such brief leisure as he and she could command should be used as an escape from immediate preoccupations, a flight to the life they always dreamed of living. Once or twice, now that this new life had actually drawn its magic circle about them, she had asked herself if she had done right; but hitherto such conjectures

had been no more than the retrospective excursions of an active fancy. Now, for the first time, it startled her a little to find how little she knew of the material foundation on which her happiness was built.

She glanced at her husband, and was again reassured by the composure of his face; yet she felt the need of more definite grounds for her reassurance.

"But doesn't this suit worry you? Why have you never spoken to me about it?"

He answered both questions at once. "I didn't speak of it at first because it *did* worry me—annoyed me, rather. But it's all ancient history now. Your correspondent must have got hold of a back number of the *Sentinel*."

She felt a quick thrill of relief. "You mean it's over? He's lost his case?"

There was a just perceptible delay in Boyne's reply. "The suit's been withdrawn—that's all."

But she persisted, as if to exonerate herself from the inward charge of being too easily put off. "Withdrawn it because he saw he had no chance?"

"Oh, he had no chance," Boyne answered.

She was still struggling with a dimly felt perplexity at the back of her thoughts.

"How long ago was it withdrawn?"

He paused, as if with a slight return of his former uncertainty. "I've just had the news now; but I've been expecting it."

"Just now—in one of your letters?"

"Yes; in one of my letters."

She made no answer, and was aware only, after a short interval of waiting, that he had risen, and, strolling across the room, had placed himself on the sofa at her side. She felt him, as he did so, pass an arm about her, she felt his hand seek hers and clasp it, and turning slowly, drawn by the warmth of his cheek, she met his smiling eyes.

"It's all right—it's all right?" she questioned, through the flood of her dissolving doubts; and "I give you my word it was never righter!" he laughed back at her, holding her close.

III

One of the strangest things she was afterward to recall out of all the next day's strangeness was the sudden and complete recovery of her sense of security.

It was in the air when she woke in her low-ceilinged, dusky room; it went with her downstairs to the breakfast-table, flashed out at her from the fire, and reduplicated itself from the flanks of the urn and the sturdy flutings of the Georgian teapot. It was as if, in some round-about way, all her diffused fears of the previous day, with their moment of sharp concentration about the newspaper article—as if this dim questioning of the future, and startled return upon the past, had between them liquidated the arrears of some haunting moral obligation. If she had indeed been careless of her husband's affairs, it was, her new state seemed to prove, because her faith in him instinctively justified such carelessness; and his right to her faith had now affirmed itself in the very face of menace and suspicion. She had never seen him more untroubled, more naturally and unconsciously himself, than after the cross-examination to which she had subjected him: it was almost as if he had been aware of her doubts, and had wanted the air cleared as much as she did.

It was as clear, thank Heaven! as the bright outer light that surprised her almost with a touch of summer when she issued from the house for her daily round of the gardens. She had left Boyne at his desk, indulging herself, as she passed the library door, by a last peep at his quiet face, where he bent, pipe in mouth, above his papers; and now she had her own morning's task to perform. The task involved, on such charmed winter days, almost as much happy loitering about the different quarters of her demesne as if spring were already at work there. There were such endless possibilities still before her, such opportunities to bring out the latent graces of the old place, without a single irrever-ent touch of alteration, that the winter was all too short to plan what spring and autumn executed. And her recovered sense of safety gave, on this particular morning, a peculiar zest to her progress through the sweet still place. She went first to the kitchen-garden, where the espaliered pear-trees drew complicated patterns on the walls, and pigeons were fluttering and preening about the silvery-slated roof of their cot. There was something wrong about the piping of the hot-house, and she was expecting an authority from Dorchester, who was to drive out between trains and make a diagnosis of the boiler. But when she dipped into the damp heat of the green-houses, among the spiced scents and waxy pinks and reds of old-fashioned exotics—even the flora of Lyng was in the note!—she learned that the great man had not arrived, and, the day being too rare to waste in an artificial atmosphere, she came out again and paced along the springy turf of the bowling-green to the gardens behind the house. At their farther end rose a grass terrace, looking across the fish-pond and yew hedges to the long house-front with its twisted chimney-stacks and blue roof angles all drenched in the pale gold moisture of the air.

Seen thus, across the level tracery of the gardens, it sent her, from open windows and hospitably smoking chimneys, the look of some warm human presence, of a mind slowly ripened on a sunny wall of experience. She had never before had such a sense of her intimacy with it, such a conviction that its secrets were all beneficent, kept, as they said to children, "for one's good," such a trust in its power to gather up her life and Ned's into the harmonious pattern of the long long story it sat there weaving in the sun.

She heard steps behind her, and turned, expecting to see the gardener accompanied by the engineer from Dorchester. But only one figure was in sight, that of a youngish slightly built man, who, for reasons she could not on the spot have given, did not remotely resemble her notion of an authority on hot-house boilers. The newcomer, on seeing her, lifted his hat, and paused with the air of a gentleman—perhaps a traveller—who wishes to make it known that his intrusion is involuntary. Lyng occasionally attracted the more cultivated traveller, and Mary half-expected to see the stranger dissemble a camera, or justify his presence by producing it. But he made no gesture of any sort, and after a moment she asked, in a tone responding to the courteous hesitation of his attitude: "Is there any one you wish to see?"

"I came to see Mr. Boyne," he answered. His intonation, rather than his accent, was faintly American, and Mary, at the note, looked at him more closely. The brim of his soft felt hat cast a shade on his face, which, thus obscured, wore to her short-sighted gaze a look of seriousness, as of a person arriving "on business," and civilly but firmly aware of his rights.

Past experience had made her equally sensible to such claims; but she was jealous of her husband's morning hours, and doubtful of his having given any one the right to intrude on them.

"Have you an appointment with my husband?" she asked.

The visitor hesitated, as if unprepared for the question.

"I think he expects me," he replied.

It was Mary's turn to hesitate. "You see this is his time for work: he never sees any one in the morning."

He looked at her a moment without answering; then, as if accepting her decision, he began to move away. As he turned, Mary saw him pause and glance up at the peaceful house-front. Something in his air suggested weariness and disappointment, the dejection of the traveller who has come from far off and whose hours are limited by the time-table. It occurred to her that if this were the case her refusal might have made his errand vain, and a sense of compunction caused her to hasten after him.

"May I ask if you have come a long way?"

He gave her the same grave look. "Yes—I have come a long way."

"Then, if you'll go to the house, no doubt my husband will see you now. You'll find him in the library."

She did not know why she had added the last phrase, except from a vague impulse to atone for her previous inhospitality. The visitor seemed about to express his thanks, but her attention was distracted by the approach of the gardener with a companion who bore all the marks of being the expert from Dorchester.

"This way," she said, waving the stranger to the house; and an instant later she had forgotten him in the absorption of her meeting with the boiler-maker.

The encounter led to such far-reaching results that the engineer ended by finding it expedient to ignore his train, and Mary was beguiled into spending the remainder of the morning in absorbed confabulation among the flower-pots. When the colloquy ended, she was surprised to find that it was nearly luncheon-time, and she half expected, as she hurried back to the house, to see her husband coming out to meet her. But she found no one in the court but an under-gardener raking the gravel, and the hall, when she entered it, was so silent that she guessed Boyne to be still at work.

Not wishing to disturb him, she turned into the drawing-room, and there, at her writing-table, lost herself in renewed calculations of the outlay to which the morning's conference had pledged her. The fact that she could permit herself such follies had not yet lost its novelty; and somehow, in contrast to the vague fears of the previous days, it now seemed an element of her recovered security, of the sense that, as Ned had said, things in general had never been "righter."

She was still luxuriating in a lavish play of figures when the parlour-maid, from the threshold, roused her with an inquiry as to the expediency of serving luncheon. It was one of their jokes that Trimmle announced luncheon as if she were divulging a state secret, and Mary, intent upon her papers, merely murmured an absentminded assent.

She felt Trimmle wavering doubtfully on the threshold, as if in rebuke of such unconsidered assent; then her retreating steps sounded down the passage, and Mary, pushing away her papers, crossed the hall and went to the library door. It was still closed, and she wavered in her turn, disliking to disturb her husband, yet anxious that he should not exceed his usual measure of work. As she stood there, balancing her impulses, Trimmle returned with the announcement of luncheon, and Mary, thus impelled, opened the library door.

Boyne was not at his desk, and she peered about her, expecting to discover him before the book-shelves, somewhere down the length of the room; but her call brought no response, and gradually it became clear to her that he was not there.

She turned back to the parlour-maid.

"Mr. Boyne must be up-stairs. Please tell him that luncheon is ready."

Trimmle appeared to hesitate between the obvious duty of obedience and an equally obvious conviction of the foolishness of the injunction laid on her. The struggle resulted in her saying: "If you please, Madam, Mr. Boyne's not up-stairs."

"Not in his room? Are you sure?"

"I'm sure, Madam."

Mary consulted the clock. "Where is he, then?"

"He's gone out," Trimmle announced, with the superior air of one who has respectfully waited for the question that a well-ordered mind would have put first.

Mary's conjecture had been right, then. Boyne must have gone to the gardens to meet her, and since she had missed him, it was clear that he had taken the shorter way by the south door, instead of going round to the court. She crossed the hall to the French window opening directly on the yew garden, but the parlour-maid, after another moment of inner conflict, decided to bring out: "Please, Madam, Mr. Boyne didn't go that way."

Mary turned back. "Where *did* he go? And when?"

"He went out of the front door, up the drive,

Madam." It was a matter of principle with Trimmle never to answer more than one question at a time.

"Up the drive? At this hour?" Mary went to the door herself, and glanced across the court through the tunnel of bare limes. But its perspective was as empty as when she had scanned it on entering.

"Did Mr. Boyne leave no message?"

Trimmle seemed to surrender herself to a last struggle with the forces of chaos.

"No, Madam. He just went out with the gentleman."

"The gentleman? What gentleman?" Mary wheeled about, as if to front this new factor.

"The gentleman who called, Madam," said Trimmle resignedly.

"When did a gentleman call? Do explain yourself, Trimmle!"

Only the fact that Mary was very hungry, and that she wanted to consult her husband about the green-houses, would have caused her to lay so unusual an injunction on her attendant; and even now she was detached enough to note in Trimmle's eye the dawning defiance of the respectful subordinate who has been pressed too hard.

"I couldn't exactly say the hour, Madam, because I didn't let the gentleman in," she replied, with an air of discreetly ignoring the irregularity of her mistress's course.

"You didn't let him in?"

"No, Madam. When the bell rang I was dressing, and Agnes——"

"Go and ask Agnes, then," said Mary.

Trimmle still wore her look of patient magnanimity. "Agnes would not know, Madam, for she had unfortunately burnt her hand in trimming the wick of the new lamp from town"—Trimmle, as Mary was aware, had always been opposed to the new lamp—"and so Mrs. Dockett sent the kitchen-maid instead."

Mary looked again at the clock. "It's after two! Go and ask the kitchen-maid if Mr. Boyne left any word."

She went into luncheon without waiting,

and Trimmle presently brought her there the kitchen-maid's statement that the gentleman had called about eleven o'clock, and that Mr. Boyne had gone out with him without leaving any message. The kitchen-maid did not even know the caller's name, for he had written it on a slip of paper, which he had folded and handed to her, with the injunction to deliver it at once to Mr. Boyne.

Mary finished her luncheon, still wondering, and when it was over, and Trimmle had brought the coffee to the drawing-room, her wonder had deepened to a first faint tinge of disquietude. It was unlike Boyne to absent himself without explanation at so unwonted an hour, and the difficulty of identifying the visitor whose summons he had apparently obeyed made his disappearance the more unaccountable. Mary Boyne's experience as the wife of a busy engineer, subject to sudden calls and compelled to keep irregular hours, had trained her to the philosophic acceptance of surprises; but since Boyne's withdrawal from business he had adopted a Benedictine regularity of life. As if to make up for the dispersed and agitated years, with their "stand-up" lunches, and dinners rattled down to the joltings of the dining-cars, he cultivated the last refinements of punctuality and monotony, discouraging his wife's fancy for the unexpected, and declaring that to a delicate taste there were infinite gradations of pleasure in the recurrences of habit.

Still, since no life can completely defend itself from the unforeseen, it was evident that all Boyne's precautions would sooner or later prove unavailable, and Mary concluded that he had cut short a tiresome visit by walking with his caller to the station, or at least accompanying him for part of the way.

This conclusion relieved her from farther preoccupation, and she went out herself to take up her conference with the gardener. Thence she walked to the village post-office, a mile or so away; and when she turned toward home the early twilight was setting in.

She had taken a foot-path across the downs,

and as Boyne, meanwhile, had probably returned from the station by the highroad, there was little likelihood of their meeting. She felt sure, however, of his having reached the house before her; so sure that, when she entered it herself, without even pausing to inquire of Trimmle, she made directly for the library. But the library was still empty, and with an unwonted exactness of visual memory she observed that the papers on her husband's desk lay precisely as they had lain when she had gone in to call him to luncheon.

Then of a sudden she was seized by a vague dread of the unknown. She had closed the door behind her on entering, and as she stood alone in the long silent room, her dread seemed to take shape and sound, to be there breathing and lurking among the shadows. Her short-sighted eyes strained through them, half-discerning an actual presence, something aloof, that watched and knew; and in the recoil from that intangible presence she threw herself on the bell-rope and gave it a sharp pull.

The sharp summons brought Trimmle in precipitately with a lamp, and Mary breathed again at this sobering reappearance of the usual.

"You may bring tea if Mr. Boyne is in," she said, to justify her ring.

"Very well, Madam. But Mr. Boyne is not in," said Trimmle, putting down the lamp.

"Not in? You mean he's come back and gone out again?"

"No, Madam. He's never been back."

The dread stirred again, and Mary knew that now it had her fast.

"Not since he went out with—the gentleman?"

"Not since he went out with the gentleman."

"But who *was* the gentleman?" Mary insisted, with the shrill note of some one trying to be heard through a confusion of noises.

"That I couldn't say, Madam." Trimmle, standing there by the lamp, seemed suddenly to grow less round and rosy, as though eclipsed by the same creeping shade of apprehension.

"But the kitchen-maid knows—wasn't it the kitchen-maid who let him in?"

"She doesn't know either, Madam, for he wrote his name on a folded paper."

Mary, through her agitation, was aware that they were both designating the unknown visitor by a vague pronoun, instead of the conventional formula which, till then, had kept their allusions within the bounds of conformity. And at the same moment her mind caught at the suggestion of the folded paper.

"But he must have a name! Where's the paper?"

She moved to the desk, and began to turn over the documents that littered it. The first that caught her eye was an unfinished letter in her husband's hand, with his pen lying across it, as though dropped there at a sudden summons.

"My dear Parvis"—who was Parvis?—"I have just received your letter announcing El-well's death, and while I suppose there is now no further risk of trouble, it might be safer——"

She tossed the sheet aside, and continued her search; but no folded paper was discoverable among the letters and pages of manuscript which had been swept together in a heap, as if by a hurried or a startled gesture.

"But the kitchen-maid *saw* him. Send her here," she commanded, wondering at her dulness in not thinking sooner of so simple a solution.

Trimmle vanished in a flash, as if thankful to be out of the room, and when she reappeared, conducting the agitated underling, Mary had regained her self-possession, and had her questions ready.

The gentleman was a stranger, yes—that she understood. But what had he said? And, above all, what had he looked like? The first question was easily enough answered, for the disconcerting reason that he had said so little—had merely asked for Mr. Boyne, and, scribbling something on a bit of paper, had requested that it should at once be carried in to him.

"Then you don't know what he wrote? You're not sure it *was* his name?"

The kitchen-maid was not sure, but supposed it was, since he had written it in answer to her inquiry as to whom she should announce.

"And when you carried the paper in to Mr. Boyne, what did he say?"

The kitchen-maid did not think that Mr. Boyne had said anything, but she could not be sure, for just as she had handed him the paper and he was opening it, she had become aware that the visitor had followed her into the library, and she had slipped out, leaving the two gentlemen together.

"But then, if you left them in the library, how do you know that they went out of the house?"

This question plunged the witness into a momentary inarticulateness, from which she was rescued by Trimmle, who, by means of ingenious circumlocutions, elicited the statement that before she could cross the hall to the back passage she had heard the two gentlemen behind her, and had seen them go out of the front door together.

"Then, if you saw the strange gentleman twice, you must be able to tell me what he looked like."

But with this final challenge to her powers of expression it became clear that the limit of the kitchen-maid's endurance had been reached. The obligation of going to the front door to "show in" a visitor was in itself so subversive of the fundamental order of things that it had thrown her faculties into hopeless disarray, and she could only stammer out, after various panting efforts: "His hat, mum, was different-like, as you might say——"

"Different? How different?" Mary flashed out, her own mind, in the same instant, leaping back to an image left on it that morning, and then lost under layers of subsequent impressions.

"His hat had a wide brim, you mean? and his face was pale—a youngish face?" Mary pressed her, with a white-lipped intensity of interrogation. But if the kitchen-maid found any adequate answer to this challenge, it was swept away for her listener down the rushing current of her own convictions. The stranger—the stranger in the garden! Why had Mary not thought of him before? She needed no one now to tell her that it was he who had called for her husband and gone away with him. But who was he, and why had Boyne obeyed him?

IV

It leaped out at her suddenly, like a grin out of the dark, that they had often called England so little—"such a confoundedly hard place to get lost in."

A confoundedly hard place to get lost in! That had been her husband's phrase. And now, with the whole machinery of official investigation sweeping its flashlights from shore to shore, and across the dividing straits; now, with Boyne's name blazing from the walls of every town and village, his portrait (how that wrung her!) hawked up and down the country like the image of a hunted criminal; now the little compact populous island, so policed, surveyed, and administered, revealed itself as a Sphinx-like guardian of abysmal mysteries, staring back into his wife's anguished eyes as if with the wicked joy of knowing something they would never know!

In the fortnight since Boyne's disappearance there had been no word of him, no trace of his movements. Even the usual misleading reports that raise expectancy in tortured bosoms had been few and fleeting. No one but the kitchen-maid had seen Boyne leave the house, and no one else had seen "the gentleman" who accompanied him. All inquiries in the neighbourhood failed to elicit the memory of a stranger's presence that day in the neighbourhood of Lyng. And no one had met Edward Boyne, either alone or in company, in any of the neighbouring villages, or on the road across the downs, or at either of the local railway-stations. The sunny English noon had swallowed him as completely as if he had gone out into Cimmerian night.

Mary, while every official means of investigation was working at its highest pressure, had ransacked her husband's papers for any trace of antecedent complications, of entanglements or obligations unknown to her, that might throw a ray into the darkness. But if any such had existed in the background of Boyne's life, they had vanished like the slip of paper on which the visitor had written his name. There remained no possible thread of guidance except—if it were indeed an exception—the letter which Boyne had apparently been in the act of writing when he received his mysterious summons. That letter, read and reread by his wife, and submitted by her to the police, yielded little enough to feed conjecture.

"I have just heard of Elwell's death, and while I suppose there is now no farther risk of trouble, it might be safer——" That was all. The "risk of trouble" was easily explained by the newspaper clipping which had apprised Mary of the suit brought against her husband by one of his associates in the Blue Star enterprise. The only new information conveyed by the letter was the fact of its showing Boyne, when he wrote it, to be still apprehensive of the results of the suit, though he had told his wife that it had been withdrawn, and though the letter itself proved that the plaintiff was dead. It took several days of cabling to fix the identity of the "Parvis" to whom the fragment was addressed, but even after these inquiries had shown him to be a Waukesha lawyer, no new facts concerning the Elwell suit were elicited. He appeared to have had no direct concern in it, but to have been conversant with the facts merely as an acquaintance, and possible intermediary; and he declared himself unable to guess with what object Boyne intended to seek his assistance.

This negative information, sole fruit of the first fortnight's search, was not increased by a jot during the slow weeks that followed. Mary knew that the investigations were still being carried on, but she had a vague sense of their gradually slackening, as the actual march of time seemed to slacken. It was as though the days, flying horror-struck from the shrouded image of the one inscrutable day, gained assurance as the distance lengthened, till at last they fell back into their normal gait. And so with the human imaginations at work on the dark event. No doubt it occupied them still, but week by week and hour by hour it grew less absorbing, took up less space, was slowly but inevitably crowded out of the foreground of consciousness by the new problems perpetually bubbling up from the cloudy caldron of human experience.

Even Mary Boyne's consciousness gradually felt the same lowering of velocity. It still swayed with the incessant oscillations of conjecture; but they were slower, more rhythmical in their beat. There were even moments of weariness when, like the victim of some poison which leaves the brain clear, but holds the body motionless, she saw herself domesticated with the Horror, accepting its perpetual presence as one of the fixed conditions of life.

These moments lengthened into hours and days, till she passed into a phase of stolid acquiescence. She watched the routine of daily life with the incurious eye of a savage on whom the meaningless processes of civilisation make but the faintest impression. She had come to regard herself as part of the routine, a spoke of the wheel, revolving with its motion; she felt almost like the furniture of the room in which she sat, an insensate object to be dusted and pushed about with the chairs and tables. And this deepening apathy held her fast at Lyng, in spite of the entreaties of friends and the usual medical recommendation of "change." Her friends supposed that her refusal to move was inspired by the belief that her husband would one day return to the spot from which he had vanished, and a beautiful legend grew up about this imaginary state of waiting. But in reality she had no such belief: the depths of anguish enclosing her were no longer lighted by flashes of hope. She was sure that Boyne would never come back, that he had gone out of her sight as completely as if Death itself had waited that day on the threshold. She had even renounced, one by one, the various theories as to his disappearance which had been advanced by the press, the police, and her own agonised imagination. In sheer lassitude her mind turned from these alternatives of hor-

ror, and sank back into the blank fact that he was gone.

No, she would never know what had become of him—no one would ever know. But the house *knew*; the library in which she spent her long lonely evenings knew. For it was here that the last scene had been enacted, here that the stranger had come, and spoken the word which had caused Boyne to rise and follow him. The floor she trod had felt his tread; the books on the shelves had seen his face; and there were moments when the intense consciousness of the old dusky walls seemed about to break out into some audible revelation of their secret. But the revelation never came, and she knew it would never come. Lyng was not one of the garrulous old houses that betray the secrets entrusted to them. Its very legend proved that it had always been the mute accomplice, the incorruptible custodian, of the mysteries it had surprised. And Mary Boyne, sitting face to face with its silence, felt the futility of seeking to break it by any human means.

V

"I don't say it *wasn't* straight, and yet I don't say it *was* straight. It was business."

Mary, at the words, lifted her head with a start, and looked intently at the speaker.

When, half an hour before, a card with "Mr. Parvis" on it had been brought up to her, she had been immediately aware that the name had been a part of her consciousness ever since she had read it at the head of Boyne's unfinished letter. In the library she had found awaiting her a small sallow man with a bald head and gold eyeglasses, and it sent a tremor through her to know that this was the person to whom her husband's last known thought had been directed.

Parvis, civilly, but without vain preamble—in the manner of a man who has his watch in his hand—had set forth the object of his visit. He had "run over" to England on business, and finding himself in the neighbourhood of

Dorchester, had not wished to leave it without paying his respects to Mrs. Boyne; and without asking her, if the occasion offered, what she meant to do about Bob Elwell's family.

The words touched the spring of some obscure dread in Mary's bosom. Did her visitor, after all, know what Boyne had meant by his unfinished phrase? She asked for an elucidation of his question, and noticed at once that he seemed surprised at her continued ignorance of the subject. Was it possible that she really knew as little as she said?

"I know nothing—you must tell me," she faltered out; and her visitor thereupon proceeded to unfold his story. It threw, even to her confused perceptions, and imperfectly initiated vision, a lurid glare on the whole hazy episode of the Blue Star Mine. Her husband had made his money in that brilliant speculation at the cost of "getting ahead" of some one less alert to seize the chance; and the victim of his ingenuity was young Robert Elwell, who had "put him on" to the Blue Star scheme.

Parvis, at Mary's first cry, had thrown her a sobering glance through his impartial glasses.

"Bob Elwell wasn't smart enough, that's all; if he had been, he might have turned round and served Boyne the same way. It's the kind of thing that happens every day in business. I guess it's what the scientists call the survival of the fittest—see?" said Mr. Parvis, evidently pleased with the aptness of his analogy.

Mary felt a physical shrinking from the next question she tried to frame: it was as though the words on her lips had a taste that nauseated her.

"But then—you accuse my husband of doing something dishonourable?"

Mr. Parvis surveyed the question dispassionately. "Oh, no, I don't. I don't even say it wasn't straight." He glanced up and down the long lines of books, as if one of them might have supplied him with the definition he sought. "I don't say it *wasn't* straight, and yet I don't say it *was* straight. It was business." After all, no definition in his category could be more comprehensive than that.

Mary sat staring at him with a look of terror. He seemed to her like the indifferent emissary of some evil power.

"But Mr. Elwell's lawyers apparently did not take your view, since I suppose the suit was withdrawn by their advice."

"Oh, yes; they knew he hadn't a leg to stand on, technically. It was when they advised him to withdraw the suit that he got desperate. You see, he'd borrowed most of the money he lost in the Blue Star, and he was up a tree. That's why he shot himself when they told him he had no show."

The horror was sweeping over Mary in great deafening waves.

"He shot himself? He killed himself because of *that?*"

"Well, he didn't kill himself, exactly. He dragged on two months before he died." Parvis emitted the statement as unemotionally as a gramophone grinding out its "record."

"You mean that he tried to kill himself, and failed? And tried again?"

"Oh, he didn't have to *try* again," said Parvis grimly.

They sat opposite each other in silence, he swinging his eyeglasses thoughtfully about his finger, she, motionless, her arms stretched along her knees in an attitude of rigid tension.

"But if you knew all this," she began at length, hardly able to force her voice above a whisper, "how is it that when I wrote you at the time of my husband's disappearance you said you didn't understand his letter?"

Parvis received this without perceptible embarrassment: "Why, I didn't understand it—strictly speaking. And it wasn't the time to talk about it, if I had. The Elwell business was settled when the suit was withdrawn. Nothing I could have told you would have helped you to find your husband."

Mary continued to scrutinise him. "Then why are you telling me now?"

Still Parvis did not hesitate. "Well, to begin with, I supposed you knew more than you appear to—I mean about the circumstances of

Elwell's death. And then people are talking of it now; the whole matter's been raked up again. And I thought if you didn't know you ought to."

She remained silent, and he continued: "You see, it's only come out lately what a bad state Elwell's affairs were in. His wife's a proud woman, and she fought on as long as she could, going out to work, and taking sewing at home when she got too sick—something with the heart, I believe. But she had his mother to look after, and the children, and she broke down under it, and finally had to ask for help. That called attention to the case, and the papers took it up, and a subscription was started. Everybody out there liked Bob Elwell, and most of the prominent names in the place are down on the list, and people began to wonder why——"

Parvis broke off to fumble in an inner pocket. "Here," he continued, "here's an account of the whole thing from the *Sentinel*—a little sensational, of course. But I guess you'd better look it over."

He held out a newspaper to Mary, who unfolded it slowly, remembering, as she did so, the evening when, in that same room, the perusal of a clipping from the *Sentinel* had first shaken the depths of her security.

As she opened the paper, her eyes, shrinking from the glaring headlines, "Widow of Boyne's Victim Forced to Appeal for Aid," ran down the column of text to two portraits inserted in it. The first was her husband's, taken from a photograph made the year they had come to England. It was the picture of him that she liked best, the one that stood on the writing-table up-stairs in her bedroom. As the eyes in the photograph met hers, she felt it would be impossible to read what was said of him, and closed her lids with the sharpness of the pain.

"I thought if you felt disposed to put your name down——" she heard Parvis continue.

She opened her eyes with an effort, and they fell on the other portrait. It was that of a youngish man, slightly built, with features somewhat blurred by the shadow of a projecting hat-brim. Where had she seen that outline before? She stared at it confusedly, her heart hammering in her ears. Then she gave a cry.

"This is the man—the man who came for my husband!"

She heard Parvis start to his feet, and was dimly aware that she had slipped backward into the corner of the sofa, and that he was bending above her in alarm. She straightened herself, and reached out for the paper, which she had dropped.

"It's the man! I should know him anywhere!" she persisted in a voice that sounded to her own ears like a scream.

Parvis's answer seemed to come to her from far off, down endless fog-muffled windings.

"Mrs. Boyne, you're not very well. Shall I call somebody? Shall I get a glass of water?"

"No, no, no!" She threw herself toward him, her hand frantically clutching the newspaper. "I tell you, it's the man! I *know* him! He spoke to me in the garden!"

Parvis took the journal from her, directing his glasses to the portrait. "It can't be, Mrs. Boyne. It's Robert Elwell."

"Robert Elwell?" Her white stare seemed to travel into space. "Then it was Robert Elwell who came for him."

"Came for Boyne? The day he went away from here?" Parvis's voice dropped as hers rose. He bent over, laying a fraternal hand on her, as if to coax her gently back into her seat. "Why, Elwell was dead! Don't you remember?"

Mary sat with her eyes fixed on the picture, unconscious of what he was saying.

"Don't you remember Boyne's unfinished letter to me—the one you found on his desk that day? It was written just after he'd heard of Elwell's death." She noticed an odd shake in Parvis's unemotional voice. "Surely you remember!" he urged her.

Yes, she remembered: that was the profoundest horror of it. Elwell had died the day before her husband's disappearance; and this was Elwell's portrait; and it was the portrait of the man who had spoken to her in the garden. She lifted her head and looked slowly about the library. The library could have borne witness that it was also the portrait of the man who had come in that day to call Boyne from his unfinished letter. Through the misty surgings of her brain she heard the faint boom of half-forgotten words—words spoken by Alida Stair on the lawn at Pangbourne before Boyne and his wife had ever seen the house at Lyng, or had imagined that they might one day live there.

"This was the man who spoke to me," she repeated.

She looked again at Parvis. He was trying to conceal his disturbance under what he probably imagined to be an expression of indulgent commiseration; but the edges of his lips were blue. "He thinks me mad; but I'm not mad," she reflected; and suddenly there flashed upon her a way of justifying her strange affirmation.

She sat quiet, controlling the quiver of her lips, and waiting till she could trust her voice; then she said, looking straight at Parvis: "Will you answer me one question, please? When was it that Robert Elwell tried to kill himself?"

"When—when?" Parvis stammered.

"Yes; the date. Please try to remember."

She saw that he was growing still more afraid of her. "I have a reason," she insisted.

"Yes, yes. Only I can't remember. About two months before, I should say."

"I want the date," she repeated.

Parvis picked up the newspaper. "We might see here," he said, still humouring her. He ran his eyes down the page. "Here it is. Last October—the——"

She caught the words from him. "The 20th, wasn't it?" With a sharp look at her, he verified. "Yes, the 20th. Then you *did* know?"

"I know now." Her gaze continued to travel past him. "Sunday, the 20th—that was the day he came first."

Parvis's voice was almost inaudible. "Came *here* first?"

"Yes."

"You saw him twice, then?"

"Yes, twice." She just breathed it at him. "He came first on the 20th of October. I remember the date because it was the day we went up Meldon Steep for the first time." She felt a faint gasp of inward laughter at the thought that but for that she might have forgotten.

Parvis continued to scrutinise her, as if trying to intercept her gaze.

"We saw him from the roof," she went on. "He came down the lime-avenue toward the house. He was dressed just as he is in that picture. My husband saw him first. He was frightened, and ran down ahead of me; but there was no one there. He had vanished."

"Elwell had vanished?" Parvis faltered.

"Yes." Their two whispers seemed to grope for each other. "I couldn't think what had happened. I see now. He *tried* to come then; but he wasn't dead enough—he couldn't reach us. He had to wait for two months to die; and then he came back again—and Ned went with him."

She nodded at Parvis with the look of triumph of a child who has worked out a difficult puzzle. But suddenly she lifted her hands with a desperate gesture, pressing them to her temples.

"Oh, my God! I sent him to Ned—I told him where to go! I sent him to this room!" she screamed.

She felt the walls of books rush toward her, like inward falling ruins; and she heard Parvis, a long way off, through the ruins, crying to her, and struggling to get at her. But she was numb to his touch, she did not know what he was saying. Through the tumult she heard but one clear note, the voice of Alida Stair, speaking on the lawn at Pangbourne.

"You won't know till afterward," it said. "You won't know till long, long afterward."

CONSEQUENCES

Willa Cather

A TRULY AMERICAN WRITER of the first half of the twentieth century, Willa (Sibert) Cather (1873–1947) is probably most associated with the western plains of Nebraska, where she set such classics as *O Pioneers!* (1913) and *My Ántonia* (1918), though she was born in Virginia and lived for some years in New York, Pittsburgh, the Southwest, Maine, and, briefly, Europe. One of her only moderately successful and now lesser-known works, *One of Ours* (1922), won the Pulitzer Prize for fiction in 1923.

Her very traditional themes and precise prose style brought her great success, though the somewhat meandering novels, largely devoid of plot, passion, and surprise, may be a bit challenging to younger readers of the present day.

Cather attended the University of Nebraska, working her way through school as a newspaper correspondent. The experience helped polish her writing skills and she soon turned to poetry and the short story form, selling them to the prestigious *McClure's Magazine*, where she accepted the position of managing editor, which she held from 1906 to 1912, though she was no great fan of the magazine's muckraking activities. In the later part of her career, the conservative views depicted in her fiction were treated unkindly by critics and she became reclusive, destroying her notebooks and correspondence.

"Consequences" was first published in the November 1915 issue of *McClure's Magazine.*

Consequences

WILLA CATHER

HENRY EASTMAN, A LAWYER, aged forty, was standing beside the Flatiron building in a driving November rainstorm, signaling frantically for a taxi. It was six-thirty, and everything on wheels was engaged. The streets were in confusion about him, the sky was in turmoil above him, and the Flatiron building, which seemed about to blow down, threw water like a mill-shoot. Suddenly, out of the brutal struggle of men and cars and machines and people tilting at each other with umbrellas, a quiet, well-mannered limousine paused before him, at the curb, and an agreeable, ruddy countenance confronted him through the open window of the car.

"Don't you want me to pick you up, Mr. Eastman? I'm running directly home now."

Eastman recognized Kier Cavenaugh, a young man of pleasure, who lived in the house on Central Park South, where he himself had an apartment.

"Don't I?" he exclaimed, bolting into the car.

"I'll risk getting your cushions wet without compunction. I came up in a taxi, but I didn't hold it. Bad economy. I thought I saw your car down on Fourteenth Street about half an hour ago."

The owner of the car smiled. He had a pleasant, round face and round eyes, and a fringe of smooth, yellow hair showed under the rim of his soft felt hat. "With a lot of little broilers fluttering into it? You did. I know some girls who work in the cheap shops down there. I happened to be down-town and I stopped and took a load of them home. I do sometimes. Saves their poor little clothes, you know. Their shoes are never any good."

Eastman looked at his rescuer. "Aren't they notoriously afraid of cars and smooth young men?" he inquired.

Cavenaugh shook his head. "They know which cars are safe and which are chancy. They put each other wise. You have to take a bunch at a time, of course. The Italian girls can never come along; their men shoot. The girls understand, all right; but their fathers don't. One gets to see queer places, sometimes, taking them home."

Eastman laughed drily. "Every time I touch the circle of your acquaintance, Cavenaugh, it's a little wider. You must know New York pretty well by this time."

"Yes, but I'm on my good behavior below Twenty-third Street," the young man replied with simplicity. "My little friends down there would give me a good character. They're wise little girls. They have grand ways with each other, a romantic code of loyalty. You can find a good many of the lost virtues among them."

The car was standing still in a traffic block at Fortieth Street, when Cavenaugh suddenly drew his face away from the window and touched Eastman's arm. "Look, please. You see that hansom with the bony gray horse—driver has a broken hat and red flannel around his throat. Can you see who is inside?"

Eastman peered out. The hansom was just cutting across the line, and the driver was making a great fuss about it, bobbing his head and waving his whip. He jerked his dripping old horse into Fortieth Street and clattered off past the Public Library grounds toward Sixth Avenue. "No, I couldn't see the passenger. Someone you know?"

"Could you see whether there was a passenger?" Cavenaugh asked.

"Why, yes. A man, I think. I saw his elbow on the apron. No driver ever behaves like that unless he has a passenger."

"Yes, I may have been mistaken," Cavenaugh murmured absent-mindedly. Ten minutes or so later, after Cavenaugh's car had turned off Fifth Avenue into Fifty-eighth Street, Eastman exclaimed, "There's your same cabby, and his cart's empty. He's headed for a drink now, I suppose." The driver in the broken hat and the red flannel neck cloth was still brandishing the whip over his old gray. He was coming from the west now, and turned down Sixth Avenue, under the elevated.

Cavenaugh's car stopped at the bachelor apartment house between Sixth and Seventh Avenues where he and Eastman lived, and they went up in the elevator together. They were still talking when the lift stopped at Cavenaugh's floor, and Eastman stepped out with him and walked down the hall, finishing his sentence while Cavenaugh found his latch-key. When he opened the door, a wave of fresh cigarette smoke greeted them. Cavenaugh stopped short and stared into his hallway. "Now how in the devil—!" he exclaimed angrily.

"Someone waiting for you? Oh, no, thanks. I wasn't coming in. I have to work to-night. Thank you, but I couldn't." Eastman nodded and went up the two flights to his own rooms.

Though Eastman did not customarily keep a servant he had this winter a man who had been lent to him by a friend who was abroad. Rollins met him at the door and took his coat and hat.

"Put out my dinner clothes, Rollins, and then get out of here until ten o'clock. I've promised to go to a supper to-night. I shan't be dining. I've had a late tea and I'm going to work until ten. You may put out some kumiss and biscuit for me."

Rollins took himself off, and Eastman settled down at the big table in his sitting-room. He had to read a lot of letters submitted as evidence in a breach of contract case, and before he got very far he found that long paragraphs in some of the letters were written in German. He had a German dictionary at his office, but none here. Rollins had gone, and anyhow, the bookstores would be closed. He remembered having seen a row of dictionaries on the lower shelf of one of Cavenaugh's bookcases. Cavenaugh had a lot of books, though he never read anything but new stuff. Eastman prudently turned down his student's lamp very low—the thing had an evil habit of smoking—and went down two flights to Cavenaugh's door.

The young man himself answered Eastman's ring. He was freshly dressed for the evening, except for a brown smoking jacket, and his yellow hair had been brushed until it shone. He hesitated as he confronted his caller, still holding the door knob, and his round eyes and smooth forehead made their best imitation of a frown. When Eastman began to apologize, Cavenaugh's manner suddenly changed. He caught his arm and jerked him into the narrow hall. "Come in, come in. Right along!" he said excitedly. "Right along," he repeated as he pushed Eastman before him into his sitting-room. "Well I'll—" he stopped short at the door and looked about his own room with an air of complete mystification. The back window was wide open and a strong wind was blowing in. Cavenaugh walked over to the window and stuck out his head, looking up and down the fire escape. When he pulled his head in, he drew down the sash.

"I had a visitor I wanted you to see," he explained with a nervous smile. "At least I thought I had. He must have gone out that way," nodding toward the window.

"Call him back. I only came to borrow a German dictionary, if you have one. Can't stay. Call him back."

Cavenaugh shook his head despondently. "No use. He's beat it. Nowhere in sight."

"He must be active. Has he left something?"

Eastman pointed to a very dirty white glove that lay on the floor under the window.

"Yes, that's his." Cavenaugh reached for his tongs, picked up the glove, and tossed it into the grate, where it quickly shriveled on the coals. Eastman felt that he had happened in upon something disagreeable, possibly something shady, and he wanted to get away at once. Cavenaugh stood staring at the fire and seemed stupid and dazed; so he repeated his request rather sternly, "I think I've seen a German dictionary down there among your books. May I have it?"

Cavenaugh blinked at him. "A German dictionary? Oh, possibly! Those were my father's. I scarcely know what there is." He put down the tongs and began to wipe his hands nervously with his handkerchief.

Eastman went over to the bookcase behind the Chesterfield, opened the door, swooped upon the book he wanted and stuck it under his arm. He felt perfectly certain now that something shady had been going on in Cavenaugh's rooms, and he saw no reason why he should come in for any hang-over. "Thanks. I'll send it back to-morrow," he said curtly as he made for the door.

Cavenaugh followed him. "Wait a moment. I wanted you to see him. You did see his glove," glancing at the grate.

Eastman laughed disagreeably. "I saw a glove. That's not evidence. Do your friends often use that means of exit? Somewhat inconvenient."

Cavenaugh gave him a startled glance. "Wouldn't you think so? For an old man, a very rickety old party? The ladders are steep, you know, and rusty." He approached the window again and put it up softly. In a moment he drew his head back with a jerk. He caught Eastman's arm and shoved him toward the window. "Hurry, please. Look! Down there." He pointed to the little patch of paved court four flights down.

The square of pavement was so small and the walls about it were so high, that it was a good deal like looking down a well. Four tall buildings backed upon the same court and made a kind of shaft, with flagstones at the bottom, and at the top a square of dark blue with some stars in it. At the bottom of the shaft Eastman saw a black figure, a man in a caped coat and a tall hat stealing cautiously around, not across the square of pavement, keeping close to the dark wall and avoiding the streak of light that fell on the flagstones from a window in the opposite house. Seen from that height he was of course fore-shortened and probably looked more shambling and decrepit than he was. He picked his way along with exaggerated care and looked like a silly old cat crossing a wet street. When he reached the gate that led into an alley way between two buildings, he felt about for the latch, opened the door a mere crack, and then shot out under the feeble lamp that burned in the brick arch over the gateway. The door closed after him.

"He'll get run in," Eastman remarked curtly, turning away from the window. "That door shouldn't be left unlocked. Any crook could come in. I'll speak to the janitor about it, if you don't mind," he added sarcastically.

"Wish you would." Cavenaugh stood brushing down the front of his jacket, first with his right hand and then with his left. "You saw him, didn't you?"

"Enough of him. Seems eccentric. I have to see a lot of buggy people. They don't take me in any more. But I'm keeping you and I'm in a hurry myself. Good night."

Cavenaugh put out his hand detainingly and started to say something; but Eastman rudely turned his back and went down the hall and out of the door. He had never felt anything shady about Cavenaugh before, and he was sorry he had gone down for the dictionary. In five minutes he was deep in his papers; but in the half hour when he was loafing before he dressed to go out, the young man's curious behavior came into his mind again.

Eastman had merely a neighborly acquaintance with Cavenaugh. He had been to a supper at the young man's rooms once, but he didn't particularly like Cavenaugh's friends; so the next time he was asked, he had another engagement. He liked Cavenaugh himself, if for nothing else than because he was so cheerful and trim and ruddy. A good complexion is always at a premium in New York, especially when it shines reassuringly on a man who does everything in the world to lose it. It encourages fellow mortals as to the inherent vigor of the human organism and the amount of bad treatment it will stand for. "Footprints that perhaps another," etc. Cavenaugh, he knew, had plenty of money. He was the son of a Pennsylvania preacher, who died soon after he discovered that his ancestral acres were full of petroleum, and Kier had come to New York to burn some of the oil. He was thirty-two and was still at it; spent his life, literally, among the breakers. His motor hit the Park every morning as if it were the first time ever. He took people out to supper every night. He went from restaurant to restaurant, sometimes to half-a-dozen in an evening. The head waiters were his hosts and their cordiality made him happy. They made a life-line for him up Broadway and down Fifth Avenue. Cavenaugh was still fresh and smooth, round and plump, with a lustre to his hair and white teeth and a clear look in his round eyes. He seemed absolutely unwearied and unimpaired; never bored and never carried away.

Eastman always smiled when he met Cavenaugh in the entrance hall, serenely going forth to or returning from gladiatorial combats with joy, or when he saw him rolling smoothly up to the door in his car in the morning after a restful night in one of the remarkable new roadhouses he was always finding. Eastman had seen a good many young men disappear on Cavenaugh's route, and he admired this young man's endurance.

To-night, for the first time, he had got a whiff of something unwholesome about the fellow—bad nerves, bad company, something on hand that he was ashamed of, a visitor old and vicious, who must have had a key to Cavenaugh's apartment, for he was evidently there when Cavenaugh returned at seven o'clock. Probably it was the same man Cavenaugh had seen in the hansom. He must have been able to let himself in, for Cavenaugh kept no man but his chauf- feur; or perhaps the janitor had been instructed to let him in. In either case, and whoever he was, it was clear enough that Cavenaugh was ashamed of him and was mixing up in question- able business of some kind.

Eastman sent Cavenaugh's book back by Rol- lins, and for the next few weeks he had no word with him beyond a casual greeting when they happened to meet in the hall or the elevator. One Sunday morning Cavenaugh telephoned up to him to ask if he could motor out to a roadhouse in Connecticut that afternoon and have supper; but when Eastman found there were to be other guests he declined.

On New Year's eve Eastman dined at the Uni- versity Club at six o'clock and hurried home before the usual manifestations of insanity had begun in the streets. When Rollins brought his smoking coat, he asked him whether he wouldn't like to get off early.

"Yes, sir. But won't you be dressing, Mr. Eastman?" he inquired.

"Not to-night." Eastman handed him a bill. "Bring some change in the morning. There'll be fees."

Rollins lost no time in putting everything to rights for the night, and Eastman couldn't help wishing that he were in such a hurry to be off somewhere himself. When he heard the hall door close softly, he wondered if there were any place, after all, that he wanted to go. From his window he looked down at the long lines of motors and taxis waiting for a signal to cross Broadway. He thought of some of their probable destinations and decided that none of those places pulled him very hard. The night was warm and wet, the air was drizzly. Vapor hung in clouds about the *Times* Building, half hid the top of it, and made a luminous haze along Broadway. While he was looking down at the army of wet, black carriage-tops and their reflected headlights and tail-lights, Eastman heard a ring at his door. He deliberated. If it were a caller, the hall porter

would have telephoned up. It must be the jani- tor. When he opened the door, there stood a rosy young man in a tuxedo, without a coat or hat.

"Pardon. Should I have telephoned? I half thought you wouldn't be in."

Eastman laughed. "Come in, Cavenaugh. You weren't sure whether you wanted company or not, eh, and you were trying to let chance decide it? That was exactly my state of mind. Let's ac- cept the verdict." When they emerged from the narrow hall into his sitting-room, he pointed out a seat by the fire to his guest. He brought a tray of decanters and soda bottles and placed it on his writing table.

Cavenaugh hesitated, standing by the fire. "Sure you weren't starting for somewhere?"

"Do I look it? No, I was just making up my mind to stick it out alone when you rang. Have one?" he picked up a tall tumbler.

"Yes, thank you. I always do."

Eastman chuckled. "Lucky boy! So will I. I had a very early dinner. New York is the most arid place on holidays," he continued as he rat- tled the ice in the glasses. "When one gets too old to hit the rapids down there, and tired of gobbling food to heathenish dance music, there is absolutely no place where you can get a chop and some milk toast in peace, unless you have strong ties of blood brotherhood on upper Fifth Avenue. But you, why aren't you starting for somewhere?"

The young man sipped his soda and shook his head as he replied:

"Oh, I couldn't get a chop, either. I know only flashy people, of course." He looked up at his host with such a grave and candid expression that Eastman decided there couldn't be any- thing very crooked about the fellow. His smooth cheeks were positively cherubic.

"Well, what's the matter with them? Aren't they flashing to-night?"

"Only the very new ones seem to flash on New Year's eve. The older ones fade away. Maybe they are hunting a chop, too."

"Well"—Eastman sat down—"holidays do dash one. I was just about to write a letter to a pair of maiden aunts in my old home town, up-state; old coasting hill, snow-covered pines, lights in the church windows. That's what you've saved me from."

Cavenaugh shook himself. "Oh, I'm sure that wouldn't have been good for you. Pardon me," he rose and took a photograph from the bookcase, a handsome man in shooting clothes. "Dudley, isn't it? Did you know him well?"

"Yes. An old friend. Terrible thing, wasn't it? I haven't got over the jolt yet."

"His suicide? Yes, terrible! Did you know his wife?"

"Slightly. Well enough to admire her very much. She must be terribly broken up. I wonder Dudley didn't think of that."

Cavenaugh replaced the photograph carefully, lit a cigarette, and standing before the fire began to smoke. "Would you mind telling me about him? I never met him, but of course I'd read a lot about him, and I can't help feeling interested. It was a queer thing."

Eastman took out his cigar case and leaned back in his deep chair. "In the days when I knew him best he hadn't any story, like the happy nations. Everything was properly arranged for him before he was born. He came into the world happy, healthy, clever, straight, with the right sort of connections and the right kind of fortune, neither too large nor too small. He helped to make the world an agreeable place to live in until he was twenty-six. Then he married as he should have married. His wife was a Californian, educated abroad. Beautiful. You have seen her picture?"

Cavenaugh nodded. "Oh, many of them."

"She was interesting, too. Though she was distinctly a person of the world, she had retained something, just enough of the large Western manner. She had the habit of authority, of calling out a special train if she needed it, of using all our ingenious mechanical contrivances lightly and easily, without over-rating them. She and Dudley knew how to live better than most people. Their house was the most charming one I have ever known in New York. You felt freedom there, and a zest of life, and safety—absolute sanctuary—from everything sordid or petty. A whole society like that would justify the creation of man and would make our planet shine with a soft, peculiar radiance among the constellations. You think I'm putting it on thick?"

The young man sighed gently. "Oh, no! One has always felt there must be people like that. I've never known any."

"They had two children, beautiful ones. After they had been married for eight years, Rosina met this Spaniard. He must have amounted to something. She wasn't a flighty woman. She came home and told Dudley how matters stood. He persuaded her to stay at home for six months and try to pull up. They were both fair-minded people, and I'm as sure as if I were the Almighty, that she did try. But at the end of the time, Rosina went quietly off to Spain, and Dudley went to hunt in the Canadian Rockies. I met his party out there. I didn't know his wife had left him and talked about her a good deal. I noticed that he never drank anything, and his light used to shine through the log chinks of his room until all hours, even after a hard day's hunting. When I got back to New York, rumors were creeping about. Dudley did not come back. He bought a ranch in Wyoming, built a big log house and kept splendid dogs and horses. One of his sisters went out to keep house for him, and the children were there when they were not in school. He had a great many visitors, and everyone who came back talked about how well Dudley kept things going.

"He put in two years out there. Then, last month, he had to come back on business. A trust fund had to be settled up, and he was administrator. I saw him at the club; same light, quick step, same gracious handshake. He was getting gray, and there was something softer in his manner; but he had a fine red tan on his face and said he found it delightful to be here in the season when everything is going hard. The Madison Avenue house had been closed since Rosina left it. He went there to get some things his sister wanted. That, of course, was the mistake. He went alone, in the afternoon, and didn't go out for dinner—found some sherry and tins of biscuit in the sideboard. He shot himself sometime that night. There were pistols in his smoking-room. They found burnt out candles beside him in the morning. The gas and electricity were shut off. I suppose there, in his own house, among his own things, it was too much for him. He left no letters."

Cavenaugh blinked and brushed the lapel of his coat. "I suppose," he said slowly, "that every suicide is logical and reasonable, if one knew all the facts."

Eastman roused himself. "No, I don't think so. I've known too many fellows who went off like that—more than I deserve, I think—and some of them were absolutely inexplicable. I can understand Dudley; but I can't see why healthy bachelors, with money enough, like ourselves, need such a device. It reminds me of what Dr. Johnson said, that the most discouraging thing about life is the number of fads and hobbies and fake religions it takes to put people through a few years of it."

"Dr. Johnson? The specialist? Oh, the old fellow!" said Cavenaugh imperturbably. "Yes, that's interesting. Still, I fancy if one knew the facts—Did you know about Wyatt?"

"I don't think so."

"You wouldn't, probably. He was just a fellow about town who spent money. He wasn't one of the *forestieri*, though. Had connections here and owned a fine old place over on Staten Island. He went in for botany, and had been all over, hunting things; rusts, I believe. He had a yacht and used to take a gay crowd down about the South Seas, botanizing. He really did botanize, I believe. I never knew such a spender—only not flashy. He helped a lot of fellows and he was awfully good to girls, the kind who come down here to get a little fun, who don't like to work and still aren't really tough, the kind you see talking hard for their dinner. Nobody knows what becomes of them, or what they get out of it, and there are hundreds of new ones every year. He helped dozens of 'em; it was he who got me cu-

rious about the little shop girls. Well, one afternoon when his tea was brought, he took prussic acid instead. He didn't leave any letters, either; people of any taste don't. They wouldn't leave any material reminder if they could help it. His lawyers found that he had just $314.72 above his debts when he died. He had planned to spend all his money, and then take his tea; he had worked it out carefully."

Eastman reached for his pipe and pushed his chair away from the fire. "That looks like a considered case, but I don't think philosophical suicides like that are common. I think they usually come from stress of feeling and are really, as the newspapers call them, desperate acts; done without a motive. You remember when Anna Karenina was under the wheels, she kept saying, 'Why am I here?'"

Cavenaugh rubbed his upper lip with his pink finger and made an effort to wrinkle his brows. "May I, please?" reaching for the whiskey. "But have you," he asked, blinking as the soda flew at him, "have you ever known, yourself, cases that were really inexplicable?"

"A few too many. I was in Washington just before Captain Jack Purden was married and I saw a good deal of him. Popular army man, fine record in the Philippines, married a charming girl with lots of money; mutual devotion. It was the gayest wedding of the winter, and they started for Japan. They stopped in San Francisco for a week and missed their boat because, as the bride wrote back to Washington, they were too happy to move. They took the next boat, were both good sailors, had exceptional weather. After they had been out for two weeks, Jack got up from his deck chair one afternoon, yawned, put down his book, and stood before his wife. 'Stop reading for a moment and look at me.' She laughed and asked him why. 'Because you happen to be good to look at.' He nodded to her, went back to the stern and was never seen again. Must have gone down to the lower deck and slipped overboard, behind the machinery. It was the luncheon hour, not many people about; steamer cutting through a soft green sea. That's one of the most baffling cases I know. His friends raked up his past, and it was as trim as a cottage garden. If he'd so much as dropped an ink spot on his fatigue uniform, they'd have found it. He wasn't emotional or moody; wasn't, indeed, very interesting; simply a good soldier, fond of all the pompous little formalities that make up a military man's life. What do you make of that, my boy?"

Cavenaugh stroked his chin. "It's very puzzling, I admit. Still, if one knew every-thing——"

"But we do know everything. His friends wanted to find something to help them out, to help the girl out, to help the case of the human creature."

"Oh, I don't mean things that people could unearth," said Cavenaugh uneasily. "But possibly there were things that couldn't be found out."

Eastman shrugged his shoulders. "It's my experience that when there are 'things' as you call them, they're very apt to be found. There is no such thing as a secret. To make any move at all one has to employ human agencies, employ at least one human agent. Even when the pirates killed the men who buried their gold for them, the bones told the story."

Cavenaugh rubbed his hands together and smiled his sunny smile.

"I like that idea. It's reassuring. If we can have no secrets, it means that we can't, after all, go so far afield as we might," he hesitated, "yes, as we might."

Eastman looked at him sourly. "Cavenaugh, when you've practised law in New York for twelve years, you find that people can't go far in any direction, except——" He thrust his forefinger sharply at the floor. "Even in that direction, few people can do anything out of the ordinary. Our range is limited. Skip a few baths, and we become personally objectionable. The slightest carelessness can rot a man's integrity or give him ptomaine poisoning. We keep up only by incessant cleansing operations, of mind and body. What we call character, is held together by all sorts of tacks and strings and glue."

Cavenaugh looked startled. "Come now, it's not so bad as that, is it? I've always thought that a serious man, like you, must know a lot of Launcelots." When Eastman only laughed, the younger man squirmed about in his chair. He spoke again hastily, as if he were embarrassed. "Your military friend may have had personal experiences, however, that his friends couldn't possibly get a line on. He may accidentally have come to a place where he saw himself in too unpleasant a light. I believe people can be chilled by a draft from outside, somewhere."

"Outside?" Eastman echoed. "Ah, you mean the far outside! Ghosts, delusions, eh?"

Cavenaugh winced. "That's putting it strong. Why not say tips from the outside? Delusions belong to a diseased mind, don't they? There are some of us who have no minds to speak of, who yet have had experiences. I've had a little something in that line myself and I don't look it, do I?"

Eastman looked at the bland countenance turned toward him. "Not exactly. What's your delusion?"

"It's not a delusion. It's a haunt."

The lawyer chuckled. "Soul of a lost Casino girl?"

"No; an old gentleman. A most unattractive old gentleman, who follows me about."

"Does he want money?"

Cavenaugh sat up straight. "No. I wish to God he wanted anything—but the pleasure of my society! I'd let him clean me out to be rid of him. He's a real article. You saw him yourself that night when you came to my rooms to borrow a dictionary, and he went down the fire-escape. You saw him down in the court."

"Well, I saw somebody down in the court, but I'm too cautious to take it for granted that I saw what you saw. Why, anyhow, should I see your haunt? If it was your friend I saw, he impressed me disagreeably. How did you pick him up?"

Cavenaugh looked gloomy. "That was queer, too. Charley Burke and I had motored out to Long Beach, about a year ago, sometime in October, I think. We had supper and stayed until late. When we were coming home, my car broke down. We had a lot of girls along who had to get back for morning rehearsals and things; so I sent them all into town in Charley's car, and he was to send a man back to tow me home. I was driving myself, and didn't want to leave my machine. We had not taken a direct road back; so I was stuck in a lonesome, woody place, no houses about. I got chilly and made a fire, and was putting in the time comfortably enough, when this old party steps up. He was in shabby evening clothes and a top hat, and had on his usual white gloves. How he got there, at three o'clock in the morning, miles from any town or railway, I'll leave it to you to figure out. *He* surely had no car. When I saw him coming up to the fire, I disliked him. He had a silly, apologetic walk. His teeth were chattering, and I asked him to sit down. He got down like a clothes-horse folding up. I offered him a cigarette, and when he took off his gloves I couldn't help noticing how knotted and spotty his hands were. He was asthmatic, and took his breath with a wheeze. 'Haven't you got any-thing—refreshing in there?' he asked, nodding at the car. When I told him I hadn't, he sighed. 'Ah, you young fellows are greedy. You drink it all up. You drink it all up, all up—up!' he kept chewing it over."

Cavenaugh paused and looked embarrassed again. "The thing that was most unpleasant is difficult to explain. The old man sat there by the fire and leered at me with a silly sort of admi-ration that was—well, more than humiliating. 'Gay boy, gay dog!' he would mutter, and when he grinned he showed his teeth, worn and yel-low—shells. I remembered that it was better to talk casually to insane people; so I remarked carelessly that I had been out with a party and got stuck.

"'Oh yes, I remember,' he said, 'Flora and Lottie and Maybelle and Marcelline, and poor Kate.'

"He had named them correctly; so I began to think I had been hitting the bright waters too hard.

"Things I drank never had seemed to make

me woody; but you can never tell when trouble is going to hit you. I pulled my hat down and tried to look as uncommunicative as possible; but he kept croaking on from time to time, like this: 'Poor Kate! Splendid arms, but dope got her. She took up with Eastern religions after she had her hair dyed. Got to going to a Swami's joint, and smoking opium. Temple of the Lotus, it was called, and the police raided it.'

"This was nonsense, of course; the young woman was in the pink of condition. I let him rave, but I decided that if something didn't come out for me pretty soon, I'd foot it across Long Island. There wasn't room enough for the two of us. I got up and took another try at my car. He hopped right after me.

"'Good car,' he wheezed, 'better than the little Ford.'

"I'd had a Ford before, but so has everybody; that was a safe guess.

"'Still,' he went on, 'that run in from Hun-tington Bay in the rain wasn't bad. Arrested for speeding, he-he.'

"It was true I had made such a run, under rather unusual circumstances, and had been ar-rested. When at last I heard my life-boat snort-ing up the road, my visitor got up, sighed, and stepped back into the shadow of the trees. I didn't wait to see what became of him, you may believe. That was visitation number one. What do you think of it?"

Cavenaugh looked at his host defiantly. East-man smiled.

"I think you'd better change your mode of life, Cavenaugh. Had many returns?" he inquired.

"Too many, by far." The young man took a turn about the room and came back to the fire. Standing by the mantel he lit another cigarette before going on with his story:

"The second visitation happened in the street, early in the evening, about eight o'clock. I was held up in a traffic block before the Plaza. My chauffeur was driving. Old Nibbs steps up out of the crowd, opens the door of my car, gets in and sits down beside me. He had on wilted evening clothes, same as before, and there was some sort of heavy scent about him. Such an un-pleasant old party! A thorough-going rotter; you knew it at once. This time he wasn't talkative, as he had been when I first saw him. He leaned back in the car as if he owned it, crossed his hands on his stick and looked out at the crowd—sort of hungrily.

"I own I really felt a loathing compassion for him. We got down the avenue slowly. I kept looking out at the mounted police. But what could I do? Have him pulled? I was afraid to. I was awfully afraid of getting him into the papers.

"'I'm going to the New Astor,' I said at last. 'Can I take you anywhere?'

"'No, thank you,' says he. 'I get out when you do. I'm due on West 44th. I'm dining to-night with Marcelline—all that is left of her!'

"He put his hand to his hat brim with a grewsome salute. Such a scandalous, foolish old face as he had! When we pulled up at the Astor, I stuck my hand in my pocket and asked him if he'd like a little loan.

"'No, thank you, but'—he leaned over and whispered, ugh!—'but save a little, save a little. Forty years from now—a little—comes in handy. Save a little.'

"His eyes fairly glittered as he made his remark. I jumped out. I'd have jumped into the North River. When he tripped off, I asked my chauffeur if he'd noticed the man who got into the car with me. He said he knew someone was with me, but he hadn't noticed just when he got in. Want to hear any more?"

Cavenaugh dropped into his chair again. His plump cheeks were a trifle more flushed than usual, but he was perfectly calm. Eastman felt that the young man believed what he was telling him.

"Of course I do. It's very interesting. I don't see quite where you are coming out though."

Cavenaugh sniffed. "No more do I. I really feel that I've been put upon. I haven't deserved it any more than any other fellow of my kind. Doesn't it impress you disagreeably?"

"Well, rather so. Has anyone else seen your friend?"

"You saw him."

"We won't count that. As I said, there's no certainty that you and I saw the same person in the court that night. Has anyone else had a look in?"

"People sense him rather than see him. He usually crops up when I'm alone or in a crowd on the street. He never approaches me when I'm with people I know, though I've seen him hanging about the doors of theatres when I come out with a party; loafing around the stage exit, under a wall; or across the street, in a doorway. To be frank, I'm not anxious to introduce him. The third time, it was I who came upon him. In November my driver, Harry, had a sudden attack of appendicitis. I took him to the Presbyterian Hospital in the car, early in the evening. When I came home, I found the old villain in my rooms. I offered him a drink, and he sat down. It was the first time I had seen him in a steady light, with his hat off."

"His face is lined like a railway map, and as to color—Lord, what a liver! His scalp grows tight to his skull, and his hair is dyed until it's perfectly dead, like a piece of black cloth."

Cavenaugh ran his fingers through his own neatly trimmed thatch, and seemed to forget where he was for a moment.

"I had a twin brother, Brian, who died when we were sixteen. I have a photograph of him on my wall, an enlargement from a Kodak of him, doing a high jump, rather good thing, full of action. It seemed to annoy the old gentleman. He kept looking at it and lifting his eyebrows, and finally he got up, tip-toed across the room, and turned the picture to the wall.

"'Poor Brian! Fine fellow, but died young,' says he.

"Next morning, there was the picture, still reversed."

"Did he stay long?" Eastman asked interestedly.

"Half an hour, by the clock."

"Did he talk?"

"Well, he rambled."

"What about?"

Cavenaugh rubbed his pale eyebrows before answering.

"About things that an old man ought to want to forget. His conversation is highly objectionable. Of course he knows me like a book; everything I've ever done or thought. But when he recalls them, he throws a bad light on them, somehow. Things that weren't much off color, look rotten. He doesn't leave one a shred of self-respect, he really doesn't. That's the amount of it." The young man whipped out his handkerchief and wiped his face.

"You mean he really talks about things that none of your friends know?"

"Oh, dear, yes! Recalls things that happened in school. Anything disagreeable. Funny thing, he always turns Brian's picture to the wall."

"Does he come often?"

"Yes, oftener, now. Of course I don't know how he gets in down-stairs. The hall boys never see him. But he has a key to my door. I don't know how he got it, but I can hear him turn it in the lock."

"Why don't you keep your driver with you, or telephone for me to come down?"

"He'd only grin and go down the fire–escape as he did before. He's often done it when Harry's come in suddenly. Everybody has to be alone sometimes, you know. Besides, I don't want anybody to see him. He has me there."

"But why not? Why do you feel responsible for him?"

Cavenaugh smiled wearily. "That's rather the point, isn't it? Why do I? But I absolutely do. That identifies him, more than his knowing all about my life and my affairs."

Eastman looked at Cavenaugh thoughtfully. "Well, I should advise you to go in for something altogether different and new, and go in for it hard; business, engineering, metallurgy, something this old fellow wouldn't be interested in. See if you can make him remember logarithms."

Cavenaugh sighed. "No, he has me there, too. People never really change; they go on being themselves. But I would never make much trou-

ble. Why can't they let me alone, damn it! I'd never hurt anybody, except, perhaps——"

"Except your old gentleman, eh?" Eastman laughed. "Seriously, Cavenaugh, if you want to shake him, I think a year on a ranch would do it. He would never be coaxed far from his favorite haunts. He would dread Montana."

Cavenaugh pursed up his lips. "So do I!"

"Oh, you think you do. Try it, and you'll find out. A gun and a horse beats all this sort of thing. Besides losing your haunt, you'd be putting ten years in the bank for yourself. I know a good ranch where they take people, if you want to try it."

"Thank you. I'll consider. Do you think I'm batty?"

"No, but I think you've been doing one sort of thing too long. You need big horizons. Get out of this."

Cavenaugh smiled meekly. He rose lazily and yawned behind his hand. "It's late, and I've taken your whole evening." He strolled over to the window and looked out. "Queer place, New York; rough on the little fellows. Don't you feel sorry for them, the girls especially? I do. What a fight they put up for a little fun! Why, even that old goat is sorry for them, the only decent thing he kept."

Eastman followed him to the door and stood in the hall, while Cavenaugh waited for the elevator. When the car came up Cavenaugh extended his pink, warm hand. "Good night."

The cage sank and his rosy countenance disappeared, his round-eyed smile being the last thing to go.

Weeks passed before Eastman saw Cavenaugh again. One morning, just as he was starting for Washington to argue a case before the Supreme Court, Cavenaugh telephoned him at his office to ask him about the Montana ranch he had recommended; said he meant to take his advice and go out there for the spring and summer.

When Eastman got back from Washington,

he saw dusty trunks, just up from the trunk room, before Cavenaugh's door. Next morning, when he stopped to see what the young man was about, he found Cavenaugh in his shirt sleeves, packing.

"I'm really going; off to-morrow night. You didn't think it of me, did you?" he asked gaily.

"Oh, I've always had hopes of you!" Eastman declared. "But you are in a hurry, it seems to me."

"Yes, I am in a hurry." Cavenaugh shot a pair of leggings into one of the open trunks. "I telegraphed your ranch people, used your name, and they said it would be all right. By the way, some of my crowd are giving a little dinner for me at Rector's to-night. Couldn't you be persuaded, as it's a farewell occasion?" Cavenaugh looked at him hopefully.

Eastman laughed and shook his head. "Sorry, Cavenaugh, but that's too gay a world for me. I've got too much work lined up before me. I wish I had time to stop and look at your guns, though. You seem to know something about guns. You've more than you'll need, but nobody can have too many good ones." He put down one of the revolvers regretfully. "I'll drop in to see you in the morning, if you're up."

"I shall be up, all right. I've warned my crowd that I'll cut away before midnight."

"You won't, though," Eastman called back over his shoulder as he hurried down-stairs.

The next morning, while Eastman was dressing, Rollins came in greatly excited.

"I'm a little late, sir. I was stopped by Harry, Mr. Cavenaugh's driver. Mr. Cavenaugh shot himself last night, sir."

Eastman dropped his vest and sat down on his shoe-box. "You're drunk, Rollins," he shouted. "He's going away to-day!"

"Yes, sir. Harry found him this morning. Ah, he's quite dead, sir. Harry's telephoned for the coroner. Harry don't know what to do with the ticket."

Eastman pulled on his coat and ran down the stairway. Cavenaugh's trunks were strapped and piled before the door. Harry was walking up and down the hall with a long green railroad ticket in his hand and a look of complete stupidity on his face.

"What shall I do about this ticket, Mr. Eastman?" he whispered. "And what about his trunks? He had me tell the transfer people to come early. They may be here any minute. Yes, sir. I brought him home in the car last night, before twelve, as cheerful as could be."

"Be quiet, Harry. Where is he?"

"In his bed, sir."

Eastman went into Cavenaugh's sleeping-room. When he came back to the sitting-room, he looked over the writing table; railway folders, time-tables, receipted bills, nothing else. He looked up for the photograph of Cavenaugh's twin brother. There it was, turned to the wall. Eastman took it down and looked at it; a boy in track clothes, half lying in the air, going over the string shoulders first, above the heads of a crowd of lads who were running and cheering. The face was somewhat blurred by the motion and the bright sunlight. Eastman put the picture back, as he found it. Had Cavenaugh entertained his visitor last night, and had the old man been more convincing than usual? "Well, at any rate, he's seen to it that the old man can't establish identity. What a soft lot they are, fellows like poor Cavenaugh!" Eastman thought of his office as a delightful place.

THE FOLLOWER AND THE CORNER SHOP

Lady Cynthia Asquith

THE DAUGHTER OF THE 11th Earl of Wemyss, Cynthia Mary Evelyn Charteris (1887–1960) was born in Wiltshire, England, and married Herbert Asquith in 1910. Herbert served in World War I and, when he returned, was too ill for regular employment so she took a job as secretary to James M. Barrie, handling his professional and personal responsibilities until his death in 1937. In gratitude for her proficiency and two decades of friendship, he left his entire estate (with the exception of Peter Pan) to her. In addition to Barrie, she had become friends with many important literary figures, including D. H. Lawrence, Hugh Walpole, Algernon Blackwood, and Arthur Machen.

Although Lady Asquith wrote novels, memoirs, essays, children's books, biographies, and excellent short stories, her major contribution to the genre of supernatural literature was as an anthologist. She called on her literary friends and acquaintances to write stories for her, notably for the seminal anthology *The Ghost Book* (1926), the first collection of 20th century ghost stories that offered readers nonsensational works by members of the literary establishment. Generally regarded as the most influential ghost story anthology of the century, it was followed by such outstanding collections as *The Black Cap* (1928), *Shudders* (1929), and *When Churchyards Yawn* (1931). Some years later, she compiled sequels to her first book with *The Second Ghost Book* (1952) and *The Third Ghost Book* (1955). The series was continued for many years after her death, edited by James Turner, Rosemary Timperley, James Hale, and others.

"The Corner Shop" was originally published in *The Ghost Book* (London, Hutchinson, 1926). "The Follower" was originally published in *My Grimmest Nightmare* (London, G. Allen & Unwin, 1935; the editorship of this anonymous anthology has frequently been attributed to Asquith but, in fact, the editor was Cecil Madden). Both stories were collected in Asquith's deservedly acclaimed collection, *This Mortal Coil* (Sauk City, WI, Arkham House, 1947).

The Follower

LADY CYNTHIA ASQUITH

MRS. MEADE HAD BEEN in the nursing home with heart trouble for three weeks, and her doctor, to whom she had confided the terror that obsessed her, had at last persuaded her to see the famous psycho-analyst, Dr. Stone. She awaited his visit in great trepidation. It would not be easy to tell him of her fantastic experiences—"hallucinations" her own doctor insisted on calling them.

A quarter of an hour before the time when she expected Dr. Stone, there was a knock on the door.

"I'm a little early, Mrs. Meade," said a smooth voice from behind the screen, "and I must ask you to forgive my fancy dress ball appearance. I was very careless with a spirit lamp and am obliged to wear this mask for some time."

As he approached her bedside, Mrs. Meade saw that her visitor's face was entirely concealed by a black mask with two small holes and a slit for his eyes and mouth.

"Now, Mrs. Meade," he said, seating himself in a chair close to the bed. "I want you to tell me all about this mysterious trouble that is thought to be affecting your physical health. Please be perfectly frank with me. When did this—shall I say obsession?—begin, and what precisely is it?"

"Very well," said Mrs. Meade. "I will try to tell you the whole story. It began years ago—when I first went to live in Regent's Park. One afternoon I was most disagreeably struck by the appearance of a man who was loafing about outside the Baker Street Tube Station. I can't tell you how strong and horrible an impression he made on me. I can only say that there was something utterly hateful about his face, with its bold, malignant eyes—lashless eyes that searched me like unshaded lights. He seemed to leer at me with a 'so there you are!' sort of look, and the queer thing was that, though I had never to my knowledge seen him and—as I say—his appearance came to me as a shock, yet it was not a shock of complete surprise. In the violent distaste I felt for him there was a faint element of—shall I say sub-sub-conscious recognition?—as though he reminded me of something I had once dreamt or imagined. I don't know! I vaguely noticed that he had on a black slouch hat and no tie but a sort of greenish muffler round his neck. Otherwise his clothes were ordinary. Like the description of Mr. Hyde, he gave an impression of deformity without any nameable malformation. His face was horrible—moistly pale like . . . like a toadstool! It's no good! I *can't* describe him! I can only repeat that the aversion he inspired in me was extraordinarily violent. I was conscious of his stare as

I hurried past him and went down the steps, and it was a great relief to disappear into the lift and be whirled away in the Tube. Though I had plenty to do that day I could not quite dismiss him from my mind, and when I returned by Tube late in the evening it was a horrid shock to find him lurking at the top of the steps just as though he were waiting for me. This time there was no doubt that he definitely leered at me, and I thought he faintly shook his head. I hurried past him. Soon I had that horrid sense of being followed and glanced over my shoulder. Sure enough, there he was—just a few paces behind! and, as I turned, he slightly raised his hat. I almost ran home, and I cannot say what a relief it was to hear my front door slam behind me. Well, I saw him the next day and the next, and practically every day. The distaste with which I recognized him became a definite shudder, and each time his cynical glance seemed to grow bolder. Several times he followed me towards my house, but never right up to the door. I made tentative inquiries at the little shops round the Tube Station, but no one seemed to have noticed him. The dread of meeting him became an absolute obsession. Soon I gave up going in the Tube and would make long detours in order to avoid that upper part of Baker Street."

"You minded him as much as all that, did you?" asked the doctor.

"Yes."

"Go on, don't let me interrupt you."

"For some time," continued Mrs. Meade, "I did not see him and then there was a hideous incident. Returning from a walk in the park one day I saw quite a large crowd just outside the gate. A little girl had been run over. An ambulance man was carrying her lifeless form, and a policeman and some women were attending to the demented mother. Amongst all those shocked and pitying faces, suddenly I saw one vile, mocking face, its familiar features horribly distorted in a gloating grin. With positive glee he pointed at the dead child and then he turned *and leered at me.*

"After this horrible encounter you may be sure I shunned Upper Baker Street, but one day, just as I was starting to walk through the park, the heaviest rain I have ever seen came on, so I rushed towards the taxis at the top of the street and jumped into the first one on the rank. A small boy opened the door for me, and, to avoid getting my hat wet, I gave him the address to give the driver. To my surprise we started off at a terrific pace. I looked up and saw a rather crouched back and a greenish muffler. The speed at which we were going was insane, and I banged on the window. The driver turned. Imagine my nightmare horror when I recognized that dreaded face, grinning at me through the glass. Heaven knows why we did not crash at once. Instead of watching the road, the creature on the box kept turning round to grin and gloat at me. We went faster and faster—whirling through the traffic. I was so sick with horror that, in spite of the appalling speed, I would at all costs have jumped out, but—struggle as I might—I could not turn the handle. I think I screamed and screamed and screamed. I was simply flung about the taxi. At last there was an appalling shock. . . .

"I can just remember the tinkle of breaking glass and the awful pain in my head—and then no more.

"When I came to, I was in a hospital where for hours I had been unconscious from concussion. I began to ask questions but could only learn that I had been picked up from the debris of a taxi which had crashed into some railings, and that it was a miracle I had not been killed. As for the driver, he had unaccountably disappeared before the police arrived and no one claimed to have seen him. The taxi bore no number and could not be identified. The police were completely baffled.

"After this I insisted on leaving the neighbourhood, and made my husband take a house in Chelsea.

"Nearly a year passed and I began to hope that I should never see him again; but I became ill, and after endless consultations a very serious operation was decided on. Everything was arranged and the evening before the date fixed I drove to the nursing home with the sinking sensation natural to the occasion. I rang the bell and the door was promptly opened by a short man. I almost screamed. In spite of the incongruous livery, *it was him!* There he stood—sickly pale as ever, and with that awful, *intimate* smile.

"In a wild panic I sprang from the door and back into the taxi which was waiting with my luggage. Directly I got home I cancelled the operation. In spite of all the Harley Street opinions, I recovered. The operation was proved unnecessary."

Mrs. Meade paused in her narrative. The listener spoke.

"Then this being—whatever he is—on this occasion may be said to have done you a good turn?" he asked.

"Yes," answered Mrs. Meade, "perhaps, but it didn't make me dread him any the less. Oh, the ghastly dreams I had!—that I had been given the anaesthetic and was thought to be unconscious, but I *wasn't*, and I saw the surgeon approach and, as he bent over me, his face was THE FACE!"

"Did you ever see him again, Mrs. Meade?"

"I'm sorry," answered the patient hastily, "but the next time I saw him, I cannot tell you about. It is still too unbearable. There are things one cannot speak about. It was then I understood why he had pointed at that dead child and leered at me out of his vile little eyes. That was a long time ago, but the dread is always with me. You see, I still have one child left—I am always looking for what I fear. I can never leave my house without expecting to see him. What if one day I should meet him in *my house*?"

"I do not think you will ever do that, Mrs. Meade."

"I suppose you think the whole thing is an illusion, Doctor Stone? And in any case I don't suppose I have been able to give any impression of what—it—he—the creature is like," sighed Mrs. Meade.

The listener rose from his chair and leant over the invalid.

"Is—his—face—like this?" he asked, and, as he spoke, he whipped off his mask.

No one who heard it will ever forget Mrs. Meade's scream.

Two nurses rushed into her room, followed by Dr. Stone, who, punctual to his appointment, had that moment arrived.

The dead woman lay on the bed.

There was no one else in the room.

The Corner Shop

LADY CYNTHIA ASQUITH

PETER WOOD'S EXECUTORS found their task a very easy one. He had left his affairs in perfect order. The only surprise yielded by his tidy writing-table was a sealed envelope on which was written, "Not wishing to be bothered by well-meaning Research Societies, I have never shown the enclosed to anyone, but after my death all are welcome to read what is, to the best of my knowledge, a true story."

The manuscript bears a date three years previous to the death of the writer, and is as follows:

I have long wished to write down an experience of my youth. I shall not attempt any diagnosis as to its nature. I draw no conclusions. I merely record certain facts. At least, as such these incidents presented themselves to my consciousness.

One evening, shortly after I had been called to the Bar, I was rather dejectedly returning to my lodgings, wishing I could afford a theater ticket, when my attention was drawn to the brightly lit window of a shop. Having an uneducated love of bric-à-brac, and remembering an unavoidable wedding present, I grasped the handle of the door which, opening with one of those cheerful clanking bells, admitted me into large rambling premises thickly crowded with all the traditional litter of a curiosity shop. Fragments of armour, pewter pots, dark, distorting mirrors, church vestments, flower pictures, brass kettles, chairs, tables, chests, chandeliers—all were here! But in spite of the heterogeneous confusion, there was none of the dingy, dusty gloom one associates with such collections. The room was brightly lit and a crackling fire leapt up the chimney. The atmosphere was warm and cheerful. Very agreeable I found it after the cold dank fog outside.

At my entrance a young woman and a child—by their resemblance obviously sisters—had risen from their two arm-chairs. Bright, bustling, gaily dressed, they were curiously unlike the type of person who usually presides over that particular sort of wares. A flower shop would have seemed a more appropriate setting.

"How wonderful of them to keep their premises so clean," I thought, as I wished them good evening.

Their smiling faces made a very pleasing impression on me; one of comfortable, serene well-being, and, though the grown-up sister was most courteous in showing me the crowded treasures and displayed knowledge and appreciation, she struck me as quite indifferent as to whether I made any purchase or not. Her manner was really more that of a custodian than of a saleswoman.

Finding a beautiful piece of Sheffield plate very moderately priced, I decided that here was the very present for my friend. The child deftly converted my purchase into a brown paper parcel. Explaining to her elder sister that I was without sufficient cash, I asked if she would take a cheque.

"Certainly," she answered, briskly producing

pen and ink. "Will you please make it out to the 'Corner Curio Shop'?"

It was with conscious reluctance that I set out into the saffron fog.

"Good evening, sir. Always pleased to see you at any time," rang out the girl's pleasant voice, a voice so agreeable that I left almost with a sense of having made a friend.

I suppose it must have been about a week later, that, as I walked home one very cold evening—fine powdery snow brushing against my face, and a cutting wind tearing down the streets, I remembered the welcoming warmth of the cheerful Corner Curio Shop, and determined to revisit it. I found myself to be in the very street, and there—yes—there was the very corner. It was with a sense of disappointment, out of all proportion to the event, that I found the shop to be wearing that baffling—so to speak, shut-eyed appearance, and saw that a piece of cardboard, on which was printed the word "Closed," hung from the door handle.

A bitter gust of wind whistled round the corner, and my wet trousers flapped dismally against my chapped ankles. I longed for the warmth and glow within, and felt annoyingly thwarted. Rather childishly—for I was certain the door was locked, I grasped the handle and shook it. To my surprise the handle turned in my hand, but not in answer to its pressure. The door was pulled open from inside, and I found myself peering into the dimly lit countenance of a very old and frail-looking little man.

"Please do come in, sir," said a gentle, rather tremulous voice, and soft footsteps shuffled away in front of me.

It is impossible to describe the altered aspect of the place. I assumed that the electric light had fused, for the darkness of the large room was only thinned by two guttering candles, and in the dim wavering light, the jumble of furniture, formerly brightly lit, now loomed towering and mysterious, and cast weird, almost menacing shadows. The fire was out, only one faintly glowering ember told that any had lately been alive. Other evidence there was none, for the grim cold of the atmosphere was such as I had never experienced. The phrase "it struck chill" is laughably inadequate. In retrospect the street seemed almost agreeable; in its biting cold there had at least been something exhilarating. The atmosphere was now as gloomy as it had previously been genial. I felt a strong impulse to leave immediately, but the surrounding darkness thinned, and I saw that the old man was busily lighting candles here and there.

"Anything I can show you, sir?" he quavered, as he spoke approaching me with a lighted taper in his hand. I now saw him comparatively distinctly, and his appearance made an indescribable impression on me. Rembrandt flitted through my mind. Who else could have suggested the strange shadows on that time-worn face? Tired is a word we lightly use. Never had I known what the word might mean, till I stared at that exhausted countenance. The ineffable, patient weariness of the withered face, the eyes—which seemed as extinct as the fire, save for a feeble glow as of some purpose. And the wan frailty of the figure!

The words "dust and ashes, dust and ashes," strayed through my brain.

On my first visit, you may remember that I had been impressed by the incongruous cleanliness of the place. The queer fancy now struck me that this old man was like an accumulation of all the dust one might have expected to see scattered over such precincts. In truth, he looked scarcely more solid than a mere conglomeration of dust that might be dispersed at a breath or a touch.

What a queer old creature to be employed by those healthy, well-to-do-looking girls! "He must," I thought, "be some old retainer kept on out of charity."

"Anything I can show you, sir?" repeated the old man. His voice had little more body than the tearing of a cobweb, and yet there was a curious, almost pleading, insistence in it, and his eyes were fixed on me in a wan yet devouring stare. I wanted to leave. Definitely I wanted to go. The proximity of this pitiable old man depressed me; I felt wretchedly dispirited, but, involuntarily murmuring "Thank you, I'll look round," I found myself following his frail form and absent-mindedly inspecting various objects temporarily illuminated by his trembling taper.

The chill silence only broken by the tired shuffle of his carpet slippers got on my nerves. "Very cold night, isn't it?" I hazarded.

"Cold is it? Cold, cold, yes, I dare say." In his grey voice was the apathy of extreme initiation.

"Been at this job long?" I asked, dully peering at an old four-poster bed.

"A long, long time." The answer came softly as a sigh, and as he spoke Time seemed no longer a matter of days, weeks, months, years, but something that stretched immeasurably. I resented the old man's exhaustion and melancholy, the infection of which was so unaccountably weighing down my own spirits.

"How long, O Lord, how long?" I said as jauntily as possible—adding, with odious jocularity—"Old age pension about due, what?" No response.

In silence we moved across to the other side of the room.

"Quaint piece that," said my guide, picking up a little grotesque frog that was lying on a shelf amongst numerous other small objects. It seemed to be made of some substance similar to jade and, rather struck by its uncouth appearance, I took it from the old man's hand. It was strikingly cold.

"I think it's rather fun," I said. "How much?"

"Half a crown, sir," whispered the old man, glancing up at my face. His voice had no more body than the sliding of dust, but in his eyes there was an unmistakable gleam of eagerness.

"Is that all? I'll have it," said I. "Don't bother to pack up old Anthony Roland. I'll put him in my pocket. Half a crown, did you say? Here it is."

In giving the old man the coin, I inadvertently touched his extended palm. I could scarcely suppress a start. I have said the frog struck cold, but its substance was tepid compared to that dessicated skin. I cannot describe the chill sensation received in that second's con-tact. "Poor old fellow!" I thought, "he's not fit to be about in this cold, lonely place. I wonder at those kind-looking girls allowing such an old wreck to struggle on. Good night," I said.

"Good night, sir; thank you, sir," quavered the feeble old voice. He closed the door behind me.

Turning my head as I breasted the driving snow, I saw his form, scarcely more solid than shadow, outlined against the candlelight. His face was pressed against the big glass pane. I imagined his tired, patient eyes peering after his vanishing customer.

Somehow I was unable to dismiss the thought of that old man from my mind. Long, long after I was in bed and courting sleep I saw that maze of wrinkles, his ravaged face and his great initiated eyes like lifeless planets, staring, staring at me, and in their steady stare there seemed a sort of question. Yes, I was unaccountably perturbed by his personality, and even after I achieved sleep my dreams were full of my strange acquaintance.

Haunted, I suppose, by a sense of his infinite tiredness, in my dream I was trying to force him to rest—to lie down. But no sooner did I succeed in laying his frail form on the four-poster bed I had noticed in the shop (only now it seemed more like a grave than a bed, and the brocade coverlet had turned into sods of turf)—than he would slip from my grasp and totteringly set forth on his rambles around the shop. On and on I chased him, down endless avenues of weird furniture, but still he eluded me, and now the dim shop seemed to stretch on and on immeasurably—to merge into an infinity of sunless, airless space until at length I myself sank breathless and exhausted on to the four-poster grave.

The next morning I received an urgent summons to my mother's sick bed, and in the anxiety of the ensuing week the episode of the Corner Curio Shop was banished from my mind. As soon as the invalid was declared out of danger, I returned to my dreary lodging. Dejectedly engaged in adding up my petty household accounts and wondering where on earth I was to find the money to pay next quarter's rent, I was agreeably surprised by a visit from an old school-fellow—at that time practically the only friend I possessed in London. He was employed by one of the best-known firms of fine art dealers and auctioneers.

After a few minutes' conversation, he rose in search of a light. My back was turned to him. I heard the sharp scratch of a match, followed by propitiating noises to his pipe. These were suddenly broken off by an exclamation.

"Good God, man!" he shouted. "Where did you get this?"

Turning round, I saw that he had snatched up my purchase of the other night, the funny little frog, whose presence on my mantelpiece I had practically forgotten.

He was holding it under the gas-jet, closely scrutinising it through a small magnifying glass, and his hands were shaking with excitement. "Where did you get this?" he repeated. "Have you any idea what it is?"

Briefly I told him that, rather than leave a shop empty-handed, I had bought the frog for half a crown.

"For half a crown?" he echoed. "My dear fellow, I can't swear to it, but I believe you've had one of those amazing pieces of luck one hears about. Unless I'm very much mistaken, this is a piece of jade of the Hsia Dynasty."

To my ignorance these words conveyed little. "Do you mean it's worth money?"

"Worth money? Phew!" he ejaculated. "Look here. Will you leave this business to me? Let me have the thing for my firm to do the best they can by you. To-day's Monday. I shall be able to get it into Thursday's auction."

Knowing I could implicitly trust my friend, I readily agreed to his proposal. Carefully enwrapping the frog in cotton-wool, he departed.

Friday morning I received the shock of my life. Shock does not necessarily imply bad news, and I can assure you that for some seconds after opening the one envelope lying on my dingy breakfast-tray, the room spun round and round me. The envelope contained an invoice from Messrs. Spunk, fine art dealers and auctioneers:

To sale of Hsia jade, £2,000, less 10 per cent. commission £1,800,

and there, neatly folded, made out to Peter Wood, Esq., was Messrs. Spunk's cheque for £1,800. For some time I was completely bewildered. My friend's words had raised hopes; hopes that my chance purchase might facilitate the payment of next quarter's rent—might even provide for a whole year's rent—but that so large a sum was involved had never even crossed my mind. Could it be true, or was it some hideous joke? Surely it was—in the trite phrase—much, much too good to be true! It was not the sort of thing that happened to oneself.

Still feeling physically dizzy, I rang up my friend. The normality of his voice and the heartiness of his congratulations convinced me as to the truth of my astounding fortune. It was no joke—no dream. I, Peter Wood, whose bank account was at present £20 overdrawn, and who possessed no securities save shares to the extent of £150, by a sheer fluke, now held in my hand a piece of paper convertible into 1,800 golden sovereigns. I sat down to think—to try to realise—to readjust. From a jumble of plans, problems, and emotions one fact emerged crystal clear. Obviously, I could not take advantage of the girl's ignorance or of her poor old caretaker's incompetence. I could not accept this amazing gift from Fate, simply because I had bought a treasure for half a crown.

Clearly I must return at least half of the sum to my unconscious benefactors. Otherwise I should feel I had robbed them almost as much as though I had broken into their shop like a thief in the night. I remember their pleasant open countenances. What fun to astonish them with the wonderful news! I felt a strong impulse to rush to the shop, but having for once a case in court, I was obliged to go to the Temple. Endorsing Messrs. Spunk's cheque, I addressed it to my bankers, and, consulting the fly-leaf of my cheque-book, made out one to the Corner Curio Shop for £900. This I placed in my pocket, determined to call at the Corner Shop on my way home.

It was late before I was free to leave the Law Courts, and on arriving at the shop, though somewhat disappointed, I was not greatly surprised to find that it was again shut, with the notice "Closed" slung over the handle. Even supposing the old caretaker to be on duty, there was no particular point in seeing him. My business was with his mistress. So, deciding to postpone my visit to the following day, I was just on the point of hurrying home, when—as though I were expected—the door opened, and there on the threshold stood the old man peering out into the darkness.

"Anything I can do for you, sir?"

His voice was even queerer than before. I now realised that I had dreaded re-encountering him, but I felt irresistibly compelled to enter. The atmosphere was as grimly cold as on my last visit. I found myself actually shivering. Several candles, obviously only just lit, were burning, and by their glimmering light I saw the old man's grey gaze questioningly fixed upon me. What a face! I had not exaggerated its weirdness. Never had I seen so singular, so striking a being. No wonder I had dreamt of him. I wished he had not opened the door.

"Anything I can show you to-night, sir?" he rather tremulously inquired.

"No, thanks. I have come about that thing you sold me the other day. I find it's of great value. Please tell your mistress that I will pay her a proper price for it tomorrow."

As I spoke there spread over the old man's face the most wonderful smile. "Smile" I use for lack of a better word; but how to convey any idea of the beauty of the indefinable expression that now transfigured that time-worn face? Tender triumph, gentle rapture! It was frost yielding to sunshine. Never before have I witnessed the thawing of thickly frozen grief—the dawn radiance of attainment. For the first time I had some inkling of the meaning of the word "beatitude." Impossible to describe the impression made on me by that transfigured face. The moment, as it were, brimmed over. Time ceased, and I became conscious of infinite things. The silence of the shop was now broken by that gathering sound of an old clock about to break into speech. I turned my head towards one of those wonderful pieces of mediæval workmanship—a Nuremberg grandfather clock. From a recess beneath its exquisitely painted face, quaint figures emerged, and while one struck a bell, others daintily stepped through a minuet. My attention was riveted by the pretty spectacle, and not till the last sounds had trembled into silence did I turn my head.

I found myself alone.

The old man had disappeared. Surprised at his leaving me, I looked all round the large room. Oddly enough, the fire, which I had supposed to be dead, had flared into unexpected life, and was now casting a cheerful glow. But neither fire nor candlelight showed any trace of the old caretaker. He had vanished.

"Hullo! Hullo!" I called interrogatively.

No answer. No sound, save the loud ticking of clocks and the busy crackling of the fire. I walked all round the room. I even looked into the four-poster bed of which I had dreamt. I then saw that there was a smaller adjoining room, and, seizing a candle, I resolved to explore it. At the far end I discerned a small staircase obviously leading up to a sort of gallery that surrounded the room. The old man must have withdrawn into some upstairs lair. I would follow him. I groped my way to the foot of the stairs, and began to ascend, but the steps creaked beneath my feet, I had a feeling of crumbling woodwork, my candle went out: cobwebs brushed against my face. To continue was most uninviting. I desisted.

After all, what did it matter? Let the old man hide himself. I had given my message. Best be gone. But the main room to which I had returned had now become quite warm and cheerful. How could I ever have thought it sinister. And it was with a distinct sense of regret that I left the shop. I felt balked. I would have liked to see more of that irradiating smile. Dear, strange, old man! How could I ever have fancied that I feared him?

The next Saturday I was free to go straight to the shop. On the way there my mind was agreeably occupied in anticipating the cordial welcome the grateful sisters were sure to give me. As the clank of the bell announced my opening of the door, the two girls, who were busily dusting their treasures, turned their heads to see who came at so unusually early an hour. Recognising me, to my surprise they bowed pleasantly, but quite casually, as though to a mere acquaintance.

With the fairy-tale bond between us, I had expected quite a different sort of greeting. I at once guessed that they had not yet heard the astounding news, and when I said "I've brought the cheque!" I saw that my surmise was correct. Their faces expressed blank uncomprehension.

"Cheque?" echoed the grown-up sister. "What cheque?"

"For the frog I bought the other day."

"The frog? What frog? I only remember you buying a piece of Sheffield plate."

I saw they knew nothing, not even of my second visit to their shop! By degrees I told them the whole story. They were bewildered with astonishment. The elder sister seemed quite dazed.

"But I can't understand it! I can't understand it!" she repeated. "Holmes isn't even supposed to admit anyone in our absence—far less to sell things. He just comes here as caretaker on the evenings when we leave early, and he's only supposed to stay till the night policeman comes on to his beat. I can't believe he let you in and never even told us he'd sold you something. It's too extraordinary! What time was it?"

"Round about seven, I should think," I answered.

"He generally leaves about half-past six," said the girl. "But I suppose the policeman must have been late."

"It was later when I came yesterday."

"Did you come again yesterday?" she asked.

Briefly I told her of my visit and the message I had left with the caretaker.

"What an incredible thing!" she exclaimed. "I can't begin to understand it; but we shall soon hear his explanation. I'm expecting him in at any moment now. He comes in every morning to sweep the floors."

At the prospect of meeting the remarkable old man again, I felt an appreciable thrill of excitement. How would he look in the strong daylight? Would he smile again?

"He's very old, isn't he?" I hazarded.

"Old? Yes, I suppose he is getting rather old; but it's a very easy job. He's a good, honest fellow. I can't understand his doing this sort of thing on the sly. I'm afraid we've been rather slack in our cataloguing lately. I wonder if he's been selling odds and ends for himself? Oh no, I can't bear to think it! By the way, can you remember whereabouts this frog was?"

I pointed to the shelf from which the caretaker had picked up the piece of jade.

"Oh, from that assortment? It's a lot I bought the other day for next to nothing, and I haven't sorted or priced them yet. I can't remember seeing a frog. Oh, what an incredible thing to happen!"

At this moment the telephone rang. She raised the receiver to her ear, and spoke down the instrument.

"Hullo! Hullo!" I heard her voice. "Yes, it's Miss Wilton speaking. Yes, Mrs. Holmes, what do you want?" There was a few seconds' pause, and then in startled tones her voice went on: "*Dead?* Dead? But how? Why? Oh, I *am* sorry!"

After a few more words she replaced the receiver and turned to us, her eyes full of tears.

"Fancy," she said. "Poor old Holmes, the caretaker, is dead. When he got home yesterday evening he complained of pain, and he died in the middle of the night. Heart failure. No one had any idea there was anything the matter with him. Oh, poor Mrs. Holmes! What will she do? We must go round and see her at once!"

Both girls were very much upset and, saying that I would soon return, I thought it best to leave. That hauntingly singular old man had made so vivid an impression upon me that I felt deeply moved by the news of his sudden death. How strange that I should have been, except for his wife, the last person to speak with him. No doubt the fatal pain had seized him in my very presence, and that was why he had left me so abruptly and without a word. Had Death already brushed against his consciousness? That ineffable irradiating smile? Was that the beginning of the peace that passes all understanding?

I returned to the Corner Curio Shop the next day. I told them all the details of the sale of the fabulous frog, and presented the cheque I had drawn out. Here I met with unexpected opposition. The sisters showed great unwillingness to accept the money. It was—they said—all mine, and they had no need of it.

"You see," explained Miss Wilton, "my father had a flare for this business amounting to a sort of genius, and made quite a large fortune. When he became too old to carry on the shop, we kept it open out of sentiment and for the sake of occupation; but we don't need to make any profit out of it."

At last I prevailed upon them to accept the money, if only to spend it on the various charities in which they were interested. It was a relief to my mind when the matter was thus settled.

The strange coincidence of the frog was a bond between us, and in the course of our amicable arguments we had become very friendly. I got into the way of dropping in quite often. In fact, I grew rather to rely on the sympathetic companionship of those two bright girls and became quite at my ease with them. I never forgot the impression made on me by the old man, and often questioned the girls about their poor caretaker, but they had nothing of much interest to tell me. They just described him as an "old dear" who had been in their father's service as long as they could remember. No further light was thrown on his sale of the frog. Naturally, they didn't like to question his widow.

One evening, when I had been having tea in the inner room with the elder sister, I picked up an album of photographs. Turning over its pages, I came on a remarkably fine likeness of the old man. There, before me, was this strange, striking countenance; but, obviously, this photograph had been taken many years before I saw him. The face was much fuller and had not yet acquired the wearied, fragile look I so vividly

remembered. But what magnificent eyes he had! Certainly there was something extraordinarily impressive about the man. I stared at the faded photograph.

"What a splendid photograph of poor old Holmes!" I said.

"Photograph of Holmes? I'd no idea there was one," she answered. "Let's see."

As I approached with the open book the younger sister looked in through the open door.

"I'm off to the movies now," she called out. "Father's just rung up to say he'll be round in about a quarter of an hour to have a look at that Sheraton sideboard."

"All right. I'll be here, and very glad to have his opinion," said Miss Wilton, taking the album from my hand. There were several photographs on the page at which I had opened the book.

"I don't see anything of old Holmes," she said.

I pointed out the photograph.

"*That!*" she exclaimed. "Why, that's my dear father!"

"Your *father?*" I gasped.

"Yes, I can't imagine two people much more unlike. It must have been very dark in the shop when you saw Holmes!"

"Yes, yes; it was very dark," I quickly said to gain time in which to think; for I felt quite bewildered with surprise. No degree of darkness could account for any such mistake. I had no moment's doubt as to the identity of him I had taken for the caretaker with the man whose photograph I now held in my hand. But what an amazing, unaccountable affair!

Her *father?* Why on earth should he have been in the shop unknown to his daughters, and for what possible purpose had he concealed his sale of the frog? And when he heard of its fabulous value, why leave the girls under the impression that it was Holmes, the dead caretaker, who had sold it?

Had he been ashamed to confess his own inadvertence? Or was it possible that the girls had never told him, wishing perhaps to keep their sudden wealth a secret? What strange family intrigue was this into which I had stumbled? If the father had determined thus to keep his actions in the dark, I had better not precipitate any exposure. Instinct bade me hold my tongue. The younger sister had announced his approaching visit. Would he recognise me?

"It's a splendid face," I said, resolving on reserve.

"Isn't it?" she said with pleased eagerness. "Isn't it clever and strong? Yes, I remember when that photograph was taken. It was just before he got religion." The girl spoke as though she regarded "religion" as a regrettable indisposition.

"Did he suddenly become very religious?"

"Yes," she said reluctantly. "Poor father! He made friends with a priest, and he became so changed. He was never the same again."

From the sort of break in the girl's voice, I guessed she thought her father's reason had been affected. Did not this explain the whole affair? On the two occasions when I saw him, was he not wandering in mind as well as in body?

"Did his religion make him unhappy?" I ventured to ask, for I was anxious to get more light on the strange being before I re-encountered him.

"Yes, dreadfully." The girl's eyes were full of tears. "You see . . . it was . . ." She hesitated, and after a glance at me went on: "There's really no reason why I shouldn't tell you. I've come to regard you as a real friend. Poor father got to think he had done very wrong. He couldn't quiet his conscience. You remember my telling you of his extraordinary flare? Well, his fortune was really founded on three marvellous strokes of business. He had the same sort of luck you had here the other day—that's why I'm telling you. It seems such an odd coincidence." She paused.

"Please go on," I urged.

"Well, you see, on three separate occasions he bought, for a few shillings, objects that were of immense value. Only—unlike you—he knew what he was about. The money he realised on their sale came as no surprise to him. . . .

Unlike you, he did not then see any obligation to make it up to the ignorant people who had thrown away fortunes. After all, most dealers wouldn't, would they?" she almost angrily asked.

"Well, father grew richer and richer. Years after, he met this priest, and then he seemed to go all sort of morbid. He came to think that our wealth was founded on what was really no better than theft. Bitterly he reproached himself for having taken advantage of those three men's ignorance and allowing them to chuck away their fortunes. Unfortunately, in each case he succeeded in discovering what had ultimately happened to those he called his 'victims.' Most unfortunately, all three men had died in destitution. This discovery made him incurably miserable. Two of these men had died without leaving any children, and no relations could be found.

"He traced the son of the third to America; but there he had died, leaving no family. So poor father could find no means of making reparation. That was what he longed for—to make reparation. This preyed and preyed on him, until—in my opinion—his poor dear mind became unhinged. As religion took stronger and stronger hold on him, he got a queer sort of notion into his head—a regular obsession—a 'complex' they would call it now. 'The next best thing to doing a good action,' he would say, '*is to provide someone else with the opportunity for doing one.* To give him his cue, so to speak. "In our sins Christ is crucified afresh." I must be the cause of three good actions corresponding to my own bad ones. In no other way can I expiate my crimes against Christ, for crimes they were——' In vain we argued with him, saying he had only done as nearly all men would have done. It had no effect. 'Other men must judge for themselves. I have done what I know to be wrong,' he would mournfully repeat. He got more and more fixed in his idea. Real religious mania it became!

"Being determined to find three human beings who would, by their good actions, as it were, *cancel* the pain caused to Divinity by what he considered his three crimes, he now busied himself in finding insignificant-looking treasures which he would offer to the public for a few shillings. Poor old father! Never shall I forget his joy when one day a man returned a piece of porcelain he had bought for five shillings and discovered to be worth £500, saying: 'I think you must have made a mistake.' Just as *you* did, bless you!

"Five years later a similar thing occurred, and he was, oh, so radiant! 'Two of Humanity's crimes cancelled,' he felt. Then came years and years of weary disappointment. 'I shall never rest until I find the third,' was what he always said." Here the girl began to cry, hiding her face behind her hands and murmuring something about "Too late, too late!"

I heard the door-bell ring.

"How he must have suffered!" I said. "I'm so glad I had the luck to be the third."

She withdrew her hands from her face and stared at me.

"And I'm so glad I'm going to meet him again," I said, as I heard footsteps approaching.

"Meet him!" she echoed in amazement, as the footsteps drew near.

"Yes, I may stay, mayn't I? I heard your sister say he was coming round now."

"Oh, I see!" she ejaculated. "*Her* father! We are only step sisters. My dear father died seven years ago."

H. P. Lovecraft

THE MOST IMPORTANT AMERICAN writer of supernatural and occult fiction during the first half of the twentieth century, H(oward) P(hillips) Lovecraft (1890–1937) was born in Providence, Rhode Island, where he lived virtually all his life. Always frail, he was reclusive and had little formal education, but read extensively, with particular emphasis on the sciences. He wrote monthly articles on astronomy for the *Providence Tribune* at the age of sixteen, then attempted fiction; his first published story, "The Alchemist," was written in 1908 but was not published until 1916. He wrote fiction for other small magazines, living in near poverty, earning his living by ghostwriting and editing the work of others until in 1923 he finally sold "Dagon" to *Weird Tales*, the top fantasy pulp magazine in America. He became a regular contributor to that magazine until his death, with only a handful of his modest sixty stories appearing in other pulps.

He was neglected as a serious writer throughout his life, with only one volume being published while he was alive: *The Shadow over Innsmouth* (1936). After his early death, two friends, August Derleth and Donald Wandrei, attempted to sell his work to commercial publishers. When they were unsuccessful, they created their own firm, Arkham House, for the sole purpose of collecting and publishing Lovecraft's stories, poems, and letters, beginning with the cornerstone work, *The Outsider and Others* (1939), and continuing with *Beyond the Wall of Sleep* (1943).

"The Terrible Old Man" was originally published in the July 1921 issue of *The Tryout*.

The Terrible Old Man

H. P. LOVECRAFT

IT WAS THE DESIGN of Angelo Ricci and Joe Czanek and Manuel Silva to call on the Terrible Old Man. This old man dwells all alone in a very ancient house on Water Street near the sea, and is reputed to be both exceedingly rich and exceedingly feeble, which forms a situation very attractive to men of the profession of Messrs. Ricci, Czanek, and Silva, for that profession was nothing less dignified than robbery.

The inhabitants of Kingsport say and think many things about the Terrible Old Man which generally keep him safe from the attention of gentlemen like Mr. Ricci and his colleagues, despite the almost certain fact that he hides a fortune of indefinite magnitude somewhere about his musty and venerable abode. He is, in truth, a very strange person, believed to have been a captain of East India clipper ships in his day; so old that no one can remember when he was young, and so taciturn that few know his real name. Among the gnarled trees in the front yard of his aged and neglected place he maintains a strange collection of large stones, oddly grouped and painted so that they resemble the idols in some obscure Eastern temple. This collection frightens away most of the small boys who love to taunt the Terrible Old Man about his long white hair and beard, or to break the small-paned windows of his dwelling with wicked missiles; but there are other things which frighten the older and more curious folk who sometimes steal up to the house to peer in through the dusty panes. These folk say that on a table in a bare room on the ground floor are many peculiar bottles, in each a small piece of lead suspended pendulum-wise from a string. And they say that the Terrible Old Man talks to these bottles, addressing them by such names as Jack, Scar-Face, Long Tom, Spanish Joe, Peters, and Mate Ellis, and that whenever he speaks to a bottle the little lead pendulum within makes certain definite vibrations as if in answer.

Those who have watched the tall, lean, Terrible Old Man in these peculiar conversations do not watch him again. But Angelo Ricci and Joe Czanek and Manuel Silva were not of Kingsport blood; they were of that new and heterogeneous alien stock which lies outside the charmed circle of New England life and traditions, and they saw in the Terrible Old Man merely a tottering, almost helpless grey-beard, who could not walk without the aid of his knotted cane, and whose thin, weak hands shook pitifully. They were really quite sorry in their way for the lonely, unpopular old fellow, whom everybody shunned, and at whom all the dogs barked singularly. But business is business, and to a robber whose soul is in his profession, there is a lure and a challenge about a very old and very feeble man who has no account at the bank, and who pays for his few necessities at the village store with Spanish gold and silver minted two centuries ago.

Messrs. Ricci, Czanek, and Silva selected the night of April 11th for their call. Mr. Ricci and Mr. Silva were to interview the poor old gentleman, whilst Mr. Czanek waited for them and their presumable metallic burden with a covered motor-car in Ship Street, by the gate in the tall rear wall of their host's grounds. Desire to avoid needless explanations in case of unexpected police intrusions prompted these plans for a quiet and unostentatious departure.

As prearranged, the three adventurers started out separately in order to prevent any evil-minded suspicions afterward. Messrs. Ricci and Silva met in Water Street by the old man's front gate, and although they did not like the way the moon shone down upon the painted stones through the budding branches of the gnarled trees, they had more important things to think about than mere idle superstition. They feared it might be unpleasant work making the Terrible Old Man loquacious concerning his hoarded gold and silver, for aged sea-captains are notably stubborn and perverse. Still, he was very old and very feeble, and there were two visitors. Messrs. Ricci and Silva were experienced in the art of making unwilling persons voluble, and the screams of a weak and exceptionally venerable man can be easily muffled. So they moved up to the one lighted window and heard the Terrible Old Man talking childishly to his bottles with pendulums. Then they donned masks and knocked politely at the weather-stained oaken door.

Waiting seemed very long to Mr. Czanek as he fidgeted restlessly in the covered motor-car by the Terrible Old Man's back gate in Ship Street. He was more than ordinarily tender-hearted, and he did not like the hideous screams he had heard in the ancient house just after the hour appointed for the deed. Had he not told his colleagues to be as gentle as possible with the pathetic old sea-captain? Very nervously he watched that narrow oaken gate in the high and ivy-clad stone wall. Frequently he consulted his watch, and wondered at the delay. Had the old man died before revealing where his treasure was hidden, and had a thorough search become necessary? Mr. Czanek did not like to wait so long in the dark in such a place. Then he sensed a soft tread or tapping on the walk inside the gate, heard a gentle fumbling at the rusty latch, and saw the narrow, heavy door swing inward. And in the pallid glow of the single dim street-lamp he strained his eyes to see what his colleagues had brought out of that sinister house which loomed so close behind. But when he looked, he did not see what he had expected; for his colleagues were not there at all, but only the Terrible Old Man leaning quietly on his knotted cane and smiling hideously. Mr. Czanek had never before noticed the colour of that man's eyes; now he saw that they were yellow.

Little things make considerable excitement in little towns, which is the reason that Kingsport people talked all that spring and summer about the three unidentifiable bodies, horribly slashed as with many cutlasses, and horribly mangled as by the tread of many cruel boot-heels, which the tide washed in. And some people even spoke of things as trivial as the deserted motor-car found in Ship Street, or certain especially inhuman cries, probably of a stray animal or migratory bird, heard in the night by wakeful citizens. But in this idle village gossip the Terrible Old Man took no interest at all. He was by nature reserved, and when one is aged and feeble, one's reserve is doubly strong. Besides, so ancient a sea-captain must have witnessed scores of things much more stirring in the far-off days of his unremembered youth.

Erckmann-Chatrian

A LONG, SUCCESSFUL, and loving relationship came to a sad and somewhat bizarre close when one of these two friends and collaborators decided that the copyright for all their works should rest with him. Emile Erckmann (1822–1899) and Alexandre Chatrian (1826–1890) met as students and began to write collaboratively in 1849. Their coauthorship methodology was probably unique in that Erckmann, clearly the creative genius behind the numerous works of fiction, wrote everything, while Chatrian took care of editing and polishing, as well as handling the messy business of publishing and dramatizations. Surviving manuscripts and papers provide evidence of their productive system. Both men were natives of Alsace-Lorraine and, while Erckmann remained there, Chatrian moved to Paris to handle their business affairs. Although their major works are unread today, their Alsatian novels provide valuable and accurate information about the events, ideas, and folklore of the time and region. Written in clear and direct prose aimed at the general reader, eschewing literary movements, styles, and fads, they were enormously popular while being largely ignored by critics. Often featuring military backgrounds, the novels were appealing to readers for their republican slant and their repudiation of imperialism and Germany. They produced many supernatural stories that were influenced by Poe and Hoffman, and it is these tales for which they are remembered today. Chatrian became ill in 1887 and ended the collaboration. Three years later, as he lay dying, he brought a lawsuit claiming full credit and ownership of all their works. He lost the suit and, although a disappointed and newly pessimistic Erckmann continued to write for several years, it was without distinction.

"The Murderer's Violin" (which has also been published as "The Spectre's Violin" and "The Violin of the Man That Was Hanged") was first published in *Histoires et Contes Fantastiques* (1849); its first appearance in English translation was in the September 1876 issue of the *Dublin University Magazine*.

The Murderer's Violin

ERCKMANN-CHATRIAN

KARL HÂFITZ HAD SPENT six years in mastering counterpoint. He had studied Haydn, Glück, Mozart, Beethoven, and Rossini; he enjoyed capital health, and was possessed of ample means which permitted him to indulge his artistic tastes—in a word, he possessed all that goes to make up the grand and beautiful in music, except that insignificant but very necessary thing—inspiration!

Every day, fired with a noble ardour, he carried to his worthy instructor, Albertus Kilian, long pieces harmonious enough, but of which every phrase was "cribbed." His master, Albertus, seated in his armchair, his feet on the fender, his elbow on a corner of the table, smoking his pipe all the time, set himself to erase, one after the other, the singular discoveries of his pupil. Karl cried with rage, he got very angry, and disputed the point; but the old master quietly opened one of his numerous music-books, and putting his finger on the passage, said:

"Look there, my boy."

Then Karl bowed his head and despaired of the future.

But one fine morning, when he had presented to his master as his own composition a fantasia of Boccherini, varied with Viotti, the good man could no longer remain silent.

"Karl," he exclaimed, "do you take me for a fool? Do you think that I cannot detect your larcenies? This is really too bad!"

And then perceiving the consternation of his pupil, he added—"Listen. I am willing to believe that your memory is to blame, and that you mistake recollection for originality, but you are growing too fat decidedly; you drink too generous a wine, and, above all, too much beer. That is what is shutting up the avenues of your intellect. You must get thinner!"

"Get thinner!"

"Yes, or give up music. You do not lack science, but ideas, and it is very simple; if you pass your whole life covering the strings of your violin with a coat of grease how can they vibrate?"

These words penetrated the depths of Hâfitz's soul.

"If it is necessary for me to get thin," exclaimed he, "I will not shrink from any sacrifice. Since matter oppresses the mind I will starve myself."

His countenance wore such an expression of heroism at that moment that Albertus was touched; he embraced his pupil and wished him every success.

The very next day Karl Hâfitz, knapsack on his back and bâton in hand, left the hotel of the Three Pigeons and the brewery sacred to King Gambrinus, and set out upon his travels.

He proceeded towards Switzerland.

Unfortunately at the end of six weeks he was much thinner, but inspiration did not come any the more readily for that.

"Can any one be more unhappy than I am?" he said. "Neither fasting nor good cheer, nor water, wine, or beer can bring me up to the necessary pitch; what have I done to deserve this? While a crowd of ignorant people produce remarkable works, I, with all my science, all my application, all my courage, cannot accomplish anything. Ah! Heaven is not good to me; it is unjust."

Communing thus with himself, he took the road from Brück to Freibourg; night was coming on; he felt weary and footsore. Just then he perceived by the light of the moon an old ruined inn half-hidden in trees on the opposite side of the way; the door was off its hinges, the small window-panes were broken, the chimney was in ruins. Nettles and briars grew around it in wild luxuriance, and the garret window scarcely topped the heather, in which the wind blew hard enough to take the horns off a cow.

Karl could also perceive through the mist that a branch of a fir-tree waved above the door.

"Well," he muttered, "the inn is not prepossessing, it is rather ill-looking indeed, but we must not judge by appearances."

So, without hesitation, he knocked at the door with his stick.

"Who is there? what do you want?" called out a rough voice within.

"Shelter and food," replied the traveller.

"Ah ha! very good."

The door opened suddenly, and Karl found himself confronted by a stout personage with square visage, grey eyes, his shoulders covered with a great-coat loosely thrown over them, and carrying an axe in his hand.

Behind this individual a fire was burning on the hearth, which lighted up the entrance to a small room and the wooden staircase, and close to the flame was crouched a pale young girl clad in a miserable brown dress with little white spots on it. She looked towards the door with an affrighted air; her black eyes had something sad and an indescribably wandering expression in them.

Karl took all this in at a glance, and instinctively grasped his stick tighter.

"Well, come in," said the man; "this is no time to keep people out of doors."

Then Karl, thinking it bad form to appear alarmed, came into the room and sat down by the hearth.

"Give me your knapsack and stick," said the man.

For the moment the pupil of Albertus trembled to his very marrow; but the knapsack was unbuckled and the stick placed in the corner, and the host was seated quietly before the fire ere he had recovered himself.

This circumstance gave him confidence.

"Landlord," said he, smiling, "I am greatly in want of my supper."

"What would you like for supper, sir?" asked the landlord.

"An omelette, some wine and cheese."

"Ha, ha! you have got an excellent appetite, but our provisions are exhausted."

"You have no cheese, then?"

"No."

"No butter, nor bread, nor milk?"

"No."

"Well, good heavens! what *have* you got?"

"We can roast some potatoes in the embers."

Just then Karl caught sight of a whole regiment of hens perched on the staircase in the gloom of all sorts, in all attitudes, some pluming themselves in the most nonchalant manner.

"But," said Hâfitz, pointing at this troop of fowls, "you must have some eggs surely?"

"We took them all to market this morning."

"Well, if the worst comes to the worst you can roast a fowl for me."

Scarcely had he spoken when the pale girl, with dishevelled hair, darted to the staircase, crying:

"No one shall touch the fowls! no one shall touch my fowls! Ho, ho, ho! God's creatures must be respected."

Her appearance was so terrible that Hâfitz hastened to say:

"No, no, the fowls shall not be touched. Let us have the potatoes. I devote myself to eating potatoes henceforth. From this moment my object in life is determined. I shall remain here three months—six months—any time that may be necessary to make me as thin as a fakir."

He expressed himself with such animation that the host cried out to the girl:

"Genovéva, Genovéva, look! The Spirit has taken possession of him; just as the other was—"

The north wind blew more fiercely outside; the fire blazed up on the hearth, and puffed great masses of grey smoke up to the ceiling. The hens appeared to dance in the reflection of the flame while the demented girl sang in a shrill voice a wild air, and the log of green wood, hissing in the midst of the fire, accompanied her with its plaintive sibilations.

Hâfitz began to fancy that he had fallen upon the den of the sorcerer Hecker; he devoured a dozen potatoes, and drank a great draught of cold water. Then he felt somewhat calmer; he noticed that the girl had left the chamber, and that only the man sat opposite to him by the hearth.

"Landlord," he said, "show me where I am to sleep."

The host lit a lamp and slowly ascended the worm-eaten staircase; he opened a heavy trapdoor with his grey head, and led Karl to a loft beneath the thatch.

"There is your bed," he said, as he deposited the lamp on the floor; "sleep well, and above all things beware of fire."

He then descended, and Hâfitz was left alone, stooping beneath the low roof in front of a great mattress covered with a sack of feathers.

He considered for a few seconds whether it would be prudent to sleep in such a place, for the man's countenance did not appear very prepossessing, particularly as, recalling his cold grey eyes, his blue lips, his wide bony forehead, his yellow hue, he suddenly recalled to mind that on the Golzenberg he had encountered three men hanging in chains, and that one of them bore a striking resemblance to the landlord; that he had also those grave eyes, the bony elbows, and that the great toe of his left foot protruded from his shoe, cracked by the rain.

He also recollected that that unhappy man named Melchior had been a musician formerly, and that he had been hanged for having murdered the landlord of the Golden Sheep with his pitcher, because he had asked him to pay his scanty reckoning.

This poor fellow's music had affected him powerfully in former days. It was fantastic, and the pupil of Albertus had envied the Bohemian; but just now when he recalled the figure on the gibbet, his tatters agitated by the night wind, and the ravens wheeling around him with discordant screams, he trembled violently, and his fears augmented when he discovered, at the farther end of the loft against the wall, a violin decorated with two faded palm-leaves.

Then indeed he was anxious to escape, but at that moment he heard the rough voice of the landlord.

"Put out that light, will you?" he cried; "go to bed. I told you particularly to be cautious about fire."

These words froze Karl; he threw himself upon the mattress and extinguished the light. Silence fell on all the house.

Now, notwithstanding his determination not to close his eyes, Hâfitz, in consequence of hearing the sighing of the wind, the cries of the night-birds, the sound of the mice pattering over the floor, towards one o'clock fell asleep; but he was awakened by a bitter, deep, and most distressing sob. He started up, a cold perspiration standing on his forehead.

He looked up, and saw crouched up beneath the angle of the roof a man. It was Melchior, the executed criminal. His hair fell down to his emaciated ribs; his chest and neck were naked. One might compare him to a skeleton of an immense grasshopper, so thin was he; a ray of moonlight entering through the narrow window gave him a ghastly blue tint, and all around him hung the long webs of spiders.

Hâfitz, speechless, with staring eyes and gaping mouth, kept gazing at this weird object, as one might be expected to gaze at Death standing at one's bedside when the last hour has come!

Suddenly the skeleton extended its long bony hand and took the violin from the wall, placed it in position against its shoulder, and began to play.

There was in this ghostly music something of the cadence with which the earth falls upon the coffin of a dearly-loved friend—something solemn as the thunder of the waterfall echoed afar by the surrounding rocks, majestic as the wild blasts of the autumn tempest in the midst of the sonorous forest trees; sometimes it was sad—sad as never-ending despair. Then, in the midst of all this, he would strike into a lively measure, persuasive, silvery as the notes of a flock of goldfinches fluttering from twig to twig. These pleasing trills soared up with an ineffable tremolo of careless happiness, only to take flight all at once, frightened away by the waltz, foolish, palpitating, bewildering—love, joy, despair—all together singing, weeping, hurrying pell-mell over the quivering strings!

And Karl, notwithstanding his extreme terror, extended his arms and exclaimed:

"Oh, great, great artist! oh, sublime genius! oh, how I lament your sad fate, to be hanged for having murdered that brute of an innkeeper who did not know a note of music!—to wander through the forest by moonlight!—never to live in the world again—and with such talents! O Heaven!"

But as he thus cried out he was interrupted by the rough tones of his host.

"Hullo up there! will you be quiet? Are you ill, or is the house on fire?"

Heavy steps ascended the staircase, a bright light shone through the chinks of the door, which was opened by a thrust of the shoulder, and the landlord appeared.

"Oh!" exclaimed Hâfitz, "what things happen here! First I am awakened by celestial music and entranced by heavenly strains; and then it all vanishes as if it were but a dream."

The innkeeper's face assumed a thoughtful expression.

"Yes, yes," he muttered, "I might have thought as much. Melchior has come to disturb your rest. He will always come. Now we have lost our night's sleep; it is no use to think of rest any more. Come along, friend; get up and smoke a pipe with me."

Karl waited no second bidding; he hastily left the room. But when he got downstairs, seeing that it was still dark night, he buried his head in his hands and remained for a long time plunged in melancholy meditation. The host relighted the fire, and taking up his position in the opposite corner of the hearth, smoked in silence.

At length the grey dawn appeared through the little diamond-shaped panes; then the cock crew, and the hens began to hop down from step to step of the staircase.

"How much do I owe you?" asked Karl, as he buckled on his knapsack and resumed his walking-staff.

"You owe us a prayer at the chapel of St. Blaise," said the man, with a curious emphasis— "one prayer for the soul of Melchior, who was hanged, and another for his *fiancée*, Genovéva, the poor idiot."

"Is that all?"

"That is all."

"Well, then, good-bye—I shall not forget."

And, indeed, the first thing that Karl did on his arrival at Freibourg was to offer up a prayer for the poor man and for the girl he had loved, and then he went to the Grape Hotel, spread his sheet of paper upon the table, and, fortified by a bottle of "rikevir," he wrote at the top of the page *The Murderer's Violin*, and then on the spot he traced the score of his first original composition.

Saki

A TROUBLED CHILDHOOD OF persecution and abuse can mold the sweetest boy into something of a monster, and H(ector) H(ugh) Munro (1870–1916) was all of that—even if he (fortunately) confined his malevolence to his stories, which are some of the cruelest and most cynical in the English language, made no less beastly by their humorous tone. Born in Burma, he was sent to England at the age of two when his mother died. He lived there with two prim, over-controlling aunts whom he tortured and murdered again and again in his fiction. After traveling abroad with his father, he returned to Burma to join the police force but, always sickly, he soon returned to London, where he had a successful career as a journalist, writing Lewis Carroll–like political sketches for *The Westminster Gazette* (collected in book form in 1902 as *The Westminster Alice*) and short stories for the same newspaper (collected in book form in 1904 as *Reginald*). He worked for several other papers, including six years as a foreign correspondent in Russia, the Balkans, and Paris. He joined the British army at the outset of World War I and was killed in France in 1916.

Munro never made clear how he came to choose the pseudonym "Saki." It is possible that it was taken from a character, the cupbearer, in *The Rubaiyat of Omar Khayyam*. It is also possible that it is a reference to a saki, a small South American monkey which is a central character in his short story "The Remoulding of Groby Lington" (contained in *The Chronicles of Clovis*, 1912).

"The Open Window" was first published in the November 18, 1911, issue of *The Westminster Gazette*. It and "Laura" were first collected in *Beasts and Super Beasts* (London, John Lane, The Bodley Head, 1914).

The Open Window

SAKI

"MY AUNT WILL BE down presently, Mr. Nuttel," said a very self-possessed young lady of fifteen; "in the meantime you must try and put up with me."

Framton Nuttel endeavoured to say the correct something which should duly flatter the niece of the moment without unduly discounting the aunt that was to come. Privately he doubted more than ever whether these formal visits on a succession of total strangers would do much towards helping the nerve cure which he was supposed to be undergoing.

"I know how it will be," his sister had said when he was preparing to migrate to this rural retreat; "you will bury yourself down there and not speak to a living soul, and your nerves will be worse than ever from moping. I shall just give you letters of introduction to all the people I know there. Some of them, as far as I can remember, were quite nice."

Framton wondered whether Mrs. Sappleton, the lady to whom he was presenting one of the letters of introduction came into the nice division.

"Do you know many of the people round here?" asked the niece, when she judged that they had had sufficient silent communion.

"Hardly a soul," said Framton. "My sister was staying here, at the rectory, you know, some four years ago, and she gave me letters of introduction to some of the people here."

He made the last statement in a tone of distinct regret.

"Then you know practically nothing about my aunt?" pursued the self-possessed young lady.

"Only her name and address," admitted the caller. He was wondering whether Mrs. Sappleton was in the married or widowed state. An undefinable something about the room seemed to suggest masculine habitation.

"Her great tragedy happened just three years ago," said the child; "that would be since your sister's time."

"Her tragedy?" asked Framton; somehow in this restful country spot tragedies seemed out of place.

"You may wonder why we keep that window wide open on an October afternoon," said the niece, indicating a large French window that opened on to a lawn.

"It is quite warm for the time of the year," said Framton; "but has that window got anything to do with the tragedy?"

"Out through that window, three years ago to a day, her husband and her two young brothers went off for their day's shooting. They never came back. In crossing the moor to their favourite snipe-shooting ground they were all three engulfed in a treacherous piece of bog. It had been that dreadful wet summer, you know, and places that were safe in other years gave way suddenly without warning. Their bodies were never recovered. That was the dreadful part of it." Here the child's voice lost its self-possessed note and became falteringly human. "Poor aunt always thinks that they will come back someday, they and the little brown spaniel that was lost with them, and walk in at that window just as they used to do. That is why the window is kept open every evening till it is quite dusk. Poor dear aunt, she has often told me how they went out, her husband with his white waterproof coat over his arm, and Ronnie, her youngest brother, singing 'Bertie, why do you bound?' as he always did to tease her, because she said it got on her nerves. Do you know, sometimes on still, quiet evenings like this, I almost get a creepy feeling that they will all walk in through that window—"

She broke off with a little shudder. It was a relief to Framton when the aunt bustled into the room with a whirl of apologies for being late in making her appearance.

"I hope Vera has been amusing you?" she said.

"She has been very interesting," said Framton.

"I hope you don't mind the open window," said Mrs. Sappleton briskly; "my husband and brothers will be home directly from shooting, and they always come in this way. They've been out for snipe in the marshes today, so they'll make a fine mess over my poor carpets. So like you menfolk, isn't it?"

She rattled on cheerfully about the shooting and the scarcity of birds, and the prospects for duck in the winter. To Framton it was all purely horrible. He made a desperate but only partially successful effort to turn the talk on to a less ghastly topic, he was conscious that his hostess was giving him only a fragment of her attention, and her eyes were constantly straying past him to the open window and the lawn beyond. It was certainly an unfortunate coincidence that he should have paid his visit on this tragic anniversary.

"The doctors agree in ordering me complete rest, an absence of mental excitement, and avoidance of anything in the nature of violent physical exercise," announced Framton, who laboured under the tolerably widespread delusion that total strangers and chance acquaintances are hungry for the least detail of one's ailments and infirmities, their cause and cure. "On the matter of diet they are not so much in agreement," he continued.

"No?" said Mrs. Sappleton, in a voice which only replaced a yawn at the last moment. Then she suddenly brightened into alert attention—but not to what Framton was saying.

"Here they are at last!" she cried. "Just in time for tea, and don't they look as if they were muddy up to the eyes!"

Framton shivered slightly and turned towards the niece with a look intended to convey sympathetic comprehension. The child was staring out through the open window with a dazed horror in her eyes. In a chill shock of nameless fear Framton swung round in his seat and looked in the same direction.

In the deepening twilight three figures were walking across the lawn towards the window, they all carried guns under their arms, and one of them was additionally burdened with a white coat hung over his shoulders. A tired brown spaniel kept close at their heels. Noiselessly they neared the house, and then a hoarse young voice chanted out of the dusk: "I said, Bertie, why do you bound?"

Framton grabbed wildly at his stick and hat; the hall door, the gravel drive, and the front gate were dimly noted stages in his headlong retreat. A cyclist coming along the road had to run into the hedge to avoid imminent collision.

"Here we are, my dear," said the bearer of the white mackintosh, coming in through the window, "fairly muddy, but most of it's dry. Who was that who bolted out as we came up?"

"A most extraordinary man, a Mr. Nuttel," said Mrs. Sappleton; "could only talk about his illnesses, and dashed off without a word of goodby or apology when you arrived. One would think he had seen a ghost."

"I expect it was the spaniel," said the niece

calmly; "he told me he had a horror of dogs. He was once hunted into a cemetery somewhere on the banks of the Ganges by a pack of pariah dogs, and had to spend the night in a newly dug grave with the creatures snarling and grinning and foaming just above him. Enough to make anyone lose their nerve."

Romance at short notice was her specialty.

Laura

SAKI

"YOU ARE NOT REALLY dying, are you?" asked Amanda.

"I have the doctor's permission to live till Tuesday," said Laura.

"But to-day is Saturday; this is serious!" gasped Amanda.

"I don't know about it being serious; it is certainly Saturday," said Laura.

"Death is always serious," said Amanda.

"I never said I was going to die. I am presumably going to leave off being Laura, but I shall go on being something. An animal of some kind, I suppose. You see, when one hasn't been very good in the life one has just lived, one reincarnates in some lower organism. And I haven't been very good, when one comes to think of it. I've been petty and mean and vindictive and all that sort of thing when circumstances have seemed to warrant it."

"Circumstances never warrant that sort of thing," said Amanda hastily.

"If you don't mind my saying so," observed Laura, "Egbert is a circumstance that would warrant any amount of that sort of thing. You're married to him—that's different; you've sworn to love, honour, and endure him: I haven't."

"I don't see what's wrong with Egbert," protested Amanda.

"Oh, I daresay the wrongness has been on my part," admitted Laura dispassionately; "he has merely been the extenuating circumstance. He made a thin, peevish kind of fuss, for instance, when I took the collie puppies from the farm out for a run the other day."

"They chased his young broods of speckled Sussex and drove two sitting hens off their nests, besides running all over the flower beds. You know how devoted he is to his poultry and garden."

"Anyhow, he needn't have gone on about it for the entire evening and then have said, 'Let's say no more about it' just when I was beginning to enjoy the discussion. That's where one of my petty vindictive revenges came in," added Laura with an unrepentant chuckle; "I turned the entire family of speckled Sussex into his seedling shed the day after the puppy episode."

"How could you?" exclaimed Amanda.

"It came quite easy," said Laura; "two of the hens pretended to be laying at the time, but I was firm."

"And we thought it was an accident!"

"You see," resumed Laura, "I really *have* some grounds for supposing that my next incarnation will be in a lower organism. I shall be an animal of some kind. On the other hand, I haven't been a bad sort in my way, so I think I may count on being a nice animal, something elegant and lively, with a love of fun. An otter, perhaps."

"I can't imagine you as an otter," said Amanda.

"Well, I don't suppose you can imagine me as an angel, if it comes to that," said Laura.

Amanda was silent. She couldn't.

"Personally I think an otter life would be rather enjoyable," continued Laura; "salmon to eat all the year round, and the satisfaction of being able to fetch the trout in their own homes without having to wait for hours till they condescend to rise to the fly you've been dangling before them; and an elegant svelte figure—"

"Think of the otter hounds," interposed Amanda; "how dreadful to be hunted and harried and finally worried to death!"

"Rather fun with half the neighbourhood looking on, and anyhow not worse than this Saturday-to-Tuesday business of dying by inches; and then I should go on into something else. If I had been a moderately good otter I suppose I should get back into human shape of some sort; probably something rather primitive—a little brown, unclothed Nubian boy, I should think."

"I wish you would be serious," sighed Amanda; "you really ought to be if you're only going to live till Tuesday."

As a matter of fact Laura died on Monday.

"So dreadfully upsetting," Amanda complained to her uncle-in-law, Sir Lulworth Quayne. "I've asked quite a lot of people down for golf and fishing, and the rhododendrons are just looking their best."

"Laura always was inconsiderate," said Sir Lulworth; "she was born during Goodwood week, with an Ambassador staying in the house who hated babies."

"She had the maddest kind of ideas," said Amanda; "do you know if there was any insanity in her family?"

"Insanity? No, I never heard of any. Her father lives in West Kensington, but I believe he's sane on all other subjects."

"She had an idea that she was going to be reincarnated as an otter," said Amanda.

"One meets with those ideas of reincarnation so frequently, even in the West," said Sir Lulworth, "that one can hardly set them down as being mad. And Laura was such an unaccountable person in this life that I should not like to lay down definite rules as to what she might be doing in an after state."

"You think she really might have passed into some animal form?" asked Amanda. She was one of those who shape their opinions rather readily from the standpoint of those around them.

Just then Egbert entered the breakfast-room, wearing an air of bereavement that Laura's demise would have been insufficient, in itself, to account for.

"Four of my speckled Sussex have been killed," he exclaimed; "the very four that were to go to the show on Friday. One of them was dragged away and eaten right in the middle of that new carnation bed that I've been to such trouble and expense over. My best flower bed and my best fowls singled out for destruction; it almost seems as if the brute that did the deed had special knowledge how to be as devastating as possible in a short space of time."

"Was it a fox, do you think?" asked Amanda.

"Sounds more like a polecat," said Sir Lulworth.

"No," said Egbert, "there were marks of webbed feet all over the place, and we followed the tracks down to the stream at the bottom of the garden; evidently an otter."

Amanda looked quickly and furtively across at Sir Lulworth.

Egbert was too agitated to eat any breakfast, and went out to superintend the strengthening of the poultry yard defences.

"I think she might at least have waited till the funeral was over," said Amanda in a scandalised voice.

"It's her own funeral, you know," said Sir Lulworth; "it's a nice point in etiquette how far one ought to show respect to one's own mortal remains."

Disregard for mortuary convention was carried to further lengths next day; during the absence of the family at the funeral ceremony the remaining survivors of the speckled Sussex were massacred. The marauder's line of retreat seemed to have embraced most of the flower beds on the lawn, but the strawberry beds in the lower garden had also suffered.

"I shall get the otter hounds to come here at the earliest possible moment," said Egbert savagely.

"On no account! You can't dream of such a thing!" exclaimed Amanda. "I mean, it wouldn't do, so soon after a funeral in the house."

"It's a case of necessity," said Egbert; "once an otter takes to that sort of thing it won't stop."

"Perhaps it will go elsewhere now there are no more fowls left," suggested Amanda.

"One would think you wanted to shield the beast," said Egbert.

"There's been so little water in the stream lately," objected Amanda; "it seems hardly sporting to hunt an animal when it has so little chance of taking refuge anywhere."

"Good gracious!" fumed Egbert, "I'm not thinking about sport. I want to have the animal killed as soon as possible."

Even Amanda's opposition weakened when, during church time on the following Sunday, the otter made its way into the house, raided half a salmon from the larder and worried it into scaly fragments on the Persian rug in Egbert's studio.

"We shall have it hiding under our beds and biting pieces out of our feet before long," said Egbert, and from what Amanda knew of this particular otter she felt that the possibility was not a remote one.

On the evening preceding the day fixed for the hunt Amanda spent a solitary hour walking by the banks of the stream, making what she imagined to be hound noises. It was charitably supposed by those who overheard her performance, that she was practising for farmyard imitations at the forth-coming village entertainment.

It was her friend and neighbour, Aurora Burret, who brought her news of the day's sport.

"Pity you weren't out; we had quite a good day. We found it at once, in the pool just below your garden."

"Did you—kill?" asked Amanda.

"Rather. A fine she-otter. Your husband got rather badly bitten in trying to 'tail it.' Poor beast, I felt quite sorry for it, it had such a human look in its eyes when it was killed. You'll call me silly, but do you know who the look reminded me of? My dear woman, what is the matter?"

When Amanda had recovered to a certain extent from her attack of nervous prostration Egbert took her to the Nile Valley to recuperate. Change of scene speedily brought about the desired recovery of health and mental balance. The escapades of an adventurous otter in search of a variation of diet were viewed in their proper light. Amanda's normally placid temperament reasserted itself. Even a hurricane of shouted curses, coming from her husband's dressing-room, in her husband's voice, but hardly in his usual vocabulary, failed to disturb her serenity as she made a leisurely toilet one evening in a Cairo hotel.

"What is the matter? What has happened?" she asked in amused curiosity.

"The little beast has thrown all my clean shirts into the bath! Wait till I catch you, you little—"

"What little beast?" asked Amanda, suppressing a desire to laugh; Egbert's language was so hopelessly inadequate to express his outraged feelings.

"A little beast of a naked brown Nubian boy," spluttered Egbert.

And now Amanda is seriously ill.

Fitz-James O'Brien

IT IS NOT IN the least surprising that Fitz-James (sometimes spelled Fitz James) O'Brien (1828–1862) was taken into New York social circles almost immediately upon his arrival from Ireland. Like Lord Byron in England, O'Brien was a charming, handsome playboy, poet, and soldier. Born Michael O'Brien in County Cork, he attended Dublin's Trinity College, then moved to London where he squandered his very considerable inheritance in a little more than two years. It was here that he began to sell stories and poems. When the money ran low, he moved to America in 1852 and changed his name. He quickly sold stories, essays, poetry, and reviews to several newspapers and such major periodicals as the *Lantern, Harper's Magazine, Putnam's Magazine, Vanity Fair,* and *Atlantic Monthly,* which published two of his most inventive and famous stories. In "The Diamond Lens," which appeared in the first issue of *Atlantic,* a man looks through a microscope and discovers a whole world in a drop of water and falls in love with a woman he sees there—a story which undoubtedly inspired the famous story by Joseph Cummings, "The Girl in the Golden Atom." "The Wondersmith" tells of a villainous toymaker whose creations come to life and kill their owners. He also wrote several plays, one of which, *The Gentleman from Ireland* (1854), reputedly was performed for twenty years. When the Civil War broke out, he joined the New York National Guard in January of 1861 and died of wounds incurred in a minor skirmish a little more than a year later.

"What Was It?" was first published in the March 1859 issue of *Harper's Magazine.* It was collected in his only book, *The Poems and Stories of Fitz-James O'Brien* (Boston, J. R. Osgood, 1881), a posthumous collection of forty-three poems and thirteen stories compiled and edited by his friend William Winter.

What Was It?

FITZ-JAMES O'BRIEN

IT IS, I CONFESS, with considerable dif-
fidence that I approach the strange narrative
which I am about to relate. The events which
I purpose detailing are of so extraordinary and
unheard-of a character that I am quite prepared
to meet with an unusual amount of incredulity
and scorn. I accept all such beforehand. I have,
I trust, the literary courage to face unbelief. I

have, after mature consideration, resolved to
narrate, in as simple and straightforward a manner as I can compass, some facts that passed
under my observation in the month of July last,
and which, in the annals of the mysteries of
physical science, are wholly unparalleled.

I live at No.——— Twenty-sixth Street, in this
city. The house is in some respects a curious one.

It has enjoyed for the last two years the reputation of being haunted. It is a large and stately residence, surrounded by what was once a garden, but which is now only a green inclosure used for bleaching clothes. The dry basin of what has been a fountain, and a few fruit-trees, ragged and unpruned, indicate that this spot, in past days, was a pleasant, shady retreat, filled with fruits and flowers and the sweet murmur of waters.

The house is very spacious. A hall of noble size leads to a vast spiral staircase winding through its center, while the various apartments are of imposing dimensions. It was built some fifteen or twenty years since by Mr. A——, the well-known New York merchant, who five years ago threw the commercial world into convulsions by a stupendous bank fraud. Mr. A——, as every one knows, escaped to Europe, and died not long after of a broken heart. Almost immediately after the news of his decease reached this country, and was verified, the report spread in Twenty-sixth Street that No. —— was haunted. Legal measures had dispossessed the widow of its former owner, and it was inhabited merely by a care taker and his wife, placed there by the house agent into whose hands it had passed for purposes of renting or sale. These people declared that they were troubled with unnatural noises. Doors were opened without any visible agency. The remnants of furniture scattered through the various rooms were, during the night, piled one upon the other by unknown hands. Invisible feet passed up and down the stairs in broad daylight, accompanied by the rustle of unseen silk dresses, and the gliding of viewless hands along the massive balusters. The care taker and his wife declared that they would live there no longer. The house agent laughed, dismissed them, and put others in their place. The noises and supernatural manifestations continued. The neighborhood caught up the story, and the house remained untenanted for three years. Several persons negotiated for it; but somehow, always before the bargain was closed, they heard the unpleasant rumors, and declined to treat any further.

It was in this state of things that my landlady—who at that time kept a boarding-house in Bleecker Street, and who wished to move farther up town—conceived the bold idea of renting No.—— Twenty-sixth Street. Happening to have in her house rather a plucky and philosophical set of boarders, she laid down her scheme before us, stating candidly everything she had heard respecting the ghostly qualities of the establishment to which she wished to remove us. With the exception of two timid persons—a sea captain and a returned Californian, who immediately gave notice that they would leave—all of Mrs. Moffat's guests declared that they would accompany her in her chivalric incursion into the abode of spirits.

Our removal was effected in the month of May, and we were all charmed with our new residence. The portion of Twenty-sixth Street where our house is situated—between Seventh and Eighth Avenues—is one of the pleasantest localities in New York. The gardens back of the houses, running down nearly to the Hudson, form, in the summer time, a perfect avenue of verdure. The air is pure and invigorating, sweeping, as it does, straight across the river from the Weehawken heights, and even the ragged garden which surrounded the house on two sides, although displaying on washing days rather too much clothesline, still gave us a piece of greensward to look at, and a cool retreat in the summer evenings, where we smoked our cigars in the dusk, and watched the fireflies flashing their dark-lanterns in the long grass.

Of course we had no sooner established ourselves at No.—— than we began to expect the ghosts. We absolutely awaited their advent with eagerness. Our dinner conversation was supernatural. One of the boarders, who had purchased Mrs. Crowe's "Night Side of Nature" for his own private delectation, was regarded as a public enemy by the entire household for not having bought twenty copies. The man led a life of supreme wretchedness while he was reading this volume. A system of espionage was established, of which he was the victim. If he incautiously laid the book down for an instant and left the room, it was immediately seized and read aloud in secret places to a select few. I found myself a person of immense importance, it having leaked out that I was tolerably well versed in the history of supernaturalism, and had once written a story, entitled "The Pot of Tulips," for *Harper's Monthly,* the foundation of which was a ghost. If a table or a wainscot panel happened to warp when we were assembled in the large drawing-room, there was an instant silence, and every one was prepared for an immediate clanking of chains and a spectral form.

After a month of psychological excitement, it was with the utmost dissatisfaction that we were forced to acknowledge that nothing in the remotest degree approaching the supernatural had manifested itself. Once the black butler asseverated that his candle had been blown out by some invisible agency while he was undressing himself for the night; but as I had more than once discovered this colored gentleman in a condition when one candle must have appeared to him like two, I thought it possible that, by going a step farther in his potations, he might have reversed his phenomenon, and seen no candle at all where he ought to have beheld one.

Things were in this state when an incident took place so awful and inexplicable in its character that my reason fairly reels at the bare memory of the occurrence. It was the tenth of July. After dinner was over I repaired with my friend, Dr. Hammond, to the garden to smoke my evening pipe. The Doctor and myself found ourselves in an unusually metaphysical mood. We lit our large meerschaums, filled with fine Turkish tobacco; we paced to and fro, conversing. A strange perversity dominated the currents of our thought. They would *not* flow through the sun-lit channels into which we strove to divert them. For some unaccountable reason they constantly diverged into dark and lonesome beds, where a continual gloom brooded. It was in vain that, after our old fashion, we flung ourselves on the shores of the East, and talked of its gay bazaars, of the splendors of the time of Haroun, of harems and golden palaces. Black afreets continually arose from the depths of our talk, and expanded, like the one the fisherman released from the copper vessel, until they blotted everything bright from our vision. Insensibly, we yielded to the occult force that swayed us, and indulged in gloomy speculation. We had talked some time upon the proneness of the human mind to mysticism, and the almost universal love of the Terrible, when Hammond suddenly said to me, "What do you consider to be the greatest element of Terror?"

The question, I own, puzzled me. That many things were terrible, I knew. Stumbling over a corpse in the dark; beholding, as I once did, a woman floating down a deep and rapid river, with wildly lifted arms, and awful, upturned face, uttering, as she sank, shrieks that rent one's heart, while we, the spectators, stood frozen at a window which overhung the river at a height of sixty feet, unable to make the slightest effort to save her, but dumbly watching her last supreme agony and her disappearance. A shattered wreck, with no life visible, encountered floating listlessly on the ocean, is a terrible object, for it suggests a huge terror, the proportions of which are veiled. But it now struck me for the first time that there must be one great and ruling embodiment of fear, a King of Terrors to which all others must succumb. What might it be? To what train of circumstances would it owe its existence?

"I confess, Hammond," I replied to my friend, "I never considered the subject before. That there must be one Something more terrible than any other thing, I feel. I cannot attempt, however, even the most vague definition."

"I am somewhat like you, Harry," he answered. "I feel my capacity to experience a terror greater than anything yet conceived by the human mind—something combining in fearful and unnatural amalgamation hitherto supposed incompatible elements. The calling of the voices in Brockden Brown's novel of 'Wieland' is awful; so is the picture of the Dweller of the Threshold, in Bulwer's 'Zanoni'; but," he added, shaking his head gloomily, "there is something more horrible still than these."

"Look here, Hammond," I rejoined, "let us drop this kind of talk, for Heaven's sake!"

"I don't know what's the matter with me to-night," he replied, "but my brain is running upon all sorts of weird and awful thoughts. I feel as if I could write a story like Hoffman to-night, if I were only master of a literary style."

"Well, if we are going to be Hoffmanesque in our talk, I'm off to bed. How sultry it is! Good night, Hammond."

"Good night, Harry. Pleasant dreams to you."

"To you, gloomy wretch, afreets, ghouls, and enchanters."

We parted, and each sought his respective chamber. I undressed quickly and got into bed, taking with me, according to my usual custom, a book, over which I generally read myself to sleep. I opened the volume as soon as I had laid my head upon the pillow, and instantly flung it to the other side of the room. It was Goudon's "History of Monsters"—a curious French work, which I had lately imported from Paris, but which, in the state of mind I had then reached, was anything but an agreeable companion. I resolved to go to sleep at once; so, turning down my gas until nothing but a little blue point of light glimmered on the top of the tube, I composed myself to rest.

The room was in total darkness. The atom of gas that still remained lighted did not illuminate a distance of three inches round the burner. I desperately drew my arm across my eyes, as if to shut out even the darkness, and tried to think of nothing. It was in vain. The confounded themes touched on by Hammond in the garden kept obtruding themselves on my brain. I battled against them. I erected ramparts of would-be blankness of intellect to keep them out. They still crowded upon me. While I was lying still as a corpse, hoping that by a perfect physical inaction I should hasten mental repose, an awful incident occurred. A Something dropped, as it seemed, from the ceiling, plumb upon my chest, and the next instant I felt two bony hands encircling my throat, endeavoring to choke me.

I am no coward, and am possessed of considerable physical strength. The suddenness of the attack, instead of stunning me, strung every nerve to its highest tension. My body acted from instinct, before my brain had time to realize the terrors of my position. In an instant I wound two muscular arms around the creature, and squeezed it, with all the strength of despair, against my chest. In a few seconds the bony hands that had fastened on my throat loosened their hold, and I was free to breathe once more. Then commenced a struggle of awful intensity. Immersed in the most profound darkness, totally ignorant of the nature of the Thing by which I was so suddenly attacked, finding my grasp slipping every moment, by reason, it seemed to me, of the entire nakedness of my assailant, bitten with sharp teeth in the shoulder, neck, and chest, having every moment to protect my throat against a pair of sinewy, agile hands, which my utmost efforts could not confine—these were a combination of circumstances to combat which required all the strength and skill and courage that I possessed.

At last, after a silent, deadly, exhausting struggle, I got my assailant under by a series of incredible efforts of strength. Once pinned, with my knee on what I made out to be its chest, I knew that I was victor. I rested for a moment to breathe. I heard the creature beneath me panting in the darkness, and felt the violent throbbing of a heart. It was apparently as exhausted as I was; that was one comfort. At this moment I remembered that I usually placed under my pillow, before going to bed, a large yellow silk pocket handkerchief, for use during the night. I felt for it instantly; it was there. In a few seconds more I had, after a fashion, pinioned the creature's arms.

I now felt tolerably secure. There was nothing more to be done but to turn on the gas, and, having first seen what my midnight assailant was like, arouse the household. I will confess to being actuated by a certain pride in not giving the alarm before; I wished to make the capture alone and unaided.

Never losing my hold for an instant, I slipped from the bed to the floor, dragging my captive with me. I had but a few steps to make to reach the gas-burner; these I made with the greatest caution, holding the creature in a grip like a vice. At last I got within arm's-length of the tiny speck of blue light which told me where the gas-burner lay. Quick as lightning I released my grasp with one hand and let on the full flood of light. Then I turned to look at my captive.

I cannot even attempt to give any definition of my sensations the instant after I turned on the gas. I suppose I must have shrieked with terror, for in less than a minute afterward my room was crowded with the inmates of the house. I shudder now as I think of that awful moment. *I saw nothing!* Yes; I had one arm firmly clasped round a breathing, panting, corporeal shape, my other hand gripped with all its strength a throat as warm, and apparently fleshly, as my own; and yet, with this living substance in my grasp, with its body pressed against my own, and all in the bright glare of a large jet of gas, I absolutely beheld nothing! Not even an outline—a vapor!

I do not, even at this hour, realize the situation in which I found myself. I cannot recall the astounding incident thoroughly. Imagination in vain tries to compass the awful paradox.

It breathed. I felt its warm breath upon my cheek. It struggled fiercely. It had hands. They clutched me. Its skin was smooth, like my own. There it lay, pressed close up against me, solid as stone—and yet utterly invisible!

I wonder that I did not faint or go mad on the instant. Some wonderful instinct must have sustained me; for, absolutely, in place of loosening my hold on the terrible Enigma, I seemed to gain an additional strength in my moment of horror, and tightened my grasp with such wonderful force that I felt the creature shivering with agony.

Just then Hammond entered my room at the head of the household. As soon as he beheld my face—which, I suppose, must have been an awful sight to look at—he hastened forward, crying, "Great heaven, Harry! what has happened?"

"Hammond! Hammond!" I cried, "come here. Oh! this is awful! I have been attacked in bed by something or other, which I have hold of; but I can't see it—I can't see it!"

Hammond, doubtless struck by the unfeigned horror expressed in my countenance, made one or two steps forward with an anxious yet puzzled expression. A very audible titter burst from the remainder of my visitors. This suppressed laughter made me furious. To laugh at a human being in my position! It was the worst species of cruelty. *Now,* I can understand why the appearance of a man struggling violently, as it would seem, with an airy nothing, and calling for assistance against a vision, should have appeared ludicrous. *Then,* so great was my rage against the mocking crowd that had I the power I would have stricken them dead where they stood.

"Hammond! Hammond!" I cried again, despairingly, "for God's sake come to me. I can hold the—the Thing but a short while longer. It is overpowering me. Help me! Help me!"

"Harry," whispered Hammond, approaching me, "you have been smoking too much."

"I swear to you, Hammond, that this is no vision," I answered, in the same low tone. "Don't you see how it shakes my whole frame with its struggles? If you don't believe me, convince yourself. Feel it—touch it."

Hammond advanced and laid his hand on the spot I indicated. A wild cry of horror burst from him. He had felt it!

In a moment he had discovered somewhere in my room a long piece of cord, and was the next instant winding it and knotting it about the body of the unseen being that I clasped in my arms.

"Harry," he said, in a hoarse, agitated voice, for, though he preserved his presence of mind, he was deeply moved, "Harry, it's all safe now. You may let go, old fellow, if you're tired. The Thing can't move."

I was utterly exhausted, and I gladly loosed my hold.

Hammond stood holding the ends of the cord that bound the Invisible, twisted round his hand, while before him, self-supporting as it were, he beheld a rope laced and interlaced, and stretching tightly round a vacant space. I never saw a man look so thoroughly stricken with awe. Nevertheless his face expressed all the courage and determination which I knew him to possess. His lips, although white, were set firmly, and one could perceive at a glance that, although stricken with fear, he was not daunted.

The confusion that ensued among the guests of the house who were witnesses of this extraordinary scene between Hammond and myself—who beheld the pantomime of binding this struggling Something—who beheld me almost sinking from physical exhaustion when my task of jailer was over—the confusion and terror that took possession of the bystanders, when they saw all this, was beyond description. The weaker ones fled from the apartment. The few who remained clustered near the door, and could not be induced to approach Hammond and his Charge. Still incredulity broke out through their terror. They had not the courage to satisfy themselves, and yet they doubted. It was in vain that I begged of some of the men to come near and convince themselves by touch of the existence in that room of a living being which was invisible. They were incredulous, but did not dare to undeceive themselves. How could a solid, living, breathing body be invisible, they asked. My reply was this. I gave a sign to Hammond, and both of us—conquering our fearful repugnance to touch the invisible creature—lifted it from the ground, manacled as it was, and took it to my bed. Its weight was about that of a boy of fourteen.

"Now, my friends," I said, as Hammond and myself held the creature suspended over the bed, "I can give you self-evident proof that here is a solid, ponderable body which, nevertheless, you cannot see. Be good enough to watch the surface of the bed attentively."

I was astonished at my own courage in treating this strange event so calmly; but I had re-covered from my first terror, and felt a sort of scientific pride in the affair which dominated every other feeling.

The eyes of the bystanders were immediately fixed on my bed. At a given signal Hammond and I let the creature fall. There was the dull sound of a heavy body alighting on a soft mass. The timbers of the bed creaked. A deep impression marked itself distinctly on the pillow, and on the bed itself. The crowd who witnessed this gave a sort of low, universal cry, and rushed from the room. Hammond and I were left alone with our Mystery.

We remained silent for some time, listening to the low, irregular breathing of the creature on the bed, and watching the rustle of the bed-clothes as it impotently struggled to free itself from confinement. Then Hammond spoke.

"Harry, this is awful."

"Aye, awful."

"But not unaccountable."

"Not unaccountable! What do you mean? Such a thing has never occurred since the birth of the world. I know not what to think, Hammond. God grant that I am not mad, and that this is not an insane fantasy!"

"Let us reason a little, Harry. Here is a solid body which we touch, but which we cannot see. The fact is so unusual that it strikes us with terror. Is there no parallel, though, for such a phenomenon? Take a piece of pure glass. It is tangible and transparent. A certain chemical coarseness is all that prevents its being so entirely transparent as to be totally invisible. It is not *theoretically impossible*, mind you, to make a glass which shall not reflect a single ray of light—a glass so pure and homogeneous in its atoms that the rays from the sun shall pass through it as they do through the air, refracted but not reflected. We do not see the air, and yet we feel it."

"That's all very well, Hammond, but these are inanimate substances. Glass does not breathe, air does not breathe. *This* thing has a heart that palpitates—a will that moves it—lungs that play, and inspire and respire."

"You forget the strange phenomena of which we have so often heard of late," answered the Doctor, gravely. "At the meetings called 'spirit circles,' invisible hands have been thrust into the hands of those persons round the table—warm, fleshly hands that seemed to pulsate with mortal life."

"What? Do you think, then, that this thing is—"

"I don't know what it is," was the solemn reply; "but please the gods I will, with your assistance, thoroughly investigate it."

We watched together, smoking many pipes, all night long, by the bedside of the unearthly being that tossed and panted until it was apparently wearied out. Then we learned by the low, regular breathing that it slept.

The next morning the house was all astir. The boarders congregated on the landing outside my room, and Hammond and myself were lions. We had to answer a thousand questions as to the state of our extraordinary prisoner, for as yet not one person in the house except ourselves could be induced to set foot in the apartment.

The creature was awake. This was evidenced by the convulsive manner in which the bedclothes were moved in its efforts to escape. There was something truly terrible in beholding, as it were, those second-hand indications of the terrible writhings and agonized struggles for liberty which themselves were invisible.

Hammond and myself had racked our brains during the long night to discover some means by which we might realize the shape and general appearance of the Enigma. As well as we could make out by passing our hands over the creature's form, its outlines and lineaments were human. There was a mouth; a round, smooth head without hair; a nose, which, however, was little elevated above the cheeks; and its hands and feet felt like those of a boy. At first we thought of placing the being on a smooth surface and tracing its outline with chalk, as shoemakers trace the outline of the foot. This plan was given up as being of no value. Such an outline would give not the slightest idea of its conformation.

A happy thought struck me. We would take a cast of it in plaster of Paris. This would give us the solid figure, and satisfy all our wishes. But how to do it? The movements of the creature would disturb the setting of the plastic covering, and distort the mold. Another thought. Why not give it chloroform? It had respiratory organs—that was evident by its breathing. Once reduced to a state of insensibility, we could do with it what we would. Doctor X—— was sent for; and after the worthy physician had recovered from the first shock of amazement, he proceeded to administer the chloroform. In three minutes afterward we were enabled to remove the fetters from the creature's body, and a well-known modeler of this city was busily engaged in covering the invisible form with the moist clay. In five minutes more we had a mold, and before evening a rough *fac simile* of the mystery. It was shaped like a man—distorted, uncouth, and horrible, but still a man. It was small, not over four feet and some inches in height, and its limbs revealed a muscular development that was unparalleled. Its face surpassed in hideousness anything I had ever seen. Gustave Doré, or Callot, or Tony Johannot, never conceived anything so horrible. There is a face in one of the latter's illustrations to "Un Voyage où il vous plaira," which somewhat approaches the countenance of this creature, but does not equal it. It was the physiognomy of what I should have fancied a ghoul to be. It looked as if it was capable of feeding on human flesh.

Having satisfied our curiosity, and bound every one in the house to secrecy, it became a question what was to be done with our Enigma. It was impossible that we should keep such a horror in our house; it was equally impossible that such an awful being should be let loose upon the world. I confess that I would have gladly voted for the creature's destruction. But who would shoulder the responsibility? Who would undertake the execution of this horrible semblance of a human being? Day after day this question was deliberated gravely. The boarders all left the house. Mrs. Moffat was in despair, and threatened Hammond and myself with all sorts of legal penalties if we did not remove the Horror. Our answer was, "We will go if you like, but we decline taking this creature with us. Remove it yourself if you please. It appeared in your house. On you the responsibility rests." To this there was, of course, no answer. Mrs. Moffat could not obtain for love or money a person who would even approach the Mystery.

The most singular part of the transaction was that we were entirely ignorant of what the creature habitually fed on. Everything in the way of nutriment that we could think of was placed before it, but was never touched. It was awful to stand by, day after day, and see the clothes toss, and hear the hard breathing, and know that it was starving.

Ten, twelve days, a fortnight passed, and it still lived. The pulsations of the heart, however, were daily growing fainter, and had now nearly ceased altogether. It was evident that the creature was dying for want of sustenance. While this terrible life struggle was going on, I felt miserable. I could not sleep of nights. Horrible as the creature was, it was pitiful to think of the pangs it was suffering.

At last it died. Hammond and I found it cold and stiff one morning in the bed. The heart had ceased to beat, the lungs to inspire. We hastened to bury it in the garden. It was a strange funeral, the dropping of that viewless corpse into the damp hole. The cast of its form I gave to Dr. X——, who keeps it in his museum in Tenth Street.

As I am on the eve of a long journey from which I may not return, I have drawn up this narrative of an event the most singular that has ever come to my knowledge.

NOTE—It was rumored that the proprietors of a well-known museum in this city had made arrangements with Dr. X—— to exhibit to the public the singular cast which Mr. Escott deposited with him. So extraordinary a history cannot fail to attract universal attention.

Alexander Woollcott

THOUGH NOT MUCH READ today, Alexander "Aleck" Woollcott (1887–1943) was a hugely influential critic in his day, both of the theater and literature, single-handedly making James Hilton's *Goodbye, Mr. Chips* and *Lost Horizon* bestsellers. Born in Phalanx, New Jersey, he became a prolific drama critic for *The New York Times* and then wrote a column titled "Shouts and Murmurs" for *The New Yorker*. His editor at the magazine was quoted as saying, "I guess he was one of the most dreadful writers who ever existed," although the great bookman Vincent Starrett selected his *While Rome Burns* as one of the fifty-two "Best Loved Books of the Twentieth Century."

He was one of the founders of the Algonquin Round Table (just as he later was one of the charter members of the Baker Street Irregulars, famously arriving at the first dinner in a hansom cab). He loved the theater and wrote two plays with fellow member George S. Kaufman, both failures. Kaufman, with Moss Hart, later wrote *The Man Who Came to Dinner* and based the titular character, Sheridan Whiteside, on Woollcott, exaggerating his best and worst characteristics. Less well known is that he also served as the inspiration for Waldo Lydecker in the noir novel and film *Laura*. Clifton Webb, who played the columnist, also toured as Whiteside in *The Man Who Came to Dinner*; Woollcott starred in a traveling company of the comedy. Although he didn't like Los Angeles, calling it "seven suburbs in search of a city," he liked being in films and had numerous small parts and cameos.

"Full Fathom Five" was presented to readers as a true story; it was originally published in the June 22, 1929, issue of *The New Yorker*.

Full Fathom Five

ALEXANDER WOOLLCOTT

THIS IS THE STORY just as I heard it the other evening—a ghost story told me as true. It seems that one chilly October night in the first decade of the present century, two sisters were motoring along a Cape Cod road, when their car broke down just before midnight and would go no further. This was in an era when such mishaps were both commoner and more hopeless than they are today. For these two, there was no chance of help until another car might chance to come by in the morning and give them a tow. Of a lodging for the night there was no hope, except a gaunt, unlighted, frame house which, with a clump of pine trees beside it, stood black in the moonlight, across a neglected stretch of frost-hardened lawn.

They yanked at its ancient bell-pull, but only a faint tinkle within made answer. They banged despairingly on the door panel, only to awaken what at first they thought was an echo, and then identified as a shutter responding antiphonally with the help of a nipping wind. This shutter was around the corner, and the ground-floor window behind it was broken and unfastened. There was enough moonlight to show that the room within was a deserted library, with a few books left on the sagging shelves and a few pieces of dilapidated furniture still standing where some departing family had left them, long before. At least the sweep of the electric flash which one of the women had brought with her showed them that on the uncarpeted floor the dust lay thick and trackless, as if no one had trod there in many a day.

They decided to bring their blankets in from the car and stretch out there on the floor until daylight, none too comfortable, perhaps, but at least sheltered from that salt and cutting wind. It was while they were lying there, trying to get to sleep, while, indeed, they had drifted halfway across the borderland, that they saw—each confirming the other's fear by a convulsive grip of the hand—saw standing at the empty fireplace, as if trying to dry himself by a fire that was not there, the wraithlike figure of a sailor, come dripping from the sea.

After an endless moment, in which neither woman breathed, one of them somehow found the strength to call out, "Who's there?" The challenge shattered the intolerable silence, and at the sound, muttering a little—they said afterwards that it was something between a groan and a whimper—the misty figure seemed to dissolve. They strained their eyes, but could see nothing between themselves and the battered mantelpiece.

Then, telling themselves (and, as one does, half believing it) that they had been dreaming, they tried again to sleep, and, indeed, did sleep until a patch of shuttered sunlight striped the morning floor. As they sat up and blinked at the gritty realism of the forsaken room, they would, I think, have laughed at their shared illusion of the night before, had it not been for something at which one of the sisters pointed with a kind of gasp. There, in the still undisturbed dust, on the spot in front of the fireplace where the apparition had seemed to stand, was a patch of water, a little, circular pool that had issued from no crack in the floor nor, as far as they could see, fallen from any point in the innocent ceiling. Near it in the surrounding dust was no footprint—their own or any other's—and in it was a piece of green that looked like seaweed. One of the women bent down and put her finger to the water, then lifted it to her tongue. The water was salty.

After that the sisters scuttled out and sat in their car, until a passerby gave them a tow to the nearest village. In its tavern at breakfast they gossiped with the proprietress about the empty house among the pine trees down the road. Oh, yes, it had been just that way for a score of years or more. Folks did say the place was spooky, haunted by a son of the family who, driven out by his father, had shipped before the mast and been drowned at sea. Some said the family had moved away because they could not stand the things they heard and saw at night.

A year later, one of the sisters told the story at a dinner party in New York. In the pause that followed a man across the table leaned forward.

"My dear lady," he said, with a smile, "I happen to be the curator of a museum where they are doing a good deal of work on submarine vegetation. In your place, I never would have left that house without taking the bit of seaweed with me."

"Of course you wouldn't," she answered tartly, "and neither did I."

It seems she had lifted it out of the water and dried it a little by pressing it against a window pane. Then she had carried it off in her pocketbook, as a souvenir. As far as she knew, it was still in an envelope in a little drawer of her desk at home. If she could find it, would he like to see it? He would. Next morning she sent it around by messenger, and a few days later it came back with a note.

"You were right," the note said, "this is seaweed. Furthermore, it may interest you to learn that it is of a rare variety which, as far as we know, grows only on dead bodies."

And that, my dears, is the story as I heard it the other evening, heard it from Alice Duer Miller who, in turn, had heard it five-and-twenty years before from Mrs. George Haven Putnam, sometime dean of Barnard College, and author of that admirable work, *The Lady*. To her I must go if—as I certainly did—I wanted more precise details. So to Mrs. Putnam I went, hat in hand and, as an inveterate reporter, showered her with questions. I wanted the names of the seaweed, of the curator, of the museum, of the two sisters, of the dead sailor, and of the nearby village on Cape Cod. I wanted a road-map marked with a cross to show the house in the grove of pines. I wanted—but the examination came to a dead stop at the sight of her obvious embarrassment. She was most graciously apologetic, but, really, what with this and what with that, she had forgotten the whole story. She could not even remember—and thus it is ever with my life in science—who it was that had told it to her.

FOOTNOTE: More recently, the Curator of the Botanical Museum in St. Louis has assured me that this tale, whispered from neighbor to neighbor across the country, has become distorted in a manner offensive to students of submarine vegetation. According to him, the visitor from the sea was seen in a house in Woods Hole, Mass. He was a son of the house who had been drowned during his honeymoon off the coast of Australia. The seaweed picked up off the dusty floor of that New England mansion was of a variety which grows only off the Australian coast. The Curator even presented me with the actual seaweed. I regard it with mingled affection and skepticism, and keep it pressed between the pages of Bullfinch's *Mythology*.

HE COMETH AND HE PASSETH BY

H. R. Wakefield

THE LAST MAJOR AUTHOR of ghost stories in the classic, old-fashioned style of M. R. James was H(erbert) R(ussell) Wakefield (1888 or 1890–1964), whose early (and best) stories were set among old ruins and involved family curses and forbidden tomes. Born in Kent, the son of the future Bishop of Birmingham, he was educated at Oxford University with a degree in history. He was a publisher from 1920 to 1930, having turned to writing as late as 1928 when his first ghost story, the much-anthologized "The Red Lodge," was inspired by a real incident in his life. He had stayed in a lovely, apparently charming old house, where he felt an inexplicable "fear without a name," as he described it, and later learned that five previous tenants had committed suicide there.

Although he wrote in other fields, such as true crime, with *The Green Bicycle Case* (1930) and *Landru: The French Bluebeard* (1936), and three undistinguished mystery novels: *Hearken to the Evidence* (1933), *Belt of Suspicion* (1936), and *Hostess of Death* (1938), it is his ghost stories for which he is remembered—although the excellence of his work exceeds his recognition. Among his outstanding collections of supernatural and occult fiction are *They Return at Evening* (1928), *Others Who Returned* (1929, published in the U.K. as *Old Man's Beard*), and *Imagine a Man in a Box* (1931); later collections are mainly reprints or comprise lesser works. In 1968, Claire Bloom starred in a BBC adaptation of Wakefield's haunted house story, "The Triumph of Death," which was first published in *Strayers from Sheol* (1961).

"He Cometh and He Passeth By" was originally published in *They Return at Evening* (London, Phillip Allen, 1928).

He Cometh and He Passeth By

H. R. WAKEFIELD

EDWARD BELLAMY SAT DOWN at his desk, untied the ribbon round a formidable bundle of papers, yawned and looked out of the window.

On that glistening evening the prospect from Stone Buildings, Lincoln's Inn, was restful and soothing. Just below the motor mowing-machine placidly "chug-chugged" as it clipped the finest turf in London. The muted murmurs from Kingsway and Holborn roamed in placidly. One sleepy pigeon was scratching its poll and ruffling its feathers in a tree opposite, two others—one coyly fleeing, the other doggedly in pursuit—strutted the greensward. "A curious rite of courtship," thought Bellamy, "but they seem to enjoy it; more than I enjoy the job of reading this brief!"

Had these infatuated fowls gazed back at Mr. Bellamy they would have seen a pair of resolute and trustworthy eyes dominating a resolute, nondescript face—one that gave an indisputable impression of kindliness, candour, and mental alacrity. No woman had etched lines upon it, nor were those deepening furrows ploughed by the highest exercise of the imagination marked thereon.

By his thirty-ninth birthday he had raised himself to the unchallenged position of the most brilliant junior at the Criminal Bar, though that is, perhaps, too flashy an epithet to describe that combination of inflexible integrity, impeccable common sense, perfect health, and tireless industry which was Edward Bellamy. A modest person, he attributed his success entirely to that "perfect health," a view not lightly to be challenged by those who spend many of their days in those Black Holes of controversy, the Law Courts of London. And he had spent eight out of the last fourteen days therein. But the result had been a signal triumph, for the Court of Criminal Appeal had taken *his* view of Mr. James Stock's motives, and had substituted ten years' penal servitude for a six-foot drop. And he was very weary—and yet here was this monstrous bundle of papers! He had just succeeded in screwing his determination to the sticking point when his telephone bell rang.

He picked up the receiver languidly, and then his face lightened.

"I know that voice. How are you, my dear Philip? Why, what's the matter? Yes, I'm doing nothing. Delighted! Brooks's at eight o'clock. Right you are!"

So Philip had not forgotten his existence. He had begun to wonder. His mind wandered back over his curious friendship with Franton. It had begun on the first morning of their first term at University, when they had both been strolling nervously about the quad. That it ever had begun was the most surprising thing about it, for superficially they had nothing in common.

Philip, the best bat at Eton, almost too decorative, with a personal charm most people found irresistible, the heir to great possessions. He, the crude product of an obscure Grammar School, destined to live precariously on his scholarships, gauche, shy, taciturn. In the ordinary way they would have graduated to different worlds, for the economic factor alone would have kept their paths all through their lives at Oxford inexorably apart. They would have had little more in common with each other than they had with their scouts. And yet they had spent a good part of almost every day together during term time, and during every vacation he had spent some time at Franton Hall, where he had had first revealed to him those many and delicate refinements of life which only great wealth, allied with traditional taste, can secure. Why had it been so? He had eventually asked Philip.

"Because," he replied, "you have a first-class brain, I have a second or third. I have always had things made too easy for me. You have had most things made too hard. *Ergo*, you have a first-class character. I haven't. I feel a sense of respectful shame towards you, my dear Teddie, which alone would keep me trotting at your heels. I feel I can rely on you as on no one else. You are at once my superior and my complement. Anyway, it has happened, why worry? Analysing such things often spoils them, it's like over-rehearsing."

And then the War—and even the Defence of Civilisation entailed subtle social distinctions.

Philip was given a commission in a regiment of cavalry (with the best will in the world Bellamy never quite understood the privileged role of the horse in the higher ranks of English society); he himself enlisted in a line regiment, and rose through his innate common sense and his unflagging capacity for finishing a job to the rank of Major, D.S.O. and bar, and a brace of wound-stripes. Philip went to Mesopotamia and was eventually invalided out through the medium of a gas-shell. His right lung seriously affected, he spent from 1917 to 1924 on a farm in Arizona.

They had written to each other occasionally—the hurried, flippant, shadow-of-death letters of the time, but somehow their friendship had dimmed and faded and become more than a little pre-War by the end of it, so that Bellamy was not more than mildly disappointed when he heard casually that Philip was back in England, yet had had but the most casual, damp letter from him.

But there had been all the old cordiality and affection in his voice over the telephone—and something more—not so pleasant to hear.

At the appointed hour he arrived in St. James's Street, and a moment later Philip came up to him.

"Now, Teddie," he said, "I know what you're thinking, I know I've been a fool and the rottenest sort of type to have acted as I have, but there is a kind of explanation."

Bellamy surrendered at once to that absurd sense of delight at being in Philip's company, and his small resentment was rent and scattered. None the less he regarded him with a veiled intentness. He was looking tired and old—forcing himself—there was something seriously the matter.

"My very dear Philip," he said, "you don't need to explain things to me. To think it is eight years since we met!"

"First of all let's order something," said Philip. "You have what you like, I don't want much, except a drink." Whereupon he selected a reasonable collation for Bellamy and a dressed crab and asparagus for himself. But he drank two Martinis in ten seconds, and these were not the first—Bellamy knew—that he had ordered since five-thirty (there *was* something wrong).

For a little while the conversation was uneasily, stalely reminiscent. Suddenly Philip blurted out, "I can't keep it in any longer. You're the only really reliable, unswerving friend I've ever had. You will help me, won't you?"

"My dear Philip," said Bellamy, touched, "I always have and always will be ready to do anything you want me to do and at any time—you know that."

"Well, then, I'll tell you my story. First of all, have you ever heard of a man called Oscar Clinton?"

"I seem to remember the name. It is somehow connected in my mind with the nineties, raptures and roses, absinthe and poses; and the *other* Oscar. I believe his name cropped up in a case I was in. I have an impression he's a wrong 'un."

"That's the man," said Philip. "He stayed with me for three months at Franton."

"Oh," said Bellamy sharply, "how was that?"

"Well, Teddie, anything the matter with one's lungs affects one's mind—not always for the worse, however. I know that's true, and it affected mine. Arizona is a moon-dim region, very lovely in its way and stark and old, but I had to leave it. You know I was always a sceptic, rather a wooden one, as I remember; well, that ancient, lonely land set my lung-polluted mind working. I used to stare and stare into the sky. One is brought right up against the vast enigmas of time and space and eternity when one lung is doing the work of two, and none too well at that."

Edward realised under what extreme tension Philip had been living, but felt that he could establish a certain control over him. He felt more in command of the situation and resolved to keep that command.

"Well," continued Philip, filling up his glass, "when I got back to England I was so frantically nervous that I could hardly speak or think. I felt insane, unclean—mentally. I felt I was going mad, and could not bear to be seen by anyone who had known me—that is why I was such a fool as not to come to you. You have your revenge! I can't tell you, Teddie, how depression roared through me! I made up my mind to die, but I had a wild desire to know to what sort of place I should go. And then I met Clinton. I had rushed up to London one day just to get the inane anodyne of noise and people, and I suppose I was more or less tight, for I walked into a club of sorts called the 'Chorazin' in Soho. The door-keeper tried to turn me out, but I pushed him aside, and then someone came up and led me to a table. It was Clinton.

"Now there is no doubt he has great hypnotic

power. He began to talk, and I at once felt calmer and started to tell him all about myself. I talked wildly for an hour, and he was so deft and delicate in his handling of me that I felt I could not leave him. He has a marvellous insight into abnormal mental—psychic—whatever you like to call them—states. Some time I'll describe what he looks like—he's certainly like no one else in the world.

"Well, the upshot was that he came down to Franton next day and stayed on. Now, I know that his motives were entirely mercenary, but none the less he saved me from suicide, and to a great extent gave back peace to my mind.

"Never could I have imagined such an irresistible and brilliant talker. Whatever he may be, he's also a poet, a profound philosopher and amazingly versatile and erudite. Also, when he likes, his charm of manner carries one away. At least, in my case it did—for a time—though he borrowed twenty pounds or more a week from me.

"And then one day my butler came to me, and with the hushed gusto appropriate to such revelations murmured that two of the maids were in the family way and that another had told him an hysterical little tale—floating in floods of tears—about how Clinton had made several attempts to force his way into her bedroom.

"Well, Teddie, that sort of thing is that sort of thing, but I felt such a performance couldn't possibly be justified, that taking advantage of a trio of rustics in his host's house was a dastardly and unforgivable outrage.

"Other people's morals are chiefly their own affair, but I had a personal responsibility towards these buxom victims—well, you can realise just how I felt.

"I had to speak about it to Clinton, and did so that night. No one ever saw him abashed. He smiled at me in a superior and patronising way, and said he quite understood that I was almost bound to hold such feudal and socially primitive views, suggesting, of course, that my chief concern in the matter was that he had infringed my *droit de seigneur* in these cases. As for him, he considered it was his duty to disseminate his

unique genius as widely as possible, and that it should be considered the highest privilege for anyone to bear his child. He had to his knowledge seventy-four offspring alive, and probably many more—the more the better for the future of humanity. But, of course, he understood and promised for the future—bowing to my rights and my prejudices—to allow me to plough my pink and white pastures—and much more to the same effect.

"Though still under his domination, I felt there was more lust than logic in these specious professions, so I made an excuse and went up to London the next day. As I left the house I picked up my letters, which I read in the car on the way up. One was a three-page *catalogue raisonné* from my tailor. Not being as dressy as all that, it seemed unexpectedly grandiose, so I paid him a visit. Well, Clinton had forged a letter from me authorising him to order clothes at my expense, and a lavish outfit had been provided.

"It then occurred to me to go to my bank to discover precisely how much I had lent Clinton during the last three months. It was four hundred and twenty pounds. All these discoveries—telescoping—caused me to review my relationship with Clinton. Suddenly I felt it had better end. I might be mediæval, intellectually costive, and the possessor of much scandalously unearned increment, but I could not believe that the pursuit and contemplation of esoteric mysteries necessarily implied the lowest possible standards of private decency. In other words, I was recovering.

"I still felt that Clinton was the most remarkable person I had ever met. I do to this day—but I felt I was unequal to squaring such magic circles.

"I told him so when I got back. He was quite charming, gentle, understanding, commiserating, and he left the next morning, after pronouncing some incantation whilst touching my forehead. I missed him very much. I believe he's the devil, but he's that sort of person.

"Once I had assured the prospective mothers of his children that they would not be sacked and that their destined contributions to the population would be a charge upon me—there is a codicil to my will to this effect—they brightened up considerably, and rather too frequently snatches of the Froth-Blowers' Anthem cruised down to me as they went about their duties. In fact, I had a discreditable impression that the Immaculate Third would have shown less lachrymose integrity had the consequences of surrender been revealed *ante factum*. Eventually a brace of male infants came to contribute their falsettos to the dirge—for whose appearance the locals have respectfully given me the credit. These brats have searching malign eyes, and when they reach the age of puberty I should not be surprised if the birth statistics for East Surrey began to show a remarkable—even a magical—rise.

"Oh, how good it is to talk to you, Teddie, and get it all off my chest! I feel almost light-hearted, as though my poor old brain had been curetted. I feel I can face and fight it now.

"Well, for the next month I drowsed and read and drowsed and read until I felt two-lunged again. And several times I almost wrote to you, but I felt such lethargy and yet such a certainty of getting quite well again that I put everything off. I was content to lie back and let that blessed healing process work its quiet kindly way with me.

"And then one day I got a letter from a friend of mine, Melrose, who was at the House when we were up. He is the Secretary of 'Ye Ancient Mysteries,' a dining club I joined before the War. It meets once a month and discusses famous mysteries of the past—the *Mary Celeste*, the McLachlan Case, and so on—with a flippant yet scholarly zeal; but that doesn't matter. Well, Melrose said that Clinton wanted to become a member, and had stressed the fact that he was a friend of mine. Melrose was a little upset, as he had heard vague rumours about Clinton. Did I think he was likely to be an acceptable member of the club?

"Well, what was I to say? On the one side of the medal were the facts that he had used my house as his stud-farm, that he had forged my name and sponged on me shamelessly. On the reverse was the fact that he was a genius and knew more about Ancient Mysteries than the rest of the world put together. But my mind was soon made up; I could not recommend him. A week later I got a letter—a charming letter, a most understanding letter from Clinton. He realised, so he said, that I had been bound to give the secretary of the Ancient Mysteries the advice I had—no doubt I considered he was not a decent person to meet my friends. He was naturally disappointed, and so on.

"How the devil, I wondered, did he know—not only that I had put my thumbs down against him, but also the very reason for which I had put them down!

"So I asked Melrose, who told me he hadn't mentioned the matter to a soul, but had discreetly removed Clinton's name from the list of candidates for election. And no one should have been any the wiser; but how much wiser Clinton was!

"A week later I got another letter from him, saying that he was leaving England for a month. He enclosed a funny little paper pattern thing, an outline cut out with scissors with a figure painted on it, a beastly-looking thing. Like this!"

And he drew a quick sketch on the table cloth.

Certainly it was unpleasant, thought Bellamy. It appeared to be a crouching figure in the posture of pursuit. The robes it wore seemed to rise and billow above its head. Its arms were long—too long—scraping the ground with curved and spiked nails. Its head was not quite human, its expression devilish and venomous. A horrid, hunting thing, its eyes encarnadined and infinitely evil, glowing animal eyes in the foul dark face. And those long vile arms—not pleasant to be in their grip. He hadn't realised Philip could draw as well as that. He straightened himself, lit a cigarette, and rallied his fighting powers. For the first time he realised, why, that Philip was in serious trouble! Just a rather beastly little sketch on a table cloth. And now it was up to him!

"Clinton told me," continued Philip, "that

this was a most powerful symbol which I should find of the greatest help in my mystical studies. I must place it against my forehead, and pronounce at the same time a certain sentence. And, Teddie, suddenly, I found myself doing so. I remember I had a sharp feeling of surprise and irritation when I found I had placarded this thing on my head and repeated this sentence."

"What was the sentence?" asked Bellamy.

"Well, that's a funny thing," said Philip. "I can't remember it, and both the slip of paper on which it was written and the paper pattern had disappeared the next morning. I remember putting them in my pocket book, but they completely vanished. And, Teddie, things haven't been the same since." He filled his glass and emptied it, lit a cigarette, and at once pressed the life from it in an ash tray and then lit another.

"Bluntly, I've been bothered, haunted perhaps is too strong a word—too pompous. It's like this. That same night I had read myself tired in the study, and about twelve o'clock I was glancing sleepily around the room when I noticed that one of the bookcases was throwing out a curious and unaccountable shadow. It seemed as if something was hiding behind the bookcase, and that this was that something's shadow. I got up and walked over to it, and it became just a bookcase shadow, rectangular and reassuring. I went to bed.

"As I turned on the light on the landing I noticed the same sort of shadow coming from the grandfather clock. I went to sleep all right, but suddenly found myself peering out of the window, and there was that shadow stretching out from the trees and in the drive. At first there was about that much of it showing," and he drew a line down the sketch on the table cloth, "about a sixth. Well, it's been a simple story since then. Every night that shadow has grown a little. It is now almost visible. And it comes out suddenly from different places. Last night it was on the wall beside the door into the Dutch Garden. I never know where I'm going to see it next."

"And how long has this been going on?" asked Bellamy.

"A month to-morrow. You sound as if you thought I was mad. I probably am."

"No, you're as sane as I am. But why don't you leave Franton and come to London?"

"And see it on the wall of the club bedroom! I've tried that, Teddie, but one's as bad as the other. Doesn't it sound ludicrous? But it isn't to me."

"Do you usually eat as little as this?" asked Bellamy.

"'And drink as much?' you were too polite to add. Well, there's more to it than indigestion, and it isn't incipient D.T. It's just I don't feel very hungry nowadays."

Bellamy got that rush of tip-toe pugnacity which had won him so many desperate cases. He had had a Highland grandmother from whom he had inherited a powerful visualising imagination, by which he got a fleeting yet authentic insight into the workings of men's minds. So now he knew in a flash how he would feel if Philip's ordeal had been his.

"Whatever it is, Philip," he said, "there are two of us now."

"Then you do believe in it," said Philip. "Sometimes I can't. On a sunny morning with starlings chattering and buses swinging up Waterloo Place—then how can such things be? But at night I know they are."

"Well," said Bellamy, after a pause, "let us look at it coldly and precisely. Ever since Clinton sent you a certain painted paper pattern you've seen a shadowed reproduction of it. Now I take it he has—as you suggested—unusual hypnotic power. He has studied mesmerism?"

"I think he's studied every bloody thing," said Philip.

"Then that's a possibility."

"Yes," agreed Philip, "it's a possibility. And I'll fight it, Teddie, now that I have you, but can you minister to a mind diseased?"

"Throw quotations to the dogs," replied Bellamy. "What one man has done another can undo—there's one for you."

"Teddie," said Philip, "will you come down to Franton to-night?"

"Yes," said Bellamy. "But why?"

"Because I want you to be with me at twelve o'clock to-night when I look out from the study window and think I see a shadow flung on the flagstones outside the drawing-room window."

"Why not stay up here for to-night?"

"Because I want to get it settled. Either I'm mad or— Will you come?"

"If you really mean to go down to-night I'll come with you."

"Well, I've ordered the car to be here by nine-fifteen," said Philip. "We'll go to your rooms, and you can pack a suitcase and we'll be there by half past ten." Suddenly he looked up sharply, his shoulders drew together and his eyes narrowed and became intent. It happened at that moment no voice was busy in the dining-room of the Brooks's Club. No doubt they were changing over at the Power Station, for the lights dimmed for a moment. It seemed to Bellamy that someone was developing wavy, wicked little films far back in his brain, and a voice suddenly whispered in his ear with a vile sort of shyness, "He cometh and he passeth by!"

As they drove down through the night they talked little. Philip drowsed and Bellamy's mind was busy. His preliminary conclusion was that Philip was neither mad nor going mad, but that he was not normal. He had always been very sensitive and highly strung, reacting too quickly and deeply to emotional stresses—and this living alone and eating nothing—the worst thing for him.

And this Clinton. He had the reputation of being an evil man of power, and such persons' hypnotic influence was absurdly underrated. He'd get on his track.

"When does Clinton get back to England?" he asked.

"If he kept to his plans he'll be back about now," said Philip sleepily.

"What are his haunts?"

"He lives near the British Museum in rooms, but he's usually to be found at the Chorazin Club after six o'clock. It's in Larn Street, just off Shaftesbury Avenue. A funny place with some funny members."

Bellamy made a note of this.

"Does he know you know me?"

"No, I think not, there's no reason why he should."

"So much the better," said Bellamy.

"Why?" asked Philip.

"Because I'm going to cultivate his acquaintance."

"Well, do look out, Teddie, he has a marvellous power of hiding the fact, but he's dangerous, and I don't want you to get into any trouble like mine."

"I'll be careful," said Bellamy.

Ten minutes later they passed the gates of the drive of Franton Manor, and Philip began glancing uneasily about him and peering sharply where the elms flung shadows. It was a perfectly still and cloudless night, with a quarter moon. It was just a quarter to eleven as they entered the house. They went up to the library on the first floor which looked out over the Dutch Garden to the Park. Franton is a typical Georgian house, with charming gardens and Park, but too big and lonely for one nervous person to inhabit, thought Bellamy.

The butler brought up sandwiches and drinks, and Bellamy thought he seemed relieved at their arrival. Philip began to eat ravenously, and gulped down two stiff whiskies. He kept looking at his watch, and his eyes were always searching the walls.

"It comes, Teddie, even when it ought to be too light for shadows."

"Now then," replied the latter, "I'm with you, and we're going to keep quite steady. It may come, but I shall not leave you until it goes and for ever." And he managed to lure Philip on to another subject, and for a time he seemed quieter, but suddenly he stiffened, and his eyes became rigid and staring. "It's there," he cried, "I know it!"

"Steady, Philip!" said Bellamy sharply. "Where?"

"Down below," he whispered, and began creeping towards the window.

Bellamy reached it first and looked down. He saw it at once, knew what it was, and set his teeth.

He heard Philip shaking and breathing heavily at his side.

"It's there," he said, "and it's complete at last!"

"Now, Philip," said Bellamy, "we're going down, and I'm going out first, and we'll settle the thing once and for all."

They went down the stairs and into the drawing-room. Bellamy turned the light on and walked quickly to the French window and began to try to open the catch. He fumbled with it for a moment.

"Let me do it," said Philip, and put his hand to the catch, and then the window opened and he stepped out.

"Come back, Philip!" cried Bellamy. As he said it the lights went dim, a fierce blast of burning air filled the room, the window came crashing back. Then through the glass Bellamy saw Philip suddenly throw up his hands, and something huge and dark lean from the wall and envelop him. He seemed to writhe for a moment in its folds. Bellamy strove madly to thrust the window open, while his soul strove to withstand the mighty and evil power he felt was crushing him, and then he saw Philip flung down with awful force, and he could hear the foul, crushing thud as his head struck the stone.

And then the window opened and Bellamy dashed out into a quiet and scented night.

At the inquest the doctor stated he was satisfied that Mr. Franton's death was due to a severe heart attack—he had never recovered from the gas, he said, and such a seizure was always possible.

"Then there are no peculiar circumstances about the case?" asked the Coroner.

The doctor hesitated. "Well, there is one thing," he said slowly. "The pupils of Mr. Franton's eyes were—well, to put it simply to the jury—instead of being round, they were drawn up so that they resembled half-moons—in a sense they were like the pupils in the eyes of a cat."

"Can you explain that?" asked the Coroner.

"No, I have never seen a similar case," replied the doctor. "But I am satisfied the cause of death was as I have stated."

Bellamy was, of course, called as a witness, but he had little to say.

About eleven o'clock on the morning after these events Bellamy rang up the Chorazin Club from his chambers and learned from the manager that Mr. Clinton had returned from abroad. A little later he got a Sloane number and arranged to lunch with Mr. Solan at the United Universities Club. And then he made a conscientious effort to estimate the chances in Rex v. Tipwinkle.

But soon he was restless and pacing the room. He could not exorcise the jeering demon which told him sniggeringly that he had failed Philip. It wasn't true, but it pricked and penetrated. But the game was not yet played out. If he had failed to save he might still avenge. He would see what Mr. Solan had to say.

The personage was awaiting him in the smoking room. Mr. Solan was an original and looked it. Just five feet and two inches—a tiny body, a mighty head with a dominating forehead studded with a pair of thrusting frontal lobes. All this covered with a thick, greying thatch. Veiled, restless little eyes, a perky, tilted, little nose and a very thin-lipped, fighting mouth from which issued the most curious, resonant, high, and piercing voice. This is a rough and ready sketch of one who is universally accepted to be the greatest living Oriental Scholar—a mystic—once upon a time a Senior Wrangler, a philosopher of European repute, a great and fascinating personality, who lived alone, save for a brace of tortoiseshell cats and a housekeeper, in Chester Terrace, Sloane Square. About every six years he published a masterly treatise on one of his special subjects; otherwise he kept to himself with the remorseless determination he brought to bear upon any subject which he considered worth serious consideration, such as the Chess Game, the works of Bach, the paintings of Van Gogh, the poems of Housman, and the short stories of P. G. Wodehouse and Austin Freeman.

He entirely approved of Bellamy, who had once secured him substantial damages in a copyright case. The damages had gone to the Society for the Prevention of Cruelty to Animals.

"And what can I do for you, my dear Bellamy?" he piped, when they were seated.

"First of all, have you ever heard of a person called Oscar Clinton? Secondly, do you know anything of the practice of sending an enemy a painted paper pattern?"

Mr. Solan smiled slightly at the first question, and ceased to smile when he heard the second.

"Yes," he said, "I have heard of both, and I advise you to have nothing whatsoever to do with either."

"Unfortunately," replied Bellamy, "I have already had to do with both. Two nights ago my best friend died—rather suddenly. Presently I will tell you how he died. But first of all, tell me something about Clinton."

"It is characteristic of him that you know so little about him," replied Mr. Solan, "for although he is one of the most dangerous and intellectually powerful men in the world he gets very little publicity nowadays. Most of the much-advertised Naughty Boys of the Nineties harmed no one but themselves—they merely canonised their own and each other's dirty linen, but Clinton was in a class by himself. He was—and no doubt still is—an accomplished corrupter, and he took, and no doubt still takes, a jocund delight in his hobby. Eventually he left England—by request—and went out East. He spent some years in a Tibetan Monastery, and then some other years in less reputable places—his career is detailed very fully in a file in my study—and then he applied his truly mighty mind to what I may loosely call magic—for what I loosely call magic, my dear Bellamy, most

certainly exists. Clinton is highly psychic, with great natural hypnotic power. He then joined an esoteric and little-known sect—Satanists—of which he eventually became High Priest. And then he returned to what we call civilisation, and has since been 'moved on' by the Civil Powers of many countries, for his forte is the extraction of money from credulous and timid individuals—usually female—by methods highly ingenious and peculiarly his own. It is a boast of his that he has never yet missed his revenge. He ought to be stamped out with the brusque ruthlessness meted out to a spreading fire in a Californian forest.

"Well, there is a short inadequate sketch of Oscar Clinton, and now about these paper patterns."

Two hours later Bellamy got up to leave. "I can lend you a good many of his books," said Mr. Solan, "and you can get the rest at Lilley's. Come to me from four till six on Wednesdays and Fridays, and I'll teach you all I think essential. Meanwhile, I will have a watch kept upon him, but I want you, my dear Bellamy, to do nothing decisive till you are qualified. It would be a pity if the Bar were to be deprived of your great gifts prematurely."

"Many thanks," said Bellamy. "I have now placed myself in your hands, and I'm in this thing till the end—some end or other."

Mr. Plank, Bellamy's clerk, had no superior in his profession, one which is the most searching test of character and adaptability. Not one of the devious and manifold tricks of his trade was unpracticed by him, and his income was twelve hundred and fifty pounds per annum, a fact which the Inland Revenue Authorities strongly suspected but were quite unable to establish. He liked Mr. Bellamy, personally well enough, financially very much indeed. It was not surprising, therefore, that many seismic recording instruments registered sharp shocks at 4 p.m. on June 12, 192—, a disturbance caused by the precipitous descent of Mr. Plank's jaw when Mr.

Bellamy instructed him to accept no more briefs for him for the next three months. "But," continued that gentleman, "here is a cheque which will, I trust, reconcile you to the fact."

Mr. Plank scrutinised the numerals and *was* reconciled.

"Taking a holiday, sir?" he asked.

"I rather doubt it," replied Bellamy. "But you might suggest to any inquisitive enquirers that that is the explanation."

"I understand, sir."

From then till midnight, with one short pause, Bellamy was occupied with a pile of exotically bound volumes. Occasionally he made a note on his writing pad. When his clock struck twelve he went to bed and read *The Wallet of Kai-Lung* till he felt sleepy enough to turn out the light.

At eight o'clock the next morning he was busy once more with an exotically bound book, and making an occasional note on his writing pad.

Three weeks later he was bidding a temporary farewell to Mr. Solan, who remarked, "I think you'll do now. You are an apt pupil; pleading has given you a command of convincing bluff, and you have sufficient psychic insight to make it possible for you to succeed. Go forth and prosper! At all times I shall be fighting for you. He will be there at nine tonight."

At a quarter past that hour Bellamy was asking the door-keeper of the Chorazin Club to tell Mr. Clinton that a Mr. Bellamy wished to see him.

Two minutes later the official reappeared and led him downstairs into an ornate and gaudy cellar decorated with violence and indiscretion— the work, he discovered later, of a neglected genius who had died of neglected cirrhosis of the liver. He was led up to a table in the corner, where someone was sitting alone.

Bellamy's first impression of Oscar Clinton remained vividly with him till his death. As he got up to greet him he could see that he was physically gigantic—six foot five at least, with a massive torso—the build of a champion wrestler. Topping it was a huge, square, domed head.

He had a white yet mottled face, thick, tense lips, the lower one protruding fantastically. His hair was clipped close, save for one twisted and oiled lock which curved down to meet his eyebrows. But what impressed Bellamy most was a pair of the hardest, most penetrating and merciless eyes—one of which seemed soaking wet and dripping slowly.

Bellamy "braced his belt about him"—he was in the presence of a power.

"Well, sir," said Clinton in a beautifully musical voice with a slight drawl, "I presume you are connected with Scotland Yard. What can I do for you?"

"No," replied Bellamy, forcing a smile, "I'm in no way connected with that valuable institution."

"Forgive the suggestion," said Clinton, "but during a somewhat adventurous career I have received so many unheralded visits from more or less polite police officials. What then, is your business?"

"I haven't any, really," said Bellamy. "It's simply that I have long been a devoted admirer of your work, the greatest imaginative work of our time in my opinion. A friend of mine mentioned casually that he had seen you going into this club, and I could not resist taking the liberty of forcing, just for a moment, my company upon you."

Clinton stared at him, and seemed not quite at his ease.

"You interest me," he said at length. "I'll tell you why. Usually I know decisively by certain methods of my own whether a person I meet comes as an enemy or a friend. These tests have failed in your case, and this, as I say, interests me. It suggests things to me. Have you been in the East?"

"No," said Bellamy.

"And made no study of its mysteries?"

"None whatever, but I can assure you I come merely as a most humble admirer. Of course, I realise you have enemies—all great men have; it is the privilege and penalty of their pre-eminence, and I know you to be a great man."

"I fancy," said Clinton, "that you are perplexed by the obstinate humidity of my left eye. It is caused by the rather heavy injection of heroin I took this afternoon. I may as well tell you I use all drugs, but am the slave of none. I take heroin when I desire to contemplate. But tell me—since you profess such an admiration for my books—which of them most meets with your approval?"

"That's a hard question," replied Bellamy, "but *A Damsel with a Dulcimer* seems to me exquisite."

Clinton smiled patronisingly.

"It has merits," he said, "but is immature. I wrote it when I was living with a Bedouin woman aged fourteen in Tunis. Bedouin women have certain natural gifts"—and here he became remarkably obscene, before returning to the subject of his works—"my own opinion is that I reached my zenith in *The Songs of Hamdonna*. Hamdonna was a delightful companion, the fruit of the raptures of an Italian gentleman and a Persian lady. She had the most naturally—the most brilliantly vicious mind of any woman I ever met. She required hardly any training. But she was unfaithful to me, and died soon after."

"The *Songs* are marvellous," said Bellamy, and he began quoting from them fluently.

Clinton listened intently. "You have a considerable gift for reciting poetry," he said. "May I offer you a drink? I was about to order one for myself."

"I'll join you on one condition—that I may be allowed to pay for both of them—to celebrate the occasion."

"Just as you like," said Clinton, tapping the table with his thumb, which was adorned with a massive jade ring curiously carved. "I always drink brandy after heroin, but you order what you please."

It may have been the whisky, it may have been the pressing nervous strain or a combination of both, which caused Bellamy now to regard the mural decorations with a much modified sangfroid. Those distorted and tortured patches of flat colour, how subtly suggestive they were of something sniggeringly evil!

"I gave Valin the subject for those panels," said Clinton. "They are meant to represent an impression of the stages in the Black Mass, but he drank away his original inspiration, and they fail to do that majestic ceremony justice."

Bellamy flinched at having his thoughts so easily read.

"I was thinking the same thing," he replied; "that unfortunate cat they're slaughtering deserved a less ludicrous memorial to its fate."

Clinton looked at him sharply and sponged his oozing eye.

"I have made these rather flamboyant references to my habits purposely. Not to impress you, but to see *how* they impressed you. Had you appeared disgusted, I should have known it was useless to pursue our acquaintanceship. All my life I have been a law unto myself, and that is probably why the Law has always shown so much interest in me. I know myself to be a being apart, one to whom the codes and conventions of the herd can never be applied. I have sampled every so-called 'vice,' including every known drug. Always, however, with an object in view. Mere purposeless debauchery is not in my character. My art, to which you have so kindly referred, must always come first. Sometimes it demands that I sleep with a negress, that I take opium or hashish; sometimes it dictates rigid asceticism, and I tell you, my friend, that if such an instruction came again to-morrow, as it has often come in the past, I could, without the slightest effort, lead a life of complete abstinence from drink, drugs, and women for an indefinite period. In other words, I have gained absolute control over my senses after the most exhaustive experiments with them. How many can say the same? Yet one does not know what life can teach till that control is established. The man of superior power—there are no such women—should not flinch from such experiments, he should seek to learn every lesson evil as well as good has to teach. So will he be able to extend and multiply his personality, but always he must remain absolute master of himself. And then he will have many strange rewards, and many secrets will be revealed to him. Some day, perhaps, I will show you some which have been revealed to me."

"Have you absolutely no regard for what is called 'morality'?" asked Bellamy.

"None whatever. If I wanted money I should pick your pocket. If I desired your wife—if you have one—I should seduce her. If someone obstructs me—something happens to him. You must understand this clearly—for I am not bragging— I do nothing purposelessly nor from what I consider a bad motive. To me 'bad' is synonymous with 'unnecessary.' I do nothing unnecessary."

"Why is revenge necessary?" asked Bellamy.

"A plausible question. Well, for one thing I like cruelty—one of my unpublished works is a defence of Super-Sadism. Then it is a warning to others, and lastly it is a vindication of my personality. All excellent reasons. Do you like my *Thus Spake Eblis*?"

"Masterly," replied Bellamy. "The perfection of prose, but, of course, its magical significance is far beyond my meagre understanding."

"My dear friend, there is only one man in Europe about whom that would not be equally true."

"Who is that?" asked Bellamy.

Clinton's eyes narrowed venomously.

"His name is Solan," he said. "One of these days, perhaps—" and he paused. "Well, now, if you like I will tell you of some of my experiences."

An hour later a monologue drew to its close.

"And now, Mr. Bellamy, what is your role in life?"

"I'm a barrister."

"Oh, so you *are* connected with the Law?"

"I hope," said Bellamy smiling, "you'll find it possible to forget it."

"It would help me to do so," replied Clinton, "if you would lend me ten pounds. I have forgotten my note-case—a frequent piece of negligence on my part—and a lady awaits me. Thanks very much. We shall meet again, I trust."

"I was just about to suggest that you dine with me one day this week?"

"This is Tuesday," said Clinton. "What about Thursday?"

"Excellent, will you meet me at the Gridiron about eight?"

"I will be there," said Clinton, mopping his eye. "Good night."

"I can understand now what happened to Franton," said Bellamy to Mr. Solan the next evening. "He is the most fascinating and catholic talker I have met. He has a wicked charm. If half to which he lays claim is true, he has packed ten lives into sixty years."

"In a sense," said Mr. Solan, "he has the best brain of any man living. He has also a marvellous histrionic sense and he is *deadly*. But he is vulnerable. On Thursday encourage him to talk of other things. He will consider you an easy victim. You must make the most of the evening—it may rather revolt you—he is sure to be suspicious at first."

"It amuses and reassures me," said Clinton at ten-fifteen on Thursday evening in Bellamy's room, "to find you have a lively appreciation of obscenity."

He brought out a snuff box, an exquisite little masterpiece with an inexpressibly vile design enamelled on the lid, from which he took a pinch of white powder which he sniffed up from the palm of his hand.

"I suppose," said Bellamy, "that all your magical lore would be quite beyond me."

"Oh yes, quite," replied Clinton, "but I can show you what sort of power a study of that lore has given me, by a little experiment. Turn round, look out of the window, and keep quite quiet till I speak to you."

It was a brooding night. In the south-west the clouds made restless, quickly shifting patterns— the heralds of coming storm. The scattered sound of the traffic in Kingsway rose and fell with the gusts of the rising wind. Bellamy found a curious picture forming in his brain. A wide lonely waste of snow and a hill with a copse of fir trees, out from which someone came running. Presently this person halted and looked back, and then out from the wood appeared another figure (of a shape he had seen before). And then the one it seemed to be pursuing began to run on, staggering through the snow, over which the Shape seemed to skim lightly and rapidly, and gain on its quarry. Then it appeared as if the one in front could go no further. He fell and rose again, and faced his pursuer. The Shape came swiftly on and flung itself hideously on the one in front, who fell to his knees. The two seemed intermingled for a moment . . .

"Well," said Clinton, "and what did you think of that?"

Bellamy poured out a whisky and soda and drained it.

"Extremely impressive," he replied. "It gave me a feeling of great horror."

"The individual whose rather painful end you have just witnessed once did me a dis-service. He was found in a remote part of Norway. Why he chose to hide himself there is rather difficult to understand."

"Cause and effect?" asked Bellamy, forcing a smile.

Clinton took another pinch of white powder.

"Possibly a mere coincidence," he replied. "And now I must go, for I have a 'date,' as they say in America, with a rather charming and profligate young woman. Could you possibly lend me a little money?"

When he had gone Bellamy washed his person very thoroughly in a hot bath, brushed his teeth with zeal, and felt a little cleaner. He tried to read in bed, but between him and Mr. Jacobs's *Night-Watchman* a bestial and persistent phantasmagoria forced its way. He dressed again, went out, and walked the streets till dawn.

Some time later Mr. Solan happened to overhear a conversation in the club smoking-room.

"I can't think what's happened to Bellamy," said one. "He does no work and is always about with that incredible swine Clinton."

"A kink somewhere, I suppose," said another, yawning. "Dirty streak probably."

"Were you referring to Mr. Edward Bellamy, a friend of mine?" asked Mr. Solan.

"We were," said one.

"Have you ever known him to do a discreditable thing?"

"Not till now," said another.

"Or a stupid thing?"

"I'll give you that," said one.

"Well," said Mr. Solan, "you have my word for it that he has not changed," and he passed on.

"Funny old devil that," said one.

"Rather shoves the breeze up me," said another. "He seems to know something. I like Bellamy, and I'll apologise to him for taking his name in vain when I see him next. But that bastard Clinton!—"

"It will have to be soon," said Mr. Solan. "I heard to-day that he will be given notice to quit any day now. Are you prepared to go through with it?"

"He's the devil incarnate," said Bellamy. "If you knew what I've been through in the last month!"

"I have a shrewd idea of it," replied Mr. Solan. "You think he trusts you completely?"

"I don't think he has any opinion of me at all, except that I lend him money whenever he wants it. Of course, I'll go through with it. Let it be Friday night. What must I do? Tell me exactly. I know that but for you I should have chucked my hand in long ago."

"My dear Bellamy, you have done marvellously well, and you will finish the business as resolutely as you have carried it through so far. Well, this is what you must do. Memorise it flawlessly."

"I will arrange it that we arrive at his rooms just about eleven o'clock. I will ring up five minutes before we leave."

"I shall be doing my part," said Mr. Solan.

Clinton was in high spirits at the Café Royal on Friday evening.

"I like you, my dear Bellamy," he observed, "not merely because you have a refined taste in pornography and have lent me a good deal of money, but for a more subtle reason. You remember when we first met I was puzzled by you. Well, I still am. There is some psychic power surrounding you. I don't mean that you are conscious of it, but there is some very powerful influence working for you. Great friends though we are, I sometimes feel that this power is hostile to myself. Anyhow, we have had many pleasant times together."

"And," replied Bellamy, "I hope we shall have many more. It has certainly been a tremendous privilege to have been permitted to enjoy so much of your company. As for that mysterious power you refer to, I am entirely unconscious of it, and as for hostility—well, I hope I've convinced you during the last month that I'm not exactly your enemy."

"You have, my dear fellow," replied Clinton. "You have been a charming and generous companion. All the same, there is an enigmatic side to you. What shall we do to-night?"

"Whatever you please," said Bellamy.

"I suggest we go round to my rooms," said Clinton, "bearing a bottle of whisky, and that I show you another little experiment. You are now sufficiently trained to make it a success."

"Just what I should have hoped for," replied Bellamy enthusiastically. "I will order the whisky now." He went out of the grill-room for a moment and had a few words with Mr. Solan over the telephone. And then he returned, paid the bill, and they drove off together.

Clinton's rooms were in a dingy street about a hundred yards from the British Museum. They were drab and melancholy, and contained nothing but the barest necessities and some books.

It was exactly eleven o'clock as Clinton took out his latchkey, and it was just exactly then that Mr. Solan unlocked the door of a curious little room leading off from his study.

Then he opened a bureau and took from it a large book bound in plain white vellum. He sat down at a table and began a bizarre procedure. He took from a folder at the end of the book a piece of what looked like crumpled tracing paper, and, every now and again consulting the quarto, drew certain symbols upon the paper, while repeating a series of short sentences in a strange tongue. The ink into which he dipped his pen for this exercise was a smoky sullen scarlet.

Presently the atmosphere of the room became intense, and charged with suspense and crisis. The symbols completed, Mr. Solan became rigid and taut, and his eyes were those of one passing into trance.

"First of all a drink, my dear Bellamy," said Clinton.

Bellamy pulled the cork and poured out two stiff pegs. Clinton drank his off. He gave the impression of being not quite at his ease.

"Some enemy of mine is working against me to-night," he said. "I feel an influence strongly. However, let us try the little experiment. Draw up your chair to the window, and do not look round till I speak."

Bellamy did as he was ordered, and peered at a dark facade across the street. Suddenly it was as if wall after wall rolled up before his eyes and passed into the sky, and he found himself gazing into a long faintly-lit room. As his eyes grew more used to the dimness he could pick out a number of recumbent figures, apparently resting on couches. And then from the middle of the room a flame seemed to leap and then another and another until there was a fiery circle playing round one of those figures, which slowly rose to its feet and turned and stared at Bellamy; and its haughty, evil face grew vast, till it was thrust, dazzling and fiery, right into his own. He put up his hands to thrust back its scorching menace—and there was the wall of the house opposite, and Clinton was saying, "Well?"

"Your power terrifies me!" said Bellamy. "Who was that One I saw?"

"The one you saw was myself," said Clinton, smiling, "during my third reincarnation, about 1750 B.C. I am the only man in the world who can perform that quite considerable feat. Give me another drink."

Bellamy got up (it was time!). Suddenly he felt invaded by a mighty reassurance. His ghostly terror left him. Something irresistible was sinking into his soul, and he knew that at the destined hour the promised succour had come to sustain him. He felt thrilled, resolute, exalted.

He had his back to Clinton as he filled the glasses and with a lightning motion he dropped a pellet into Clinton's which fizzed like a tiny comet down through the bubbles and was gone.

"Here's to many more pleasant evenings," said Clinton. "You're a brave man, Bellamy," he exclaimed, putting the glass to his lips. "For what you have seen might well appal the devil!"

"I'm not afraid because I trust you," replied Bellamy.

"By Eblis, this is a strong one," said Clinton, peering into his glass.

"Same as usual," said Bellamy, laughing. "Tell me something. A man I knew who'd been many years in the East told me about some race out there who cut out paper patterns and paint them and sent them to their enemies. Have you ever heard of anything of the sort?"

Clinton dropped his glass on the table sharply. He did not answer for a moment, but shifted uneasily in his chair.

"Who was this friend of yours?" he asked, in a voice already slightly thick.

"A chap called Bond," said Bellamy.

"Yes, I've heard of that charming practice. In fact, I can cut them myself."

"Really, how's it done? I should be fascinated to see it."

Clinton's eyes blinked and his head nodded.

"I'll show you one," he said, "but it's dangerous and you must be very careful. Go to the bottom drawer of that bureau and bring me the piece of straw paper you'll find there. And there are some scissors on the writing table and two crayons in the tray." Bellamy brought them to him.

"Now," said Clinton, "this thing, as I say, is dangerous. If I wasn't drunk I wouldn't do it. And why am I drunk?" He leaned back in his chair and put his hand over his eyes. And then he sat up and, taking the scissors, began running them with extreme dexterity round the paper. And then he made some marks with the coloured pencils.

The final result of these actions was not unfamiliar in appearance to Bellamy.

"There you are," said Clinton. "That, my dear Bellamy, is potentially the most deadly little piece of paper in the world. Would you please take it to the fireplace and burn it to ashes?"

Bellamy burnt a piece of paper to ashes.

Clinton's head had dropped into his hands.

"Another drink?" asked Bellamy.

"My God, no," said Clinton, yawning and reeling in his chair. And then his head went down again. Bellamy went up to him and shook him. His right hand hovered a second over Clinton's coat pocket.

"Wake up," he said. "I want to know what could make that piece of paper actually deadly?"

Clinton looked up blearily at him and then rallied slightly.

"You'd like to know, wouldn't you?"

"Yes," said Bellamy. "Tell me."

"Just repeating six words," said Clinton, "but I shall not repeat them." Suddenly his eyes became intent and fixed on a corner of the room.

"What's that?" he asked sharply. "There! there! there! in the corner." Bellamy felt again the presence of a power. The air of the room seemed rent and sparking.

"That, Clinton," he said, "is the spirit of Philip Franton, whom you murdered." And then he sprang at Clinton, who was staggering from the chair. He seized him and pressed a little piece of paper fiercely to his forehead.

"Now, Clinton," he cried, "say those words!"

And then Clinton rose to his feet, and his face was working hideously. His eyes seemed bursting from his head, their pupils stretched and curved, foam streamed from his lips. He flung his hands above his head and cried in a voice of agony:

"He cometh and he passeth by!"

And then he crashed to the floor.

As Bellamy moved towards the door the lights went dim, in from the window poured a burning wind, and then from the wall in the corner a shadow began to grow. When he saw it, swift icy ripples poured through him. It grew and grew, and began to lean down towards the figure on the floor. As Bellamy took a last look back it was just touching it. He shuddered, opened the door, closed it quickly, and ran down the stairs and out into the night.

THURNLEY ABBEY

Perceval Landon

ALTHOUGH HIS MAJOR WORK was writing about the virtually unknown regions of Tibet and Nepal in the early years of the nineteenth century, Perceval Landon (1868–1927) is the author of this masterpiece, which has been called one of the three most terrifying stories in the English language. Due to its fame and brilliant portrayal of dread and the sense of waking nightmare, it has been frequently anthologized.

Landon was born into a prominent family (a relation was Spencer Perceval, the only British Prime Minister ever to have been assassinated). After graduating from Hertford College, Oxford, he became a barrister. More interested in adventure and journalism, however, he became a special correspondent to *The Times* (London), covering the Boer War in South Africa (1899–1900), then serving as private secretary to the Governor of New South Wales (1900–1903), after which he took on the role of special correspondent for *The Daily Mail* in China, Japan, and Siberia (1903). His reportage on the 1903–1904 British mission to Tibet, led by Col. Sir Francis E. Younghusband, which he accompanied, led to his important book, *The Opening of Tibet* (1905), in which he provides a narrative of the march but also describes what Western eyes first saw. Often political in tone (Landon was powerfully British in his attitudes and judgments), the book also offered insight into the daily lives of Tibetans, including their religion, manners, and customs. His familiarity and expertise in the region resulted in such further books as *Lhasa: An Account of the Country and People of Central Tibet* (1905), *Under the Sun: Impressions of Indian Cities* (1906), *1857: In Commemoration of the 50th Anniversary of the Indian Mutiny* (1907), and *Nepal* (1928). The very few works of supernatural fiction that Landon produced in his lifetime were collected in a single volume, *Raw Edges* (1908).

"Thurnley Abbey" was first published in *Raw Edges: Studies and Stories of These Days* (London, William Heinemann, 1908).

Thurnley Abbey

PERCEVAL LANDON

THREE YEARS AGO I was on my way out to the East, and as an extra day in London was of some importance, I took the Friday evening mail-train to Brindisi instead of the usual Thursday morning Marseilles express. Many people shrink from the long forty-eight-hour train journey through Europe, and the subsequent rush across the Mediterranean on the nineteen-knot *Isis* or *Osiris*; but there is really very little discomfort on either the train or the mail-boat, and unless there is actually nothing for me to do, I always like to save the extra day and a half in London before I say goodbye to her for one of my longer tramps. This time—it was early, I remember, in the shipping season, probably about the beginning of September—there were few passengers, and I had a compartment in the P. & O. Indian express to myself all the way from Calais. All Sunday I watched the blue waves dimpling the Adriatic, and the pale rosemary along the cuttings; the plain white towns, with their flat roofs and their bold "duomos," and the grey-green gnarled olive orchards of Apulia. The journey was just like any other. We ate in the dining-car as often and as long as we decently could. We slept after luncheon; we dawdled the afternoon away with yellow-backed novels; sometimes we exchanged platitudes in the smoking-room, and it was there that I met Alastair Colvin.

Colvin was a man of middle height, with a resolute, well-cut jaw; his hair was turning grey; his moustache was sun-whitened, otherwise he was clean-shaven—obviously a gentleman, and obviously also a pre-occupied man. He had no great wit. When spoken to, he made the usual remarks in the right way, and I dare say he refrained from banalities only because he spoke less than the rest of us; most of the time he buried himself in the Wagon-lit Company's time-table, but seemed unable to concentrate his attention on any one page of it. He found that I had been over the Siberian railway, and for a quarter of an hour he discussed it with me. Then he lost interest in it, and rose to go to his compartment. But he came back again very soon, and seemed glad to pick up the conversation again.

Of course this did not seem to me to be of any importance. Most travellers by train become a trifle infirm of purpose after thirty-six hours' rattling. But Colvin's restless way I noticed in somewhat marked contrast with the man's personal importance and dignity; especially ill suited was it to his finely made large hand with strong, broad, regular nails and its few lines. As I looked at his hand I noticed a long, deep, and recent scar of ragged shape. However, it is absurd to pretend that I thought anything was unusual. I went off at five o'clock on Sunday afternoon to sleep away the hour or two that had still to be got through before we arrived at Brindisi.

Once there, we few passengers transhipped our hand baggage, verified our berths—there were only a score of us in all—and then, after an aimless ramble of half an hour in Brindisi, we returned to dinner at the Hotel International, not wholly surprised that the town had been the death of Virgil. If I remember rightly, there is a gaily painted hall at the International—I do not wish to advertise anything, but there is no other place in Brindisi at which to await the coming of the mails—and after dinner I was looking with awe at a trellis overgrown with blue vines, when Colvin moved across the room to my table. He picked up *Il Secolo*, but almost immediately gave up the pretence of reading it. He turned squarely to me and said:

"Would you do me a favour?"

One doesn't do favours to stray acquaintances on Continental expresses without knowing something more of them than I knew of Colvin. But I smiled in a noncommittal way, and asked him what he wanted. I wasn't wrong in part of my estimate of him; he said bluntly:

"Will you let me sleep in your cabin on the *Osiris*?" And he coloured a little as he said it.

Now, there is nothing more tiresome than having to put up with a stable-companion at sea, and I asked him rather pointedly:

"Surely there is room for all of us?" I thought that perhaps he had been partnered off with some mangy Levantine, and wanted to escape from him at all hazards.

Colvin, still somewhat confused, said: "Yes; I am in a cabin by myself. But you would do me the greatest favour if you would allow me to share yours."

This was all very well, but, besides the fact that I always sleep better when alone, there had been some recent thefts on board English liners, and I hesitated, frank and honest and self-conscious as Colvin was. Just then the mail-train came in with a clatter and a rush of escaping steam, and I asked him to see me again about it on the boat when we started. He answered me curtly—I suppose he saw the mistrust in my manner—"I am a member of

White's." I smiled to myself as he said it, but I remembered in a moment that the man—if he were really what he claimed to be, and I make no doubt that he was—must have been sorely put to it before he urged the fact as a guarantee of his respectability to a total stranger at a Brindisi hotel.

That evening, as we cleared the red and green harbour-lights of Brindisi, Colvin explained. This is his story in his own words.

"When I was travelling in India some years ago, I made the acquaintance of a youngish man in the Woods and Forests. We camped out together for a week, and I found him a pleasant companion. John Broughton was a light-hearted soul when off duty, but a steady and capable man in any of the small emergencies that continually arise in that department. He was liked and trusted by the natives, and though a trifle over-pleased with himself when he escaped to civilisation at Simla or Calcutta, Broughton's future was well assured in Government service, when a fair-sized estate was unexpectedly left to him, and he joyfully shook the dust of the Indian plains from his feet and returned to England. For five years he drifted about London. I saw him now and then. We dined together about every eighteen months, and I could trace pretty exactly the gradual sickening of Broughton with a merely idle life. He then set out on a couple of long voyages, returned as restless as before, and at last told me that he had decided to marry and settle down at his place, Thurnley Abbey, which had long been empty. He spoke about looking after the property and standing for his constituency in the usual way. Vivien Wilde, his *fiancée*, had, I suppose, begun to take him in hand. She was a pretty girl with a deal of fair hair and rather an exclusive manner; deeply religious in a narrow school, she was still kindly and high-spirited, and I thought that Broughton was in luck. He was quite happy and full of information about his future.

"Among other things, I asked him about Thurnley Abbey. He confessed that he hardly knew the place. The last tenant, a man called Clarke, had lived in one wing for fifteen years and seen no one. He had been a miser and a hermit. It was the rarest thing for a light to be seen at the Abbey after dark. Only the barest necessities of life were ordered, and the tenant himself received them at the side-door. His one half-caste manservant, after a month's stay in the house, had abruptly left without warning, and had returned to the Southern States. One thing Broughton complained bitterly about: Clarke had wilfully spread the rumour among the villagers that the Abbey was haunted, and had even condescended to play childish tricks with spirit-lamps and salt in order to scare trespassers away at night. He had been detected in the act of this tomfoolery, but the story spread, and no one, said Broughton, would venture near the house except in broad daylight. The hauntedness of Thurnley Abbey was now, he said with a grin, part of the gospel of the countryside, but he and his young wife were going to change all that. Would I propose myself any time I liked? I, of course, said I would, and equally, of course, intended to do nothing of the sort without a definite invitation.

"The house was put in thorough repair, though not a stick of the old furniture and tapestry were removed. Floors and ceilings were relaid: the roof was made watertight again, and the dust of half a century was scoured out. He showed me some photographs of the place. It was called an Abbey, though as a matter of fact it had been only the infirmary of the long-vanished Abbey of Clouster some five miles away. The larger part of the building remained as it had been in pre-Reformation days, but a wing had been added in Jacobean times, and that part of the house had been kept in something like repair by Mr. Clarke. He had in both the ground and first floors set a heavy timber door, strongly barred with iron, in the passage between the earlier and the Jacobean parts of the house, and had entirely neglected the former. So there had been a good deal of work to be done.

"Broughton, whom I saw in London two or three times about this period, made a deal of fun over the positive refusal of the workmen to remain after sundown. Even after the electric light had been put into every room, nothing would induce them to remain, though, as Broughton observed, electric light was death on ghosts. The legend of the Abbey's ghosts had gone far and wide, and the men would take no risks. They went home in batches of five and six, and even during the daylight hours there was an inordinate amount of talking between one and another, if either happened to be out of sight of his companion. On the whole, though nothing of any sort or kind had been conjured up even by their heated imaginations during their five months' work upon the Abbey, the belief in the ghosts was rather strengthened than otherwise in Thurnley because of the men's confessed nervousness, and local tradition declared itself in favour of the ghost of an immured nun.

" 'Good old nun!' said Broughton.

"I asked him whether in general he believed in the possibility of ghosts, and, rather to my surprise, he said that he couldn't say he entirely disbelieved in them. A man in India had told him one morning in camp that he believed that his mother was dead in England, as her vision had come to his tent the night before. He had not been alarmed, but had said nothing, and the figure vanished again. As a matter of fact, the next possible dak-walla brought on a telegram announcing the mother's death. 'There the thing was,' said Broughton. But at Thurnley he was practical enough. He roundly cursed the idiotic selfishness of Clarke, whose silly antics had caused all the inconvenience. At the same time, he couldn't refuse to sympathise to some extent with the ignorant workmen. 'My own idea,' said he, 'is that if a ghost ever does come in one's way, one ought to speak to it.'

"I agreed. Little as I knew of the ghost world and its conventions, I had always remembered that a spook was in honour bound to wait to be spoken to. It didn't seem much to do, and I felt that the sound of one's own voice would at any rate reassure oneself as to one's wakefulness. But there are few ghosts outside Europe—few, that is, that a white man can see—and I had never been troubled with any. However, as I have said, I told Broughton that I agreed.

"So the wedding took place, and I went to it in a tall hat which I bought for the occasion, and the new Mrs. Broughton smiled very nicely at me afterwards. As it had to happen, I took the Orient Express that evening and was not in England again for nearly six months. Just before I came back I got a letter from Broughton. He asked if I could see him in London or come to Thurnley, as he thought I should be better able to help him than anyone else he knew. His wife sent a nice message to me at the end, so I was reassured about at least one thing. I wrote from Budapest that I would come and see him at Thurnley two days after my arrival in London, and as I sauntered out of the Pannonia into the Kerepesi Utcza to post my letters, I wondered of what earthly service I could be to Broughton. I had been out with him after tiger on foot, and I could imagine few men better able at a pinch to manage their own business. However, I had nothing to do, so after dealing with some small accumulations of business during my absence, I packed a kit-bag and departed to Euston.

"I was met by Broughton's great limousine at Thurnley Road station, and after a drive of nearly seven miles we echoed through the sleepy streets of Thurnley village, into which the main gates of the park thrust themselves, splendid with pillars and spread-eagles and tom-cats rampant atop of them. I never was a herald, but I know that the Broughtons have the right to supporters—Heaven knows why! From the gates a quadruple avenue of beech-trees led inwards for a quarter of a mile. Beneath them a neat strip of fine turf edged the road and ran back until the poison of the dead beech-leaves killed it under the trees. There were many wheel-tracks on the road, and a comfortable little pony trap jogged past me laden with a country parson and his wife and daughter. Evidently there was some garden party going on at the Abbey. The road dropped away to the right at the end of the avenue, and I could see the Abbey across a wide pasturage and a broad lawn thickly dotted with guests.

"The end of the building was plain. It must have been almost mercilessly austere when it was first built, but time had crumbled the edges and toned the stone down to an orange-lichened grey wherever it showed behind its curtain of magnolia, jasmine, and ivy. Farther on was the three-storied Jacobean house, tall and handsome. There had not been the slightest attempt to adapt the one to the other, but the kindly ivy had glossed over the touching-point. There was a tall flèche in the middle of the building, surmounting a small bell tower. Behind the house there rose the mountainous verdure of Spanish chestnuts all the way up the hill.

"Broughton had seen me coming from afar, and walked across from his other guests to welcome me before turning me over to the butler's care. This man was sandy-haired and rather inclined to be talkative. He could, however, answer hardly any questions about the house; he had, he said, only been there three weeks. Mindful of what Broughton had told me, I made no inquiries about ghosts, though the room into which I was shown might have justified anything. It was a very large low room with oak beams projecting from the white ceiling. Every inch of the walls, including the doors, was covered with tapestry, and a remarkably fine Italian fourpost bedstead, heavily draped, added to the darkness and dignity of the place. All the furniture was old, well made, and dark. Underfoot there was a plain green pile carpet, the only new thing about the room except the electric light fittings and the jugs and basins. Even the looking-glass on the dressing-table was an old pyramidal Venetian glass set in heavy repoussé frame of tarnished silver.

"After a few minutes' cleaning up, I went downstairs and out upon the lawn, where I greeted my hostess. The people gathered there were of the usual country type, all anxious to be pleased and roundly curious as to the new master of the Abbey. Rather to my surprise, and quite to my pleasure, I rediscovered Glenham, whom I had known well in the old days in Barotseland: he lived quite close, as, he remarked with a grin, I ought to have known. 'But,' he added, 'I don't live in a place like this.' He swept his hand to the long, low lines of the Abbey in obvious admiration, and then, to my intense interest, muttered beneath his breath, 'Thank God!' He saw that I had overheard him, and turning to me said decidedly, 'Yes, "thank God" I said, and I meant it. I wouldn't live at the Abbey for all Broughton's money.'

" 'But surely,' I demurred, 'you know that old Clarke was discovered in the very act of setting light on his bug-a-boos?'

"Glenham shrugged his shoulders. 'Yes, I know about that. But there is something wrong with the place still. All I can say is that Broughton is a different man since he has lived there. I don't believe that he will remain much longer. But—you're staying here?—well, you'll hear all about it to-night. There's a big dinner, I understand.' The conversation turned off to old reminiscences, and Glenham soon after had to go.

"Before I went to dress that evening I had twenty minutes' talk with Broughton in his library. There was no doubt that the man was altered, gravely altered. He was nervous and fidgety, and I found him looking at me only when my eye was off him. I naturally asked him what he wanted of me. I told him I would do anything I could, but that I couldn't conceive what he lacked that I could provide. He said with a lustreless smile that there was, however, something, and that he would tell me the following morning. It struck me that he was somehow ashamed of himself, and perhaps ashamed of the part he was asking me to play. However, I dismissed the subject from my mind and went up to dress in my palatial room. As I shut the door a draught blew out the Queen of Sheba from the wall, and I noticed that the tapestries were not fastened to the wall at the bottom. I have always held very practical views about spooks, and it has often seemed to me that the slow waving in firelight of loose tapestry upon a wall would account for ninety-nine per cent of the stories one hears. Certainly the dignified undulation of this lady with her attendants and huntsmen—one of whom was untidily cutting the throat of a fallow deer upon the very steps on which King Solomon, a grey-faced Flemish nobleman with the order of the Golden Fleece, awaited his fair visitor—gave colour to my hypothesis.

"Nothing much happened at dinner. The people were very much like those of the garden party. A young woman next me seemed anxious to know what was being read in London. As she was far more familiar than I with the most recent magazines and literary supplements, I found salvation in being myself instructed in the tendencies of modern fiction. All true art, she said, was shot through and through with melancholy. How vulgar were the attempts at wit that marked so many modern books! From the beginning of literature it had always been tragedy that embodied the highest attainment of every age. To call such works morbid merely begged the question. No thoughtful man—she looked sternly at me through the steel rim of her glasses—could fail to agree with me. Of course, as one would, I immediately and properly said that I slept with Pett Ridge and Jacobs under my pillow at night, and that if *Jorrocks* weren't quite so large and cornery, I would add him to the company. She hadn't read any of them, so I was saved—for a time. But I remember grimly that she said that the dearest wish of her life was to be in some awful and soul-freezing situation of horror, and I remember that she dealt hardly with the hero of Nat Paynter's vampire story, between nibbles at her brown-bread ice. She was a cheerless soul, and I couldn't help thinking that if there were many such in the neighbourhood, it was not surprising that old Glenham had been stuffed with some nonsense or other about the Abbey. Yet nothing could well have been less creepy than the glitter of silver and glass, and the subdued lights and cackle of conversation all round the dinner-table.

"After the ladies had gone I found myself talking to the rural dean. He was a thin, ear-nest man, who at once turned the conversation to old Clarke's buffooneries. But, he said, Mr. Broughton had introduced such a new and cheerful spirit, not only into the Abbey, but, he might say, into the whole neighbourhood, that he had great hopes that the ignorant superstitions of the past were from henceforth destined to oblivion. Thereupon his other neighbour, a portly gentleman of independent means and position, audibly remarked 'Amen,' which damped the rural dean, and we talked to partridges past, partridges present, and pheasants to come. At the other end of the table Broughton sat with a couple of his friends, red-faced hunting men. Once I noticed that they were discussing me, but I paid no attention to it at the time. I remembered it a few hours later.

"By eleven all the guests were gone, and Broughton, his wife, and I were alone together under the fine plaster ceiling of the Jacobean drawing-room. Mrs. Broughton talked about one or two of the neighbours, and then, with a smile, said that she knew I would excuse her, shook hands with me, and went off to bed. I am not very good at analysing things, but I felt that she talked a little uncomfortably and with a suspicion of effort, smiled rather conventionally, and was obviously glad to go. These things seem trifling enough to repeat, but I had throughout the faint feeling that everything was not quite square. Under the circumstances, this was enough to set me wondering what on earth the service could be that I was to render—wondering also whether the whole business were not some ill-advised jest in order to make me come down from London for a mere shooting-party.

"Broughton said little after she had gone. But he was evidently labouring to bring the conversation round to the so-called haunting of the Abbey. As soon as I saw this, of course I asked him directly about it. He then seemed at once to lose interest in the matter. There was no doubt about it: Broughton was somehow a changed man, and to my mind he had changed in no way for the better. Mrs. Broughton seemed no sufficient cause. He was clearly very fond of her, and she of him. I reminded him that he was going to tell me what I could do for him in the morning, pleaded my journey, lighted a candle, and went upstairs with him. At the end of the passage leading into the old house he grinned weakly and said, 'Mind, if you see a ghost, do talk to it; you said you would.' He stood irresolutely a moment and then turned away. At the door of his dressing-room he paused once more: 'I'm here,' he called out, 'if you should want anything. Good night,' and he shut the door.

"I went along the passage to my room, undressed, switched on a lamp beside my bed, read a few pages of *The Jungle Book,* and then, more than ready for sleep, turned the light off and went fast asleep.

"Three hours later I woke up. There was not a breath of wind outside. There was not even a flicker of light from the fireplace. As I lay there, an ash tinkled slightly as it cooled, but there was hardly a gleam of the dullest red in the grate. An owl cried among the silent Spanish chestnuts on the slope outside. I idly reviewed the events of the day, hoping that I should fall off to sleep again before I reached dinner. But at the end I seemed as wakeful as ever. There was no help for it. I must read my *Jungle Book* again till I felt ready to go off, so I fumbled for the pear at the end of the cord that hung down inside the bed, and I switched on the bedside lamp. The sudden glory dazzled me for a moment. I felt under my pillow for my book with half-shut eyes. Then, growing used to the light, I happened to look down to the foot of my bed.

"I can never tell you really when happened then. Nothing I could ever confess in the most abject words could even faintly picture to you what I felt. I know that my heart stopped dead, and my throat shut automatically. In one instinctive movement I crouched back up against the head-boards of the bed, staring at the horror. The movement set my heart going again, and the sweat dripped from every pore. I am not a particularly religious man, but I had always believed that God would never allow any supernatural appearance to present itself to man in such a guise and in such circumstances that harm, either bodily or mental, could result to him. I can only tell you that at the moment both my life and my reason rocked unsteadily on their seats."

The other *Osiris* passengers had gone to bed. Only he and I remained leaning over the starboard railing, which rattled uneasily now and then under the fierce vibration of the over-engined mail-boat. Far over, there were the lights of a few fishing-smacks riding out the night, and a great rush of white combing and seething water fell out and away from us overside.

At last Colvin went on:

"Leaning over the foot of my bed, looking at me, was a figure swathed in a rotten and tattered veiling. This shroud passed over the head, but left both eyes and the right side of the face bare. It then followed the line of the arm down to where the hand grasped the bed-end. The face was not entirely that of a skull, though the eyes and the flesh of the face were totally gone. There was a thin, dry skin drawn tightly over the features, and there was some skin left on the hand. One wisp of hair crossed the forehead. It was perfectly still. I looked at it, and it looked at me, and my brains turned dry and hot in my head. I had still got the pear of the electric lamp in my hand, and I played idly with it; only I dared not turn the light out again. I shut my eyes, only to open them in a hideous terror the same second. The thing had not moved. My heart was thumping, and the sweat cooled me as it evaporated. Another cinder tinkled in the grate, and a panel creaked in the wall.

"My reason failed me. For twenty minutes, or twenty seconds, I was able to think of nothing else but this awful figure, till there came, hurtling through the empty channels of my senses, the remembrances that Broughton and his friends had discussed me furtively at dinner. The dim possibility of its being a hoax stole gratefully into my unhappy mind, and once there, one's pluck came creeping back along a thousand tiny veins. My first sensation was one of blind unreasoning thankfulness that my brain was going to stand the trial. I am not a timid man, but the best of us needs some human handle to steady him in time of extremity, and in this faint but growing hope that after all it might be only a brutal hoax, I found the fulcrum that I needed. At last I moved.

"How I managed to do it I cannot tell you, but with one spring towards the foot of the bed I got within arm's-length and struck out one fearful blow with my fist at the thing. It crumbled under it, and my hand was cut to the bone. With a sickening revulsion after my terror, I dropped half-fainting across the end of the bed. So it was merely a foul trick after all. No doubt the trick had been played many a time before: no doubt Broughton and his friends had had some large bet among themselves as to what I should do when I discovered the gruesome thing. From my state of abject terror I found myself transported into an insensate anger. I shouted curses upon Broughton. I dived rather than climbed over the bed-end of the sofa. I tore at the robed skeleton—how well the whole thing had been carried out, I thought—I broke the skull against the floor, and stamped upon its dry bones. I flung the head away under the bed, and rent the brittle bones of the trunk in pieces. I snapped the thin thigh-bones across my knee, and flung them in different directions. The shin-bones I set up against a stool and broke with my heel. I raged like a Berserker against the loathly thing, and stripped the ribs from the backbone and slung the breastbone against the cupboard. My fury increased as the work of destruction went on. I tore the frail rotten veil into twenty pieces, and the dust went up over everything, over the clean blotting-paper and the silver inkstand. At last my work was done. There was but a raffle of broken bones and strips of parchment and crumbling wool. Then, picking up a piece of the skull—it was the cheek and temple bone of the right side, I remember—I opened the door and went down the passage to Broughton's dressing-room. I remember still how my sweat-dripping pyjamas clung to me as I walked. At the door I kicked and entered.

"Broughton was in bed. He had already turned the light on and seemed shrunken and horrified. For a moment he could hardly pull himself together. Then I spoke. I don't know what I said. Only I know that from a heart full and over-full with hatred and contempt, spurred on by shame of my own recent cowardice, I let my tongue run on. He answered nothing. I was amazed at my own fluency. My hair still clung lankily to my wet temples, my hand was bleeding profusely, and I must have looked a strange sight. Broughton huddled himself up at the head of the bed just as I had. Still he made no answer, no defence. He seemed preoccupied with something besides my reproaches, and once or twice moistened his lips with his tongue. But he could say nothing though he moved his hands now and then, just as a baby who cannot speak moves its hands.

"At last the door into Mrs. Broughton's rooms opened and she came in, white and terrified. 'What is it? What is it? Oh, in God's name! what is it?' she cried again and again, and then she went up to her husband and sat on the bed in her night-dress, and the two faced me. I told her what the matter was. I spared her husband not a word for her presence there. Yet he seemed hardly to understand. I told the pair that I had spoiled their cowardly joke for them. Broughton looked up.

" 'I have smashed the foul thing into a hundred pieces,' I said. Broughton licked his lips again and his mouth worked. 'By God!' I shouted, 'it would serve you right if I thrashed you within an inch of your life. I will take care that not a decent man or woman of my acquaintance ever speaks to you again. And there,' I added, throwing the broken piece of the skull upon the floor beside his bed, 'there is a souvenir for you, of your damned work to-night!'

"Broughton saw the bone, and in a moment

it was his turn to frighten me. He squealed like a hare caught in a trap. He screamed and screamed till Mrs. Broughton, almost as bewildered as myself, held on to him and coaxed him like a child to be quiet. But Broughton—and as he moved I thought that ten minutes ago I perhaps looked as terribly ill as he did—thrust her from him, and scrambled out of bed on to the floor, and still screaming put out his hand to the bone. It had blood on it from my hand. He paid no attention to me whatever. In truth I said nothing. This was a new turn indeed to the horrors of the evening. He rose from the floor with the bone in his hand and stood silent. He seemed to be listening. 'Time, time, perhaps,' he muttered, and almost at the same moment fell at full length on the carpet, cutting his head against the fender. The bone flew from his hand and came to rest near the door. I picked Broughton up, haggard and broken, with blood over his face. He whispered hoarsely and quickly, 'Listen, listen!' We listened.

"After ten seconds' utter quiet, I seemed to hear something. I could not be sure, but at last there was no doubt. There was a quiet sound as one moving along the passage. Little regular steps came towards us over the hard oak flooring. Broughton moved to where his wife sat, white and speechless, on the bed, and pressed her face into his shoulder.

"Then, the last thing that I could see as he turned the light out, he fell forward with his own head pressed into the pillow of the bed. Something in their company, something in their cowardice, helped me, and I faced the open doorway of the room, which was outlined fairly clearly against the dimly lighted passage. I put out one hand and touched Mrs. Broughton's shoulder in the darkness. But at the last moment I too failed. I sank on my knees and put my face in the bed. Only we all heard. The footsteps came to the door and there they stopped. The piece of bone was lying a yard inside the door. There was a rustle of moving stuff, and the thing was in the room. Mrs. Broughton was silent: I could hear Broughton's voice praying, muffled in the pil-

low: I was cursing my own cowardice. Then the steps moved out again on the oak boards of the passage, and I heard the sounds dying away. In a flash of remorse I went to the door and looked out. At the end of the corridor I thought I saw something that moved away. A moment later the passage was empty. I stood with my forehead against the jamb of the door almost physically sick.

" 'You can turn the light on,' I said, and there was an answering flare. There was no bone at my feet. Mrs. Broughton had fainted. Broughton was almost useless, and it took me ten minutes to bring her to. Broughton only said one thing worth remembering. For the most part he went on muttering prayers. But I was glad afterwards to recollect that he had said that thing. He said in a colourless voice, half as a question, half as a reproach, 'You didn't speak to her.'

"We spent the remainder of the night together. Mrs. Broughton actually fell off into a kind of sleep before dawn, but she suffered so horribly in her dreams that I shook her into consciousness again. Never was dawn so long in coming. Three or four times Broughton spoke to himself. Mrs. Broughton would then just tighten her hold on his arm, but she could say nothing. As for me, I can honestly say that I grew worse as the hours passed and the light strengthened. The two violent reactions had battered down my steadiness of view, and I felt that the foundations of my life had been built upon the sand. I said nothing, and after binding up my hand with a towel, I did not move. It was better so. They helped me and I helped them, and we all three knew that our reason had gone very near to ruin that night. At last, when the light came in pretty strongly, and the birds outside were chattering and singing, we felt that we must do something. Yet we never moved. You might have thought that we should particularly dislike being found as we were by the servants: yet nothing of that kind mattered a straw, and an overpowering listlessness bound us as we sat, until Chapman, Broughton's man, actually knocked and opened the door. None of us moved. Broughton, speaking hardly and stiffly, said, 'Chapman, you can come back in five minutes.' Chapman was a discreet man, but it would have made no difference to us if he had carried his news to the 'room' at once.

"We looked at each other and I said I must go back. I meant to wait outside till Chapman returned. I simply dared not re-enter my bedroom alone. Broughton roused himself and said that he would come with me. Mrs. Broughton agreed to remain in her own room for five minutes if the blinds were drawn up and all the doors left open.

"So Broughton and I, leaning stiffly one against the other, went down to my room.

By the morning light that filtered past the blinds we could see our way, and I released the blinds. There was nothing wrong with the room from end to end, except smears of my own blood on the end of the bed, on the sofa, and on the carpet where I had torn the thing to pieces."

Colvin had finished his story. There was nothing to say. Seven bells stuttered out from the fo'c'sle, and the answering cry wailed through the darkness. I took him downstairs.

"Of course I am much better now, but it is a kindness of you to let me sleep in your cabin."

THE FEMALE OF THE SPECIES

THE WOMAN'S GHOST STORY

Algernon Blackwood

RATED BY H. P. LOVECRAFT as "the one absolute and unquestioned master of weird atmosphere," Algernon Blackwood (1869–1951) was born in London and educated at Wellington College, the Moravian Brotherhood, and Edinburgh University, studying Oriental religions and the occult, and joining several occult societies. He moved to Canada at the age of twenty and worked a farm, then ran a hotel before moving to New York as a newspaper reporter for *The New York Sun* and *The New York Times*. He returned to England at the age of thirty-six to become a prolific full-time writer, producing more than a dozen short story collections and sixteen novels about ghosts and other supernatural entities. An important characteristic of his work is that it is generally about an average person caught up in extrasensory experiences, rather than a bizarre Gothic eccentric who has gone looking for trouble. Blackwood is probably best known for his many stories about the psychic detective John Silence, some of which were collected in the eponymous *John Silence: Physician Extraordinary* (1908). These tales had originally been submitted to his publisher as essays recounting his own true-life experiences, but he was persuaded to turn them into fictional works. Silence is a stand-in for the author, then, which contributes to the intensity of the suspense.

His most famous non-Silence stories are the often-anthologized horror tales "The Willows" (1907) and "The Wendigo" (1910). He also wrote an autobiography of his early years, *Episodes Before Thirty* (1923).

"The Woman's Ghost Story" was first published in book form in *The Listener and Other Stories* (London, Eveleigh Nash, 1907).

The Woman's Ghost Story

ALGERNON BLACKWOOD

"YES," SHE SAID, from her seat in the dark corner, "I'll tell you an experience if you care to listen. And, what's more, I'll tell it briefly, without trimmings—I mean without unessentials. That's a thing story-tellers never do, you know," she laughed. "They drag in all the unessentials and leave their listeners to disentangle; but I'll give you just the essentials, and you can

make of it what you please. But on one condition: that at the end you ask no questions, because I can't explain it and have no wish to."

We agreed. We were all serious. After listening to a dozen prolix stories from people who merely wished to "talk" but had nothing to tell, we wanted "essentials."

"In those days," she began, feeling from the

quality of our silence that we were with her, "in those days I was interested in psychic things, and had arranged to sit up alone in a haunted house in the middle of London. It was a cheap and dingy lodging-house in a mean street, unfurnished. I had already made a preliminary examination in daylight that afternoon, and the keys from the caretaker, who lived next door, were in my pocket. The story was a good one—satisfied me, at any rate, that it was worth investigating; and I won't weary you with details as to the woman's murder and all the tiresome elaboration as to *why* the place was *alive*. Enough that it was.

"I was a good deal bored, therefore, to see a man, whom I took to be the talkative old caretaker, waiting for me on the steps when I went in at 11 p.m., for I had sufficiently explained that I wished to be there alone for the night.

" 'I wished to show you *the* room,' he mumbled, and of course I couldn't exactly refuse, having tipped him for the temporary loan of a chair and table.

" 'Come in, then, and let's be quick,' I said.

"We went in, he shuffling after me through the unlighted hall up to the first floor where the murder had taken place, and I prepared myself to hear his inevitable account before turning him out with the half-crown his persistence had earned. After lighting the gas I sat down in the arm-chair he had provided—a faded, brown plush arm-chair—and turned for the first time to face him and get through with the performance as quickly as possible. And it was in that instant I got my first shock. The man was *not* the caretaker. It was not the old fool, Carey, I had interviewed earlier in the day and made my plans with. My heart gave a horrid jump.

" 'Now who are *you*, pray?' I said. 'You're not Carey, the man I arranged with this afternoon. Who are you?'

"I felt uncomfortable, as you may imagine. I was a 'psychical researcher,' and a young woman of new tendencies, and proud of my liberty, but I did not care to find myself in an empty house with a stranger. Something of my confidence left me. Confidence with women, you know, is all humbug after a certain point. Or perhaps you don't know, for most of you are men. But anyhow my pluck ebbed in a quick rush, and I felt afraid.

" 'Who are you?' I repeated quickly and nervously. The fellow was well dressed, youngish and good-looking, but with a face of great sadness. I myself was barely thirty. I am giving you essentials, or I would not mention it. Out of quite ordinary things comes this story. I think that's why it has value.

" 'No,' he said; 'I'm the man who was frightened to death.'

"His voice and his words ran through me like a knife, and I felt ready to drop. In my pocket was the book I had bought to make notes in. I felt the pencil sticking in the socket. I felt, too, the extra warm things I had put on to sit up in, as no bed or sofa was available—a hundred things dashed through my mind, foolishly and without sequence or meaning, as the way is when one is really frightened. Unessentials leaped up and puzzled me, and I thought of what the papers might say if it came out, and what my 'smart' brother-in-law would think, and whether it would be told that I had cigarettes in my pocket, and was a free-thinker.

" 'The man who was frightened to death!' I repeated aghast.

" 'That's me,' he said stupidly.

"I stared at him just as you would have done—any one of you men now listening to me—and felt my life ebbing and flowing like a sort of hot fluid. You needn't laugh! That's how I felt. Small things, you know, touch the mind with great earnestness when terror is there—*real terror*. But I might have been at a middle-class tea-party, for all the ideas I had: they were so ordinary!

" 'But I thought you were the caretaker I tipped this afternoon to let me sleep here!' I gasped. 'Did—did Carey send you to meet me?'

" 'No,' he replied in a voice that touched my boots somehow. 'I am the man who was frightened to death. And what is more, I am frightened *now*!'

" 'So am I!' I managed to utter, speaking instinctively. 'I'm simply terrified.'

" 'Yes,' he replied in that same odd voice that seemed to sound within me. 'But you are still in the flesh, and I—*am not!*'

"I felt the need for vigorous self-assertion. I stood up in that empty, unfurnished room, digging the nails into my palms and clenching my teeth. I was determined to assert my individuality and my courage as a new woman and a free soul.

" 'You mean to say you are not in the flesh!' I gasped. 'What in the world are you talking about?'

"The silence of the night swallowed up my voice. For the first time I realized that darkness was over the city; that dust lay upon the stairs; that the floor above was untenanted and the floor below empty. I was alone in an unoccupied and haunted house, unprotected, and a woman. I chilled. I heard the wind round the house, and knew the stars were hidden. My thoughts rushed to policemen and omnibuses, and everything that was useful and comforting. I suddenly realized what a fool I was to come to such a house alone. I was icily afraid. I thought the end of my life had come. I was an utter fool to go in for psychical research when I had not the necessary nerve.

" 'Good God!' I gasped. 'If you're not Carey, the man I arranged with, who are you?'

"I was really stiff with terror. The man moved slowly towards me across the empty room. I held out my arm to stop him, getting up out of my chair at the same moment, and he came to halt just opposite to me, a smile on his worn, sad face.

" 'I told you who I am,' he repeated quietly with a sigh, looking at me with the saddest eyes I have ever seen, 'and I am frightened *still.*'

"By this time I was convinced that I was entertaining either a rogue or a madman, and I cursed my stupidity in bringing the man in without having seen his face. My mind was quickly made up, and I knew what to do. Ghosts and psychic phenomena flew to the winds. If I angered the creature my life might pay the price.

I must humor him till I got to the door, and then race for the street. I stood bolt upright and faced him. We were about of a height, and I was a strong, athletic woman who played hockey in winter and climbed Alps in summer. My hand itched for a stick, but I had none.

" 'Now, of course, I remember,' I said with a sort of stiff smile that was very hard to force. 'Now I remember your case and the wonderful way you behaved. . . .'

"The man stared at me stupidly, turning his head to watch me as I backed more and more quickly to the door. But when his face broke into a smile I could control myself no longer. I reached the door in a run, and shot out on to the landing. Like a fool, I turned the wrong way, and stumbled over the stairs leading to the next story. But it was too late to change. The man was after me, I was sure, though no sound of footsteps came; and I dashed up the next flight, tearing my skirt and banging my ribs in the darkness, and rushed headlong into the first room I came to. Luckily the door stood ajar, and, still more fortunate, there was a key in the lock. In a second I had slammed the door, flung my whole weight against it, and turned the key.

"I was safe, but my heart was beating like a drum. A second later it seemed to stop altogether, for I saw that there was some one else in the room besides myself. A man's figure stood between me and the windows, where the street lamps gave just enough light to outline his shape against the glass. I'm a plucky woman, you know, for even then I didn't give up hope, but I may tell you that I have never felt so vilely frightened in all my born days. I had locked myself in with him!

"The man leaned against the window, watching me where I lay in a collapsed heap upon the floor. So there were two men in the house with me, I reflected. Perhaps other rooms were occupied too! What could it all mean? But, as I stared something changed in the room, or in me—hard to say which—and I realized my mistake, so that my fear, which had so far been physical, at once altered its character and became *psychical*. I became afraid in my soul instead of in my heart, and I knew immediately who this man was.

" 'How in the world did you get up here?' I stammered to him across the empty room, amazement momentarily stemming my fear.

" 'Now, let me tell you,' he began, in that odd faraway voice of his that went down my spine like a knife. 'I'm in different space, for one thing, and you'd find me in any room you went into; for according to your way of measuring, I'm *all over the house.* Space is a bodily condition, but I am out of the body, and am not affected by space. It's my condition that keeps me here. I want something to change my condition for me, for then I could get away. What I want is sympathy. Or, really, more than sympathy; I want affection—I want *love!*'

"While he was speaking I gathered myself slowly upon my feet. I wanted to scream and cry and laugh all at once, but I only succeeded in sighing, for my emotion was exhausted and a numbness was coming over me. I felt for the matches in my pocket and made a movement towards the gas jet.

" 'I should be much happier if you didn't light the gas,' he said at once, 'for the vibrations of your light hurt me a good deal. You need not be afraid that I shall injure you. I can't touch your body to begin with, for there's a great gulf fixed, you know; and really this half-light suits me best. Now, let me continue what I was trying to say before. You know, so many people have come to this house to see me, and most of them have seen me, and one and all have been terrified. If only, oh, if only some one would be *not* terrified, but kind and loving to me! Then, you see, I might be able to change my condition and get away.'

"His voice was so sad that I felt tears start somewhere at the back of my eyes; but fear kept all else in check, and I stood shaking and cold as I listened to him.

" 'Who are you then? Of course Carey didn't send you, I know now,' I managed to utter. My thoughts scattered dreadfully and I could think of nothing to say. I was afraid of a stroke.

" 'I know nothing about Carey, or who he is,' continued the man quietly, 'and the name my body had I have forgotten, thank God; but I am the man who was frightened to death in this house ten years ago, and I have been frightened ever since, and am frightened still; for the succession of cruel and curious people who come to this house to see the ghost, and thus keep alive its atmosphere of terror, only helps to render my condition worse. If only some one would be kind to me—*laugh,* speak gently and rationally with me, cry if they like, pity, comfort, soothe me—anything but come here in curiosity and tremble as you are now doing in that corner. Now, madam, won't you take pity on me?' His voice rose to a dreadful cry. 'Won't you step out into the middle of the room and try to love me a little?'

"A horrible laughter came gurgling up in my throat as I heard him, but the sense of pity was stronger than the laughter, and I found myself actually leaving the support of the wall and approaching the center of the floor.

" 'By God!' he cried, at once straightening up against the window, 'you have done a kind act. That's the first attempt at sympathy that has been shown me since I died, and I feel better already. In life, you know, I was a misanthrope. Everything went wrong with me, and I came to hate my fellow men so much that I couldn't bear to see them even. Of course, like begets like, and this hate was returned. Finally I suffered from horrible delusions, and my room became haunted with demons that laughed and grimaced, and one night I ran into a whole cluster of them near the bed—and the fright stopped my heart and killed me. It's hate and remorse, as much as terror, that clogs me so thickly and keeps me here. If only some one could feel pity, and sympathy, and perhaps a little love for me, I could get away and be happy. When you came this afternoon to see over the house I watched you, and a little hope came to me for the first time. I saw you had courage, originality, resource—*love.* If only I could touch your heart, without frightening you, I knew I could perhaps tap that love you have stored up in your being there, and thus borrow the wings for my escape!'

"Now I must confess my heart began to ache a little, as fear left me and the man's words sank their sad meaning into me. Still, the whole affair was so incredible, and so touched with unholy quality, and the story of a woman's murder I had come to investigate had so obviously nothing to do with this thing, that I felt myself in a kind of wild dream that seemed likely to stop at any moment and leave me somewhere in bed after a nightmare.

"Moreover, his words possessed me to such an extent that I found it impossible to reflect upon anything else at all, or to consider adequately any ways or means of action or escape.

"I moved a little nearer to him in the gloom, horribly frightened, of course, but with the beginnings of a strange determination in my heart.

" 'You women,' he continued, his voice plainly thrilling at my approach, 'you wonderful women, to whom life often brings no opportunity of spending your great love, oh, if you only could know how many of *us* simply yearn for it! It would save our souls, if but you knew. Few might find the chance that you now have, but if you only spent your love freely, without definite object, just letting it flow openly for all who need, you would reach hundreds and thousands of souls like me, and *release us!* Oh, madam, I ask you again to feel with me, to be kind and gentle—and if you can to love me a little!'

"My heart did leap within me and this time the tears did come, for I could not restrain them. I laughed too, for the way he called me 'madam' sounded so odd, here in this empty room at midnight in a London street, but my laughter stopped dead and merged in a flood of weeping when I saw how my change of feeling affected him. He had left his place by the window and was kneeling on the floor at my feet, his hands stretched out towards me, and the first signs of a kind of glory about his head.

" 'Put your arms round me and kiss me, for the love of God!' he cried. 'Kiss me, oh, kiss me, and I shall be freed! You have done so much already—now do this!'

"I stuck there, hesitating, shaking, my determination on the verge of action, yet not quite able to compass it. But the terror had almost gone.

" 'Forget that I'm a man and you're a woman,' he continued in the most beseeching voice I ever heard. 'Forget that I'm a ghost, and come out boldly and press me to you with a great kiss, and let your love flow into me. Forget yourself just for one minute and do a brave thing! Oh, love me, *love me, love me*! and I shall be free!'

"The words, or the deep force they somehow released in the center of my being, stirred me profoundly, and an emotion infinitely greater than fear surged up over me and carried me with it across the edge of action. Without hesitation I took two steps forward towards him where he knelt, and held out my arms. Pity and love were in my heart at that moment, genuine pity, I swear, and genuine love. I forgot myself and my little tremblings in a great desire to help another soul.

" 'I love you! poor, aching, unhappy thing! I love you,' I cried through hot tears; 'and I am not the least bit afraid in the world.'

"The man uttered a curious sound, like laughter, yet not laughter, and turned his face up to me. The light from the street below fell on it, but there was another light, too, shining all round it that seemed to come from the eyes and skin. He rose to his feet and met me, and in that second I folded him to my breast and kissed him full on the lips again and again."

All our pipes had gone out, and not even a skirt rustled in that dark studio as the story-teller paused a moment to steady her voice, and put a hand softly up to her eyes before going on again.

"Now, what can I say, and how can I describe to you, all you skeptical men sitting there with pipes in your mouths, the amazing sensation I experienced of holding an intangible, impalpable thing so closely to my heart that it touched my body with equal pressure all the way down, and then melted away somewhere into my very being? For it was like seizing a rush of cool wind and feeling a touch of burning fire the moment it had struck its swift blow and passed on. A series of shocks ran all over and all through me; a momentary ecstasy of flaming sweetness and wonder thrilled down into me; my heart gave another great leap—and then I was alone.

"The room was empty. I turned on the gas and struck a match to prove it. All fear had left me, and something was singing round me in the air and in my heart like the joy of a spring morning in youth. Not all the devils or shadows or hauntings in the world could then have caused me a single tremor.

"I unlocked the door and went all over the dark house, even into kitchen and cellar and up among the ghostly attics. But the house was empty. Something had left it. I lingered a short hour, analyzing, thinking, wondering—you can guess what and how, perhaps, but I won't detail, for I promised only essentials, remember—and then went out to sleep the remainder of the night in my own flat, locking the door behind me upon a house no longer haunted.

"But my uncle, Sir Henry, the owner of the house, required an account of my adventure, and of course I was in duty bound to give him some kind of a true story. Before I could begin, however, he held up his hand to stop me.

" 'First,' he said, 'I wish to tell you a little deception I ventured to practice on you. So many people have been to that house and seen the ghost that I came to think the story acted on their imaginations, and I wished to make a better test. So I invented for their benefit another story, with the idea that if you did see anything I could be sure it was not due merely to an excited imagination.'

" 'Then what you told me about a woman having been murdered, and all that, was not the true story of the haunting?'

" 'It was not. The true story is that a cousin of mine went mad in that house, and killed himself in a fit of morbid terror following upon years of miserable hypochondriasis. It is his figure that investigators see.'

" 'That explains, then,' I gasped—

" 'Explains what?'

"I thought of that poor struggling soul, longing all these years for escape, and determined to keep my story for the present to myself.

" 'Explains, I mean, why I did not see the ghost of the murdered woman,' I concluded.

" 'Precisely,' said Sir Henry, 'and why, if you had seen anything, it would have had value, inasmuch as it could not have been caused by the imagination working upon a story you already knew.' "

Victor Rousseau

LIKE MOST PROLIFIC PULP writers, Victor Rousseau (Emanuel) (1879–1960) wrote in a wide range of genres, including mysteries, historical fiction, and westerns, with several of these serving as the source for silent films, including *West of the Rainbow's End* (1926), *Hi-Jacking Rustlers* (1926), *Prince of the Plains* (1927), *A Wanderer of the West* (1927) (the latter two featuring the great silent star Tex Maynard), *Trailin' Back* (1928), and *The Devil's Tower* (1928). Emanuel began his career as a journalist, first as a reporter for the New York *World,* then as an editor for *Harper's Weekly,* before becoming a full-time fiction writer, mainly for the pulps. Most of his stories in the United States appeared as Victor Rousseau and, in England as H. M. Egbert; he also used the pseudonym Lewis Merrill. Under the house name John Grange, he created the superhero Jim Anthony in *Super-Detective* magazine to compete with Doc Savage. Blessed with great wealth and many superpowers, Anthony battled supervillains in the first ten episodes, then became more of a hard-boiled private detective. The series lasted for only twenty-five issues from 1940 to 1943. Emanuel wrote the first three novels and probably the next twelve; the final ten were written by Robert Leslie Bellem and W. T. Ballard.

It is in the fantasy, science fiction, and supernatural genres in which Emanuel found his greatest success, producing such novels as *The Sea Demons* (1916), in which transparent creatures invade England; *The Messiah of the Cylinder* (1917), which portrayed a totalitarian future; and *Fruit of the Lamp* (1918, published in the U.K. in 1925 as *Mrs. Aladdin*), in which a young man acquires an ancient lamp with a beautiful female genie. Although *Ghost Stories* magazine published a great deal of pedestrian fiction, it carried the very good series by Emanuel about Dr. Martinus, Occultist, a psychic detective in the style of William Hope Hodgson's Carnacki and Algernon Blackwood's John Silence; another psychic investigator, Dr. Ivan Brodsky, was created for *Weird Tales,* running in 1926 and 1927.

"The Angel of the Marne" was originally published in the July 1929 issue of *Ghost Stories.*

The Angel of the Marne

VICTOR ROUSSEAU

THE QUAINT OLD MARKET-PLACE of Rouen basked drowsily in the sunshine of a late afternoon in May. Nearby, a group of people were taking their dinner at one of the little sidewalk cafés, happily undisturbed by the passers-by. Overhead arched the blue, serene sky of Normandy.

Such was the scene of my chance meeting with Captain Philippe Roget, famous war ace. I had not seen him since the Legion held its convention "over there," and then we had chatted for only a few minutes, for we had never been intimate. During the War I had held the minor post of liaison officer at the Headquarters of Captain Roget's brigade.

In view of the fact that I had arrived in

France on business hardly twenty-four hours before, the Captain was probably the last person I had expected to see.

Yet there he was, left sleeve hanging empty, the right hand clutching a bouquet of magnificent roses, whose fragrance scented the air all about us. At the sight of me he uttered an exclamation of delight, and, laying the flowers upon a nearby table, gripped my hand in his with utmost cordiality.

"But how does this happen, my dear Captain Sewell?" he inquired. "Let us sit down. I have an hour, and intended dining here. And you?"

I confessed that I had not dined, and we took possession of one of the little tables without more ado.

"But you have not told me what brings you here," said Roget, when we had given our order.

I explained my business briefly, adding that I was to see an important customer of my firm the following morning.

"And you?" I asked. "Those flowers give you away, Captain Roget. I hope the lady is very charming?"

There was a strange glint in Roget's eyes.

"The most charming and wonderful woman in the world," he answered. "One whom I am proud to love and serve."

"That's good," I answered lightly. "I congratulate you with all my heart, my dear Captain." My tone belied my really deep sincerity, for I knew that the woman who had won Captain Philippe Roget's heart was fortunate indeed.

Tall, handsome, in spite of the grey at his temples, he wore his empty sleeve like a badge of courage and seemed, in every way, a hero out of romance. During the War he had performed deeds of incredible daring, including the one that had cost him his arm. In the first days of the conflict, when the French, surprised by the German invasion of Belgium, were falling back in confusion all along the frontiers, Roget had been entrusted with dispatches whose delivery meant the salvation of the French armies; their non-delivery, ruin and defeat.

They were sent to General Joffre by the commander of a French army corps, already cut off on all sides and offering hopeless resistance to overwhelming numbers. They contained vital information as to the disposition of the German forces which seemed likely to entrap half the armies of the Republic.

Alone in his plane, Philippe Roget had been sent by night from the encircled troops, with orders to reach French Headquarters or die in the attempt.

Philippe had reached Headquarters and placed the communication in the hands of Joffre, thereby making it possible for the scattered French armies to unite into the line that later snatched victory out of defeat at the Battle of the Marne.

Later, as a one-armed flyer—for France was in urgent need of so brave a son—he had covered himself with glory, escaping death time after time by a veritable miracle.

So, looking at him, I felt that this lady for whom he was bringing his roses was certainly to be congratulated.

As we ate, we talked for the most part of impersonal affairs, guardedly skirting all references to the War—as ex-soldiers do when they meet. So much is taken for granted; so many experiences have been identical, that there is usually surprisingly little to talk about. Besides, Captain Philippe's thoughts were still on the lady—I could tell by the way he kept glancing at the flowers.

"I hope I'm not detaining you," I said at length. "This engagement of yours——"

"No, not at all, Captain Sewell," he answered. "She is in no hurry, and I am not of much consequence to her."

"But surely you must be," I returned. I thought he must be jesting. But there was no levity in Philippe Roget's clear blue eyes.

"It is an old affair," he answered absently. Then he turned toward me. "I have never told you of my experiences when I was sent from the front with those dispatches for General Joffre," he said. "I have rarely ever spoken of them. Do you believe in miracles, Sewell?"

I hesitated. I remembered that Captain Philippe had been what few of the army officers were in those days, a fervently religious man. I did not know what to say.

"Modern science seems to be taking a more tolerant attitude toward the supernatural," I parried.

"But suppose we do not call it the supernatural," suggested Philippe. "Suppose we regard it as coming within the domain of natural law, of science—all these things that are slowly forcing belief upon the sceptics and materialists of the past generation?"

"Spiritualism and table tipping, for instance?" I ventured.

A look of unutterable disgust came over Philippe Roget's clear-cut features.

"Bah, pranks of dead diabolists!" he retorted. "Throwers of pots and pans in haunted kitchens! No, those are not miracles, Sewell. I spoke of something different—the direct intervention, by Divine permission, of the souls of the illustrious dead!"

I was silent. Philippe Roget was sitting up very straight and looking across at the sculptured figure of a woman in the centre of the square. The statue seemed to have taken on a sort of radiance in the translucent light of the summer evening.

"I was a sceptic when I started on that mission, Sewell," said Philippe, turning to me again. "But I arrived at my journey's end convinced that I had been used by an all-powerful Being for the salvation of France and the glory of God. I should like your permission to tell you about it."

This is what he told me:

Those last days in the Vosges were terrible ones for us. We had gone forward with so much confidence, not knowing that the utmost valour is impotent against machine-guns and high-powered modern artillery. A third of our army had been killed. The bodies strewed the earth everywhere. The Germans were closing in on us, and a reconnaissance by the cavalry showed that the enemy had cut off all our roads of retreat.

In that expedition the flower of our horsemen were mowed down by hidden machine-guns. It was not war, it was massacre!

There were only six of us aviators with the army corps, for nobody had guessed the part that airplanes were destined to play. Three of our fliers, venturing too low, had been shot down by German cannon. A fourth had lost his life in combat with a whole squadron of Taubes. There remained only myself and another, and it was we whom the General summoned to him that day.

"You are to fly to French Headquarters with dispatches, Captain Roget," he said to me. "Lieutenant Arnault, with his plane, will accompany you. His mission will be to protect you against the attacks of hostile aircraft. He will sacrifice his life to that end, if necessary. But you yourself will avoid all action, if possible; and if he is shot down, you will make no attempt to avenge him."

"*Bien, mon Général*," I answered. It was all a part of the game of war, and one had to obey.

"We do not know where Joffre's headquarters are, but you will fly to——" He then gave me detailed instructions. "These dispatches will inform him that we are cut off by a force seven times our superior. Furthermore, they will make it clear to him that the main German thrust is coming in this direction, and that the enemy are overwhelmingly strong. If these dispatches do not reach Joffre, he cannot learn the enemy's strategical position—until it is too late.

"I wish it might be possible for you to wait until night, but every hour's delay makes our position more dangerous." The General handed me the package. "If you are shot down, let your last act be to destroy these papers. I have given you the gist of the information they contain, so that, if you yourself manage to escape, you can transmit it to the commander-in-chief. That is all, gentlemen. You will start immediately."

Lieutenant Arnault and I saluted, and left the office. There was no tarmac, not even a level field for taking off. All that was to come later in the War. We had just three mechanics, and as quickly as possible they got our two Nieuports into flying condition. The Anzani engines were tuned up till they were warm and the tanks filled to the brim with petrol. At last we were off, rising above the field of battle.

What a field! At a height of five thousand feet we first began to see the disposition of the enemy forces. They were all around us. Puffs of white smoke showed where the ring of artillery was closing in. Here were hastily dug trenches, with swaths of dead lying before them. There we could see where the battle was still in progress; long lines of lorries traversed the roads, with the German shells bursting beside them; and columns of soldiers, wearing the blue tunics and red trousers of those early days, were moving forward.

Almost immediately we saw four Taubes rising from somewhere along the German lines and making toward us.

The Nieuport was at that time reputed the fastest plane in the air, and we had a good chance of outflying our opponents. Though we were both burning with eagerness to turn and fight, the recollections of our instructions restrained us. I headed my machine westward, and Lieutenant Arnault took up his flying position behind and above me, ready to protect me.

I let the enemy overhaul us slightly, confident in the flying powers of my machine. Meanwhile I let the engine warm up to the limit; then I opened the throttle to the full extent and rushed on. Two minutes later I looked back and saw that we had increased our lead over the Taubes. There was nothing to fear. I laughed exultantly. We were safe now.

But not for long! Two minutes later three black dots appeared out of the clouds a mile ahead of us. They came down in a swift glide, and I saw the hated stripes and crosses of the Germans on their fuselages as the sun glinted on them.

We were cut off; but now we were two to three. Our Nieuports were among the first French planes to be equipped with machine-guns and if we had to fight, we would be able to give a very good account of ourselves.

As the two foremost Taubes shot toward us, Arnault rushed past me overhead and engaged in a brisk machine-gun duel with them. Firing at pointblank range, it was almost impossible for anyone to miss. I shouted as I saw one of the Germans side-slip, and then go weaving down in a steep nose-dive that ended on the ground nearly two miles beneath.

The next instant flames burst from Lieutenant Arnault's motor. I saw him frantically leaning forward in the cockpit; then, to my horror, the flames leaped toward him.

His end was only a matter of moments now, but he sat there, still working the controls, while the Nieuport seemed to stagger in the air like a wounded bird, and then, nosing down, followed the German to destruction.

The Taube that had shot Arnault down followed, still pouring lead into its doomed victim. I do not blame the German. Those were the instructions that the airmen of both sides received, although many of us French and you Americans refused to fire upon a stricken enemy. I saw poor Arnault fling up his hand in a last gesture of defeat.

Then a wonderful thing happened. The upward rush of air drove the flames away from my comrade, so that they streamed up behind the descending plane like a comet's tail. Suddenly I saw Arnault raise his gun and aim straight into the fuselage of his pursuer, who, thinking him done for, had swooped perilously close. Fearfully burned, and doubtless riddled with lead, Arnault had proved himself a true soldier of France.

The pilot of the second plane slumped in the cockpit. The Taube dropped sidewise, and began nose-diving after the Nieuport. I saw the two doomed ships weave their headlong course downward until they disappeared in the wake of the first one.

Arnault was dead, but he had taken two German planes with him, and he had died for me.

That was my thought as, mad for revenge, I swung to meet the third Taube, which was now swooping down upon me. I had been told to avoid a fight if possible, but it was no longer possible, and even had it been, I doubt whether I could have obeyed. There are some situations where the elemental human instinct takes command; and when a man's comrade has been killed almost at his side—well, that is one of them!

A shower of bullets cut holes in my left wing. I banked, and received another burst that shattered my windshield and swept half the instruments from the board.

Immelmann had not then invented the famous manoeuvre, but I made it, my friend—made it because I could see no other way to escape destruction. As that cursed Boche rode my tail and splintered rudder and elevators, I made a steep zoom upward and a wing-over turn that reversed the situation and brought him within my range.

One blast from my gun, and I had sent him to flaming hell!

The road was clear, but by this time the four Taubes that had started in pursuit of us were opening fire. So engrossed had I been with my last encounter that the first I was aware of them was when I felt a sharp sting in my arm and saw the blood running. I glanced back, and realized that I had no chance save in instant flight. I thought of nothing now save my precious dispatches.

The mad rage died in me. I shot forward with wide-open throttle, though not before a second bullet had scored its way through my shoulder. Ahead of me lay a heavy cloud-bank. I made it, shot through it, zoomed, and saw that my pursuers were hopelessly behind me. Beneath lay the heavy wooded and mountainous country of the Vosges. Somewhere on the other side were the French battle-lines, or perhaps more Germans—who knew?

I was losing blood fast; my head was dizzy; I knew that I could not keep on much longer. If I encountered another Taube, I was doomed, for my left arm was helpless, and it was all I could do to manipulate the controls. Fortunately it was well on in the afternoon, and the day was dying out in a drizzle of rain and fog which made the visibility poor.

Somewhere on the other side of those mountains—but I could not go on. I must land, rest and try to bandage my wounds. Otherwise I should never be able to reach French Headquarters.

Underneath me I saw a break in the forest. A little mountain village seemed to be nestling in a clearing; there was the spire of a tall church, rising into the air.

I circled, side-slipped, exerting all my will-power to prevent lapsing into unconsciousness. Somehow I succeeded in making the landing on a bumpy field not far from the church, with a fringe of forest between myself and the village, and with the plane still in serviceable condition.

I groped for my first-aid bandage, but instead, I must have fainted, for I knew nothing for some time thereafter.

It was the caressing touch of a soft hand upon my forehead that brought me back to consciousness. I opened my eyes and stared. A young girl was bending over me, her face transfigured with such infinite compassion that I could only marvel at its wondrous sweetness and serenity. Surprising, too, was the taste of some cordial on my lips.

I looked about me. I was sitting with my back against the fuselage of the plane, which lay at the extreme edge of the woods, hidden from observation by a tall hedge which offered an effective barrier to any one passing along the road near the church. It almost seemed to me that the girl must have wheeled the machine into that position, for I had come down out in the open.

I looked at my companion again. It was dusk and I could just make out that she was dressed in some sort of peasant costume. She was not a peasant type, however, but looked rather like the daughter of some small landed proprietor in the vicinity.

"You are safe here," she whispered, as I opened my lips to speak, "but you must be careful. The Germans are in possession of the village beyond that strip of trees. Fortunately they feel entirely secure and it is not likely that the noise of your motor—if they heard it at all—has caused any alarm."

I groaned. The invaders must have penetrated very far into the heart of France.

As if she understood what was passing in my mind, the girl smiled.

"France has been invaded many times before," she said, "but she has always conquered in the end. Have no fear! The Boche will meet with a terrible blow that will send him reeling back to the Rhine. But ah, my poor country!"

She pressed her hand to her heart, and her face was the picture of grief as she spoke. All the woes of my poor country seemed mirrored there.

I was feeling much stronger, and looking down, I saw that my wounds had been bandaged. As the cordial the girl had given me began to take effect, life coursed through me again and I thought at once of my dispatches.

"I owe you a thousand thanks, Mademoiselle," I said. "But now I must get on. I am bearing important dispatches for General Joffre. I have lost too much time already. Do you know how far the German lines extend?"

"Far into the heart of France," she answered. "The outposts are at Vitry."

"But that is a hundred miles away!" I cried.

"The Boche has advanced fast. But have courage, my friend. Five miles beyond Vitry you will find the French outposts, and twelve miles back of there, at Villerons-sur-Yser, General Joffre sleeps tonight."

"How do you know?" I cried.

She smiled sadly.

"The Boches in our village are indiscreet," she answered. "They think we poor peasants are too simple to understand them, especially when they speak their own language. This is the headquarters of an army corps, and little goes on here that is unknown to us. Also, we have means of communicating with our friends."

"I thank you a thousand times, Mademoiselle," I answered. "Now I must be getting on."

But I stopped, frozen with horror, for at that moment I heard the tramp of feet, a sharp, gut-tural command—and then I saw a whole company of German soldiers emerge from the forest and move along the road in marching order.

I made a quick movement toward the plane. My first impulse was to try to start it before the column was upon us, though I knew beforehand the futility of such an attempt.

But the girl restrained me. Laying a gentle hand upon my arm, she seemed to arrest all my powers of movement.

Paralyzed with fear for my beloved country, I could only stand there beside her, watching those men in the hated uniform moving, moving toward us. The road ran close beside the hedge of furze, and it was not so dark but that they were bound to see us, when they turned their eyes in our direction.

Tramp, tramp! At least we might have lain down, grovelled on the earth, hoping thus to escape notice. But the girl stood proudly erect, her sensitive nostrils dilating with scorn as she watched the invaders. And, even though the paralysis that had momentarily gripped my muscles had passed away—even though everything was at stake—*I could not crouch.*

I, a French soldier, could not grovel on the ground to escape the notice of those arrogant invaders, marching, marching on, their feet making heavy contact with the earth, the metal parts of their equipment clanking as they moved. And so I waited for death, too proud to hide or run.

The Germans were only a few feet away, on the opposite side of the hedge, and still we two stood there. The girl's hands were clenched, and her face now bore a look of inspired scorn, almost as if she had been some ancient prophetess.

Then from the trees appeared the form of an officer on horseback. He took up his position in advance of the column, on the side nearer to us—so near that scarcely six feet separated us from him. I gripped my pistol, and, as I did so, my companion turned her face and looked at me. She smiled and shook her head ever so little.

The officer was abreast of us—merciful heaven, he was almost near enough to touch the girl!

Then the man turned his face, and I saw his eyes meet my companion's.

He did not see her!

I saw him shiver and glare wildly about him, as his horse reared and snorted. He shouted and brought his whip down heavily upon the animal's shoulders. It broke into a mad gallop, and so man and horse passed us, the man pulling at the reins and swearing, and the horse a-quiver, as if terrified by something more than the lash.

Tramp, tramp! The company was passing us. It was passing out of sight along the road. I looked at my companion. That gentle smile was on her lips again, and her eyes were raised to heaven.

Then, for the first time, a feeling of superstitious awe overcame me. Sceptic though I was, I wondered whether the girl had not invoked some divine power that had protected us.

I trembled. The reaction from our imminent danger almost unnerved me. I had feared for my companion, no less than for myself. I knew that, had she been discovered, she would have been shot, along with probably half her village.

She laid her hand upon my shoulder, and its caressing touch seemed to calm me.

"Yes, you must go, soldier of France," she said. "But before you go, let us pray, here in the shadow of that great church yonder. It is a famous shrine, where many miraculous things have happened. Will you join your prayers with mine, for France?"

Looking into her clear eyes, I could not lie to her.

"Mademoiselle," I stammered, "I must tell you—I am an unbeliever. That will shock you terribly——"

"No, Monsieur, it does not shock me at all," she answered, though there was a wistful look on her face. "I know that many men, and women too, no longer believe. But Our Lord does not despise those who stumble helplessly in the darkness. One day He will bring them all to Himself. And——" Here her voice rang out like a silver flute, with astonishing force and rhythm, "He will work wonderful things for our beloved France. The invader shall be hurled back and brought low in the dust!

"Pray with me, soldier," she said softly.

I knelt beside her on the damp meadow, and repeated the words that came from her lips. Simple and eloquent they were. A prayer that God would show His mercies to our beloved country, that right should triumph, that the dreadful flow of blood should cease as soon as His wrath was satisfied. . . .

And then she prayed for me—prayed that I might come safe through all the perils of the war, and that I should be led to acknowledge Him as the author of my being, and my salvation.

I confess my eyes were wet when we stood up. Something was stirring in me. I, who had hitherto scoffed at things spiritual, felt that a gate had been opened in me somewhere, that I was stumbling out of darkness into sunshine.

"Now, soldier!" said the girl.

I took her hands in mine.

"Mademoiselle, will you not tell me your name," I asked, "so that, after the war is ended, I may find you again and thank you for your heroism? I shall mention it to General Joffre. Your name, please, and that of this village?"

That tremulous, faint smile played about her lips again.

"Monsieur, the praise of men means little," she answered. "You will know me some day. But not—now. It is better that I should not answer your questions. Farewell, Monsieur."

Her hands hovered above my head like a benediction. Then, with a new strength, as though my wounds did not exist, I leaped into the cockpit. The girl's white fingers touched the propeller and the engine started with a roar. The next instant she was no longer there.

Dark though it had grown, I still could not believe that she had run from me. I should have seen her go. . . . No, she had vanished utterly.

I knew then—yes, I *knew* that she had been a spirit of good, sent by the Heavenly Powers to help a poor, wounded soldier, and to save France. All my scepticism fell from me. I uttered a silent prayer, asking forgiveness for my past doubts.

In a minute or two I opened the throttle wide enough to send the wheels over the furrows that acted as chocks. I taxied the length of the field, and took the air just as two German sentries came running out of the wood, shouting hoarse challenges.

I shouted back above the roaring motor, heard the snap of their rifles and felt a bullet fan my face. Then I was soaring high above the tree-tops and winging my way toward Vitry.

Late that night I descended at the headquarters of General Joffre. I had flown unmolested over regions infested by the invaders. I had seen squadrons of hostile planes aloft, but they must have thought it impossible that I could be an enemy, so far from my own base, for they had paid no attention to me.

I had flown high above belching cannon, over battlefields where Boche and Frenchman still contested in bitter frenzy. And so, at last, I had dropped miraculously at Villerons-sur-Yser.

Miraculously, I say, for, flying in the night, I had had nothing to guide me except the consciousness that I was not alone. Yes, even up there in the air I had had the sense of guidance.

Some unknown power seemed to direct my flight and a few minutes after I landed, I was standing in the presence of Joffre. He took my dispatches and read them.

His self-command was superb, for it would have been impossible for any Frenchman to have read those dispatches unmoved. They told him of a peril he had not suspected, and of the destruction of a part of his army; but they showed him the way to that concentration that was to save France at the Battle of the Marne.

He held an anxious discussion with his staff, seeming to have forgotten me. Unheeded, I stood there while messages were sent over the telephone, and motor cyclists went thundering off through the night. The feeling of strength that had sustained me had disappeared, now that my task was done, and I was feeling desperately weak.

Suddenly I grew aware that Joffre was speaking to me, and with an effort I stood upright at attention.

"You have been wounded, Captain Roget? You must go to the hospital and receive attention at once. Your deed shall not be forgotten."

That was almost the last thing that I remembered. I must have collapsed, for I was only dimly conscious of being placed in an ambulance, of jolting mile after mile that night, and the next day, and the next night.

But afterward, when I opened my eyes to full consciousness again, to find myself a cripple (Philippe touched his empty sleeve), it was to receive the news of the glorious victory of the Marne.

My delivery of those dispatches had saved France, and I was not forgotten, as Joffre had promised.

But I could not accept praise for myself alone. I wanted to render homage to my protector, whether spirit or human. And that, strangely enough, was the most difficult thing in the world to do.

You see, all this time I had been wavering between two convictions. However sure I had been of the girl's actual presence, I could not help believing at times that I must have been the victim of an hallucination due to my wounds. Nevertheless, I was convinced that the girl's existence had not been a dream. I *had* seen her beyond doubt.

But to tell the highly sceptical French officers that I had been saved by a spirit would have been simply to invite ridicule. And, if the girl had been human, I did not know her name, nor the name of her village.

In time I became friendly with old Colonel Chabot, the commander of the hospital. To him I spoke of the affair, and of my perplexities. He was a sincerely religious man, graver than the ordinary type of soldier, and he heard my story in sympathetic silence.

"Never mind the girl for the moment, my dear Roget," he said finally. "This village—can you not describe it?"

"Impossible," I answered. "You see, it was

dark, and it was hidden from me by the belt of trees. All I saw was the church."

"Ah, yes, the church! Can you describe this church, then?"

I had thought that I had taken little enough notice of the church, but now, of a sudden, the whole appearance of it came back into my mind. I described it to him in detail; it was almost as if I was being prompted in what I said.

Chabot interrupted me to ask numerous questions, growing more and more excited the while. Suddenly he clapped me on the shoulder.

"Enough, my boy, enough!" he exclaimed. "Tell that to your priest—tell it to those who have the wit to understand, but do not tell it to the Government—not now!"

"But—but—what do you mean?" I stammered.

"I mean——" Coolly and quietly old Chabot explained the miracle.

That was the story that I gleaned from my erstwhile war comrade, Captain Philippe Roget, at the little café opposite the statue in the square in Rouen. But what Chabot had told him he did not explain to me.

"I shall show you in a few moments, my dear Sewell," said Philippe. "Come, let us settle our bill, for it is growing late, and, as I told you, I have an appointment with a lady."

"And I am willing to hazard," I answered, "that the lady is the girl who saved you from the Boches in that unknown village. I'll wager she turned out to be no spirit, but a girl of flesh and blood, who slipped away from you in the darkness, once her mission was done.

"And further," I added, warming up to my theme, and feeling the romance of it, "she was probably a lady of gentle breeding, who had somehow become entrapped in this village of the Vosges, and, fearing to disclose her rank to the Germans, had lived there when they occupied the town, in the guise of a peasant, helping her country in that way."

Philippe Roget smiled, an enigmatical smile that conveyed the impression that I was very wide of the mark. We settled the bill, and then he turned to me.

"Would you like to meet this lady of mine?" he asked, taking up his roses.

"With all my heart," I answered. "I am sure she is in every way worthy of the homage you have paid her. And I hope that the day is not far distant when your loyalty will be rewarded."

"You are very dense, my dear Sewell," was all that Philippe answered.

With the roses in his right hand, he motioned me to join him, and together we walked forth into the softness of the May evening. The old houses about the square loomed up picturesquely in the twilight. I was thinking of the many famous persons who had lived in Rouen, of the stirring part the quaint town had played in history. The very air about us seemed astir with romance. . . .

The square was nearly empty, but there were a few persons passing to and fro, and clustered around the statue there was a little group of people, some of whom were kneeling. A woman in the garb of mourning, her hands clasped, was praying aloud in a quavering voice, while the tears streamed down her cheeks.

As we drew nearer, I saw a young girl approach, make a genuflexion, and lay a handful of wild flowers at the feet of the sculptured figure.

Then I saw that the statue was wreathed with roses, lilies, hothouse flowers, and that its base was heaped with floral offerings.

Captain Philippe Roget took off his hat, and mechanically I did the same. Then, to my astonishment—for I had not yet guessed what his purpose was—he fell upon his knees, and reverently placed the spray of roses upon the base of the statue. His lips moved in prayer.

I stood there, watching him, and of a sudden the truth dawned upon me with almost blinding clarity. I watched in amazement, and I looked up at the noble face of the young girl chiselled in stone. I knew.

Philippe Roget rose to his feet.

"That village I spoke of," he said, "was named Domrémy."

And this was May 30th—the day on which the English had burned Joan of Domrémy as a sorceress, on this very site—the Rouen market-place—almost five hundred years before.

"You understand?" whispered Philippe to me.

"I understand," I answered in a low voice.

"They call her the Guide of France," he said quietly. "I believe that it was she who came to me in the hour of my country's gravest peril, to save France through me—and to save my soul."

And to that I was silent.

Olivia Howard Dunbar

OF THE MANY CAUSES of which Olivia Howard Dunbar (1873–1953) became an advocate, most were of a liberal bent, notably her support of women's suffrage, her benign attitude toward lesbianism and single-sex couples embracing motherhood, and, along with her husband, Ridgeley Torrence, the poetry editor of *The New Republic*, her involvement with black rights. She was also a powerful voice for ghost stories, especially those written by women.

Born in West Bridgewater, Massachusetts, she received a B.A. from Smith College and moved to New York City in 1896 to become an editor at the New York *World*. She resigned six years later to become a prolific freelance writer of short stories and articles for such publications as *Lippincott's, Harper's, The Century, Scribner's,* and other leading periodicals of the day. She married Torrence in 1914 and the couple became popular and influential members of the literary community of the city. Dunbar's attitude toward ghost stories, outlined in a piece she wrote for *The Dial* in 1905 calling for a renaissance of the genre, was that they should deviate from the M. R. James school of slowly unfolding tales of old scholars and antiquarians in dark churches and libraries and instead involve women and children in more naturalistic literature. Among her most enduring works are "The Long Chamber," in which a clearly superior woman subjugates herself to her husband, "The Dream-Baby," which tacitly accepts a lesbian couple, and "The Sycamore," in which a young woman lives mainly to support her husband's career.

"The Shell of Sense" was originally published in the December 1908 issue of *Harper's Magazine*.

The Shell of Sense

OLIVIA HOWARD DUNBAR

IT WAS INTOLERABLY UNCHANGED, the dim, dark-toned room. In an agony of recognition my glance ran from one to another of the comfortable, familiar things that my earthly life had been passed among. Incredibly distant from it all as I essentially was, I noted sharply that the very gaps that I myself had left in my bookshelves still stood unfilled; that the delicate fingers of the ferns that I had tended were still stretched futilely toward the light; that the soft agreeable chuckle of my own little clock, like some elderly woman with whom conversation has become automatic, was undiminished.

Unchanged—or so it seemed at first. But there were certain trivial differences that shortly smote me. The windows were closed too tightly;

for I had always kept the house very cool, although I had known that Theresa preferred warm rooms. And my work-basket was in disorder; it was preposterous that so small a thing should hurt me so. Then, for this was my first experience of the shadow-folded transition, the odd alteration of my emotions bewildered me. For at one moment the place seemed so humanly familiar, so distinctly my own proper envelope, that for love of it I could have laid my cheek against the wall; while in the next I was miserably conscious of strange new shrillnesses. How could they be endured—and had I ever endured them?—those harsh influences that I now perceived at the window; light and color so blinding that they obscured the form of the wind, tumult so discordant that one could scarcely hear the roses open in the garden below?

But Theresa did not seem to mind any of these things. Disorder, it is true, the dear child had never minded. She was sitting all this time at my desk—at *my* desk—occupied, I could only too easily surmise how. In the light of my own habits of precision it was plain that that sombre correspondence should have been attended to before; but I believe that I did not really reproach Theresa, for I knew that her notes, when she did write them, were perhaps less perfunctory than mine. She finished the last one as I watched her, and added it to the heap of black-bordered envelopes that lay on the desk. Poor girl! I saw now that they had cost her tears. Yet, living beside her day after day, year after year, I had never discovered what deep tenderness my sister possessed. Toward each other it had been our habit to display only a temperate affection, and I remember having always thought it distinctly fortunate for Theresa, since she was denied my happiness, that she could live so easily and pleasantly without emotions of the devastating sort. . . . And now, for the first time, I was really to behold her. . . . Could it be Theresa, after all, this tangle of subdued turbulences? Let no one suppose that it is an easy thing to bear, the relentlessly lucid understanding that I then first exercised; or that,

in its first enfranchisement, the timid vision does not yearn for its old screens and mists.

Suddenly, as Theresa sat there, her head, filled with its tender thoughts of me, held in her gentle hands, I felt Allan's step on the carpeted stair outside. Theresa felt it, too,—but how? for it was not audible. She gave a start, swept the black envelopes out of sight, and pretended to be writing in a little book. Then I forgot to watch her any longer in my absorption in Allan's coming. It was he, of course, that I was awaiting. It was for him that I had made this first lonely, frightened effort to return, to recover. . . . It was not that I had supposed he would allow himself to recognize my presence, for I had long been sufficiently familiar with his hard and fast denials of the invisible. He was so reasonable always, so sane—so blindfolded. But I had hoped that because of his very rejection of the ether that now contained me I could perhaps all the more safely, the more secretly, watch him, linger near him. He was near now, very near—but why did Theresa, sitting there in the room that had never belonged to her, appropriate for herself his coming? It was so manifestly I who had drawn him, I whom he had come to seek.

The door was ajar. He knocked softly at it. "Are you there, Theresa?" he called. He expected to find her, then, there in my room? I shrank back, fearing, almost, to stay.

"I shall have finished in a moment," Theresa told him, and he sat down to wait for her.

No spirit still unreleased can understand the pang that I felt with Allan sitting almost within my touch. Almost irresistibly the wish beset me to let him for an instant feel my nearness. Then I checked myself, remembering—oh, absurd, piteous human fears!—that my too unguarded closeness might alarm him. It was not so remote a time that I myself had known them, those blind, uncouth timidities. I came, therefore, somewhat nearer—but I did not touch him. I merely leaned toward him and with incredible softness whispered his name. That much I could not have forborne; the spell of life was still too strong in me.

But it gave him no comfort, no delight. "Theresa!" he called, in a voice dreadful with alarm—and in that instant the last veil fell, and desperately, scarce believingly, I beheld how it stood between them, those two.

She turned to him that gentle look of hers.

"Forgive me," came from him hoarsely. "But I had suddenly the most—unaccountable sensation. Can there be too many windows open? There is such a—chill—about."

"There are no windows open," Theresa assured him. "I took care to shut out the chill. You are not well, Allan!"

"Perhaps not." He embraced the suggestion. "And yet I feel no illness apart from this abominable sensation that persists—persists. . . . Theresa, you must tell me: do I fancy it, or do you, too, feel—something—strange here?"

"Oh, there is something very strange here," she half sobbed. "There always will be."

"Good heavens, child, I didn't mean that!" He rose and stood looking about him. "I know, of course, that you have your beliefs, and I respect them, but you know equally well that I have nothing of the sort! So—don't let us conjure up anything inexplicable."

I stayed impalpably, imponderably near him. Wretched and bereft though I was, I could not have left him while he stood denying me.

"What I mean," he went on, in his low, distinct voice, "is a special, an almost ominous sense of cold. Upon my soul, Theresa,"—he paused—"if I *were* superstitious, if I *were* a woman, I should probably imagine it to seem—a presence!"

He spoke the last word very faintly, but Theresa shrank from it nevertheless.

"*Don't* say that, Allan!" she cried out. "Don't think it, I beg of you! I've tried so hard myself not to think it—and you must help me. You know it is only perturbed, uneasy spirits that wander. With her it is quite different. She has always been so happy—she must still be."

I listened, stunned, to Theresa's sweet dogmatism. From what blind distances came her confident misapprehensions, how dense, both for her and for Allan, was the separating vapor!

Allan frowned. "Don't take me literally, Theresa," he explained; and I, who a moment before had almost touched him, now held myself aloof and heard him with a strange untried pity, new born in me. "I'm not speaking of what you call—spirits. It's something much more terrible." He allowed his head to sink heavily on his chest. "If I did not positively know that I had never done her any harm, I should suppose myself to be suffering from guilt, from remorse. . . . Theresa, you know better than I, perhaps. Was she content, always? Did she believe in me?"

"Believe in you?—when she knew you to be so good!—when you adored her!"

"She thought that? She said it? Then what in Heaven's name ails me?—unless it is all as you believe, Theresa, and she knows now what she didn't know then, poor dear, and minds——"

"Minds what? What do you mean, Allan?"

I, who with my perhaps illegitimate advantage saw so clear, knew that he had not meant to tell her: I did him that justice, even in my first jealousy. If I had not tortured him so by clinging near him, he would not have told her. But the moment came, and overflowed, and he did tell her—passionate, tumultuous story that it was. During all our life together, Allan's and mine, he had spared me, had kept me wrapped in the white cloak of an unblemished loyalty. But it would have been kinder, I now bitterly thought, if, like many husbands, he had years ago found for the story he now poured forth some clandestine listener; I should not have known. But he was faithful and good, and so he waited till I, mute and chained, was there to hear him. So well did I know him, as I thought, so thoroughly had he once been mine, that I saw it in his eyes, heard it in his voice, before the words came. And yet, when it came, it lashed me with the whips of an unbearable humiliation. For I, his wife, had not known how greatly he could love.

And that Theresa, soft little traitor, should, in her still way, have cared too! Where was the iron in her, I moaned within my stricken spirit, where the steadfastness? From the moment he bade her, she turned her soft little petals up to him—and my last delusion was spent. It was intolerable; and none the less so that in another moment she had, prompted by some belated thought of me, renounced him. Allan was hers, yet she put him from her; and it was my part to watch them both.

Then in the anguish of it all I remembered, awkward, untutored spirit that I was, that I now had the Great Recourse. Whatever human things were unbearable, I had no need to bear. I ceased, therefore, to make the effort that kept me with them. The pitiless poignancy was dulled, the sounds and the light ceased, the lovers faded from me, and again I was mercifully drawn into the dim, infinite spaces.

There followed a period whose length I cannot measure and during which I was able to make no progress in the difficult, dizzying experience of release. "Earth-bound" my jealousy relentlessly kept me. Though my two dear ones had forsworn each other, I could not trust them, for theirs seemed to me an affectation of a more than mortal magnanimity. Without a ghostly sentinel to prick them with sharp fears and recollections, who could believe that they would keep to it? Of the efficacy of my own vigilance, so long as I might choose to exercise it, I could have no doubt, for I had by this time come to have a dreadful exultation in the new power that lived in me. Repeated delicate experiment had taught me how a touch or a breath, a wish or a whisper, could control Allan's acts, could keep him from Theresa. I could manifest myself as palely, as transiently, as a thought. I could produce the merest necessary flicker, like the shadow of a just-opened leaf, on his trembling, tortured consciousness. And these unrealized perceptions of me he interpreted, as I had known that he would, as his soul's inevitable penance. He had come to believe that he had done evil in silently loving

Theresa all these years, and it was my vengeance to allow him to believe this, to prod him ever to believe it afresh.

I am conscious that this frame of mind was not continuous in me. For I remember, too, that when Allan and Theresa were safely apart and sufficiently miserable I loved them as dearly as I ever had, more dearly perhaps. For it was impossible that I should not perceive, in my new emancipation, that they were, each of them, something more and greater than the two beings I had once ignorantly pictured them. For years they had practiced a selflessness of which I could once scarcely have conceived, and which even now I could only admire without entering into its mystery. While I had lived solely for myself, these two divine creatures had lived exquisitely for me. They had granted me everything, themselves nothing. For my undeserving sake their lives had been a constant torment of renunciation—a torment they had not sought to alleviate by the exchange of a single glance of understanding. There were even marvelous moments when, from the depths of my newly informed heart, I pitied them—poor creatures, who, withheld from the infinite solaces that I had come to know, were still utterly within that

Shell of sense
So frail, so piteously contrived for pain.

Within it, yes; yet exercising qualities that so sublimely transcended it. Yet the shy, hesitating compassion that thus had birth in me was far from being able to defeat the earlier, earthlier emotion. The two, I recognized, were in a sort of conflict; and I, regarding it, assumed that the conflict would never end; that for years, as Allan and Theresa reckoned time, I should be obliged to withhold myself from the great spaces and linger suffering, grudging, shamed, where they lingered.

It can never have been explained, I suppose, what, to devitalized perception such as mine, the contact of mortal beings with each other appears to be. Once to have exercised this sense-freed perception is to realize that the gift of prophecy, although the subject of such frequent marvel, is no longer mysterious. The merest glance of our sensitive and uncloyed vision can detect the strength of the relation between two beings, and therefore instantly calculate its duration. If you see a heavy weight suspended from a slender string, you can know, without any wizardry, that in a few moments the string will snap; well, such, if you admit the analogy, is prophecy, is foreknowledge. And it was thus that I saw it with Theresa and Allan. For it was perfectly visible to me that they would very little longer have the strength to preserve, near each other, the denuded impersonal relation that they, and that I, behind them, insisted on; and that they would have to separate. It was my sister, perhaps the more sensitive, who first realized this. It had now become possible for me to observe them almost constantly, the effort necessary to visit them had so greatly diminished; so that I watched her, poor, anguished girl, prepare to leave him. I saw each reluctant movement that she made. I saw her eyes, worn from self-searching; I heard her step grown timid from inexplicable fears; I entered her very heart and heard its pitiful, wild beating. And still I did not interfere.

For at this time I had a wonderful, almost demoniacal sense of disposing of matters to suit my own selfish will. At any moment I could have checked their miseries, could have restored happiness and peace. Yet it gave me, and I could weep to admit it, a monstrous joy to know that Theresa thought she was leaving Allan of her own free intention, when it was I who was contriving, arranging, insisting. . . . And yet she wretchedly felt my presence near her; I am certain of that.

A few days before the time of her intended departure my sister told Allan that she must speak with him after dinner. Our beautiful old house branched out from a circular hall with great arched doors at either end; and it was through the rear doorway that always in sum-

mer, after dinner, we passed out into the garden adjoining. As usual, therefore, when the hour came, Theresa led the way. That dreadful daytime brilliance that in my present state I found so hard to endure was now becoming softer. A delicate, capricious twilight breeze danced inconsequently through languidly whispering leaves. Lovely pale flowers blossomed like little moons in the dusk, and over them the breath of mignonette hung heavily. It was a perfect place—and it had so long been ours, Allan's and mine. It made me restless and a little wicked that those two should be there together now.

For a little they walked about together, speaking of common, daily things. Then suddenly Theresa burst out:

"I am going away, Allan. I have stayed to do everything that needed to be done. Now your mother will be here to care for you, and it is time for me to go."

He stared at her and stood still. Theresa had been there so long, she so definitely, to his mind, belonged there. And she was, as I also had jealously known, so lovely there, the small, dark, dainty creature, in the old hall, on the wide staircases, in the garden. . . . Life there without Theresa, even the intentionally remote, the perpetually renounced Theresa—he had not dreamed of it, he could not, so suddenly, conceive of it.

"Sit here," he said, and drew her down beside him on a bench, "and tell me what it means, why you are going. Is it because of something that I have been—have done?"

She hesitated. I wondered if she would dare tell him. She looked out and away from him, and he waited long for her to speak.

The pale stars were sliding into their places. The whispering of the leaves was almost hushed. All about them it was still and shadowy and sweet. It was that wonderful moment when, for lack of a visible horizon, the not yet darkened world seems infinitely greater—a moment when anything can happen, anything be believed in. To me, watching, listening, hovering, there came a dreadful purpose and a dreadful courage. Suppose for one moment, Theresa should not only feel, but *see* me—would she dare to tell him then?

There came a brief space of terrible effort, all my fluttering, uncertain forces strained to the utmost. The instant of my struggle was endlessly long and the transition seemed to take place outside me—as one sitting in a train, motionless, sees the leagues of earth float by. And then, in a bright, terrible flash I knew I had achieved it—I had *attained visibility*. Shuddering, insubstantial, but luminously apparent, I stood there before them. And for the instant that I maintained the visible state I looked straight into Theresa's soul.

She gave a cry. And then, thing of silly, cruel impulses that I was, I saw what I had done. The very thing that I wished to avert I had precipitated. For Allan, in his sudden terror and pity, had bent and caught her in his arms. For the first time they were together; and it was I who had brought them.

Then, to his whispered urging to tell the reason of her cry, Theresa said:

"Frances was here. You did not see her, standing there, under the lilacs, with no smile on her face?"

"My dear, my dear!" was all that Allan said. I had so long now lived invisibly with them, he knew that she was right.

"I suppose you know what it means?" she asked him, calmly.

"Dear Theresa," Allan said, slowly, "if you and I should go away somewhere, could we not evade all this ghostliness? And will you come with me?"

"Distance would not banish her," my sister confidently asserted. And then she said, softly: "Have you thought what a lonely, awesome thing it must be to be so newly dead? Pity her, Allan. We who are warm and alive should pity her. She loves you still—that is the meaning of it all, you know—and she wants us to understand that for that reason we must keep apart. Oh, it was so plain in her white face as she stood there. And you did not see her?"

"It was your face that I saw," Allan solemnly

told her—oh, how different he had grown from the Allan that I had known!—"and yours is the only face that I shall ever see." And again he drew her to him.

She sprang from him. "You are defying her, Allan!" she cried. "And you must not. It is her right to keep us apart, if she wishes. It must be as she insists. I shall go, as I told you. And, Allan, I beg of you, leave me the courage to do as she demands!"

They stood facing each other in the deep dusk, and the wounds that I had dealt them gaped red and accusing. "We must pity her," Theresa had said. And as I remembered that extraordinary speech, and saw the agony in her face, and the greater agony in Allan's, there came the great irreparable cleavage between mortality and me. In a swift, merciful flame the last of my mortal emotions—gross and tenacious they must have been—was consumed. My cold grasp of Allan loosened and a new unearthly love of him bloomed in my heart.

I was now, however, in a difficulty with which my experience in the newer state was scarcely sufficient to deal. How could I make it plain to Allan and Theresa that I wished to bring them together, to heal the wounds that I had made?

Pityingly, remorsefully, I lingered near them all that night and the next day. And by that time had brought myself to the point of a great determination. In the little time that was left, before Theresa should be gone and Allan bereft and desolate, I saw the one way that lay open to me to convince them of my acquiescence in their destiny.

In the deepest darkness and silence of the next night I made a greater effort than it will ever be necessary for me to make again. When they think of me, Allan and Theresa, I pray now that they will recall what I did that night, and that my thousand frustrations and selfishnesses may shrivel and be blown from their indulgent memories.

Yet the following morning, as she had planned, Theresa appeared at breakfast dressed for her journey. Above in her room there were the sounds of departure. They spoke little during the brief meal, but when it was ended Allan said:

"Theresa, there is half an hour before you go. Will you come upstairs with me? I had a dream that I must tell you of."

"Allan!" She looked at him, frightened, but went with him. "It was of Frances you dreamed," she said, quietly, as they entered the library together.

"Did I say it was a dream? But I was awake—thoroughly awake. I had not been sleeping well, and I heard, twice, the striking of the clock. And as I lay there, looking out at the stars, and thinking—thinking of you, Theresa—she came to me, stood there before me, in my room. It was no sheeted specter, you understand; it was Frances, literally she. In some inexplicable fashion I seemed to be aware that she wanted to make me know something, and I waited, watching her face. After a few moments it came. She did not speak, precisely. That is, I am sure I heard no sound. Yet the words that came from her were definite enough. She said: 'Don't let Theresa leave you. Take her and keep her.' Then she went away. Was that a dream?"

"I had not meant to tell you," Theresa eagerly answered, "but now I must. It is too wonderful. What time did your clock strike, Allan?"

"One, the last time."

"Yes; it was then that I awoke. And she had been with me. I had not seen her, but her arm had been about me and her kiss was on my cheek. Oh. I knew; it was unmistakable. And the sound of her voice was with me."

"Then she bade you, too——"

"Yes, to stay with you. I am glad we told each other." She smiled tearfully and began to fasten her wrap.

"But you are not going—*now!*" Allan cried. "You know that you cannot, now that she has asked you to stay."

"Then you believe, as I do, that it was she?" Theresa demanded.

"I can never understand, but I know," he answered her. "And now you will not go?"

I am freed. There will be no further semblance of me in my old home, no sound of my voice, no dimmest echo of my earthly self. They have no further need of me, the two that I have brought together. Theirs is the fullest joy that the dwellers in the shell of sense can know. Mine is the transcendent joy of the unseen spaces.

THE AVENGING OF ANN LEETE

Marjorie Bowen

AS THE AUTHOR OF more than one hundred fifty books and count-less short stories, Gabrielle Margaret Vere Long (née Campbell) (1886–1952) used numerous pseudonyms, writing mainly ghost stories as Marjorie Bowen. She was born to deeply poor parents on Hayling Island, Hampshire, a situation made worse when her father abandoned the family. To help assist her sister and profligate, unstable mother, she began to write and had her first novel published when she was only sixteen, immediately becoming the prime supporter of her small family. Her dark and unhappy early years led her to produce a plethora of fictional works with Gothic overtones. While many were hastily written potboil-ers, she often wrote finely crafted tales that remain highly readable and popu-lar today. Her seemingly inexhaustible imagination and smooth, accessible style made her popular with readers while also earning the praise of such significant critics of her time as Rebecca West, William Roughead, Graham Greene, and Will Cuppy.

"The Avenging of Ann Leete" was originally published in *Seeing Life! and Other Stories* (London, Hurst & Blackett, 1923; the collection was published in the United States two years later).

The Avenging of Ann Leete

MARJORIE BOWEN

THIS IS A QUEER story, the more queer for the interpretation of passions of strong human heat that has been put upon it, and for glimpses of other motives and doings, not, it would seem, human at all.

The whole thing is seen vaguely, brokenly, a snatch here and there; one tells the tale, strangely another exclaims amaze, a third points out a scene, a fourth has a dim memory of a circumstance, a nine-days' (or less) wonder, an old print helps, the name on a mural tablet in a deserted church pinches the heart with a sense of confirmation, and so you have your story. When all is said it remains a queer tale.

It is seventy years odd ago, so dating back from this present year of 1845 you come to nearly midway in the last century when conditions were vastly different from what they are now.

The scene is in Glasgow, and there are three points from which we start, all leading us to the heart of our tale.

The first is the portrait of a woman that hangs in the parlour of a respectable banker. He believes it to be the likeness of some connexion of his wife's, dead this many a year, but he does not know much about it. Some while ago it was discovered in a lumberroom, and he keeps it for the pallid beauty of the canvas, which is much faded and rubbed.

Since, as a young man, I first had the privilege of my worthy friend's acquaintance, I have always felt a strange interest in this picture; and, in that peculiar way that the imagination will seize on trifles, I was always fascinated by the dress of the lady. This is of dark-green very fine silk, an uncommon colour to use in a portrait, and, perhaps, in a lady's dress. It is very plain, with a little scarf of a striped Roman pattern, and her hair is drawn up over a pillow in the antique mode. Her face is expressionless, yet strange, the upper lip very thin, the lower very full, the light brown eyes set under brows that slant. I cannot tell why this picture was always to me full of such a great attraction, but I used to think of it a vast deal, and often to note, secretly, that never had I chanced to meet in real life, or in any other painting, a lady in a dark-green silk dress.

In the corner of the canvas is a little device, put in a diamond, as a gentlewoman might bear arms, yet with no pretensions to heraldry, just three little birds, the topmost with a flower in its beak.

It was not so long ago that I came upon the second clue that leads into the story, and that was a mural tablet in an old church near the Rutherglen Road, a church that has lately fallen into disrepute or neglect, for it was deserted and impoverished. But I was assured that a generation ago it had been a most famous place of worship, fashionable and well frequented by the better sort.

The mural tablet was to one "Ann Leete,"

and there was just the date (seventy-odd years old) given with what seemed a sinister brevity.

And underneath the lettering, lightly cut on the time-stained marble, was the same device as that on the portrait of the lady in the green silk dress.

I was curious enough to make inquiries, but no one seemed to know anything of, or wished to talk about, Ann Leete.

It was all so long ago, I was told, and there was no one now in the parish of the name of Leete.

And all who had been acquainted with the family of Leete seemed to be dead or gone away. The parish register (my curiosity went so far as an inspection of this) yielded me no more information than the mural tablet.

I spoke to my friend the banker, and he said he thought that his wife had had some cousins by the name of Leete, and that there was some tale of a scandal or great misfortune attached to them which was the reason of a sort of ban on their name so that it had never been mentioned.

When I told him I thought the portrait of the lady in the dark-green silk might picture a certain Ann Leete he appeared uneasy and even desirous of having the likeness removed, which roused in me the suspicion that he knew something of the name, and that not pleasant. But it seemed to me indelicate and perhaps useless to question him.

It was a year or so after this incident that my business, which was that of silversmith and jeweller, put into my hands a third clue. One of my apprentices came to me with a rare piece of work which had been left at the shop for repair.

It was a thin medal of the purest gold, on which was set in fresh-water pearls, rubies, and cairngorms the device of the three birds, the plumage being most skilfully wrought in the bright jewels and the flower held by the topmost creature accurately designed in pearls.

It was one of these pearls that was missing, and I had some difficulty in matching its soft lustre.

An elderly lady called for the ornament, the same person who had left it. I saw her myself, and ventured to admire and praise the workmanship of the medal.

"Oh," she said, "it was worked by a very famous jeweller, my great-uncle, and he has a peculiar regard for it—indeed I believe it has never before been out of his possession, but he was so greatly grieved by the loss of the pearl that he would not rest until I offered to take it to be repaired. He is, you will understand," she added, with a smile, "a very old man. He must have made that jewellery—why—seventy-odd years ago."

Seventy-odd years ago—that would bring one back to the date on the tablet to Ann Leete, to the period of the portrait.

"I have seen this device before," I remarked, "on the likeness of a lady and on the mural inscription in memory of a certain Ann Leete." Again this name appeared to make an unpleasant impression.

My customer took her packet hastily.

"It is associated with something dreadful," she said quickly. "We do not speak of it—a very old story. I did not know anyone had heard of it——"

"I certainly have not," I assured her. "I came to Glasgow not so long ago, as apprentice to this business of my uncle's which now I own."

"But you have seen a portrait?" she asked.

"Yes, in the house of a friend of mine."

"This is queer. We did not know that any existed. Yet my great-uncle does speak of one—in a green silk dress."

"In a green silk dress," I confirmed.

The lady appeared amazed.

"But it is better to let the matter rest," she decided. "My relative, you will realize, is very old—nearly, sir, a hundred years old, and his wits wander and he tells queer tales. It was all very strange and horrible, but one cannot tell how much my old uncle dreams."

"I should not think to disturb him," I replied.

But my customer hesitated.

"If you know of this portrait—perhaps he

should be told; he laments after it so much, and we have always believed it an hallucination——"

She returned the packet containing the medal.

"Perhaps," she added dubiously, "you are interested enough to take this back to my relative yourself and judge what you shall or shall not tell him?"

I eagerly accepted the offer, and the lady gave me the name and residence of the old man who, although possessed of considerable means, had lived for the past fifty years in the greatest seclusion in that lonely part of the town beyond the Rutherglen Road and near to the Green, the once pretty and fashionable resort for youth and pleasure, but now a deserted and desolate region. Here, on the first opportunity, I took my way, and found myself well out into the country, nearly at the river, before I reached the lonely mansion of Eneas Bretton, as the ancient jeweller was called.

A ferocious dog troubled my entrance in the dark overgrown garden where the black glossy laurels and bays strangled the few flowers, and a grim woman, in an old-fashioned mutch or cap, at length answered my repeated peals at the rusty chain bell.

It was not without considerable trouble that I was admitted into the presence of Mr. Bretton, and only, I think, by the display of the jewel and the refusal to give it into any hands but those of its owner.

The ancient jeweller was seated on a southern terrace that received the faint and fitful rays of the September sun. He was wrapped in shawls that disguised his natural form, and a fur and leather cap was fastened under his chin.

I had the impression that he had been a fine man, of a vigorous and handsome appearance; even now, in the extreme of decay, he showed a certain grandeur of line and carriage, a certain majestic power in his personality. Though extremely feeble, I did not take him to be imbecile nor greatly wanting in his faculties.

He received me courteously, though obviously ill-used to strangers.

I had, he said, a claim on him as a fellow craftsman, and he was good enough to commend the fashion in which I had repaired his medal.

This, as soon as he had unwrapped, he fastened to a fine gold chain he drew from his breast, and slipped inside his heavy clothing.

"A pretty trinket," I said, "and of an unusual design."

"I fashioned it myself," he answered, "over seventy years ago. The year before, sir, she died."

"Ann Leete?" I ventured.

The ancient man was not in the least surprised at the use of this name.

"It is a long time since I heard those words with any but my inner ear," he murmured; "to be sure, I grow very old. You'll not remember Ann Leete?" he added wistfully.

"I take it she died before I was born," I answered.

He peered at me.

"Ah, yes, you are still a young man, though your hair is grey."

I noticed now that he wore a small tartan scarf inside his coat and shawl; this fact gave me a peculiar, almost unpleasant shudder.

"I know this about Ann Leete—she had a dark-green silk dress. And a Roman or tartan scarf."

He touched the wisp of bright-coloured silk across his chest.

"This is it. She had her likeness taken so— but it was lost."

"It is preserved," I answered. "And I know where it is. I might, if you desired, bring you to a sight of it."

He turned his grand old face to me with a civil inclination of his massive head.

"That would be very courteous of you, sir, and a pleasure to me. You must not think," he added with dignity, "that the lady has forsaken me or that I do not often see her. Indeed, she comes to me more frequently than before. But it would delight me to have the painting of her to console the hours of her absence."

I reflected what his relative had said about the weakness of his wits, and recalled his great age, which one was apt to forget in face of his composure and reasonableness.

He appeared now to doze and to take no further notice of my presence, so I left him.

He had a strange look of lifelessness as he slumbered there in the faintest rays of the cloudy autumn sun.

I reflected how lightly the spirit must dwell in this ancient frame, how easily it must take flight into the past, how soon into eternity.

It did not cost me much persuasion to induce my friend, the banker, to lend me the portrait of Ann Leete, particularly as the canvas had been again sent up to the attics.

"Do *you* know the story?" I asked him.

He replied that he had heard something; that the case had made a great stir at the time; that it was all very confused and amazing, and that he did not desire to discuss the matter.

I hired a carriage and took the canvas to the house of Eneas Bretton.

He was again on the terrace, enjoying with a sort of calm eagerness the last warmth of the failing sun.

His two servants brought in the picture and placed it on a chair at his side.

He gazed at the painted face with the greatest serenity.

"That is she," he said, "but I am glad to think that she looks happier now, sir. She still wears that dark-green silk. I never see her in any other garment."

"A beautiful woman," I remarked quietly, not wishing to agitate or disturb his reflections, which were clearly detached from any considerations of time and space.

"I have always thought so," he answered gently, "but I, sir, have peculiar faculties. I saw her, and see her still as a spirit. I loved her as a spirit. Yet our bodily union was necessary for our complete happiness. And in that my darling and I were balked."

"By death?" I suggested, for I knew that the word had no terrors for him.

"By death," he agreed, "who will soon be forced to unite us again."

"But not in the body," I said.

"How, sir, do you know that?" he smiled. "We have but finite minds. I think we have but little conception of the marvellous future."

"Tell me," I urged, "how you lost Ann Leete."

His dim, heavy-lidded, many-wrinkled eyes flickered a glance over me.

"She was murdered," he said.

I could not forbear a shudder.

"That fragile girl!" I exclaimed. My blood had always run cool and thin, and I detested deeds of violence; my even mind could not grasp the idea of the murder of women save as a monstrous enormity.

I looked at the portrait, and it seemed to me that I had always known that it was the likeness of a creature doomed.

"Seventy years ago and more," continued Eneas Bretton, "since when she has wandered lonely betwixt time and eternity, waiting for me. But very soon I shall join her, and then, sir, we shall go where there is no recollection of the evil things of this earth."

By degrees he told me the story, not in any clear sequence, nor at any one time, nor without intervals of sleep and pauses of dreaming, nor without assistance from his servants and his great-niece and her husband, who were his frequent visitors.

Yet it was from his own lips and when we were alone together that I learned all that was really vital in the tale.

He required very frequent attendance; although all human passion was at the utmost ebb with him, he had, he said, a kind of regard for me in that I had brought him his lady's portrait, and he told me things of which he had never spoken to any human being before. I say human on purpose because of his intense belief that he was, and always had been, in communication with powers not of this earth.

In these words I put together his tale.

As a young man, said Eneas Bretton, I was healthy, prosperous, and happy.

My family had been goldsmiths as long as

there was any record of their existence, and I was an enthusiast in this craft, grave, withal, and studious, over-fond of books and meditation. I do not know how or when I first met Ann Leete.

To me she was always there like the sun; I think I have known her all my life, but perhaps my memory fails.

Her father was a lawyer and she an only child, and though her social station was considered superior to mine, I had far more in the way of worldly goods, so there was no earthly obstacle to our union.

The powers of evil, however, fought against us; I had feared this from the first, as our happiness was the complete circle ever hateful to fiends and devils who try to break the mystic symbol.

The mistress of my soul attracted the lustful attention of a young doctor, Rob Patterson, who had a certain false charm of person, not real comeliness, but a trick of colour, of carriage, and a fine taste in clothes.

His admiration was whetted by her coldness and his intense dislike of me.

We came to scenes in which he derided me as no gentleman, but a beggarly tradesman, and I scorned him as an idle voluptuary designing a woman's ruin for the crude pleasure of the gratification of fleeting passions.

For the fellow made not even any pretence of being able to support a wife, and was of that rake-helly temperament that made an open mock of matrimony.

Although he was but a medical student, he was of what they call noble birth, and his family, though decayed, possessed considerable social power, so that his bold pursuit of Ann Leete and his insolent flaunting of me had some licence, the more so that he did not lack tact and address in his manner and conduct.

Our marriage could have stopped this persecution, or given the right to publicly resent it, but my darling would not leave her father, who was of a melancholy and querulous disposition.

It was shortly before her twenty-first birthday, for which I had made her the jewel I now wear (the device being the crest of her mother's family and one for which she had a great affection), that her father died suddenly. His last thoughts were of her, for he had this very picture painted for her birthday gift. Finding herself thus unprotected and her affairs in some confusion, she declared her intention of retiring to some distant relative in the Highlands until decorum permitted of our marriage.

And upon my opposing myself to this scheme of separation and delay she was pleased to fall out with me, declaring that I was as importunate as Dr. Patterson, and that I, as well as he, should be kept in ignorance of her retreat.

I had, however, great hopes of inducing her to change this resolution, and, it being then fair spring weather, engaged her to walk with me on the Green, beyond the city, to discuss our future.

I was an orphan like herself, and we had now no common meeting-place suitable to her reputation and my respect.

By reason of a pressure of work, to which by temperament and training I was ever attentive, I was a few moments late at the tryst on the Green, which I found, as usual, empty; but it was a lovely afternoon of May, very still and serene, like the smile of satisfied love.

I paced about, looking for my darling.

Although she was in mourning, she had promised me to wear the dark-green silk I so admired under her black cloak, and I looked for this colour among the brighter greens of the trees and bushes.

She did not appear, and my heart was chilled with the fear that she was offended with me and therefore would not come, and an even deeper dread that she might, in vexation, have fled to her unknown retreat.

This thought was sending me hot-foot to seek her at her house, when I saw Rob Patterson coming across the close-shaven grass of the Green.

I remembered that the cheerful sun seemed to me to be at this moment darkened, not by any natural clouds or mists, but as it is during an eclipse, and that the fresh trees and innocent flowers took on a ghastly and withered look.

It may appear a trivial detail, but I recall so clearly—his habit, which was of a luxury beyond his means, fine grey broadcloth with a deep edging of embroidery in gold thread, little suited to his profession.

As he saw me he cocked his hat over his eyes, but took no notice of my appearance, and I turned away, not being wishful of any encounter with this gentleman while my spirit was in a tumult.

I went at once to my darling's house, and learnt from her maid that she had left home two hours previously.

I do not wish to dwell on this part of my tale—indeed, I could not, it becomes very confused to me.

The salient facts are these—that no one saw Ann Leete in bodily form again.

And no one could account for her disappearance; yet no great comment was aroused by this, because there was no one to take much interest in her, and it was commonly believed that she had disappeared from the importunity of her lovers, the more so as Rob Patterson swore that the day of her disappearance he had had an interview with her in which she had avowed her intention of going where no one could discover her. This, in a fashion, was confirmed by what she had told me, and I was the more inclined to believe it, as my inner senses told me that she was not dead.

Six months of bitter search, of sad uneasiness, that remain in my memory blurred to one pain, and then, one autumn evening, as I came home late and dispirited, I saw her before me in the gloaming, tripping up the street, wearing her dark-green silk dress and tartan or Roman scarf.

I did not see her face as she disappeared before I could gain on her, but she held to her side one hand, and between the long fingers I saw the haft of a surgeon's knife.

I knew then that she was dead.

And I knew that Rob Patterson had killed her.

Although it was well known that my family were all ghost-seers, to speak in this case was to be laughed at and reprimanded.

I had no single shred of evidence against Dr. Patterson.

But I resolved that I would use what powers I possessed to make him disclose his crime.

And this is how it befell.

In those days, in Glasgow, it was compulsory to attend some place of worship on the Sabbath, the observation of the holy day being enforced with peculiar strictness, and none being allowed to show themselves in any public place during the hours of the church services, and to this end inspectors and overseers were employed to patrol the streets on a Sabbath and take down the names of those who might be found loitering there.

But few were the defaulters, Glasgow on a Sunday being as bare as the Arabian desert.

Rob Patterson and I both attended the church in Rutherglen Road, towards the Green and the river.

And the Sunday after I had seen the phantom of Ann Leete, I changed my usual place and seated myself behind this young man.

My intention was to so work on his spirit as to cause him to make public confession of his crime. And I crouched there behind him with a concentration of hate and fury, forcing my will on his during the whole of the long service.

I noticed he was pale, and that he glanced several times behind him, but he did not change his place or open his lips; but presently his head fell forward on his arms as if he was praying, and I took him to be in a kind of swoon brought on by the resistance of his spirit against mine.

I did not for this cease to pursue him. I was, indeed, as if in an exaltation, and I thought my soul had his soul by the throat, somewhere above our heads, and was shouting out: "Confess! Confess!"

One o'clock struck and he rose with the rest of the congregation, but in a dazed kind of fashion. It was almost side by side that we issued from the church door.

As the stream of people came into the street they were stopped by a little procession that came down the road.

All immediately recognized two of the inspectors employed to search the Sunday streets for defaulters from church attendance, followed by several citizens who appeared to have left their homes in haste and confusion.

These people carried between them a rude bundle which some compassionate hand had covered with a white linen cloth. Below this fell a swathe of dark-green silk and the end of a Roman scarf.

I stepped up to the rough bier.

"You have found Ann Leete," I said.

"It is a dead woman," one answered me. "We know not her name."

I did not need to raise the cloth. The congregation was gathering round us, and amongst them was Rob Patterson.

"Tell me, who was her promised husband, how you found her," I said.

And one of the inspectors answered:

"Near here, on the Green, where the wall bounds the grass, we saw, just now, the young surgeon, Rob Patterson, lying on the sward, and put his name in our books, besides approaching him to inquire the reason of his absence from church. But he, without excuse for his offence, rose from the ground, exclaiming: 'I am a miserable man! Look in the water!'

"With that he crossed a stile that leads to the river and disappeared, and we, going down to the water, found the dead woman, deep tangled between the willows and the weeds——"

"And," added the other inspector gravely, "tangled in her clothes is a surgeon's knife."

"Which," said the former speaker, "perhaps Dr. Patterson can explain, since I perceive he is among this congregation—he must have found some quick way round to have got here before us."

Upon this all eyes turned on the surgeon, but more with amaze than reproach.

And he, with a confident air, said:

"It is known to all these good people that I have been in the church the whole of the morn-ing, especially to Eneas Bretton, who sat behind me, and, I dare swear, never took his eyes from me during the whole of the service."

"Ay, your *body* was there," I said.

With that he laughed angrily, and mingling with the crowd passed on his way.

You may believe there was a great stir; the theory put abroad was that Ann Leete had been kept a prisoner in a solitary, ruined hut there was by the river, and then, in fury or fear, slain by her jailer and cast into the river.

To me all this is black. I only know that she was murdered by Rob Patterson.

He was arrested and tried on the circuit.

He there proved, beyond all cavil, that he had been in the church from the beginning of the service to the end of it; his alibi was perfect. But the two inspectors never wavered in their tale of seeing him on the Green, of his self-accusation in his exclamation; he was very well known to them; and they showed his name written in their books.

He was acquitted by the tribunal of man, but a higher power condemned him.

Shortly after he died by his own hand, which God armed and turned against him.

This mystery, as it was called, was never solved to the public satisfaction, but I know that I sent Rob Patterson's soul out of his body to betray his guilt, and to procure my darling Christian burial.

This was the tale Eneas Bretton, that ancient man, told me, on the old terrace, as he sat opposite the picture of Ann Leete.

"You must think what you will," he concluded. "They will tell you that the shock unsettled my wits, or even that I was always crazed. As they would tell you that I dream when I say that I see Ann Leete now, and babble when I talk of my happiness with her for fifty years."

He smiled faintly; a deeper glory than that of the autumn sunshine seemed to rest on him.

"Explain it yourself, sir. What was it those inspectors saw on the Green?"

He slightly raised himself in his chair and peered over my shoulder.

"And what is this," he asked triumphantly, in the voice of a young man, "coming towards us now?"

I rose; I looked over my shoulder.

Through the gloom I saw a dark-green silk gown, a woman's form, a pale hand beckoning.

My impulse was to fly from the spot, but a happy sigh from my companion reproved my cowardice. I looked at the ancient man whose whole figure appeared lapped in warm light, and as the apparition of the woman moved into this glow, which seemed too glorious for the fading sunshine, I heard his last breath flow from his body with a glad cry. I had not answered his questions; I never can.

BEATEN TO A PULP

THE DEAD-WAGON

Greye La Spina

LARGELY UNREMEMBERED TODAY, (FANNY) Greye La Spina (1880–1969), née Bragg, was one of the most popular writers in the 1920s and early 1930s for *Weird Tales,* for which she wrote very creepy short stories and serialized four novels: *Invaders from the Dark* (1925), *The Gargoyle* (1925), *Fettered* (1926), and *The Portal to Power* (1930–1931).

Born to a Methodist minister in Wakefield, Massachusetts, she married in 1898 and had a daughter two years later; her husband died the following year. She remarried in 1910 to Robert La Spina, Barone di Savuto, who was descended from Russian aristocracy. She became a news photographer (one of the first women in the profession), was a typist for other writers, and became a master weaver, winning prizes for her tapestries and rugs.

Her writing career began early when she produced her own newspaper at the age of ten, publishing her poems and local gossip and selling copies to her neighbors. While still a teenager, she won a literary contest and saw her story published in *Connecticut Magazine.* Her first story in the supernatural area was a werewolf tale, "Wolf of the Steppes," which she sent to *Popular Magazine,* a general interest pulp. When Street & Smith started a new pulp devoted to weird and supernatural fiction, her story was selected as the lead story of the first issue of *Thrill Book* (March 1, 1919). She wrote several more stories for the short-lived magazine, both under her own name and a pseudonym; her work appeared in the last issue as well. She wrote for many other magazines after that, both as Greye La Spina and Isra Putnam, including the prestigious *Black Mask, All-Story, Action Stories, Ten-Story Book,* and *Weird Tales,* where her career flourished. Her only book did not appear until 1960, when Arkham House published a hardcover edition of her werewolf novel, *Invaders from the Dark.*

"The Dead-Wagon" was originally published in the September 1927 issue of *Weird Tales.*

The Dead-Wagon

GREYE LA SPINA

I

"Someone's been chalking up the front door." The speaker stepped off the terrace into the library through the open French window.

From his padded armchair Lord Melverson rose with an involuntary exclamation of startled dismay.

"Chalking the great door?" he echoed, an unmistakable tremor in his restrained voice. His aristocratic, clean-shaven old face showed pallid in the soft light of the shaded candles.

"Oh, nothing that can do any harm to the carving. Perhaps I am mistaken—it's coming on dusk—but it seemed to be a great cross in red, chalked high up on the top panel of the door. You know—the Great Plague panel."

"Good God!" ejaculated the older man weakly.

Young Dinsmore met his prospective father-in-law's anxious eyes with a face that betrayed his astonishment. He could not avoid marveling at the reception of what certainly seemed, on the surface, a trifling matter.

To be sure, the wonderfully carved door that, with reinforcement of hand-wrought iron, guarded the entrance to Melverson Abbey was well worth any amount of care. Lord Melverson's ill-concealed agitation would have been excusable had a tourist cut vandal initials on that admirable example of early carving. But to make such a fuss over a bit of red chalk that a servant could wipe off in a moment without injury to the panel—Kenneth felt slightly superior to such anxiety on the part of Arline's father.

Lord Melverson steadied himself with one hand against the library table.

"Was there—did you notice—anything else—besides the cross?"

"Why, I don't think there was anything else. Of course, I didn't look particularly. I had no idea you'd be so—interested," returned the young American.

"I think I'll go out and take a look at it myself. You may have imagined you saw some things, in the dusk," murmured Lord Melverson, half to himself.

"May I come?" inquired Dinsmore, vaguely disturbed at the very apparent discomposure of his usually imperturbable host.

Lord Melverson nodded. "I suppose you'll have to hear the whole story sooner or later, anyway," he acquiesced as he led the way.

His words set Kenneth's heart to beating madly. They meant but one thing: Arline's father was not averse to his suit. As for Arline, no one could be sure of such a little coquette. And yet—the young American could have sworn there was more than ordinary kindness in her eyes the day she smiled a confirmation of her father's invitation to Melverson Abbey. It was that vague promise that had brought Kenneth Dinsmore from New York to England.

A moment later, the American was staring, with straining eyes that registered utter astonishment, at the famous carved door that formed the principal entrance to the abbey. He would have been willing to swear that no one could have approached that door without having been seen from the library windows; yet in the few seconds of time that had elapsed between his first and second observation of the panel, an addition had been made to the chalk marks.

The Melverson panels are well known in the annals of historic carvings. There is a large lower panel showing the Great Fire of London. Above this are six half-panels portraying important scenes in London's history. And running across the very top is a large panel which shows a London street during the Great Plague of 1664.

This panel shows houses on either side of a narrow street yawning vacantly, great crosses upon their doors. Before one in the foreground is a rude wooden cart drawn by a lean nag and driven by a saturnine individual with leering face. This cart carries a gruesome load; it is piled high with bodies. Accounts vary oddly as to the number of bodies in the cart; earlier descriptions of the panel give a smaller number than the later ones, an item much speculated upon by connoisseurs of old carvings. The *tout ensemble* of the bas-relief greatly resembles the famous Hogarth picture of a similar scene.

Before this great door Kenneth stood, staring at a red-chalked legend traced across the rough surface of the carved figures on the upper panel. "God have mercy upon us!" it read. What did it mean? Who had managed to trace, unseen, those words of despairing supplication upon the old door?

And suddenly the young man's wonderment was rudely disturbed. Lord Melverson lurched away from the great door like a drunken man, a groan forcing its way from between his parched lips. The old man's hands had flown to his face, covering his eyes as though to shut out some horrid and unwelcome sight.

"Kenneth, you have heard the story! This is

some thoughtless jest of yours! Tell me it is, boy! Tell me that your hand traced these fatal words!"

Dinsmore's sympathy was keenly aroused by the old nobleman's intense gravity and anxiety, but he was forced to deny the pitifully pleading accusation.

"Sorry, sir, but I found the red cross just as I told you. As for the writing below, I must admit—"

"Ah! Then you *did* put *that* there? It was you who did it, then? Thank God! Thank God!"

"No, no, I hadn't finished. I was only wondering how anyone could have slipped past us and have written this, unseen. I'm sure," puzzled, "there was nothing here but the red cross when I told you about it first, sir."

"Then you haven't heard—no one has told you that old legend? The story of the Melverson curse?"

"This is the first I've heard of it, I assure you."

"And you positively deny writing that, as a bit of a joke?"

"Come, sir, it's not like you to accuse me of such a silly piece of cheap trickery," Kenneth retorted, somewhat indignantly.

"Forgive me, boy. I—I should not have said that but—I am agitated. Will you tell me"—his voice grew tenser—"look closely, for God's sake, Kenneth!—*how many bodies are there in the wagon?*"

Dinsmore could not help throwing a keen glance at his future father-in-law, who now stood with averted face, one hand shielding his eyes as though he dared not ascertain for himself that which he asked another in a voice so full of shrinking dread. Then the American stepped closer to the door and examined the upper panel closely, while the soft dusk closed down upon it.

"There are eleven bodies," he said finally.

"Kenneth! Look carefully! More depends upon your reply than you can be aware. Are you sure there are only eleven?"

"There are only eleven, sir. I'm positive of it."

"Don't make a mistake, for pity's sake!"

"Surely my eyesight hasn't been seriously

impaired since this morning, when I bagged my share of birds," laughed the young man, in a vain effort to throw off the gloomy depression that seemed to have settled down upon him from the mere propinquity of the other.

"Thank God! Then there is still time," murmured the owner of the abbey brokenly, drawing a deep, shivering sigh of relief. "Let us return to the house, my boy." His voice had lost its usually light ironical inflection and had acquired a heaviness foreign to it.

Kenneth contracted his brows at Lord Melverson's dragging steps. One would almost have thought the old man physically affected by what appeared to be a powerful shock.

Once back in the library, Lord Melverson collapsed into the nearest chair, his breath coming in short, forced jerks. Wordlessly he indicated the bell-pull dangling against the wall out of his reach.

Kenneth jerked the cord. After a moment, during which the young man hastily poured a glassful of water and carried it to his host, the butler came into the room.

At sight of his beloved master in such a condition of pitiful collapse, the gray-haired old servitor was galvanized into action. He flew across the room to the desk, opened a drawer, picked up a bottle, shook a tablet out into his hand, flew back.

He administered the medicine to his master, who sipped the water brought by Kenneth with a grateful smile that included his guest and his servant.

Jenning shook his head sadly, compressing his lips, as Lord Melverson leaned back exhausted in his chair, face grayish, lids drooping over weary eyes.

Kenneth touched the old servant's arm to attract his attention. Then he tapped his left breast and lifted his eyebrows questioningly. An affirmative nod was his reply. Heart trouble! Brought on by the old gentleman's agitation over a chalk mark on his front door! There was a mystery somewhere, and the very idea stimulated curiosity. And had not Lord Melverson

said, "You will have to know, sooner or later"? Know what? What strange thing lay back of a red cross and a prayer to heaven, chalked upon the great Melverson portal?

II

Lord Melverson stirred ever so little and spoke with effort. "Send one of the men out to clean the upper panel of the front door, Jenning," he ordered tonelessly.

Jenning threw up one hand to cover his horrified mouth and stifle an exclamation. His faded blue eyes peered at his master from under pale eyebrows as he stared with dreadful incredulity.

"It isn't the red cross, m'lord? Oh, no, it cannot be the red cross?" he stammered.

The thrill of affection in that cracked old voice told a little something of how much his master meant to the old family retainer.

"It seems to be a cross, chalked in red," admitted Melverson with patent reluctance, raising dull eyes to the staring ones fixed upon him with consternation.

"Oh, m'lord, not the red cross! And—was the warning there? Yes? Did you count them? *How many were there?*"

Terrible foreboding, shrinking reluctance, rang in that inquiry, so utterly strange and incomprehensible. Kenneth felt his blood congeal in his veins with the horrid mystery of it.

Lord Melverson and his retainer exchanged a significant glance that did not escape the young American's attention. The answer to Jenning's question was cryptic but not more so than the inquiry.

"The same as before, Jenning. That is all—as yet."

Kenneth's curiosity flamed up anew. What could that mean? Could Jenning have been inquiring how many bodies were in the cart? There would be eleven, of course. How could there be more, or less, when the wood-carver had made them eleven, for all time?

The old servant retired from the room, dragging one slow foot after the other as though he had suddenly aged more than his fast-whitening hairs warranted.

In his capacious armchair, fingers opening and closing nervously upon the polished leather that upholstered it, Lord Melverson leaned back wearily, his eyes wide open but fixed unseeingly upon the library walls with their great paintings in oil of bygone Melversons.

"Kenneth!" Lord Melverson sought his guest's eyes with an expression of apology on his face that was painfully forced to the surface of the clouded atmosphere of dread and heaviness in which the old nobleman seemed steeped. "I presume you are wondering over the to-do about a chalk mark on my door? It—it made me think—of an old family tradition—and disturbed me a little.

"There's just one thing I want to ask you, my boy. Arline must not know that I had this little attack of heart-failure. I've kept it from her for years and I don't want her disturbed about me. And Kenneth, Arline has never been told the family legend. Don't tell her about the cross— the chalk marks on my door." His voice was intensely grave. "I have your word, my boy? Thank you. Some day I'll tell you the whole story."

"Has it anything to do with the quaint verse in raised gilded letters over the fireplace in the dining-hall?" questioned Kenneth.

He quoted it:

"Melverson's first-born will die early away;
Melverson's daughters will wed in gray;
Melverson's curse must Melverson pay,
Or Melverson Abbey will ownerless stay."

"Sounds like doggerel, doesn't it, lad? Well, that's the ancient curse. Foolish? Perhaps it is— perhaps it is. Yet—I am a second son myself; my brother Guy died before his majority."

"Coincidence, don't you think, sir?"

Lord Melverson smiled wryly, unutterable weariness in his old eyes. "Possibly—but a chain of coincidences, then. You—you don't believe there could be anything in it, do you, Kenneth?

Would you marry the daughter of a house with such a curse on it, knowing that it was part of your wife's dowry? Knowing that your first-born son must die before his majority?"

The American laughed light-heartedly.

"I don't think I'd care to answer such a suppositious question, sir. I can't admit such a possibility. I'm far too matter-of-fact, you see."

"But would you?" persistently, doggedly.

"I don't believe a word of it," sturdily. "It's just one of those foolish superstitions that people have permitted to influence them from time immemorial. I refuse to credit it."

Did Kenneth imagine it, or did Lord Melverson heave a deep, carefully repressed sigh of relief?

"Hardly worth while to go over the old tradition, is it?" he asked eagerly. "You wouldn't believe it, anyway. And probably it is just superstition, as you say. Ring for Jenning again, will you? Or—do you want to lend me your arm, my boy? I—I feel a bit shaky yet. I rather think bed will be the best place for me."

III

After Kenneth had bidden Lord Melverson good-night, he got out his pipe and sat by his window smoking. Tomorrow, he decided, he would try his fate; if he could only get Arline away where they could be alone. Little witch, how she managed always to have someone else around! Tomorrow he would know from her own lips whether or not he must return to America alone.

The clock struck midnight. Following close upon its cadences, a voice sounded on the still night, a voice raucous, grating, disagreeable. The words were indistinguishable and followed by a hard chuckle that was distinctly not expressive of mirth; far from it, the sound made Kenneth shake back his shoulders quickly in an instinctive effort to throw off the dismal effect of that laugh.

"Charming music!" observed he to himself, as he leaned from his window.

Wheels began to grate and crunch through the graveled road that led around the abbey. The full moon threw her clear light upon the space directly under Kenneth's window. He could distinguish every object as distinctly, it seemed to him, as in broad daylight. He listened and watched, a strange tenseness upon him. It was as though he waited for something terrible which yet must be; some unknown peril that threatened vaguely but none the less dreadfully.

The noise of the wheels grew louder. Then came a cautious, scraping sound from the window of a room close at hand. Kenneth decided that it was Lord Melverson's room. His host, hearing the horrid laughter that had been flung dismally upon the soft night air, had removed the screen from his window, the better to view the night visitor with the ugly chuckle.

The grinding of wheels grew louder. And then there slid into the full length of the moon a rude cart drawn by a lean, dappled nag and driven by a hunched-up individual who drew rein as the wagon came directly under Lord Melverson's window.

From the shadow of his room, Kenneth stared, open-eyed. There was something intolerably appalling about that strange equipage and its hunched-up driver, something that set his teeth sharply on edge and lifted his hair stiffly on his head. He did not want to look, but something pushed him forward and he was obliged to.

With a quick motion of his head, the driver turned a saturnine face to the moon's rays, revealing glittering eyes that shone with terrible, concentrated malignancy. The thinly curling lips parted. The cry Kenneth had heard a few minutes earlier rang—or rather, grated—on the American's ear. This time the words were plainer; plainer to the ear, although not to the sense—for what sense could they have? he reasoned as he heard them.

"Bring out your dead! Bring out your dead!"

A stifled groan. That was Lord Melverson, thought Kenneth, straining his eyes to watch the strange scene below.

For suddenly there rose from out of the shadow of the abbey's great gray walls two figures bearing between them a burden. They carried it to the cart and with an effort lifted it, to toss it carelessly upon the grisly contents of that horrid wagon—contents that Kenneth now noted for the first time with starting eyes and prickling skin. And as the white face of the body lay upturned to the moon, a terrible cry wailed out from Lord Melverson's apartment, a cry of anguish and despair. For the moon's light picked out the features of that dead so callously tossed upon the gruesome pile.

"Oh, Albert, Albert, my son, my son!"

Kenneth leaned from his window and peered toward that of his host. From above the sill protruded two clasped hands; between them lay the white head of the old man. Had he fainted? Or had he had another attack of heart-failure?

The driver in the roadway below chuckled malignantly, and pulled at his horse's reins. The lean, dappled nag started up patiently in answer, and the cart passed slowly out of sight, wheels biting deep into the road-bed. And as it went out of sight among the deep shadows cast by the thickly wooded park, that harsh chuckle floated back again to the American's ears, thrilling him with horror of that detestable individual.

The hypnotic influence of that malignant glance had so chained Kenneth to the spot that for the moment he could not go to the assistance of Lord Melverson. But he found that he had been anticipated; as he reached his door, Jenning was already disappearing into his host's room. Kenneth retreated, unseen; perhaps he would do better to wait until he was called. It might well be that the drama he had seen enacted was not meant for his eyes and ears.

After all, had he seen or heard anything? Or was he the victim of a nightmare that had awakened him at its end? Kenneth shrugged his shoulders. He would know in the morning. Unless it rained hard in the meantime, the wheels of the cart would have left their mark on the gravel. If he had not dreamed, he would find the ruts made by those broad, ancient-looking wheels.

He could not sleep, however, until he heard Jenning leave his master's room. Opening the door softly, he inquired how Lord Melverson was. The old servitor flung a suspicious glance at him.

"I heard him cry out," explained Kenneth, seeing that the old man was averse to any explanation on his own side. "I hope it is nothing serious?"

"Nothing," replied Jenning restrainedly. But Dinsmore could have sworn that bright tears glittered in the old retainer's faded blue eyes and that the old mouth was compressed as though to hold back an outburst of powerful emotion.

Arline Melverson, her face slightly clouded, reported that her father had slept poorly the night before and would breakfast in his own room. She herself came down in riding-habit and vouchsafed the welcome information that she had ordered a horse saddled for Kenneth, if he cared to ride with her. Despite his desire to be alone with her, the American felt that he ought to remain at the abbey, where he might be of service to Lord Melverson. But inclination overpowered intuition, and after breakfast he got into riding-togs.

"I believe I'm still dreaming," he thought to himself as he rode back to the abbey at lunch-time, his horse crowding against Arline's as he reached happily over to touch her hand every little while. "Only this dream isn't a nightmare."

Instinctively his glance sought the graveled road where the dead-cart of the night before had, under his very eyes, ground its heavy wheels into the ground. The road was smooth and rutless. After all, then, he had dreamed and had undoubtedly been awakened by Lord Melverson's cry as the old man fainted. The dream had been so vivid that Kenneth could hardly believe his eyes when he looked at the smooth roadway, but his new happiness soon chased his bewilderment away.

As the young people dismounted before the door, Jenning appeared upon the threshold. The old man's lined face was turned almost with terror upon his young mistress. His lips worked as though he would speak but could not. His eyes sought the other man's as if in supplication.

"What's the matter, Jenning?"

"Master Albert, Mr. Dinsmore! M'lord's first-born son!"

"What is it?" Arline echoed. "Is my brother here?"

"I can't tell her, sir," the major-domo implored of Kenneth. "Take her to Lord Melverson, sir, I beg of you. He can tell her better than I."

Kenneth did not take Arline to her father. The girl fled across the great hall as if whipped by a thousand fears. Kenneth turned to Jenning with a question in his eyes.

Down the old man's face tears ran freely. His wrinkled hands worked nervously together. "He fell, sir. Something broke on his plane. He died last night, sir, a bit after midnight. The telegram came this morning, just after you and Miss Arline went."

Kenneth, one hand pressed bewildered to his forehead, walked aimlessly through that house of sorrow. Albert Melverson had fallen from his plane and died, the previous night. Had that dream, that nightmare, been a warning? Had it perhaps been so vivid in Lord Melverson's imagination that the scene had been telepathically reproduced before the American's own eyes?

Although puzzled and disturbed beyond words, Kenneth realized that the matter must rest in abeyance until Lord Melverson should of his own free will explain it.

In the meantime there would be Arline to comfort, his sweetheart, who had just lost her dearly beloved and only brother.

IV

Two months had hardly passed after Albert's death before Lord Melverson broached the subject of his daughter's marriage.

"It's this way, my boy. I'm an old man and far from well of late. I'd like to know that Arline was in safe keeping, Kenneth," and he laid an affectionate hand on the young man's shoulder.

Kenneth was deeply affected. "Thank you, sir. I promise you I shall do my utmost to make her happy."

"I know you will. I want you to speak to Arline about an early wedding. Tell her I want to see her married before—before I have to leave. I have a very powerful reason that I cannot tell you, my boy, for Arline to marry soon. I want to live to see my grandson at her knee, lad. And unless you two marry soon, I shall be powerless to prevent—that is, I shall be unable to do something for you both that has been much in my mind of late. It is vital that you marry soon, Kenneth. More I cannot say."

"You don't need to say more. I'll speak to Arline today. You understand, sir, that my only motive in not urging marriage upon her now has been your recent bereavement?"

"Of course. But Arline is too young, too volatile, to allow even such a loss to weigh permanently upon her spirits. I think she will yield to you, especially if you make it plain that I want it to be so."

Kenneth sought Arline thoughtfully. Lord Melverson's words impressed him almost painfully. There was much behind them, much that he realized he could not yet demand an explanation of. But the strength of Lord Melverson's request made him surer when he asked Arline to set an early date for their marriage.

"I am ready if Father does not consider it disrespectful to Albert's memory, Kenneth. You know, dear, we intended to marry soon, anyway. And I think Albert will be happier to know that I did not let his going matter. You understand, don't you? Besides, I feel that he is here with us in the abbey, with Father and me.

"But there is one thing, dear, that I shall insist upon. I think too much of my brother to lay aside the light mourning that Father permitted me to wear instead of heavy black. So if you

want me to marry you soon, dear, you must wed a bride in gray."

Into Kenneth's mind flashed one line of the Melverson curse:

"Melverson's daughters will wed in gray."

Could there be something in it, after all? Common sense answered scornfully: No!

Four months after Albert Melverson had fallen to his death, his sister Arline—gray-clad like a gentle dove—put her hand into that of Kenneth Dinsmore, while Lord Melverson, his lips twitching as he strove to maintain his composure, gave the bride away.

A honeymoon trip that consumed many months took the young people to America as well as to the Continent, as the groom could hardly wait to present his lovely young wife to his family. Then, pursuant to Lord Melverson's wishes, the bridal pair returned to Melverson Abbey, that the future heir might be born under the ancestral roof.

V

Little Albert became the apple of his grandfather's eye. The old gentleman spent hours watching the cradle the first few months of his grandson's life, and then again other hours in fondly guiding the little fellow's first steps.

But always in the background of this apparently ideally happy family lurked a black shadow. Jenning, his pale eyes full of foreboding, was always stealing terrified looks in secret at the panel of the great door. Kenneth grew almost to hate the poor old man, merely because he knew that Jenning believed implicitly in the family curse.

"Confound the man! He'll bring it upon us by thinking about it," growled the young father one morning as he looked out of the window of the breakfast room, where he had been eating a belated meal.

Little Albert, toddling with exaggerated precaution from his mother's outstretched hands to those of his grandfather, happened to look up.

He saw his father; laughed and crowed lustily. Dinsmore waved his hand.

"Go to it, young chap. You'll be a great walker some day," he called facetiously.

Lord Melverson looked around, a pleased smile on his face. Plainly, he agreed to the full with his son-in-law's sentiments.

As usual, entered that black-garbed figure, the presentment of woe: Jenning. Into the center of the happy little circle he came, his eyes seeking the old nobleman's.

"M'lord! Would your lordship please take a look?" stammered Jenning, his roving eyes going from the young father to the young mother, then back to the grandfather again, as if in an agony of uncertainty.

Lord Melverson straightened up slowly and carefully from his bent position over the side of a great wicker chair. He motioned Jenning silently ahead of him. The old butler retraced his footsteps, his master following close upon his heels. They disappeared around the corner of the building.

"Now, what on earth are they up to?" wondered Kenneth. His brow contracted. There had been something vaguely suspicious about Lord Melverson's air. "I've half a mind to follow them."

"Kenneth!" Arline's cry was wrung agonizingly from her.

Kenneth whirled about quickly, but too late to do anything. The baby, toddling to his mother's arms, missed a step, slipped, fell. The tender little head crashed against the granite coping at the edge of the terrace.

And even then Kenneth did not realize what it all meant. It was not until late that night that he suddenly understood that the Melverson curse was not silly tradition, but a terrible blight upon the happiness of the Melverson family, root and branch.

He had left Arline under the influence of a sleeping-potion. Her nerves had gone back on her after the day's strain and the knowledge that her baby might not live out the night. A competent nurse and a skilled physician had taken over

the case. Specialists were coming down from London as fast as a special train would bring them. Kenneth felt that his presence in the sickroom would be more hindrance than help.

He went down to the library where his father-in-law sat grimly, silently, expectantly, a strangely fixed expression of determination on his fine old face. Lord Melverson had drawn a handkerchief from his pocket. And then Kenneth suddenly knew, where before he had only imagined. For the old man's fine cambric kerchief was streaked with red, red that the unhappy young father knew must have been wiped from the upper panel of the great door that very morning. *The baby, Kenneth's first-born son, was doomed.*

"Why didn't you tell me? You hid it from me," he accused his wife's father, bitterly.

"I thought I was doing it for the best, Kenneth," the older man defended himself sadly.

"But if you had told me, I would never have left him alone for a single moment. I would have been beside him to have saved him when he fell."

"You *know* that if he had not fallen, something else would have happened to him, something unforeseen."

"Oh yes, I know, now, when it is too late. My little boy! My Arline's first-born! The first-born of Melverson!" fiercely. "Why didn't you tell me that the Melverson curse would follow my wife? That it would strike down her first-born boy?"

"And would that have deterred you from marrying Arline?" inquired Arline's father, very gently. "You know it wouldn't, Kenneth. I tried to put a hypothetical case to you once, but you replied that you refused to consider the mere possibility. What was I to do? I will confess that I have suffered, thinking that I should have insisted upon your reading the family records before you married Arline—then you could have decided for yourself."

"Does Arline know?"

"No. I've shielded her from the knowledge, Kenneth."

"I can't forgive you for not letting me know. It might have saved Albert's life. If Arline, too, had known—"

"Why should I have told her something that would have cast a shadow over her young life, Kenneth? Are you reproaching me because I have tried to keep her happy?"

"Oh, Father, I didn't mean to reproach you. I'm sorry. You must understand that I'm half mad with the pain of what's happened, not only on account of the little fellow, but for Arline. Oh, if there were only some way of saving him! How I would bless the being who would tell me how to save him!"

Lord Melverson, still with that strange glow in his eyes, rose slowly to his feet.

"There is a way, I believe," said he. "But don't put too much stress on what may be but a groundless hope on my part. I have had an idea for some time that I shall put into expression to-night, Kenneth. I've been thinking it over since I felt that I had wronged you in not pressing home the reality of the Melverson curse. If my idea is a good one, our little Albert is saved. And not only he, but I too shall have broken the curse, rendered it impotent for ever." His eyes shone with fervor.

"Is it anything I can do?" the young father begged.

"Nothing. Unless, perhaps, you want to read the old manuscript in my desk drawer. It tells why we Melversons have been cursed since the days of the Great Plague of 1664.

"Just before midnight, be in little Albert's room. If he is no better when the clock strikes twelve, Kenneth—why, then, my plan will have been a poor one. But I shall have done all I can do; have given all that lies in my power to give, in my attempt to wipe out the wrong I have inadvertently done you."

Kenneth pressed the hand outstretched to him.

"You've been a good husband to my girl, Kenneth, lad. You've made her happy. And, in case anything were to happen to me, will you tell Arline that I am perfectly contented if only our little one recovers? I want no vain regrets," stressed Lord Melverson emphatically, as he released Kenneth's hand and turned to leave the room.

"What could happen?"

"Oh, nothing. That is—you know I've had several severe heart attacks of late," returned Arline's father vaguely.

VI

Kenneth, alone, went to his father-in-law's desk and drew out the stained and yellow manuscript. Sitting in a chair before the desk, he laid the ancient sheets before him and pored over the story of the Melverson curse. He thought it might take his mind off the tragedy slowly playing to a close in the hushed room upstairs.

Back in 1664, the then Lord Melverson fell madly in love with the charming daughter of a goldsmith. She was an only child, very lovely to look upon and as good as she was fair, and she dearly loved the rollicking young nobleman. But a Melverson of Melverson Abbey, though he could love, could not wed a child of the people. Charles Melverson pleaded with the lovely girl to elope with him, without the sanction of her church.

But the damsel, being of lofty soul, called her father and related all to him. Then she turned her fair shoulder indifferently upon her astonished and chagrined suitor and left him, while the goldsmith laughed saturninely in the would-be seducer's face.

A Melverson was not one to let such a matter rest quietly, however, especially as he was deeply enamored of the lady. He sent pleading letters, threatening to take his own life. He attempted to force himself into the lady's presence. At last, he met her one day as she returned from church, caught her up, and fled with her on his swift charger.

Still she remained obdurate, although love for him was eating her wounded heart. Receive him she must, but she continued to refuse him so little a favor as a single word.

Despairing of winning her by gentle means, Charles Melverson determined upon foul.

It was the terrible winter of 1664–5. The Black Death, sweeping through London and out into the countryside, was taking dreadful toll of lives. Hundreds of bodies were daily tumbled carelessly into the common trenches by hardened men who dared the horrors of the plague for the big pay offered those who played the part of grave-digger. And at the very moment when Melverson had arrived at his evil decision, the goldsmith staggered into the abbey grounds after a long search for his ravished daughter, to fall under the very window where she had retreated in the last stand for her maiden virtue.

Retainers without shouted at one another to beware the plague-stricken man. Their shouts distracted the maiden. She looked down and beheld her father dying, suffering the last throes of the dreaded pestilence.

Coldly and proudly she demanded freedom to go down to her dying parent. Melverson refused the request; in a flash of insight he knew what she would do with her liberty. She would fling herself desperately beside the dying man; she would hold his blackening body against her own warm young breast; she would deliberately drink in his plague-laden breath with her sweet, fresh lips.

Lifting fast-glazing eyes, the goldsmith saw his daughter, apparently clasped fast in her lover's arms. How was he to have known that her frantic struggles had been in vain? With his last breath he cursed the Melversons, root and branch, lifting discolored hands to the brazen, glowing sky lowering upon him. Then, "And may the demon of the plague grant that I may come back as long as a Melverson draws breath, to steal away his first-born son!" he cried. With a groan, he died.

And then, thanks to the strange heart of woman, Charles Melverson unexpectedly won what he had believed lost to him for ever, for he could not have forced his will upon that orphaned and sorrowful maiden. The goldsmith's daughter turned upon him limpid eyes that wept for him and for her father, too.

"It is too much to ask that you should suffer alone what my poor father has called down upon your house," she said to him, with unexpected gentleness. "He would forgive you, could he know that I have been safe in your keeping. I must ask you, then, to take all I have to give, if by so doing you believe the shadow of the curse will be lightened—for you, at least."

Touched to his very heart by her magnanimity, Charles Melverson released her from his arms, knelt at her feet, kissed her hand, and swore that until he could fetch her from the church, his lawful wedded wife, he would neither eat nor sleep.

But—the curse remained. Down through the centuries it had worked its evil way, and no one seemed to have found a way of eluding it. Upon the last pages of the old manuscript were noted, in differing chirography, the death dates of one Melverson after another, after each the terribly illuminating note: "First-born son. Died before his majority."

And last of all, in the handwriting of Lord Melverson, was written the name of that Albert for whom Kenneth Dinsmore's son had been named. Must another Albert follow that other so soon?

VII

Kenneth tossed the stained papers back into the drawer and shut them from sight. There was something sinister about them. He felt as if his very hands had been polluted by their touch. Then he glanced at the clock. It was on the point of striking midnight. He remembered Lord Melverson's request, and ran quickly upstairs to his little dying son's room.

Arline was already at the child's side; she had wakened and would not be denied. Nurse and physician stood in the background, their faces showing plainly the hopelessness of the case.

On his little pillow, the poor baby drew short,

painful gasps, little fists clenched against his breast. A few short moments, thought Kenneth, would determine his first-born's life or death. And it would be death, unless Lord Melverson had discovered how to break the potency of the Melverson curse.

Torn between wife and child, the young father dared not hope, for fear his hope might be shattered. As for Arline, he saw that her eyes already registered despair; already she had, in anticipation, given up her child, her baby, her first-born.

What was that? The sound of heavy, broad-rimmed wheels crunching through the gravel of the roadway; the call of a mocking voice that set Kenneth's teeth on edge with impotent fury.

He went unobtrusively to the window and looked out. After all, he could not be expected to stand by the bed, watching his little son die. And he had to see, at all costs, that nightmare dead-cart with its ghastly freight; he had to know whether or not he had dreamed it, or had seen it truly, on the night before Albert Melverson's death.

Coming out of the shadows of the enveloping trees, rumbled the dead-wagon with its hunched-up driver. Kenneth's hair rose with a prickling sensation on his scalp. He turned to glance back into the room. No, he was not dreaming; he had not dreamed before; it was real—as real as such a ghastly thing could well be.

On, on it came. And then the hateful driver lifted his malignant face to the full light of the moon. His challenging glance met the young father's intent gaze with a scoffing, triumphant smile, a smile of satisfied hatred. The thin lips parted, and their grating cry fell another time upon the heavy silence of the night.

"Bring out your dead!"

As that ominous cry pounded against his ears, Kenneth Dinsmore heard yet another sound: it was the sharp explosion of a revolver.

He stared from the window with straining eyes. Useless to return to the baby's bedside; would not those ghostly pall-bearers emerge from the shadows now, bearing with them the tiny body of his first-born?

They came. But they were carrying what seemed to be a heavy burden. That was no child's tiny form they tossed with hideous upward grins upon the dead-cart.

"Kenneth! Come here!"

It was Arline's voice, with a thrilling undertone of thankfulness in it that whirled Kenneth from the window to her side, all else forgotten.

"Look! He is breathing easier. Doctor, look! Tell me, doesn't he seem better?"

Doctor and nurse exchanged mystified, incredulous glances. It was plain that neither had heard or seen anything out of the ordinary that night, but that the baby's sudden turn for the better had astonished them both.

"I consider it little short of a miracle," pronounced the medical man, after a short examination of the sleeping child. "Madam, your child will live. I congratulate you both."

"Oh, I must tell Father, Kenneth. He will be *so* happy. Dear Father!"

The cold hand of certain knowledge squeezed Kenneth's heart. "If anything should happen to me," Lord Melverson had said. What did that revolver shot mean? What had meant that body the ghostly pall-bearers had carried to the dead-wagon?

A light tap came at the door. The nurse opened it, then turned and beckoned to Kenneth.

"He's gone, Mr. Dinsmore. Break it to her easy, sir—but it's proud of him she ought to be." His voice trembled, broke. "Twas not the little master *they* carried away in the accursed dead-cart, thanks to him. I tried to stop him, sir; forgive me, I loved him! But he *would* make the sacrifice; he said it was worth trying. And so—he—did—it. But—*he's broken the curse, sir, he's broken the curse!*"

A SOUL WITH TWO BODIES

Urann Thayer

URANN THAYER APPEARS TO be as much of a ghost as the disappearing character in this story. The byline is almost certainly a pseudonym, very possibly for William Rollins, Jr. (1897–1950), who also wrote for *Ghost Stories* magazine under the pseudonym O'Connor Stacy. The deduction that leads to Rollins as the true author is that his full name was William Stacy Uran Rollins, which seems a pretty strong clue, as Uran or Urann are extremely uncommon names. Rollins wrote for several mystery magazines, most notably *Black Mask*, for which he wrote twenty-one stories. He also wrote several novels under his own name, including *Midnight Treasure* (1929), *The Wall of Men* (1938), and *The Ring and the Lamp* (1947), as well as one mystery novel as Stacy, *Murder at Cypress Hall* (1933), along with short stories for such pulps as *Clues* and *Mystery Stories*. There were three stories by Stacy in *Ghost Stories* and four by Urann Thayer, the only four stories known under this name.

Much of this information—and speculation—is the result of research by the outstanding scholar of supernatural fiction, Mike Ashley.

"A Soul with Two Bodies" was originally published in the February and March 1928 issues of *Ghost Stories*.

A Soul with Two Bodies

URANN THAYER

THIS LETTER, my dear wife, or at least my part of it, is going to be extremely short, since I gave you all my personal news yesterday. For the rest, I am enclosing the strangest, most horrible document it has ever been my fortune to read.

I told you yesterday how we stopped at this little village in the Dolomite Mountains, in the shadow of a great and gloomy chateau; I told you too, about our host's daughter, the charming girl Myra—how pale and beaten she looks, and how she shrank from the sight of strangers and uttered a pitiful cry when we said we were Americans.

Well, now I understand why. Today, George and I climbed up to the chateau, against the earnest entreaty of our aged host, who shuddered at the mere suggestion; for a vivid description of the place, inside and out, I refer you to the ill-fortuned writer of the enclosed, who can far surpass my poor descriptive powers.

We examined the whole chateau, which was deserted by its Austrian owners when the Italians conquered this country, and finally we arrived in a deep sort of cellar, where, upon opening a thick old door, we found ourselves in the family vaults. We were about to retreat, when George grasped my arm.

"My God! will you look here!" he whispered.

Holding my candle high, I crossed the stone floor, to see, laid side by side, two open caskets, both tenanted! Due to the dryness of the vault, the bodies were fairly well preserved, and we lowered our candles to look at them more closely.

One was a young man, English or American, and with a face that was extraordinarily good-looking, but sensitive and imaginative. On looking closer, I was astonished to see his body was tightly bound, hand and foot.

The other's face—well, once again I refer you to the tragic document, the writer of which had sad reasons for being able to describe it vividly. I'll say this much, though: even in death, it was so repulsive, so demoniacally powerful looking, that I instinctively backed away when I saw it. One arm fell limply out of this second coffin, and on the stone floor beside it lay a revolver.

Near to the caskets was an ancient table and a rickety old chair, and under a candle, long ago burnt to the table's edge, lay a thick bunch of folded paper. This we took up and glanced over—and before long, the subtle horror of that chateau over our heads was making our flesh creep, while the terrible experiences of the unhappy writer were sending thrills of fear through us, such as I, at any rate, had never before experienced.

And I think that even you, dearest, in far-away America, surrounded though you are by the comforts and reality of the city, must share our horror as you sit by your electric lamp, turning these pages. But I'll let the document speak for itself:

It's all over now—and I loved life so much! I'd hoped for so much! It's hard, when one is young, filled with the hot blood and ambitions of youth, to die by his own hand!

But it's *not* by my own hand, and that is why I must die! It is *his* hand, long, strong with the strength of the devil, snake-like; to look at it turns one's stomach; to think of carrying it through life makes me faint with horror! No, no! The best thing that hand can do is turn the muzzle of this gun against that hideous head and end it all.

I have already laid my dead body in one casket. Now I shall lie myself—if I can still use that word "myself"—in the other; and in a moment it will be over. Perhaps some kind person will chance upon this foul place in years to come and bury myself—or myselves—as I should be buried. And perhaps, if that person comes before *she* dies, he will read this and explain it all to her, and then, maybe, she will understand. God grant that may be true—if He has not deserted me altogether. Anyhow, it is for that reason that I set this all down before I leave the world forever.

If I had never wandered away from my fellow-soldiers that night, I should never have seen this chateau, this stronghold of all that is hellish, and this terrible fate would not have fallen upon me; it was the summer of 1918, an August night, while I was serving, along with a small detachment of American troops, with the Italian army in the mountainous neighbourhood slightly north-west of the famous Monte Grappa.

It was a quiet sector, and there had been scarcely any action since my arrival two months earlier. This night, however, we took part in a small skirmish; and in the confusion that followed, I became separated from my detachment.

The stars were shining quite brightly, but there was no moon; and knowing next to nothing about astronomy, I was completely ignorant of the direction I must take to return to my buddies. I wandered through the deep valley, beneath the far-away peaks of the Dolomites, which I could make out, standing black against the spangled sky, and finally, after a couple of hours, I struck a mule path that climbed easily along the sides of the mountains. I hoped it would lead me to our lines.

I followed this for another hour, making my way slowly, as in places, right at my side, it dropped, sheer, to the silent and invisible valley-bed a thousand feet below. Always I was on the alert for the enemy; always I hoped against hope that another turn around the mountains would take me in sight of my friends. And I kept on, plodding wearily, until at last a sharp turn did show me something unexpected—but not the camp of my friends.

It was a chateau, a hundred yards ahead of me, rising majestic and black against the mountain that dropped away behind it. Not one light shone in its innumerable dark windows; not a sound, no sign of life, disturbed its gloomy grandeur. And I decided that its owners, like most of the wealthy families that lived along the various fronts, had deserted their home to await, in healthier climes, the coming of peace, leaving the surrounding peasants, who had little to lose, to stay and keep guard.

I advanced toward the chateau, for want of a better direction to take, and reaching the high iron gate that opened into the courtyard, I suddenly paused. There was no hope of finding my detachment before daylight, I thought, and this place seemed deserted. Then why not break in, if I could, and try to find a comfortable bed for the night, instead of sleeping on an uncomfortable rocky couch, and taking a chance of being caught by the Austrian patrol, if I had crossed into their lines?

Since that night, I've often wondered what fiend of hell put that thought in my head; for surely mere chance could not have ordered the terrible fate that was standing in wait for me!

The great gate was locked; but the wall, which was about fifteen feet high, had been so roughened by time that it was an easy matter to find a foothold. And making my way up with difficulty, I reached the top and dropped to the other side, into a high black courtyard, similar to those of ancient strongholds, only on a smaller scale.

The crack of my feet as they struck the ancient stone paving echoed loudly against the three walls that rose around me to twice my height, and against the building itself, looming dark and silent in back of me. I whirled around to look at the chateau, feeling sure that if anybody were inside, he must have been awakened by the noise, and appear.

But the long French windows directly ahead of me returned my stare, blank and empty, and above them other lines of windows were equally dark and still. If anybody stood in the dark rooms behind them, he kept well out of sight as he watched me.

That was the uneasy thought that entered my head. I can't say why, for before this an empty house had meant an empty house to me, and nothing more. I suppose its grandeur and its gloominess and the fact that it stood in the loneliness of the mountains, caused that eerie feeling to creep over me. I even turned to look once more at the high walls, half contemplating climbing over them again and taking a chance on meeting the Austrian patrol—and somehow I felt my heart sink when I realized it was impossible to climb from this side.

Although the outside had been allowed to crumble away, the inside had been plastered smooth within the last generation, and there was no chance of gaining a foothold here.

However, I shrugged my shoulders, wheeled about, and started for the great iron door ahead of me, the sound of my feet ringing against the flags and echoing against the dark, silent front of the building, that rose high up, to where several uneven turrets vied with the mountain crags behind them, cutting the night sky with awe-inspiring gloom. Grasping the big iron ring that served as the door's handle, I twisted it, and was pleasantly surprised to find the door slowly open, though it creaked and squeaked in protest till its cries rang through the whole dark building. I entered and lit a match.

A great hall sprang into sight. On its walls I saw lines of crossed swords and shields of beaten silver, gleaming in the faint light, becoming fainter farther along the hall, till finally they were swallowed in the gloom. Ahead of me, so far away I could scarcely make it out in the flickering light and shadows, rose the grand staircase, leading to the floor above.

As the match died out, I crossed the floor of mosaic pavements, walking unconsciously on tip-toe; and even that muffled tread whispered against the far walls about me. I reached the stairs quicker than I expected, and my toe rapped against the lowest step. A hollow echo rose through the gloom, beating against the walls of the empty halls over my head. I stopped a moment. Was there the sound of a light step, directly above me? I listened, holding my breath.

But if there *was* somebody there, he, too, was standing very still and listening to me.

I waited a while longer, and then cursing myself for an imaginative coward, and deciding to prove myself wrong, once and for all, I rushed up the stairs, the sound of my feet beating hollowly against the walls of a hundred empty rooms. I whirled around at the landing, and ran up the remaining steps, two at a time; and then grabbing my match-box and striking a match quickly, I held it high.

I saw another great hall, similar to the one below. Its high ceiling scarcely appeared in my tiny light, and the walls for the most part disappeared in the dense shadows. And there was nobody in sight.

Lighting match after match, I turned to the right and allowed chance to direct my reverberating footsteps, the sound of which I no longer attempted to deaden. The few furnishings of that bare hall sprang into sight as I passed—an ancient chair or two, a richly-carved strong box—and finally I arrived at a high doorway, leading into a suite of rooms.

Entering this, I passed through a barely furnished living-room and into a smaller dressing-room, whose narrow walls muffled the sound of my feet; at last, I entered a fair-sized bedroom.

Here was a bed. A bed! If you could understand what that meant to a man who for over a year had considered himself lucky if he slept on a cot! I threw myself down on it, sank into its luxurious softness, and closed my eyes for sleep.

But sleep did not come. Instead, I lay in that darkness, and a queer, unpleasant heaviness weighted down my eyes and numbed my brain; but I did not sleep. From some village in the valley, directly below the chateau, rose the clear, rounded note of a church bell, ringing the hour.

One . . . two . . . !

And the heaviness crept over me. Like a silent, invisible cloud, entering the room, filled with the dust of some sleep-producing drug, that unpleasant sensation passed over me, soothing my body. I fought against it; and finally I forced my eyes open.

And then I knew I was not alone in that room. I turned my eyes to right and left, my body being too sluggish to move my head. I could see nobody, and I could hear nothing in that intense stillness. Yet I knew that another presence was in that darkness beside my bed; and more than that, I knew he was watching me.

I forced my head to turn, to look farther; and then I saw them—two eyes, staring steadily at my face! And when they caught my gaze, they held me, like a grim spider clutching his prey.

I could not turn my eyes away. His eyes seemed to stand out of the darkness, alone, silently boring into me. A faintness passed over me. Queer noises commenced whispering in my brain.

My resistance became less and less. Already, evil dreams were popping into my brain as I lay there, motionless as a corpse. Weird faces appeared, vivid, terrible. They spoke to me. I was conversing with them—out in a deathlike plain of darkness and endless space, we were floating, floating, floating!

I sat upright. The terrible shriek that had waked me was dying away, vibrating through the empty rooms around me—dying away, till nothing was left but that oppressive silence.

I was wide awake now, and I knew the room was free from any presence save my own. Had I dreamed it, or *had* there been somebody here? And if so, whereabout in this great chateau was he waiting so silently?

I sat up; and then—then I was once more

aware of the presence; not in the room now, but somewhere in the chateau. And I knew that wherever he stood, those terrible eyes were turned again toward me, and through walls and ceilings, their power was concentrated against my body. A sluggishness crept over me; those noises commenced whispering once more in my brain, as, sitting there, my eyelids dropped heavily over my eyes.

But, distant by several rooms, the power was not so great now; and throwing it off with one tremendous effort, I rose to my feet and commenced tip-toeing through the series of chambers, until finally I knew I stood at the entrance to the great hall. For, though I could neither see nor hear anything, the very thinness of the air around me showed the immense size and barrenness of the place.

I walked quietly to the centre of the hall, and then stood, listening. Everything was still, still as the grave; but what was that odour of something burning, something unpleasant and overpowering? Sniffing in all directions, I finally figured it came from somewhere above me, and lighting a match glanced at the two huge staircases, side by side, one of which descended, its steps becoming less and less clear, until finally it plunged into the gloom of the floor below, and the other rising through a like impenetrable gloom to the floor above.

I headed for this, creeping up the steps slowly and quietly. At the landing I turned and glanced along the hallway of the floor to which I was climbing—to see, far down it, a faint streak of light, coming from some room at the end of a suite. I tip-toed up and along the hall to the doorway. Here, beyond a darkened room, I could see a pair of closely drawn portières, through which the light scarcely filtered and behind which I could hear a deep, monotonous voice. I made my way to this and pulled the velvet cautiously aside, and a queer shiver passed over my body.

A girl faced me, the most charming, soft-haired girl I had ever seen. She stood in the centre of the floor, her body swaying, her gorgeous white throat thrown back. And in her wide-open violet-blue eyes, there was a look of horror such as I hope never again to see.

She seemed to be staring at me. But in reality, she saw nothing. Those beautiful eyes were glazed with a hypnotic influence; with all her power she tried to hold her head averted—from him.

Him! How shall I describe the man, the thing, that towered over her, not moving a muscle, just regarding her, steadily . . . steadily . . . waiting until she was forced to turn her eyes to his, when she would be completely subdued? How *can* I describe him now, as I sit in the darkness and the silence of this vault, beaten at last by him; as I actually employ those bulging eyes of his and those long, hideous fingers to write this document? But you who discover this—if ever in years to come these papers are found—gaze upon him, as he lies in his coffin—if his body has not mouldered away—look into those hideous, bulging eyes, glazed by death, and think of how they looked to me, and to her, with all the power of his hellish mind behind them!

He stood, towering in a long, black cloak. Somewhere, a cigarette he had laid down was burning, and from that cigarette came the queer, exotic odour I had noted. I heard the monster speak to the girl in German, a language I understood fairly well. His voice was low, monotonous, terrible; it repulsed one, and at the same time, fascinated with its hypnotic power.

"Remember, Myra, I am not forcing you. But you want to come to me, Myra; you want to come to me and stay with me forever and ever," he said slowly.

"I don't! I don't!" she gasped, hoarsely. "Let me go, *mein Graf*! Let me go back down to the village!"

"You will never want to go down to the village again, Myra," he droned, hypnotically. "Once you have turned again and looked into my eyes, you will want to be with me always. Turn and look at me, Myra. Turn and look at me!"

Her head moved slowly, drawn by that terrible power. I could see her delicately tipped nose in profile. But now her pretty red lips parted in one last feeble effort.

"I'll scream again," she whispered. "I'll wake whoever is downstairs!"

"No, you won't, Myra," replied that slow, monotonous voice. "You can't scream now. And besides, I have put him to sleep, and it would be no good." He glided a step closer. "Turn, Myra," he droned. "Turn to me . . . turn . . . turn . . ."

And completely overpowered, she turned to face him.

Up till this time I had watched, fascinated, almost conquered myself by the power he exercised over the girl. Now, however, I suddenly pulled myself together, ready to spring on him.

I did not move an inch; I had not as yet made the slightest sound. But that very thought and exertion of will on my part seemed to penetrate his silent smooth-flowing will, to strike a discordant note.

Slowly, those terrible, bulging eyes left the face of the girl before him. His head turned, slowly—slowly—until finally those eyes rested on the spot where I hid. I knew he could not see me; but I could feel powerful, hypnotic waves steal over me, weave around me, as a spider weaves his web around a helpless fly.

There was a scream from the released girl. I heard her slip through the far side of the portières, I knew that for one brief instant she stopped and gazed into my face while my eyes remained rigidly before me. I heard her light feet fly down the stairs . . . growing fainter . . . fainter. A door, far below us, opened and slammed. The echoes died away on the walls around us, and everything was still again.

And he stood before me motionless, tall, powerful, his face emaciated and ghastly pale; and those bulging eyes, like glinting steel, gazed into mine. Everything before me grew faint and grey, save those eyes. They seemed to float by themselves in a cloudy darkness, like two mystic stars. The dark whispering commenced again in my brain. I felt myself swaying. And now those eyes were drawing nearer, as he approached.

Whether, in commanding his limbs to move

toward me, he distracted some of the power concentrated upon me, I don't know. But suddenly a flicker of strength returned to me.

Quickly, almost mechanically, my hand shot to my belt. My army gun flashed up. There was a thundering report, though I do not recall pulling the trigger.

The man stopped. His terrible eyes seemed to bulge farther than ever. For a moment he stood, staring at me.

"*You're going now,*" he said, "*but you'll come back.*" The words came out in English—low, guttural, and lifeless. I could have sworn that life had already passed from the loathsome body, and that he was speaking from Beyond. But once more the monotonous sound came through his repulsive, voluptuous lips:

"*It's not the end for you. You're coming back—and I'll be waiting!*" Then he collapsed in a heap.

Cold dawn was stealing through the barred windows as I hurried down the stairs. A quick search in the rear of the building showed me an unlocked door, by which the girl probably escaped. I slipped through this, and discovering the direction to our lines by the faint light in the east, I was able to make my way back to my comrades before the sun rose.

God, how sweet the fresh air seemed, after the heavy, drugged air of that dark chateau! How beautiful and safe seemed the bodies of my comrades, sleeping in the dugout here! One thing was certain, I thought, as I made my way on tip-toe to my own bunk and sank down on it: whatever happened in the future, I should never go back to that fiendish place! Never, I thought, never!

And as that thought flashed through my brain, I stooped down to unwind my puttees—and met the eyes of my buddy, Fred Vincent. His look seemed odd.

"Did you whisper something to me?" he asked in a low voice, after staring at me a second.

I shook my head. Fred sat up, rubbed his eyes as if trying to waken himself, and then turned and regarded me with an odd look.

"It's funny," he said, still in a low voice, "but

it seemed as if—as if somebody rather terrible to look at was leaning over my bed. And he put his lips to my ear and whispered, ever so clear: '*Tell him, it's not the end!*' he whispered. '*Tell him, he's coming back . . . and I'll be waiting!*'"

The Armistice came, and two months later found me in Paris, employed as a representative of an American automobile concern. I succeeded in my work beyond my best hopes, and at the end of another year, I was a fairly prosperous man, with rooms in a fine, up-to-date apartment on the Boulevard Raspail.

I remember sitting by the window in my living-room on the sixth floor, early one evening. Below me gleamed the stationary street lamps and the moving, criss-crossing lamps of the continual line of automobiles; the noise rose to my window with a muffled roar. It was all so snappy, so modern and safe! But my thoughts drifted away to that gloomy chateau, rising in the silence of the forests of the Dolomite Mountains. It was all so far away, I thought; so impossible. Even the beautiful child of the violet-blue eyes and the maddening white throat seemed unreal. It was a dream, a hideous nightmare, in which an angel flitted for a brief moment.

I remember that that was on the fifteenth of December, because the same evening was the never-to-be-forgotten evening I spent with the Dawsons.

There were about ten of us there, all members of the American business colony; and after dinner we moved to the drawing-room, where we sat about our coffee, drinking and chatting.

Somehow, the conversation turned to Spiritualism, and practically everyone scoffed at it. Pretty Helen Purcell, however, had a doubtful word to say in its defence.

"There's nothing in it, I know," she said with a laugh. "But have you ever been to a séance? They may be fake, but they're terribly thrilling!"

"I know they are! Awfully eerie!" Jane Dawson, our hostess, jumped to her feet. "Let's rig one up!" she cried. "Come on, Professor Fallow, you be our medium! I'm sure you've got a lot of psychic waves, or static, or whatever you call it!"

We all burst into laughter, and old Doctor Fallow, an exchange professor at the Sorbonne, rose to his feet. He was a thin, dried-up man, capable of saying extraordinarily funny things in a very solemn voice.

"I feel extremely psychic tonight," he said, in a slow pompous voice. "I feel a queer, crawling sensation along my body which must be spirit fingers—though till now I simply took it to be my winter underwear that I put on today for the first time."

While the laughter died away, he seated himself at the far end of the room, before a table. All lights, save a lamp directly beside him, were extinguished. Then, in the hush that followed, Fallow placed his finger-tips on the table and stared before him, into space.

"Communication for Mr. Dawson," he commenced, solemnly, "from Moses—Abe Moses, late of Grand Street, New York. He says to pay that last instalment on your piano to his wife, or he'll get the spirit law after you!"

"Good!" cried Dawson, in the laugh that followed. "What's his wife's name?"

There was a long pause. The old man continued to stare solemnly before him, but—did a shudder pass over his body, leaving his face paler, even, than usual? For a minute we waited for an answer, but no answer came.

"I say!" Dawson demanded again. "Why don't you tell me her name? I can't make out a cheque unless I know it, you know!"

Again a long silence followed. Then the old man's lips moved—moved tightly over his teeth, like a dead man's.

"*Myra,*" he said, his voice hoarse and lifeless.

For some reason, a shudder passed over me. I heard Dawson's jovial voice, coming out of the darkness around us.

"Myra?" he cried. "That's a pretty name for a piano salesman's wife!"

The old man did not heed him. He stared directly before him, and once more those lips moved.

"*Myra . . . look at me, Myra . . . look at me, and you will be calm . . . calm . . . calm . . .*" The voice, very faint, was a terrible monotone now. It did not seem to come from the man's lips, but rather from far down within him, like a far-away voice, overheard as it addressed another person in confidential tones. The room was quiet now, and the people sitting in the darkness around me grew tense.

As for me, I sat there, feeling that creeping sensation, which the old man had laughed at a few minutes earlier, crawling up my back. Myra! The name of that far-away Austrian girl! Could there be any connection? And those words and the voice—how strangely familiar they sounded, calling to me from a near-forgotten past, through those dried-up lips! But now he spoke again.

"*Myra . . .*" sounded that lifeless, muffled voice. "*Don't scream, Myra . . . you can't wake him . . . he sleeps, until I am ready for him.*"

One of the women choked back a hysterical laugh. I saw Jim Edgemere, a consulate man, half rise to his feet.

"Better cut it, Doctor Fallow," he snapped. "You're too good an actor for the girls!" but his wife pulled him back again.

A long silence followed the interruption, a terrible silence in which no one stirred. The old man continued to stare before him, motionless, unseeing. His outstretched fingers did not move; his lips did not move; it almost seemed as if he did not breathe.

Then, slowly, his head turned, as if on a pivot. His eyes, no longer lifeless, bulged out, a terrible light in them, until I heard the woman beside me draw in her breath with fear. Slowly, slowly, his head turned, until, finally, those eyes rested on mine in the half light—and my heart stopped beating a moment, as I thought I saw *another's* eyes, gazing through his at me!

An evil smile, like the smile of a dead body, curved the lips; and now he spoke again, this time loudly, and directly to myself.

"*It's not the end for you,*" he said. "*You're coming back . . . and I am waiting for you. . . .*"

There was a scream, and Helen Purcell fell in a dead faint. Immediately the lights were switched on, and young Doctor Palmer rushed to her side and commenced chafing her wrists. She opened her eyes, to our immense relief; and at that very moment, a cry from our hostess caused us to whirl about.

"Look!" she gasped. "Professor Fallow!" She pointed to where the old man slumped, a crumpled heap, across the table.

In a moment the young doctor was at his side. He chafed his wrists for a moment, as he had the girl's. Then, suddenly stopping, he lifted the man's head and examined him carefully. Finally he glanced up.

Jim Edgemere intercepted the grave look on the doctor's face.

"Is he—dead?" he asked, in a low voice.

For answer, the doctor stared at the motionless body in a puzzled fashion. Finally he looked up.

"If—if I did not feel it would be the remark of a madman," he said, in repressed tones, "I would say he has been dead ten minutes!"

I walked home that night, a terrible fear clutching at me. Could it be true that this power, this Influence, not only was able to reach beyond the grave, but stretch beyond mountains, beyond national borders, like a terrible Hand, stretching out silently to grasp me? I glanced around at the broad, busy Champs Elysées, as I hurried down it, at the lighted bridge of the Concorde as I crossed it. It was absurd, I decided! How could this power, whatever its strength, force me to return to that lonely country and chateau, where it held sway? And I laughed to myself.

And as I laughed, a picture suddenly flashed across my brain—the picture of a beautiful girl with violet-blue eyes. It was startlingly vivid, all the more startling, because I had remembered her only vaguely all this time. And as I pictured that charming face, that gorgeous throat, a vague uneasiness crept over me. It was as if some devilishly keen opponent had discovered a weak spot in my armour, which I myself did not know existed. Had I unconsciously been wounded by an arrow from young love's bow?

"But what difference could that make to *him?*" I said, half aloud, as, entering my apartment building, I stepped into the automatic elevator and mounted to the sixth floor. Striding down the long dark corridor to my own rooms, the sound of my feet muffled in the thick plush carpet, I reached my door and unlocked it. Whatever happened, there was one thing I was willing to swear to: in no circumstances would I ever again go to that mysterious chateau; never, never again.

And throwing open the door, I stepped into the dark, empty living-room of my apartment.

"I won't give in!" I cried aloud, clenching my fists to steel myself. "I won't!" And the echo of my words beat against the dark walls around me. Those words gave me strength, and undressing and jumping into bed, I succeeded in controlling my thoughts long enough to get to sleep.

With the morning, however, came a horrible realization. Dull memories of tortured dreams rose in my mind, and although I tried to laugh it off, I knew deep inside that I had entered upon a struggle—a struggle with a powerful, evil Mind, released from its body. For over a year that Mind had probably hovered over me, hunting for a point of attack; and yesterday evening, through the poor old professor's mind, it had found an opening. Fear had entered my consciousness; and through fear, it hoped gradually to gain control of me, to overpower me.

And so it proved true. As I sat at my desk in my busy office or walked the crowded streets, always that thought remained at the back of my head—the thought of *him.* And as the thought jumped into my consciousness, more and more that Mind seized at the opening, drilled into me, trying to weaken my resistance. As I thought of *him,* so I thought more and more of *her,* the soft-skinned peasant girl of the violet-blue eyes. In the daytime, I saw her beautiful, innocent face always before me, and in the night, she was always in my dreams. Somehow, terrible as it seems, the two went together in my thoughts:

the personification of Evil. It almost seemed as though *he* thrust the memory of her before me, and thus weakened my resistance.

I became nervous and jumpy; my face grew pale and haggard-looking. But I fought; fought with all my strength and reason, so that never was *he* able to gain, even for a moment, that complete power over me that *he* wanted—the power which, I knew, meant the end. So long as I strode the gay streets or sat in the noisy cafés of Paris, I felt myself protected by a force *he* was unable to combat; for that force lay in the hard reality that surrounded my senses; crowds, lights, laughter . . . so different from the mystic gloominess of that chateau in the Dolomites, where he held sway.

"Never will I go where *he* can get me absolutely in his power!" I said to myself, as I sat before a crowded café one evening in late summer. I brought my glass of *anisette* to my lips, holding it tight in my fingers, for nowadays my hand trembled more and more. "*He* is mad to imagine I would be such a fool!" I laughed to myself, and stopped abruptly. Almost, it seemed, I saw *her* in the flesh, standing in the street before me, regarding me with sad, beseeching eyes. I jumped up and ran out a few steps, and found I had been staring at a shrunken old woman who was selling newspapers.

That night, feeling more nervous than ever, I dropped into the Alhambra music-hall, hoping to be calmed and amused by a good show. There was a mind-reading act on when I entered, one of those acts wherein a man sits blindfolded in the centre of the stage, his aide points haphazardly to someone in the audience, and the mind-reader then tells the world about that man's private life. Having always believed that the person chosen from the audience was picked out before the performance began, I dropped into my seat in the back of the darkened theatre, smiling at the credulity of the people around me.

A sheepish-looking man was standing in the middle of the house, the aide having pointed him out, and the blindfolded reader was telling him what he already knew rather well. "Your wife's name is Vivienne. Her age is forty-three, though you've been thinking it's thirty-eight, and you have two children, a boy named Jacques and a girl named . . ." Here he hesitated, for a long time, while he sat motionless in the silence of the house. His aide turned with a look of surprise. The audience stirred uneasily, and then settled back into a puzzled silence. At last he spoke, very, very slowly. "And a girl named . . . Myra!"

There was a gleeful laugh from the man in the audience. Distinctly the patrons heard him say: "*Non! Elle s'appelle Louise!*" and the whole house broke into a roar of laughter.

The laughter died away. The mind-reader sat, still blindfolded, his body tense and motionless. I saw his helper scratch his head in perplexity. Then the reader spoke, and his words came slow and forced. His voice had a strange quality. "Myra, the name *is* Myra!" he said. "I see it standing before me, written in fire!" There was a long pause. "I feel," he said, uncertainly, "some influence, which has come in this house . . ."

He stood up; came to the edge of the stage, without removing the cloth from his eyes. The house was hushed expectantly. Finally he spoke again, in a clear, hard voice, but very slowly.

"Someone is calling. I hear it faint, far, away . . . A woman's voice, calling for help through the darkness . . . Her voice is tragic, helpless . . ." Again he stopped. The audience was breathless with attention, while I sat, the sweat pouring off my face, every nerve taut and quivering. A whole minute passed before he continued in the same slow, deliberate voice. "There is a man in the audience, a man who has just come in . . . an American who fought on the Italian front. Will he stand up?"

There was a swish of moving bodies, and everybody looked right and left and behind them. Scarcely realizing what I did, I forced myself to rise to my feet. Immediately all eyes were turned upon me. The reader, who could neither see nor hear me, turned in my direction.

"You know a girl named Myra?" he asked, low but clearly.

"Yes." The word came out hoarsely, scarcely more than a whisper.

"She is calling to you. I hear her clearer now," he went on in a slow unnatural voice. "It is like a voice from down in a deep, dark valley, calling to the light, helplessly, pitifully. I can hear the words now . . ." He hesitated a moment. "*If you remember, come! Help me! Help me! . . .* I can hear no more."

He stopped. A woman shrieked hysterically. Somewhere behind the scenes, a cautious manager gave orders. The curtain rolled down; lights flashed on.

The cynosure of several thousand eyes, I made my way to the aisle and strode back to the exit, forcing myself to walk steadily. Once outside, I slipped away from any curious members of the audience, and reaching the Café de la Paix, I threw myself into a sidewalk seat and mechanically ordered a fine champagne. While I drank with trembling fingers, I seemed to see her before me, more vividly than ever, her slender body, her smooth, heart-breaking throat, and her violet-blue eyes, gazing solemnly and reproachfully into mine. She was in danger, and she called to me. To *me,* whom she had seen only in a flash, and yet that flash had been so vivid to her that it enabled her to call across the night, to me. As, with fast-beating heart, I thought of this, another thought whispered to me in the back of my brain: "Was it really *she* who called? Or could it be a ruse?"

For a long time I sat there in the crowds and lights of that most famous of all cafés, staring into the great square of honking autos, sauntering crowds, newswomen, policemen—the noisy safe reality where *he* could not come, where millions of prosaic people created a matter-of-fact bulwark that strengthened my resistance and thwarted him. And outside that bulwark, in the darkness beyond these safe borders, was *he* waiting?

For my answer, my vision flashed across the night-covered mountains to the great and gloomy chateau, to the dark, silent rooms, where *he* held sway. And, as if *he* waited there, watching me across the darkness, chuckling at this new hold *he* had on me, I felt a shudder pass through my entire body.

For a long time I sat there, always seeing those violet-blue eyes before me, imploring, reproachful; hearing those words ring over and over in my brain: "*If you remember, come! Help me! Help me!*"

I slipped a five franc note under my glass and, jumping up, I called a taxi. Half an hour later I had thrown a few things in my suitcase, and was speeding down the Gare de Lyon, where I bought a ticket and succeeded in hopping onto the Turin express just as it was leaving the station.

I would not go to the chateau alone. Never! I would go to the village below it, seek information concerning the girl and, if necessary, lead a good-sized posse up to that stronghold of dark evil and rescue her. That, anyhow, is what I thought at the time.

Late the next afternoon I was in the train, chugging north to these mountains in the heart of which I now am. It was a muggy day, with the setting sun struggling rather unsuccessfully to burn its way through the thick clouds. I sat by the window of my compartment, gazing at the passing mountains, that became higher and more rugged as we sped on.

In this little old train, each car was divided into a half-dozen compartments, each separate from the other. A door on each side lets you out at your station but is locked when the train is moving, while two seats, long enough for four persons each, run from door to door and face each other. There were only two old gentlemen in my compartment, sitting opposite each other by the door at the far end. They were pleasant, ordinary looking people, and I paid little attention to them, since they passed the time chatting together in Italian, which I do not understand.

After an hour or two of the journey the conversation died down. I glanced over to see that the man on the same side as myself had fallen asleep where he sat, his limp body jogging up and down as the train bumped along. The gentleman opposite him, too, was blinking drowsily.

They began to affect me. I turned back to view the scenery which, with the coming of darkness, was fast becoming gloomier. Higher and higher rose the sinister mountains, majestic and awe-inspiring. I sank back, half closing my eyes.

Slowly, a queer sensation crept over me, making my body tingle. I steeled myself against it, for I recognised it. But it was strong now, stronger than I had ever known it. I kept my eyes on the window, desperately trying to force an impression of the passing scenery to register on my brain and crowd out the other. But the feeling grew stronger, silently seeping into my consciousness. Like the rhythmic sound of the train's wheels, which was all I could now hear, it crept over me, as if to overpower me.

I turned my eyes away from the scenery, back to the compartment in which I sat. The man who sat on the same side as myself slept peacefully, half reclining in his corner. I glanced at the man opposite him, and suppressed a shiver. His old, shrivelled, kindly face was turned toward me and he was looking at me. But those eyes that bulged out, staring at me, they were not his. They were huge, repulsive, and fixed on me intently in the silence of that compartment. He did not speak; he did not move. He simply gazed with a terrible unblinking stare.

And now, while I sat there unable to make a sound, he commenced to move toward me. Grasping the edge of the cushioned seat with his aged hands, he started slowly sliding along, toward the seat directly opposite mine, where our knees must touch. I clenched my fists; I wet my lips. But I was helpless.

The train gave a lurch. The man in the corner awoke. At the same time the other man's body lurched sideways. He recovered his balance and commenced rubbing his eyes, and when he took his hands away, I saw only the kindly eyes of the old gentleman.

His companion said something, obviously about their having dropped off to sleep, and they both laughed and went on with their conversation. But I sat there trying to regain my control, which I had nearly lost, and I alone knew what losing my control would mean *now*! Had I been dreaming, or were those *his* eyes? And if they were his eyes, looking through the kindly face of the sleeping old man, did it mean his power grew as I neared the fastness of his gloomy home? One more incident served to strengthen this belief in his growing power. It was an incident that unnerved me almost to the extent of giving up my plan.

Late that afternoon we reached the village of Schio, nestled in the foothills of the Dolomites, where I learned that an automobile habitually met the evening train. This automobile served as a bus, driving along the highway that wound up through the mountains, past the small and infrequent hamlets. The car was a closed limousine and although there was room for three on the big seat, one of the old men insisted upon taking the pull-down seat facing his friend, so that we were placed rather similarly to our positions in the train. And thus we sat, the pull-down seat opposite me empty, and we sped along, down the straight road for five hundred metres and then commenced winding up the tortuous mountain path. The sky was still cloudy and the peaks that rose above us flung great shadows across the darkening valley. As we mounted, the road tunnelled more often through the rugged rock formations, sometimes only for the distance of a yard or so, at other times leaving us in utter darkness for some moments.

It was just before we passed through the longest of these tunnels, that one of my companions, with whom I had laughingly attempted to carry on a conversation in two languages, offered his friend and myself a cigarette. We took them, and all three of us lit up. Just then the car shot into that long dark tunnel. Everything was as dark as pitch, and the sound of the engine roared hollowly around us. For all that, we continued our half-successful attempt to make ourselves understood in French and Italian, shouting to one another in the direction of the jerking cigarette ends.

Finally, we gave it up as a bad job, and I settled back in my seat, and suddenly felt my scalp tingle with fear. Before we drove into the tunnel there had been three of us inside the car, smoking cigarettes. Now, as I sat back, I could see the glowing ends of four cigarettes. The fourth was directly opposite myself, and from it came the queer pungent odour of the dead Austrian's cigarettes.

I clapped my hands to my eyes, fighting back the fear that possessed me, and when I removed them, we had shot out into the light of the dying day. Dim as it was, I could see that the seat before me was empty, and there were but three lighted cigarettes.

I breathed a sigh of relief, forcing myself to believe that it was the hallucination of an overwrought brain. Then my attention was attracted by the man beside me, tapping my shoulder. He was looking round in a puzzled fashion, shaking his head in annoyance. "*Fuma!*" he exclaimed. "*Dové?*"

I shrugged my shoulders, but once more my heart shrank, for he, too, had smelt it. Had *he*, then, gained that much more power, the power of materializing to a degree where *he* could actually sit smoking in the darkness, as we penetrated further into his silent country?

As the shadows deepened, as night slowly blotted out even the bare rocks that we shot by, until only the leaping headlights of the car showed the lonely road we traversed, I struggled with a terrible fear: the fear of the supernatural, the fear of a horrible, unknowable death. If only I could have known how much more terrible than my wildest fears would be the doom that awaited me. If only I had followed that inner voice which whispered: "Turn back. Turn back!" As it was, I had not reached a decision when the speeding car slowed down and stopped. The driver turned and pulled down the little window.

"*Ecco, signore!*" he said, looking at me, "here is where you get off."

Instinctively, I glanced beyond the car to where the powerful searchlights shot down the road a hundred yards. On the left of the road was a sheer drop into the black valley far below: on the right rose the perpendicular rocks, bare and rugged, with gnarled, leafless growth springing out of them and shining vividly in the glare. A hundred yards beyond, a small break in the right hand wall of rocks showed a path gently falling away until it was swallowed by the shadows. That path, I knew, led around the deserted mountainside to the great old chateau.

I got out and yanked my suitcase from under the seat and, with a smile, held out my hand to my companions. But when I noted their expressions, as they saw where I was getting off, I think that the smile left my lips.

"*Non è buono,*" said one; and I read fear in his large, old eyes. "It is not good! Down beyond that mountain pass is a terrible——" He had stretched out his hand, pointing along the little road. But suddenly his friend scowled, and immediately his hand dropped. With feigned smiles, but suspicion in their eyes, they said goodbye. After all, I reasoned, what did they know about me, who I was, or what I was doing here?

A moment later, the car started up, gathered speed, and the two powerful lights shot ahead of it farther and farther away, until finally the machine whirled around a corner and was lost to sight altogether. For a moment I stood silently gazing into the darkness where it had disappeared, feeling very much alone, feeling my heart heavy with a foreknowledge of evil. Already, in that dark valley, I seemed to sense that Mind, motionless, silent, but pervading this gloomy country with the calm of undisputed power. I had to go on, ever closer to *its* stronghold, passing under its very windows, before I could reach the village.

"But what can he do if you don't go in the chateau?" I muttered as I picked up my suitcase and started off. At that moment I was mighty certain that I would not go inside without a dozen other men. Taking my flashlight in my free hand, I headed along the road and turned down the path that led through the mountain pass.

The air was heavy; the sky overcast; above and below me the whole world was a black void through which I walked alone. Ahead of me glowed the small circle of flaring light cast by my torch and visible, I imagine, for miles across the valley. It was difficult going as the path became smaller until it degenerated into a mule path, winding around the mountains, a path which I immediately recognized as the one I had stumbled onto that damnable night two years before. This I kept to, feeling the utter desolation of the country around me, hearing the metallic click of my heels as they knocked against the loose stones, and the hollow echo of each step. Then, suddenly, I realised I was hearing another sound, similar to the one I was making. I lifted my flash, and the light shot up the path. An old peasant was in front of me, headed in the same direction as myself. His back was bent, and in his hand he held a stout stick which he used as a cane. By the snail-like speed of his advance and the cautious way he felt the ground before he took a step, I knew that he was blind. Before I had taken three steps, I knew his keen ears had heard me; for he halted, half turned and, drawing himself up, pressed against the overhanging rocks to let me pass.

I hurried on, until, just before reaching his side, I was struck with astonishment. I saw that he was taller than myself while, despite his aged appearance, his toil-worn body was extremely powerful.

"God be with you," I said in the Provençal dialect, that being my nearest approach to Italian.

"God be with you." His reply, low and gruff, was with a German guttural. It rumbled hollowly in the still air around us, lifeless as his cold, lifeless eyes that stared unseeingly into the darkness beyond.

As I passed him my hand inadvertently brushed his smock, and an odd quiver shot through my entire body. Clenching my teeth to force myself to be calm, I strode on. For a minute I could hear nothing but the clink of my heels and the clatter of the pebbles they disturbed. Then I heard him turn and recommence his journey after me. But now, instead of the slow, cautious pace, his step had quickened.

Tap . . . tap . . . tap. The sound of that stick on the stones sent a weird, hollow echo across the deep, still valley beside us. *Tap . . . tap . . . tap.* It hurried after me with incredible speed. And I, hurrying my own pace, felt my heart growing heavy within me. Somehow, I seemed to know that in that blind man was centred the malign influence that meant the end. Somehow, I felt it was not a man following me, but a fiend in man's form!

I sped around a bend on the run and saw, straight ahead of me, a lone, black turret, outlined like an evil sign against the sky. I had reached the chateau.

The sound of the man following me was lost behind the bend in the cliff as I made my way toward that dark building. In its place I heard the moaning of the rising wind, sighing through the invisible trees above me, and I hurried on. Somehow, I felt that if I could pass that chateau before the blind man caught up, I would be able to continue safely on to the village. I broke into as fast a run as the narrow, treacherous path would allow. Nearer, nearer the chateau; and then . . .

Tap . . . tap . . . tap. He had rounded the bend. I whirled my light around and saw his bent body moving jerkily toward me. He stopped; not because of the light, which he could not see, but because his keen ears told him I was standing still. He straightened his bent body and peered forward, his sightless eyes turned in my direction. For all the world he looked like a beast, scenting its prey. Then he bent over and started again, and God! the speed with which he now approached me was something more than human. It was as if he, too, felt that all was lost to him should I pass the chateau.

I ran along the path that led around the back of the building to the village. I reached the chateau, hearing him come closer and closer. I sped alongside the wall—nearly passed it. Then, suddenly, I tripped and fell. He was almost upon me. My head in a whirl, with only the thought of escaping in my mind, I jumped up, saw a big door beside me and, pulling it open, I ran inside. Standing on my toes, scarcely breathing,

I waited in terrible silence and blackness while, slowly, the horrible realisation dawned upon me that I had entered the chateau where the fiend himself was waiting for me.

Meanwhile, the old man neared the door; he was moving stealthily now. Even had I not been able to hear the low *tap, tap, tap* of his stick, I would have known of his approach by the subtle horror that crept over me. Who was this old man? It was not *he,* that I knew. More likely it was some strong-bodied, weak-minded peasant that the fiend was able to enter and control.

Tap, tap, tap . . . tap . . . tap . . . tap.

He halted, directly beside the door, and listened. Though we were separated by the thick, closed door, I could almost see him standing there, listening for my tell-tale sound. Then, although I could neither see nor hear anything, I knew the door was slowly opening.

I switched on my light and felt my way down a long corridor. Under my feet was a thick plush carpet that I knew must deaden the sound to even his keen ears. I followed it until finally I stepped into the huge entrance hall where, far ahead of me, I could see the grand staircase rising above my circle of light, into the darkness of the landing. I tip-toed on till I was about a dozen feet from the door; then I turned about, and what I saw caused the flashlight to slip from my fingers while I stifled a shriek. The ghostly figure of the old man was advancing silently toward me, and it was surrounded by a strange, unearthly light. Now he reached the end of the corridor; he felt around; he seemed to know he stood at the opening to the main hall. Then he straightened his strong body. His sightless eyes turned in my direction, and he listened. How tense a moment it was. For a long time we faced each other, neither moving a muscle, while he waited for the slightest sound, like a spider ready to pounce upon its prey. I felt my heart pound within me until it seemed he must hear it. If only I could pass him. If I could slip into that corridor again, I could flee from the chateau. I would be safe.

He was standing just inside the doorway, about ten feet from me. Clenching my fists, scarcely daring to breathe, I started tip-toeing toward the corridor. Nearer I moved to him, my eyes always on his face. Then, just as I came abreast of him, I felt my heart shudder. For, while I watched him, I was suddenly aware of a horrible transformation. Those eyes, till now bleary and sightless, could see me.

With an exclamation, I broke into a run; but before I had taken three steps, I felt a sharp blow on the back of my head as he hurled his heavy stick after me. Half dazed, I staggered back, and fell into his strong arms.

How shall I explain the sensations of my stunned mind? I offered no resistance, partly because of the blow that had weakened me, but partly, too, because I knew there was no hope. And, limp and half alive, I felt those arms, supernaturally strong now, lift me like a babe. In a state approaching coma, I knew I was being carried up a flight of stairs, up another and along a black corridor. I knew I was in a darkened room now, and I felt myself gently laid on the floor, alongside another body which, without even seeing it, I knew to be that of the dead *Graf,* untouched by time, and lying in exactly the same position in which it had fallen, two years before.

Strong fingers bound me with a thick cord in the darkness; bound me so that I could move neither hand nor foot. Then my helpless body was rolled on its side, till I knew I was face to face with the Count, a foot away.

As my head cleared, I heard the old man rise in the darkness. His work was done, and he left the room. I heard him patter down the stairs. The sound of his feet died away in the distance. Far, far below me now, I could hear his stick feeling its blind way along the pebbles of the path beneath the windows. It grew fainter, fainter . . . and then all was still as death.

I lay there, wondering if this was the end planned for me—to die of starvation beside the body of the man I had killed; or had that fiendish mind evolved some scheme for punishment, even more horrible?

Then I knew I was not alone. Somewhere in that room, *he* was watching me. That terrible, sinking sensation, that ghastly pulling at the heart, which I knew so well, had come over my body stronger than ever before. And then, finally, I understood.

Having led the old man safely away, *he* had left that borrowed body; and now, for the first time, his evil spirit had re-entered his own body and, lying outstretched alongside me, he was gazing at me through those dead eyes, stronger than ever now, for his own body offered no resistance such as another's would. He did not move; he made no sound. But I knew those dead eyes gazed into mine, steadily, unblinkingly.

I felt that faintness steal over me; noises commenced humming, in my ears, growing louder. I clenched my fists and fought against it. I forced visions of far away, safe Paris to my mind. I was sitting at the Café de la Paix. Street lamps, lighted music halls were around me. Glaring headlights of a thousand automobiles flashed across the square, while the cars honked their ways through the masses of people who were shouting, laughing, singing. What did I care for dark valleys and mystic chateaux, still and deserted? They were all so far away . . .

Ah, no they weren't. I lay bound hand and foot in one, and in the tomb-like blackness and silence of this room, those poisonous eyes bored into mine, weakening me. Nausea crept over me. Grey specks flashed across my vision like an endless hurricane. Something rang, *rang,* RANG, like a terrible gong of death. And all the time I felt that terrible strain, as if my heart were being pulled out of me.

Somebody chuckled. I listened, and knew with horror that it was myself. Again a loud, mad laugh. And now I was talking. I was a hundred people, talking, laughing, cursing, while always those motionless eyes pulled at my heart strings. Suddenly something inside me snapped. I heard a sickening rattle in my own throat. And then came darkness . . .

"Signore!" Far away, a girl's voice called to me. I opened my eyes. The window shades were

drawn and it was dark in the room, but I could see that the dawn had come again.

"*Signore! Signore!*" the girl called again, her voice quivering with fear. I sat up and was overjoyed to find I was untied. I listened for the sweet voice, which I knew was the voice of that charming Austrian girl, calling to me in Italian. I rose to my feet.

Free! I was free, I thought. Not only free, but I felt a strange power course through my body that had always been only too delicate. I strode out of the room and ran quickly down the stairs. In the hall I stopped only to pick up my flashlight, which was lying where I had dropped it the night before.

I heard the girl calling again. She was coming toward me, along a pitch-dark corridor at the rear. I ran to meet her, flashing my light upon her. God, how beautiful she was, though her face was white as marble, and her violet-blue eyes wide with fear. She raised her hand to protect her eyes from the glaring light and then took it away, trying to penetrate the darkness where I stood.

"It—it is the young man who came before?" she whispered hesitantly. "The American or Englishman who save me?"

"It is," I replied. "And for two years he has dreamed of seeing you again."

A relieved smile lit her face. "I knew it was you," she whispered. "When my old grandfather told me of the foreigner who passed him on the path, I—I somehow was sure it was you. And when——" and now her smile died away— "when he told me of the queer feeling that rushed over him afterwards, as if a devil had entered his body, and how he had a vague memory of entering the chateau, but could really remember nothing clearly till he stood before his own door in the village, then I knew *he*—" she shuddered as she formed the word with her lips, "—had done his work; and I was afraid. I slipped away from the house before dawn, and I have been searching, searching——" Her voice died away, and she dropped her eyes.

I took a step toward her. "You braved everything to come to my aid?"

She nodded.

"You see," she whispered, "I felt partly to blame. The night before last I dreamed of you. I dreamed I was calling to you. And yet, I was afraid to have you come. It was as if somebody stood over my bed and forced me."

I remembered the mind-reader in the theatre. Taking her hand in mine, I gently pressed her fingers. I felt her shudder. "Come," she whispered, "we must get away from this place, from *him*!"

"There's nothing to fear," I replied softly. I drew her close and we walked together into the entrance hall, toward the outer door of the chateau, toward happiness and freedom. "He has lost his power. I know it, because I feel free."

But now her whole body was trembling. "No, no!" she gasped. "He is here! He is near us! I . . ."

We were passing near one of the long narrow windows that lighted the gloomy hall and she was walking close by my side. Suddenly she turned to look at me, and her words ended in a shriek as she tore herself free from my hold. Astounded, I saw her stare at my face. In her eyes I could read a terror even greater than on that night when I first saw her. Her fingers rose as if to make the sign of the cross; and then, before it was completed, she swayed and sank at my feet in a faint.

I stared down at her, stunned. Slowly I lifted my eyes to a tall mirror before me, while a tremendous fear crept over my body, leaving me cold. Then I saw the image reflected there, and recoiled as if from a snake.

Staring out of that long glass at me was the hideous face of the dead Count!

Having overpowered me, as I lay bound on the floor, he had transferred my mind, my soul, to his own dead body. That was his ghastly revenge.

What can I say of my feelings as I gazed at the loathsome thing that was now myself? What words can express the horror as, tottering up to the room beyond the portières, I turned the light upon the bound body that was mine, and yet no longer mine, lying limp and lifeless, the eyes closed in a soulless slumber. In a daze I staggered down to the hall, and stared at the beautiful girl who moaned as she lay there, still unconscious. Then, as I watched her, a new sensation crept over me—an evil desire, a burning love for the girl that was worse than hate. Then I experienced the final culminating horror. I knew that the very evil that was his was creeping over my soul, trying to conquer the last vestige of the pitiful thing that was me.

Little remains to be told. The last hope was gone, and I knew it. I knew I must act, and act quickly, before my soul succumbed completely to this Evil Thing.

There is something ludicrous about carrying one's own body down a long flight of wide, dark stairs; but there was something pitiful, too. The face looked so white and lifeless, so much more completely dead than any corpse I had ever seen. With the aid of my light, I finally arrived down here, in the vaults. I found two empty caskets which I laid side by side, and in one I gently deposited the pitiful thing that was me. From the pocket I took paper and pen which I always carried with me and now, seated on an old chair by an ancient table, the candle lighted beside me, I am hurrying to finish this document. Stronger and stronger grows the power of evil within me, and if it gained the upper hand, it would thwart my plans. For it wishes to live to carry out its fiendish will.

But I am still the stronger of the two; and now my tale is finished. With this long, hairy hand, which has written these words for me, I will take my old army revolver, and after I have laid myself in the empty coffin, I shall turn the muzzle against this evil hideous head, and thus thwart him in the end.

Far above me I hear hurried footsteps, running down the stairs and out of this haunt of hell. She has awakened, and is flying from me, flying from the evil Thing that she thinks I am. You need not fear me, Myra. I shall never follow you. Soon I shall be far from you, far from this world, forever and ever. Goodbye, sweet child. And may God bless you for your brave attempt to save me.

How still that body lies . . . It was me, once . . . Me? Who is "me"?

Soon there shall be nothing but two bodies, lying side by side, rotting through eternity.

THE GHOSTS OF STEAMBOAT COULEE

Arthur J. Burks

UNUSUALLY FOR A WRITER for the pulp magazines of the 1920s and 1930s, many of the stories by Arthur J. Burks (1898–1974) were less plot-driven than those of his contemporaries, using instead a sense of mood to create terror, and never more tellingly than in his supernatural tales. Born in Waterville, Washington, Burks had two primary careers, in the military, and as a prolific pulp writer. After serving in World War I, promotions made him an aide to General Smedley D. Butler in 1924; he resigned in 1928 to become a full-time writer, but rejoined the Marines when World War II broke out, supervising the basic training of nearly one-third of all Marines engaged in the war, and retiring as a lieutenant colonel. Although he had started writing at the age of twenty while a lieutenant, it is in the 1930s that he earned the title "The Speed Merchant of the Pulps," producing between one and two million words a year for more than a decade. Unlike other hyperprolific authors like Walter B. Gibson (as Maxwell Grant) and Lester Dent (as Kenneth Robeson), who wrote novels about The Shadow and Doc Savage, respectively, Burks rarely wrote novels and had few series characters, keeping to original short stories in virtually every genre, notably horror, mystery, aviation, science fiction, adventure, fantasy, and romance (the last under the pseudonym Esther Critchfield). He wrote about what it was like to write at such a furious pace for *Writers Digest,* noting that he once had eleven stories in a single magazine under eleven different names. He had the reputation among other pulp writers (and editors) of being able to select any inanimate object in a room and write a thrilling story about it.

"The Ghosts of Steamboat Coulee" was first published in the May 1926 issue of *Weird Tales.*

The Ghosts
of Steamboat Coulee

ARTHUR J. BURKS

A HEARTLESS BRAKEMAN discovered me and kicked me off the train at Palisades. I didn't care greatly. As well be dropped here in Moses Coulee like a bag of spoiled meal as farther up the line. When a man knows he has but a short time to live, what does it matter? Had I not been endowed with a large modicum of my beloved father's stubbornness I believe I should

long since have crawled away into some hole, like a mongrel cur, to die. There was no chance to cheat the Grim Reaper. That had been settled long ago, when, without a gas mask, I had gone through a certain little town in Flanders.

My lungs were just about done. Don't think I am making a bid for sympathy.

I am telling this to explain my actions in

those things which came later—to alibi myself of the charge of cowardice.

After leaving the train at Palisades I looked up and down the coulee. Where to go? I hadn't the slightest idea. Wenatchee lay far behind me, at the edge of the mighty Columbia River. I had found this thriving little city unsympathetic and not particularly hospitable. I couldn't, therefore, retrace my steps. Besides, I never have liked to go back over lost ground. I saw the train which had dropped me crawl like a snake up the steep incline which led out of the coulee. I hadn't the strength to follow. I knew that I could never make the climb.

So, wearily, I trudged out to the road and headed farther into the coulee, to come, some hours later, to another cul-de-sac. It was another (to me impossible) incline, this time a wagon road. I have since learned that this road leads, via a series of three huge terraces bridged by steep inclines, out of Moses Coulee. It is called the Three Devils—don't ask me why, for it was named by the Siwash Indians.

At the foot of this road, and some half-mile from where it began to climb, I saw a small farmhouse, from the chimney of which a spiral of blue smoke rose lazily. Here were folks, country folks, upon whose hospitality I had long ago learned to rely. Grimy with the dust of the trail, damp with perspiration, red spots dancing in the air before my eyes because of the unaccustomed exertion to which I had compelled myself, I turned aside and presently knocked at the door of the farmhouse.

A kindly housewife answered my knock and bade me enter. I was shortly told to seat myself at the table. When I had finished eating I arose and was about to ask her what I might do in payment for the meal, when I was seized with a fit of coughing which left me faint and trembling; and I had barely composed myself when the woman's husband and a half-grown boy entered the house silently and looked at me.

"How come a man as sick as you is out on the road afoot like this?" demanded the man.

I studied the three carefully before replying.

Nothing squeamish about them. Knew something of the rough spots of life, all of them. I knew this at once. So I told them my story, and that I had neither friends nor family, nor abode. While I talked they exchanged glances with one another, and when I had finished the husband looked at me steadily for a long moment.

"Is there a chance for you to get well?" he asked finally.

"I am afraid not." I tried to make my voice sound cheerful.

"Would you like to find a place where nobody'd bother you? A place where you could loaf along about as you wished until your time came?"

I didn't exactly like the way he put it; but that was just about all there was left to me, and, to date, even that had been denied me.

I nodded in answer to the question. The man strode to the door and pointed.

"See there?" he asked. "That's the road you came here on, against that one hundred-foot cliff. Opposite that cliff, back of my house, is another cliff, three hundred feet high. Matter of fact, my place is almost surrounded by cliffs, don't need to build fences, except where the coulee opens away toward the Columbia River, which is some lot of miles away from here. Cliffs both sides of it, all the way down. No other exit, except there!"

As he spoke he swung his extended forearm straight toward the cliff to the north.

"See what looks like a great black shadow against the face of the cliff, right where she turns to form the curve of the coulee?"

"Yes, I see it."

"Well, that ain't a shadow. That's the entrance to another and smaller coulee which opens into this one. It is called Steamboat Coulee, and if you look sharp you can see why."

I studied that black shadow as he pointed, carefully, running my eyes over the face of the cliff. Then I exclaimed suddenly, so unexpectedly did I discover the reason for the name given the coulee. Right at the base of that black shadow was a great pile of stone, its color all but blending with the mother cliff unless one looked closely; and this mass of solid rock, from where we stood in the doorway of the farmhouse, looked like a great steamboat slowly emerging from the cleft in the giant walls!

"Good Lord!" I exclaimed. "If I didn't know better I would swear that was a boat under steam!"

"It's fooled a lot of folks," returned the farmer dryly. "Well, that coulee entrance is on my land, so I guess I have a right to make this proposition to you. Back inside that coulee about two miles is a log cabin that could easy be made livable. Just the place for you, and I could send in what little food you would need. It's kind of cool at night, but in the daytime the sun makes the coulee as hot as an oven, and you could loaf all day in the heat. There are plenty of big rocks there to flop on and—who knows?—maybe you'd even get well!"

"And nobody owns the house?" I inquired.

"Yes, I own it. I used to live in it myself."

"Why did you move?" I felt as a fellow must feel when he looks a gift horse in the face, but to save me I could not forbear asking the question.

"Well," he said finally, "all my land lies out here in Moses Coulee, and when I lived there I could not keep my eye on it. I have large melon patches down toward Steamboat, and if there isn't someone here when the Siwashes drift though to their potlatch on Badger Mountain, outside, the damn Indians would steal all the melons. So we moved out here."

The explanation sounded reasonable enough; but it left me unsatisfied. I had been moodily gazing at that black shadow on the cliff which was the entrance to Steamboat Coulee, and while I stared it had come to me that the huge maw looked oddly like a great open mouth that might take one in and leave no trace. There was something menacing about it, distant though it was. I felt that this unexplainable aura would become more depressing as one approached the coulee. I had begun to distrust these people, too. The woman and the son talked too little, even for people who lived much alone.

The sun was weltering, deepening the shadow

at the mouth of Steamboat. At the two irregular edges of the shadow there hung a weirdly shimmering blue haze.

I blamed morbid fancies to my sickness. I began to reason with myself. Here was I, a grown man, looking a gift horse in the mouth, questioning the motives of kindly people who were only giving me a chance to die under cover like a human being—near to, if not among, friends.

I swallowed my forebodings and turned to the man. Beyond him, over his shoulder, I looked into the eyes of the woman, who, arms akimbo, was standing in the half-shadow beyond the door, gravely awaiting my answer. Confound it! Why couldn't she say something? Beside her stood the boy, also noting me gravely. As my eyes went to the boy his tongue crept forth from his mouth slowly and described a circle, moistening his lips. My morbid fancy saw something sinister even in this, for I was minded of a cat that looks expectantly at a saucer of cream. I jerked my head around to meet the eyes of the man, and he, too, was regarding me gravely.

"I thank you, sir," I said, as politely as I could; "you are very kind. I accept your offer with great pleasure. May I know to whom I am indebted for this unusually benevolent service?"

Again that queer hesitation before the answer. When it came the tones were strangely harsh, almost a rebuke.

"What difference does a name make? We don't go much on last names here. That there is Reuben, my boy, and this is my wife, Hildreth. My own name is Plone. You can tell us what to call you, if you wish; but it don't make much difference if you don't care to."

"My name is Harold Skidmore, late of the U. S. Army. Once more allow me to thank you, then I shall go into my new home before it gets so dark I can't find it."

"That's all right. Reuben will go along and show you the place. Hillie, put up a sack of grub for Skidmore. Enough to last him a couple of days. He'll probably be too sore from his walk to come out for more before that—and we may be too busy to take any in to him."

The woman dropped her arms to her side and moved into the kitchen to do the bidding of Plone. Plone! What an odd name for a man! I studied him as, apparently having forgotten me, he stared moodily down the haze-filled coulee. I tried to see what his eyes were seeking, but all I could tell was that he watched the road by which I had come to this place—watched it carefully and in silence, as though he expected other visitors to come around the bend which leads to the Three Devils. He did not turn back to me again; and when, ten minutes or so later, Reuben touched my arm and started off in the direction of Steamboat, Plone was still staring down the road.

I looked back after we had left the house well behind, and he was watching me now, while his taciturn wife stood motionless beside him, with her arms akimbo. Looking at the two made me feel strangely uncomfortable again, so I turned back and tried to engage Reuben in conversation. As soon as I spoke he quickened his stride so that it took all my breath to keep pace.

I had a chance to study the territory over which we traveled. Back in my mind I remembered Plone's remark about his melon patches, and looked about for sight of them. We were halfway to the Steamboat Coulee entrance, yet I hadn't seen a melon patch or anything that remotely resembled one. Though I knew absolutely nothing about farming, I would have sworn that this ground hadn't been cultivated for many years. It had been plowed once upon a time, but the plowing had been almost obliterated by scattered growths of wild hollyhocks, heavy with their fiery blooms. Plone's farm was nothing but a desert on the coulee floor.

But we were approaching Steamboat Coulee entrance, and the nearer we strode the less I liked the bargain I had made, for the entrance looked more like a huge mouth than ever. But those red spots were dancing before my eyes again and may have helped me to imagine things. When we reached the entrance its mouth-like appearance was not so pronounced, and the rock which had looked like a steamboat did not resemble a steamboat at all. The floor of this coulee was a dry stream-bed which, when the spring freshets came, must have been a roaring torrent.

Before entering the coulee behind Reuben I looked back at the house of Plone, and shouted in amazement.

"Reuben! Where is the house? I can see all of that end of the coulee, and your house is not in sight!"

"We come over a rise, a high one, that's all," he replied carelessly; "if we go back a piece we can see the house. Only we ain't got time. I want to show you the cabin and get back before dark. This coulee ain't nice to get caught in after dark."

"It isn't?" I questioned. "Why not?"

But Reuben had begun the entrance to Steamboat Coulee and did not answer. I was very hesitant about following him now, for I knew that he had lied to me. We hadn't come over any rise, and I should have been able to see the farmhouse! What had happened to my eyes? Were they, like my lungs, failing me? I stopped dead still, there in the bottom of that dry stream-bed. Reuben stopped, ahead of me, and looked silently back. He smiled at me insolently, a sort of challenging smile. Just stood there smiling. What else could I do? I strode on after Reuben.

I liked this coulee less and less as we went deeper into it. Walls rose straight on either hand, and they were so close that they seemed to be pressing over upon me. The stream-bed narrowed and deepened. On its banks grew thickets of wild willow, interspersed with clumps of squawberry bushes laden with pink fruit. Behind these thickets arose the talus slope of shell-rock.

I studied the slopes for signs of pathways which might lead out of this coulee in case a heavy rain should fill the stream-bed and cut off my retreat by the usual way, but saw none. I saw instead something that filled me with a sudden feeling of dread, causing a sharp constriction of my throat. It was just a mottled mass on a large rock; but as I looked at it the mass moved, untwisted itself, and a huge snake glided out of sight in the rocks.

"Reuben," I called, "are there many snakes in this coulee?"

"Thousands!" he replied without looking back. "Rattlers, blue racers, and bull whips—but mostly rattlers. Keep your shanty closed at night and stay in the stream-bed in the daytime and they won't be any danger to you!"

Well, I was terribly tired, else I would have turned around and quitted this coulee—yes, though I fell dead from exhaustion ten minutes later. As it was I followed Reuben, who turned aside finally and climbed out of the stream-bed. I followed him and stood upon a trail which led down a gloomy aisle into a thicket of willows. Heavy shadows hung in this moody aisle, but through these I could make out the outline of a squatty log cabin.

Ten minutes later I had a fire going in the cracked stove which the house boasted, and its light was driving away the shadows in the corners. There was one chair in the house, and a rough bed against the wall. The board floor was well laid—no cracks through which venturesome rattlers might come. I made sure of this before I would let Reuben get away, and that the door could be closed and bolted.

"Well," said Reuben, who had stood by while I put the place rapidly to rights, "you'll be all right now. Snug as a bug in a rug—if you ain't afraid of ghosts!"

His hand had dropped to the door-knob as he began to talk, and when he had uttered this last sinister sentence he opened the door and slipped out before I could stop him. Those last six words had sent a chill through my whole body. In a frenzy of fear which I could not explain, I rushed to the door and looked out, intending to call Reuben back.

I swear he hadn't had time to reach the stream-bed and drop into it out of sight; but when I looked out he was nowhere to be seen, and when I shouted his name until the echoes rang to right and left through the coulee, there was no answer! He must have fairly flown out of that thicket!

I closed the door and barred it, placed the chair-back under the door-knob, and sat down upon the edge of the bed, gazing into the fire.

What sort of place had I wandered into?

For a time the rustling of the wind through the willows outside the log cabin was my only answer. Then a gritty grating sound beneath the floor, slow and intermittent, told me that a huge snake, sluggish with the coolness of the evening, was crawling there and was at that moment scraping alongside one of the timbers which supported the floor.

I was safe from these, thank God!

The feeling of security which now descended upon me, together with the cheery roaring of the fire in the stove, almost lulled me to sleep. My eyes were closing wearily and my head was sinking upon my breast. . . .

A cry that the wildest imagination would never have expected to hear in this place, came suddenly from somewhere in the darkness outside.

It was a cry as of a little baby that awakes in the night and begs plaintively to be fed. And it came from somewhere out there in the shell-rock of the talus slopes.

Merciful heaven! How did it happen that a wee small child such as I guessed this to be had wandered out into the darkness of the coulee? Whence had it come? Were there other inhabitants in Steamboat? But Plone had told me that there were not. Then how explain that eery cry? A possible explanation, inspired by frayed nerves, came to me, and froze the marrow in my bones before I could reason myself out of it.

"If you ain't afraid of ghosts!"

What had Reuben of the unknown surname meant by this remark? And by what means had he so swiftly disappeared after he had quitted my new home?

Just as I asked myself the question, that wailing cry came again, from about the same place, as near as I could judge, on the talus slope in the rear of my cabin. Unmistakably the cry of a lost baby, demanding by every means of expression in its power, the attention of its mother. Out there alone and frightened in the darkness, in the heart of Steamboat Coulee, which Reuben had told me was infested by great numbers of snakes, at least one kind of which was venomous enough to slay.

Dread tugged at my throat. My tongue became dry in my mouth, cleaving to the palate. I knew before I opened the door that the coulee was now as dark as Erebus, and the moving about would be like groping in some gigantic pocket. But there was a feeble child out there on the talus slope, lost in the darkness, wailing for its mother. And I prided myself upon being at least the semblance of a man.

Mentally girding myself, I strode to the door and flung it open. A miasmatic mist came in immediately, cold as the breath from a sunless marsh, chilling me anew. Instinctively I closed the door as if to shut out some loathsome presence—I knew not what. The heat of the fire absorbed the wisps of vapor that had entered. I leaned against the door, panting with a nameless terror, when, from the talus slope outside, plain through the darkness came again that eery wailing.

Gulping swiftly, swallowing my terrible fear, I closed my eyes and flung the door wide open. Nor did I close it until I stood outside and opened my eyes against an opaque blanket of darkness. When Plone had told me the coulee was cold after nightfall, he had not exaggerated. It was as cold as the inside of a tomb.

The crying of the babe came again, from directly behind my cabin. The cliff bulked large there, while above its rim, high up, I made out the soft twinkling of a pale star or two.

Before my courage should fail me and send me back into the cheery cabin, thrice cheery now that I was outside it, I ran swiftly around the cabin, not stopping until I had begun to clamber up the talus slope, guided by my memory of whence that wailing cry had come. The

shell-rock shifted beneath me, and I could hear the shale go clattering down among the brush about the bases of the willows below. I kept on climbing.

Once I almost fell when I stepped upon something round, which writhed beneath my foot, causing me to jump straight into the air with a half-suppressed cry of fear. I was glad now that the coulee was cold after nightfall, else the snake could have struck me a death-blow. The cold, however, made the vile creature sluggish.

When I thought I had climbed far enough I bent over and tried to pierce the heavy gloom, searching the talus intently for a glimpse of white—white which should discover to me the clothing of the baby which I sought. Failing in this, I remained quiet, waiting for the cry to come again. I waited amid a silence that could almost be felt, a silence lasting so long that I began to dread a repetition of that cry. What if there were no baby—flesh and blood, that is? Reuben had spoken of ghosts. Utter nonsense! No grown man believes in ghosts! And if I didn't find the child before long the little tot might die of the cold. Where had the child gone? Why this eery silence? Why didn't the child cry again? It was almost as though it had found that which it sought, there in the darkness. The cry had spoken eloquently of a desire for sustenance.

If the child did not cry, what was I to believe? Who, or what, was suckling the baby out on the cold talus slope?

I became as a man turned to stone when the eery cry came again. It was not a baby's whimper, starting low and increasing in volume; it was a full-grown wail as it issued from the unseen mouth. And it came from at least a hundred feet higher up on the talus! I, a grown man, had stumbled heavily in the scramble to reach this height; yet a baby so small that it wailed for its milk had crept a hundred feet farther up the slope! It was beyond all reason; weird beyond the wildest imagination. But undoubtedly the wailing of a babe.

I did not believe in ghosts. I studied the spot whence the wail issued, but could see no blotch of white. Only two lambent dots, set close together, glowing like resting fireflies among the shale. I saw them for a second only. Undoubtedly mating fireflies, and they had flown.

I began to climb once more, moving steadily toward the spot where I had heard the cry.

I stopped again when the shell-rock above me began to flow downward as though something, or somebody, had started it moving. What, in God's name, was up there at the base of the cliff? Slowly, my heart in my mouth, I climbed on.

There was a rush, as of an unseen body, along the face of the talus. I could hear the contact of light feet on the shale; but the points of contact were unbelievably far apart. No baby in the world could have stepped so far—or jumped. Of course the cry might have come from a half-witted grown person; but I did not believe it.

The cry again, sharp and clear; but at least two hundred yards up the coulee from where I stood, and on about a level with me. Should I follow or not? Did some nocturnal animal carry the babe in its teeth? It might be; I had heard of such things, and had read the myth of Romulus and Remus. Distorted fantasies? Perhaps; but show me a man who can think coolly while standing on the talus slopes of Steamboat after dark, and I will show you a man without nerves.

Once more I took up the chase. I had almost reached the spot whence the cry had come last, when I saw again those twin balls of lambent flame. They seemed to blink at me—off and on, off and on.

I bent over to pick up a bit of shale to hurl at the dots, when, almost in my ears, that cry came once more; but this time the cry ended in a spitting snarl as of a tom-cat when possession of food is disputed!

With all my might I hurled the bit of shale I had lifted, straight at those dots of flame. At the same time I gave utterance to a yell that set the echoes rolling the length and breadth of the coulee. The echoes had not died away when

the coulee was filled until it rang with that eery wailing—as though a hundred babies cried for mothers who did not come!

Then I knew!

Bobcats! The coulee was alive with them! I was alone on the talus, two hundred yards from the safe haven of my cabin, and though I knew that one alone would not attack a man in the open, I had never heard whether they hunted in groups. For all I knew they might. At imminent risk of breaking my neck, I hurled myself down the slope and into the thicket of willows at the base. Through these and into the dry stream-bed I blundered, still running. I kept this mad pace until I had reached the approximate point where the trail led to my cabin, climbed the bank of the dry stream and sought for the aisle through the willows.

Though I searched carefully for a hundred yards on each hand I could not find the path. And I feared to enter the willow thicket and beat about. The ominous wailing had stopped suddenly, as though at a signal, and I believed that the bobcats had taken to the trees at the foot of the talus. I studied the dark shadows for dots of flame in pairs, but could see none. I knew from reading about them that bobcats have been known to drop on solitary travelers from the limbs of trees. Their sudden silence was weighted with ponderous menace.

I was afraid—afraid! Scared as I had never been in my life before—and I had gone through a certain town in Flanders without a gas mask.

Why the sudden, eery silence? I would have welcomed that vast chorus of wailing, had it begun again.

When I crept back to the bank of the stream-bed a pale moon had risen, partly dispelling the shadows in Steamboat Coulee. The sand in the stream-bed glistened frostily in the moonlight, making me think of the blinking eyes of a multitude of toads.

Where, in Steamboat, was the cabin with its cheery fire? I had closed the door to keep my courage from failing me, and now there was no light to guide me.

I sat down on the high bank, half sidewise so that I could watch the shadows among the willows, and tried mentally to retrace my steps, hoping that I could reason out the exact location of the cabin in the thicket.

Sitting as I was, I could see for a hundred yards or so down the stream-bed. I studied its almost straight course for a moment or two, for no reason that I can assign. I saw a black shadow dart across the open space, swift as a breath of wind, and disappear in the thicket on the opposite side. It was larger than a cat, smaller than the average dog. A bobcat had changed its base hurriedly, and in silence.

Silence! That was the thing that was now weighing upon me, more even than thought of my failure to locate the little cabin. Why had the cats stopped their wailing so suddenly, as though they waited for something? This thought deepened my feeling of dread. If the cats were waiting, for what were they waiting?

Then I breathed a sigh of relief. For, coming around a bend in the stream-bed, there strode swiftly toward me the figure of a man. He was a big man who looked straight before him. He walked as a countryman walks when he hurries home to a late supper. Then there were other people in this coulee, after all! Plone, like Reuben, had lied.

But what puzzled me about this newcomer was his style of dress. He was garbed after the manner of the first pioneers who had come into this country from the East. From his high-topped boots, into which his trousers were tucked loosely, to his broad-brimmed hat, he was dressed after the manner of those people who had vanished from this country more than a decade before my time. An old prospector evidently, who had clung to the habiliments of his younger days. But he did not walk like an old man; rather he strode, straight-limbed and erect, like a man in his early thirties. There was a homely touch about him, though, picturesque as he was; for he smoked a corn-cob pipe, from the bowl of which a spiral of blue smoke eddied into the chill night air. I knew from this that,

if I called him, his greeting in return would be bluffly friendly.

I waited for him to come closer, hoping that he would notice me first. As he approached I noticed with a start that two huge revolvers, the holsters tied back, swung low upon his hips. People now days did not carry firearms openly. In an instant I had decided to let this stranger pass, even though I spent the remainder of the night on the bank of the dry stream. Sight of those weapons had filled me with a new and different kind of dread.

Then I started as another figure, also of a man, came around the self-same bend of the watercourse, for there was something oddly familiar about that other figure. He moved swiftly, his body almost bent double as he hurried forward. As he came around the bend and saw the first man who had come into my range of vision, he bent lower still.

As he did so the moonlight glowed dully on something that he carried in the crook of his arm. I knew instantly that what he carried was a rifle. Once more that chill along my spine, for there was no mistaking his attitude.

He was stalking the first man.

It did not take his next action to prove this to me. I knew it, even as the second man knelt swiftly in the sand of the watercourse and flung the rifle to his shoulder, its muzzle pointing at the man approaching me.

As the kneeling man aimed the deadly weapon, his head was drawn back and the moonlight shone for a moment on his face. I cried out, loudly and in terrible fear, as much to warn the unconscious man as in surprise at my discovery. For the man with the rifle was my Moses Coulee benefactor—Plone.

Again I cried out, this time with all the power of my shattered lungs. And the man ahead, all unconscious of the impending death at his heels, paid me absolutely no attention. He was no more than twenty yards from me when I shouted, yet he did not turn his head. For all the attention he paid me I might as well have remained silent. It was as though he were stone-deaf.

As this thought came to me the first man raised his head and looked directly into my eyes, and through and beyond me as though I had not been there. I saw his eyes plainly, and in them was no sign that he noted my presence.

I shouted again, waving my arms wildly. Perhaps he could not see me because of the shadows at my back. Still he did not see me. I whirled to the kneeling man, just as a sheet of yellow flame leaped from the muzzle of his rifle. The first man was right in front of me when the bullet struck him. He stopped, dead in his tracks. I guessed that the bullet had struck him at the base of the skull. Even so, he whirled swiftly, and both his guns were out. But he could not raise them to fire. He slumped forward limply, and sprawled in the sand.

I had not heard the report of the rifle, for simultaneously with that spurt of flame the bobcats had begun their wailing once more, drowning out the sound.

I, unable to prevent it or give a warning, had seen a cold-blooded murder enacted. There before me in the sand was the proof of it. I half arose, intending to run to the fallen man to see if he still lived. But when I saw Plone arise leisurely from his knees and come forward I drew back in the shadow again. Plone was a killer, and I had seen him make his kill. If he knew that his evil deed had been witnessed he would have no compunction about another killing, and even to me, whose life was destined to be short, life was still sweet.

I drew back and waited.

Plone stopped above the fallen man and looked down. Then he opened the breech of his rifle and coolly blew the smoke from the bore. He kicked the fallen man, and I saw his lips move as though he whispered something. He took the two pistols, shrugged his shoulders and turned away, walking swiftly back the way he had come, carrying his rifle in the crook of his arm. The murdered man he left to the creatures of the night.

Well, the man was dead, no doubt about that. But the sand was deep and I could bury him. I watched until Plone reached the turn in the watercourse, where he seemed to vanish as though the earth had opened and swallowed him.

Then I dropped into the stream-bed and strode to the fallen man, stooped over him to see that he no longer breathed—and drew back with a cry of horror. For what looked up at me was not the face of a man newly slain; but the sightless eyes of a grinning, aged skull.

As I stared in unbelief, the perspiration starting from every pore, the skull seemed to fade slowly away before my eyes, and in a matter of seconds there was nothing before me but the shifting sand, upon which there was not even a depression where a body had fallen!

Add to this uncanny happening the myriad-tongued caterwauling of the bobcats on the talus—crying as of babies lost in the night—and you can faintly guess at the state of my nerves. But I could not believe my eyes. Something was wrong, said reason. So I stooped again and ran my hand hurriedly over the sand where I had seen the body. Surely I could not have been mistaken!

Frantically, unable to believe it all hallucination, I ran my fingers deep into the sand. At once they brought up against something solid which, for many minutes, I found myself without the courage to uncover. I conquered this fear, finally, and began to dig.

Soon there lay before me, in the shallow grave, a fleshless skeleton. This in itself did not bother me, for I have seen many such, and in Flanders I have slept peacefully with dead buddies all around me. But, while digging near the skull of my find, I had unearthed something else which had been fairly well preserved in the dry sand.

It was a rotting corn-cob pipe, with black, corroded bowl!

With a cry whose echoes could be heard in the coulee even through the wailing of the bobcats, I sprang to my feet and ran, staggering, down the watercourse, in the direction I had come before darkness with Reuben.

Long before I had reached it my poor body

failed me and I fell to the sandy floor, coughing my lungs away, while scarlet stains wetted the sands near my mouth.

When I awoke in the sand the sun was shining. Some sixth sense told me to remain motionless, warning me that all was not well. Without moving my head I rolled my eyes until I could see ahead in the direction I had fallen. In falling my right hand had been flung out full length, fingers extended.

Imagine my fear and horror when I saw, coiled up within six inches of my hand, a huge rattlesnake! His head was poised above the coil, while just behind it, against the other arc of the vicious circle, the tip of the creature's tail, adorned with an inch or more of rattles, hummed its fearful warning.

With all my power I sprang back and upward. At the same time the bullet head, unbelievably swift, flashed toward my hand and—thank God!—safely beneath it! Stretched helplessly now to its full length, the creature's mouth, with its forked tongue, had stopped within a scant two inches of where my face had been.

Before the rattler could return and coil again I had stepped upon the bullet head, grinding it deep into the sand, and when the tail whipped frantically against my leg I seized it and hurled the reptile with all my might, out of the stream-bed into the shell-rock. Even as I did it I wondered where I had found the courage; and what had kept me from moving while unconscious. Had I moved I might never have awakened.

The sun was directly overhead. I had lost my sense of direction during last night's rambles among the shale, and could not figure out which way I should go to win free of this coulee. Then I remembered the direction Plone had taken, and set out to trace his footsteps, but there was none! I could not understand it, for I had seen Plone quite plainly in the moonlight.

I passed around the bend where he had disappeared and continued on. When, ten minutes later, I came to the shallow grave, with its aged skeleton, which had so taken away my nerve last night, I did not know where I was. I had been sure that this grave was in the opposite direction. But Plone must have known the way out—I knew that he lived on the floor of Moses Coulee, into which Steamboat debouched.

I kept on moving. If, as I now believed, I had been in error in the location of the grave, then my log cabin lay ahead of me. I climbed the bank of the dry stream and continued my hike, keeping well away from the thickets for fear of snakes. With the sun high in the heavens, turning the coulee into a furnace, the snakes came out by hundreds to stretch in the shade, and as I passed, they coiled and warned me away with myriad warnings. I did not trespass upon their holdings.

After I had plodded along for fully an hour I knew that I must be quite close to the rock which gives Steamboat its name; but still I had not found the pathway leading to the log cabin. Evidently I had already passed it.

Even as I had this thought I came upon a path leading into the shadows of the willow thicket—a path that seemed familiar, even though, from the stream-bed, I could not see the cabin. With a sigh, and much surprised that I had, last night, traveled so far, I turned into this path and increased my pace.

I came shortly to pause, chilled even though the sun was shining. For at the end of the mossy trail there was no cabin; but a cleared plot of ground adorned with aged mounds and rough-hewn crosses! Rocks were scattered profusely over the mounds and, I guessed, had been placed to foil the creatures which otherwise would have despoiled the bodies resting there. There was a great overhang of the cliff wall, bulging out over the little graveyard, and from the overhang came a steady drip of moisture. Slimy water lay motionless in a pool in the center of the plot. Mossy green were the stones. Mud-puppies scurried into the deeps as I stopped and stared, turning the water to a pool of slime.

How uneasy I felt in this place! Why had such a remote location been chosen as a cemetery, hidden away here from the brightness of God's sunshine? Nothing but shadow-filled silence, except for the dripping of the water from the overhang.

I hurried back to the stream-bed and continued on my way.

Another hour passed, during which, my body racked with continual coughing, I suffered the torments of the damned. Those red dots were dancing before my eyes again, and nothing looked natural to me. The snakes seemed to waver grotesquely—twisting, writhing, coiling. Here, on the cliff, was a row of ponderous palisades; but they seemed to be ever buckling and bending, as though shaken by an earthquake.

Then, far ahead, I saw the rock at the entrance. With a sob of joy I began to run—only to stop when I reached the pile, with a cry of hopelessness and despair. For the rock, unscalable even to one who possessed the strength to climb, now filled the coulee from lip to lip, while on my side of the pile there nestled a little lake, clear and pellucid, into which I could look, straight down, for what I guessed must have been all of twenty feet!

Some great shifting of the walls, during the night, had blocked the entrance, entombing me in Steamboat Coulee with all its nameless horrors!

There was no one to see me, so I flung myself down at the edge of the pool and wept weakly.

After a time I regained control of my frayed nerves, arose to my knees, and bathed my throbbing temples. Sometime, somehow, I reasoned, Plone would find a way to reach me. There was nothing to do now but return and search again for my cabin. Plone had hinted that he would be in after a day or two with supplies for me if I did not come out for them—and I felt that he would know how to get in by some other way. He had lived in the coulee and should know his way about.

Wearily I began the return march. It never occurred to me to note that the sun went ahead of me on its journey into the west. I can only blame my physical condition for not noting this.

Had I done so I would have realized at once that I had gone in the wrong direction in the first place, and that straight ahead of me lay freedom. I had gone to the head of the coulee, straight in from Steamboat Rock, and when I found the coulee blocked at the end had thought the entrance closed against me.

But I did not note the sun.

I strode wearily on, and found the cabin with ridiculous ease. Inside, calmly awaiting my coming, sat Hildreth, the wife of Plone! She said nothing when I opened the door, just sat on the only chair in the house and looked at me. I spoke to her, thanking her for the sack of provisions which I saw on the rickety shelf on the wall beyond the door. Still she said nothing. Just stared at me, unblinking.

I asked her about leaving this place and she shook her head, as though she did not understand.

"For God's sake, Hildreth!" I cried. "Can't you speak?"

For it had come to me that I had never heard her speak. When I had first entered the farmhouse she had placed a meal for me, and had bidden me eat. But I remembered now that she had done so by gestures.

In answer now to my question she opened her mouth and pointed into it with her forefinger. Hildreth, the wife of Plone, had no tongue!

Did you ever hear a tongueless person try to speak? It is terrible. For after this all-meaning gesture there came a raucous croak from the mouth of Hildreth—wordless, gurgling, altogether meaningless.

I understood no word; but the eyes of the woman, strangely glowing now, were eloquent. She was trying to warn me of something, and stamped her foot impatiently when I did not understand. I saw her foot move as she stamped it—but failed to notice at the time that the contact of her foot with the board floor made no noise! Later I remembered it.

When I shook my head she arose from her chair and strode to the door, flinging it wide.

Then she pointed up the coulee in the direction I had just come. Again that raucous croak, still meaningless. Once more I shook my head.

What was there, up that coulee, that menaced me?

I was filled with dread of the unknown, wished with all my soul that I could understand what this woman was trying to say. What was there up the coulee, about which she strove to tell me?

All I could think of was a hidden graveyard, dotted with rotting crosses and, in the center of the plot, a pool in which slimy mud-puppies played, hidden forever from the light of the sun.

I shivered as the picture came back to me.

Then I stepped back, to search about the place for paper, so that, with the aid of a pencil which I possessed, she might write what she had to tell me. I found it and turned back to the woman, who had watched me gravely while I searched. Noting the paper she shook her head, telling me mutely that she could not write.

Then Plone, his face as dark as a thundercloud, stood in the doorway! To me he paid no attention. His eyes, glowering below heavy brows, burned as he stared at the woman. In her eyes I could read fright unutterable. She gave one frightened croak and turned to flee. But she could not go far, for she fled toward the bare wall opposite the open door. Plone leaped after her, while I jumped forward to fling him aside.

Imagine my horror when Hildreth touched the wall—and vanished through it as though there had been no wall! I caught a glimpse of the wall, not a breach on it, before Plone, too, plunged through and was gone!

To me now came an inkling of what it all meant. Now I understood, or thought I did, the mystery of the disappearing farmhouse. Was this land into which I stumbled a land of wraiths and shadows? A land of restless dead people? Why?

Trembling in every fiber of my being I strode to the wall where Plone and his wife had gone through, and ran my hand over the rough walls. They were as solid, almost, as the day the cabin had been built. To me this was a great relief. I should not have been surprised had the wall also proved to be things of shadow-substance, letting me through to stand amazed upon the shell-rock behind the cabin.

Here was one place in the coulee of shadows that was real.

I went to the door, locked and barred it. Then I returned and lighted the stove to disperse the unnatural chill that hovered in the room. After this I searched out my food and wolfed some of it ravenously. Another thought came to me: if Reuben, Plone, and Hildreth were nothing but shadows, where had I procured this food, which was real enough and well cooked? Somewhere in my adventures since being kicked off the train at Palisades there was a great gap, bridged only by fantasies and hallucinations. What had happened, really, in that blank space?

Having eaten, I stepped to the door and looked out. If I again went forth into the streambed in an attempt to get out of the coulee, I should never reach it before dark. What would it mean to my tired reason to be caught in the open, in the midst of this coulee, for another terrible night? I could not do it.

Again I secured the door. Nothing *real* could get in to bother me—and even now I reasoned myself out of positive belief in ghosts. The hallucinations which had so terrified me had undoubtedly been born of my sickness.

Convinced of this at last I lay down on the rough cot and went to sleep.

When I awoke suddenly in the night, the fire had burned very low and a heavy chill possessed the cabin. I had a feeling that I was not the only occupant, but striving to pierce the gloom in the cabin's corners, I could see nothing.

What was that?

In the farthest corner I saw the pale, ghostly lineaments of a woman! Just the face, shimmering there in the gloom, oddly, but neither body nor substance. The face of Hildreth, wife of Plone! Then her hands, no arms visible, came up before her face and began to gesture. Her mouth opened and I imagined I again heard the raucous croak of the tongueless. Again her eyes were eloquent mutely giving a warning which I could not understand.

Fear seizing me in its terrible grip, I leaped from my bed and threw wood on the fire, hoping to dispel this silent shadow. When the light flared up the head shimmered swiftly and began to fade away; but not before I saw a pair of hands come from nowhere and fasten themselves below that head, about where the neck should have been. Hands that were gnarled and calloused from toil on an unproductive farm—the work-torn hands of the killer, Plone!

Then the weird picture vanished and I was alone with my fantasies.

I had scarcely returned to my seat on the bed, sitting well back against the wall so that my back was against something solid, when the wailing of lost babies broke out again on the talus slopes outside. I had expected this to happen after nightfall; but the reality left me weak and shivering, even though I knew that the animals that uttered the mournful wails were flesh and blood. The wailing of bobcats, no matter how often it is heard, always brings a chill that is hard to reason away. Nature certainly prepared weird natural protections for some of her creatures!

Then the wailing stopped suddenly. And the silence was more nerve-devastating than the eery wailing.

Nothing for many minutes. Then the rattle of sliding talus, as the shale glided into the underbrush.

This stopped, and a terrible silence pressed down upon me.

Then my cabin shook with the force of the wind that suddenly swooped through the coulee. It rattled through the eaves, shook the door on its hinges, while the patter-patter on the roof told me of showers of sand which the wind had scooped up from the bed of the dry stream. The wind was terrific, I thought; but ever it increased in power and violence.

The patter on the roof and the rattle in the eaves began to take on a new significance; for the patter sounded like the scamper of baby feet above my head, while the wailing about the eaves sounded like the screaming of people who are tongueless. The door bellied inward against the chair-back as though many hands were pressed against it from outside, seeking entrance. Yet I knew that there was no one outside.

Then, faint and feeble through the roaring of the wind, I caught that eery cry in the night. It was the despairing voice of a woman, and she was calling aloud, hopelessly, for help! I shivered and tried not to hear. But the cry came again, nearer now, as though the woman moved toward me on leaden feet.

No man, fear the shadows as he might, could ignore that pitiful plea and call himself a man.

I gritted my teeth and ran to the door, flinging it open. A veritable sea of flying sand swept past me; but through the increased roar came plainly that cry for help. I left the door open this time, so that the light would stream out and guide my return.

On the bank of the dry stream I stopped.

I heard the slamming of a door behind me. I turned back. The door opened a bit and a face looked out—the leering, now malevolent, face of Reuben, the son of Plone! As I saw him he jerked back, closing the door again, shutting out the light.

Even as the wailing of the bobcats had stopped, so, now, stopped the wind. And before and below me I saw Hildreth, wife of Plone, fighting for her very life with her brutal husband! She was groveling on her knees at his feet—his hands were about her throat. As she begged for mercy I could understand her words. She had a tongue, after all! Then Plone, holding Hildreth with his left hand, raised his right and crooking it like a fearful talon, poised it above the face of Hildreth.

He did a ghastly, unbelievable thing. I cannot tell it. But when his hand came away her words were meaningless, gurgling—the raucous croaking of a person who has no tongue.

Forgetting what I had before experienced, frenzied with horror at what Plone had done, I leaped into the dry stream and ran forward—to bring up short in the middle of the sandy open space.

For I was all alone—no Hildreth, the tongueless—no Plone with the calloused hands! Once more an hallucination had betrayed me.

Screaming in fear I sprang out of the stream-bed and rushed to the cabin, crashing against the door in my frenzy, with all my weight.

The door did not open. Rather it bellied inward, slightly, as though someone held against my efforts inside!

Who, or what, was inside?

Too late, now, I guessed what the wraith of Hildreth had tried to tell me. Going back in my memory I watched her lips move again. And as they moved I read the words she would have uttered. As plain as though she had spoken I now understood the warning.

"As you value the reason God has given you—*do not leave this cabin tonight!*"

I understood now, as, panting with my exertions, I pressed my weight against the door that would not give—except slightly.

For from inside the log cabin, faint as the sighing of a spring zephyr, came the faintest sound as of someone breathing!

What was coming to me out of the night? That against which the wraith of Hildreth had tried to warn me?

My eyes must have been very wide, had there been anyone to see. My body chilled with fear—afraid to force in the door and see what it was inside that breathed expectantly—afraid to face about and keep my eyes upon the stream-bed where I had seen Hildreth battle for her life against her spouse.

Choosing between the two fears as a desperate person chooses between two evils, I turned with my back against the jamb of the door and stared toward the dry stream.

At once there came to me the odor of burning tobacco! Someone was near me, someone who smoked; but who it was there was no way for me to learn. The door behind me shook slightly, so I darted to the corner of the cabin where I could see both the dry stream and the door.

Silence for many minutes, during which I would have welcomed the eery wailing of the bobcats on the shell-rock.

Then the door of my cabin opened and out walked a stranger! He was dressed very much as had been the man whom I had seen fall before the murderous rifle of Plone last night. But he was older, stooped slightly under the weight of years. I heard him sigh softly, as a man sighs whose stomach is comfortably filled with food.

He walked toward the stream-bed, following the path through the thicket. He had almost reached the lip of the dry stream when another figure followed him from the cabin—and that figure was Reuben, the malevolent son of Plone! Reuben, as his father had stalked that other unfortunate, stalked the stranger. More pungent now the odor of burning tobacco, though the stooped one was not smoking. The latter passed a clump of service berry bushes and paused on the lip of the dry stream. He had scarcely halted when, out of the clump of service berries, stepped Plone himself, moving stealthily, like a cat that stalks a helpless, unsuspecting bird!

The older man half turned as though he heard some slight sound, when Plone, with the silent fury of the bobcat making a kill, leaped upon his back and bore him to the ground, where the two of them, fighting and clawing, rolled into the sand below.

Plone was smoking an evil-smelling pipe.

Reuben began to run when his father closed with the stranger, and I was right at his heels when he leaped over the edge to stop beside the silent combatants. Then he bent to assist his father.

The end was speedy. For what chance has an aged man, taken by surprise, against two determined killers? They slew him there in the sand, while I, my limbs inert because of my fright, looked on, horror holding me mute when I would have screamed aloud.

Their bloody purpose accomplished, Reuben and Plone methodically began to turn the pockets of the dead man inside out. The contents of these they divided between themselves.

This finished, in silence, the murderers, taking each an arm of the dead man, began to drag the body up the sandy stretch toward the end of the coulee—the closed end.

Still I stood, as one transfixed.

Then I became conscious of a low, heart-breaking sobbing at my side. Turning, I saw the figure of Hildreth standing there, tragedy easily readable in her eyes, wringing her hands as her eyes followed the pleading gesture, calling the two who dragged the body.

Then she began to follow them along the stream-bed, dodging from thicket to thicket on the bank as though she screened her movements from Plone and Reuben. I watched her until her wraithlike form blended with the shadows in the thickets and disappeared from view.

As I watched her go, and saw the figures of Plone and Reuben passing around a sharp bend in the dry stream, there came back to my memory a mental picture of a graveyard located in perpetual shadow, adorned with rotting crosses upon which no names were written. Slimy stones at the edge of a muddy pool populated by serpentine mud-puppies.

Turning then, I hurried back to the cabin, whose door now stood open—to pause as the threshold, staring in. At a table in the center of the room—a table loaded with things to eat, fresh and steaming from the stove—sat another stranger, this time a man dressed after the manner of city folk. His clothing bespoke wealth and refinement, while his manner of eating told that he was accustomed to choicer food than that of which necessity now compelled him to eat. Daintily he picked over the viands, sorting judiciously, while near the stove stood Hildreth, her eyes wide with fright and wordless entreaty.

Reuben stood in a darkened corner and his eyes never left the figure of the stranger at the table. As he stared at this one I saw his tongue come forth from his mouth and describe a circle, moistening his lips, anticipatory, like a cat that watches a saucer of cream.

Plone, too, was silently watching, standing just inside the door, with his back toward me. As I watched him he moved slightly, edging toward the table.

Then Plone was upon the stranger, a carving knife, snatched from the table, in his hand.

But why continue? I had seen this same scene, slightly varied, but a few minutes before, in the sand of the dry stream.

I watched them rifle the clothes of the dead man, stepped aside as they dragged the body forth and away, up the coulee. For where is the hand that can halt the passing of shadows?

For hours I watched, there beside the cabin, while Reuben and Plone carried forward their ghastly work. Many times during those hours did I see them make their kill. Ever it was Plone who commanded, ever it was Reuben who stood at his father's side to assist. Ever it was Hildreth who raised her hand or her voice in protest.

Then, suddenly, she was back in the cabin with Reuben and Plone. She told the latter something, gesturing vehemently as she spoke. These gestures were simple, easy to understand. For she pointed back down the coulee, in the direction of Steamboat Rock. Somehow I knew that what she tried to tell him was that she had gone forth and told the authorities what he and Reuben had done. Plone's face became black with wrath. Reuben's turned to the pasty gray of fear which is unbounded. Both sprang to the door and stared down the coulee. Then Plone leaped back to Hildreth, striking her in the face. She fell to the floor, groveling. He dragged her into the trail, along it to the stream-bed.

There, while I watched, was repeated that terrible scene I had witnessed once before. The pleading of Hildreth, the motion before her face of Plone's hand, crooked like a great talon. Then her gurgling scream which told that her mouth was empty of the tongue!

Reuben advanced to the lip of the dry stream as Plone fought with Reuben's mother. He paid them no heed, however, but shaded his eyes with his hand as he gazed into the west in the direction of Steamboat Rock. Then he gestured excitedly to Plone, pointing down the coulee.

But Plone was all activity at once. With Reuben at his heels and Hildreth stumbling farther in the rear, they rushed to the cabin and began to throw rough packs together, one each for Reuben and Plone.

But in the midst of their activities they paused and stared at the doorway where I stood. Then, slowly, though no one stood there except myself, they raised their hands above their heads, while Hildreth crouched in a corner, wild-eyed, whimpering.

Plone and Reuben suddenly lurched toward me, haltingly, as though propelled by invisible hands. Their hands were at their sides now as though bound there securely by ropes. Outside they came, walking oddly with their hands still at their sides.

They stopped beneath a tree which had one bare limb, high up from the ground—a strong limb, white as a ghost in the moonlight. Reuben and Plone looked upward at this limb, and both their faces were gray. Hildreth came out and stood near by, also looking up, wringing her hands, grief marring her face that might once have been beautiful.

Reuben and Plone looked at each other and nodded. Then they looked mutely at Hildreth, as though asking her forgiveness. After this they turned and nodded toward no one that I could see, as though they gestured to unseen hangmen.

I cried aloud, even though I had seen what was to come, as both Plone and Reuben sprang straight into the air to an unbelievable height, to pause midway to that bare limb; their necks twisted at odd angles, their bodies writhing grotesquely.

I watched until the writhing stopped, until the bodies merely swayed as though played upon by vagrant breezes sweeping in from the sandy dry stream.

Then, for the last time, I heard the piercing, wordless shriek of a tongueless woman. I swerved to look for Hildreth, and saw a misty, wraithlike shadow disappear among the willows, flashing swiftly out of sight up the coulee.

Hildreth had gone, and I was alone, swaying weakly, nauseated, staring crazily up to two bodies which oscillated as though played upon by vagrant breezes.

Then the bodies faded slowly away as my knees began to buckle under me. I sank to the ground before the cabin, and darkness descended once more.

When I regained consciousness I opened my eyes, expecting to see those swaying bodies in the air above me. There were no bodies. Then I noted that my wrists were close together, held in place by manacles of shining steel.

From the cabin behind me came the sound of voices—voices of men who talked as they ate—noisily. Behind the cabin I could hear the impatient stamping of horses.

I lay there dully, trying to understand it all.

Then two men came out of the cabin toward me. One of them chewed busily upon a bit of wood in lieu of a toothpick. Upon the mottled vest of this one glistened a star, emblem of the sheriff. The second man I knew to be his deputy.

"He's awake, I see, Al," said the first man as he looked at me.

"So I see," said the man addressed as Al.

Then the sheriff bent over me.

"Ready to talk, young man?" he demanded.

It must have mystified this one greatly when I leaped suddenly to my feet and ran my hands over him swiftly. How could they guess what it meant to me to learn that these two were flesh and blood?

"Thank God!" I cried. Then I began to tremble so violently that the man called Al supported me with a burly arm about my shoulders. As he did so his eyes met those of the sheriff and a meaning glance passed between them.

The sheriff passed around the cabin, returning almost at once with three horses, saddled and bridled for the trail. The third horse was for me. Weakly, aided by Al, I mounted.

Then we clambered down into the dry stream and started toward Steamboat Rock.

I found my voice.

"For what am I wanted, Sheriff?" I asked.

"For burglarious entry, son," he replied, not

unkindly. "You went into a house in Palisades, while the owner and his wife were working in the fields, and stole every bit of food you could lay your hands on. There's no use denying it, for we found the sack you brought it away in, right in that there cabin!"

"But Hildreth, the wife of Plone, gave me the food!" I cried. "I didn't steal it!"

"Hildreth? Plone?" The sheriff fairly shouted the two names.

Then he turned and stared at his deputy—again that meaning exchange of glances. The sheriff regained control of himself.

"This Hildreth and Plone," he began, hesitating strangely, "did they have a son, a half-grown boy?"

"Yes! Yes!" I cried eagerly. "The boy's name was Reuben! He led me into Steamboat Coulee!"

Then I told them my story, from beginning to end, sparing none of the unbelievable details. When I had finished, the two of them turned in their saddles and looked back into the coulee, toward the now invisible log cabin we had left. The deputy shook his head, muttering, while the sheriff removed his hat and scratched his head. He spat judiciously into the sand of the dry stream before he spoke.

"Son," he said finally, "if I didn't know you was a stranger here I would swear that you was crazy as a loon. There ain't a darn thing real that you saw or heard, except the rattlesnakes and the bobcats!"

I interrupted him eagerly.

"But what about Plone, Hildreth, and Reuben?"

"Plone and Reuben," he replied, "were hanged fifteen years ago! Right beside that cabin where we found you! Hildreth went crazy and ran away into the coulee. She was never seen again."

I waited, breathless, for the sheriff to continue.

"Plone and Reuben," he went on, "were the real bogy men of this coulee in the early days. They lived in that log cabin. Reuben used to lure strangers in there, where the two of them murdered the wanderers and robbed their dead bodies, burying them afterward in a gruesome graveyard farther inside Steamboat Coulee. Hildreth, so the story goes, tried to prevent these murders; but was unable to do so. Finally she reported to the pioneer authorities—and Plone cut her tongue out as punishment for the betrayal. God knows how many unsuspecting travelers the two made away with before they were found out and strung up without trial!"

"But how about Plone's farm in Moses Coulee, outside Steamboat, and the farmhouse where I met the family?"

"It's mine," replied the sheriff. "There's never been a house on it to my knowledge. I foreclosed on it for the taxes, and the blasted land is so poor that even the rattlesnakes starve while they are crawling across it!"

"But I saw it as plainly as I see you!"

"But you're a sick man, ain't you? You never went near the place where you say the house was. We followed your footprints, and they left the main road at the foot of the Three Devils, from which they went straight as a die, to the mouth of Steamboat Coulee! They was easy to follow, and if I hadn't had another case on I'd have picked you up before you ever could have reached the cabin!"

Would to God that he had! It would have saved me many a weird and terrifying nightmare in the nights which have followed.

There the matter ended—seemingly. The sheriff, not a bad fellow at all, put me in the way of work which, keeping me much in the open beneath God's purifying sunshine, is slowly but surely mending my ravished lungs. After a while, there will come a day when I shall no longer be a sick man.

But often I raise my eyes from my work, allowing them to wander, against my will, in the direction of that shadow against the walls of Moses Coulee—that shadow out of which seems slowly to float the stony likeness of a steamboat under reduced power. And I wonder.

Thorp McClusky

THORP MCCLUSKY (1906–1975) enjoys a modest reputation as the author of about forty short stories for the pulps, mostly in the horror category, occasionally for the prestigious *Weird Tales,* though he also wrote westerns and mysteries. He studied music at Syracuse University but spent most of his life as a freelance writer in New Jersey. As is true for most journalists and fiction authors who don't enjoy great success in a single literary genre or special field of expertise, McClusky wrote both fiction and nonfiction in wildly disparate areas. Among his best-known works are the serial *Loot of Vampires,* published in book form in 1975, and the frequently reprinted "The Crawling Horror" (1936). He used a variety of pseudonyms, including L. MacKay Phelps, Thorp McClosky, Otis Cameron, and Larry Freud.

Among his juveniles are *Chuck Malloy Railroad Detective on the Streamliner* (Big Little Book, 1938) and *Calling W-1-X-Y-Z Jimmy Kean and the Radio Spies* (Better Little Book, 1939). Most of his pulp fiction was published in the 1930s and 1940s, after which he mainly produced journalism for *The Saturday Evening Post, Man's Magazine,* and others. His single nonfiction book was *Your Health and Chiropractic* (1957). He also served as the editor of *Motor* magazine.

If "The Considerate Hosts" is not his most anthologized work, then that honor must go to "While Zombies Walked" (1939), the uncredited inspiration for the B movie *Revenge of the Zombies* (1943) that starred John Carradine, Robert Lowery, Gale Storm, and Mantan Morland.

"The Considerate Hosts" was first published in the December 1939 issue of *Weird Tales.*

The Considerate Hosts

THORP MCCLUSKY

MIDNIGHT.

It was raining, abysmally. Not the kind of
rain in which people sometimes fondly say they
like to walk, but rain that was heavy and pitiless,
like the rain that fell in France during the war.
The road, unrolling slowly beneath Marvin's
headlights, glistened like the flank of a great
blacksnake; almost Marvin expected it to writhe

out from beneath the wheels of his car. Marvin's
small coupé was the only man-made thing that
moved through the seething night.

Within the car, however, it was like a snug
little cave. Marvin might almost have been in a
theater, unconcernedly watching some somber
drama in which he could revel without really
being touched. His sensation was almost one of

creepiness; it was incredible that he could be so close to the rain and still so warm and dry. He hoped devoutly that he would not have a flat tire on a night like this!

Ahead a tiny red pinpoint appeared at the side of the road, grew swiftly, then faded in the car's glare to the bull's-eye of a lantern, swinging in the gloved fist of a big man in a streaming rubber coat. Marvin automatically braked the car and rolled the right-hand window down a little way as he saw the big man come splashing toward him.

"Bridge's washed away," the big man said. "Where you going, Mister?"

"Felders, damn it!"

"You'll have to go around by Little Rock Falls. Take your left up that road. It's a county road, but it's passable. Take your right after you cross Little Rock Falls bridge. It'll bring you into Felders."

Marvin swore. The trooper's face, black behind the ribbons of water dripping from his hat, laughed.

"It's a bad night, Mister."

"Gosh, yes! Isn't it!"

Well, if he must detour, he must detour. What a night to crawl for miles along a rutty back road!

Rutty was no word for it. Every few feet Marvin's car plunged into water-filled holes, gouged out from beneath by the settling of the light roadbed. The sharp, cutting sound of loose stone against the tires was audible even above the hiss of the rain.

Four miles, and Marvin's motor began to sputter and cough. Another mile, and it surrendered entirely. The ignition was soaked; the car would not budge.

Marvin peered through the moisture-streaked windows, and, vaguely, like blacker masses beyond the road, he sensed the presence of thickly clustered trees. The car had stopped in the middle of a little patch of woods. "Judas!" Marvin thought disgustedly. "What a swell place to get stalled!" He switched off the lights to save the battery.

He saw the glimmer then, through the intervening trees, indistinct in the depths of rain.

Where there was a light there was certainly a house, and perhaps a telephone. Marvin pulled his hat tightly down upon his head, clasped his coat collar up around his ears, got out of the car, pushed the small coupé over on the shoulder of the road, and ran for the light.

The house stood perhaps twenty feet back from the road, and the light shone from a front-room window. As he plowed through the muddy yard—there was no sidewalk—Marvin noticed a second stalled car—a big sedan—standing black and deserted a little way down the road.

The rain was beating him, soaking him to the skin; he pounded on the house door like an impatient sheriff. Almost instantly the door swung open, and Marvin saw a man and a woman standing just inside, in a little hallway that led directly into a well-lighted living-room.

The hallway itself was quite dark. And the man and woman were standing close together, almost as though they might be endeavoring to hide something behind them. But Marvin, wholly preoccupied with his own plight, failed to observe how unusual it must be for these two rural people to be up and about, fully dressed, long after midnight.

Partly shielded from the rain by the little overhang above the door, Marvin took off his dripping hat and urgently explained his plight.

"My car. Won't go. Wires wet, I guess. I wonder if you'd let me use your phone? I might be able to get somebody to come out from Little Rock Falls. I'm sorry that I had to——"

"That's all right," the man said. "Come inside. When you knocked at the door you startled us. We—we really hadn't—well, you know how it is, in the middle of the night and all. But come in."

"We'll have to think this out differently, John," the woman said suddenly.

Think what out differently? thought Marvin absently.

Marvin muttered something about you never can be too careful about strangers, what with so many hold-ups and all. And, oddly, he sensed that in the half darkness the man and woman smiled briefly at each other, as though they shared some secret that made any conception of physical danger to themselves quietly, mildly amusing.

"We weren't thinking of you in that way," the man reassured Marvin. "Come into the living-room."

The living-room of that house was—just ordinary. Two over-stuffed chairs, a davenport, a bookcase. Nothing particularly modern about the room. Not elaborate, but adequate.

In the brighter light Marvin looked at his hosts. The man was around forty years of age, the woman considerably younger, twenty-eight, or perhaps thirty. And there was something definitely attractive about them. It was not their appearance so much, for in appearance they were merely ordinary people; the woman was almost painfully plain. But they moved and talked with a curious singleness of purpose. They reminded Marvin of a pair of gray doves.

Marvin looked around the room until he saw the telephone in a corner, and he noticed with some surprise that it was one of the old-style, coffee-grinder affairs. The man was watching him with peculiar intentness.

"We haven't tried to use the telephone tonight," he told Marvin abruptly, "but I'm afraid it won't work."

"I don't see how it can work," the woman added.

Marvin took the receiver off the hook and rotated the little crank. No answer from Central. He tried again, several times, but the line remained dead.

The man nodded his head slowly. "I didn't think it would work," he said, then.

"Wires down or something, I suppose," Marvin hazarded. "Funny thing, I haven't seen one of those old-style phones in years. Didn't think they used 'em any more."

"You're out in the sticks now," the man laughed. He glanced from the window at the almost opaque sheets of rain falling outside.

"You might as well stay here a little while. While you're with us you'll have the illusion, at least, that you're in a comfortable house."

What on earth is he talking about? Marvin asked himself. Is he just a little bit off, maybe? That last sounded like nonsense.

Suddenly the woman spoke.

"He'd better go, John. He can't stay here too long, you know. It would be horrible if someone took his license number and people—jumped to conclusions afterward. No one should know that he stopped here."

The man looked thoughtfully at Marvin.

"Yes, dear, you're right. I hadn't thought that far ahead. I'm afraid, sir, that you'll have to leave," he told Marvin. "Something extremely strange——"

Marvin bristled angrily, and buttoned his coat with an air of affronted dignity.

"I'll go," he said shortly. "I realize perfectly that I'm an intruder. You should not have let me in. After you let me in I began to expect ordinary human courtesy from you. I was mistaken. Good night."

The man stopped him. He seemed very much distressed.

"Just a moment. Don't go until we explain. We have never been considered discourteous before. But tonight—tonight . . .

"I must introduce myself. I am John Reed, and this is my wife, Grace."

He paused significantly, as though that explained everything, but Marvin merely shook his head. "My name's Marvin Phelps, but that's nothing to you. All this talk seems pretty needless."

The man coughed nervously. "Please understand. We're only asking you to go for your own good."

"Oh, sure," Marvin said. "Sure. I understand perfectly. Good night."

The man hesitated. "You see," he said slowly, "things aren't as they seem. We're really ghosts."

"You don't say!"

"My husband is quite right," the woman said loyally. "We've been dead twenty-one years."

"Twenty-two years next October," the man added, after a moment's calculation. "It's a long time."

"Well, I never heard such hooey!" Marvin babbled. "Kindly step away from that door, Mister, and let me out of here before I swing from the heels."

"I know it sounds odd," the man admitted, without moving, "and I hope that you will realize that it's from no choosing of mine that I have to explain. Nevertheless, I was electrocuted, twenty-one years ago, for the murder of the Chairman of the School Board, over in Little Rock Falls. Notice how my head is shaved, and my split trouser-leg? The fact is, that whenever we materialize we have to appear exactly as we were in our last moment of life. It's a restriction on us."

Screwy, certainly screwy. And yet Marvin hazily remembered that School Board affair. Yes, the murderer *had* been a fellow named Reed. The wife had committed suicide a few days after burial of her husband's body.

It was such an odd insanity. Why, they *both* believed it. They even dressed the part. That odd dress the woman was wearing. Way out of date. And the man's slit trouser-leg. The screwy cluck had even shaved a little patch on his head, too, and his shirt was open at the throat.

They didn't look dangerous, but you never can tell. Better humor them, and get out of here as quick as I can.

Marvin cleared his throat.

"If I were you—why, say, I'd have lots of fun materializing. I'd be at it every night. Build up a reputation for myself."

The man looked disgusted. "I should kick you out of doors," he remarked bitterly. "I'm trying to give you a decent explanation, and you keep making fun of me."

"Don't bother with him, John," the wife exclaimed. "It's getting late."

"Mr. Phelps," the self-styled ghost doggedly persisted, ignoring the woman's interruption, "perhaps you noticed a car stalled on the side of the road as you came into our yard. Well,

that car, Mr. Phelps, belongs to Lieutenant-Governor Lyons, of Felders, who prosecuted me for that murder and won a conviction, although he knew that I was innocent. Of course he wasn't Lieutenant-Governor then; he was only County Prosecutor. . . .

"That was a political murder, and Lyons knew it. But at that time he still had his way to make in the world—and circumstances pointed toward me. For example, the body of the slain man was found in the ditch just beyond my house. The body had been robbed. The murderer had thrown the victim's pocket-book and watch under our front steps. Lyons said that I had *hidden* them there—though obviously I'd never have done a suicidal thing like that, had I really been the murderer. Lyons knew that, too—but he had to burn somebody.

"What really convicted me was the fact that my contract to teach had not been renewed that spring. It gave Lyons a ready-made motive to pin on me.

"So he framed me. They tried, sentenced, and electrocuted me, all very neatly and legally. Three days after I was buried, my wife committed suicide."

Though Marvin was a trifle afraid, he was nevertheless beginning to enjoy himself. Boy, what a story to tell the gang! If only they'd believe him!

"I can't understand," he pointed out slyly, "how you can be so free with this house if, as you say, you've been dead twenty-one years or so. Don't the present owners or occupants object? If I lived here I certainly wouldn't turn the place over to a couple of ghosts—especially on a night like this!"

The man answered readily, "I told you that things are not as they seem. This house has not been lived in since Grace died. It's not a very modern house, anyway—and people have natural prejudices. At this very moment you are standing in an empty room. Those windows are broken. The wallpaper has peeled away, and half the plaster has fallen off the walls. There is really no light in the house. If things appeared to you as they really are you could not see your hand in front of your face."

Marvin felt in his pocket for his cigarettes. "Well," he said, "you seem to know all the answers. Have a cigarette. Or don't ghosts smoke?"

The man extended his hand. "Thanks," he replied. "This is an unexpected pleasure. You'll notice that although there are ash-trays about the room there are no cigarettes or tobacco. Grace never smoked, and when they took me to jail she brought all my tobacco there to me. Of course, as I pointed out before, you see this room exactly as it was at the time she killed herself. She's wearing the same dress, for example. There's a certain form about these things, you know."

Marvin lit the cigarettes. "Well!" he exclaimed. "Brother, you certainly seem to think of everything! Though I can't understand, even yet, why you want me to get out of here. I should think that after you've gone to all this trouble, arranging your effects and so on, you'd want somebody to haunt."

The woman laughed dryly.

"Oh, you're not the man we want to haunt, Mr. Phelps. You came along quite by accident; we hadn't counted on you at all. No, Mr. Lyons is the man we're interested in."

"He's out in the hall now," the man said suddenly. He jerked his head toward the door through which Marvin had come. And all at once all this didn't seem half so funny to Marvin as it had seemed a moment before.

"You see," the woman went on quickly, "this house of ours is on a back road. Nobody ever travels this way. We've been trying for years to— to haunt Mr. Lyons, but we've had very little success. He lives in Felders, and we're pitifully weak when we go to Felders. We're strongest when we're in this house, perhaps because we lived here so long.

"But tonight, when the bridge went out, we knew that our opportunity had arrived. We knew that Mr. Lyons was not in Felders, and we knew that he would have to take this detour in order to get home.

"We felt very strongly that Mr. Lyons would be unable to pass this house tonight.

"It turned out as we had hoped. Mr. Lyons had trouble with his car, exactly as you did, and he came straight to this house to ask if he might use the telephone. Perhaps he had forgotten us, years ago—twenty-one years is a long time. Perhaps he was confused by the rain, and didn't know exactly where he was.

"He fainted, Mr. Phelps, the instant he recognized us. We have known for a long time that his heart is weak, and we had hoped that seeing us would frighten him to death, but he is still alive. Of course while he is unconscious we can do nothing more. Actually, we're almost impalpable. If you weren't so convinced that we are real you could pass your hand right through us.

"We decided to wait until Mr. Lyons regained consciousness and then to frighten him again. We even discussed beating him to death with one of those non-existent chairs you think you see. You understand, his body would be unmarked; he would really die of terror. We were still discussing what to do when you came along.

"We realized at once how embarrassing it might prove for you if Mr. Lyons' body were found in this house tomorrow and the police learned that you were also in the house. That's why we want you to go."

"Well," Marvin said bluntly, "I don't see how I can get my car away from here. It won't run, and if I walk to Little Rock Falls and get somebody to come back here with me the damage'll be done."

"Yes," the man admitted thoughtfully. "It's a problem."

For several minutes they stood like a tableau, without speaking. Marvin was uneasily wondering: Did these people really have old Lyons tied up in the hallway; were they really planning to murder the man? The big car standing out beside the road belonged to *somebody*. . . .

Marvin coughed discreetly.

"Well, it seems to me, my dear shades," he said, "that unless you are perfectly willing to put me into what might turn out to be a very unpleasant position you'll have to let your vengeance ride, for tonight, anyway."

"There'll never be another opportunity like this," the man pointed out. "That bridge won't go again in ten lifetimes."

"We don't want the young man to suffer though, John."

"It seems to me," Marvin suggested, "as though this revenge idea of yours is overdone, anyway. Murdering Lyons won't really do you any good, you know."

"It's the customary thing when a wrong has been done," the man protested.

"Well, maybe," Marvin argued, and all the time he was wondering whether he were really facing a madman who might be dangerous or whether he were at home dreaming in bed; "but I'm not so sure about that. Hauntings are pretty infrequent, you must admit. I'd say that shows that a lot of ghosts really don't care much about the vengeance angle, despite all you say. I think that if you check on it carefully you'll find that a great many ghosts realize that revenge isn't so much. It's really the thinking about revenge, and the planning it, that's all the fun. Now, for the sake of argument, what good would it do you to put old Lyons away? Why, you'd hardly have any incentive to be ghosts any more. But if you let him go, why, say, any time you wanted to, you could start to scheme up a good scare for him, and begin to calculate how it would work, and time would fly like everything. And on top of all that, if anything happened to me on account of tonight, it would be just too bad for you. *You'd* be haunted, really. It's a bad rule that doesn't work two ways."

The woman looked at her husband. "He's right, John," she said tremulously. "We'd better let Lyons go."

The man nodded. He looked worried.

He spoke very stiffly to Marvin. "I don't agree entirely with all you've said," he pointed out, "but I admit that in order to protect you we'll have to let Lyons go. If you'll give me a hand we'll carry him out and put him in his car."

"Actually, I suppose, I'll be doing all the work."

"Yes," the man agreed, "you will."

They went into the little hall, and there, to Marvin's complete astonishment, crumpled on the floor lay old Lyons. Marvin recognized him easily from the newspaper photographs he had seen.

"Hard-looking duffer, isn't he?" Marvin said, trying to stifle a tremor in his voice.

The man nodded without speaking.

Together, Marvin watching the man narrowly, they carried the lax body out through the rain and put it into the big sedan. When the job was done the man stood silently for a moment, looking up into the black invisible clouds.

"It's clearing," he said matter-of-factly. "In an hour it'll be over."

"My wife'll kill me when I get home," Marvin said.

The man made a little clucking sound. "Maybe if you wiped your ignition now your car'd start. It's had a chance to dry a little."

"I'll try it," Marvin said. He opened the hood and wiped the distributor cap and points and around the spark plugs with his handkerchief. He got in the car and stepped on the starter, and the motor caught almost immediately.

The man stepped toward the door, and Marvin doubled his right fist, ready for anything. But then the man stopped.

"Well, I suppose you'd better be going along," he said. "Good night."

"Good night," Marvin said. "And thanks. I'll stop by one of these days and say hello."

"You wouldn't find us in," the man said simply.

By Heaven, he *is* nuts, Marvin thought. "Listen, brother," he said earnestly, "you aren't going to do anything funny to old Lyons after I'm gone?"

The other shook his head. "No. Don't worry."

Marvin let in the clutch and stepped on the gas. He wanted to get out of there as quickly as possible.

In Little Rock Falls he went into an all-night lunch and telephoned the police that there was an unconscious man sitting in a car three or four miles back on the detour. Then he drove home.

Early the next morning, on his way to work, he drove back over the detour.

He kept watching for the little house, and when it came in sight he recognized it easily from the contour of the rooms and the spacing of the windows and the little overhang above the door.

But as he came closer he saw that it was deserted. The windows were out, the steps had fallen in. The clapboards were gray and weatherbeaten, and naked rafters showed through holes in the roof.

Marvin stopped his car and sat there beside the road for a little while, his face oddly pale. Finally he got out of the car and walked over to the house and went inside.

There was not one single stick of furniture in the rooms. Jagged scars showed in the ceilings where the electric fixtures had been torn away. The house had been wrecked years before by vandals, by neglect, by the merciless wearing of the sun and the rain.

In shape alone were the hallway and living-room as Marvin remembered them. "*There,*" he thought, "is where the bookcases were. The table was *there*—the davenport *there.*"

Suddenly he stooped, and stared at the dusty boards and underfoot.

On the naked floor lay the butt of a cigarette. And, a half-dozen feet away, lay another cigarette that had not been smoked—that had not even been lighted!

Marvin turned around blindly, and, like an automaton, walked out of that house.

Three days later he read in the newspapers that Lieutenant-Governor Lyons was dead. The Lieutenant-Governor had collapsed, the item continued, while driving his own car home from the state capital the night the Felders bridge was washed out. The death was attributed to heart disease. . . .

After all, Lyons was not a young man.

So Marvin Phelps knew that, even though his considerate ghostly hosts had voluntarily relinquished their vengeance, blind, impartial nature had meted out justice. And, in a strange way, he felt glad that that was so, glad that Grace and John Reed had left to Fate the punishment they had planned to impose with their own ghostly hands. . . .

THE FIFTH CANDLE

Cyril Mand

"THE FIFTH CANDLE" appears to be the only short story written in the name of Cyril Mand, the pseudonym of George R. Hahn (1923?–1971) and Richard Levin, although in January/February 1939 a "Cyril Mand" piece titled "The Arts of Hantoc" was published in an amateur fanzine titled *Fantascience Digest* published by Robert Madle.

No information could be discovered about Levin, nor could I track down any information about Hahn beyond the fact that he published two science fiction stories, "Gangway for Homer" in the Spring 1942 issue of *Science Fiction Quarterly* and "The Round Peg" in 1957 in *Future Science Fiction.*

"The Fifth Candle" has been frequently anthologized. It was originally published in the January 1939 issue of *Weird Tales.*

The Fifth Candle

CYRIL MAND

I fled, and cried out Death;
Hell trembled at the hideous name, and sighed
From all her caves, and back resounded Death.
—MILTON: *Paradise Lost.*

LAUGHABLE—ISN'T IT?—that one so cynical and unbelieving as I should sit here, quivering and shaking in fear of a specter; that I should cower in dread, listening to the inexorable ticking of the remorseless clock. Amusing, indeed, that I should know terror.

And yet five years ago when we sat at this table, we five Brunof brothers, the way we laughed! The pall of stale, blue cigarette smoke that hung over us was an exotic mask for the strident laughter that echoed and re-echoed through it. The dim electric light filtered through its mistiness, centering upon the figure of the Old Man at the head of the table, frothing in fury. We were taunting him—perhaps a little too much, for of a sudden he calmed. His face became grim, almost imposing in spite of the tracks of illness and age. His thin falsetto voice took on tone.

"So be it then! You, my evil sons—you who instead of filial love and respect have given me affront and irreverence—you who have repeatedly brought disgrace upon my name—you who have been profligates, who through your squandering have nearly ruined me—you who have brought me to death's door—you shall now pay for your flagrancy.

"I was born in Russia—not the gay, carefree Russia of Moscow or Saint Petersburg but the silent, frigid Russia of the Kirghiz levels. The knowledge that for centuries has been the lore of these steppes was born into me. Jeer if you want to. My years of study in the occult have not caused you alarm thus far. Let them not trouble you now.

"Look at that candelabrum with its five candles. I die tonight. But every year on this day, March 21, at this hour, eight o'clock, I shall return to this room to light a candle in that candelabrum. And as each candle burns itself down and flickers and dies, so shall one of you weaken and die. May this be my legacy to you, my evil sons!"

He retired beyond the scope of the haze-diffused light into the black yawn of the hallway, leaving us laughing and hurling gibes at his retreating figure. Later, we did not laugh so much, when we went into his somber walnut-paneled room and found his shriveled body at the desk, his lifeless head with beady eyes glazed in death, pillowed on the crumpled pages of one of his evil Russian volumes.

The Old Man left the house to all of us, together. Because of this, and also of our lack of money, March 21 of the next year found us all, but one, Sergei, seated at the table at dinner. The odors and harsh clatter of dinnertime jarred against the calm placidity of approaching spring. We were laughing again. Ivan, who always did seem like a younger and more droll edition of myself, had remembered the anniversary of the curse. With mock ceremony he had abstained from lighting one of the candles in the candelabrum and had made us leave the chair at the head of the table vacant. Now we sat listening to his ribald jests at the Old Man's expense.

"Be patient, brothers. But four and one-half minutes more," he said, glancing at the huge, gold-handed Peter the First clock at the side of the room, "and we shall be again honored by the presence of our esteemed father. And who shall be the first he takes back with him? Certainly not me—the youngest. Probably you, Alexei," he grinned at me. "He always did hate you most. Ever fleering him in your nice quiet way. Sneering. Laughing up your sleeve at him and his distemper. And then, too, you are the oldest of us. You're first in line. Boris, why don't you pray for him a bit? A religious cove like you ought to be able to really go to town on his black soul.

"Ah, it's time for our phantom. It's eight o'clock. Hello, Old Man." He rose, bowing to an imaginary figure at the door. "How are you? How's it back there in Hades? You *did* go there. Sit right dow——" His speech died off.

The chamber darkened. A queer, spectral haze filled the room. It swished and swirled, yet ever contracted toward a single point—the chair at the head of the table. We gazed, stupefied. It became a shape. The shape became—a man. There could be no mistake. The shriveled figure; the wolfish head with its piercing, beady eyes, hawk-like nose, bulging forehead, and parchment cheeks—it was the Old Man!

We stared aghast. Ivan staggered back. Boris crossed himself. Dmitri and I just sat, unnerved, frozen into impotency. The Old Man stood up. He slowly extended his fleshless hand toward the malefically scintillating candelabrum on the table. The unlit candle flared into life! His well-remembered falsetto came as of old, seeming strangely melancholy.

"Even as this candle burns down and flickers and dies, so shall you weaken and die, Ivan."

Ivan gasped. Dmitri's oath shattered the silence as he leaped up and reached for the fowling-piece over the mantel. He grasped it and fired blindly as he turned. The detonation echoed back and forth in the narrow confines of the room. The air was polluted by gun smoke and the bitter tang of exploded powder. The candle sputtered, undulated, and flamed on. The smoke cleared slowly. The misty figure of the Old Man was gone. And on the floor, thrashing frantically, lay Ivan, blood spurting from a wound in his chest.

We rushed to him; all except Boris, who stood, devoutly blind eyes fixed on the ceiling, muttering monotonous prayer. Dmitri cursed himself violently. It was a mortal wound. We bandaged him in vain. His life ebbed out with his blood. And as he breathed out his last, the lone candle flickered and went out.

The trial was a nightmare. Of course, we three brothers stood firmly behind Dmitri. Sergei was the real mainstay, though. He saw to the selecting and the hiring of the lawyers, and the various other matters of Dmitri's defense. As a prosperous business man his influence and money aided us immeasurably. Throughout Dmitri's successive convictions for first degree murder, it was always Sergei who secured another appeal and carried the case to a still higher court while the months dragged along. But it was all futile. Dmitri and Ivan had always been utter opposites in character. As a result, they had had violent and frequent quarrels. It was these clashes of opposing wills—in reality unimportant, but to the world highly significant—that were now continually flaunted before the jury. At each trial we repeated the story of the Old Man's curse and the part it had played in Ivan's death—and were laughed down as liars, lunatics, or both. We only succeeded in making our case ridiculous and in tying tighter the noose around Dmitri's neck. We fought on in vain.

In the heat of litigation we almost forgot the shadow that hung over us too. And yet the sands were running low.

Finally, the inevitable occurred. On January 30, the highest court of the state set the date of execution by hanging for the week of March 17. The governor refused a reprieve. We could do no more. We gave up the fight and went home.

On the night of March 21, a few minutes after eight o'clock, at the same time that three brothers sitting at dinner watched a lone candle flicker and burn out, Dmitri Brunof at the state penitentiary was executed for murder in the first degree.

Boris was really frightened now. According to age he was next to go after Dmitri. He lived in a mortal funk of terror. For a time he turned to religion as a means of escape. The pageantry and ceremonies of the Church imparted to him an illusion of power and protection. However, religion was not the thing for him now. It had an undue influence on his mind, battered as it was by repeated shock and terror; and his inherent mysticism was intensified by it to a stark fanaticism.

His superstitions, too, were magnified and stimulated. He grew into an unreasoning dread of the dark. He became the victim of charlatans and fakes. He spent his money on occult remedies and charms. Any exhibition of seemingly supernatural power awed and frightened him.

And then at a stage show of Edward Rentmore, the English wizard, he went into hysterics. This and the notoriety we had achieved through our evidence at Dmitri's trial were enough to gain us Rentmore's attention. Besides being an illusionist, he had gained quite a degree of fame as a medium. To Boris, whom he now befriended, he was another bulwark against the power of the Old Man. Under his influence Boris became an adherent of spiritualism. He developed into an actual disciple of Rentmore. And finally Rentmore brought his mind to bear upon his underling's problem. As was natural to him, considering his vocation, he decided that the best protection against the Old Man would be to fight him with his own weapon—the occult. And so, during the time remaining till March 21 Boris and Rentmore were engaged in preparing for the destruction of the Old Man on the night of his appearance. They sat up far into the night poring over the Old Man's malefic Russian volumes. It was in that dimly-lit library that they learned to develop their innate mind-forces. Sergei and I just waited, watching skeptically, grimly amused.

On March 21 at dinner, Rentmore, Boris, Sergei, and I were seated at the table. It was almost eight o'clock. The dim, inadequate light illuminated us feebly: Sergei, white face twisted into a cynical smile; Boris, nervously confident; and Rentmore, his sallow, yellow face frozen into a featureless impenetrability.

We were hardly surprised when that unearthly mist came and condensed, forming the shape of the Old Man. Sergei and I sat as if drugged, detachedly curious as spectators, conscious of the seething ferment of battle around us. We *felt* that struggle—mind against mind, will against will, knowledge against knowledge.

Then, as the beat of the hostile wills fell upon it, the form of the Old Man seemed to blur, diffuse, go queerly out of focus. We were winning! My detachedness vanished. I felt jubilant. The shadow that hung over us was lifting. But no! The figure of the Old Man once more took on its sharp, well-defined lines. Inexorably his arm reached out. Slowly, almost as if reluctantly, the candle in the candelabrum flamed up in response to that outstretched, withered hand. That thin statement of doom once more shrilled through the air.

"Even as this candle burns down and flickers and dies, so shall you weaken and die, Boris."

We stared at the candle, fascinated—not even noticing in what manner the Old Man went. The Peter the First clock ticked on, its golden hands slicing time and life, slowly and deliberately. The candle burned with a steady, even flame. Minutes passed. Rentmore lay in an exhausted stupor. The flame flickered, danced wildly as some slight current of air twisted it askew. It steadied, then flickered again. For a moment it writhed fitfully, sputtering.

Boris screamed—a long, agonized shriek. He started up, with one hand sweeping the candelabrum from the table, with the other fumbling at the insecurely mounted light-button. Then, suddenly, he choked, gasped, as if suffocating. The candelabrum seemed to cling to his hand. His twisted face mimicked our horror.

He slumped to the floor, breaking that lethal current of electricity, a grotesque heap of death. The candelabrum slipped from his hand, its clatter muffled by the exotic thickness of the Khivan rug.

Sergei had always been the cleverest one of us. He was practical, and besides his native cunning he possessed a good amount of real intelligence. Therefore, to him, of all the brothers, had passed the administration of our affairs. And certainly he had always done well in this capacity.

Whenever he had a problem, either personal or of business, he sat down alone in a half-dark room and there analyzed, speculated, and made and discarded schemes until he was sure he had the correct solution. It was this that he did now. The day after Boris' death he sat for a long time in the huge, half-lit dining-room, staring with perplexed eyes and knit brows at the candelabrum. It was long after I had gone to a sleepless bed that I heard him tread heavily up to his room.

The next morning he gave me his solution as I knew he would. "It seems that just two things are menacing us—the Old Man and the candelabrum. It is these two things that we must fight against if we want to survive. The Old Man is, of course, beyond our reach. However, the candelabrum——" His hand had knocked over a glass of water. He regarded the weaving track of the spilled liquid. "It is of solid gold and valuable. This afternoon when I go to the city I shall take it with me. At the Government mint I shall sell it as old gold. Within a week, probably, it will be melted down and stamped into coins. The coins will circulate and by March 21 the candelabrum will be scattered all over the country. Then let us see how our esteemed father will take the loss of his precious candelabrum. In his present state he can hardly curse another of the things. Yes, I think we are safe. . . ."

I rather agreed with him. I rejoiced now as in the old days Ivan, Dmitri, Boris, and I had rejoiced together in having a brother gifted with that elusive thing—common sense. I was confident that Sergei's canniness had saved us. The candelabrum was duly sold and, as our inquiries a few months later proved, melted down. Thus with the material threat of the curse removed, our fears vanished. We joked again, if rather grimly, of the Old Man. We mocked once more—mimicking the Old Man's falsetto voice. We speculated endlessly as to what the Old Man would do when he failed to find the candelabrum when he came to light it—or did he know already? We laughed again. . . . The days and weeks and months passed quickly, unclouded.

March 21 found me at a friend's house. Sergei was traveling again on one of his business trips, and I had no desire to be present alone when the Old Man came to light the candle in the vanished candelabrum. The day, the evening, and even the eighth hour passed easily. My friend and I chatted, supped, and played chess. Finally we went to bed.

I dropped off to sleep almost immediately. And then—out of the forefront of oblivion, as if he had been waiting for me, came the Old Man. The black nothingness behind him became a swirling mist that advanced and settled down around us. I was seated at the table. I looked wildly about me. There at the side the Peter the First clock marked eight o'clock. The candelabrum occupied the center of the table. And as the candle in it flared into life, the Old Man's words came to me.

"Even as this candle burns down and flickers out, so shall you weaken and die, Sergei."

I awoke shrieking at the gray dawn.

I dressed hurriedly, rushed downstairs, and seized the newspaper. The front page was smeared with a flamboyantly written and detailed account of a railway wreck. I read it through carefully. Among the killed was—Sergei Brunof. I looked for the time of the crash, strangely calm now. Yes, it had happened just after eight.

For two weeks I could not bring myself to go to the mansion. Not only was it the fear of that lonely old building with its charnel atmosphere, but also melancholy that kept me away. I knew how sad it would be to live there with the shades of vanished lives and muted laughter. The phantoms of my four brothers and the Old Man still peopled those silent rooms and empty halls.

Finally I did again venture into the dark oppressiveness of the house. And then in the dining-room I received another shock. There on the table where it had always stood before, and where I had seen it in the dream, was the candelabrum. Ridiculous, fantastic, impossible! And yet there it was, its dull golden glitter mocking me! I was stricken, bemazed—and yet really I knew that I had expected some such thing. So I just left it there.

And so it stood there throughout the year. Every day I sat at the table and ate my lonely meals, watching it cautiously, as if it were a live, malevolent being. I think I went a little mad watching it. It seemed to hypnotize me, too. It possessed an eery power over my mind. It drew me from whatever I was doing at times. I sat and gazed at it for hours. I mused endlessly as to what strange hands had hammered it again to its old shape, what weird tools had again formed its graceful branches. And all the time it seemed to be possessed of that same unearthly sentience. I could hardly bear even to dust it. I tried a few times to escape its evil spell. I went away—only to leave abruptly wherever I was, lured back to the dank old house and the glittering candelabrum. I lost contact with all humans. My supplies were sent out from the city by a boy who seemed to fear me as if I were the devil himself. I hardly ate. I just watched it. It seemed the only real thing in a house of mist and indistinctness. Vague and unrelated thoughts crept into my mind. I felt strangely confused and bewildered. It inspired me with an irrational and insatiable longing for something—I don't know what. I took to stalking the long, gloomy corridors in a frenzied search for the non-existent.

Today, cold fear jelled my panic into a sort of blunt insensibility when I realized that it was March 21. I sat all day at the table in a dull stupor, staring with dead, vacant eyes at the golden candelabrum.

Suddenly the desire to set this tale on paper came to me. The reaction to my apathy set in. Of a sudden I was full of a nervous, driving energy. For the past hour I have been sitting here writing. I am glad that I have been able to finish in time. The hour for the fifth candle draws near.

Ivan, Dmitri, Sergei, Boris—they are all gone. The Old Man took them. And certainly he will take me, too. Perhaps it will be just as well if I join them. I'll be back among my own. Dust to dust. . . .

It is after eight already. The candelabrum is empty of candles. I wonder, will he bring one. . . .

August Derleth
and Mark Schorer

ONE OF THE GIANTS in the field of supernatural fiction, August William Derleth (1909–1971) was born in Sauk City, Wisconsin, where he remained his entire life. He received a B.A. from the University of Wisconsin in 1930, by which time he had already begun to sell horror stories to *Weird Tales* (the first appearing in 1926) and other pulp magazines. During his lifetime, he wrote more than three thousand stories and articles, and published more than a hundred books, including detective stories (featuring Judge Peck and an American Sherlock Holmes clone, Solar Pons), supernatural stories, and what he regarded as his serious fiction: a very lengthy series of books, stories, poems, journals, etc., about life in his small town, which he renamed Sac Prairie.

Derleth's boyhood friend and frequent collaborator, Mark Schorer (1908–1977), was born in the same town and attended the same university. He published his first novel, *A House Too Old* (1935), about Wisconsin life, while still a graduate student. He went on to a distinguished career as a scholar, critic, writer, and educator, holding positions at Dartmouth, Harvard, and the University of California, Berkeley. He won three Guggenheim scholarships and a Fulbright professorship to the University of Pisa. In addition to writing for the pulps, he sold many short stories to such magazines as *The New Yorker, Esquire,* and *The Atlantic Monthly,* but his most important work was his biography, *Sinclair Lewis: An American Life* (1961). He was elected to the American Academy of Arts and Sciences.

"The Return of Andrew Bentley" was first published in the September 1933 issue of *Weird Tales*; it was first collected in *Colonel Markesan and Less Pleasant People* (Sauk City, Wisconsin, Arkham House, 1966).

The Return
of Andrew Bentley

AUGUST DERLETH AND MARK SCHORER

IT IS WITH CONSIDERABLE hesita-
tion that I here chronicle the strange incidents
which marked my short stay at the old Wilder
homestead on the banks of the Wisconsin River
not far from the rustic village of Sac Prairie. My

reluctance is not entirely dispelled by the conviction that some record of these events should
emphatically be made, if only to stop the circula-
tion of unfounded rumors which have come into
being since my departure from the vicinity.

The singular chain of events began with a peremptory letter from my aging uncle, Amos Wilder, ordering me to appear at the homestead, where he was then living with a housekeeper and a caretaker. Communications from my Uncle Amos were not only exceedingly rare, but usually tinged with biting and withering comments about my profession of letters, which he held in great scorn. Previous to this note, we had not seen each other for over four years. His curt note hinted that there was something of vital importance to both of us which he wished to take up with me, and though I had no inkling of what this might be, I did not hesitate to go.

The old house was not large. It stood well back in the rambling grounds, its white surface mottled by the shadows of leafy branches in the warm sunlight of the day on which I arrived. Green shutters crowded upon the windows, and the door was tightly closed, despite the day's somnolent warmth. The river was cerulean and silver in the immediate background, and farther beyond, the bluffs on the other side of the river rose from behind the trees and were lost in the blue haze of distance to the north and south.

My uncle had grown incredibly old, and now hobbled about with the aid of a cane. On the morning of my arrival he was dressed in a long, ragged black robe that trailed along the floor; beneath this garment he wore a threadbare black jersey and a pair of shabby trousers. His hair was unkempt, and on his chin was a rough beard, masking his thin, sardonic mouth. His eyes, however, had lost none of their fire, and I felt his disapproval of me as clearly as ever. His expression was that of a man who is faced with an unpleasant but necessary task.

At last, after a rude scrutiny, he began to speak, having first made certain that no one lurked within earshot.

"It's hardly necessary for me to say I'm not too certain I've done a wise thing in choosing you," he began. "I've always considered you somewhat of a milksop, and you've done nothing to change my opinion."

He watched my face closely as he spoke, to detect any resentment that I might feel; but I had heard this kind of speech from him too often before to feel any active anger. He sensed this, apparently, for he went on abruptly.

"I'm going to leave everything I've got to you, but there'll be a condition. You'll have to spend most of your time here, make this your home, of course, and there are one or two other small things you'll have to see to. Mind, I'm not putting anything in my will; I want only your word. Do you think you can give it? Think you can say, 'Yes' to my terms?"

He paused, and I said, "I see no reason why I shouldn't—if you can guarantee that your terms won't interfere with my writing."

My uncle smiled and shook his head as if in exasperation. "Nothing is easier," he replied curtly. "Your time for writing will be virtually unlimited."

"What do you want me to do?" I asked.

"Spend most of your time here, as I said before. Let no day go by during which you do not examine the vault behind the house. My body will lie there, and the vault will be sealed; I want to know that I can depend upon you to prevent anything from entering that vault. If at any time you discover that some one has been tampering, you will find written instructions for your further procedure in my library desk. Will you promise me to attend to these things without too much curiosity concerning them?"

I promised without the slightest hesitation, though there were perplexing thoughts crowding upon my mind.

Amos Wilder turned away, his eyes glittering. Then he looked through the window directly opposite me and began to chuckle in a curiously guttural tone. At last he said, his eyes fixed upon a patch of blue sky beyond the tree near the window, "Good. I'll block him yet! Amos Wilder is still a match for you—do you hear, Andrew?"

What his words might portend I had no means of knowing, for he turned abruptly to me and said in his clipped, curt way, "You must go now, Ellis. I shall not see you again." With that, he left the room, and as if by magic, old Jacob

Kinney, the caretaker, appeared to show me from the grounds, his lugubrious face regarding me with apologetic eyes from the doorway through which his master had so abruptly vanished but a moment before.

My uncle's strange words puzzled me, and it occurred to me that the old man was losing his mind. That I then did him an injustice I subsequently learned, but at the time all evidence pointed to mental derangement. I finally contented myself with this explanation, though it did not account for the old man's obvious rationality during most of the conversation. Two points struck me: my uncle had put particular stress upon the suggestion that something might enter his vault. And secondly, what was the meaning of his last words, and to whom was my uncle referring when he said, "I'll block him yet!" and "Amos Wilder is still a match for you—do you hear, Andrew?" Conjecture, however, was futile; for, since I knew very little of my uncle's personal affairs, any guesses I might have made as to his obscure references, if indeed he was not losing his mind, would be fruitless.

I left the old homestead that day in May only to find myself back there again within forty-eight hours, summoned by Thomas Weatherbee of Sac Prairie, my uncle's solicitor, whose short telegram apprising me of Amos Wilder's death reached me within three hours of my return to the St. Louis apartment which served me as my temporary home. My shock at the news of his sudden death was heightened when I learned that the circumstances surrounding his decease indicated suicide.

Weatherbee told me the circumstances of my uncle's singular death. It appeared that Jacob Kinney had found the old man in the very room in which he and I had discussed his wishes only a day before. He was seated at the table, apparently asleep. One hand still grasped a pen, and before him lay a sheet of note-paper upon which he had written my name and address, nothing more. It was presumed at first that he had had a heart attack, but a medical examination had brought forth the suspicion that the old man had

made away with himself by taking an overdose of veronal. There was, however, considerable reluctance to presume suicide, for an overdose of veronal might just as likely be accident as suicide. Eventually a coroner's jury decided that my uncle had met his death by accident, but from the first I was convinced that Amos Wilder had killed himself. In the light of subsequent events and of his own cryptic words to me, "I shall not see you again," my suspicion was, I feel, justified, though no definite and conclusive evidence emerged.

My uncle was buried, as he had wished, in the long-disused family vault behind the house, and the vault was sealed from the outside with due ceremony and in the presence of witnesses. The reading of the will was a short affair, for excepting bequests made to the housekeeper and caretaker, I inherited everything. My living was thus assured, and as my uncle had said, I found the future holding many hours of leisure in which to pursue letters.

And yet, despite the apparent rosiness of the outlook, there was from the first a peculiar restraint upon my living in the old homestead. It was indefinable and strange, and numerous small incidents occurred to supplement this odd impression. First old Jacob Kinney wanted to leave. With great effort I persuaded him to stay, and dragged from him his reason for wanting to go.

"There've been mighty strange things a-goin' on about this house, Mr. Wilder, all the time your uncle was alive—and I'm afraid things'll be goin' on again after a bit."

More than that cryptic utterance I could not get out of him. I took the liberty shortly after to repeat Kinney's words to the housekeeper, Mrs. Seldon. The startled expression that passed over her countenance did not escape me, and her immediate assurance that Jake Kinney was in his dotage did not entirely reassure me.

Then there was the daily function of examining the seal on the vault. The absurdity of my uncle's request began to grow on me, and my task, trivial as it was, became daily more irritating. Yet, having given my promise, I could do no more than fulfill it.

On the third night following my uncle's interment, my sleep was troubled by a recurrent dream which gave me no little thought when I remembered its persistence on the following day. I dreamed that my Uncle Amos stood before me, clad as I had last seen him on the visit just preceding his strange death. He regarded me with his beady eyes, and then abruptly said in a mournful and yet urgent voice, "You must bring Burkhardt back here. He forgot to protect me against them. You must get him to do so. If he will not, then see those books on the second shelf of the seventh compartment of my library."

This dream was repeated several times, and it had a perfectly logical basis, which was briefly this: My uncle was buried by Father Burkhardt, the Sac Prairie parish priest, who was not satisfied with the findings of the coroner's jury, and consequently, in the belief that Amos Wilder had killed himself, had refused to bless the grave of a suicide. Yet, what the dream-shape of the night before had obviously meant when he spoke of what Father Burkhardt had forgotten to do, was the blessing of the grave.

I spent some time mulling over this solution of the dream, and at length went to see the priest. My efforts, however, were futile. The old man explained his attitude with great patience, and I was forced to agree with him.

On the following night the dream recurred, and in consequence, since a visit to Father Burkhardt had already failed to achieve the desired effect, I turned, impelled largely by curiosity, to the books on the second shelf of the seventh compartment indicated by the dream-figure of my uncle. From the moment that I opened the first of those books, the entire complexion of the occurrences at the homestead changed inexplicably, and I found myself involved in a chain of incidents, the singularity of which continues to impress me even as I write at this late date. For the books on the second shelf of the seventh compartment in my dead uncle's library

were books on black magic—books long out of print, and apparently centuries old, for in many of them the print had faded almost to illegibility.

The Latin in which most of the books were written was not easily translated, but fortunately it was not necessary for me to search long for the portions indicated by my uncle, for in each book paragraphs were marked for my attention. The subjects of the marked portions were strangely similar. After some difficulty I succeeded in translating the first indicated paragraph to catch my eye. "For Protection from Things That Walk in the Night," it read. "There are many things stalking abroad by darkness, perhaps ghouls, perhaps evil demons lured from outer space by man's own ignorance, perhaps souls isolated in space, havenless and alone, and yet strongly attached to the things of this earth. Let no bodies be exposed to their evil wrath. Let there be all manner of protection for vaults and graves, for the dead as well as the living; for ghouls, incubi, and succubi haunt the near places as well as the far, and seek always to quench the fire of their unholy desire. . . . Take blessed water from a church and mix it with the blood of a young babe, be it ever so small a measure, and with this cross the grave or the door of the vault thrice at the full of the moon."

If this was what my Uncle Amos desired me to do, I knew at once that the task had devolved upon the wrong man; for I could certainly not see myself going about collecting holy water and the blood of a young child and then performing ridiculous rites over the vault with an odious mixture of the two. I put the books aside and returned to my work, which seemed suddenly more inviting than it had ever been before.

Yet what I had read disturbed me, and the suggestion that my uncle had come to believe in the power of black magic—perhaps even more than this, for all I knew—was extremely distasteful to me. In consequence, my writing suffered, and immediately after my supper that evening, I went for a long walk on the river bank.

A half-moon high in the sky made the countryside bright and clear, and since the night was balmy and made doubly inviting by the sweet mystery of night sounds—the gasping and gurgling of the water, the splashing of distant fish, the muted cries of night-birds, particularly the *peet, peet* of the nighthawk and the eery call of the whippoorwill, and the countless mysterious sounds from the underbrush in the river bottoms—I extended my walk much farther than I had originally intended; so that it was shortly after midnight when I approached the house again, and the moon was close upon the western horizon.

As I came quietly along in the now still night, my eye caught a movement in the shadowy distance. The movement had come from the region of the large old elm which pressed close upon the house near the library window, and it was upon this tree that I now fixed my eyes. I had not long to wait, for presently a shadow detached itself from the giant bole and went slowly around the house toward the darkness behind. I could see the figure quite clearly, though I did not once catch sight of its face, despite the fact that the man, for man it was, wore no hat. He walked with a slight limp, and wore a long black cape. He was near medium height, but quite bent, so that his back was unnaturally hunched. His hands were strikingly white in the fading light of the moon, and he walked with a peculiar flaffing motion, despite his obvious limp. He passed beyond the house with me at his heels, for I was determined to ascertain if possible what design had brought him to the old house.

I lost sight of him for a few moments while I gained the shelter of the house, but in a minute I saw him again, and with a gasp of astonishment realized that he was making directly for the vault in which my Uncle Amos lay buried. I stifled an impulse to shout at him, and made my way cautiously in the shadow of a row of lilac bushes toward the vault, before which he was now standing. The darkness here was intense, owing to the fact that the trees from the surrounding copse pressed close upon this corner of the estate; yet I could see from my crouching position that the mysterious intruder was fumbling with the seals of the vault. My purpose in following him so closely was to collar him while he was engaged with the seals, but this design was now for the moment thwarted by his stepping back to survey the surface of the vault door. He remained standing in silence for some while, and I had almost decided that it might be just as easy to capture him in this position, when he moved forward once more. But this time he did not fumble with the seals. Instead, he seemed to flatten himself against the door of the vault. Then, incredible as it may seem, his figure began to grow smaller, to shrink, save for his gaunt and gleaming white fingers and arms!

With a strangled gasp, I sprang forward.

My memory at this point is not quite clear. I remember seizing the outstretched fingers of the man at the vault door, feeling something within my grasp. Then something struck me at the same moment that the intruder whirled and leaped away. I had the fleeting impression that a second person had leaped upon me from behind. I went down like a log.

I came to my senses not quite an hour later, and lay for a moment recalling what had happened. I remembered having made a snatch at the intruder's fingers, and being struck. There was an appreciable soreness of the head, and a sensitive bruise on my forehead when finally I felt for it. But what most drew my attention was the thing that I held tightly in my left hand, the hand which had grasped at the strangely white fingers of the creature pressed against the door of the Wilder vault. I had felt it within my grasp from the first moment of consciousness, but from its roughness, I had taken it for a small twig caught up from the lawn. In consequence, it was not until I reached the security of the house that I looked at it. I threw it upon the table in the dim glow of the table lamp—and almost fell in my utter amazement; for the thing I had held in my hand was a fragment of human bone—the unmistakable first two joints of the little finger!

This discovery loosed a flood of futile conjectures. Was it after all a man I had surprised at the vault, or was it—something else? . . . That my uncle was in some way vitally concerned now became apparent, if it had not been entirely so before. The fact that Amos Wilder had looked for some such interruption of his repose in the old vault led me to believe that whatever he feared derived from some source in the past. Accordingly, I gave up all conjecture for the time, and promised myself that in the morning I would set on foot inquiries designed to make me familiar with my secluded uncle's past life.

I was destined to receive a shock in the morning. Determined to prosecute my curiosity concerning my uncle without loss of time, I summoned Jacob Kinney, whose surliness had noticeably increased during the few days I had been at the old Wilder house. Instead of asking directly about my uncle, I began with a short account of the figure I had seen outside the preceding night.

"I was out quite late last night, Jake," I began, "and when I came home I noticed a stranger on the grounds."

Kinney's eyebrows shot up in undisguised curiosity, but he said nothing, though he began to exhibit signs of uneasiness which did not escape my notice.

"He was about five feet tall, I should say, and wore no hat," I went on. "He wore a long black cape, and walked with a slight limp."

Abruptly Kinney came to his feet, his eyes wide with fear. "What's that you say?" he demanded hoarsely. "Walked with a limp—wore a cape?"

I nodded, and would have continued my narrative, had not Kinney cut in.

"My God!" he exclaimed. "Andrew Bentley's back!"

"Who's Andrew Bentley?" I asked.

But Kinney did not hear. He had whirled abruptly and run from the room as fast as his feeble legs would allow him to go. My astonishment knew no bounds, nor did subsequent events in any way lessen it; for Jacob Kinney ran not only from the house, but from the grounds, and his flight was climaxed shortly after by the appearance of a begrimed youth representing himself as the old man's nephew, who came for "Uncle Jake's things." From him I learned that Kinney was leaving his position at once, and would forfeit any wages due him, plus any amount I thought fit to recompense me for his precipitate flight.

Kinney's unaccountable action served only to sharpen my already keen interest, and I descended upon Mrs. Seldon post-haste. But the information which she was able to offer me was meager indeed. Andrew Bentley had arrived in the neighborhood only a few years back. He and my uncle had immediately become friends, and the friendship, despite an appearance of strain, had ended only when Bentley mysteriously disappeared about a year ago. She confirmed my description of the figure I had seen as that of Bentley. Mrs. Seldon, too, was inexplicably agitated, and when I sought to probe for the source of this agitation she said only that there were some very strange stories extant about Bentley, and about my uncle as well, and that most of the people in the neighborhood had been relieved of a great fear when Bentley disappeared from the farm adjoining the Wilder estate. This farm, which he had inhabited for the years of his residence, but had not worked, and had yet always managed to exist without trouble, was now uninhabited. This, together with a passing hint that Thomas Weatherbee might be able to add something, was the sum of what Mrs. Seldon knew.

I lost no time in telephoning Weatherbee and making an appointment for that afternoon. On the way to the attorney's office I had ample time to think over the events of the last ten days. That it was Andrew Bentley whom my Uncle Amos had referred to when he spoke so cryptically with me before his death, I had no longer any doubt. Evidently then, he, too, feared his strange neighbor, but how he hoped to thwart any attempt that Bentley might make to get the body—for what reason he might want it I could not guess—with black magic, was beyond my comprehension.

Thomas Weatherbee was a short and rather insignificant man, but his attitude was conducive to business, and he made clear to me that he had only a limited time at my disposal. I came directly to the matter of Andrew Bentley.

"Andrew Bentley," began Weatherbee with some reluctance, "was a man with whom I had no dealings, with whom I cared to have none. I have seldom met any one whose mere presence was so innately evil. Your uncle took up with him, it is true, but I believe he regretted it to the end of his days."

"What exactly was wrong with Bentley?" I cut in.

Weatherbee smiled grimly, regarded me speculatively for a moment or two, and said, "Bentley was an avowed sorcerer."

"Oh, come," I said; "that sort of thing isn't believed in any more." But a horrible suspicion began to grow in my mind.

"Perhaps not generally," replied Weatherbee at once. "But I can assure you that most of us around here believe in the power of black magic after even so short an acquaintance as ours with Andrew Bentley. Consider for a moment that you have spent the greater part of your life in a modern city, away from the countrysides where such beliefs flourish, Wilder."

He stopped with an abrupt gesture, and took a portfolio from a cabinet. From this he took a photograph, looked at it with a slight curl of disgust on his lips, and passed it over to me.

It was a snapshot, apparently made surreptitiously, of Andrew Bentley, and it had been taken evidently at considerable risk after sunset, for the general appearance of the picture led me to assume that its vagueness was caused by the haziness of dusk—a supposition which Weatherbee confirmed. The figure, however, was quite clear, save for blurred arms, which had evidently been moving during the exposure, and for the head. The view had been taken from the side, and showed Andrew Bentley, certainly identified for me by the long cape he wore, standing as if in conversation with some one. Yet it struck me as strange that Bentley could have stood quietly during the exposure with no incentive to do so, and I commented upon it at once.

Weatherbee looked at me queerly. "Wilder," he said, "there was another person there—or should I say *thing*? And this thing was directly in line with the lens, for he was standing very close to Bentley—and yet, there is nothing on the snapshot, nor is there any evidence on the exposed negative itself that any one stood there; for, as you can see, the landscape is unbroken."

It was as he said.

"But this other person," I put in. "He was seen, and yet does not appear. Apparently the camera was out of focus, or the film was defective."

"On the contrary. There are logical explanations for the nonappearance of something on a film. You can't photograph a dream. And you can't photograph something that has no material form—I say *material* advisedly—even though our own eyes give that thing a physical being."

"What do you mean?"

"Father Burkhardt would call it a familiar," he said, clipping his words. "A familiar, in case you don't know, is an evil spirit summoned by a sorcerer to wait upon his desires. That tall, gaunt man was never seen by day—always by night, and never without Bentley. I can give you no more of my time now, but if you can bring yourself to accept what I have to say at face value, I'll be glad to see you again."

My interview with Thomas Weatherbee left me considerably shaken, and I found myself discarding all my previously formed beliefs regarding black magic. I went immediately to my late uncle's store of books, and began to read through them for further information, in the hope that something I might learn would enable me to meet Andrew Bentley on more equal footing, should he choose to call.

I read until far into the night, and what inconceivable knowledge I assimilated lingers clearly in my mind as I write. I read of age-old horror summoned from the abyss by the ignorance of men, of cosmic ghouls that roamed the ether in search of prey, and of countless things that walk by night. There were many legends of familiars, ghastly demons called forth from the depths at the whims of long-dead sorcerers; and it was significant that each legend had been heavily scored along the margins, and in one case the name "Andrew Bentley" was written in my uncle's hand. In another place my uncle had written, "We are fools to play with powers of whose scope even the wisest of us has no knowledge!"

It was at this point that it occurred to me that my uncle had left a letter of sealed instructions for me in case the vault was tampered with. This letter was to be in the library desk, where I found it with little trouble, a long, legal-looking envelope with my name inscribed very formally. The handwriting was undoubtedly my uncle's, and the letter within was the thing that finally dispelled all doubt from my mind as to the reality of the sorcery that had been and was still being practiced near the Wilder homestead; for it made clear what had happened between my uncle and Andrew Bentley—and that other.

My Dear Ellis:

If indeed they have come for me, as they must have if you read this, there is but one thing you can do. Bentley's body must be found and utterly destroyed; surely there cannot be much left of it now. Perhaps you have seen him in the night when he walks— as I have. He is not alive. I know, because I killed him a year ago—stabbed him with your grandfather's hunting-knife—which must yet lie in his black skeleton.

I think both Burkhardt and Weatherbee suspected that I aided Bentley to his black rites, but that was long before I dreamed of what depths of evil lurked in his soul. And when he began to hound me so, when he brought forward that other, that hellish thing he had conjured up from the nethermost places of evil—could I do otherwise than rid myself of his evil presence? My mind was at stake—and yes, my body. When you read this, only my body is at stake. For they want it—conceive if you can the ghastly irony of

my lifeless body given an awful new existence by being inhabited by Bentley's familiar!

The body—Bentley's body—I put it in the vault, but that other removed it and hid it somewhere on the grounds. I have not been able to find it, and this past year has been a living hell for me—they have hounded me nightly, and though I can protect myself from them, I cannot stop them from appearing to taunt me. And when I am dead, my protection must come from you. But I hope that Burkhardt will have closed his eyes and blessed the vault, for this I think will be strong enough to keep them away—and yet, I cannot tell.

And perhaps even this is being read too late—for if once they have my body, destroy me, too, with Bentley's remains—by fire.

Amos Wilder.

I put down this letter and sat for a moment in silence. But what thoughts crowded upon my mind were interrupted by an odd sound from outside the window, a sound that was unnaturally striking in the still night. I glanced at my watch; it was one o'clock in the morning. Then I turned out the small reading-lamp and moved quietly toward the window, immediately beyond which stood the giant elm beneath which on the previous night I had first seen the ghostly figure of Andrew Bentley—for since he had been killed a year before, what I had seen could have been none other than his specter.

Then a thought struck me that paralyzed me with horror. Suppose I had been struck by *that other*? It seemed to me that the blow which had knocked me out had been struck from behind. At the same instant my eyes caught sight of the faintest movement beyond the window. The moon hung in a hazy sky and threw a faint illumination about the tree, despite the fairly heavy shadow of its overhanging limbs. There was a man pressed close to the bole of the tree, and even as I looked another seemed to rise up out of the ground at his side. And the second man was Andrew Bentley! I looked again at the first, and saw a tall, gaunt figure with malevolent red eyes, *through* whom I could see the line of moonlight and shadow on the lawn beyond the tree. They stood there together for only a moment, and then went quickly around the house—toward the vault!

From that instant events moved rapidly to a climax.

My eyes fixed themselves upon that place in the ground from which the figure of Andrew Bentley had sprung, and saw there an opening in the trunk of the old tree—for the elm was hollow, and its bole held the remains of Andrew Bentley! Small wonder that my uncle had been haunted by the presence of the man he had killed, when his remains were hidden in the tree near the library window!

But I stood there only for a fraction of a minute. Then I went quickly to the telephone, and after an agonizing delay got Weatherbee on the wire and asked him to come out at once, hinting enough of what was happening to gain his assent. I suggested also that he bring Father Burkhardt along, and this he promised to do.

Then I slipped silently from the house into the shadowy garden. I think the sight of those two unholy figures hovering about the door of the vault was too much for me, for I launched myself at them, heedless of my danger. But realization came almost instantly, for Andrew Bentley did not even turn at my appearance. Instead, the other looked abruptly around, fixed me with his red and fiery eyes, smiled wickedly so that his leathery face was weirdly creased, and leisurely watched my approach. Instinct, I believe, whirled me about and sent me flying from the garden.

The thing was somewhat surprised at my abrupt bolt, and this momentary hesitation on its part I continue to believe is responsible for my being alive to write this. For I knew that I was flying for my life, and I ran with the utmost speed of which I was capable. A fleeting glance showed me that the thing loped after me, a weirdly flaffing shape seeming to come with the wind in the moonlight night, and struck shuddery horror into my heart.

I made for the river, because I remembered reading in one of my uncle's old books that certain familiars could not cross water unless accompanied by those whose sorcery had summoned them to earth. I leaped into the cold water, tense with the hope that the thing behind could not follow.

It could not.

I saw it raging up and down along the river bank, impotent and furious at my fortunate escape, while I kept myself afloat in mid-current. The current carried me rapidly downstream, and I kept my eyes fixed upon the thing I had eluded until it turned and sped back toward the vault. Only when I was completely out of its sight did I make for the bank once more.

I ran madly down the road along which Weatherbee and the priest must come, flinging off some of my wet clothes as I went. What was happening at the vault I did not know—at the moment my only thought was temporary safety from the thing whose power I had so thoughtlessly challenged.

I had gone perhaps a half-mile beyond the estate when the headlights of Weatherbee's car swept around a curve and outlined me in the road. The car ground to an emergency stop, and Weatherbee's voice called out. I jumped into the car, and explained as rapidly as I could what had happened.

Father Burkhardt regarded me quizzically, half smiling.

"You've had a narrow escape, my boy," he said, "a very narrow escape. Now if only we can get to the vault before they succeed in their evil design. Such a fate is too harsh a punishment even for the sins of Amos Wilder."

He shuddered as he spoke, and Weatherbee's face was grim.

None of us wasted a moment when the car came to a stop near the house. Father Burkhardt, despite his age, led the way, marshaling us behind him, for he went ahead with a crucifix extended.

But even he faltered at the horrifying sight that met our eyes when we rounded the house and came into the garden. For the vault was open, and from it emerged the skeletal Bentley and his familiar, and between them they dragged the lifeless body of my Uncle Amos! Burkhardt's hesitation, however, was only momentary, for he ran forward immediately; nor were Weatherbee and I far behind.

At the same moment the two at the vault caught sight of us. With a shrill scream, the tall, gaunt thing loosed his hold of the corpse and launched himself forward. But the crucifix served us well, for the thing fell shuddering away from it. Father Burkhardt immediately pressed his advantage, and following his sharp command, Weatherbee and I rushed at Bentley, who had up to this moment remained beside the corpse, still keeping hold of one dead arm.

But at our advance, Bentley wavered a moment, and then turned and took flight, dodging nimbly past us and running for the house. We were at his heels, and saw him when he vanished in the deep shadows of the tree near the library window.

Father Burkhardt presently made his appearance, walking warily, for the thing was still at bay but eager to attack.

"Find the bones," directed the priest. "They're in the tree, I suspect."

I bent obediently, and presently my searching hand encountered a scooped-out hollow in the trunk just above the opening at the base of the tree. In this lay the skeleton of Andrew Bentley, together with the weapon by which he had met his death, and here it had lain ever since the thing Bentley had summoned from the depths had removed the sorcerer's body from the old vault. Small wonder that it had never been discovered!

Father Burkhardt stood protectingly close while Weatherbee and I prepared a pyre to consume the remains of the sorcerer.

"But what can we do about that?" I asked once, pointing to the familiar that now raged in baffled fury just beyond us.

"We need not bother about that," said the priest. "He is held to earth only by the body of the man who summoned him from below. When once that body is destroyed, he must return. That's why they were after your uncle's body. If the familiar could inhabit a body fresh from a new grave, he could walk by day as well as by night, and need have no fear of having to return."

Once or twice the thing did rush at us—but each time its charge was arrested by the power of that crucifix held unfalteringly aloft by Father Burkhardt, and each time the thing shrank away, wailing.

It was over at last, but not without a short period of ghastly doubt. The remains of Andrew Bentley were reduced to ashes, utterly destroyed, and yet the thing Bentley had called from outside lingered beyond us, strangely quiet now, regarding us malevolently.

"I don't understand," admitted Father Burkhardt at last. "Now that Bentley's ashes alone remain, the thing should go back into the depths."

But if the priest did not understand, I did. Abruptly I ran to the library window, raised it as far as it would go, and scrambled into the room. In a moment I emerged, bearing the fragment of Bentley's little finger which I had snatched from the skeletal hand the night before. I threw it into the flames already dying down in the shadow of the tree.

In a moment it had caught fire, and at the same instant the thing hovering near gave a chilling scream of pain and fury, pushed madly toward us, and then abruptly shot into space and vanished like the last fragment of an unholy, ghastly nightmare.

"*Requiescat in pace,*" said Father Burkhardt softly, looking at the ashes at our feet. But the dubious expression in his eyes conveyed his belief that for the now-released spirit of Andrew Bentley a greater and longer torture had just begun.

M. L. Humphreys

M. L. HUMPHREYS APPEARS to be one of the many obscure writers who worked briefly in the pulps. Or perhaps the name is a pseudonym, used once and discarded. I could find nothing about this author beyond the fact that this story, the only one I could locate with this byline, was selected by H. P. Lovecraft in 1929 and 1930, when he compiled a list of significant horror stories, incorporating both literary fiction and popular stories. The list was published as *H. P. Lovecraft's Favorite Weird Tales: The Roots of Modern Horror,* and the criterion for being included was that the stories must have "the greatest amount of truly cosmic horror and macabre convincingness."

"The Floor Above" was originally published in the May 1923 issue of *Weird Tales.*

The Floor Above

M. L. HUMPHREYS

SEPTEMBER 17, 1922.—I sat down to breakfast this morning with a good appetite. The heat seemed over, and a cool wind blew in from my garden, where chrysanthemums were already budding. The sunshine streamed into the room and fell pleasantly on Mrs. O'Brien's broad face as she brought in the eggs and coffee. For a supposedly lonely old bachelor the world seemed to me a pretty good place. I was buttering my third set of waffles when the housekeeper again appeared, this time with the mail.

I glanced carelessly at the three or four letters beside my plate. One of them bore a strangely familiar handwriting. I gazed at it a minute, then seized it with a beating heart. Tears almost came into my eyes. There was no doubt about it—it was Arthur Barker's handwriting! Shaky and changed, to be sure, but ten years have passed since I have seen Arthur, or, rather, since his mysterious disappearance.

For ten years I have not had a word from him. His people know no more than I what has become of him, and long ago we gave him up for dead. He vanished without leaving a trace behind him. It seemed to me, too, that with him vanished the last shreds of my youth. For Arthur was my dearest friend in that happy time. We were boon companions, and many a mad prank we played together.

And now, after ten years of silence, Arthur was writing to me!

The envelope was postmarked Baltimore. Almost reluctantly—for I feared what it might contain—I passed my finger under the flap and opened it. It held a single sheet of paper torn from a pad. But it was Arthur's writing:

Dear Tom:
    Old man, can you run down to see me for a few days? I'm afraid I'm in a bad way.

                          Arthur.

Scrawled across the bottom was the address, 536 N. Marathon Street.

I have often visited Baltimore, but I can not recall a street of that name.

Of course I shall go . . . But what a strange letter after ten years! There is something almost uncanny about it.

I shall go tomorrow evening. I can not possibly get off before then.

September 18—I am leaving tonight. Mrs. O'Brien has packed my two suitcases, and everything is in readiness for my departure. Ten minutes ago I handed her the keys and she went off tearfully. She has been sniffling all day and I have been perplexed, for a curious thing occurred this morning.

It was about Arthur's letter. Yesterday, when I had finished reading it, I took it to my desk and placed it in a small compartment together with other personal papers. I remember distinctly that it was on top, with a lavender card from my sister directly underneath. This morning I went to get it. It was gone.

There was the lavender card exactly where I had seen it, but Arthur's letter had completely disappeared. I turned everything upside down, then called Mrs. O'Brien and we both searched, but in vain. Mrs. O'Brien, in spite of all I could say, took it upon herself to feel that I suspected her . . . But what could have become of it? Fortunately I remembered the address.

September 19—I have arrived. I have seen Arthur. Even now he is in the next room and I am supposed to be preparing for bed. But something tells me I shall not sleep a wink this night. I am strangely wrought up, though there is not the shadow of an excuse for my excitement. I should be rejoicing to have found my friend again. And yet—

I reached Baltimore this morning at eleven o'clock. The day was warm and beautiful, and I loitered outside the station a few minutes before calling a taxi. The driver seemed well acquainted with the street I gave him, and we rolled off across the bridge.

As I drew near my destination, I began to feel anxious and afraid. But the ride lasted longer than I expected—Marathon Street seemed to be located in the suburbs of the city. At last we turned into a dusty street, paved only in patches and lined with linden and aspen trees. The fallen leaves crunched beneath the tires. The September sun beat down with a white intensity. The taxi drew up before a house in the middle of a block that boasted not more than six dwellings. On each side of the house was a vacant lot, and it was set far back at the end of a long narrow yard crowded with trees.

I paid the driver, opened the gate, and went in. The trees were so thick that not until I was half-way up the path did I get a good view of the house. It was three stories high, built of brick, in fairly good repair, but lonely and deserted-looking. The blinds were closed in all of the windows with the exception of two, one on the first, one on the second floor. Not a sign of life anywhere, not a cat nor a milk-bottle to break the monotony of leaves that carpeted the porch.

But, overcoming my feeling of uneasiness, I resolutely set my suitcases on the porch, caught at the old-fashioned bell, and gave an energetic jerk. A startling peal jangled through the silence. I waited, but there was no answer.

After a minute I rang again. Then from the interior I heard a queer dragging sound, as if some one was coming slowly down the hall. The knob was turned and the door opened. I saw before me an old woman, wrinkled, withered, and filmy-eyed, who leaned on a crutch.

"Does Mr. Barker live here?" I asked.

She nodded, staring at me in a curious way, but made no move to invite me in.

"Well, I've come to see him," I said. "I'm a friend of his. He sent for me."

At that she drew slightly aside.

"He's upstairs," she said in a cracked voice that was little more than a whisper. "I can't show you up. Hain't been up a stair now in ten years."

"That's all right," I replied, and, seizing my suitcases, I strode down the long hall.

"At the head of the steps," came the whispering voice behind me. "The door at the end of the hall."

I climbed the cold dark stairway, passed along the short hall at the top, and stood before a closed door. I knocked.

"Come in." It was Arthur's voice, and yet— not his.

I opened the door and saw Arthur sitting on a couch, his shoulders hunched over, his eyes raised to mine.

After all, ten years had not changed him so much. As I remembered him, he was of medium height, inclined to be stout, and ruddy-faced, with keen gray eyes. He was still stout, but had lost his color and his eyes had dulled.

"And where have you been all this time?" I demanded, when the first greetings were over.

"Here," he answered.

"In this house?"

"Yes."

"But why didn't you let us hear from you?"

He seemed to be making an effort to speak.

"What did it matter? I didn't suppose any one cared."

Perhaps it was my imagination, but I could not get rid of the thought that Arthur's pale eyes, fixed tenaciously upon my face, were trying to tell me something, something quite different from what his lips said.

I felt chilled. Although the blinds were open, the room was almost darkened by the branches of the trees that pressed against the window. Arthur had not given me his hand, had seemed troubled to know how to make me welcome. Yet of one thing I was certain: He needed me and he wanted me to know he needed me.

As I took a chair I glanced about the room. It was a typical lodging-house room, medium-sized, with flowered wallpaper, worn matting, nondescript rugs, a wash-stand in one corner, a chiffonier in another, a table in the center, two or three chairs, and the couch which evidently served Arthur as a bed. But it was cold, strangely cold for such a warm day.

Arthur's eyes had wandered uneasily to my suitcases. He made an effort to drag himself to his feet.

"Your room is back here," he said, with a motion of his thumb.

"No, wait," I protested. "Let's talk about yourself first. What's wrong?"

"I've been sick."

"Haven't you a doctor? If not, I'll get one."

At this he started up with the first sign of animation he had shown.

"No, Tom, don't do it. Doctors can't help me now. Besides, I hate them. I'm afraid of them."

His voice trailed away, and I took pity on his agitation. I decided to let the question of doctors drop for the moment.

"As you say," I assented carelessly.

Without more ado, I followed him into my room, which adjoined his and was furnished in much the same fashion. But there were two windows, one on each side, looking out on the vacant lots. Consequently there was more light, for which I was thankful. In a far corner I noticed a door, heavily bolted.

"There's one more room," said Arthur, as I deposited my belongings, "one that you'll like. But we'll have to go through the bathroom."

Groping our way through the musty bathroom, in which a tiny jet of gas was flickering, we stepped into a large, almost luxurious chamber. It was a library, well-furnished, carpeted, and surrounded by shelves fairly bulging with books. But for the chilliness and bad light, it was perfect. As I moved about, Arthur followed me with his eyes.

"There are some rare works on botany—"

I had already discovered them, a set of books that I would have given much to own. I could not contain my joy.

"You won't be so bored browsing around in here—"

In spite of my preoccupation, I pricked up my ears. In that monotonous voice there was no sympathy with my joy. It was cold and tired.

When I had satisfied my curiosity we returned to the front room, and Arthur flung himself, or rather fell, upon the couch. It was nearly five o'clock and quite dark. As I lighted the gas, I heard a sound below as of somebody thumping on the wall.

"That's the old woman," Arthur explained. "She cooks my meals, but she's too lame to bring them up."

He made a feeble attempt at rising, but I saw he was worn out.

"Don't stir," I warned him. "I'll bring up your food tonight."

To my surprise, I found the dinner appetizing and well-cooked, and, in spite of the fact that I did not like the looks of the old woman, I ate with relish. Arthur barely touched a few spoonfuls of soup to his lips and absently crumbled some bread in his plate.

Directly I had carried off the dishes, he wrapped his reddish-brown dressing gown about him, stretched out at full length on the couch, and asked me to turn out the gas. When I had complied with his request, I again heard his weak voice asking if I had everything I needed.

"Everything," I assured him, and then there was unbroken silence.

I went to my room, finally, closed the door, and here I am sitting restlessly between the two back windows that look out on the vacant lots.

I have unpacked my clothes and turned down the bed, but I can not make up my mind to retire. If the truth be told, I hate to put out the light. . . . There is something disturbing in the way the dry leaves tap on the panes. And my heart is sad when I think of Arthur.

I have found my old friend, but he is no longer my old friend. Why does he fix his pale eyes so strangely on my face? What does he wish to tell me?

But these are morbid thoughts. I will put them out of my head. I will go to bed and get a good night's rest. And tomorrow I will wake up finding everything right and as it should be.

September 26—I have been here a week today, and have settled down to this queer existence as if I had never known another. The day after my arrival I discovered that the third volume of the botanical series was done in Latin, which I have set myself the task of translating. It is absorbing work, and when I have buried myself in one of the deep chairs by the library table, the hours fly fast.

For health's sake I force myself to walk a few miles every day. I have tried to prevail on Arthur to do likewise, but he, who used to be so active, now refuses to budge from the house. No wonder he is literally blue! For it is a fact that his complexion, and the shadows about his eyes and temples, are decidedly blue.

What does he do with himself all day? Whenever I enter his room, he is lying on the couch, a book beside him, which he never reads. He does not seem to suffer pain, for he never complains. After several ineffectual attempts to get medical aid for him, I have given up mentioning the subject of doctor. I feel that his trouble is more mental than physical.

September 28—A rainy day. It has been coming down in floods since dawn. And I got a queer turn this afternoon.

As I could not get out for my walk, I spent the morning staging a general house-cleaning. It was time! Dust and dirt everywhere. The bathroom, which has no window and is lighted by gas, was fairly overrun with water-bugs and roaches. Of course I did not penetrate to Arthur's room, but I heard no sound from him as I swept and dusted.

I made a good dinner and settled down in the library, feeling quite cozy. The rain came down steadily and it had grown so cold I decided to make a fire later on. But once I had gathered my tablets and notebooks about me I forgot the cold.

I remember I was on the subject of the *Aster trifolium*, a rare variety seldom found in this country. Turning a page, I came upon a specimen of this very variety, dried, pressed flat, and pasted to the margin. Above it, in Arthur's handwriting, I read: *September 27, 1912.*

I was bending close to examine it, when I felt a vague fear. It seemed to me that some one was in the room and was watching me. Yet I had not heard the door open, nor seen any one enter. I turned sharply and saw Arthur, wrapped in his reddish-brown dressing-gown, standing at my very elbow.

He was smiling—smiling for the first time since my arrival, and his dull eyes were bright. But I did not like that smile. In spite of myself I jerked away from him. He pointed at the aster.

"It grew in the front yard under a linden tree. I found it yesterday."

"Yesterday!" I shouted, my nerves on edge. "Good Lord, man! Look! It was ten years ago!"

The smile faded from his face.

"Ten years ago," he repeated thickly. *"Ten years ago?"*

. . .

Five o'clock. Dusk is falling. O God! What has come over me? Am I the same man that went out of this house three hours ago? And what has happened? . . .

I had a splendid walk, and was striding homeward in a fine glow. But as I turned the corner and came in sight of the house, it was as if I looked at death itself. I could hardly drag myself up the stairs, and when I peered into the shadowy chamber, and saw the man hunched up on the couch, with his eyes fixed intently on my face, I could have screamed like a woman. I wanted to fly, to rush out into the clear cold air and run—to run and never come back! But I controlled myself, forced my feet to carry me to my room.

There is a weight of hopelessness at my heart. The darkness is advancing, swallowing up everything, but I have not the will to light the gas. . . .

Now there is a flicker in the front room. I am a fool; I must pull myself together. Arthur is lighting up, and downstairs I can hear the thumping that announces dinner. . . .

It is a queer thought that comes to me now, but it is odd I have not noticed it before. We are about to sit down to our evening meal. Arthur will eat practically nothing, for he has no appetite. Yet he remains stout. It can not be healthy fat, but even at that it seems to me that a man who eats as little as he does would become a living skeleton.

October 5—Positively, I must see a doctor about myself, or soon I shall be a nervous wreck. I am acting like a child. Last night I lost all control and played the coward.

I had gone to bed early, tired out from a hard day's work. It was raining again, and as I lay in bed I watched the little rivulets trickling down the panes. Lulled by the sighing of the wind among the leaves, I fell asleep.

I awoke (how long afterward I can not say) to feel a cold hand laid on my arm. For a moment I lay paralyzed with terror. I would have cried aloud, but I had no voice. At last I managed to sit up, to shake the hand off. I reached for the matches and lighted the gas.

It was Arthur who stood by my bed—Arthur wrapped in his eternal reddish-brown dressing-gown. He was excited. His blue face had a yellow tinge, and his eyes gleamed in the light.

"Listen!" he whispered.

I listened but heard nothing.

"Don't you hear it?" he gasped, and he pointed upward.

"Upstairs?" I stammered. "Is there somebody upstairs?"

I strained my ears, and at last I fancied I could hear a fugitive sound like the light tapping of footsteps.

"It must be somebody walking about up there," I suggested.

"No!" he cried in a sharp rasping voice. "No! It is nobody walking about up there!"

And he fled into his room.

For a long time I lay trembling, afraid to move. But at last, fearing for Arthur, I got up and crept to his door. He was lying on the couch, with his face in the moonlight, apparently asleep.

October 6—I had a talk with Arthur today. Yesterday I could not bring myself to speak of the previous night's happening, but all of this nonsense must be cleared away.

We were in the library. A fire was burning in the grate, and Arthur had his feet on the fender. The slippers he wears are as objectionable to me as his dressing-gown. They are felt slippers, old and worn, and frayed around the edges as if they had been gnawed by rats. I can not imagine why he does not get a new pair.

"Say, old man," I began abruptly, "do you own this house?"

He nodded.

"Don't you rent any of it?"

"Downstairs—to Mrs. Harlan."

"But upstairs?"

He hesitated, then shook his head.

"No, it's inconvenient. There's only a peculiar way to get upstairs."

I was struck by this.

"By Jove! you're right. Where's the staircase?"

He looked me full in the eyes.

"Don't you remember seeing a bolted door in a corner of your room? The staircase runs from that door."

I did remember it, and somehow the memory made me uncomfortable. I said no more and decided not to refer to what had happened that night. It occurred to me that Arthur might have been walking in his sleep.

October 8—When I went for my walk on Tuesday I dropped in and saw Doctor Lorraine, who is an old friend. He expressed some surprise at my rundown condition and wrote me a prescription.

I am planning to go home next week. How pleasant it will be to walk in my garden and listen to Mrs. O'Brien singing in the kitchen!

October 9—Perhaps I had better postpone my trip. I casually mentioned it to Arthur this morning.

He was lying relaxed on the sofa, but when I spoke of leaving he sat up as straight as a bolt. His eyes fairly blazed.

"No, Tom, don't go!" There was terror in his voice, and such pleading that it wrung my heart.

"You've stood it alone here ten years," I protested. "And now—"

"It's not that," he said. "But if you go, you will never come back."

"Is that all the faith you have in me?"

"I've got faith, Tom. But if you go, you'll never come back."

I decided that I must humor the vagaries of a sick man.

"All right," I agreed. "I'll not go. Anyway, not for some time."

October 12—What is it that hangs over this house like a cloud? For I can no longer deny that there *is* something—something indescribably oppressive. It seems to pervade the whole neighborhood.

Are all the houses on this block vacant? If not, why do I never see children playing in the street? Why are passers-by so rare? And why, when from the front window I do catch a glimpse of one, is he hastening away as fast as possible?

I am feeling blue again. I know that I need a change, and this morning I told Arthur definitely that I was going.

To my surprise, he made no objection. In fact, he murmured a word of assent and smiled. He smiled as he smiled in the library that morning when he pointed at the *Aster trifolium*. And I don't like that smile. Anyway, it is settled. I shall go next week, Thursday, the 19th.

October 13—I had a strange dream last night. Or was it a dream? It was so vivid. . . . All day long I have been seeing it over and over again.

In my dream I thought that I was lying there in my bed. The moon was shining brightly into the room, so that each piece of furniture stood out distinctly. The bureau is so placed that when I am lying on my back, with my head high on the pillow, I can see full into the mirror.

I thought I was lying in this manner and staring into the mirror. In this way I saw the bolted door in the far corner of the room. I tried to keep my mind off it, to think of something else, but it drew my eyes like a magnet.

It seemed to me that some one was in the room, a vague figure that I could not recognize. It approached the door and caught at the bolts. It dragged at them and struggled, but in vain—they would not give way.

Then it turned and showed me its agonized face. It was Arthur! I recognized his reddish-brown dressing-gown.

I sat up in bed and cried to him, but he was gone. I ran to his room, and there he was, stretched out in the moonlight, asleep. It must have been a dream.

October 15—We are having Indian Summer weather now—almost oppressively warm. I have been wandering about all day, unable to settle down to anything. This morning I felt so lonesome that when I took the breakfast dishes down, I tried to strike up a conversation with Mrs. Harlan.

Hitherto I have found her as solemn and uncommunicative as the Sphinx, but as she took the tray from my hands, her wrinkles broke into the semblance of a smile. Positively at that moment it seemed to me that she resembled Arthur. Was it her smile, or the expression of her eyes? Has she, also, something to tell me?

"Don't you get lonesome here?" I asked her sympathetically.

She shook her head. "No, sir, I'm used to it now. I couldn't stand it anywhere else."

"And do you expect to go on living here the rest of your life?"

"That may not be very long, sir," she said, and smiled again.

Her words were simple enough, but the way she looked at me when she uttered them seemed to give them a double meaning. She hobbled away, and I went upstairs and wrote Mrs. O'Brien to expect me early on the morning of the 19th.

October 18—Ten a.m.—Am catching the twelve o'clock train tonight. Thank God, I had the resolution to get away! I believe another week of this life would drive me mad. And perhaps Arthur is right—perhaps I shall never come back.

I ask myself if I have become such a weakling as that, to desert him when he needs me most. I don't know. I don't recognize myself any longer. . . .

But of course I will be back. There is the translation, for one thing, which is coming along famously. I could never forgive myself for dropping it at the most vital point.

As for Arthur, when I return I intend to give in to him no longer. I will make myself master here and cure him against his will. Fresh air, change of scene, a good doctor, these are the things he needs.

But what is his malady? Is it the influence of this house that has fallen on him like a blight? One might imagine so, since it is having the same effect on me.

Yes, I have reached that point where I no longer sleep. At night I lie awake and try to keep my eyes off the mirror across the room. But in the end I always find myself staring into it—watching the door with the heavy bolts. I long to rise from the bed and draw back the bolts, but I'm afraid.

How slowly the day goes by! The night will never come!

Nine p.m.—Have packed my suitcases and put the room in order. Arthur must be asleep. . . . I'm afraid the parting from him will be painful. I shall leave here at eleven o'clock in order to give myself plenty of time . . . It is beginning to rain. . . .

October 19—At last! It has come! I am mad! I knew it! I felt it creeping on me all the time! Have I not lived in this house a month? Have I not seen? . . . To have seen what I have seen, to have lived for a month as I have lived, one must be mad. . . .

It was ten o'clock. I was waiting impatiently for the last hour to pass. I had seated myself in a rocking-chair by the bed, my suitcases beside me, my back to the mirror. The rain no longer fell. I must have dozed off.

But all at once I was wide awake, my heart beating furiously. Something had touched me. I leapt to my feet, and, as I turned sharply, my eyes fell upon the mirror. In it I saw the door just as I had seen it the other night, and the figure fumbling with the bolt. I wheeled around, but there was nothing there.

I told myself that I was dreaming again, that Arthur was asleep in his bed. But I trembled as I opened the door of his room and peered in. The room was empty, the bed not even crumpled. Lighting a match, I groped my way through the bathroom into the library.

The moon had come from under a cloud and was pouring in a silvery flood through the windows, but Arthur was not there. I stumbled back into my room.

The moon was there, too . . . And the door, the door in the corner was half open. The bolt had been drawn. In the darkness I could just make out a flight of steps that wound upward.

I could no longer hesitate. Striking another match, I climbed the back stairway.

When I reached the top I found myself in total darkness, for the blinds were tightly closed. Realizing that the room was probably a duplicate of the one below, I felt along the wall until I came to the gas jet. For a moment the flame flickered, then burned bright and clear.

O God! what was it I saw? A table, thick with dust, and something wrapped in a reddish-brown dressing-gown, that sat with its elbows propped upon it.

How long had it been sitting there, that it had grown more dry than the dust upon the table! For how many thousands of days and nights had the flesh rotted from that grinning skull!

In its bony fingers it still clutched a pencil. In front of it lay a sheet of scratched paper, yellow with age. With trembling fingers I brushed away the dust. It was dated October 19, 1912. It read:

"Dear Tom:

"Old man, can you run down to see me for a few days? I'm afraid I'm in a bad way—"

SCHOOL FOR THE UNSPEAKABLE

Manly Wade Wellman

MANLY WADE WELLMAN (1903–1986) began writing in the 1920s, mainly in the horror field. By the 1930s, he was selling stories to the leading pulps in the genre: *Weird Tales, Wonder Stories,* and *Astounding Stories.* He had three series running simultaneously in *Weird Tales*: Silver John, also known as John the Balladeer, the backwoods minstrel with a silver-stringed guitar; John Thunstone, the New York playboy and adventurer who was also a psychic detective; and Judge Keith Hilary Persuivant, an elderly occult detective, written under the pseudonym Gans T. Fields.

His short story, "A Star for a Warrior," won the Best Story of the Year award from *Ellery Queen Mystery Magazine* in 1946, beating out William Faulkner, who wrote an angry letter of protest. Other major honors include Lifetime Achievement Awards from the World Fantasy Writers (1980) and the British Fantasy Writers (1986), and the World Fantasy Award for Best Collection for *Worse Things Waiting* (1975).

Several stories have been adapted for television, including "The Valley Was Still" for *The Twilight Zone* (1961), "The Devil Is Not Mocked" for *Night Gallery* (1971), and two episodes of *Lights Out,* "Larroes Catch Meddlers" (1951) and "School for the Unspeakable" (1952).

Wellman also wrote for the comic books, producing the first Captain Marvel issue for Fawcett Publishers. When D.C. Comics sued Fawcett for plagiarizing their Superman character, Wellman testified against Fawcett, and D.C. won the case after three years of litigation.

"School for the Unspeakable" was originally published in the September 1937 issue of *Weird Tales.*

School for the Unspeakable

MANLY WADE WELLMAN

BART SETWICK DROPPED OFF the train at Carrington and stood for a moment on the station platform, an honest-faced, well-knit lad in tweeds. This little town and its famous school would be his home for the next eight months; but which way to the school? The sun had set, and he could barely see the shop signs across Carrington's modest main street.

He hesitated, and a soft voice spoke at his very elbow:

"Are you for the school?"

Startled, Bart Setwick wheeled. In the gray twilight stood another youth, smiling thinly and waiting as if for an answer. The stranger was all of nineteen years old—that meant maturity to young Setwick, who was fifteen—and his pale face had shrewd lines to it. His tall, shambling body was clad in high-necked jersey and unfashionably tight trousers. Bart Setwick skimmed him with the quick, appraising eye of young America.

"I just got here," he replied. "My name's Setwick."

"Mine's Hoag." Out came a slender hand. Setwick took it and found it froggy-cold, with a suggestion of steel-wire muscles. "Glad to meet you. I came down on the chance someone would drop off the train. Let me give you a lift to the school."

Hoag turned away, felinely light for all his ungainliness, and led his new acquaintance around the corner of the little wooden railway station. Behind the structure, half hidden in its shadow, stood a shabby buggy with a lean bay horse in the shafts.

"Get in," invited Hoag, but Bart Setwick paused for a moment. His generation was not used to such vehicles. Hoag chuckled and said, "Oh, this is only a school wrinkle. We run to funny customs. Get in."

Setwick obeyed. "How about my trunk?"

"Leave it." The taller youth swung himself in beside Setwick and took the reins. "You'll not need it tonight."

He snapped his tongue and the bay horse stirred, drew them around and off down a bush-lined side road. Its hoof-beats were oddly muffled.

They turned a corner, another, and came into open country. The lights of Carrington, newly kindled against the night, hung behind like a constellation settled down to Earth. Setwick felt a hint of chill that did not seem to fit the September evening.

"How far is the school from town?" he asked.

"Four or five miles," Hoag replied in his hushed voice. "That was deliberate on the part of the founders—they wanted to make it hard for the students to get to town for larks. It forced us to dig up our own amusements." The pale face creased in a faint smile, as if this were a pleasantry. "There's just a few of the right sort on hand tonight. By the way, what did you get sent out for?"

Setwick frowned his mystification. "Why, to go to school. Dad sent me."

"But what for? Don't you know that this is a high-class prison prep? Half of us are lunkheads that need poking along, the other half are fellows who got in scandals somewhere else. Like me." Again Hoag smiled.

Setwick began to dislike his companion. They rolled a mile or so in silence before Hoag again asked a question:

"Do you go to church, Setwick?"

The new boy was afraid to appear priggish, and made a careless show with, "Not very often."

"Can you recite anything from the Bible?" Hoag's soft voice took on an anxious tinge.

"Not that I know of."

"Good," was the almost hearty response. "As I was saying, there's only a few of us at the school tonight—only three, to be exact. And we don't like Bible-quoters."

Setwick laughed, trying to appear sage and cynical. "Isn't Satan reputed to quote the Bible to his own——"

"What do you know about Satan?" interrupted Hoag. He turned full on Setwick, studying him with intent, dark eyes. Then, as if answering his own question: "Little enough, I'll bet. Would you like to know about him?"

"Sure I would," replied Setwick, wondering what the joke would be.

"I'll teach you after a while," Hoag promised cryptically, and silence fell again.

Half a moon was well up as they came in sight of a dark jumble of buildings.

"Here we are," announced Hoag, and then, throwing back his head, he emitted a wild, wordless howl that made Setwick almost jump out of the buggy. "That's to let the others know we're coming," he explained. "Listen!"

Back came a seeming echo of the howl, shrill, faint, and eery. The horse wavered in its muffled trot, and Hoag clucked it back into step. They turned in at a driveway well grown up in weeds, and two minutes more brought them up to the rear of the closest building. It was dim gray in the wash of moonbeams, with blank inky rectangles for windows. Nowhere was there a light, but as the buggy came to a halt Setwick saw a young head pop out of a window on the lower floor.

"Here already, Hoag?" came a high, reedy voice.

"Yes," answered the youth at the reins, "and I've brought a new man with me."

Thrilling a bit to hear himself called a man, Setwick alighted.

"His name's Setwick," went on Hoag. "Meet Andoff, Setwick. A great friend of mine."

Andoff flourished a hand in greeting and scrambled out over the window-sill. He was chubby and squat and even paler than Hoag, with a low forehead beneath lank, wet-looking hair, and black eyes set wide apart in a fat, stupid-looking face. His shabby jacket was too tight for him, and beneath worn knickers his legs and feet were bare. He might have been an overgrown thirteen or an undeveloped eighteen.

"Felcher ought to be along in half a second," he volunteered.

"Entertain Setwick while I put up the buggy," Hoag directed him.

Andoff nodded, and Hoag gathered the lines in his hands, but paused for a final word.

"No funny business yet, Andoff," he cautioned seriously. "Setwick, don't let this lard-bladder rag you or tell you wild stories until I come back."

Andoff laughed shrilly. "No, no wild stories," he promised. "You'll do the talking, Hoag."

The buggy trundled away, and Andoff swung his fat, grinning face to the new arrival.

"Here comes Felcher," he announced. "Felcher, meet Setwick."

Another boy had bobbed up, it seemed, from nowhere. Setwick had not seen him come around the corner of the building, or slip out of a door or window. He was probably as old as Hoag, or older, but so small as to be almost a dwarf, and frail to boot. His most notable characteristic was his hairiness. A great mop covered his head, bushed over his neck and ears, and hung unkemptly to his bright, deep-set eyes. His lips and cheeks were spread with a rank down, and a curly thatch peeped through the unbuttoned collar of his soiled white shirt. The hand he offered Setwick was almost simian in its shagginess and in the hardness of its palm. Too, it was cold and damp. Setwick remembered the same thing of Hoag's handclasp.

"We're the only ones here so far," Felcher remarked. His voice, surprisingly deep and strong for so small a creature, rang like a great bell.

"Isn't even the head-master here?" inquired Setwick, and at that the other two began to laugh uproariously, Andoff's fife-squeal rendering an obbligato to Felcher's bell-boom. Hoag, returning, asked what the fun was.

"Setwick asks," groaned Felcher, "why the head-master isn't here to welcome him."

More fife-laughter and bell-laughter.

"I doubt if Setwick would think the answer was funny," Hoag commented, and then chuckled softly himself.

Setwick, who had been well brought up, began to grow nettled.

"Tell me about it," he urged, in what he hoped was a bleak tone, "and I'll join your chorus of mirth."

Felcher and Andoff gazed at him with eyes strangely eager and yearning. Then they faced Hoag.

"Let's tell him," they both said at once, but Hoag shook his head.

"Not yet. One thing at a time. Let's have the song first."

They began to sing. The first verse of their offering was obscene, with no pretense of humor to redeem it. Setwick had never been squeamish, but he found himself definitely repelled. The second verse seemed less objectionable, but it hardly made sense:

All they tried to teach here
Now goes untaught.
Ready, steady, each here,
Knowledge we sought.

What they called disaster
Killed us not, O master!
Rule us, we beseech here,
Eye, hand, and thought.

It was something like a hymn, Setwick decided; but before what altar would such hymns be sung? Hoag must have read that question in his mind.

"You mentioned Satan in the buggy on the way out," he recalled, his knowing face hanging like a mask in the half-dimness close to Setwick. "Well, that was a Satanist song."

"It was? Who made it?"

"I did," Hoag informed him. "How do you like it?"

Setwick made no answer. He tried to sense mockery in Hoag's voice, but could not find it. "What," he asked finally, "does all this Satanist singing have to do with the head-master?"

"A lot," came back Felcher deeply, and "A lot," squealed Andoff.

Hoag gazed from one of his friends to the others, and for the first time he smiled broadly. It gave him a toothy look.

"I believe," he ventured quietly but weightily, "that we might as well let Setwick in on the secret of our little circle."

Here it would begin, the new boy decided—the school hazing of which he had heard and read so much. He had anticipated such things with something of excitement, even eagerness, but now he wanted none of them. He did not like his three companions, and he did not like the way they approached whatever it was they intended to do. He moved backward a pace or two, as if to retreat.

Swift as darting birds, Hoag and Andoff closed in at either elbow. Their chill hands clutched him and suddenly he felt light-headed and sick. Things that had been clear in the moonlight went hazy and distorted.

"Come on and sit down, Setwick," invited Hoag, as though from a great distance. His voice

did not grow loud or harsh, but it embodied real menace. "Sit on that window-sill. Or would you like us to carry you?"

At the moment Setwick wanted only to be free of their touch, and so he walked unresistingly to the sill and scrambled up on it. Behind him was the blackness of an unknown chamber, and at his knees gathered the three who seemed so eager to tell him their private joke.

"The head-master was a proper churchgoer," began Hoag, as though he were the spokesman for the group. "He didn't have any use for devils or devil-worship. Went on record against them when he addressed us in chapel. That was what started us."

"Right," nodded Andoff, turning up his fat, larval face. "Anything he outlawed, we wanted to do. Isn't that logic?"

"Logic and reason," wound up Felcher. His hairy right hand twiddled on the sill near Setwick's thigh. In the moonlight it looked like a big, nervous spider.

Hoag resumed. "I don't know of any prohibition of his it was easier or more fun to break."

Setwick found that his mouth had gone dry. His tongue could barely moisten his lips. "You mean," he said, "that you began to worship devils?"

Hoag nodded happily, like a teacher at an apt pupil. "One vacation I got a book on the cult. The three of us studied it, then began ceremonies. We learned the charms and spells, forward and backward——"

"They're twice as good backward," put in Felcher, and Andoff giggled.

"Have you any idea, Setwick," Hoag almost cooed, "what it was that appeared in our study the first time we burned wine and sulfur, with the proper words spoken over them?"

Setwick did not want to know. He clenched his teeth. "If you're trying to scare me," he managed to growl out, "it certainly isn't going to work."

All three laughed once more, and began to chatter out their protestations of good faith.

"I swear that we're telling the truth, Setwick," Hoag assured him. "Do you want to hear it, or don't you?"

Setwick had very little choice in the matter, and he realized it. "Oh, go ahead," he capitulated, wondering how it would do to crawl backward from the sill into the darkness of the room.

Hoag leaned toward him, with the air as of one confiding. "The head-master caught us. Caught us red-handed."

"Book open, fire burning," chanted Felcher.

"He had something very fine to say about the vengeance of heaven," Hoag went on. "We got to laughing at him. He worked up a frenzy. Finally he tried to take heaven's vengeance into his own hands—tried to visit it on us, in a very primitive way. But it didn't work."

Andoff was laughing immoderately, his fat arms across his bent belly.

"He thought it worked," he supplemented between high gurgles, "but it didn't."

"Nobody could kill us," Felcher added. "Not after the oaths we'd taken, and the promises that had been made us."

"What promises?" demanded Setwick, who was struggling hard not to believe. "Who made you any promises?"

"Those we worshipped," Felcher told him. If he was simulating earnestness, it was a supreme bit of acting. Setwick, realizing this, was more daunted than he cared to show.

"When did all these things happen?" was his next question.

"When?" echoed Hoag. "Oh, years and years ago."

"Years and years ago," repeated Andoff.

"Long before you were born," Felcher assured him.

They were standing close together, their backs to the moon that shone in Setwick's face. He could not see their expressions clearly. But their three voices—Hoag's soft, Felcher's deep and vibrant, Andoff's high and squeaky—were absolutely serious.

"I know what you're arguing within yourself," Hoag announced somewhat smugly. "How can we, who talk about those many past years, seem so young? That calls for an explanation, I'll admit." He paused, as if choosing words. "Time—for us—stands still. It came to a halt on that very night, Setwick; the night our head-master tried to put an end to our worship."

"And to us," smirked the gross-bodied Andoff, with his usual air of self-congratulation at capping one of Hoag's statements.

"The worship goes on," pronounced Felcher, in the same chanting manner that he had affected once before. "The worship goes on, and we go on, too."

"Which brings us to the point," Hoag came in briskly. "Do you want to throw in with us, Setwick?—make the fourth of this lively little party?"

"No, I don't," snapped Setwick vehemently.

They fell silent, and gave back a little—a trio of bizarre silhouettes against the pale moon-glow. Setwick could see the flash of their staring eyes among the shadows of their faces. He knew that he was afraid, but hid his fear. Pluckily he dropped from the sill to the ground. Dew from the grass spattered his sock-clad ankles between oxfords and trouser-cuffs.

"I guess it's my turn to talk," he told them levelly. "I'll make it short. I don't like you, nor anything you've said. And I'm getting out of here."

"We won't let you," said Hoag, hushed but emphatic.

"We won't let you," murmured Andoff and Felcher together, as though they had rehearsed it a thousand times.

Setwick clenched his fists. His father had taught him to box. He took a quick, smooth stride toward Hoag and hit him hard in the face. Next moment all three had flung themselves upon him. They did not seem to strike or grapple or tug, but he went down under their assault. The shoulders of his tweed coat wallowed in sand, and he smelled crushed weeds. Hoag, on top of him, pinioned his arms with a knee on each bicep. Felcher and Andoff were stooping close.

Glaring up in helpless rage, Setwick knew once and for all that this was no schoolboy prank. Never did practical jokers gather around their victim with such staring, green-gleaming eyes, such drawn jowls, such quivering lips.

Hoag bared white fangs. His pointed tongue quested once over them.

"Knife!" he muttered, and Felcher fumbled in a pocket, then passed him something that sparkled in the moonlight.

Hoag's lean hand reached for it, then whipped back. Hoag had lifted his eyes to something beyond the huddle. He choked and whimpered inarticulately, sprang up from Setwick's laboring chest, and fell back in awkward haste. The others followed his shocked stare, then as suddenly cowered and retreated in turn.

"It's the master!" wailed Andoff.

"Yes," roared a gruff new voice. "Your old head-master—and I've come back to master *you*!"

Rising upon one elbow, the prostrate Setwick saw what they had seen—a tall, thick-bodied figure in a long dark coat, topped with a square, distorted face and a tousle of white locks. Its eyes glittered with their own pale, hard light. As it advanced slowly and heavily it emitted a snigger of murderous joy. Even at first glance Setwick was aware that it cast no shadow.

"I am in time," mouthed the newcomer. "You were going to kill this poor boy."

Hoag had recovered and made a stand. "Kill him?" he quavered, seeming to fawn before the threatening presence. "No. We'd have given him life——"

"You call it life?" trumpeted the long-coated one. "You'd have sucked out his blood to teem your own dead veins, damned him to your filthy condition. But I'm here to prevent you!"

A finger pointed, huge and knuckly, and then came a torrent of language. To the nerve-stunned Setwick it sounded like a bit from the New Testament, or perhaps from the Book of Common Prayer. All at once he remembered Hoag's avowed dislike for such quotations.

His three erstwhile assailants reeled as if before a high wind that chilled or scorched. "No, no! Don't!" they begged wretchedly.

The square old face gaped open and spewed merciless laughter. The knuckly finger traced a cross in the air, and the trio wailed in chorus as though the sign had been drawn upon their flesh with a tongue of flame.

Hoag dropped to his knees. "Don't!" he sobbed.

"I have power," mocked their tormenter. "During years shut up I won it, and now I'll use it." Again a triumphant burst of mirth. "I know you're damned and can't be killed, but you can be tortured! I'll make you crawl like worms before I'm done with you!"

Setwick gained his shaky feet. The long coat and the blocky head leaned toward him.

"Run, you!" dinned a rough roar in his ears. "Get out of here—and thank God for the chance!"

Setwick ran, staggering. He blundered through the weeds of the driveway, gained the road beyond. In the distance gleamed the lights of Carrington. As he turned his face toward them and quickened his pace he began to weep, chokingly, hysterically, exhaustingly.

He did not stop running until he reached the platform in front of the station. A clock across the street struck ten, in a deep voice not unlike Felcher's. Setwick breathed deeply, fished out his handkerchief and mopped his face. His hand was quivering like a grass stalk in a breeze.

"Beg pardon!" came a cheery hail. "You must be Setwick."

As once before on this same platform, he whirled around with startled speed. Within touch of him stood a broad-shouldered man of thirty or so, with horn-rimmed spectacles. He wore a neat Norfolk jacket and flannels. A short briar pipe was clamped in a good-humored mouth.

"I'm Collins, one of the masters at the school," he introduced himself. "If you're Setwick, you've had us worried. We expected you on that seven o'clock train, you know. I dropped down to see if I couldn't trace you."

Setwick found a little of his lost wind. "But I've—been to the school," he mumbled protestingly. His hand, still trembling, gestured vaguely along the way he had come.

Collins threw back his head and laughed, then apologized.

"Sorry," he said. "It's no joke if you really had all that walk for nothing. Why, that old place is deserted—used to be a catch-all for incorrigible rich boys. They closed it about fifty years ago, when the head-master went mad and killed three of his pupils. As a matter of coincidence, the master himself died just this afternoon, in the state hospital for the insane."

A. V. Milyer

NO INFORMATION IS AVAILABLE about A. V. Milyer. "Mordecai's Pipe" appears to be the only story written by anyone with this name, and it is not impossible that this name is a one-time pseudonym of another pulp writer—an extremely common practice during the height of the pulp era, in the 1920s and 1930s.

The story has been interpreted to suggest that somehow the eponymous pipe came to life. A more likely explanation for the events that come to pass is that an outside agent, certainly a ghost, was responsible. But you may decide for yourself.

"Mordecai's Pipe" was originally published in the June 1936 issue of *Weird Tales*.

Mordecai's Pipe

A. V. MILYER

"JANUARY 7 — McNally sent the pipe today. I found it waiting when I returned home from the office this evening. Oh, it's quite an ordinary-looking pipe; a four-inch stem, badly chewed around the mouthpiece, and a large, round bowl, worn smooth and dark from constant handling. One would never think to look at it that it had had such a gruesome past.

"But McNally swears that it was the one cherished possession of old Peter Mordecai, the fellow they executed at the state prison last week. And what a malevolent old devil *he* must have been! Seems that all the other prisoners shunned him as they would a plague—but then who wouldn't shun a man who's killed four children and used their bodies for God-only-knows what crazy rites? Not that the absence of fellow-ship worried Mordecai, though; for they say that he even refused to speak to guards, silencing their attempts with that wolfish snarl that the newspapers made so much of.

"Oh, how plainly I can see him—smoking his pipe as he grins over the mangled bodies of his victims; smoking it throughout the endless days at the death-house; even smoking it as he takes that last, brief walk to the gallows. I can see him on the very scaffold, shoving his pipe at McNally with a muttered 'Here, Warden,' and a rotten, knowing leer as though he were in possession of some filthy secret.

"Is it any wonder that McNally didn't want it? Is it any wonder that, knowing of my bad taste for gruesome curios, he sent it along to me? I'm sure that no one, however morbid, could desire a more macabre souvenir than this, the pipe of Mordecai.

"It's odd how past events can cast a sinister light upon perfectly innocent objects. This pipe, now—just because of old Mordecai's devil-ish malevolence, his unearthly hate of all man-kind—it repels and fascinates me at the same time. Oh, the power of the human mind is un-limited.

"But enough of this! First thing you know I'll be seeing old Mordecai himself in one of the shadowy corners of my little study here. Too much imagination is a bad thing. . . ."

Pettigrew laid down his pen, pushed back the voluminous diary that was his sole emotional outlet, and gazed fixedly at the battered old briar that lay on the desk before him. He quivered perceptibly as the odd little thought grew in his mind; the thought that told him to smoke the pipe.

With a wry half-smile at his own queerness he tried to dismiss the thought, but it persisted. Smoke the pipe—the pipe that a madman's lips had last caressed; the pipe that murdering fin-gers had last fondled. How novel it would be!

How utterly fantastic! The normal element in Pettigrew's mind whispered "No!"; the morbid strain shouted "Yes!"

Pettigrew found himself reaching slowly for the humidor that rested at his left elbow. He picked up the battered briar and carefully packed the hard-coated interior of the bowl with his private mixture of fragrant tobaccos. Then, with an involuntary shudder of disgust at his au-dacity, he thrust the bitten mouthpiece into his mouth and carefully applied a match.

As he expelled the first blue smoke-cloud from his lungs, Pettigrew reflected with amuse-ment upon the shocked amazement his friends would register if he told them of his rather ghastly experiment. He was suddenly brought back to the present by a momentary twinge of pain. He had, it seemed, pinched a portion of his soft mouth-tissue between stem and teeth so that it bled. With a grimace at his own ner-vousness, he replaced the pipe and again inhaled deeply. Odd that the pipe should seem so un-wieldy, almost as if unseen fingers were tugging at it!

The blinding suddenness of the flash of red-hot agony brought Pettigrew to his feet in a mad leap that upset his chair with a crash. Like a puppet on a string he caromed madly about the room, knocking over lamps and furniture in a sudden fight for breath. His throat was gripped by a constricting band of fire that filled it with hellish, strangling pain—a grip that made his brain spin and roar in an insane cacophony. His clawing fingers were tearing wildly at his con-torted mouth when he finally crashed to the floor.

Doctor Clayton, from his crouched position over Pettigrew's sprawled body, beckoned to Sergeant McCullough.

"Of all the damn-fool ways to die!" growled the doctor, pointing to the gaping jaws that helped make a grotesque mockery of the em-purpled thing that had once been a human face.

"It's a pipe—you can barely see part of the bowl there at the top of his throat. But how in God's name could a fellow possibly swallow a pipe— stem first, at that? McCullough, if it weren't all so damned ridiculous I'd swear that someone *rammed* it down the poor devil's throat!"

HE WALKED BY DAY

Julius Long

JULIUS W. LONG (1907–1955) was mainly a writer of detective stories, but he was a great fan of supernatural fiction, writing enthusiastic letters to *Weird Tales* while writing for other publications. He was born in Ohio, received a law degree, and was admitted to the Ohio bar, where he practiced. A collector of guns (at one time he owned the only Tokerev 7.62 ever offered for sale in *The American Rifleman*), his extensive knowledge of firearms was often apparent in his articles for *Field and Stream* as well as in his crime and mystery stories.

Long wrote many different types of fiction for about thirty magazines, most importantly ghost and fantastic stories for the top magazine in the genre, *Weird Tales*, to which he contributed nine stories in the 1930s, and mystery stories for *Black Mask, Detective Story, Dime Detective, Dime Story, The Shadow,* and *Strange Detective Tales*. One of his *Black Mask* stories, "Carnie Kill" (1945), was selected for *Best Detective Stories of the Year* (1946). He wrote only one novel, *Keep the Coffins Coming* (1947), a murder mystery involving a beautiful woman, her millionaire father, a Communist leader, a German scientist, and several gorillas. One of his short stories served as the basis for the motion picture *The Judge* (1949); it was released in Great Britain as *The Gambler*. The story of a crooked lawyer who blackmails his client into killing his wife, it was directed by Elmer Clifton, produced by Anson Bond, with a screenplay by Samuel Newman, Clifton, and Bond. It starred Milburn Stone, Katherine DeMille, Paul Guilfoyle, and Stanley Waxman.

"He Walked by Day" was published in the June 1934 issue of *Weird Tales*.

He Walked by Day

JULIUS LONG

FRIEDENBURG, OHIO, sleeps between the muddy waters of the Miami River and the rusty track of a little-used spur of the Big Four. It suddenly became important to us because of its strategic position. It bisected a road which we were to surface with tar. The materials were to come by way of the spur and to be unloaded at the tiny yard.

We began work on a Monday morning. I was watching the tar distributer while it pumped tar from the car, when I felt a tap upon my back. I turned about, and when I beheld the individual who had tapped me, I actually jumped.

I have never, before or since, encountered such a singular figure. He was at least seven feet tall, and he seemed even taller than that because of the uncommon slenderness of his frame. He looked as if he had never been warmed by the rays of the sun, but confined all his life in a dank and dismal cellar. I concluded that he had been the prey of some insidious, etiolating disease. Certainly, I thought, nothing else could account for his ashen complexion. It seemed that not blood, but shadows passed through his veins.

"Do you want to see me?" I asked.

"Are you the road feller?"

"Yes."

"I want a job. My mother's sick. I have her to keep. Won't you please give me a job?"

We really didn't need another man, but I was interested in this pallid giant with his staring, gray eyes. I called to Juggy, my foreman.

"Do you think we can find a place for this fellow?" I asked.

Juggy stared incredulously. "He looks like he'd break in two."

"I'm stronger'n anyone," said the youth.

He looked about, and his eyes fell on the Mack, which had just been loaded with six tons of gravel. He walked over to it, reached down and seized the hub of a front wheel. To our utter amazement, the wheel was slowly lifted from the ground. When it was raised to a height of eight or nine inches, the youth looked inquiringly in our direction. We must have appeared sufficiently awed, for he dropped the wheel with an abruptness that evoked a yell from the driver, who thought his tire would blow out.

"We can certainly use this fellow," I said, and Juggy agreed.

"What's your name, Shadow?" he demanded.

"Karl Rand," said the boy, but "Shadow" stuck to him, as far as the crew was concerned.

We put him to work at once, and he slaved all morning, accomplishing tasks that we ordinarily assigned two or three men to do.

We were on the road at lunchtime, some miles from Friedenburg. I recalled that Shadow had not brought his lunch.

"You can take mine," I said. "I'll drive in to the village and eat."

"I never eat none," was Shadow's astonishing remark.

"You never eat!" The crew had heard his as-

777

sertion, and there was an amused crowd about him at once. I fancied that he was pleased to have an audience.

"No, I never eat," he repeated. "You see"—he lowered his voice—"you see, I'm a ghost!"

We exchanged glances. So Shadow was psychopathic. We shrugged our shoulders.

"Whose ghost are you?" gibed Juggy. "Napoleon's?"

"Oh, no. I'm my own ghost. You see, I'm dead."

"Ah!" This was all Juggy could say. For once, the arch-kidder was nonplussed.

"That's why I'm so strong," added Shadow.

"How long have you been dead?" I asked.

"Six years. I was fifteen years old then."

"Tell us how it happened. Did you die a natural death, or were you killed trying to lift a fast freight off the track?" This question was asked by Juggy, who was slowly recovering.

"It was in the cave," answered Shadow solemnly. "I slipped and fell over a bank. I cracked my head on the floor. I've been a ghost ever since."

"Then why do you walk by day instead of by night?"

"I got to keep my mother."

Shadow looked so sincere, so pathetic when he made this answer, that we left off teasing him. I tried to make him eat my lunch, but he would have none of it. I expected to see him collapse that afternoon, but he worked steadily and showed no sign of tiring. We didn't know what to make of him. I confess that I was a little afraid in his presence. After all, a madman with almost superhuman strength is a dangerous character. But Shadow seemed perfectly harmless and docile.

When we had returned to our boarding-house that night, we plied our landlord with questions about Karl Rand. He drew himself up authoritatively, and lectured for some minutes upon Shadow's idiosyncrasies.

"The boy first started telling that story about six years ago," he said. "He never was right in his head, and nobody paid much attention to him at first. He said he'd fallen and busted his head in a cave, but everybody knows they ain't no caves hereabouts. I don't know what put that idea in his head. But Karl's stuck to it ever since, and I 'spect they's lots of folks round Friedenburg that's growed to believe him—more'n admits they do."

That evening, I patronized the village barber shop, and was careful to introduce Karl's name into the conversation. "All I can say is," said the barber solemnly, "that his hair ain't growed any in the last six years, and they was nary a whisker on his chin. No, sir, nary a whisker on his chin."

This did not strike me as so tremendously odd, for I had previously heard of cases of such arrested growth. However, I went to sleep that night thinking about Shadow.

The next morning, the strange youth appeared on time and rode with the crew to the job.

"Did you eat well?" Juggy asked him.

Shadow shook his head. "I never eat none."

The crew half believed him.

Early in the morning, Steve Bradshaw, the nozzle man on the tar distributer, burned his hand badly. I hurried him in to see the village doctor. When he had dressed Steve's hand, I took advantage of my opportunity and made inquiries about Shadow.

"Karl's got me stumped," said the country practitioner. "I confess I can't understand it. Of course, he won't let me get close enough to him to look at him, but it don't take an examination to tell there's something abnormal about him."

"I wonder what could have given him the idea that he's his own ghost," I said.

"I'm not sure, but I think what put it in his head was the things people used to say to him when he was a kid. He always looked like a ghost, and everybody kidded him about it. I kind of think that's what gave him the notion."

"Has he changed at all in the last six years?"

"Not a bit. He was as tall six years ago as he is today. I think that his abnormal growth might have had something to do with the stunting of his mind. But I don't know for sure."

I had to take Steve's place on the tar distributer during the next four days, and I watched Shadow pretty closely. He never ate any lunch, but he would sit with us while we devoured ours. Juggy could not resist the temptation to joke at his expense.

"There was a ghost back in my home town," Juggy once told him. "Mary Jenkens was an awful pretty woman when she was living, and when she was a girl, every fellow in town wanted to marry her. Jim Jenkens finally led her down the aisle, and we was all jealous—especially Joe Garver. He was broke up awful. Mary hadn't no more'n come back from the Falls when Joe was trying to make up to her. She wouldn't have nothing to do with him. Joe was hurt bad.

"A year after she was married, Mary took sick and died. Jim Jenkens was awful put out about it. He didn't act right from then on. He got to imagining things. He got suspicious of Joe.

"'What you got to worry about?' people would ask him. 'Mary's dead. There can't no harm come to her now.'

"But Jim didn't feel that way. Joe heard about it, and he got to teasing Jim.

"'I was out with Mary's ghost last night,' he would say. And Jim got to believing him. One night, he lays low for Joe and shoots him with both barrels. 'He was goin' to meet my wife!' Jim told the judge."

"Did they give him the chair?" I asked.

"No, they gave him life in the state hospital."

Shadow remained impervious to Juggy's yarns, which were told for his special benefit. During this time, I noticed something decidedly strange about the boy, but I kept my own counsel. After all, a contractor can not keep the respect of his men if he appears too credulous.

One day Juggy voiced my suspicions for me. "You know," he said, "I never saw that kid sweat. It's uncanny. It's ninety in the shade today, and Shadow ain't got a drop of perspiration on his face. Look at his shirt. Dry as if he'd just put it on."

Everyone in the crew noticed this. I think we all became uneasy in Shadow's presence.

One morning he didn't show up for work. We waited a few minutes and left without him. When the trucks came in with their second load of gravel, the drivers told us that Shadow's mother had died during the night. This news cast a gloom over the crew. We all sympathized with the youth.

"I wish I hadn't kidded him," said Juggy.

We all put in an appearance that evening at Shadow's little cottage, and I think he was tremendously gratified. "I won't be working no more," he told me. "There ain't no need for me now."

I couldn't afford to lay off the crew for the funeral, but I did go myself. I even accompanied Shadow to the cemetery.

We watched while the grave was being filled. There were many others there, for one of the chief delights in a rural community is to see how the mourners "take on" at a funeral. Moreover, their interest in Karl Rand was deeper. He had said he was going back to his cave, that he would never again walk by day. The villagers, as well as myself, wanted to see what would happen.

When the grave was filled, Shadow turned to me, eyed me pathetically a moment, then walked from the grave. Silently, we watched him set out across the field. Two mischievous boys disobeyed the entreaties of their parents, and set out after him.

They returned to the village an hour later with a strange and incredible story. They had seen Karl disappear into the ground. The earth had literally swallowed him up. The youngsters were terribly frightened. It was thought that Karl had done something to scare them, and their imaginations had got the better of them.

But the next day they were asked to lead a group of the more curious to the spot where Karl had vanished. He had not returned, and they were worried.

In a ravine two miles from the village, the

party discovered a small but penetrable entrance to a cave. Its existence had never been dreamed of by the farmer who owned the land. (He has since then opened it up for tourists, and it is known as Ghost Cave.)

Someone in the party had thoughtfully brought an electric searchlight, and the party squeezed its way into the cave. Exploration revealed a labyrinth of caverns of exquisite beauty. But the explorers were oblivious to the esthetics of the cave; they thought only of Karl and his weird story.

After circuitous ramblings, they came to a sudden drop in the floor. At the base of this precipice they beheld a skeleton.

The coroner and the sheriff were duly summoned. The sheriff invited me to accompany him.

I regret that I can not describe the gruesome, awesome feeling that came over me as I made my way through those caverns. Within their chambers the human voice is given a peculiar, sepulchral sound. But perhaps it was the knowledge of Karl's bizarre story, his unaccountable disappearance that inspired me with such awe, such thoughts.

The skeleton gave me a shock, for it was a skeleton of a man *seven feet tall!* There was no mistake about this; the coroner was positive.

The skull had been fractured, apparently by a fall over the bank. It was I who discovered the hat near by. It was rotted with decay, but in the leather band were plainly discernible the crudely penned initials, "K. R."

I felt suddenly weak. The sheriff noticed my nervousness. "What's the matter, have you seen a ghost?"

I laughed nervously and affected nonchalance. With the best off-hand manner I could command, I told him of Karl Rand. He was not impressed.

"You don't—?" He did not wish to insult my intelligence by finishing his question.

At this moment, the coroner looked up and commented: "This skeleton has been here about six years, I'd say."

I was not courageous enough to acknowledge my suspicions, but the villagers were outspoken. The skeleton, they declared, was that of Karl Rand. The coroner and the sheriff were incredulous, but, politicians both, they displayed some sympathy with this view.

My friend, the sheriff, discussed the matter privately with me some days later. His theory was that Karl had discovered the cave, wandered inside and come upon the corpse of some unfortunate who had preceded him. He had been so excited by his discovery that his hat had fallen down beside the body. Later, aided by the remarks of the villagers about his ghostliness, he had fashioned his own legend.

This, of course, may be true. But the people of Friedenburg are not convinced by this explanation, and neither am I. For the identity of the skeleton has never been determined, and Karl Rand has never since been seen to walk by day.

Dale Clark

ALTHOUGH HE WROTE IN numerous genres, Dale Clark, the pseudonym of Ronal Kayser (1905–1988), is best known for his many mystery, crime, and detective stories. Born in a small town in the Midwest, he took such disparate jobs at various times as a lumberyard worker, reporter, private detective, house-to-house salesman, editor, and creative writing teacher, but remained throughout his adult life a prolific writer.

In addition to more than a half-dozen mystery novels—*Focus on Murder* (1943), *The Narrow Cell* (1944), *The Red Rods* (1946), *A Run for the Money* (1949), *Mambo to Murder* (1955), *Death Wore Fins* (1959), and *Country Coffin* (1961)—Clark wrote more than four hundred stories for both the pulps and the more prestigious slick magazines such as *Collier's*, *Liberty*, and *This Week*. Many of his tales of horror and the supernatural were written and published under his real name.

Many of his stories are set in Southern California, where he spent most of his writing life. Although he inevitably created a wide range of characters, an unusually high percentage of them have an interest in contemporary technology. A forest ranger's station is jammed full of highly technical devices; Doc Judson, a detective-cum-criminalist, speaks frequently of the need for scientific methodology, though it is mainly limited to ballistics; the best-named of Clark's series characters, Highland Park Price (High Price), has amassed a collection of high-tech toys which seldom work because he was too cheap to buy new ones or reputable brands. In these comical private eye yarns, High Price gouges his clients, frequently using blackmail.

"Behind the Screen" was published in the April 1934 issue of *Weird Tales*.

Behind the Screen

DALE CLARK

SIGHT OF THE POLICE officer at the corner roused Catlin from his delirious frenzy like a spray of cold water. He stopped short; he gasped, almost expelling the cigarette from his mouth. The lifting red haze of anger and dismay left him sober and shivering, and a little stunned. He stared stupidly up the dingy Chinatown street into which the first rays of the morning were stealing. He had run many blocks, perhaps miles, to reach the heart of this dismal and unsavory quarter. But why? He could not say. Somnambulistic fumes clouded his mind; he could remember only plunging on madly and blindly without having noticed either his direction or the breaking of day overhead. It was as if some invisible power had guided his flight. Aroused now, Catlin found his situation inexpressibly terrifying. And after a glance at the slit trouser leg, where the recently shaved flesh showed a bald and chalky white, he shrank into the doorway under the sign of Lung Wei.

To Catlin's surprize, the latch yielded under his fumbling hand. Inside, he stood stock-still, puffing hard at the cigarette and staring warily about the shop. A melancholy light leaking through the small, dust-coated window quickly melted and died in the pervading murky gloom. But a faint and nebulous glow spread from an Oriental screen stretched across the rear of the long, narrow, low room. The screen was of some translucent and gauzy stuff; it had the color of silver, and shimmered with a rosy iridescence as minute ripples stirred the gossamer surface.

Behind the screen, a single candle burned with a wan and discouraged flame; its dim glimmer fell in crepuscular half-tones upon a robed figure slumbering in a cane chair. That, too, was behind the gauzy curtain.

Catlin wet his lips nervously. An uneasy sensation overpowered him: it was that he had been here before. But that, of course, could not be. His mind was playing tricks again. . . . Then he smiled harshly.

It was the odor he had recognized. There was in the shop a smell of dead incense, dry and musty and blended with the peculiar trail of opium. The musky taste in the air resembled that which he had often detected in his wife's room—she was a narcotic addict.

It was only the odor; it could be nothing more.

On tiptoe, without making a sound, he advanced into the shadows and inspected the squat show-cases and counters ranged along the low walls. He saw tiny figurines of wood and jade, vases and jars of porcelain, cabinets, sandals, and embroidered cloths. But there was nothing he could convert into money without much difficulty.

He glided toward the screen. (He had become marvelously adept in muffling his footfalls, these past few hours.)

Nevertheless, the figure in the chair behind the screen stirred, and looked around, and arose. He was Chinese, and very old. He came close to the diaphanous gauze, smiling a strange and enigmatic smile.

"Ah, here you are!" he said. "At last."

This Lung Wei wore a black skull-cap, and had gathered about his thin shoulders a stiff, richly brocaded crimson robe. Above the robe, his thin, wrinkled, clean-shaven face had in its expression the delicacy of ancient and yellowed lace. It was, in fact, an expression too delicate, too indefinable, for analysis; it was bland, inscrutable, and mystic as well.

Staring, Catlin forgot that he had been about to hurl himself through the screen. It struck him that there was something dimly familiar in that countenance; he might have glimpsed Lung Wei in a crowd once, or it might have been only in a dream.

"Yes," he faltered, confused.

"I knew you'd come," the Oriental said. He spoke without any accent, with the merest sibilant slurring of syllables. "You see, I have waited so patiently!"

Catlin reflected. Concealed as he stood in the shadows—and seen through the screen, too—he decided that the Chinaman had mistaken him for someone else.

"Well, here I am!" he parried gruffly. It could be no harm, this little game.

Lung Wei arched his eyebrows. "You are not afraid, young sir?" he asked softly.

Catlin puffed his cigarette. "No," he said with a laugh. "Not at all. Of course not."

"That is well." The Oriental removed his hands from the sleeves of the robe, extending them in a curious gesture of—was it appeal? Or perhaps invitation. The outspread fingers looked quite as tenuous and pale as the gossamer screen itself. "You must believe this," he said, "that I want only to help you."

Catlin did not say anything, but his heart began to beat with a furious, groping hope. Decidedly, this became interesting!

Lung Wei regarded him steadily through the shimmering curtain. "That is why I waited so long. I thought that I might be of some service to you." The delicate, unknowable smile played upon his worn and yellowed face. "Do you find that hard to understand? You—you are so very young! That was what impressed me at the first—your so-blind youth. I wonder what you thought of me. Perhaps that I was so very old, eh? Or perhaps you did not think at all?"

The musing voice dripped away into placid silence. Catlin leaned watchfully against a show-case, filling his lungs with the cigarette smoke and letting it drift from his nostrils. He said nothing. There was nothing to say.

"You do not understand, do you?" the Oriental murmured.

Catlin watched the candle brighten, watched a ripple of ruby cross the screen.

"No," he said at last.

"But that is natural." Lung Wei bobbed his head sagely. "It is confusing. One is not exactly prepared. And then, you left in such haste. You have had no time to think."

Cold perspiration cropped forth on Catlin's face at these soft, sibilant words. Some divining sixth sense warned him of an inexplicable peril.

"No!" he exclaimed roughly. "I—that is, you—both of us—why, it's all a mistake! I'm not the man, whoever he is, you were waiting for; I came in to"—he hesitated—"to the wrong shop!"

But with his enigmatic and relentless smile, the old Chinaman said: "In that case, you had better go back. If you think I can help you when you have returned to the prison——"

With a strangled cry, Catlin started toward the screen. He raised his clenched fist.

"So you know!" he panted.

Then, and at the moment he was about to dash aside the shimmering veil, a dazzling light burst within his disordered mind; he stopped short, and the fist dropped numbly to his side.

"But then," he faltered, "if you knew—what you said about helping me——?"

He peered at the face of Lung Wei, serene and bland behind the gauze.

"It's a trick!" he said hoarsely. "A Chinese trick!"

Lung Wei laughed musically. It was not a laugh of amusement or of scorn; there was perhaps a note of pity in it.

"You do not understand, young sir," the liquid voice said.

"No," Catlin muttered.

He felt strangely dizzy. That was the sheen of the candlelight flickering on the glistening gossamer; that, and the smell of the dead incense crawling into his lungs and into his very blood.

He began to walk to and fro in front of the curtain. Presently he said slowly, "There is one solution. This man I killed—you knew him, is that it? He might have been your enemy. Let us say, he belonged to a rival Tong. That is why you offer me your help?"

He stared interrogatively at the veil. But the face of the Chinaman remained impassive, like a sheet of parchment wrinkled into indecipherable lines.

Catlin made an apologetic gesture, an opening and falling of his hands. "I do not expect you to commit yourself," he said hurriedly. "It does not matter. The thing is, I must get away. I need money. Clothes." He looked despairingly at the slit trouser leg. "I can't go far, like this."

"It is not that," Lung Wei said. "You will have to tell me exactly what happened. Otherwise—I am sorry. There would be nothing I could do."

Catlin took a long pull at the cigarette.

"I know what you mean," he muttered. "You are afraid. You needn't be. They can't trace me here. No one has seen me since I escaped. No one at all."

"We are talking at cross-purposes," Lung Wei said. "If you will tell me exactly how it was—then, it may be, I can help."

"I am at your mercy," Catlin muttered. "I will try to remember. It is not very clear—there are things I can recall perfectly, and other parts of it that are quite gone."

Lung Wei made again that gesture of appeal—of sympathy, it might have been—with his hands outspread, the fingers like pale smoke,

the palms dark shadows. "It is for your good, young sir."

Catlin shivered. "The worst was when the priest put the oil, the peculiar oil, over my eyes. And on my fingers. That happened, you understand, in the cell. It was because I could not stand any more! I rolled the cigarette. And when I licked it, at the same time I dropped onto my tongue the wad of cigarette papers."

He looked through the screen into the Oriental's face.

"The pellet tasted bitter. In your country, you know about that. You may have saturated paper, or a cloth with a drug? That is the way Blossom—my wife—smuggled this stuff to me."

He stood silent, thinking, watching the smoke drift upward from his lips into the dry, dead-scented air.

"I did not intend to kill that man," he said at last. "I am a respectable man, a chemist. And I could not earn money enough for her—for Blossom—to buy that stuff. That was how she met Trent, Billy Trent, met him in one of those dens where they smoke it. They put their heads together and told me how I could get it for them. It was Trent's gun I used. They waited outside in his automobile and I went in; they sent me in because the dealer would not know me. But I did not intend to kill him."

He resumed his pacing in front of the screen.

"The police were continually after me, continually asking me who had been in the car. They even promised to commute the sentence to life imprisonment if I'd tell where I got the gun. That was why Blossom brought me the cigarette papers—so at the last I wouldn't lose my nerve and confess. Being doped, you see, I could go to the chair without any fear. I swallowed the wad, the whole pellet, all that she had brought me.

"I could feel it burning in my stomach. I wasn't used to that sort of thing, and for a while I was afraid it wouldn't take hold soon enough. The warden had come in. I tried to put him off, asking for a match to light the cigarette. He didn't have one. Perhaps he saw through me. I had been sitting on the edge of the bunk; I got up and went over to the wash-stand to the candles, those candles the priest was burning.

"I remember he said something horrified. Then it happened. As I straightened up from the candles, with the first puff I became all at once sick. The dose must have been a big one. I staggered. I could feel and hear the bones in my head grinding and crunching upon them-selves. When I opened my eyes, I was lying on the floor. I sat up and looked around. The priest was kneeling there in front of his candles, pray-ing. His robe made it look like he was kneeling in a pool of black water, the robe spilled around his knees. The warden was gone."

Catlin flung back his head and laughed, filling the shop with the reverberations of his laughter.

"I suppose he had run to get the prison doc-tor, making sure I shouldn't cheat the chair, after all!"

He lowered his voice.

"You won't believe it," he said, "but he had left the cell door open. I crept there, on my hands and knees, so as not to disturb the priest. And the corridor was empty. I closed my eyes and opened them again to make sure.

"So I went out. I walked down the corridor, and down the stair, and so into the prison yard. You understand, all this was in the dark, before sunrise. I waited there beside the death-house wall. After a while they opened the gate to let in a car—newspaper men coming to cover the ex-ecution—and I ran out through the open gate. No one saw me."

He looked fixedly at the man behind the screen of gauze.

"It was as simple as that," he said insistently. "It was as easy as coming in here, coming into your shop."

"Of course," said Lung Wei. "Proceed."

"I went straight home," Catlin muttered. "I thought that the three of us—Blossom, and Trent, and I—could think of some safe place for

me. I remember fancying how, afterward, we'd all laugh about the way that drug fooled the war-den. I was quite happy about it."

The Chinaman gave him a curious glance. "Did you walk?" he asked.

Catlin became confused. "I don't know," he stammered. "I can't remember—the drug, you see—I suppose I took a street-car. It is quite a long way. I suppose that is what I did. I am per-fectly sure no one noticed me, however it was."

The Oriental said, "But it is important, young sir. Can't you think?"

"I got there, anyway," Catlin told him. "I rang the bell—rang it again and again. And Blossom didn't answer. I waited there on the porch, smoking, and trying to think what to do next. And then a car—Trent's car—stopped out in front, and those two came up onto the porch together."

His voice trembled.

"They were in evening clothes. They had been to some club or other. On the night I was to die, you see, it had been that way with them. They had been dancing and drinking. I smelled the liquor on them when I went up and spoke to her."

The eyes of the Oriental burned with a strange eagerness. "So, young sir——?"

"She did not even hear me!" Catlin declared. He avoided the gaze of Lung Wei, and contin-ued wearily:

"They had eyes and ears only for each other. Without noticing me, they fell into each other's arms."

He began to laugh shakily. "Perhaps I should have killed them both! On the contrary, I was glad to escape. I was like an animal crawling away to lick its hurt in silence. Besides, would they have helped me? They would only have no-tified the police!" Then he added, almost calmly, "But, as they did not see me, there is no danger from that source."

"That is true," said Lung Wei. He appeared to reflect; his pointed yellow chin rested upon the gathered collar of the brocade robe, and his eyes were lowered.

"Your cigarette," he said at last.

"What did you say?" Catlin asked.

He stared at the screen, which had grown suddenly brighter, with a myriad of little colored glints flashing upon its shining surface. The candle in the background burned no better than before. . . . The gossamer seemed to quiver and glow with a luminous life of its own.

He looked down at the cigarette. The steady white wisp rose in a spiral from its end, from the little molten tip; and he had been smoking it for so long, for hours perhaps.

"Did I roll another?" he asked in bewilderment. "I don't remember that."

"If you will observe its odor," said the liquid Oriental voice of Lung Wei. "That is not a drug, young sir. I, who am used to such things, recognize the presence of a poison——"

"*Poison!*" cried Catlin in a dry sob. "Then she—then that is why—but *that* would mean——"

The words stumbled and blurred into a groan as Catlin reeled back from the thought. He stared blankly into that shimmering veil of gauze. And now it blazed up in pitiless molten brilliance; it extended to titanic proportions; it became a scroll of fire. His confused eyes beheld incandescent suns wheeling in its argent depths. He cowered in a funnel of searing light. His flesh seemed to shrivel in that glare, his breath clotted in his throat, and a fierce whining, crackling sound thrashed and gibbered about his ears. The suns rushed past him, the curtain enfolded him and drew him into a weird spaceland where the myriad lights receded to pin-points. This sudden darkness was more terrible than the intolerable light had been. With a cry of despair he plunged ahead, striking madly with both fists.

Then he realized that he was fighting the little gauze screen. The gossamer was cool, like a stream of water passing over his hands. It tore with a strange tinkling sound, a patter of distant bells.

It lay in a cloud of crumpled silver at his feet. The little jeweled particles in the fabric winked in the candle-light.

Catlin raised his eyes to the face of Lung Wei.

A chill seized him; the next moment, a fever came stinging through his veins. Without the screen to veil it, the face was——

"I remember you, now," he said. "You are the man I killed."

The Oriental smiled his enigmatic, mystic smile.

"That is so," replied the imperturbable yellow man. "You understand, then. Are you ready?"

"Ready?" Catlin faltered.

"To go," said Lung Wei.

Catlin nodded. Lung Wei blew out the candle, and walked out of the shop, and the younger man followed.

There was a long moment in which Lung Wei locked the door of his establishment, and in which Catlin stood gazing into the street. The sun was well up, now, and a thin trickle of traffic stirred upon the pavement. A milk-wagon clattered over the street-car rails. A fruit peddler went by, his legs scissoring between the shafts of his cart. Away off in the city a factory whistle blew.

Catlin touched the brocaded sleeve of Lung Wei.

"Which way?" he asked.

MODERN MASTERS

M. Rickert

MARY RICKERT (1959–), who was born, raised, and still lives in Wisconsin, decided to use only her initial M as a byline because she was in the process of writing stories with a male voice and didn't want to "break the fiction," as she said in an interview. The decision has worked well for her, as her meticulously crafted stories are as gender-neutral as any in the supernatural genre. Her first story, "The Girl Who Ate Butterflies," was published in the August 1999 issue of *The Magazine of Fantasy and Science Fiction*, where most of her work has appeared. She has produced work in a wide range of fields, including science fiction, fantasy, horror, and magic realism, but it is her retelling of Greek myths, often in a startlingly unsettling way, for which she became best known.

A comparative newcomer to the writing world (she had wanted to be a painter), Rickert has already been nominated for and won several major awards. "Journey into the Kingdom" was nominated for a Nebula Award for the best novelette of 2006, was nominated for an International Horror Guild Award, and won the 2007 World Fantasy Award for Best Short Fiction. *Map of Dreams* (2006) won the World Fantasy Award for Best Collection and the Locus Award for Best Collection; the title story was nominated for the World Fantasy Award for Best Novella.

"Journey into the Kingdom" was originally published in the May 2006 issue of *The Magazine of Fantasy and Science Fiction*.

Journey into the Kingdom

M. RICKERT

THE FIRST PAINTING WAS of an egg, the pale ovoid produced with faint strokes of pink, blue, and violet to create the illusion of white. After that there were two apples, a pear, an avocado, and finally, an empty plate on a white tablecloth before a window covered with gauzy curtains, a single fly nestled in a fold at the top right corner. The series was titled "Journey into the Kingdom."

On a small table beneath the avocado there was a black binder, an unevenly cut rectangle of white paper with the words "Artist's Statement" in neat, square, handwritten letters taped to the front. Balancing the porcelain cup and saucer with one hand, Alex picked up the binder and took it with him to a small table against the wall toward the back of the coffee shop, where he opened it, thinking it might be interesting to read something besides the newspaper for once, though he almost abandoned the idea when he saw that the page before him was handwritten in the same neat letters as on the cover. But the title intrigued him.

AN IMITATION LIFE

Though I always enjoyed my crayons and watercolors, I was not a particularly artistic child. I produced the usual assortment of stick figures and houses with dripping yellow suns. I was an avid collector of seashells and sea glass and much preferred to be outdoors, throwing stones at seagulls (please, no haranguing from animal rights activists, I have long since outgrown this) or playing with my imaginary friends to sitting quietly in the salt rooms of the keeper's house, making pictures at the big wooden kitchen table while my mother, in her black dress, kneaded bread and sang the old French songs between her duties as lighthouse keeper, watcher over the waves, beacon for the lost, governess of the dead.

The first ghost to come to my mother was my own father who had set out the day previous in the small boat heading to the mainland for supplies such as string and rice, and also bags of soil, which, in years past, we emptied into crevices between the rocks and planted with seeds, a makeshift garden and a "brave attempt," as my father called it, referring to the barren stone we lived on.

We did not expect him for several days so my mother was surprised when he returned in a storm, dripping wet icicles from his mustache and behaving strangely, repeating over and over again, "It is lost, my dear Maggie, the garden is at the bottom of the sea."

My mother fixed him hot tea but he refused it, she begged him to take off the wet clothes and

retire with her, to their feather bed piled with quilts, but he said, "Tend the light, don't waste your time with me." So my mother, a worried expression on her face, left our little keeper's house and walked against the gale to the lighthouse, not realizing that she left me with a ghost, melting before the fire into a great puddle, which was all that was left of him upon her return. She searched frantically while I kept pointing at the puddle and insisting it was he. Eventually she tied on her cape and went out into the storm, calling his name. I thought that, surely, I would become orphaned that night.

But my mother lived, though she took to her bed and left me to tend the lamp and receive the news of the discovery of my father's wrecked boat, found on the rocky shoals, still clutching in his frozen hand a bag of soil, which was given to me, and which I brought to my mother though she would not take the offering.

For one so young, my chores were immense. I tended the lamp, and kept our own hearth fire going too. I made broth and tea for my mother, which she only gradually took, and I planted that small bag of soil by the door to our little house, savoring the rich scent, wondering if those who lived with it all the time appreciated its perfume or not.

I did not really expect anything to grow, though I hoped that the seagulls might drop some seeds or the ocean deposit some small thing. I was surprised when, only weeks later, I discovered the tiniest shoots of green, which I told my mother about. She was not impressed. By that point, she would spend part of the day sitting up in bed, mending my father's socks and moaning, "Agatha, whatever are we going to do?" I did not wish to worry her, so I told her lies about women from the mainland coming to help, men taking turns with the light. "But they are so quiet. I never hear anyone."

"No one wants to disturb you," I said. "They whisper and walk on tiptoe."

It was only when I opened the keeper's door so many uncounted weeks later, and saw, spread before me, embedded throughout the rock (even in crevices where I had planted no soil) tiny pink, purple, and white flowers, their stems shuddering in the salty wind, that I insisted my mother get out of bed.

She was resistant at first. But I begged and cajoled, promised her it would be worth her effort. "The fairies have planted flowers for us," I said, this being the only explanation or description I could think of for the infinitesimal blossoms everywhere.

Reluctantly, she followed me through the small living room and kitchen, observing that, "the ladies have done a fairly good job of keeping the place neat." She hesitated before the open door. The bright sun and salty scent of the sea, as well as the loud sound of waves washing all around us, seemed to astound her, but then she squinted, glanced at me, and stepped through the door to observe the miracle of the fairies' flowers.

Never had the rock seen such color, never had it known such bloom! My mother walked out, barefoot, and said, "Forget-me-nots, these are forget-me-nots. But where . . . ?"

I told her that I didn't understand it myself, how I had planted the small bag of soil found clutched in my father's hand but had not really expected it to come to much, and certainly not to all of this, waving my arm over the expanse, the flowers having grown in soilless crevices and cracks, covering our entire little island of stone.

My mother turned to me and said, "These are not from the fairies, they are from him." Then she started crying, a reaction I had not expected and tried to talk her out of, but she said, "No, Agatha, leave me alone."

She stood out there for quite a while, weeping as she walked amongst the flowers. Later, after she came inside and said, "Where are all the helpers today?" I shrugged and avoided more questions by going outside myself, where I discovered scarlet spots amongst the bloom. My mother had been bedridden for so long, her feet had gone soft again. For days she left tiny teardrop shapes of blood in her step, which I surreptitiously wiped up, not wanting to draw any

attention to the fact, for fear it would dismay her. She picked several of the forget-me-not blossoms and pressed them between the heavy pages of her book of myths and folklore. Not long after that, a terrible storm blew in, rocking our little house, challenging our resolve, and taking with it all the flowers. Once again our rock was barren. I worried what effect this would have on my mother but she merely sighed, shrugged, and said, "They were beautiful, weren't they, Agatha?"

So passed my childhood: a great deal of solitude, the occasional life-threatening adventure, the drudgery of work, and all around me the great wide sea with its myriad secrets and reasons, the lost we saved, those we didn't. And the ghosts, brought to us by my father, though we never understood clearly his purpose, as they only stood before the fire, dripping and melting like something made of wax, bemoaning what was lost (a fine boat, a lady love, a dream of the sea, a pocketful of jewels, a wife and children, a carving on bone, a song, its lyrics forgotten). We tried to provide what comfort we could, listening, nodding, there was little else we could do, they refused tea or blankets, they seemed only to want to stand by the fire, mourning their death, as my father stood sentry beside them, melting into salty puddles that we mopped up with clean rags, wrung out into the ocean, saying what we fashioned as prayer, or reciting lines of Irish poetry.

Though I know now that this is not a usual childhood, it was usual for me, and it did not veer from this course until my mother's hair had gone quite gray and I was a young woman, when my father brought us a different sort of ghost entirely, a handsome young man, his eyes the same blue-green as summer. His hair was of indeterminate color, wet curls that hung to his shoulders. Dressed simply, like any dead sailor, he carried about him an air of being educated more by art than by water, a suspicion soon confirmed for me when he refused an offering of tea by saying, "No, I will not, cannot drink your liquid offered without first asking for a kiss, ah a kiss is all the liquid I desire, come succor me with your lips."

Naturally, I blushed and, just as naturally, when my mother went to check on the lamp, and my father had melted into a mustached puddle, I kissed him. Though I should have been warned by the icy chill, as certainly I should have been warned by the fact of my own father, a mere puddle at the hearth, it was my first kiss and it did not feel deadly to me at all, not dangerous, not spectral, most certainly not spectral, though I did experience a certain pleasant floating sensation in its wake.

My mother was surprised, upon her return, to find the lad still standing, as vigorous as any living man, beside my father's puddle. We were both surprised that he remained throughout the night, regaling us with stories of the wild sea populated by whales, mermaids, and sharks; mesmerizing us with descriptions of the "bottom of the world" as he called it, embedded with strange purple rocks, pink shells spewing pearls, and the seaweed tendrils of sea witches' hair. We were both surprised that, when the black of night turned to the gray hue of morning, he bowed to each of us (turned fully toward me, so that I could receive his wink), promised he would return, and then left, walking out the door like any regular fellow. So convincing was he that my mother and I opened the door to see where he had gone, scanning the rock and the inky sea before we accepted that, as odd as it seemed, as vigorous his demeanor, he was a ghost most certainly.

"Or something of that nature," said my mother. "Strange that he didn't melt like the others." She squinted at me and I turned away from her before she could see my blush. "We shouldn't have let him keep us up all night," she said. "We aren't dead. We need our sleep."

Sleep? Sleep? I could not sleep, feeling as I did his cool lips on mine, the power of his kiss, as though he breathed out of me some dark aspect that had weighed inside me. I told my mother that she could sleep. I would take care of everything. She protested, but using the past as

reassurance (she had long since discovered that I had run the place while she convalesced after my father's death), finally agreed.

I was happy to have her tucked safely in bed. I was happy to know that her curious eyes were closed. I did all the tasks necessary to keep the place in good order. Not even then, in all my girlish giddiness, did I forget the lamp. I am embarrassed to admit, however, it was well past four o'clock before I remembered my father's puddle, which by that time had been much dissipated. I wiped up the small amount of water and wrung him out over the sea, saying only as prayer, "Father, forgive me. Oh, bring him back to me." (Meaning, alas for me, a foolish girl, the boy who kissed me and not my own dear father.)

And that night, he did come back, knocking on the door like any living man, carrying in his wet hands a bouquet of pink coral which he presented to me, and a small white stone, shaped like a star, which he gave to my mother.

"Is there no one else with you?" she asked.

"I'm sorry, there is not," he said.

My mother began to busy herself in the kitchen, leaving the two of us alone. I could hear her in there, moving things about, opening cupboards, sweeping the already swept floor. It was my own carelessness that had caused my father's absence, I was sure of that; had I sponged him up sooner, had I prayed for him more sincerely, and not just for the satisfaction of my own desire, he would be here this night. I felt terrible about this, but then I looked into his eyes, those beautiful sea-colored eyes, and I could not help it, my body thrilled at his look. Is this love? I thought. Will he kiss me twice? When it seemed as if, without even wasting time with words, he was about to do so, leaning toward me with parted lips from which exhaled the scent of salt water, my mother stepped into the room, clearing her throat, holding the broom before her, as if thinking she might use it as a weapon.

"We don't really know anything about you," she said.

To begin with, my name is Ezekiel. My mother was fond of saints and the Bible and such. She died shortly after giving birth to me, her first and only child. I was raised by my father, on the island of Murano. Perhaps you have heard of it? Murano glass? We are famous for it throughout the world. My father, himself, was a talented glassmaker. Anything imagined, he could shape into glass. Glass birds, tiny glass bees, glass seashells, even glass tears (an art he perfected while I was an infant), and what my father knew, he taught to me.

Naturally, I eventually surpassed him in skill. Forgive me, but there is no humble way to say it. At any rate, my father had taught me and encouraged my talent all my life. I did not see when his enthusiasm began to sour. I was excited and pleased at what I could produce. I thought he would feel the same for me as I had felt for him, when, as a child, I sat on the footstool in his studio and applauded each glass wing, each hard teardrop.

Alas, it was not to be. My father grew jealous of me. My own father! At night he snuck into our studio and broke my birds, my little glass cakes. In the morning he pretended dismay and instructed me further on keeping air bubbles out of my work. He did not guess that I knew the dismal truth.

I determined to leave him, to sail away to some other place to make my home. My father begged me to stay, "Whatever will you do? How will you make your way in this world?"

I told him my true intention, not being clever enough to lie. "This is not the only place in the world with fire and sand," I said. "I intend to make glass."

He promised me it would be a death sentence. At the time I took this to be only his confused, fatherly concern. I did not perceive it as a threat.

It is true that the secret to glassmaking was meant to remain on Murano. It is true that the entire populace believed this trade, and only this trade, kept them fed and clothed. Finally, it is true that they passed the law (many years before my father confronted me with it) that anyone who dared attempt to take the secret of glassmaking off the island would suffer the penalty of death. All of this is true.

But what's also true is that I was a prisoner in my own home, tortured by my own father, who pretended to be a humble, kind glassmaker, but who, night after night, broke my creations and then, each morning, denied my accusations, his sweet old face mustached and whiskered, all the expression of dismay and sorrow.

This is madness, I reasoned. How else could I survive? One of us had to leave or die. I chose the gentler course.

We had, in our possession, only a small boat, used for trips that never veered far from shore. Gathering mussels, visiting neighbors, occasionally my father liked to sit in it and smoke a pipe while watching the sun set. He'd light a lantern and come home, smelling of the sea, boil us a pot of soup, a melancholic, completely innocent air about him, only later to sneak about his breaking work.

This small boat is what I took for my voyage across the sea. I also took some fishing supplies, a rope, dried cod he'd stored for winter, a blanket, and several jugs of red wine, given to us by the baker, whose daughter, I do believe, fancied me. For you, who have lived so long on this anchored rock, my folly must be apparent. Was it folly? It was. But what else was I to do? Day after day make my perfect art only to have my father, night after night, destroy it? He would destroy me!

I left in the dark, when the ocean is like ink and the sky is black glass with thousands of air bubbles. Air bubbles, indeed. I breathed my freedom in the salty sea air. I chose stars to follow. Foolishly, I had no clear sense of my passage and had only planned my escape.

Of course, knowing what I do now about the ocean, it is a wonder I survived the first night, much less seven. It was on the eighth morning that I saw the distant sail, and, hopelessly drunk and sunburned, as well as lost, began the desperate task of rowing toward it, another folly as I'm sure you'd agree, understanding how distant the horizon is. Luckily for me, or so I thought, the ship headed in my direction and after a few more days it was close enough that I began to believe in my life again.

Alas, this ship was owned by a rich friend of my father's, a woman who had commissioned him to create a glass castle with a glass garden and glass fountain, tiny glass swans, a glass king and queen, a baby glass princess, and glass trees with golden glass apples, all for the amusement of her granddaughter (who, it must be said, had fingers like sausages and broke half of the figurines before her next birthday). This silly woman was only too happy to let my father use her ship, she was only too pleased to pay the ship's crew, all with the air of helping my father, when, in truth, it simply amused her to be involved in such drama. She said she did it for Murano, but in truth, she did it for the story.

It wasn't until I had been rescued, and hoisted on board, that my father revealed himself to me. He spread his arms wide, all great show for the crew, hugged me and even wept, but convincing as was his act, I knew he intended to destroy me.

These are terrible choices no son should have to make, but that night, as my father slept and the ship rocked its weary way back to Murano where I would likely be hung or possibly sentenced to live with my own enemy, my father, I slit the old man's throat. Though he opened his eyes, I do not believe he saw me, but was already entering the distant kingdom.

You ladies look quite aghast. I cannot blame you. Perhaps I should have chosen my own death instead, but I was a young man, and I wanted to live. Even after everything I had gone through, I wanted life.

Alas, it was not to be. I knew there would be trouble and accusation if my father were found with his throat slit, but none at all if he just disappeared in the night, as so often happens on large ships. Many a traveler has simply fallen overboard, never to be heard from again, and my father had already displayed a lack of seafaring savvy to rival my own.

I wrapped him up in the now-bloody blanket but although he was a small man, the effect was still that of a body, so I realized I would have to bend and fold him into a rucksack. You wince, but do not worry, he was certainly dead by this time.

I will not bore you with the details of my passage, hiding and sneaking with my dismal load. Suffice it to say that it took a while for me to at last be standing shipside, and I thought then that all danger had passed.

Remember, I was already quite weakened by my days adrift, and the matter of taking care of this business with my father had only fatigued me further. Certain that I was finally at the end of my task, I grew careless. He was much heavier than he had ever appeared to be. It took all my strength to hoist the rucksack, and (to get the sad, pitiable truth over with as quickly as possible) when I heaved that rucksack, the cord became entangled on my wrist, and yes, dear ladies, I went over with it, to the bottom of the world. There I remained until your own dear father, your husband, found me and brought me to this place, where, for the first time in my life, I feel safe, and, though I am dead, blessed.

Later, after my mother had tended the lamp while Ezekiel and I shared the kisses that left me breathless, she asked him to leave, saying that I needed my sleep. I protested, of course, but she insisted. I walked my ghost to the door, just as I think any girl would do in a similar situation, and there, for the first time, he kissed me in full view of my mother, not so passionate as those kisses that had preceded it, but effective nonetheless.

But after he was gone, even as I still blushed, my mother spoke in a grim voice, "Don't encourage him, Agatha."

"Why?" I asked, my body trembling with the

impact of his affection and my mother's scorn, as though the two emotions met in me and quaked there. "What don't you like about him?"

"He's dead," she said, "there's that for a start."

"What about Daddy? He's dead too, and you've been loving him all this time."

My mother shook her head. "Agatha, it isn't the same thing. Think about what this boy told you tonight. He murdered his own father."

"I can't believe you'd use that against him. You heard what he said. He was just defending himself."

"But Agatha, it isn't what's said that is always the most telling. Don't you know that? Have I really raised you to be so gullible?"

"I am not gullible. I'm in love."

"I forbid it."

Certainly no three words, spoken by a parent, can do more to solidify love than these. It was no use arguing. What would be the point? She, this woman who had loved no one but a puddle for so long, could never understand what was going through my heart. Without more argument, I went to bed, though I slept fitfully, feeling torn from my life in every way, while my mother stayed up reading, I later surmised, from her book of myths. In the morning I found her sitting at the kitchen table, the great volume before her. She looked up at me with dark circled eyes, then, without salutation, began reading, her voice, ominous.

"There are many kinds of ghosts. There are the ghosts that move things, slam doors and drawers, throw silverware about the house. There are the ghosts (usually of small children) that play in dark corners with spools of thread and frighten family pets. There are the weeping and wailing ghosts. There are the ghosts who know that they are dead, and those who do not. There are tree ghosts, those who spend their afterlife in a particular tree (a clue for such a resident might be bite marks on fallen fruit). There are ghosts trapped forever at the hour of their death (I saw one like this once, in an old movie theater bathroom, hanging from the ceiling).

There are melting ghosts (we know about these, don't we?), usually victims of drowning. And there are breath-stealing ghosts. These, sometimes mistaken for the grosser vampire, sustain a sort of half-life by stealing breath from the living. They can be any age, but are usually teenagers and young adults, often at that selfish stage when they died. These ghosts greedily go about sucking the breath out of the living. This can be done by swallowing the lingered breath from unwashed cups, or, most effectively of all, through a kiss. Though these ghosts can often be quite seductively charming, they are some of the most dangerous. Each life has only a certain amount of breath within it and these ghosts are said to steal an infinite amount with each swallow. The effect is such that the ghost, while it never lives again, begins to do a fairly good imitation of life, while its victims (those whose breath it steals) edge ever closer to their own death."

My mother looked up at me triumphantly and I stormed out of the house, only to be confronted with the sea all around me, as desolate as my heart.

That night, when he came, knocking on the door, she did not answer it and forbade me to do so.

"It doesn't matter," I taunted, "he's a ghost. He doesn't need doors."

"No, you're wrong," she said, "he's taken so much of your breath that he's not entirely spectral. He can't move through walls any longer. He needs you, but he doesn't care about you at all, don't you get that, Agatha?"

"Agatha? Are you home? Agatha? Why don't you come? Agatha?"

I couldn't bear it. I began to weep.

"I know this is hard," my mother said, "but it must be done. Listen, his voice is already growing faint. We just have to get through this night."

"What about the lamp?" I said.

"What?"

But she knew what I meant. Her expression betrayed her. "Don't you need to check on the lamp?"

"Agatha? Have I done something wrong?"

My mother stared at the door, and then turned to me, the dark circles under her eyes giving her the look of a beaten woman. "The lamp is fine."

I spun on my heels and went into my small room, slammed the door behind me. My mother, a smart woman, was not used to thinking like a warden. She had forgotten about my window. By the time I hoisted myself down from it, Ezekiel was standing on the rocky shore, surveying the dark ocean before him. He had already lost some of his life-like luster, particularly below his knees where I could almost see through him. "Ezekiel," I said. He turned and I gasped at the change in his visage, the cavernous look of his eyes, the skeletal stretch at his jaw. Seeing my shocked expression, he nodded and spread his arms open, as if to say, yes, this is what has become of me. I ran into those open arms and embraced him, though he creaked like something made of old wood. He bent down, pressing his cold lips against mine until they were no longer cold but burning like a fire.

We spent that night together and I did not mind the shattering wind with its salt bite on my skin, and I did not care when the lamp went out and the sea roiled beneath a black sky, and I did not worry about the dead weeping on the rocky shore, or the lightness I felt as though I were floating beside my lover, and when morning came, revealing the dead all around us, I followed him into the water, I followed him to the bottom of the sea, where he turned to me and said, "What have you done? Are you stupid? Don't you realize? You're no good to me dead!"

So, sadly, like many a daughter, I learned that my mother had been right after all, and when I returned to her, dripping with saltwater and seaweed, tiny fish corpses dropping from my hair, she embraced me. Seeing my state, weeping, she kissed me on the lips, our mouths open. I drank from her, sweet breath, until I was filled and she collapsed to the floor, my mother in her black dress, like a crushed funeral flower.

I had no time for mourning. The lamp had been out for hours. Ships had crashed and men had died. Outside the sun sparkled on the sea. People would be coming soon to find out what had happened.

I took our small boat and rowed away from there. Many hours later, I docked in a seaside town and hitchhiked to another, until eventually I was as far from my home as I could be and still be near my ocean.

I had a difficult time of it for a while. People are generally suspicious of someone with no past and little future. I lived on the street and had to beg for jobs cleaning toilets and scrubbing floors, only through time and reputation working up to my current situation, finally getting my own little apartment, small and dark, so different from when I was the lighthouse keeper's daughter and the ocean was my yard.

One day, after having passed it for months without a thought, I went into the art supply store, and bought a canvas, paint, and two paintbrushes. I paid for it with my tip money, counting it out for the clerk whose expression suggested I was placing turds in her palm instead of pennies. I went home and hammered a nail into the wall, hung the canvas on it, and began to paint. Like many a creative person I seem to have found some solace for the unfortunate happenings of my young life (and death) in art.

I live simply and virginally, never taking breath through a kiss. This is the vow I made, and I have kept it. Yes, some days I am weakened, and tempted to restore my vigor with such an easy solution, but instead I hold the empty cups to my face, I breathe in, I breathe everything, the breath of old men, breath of young, sweet breath, sour breath, breath of lipstick, breath of smoke. It is not, really, a way to live, but this is not, really, a life.

For several seconds after Alex finished reading the remarkable account, his gaze remained transfixed on the page. Finally, he looked up, blinked in the dim coffee shop light, and closed the black binder.

Several baristas stood behind the counter busily jostling around each other with porcelain cups, teapots, bags of beans. One of them, a short girl with red and green hair that spiked around her like some otherworld halo, stood by the sink, stacking dirty plates and cups. When she saw him watching, she smiled. It wasn't a true smile, not that it was mocking, but rather, the girl with the Christmas hair smiled like someone who had either forgotten happiness entirely, or never known it at all. In response, Alex nodded at her, and to his surprise, she came over, carrying a dirty rag and a spray bottle.

"Did you read all of it?" she said as she squirted the table beside him and began to wipe it with the dingy towel.

Alex winced at the unpleasant odor of the cleaning fluid, nodded, and then, seeing that the girl wasn't really paying any attention, said, "Yes." He glanced at the wall where the paintings were hung.

"So what'd you think?"

The girl stood there, grinning that sad grin, right next to him now with her noxious bottle and dirty rag, one hip jutted out in a way he found oddly sexual. He opened his mouth to speak, gestured toward the paintings, and then at the book before him. "I, I have to meet her," he said, tapping the book, "this is remarkable."

"But what do you think about the paintings?"

Once more he glanced at the wall where they hung. He shook his head, "No," he said, "it's this," tapping the book again.

She smiled, a true smile, cocked her head, and put out her hand, "Agatha," she said.

Alex felt like his head was spinning. He shook the girl's hand. It was unexpectedly tiny, like that of a child's, and he gripped it too tightly at first. Glancing at the counter, she pulled out a chair and sat down in front of him.

"I can only talk for a little while. Marnie is the manager today and she's on the rag or something all the time, but she's downstairs right now, checking in an order."

"You," he brushed the binder with the tip of his fingers, as if caressing something holy, "you wrote this?"

She nodded, bowed her head slightly, shrugged, and suddenly earnest, leaned across the table, elbowing his empty cup as she did. "Nobody bothers to read it. I've seen a few people pick it up but you're the first one to read the whole thing."

Alex leaned back, frowning.

She rolled her eyes, which, he noticed, were a lovely shade of lavender, lined darkly in black.

"See, I was trying to do something different. This is the whole point," she jabbed at the book, and he felt immediately protective of it, "I was trying to put a story in a place where people don't usually expect one. Don't you think we've gotten awful complacent in our society about story? Like it all the time has to go a certain way and even be only in certain places. That's what this is all about. The paintings are a foil. But you get that, don't you? Do you know," she leaned so close to him, he could smell her breath, which he thought was strangely sweet, "someone actually offered to buy the fly painting?" Her mouth dropped open, she shook her head and rolled those lovely lavender eyes. "I mean, what the fuck? Doesn't he know it sucks?"

Alex wasn't sure what to do. She seemed to be leaning near to his cup. Leaning over it, Alex realized. He opened his mouth, not having any idea what to say.

Just then another barista, the one who wore scarves all the time and had an imperious air about her, as though she didn't really belong there but was doing research or something, walked past. Agatha glanced at her. "I gotta go." She stood up. "You finished with this?" she asked, touching his cup.

Though he hadn't yet had his free refill, Alex nodded.

"It was nice talking to you," she said. "Just goes to show, doesn't it?"

Alex had no idea what she was talking about. He nodded halfheartedly, hoping comprehension would follow, but when it didn't, he raised his eyebrows at her instead.

She laughed. "I mean you don't look anything like the kind of person who would understand my stuff."

"Well, you don't look much like Agatha," he said.

"But I am Agatha," she murmured as she turned away from him, picking up an empty cup and saucer from a nearby table.

Alex watched her walk to the tiny sink at the end of the counter. She set the cups and saucers down. She rinsed the saucers and placed them in the gray bucket they used for carrying dirty dishes to the back. She reached for a cup, and then looked at him.

He quickly looked down at the black binder, picked it up, pushed his chair in, and headed toward the front of the shop. He stopped to look at the paintings. They were fine, boring, but fine little paintings that had no connection to what he'd read. He didn't linger over them for long. He was almost to the door when she was beside him, saying, "I'll take that." He couldn't even fake innocence. He shrugged and handed her the binder.

"I'm flattered, really," she said. But she didn't try to continue the conversation. She set the book down on the table beneath the painting of the avocado. He watched her pick up an empty cup and bring it toward her face, breathing in the lingered breath that remained. She looked up suddenly, caught him watching, frowned, and turned away.

Alex understood. She wasn't what he'd been expecting either. But when love arrives it doesn't always appear as expected. He couldn't just ignore it. He couldn't pretend it hadn't happened. He walked out of the coffee shop into the afternoon sunshine.

Of course, there were problems, her not being alive for one. But Alex was not a man of prejudice.

He was patient besides. He stood in the art supply store for hours, pretending particular in-

terest in the anatomical hinged figurines of sexless men and women in the front window, before she walked past, her hair glowing like a forest fire.

"Agatha," he called.

She turned, frowned, and continued walking. He had to take little running steps to catch up. "Hi," he said. He saw that she was biting her lower lip. "You just getting off work?"

She stopped walking right in front of the bank, which was closed by then, and squinted up at him.

"Alex," he said. "I was talking to you today at the coffee shop."

"I know who you are."

Her tone was angry. He couldn't understand it. Had he insulted her somehow?

"I don't have Alzheimer's. I remember you."

He nodded. This was harder than he had expected.

"What do you want?" she said.

Her tone was really downright hostile. He shrugged. "I just thought we could, you know, talk."

She shook her head. "Listen, I'm happy that you liked my story."

"I did," he said, nodding, "it was great."

"But what would we talk about? You and me?"

Alex shifted beneath her lavender gaze. He licked his lips. She wasn't even looking at him, but glancing around him and across the street. "I don't care if it does mean I'll die sooner," he said. "I want to give you a kiss."

Her mouth dropped open.

"Is something wrong?"

She turned and ran. She wore one red sneaker and one green. They matched her hair.

As Alex walked back to his car, parked in front of the coffee shop, he tried to talk himself into not feeling so bad about the way things went. He hadn't always been like this. He used to be able to talk to people. Even women. Okay, he had never been suave, he knew that, but he'd been a regular guy. Certainly no one had ever run away from him before. But after Tessie died, people changed. Of course, this made sense, initially. He was in mourning, even if he didn't cry (something the doctor told him not to worry about because one day, probably when he least expected it, the tears would fall). He was obviously in pain. People were very nice. They talked to him in hushed tones. Touched him, gently. Even men tapped him with their fingertips. All this gentle touching had been augmented by vigorous hugs. People either touched him as if he would break, or hugged him as if he had already broken and only the vigor of the embrace kept him intact.

For the longest time there had been all this activity around him. People called, sent chatty e-mails, even handwritten letters, cards with flowers on them and prayers. People brought over casseroles, and bread, Jell-O with fruit in it. (Nobody brought chocolate chip cookies, which he might have actually eaten.)

To Alex's surprise, once Tessie had died, it felt as though a great weight had been lifted from him, but instead of appreciating the feeling, the freedom of being lightened of the burden of his wife's dying body, he felt in danger of floating away or disappearing. Could it be possible, he wondered, that Tessie's body, even when she was mostly bones and barely breath, was all that kept him real? Was it possible that he would have to live like this, held to life by some strange force but never a part of it again? These questions led Alex to the brief period where he'd experimented with becoming a Hare Krishna, shaved his head, dressed in orange robes, and took up dancing in the park. Alex wasn't sure but he thought that was when people started treating him as if he were strange, and even after he grew his hair out and started wearing regular clothes again, people continued to treat him strangely.

And, Alex had to admit, as he inserted his key into the lock of his car, he'd forgotten how to behave. How to be normal, he guessed.

You just don't go read something somebody wrote and decide you love her, he scolded him-

self as he eased into traffic. You don't just go falling in love with breath-stealing ghosts. People don't do that.

Alex did not go to the coffee shop the next day, or the day after that, but it was the only coffee shop in town, and had the best coffee in the state. They roasted the beans right there. Freshness like that can't be faked.

It was awkward for him to see her behind the counter, over by the dirty cups, of course. But when she looked up at him, he attempted a kind smile, then looked away.

He wasn't there to bother her. He ordered French Roast in a cup to go, even though he hated to drink out of paper, paid for it, dropped the change into the tip jar, and left without any further interaction with her.

He walked to the park, where he sat on a bench and watched a woman with two small boys feed white bread to the ducks. This was illegal because the ducks would eat all the bread offered to them, they had no sense of appetite, or being full, and they would eat until their stomachs exploded. Or something like that. Alex couldn't exactly remember. He was pretty sure it killed them. But Alex couldn't decide what to do. Should he go tell that lady and those two little boys that they were killing the ducks? How would that make them feel, especially as they were now triumphantly shaking out the empty bag, the ducks crowded around them, one of the boys squealing with delight? Maybe he should just tell her, quietly. But she looked so happy. Maybe she'd been having a hard time of it. He saw those mothers on *Oprah*, saying what a hard job it was, and maybe she'd had that kind of morning, even screaming at the kids, and then she got this idea, to take them to the park and feed the ducks and now she felt good about what she'd done and maybe she was thinking that she wasn't such a bad mom after all, and if Alex told her she was killing the ducks, would it stop the ducks from dying or just stop her from feeling happiness? Alex sighed. He couldn't decide what to do. The ducks were happy, the lady was happy, and one of the boys was happy. The other one looked sort of terrified. She picked him up and they walked away together, she, carrying the boy who waved the empty bag like a balloon, the other one skipping after them, a few ducks hobbling behind.

For three days Alex ordered his coffee to go and drank it in the park. On the fourth day, Agatha wasn't anywhere that he could see and he surmised that it was her day off so he sat at his favorite table in the back. But on the fifth day, even though he didn't see her again, and it made sense that she'd have two days off in a row, he ordered his coffee to go and took it to the park. He'd grown to like sitting on the bench watching strolling park visitors, the running children, the dangerously fat ducks.

He had no idea she would be there and he felt himself blush when he saw her coming down the path that passed right in front of him. He stared deeply into his cup and fought the compulsion to run. He couldn't help it, though. Just as the toes of her red and green sneakers came into view he looked up. I'm not going to hurt you, he thought, and then, he smiled, that false smile he'd been practicing on her and, incredibly, she smiled back! Also, falsely, he assumed, but he couldn't blame her for that.

She looked down the path and he followed her gaze, seeing that, though the path around the duck pond was lined with benches every fifty feet or so, all of them were taken. She sighed. "Mind if I sit here?"

He scooted over and she sat down, slowly. He glanced at her profile. She looked worn out, he decided. Her lavender eyes flickered toward him, and he looked into his cup again. It made sense that she would be tired, he thought, if she'd been off work for two days, she'd also been going that long without stealing breath from cups. "Want some?" he said, offering his.

She looked startled, pleased, and then, falsely unconcerned. She peered over the edge of his cup, shrugged, and said, "Okay, yeah, sure."

He handed it to her and politely watched the ducks so she could have some semblance of privacy with it. After a while she said thanks and handed it back to him. He nodded and stole a look at her profile again. It pleased him that her color already looked better. His breath had done that!

"Sorry about the other day," she said, "I was just . . ."

They waited together but she didn't finish the sentence.

"It's okay," he said, "I know I'm weird."

"No, you're, well—" she smiled, glanced at him, shrugged. "It isn't that. I like weird people. I'm weird. But, I mean, I'm not dead, okay? You kind of freaked me out with that."

He nodded. "Would you like to go out with me sometime?" Inwardly, he groaned. He couldn't believe he just said that.

"Listen, Alex?"

He nodded. Stop nodding, he told himself. Stop acting like a bobblehead.

"Why don't you tell me a little about yourself?"

So he told her. How he'd been coming to the park lately, watching people overfeed the ducks, wondering if he should tell them what they were doing but they all looked so happy doing it, and the ducks looked happy too, and he wasn't sure anyway, what if he was wrong, what if he told everyone to stop feeding bread to the ducks and it turned out it did them no harm and how would he know? Would they explode like balloons, or would it be more like how it had been when his wife died, a slow painful death, eating her away inside, and how he used to come here, when he was a monk, well, not really a monk, he'd never gotten ordained or anything, but he'd been trying the idea on for a while and how he used to sing and spin in circles and how it felt a lot like what he'd remembered of happiness but he could never be sure because a remembered emotion is like a remembered taste, it's never really there. And then, one day, a real monk came and watched him spinning in circles and singing nonsense, and he just stood and watched Alex, which made him self-conscious because he didn't really know what he was doing, and the monk started laughing, which made Alex stop and the monk said, "Why'd you stop?" And Alex said, "I don't know what I'm doing." And the monk nodded, as if this was a very wise thing to say and this, just this monk with his round bald head and wire-rimmed spectacles, in his simple orange robe (not at all like the orange-dyed sheet Alex was wearing) nodding when Alex said, "I don't know what I'm doing," made Alex cry and he and the monk sat down under that tree, and the monk (whose name was Ron) told him about Kali, the goddess who is both womb and grave. Alex felt like it was the first thing anyone had said to him that made sense since Tessie died and after that he stopped coming to the park, until just recently, and let his hair grow out again and stopped wearing his robe. Before she'd died, he'd been one of the lucky ones, or so he'd thought, because he made a small fortune in a dot com, and actually got out of it before it all went belly up while so many people he knew lost everything but then Tessie came home from her doctor's appointment, not pregnant, but with cancer, and he realized he wasn't lucky at all. They met in high school and were together until she died, at home, practically blind by that time and she made him promise he wouldn't just give up on life. So he began living this sort of half-life, but he wasn't unhappy or depressed, he didn't want her to think that, he just wasn't sure. "I sort of lost confidence in life," he said. "It's like I don't believe in it anymore. Not like suicide, but I mean, like the whole thing, all of it isn't real somehow. Sometimes I feel like it's all a dream, or a long nightmare that I can never wake up from. It's made me odd, I guess."

She bit her lower lip, glanced longingly at his cup.

"Here," Alex said, "I'm done anyway."

She took it and lifted it toward her face, breathing in, he was sure of it, and only after she was finished, drinking the coffee. They sat like that in silence for a while and then they just started talking about everything, just as Alex had hoped they would. She told him how she had grown up living near the ocean, and her father had died young, and then her mother had

too, and she had a boyfriend, her first love, who broke her heart, but the story she wrote was just a story, a story about her life, her dream life, the way she felt inside, like he did, as though somehow life was a dream. Even though everyone thought she was a painter (because he was the only one who read it, he was the only one who got it), she was a writer, not a painter, and stories seemed more real to her than life. At a certain point he offered to take the empty cup and throw it in the trash but she said she liked to peel off the wax, and then began doing so. Alex politely ignored the divergent ways she found to continue drinking his breath. He didn't want to embarrass her.

They finally stood up and stretched, walked through the park together and grew quiet, with the awkwardness of new friends. "You want a ride?" he said, pointing at his car.

She declined, which was a disappointment to Alex but he determined not to let it ruin his good mood. He was willing to leave it at that, to accept what had happened between them that afternoon as a moment of grace to be treasured and expect nothing more from it, when she said, "What are you doing next Tuesday?" They made a date, well, not a date, Alex reminded himself, an arrangement, to meet the following Tuesday in the park, which they did, and there followed many wonderful Tuesdays. They did not kiss. They were friends. Of course Alex still loved her. He loved her more. But he didn't bother her with all that and it was in the spirit of friendship that he suggested (after weeks of Tuesdays in the park) that the following Tuesday she come for dinner, "nothing fancy," he promised when he saw the slight hesitation on her face.

But when she said yes, he couldn't help it; he started making big plans for the night.

Naturally, things were awkward when she arrived. He offered to take her sweater, a lumpy looking thing in wild shades of orange, lime green, and purple. He should have just let her throw it across the couch, that would have been the casual non-datelike thing to do, but she handed it to him and then, wiping her hand through her hair, which, by candlelight looked like bloody grass, cased his place with those lavender eyes, deeply shadowed as though she hadn't slept for weeks.

He could see she was freaked out by the candles. He hadn't gone crazy or anything. They were just a couple of small candles, not even purchased from the store in the mall, but bought at the grocery store, unscented. "I like candles," he said, sounding defensive even to his own ears.

She smirked, as if she didn't believe him, and then spun away on the toes of her red sneaker and her green one, and plopped down on the couch. She looked absolutely exhausted. This was not a complete surprise to Alex. It had been a part of his plan, actually, but he felt bad for her just the same.

He kept dinner simple, lasagna, a green salad, chocolate cake for dessert. They didn't eat in the dining room. That would have been too formal. Instead they ate in the living room, she sitting on the couch, and he on the floor, their plates on the coffee table, watching a DVD of *I Love Lucy* episodes, a mutual like they had discovered. (Though her description of watching *I Love Lucy* reruns as a child did not gel with his picture of her in the crooked keeper's house, offering tea to melting ghosts, he didn't linger over the inconsistency.) Alex offered her plenty to drink but he wouldn't let her come into the kitchen, or get anywhere near his cup. He felt bad about this, horrible, in fact, but he tried to stay focused on the bigger picture.

After picking at her cake for a while, Agatha set the plate down, leaned back into the gray throw pillows, and closed her eyes.

Alex watched her. He didn't think about anything, he just watched her. Then he got up very quietly so as not to disturb her and went into the kitchen where he, carefully, quietly opened the drawer in which he had stored the supplies. Coming up from behind, eyeing her red and green hair, he moved quickly. She turned toward him, cursing loudly, her eyes wide and frightened, as he pressed her head to her knees, pulled her arms behind her back (to the accompaniment of a sickening crack, and her scream), pressed the wrists together and wrapped them with the rope. She struggled in spite of her weakened state, her legs flailing, kicking the coffee table. The plate with the chocolate cake flew off it and landed on the beige rug and her screams escalated into a horrible noise, unlike anything Alex had ever heard before. Luckily, Alex was prepared with the duct tape, which he slapped across her mouth. By that time he was rather exhausted himself. But she stood up and began to run, awkwardly, across the room. It broke his heart to see her this way. He grabbed her from behind. She kicked and squirmed but she was quite a small person and it was easy for him to get her legs tied.

"Is that too tight?" he asked.

She looked at him with wide eyes. As if he were the ghost.

"I don't want you to be uncomfortable."

She shook her head. Tried to speak, but only produced muffled sounds.

"I can take that off," he said, pointing at the duct tape. "But you have to promise me you won't scream. If you scream, I'll just put it on, and I won't take it off again. Though, you should know, ever since Tessie died I have these vivid dreams and nightmares, and I wake up screaming a lot. None of my neighbors has ever done anything about it. Nobody's called the police to report it, and nobody has even asked me if there's a problem. That's how it is amongst the living. Okay?"

She nodded.

He picked at the edge of the tape with his fingertips and when he got a good hold of it, he pulled fast. It made a loud ripping sound. She grunted and gasped, tears falling down her cheeks as she licked her lips.

"I'm really sorry about this," Alex said. "I just couldn't think of another way."

She began to curse, a string of expletives quickly swallowed by her weeping, until finally she managed to ask, "Alex, what are you doing?"

He sighed. "I know it's true, okay? I see the way you are, how tired you get and I know why.

I know that you're a breath-stealer. I want you to understand that I know that about you, and I love you and you don't have to keep pretending with me, okay?"

She looked around the room, as if trying to find something to focus on. "Listen, Alex," she said, "Listen to me. I get tired all the time 'cause I'm sick. I didn't want to tell you, after what you told me about your wife. I thought it would be too upsetting for you. That's it. That's why I get tired all the time."

"No," he said, softly, "you're a ghost."

"I am not dead," she said, shaking her head so hard that her tears splashed his face. "I am not dead," she said over and over again, louder and louder until Alex felt forced to tape her mouth shut once more.

"I know you're afraid. Love can be frightening. Do you think I'm not scared? Of course I'm scared. Look what happened with Tessie. I know you're scared too. You're worried I'll turn out to be like Ezekiel, but I'm not like him, okay? I'm not going to hurt you. And I even finally figured out that you're scared 'cause of what happened with your mom. Of course you are. But you have to understand. That's a risk I'm willing to take. Maybe we'll have one night together or only one hour, or a minute. I don't know. I have good genes though. My parents, both of them, are still alive, okay? Even my grandmother only died a few years ago. There's a good chance I have a lot, and I mean a lot, of breath in me. But if I don't, don't you see, I'd rather spend a short time with you, than no time at all?"

He couldn't bear it, he couldn't bear the way she looked at him as if he were a monster when he carried her to the couch. "Are you cold?"

She just stared at him.

"Do you want to watch more *I Love Lucy*? Or a movie?"

She wouldn't respond. She could be so stubborn.

He decided on *Annie Hall*. "Do you like Woody Allen?" She just stared at him, her eyes filled with accusation. "It's a love story," he said, turning away from her to insert the DVD.

He turned it on for her, then placed the remote control in her lap, which he realized was a stupid thing to do, since her hands were still tied behind her back, and he was fairly certain that, had her mouth not been taped shut, she'd be giving him that slack-jawed look of hers. She wasn't making any of this very easy. He picked the dish up off the floor, and the silverware, bringing them into the kitchen, where he washed them and the pots and pans, put aluminum foil on the leftover lasagna and put it into the refrigerator. After he finished sweeping the floor, he sat and watched the movie with her. He forgot about the sad ending. He always thought of it as a romantic comedy, never remembering the sad end. He turned off the TV and said, "I think it's late enough now. I think we'll be all right." She looked at him quizzically.

First Alex went out to his car and popped the trunk, then he went back inside where he found poor Agatha squirming across the floor. Trying to escape, apparently. He walked past her, got the throw blanket from the couch and laid it on the floor beside her, rolled her into it even as she squirmed and bucked. "Agatha, just try to relax," he said, but she didn't. Stubborn, stubborn, she could be so stubborn.

He threw her over his shoulder. He was not accustomed to carrying much weight and immediately felt the stress, all the way down his back to his knees. He shut the apartment door behind him and didn't worry about locking it. He lived in a safe neighborhood.

When they got to the car, he put her into the trunk, only then taking the blanket away from her beautiful face. "Don't worry, it won't be long," he said as he closed the hood.

He looked through his CDs, trying to choose something she would like, just in case the sound carried into the trunk, but he couldn't figure out what would be appropriate so he finally decided just to drive in silence.

It took about twenty minutes to get to the beach; it was late, and there was little traffic. Still, the ride gave him an opportunity to reflect on what he was doing. By the time he pulled up next to the pier, he had reassured himself that it was the right thing to do, even though it looked like the wrong thing.

He'd made a good choice, deciding on this place. He and Tessie used to park here, and he was amazed that it had apparently remained undiscovered by others seeking dark escape.

When he got out of the car he took a deep breath of the salt air and stood, for a moment, staring at the black waves, listening to their crash and murmur. Then he went around to the back and opened up the trunk. He looked over his shoulder, just to be sure. If someone were to discover him like this, his actions would be misinterpreted. The coast was clear, however. He wanted to carry Agatha in his arms, like a bride. Every time he had pictured it, he had seen it that way, but she was struggling again so he had to throw her over his shoulder where she continued to struggle. Well, she was stubborn, but he was too, that was part of the beauty of it, really. But it made it difficult to walk, and it was windier on the pier, also wet. All in all it was a precarious, unpleasant journey to the end.

He had prepared a little speech but she struggled against him so hard, like a hooked fish, that all he could manage to say was, "I love you," barely focusing on the wild expression in her face, the wild eyes, before he threw her in and she sank, and then bobbed up like a cork, only her head above the black waves, those eyes of hers, locked on his, and they remained that way, as he turned away from the edge of the pier and walked down the long plank, feeling lighter, but not in a good way. He felt those eyes, watching him, in the car as he flipped restlessly from station to station, those eyes, watching him, when he returned home, and saw the clutter of their night together, the burned-down candles, the covers to the *I Love Lucy* and *Annie Hall* DVDs on the floor, her crazy sweater on the dining room table, those eyes, watching him, and suddenly Alex was cold, so cold his teeth were chattering and he was shivering but sweating besides. The black water rolled over those eyes and closed them and he ran to the bathroom and

only just made it in time, throwing up everything he'd eaten, collapsing to the floor, weeping, *What have I done? What was I thinking?*

He would have stayed there like that, he determined, until they came for him and carted him away, but after a while he became aware of the foul taste in his mouth. He stood up, rinsed it out, brushed his teeth and tongue, changed out of his clothes, and went to bed, where, after a good deal more crying, and trying to figure out exactly what had happened to his mind, he was amazed to find himself falling into a deep darkness like the water, from which, he expected, he would never rise.

But then he was lying there, with his eyes closed, somewhere between sleep and waking, and he realized he'd been like this for some time. Though he was fairly certain he had fallen asleep, something had woken him. In this half state, he'd been listening to the sound he finally recognized as dripping water. He hated it when he didn't turn the faucet tight. He tried to ignore it, but the dripping persisted. So confused was he that he even thought he felt a splash on his hand and another on his forehead. He opened one eye, then the other.

She stood there, dripping wet, her hair plastered darkly around her face, her eyes smudged black. "I found a sharp rock at the bottom of the world," she said and she raised her arms. He thought she was going to strike him, but instead she showed him the cut rope dangling there.

He nodded. He could not speak.

She cocked her head, smiled, and said, "Okay, you were right. You were right about everything. Got any room in there?"

He nodded. She peeled off the wet T-shirt and let it drop to the floor, revealing her small breasts white as the moon, unbuttoned and unzipped her jeans, wiggling seductively out of the tight wet fabric, taking her panties off at the same time. He saw when she lifted her feet that the rope was no longer around them and she was already transparent below the knees. When she pulled back the covers he smelled the odd odor of saltwater and mud, as if she were both fresh and loamy. He scooted over, but only far enough that when she eased in beside him, he could hold her, wrap her wet cold skin in his arms, knowing that he was offering her everything, everything he had to give, and that she had come to take it.

"You took a big risk back there," she said.

He nodded.

She pressed her lips against his and he felt himself growing lighter, as if all his life he'd been weighed down by this extra breath, and her lips were cold but they grew warmer and warmer and the heat between them created a steam until she burned him and still, they kissed, all the while Alex thinking, I love you, I love you, I love you, until, finally, he could think it no more, his head was as light as his body, lying beside her, hot flesh to hot flesh, the cinder of his mind could no longer make sense of it, and he hoped, as he fell into a black place like no other he'd ever been in before, that this was really happening, that she was really here, and the suffering he'd felt for so long was finally over.

MR. SAUL

H. R. F. Keating

ONE OF THE MOST honored mystery writers of the twentieth century, H(enry) R(eymond) F(itzwalter) Keating (1926–2011) created the popular Bombay detective, Inspector Ganesh Ghote, in *The Perfect Murder* (1964), which won a Gold Dagger from the British Crime Writers' Association (CWA) and was nominated for an Edgar Allan Poe Award by the Mystery Writers of America; the modest policeman appeared in twenty-five subsequent novels. Keating has produced more than fifty mystery novels, several non-mysteries, short story collections, and a half-dozen reference books, including *Sherlock Holmes: The Man and His World* (1979), *Crime and Mystery: The 100 Best Books* (1987), and a biography of Agatha Christie titled *Agatha Christie: First Lady of Crime* (1977).

Born in East Sussex, England, Keating wrote his first story at the age of eight. After graduating from Trinity College, Dublin, he served in the army and moved to London to work as a journalist on the *Daily Telegraph* and later was the mystery reviewer for *The Times* for fifteen years. He married the actress Sheila Mitchell in 1953. He served as chairman of the CWA (1970–71), chairman of the Society of Authors (1983–1984), president of the prestigious Detection Club (1985–2000), and was a Fellow of the Royal Society of Literature. In 1996 the CWA awarded him its highest honor, the Cartier Diamond Dagger for outstanding services to crime literature.

"Mr. Saul" was originally published in *The Thirteenth Ghost Book*, edited by James Hale (London, Barrie & Jenkins, 1977).

Mr. Saul

H. R. F. KEATING

IT BEGAN IN TEWKESBURY. Mr. Saul had not exactly gone there of his own free will. Visiting an ancient romantic West Country town was not what Mr. Saul would have done if he had been, as the poet says, master of his fate and captain of his soul. But he had known ever since he had first set eyes, at a "hop" in a wartime canteen nearly thirty-five years before, on Gwennie Peters, as she was then, a lively Corporal in the ATS, that the mastership and captaincy of that seaworthy but indisputably coastal craft was in other hands. A quiet pint or two at the pub was Mr. Saul's idea of an outing and a deck-chair facing the briny his notion of a holiday. But Gwennie Saul was a creature of romance, despite a now hardly romantic appearance, and for her it was visiting and savouring places of romance that time free from the everyday round should be consecrated to. And battles long ago.

But Mr. Saul was happy enough to wander along in her wake, and she knew him well enough to be able to calculate to within ten minutes the time when castle or keep, hallowed abbey or craggy moorland view should be abandoned in favour of the weight off the feet and the glass in the hand. And then she let him have his pleasures entirely cheerfully and joined him in them (lager and lime in summer, rum and Coke in winter) wholeheartedly.

So, that day in August brought them to Tewkesbury and they went into the wonderful old Abbey church and Gwennie Saul breathed in the calm of its cool stonework, airy vaulted roof, and dimly radiant stained glass and then scuttered delightedly round its monuments, while Mr. Saul sat in a pew near the entrance doors and wondered whether it would be all right to light up a pipe. And when his wife came clattering back down the whole length of the stone-floored nave to tell him there was "something you've really got to see, you've got to" he ambled down with her uncomplainingly and looked long and steadily at the gruesome effigy of a monk in a state of partial decay with a frog on his neck, a beetle on his arm, and a mouse at work on the tummy. But Mr. Saul was never put out by any of the more grisly and blood-spattered aspects of his wife's passion for the past. "That's a mouse," he commented. "You can see it's a mouse."

Then, after they had made sure the car was still all right in the municipal car park, they looked over the Mill and stared down into the tumbling waters of its race and Mrs. Saul, consulting the little guide-book she had bought, wondered out loud whether she would be able to find a copy of Mrs. Craik's old novel *John Halifax Gentleman* in her local library "if it's got all the places we've seen in it, I mean it'd be an added interest, wouldn't it?"

"I dare say," Mr. Saul agreed.

Then they had lunch at the old post-inn visited by the immortal travellers of Dickens' *Pickwick Papers*, and with a board up outside to prove it. Mr. Saul waited patiently while his wife read every word of this, and grunted sagely at each ooh or ah. And afterwards they strolled along to the town's little museum and Mr. Saul peered when Mrs. Saul peered and looked upwards when she looked up and uncomplainingly mounted the narrow stairs to the small first-floor rooms behind her despite the way his not inconsiderable lunch was lying on his stomach.

And in one of those upper rooms Mrs. Saul found the panorama of the Battle of Tewkesbury, May 4, 1471, made out of cunningly painted toy soldiers by the local Boy Scouts to commemorate the Coronation. It entranced her. There was nothing she loved more than a battle, if it was sufficiently long ago, and this was certainly that, and it had wonderful pennons carried on high with quarterings and lions rampant gules and heaven knows what and knights in armour at the full charge and little notices telling you what was happening with marvellous old names on them, the Lords Wenlock and St. John, William Viscount de Beaumont, Jasper Tudor Earl of Pembroke, Sir Robert Whittingham, Sir John Lewkenor.

She was so enthusiastic indeed that the attendant that day, a fellow who in the ordinary way had a somewhat jaundiced view of tourists, actually spoke to her. "The site of the battle's not far out of the town," he said. "You can go there easily if you've got a car. Not much to see, but perhaps you'll be interested." Mrs. Saul said that she was. "The actual place," she said to her husband. "Standing there, only fancy."

"Yes," said Mr. Saul.

So off they went straight away. Luckily the car had been in the shade and wasn't too hot inside, and without much difficulty—there was a signpost or two—they found the area.

"Stop. Stop the car," Mrs. Saul hallooed.

Obediently Mr. Saul drew into a gateway and carefully parked.

"Oh, it'd be sacrilege to go down there in a car," Mrs. Saul explained, even though "down there" was to the unseeing eye no more than two or three very green-looking fields and some neatly cropped hedges.

So out they got and, despite the sun, Mr. Saul, a portly figure, walked with his wife—she kept darting ahead, but always stopped and waited for him—down to the place, as far as they could make out, where the actual armed encounter had occurred all those many years before. And there, "at the very spot," Mrs. Saul was in her element. She had run on a bit at the end. She hadn't been able to stop herself. And when Mr. Saul arrived, sweating a little and rather red in the face, still plainly feeling the effects of that large lunch, she was triumphant.

"I can see it all," she exclaimed, her voice ringing out over the somnolent fields. "There's the King—Edward the Fourth, you know, or was it Fifth, no, Fourth—with all his forces coming galloping down that way, and the Earl of Warwick, the Kingmaker—no, he'd been killed already in another battle just before, we could go to that some day, it's only at Barnet, not far from London—well, the other lot then, Queen Margaret's lot, they'd come charging this way. And there, just about there I think, they'd meet and gore, gore would stain all that little stream that goes under the bridge now. Gore."

She turned to Mr. Saul to receive his customary appreciation.

Mr. Saul had turned a terrible whitish-grey. He looked as if every drop of blood he possessed had taken refuge in his heart. His very clothes seemed all of a sudden to be hanging from his stout body as if they had been draped there.

It had cast rather a blight over the day. Of course, Mrs. Saul had got him back to the car, though he had been a leaden weight on her arm at first, and after a quarter of an hour or so he had been fit to drive, more or less. But the heart had gone out of him and instead of the pleasant couple of hours at a pub they had been thinking of—they had seen a place called the Berkeley Arms in the morning that had looked ideal, good beer for him, oak beams and tottering gable-ends for her—he settled for a strong cup of tea and making straight for the next hotel on their route.

He had been able to tell her little about the mysterious attack. Only that it wasn't the sun, and it wasn't his inside. "I just suddenly came over queer," he said. "I don't know why. I don't want to talk about it." And only looking back long afterwards did Mrs. Saul come to see that that moment was the terrible beginning of it all.

But at the time the incident seemed perfectly insignificant. As, really, did the business of the Townswomen's Guild lecture some four or five months later. Mrs. Saul liked to go to her nearest guild when the speaker had any vaguely historical subject, and when a meeting occurred in bad weather she would tell her husband that he could come too and drive her back afterwards. Mr. Saul never complained at the loss of his couple of hours at the pub on such occasions. "She keeps me very comfortable," he would say to his cronies there, "so if I have to turn out for her once in a way, well, fair's fair." And on this particular night, with a lecture entitled "Clothing Through the Ages" and a cold rain sleeting down, Mrs. Saul had no hesitation in calling on his services.

The lecturer, a lady with more enthusiasm than platform skill, all too apt to signal for the next slide earlier than she meant to, suited Mrs. Saul down to the ground, and Mr. Saul beside her sat in the darkened hall with eyelids gradually drooping, thinking, as he liked to do, about nothing much. They had reached the late medieval period and, for once, the correct picture had come up on the screen the right way up at the time it was wanted. It was of a fashionably dressed nobleman of the period and the lecturer happily pointed out his pelisse and drew attention to its long exaggerated sleeves almost touching the ground. And then she came to deal with his headgear.

"It's what we call a capuchon," she said, in her clear ringing voice. "From the French, meaning 'hood' or 'cowl.' Capuchon."

There was an appreciative murmur at such erudition.

"And you see now," the lecturer continued, "that the tail of the capuchon has also become

much exaggerated, like the sleeves of the pelisse, so much so that it winds right round his neck and even trails down to the ground. This piece was called . . . was named . . . Oh dear, silly me, I've quite forgotten what it was called, but . . ."

Then from the audience in the dark, from indeed right beside Mrs. Saul, there came a growling masculine voice.

"Liripipe," it said.

"Ah, yes, quite right. Thank you, sir. How very clever of you to know. The liripipe. Next picture, please."

The evening after, Mrs. Saul asked him about it. "I looked it up in the dictionary," she said, "after Mrs. Anstruther who dropped in for coffee wanted to know how you knew, and it's not there. Not at all. How ever did you do it?"

But Mr. Saul was not at all as pleased as she had expected him to be with her praise. Indeed, at first he attempted to deny he had spoken at all, but, when his wife cheerfully insisted, all he would say was that he just knew it, "that's all, I just knew, don't keep nagging at me, Gwennie."

Which was a little hard on Mrs. Saul who, though she bustled her husband about often enough, was by no means a nagger. Perhaps the unjust accusation was the reason she could not put the liripipe incident, trifling though it was, quite out of her mind.

And when, the following Easter, there was "that funny thing at the castle" when they went to Warwick the liripipe affair came back to her all the more insistently.

The trip to Warwick was their Easter jaunt and it seemed to be going very successfully. They had done the historic houses of the town, medieval, Tudor, seventeenth century, and Georgian, and had visited each of the two remaining town gates as well as the shire-hall and had recovered from all that exertion with a splendid lunch at a nice old pub—lamb with mint sauce and peas and plenty of really crisp roast potatoes—and were going to devote the whole of the afternoon to the castle. And all still seemed to be going well then. Although the climb up was stiff, after all that lunch, Mr. Saul made, as usual, no protests and once looking out at the lazily turning River Avon below he agreed comfortably that it was "a picture, a real picture." Then they began to explore the building itself with the aid of a small guide-book, though guides and maps generally seemed rather to fox Mrs. Saul who never could grasp that North need not always be at the top of the page. And here what she afterwards thought of as "that funny thing at the castle" occurred.

It was nothing very much.

"Now we'll go to Guy's Tower," she said, peering at the guide's sketch-plan. "That's this way."

"No," said Mr. Saul, who had been standing patiently a yard or two away. "Guy's Tower's over here."

And he turned in precisely the opposite direction and walked off.

A little surprised, because really she had never before known him to take the initiative on any of their expeditions, and a little nettled too, because after all he hadn't seen the guide and he'd never been to Warwick before, Mrs. Saul, after a moment standing where she was, not quite dumb-struck but decidedly put out, hurried off after him to put him right.

Only to find, when she caught him up, that outside the part of the building beside which he was standing was a large plain notice saying "Guy's Tower."

"Well," she said, "who's the clever one then? Fancy you knowing which tower was which when I'd got the guide wrong way up as per usual."

But once more Mr. Saul did not seem pleased by the flattery. In fact he seemed quite put out by the whole incident and, for almost the first time in Mrs. Saul's experience, omitted to utter even a word of appreciation when she drew a vivid verbal picture of defenders on the tower roof pouring hot pitch on to attackers below.

So this again was something she remembered.

Then came the really quite unpleasant scene with the visiting author.

That was early in the following autumn. The Townswomen's Guild speaker that month was Mrs. Saul's own recommendation, a novelist who had written a book about the underside of Victorian London, a work she had greatly admired for its unsparing picture of the seamy depths of the great metropolis. She had even volunteered, since the lecturer lived in the country, to put him up for the night afterwards. The unpleasant scene occurred the next morning.

The author, a bristly bearded fellow so well pleased with himself that he vigorously elaborated on the misdoings of the Victorians even at the breakfast table, was busy regaling his host and hostess with a minutely particularized account of a visit by a *roué* to a house of ill-fame.

"Then the fellow said to the girl: 'My dear, I shan't let you go from this room until you have taken off your chemise.' That's the sole undergarment girls of that sort wore in those days, you know. It was a sort of shoulder-length petticoat."

"It wasn't."

Mr. Saul, always bleary at breakfast, had hardly spoken before, other than to wish their distinguished guest a muffled good-morning. But now he had looked up from his bacon and egg and spoken to some purpose.

"I—I beg your pardon," said the author, a little more sharply than was strictly polite, but he was a touchy chap.

"A chemise," Mr. Saul said. "It isn't that. It's something that goes round a book, a prayer-book, ladies carry them in their bags. You have to have a chemise to protect something as precious as a book."

"If you'll excuse me," the author replied, "I can assure you what you've said is totally wrong. A chemise was an undergarment, I'm telling you, an undergarment."

"It went round a book," Mr. Saul almost bellowed back.

And then, as if he had been sleep-walking and had been woken by the loud sound of his own voice, he jerked his head up, looked at the author as if he couldn't understand what he was doing there and, muttering what might have been an apology, bolted from the room.

Mrs. Saul had quite a time smoothing down her distinguished guest. And afterwards—Mr. Saul had gone off to work without another word—she was so upset by it all, and especially by her husband's tone of absolute certainty, that she went specially down to the borough library and, rather daringly, sought the help of the young man in the reference room. Luckily he turned out to be most helpful and, consulting all sorts of big volumes together, they discovered that both sides of the quarrel had been in the right. Yes, a chemise was "a woman's loose-fitting undergarment formerly called a shift" but in medieval times the same word had apparently meant both a containing wall used in fortification and "an embroidered cover for a book of devotions."

It puzzled Gwennie Saul immensely. How could her hubby, who never even opened so much as a crime story, have known this obscure fact? But she could find no answer. And, after her snubs at Warwick and when she had asked him how he had known what a liripipe was—they had looked that up, too, and Mr. Saul again had been quite correct—she did not dare tackle him now. It would be quite enough, she guessed, to send him into one of his moods. And these were, she came to see now, quite a new thing with him. He had never until the autumn after their West Country tour been moody, quite the contrary. But nowadays she would frequently find him sitting, for instance, staring at the TV with no picture at all on the screen. And the time he spent in the loo at weekends . . .

It was all rather worrying. But not, really, so upsetting as to make it worthwhile to do anything about it. Just one of life's little miseries.

And before very much longer she got her explanation. About a fortnight before Christmas Mr. Saul came home one night looking rotten, and at once she knew that he had got the flu which had been raging at the works for weeks.

Got it he had too, as badly as any illness he had had in all their married life. He had developed complications, the doctor said, and within forty-eight hours he was delirious.

That was when she discovered his secret.

Because the stout sweating man who lay in their familiar bed moaning, tossing, and turning and talking in long wild gabbled bursts was not the man she had married at all. For almost all the time quite plainly he was someone else. He spoke with quite a different accent, a West Country one, she could tell. But that was not all. He used words she had never heard and he spoke about customs she hardly knew of, and when she did recognize any of them she realized that they all dated from long, long ago. Parts of lectures she had been to at the Townswomen's Guild came back to her, including the one on clothes through the ages, and memories of books she had read, the historical romances which Mr. Saul would never so much as glance at. And eventually she was convinced that the life which the man on the bed, who looked just like her husband only more ill than she had ever seen him, was babbling about had been lived in the West Country, somewhere near Tewkesbury for the most part, and in the time of the Wars of the Roses.

She even learnt the man's Christian name. It was Bennet.

And she learnt now, too, why Mr. Saul had known his way about Warwick Castle. It was because Bennet had been there. Bit by bit it came tumbling out, and bit by bit she pieced it together, sitting half-awake in the armchair in the bedroom while the sick man in the bed dozed and groaned. Bennet had lived a quiet life working on the land, she gathered, and had had a wife, Alison—she felt an odd stir of jealousy when she worked that out—and two children, a boy and a girl, whom he had loved.

Again here Gwennie Saul felt a pang of desolation. But children they had not had, and that was all there was to it.

Bennet, though, had had his children and his wife. But he had fallen in love with another woman. A beautiful one, too, if the meandering voice of the man in the bed was to be believed. A red-haired creature above his station. And an outcomer. Some sort of foreigner. And because of her, whether to separate himself from her or to follow her Mrs. Saul was not clear, Bennet had turned soldier. He had become one of the Earl of Warwick's men and had gone each day to Holme Castle, the earl's house near Tewkesbury, and there with his fellow men-at-arms he had been allowed as much meat as he could carry away on his dagger.

Her hubby spearing up meat on a dagger. Her hubby a man crazed with love.   -

Then, the night before the antibiotic the doctor had prescribed brought Mr. Saul's temperature down at last, his wife found out how Bennet had died.

It was at the Battle of Tewkesbury, the very battle whose site they had happily visited some fifteen months before. Where she had enthusiastically described to him how the King's forces must have come this way and the rebels supporting Queen Margaret and the already dead Earl of Warwick must have come that way.

He had been one of those rebels. No wonder her poor contented hubby had been struck down in that extraordinary way when they had stood at the very spot. No wonder at all.

And the battle as he had seen it—as Bennet had seen it—had been a very different affair from that depicted in the Boy Scouts' panorama and remembered, more or less, by her. It had not been at all a clear event, with the Duke of Somerset's men advancing in a neat formation here and being attacked from the flank by two hundred lances in a neat formation there. The battle, for Bennet, had been hours of waiting in the chill of that night of May 3 and the slow dawn of the next day, and then there had been the distant solitary boom of cannon and a few heavy cannonballs falling lazily on to the shallow entrenchments not far to his left and leaving men mangled there. And soon after volleys of arrows had come whining down at them, thudding into the earth, and into his fellow soldiers. Flight arrows, Bennet had called them, and only afterwards down at the library did she find out that there had been flight arrows, which could kill at two hundred yards and more, and sheaf arrows, shorter and heavier-headed, which were used sometimes at point-blank range. And at last there had been armed men running towards Bennet and his fellows, unrecognizable as foe or friend without any standard carried above them, and they had not known whether to fight them or to welcome them.

So even when Bennet had seen a long bill coming straight at him, its point glinting in the fresh morning sun and its hook moving from side to side as the charging man holding it swayed as he ran, he had done nothing to parry the blow. "I seen her glister by my face," said that West Country voice, "and then 'twas dark."

Mrs. Saul had not liked, while her husband was still weak, to say anything about what he had babbled out in his delirium. But eventually, choosing her time carefully, she told him everything, only not being able to bring herself somehow to mention his wife, Alison, and, much less, the red-haired beauty whom he had called Ghislaine as far as she could tell. She had looked up names that sounded like what he had shouted out, in something called *A Book of Names* in the library and this was what had seemed to fit best.

And Mr. Saul had admitted, getting rather hot under the collar, that what she had pieced together was, despite everything, true. He had, ever since their fateful chance visit to the Field of Tewkesbury, been increasingly aware that inside his everyday comfortable body another person also lived. Bennet. The Wars of the Roses follower of the Earl of Warwick. But it was plain that he much disliked having to speak about it all. He hated the interruption of this distant different person into his contented state of existence.

So Mrs. Saul never mentioned the subject again. And she thought, as New Year came and went and as her hubby at last threw off the consequences of his bad bout and went back to work, that his fits of moodiness were little by little getting fewer and fewer and lasting a shorter time.

Perhaps, she said to herself—because she dared tell no one of the extraordinary thing that had happened to Mr. Saul—perhaps Bennet, finding himself not welcome, was gradually taking his departure.

And so it might have been, except for Mrs. Carfax up the other end of the road.

Mrs. Saul had never much liked Mrs. Carfax, "stuck up thing," and now she was to have cause to like her a great deal less. Yet Mrs. Carfax was really a totally innocent party in the whole business. All she did was to acquire an au pair, the first lady in the road to be so bold. And as she had two small children and her husband was in a good job she could almost be excused such an uppity move. But the au pair—she was French—had long and beautiful red hair and her name, it turned out, was Ghislaine.

The Sauls chanced to meet her only several weeks after her arrival. It was a chill night towards the end of February and Mrs. Saul had asked her husband to come with her to the Townswomen's Guild—the lecture subject was "The Edwardians" and so was perfectly safe— and it turned out that Mrs. Carfax had decided to go too and had taken with her the au pair. "I thought it would be nice for her to have some social life while she's here. Her name's Ghislaine, you know, so aristocratic."

Mrs. Saul had felt that as a knock-down blow. She tried to tell herself in a panic of hope that her husband, who certainly had been looking sleepily content as usual, had not heard. But when she shot an anxious glance at him she knew that she had not had that immense piece of luck.

Mr. Saul was almost as white-faced as he had been that time at Tewkesbury.

He said nothing however. And neither did Mrs. Saul, then or later. She was certainly not going to risk stirring anything up by telling him she knew how mad for love of another Ghislaine had once been Bennet, that medieval man.

But she could not have missed the way her husband after that evening took to stepping out into the front garden at all likely and unlikely times of day. And seeing how when he was there he kept peering into the distance up the road, and flushed red with guilt if she came out and spoke to him. Nor could she have missed the way he stopped altogether going round to the pub. And she could not have missed either his loss of appetite, the husband who had hardly once failed to clear meat plate and pudding plate at any meal during their whole life together.

But within two months of the night of that "Edwardians" meeting Mr. Saul had grown thin.

Once, about the middle of April, when she had chanced to come home from a visit to her sister earlier than she had expected, as she turned into the road on her way from the Tube station she caught him actually hiding in the shadow of a big hydrangea in the Carfaxes' garden. She had been on the point of marching in at the gate and accusing him—she felt such bitter and unaccustomed anger—but in the dying evening light she glimpsed his face then, and the expression on it was so drawn, so despairing, that in an instant her own scathing jealousy was submerged in a welling-up of pure pity.

She waited there, as dusk thickened, standing just where she was and thinking and thinking what she could do to help him, and knowing there was nothing, until with a shattering crude roar of sound a young man on a motorbike drew up outside the house and went to the door and rang the bell. And then the red-haired au pair came out, got on the back of the machine, and went roaring off, her arms round the rider. And Mrs. Saul watched her husband come creeping out of the Carfaxes' gate then and drag himself towards their house, and all she could do when she got back in her turn was to pretend she thought he was happy watching TV when all along she knew he was crouching there in the front room without the light on even, like an animal gnawed at by a pain it cannot understand.

"There's no way out, there's no way out," she kept murmuring to herself as she stood at the sink in the kitchen with the tears trickling unstoppably down her face.

But there was a way out.

In the days after that incident Mr. Saul grew evidently worse. He hardly spoke in the house at all, only answering a direct question and that only if it was almost shouted at him. And he became terribly, appallingly restless. He never sat in one chair for more than two or three minutes, and when he was up he prowled about the place like a lion constricted in a stale-smelling cage. And then he took to going out in the car, without the least explanation. The first time he did so Mrs. Saul actually went sneaking along the road to the Carfaxes to see if he had gone there taking the car as a way of deceiving her. But he had not. The family was at home, she could see through the as yet uncurtained windows, and presumably Ghislaine was out with the boy with the motorbike. So she had had to go trailing back home and wait in misery. And Mr. Saul had not come back till two-thirty in the morning.

Soon this became a regular thing. And there was still nothing Mrs. Saul could do about it, only go to bed at much the usual time in case he came back then, and lie there worrying and clutching the sheet and waiting and waiting.

And on the night of May the third, or the morning of May the fourth by a punctilious count, Mr. Saul did not come back.

The car had crashed, they told her later. He had been alone in it. No other vehicle was involved. But the smash had reduced the car to a mass of tangled metal.

As it happened, their own doctor had been the one called to the scene.

"He would have gone instantly, you know," he said to Mrs. Saul with clumsy tact when they broke the news to her. "A piece of metal must have pierced right to the brain. Don't know what. Something long and pointed. Wasn't anywhere to be seen when I got to him. But it would have meant he knew nothing, you know. Everything would have just gone suddenly dark for him. Suddenly dark."

Chet Williamson

NOTED FOR OUTSTANDING CHARACTERIZATIONS in his novels and short stories, which have been compared with the work of Shirley Jackson, Chester Carlton (Chet) Williamson (1948–) is a prolific author, mainly of horror and supernatural fiction. He also has had a successful career as a musician and an actor with a lifetime membership in Actors' Equity. Born in Lancaster, Pennsylvania, he received his B.S. from Indiana University of Pennsylvania, and became a teacher in Cleveland before becoming a professional actor. He turned to full-time freelance writing in 1986 and has written more than a hundred short stories for such publications as *The New Yorker*, *Playboy*, *The Twilight Zone*, *The Magazine of Fantasy and Science Fiction*, *Alfred Hitchcock's Mystery Magazine*, and *Esquire*. He also has written twenty novels, beginning with *Soulstorm* (1986), and a psychological suspense play, *Revenant*. Among his numerous awards are the International Horror Guild Award for Best Short Story Collection for *Figures in Rain: Weird and Ghostly Tales* (2002), two nominations for the World Fantasy Award, six for the Bram Stoker Award by the Horror Writers Association, and an Edgar Allan Poe Award nomination by the Mystery Writers of America for Best Short Story for "Season Pass" (1985). Many readers believe that Williamson's finest work was in his "Searchers" trilogy: *City of Iron* (1998), *Empire of Dust* (1998), and *Siege of Stone* (1999), an *X-Files*–type series with the basic premise being that three CIA operatives are asked by a rogue CIA director to investigate paranormal activities—not to find out the truth, but to debunk the claims.

"Coventry Carol" was originally published in *Ghosts*, edited by Peter Straub (Brooklandville, MD, Borderlands Press, 1995).

Coventry Carol

CHET WILLIAMSON

Lully, lulla, thou little tiny child,
By, by, lully, lullay.

I

After it happened, Richard was unable to eat grapes. He bought a bunch at a farmers' market, and set the bag on the car seat next to him, planning to munch on them as he drove home. But when his teeth pierced the resilient green skin and the juice burst tartly over his tongue, the image came immediately to mind of what had been floating there in the toilet bowl only a few weeks before. He pulled the car onto the shoulder, spit out the grape, and gagged, but was able to keep from vomiting. Then he hurled the grapes into the bushes for the rabbits, the groundhogs, the deer. For simpler animals, whose minds did not make such tenuous connections, such fine distinctions of taste.

For the primitive.

II

Both he and Donna had wanted the baby. It was time. They were in their mid-thirties, and the tales of complicated pregnancies haunted their age group as Hansel and Gretel's witch haunted young children. Hydrocephaly, brain damage, and worse, all because of the waiting. There was, Donna once joked, a price to be paid for living in the bygone Age of Me.

The timing was right in other ways too. Richard had just been made a full professor, and the market research firm where Donna had worked for the past six years was gearing down, so that her departure would save the necessity of firing a colleague, and odds were good, she was told, that in a year or two, when she was ready to return to a job, there would be a job to return to.

Two weeks after they discovered Donna was pregnant, they started on the nursery. Their farmhouse, which they had bought in their early twenties, had transformed over the years, changing as they grew older. In the first few years they had worked only on the kitchen, their bedroom, and their bath, leaving the rest of the building to its previous squalor, so that if, in one of the many parties of those early years, a joint fell burning and unnoticed to the floor, or a beer can spilled, or a bottle of Cribari shattered, it was of no account. The room would be redone someday.

And as they and their circle of friends aged and changed, left Cribari and Bud in cans to the closets of college memories, grew to be more careful with burning drugs of all kinds, started to marry and have children and divorce, to solidify and melt and rethicken, so did the parties and the house change. Carpets covered the planks too scarred to refinish, furniture of wood and glass and chrome replaced the overstuffed monstrosities that had sponged up little less beer than their occupants had drunk. Unframed film posters fell like dead leaves before the winter white walls, the stark muted graphics.

The farmhouse was different from when they had moved in, but it was, then and now, theirs. Only two rooms on the third floor and one on the second remained untouched, and it was that second floor room they worked on, sanding, scrubbing, cleaning, painting, preparing it for the child who would soon arrive.

They were painting the evening it happened, listening to an old Crosby, Stills, and Nash tape on the remote speaker. The music was punctuated by the slap of the rollers, and at times their motion fit the music's cadence, making Richard smile, then concentrate again on the rough plaster, putting his weight heavily against the roller so that the paint filled the crannies, lightened the dark tiny valleys.

He became aware that Donna's roller was silent, and turned to look at her. She was sitting on the floor, her back propped against an unpainted wall, her legs splayed out in front of her. She had pulled the sweatband from around her brow so that her ash blonde hair hung loose, and she was twisting the band in her hands. Her lip shook, and tears dropped from her cheeks onto the front of her old, faded blue work shirt. She looked like a handcuffed prisoner, alone and miserable.

"Donna?" he said. "Honey, what's wrong?" He set his roller carefully in its tray, and knelt in front of her, hoping that it was anticipation and anxiety that had brought her down rather than pain.

She shook her head angrily, and he felt his stomach tense. These were not tears of joy.

"Donna?"

She opened her lips and took several deep, slow breaths through her teeth. At last she looked at him challengingly. "I'll be all right."

"What is it?"

"I'm *scared*. Okay?"

Her antagonism made him uncomfortable. "Scared?" he muttered.

"Yes, scared. May I be scared?"

"Well . . . well, sure. I'm scared too, honey. Of the responsibility, the . . . the changes it's going to mean. . . ."

"You would be." Her words were cold.

"What?"

"I'm scared for the baby," she said quietly. "And you're afraid you're going to have your life style cramped."

"Donna, how can you say that? I *want* this baby, and you . . ."

She broke down then, and her arms went out to him, so that he gathered her in and held her tightly. "I'm sorry, Rick," she cried, "but something's wrong, something *is, I know* it. . . ."

"Okay, relax, relax," he crooned. "Have you told the doctor?"

"Yes, yes, he says it's nothing, that nothing's wrong."

"Have you been spotting?"

"No."

"Cramps, pains?"

"No . . . twinges. It's just, oh God, a *feeling*. It sounds so stupid, so foolish, but it's *there*."

He continued to hold her. "You know," he said slowly, "you can't go through the whole pregnancy like this."

"I don't think I can have a healthy baby," she said with a sincerity that chilled him.

"That's ridiculous. Don't say that."

"But all we did over the years. The grass, Christ, we did acid a couple of times, and the coke. . . ."

"We're not doing it *now*, and we won't any more, and that's what's important."

"And the abortion," she added desperately, "when we couldn't afford . . ."

He cut her off. "The doctor knows all about that, and it doesn't mean a thing. You heard him say that it would have no effect at all on this baby."

"Yeah. I heard."

"Donna, expectant mothers worry all the

time. They worry if they drink coffee, they worry if they smoke, it's only natural."

"I know all that, I just . . ." She paused, her eyes far away. "I want this baby so much. I want to hold it and love it and watch it grow, and sing lullabies to it. I want everything I did in the past to stop, and to start everything over with this baby, have everything new, forget everything I did and was. . . ."

"Hey," Richard interrupted, "you don't have to feel guilty about a thing."

She looked at him and smiled. "If I don't, Richard, who will?"

"Donna . . ."

"You have to take responsibility sometime."

"And we will. We *are*. But don't get upset before anything happens. Seven months is a long time, honey."

"I know. All right. Forget it then. Let's get back to work."

They started painting again. The CS&N tape ended, and after a while Richard heard Donna humming a tune. "Pretty," he said.

She stopped. "Hmm?"

"The song. You were humming."

"Was I?"

"Coventry Carol," he said, renewing the supply of paint on his roller. He sang in a light baritone.

"Lully, lulla, thou little tiny child,
By, by, lully, lullay."

"Is that the name of it?" she asked. "I must have heard it on the radio." It was a month before Christmas, and the airwaves were filled with carols. Richard sang on.

"Oh sisters two, how may we do
For to preserve this day
This poor youngling for whom we do sing
By, by, lully, lullay."

She hummed as he sang, and when they'd finished the Coventry Carol, they sang others,

sacred and secular—"Oh Come, All Ye Faithful," "Up on the Housetop," "What Child Is This?" and "The First Noel." Finally Donna set down her roller. "Be right back," she said.

"How about bringing me back a beer?" Richard asked.

"You got it."

He heard her walking unhurriedly down the hall, heard the door to the bathroom close. He worked on, and found himself softly singing the Coventry Carol once more. It was no wonder, he thought. The tune was haunting, though melancholy for a Christmas song. There was sadness in it, as though its composer had kept in mind the ultimate destiny of the newborn child.

Then Donna screamed.

The sound froze him for a heartbeat, and he dropped the roller with a wet slap onto the floor, leaped from the ladder, and ran out the door, down the hall, where he threw open the door of the large guest bath.

His wife lay on the cold white tiles, her jeans and underwear in a tangle around her knees. Her body, shaking with sobs, was hunched embryonically, and her hands were buried between her thighs, as if striving to hold something in. A few watery drops of blood dotted the floor.

"I knew it, I told you," she gasped. "It's gone, I lost it, oh, Rick, I lost it. . . ."

He knelt beside her and smoothed the wet hair back from her hot forehead, whispering, "Shh, shh," not wanting to look into the toilet bowl, unable not to.

It was there. He could barely make it out, floating in a gelatinous cloud of blood and pus. The deep yellow urine darkened it further, a tiny, monstrous fish swimming in some underground sea.

My daughter. My son.

He wanted to vomit, but he kept it down, although the taste of bile was strong at the back of his throat. He started to reach for the flush handle automatically, as he would to flush down a spider, a wriggling centipede, a battered fly, then stopped, realizing that it was neither fly nor fish, but something that was to have been human, that was to have been—that *was*—his child. So he closed the lid, and turned his attention back to Donna.

"Come on, can you get to the bedroom?" His voice was thick with sorrow.

Hers was thinned by tears. "I think . . . think so."

"Ought to lie down," he said, getting an arm beneath her. "You lie down and I'll call the doctor."

"Oh, Rick . . ."

"Now, it's all right, it's over . . ."

"I *lost* it."

"It's done, it's over now, just relax."

She leaned against him as they went down the hall into their room, her feet dragging, stumbling across the carpet.

"I knew it, *knew* it, all my fault . . ."

"Shh. It's not, Donna."

"Oh yes, yes it is."

He helped her take off her paint-spattered shirt and kick off her jeans. Tenderly he lowered her back against the pillow and stepped into the adjoining bath, where he took a lavender towel from a high, fluffy stack. When he came back into the bedroom a wave of love shook him as he saw her lying there clad only in an old t-shirt, her lower half bare and vulnerable as a child's. He tucked the towel beneath her hips and drew the sheet over her.

"Some water?" he asked. She looked at him strangely. "Some water to drink?" he explained. She shook her head no. Tears pooled in her eyes as she stared at the ceiling. "All right. You rest. You just rest now, and I'll call the doctor." He could have used the phone by the bed, but he didn't want her to hear him say that she'd lost the baby.

Richard kissed her forehead, tucked in her sheet, and left the room. On his way to the downstairs telephone, he passed the open door of the guest bath and stopped, looking in at the stained tiles and grout, the closed lid of the toilet bowl, and wondered what he should do.

Then he knew, knew what the doctors and the laboratories would want, knew what they would want to see so that they could find out what went wrong, so that maybe he and Donna could try again and have a baby, a *real* baby, and not what floated, dead, in the cloudy water, not what he would now have to preserve, to save for study, dissection.

My child. Stained sections on a microscope slide.

"So be it," he whispered aloud, remembering burying his first dog, scooping his dead goldfish from the smooth surface of the fish bowl. "So be it."

With a soft pop, he pulled a paper cup from the wall dispenser, then knelt and lifted the lid. It was there, as he knew and feared it would be, drifting against the white porcelain, still shrouded in its coverlet of thick blood and fluid, perhaps still dreaming that it was safely ensconced in its amniotic home.

Even now it was swimming, wasn't it, so unbelievably tiny, and yet a person. . . . *There*, did the little arms move? Arms or paddles, but yes, there were fingers, or the buds that would have been fingers, weren't there? Like a fly, oh certainly no bigger than a fly, and the limbs *did* move, yes, there *again*, and it *was* swimming, or trying to, wriggling like a tadpole, and wasn't it still alive, oh yes, of *course* it was, and he could save it now, and put it back where it could grow, couldn't he? Of course he could, he was the *father*, and he *could*, of course, of course . . .

Oh sisters two, how may we do
For to preserve this day
This poor youngling . . .

In a bottle, he thought suddenly, coldly, damning fantasies and accepting the real. *Preserved in a bottle.*

He dipped the cup into the water, pulled it against the side until what he wanted was surrounded by the paper, and then lifted it up out of the bowl, pressing the flush lever so that the urine and detritus whirled and sank away, and the water was fresh and clear again.

He carried the cup with the fetus down to the kitchen, put aluminum foil over the top, and placed it at the back of the refrigerator, next to the tray of baking soda, gray with age. As he dialed the doctor's number, he found that he was humming the Coventry Carol again.

III

"It's best that it happened," Richard said.

"I can't believe that."

"You know what he said—it would have been impossible to carry it to term, and if it *had* been born . . ." He left it unfinished and sipped his wine. It was the evening of the day Richard had thrown away the grapes. The fetus had disappeared into a laboratory, and was no doubt destroyed by now. Donna had recovered completely, at least physically. They had hardly spoken about it. He did not want to force her. The doctor told him in private not to push it, that she seemed extremely depressed (as if he couldn't tell), and that it would be best to let her come to terms with what had happened on her own schedule.

Tonight he had finally talked her into a glass of wine, which had loosened her tight facade enough for her to say, slowly and carefully, "Well, I really did it, didn't I?"

Nature's way, Richard had replied, spoonfeeding the words the doctor had given him. Donna would not accept them, would accept nothing but the concept that her sins had found her out, and destroyed her child. "I wouldn't have cared," she said, "if it *had* been a monster. I would've loved it."

Richard could say nothing in response.

"Would you?" she asked him.

"What?"

"Have loved it? If it hadn't been right?"

"It still would have been my child," he answered, too glibly.

"Until I killed it," she said.

"You didn't do any such thing."

"What I did killed it."

"That's stupid. There's no way to know that," he said.

"So there's no way to refute it," she replied. "Damned if I do, damned if I don't. And my poor little baby is damned forever."

"Stop talking like that. It was a . . . a mistake, that's all, just a genetic fluke, Donna. It could have been as much *my* fault as yours, for Christ's sake. It *never* would've been a baby—odds are it couldn't have survived a minute out of the womb."

She grew pale as he talked, but he couldn't stop. He had to tell her what he'd been thinking, what he'd been aching to say. "You did *nothing.* Things *happen,* things like this *happen* to mothers who've never smoked a cigarette or had a beer. It could've been something that's been in you or me since we were *born,* something the goddam factories put into the air or water or food that just didn't *agree* with you, it could've been so goddam *many* things, Donna. So stop. Please. Just stop killing yourself over what you couldn't help. Let's just think ahead. To the next one."

The look she gave him was cold, foreign, one he had never seen on her face. "There isn't going to be a next one."

"But . . . but there's no reason we . . ."

"No more," she said. "We can still fuck"— he blanched at the harshness of the word in her mouth—"but not for a baby. I won't do this again. I mean it."

"But nothing says that this would happen again."

"I won't take the chance."

"Life's *full* of chances, Donna. From the minute . . ." He stopped.

"From the minute you're born," she finished for him.

"Yes. From the minute you're born."

"I'm sorry, Rick."

"We should see someone."

"No, there's no point."

"A counselor, a . . ."

"A psychiatrist?"

"Maybe. Donna, I know, I know it was hard to lose it, it was hard for me too, but you can't let it rule your life."

"It won't. Just maybe the one small part of it, that's all."

Richard felt exhausted, unable to prolong their verbal skirmish. Her defenses seemed impregnable anyway, at least for now. In time, he thought, reason, the reason *he* possessed, might prevail. But not now. Not so soon.

That night, in bed, he put his arm around her and she moved into his warmth, but they did not make love, and he wondered if they ever would again.

Long after midnight, Richard awoke, conscious of Donna sitting up in bed next to him. Even in the dark, he could sense her tension, her attitude of expectant listening. "Donna?"

"Shh."

"What is it?"

"Listen." Her voice shook with excitement. Slowly he began to be aware of an alien sound just on the edge of audibility, similar to the tiny cracks and pings of expanding and cooling heat ducts that he spent the evenings of October getting used to. But this new sound seemed non-metallic, liquid in nature. It was nothing so simple as a drip, but it *was* rhythmic, a steady, constant *surge* of sound, like waves on a shore, though they were five hundred miles from the nearest beach. It was haunting, soothing, restful, and Richard thought there was a familiarity to it. It was tantalizing, elusive, and he knew that if he could only think back, think back *far* enough . . .

The furnace kicked on, and its barreling *whoosh* swept the sound and the nearly grasped memory far away. "Damn!" Donna cried. "Oh *damn* it!" Beside her, Richard shook his head as though coming out of a dream. "You heard it?" she said, switching on the lamp, barely blinking at its sudden glare.

"Yeah. Sure I did."

"What *was* it?"

"I'm . . . not sure."

"Where was it coming from?"

And he knew. Even though the sound seemed to lack any positive direction, he knew its source.

"The bath," she whispered, saying what he would not. "The guest bath." She turned as he nodded agreement, and stepped onto the cold wooden floor. Without pausing for a robe, she left the room and moved down the hall. He followed her.

When he arrived at the guest bath, she was already inside. The bright fluorescents had flickered into life, but their hum and the muffled rush of the furnace could not quell the other sound, that deep roar of moving fluids, the ebb and flow of the thick, heavy juices of life, all the churning activity of the womb. It was impossible to remember it, but he knew it could be nothing else.

"Oh my God," said Donna. "It's the baby."

The closed lid of the toilet started to rattle, lightly at first, then began to chatter like a giant bridgework, rising so high that he almost, but not quite, got a glimpse of what was inside. He walked past Donna and stood beside the clattering bowl, staring down at it, the surging sound all around him now.

"Open it," she said hollowly.

He began to reach down, but before his fingers could touch the vibrating lid, it snapped open like a hungry mouth, startling him, making him stumble backwards into his wife. The lid stayed open, showing them the water inside.

It was as black as ink, the unrelieved black of midnight cellars. As they watched, it started to slowly swirl and sink soundlessly downward, and more water, just as black, entered from under the rim to pour down, dance and turn and sink, over and over again, the sound of it lost in the pulse of the thicker liquids, that cacophony which poured over them, drowning their senses.

"Stop," Richard said, or thought he said, as he could not hear his voice. "Stop!" he cried again, and this time it was thinly audible. Now he shrieked, "*Stop!*" and it cut the surging, parted the liquid waves of sound that deafened them, and the waters stopped pouring, the roar of fluid, of heartbeat, of life force quieted, leaving them in a flat, dead silence, a silence in which he *saw*.

It could have lasted only a split second, but in its brief space the bathroom winked from sight, and in its place was a face, huge and malformed. It was the face of a beast, yet a beast of *potential*. It was as primitive in form as a child's drawing, yet the texture of the flesh was rich, finely grained, highly defined, viewed with perfect clarity. It was crowned by a vast and fleshy dome, bisected by a line of demarcation that could only be there to divide the hemispheres of its massive brain. The lower half of the face was composed of folds and wrinkles, out of which Richard could define loops of flexed muscle parodying a nose, and, beneath it, a broad, mountainous ridge that split the face from side to side, sinking at the edges into a countenance-spanning frown. On those hummocky sides of the primitive face hung two pouches, with a pit in each, that Richard knew would be eyes. They were not now. The thing was blind, though he felt it saw nonetheless, and his fear at seeing the thing was dwarfed by the realization that he in turn was seen.

He gasped and drew back, and the vision vanished. Once again the whiteness of the bathroom was all around him, and he heard no sounds but his own ragged breathing, the rumble of the furnace, the voice of Donna beside him.

"Did you *see?*" she said, as though she still could.

"See what?" he asked, praying she'd say the water, or the lid jiggling, hoping against hope that she had not seen what he had. If so, it had to have been real. They could not both be mad.

She shattered his hopes forever. "The face." There was unimaginable awe in her words. "It was the baby. I saw it."

So simply, he realized that she must be right. The face of a fetus, unborn, undeveloped, primitive in the extreme, little different from the fetus of beast or fish or fowl. How long, he tried to recall, before a fetus shows traces of being mammalian? And how much longer after that until displaying signs of humanity? Longer, surely, than eight weeks.

Oh, dear Christ, what had happened here? What had died? And what still, impossibly, lived?

IV

When Richard and Donna looked at the water in the bowl, it was perfectly clear and still. Indeed, there was not a thing in the bathroom to ascertain the sounds and sights they had experienced. It was as though they had undergone the same delusion, though Richard found that theory so unlikely as to be impossible. He had seen what he had seen, heard what he had heard, and that it had been a delusion occurred to him only momentarily.

The later manifestations, though, were quick and short and sharp, like jabs of temper, angry releases of ghostly frustration. The first of them occurred when he and Donna sat at the kitchen table, drinking instant coffee, trying to determine what had happened in the guest bath and why.

"It was the baby," Donna said with rigid certainty.

"It couldn't have been."

"You saw it."

"I saw *something*."

"It *was* the baby."

"Donna, the baby's dead. It *died*. I *don't* believe in ghosts."

"How else can you explain it?"

"It can't . . ."

"*Listen*," she said. "I don't believe either . . . *didn't*, at least. But if ghosts are supposed to result from violent things that happen, from . . . from *traumatization*, well, *God*, can you imagine anything more traumatic than being stillborn? Being yanked out of the only place in the world where you can survive?"

"So what are you saying? That . . . that somehow this thing that wasn't even *born*, that was never even alive, that never had"—he felt absurd saying it—"a *soul*, has come back as a ghost to flush our goddam *toilet*?"

He laughed at his words, and as he did his untouched coffee mug tipped over, pouring a half-cup of scalding liquid onto his stomach, groin, and thighs. The thin robe he wore offered no protection, and he gasped and stood up, letting the steaming brew drip off of him, trying not to cry out.

Donna, shocked, leaned toward him as if wanting to help but not knowing how. In a few seconds, after the first searing pains were over, he opened the robe. The flesh of his loins was bright red, but there were no blisters. He took a jar of cold water from the refrigerator, poured some into his cupped hand, and patted it on his skin. "Bastard," he whispered fervently. "How the . . ." He stopped, knowing the only answer.

"*It* did it," Donna said. "Because you laughed."

It took Richard a moment to speak again. "I'm going to bed," he said, wrapping the wet robe around him. "We'll talk about this in the morning."

The morning came slowly. Richard lay awake, listening for noises, his eyes staring at the false lights of the darkness, seeing that bulbous face in his memory. When daylight came, they did not speak of the night before, and Richard kept one hand firmly on his coffee mug.

Nothing happened for a week. Donna seemed exhausted and slept well, but Richard took a long time to get to sleep, and when he did, his night was haunted by disquieting dreams he could not remember in the morning.

Donna had said nothing about going back to work, and Richard brought it up only once. She dismissed it rather flippantly, which annoyed him. Mortgage payments were not small, and it seemed to him a waste to have her idle at home. Still, he remembered what the doctor had said, and did not press her.

A heavy snow storm blew up the following Thursday, and rapid changes in temperature crusted the white-covered roof with ice. A warm front came into the area on Saturday, and the snow beneath the ice melted. Unable to drip off the roof because of the ice dam above the spoutings, the chill water trickled beneath the eaves,

down into the walls, and ultimately dripped from beneath the interior window sills. It had happened one previous winter, and Richard and Donna grudgingly packed towels beneath the sills, bundled up, and went outside. Richard took a hatchet and ladder from one of the outbuildings, wedged the ladder into the snow, and climbed up to the edge of the two-storey high roof, where he began to hack long chunks of ice from above the rusty spouting. Donna stood below, watching from a distance of a few yards, her booted feet wedged firmly in eighteen inches of snow.

Richard was leaning far to his left, trying to minimize the number of times he had to descend and shift the ladder, when the house suddenly seemed to slew to his left. The sensation lasted only a moment, and he knew he was falling, the ladder with him. He pushed back and away, thinking only that he must not smash into the house. He felt his body leave the ladder, float dizzily, and fall. The impact as he hit the ice made a sharp *crack*, and he was still, lying on his side in the snow beneath the icy crust.

"Richard!" Donna cried, wading toward him. "Richard! Don't move!"

He had no intention of doing so until he knew he was capable of it. His heart was ratcheting, yet he felt curiously alive, as though he had just stepped from a particularly invigorating roller coaster ride. "I'm . . . I'm all right. I think I'm all right." He tried a few tentative movements. There was no pain. "I'm okay." He struggled through the thick snow to his feet. "What the hell happened?"

The ladder lay where it had fallen, the base at least twenty feet from where it had been solidly rooted in the snow.

"My God," he whispered. "What on earth . . ."

"It didn't fall," Donna said. "It was just like it . . . like it was pulled out of the snow and thrown away. Like some invisible hand."

"That's impossible," he said thickly.

"Look. Look for yourself."

He saw that she was right. Had he merely overbalanced, the ladder's base would have been next to the holes in the snow. As it was . . .

"This is crazy," he said. "Some freak, that's all. The way it hit, it bounced or something. Just some freak."

"Don't do any more. Let's go inside."

He looked at the ladder, then up at the roof, from which he had chipped well over half of the ice. There should be space for the melting water to drain off now. Yes, he told himself, there *should* be.

"Please, Richard." Donna took his arm. "I love you. I don't want you hurt."

He let her lead him into the house.

The next evening he was taking a shower when Donna came into the bathroom to get a pair of tweezers. As she opened the door to leave, the shower caddy, laden with several pounds of soaps, shampoos, and rinses, tore loose from the tile and fell, hitting Richard sharply in the back of the neck. When they looked, they found the adhesive had not dried out.

On Sunday, Richard was in the den writing a letter at the roll-top desk, and Donna was standing by the bookcase. The heavy roll-top, contrary to all the laws of physics, came crashing down, striking the typewriter that Richard had pulled toward the desk's edge. It was all that kept his wrists from being crushed.

Donna held him while he trembled and laughed simultaneously, but neither one of them said anything about the baby that had been lost. For Richard to suggest it would have meant admitting that something totally inexplicable and irrational was intruding into their lives. He could not admit to that, not after the night he had laughed at Donna for suggesting what he had considered to be the fantasy of a semi-hysterical woman. Now, he was unsure enough that he could not speak of it.

V

When Richard returned from his classes Monday afternoon, Donna was gone. She had taken the Accord, a great many of her clothes, and several thousand dollars, he later learned, from her personal savings account. She had left behind a letter, written in her sharp, slanting script:

Dear Rick,

I'm sorry that I have to do this, but I think it's for the best for everybody. For you, for me, for the baby.

Maybe you'll think I'm crazy, but the baby's still alive, I know. Somehow, somewhere, and it's still bound to me. It's got to be. It's too small to survive on its own. So I'm leaving, and I think it will come with me, and then you'll be safe. It can do things, Rick. It can make things happen, and I'm afraid it will hurt you. Going away is the only answer. I owe it to you, and I owe it to the baby.

I didn't tell you before, because I thought you'd laugh at me, but I honestly feel as though I've never lost it. After the miscarriage, I still felt (and feel) as though I was still pregnant, still carrying it inside me. So I'm taking it away. Please try to understand and try to forgive me. And please don't look for me. I'll be all right. I'm not crazy, Rick, and I say that knowing that that's what crazy people always say. I'm not crazy, but I am special, and if that's delusions of grandeur, so be it, but there's got to be some purpose behind all this. I don't know when I'll come back, but I will come back, Rick. I love you, darling. Merry Christmas.

Donna

He put down the letter, poured himself a scotch, sat down, and listened to the silence. The house felt empty, lifeless. Had there been any kind of entity there, it was gone now. Gone with Donna.

He stood, encased by quiet, and turned on the amplifier, hitting the scan switch and letting the first station click in. It was a choir singing Christmas music, and he half-moaned, half-laughed as he identified it as the Coventry Carol. So fitting, he thought. His *soul* felt like Coventry, the latter-day Coventry, bombed, a shambles, wooden skeletons poking their fingers up through smoky rubble.

He listened. They were singing the final verse.

That woe is me, poor child, for thee,
And ever mourn and say:
For thy parting, neither say nor sing
By, by, lully lullay.

He kept listening until he fell asleep. He did not dream.

VI

Parsons finished reading the letter. He stuck out his lower lip, tapped the paper with the knuckles of his right hand, set it down, and looked at Richard. "She's disturbed," he said.

"No shit, Sherlock," Richard responded bitterly.

"What did you expect me to say? You want a complete case history neatly labeled and explained?"

"You're the psychiatrist."

"I'm not a goddam psychiatrist, I'm a goddam psychologist."

"So what the hell does the psychologist have to say?"

"Little more than you can figure out with common sense. Donna was very upset by the miscarriage, and when these incidents began happening, she interpreted it as a sign that the baby—or the life force, call it, that had been the baby—had somehow survived. Isn't that what *you* think?"

"I suppose so."

Parsons was silent for a moment. He eyed Richard carefully. "Now what do you *believe*?"

"There's a difference?"

"You bet."

Richard sighed. "Everything seems *too* coincidental. Why did these things all start to happen at once? And what about that thing . . . those noises and everything in the guest bath? We *both* saw it."

"You *thought* you both saw it."

"Oh, come on, John, I know when . . ."

"Hold it. I didn't say you *didn't* see it. I think maybe you did."

"What?"

"You want an answer. Okay. I'll give you an answer that isn't completely rational, but one that has nothing to do with ghosts. You're not going to find it in any textbook, but that doesn't mean it's not possible. It just means it's not proven. Hell, it's not even seriously proposed."

"What are you talking about?"

"Look, when these things happened, the coffee cup, the ladder, the desk, where was Donna?"

Richard thought for a second. "There with me."

"Each time?"

"Yes. Why?"

"All right. This may be hard. Do you think that Donna felt angry with you? I mean about losing the baby?"

"I . . . I don't know. She may have."

"You said you argued about responsibility."

"Well, yes . . ."

"Isn't it possible that she may have blamed you for the things she feared? The side effects, and what might have caused them?"

"I don't know."

"You think she may have wanted you to *share* that responsibility? And when you didn't, when you said that there was nothing to feel guilty about, she thought you were trying to cop out, leaving her to take the consequences?"

"Look, John!" Richard half rose to his feet.

"Relax, Richard, I'm not saying that it's true, I'm just asking if Donna might not have seen it that way." Richard sat back, slowly. "Well? Could she have?"

"I suppose . . . . it's possible."

"So then," Parsons went on, "she loses the baby, blames herself, but blames you as well, and then strikes out at you."

"Strikes out? How?"

"Call it telekinesis if you like. Everything's got to have a name, doesn't it? What happened in the bathroom was something she projected.

From her mind to yours. *She* knocked over the ladder, spilled the coffee, slammed the desk."

"Jesus Christ, John, you're supposed to be a *scientist*. How can you spout this shit?"

"Richard, the more I study the mind, the more I learn I don't know. Now, I *do* have limits. Ghosts are out, as are demons. No magic spells. Astrology is crap. Lumps on heads, crystals, channeling, ouija boards, it's all bullshit. But what the mind can do isn't."

"You mean you think that Donna made me see and hear it all? That she . . . she attacked me with her mind? Knocked over that ladder without touching it?"

"I think it's possible. Highly improbable, but possible."

"All right, look. Assuming she could, *why* would she? Why try to hurt me? She *loves* me, John. She says so in the letter, and I believe it. I know she does."

"If she's behind all this, Richard, it isn't her conscious mind that's doing it. It's her subconscious. And there, deep down in that pit of primitive irrationality, she may very well hate your guts. And instead of accepting her own hostility toward you, she projects it into the baby. The *fetus*, I guess I should say."

Richard barked a laugh. "But how can she do that? Turn her baby—what she *thinks* is her baby—into a . . . a monster?"

"Maybe it just gives her more to take responsibility for."

Richard stood up, walked to the window, and looked out at the snow-covered quadrangle, where the down- and wool-wrapped students passed like purposeful bears. "So what do I do?" he wondered aloud.

"Do you know where she could have gone?"

Richard shook his head. "Her parents are dead. She was an only child. John," he said, turning to Parsons, "what do I do?"

"The only thing you can. Wait. Leave her alone."

". . . and she'll come home."

"Probably. When she finds there *is* no baby. That she isn't still pregnant."

"Do you think . . . when she has a period?"

"Maybe that soon. Or maybe she'll ignore it. Could be a full seven months. Or more. Whenever she realizes that there's nothing there to come to term."

Richard swallowed heavily. "What you said about the mind. Do you think . . . could it be possible that . . ."

"I know what you're thinking. And no, it's *not* possible. You can't get around biology, Richard. Donna lost her baby. That's all there is to it. She'll be back. And she'll come back alone."

VII

Donna came back in July, in the middle of a summer so hot and dry that the grass around the farmhouse had yellowed, then browned to the color of dead leaves, crackling like melting ice when Richard walked on it.

He was sitting on the front porch, drifting back and forth on the rusty metal glider, a vodka and tonic dripping condensation onto his bare leg, when she drove down the driveway in the Accord. She parked, but didn't get out of the car right away. She sat there for a minute, watching him watching her. Then she opened the door, walked up the path, and stood at the bottom of the porch steps. He noticed her hands were empty, her belly flat. She looked as though she had lost weight. Her color was bad, her eyes tired, her cheeks as hollow as his stomach felt. "Hi," she said, with barely a trace of emotion.

He looked at her and nodded. Twice.

"Aren't you glad to see me?" Now there was, he thought, just a touch of pleading.

"You didn't write," he said. "Or call. Seven months and not a word from you."

She tried to smile. "I thought you'd try to find me. I didn't want you to."

"I didn't try. If I would have, I could have. A detective could have traced the car, followed you."

"Thank you."

"For what?"

"For not trying. For leaving me alone." She stepped onto the porch and sat next to him on the glider. "Aren't you going to hug me?"

Slowly, he set down his drink and embraced her. His arms felt stiff and heavy as they touched her, but the contact changed his mood immediately, as a spark of power lights a dusty and long extinguished lamp. He held her tightly, buried his face against her shoulder, and began to cry.

"Oh, Rick," she said, putting her arms around him and hugging him tightly. "Oh, Richard." Her eyes teared. Her nose began to run. "I did miss you."

"I didn't know," Richard said through his crying. "I just didn't know. You could have been dead. I didn't know if you'd ever come back."

"I'd always come back. You knew I'd come back."

"You were so upset," he went on. "I thought you might even . . . hurt yourself."

"Oh no. Never that. Never that. Shh. Shh, darling. I'm home now. I'm home and I love you, and everything's all right. More than all right."

He cried some more, and Donna kept holding him, lightly crying as well. "Where were you?" he finally asked. "Where did you go?"

"Ohio. A small town near Akron. I just drove until I found a place that felt right. A boarding house. An older lady had it. She was very nice. I helped her with the housework and things until . . ."

She paused. In the heat, Richard felt very cold. "Until . . . you came home."

"Yes." Donna nodded. "Until then." She took her arms from around him, stood up, leaned on the porch railing. "Rick, remember my letter?" she asked quietly. "What I said I thought was happening?"

He nodded, smiling to drive away the specters.

"I was right, Richard. What I thought was happening? It happened."

He would not stop smiling. If he stopped smiling, he would let the monsters in. "No, Donna. The baby died. We *lost* the baby." He smiled, being rational.

Donna smiled back. "It's in the car."

He shook his head. He smiled. How he smiled. "No."

"Come look. See for yourself." She reached out her hand and took his, drawing him to his feet. Together they walked down the chipped and flaking wooden steps, down the path to the Accord. "It was sleeping on the way in," she said.

"It," Richard parroted.

"I don't know whether it's a boy or a girl. I can't really tell. Not yet."

"Donna . . ."

"Shh." They were at the car, and Donna leaned over and looked into the back seat. "Look," she said.

Richard looked.

He did not see it at first, but as Donna's grip tightened on his hand, something swam into view, hiding the faded blue vinyl. Its outline was a pair of joined ovals, one larger than the other, with four protuberances he tentatively identified as arms and legs. They were round and fat, and, like the trunk and head, pink in color. His breath locked in his throat as he heard her ask gently, "There, do you see it?"

"Donna . . . no . . ."

"Yes you do. I can see you do."

"Donna . . ."

"It's very quiet. Very good. It doesn't eat, but it loves to be sung to, talked to."

"Donna, it's . . . it's not there. Not really. You created it."

"Of course, Richard. *We* created it. Together. It's our baby."

"It is not there, Donna."

"You can't say that. You can't believe it. You see it. It's what we did. It's *us*, Richard, it's part of us. It's who we are, and what we've done." She looked down at the shadowy form, which was growing ever more distinct. "So we have to take care of it." She rested a hand on Richard's shoulder. "Let's go inside now. Into our house."

She turned and started to walk up the path. When she saw him hesitate, looking at her and then at what lay in the back seat, she gave a little bell of a laugh. "We don't have to take it," she said. "It'll be inside before we are."

She was right. When they entered the living-room, it was lying on the sofa, half-seen, like some plump fruit shrouded by leaves and branches. Donna looked down at it lovingly, then walked around the room, touching familiar things. "You've kept the house nice, Rick. Everything looks so clean. We'll be happy now." She smiled at him. "I think I'll get my bags. I won't really feel at home until I'm unpacked."

Richard continued to gaze at the shape, seeing it float on the brown brocade as he'd seen a similar shape float in water, dark and lambent. "I'll . . . I'll help you," he said huskily.

"No. You stay here." She embraced him from behind. "Sing to it, Richard. It loves that."

He felt her kiss his hair, then listened to her retreating footsteps, the screen door slamming shut on its weary spring, the boards of the porch creaking under her weight.

It did not disappear, did not vanish in her ab- sence as he had thought it might. It remained on the couch, its outline firm. *How strong can she be, how strong?*

And then the other thought intruded:

How strong have I become?

Parson's mysteries of mind swept through him, and he wondered what cancer had clamped his brain, what sickness, what maleficent suggestion had given him the power to conjure this thing that shared his house, his wife's love, and, ultimately, his own affections.

The plumpness on the sofa moved as if trying to give an answer, and the appendages twitched, stroked through unseen waves, extended toward him as if to say:

Love me. I am here, am yours. Love me.

He looked at his baby, and found himself humming, very gently, very quietly. It was a carol, a carol and a lullaby.

I am yours. Love me, it said to him.

He would. Helpless, bound, he knew he would.

Permissions Acknowledgments

"Mr. Arcularis" by Conrad Aiken from *Harper's* 1931. Copyright © 1931 by Conrad Aiken. Renewed. Reprinted by permission of Brandt & Hochman Literary Agents, Inc.

"The Night Wire" by H. F. Arnold from *Weird Tales*, September 1926. Copyright © 1926 by Popular Fiction Publishing Co. Renewed. Reprinted by permission of Weird Tales Ltd.

"Legal Rites" by Isaac Asimov and James MacCreigh from *Weird Tales*, September 1950. Copyright © 1950 by Isaac Asimov and Frederick Pohl. Renewed. Reprinted by permission of the Trident Media Group and Curtis Brown Ltd.

"The Corner Shop" by Cynthia Asquith from *The Ghost Book*, edited by Cynthia Asquith. London, Hutchinson, 1926. Copyright © 1926 by Cynthia Asquith. Renewed. Reprinted by permission of Roland Asquith.

"The Follower" by Cynthia Asquith from *My Grimmest Nightmare*, London, G. Allen & Unwin, 1935. Copyright © 1935 by Cynthia Asquith. Renewed. Reprinted by permission of Roland Asquith.

"Song of the Dead" by Wyatt Blassingame from *Dime Mystery Magazine*, March 1935. Copyright © 1935 by Popular Publications, Inc. Copyright renewed 1963 and assigned to Argosy Communications, Inc. All rights reserved. Reprinted by arrangement with Argosy Communications, Inc.

"The House in Half Moon Street" by Hector Bolitho from *The House in Half Moon Street* by Hector Bolitho, London, Cobden-Sanderson, 1935. Copyright © 1935 by Hector Bolitho. Renewed. Reprinted by permission of The Alfred and Isabel Marian Reed Trust.

"The Avenging of Ann Leete" by Marjorie Bowen from *Seeing Life! And Other Stories* by Marjorie Bowen, London, Hurst & Blackett, 1923. Copyright © 1923 by Gabrielle Margaret Vere Long. Renewed. Reprinted by permission of Sharon Eden.

"The Ghosts of Steamboat Coulee" by Arthur J. Burks from *Weird Tales*, May 1926. Copyright © 1966 by Arkham House; from *Black Medicine*, Sauk City, WI, Arkham House, 1966. Reprinted by permission of Arkham House.

"Playmates" by A. M. Burrage from *Some Ghost Stories* by A. M. Burrage, London, Cecil Palmer, 1927. Copyright © 1927 by A. M. Burrage. Renewed. Reprinted by permission of J. S. F. Burrage.

"Just Behind You" by Ramsey Campbell from *Poe's Progeny*, edited by Gary Fry, Bradford, U.K., Gray Friar Press, 2005. Copyright © 2005 by Ramsey Campbell. Reprinted by permission of the author.

"Behind the Screen" by Dale Clark from *Weird Tales*, April 1934. Copyright © 1934 by Popular Fiction Publishing Co. Renewed. Reprinted by permission of Weird Tales Ltd.

"Death Must Die" by Albert E. Cowdrey from *The Magazine of Fantasy and Science Fiction*, November/December 2010. Copyright © 2010 by Albert E. Cowdrey. Reprinted by permission of the author.

"Punch and Judy" by Frederick Cowles from *Star Book of Horror No. 1*, 1975. Copyright © 1975 by Michael W. Cowles. Reprinted by permission of Michael W. Cowles.

"Pacific 421" by August Derleth from *Weird Tales*, September 1944 and *Something Near* by Au-

gust Derleth, Sauk City, WI, Arkham House, 1945. Copyright © 1945 by Arkham House. Reprinted by permission of Arkham House.

"The Return of Andrew Bentley" by August Derleth and Mark Schorer from *Weird Tales*, September 1933 and *Colonel Markesan and Less Pleasant People*, Sauk City, WI, Arkham House, 1966. Copyright © 1966 by Arkham House. Reprinted by permission of Arkham House.

"Death's Warm Fireside" by Paul Ernst from *Dime Mystery Magazine*, March 1936. Copyright © 1936 by Popular Publications, Inc. Copyright © renewed 1964 and assigned to Argosy Communications, Inc. All rights reserved. Reprinted by arrangement with Argosy Communications, Inc.

"The Lost Boy of the Ozarks" by Steve Friedman from *Backpacker*, November 2009. Copyright © 2009 by Steve Friedman. Reprinted by permission of the author.

"The Floor Above" by M. L. Humphreys from *Weird Tales*, May 1923. Copyright © 1923 by Rural Publications. Renewed. Reprinted by permission of Weird Tales Ltd.

"Mr. Saul" by H. R. F. Keating from *The Thirteenth Ghost Book*, edited by James Hale, London, Barrie & Jenkins, 1977. Copyright © 1977 by H. R. F. Keating. Reprinted by permission of the author.

"The Advent Reunion" by Andrew Klavan from *Ellery Queen Mystery Magazine*, January 2011. Copyright © 2011 by Amalgamated Metaphor. Reprinted by permission of the author.

"The Dead-Wagon" by Greye La Spina from *Weird Tales*, September 1927. Copyright © 1927 by Popular Fiction Publishing Co. Renewed. Reprinted by permission of Weird Tales Ltd.

"Smoke Ghost" by Fritz Leiber from *Unknown*, October 1941. Copyright © 1941 by Fritz Leiber. Renewed. Reprinted by permission of Richard Curtis Associates, Inc.

"He Walked by Day" by Julius Long from *Weird Tales*, June 1934. Copyright © 1934 by Popular Fiction Publishing Co. Renewed. Reprinted by permission of Weird Tales Ltd.

"The Fifth Candle" by Cyril Mand from *Weird Tales*, January 1939. Copyright © 1939 by Popular Fiction Publishing Co. Renewed. Reprinted by permission of Weird Tales Ltd.

"The Considerate Hosts" by Thorp McClusky from *Weird Tales*, December 1939. Copyright © 1939 by Popular Fiction Publishing Co. Renewed. Reprinted by permission of Weird Tales Ltd.

"Mordecai's Pipe" by A.V. Milyer from *Weird Tales*, June 1936. Copyright © 1936 by Popular Fiction Publishing Co. Renewed. Reprinted by permission of Weird Tales Ltd.

"But at My Back I Always Hear" by David Morrell from *Shadows 6*, edited by Charles L. Grant, New York, Doubleday, 1983. Copyright © 1983 by David Morrell. Reprinted by permission of the author.

"Night-Side" by Joyce Carol Oates from *Night-Side* by Joyce Carol Oates, New York, Vanguard Press, 1977. Copyright © 1977 by Ontario Review, Inc. Reprinted by permission of the author and John Hawkins and Associates, Inc.

"Thing of Darkness" by G. G. Pendarves from *Weird Tales*, August 1937. Copyright © 1937 by Popular Fiction Publishing Co. Renewed. Reprinted by permission of Weird Tales Ltd.

"Make-Believe" by Michael Reaves from *The Magazine of Fantasy and Science Fiction*, March/April 2010. Copyright © 2010 by Michael Reaves. Reprinted by permission of the author.

"Journey into the Kingdom" by M. Rickert from *The Magazine of Fantasy and Science Fiction*, May 2006. Copyright © 2006 by M. Rickert. Reprinted by permission of the author.

"They Found My Grave" by Joseph Shearing from *Orange Blossoms* by Joseph Shearing, London, Heinemann, 1938. Copyright © 1938 by Gabrielle Margaret Vere Long. Renewed. Reprinted by permission of Sharon Eden.

"The Midnight El" by Robert Weinberg from *Return to the Twilight Zone*, edited by Carol Ser-

ALSO EDITED BY OTTO PENZLER

THE BLACK LIZARD BIG BOOK OF PULPS
The Best Crime Stories from the Pulps During Their Golden Age—
The '20s, '30s, & '40s

Weighing in at over a thousand pages, containing more than fifty stories and two novels, this book is big, baby, bigger and more powerful than a freight train—a bullet couldn't pass through it. Here are the best stories and every major writer who ever appeared in celebrated pulps like *Black Mask*, *Dime Detective*, *Detective Fiction Weekly*, and more. These are the classic tales that created the genre and gave birth to hard-hitting detectives who smoke criminals like cheap cigars; sultry dames whose looks are as lethal as a dagger to the chest; and gin-soaked hideouts where conversations are just preludes to murder. This is crime fiction at its gritty best.

Crime Fiction

THE BLACK LIZARD BIG BOOK OF
BLACK MASK STORIES

The Greatest Crime Fiction from
the Legendary Magazine

An unstoppable anthology of crime stories culled from *Black Mask*, the magazine where the first hard-boiled detective story, which was written by Carroll John Daly, appeared. It was the slum in which Dashiell Hammett, Raymond Chandler, Horace McCoy, Cornell Woolrich, John D. MacDonald all got their start. It was the home of stories with titles like "Murder *Is* Bad Luck," "Ten Carats of Lead," "Diamonds Mean Death," and "Drop Dead Twice." Also here is *The Maltese Falcon* as it originally appeared in the magazine. Crime writing gets no better than this.

Crime Fiction

THE BIG BOOK OF ADVENTURE STORIES

The Most Daring, Dangerous, and Death-Defying Collection of Adventure Tales
Ever Captured in One Mammoth Volume

Everyone loves adventure, and Otto Penzler has collected the best adventure stories of all time into one awe-inspiring volume. With stories by Jack London, O. Henry, H. Rider Haggard, Alistair MacLean, Talbot Mundy, Cornell Woolrich, and many others, this wide-reaching and fascinating volume contains some of the best characters from the most thrilling adventure tales, including The Cisco Kid; Sheena, Queen of the Jungle; Bulldog Drummond; Tarzan; The Scarlet Pimpernel; Conan the Barbarian; Hopalong Cassidy; King Kong; Zorro; and The Spider. Divided into sections that embody the greatest themes of the genre—Sword & Sorcery; Megalomania Rules; Man vs. Nature; Island Paradise; Sand and Sun; Something Feels Funny; Go West, Young Man; Future Shock; I Spy; Yellow Peril; In Darkest Africa—it is destined to be the greatest collection of adventure stories ever compiled.

Fiction

THE VAMPIRE ARCHIVES
The Most Complete Volume of Vampire Tales
Ever Published

The Vampire Archives is the biggest, hungriest, undeadliest collection of vampire stories, as well as the most comprehensive bibliography of vampire fiction ever assembled. Whether imagined by Bram Stoker or Anne Rice, vampires are part of the human lexicon and as old as blood itself. They are your neighbors, your friends, and they are always lurking. Now Otto Penzler has compiled the darkest, the scariest, and by far the most evil collection of vampire stories ever. With over eighty stories, including the works of Stephen King and D. H. Lawrence, alongside Lord Byron and Tanith Lee, not to mention Edgar Allan Poe and Harlan Ellison, it will drive a stake through the heart of any other collection out there.

Fiction

ALSO AVAILABLE IN MASS-MARKET VOLUMES:

BLOODSUCKERS
The Vampire Archives, Volume 1
Including stories by Stephen King, Dan Simmons, and
Bram Stoker

FANGS
The Vampire Archives, Volume 2
Including stories by Clive Barker, Anne Rice, and
Arthur Conan Doyle

COFFINS
The Vampire Archives, Volume 3
Including stories by Harlan Ellison, Robert Bloch, and
Edgar Allan Poe

ZOMBIES! ZOMBIES! ZOMBIES!

The legendary editor of *The Vampire Archives* now brings us *Zombies! Zombies! Zombies!*, an unstoppable anthology of the living dead. These superstars of horror are everywhere, storming the world of print and visual media. Their endless march will never be stopped. It's the Zombie Zeitgeist! Now, with his wide sweep of knowledge and keen eye for great storytelling, Otto Penzler offers a remarkable catalog of zombie literature. From world-renowned authors like Stephen King, Joe R. Lansdale, Robert McCammon, Robert E. Howard, and Richard Matheson to the writer who started it all, W. B. Seabrook, *Zombies! Zombies! Zombies!* is the darkest, the living-deadliest, scariest, and—dare we say—tasteful collection of the wandering zombie horde ever assembled. Its relentless pages will devour horror fans from coast to coast.

Fiction

AGENTS OF TREACHERY

Never Before Published Spy Fiction from
Today's Most Exciting Writers

For the first time ever, Otto Penzler has handpicked some of the most respected and best-selling thriller writers working today for a riveting collection of spy fiction. From first to last, this stellar collection signals mission accomplished. Featuring: Lee Child with an incredible look at the formation of a special ops team; James Grady writing about an Arab undercover FBI agent with an active cell; Joseph Finder riffing on a Boston architect who's convinced that his Persian neighbors are up to no good; John Lawton concocting a Len Deighton-esque story about British intelligence; Stephen Hunter thrilling us with a tale about a World War II brigade; and much more.

Spy Fiction

VINTAGE CRIME/BLACK LIZARD
Available wherever books are sold.
www.weeklylizard.com
www.randomhouse.com